GREEN EARTH

Books by Frederick Manfred

THE GOLDEN BOWL, 1944
BOY ALMIGHTY, 1945
THIS IS THE YEAR, 1947
THE CHOKECHERRY TREE, 1948
THE PRIMITIVE, 1949
THE BROTHER, 1950
THE GIANT, 1951
LORD GRIZZLY, 1954
MORNING RED, 1956
RIDERS OF JUDGMENT, 1957
CONQUERING HORSE, 1959
ARROW OF LOVE, stories, 1961
WANDERLUST, trilogy, 1962*
SCARLET PLUME, 1964
THE SECRET PLACE, 1965**
WINTER COUNT, poems, 1966
KING OF SPADES, 1966
APPLES OF PARADISE, stories, 1968
EDEN PRAIRIE, 1968
CONVERSATIONS, 1974***
MILK OF WOLVES, 1976
THE MANLY-HEARTED WOMAN, 1976
GREEN EARTH, 1977

*A new revised version of a trilogy that was originally published in three separate volumes, *The Primitive, The Brother, The Giant*. Mr. Manfred wrote under the pen name of Feike Feikema from 1944 through 1951.

**Originally published in hardback as *The Man Who Looked like the Prince of Wales;* reprinted in paperback as *The Secret Place*.

***Moderated by John R. Milton.

GREEN EARTH

a novel by Frederick Manfred

Who can see the green earth anymore
as she was by the sources of Time?
—Matthew Arnold

Crown Publishers, Inc. New York

Any resemblance of any character in this work of fiction to any person in real life, alive or dead, or yet to come, is purely coincidental. This book is altogether the work of the imagination.

Printed in the United States of America

Published simultaneously in Canada by General Publishing Company Limited

Designed by Rhea Braunstein

Library of Congress Cataloging in Publication Data

Manfred, Frederick Feikema, 1912-
Green earth.

I. Title.
PZ3.M313705Gr5 [PS3525.A52233] 813'.5'4
ISBN 0-517-52985-8 77-5707

Manfred

Preface

I visited my uncle and aunt on the farm shortly after my first novel was published. It was on a Sunday, and I went to church with them. After the service, their minister stopped me as he shook hands with departing parishioners and asked me how it felt to have written a best seller.

"Best seller?" I exclaimed. "Where'd you get that idea?"

The minister said, "With all that filth and dirty sex in it, it's bound to sell, isn't it?"

"Not any more than all that filth in the Bible might sell it."

"Oh, but the Bible is God's word."

"Did you buy a copy of my book?"

"No. Your uncle let me read his copy."

"Domeny, a friend of mine once advised me that I should never pay attention to criticism unless it came from someone who'd bought my book."

Later that evening at supper, as everything was going along smoothly, food being passed around the table, mean gossip kept to a minimum, proper thanks given for the good summer just passed . . . Aunt suddenly said, "Yes, I read your book too."

Silence.

"Domeny's right. That scene there by the crick, what that Maury done there to that Kirsten, that's awful. It's pure filth. How can you, Alice's boy, write such about such things?"

"And I'm not my father's son?"

All eyes down the long table fixed on me for a second, then went back to concentrating on the food.

Aunt sat up very straight at her end of the table. Her blue eyes flashed. "Are you ashamed of your mother?"

"I loved her."

"Well then?"

"She would want me to tell the truth according to my own lights. Rather than be a hypocrite. Pretend to be something I am not."

"I still think you didn't have to write that stuff about them two there by the crick."

Uncle raised his graying head. He held it partly sideways as if trimming his sails to the solar wind coming from Aunt's burning eyes. His blue eyes just barely dared to look into mine for a moment. "That's right, Fred. You didn't have to write that stuff. It's not Christian Reformed."

I decided not to raise a fuss. My cousins around the table were too young to understand what I was up to. I said instead, "Tante, you always make the most wonderful pies. Better than my mother even. This lemon meringue is num num."

After a bit Aunt had to smile a little. "Now you're buttering me up, Fred." Aunt had often been jealous of the way her husband's older sister could cook.

"But this pie is good, Tante. It almost evaporates in your mouth."

"Well, I try my best," Aunt said.

At six o'clock the menfolks went to the barn. Uncle milked some twenty cows six on six, six o'clock in the morning and six o'clock at night. The cows gave more if milked every twelve hours right on the dot. Uncle and his tall slim son attached the milking machines while I stood well back of the gutter and watched.

Once the milking machines were going, Uncle had time for talk. "Say," he said, shaking his head gravely in admiration, looking me directly in the eye, "some of those passages there in your book, man, they surely was good. About how the dust blew around. And how the earth was cracked. And yet how the people hung on. How they wouldn't give up. That surely was good. Just the way it was. Yes, everything was good in it. Even that passage by the crick there, where you tell about what that boy done to that girl, that was all just the way it was."

I was surprised, and showed it. "Hey, Uncle, where were you at the supper table when Aunt jumped me about that crick passage?"

He waved that off. "Oh, I just said that to quiet her down. Womenfolks and ministers all think alike about them things and there ain't much you can do about it. But we here in the barn now, we menfolks, we can speak plain. Now, you take that passage where . . . . "

Frederick Manfred

BOOK ONE

Lady of the House

To
ALICE
mother
January 3, 1891; April 19, 1929

Ada ❦ 1

IT WAS THE Sunday before Christmas, 1909. The Alfred Englekings were having supper. It was a simple meal: rice with milk and brown sugar, black rye bread with butter, and green tea.

The Englekings didn't eat big meals on Sunday. A good Christian wasn't supposed to indulge himself on Sunday or do any work on Sunday except what was strictly necessary to keep body and soul together. The Lord's Day had to be spent in soul-searching and prayer and divine worship. There was to be absolutely no fun.

After church that afternoon Pa and Ma'd had an argument. They were still looking black at each other across the supper table. The four children ate their rice in silence.

The table stood against the east wall between two windows. Pa sat on the north side near his corner, with Baby Sherman in a high chair beside him. Ma sat on the west side, not too far from the stove. Ada, the oldest, sat next to Ma. Joan, eight, and John, fourteen, sat across from Pa. Behind Joan and John was the cistern pump and a sink with a pail of water standing beside it.

A kerosene lamp shed a soft yellow light on the wall above the table. The clock next to the lamp showed a few minutes past six. Higher on the wall hung a weather clock. The old lady with the bad weather clothes had just come out of her door, while the old man with the good weather clothes had retreated into his door.

Ada wasn't hungry. Fighting always upset her. Pa didn't like it that she had a date with Alvin Ravenhorse that night. Pa said she was still too young to think of getting married. That had set the dolls to dancing. She'd been seeing Alvin every Sunday night since the past summer. Pa allowed her only an hour with Alvin after catechism, on stiff chairs in the parlor in the winter. At nine-thirty sharp Pa let Ada know it was time for Alvin to leave. Alvin was the catch of the church.

Pa buttoned up his black knit jacket. "John, put a little wood on the fire. It must be near zero outside."

"I'll do it," Ada said.

"No. I said for John to do it."

John took yet another mouthful of rice before putting down his spoon.

Ma abruptly pushed back her chair and got to her feet. "I'll do it." Ma was tall and billowy. "When the master speaks, we'd all better jump to attention."

Pa stiffened. His high-back swivel chair squeaked. For a fleeting moment his struggle to be patient with his wife gave his hollow gray face an almost bland expression. Then his light blue eyes turned a light gray. He gave John a shriveling look. His brown moustache twitched. Usually he and John tended to be pretty good friends.

Ma opened the front of the shining black stove, and holding back her dress over her lap put in several chunks of ash wood. Light from the jumping fire touched the rhinestones in her pompadour comb. The rhinestones glittered each time she reached down, matching the gray eyes behind her gold-rimmed glasses. Over the years a perpetual frown had deepened a crease between her eyes. "Almost nineteen and she still mayn't have a steady boyfriend. When all her friends are getting married. All." Ma let the stove lid drop shut. "I raised my daughter right and I trust her."

The slamming sound made every head at the table lower a notch.

Ma sat down, haughty. Her corset squeaked. "I wonder how old I was when you first began to date me, hah?"

Pa pushed his bowl of rice away. "Wife."

"I suppose you'd say no even if that young candidate minister, Paul Brook, was to date her, hah?"

Pa placed his long hands flat on the table in front of him. "So now it comes out that you don't like Alvin Ravenhorse either?"

Ma choked to herself in her large fleshes. "For a daughter of mine, no, Alvin Ravenhorse is not good enough. But Domeny Brook would be."

Ada stared down at her rice. A pale red-gold hair hung in her eyes. Carefully she brushed it back in place.

Ma just couldn't resist sticking it into Pa that he'd been a poor carpenter when they got married in the Old Country, while she, Joan Alderling, came from a better class of people. The truth was of course that Pa's people a generation before had been important people in East Friesland, Germany. Great John Engleking, Pa's father, had been the baron of a district known as Lengen. Great John had defied Bismarck and had had to escape across the Dollart into West Friesland, The Netherlands, with his wife Adelheid and three children, Big John and Alfred and daughter Alberta. When the truth was also that Ma's mother had emigrated from East Friesland with the Englekings as a servant girl, and that it had only been because of her blond beauty that a Henry Alderling had married her.

John threw back his blond forelock and wondered out loud, "Why can't Ade pick her own man? When she's going to live with him and not with us."

Pa suddenly stood up, sending his chair cracking against a tobacco stand in the corner. "That's enough of that now!" Pa had learned that if he suddenly stood up to his full height, six foot two, it ended all argument.

After glaring down at each head in turn, Pa reached back for his swivel chair and sat down again.

Spoons clicked lightly in bowls.

"Adelheid is also a daughter of mine, you know," Pa said to Ma. "And I don't want her to come home with her pants on over her head."

Joan choked back a giggle.

Pa fixed his eyes on Joan. "And that goes for you too, Joanie."

Ma said, "What? And Joan's only eight years old?"

"There is to be no daughter in this family heavy with child before she's married." Pa gave Joan another hard look.

Ma let out a loud scoff. "Now you can electrocute me, because I've heard everything. Talking like that to a little child."

"She likes to sit too much with her legs up in the air already."

"What?!"

"I'll say it again." Pa looked first at Ada, then at Joan. "You'll get no one hundred dollar wedding present from me if you come home with your pants on over your head. You hear?"

It was John's turn to choke back his feelings.

"Still you kids! It's nothing to laugh at."

Spoons again clicked lightly in bowls.

Baby Sherman held out a pink hand toward the window. His little dumpling fingers were outspread in primitive baby eloquence. "Da?"

Ada looked up. Large snowflakes were drifting down through the shaft of light where it streamed into the darkness outside. "It's snowing."

Everyone looked out of the window.

"Well, we can use the snow," Pa said. "Make the house warmer. The Lord's will."

Ma said nothing. The idea that the Lord might be worrying about what Pa might want in the way of weather was crazy.

Ada wished she could do something to make Pa and Ma get along better. Pa'd never been able to do anything right for Ma. One of the conditions Ma made before agreeing to come to America was that they had to have a house of their own. She was accustomed to a well-to-do manner of living and she at least was going to have that in return for going across an ocean to live in a wilderness full of wild savages. Pa hated being beholden to anyone, yet for her sake went into debt. He first took day labor in America, which included removing dung from the outdoor privies of the rich. Later he got a job laying cement walks for the town of Jerusalem in northwest Iowa. Winters he made both wooden and leather shoes to order in his little barn by the alley. Ma never allowed Pa a moment's rest, not even on a rainy day when he couldn't lay cement. "Well, Alfred, must this day pass with no work done, hah?"

Baby Sherman raised his dumpling hand to the ceiling. "Da?" Was that where the snow came from?

Ada smiled. She loved her baby brother. "Yes, like manna from heaven."

"Man?"

Ada's smile widened. "Yes, you're Papa's little man."

"And Mama's treasure," Ma quickly put in. Tears gathered in the corners of Ma's eyes.

Pa looked at Ada's plate. "Is that all you can eat?"

John had to laugh. "You can't eat when you're in love, you know."

Ada could feel pink spreading over her cheeks. She bit her tongue. Yes, she was in love. And her not being very hungry did have something to do with it all right. But it was also that her new Ladyship Abdominal Model corset was too tight. Ada had asked John to lace it up for her in back that morning and all day long she'd felt full. A small waist might be a sign of beauty, like the mail order catalog said, but it was also a trial. Ada thought to herself: "I feel like I'm corseted down to the last gasp."

Snowflakes as big as cabbage butterflies continued to drift through the shaft of amber light outside.

Ada thought to herself, "When I get married, it's going to be different in my family. I'm going to be an understanding wife. Alvin is a hard worker. And, thank God, he's handsome like Pa." It was true that Alvin liked to tell dirty stories once in a while, but Ada was sure she could cure him of that. Once he became a father, he'd have to think of the children.

Just so Alvin wouldn't turn out to be as strict as Pa. Maybe if she were warm to Alvin, and patient with him, he'd be a gentle father, let the kids have a little fun once in a while so long as it was innocent. Like Pa should've let her have the time she went roller-skating with Minnie Alfredson at the city rink. She and Minnie didn't go there looking for dates. They went there to skate by themselves. Skating was so heavenly. For once her long feet came in handy. They helped her take the sidestepping turns at the end of the rink. She hadn't known Alvin would show up at the rink. She was as surprised as anybody. But there Alvin was. And wouldn't you know it, but on that one particular night Pa had begun to worry about her that she'd been gone so long visiting Minnie. And Pa had looked for her, and found her floating, arms cross-linked, with Alvin in long lovely swoops up and down the roller rink. Then Pa shamed her something awful. He stepped onto the rink, right in the middle of all the flying skaters, and told her to come home with him. Alvin hadn't helped much either when he turned out to be such a sheep around Pa.

"Nah," Pa said as he reached for the old black family Bible on the shelf above him, "you've all had sufficient then? Ada?" Pa glanced at her bowl. "No leftovers in this family, you know."

"I'll put what's left of my rice in the pantry and eat it before I go to bed tonight, Pa."

"All right." Pa adjusted the reflector behind the lamp chimney until its beam of sharp light fell on the open pages of the Bible. Pa threw a last look around under thick brown brows and then began reading from the last chapter of The Song of Solomon. "O that thou wert as my brother, that sucked the breasts of my mother! when I should find thee without, I would kiss thee; yea, I should not be despised."

There was another giggle from Joan.

Pa almost looked up. "I would lead thee and bring thee into my mother's house, who would instruct me: I would cause thee to drink of spice wine of the juice of my pomegranate."

Ada listened. Such rich passages. Yes, she and Alvin wouldn't live as strict as Pa and Ma did. She and Alvin would have more of the juicy enjoying of life, of the pomegranate, whatever that was.

Ada had one regret about Alvin. Alvin was not as smart as Pa. Pa read a lot. It made Ma awfully jealous that Reverend Carpenter sometimes liked to come over in the evening to visit with Pa. Pa had such a rich mind, he said. Only trouble was, Pa had trouble expressing his best thoughts. After Reverend Carpenter left, Pa would often think of what he should have said. To make sure that his thoughts weren't lost, Pa would write them down, little impromptu essays written in a neat black pencil script on lined linen paper. When Domeny learned of the little essays, he asked Pa to let him see them. Pa was reluctant, but in the end he let Domeny read them. Domeny sometimes took the little essays and built up a sermon around them. That was all right with Pa. But he told Domeny that he must never mention it to Ma, as Ma would figure out a way to use it against him in a pinch. So there Pa often sat on Sunday in his pew by the side door, colored light from the high windows streaming down on his graying brown head, listening to his own ideas being expounded from the pulpit.

"Love is as strong as death," Pa read. "Jealousy is as cruel as the grave: the coals thereof are coals of fire, which hath a most vehement flame."

Looking up, Ada saw that Joan and John were trying not to look at each other while Pa was reading to make sure they wouldn't burst out laughing.

Ada hoped Pa could finish the reading before the kids exploded. She could feel a bubble of some kind trying to rise up in her own innards. The tighter the lid on the teakettle the more surely the lid would blow off. Pa's clear solemn voice made it all the worse. Ada had often wondered why The Song was in the Bible at all. The words were the words of ardent lovers. The reading of it could sometimes set off the whole catechism class to tittering.

"Many waters cannot quench love, neither can the floods drown it: if a man would give all the substance of his house for love, it would utterly be condemned."

By the way Pa leaned over as he read, it could be seen that Pa was aware that that old devil, Laughter, was sitting at his table.

"We have a little sister, and she hath no breasts: what shall we do for our sister in the day when she shall be spoken for?"

Joan and John pinched their eyes tight shut.

"I am a wall and my breasts are like towers."

Joan and John both threw a quick look at Ada's full bosom.

Ada frowned severely at them.

Joan clapped a hand to her mouth. Breath squeaked through her fingers.

"Ssst!" Ma hissed.

A single kernel of rice shot through Joan's plump fingers.

That did it. John exploded into helpless laughter.

"Make haste, my beloved, and be thou like to a roe, or to a young hart, upon the mountains of spices." Pa closed the Bible with a loud clap, then gave the three of them a blazing look. "What was the last word?"

"Da," Baby Sherman said.

That made it all the worse, and Joan finally fell laughing off her chair.

Ma got caught up in the silly insanity of it then, too, and laughed.

"What was the last word read?"

Ada swallowed. And swallowed. "Spices," she squeaked. "And I'm sorry, Pa. But you don't have to worry about me coming home with my pants on over my head."

"That's better," Pa said.

Ada's saying it out loud helped. Joan and John could now quit laughing. Slowly they simmered down.

"Na," Pa said, catching them all up with a sweep of his light blue eyes, "let us give thanks to our heavenly Father." Placing his elbows on the table, folding his hands, he rested his forehead on his knuckles. "Oh Lord of the endless skies, in thy infinite mercy look down upon us here, miserable worms that we are, and accept, if thou wilt, our grateful thanks for this food that thou hast given us."

The stove behind Ma cracked with new heat.

Ma breathed heavily through her fat button of a nose on her side of the table.

"Protect our fragile and oh so easily broken bodies from harm. Let sickness stay away from our door. All this we ask in Jesus' name, who died for our sins. Amen."

John followed with his little prayer. "Lord, we thank thee for this food. Amen." Then came Joan. "Lord, we thank thee for this food. Amen."

Ada, then Ma, slowly let their eyes open.

"Da," Baby Sherman said.

"Yes, that's right," Ma murmured, leaning over to kiss him. "You're a good boy."

Ada ❦ 2

ADA SWEPT HER blue cape up around her shoulders. "By, Pa, Ma."

Pa looked up from where he was reading Calvin's *Institutes* in his black rocker. His legs were crossed and one of his slippers had let go at the heel and hung from his big toe. "Be home on time now."

"Yes, Pa."

Ma looked up from her rocker. "What about your feet?"

Ada lifted a foot from under her blue dress. "See? My new buckle arctic boots from Sears Roebuck."

"Bye, then."

Ada closed the door behind her. One hand on the porch pillar, she stepped down off the stoop. She turned up the walk toward church. A light dusting of snow lay caught in the sidewalk cracks. Yellow windows along the block lighted her way. Ahead on the corner near church a single gaslight glowed in its white globe.

Tonight on the way back from catechism Alvin would try to kiss her again. Alvin was getting to be pretty bold lately and twice she'd had to hold him off. She resnugged her hands in her fur muff. She rubbed her chin against the beaver collar of her blue cape.

Ada hoped Alvin would like the Christmas present she'd made for him, a fancy satin puff tie, red and light blue, to match his blue suit. She wondered what kind of gift he was getting for her. She hoped it would finally be their engagement ring, a small rose diamond, with maybe an opal on either side to set it off. The tight jostling of her innards inside her corset gave her a voluptuous feeling.

She turned the corner under the gaslight and headed for their stark white church. Some boys were talking inside the darkness of the wide horse barn door. Behind them a stalled trotter let go with a low whinny.

Just as she reached the crosswalk a horse and buggy came whizzing out of the falling snow and almost ran her down. She caught a glimpse of the driver. Fluit Stokes. The fellow with all those sores on his hands always. "Watch out where you're going, you crazy fool."

With a vicious haul on the lines, so hard that his horse reared up pawing the air, Fluit pulled up beside some other buggies. Before his horse could come down on all fours again, Fluit with a leap was already out of his buggy and unhitching his horse.

"What's the big rush, Fluit?" one of the boys in the barn called.

"That damned Tress of mine has been stepping out on me. And I know who with too. That son of a bitch. I'm going to collar that miserable weasel tonight and shake the ball bearings right out of him."

Ada thought such talk awful. On the churchyard yet too. She hoped brother John wouldn't get mixed up with fellows like Fluit.

Ada took the side door into the annex. On Sunday night the janitor closed off the annex from the main part of the church with a set of dividers. Under a single gas jet lamp the annex made for a cozy meeting place. There was a brisk smell of drying oak benches.

She was just barely in time. Most of the benches were already filled. The big copper clock on the wall showed two minutes to eight. Those boys out in the barn had better hurry if they didn't want to be late.

She looked for Alvin. Then she spotted Minnie Alfredson, sitting at the end of the third row. Ada rustled over. Minnie saw her coming, smiled, and slid up the oak bench a ways to make room for her. Minnie was a doll of a girl, dainty where Ada was tall.

Minnie gave her a sly green smile. "Alvin ain't here yet."

"Can't you let me find out for myself?"

The bunch from the horse barn banged in, stomping snow off their boots, shaking open their fur coats. The loudest was Fluit. He looked boldly up and down the rows, trying to find the fellow who was beating his time with his girl. Apparently the fellow was absent. Fluit next gave his girl, Tressa Applethorn, a black look. Then he sat down with a loud thump.

Reverend Carpenter appeared silently in front of them. He had a way of suddenly appearing like an apparition. He was a short man and for young people's catechism usually wore a gray suit and a subdued red tie. His head, small in back, was big in front, with a wide brow, a wide mouth with thin lips, and wide half-closed gray eyes. He was fifty and had no children. It was said of his lady wife that she couldn't have children. He took up his post directly in front of the catechism class. He liked to get close to his young folk. He glanced at his pocket watch, checked it with the big copper church clock. Right on the dot. He cleared his throat. "Shall we have a word of prayer?"

Ada bowed her head. Where was Alvin? Sick? She hoped not. Ada began to feel a lightness of breath. She feared the lightness of breath might have something to do with her heart. She remembered how faint she used to feel when she had those growing pains in her knees. Reverend Carpenter finally finished praying, and she opened her eyes. Still no Alvin at the door.

Some ten minutes into the catechism, Domeny had a casual question. "Well, Mr. Stokes, I see you sitting there thinking hard about something. Perhaps you can tell us what shape the world is in today."

"Rotten!" Fluit blurted. "Plumb rotten, that's what I say."

Domeny's brows climbed his forehead. "Really? Completely so?"

"Yessir. And it's getting worse by the minute."

There was no laughter. Everybody knew about Tressa's two-timing.

"I take it then you do not quite go along with the president of the local Optimist Club who said the other day that the universe was perfect and that it was getting better by the minute."

Ada was the first to catch the point, and she laughed aloud, merrily.

Reverend Carpenter threw her an appreciative look.

The rest caught on then too. So did Fluit, who turned red.

Someone began stomping snow off his boots outside the door.

Ada turned her head a little, looking past the gray ostrich feather on Minnie's black hat. That had to be Alvin.

The door cracked open an inch. One blue eye peered in.

"Come in, Mr. Ravenhorse," Reverend Carpenter said quietly. "Glad to have you with us even if it is a little late."

Alvin stepped in, handsome face pale, eyes sheepish. Alvin filled the whole doorway with his tall frame. He was taller than Pa. He slipped out of his coonskin coat one arm at a time, and carrying it over an arm, slunk to a seat up front. It was across from where Ada sat.

"Perhaps we should get Mr. Ravenhorse's opinion." Reverend Carpenter bent a smiling look at Alvin. "Can you tell us what shape the world is in today?"

Alvin threw Domeny a look; then looked at his hands.

Ada sat up straighter. Other times when Alvin came late he'd enter the annex with an assured smile, knowing he'd be forgiven because of his mean boss, fat Bart Stoneman, a worldling farmer who made brutes out of his wife and children and who liked to torment his help by always finding some last minute thing to do.

When Alvin continued to sit hunched up, eyes down, Reverend Carpenter wisely switched his attention to a hand raised in the back row.

Ada stared at Alvin. What in God's name had happened to him? Had he finally struck his boss because he just couldn't stand slaving for him any more?

Minnie sensed something was wrong too. Her sly look vanished.

It took hours before Domeny ended the class with a closing prayer. It seemed to take almost as long for everybody to get on their clothes and leave.

And still Alvin sat alone, all hunkered up, looking down at his hands, unable to look at Ada. In the gaslight his thin face looked a fright.

Ada sidled toward him between the benches.

He sensed her coming. He cringed, a black forelock falling across his forehead.

"Alvin?"

He made a squeaking sound.

"What's the matter with you, Alvin? Are you sick?"

He threw her a tortured look.

"What is it, Alvin?"

Alvin groaned.

Ada turned and threw Domeny a puzzled look.

Domeny took a tentative step toward them; then thought the better of it. It was best if Ada and Alvin worked out the trouble themselves.

Ada sat down beside Alvin and placed a soft hand on his arm.

Alvin leaped to his feet. "Let's get out of here." He threw her a wild look. "Outside!"

"Of course, Alvin."

He jerked on his coonskin coat, face averted. He felt twice in his pockets for his fur cap and fur mittens before finding them. Then, mittens in one hand and cap in the other, he bungled out of the bench and headed for the door, not once looking back to see if Ada was following him.

"Good night, Alvin," Reverend Carpenter said. "Good night, Ada."

Alvin said nothing. He stepped through the door into the night.

Ada tried to make up for Alvin's behavior with a pleading smile. "Good night, Domeny."

Outside the snow was falling thicker. A good two inches of it had accumulated on the churchyard. It softened the sound of stomping horses, of young male voices joshing each other, of young girls laughing past their muffs as they formed twos and threes down the walk. Several of the girls hastened out to the four-hole privy behind the church. The carbide lights on the buggies provided the only light.

Ada caught Alvin by the elbow. "What—is—wrong?"

Alvin sobbed; got on top of it. "I wish I could tell you."

Ada's heart beat funny in her throat. "Come, let's start walking home. We can talk about it there."

"But I can't talk to you about it in your house."

It was something really serious then. The big soft flakes fell around them as buoyant as pullet feathers.

Alvin grabbed her by the elbow in turn. "Let me go get my horse and we'll ride around in my buggy for a while."

Ada freed her arm. "You know Pa won't approve of that. He said I was never to go gallivanting through town with the rest of the bunch."

"On our last date, what difference does it make, since after tonight we won't have to worry about what your pa thinks of me."

Ada stopped on the walk. "Alvin, are you trying to tell me you don't love me any more?" Ada stood very stiff and straight. "Because if you are, I want to know about it right here and now."

"Oh God, of course I love you, Ada."

"Then what is it?"

Alvin bent over.

"Alvin. You know you can tell me anything. Anything."

"Not this. You don't know what you're saying. You don't know."

It was pitch dark where they stood. The clopping of fast horses and the crinching of buggy wheel rims on the fresh snow gradually died away. Ada's heart beat so light she was afraid she was going to faint.

"Please, Ada. Come sit with me in my buggy a minute. Under my lap robe. And talk. Because I can't tell you in your house with your father hanging around."

"All right, Alvin. But only for a few minutes."

"That's better. Oh God, yes." He hurried her over to his buggy.

Ada let herself be helped up over the high front wheel and into the seat. Alvin hopped up beside her and bundled them both under a black bearskin robe. All they could see of each other was their faces, pale lemon ovals a foot apart.

Ada's heart beat a strange tiptoe in her throat.

Alvin slipped an arm around her. He clung to her.

"Alvin?"

Alvin looked down. "Oh, girl, I can't. You'll never forgive me."

"In that case maybe I better start for home then."

"No. Wait. Please." He clung to her. "Ada, what I did . . . "

"Alvin, perhaps you should first talk to the Lord about it."

Alvin abruptly let go of her and got out from under the robe. "You stay here. I'm gonna get Duke. You've got to let me take you for a spin around town on our last date. It's silly to be sitting here without a horse in front."

Ada took a deep breath. If it was going to be the last time then maybe Pa wouldn't say too much. "All right, Alvin. This once."

Alvin quick got out his black pacer and hitched him up to the buggy. Duke didn't fancy the falling snow and snorted at it. Alvin hopped in; and they were off on two wheels.

"Not so fast now, Alvin. Going fast always makes me feel faint."

"Hah!" With a snap, Alvin lapped the reins hard across Duke's rolling butt. They spun toward the main drag. Soon they were sparkling past the courthouse where all the other young folks in their buggies were showing off racing with each other. Three times they went spanking up and down Main Street under the globes of light. Duke held his head high. His overhead checkrein hung slack.

Finally Ada said, "I think by now just about everybody has seen us, Alvin. So you can take me home. And please slow down."

Alvin sobbed. He hauled back on the lines and Duke slowed to a moderate pace. Alvin took a side street home to Ada's house.

Duke knew the Engleking hitching post with its iron ring and stopped in front of it. Alvin wound the lines around the whip in the whipsocket. Falling snow softened the orange light in the Engleking bay window.

"Well, Alvin?"

It exploded out of him. "Ada, I knocked up the hired girl."

Ada's cheeks chilled over. It moved down into her neck. Dear Lord. He'd done it then with someone else. Did it while still engaged to her. She had no idea at all what he was like that way. He'd shared that precious part of himself with another girl. Someone who didn't even go to their church.

"It was like this, see. Matty sleeps in a room at the head of the stairs. She always leaves the door open so I can see her reading in bed with her knees up. Under the quilts of course—"

"Alvin, I don't care to hear any more."

"Well, Ada, you always said yourself that your pa should've let us see each other more often. And not just for that measly half hour after catechism either." Alvin groaned. "Oh, if you would've only let me kiss you once in a while. Because I finally just couldn't help myself, and so one night I just went in there and blew her lamp out."

"Don't blame my father for it, Alvin."

"But it's true just the same, Ada."

"Oh, Alvin, that you couldn't wait. Couldn't leave it alone."

Alvin cried. "I know. I know."

Ada found herself sucking for air. If she didn't hurry and get her corset off she was going to faint right there in the buggy. Then the Lord only knew what might happen.

"Oh, Ada, maybe I ought to tell Matty I can't marry her. That it's as much her fault as mine she got knocked up."

"You can't do that."

Alvin hid his face. His voice came muffled through his fingers. "Now I'll never be able to marry you. When I love you so."

Ada spoke through dry lips. "You belong to another woman now and you must not think of me that way any more."

Of a sudden Alvin's arms were around her, and he was hugging her, and sobbing on her neck between the fur of her cape and the edge of her blond hair.

"Alvin. Please. You mussent."

"I don't deserve it, but, Ada, I've just got to touch you once." Next of a sudden Alvin had his mitten off, and then under her long dress his hand slid up into her lap. "Just once." His hand found where her union suit was buttoned in front just under the edge of her corset.

"Alvin! Why!" She let go of her muff and with both hands sought to restrain him. "I'm not yours to touch now."

Alvin began to cry again. His hand fell lax. "I lost you."

"You certainly did for sure now." She pushed his hand away.

"Your father didn't like me anyway. So maybe it's all for the best."

Ada retrieved her muff.

"He never thought I was good enough for you anyway."

Ada had enough. She flipped the robe back, and placing her buckle boot precisely on the rubber step swept to the ground, her blue cape flowing and lifting up. Snowflakes catching in her eyelashes, she marched up the walk, and without looking back entered the house.

Heat from the hard-coal burner touched her brow like a warm fatherly hand. The smell of eau de cologne and homemade bread was reassuring.

Pa and Ma were still up. A rose lamp glowed on the little table between them. The children were in bed.

Ma caught on right away. "Child, you're covered with snow."

Pa looked at his watch. "And you're late."

Ada slowly settled in the nearest chair. Tearless until then, she let herself cry. She didn't bother to hide her face.

"Speak up, daughter," Pa said. "Is it something we should know?"

Ma got mad again. "Must you always be tearing at your daughter so?"

Pa said evenly, "I think I have a right to ask my daughter what she's crying about after she comes home from her date."

"And if she doesn't want to tell you?"

In the midst of her tears Ada gathered that her mother thought that the worst had happened. Ada stood up. "You'd both probably like to know that I won't be seeing Alvin any more. Ever."

Ma lifted her nose. "He didn't get fresh with you?"

"He got fresh with the hired girl where he works."

"What!"

"Yes, he knocked her up"—Ada choked over Alvin's rough language—"and now he's got to marry her."

"Well!" Ma exclaimed. "Of all the crazy things."

Pa let his eyes close.

Ma had to stick it into Pa yet once more. "Well, Baron Engleking, Emptier of Privies, what do you say now about us having to raise our children in this wilderness full of wild boars, hah?"

Ada took off her cape. "And now if you'll excuse me, I'm going to take off this corset. I can hardly breathe." Ada marched upstairs.

Ada ❦ 3

IN THE NEXT days Pa was the one to show some true understanding. He even had a kind word for Alvin. Alvin had at least been an honorable man to stick by the girl he'd got into a family way. Some men, when they realized they'd got a girl in trouble, just skipped the country, went West to take the mischief cure.

Ma couldn't find anything good to say. "That poor hired girl, a lot she has yet to learn, hoo." Ma spoke in the manner of an old complaining brood hen. "A girl can catch a man with face powder all right, oh yes. But to hold a man, then she better know how to use baking powder."

Ada went about her chores numbed. From Minnie she heard about Alvin and Matty's shotgun wedding, about the wild chivaree, how the newlyweds went to Sioux City for their honeymoon, how their boss Bart Stoneman surprised them by offering them an adjoining eighty to rent.

Late in January, when Pa saw that Ada was still taking it hard, he decided to send her to her cousins near Bonnie for a month. His brother John Engleking, married a second time to a widow with one child, had a raft of kids, more than a dozen, most of them still home helping him farm a section of land. Cousin Allie was Ada's age. She'd make her good company. The whole family was on the hearty side and liked to tell jokes.

Once Ada was aboard the train, she was glad she'd left home. She wouldn't have to listen to the endless bickering between Pa and Ma. Pa and Ma were getting to be like the old couple in the weather clock, each with his own door and cool and distant to the other.

Ada had to change trains in Maurice, walking from the Northwestern depot over to the Cannonball depot, where after a half-hour wait she caught the train for Bonnie. When she stepped down off the train at Bonnie at 9:07 P.M., Cousin Fat John was there to pick her up. Pa had telegraphed ahead.

Fat John greeted her with a happy smile. She'd seen Fat John several times at Engleking reunions and had remarked on what a big man he'd become. In his fur coat he reminded her of a big fat bear. Ada liked Fat John. He had a way of saying the unexpected. And he never embarrassed her by remarking on her height. He was the proper heir to the Engleking line all right. Fat John gave her a limp handshake. "Hi."

The weak handshake was the only thing about Fat John she didn't like. Ada recalled that Pa sometimes wondered why it was that the whole batch of Bonnie Englekings never shook hands firmly like a man. It was as if they didn't trust the custom. "Well, John, you look good."

"Maybe Bonnie is a good town for a man down on his luck."

The Bonnie Englekings had once lived in Jerusalem where Uncle Big John had made a living as a livestock commissioner. Uncle Big John hadn't done too well as a commissioner. Thus when his first wife Sarah Rigging died, and he was left with four children, he decided to pull up stakes and start over.

Land agents told him to go where the West Frisian emigrants were settling. The West Frisians were the boys who knew how to make a go of it. They knew one should buy overflow land along a river, having learned how to farm wet ground back in the Old Country. They were all moving into the Bonnie area along the Big Rock and Little Rock rivers. When Uncle Big John got a chance to rent a section of lowlands east of Bonnie, he moved the whole family over by freight car.

The one-eyed locomotive gave a couple of hoarse coughs. Instantly couplings clanged down the line, and then, huffing slowly faster, its iron wheels anguishingly loud, the train pulled out.

Fat John helped Ada into his buggy. He put her suitcase in back. He neatly looped the hitching strap on a hame with a slipknot. He turned up the carbide lights. Then, with a heave that tipped the buggy toward him, he got in beside Ada. He tucked them both in under a horsehide, snug and close. Picking up the black lines with one hand and giving the buggy whip a smart whistling snap with his other hand, he said quietly, "All right, Fly, old girl, let's head for oats and home."

And they did fly. Fly was a long-legged black trotter. In full stride she leaned up off the ground. A cluster of street lights sailed by, a large pale lemon globe above with four little lemon globes beneath. Ada caught but a brief glimpse of Bonnie's main street, a two-story hotel, a redstone department store, a red brick bank.

When they turned east out of the south end of town, they quartered into a northeast wind and Ada had to hold up her fur muff against it.

Fat John said, "Yeh, by morning it'll be way below zero."

Past the edge of her muff Ada caught a glimpse of Fat John's face. His fat cheeks glowed with a healthy red. He was too fat to get cold.

Fly stroked along with a vigorous diagonal gait. When a wheel hit a frozen rut, its rim rang out in a vibrating alto.

Every now and then Fly would lift her flowing black tail a little and let go with a series of little toots. The smell of thoroughly fermented oats drifted back toward them in waves. Sometimes there was the hint of moisture in the smell, as of a fine mist. Ada had to hold her breath in her muff until the string of tootlings was finished.

When it happened for about the fourth time, Fat John finally remarked, "Yep, it don't pay to wear glasses behind a horse that breaks wind."

Ada first choked; then laughed aloud, merrily.

They made the two miles in seven minutes flat. Fly of herself turned into the Engleking lane angling off the road and headed for some willows in a draw and then for the lights of a small compact house.

Fat John pulled up by the front door. Before he could get down to help her, the porch door opened and another big Engleking boy stepped out. It was Cousin Sherm. He too had the nickname of Fat.

"Hope you brought some warm weather with you from the south."

Ada said brightly, "I took some along in my muff."

"Then I'm afraid it's gonna get a lot colder before it gets warmer." Fat Sherm picked her suitcase out of the back of the buggy. "C'mon in. Mem's got the hot chocolate ready."

Fat John saluted and drove on to unhitch Fly.

Fat Sherm led the way inside. There was a smell of just butchered hog fat in the house, freshly fried. There was also the sourish smell of bread. Near the door coals in a big nickel-plated base burner glowed pink just below slow intense blue flames. A black mantel clock on a bookcase showed twenty-five after nine.

Except for the little ones, and someone busy in the kitchen, the Englekings were all waiting around a long table: Uncle Big John at the head with a reddish spade beard hiding half of his chest, Aunt Josephine across from him heavy with child again, Big Paul every bit as huge as Fat John and Fat Sherm, Geer long-armed and surprisingly slender, and little Richard with blond hair like a flow of coarse gold.

Ada stepped around to Uncle John and held out her hand. "Hello, Uncle. Pa said to send you his greetings."

Uncle Big John took her hand like it might be an apple. No pressure. With a single bold glance he read her to the core. And right away liked what he saw. A smile stirred under his vast red beard and big red nose. "Thank you."

Ada held a hand to Aunt Josephine. "And Ma said to send you her compliments."

Aunt Josephine liked what she saw too. "Welcome."

There was an air around the long table that the differences between the two heads of the Engleking families, lanky Alfred and burly John, had been discussed. Alfred was strict religious like Calvin, Big John was hearty religious like Luther. Where Alfred was inclined to be overly conscientious, Big John was quite satisfied with himself. There was also the dark memory between them that when Big John was livestock commissioner, Alfred often had to haul him out of the saloon, drunk, and bring him home. Ada recalled Ma didn't like Big John at all. Ma said he was filthy from chewing tobacco and that he spit brown splotches all over everywhere. Ma claimed that Big John had never worked a day in his life and that he ran things in a lordly way.

Aunt Josephine called to the kitchen. "Bring out the treat."

Two very blond women came out, Cousin Allie carrying a huge steaming pitcher of hot chocolate and Cousin Ada carrying a tray of cups.

Ada was surprised to see her namesake. She had heard that Cousin Ada had separated from her husband, Barry Simmons, because she'd caught him running around with other women, but Ada didn't expect to see her living with her folks again. Her cousin's baby, Frances, had to be somewhere in the house then. How sad.

Cousin Ada set the cups down. She was a good half foot shorter than Ada, and heavy like her brothers. She brushed back a sliding strand of gold hair. A smile worked in her glum face.

Ada threw her arms around her sad cousin and gave her a warm hug. "I've thought about you so often."

"Holy cats, I didn't know the bad news had worked that far south."

Allie, having set the hot pitcher on the table, touched Ada on the elbow. "Hi." Allie was taller than her sister, and quite a beauty, a real cream-fed kewpie doll. She was the first child born to the Big John and Josephine union.

Ada held out a hand. "Allie, you look so happy."

Allie gave her a smile that only someone in love could give.

Fat John came in. He took off his fur coat and hung it behind the door. He came forward rubbing his short broad hands. "Well, Ada, why don't you sit down? Or are we short a chair?"

Ada found a chair between Cousin Ada and Allie.

Uncle Big John, stroking his red beard, looked upon Fat John, his son and heir, with pleasure.

Ada spotted a strange face. He had lean cheeks and dark hair. In the midst of all the other gold-headed Englekings, he stuck out like a blackbird in a flock of orioles. "And who is this?"

Aunt Josephine looked surprised. "You've never met my first born? From my first marriage?"

"No. He never came to the family reunions."

"Well, that's easily fixed. Ada, meet my son Wilmer Youngman."

Wilmer shook hands firmly.

Sipping her hot chocolate, Ada began to wonder about something. "Tante, in such a small house, where in the world do you folks all sleep?"

"We manage," Aunt Josephine said. "We pack the boys in one room and the girls in the other."

"And the little ones?"

"We put them up in a little storeroom at the head of the stairs."

Big Paul wiped chocolate from his lips with the back of his broad hand. "In the wintertime it ain't too bad sleeping five in a bed." He gave Ada a sidelong smile. "At least the three in the middle don't freeze."

What a crew. And all of them her relations. "I see all you boys go to the same barber. Somebody local in Bonnie?"

"It's a local barber all right." Fat John nodded toward his father. "He knows only one style. Sheep clippers all around with a pisspot over your head."

Uncle Big John said, "I save a lot of quarters that way."

It fell out before Ada could bite on her tongue. "You folks seem to have a lot more fun that we do in our family."

Uncle Big John lifted a bronze eyebrow. "So, your father's still eating his heart out over his debts then, eh?"

"Yes."

"Poor Alfred. He took that business of escaping from Bismarck harder than I did. He was only a little boy at the time, you know, and was scared to death of the soldiers chasing us, and of that storm on the Dollart, and of how we almost went down in our little boat. He probably doesn't remember that we once had it real good in East Friesland. All he remembers is the running away and all the poverty in Holland afterwards. That's why we all finally came over to America. To have it good again here someday." Uncle Big John combed his red beard with sure fingers. "And we will. It's in our blood. And it is our right."

It came to Ada that probably the reason why Uncle Big John and his older children didn't shake hands American style was that they came from a higher station in life in the Old Country. Back there Grampa Great John had never had to shake hands. Barons didn't shake hands.

Allie asked, "Don't you have any gay old times in your house at all?"

"Not really," Ada said.

All blue eyes stared at her. Everyone took a sip of chocolate.

"Oh, we get along all right. You know. It's just that the way we live is different. Pa is a wonderful man."

Fat Sherm had an impish smile on his lips. "Yeh, just about anything goes here. In fact there's only one thing we don't do here, and that's fart out loud."

The boys all laughed. Though Uncle Big John sat as if he hadn't heard.

Aunt Josephine looked pretty black at Fat Sherm. "Fooey!" Then she looked at Uncle Big John. Couldn't he control his children like she controlled her Wilmer? "Scandalous."

Fat Sherm didn't care. "But it's true though, ain't it, Ma?"

Aunt Josephine was somewhat appeased that Fat Sherm should call her "Ma." "Around the girls some decency please."

Ada began to feel tight in her corset. That kind of gay old time she didn't want.

Uncle Big John stroked his red beard. "Nah, is there any more chocolary?"

"Enough for one more cup."

Hot chocolate down, everybody got ready to go to bed. The boys went out onto the yard a ways to relieve themselves, while the women scurried out to the cold privy in back.

The girls' room was so small there was just enough room for one big bed. The storeroom where the little ones slept was even smaller, just barely enough room for a three-quarter bed. In the dim night light Ada couldn't get over the sight of all those little gold heads sticking out of the thick blanket in various attitudes of sweet sleep.

It was decided that Allie should sleep in the middle between the two Adas. The three girls spoke low together, sometimes whispering, to make sure the boys couldn't hear them. There was an occasional sound of horseplay from the boys' room.

Ada noticed as they undressed that Cousin Ada was wearing draining rags. That also helped explain why she was so owly. Ada had noticed that she herself could sometimes be a trace crabby during those five days.

Cousin Ada blew out the lamp.

It wasn't long before the tight upstairs became fragrant with the Engleking smell, fleshy, a hint of sweat part-sweet, part-sour.

Allie in the middle every now and then giggled a little. The fleshy part of her arm where it touched Ada was hot.

All of a sudden Cousin Ada from the other side of the bed asked in a sharp whisper, "Allie, has Willie Alfredson popped the question yet?"

"What question?"

"That he'll marry you, you dumb nut."

"No."

Cousin Ada snorted. "Well, all I can say is, you're a damn fool to be letting Willie do it to you before you've got your permit."

"You're just jealous."

"Jealous my ass. Suppose you get a baby, think he'll marry you?"

"Sure."

"Hmp! I know men. Barry didn't me. Pa had to make him."

"Maybe Pa can help me then too, if it comes to that."

"And have Willie hate you for the rest of your life? No, you're better off saying no now, be hard to get. Because if you no him off now, he'll later on think he's got a prize in you. Instead of a burden."

Allie laughed low to herself. It was quite clear she didn't care for her sister's advice.

"You're playing with fire, you know."

"Maybe danger is s'posed to go with fun."

"I'll talk to you again when you're screaming your head off the night your baby comes."

"But it feels so good."

"Famous last words."

Again a dull feeling arose in Ada's stomach. Her girl cousins talking about doing it and getting a baby . . . my goodness. Here she'd been sent to the Bonnie Englekings to try and forget what Alvin had done to that hired girl, Matty.

Ada groaned inwardly. "Oh, Alvin," she thought, "and here I'd been saving myself for you, that precious untouched jewel of oneself that belongs to the Lord."

Cousin Ada lifted her head from her pillow. "Something the matter, Ada?"

Ada caught her breath. Had she talked out loud? She didn't want the Englekings in Bonnie to know what Alvin had tried to do to her.

"Ada?"

"It's nothing."

"You're squirming around there like you're gonna give birth."

"Oh, nothing like that."

Cousin Ada nuzzled down in her pillow. "You better not. It's already pretty crowded in this bed."

Ada thought: "My, they sure can't leave it alone, can they. They're always scratching at that sore. No wonder it's been said of the Englekings that they're descended from 'a race of stingers whose god is Ing.' Swordsmen."

Slowly sleep took over in the packed little house. There were various choruses of snores under the low peaked ceilings.

As Ada drifted off to sleep, she could still feel the place on her leg where Alvin had touched her.

Bright and early Ada got up with the family the next morning. The girls prepared the breakfast while the menfolks chored in the barn. Ada's job was to help cute little Sadie set the table.

When they all sat down to eat, with the pulldown lamp spreading orange light over the center of the long table, Ada was startled to see Cousin Ada carry in a great platter of steak and bacon and sausage, even some river carp, while Allie came in with a wide plate full of tottering stacks of bread. The meat and the bread were set directly in front of Uncle Big John. There were also several dishes of butter, pitchers of milk and cream, and a tall gray pot of steaming coffee. It was the board of a baron all right. The Bonnie Englekings sure ate good. It was a lot different from Pa's humble board back home.

Uncle Big John sat at the head of the table in his high-back swivel chair like a lord. Aunt Josephine sat at the other end of the table in a smaller armchair like a lady. The boys sat in a row on the side nearest the door and the girls sat on the side nearest the kitchen. The youngest child lolled in a high chair next to Aunt Josephine and Cousin Ada's little girl, Frances, sat in another high chair between Cousin Ada and Allie.

First there was a long formal prayer in which the head of the house asked for a blessing on the food and on the work to be done that day. After the solemn "Amen," the children from thirteen on down parroted a child's little prayer, somewhat telescoped by usage."LordblessthisfoodmysoultokeepAmen."

"Nah," Uncle Big John pronounced, "each to his full satisfaction." He tucked his beard under a linen bib, picked up the platter of meat, helped himself to two steaks, a sausage, bacon, then passed the platter on to his oldest son. Fat John in turn helped himself to three steaks, two sausages, bacon, a hunk of carp, then passed it on to the next oldest. The meat platter slowly went down the line. Next came the bread and butter.

By the time the meat platter got to where stepson Wilmer Youngman sat, there wasn't much left: one little carp, four sausages, and several wisps of bacon. Wilmer viewed the remains with a wry smile. "I can see already that if I'm to share what's left with Mem and the girls, we're gonna have to have another miracle of the feeding of the five thousand. And this time with only one fish."

Wilmer's remark came at exactly the wrong moment. Fat John had just filled his mouth with steak and bread. A sudden intake of breath sucked the food partway down his throat. He began to choke. He tried to cough it up; couldn't. He tried with a deeper indrawn breath, which made it all the worse. He turned purple behind the ears.

Ada looked on with alarm. Getting a piece of meat down one's Sunday pipe wasn't something to laugh about.

Uncle Big John's eyes opened like big blue Frisian saucers. Then, pushing back his chair, Uncle Big John raised a hairy hand, along with a vast paunch of a belly, and came down with a whack on Fat John's back strong enough to bowl over a buffalo.

Out popped the obstruction.

Uncle Big John asked, "Better now?"

"Yeh," Fat John managed to gasp. "Thanks."

"That was a near thing, boy."

"Yeh." When he became a normal pink again, Fat John gave them all a rueful smile. "Like I said before, I don't like no jokes at the table when I'm eating."

Uncle Big John quirked a big bronze eyebrow at Ada. "Any of your family have trouble with choking?"

Ada shook her head. "No, Uncle John, not one."

"Hmm. Must come from my first wife Sarah's side then. I once heard they were a family of chokers. Bad throats."

Fat John cut himself another square of meat as well as broke off a good chunk of bread. With a quiet smile he said, "Trouble really is, we're a family of jokers, not chokers." Then he loaded in the same amount as before.

Uncle Big John read a passage from the old leather family Bible. "There was a man in the land of Uz, whose name was Job; and that man was perfect and upright, and one that feared God, and eschewed evil. And there was born unto him seven sons and three daughters. His substance also was seven thousand sheep, and three thousand camels, and five hundred yoke of oxen, and five hundred she asses, and a very great household; so that this man was the greatest of all the men of the east."

Uncle Big John prayed, thanking Jehovah for the wonderful increase of his own family, as well as for the bountiful increase of his possessions. Uncle Big John also had some sage advice for the Lord. Those poachers who'd shot some deer in his upper pasture, and those Coopers who were thinking of breaking away from the Little Church to set up their own Protestant Little Church, and the Kaiser who still persecuted the East Frisians in Germany, and the heathen in China who still persisted in killing the missionaries sent to save them, and those mockers in the back of the church on Sunday who during long prayer shot paper wads over onto the girls' side—all such evil doers should be given a good searing in hell, oh Lord. "In Jesus' name we ask it. Amen."

"Lordthanktheeforthisfoodmybodytostrengthen Amen."

Uncle Big John pushed back in his chair. He got out his heavy curved black pipe from his smoking stand and lit up. Then like a king, stroking his red beard, he sat back, ready to give the orders for the day.

Fat John was the first to get to his feet and stand before him.

"Fat, you take Geer and butcher us a steer today. Ma says we're almost out of fresh meat again."

"Will do." Fat John crooked a finger at Geer and together they went out on the porch and put on their sheepskin coats and boots and disappeared in the direction of the barn.

"Sherman, Paul, you two can haul in some hay from that stack back in the slough. Two loads."

"All right, Pa."

Cousin Ada was next to stand before the head of the house.

"Ada, daughter, you know that so long as you live under my roof—"

"—I'm to do my share of the family work. Yes, I know, Pa."

"Good. Then you and Allie go to your mother for your orders."

The last was stepson Wilmer. But he didn't go stand in front of the king of the Englekings. He waited beside his chair.

"Wilmer."

"Yes."

"Go to your mother for your orders."

Aunt Josephine loved both her autocrat husband and her fatherless son. Her thin lips twitched as she smoothed her green apron over her mound of a belly. "Wilmer, I'm sure Pa's got something for you to do."

Wilmer's gray eyes glinted. He didn't think much of his stepfather's feudal folderol. "Well, Pa?"

To have his stepson call him "Pa" always slowed the old heavy-bellied head of the house. Working his lips as if he were chewing on a tough piece of gristle, Uncle Big John said slowly, "Well, maybe you can harness Swifty for me and bring her up to the door."

"Can I drive you to town, Pa? For once? As a kind of a favor?"

"No."

Wilmer nodded. "I can stay home and do the dirty work. Hah?"

Uncle Big John's red beard ruffed up in anger. "I said, no."

"I won't bother you uptown. I'll stay in the buggy."

"Wilmer!" Aunt Josephine warned. "Do what Pa says."

"All right." Wilmer put on his sheepskin coat, winter cap, red buckle boots, and left the house.

Ada was furious with her uncle. The big Pharisee. Everybody knew why Uncle Big John wanted to go to town alone. It was to tank up at the saloon. Pa said he still sometimes got so deep in his cups that had it not been for his mare, Swifty, he'd not have got home safe. And when Swifty arrived on the yard, she'd stop in front of the house to let Uncle Big John roll out, wait long enough to make sure he'd made it to the door, then head for the barn, where the boys, usually Wilmer, would unhitch her and stall her. Pa said Swifty was a very smart horse. When Uncle Big John sometimes took the train to Sioux City, he'd send Swifty home by herself. When people would try to catch Swifty, she'd just swing out of the way and speed past them.

At last, pipe out, Uncle Big John clapped out the ash, and got out a horehound-colored plug of tobacco and bit off a corner of it. He thrust the bite into the pocket of his cheek. Then he rose ponderously to his feet, grunted himself into his coonskin coat, and went out on the porch step to await his horse and buggy.

No one dared to say a word. All went quietly about their work. The little children, once they were dressed for school, left with low good-byes.

Ada helped her cousins clean off the breakfast table. She felt homesick. This was not the kind of family life she was used to at all.

When the dishes were out of the way, Cousin Ada asked Ada to come along and help her clean the cream separator and the pails in the milkshed. Ada slipped on a borrowed mackinaw and in her own arctic boots followed her cousin out to a little white shack a dozen steps from the house. Each carried a teakettle of boiling water.

The sun was just up, pink and cold. Occasional snow crystals glinted down out of the blue sky.

Cousin Ada glanced at the thermometer hanging in the shade of the milkhouse. "32° below. Whew!"

The two girls pushed into the milkshed. There was a smell of old cottage cheese under the low ceiling.

Cousin Ada began to take the cream separator apart, unscrewing the bowl and taking out the tins. Ada poured some hot water into the milk tank.

Cousin Ada'd worked in silence for a while, then of a sudden said, "Sometimes I'm sorry I divorced Barry."

Ada gasped. "I thought you were just separated from him."

"No, we got a divorce all right. In Rock Falls. It was hushed up." Cousin Ada gave her a twisted smile. "Oh, divorce is not nearly as awful as it's cracked up to be. Once you've got to do it, you do it."

Ada thought of Alvin. Suppose she'd married Alvin the past winter and then later it had come out that Alvin had done it to that hired girl Matty. Would she have divorced him? Awful as it was, she was inclined to think she might have forgiven him.

Cousin Ada said, "Yes, there's never any fun in it for the woman. Hold this cover for me a minute, will you?"

The moment her fingers touched the cold metal cover Ada had to go visit the privy. "Excuse me, but I've got to go somewheres quick."

"Don't sit out there too long or you'll freeze your butt."

On the way back from the outhouse, Ada thought she heard someone playing a harmonica. The sun's reflection on something in a nearby weeping willow caught her eye. It was near the top. Shading her eyes, she finally made it out. A harmonica. Her ears had heard right. Someone had tossed it up there and it had somehow accidentally got hooked on a tiny twig. The light north wind caught it just right to stir up its reeds, low and sad.

When she reentered the milkshed, Ada asked, "Who threw that harmonica up in the willow there?"

Cousin Ada swished the separator tins around in a pan of steaming water. "Fat John. We got him one for his birthday last year, and one hot Sunday afternoon he decided he was going to learn to play it. He sat for an hour in the privy trying to get the hang of it. But when it wouldn't come to him, he finally pulled up his pants and threw the harmonica away. It happened to land up there."

Ada could just see Fat John. It was just like him. "Couldn't somebody else in the family play it?"

"Nobody else was interested."

"Too bad."

"Well, if you're so anxious to hear someone play it, maybe we should get Big Alf to come over and blow on it. He's good at it, he is."

"Who's Big Alf?"

"One of the Alfredson boys. Works for George Pullman north of here."

"You sound like you like this Alf."

"I do," Cousin Ada said flatly. "I'd been better off marrying him."

"Why didn't you?"

"He never asked me. He hangs around with a crowd that goes to country dances, so I didn't get to see him much." Cousin Ada shook her head. "Besides, he probably thought I was too short and fat for him." Cousin Ada allowed herself a mite of a smile. "Man, is he long-geared."

Ada was intrigued. "Taller than me?"

"Than you? Ha. By almost a foot."

There was the sound of some cursing and pounding out on the yard, and of some animal kicking wildly in its harness.

Both girls peered through the door to have a look.

There were Fat John and Geer tussling with a gray mule and behind the mule on the ground with its throat just slit lay a bleeding red steer.

It took several moments for the girls to understand what was going on. The rear feet of the steer were trussed up on a singletree. A rope was tied to the singletree and it led to an overhead pulley in the alley of the granary and then out to another singletree hitched to the mule. Fat John and Geer were trying to get the mule to pull the steer up off the ground so that, head down, its carcass could bleed. Geer was hauling away at the mule by the bridle and Fat John was whaling away at the mule over its butt with a two-by-four. But the more Fat John pounded the gray mule over the more it hung back. Every now and then the mule let go with a violent vicious kick at Fat John, with both rear heels cunningly trying to catch Fat John just as he was at the top of his swing.

"That poor creature," Ada whispered.

"No room for slackers on this place," Cousin Ada said.

Ada thought: "Yes, except for Uncle Big John."

Fat John finally got ticked in the belly by a flying hoof. That did it. Fat John turned a dark red. He dropped the two-by-four, came around in front of the gray mule, and, balling a fist, gave it a pound over its brain. The mule fell down as if struck by a sledgehammer. The falling down jerked the bridle out of Geer's hand. Then, still in a silent thick rage, gnashing his big white teeth, Fat John reached down and grabbed the mule by the bridle and began pulling it in the direction he'd wanted it to go in the first place. The rope to the steer tightened and, miracle of miracles, the steer came up off the ground. When the steer was high enough, Fat John growled between set teeth, "Geer, take a hitch on the rope there. I think we got her where we want her after all."

Geer wrapped the rope around the handle of the granary door.

"That's better." Fat John let go of the mule's bridle and the mule fell to the ground, still stunned.

"Wow!" Geer said, marveling at Fat John's show of power.

"Yeh," Fat John said, slapping his mittens. "I made up my mind Gertie was going to help us even if I had to pull her myself to do it."

Ada burst out laughing. The idea of Fat John making an unconscious Gertie pull up the steer, when he could just as well have pulled up the steer himself in the first place, was pure Fat John. The laughing finally caught Ada so in the side she had to bend over to relieve herself of it.

Cousin Ada resented the laughter. "I don't see what's so funny."

"You don't? Wait'll I tell Pa. Ha-ha-ha. He'll laugh his head off."

"That's not the way I heard it. He never laughs."

That night at nine the family gathered around the long table for a doughnut and a cup of chocolate. The old king sat in his place at the head of the table. His nose was red. Whiffs of alcohol-sopped flesh emanated from his hoary beard.

There was some serious joshing going on between Fat Sherm and Fat John. Fat Sherm resented it that Uncle Big John had declared that Fat John was probably as strong as Samson in the Bible.

Fat Sherm said, "Someday you'll run into a she-mule that'll cut you down to size."

Geer was still smiling to himself in memory. "Gertie just about cut him down this morning as it was. That last kick of hers was a pretty close shave."

Fat John ran a hand over where Gertie's hoof had grazed him.

"You should've seen it," Geer went on. "Even if Gertie had been of a mind to, she couldn't have pulled up that steer any faster than Fat did."

"Hoh!" Fat Sherm scoffed. "That strong Fat ain't."

Blond Geer loved Fat John. He measured Fat Sherm with level eyes. "I'll bet you he can beat you and anybody else you can name pulling on a broomstick."

"Never."

"I dare yuh."

"How about Big Paul and me?"

"The dare still stands."

"Okay. If Fat John is willing."

"Fat?"

Fat John took another bite of his doughnut and pretended to consider the dare. He sipped some steaming chocolate. Then he carefully wiped his lips clean. "All right. But we better use a fork handle. A broom handle will snap in two."

Wilmer laughed. "With all that lard hanging on both sides, you better use a singletree."

Aunt Josephine flashed Wilmer a warning look.

Fat John saw the glance. "It's all right, Mem. Wilmer's right." Fat John gave his belly a slap. "We're all too fat." He smiled at Geer. "There's a manure fork outside the front door there."

Geer got the fork. Coming back into the house, he had a shocked look on his face. "You know how cold it is out there?"

Fat John got to his feet. "Thirty at least."

"Thirty-eight below. Imagine what it'll be by morning."

Uncle Big John immediately began to button up his black vest. "Wilmer, more coal in the base burner. And more cobs in the kitchen stove."

Wilmer did as he was told, a hostile smile on his mobile lips.

Fat Sherm took the fork and settled down on an oval rug. "Paul, get down here with me."

"Not on my new rag rug," Aunt Josephine cried. "You'll tear it to pieces with your comical stunts."

Uncle Big John agreed. "Over there on the bare linoleum."

Fat Sherm and Big Paul took up positions opposite Fat John with the fork handle between them. Fat Sherm placed the soles of his two shoes against the sole of Fat John's right shoe and Big Paul placed the soles of his two shoes against the sole of Fat John's left shoe. Holding the fork handle level between them just above their toes, Fat Sherm got a grip on the handle near Fat John's right hand and Big Paul got a grip near Fat John's left hand.

Uncle Big John rolled up closer in his swivel chair to be the judge. "All set?"

"Yup," all three grunted.

"All right. One, two, three, pull!"

The three boars leaned back for all they were worth. They strained. They fought to keep their knees from buckling. Faces turned a mottled red. The fork tines glittered in the yellow light. Calluses crinched on the shiny handle. Overalls tightened to the breaking point over fat oblong hams. There were groans. Once a compressed fart.

At last the butts of both Big Paul and Fat Sherm slowly came off the floor, one inch, two inches.

Fat John gave yet another massive pull and Big Paul and Fat Sherm came to their feet on the run.

"He's like Samson all right," Uncle Big John pronounced.

Fat Sherm's sulky lips pushed out. He took the fork from the other two. "You don't pull fair, Fat."

Fat John got to his feet. "How so?"

"Letting one like that. You know that always makes me laugh."

"Better check your own shirttail. First to notice it is last to admit it."

Fat Sherm reddened all over once again. He stood with the manure fork in his hands. The tines glittered in the lamplight.

Fat John settled in his chair. "C'mon, Fat, take a load off your feet."

"No." Fat Sherm reached over Fat John with the fork and speared up a doughnut from the pile on the cookie dish.

"Nah, nah," Aunt Josephine scolded. "What will Ada think?"

Fat Sherm plucked the doughnut off the fork tine with his teeth. "I don't care what she thinks."

Uncle Big John didn't like it either. "You know where that fork's been. Take it outdoors, Sherman."

Still sulking, Fat Sherm set it to one side in the kitchen.

Wilmer stretched. "Guess it's about time to go see if the stars are still in place." Wilmer picked up the fork and took it outside with him.

Ada sat with a smile on her face. What a funny family these Bonnie Englekings were.

A few minutes later Wilmer came back inside. As he closed the door behind him, he involuntarily shivered.

Ada saw the shiver. "Is it really that cold out there?"

"Ada, it's so cold out there that the water I just passed froze into a rainbow before it could hit the ground. And if you don't believe me, go have a look. It's standing there just outside the door."

Ada had to laugh and laugh. She finally laughed so hard she slid out of her chair onto the linoleum floor.

"Well, well," Uncle Big John said with a smile, "someone from my brother's family can actually laugh a little."

"Yeh," Cousin Ada said, "from the way she acted when she first got here, I didn't think she knew what a pisser was."

"Nah, nah," Aunt Josephine said, "mind your manners."

Fat John wiggled his ears. "What you meant was, you didn't think she knew what a coupling pin was. That's a little more decent."

Ada ❦ 4

SATURDAY NIGHT THE Engleking gang piled into a carriage and drove up the back road to the Stallings' a mile and a half to the north. The Stallings bunch had invited the neighborhood young over for a shindig. John, Sherm, Paul, and Geer rode up in front; Cousin Ada, Allie, and Ada sat in back. Wilmer didn't come along. He had a date with a neighbor girl. It wasn't very cold out, about twenty above, and everybody rode warm in their sheepskins and muffs.

Two lanterns burned on the Stallings' yard, one by the house and the other by the barn. Various rigs were lined up along the feedlot fence. Fat John tied their team at the end of the line. Up in the haymow someone was playing the harmonica as though to a long lost friend.

The Englekings entered the barn and headed down an alley toward a wooden ladder. Because of all the stomping above, the air below was filled with hay dust. Coughing, the Englekings climbed the ladder one after the other up into the haymow.

A half dozen lanterns lighted the whole loft. Raw wood rafters, dulled by time, angled starkly up toward an iron hay-carrier rail under the peak. Hay as well as shoe leather had polished the old fir floor to a glossy brown. Here and there beads of hard rosin gleamed like carnelian. The old wood smelled like pressed wild roses.

Young girls sat on improvised benches under the angled rafters. Young men stood around in groups, smoking, telling stories.

Four couples were out on the floor whirling through the set turns of a square skip tune known as "Two Old Maids." An old man with a gobbler neck was calling the dance while a tall young man was whumpfing it up on a long silver harmonica.

Ada drew back. "But this is dancing."

"Sure," Fat Sherm said, "what did you think it was."

"But you said a shindig."

"Sure," Fat Sherm said, making a motion as though to kick her in the shins, "what else?"

"I thought it would be just something where we'd play parlor games. And maybe you boys would play your stunts. Maybe even have a good serious talk before the evening was over. And then of course refreshments."

Fat Sherm laughed. "Oh, there'll be refreshments all right. Those boys over there ain't just telling stories."

Ada paled. "You mean . . . whiskey?"

"Oh no. We don't drink." Fat Sherm snickered cynical. "Pa already does enough of that for our family."

Ada was sorry she asked. "I think I better leave. I'll walk home."

Cousin Ada took her by the arm. "Oh, come on now. Are you really that afraid of your pa?"

"I'm more afraid of my Maker."

"Same difference."

Ada caught the pun. Cousin Ada sure had a sharp tongue. "Isn't this the kind of place where you met Barry Simmons?"

"Oh, Ada, don't be such a damp rag now, for catsakes. Enjoy life. It's so much fun to have two legs."

The whumpfing on the harmonica worked on Ada. She found herself looking at the tall musician blowing away. She noted his wavy ink-black hair, his strong pink nose, and, when he opened them for a fleeting moment between phrases, his deep-set gray eyes.

Cousin Ada saw where she was looking. "Isn't he a good player? I sure wish I would've waited for him. Alfred Alfredson."

"He can play all right."

"You should see him skip the squares when Old Wickett saws on the squeakbox. Those long legs of his work like flying scissors."

Allie was looking at Big Alf too. "He's even better on skates. Like his cousin Willie."

Ada threw Allie a guarded look. "You mean the Willie that . . . "

"Yes. That one." Allie's tongue showed pink for a moment.

Ada shivered. Riding in a buggy with a man it always wound up with him trying to get into one's pants. Ada put her nose in her muff.

Big Alf swung into a new tune and Old Wickett called it out:

"Dive for the oyster, hump, hump,
Dive for the clam, hump, hump,
Down and up, up."

Cousin Ada and Allie were invited out onto the slick floor by local boys. Fat John and Fat Sherm next sought out partners. Ada saw that the Bonnie people liked her cousins. That was certainly a lot different from home. There only the church people had time for Pa's family.

Quickly four squares were formed. The brown hay floor creaked, emitted puffs of straw dust from between its cracks, swayed in the center when the heavy Englekings all happened to gyrate near each other on the turns.

The smell of dried wild roses became stronger than ever.

Ada sat down on a plank bench. She would have to suffer through it somehow. Oh, Pa. Already she feared his piercing look.

The two Stallings boys across the haymow had been eyeing Ada and when they saw her sitting alone they decided to try their luck. They shallied up to her, blond heads lowered a little, raw hands at their pockets by the thumbs. They were powerful louts, broad and thick through the shoulders.

The taller one spoke first. "I'm Bart Stallings. How about making up a fifth square with us?"

"I don't dance. My feet are too big."

The other Stallings thought her a card. "I'm Hector. My feet are too big too. Dance with me if you don't fancy my brother."

"No. Really. I don't dance."

"You're kidding us."

"No. Honest. I don't even know how."

"It's easy. Just keep your head up like you've been checkreined. And keep your feet on the floor. That's all there is to it."

Ada could feel her face whiten back over her cheeks.

Old Wickett's fipple voice rose an octave. It pierced through the loud stomping of leather soles:

"Circle four in the middle of the floor.
Dive for your oyster and down you go."

Ada decided the best thing to do was just to leave and hope to find some high-minded person up at the house. She stood up so quickly her blue cape swirled up and away from her shoulders.

The shorter Stallings fell back a step. "Jesus, I'd heard you was tall. Why, you're taller than my brother Bart here."

Ada flinched inside her tight corset. Somehow she managed to say gently, "It's probably just my high heels."

Hector quickly recovered. "Oh, but I don't mind. The bigger you are the more you can do."

"Sorry."

Bart took her familiarly by the arm. "I don't mind 'em tall either."

Ada firmly withdrew her arm.

"What's going on here?" a winning male voice asked.

Ada had to look up. It was the black-haired harmonica player, Alfred Alfredson. It took her a moment to realize that while she'd been fending off the Stallings boys, the music had changed. Old Wickett was now working the fiddle and someone else was calling the squares.

The Stallings resented the butting in. "You keep out of this, Alf."

"I still say, what's going on here?"

Ada said, "I don't believe in dancing."

"Well now, lady, this really ain't dancing, you know." Alfred smiled down at her. "It's only skipping."

Ada gave Alfred a slow measuring look. "Sir, you know very well that in the eyes of the Lord there really is no difference."

Alfred's deep-set eyes took on the light blue intensity of coal fire. "But what if I think both dancing and skipping are okay?"

"Both are of the world."

"How come then so many of your Little Churchers are here?" Alfred waved a long arm at the skippers. "The Pipps, the Lemons, the Tammings, the Ettens, the Fabers, the Coopers—they're all here."

"I can't speak for them. What church do you go to again?"

"I go to the Congregational. With the George Pullmans. When they go."

"When they go. Why, you heathen you."

Alfred burned another look at her. "Lady, you're going to be a mighty surprised little gal come Judgment Day when you discover there'll be as many Congregationalists up in heaven as Little Churchers."

"Then you approve of wild goings-on?"

"Lady, there ain't a woman in the world I can't look in the eye. I've kept my nose clean. And I'm proud to be able to say it, too."

Ada thought: "Good." Ada liked having to look up to him. He appeared to be even taller than Alvin. For once she felt dainty.

Bart again took Ada possessively by the arm. "First come first served. That makes Ada mine."

Ada once more withdrew her arm, this time with a flash of anger. "I shouldn't have come here in the first place. I didn't know what a shindig was. I'm sorry, but dancing and drinking are against my religion."

Bart gave her a mocking look. "What do you do for fun?"

"Sing."

"Sing?"

"Yes. I love my Lord and I take delight in singing his praises."

The Stallings boys fell off a step. They stared at her.

Ada pushed her arm all the way through her muff and grabbing hold of the top rung of the ladder started to go down.

"Let me help you," Alfred said in a kinder voice.

"I can manage it."

"You sure?"

"Yes. Thank you just the same."

Alfred watched her climb down. "Bye."

"Bye."

Ada hit the floor below in the alley. Old hay crinched underfoot. Puffs of a faded alfalfa bouquet rose around her. The lantern light gave the wooden stanchions the look of pillars of gold.

Ada stood in thought. The violin whined and moaned upstairs. The caller intoned his do-si-dos. Feet stomped and skirted at the corners.

In the vague lantern light she spotted an old chair in a harness room on her right. She pushed through a swing-door, careful not to let it touch her dress, stepped over some fallen horse collars, and then, brushing off the chair with her muff and snapping the muff free of dust, carefully sat down.

She sat alone, resigned. The dancers upstairs danced to a tune called "Shoot That Pretty Girl Through To Me." She could just make out in the semidark a huge spiderweb stretching from a harness peg to a hame knob. Dust particles in the old web glowed like old burned-out stars. There was a soft smell in the air of old shriveled leather.

When the Engleking gang arrived home at one o'clock, they found Uncle Big John and Aunt Josephine still up, toasting their feet on the nickel railing of the hard-coal burner. Uncle Big John was reading some poetry by Gysbert Japicx and Aunt Josephine was reading the church weekly *The Watchman*. Both looked at the clock when the bunch trooped in.

Uncle Big John placed his book upside down over his knee. "Well, did you all have a good time?"

Fat Sherm held his hands out over the stove. "All except Ada."

"Oh?" Uncle Big John quirked a grizzly look at Ada. "And why not her?"

"She says having a good time is against her religion."

"Is her religion so different from ours?"

Ada said, "I hope not."

Uncle Big John fixed her with a piercing look. "So, you're too good for our Bonnie parties, eh?"

"I don't approve of dancing."

"Why not?"

"It may lead to the temptation of the flesh." Ada stood by the stove.

"Didn't King David once dance up before the Lord into Jerusalem?"

"That was for those times. And it was for joy."

"Then when young people dance these days it isn't for joy?"

Ada didn't know how to answer that. Her uncle continued to surprise her. He was smart.

"The Bible is wrong then when it tells us to 'praise Him with the timbrel and dance'?"

"Where does it say that?" Ada took comfort in the warmth of the stove.

"Psalm 150."

"Dancing the way they do now, I still think it's sinful."

Uncle Big John shook his head. "That's where your father and I part company. I happen to believe that God gave us a body to enjoy ourselves in, so long as we don't abuse it. And I'm afraid your father doesn't think much of this gift—" Uncle Big John struck his chest a clap—"our body."

That was a good point.

Uncle Big John said, "Your father . . . you couldn't get him to loosen up and have a little fun. He was like a clock that had been wound up too tight."

Ada shifted ground. "Then you don't think pouring poison into this gift from God is wrong?"

"Hmm." Uncle Big John reddened a little just above his great beard. "In that miracle of the marriage feast, I wonder how Jesus explained to His Father all that extra wine he made for the guests?"

Ada came up with a counter text. " 'Behold a gluttonous man, and a wine bibber, a friend of publicans and sinners.' "

An old smile moved in Uncle Big John's red beard. "But that was said by the Pharisees, when they pointed a finger at Christ for partaking of wine on occasion."

"Where does it say that?"

"Luke 7, verses 30 to 35." Uncle Big John's beady eyes fastened on her bosom for a moment.

Fat John stepped into the living room. He sensed instantly that an argument was going on. "I hope you guys haven't been ragging Ada. It's her business if she doesn't care to dance."

Cousin Ada couldn't resist getting in one last stinger. "Ada, why don't you join the Catholic Church and become a nun?"

Fat John growled, "I said not to rag Ada."

Uncle Big John slowly ran his tuber fingers through his beard. "The trouble with my brother Alfred is, he's taken the vow of the Nazarite, so that he can't even eat moist grapes, let alone raisins."

Ada glanced at the book her uncle was reading. "Is that what that book teaches?"

"Gysbert Japicx? Oh no. Gysbert tells of Raemer, who hungers to go out into the country where he can find simple and honest people."

"Now, Pa," Fat John warned.

The next day, around sunset, as Ada was crossing the yard with a bucket of eggs, she was startled to hear harmonica music again. She looked over at the willow. But the sound wasn't coming from there. It was coming from behind her.

She turned around, her boots making a nubbing sound on the frozen ground. There down the back north road came a horse and buggy.

Alfred Alfredson. The playing had his peculiar style. She remembered that the boys had mentioned Alfred liked to drop by on his Sunday off.

The spanking buggy rolled through a dip in the back road and half disappeared; after a moment rose to view again. It was Alfred all right. He had spotted her crossing the yard with a bucket of eggs and had quick whipped out his harmonica and had begun playing for her benefit.

She was afraid she was going to faint. Ever since she'd had growing pains at twelve, she'd every now and then felt a lightness of breath. She'd felt it when she first started seeing Alvin.

She thought to herself: "He better not catch me standing here in the middle of the yard." She tucked her nose under her shawl and scurried into the kitchen.

Cousin Ada was standing by the window. She had parted the curtains with a finger and was peering out. "There's your boyfriend and his fast stepper Daise, Ada."

It slipped out before Ada could bite her tongue. " Wonder what that silly fool wants around here?"

"Listen. Hear him playing the harmonica? There's your answer."

Allie came floating into the kitchen. She too peered out through the parted curtains. "I wish Willie could play like that."

Ada finally had to have another look at this Alfred Alfredson.

One of the boys had heard Alfred coming and had opened the gate for him. Alfred rolled through, still playing his harmonica, his long fingers opening and closing like the bill of a pelican. The hard pop pop pop of the trotter's hooves hitting the frozen ground underscored the playing like an accompaniment on a snare drum.

"Look at him," Cousin Ada said. "All duded up. Even his horse."

Alfred was wearing a black hat, black tie, black suit, and tan coonskin coat. His roan mare had been gotten up stylish too, with a gleaming black harness, and high hames sticking up like a pair of silver horns. A motley array of celluloid rings spangled Daise's checkrein. The rose sunset mellowed the colors of the rings: maroon and white and blue and yellow. Alfred had tied the lines around the stock of the whip in the whipsocket and let Daise run free. The horse breasted straight for the house door.

Ada listened. That tune. It was almost blasphemy.

Cousin Ada gave her a sour look. "I'd consider myself a pretty darn lucky woman if he was calling on me. Enough so that I wouldn't laugh at him."

"Maybe he's coming to see you."

"Not a chance."

Yes. Alfred was trying to shine up to her all right, playing that hymn, "Ninety and Nine," instead of one of his skip tunes.

Daise pulled up at the hitching post outside the front door. Then Daise lowered her head. She'd come to the end of a stint well done.

Alfred spotted the girls in the window. It made him plumpf his long fingers with even more of a flourish.

Allie caught on too. "Why," she cried, and she started to laugh, "Alf's playing a hymn for you, Ada. Has he ever set his cap for you."

Cousin Ada let the curtains fall. "A soft answer turneth away wrath."

Allie hugged Ada. "Well, aren't you going to ask him in?"

"He can knock first," Ada said. "If he's coming to see me."

"Atta girl, Ada," Cousin Ada said. "Play hard to get. I wisht I had."

Allie gave Ada another hug. "Wait till he gives you a hickey. That'll change your tune. Especially if he gives you one under the ear."

Ada had never heard of a hickey. But she wasn't going to admit it.

The harmonica fell silent. Allie took another peek through the curtains. "Oh, shucks, he's going out to the barn first."

"Maybe he won't even come in the house," Ada said.

"Oh, he'll come in the house all right," Cousin Ada snorted. "When it's time to eat. Sundays there's always a lot of hired men running around the country looking for a free meal on their day off."

"Speaking of free meals," Aunt Josephine said suddenly in the doorway behind them, a hand supporting her belly, "the boys will soon be in from chorsing. Get busy."

"Ya, Ma."

After Aunt Josephine left, Cousin Ada explained, "Sunday or not, milking's always started right on the dot. Six on six. Pa'll even cheat a little when he gives thanks so as to start the milking on time."

"Why must it be so precise?"

"If you don't milk a cow regular hours, she'll dry up on you."

Cousin Ada got out a quarter of a hog and began cleavering out a row of pork chops on a meatboard. Allie got the potatoes out of the cellar and began peeling them. And Ada cut bread on the breadboard, slice after slice, until she'd built up three mounds each a foot high. Ada noted that her aunt's bread smelled about as sour as her own mother's bread. It wasn't at all appetizing. Some of it was still lumpy with wet dough. Someday, when she was the mother in her own home, Ada resolved she'd have bread as light as a sponge.

The lamps were lighted when Alfred entered the house with the boys at five. The several golden flames gave the old house cozy shadows. Young faces took on shadows and old faces appeared young. The voices of the little children were like the cooing of doves about to be given grain.

As the family gathered around the table, Ada lingered behind in the kitchen. She still felt light in her chest.

"Niece?" Uncle Big John called. "We're waiting."

"Coming."

Brushing down her blue dress, Ada moved to her place next to the girls at the foot of the table. She avoided looking over at where Alfred sat in the guest's chair to the right of Uncle Big John.

"Well, niece." Uncle Big John bent a wise bearded smile her way. "Aren't you going to say hello to the company?"

"Hi," Alfred said across to her.

Ada gave Alfred a brief look and a nod.

Uncle Big John asked the blessing.

After the last amen, as Ada opened her eyes, she couldn't resist another look at Alfred. His dark head stood out among all the pink blond heads like a black sheep amongst pure white sheep. He was every bit as dark as stepson Wilmer Youngman. Under that black wavy hair Alfred's cheeks and strong jaw had the look of hard red winter apples.

Ada finally caught eyes with Alfred when they were well into the supper, and then she discovered he was about as flustered as she was. He immediately looked down at his plate.

It was going on six and everybody ate in a hurry and in silence.

When all had finished, Uncle Big John chose a short psalm to read. "The Lord is my shepherd, I shall not want." And for once in his prayer he skipped giving the Lord advice on how to run His various projects on earth. By six the big boys were out of the house and milking.

Alfred lingered behind. Uncle Big John wanted someone to talk to over a pipe of tobacco. The two of them turned their chairs to face the slow blue flames in the hard-coal burner.

The girls finished cleaning up in the kitchen at about the same time that the boys finished separating the milk in the milkhouse. It was still an hour before catechism, and except for Ada, everyone gathered around the blue-titted fire in the base burner. There was a lot of lively joshing, about who was going to catechism, as well as who was stepping out with whom afterwards.

Ada still lingered in the kitchen. She decided Aunt Josephine's tumblers could use some extra polishing. She held the glasses up to the light one by one looking for smudges.

A footstep sounded on the linoleum behind her. "Well," a winning male voice said, "I see my lady does as my lady is."

A bubble caught square in her throat.

"I sure like to see a lady who doesn't mind a little work. Not one of your lazy lizzies. Fol-de-rol."

Ada had to smile. She carefully set a tumbler in its proper place. She turned to face Alfred. "Aren't you a little lost visiting Little Churchers on a Sunday?"

"What do you think I should be doing on Sunday?"

"I don't know. Go to your pool hall maybe."

"Baseball on Sunday, maybe. But a poolroom bum, nope, not me."

Ada frowned. And frowning, she got control of herself. Baseball? "Do you really play ball on Sunday?"

"Nope. Not good enough. I got a good curve, but I'm too slow afoot. Ever since I stuck a hay knife into my knee." Alfred patted his right knee.

"How did that happen?"

"It was my own fault." Alfred relaxed. "Shouldn't work outdoors when it's thirty below. But you know how it is when you're a kid. I had to go. Wal, I was sawing off a hunk of this haystack, when all of a sudden the hay knife hit a piece of ice. So I decided to really jab the hay knife down through it, and then, just as I started the knife down, a gust of wind caught me and I missed the groove, and ran the point of the hay knife right down into my knee here instead. Wicked fish-teeth edge going right through the overall and into the bone. It stuck in hard there too, tight. I had to give it two big yanks to jerk it out. And then, gotske, did it bleed. I bled like a stuck hog."

"What did you do then?"

"I wrapped my belt around my leg and hopped home on one foot as fast as I could. Doc had to put in twenty-eight stitches."

"You don't limp now though."

"I was lucky. But I can't run worth a lick."

"Maybe that was the Lord's way of letting you know you shouldn't play baseball on Sunday."

"Could be. Though it's sure funny there ain't been any more fellows sticking a hay knife into their knee."

Ada liked Alfred's openhanded manner. He might sound a bit simple, but through it all there ran the suggestion of a slow country smile.

"Say, Ada, the reason I came in here is" — Alfred's long face turned pink— "well, how about my lady riding with me to catechism tonight?"

"But I thought you were a Congregationalist?"

"I am. But this once it won't hurt to go to your church, will it?"

"Well, I don't know. My father doesn't like it if I go riding around in buggies with young men on Sunday night."

Alfred's high nose lifted a little. His eyes slowly became a sharp gray. "How did your pa and ma manage to get married without getting acquainted?"

Ada had to laugh. Yes, just when had Pa courted Ma?

"Well?"

"Alfred, it's just that Pa doesn't know you and when I tell him I went out riding with a strange boy in Bonnie, he'll—

"—think the worst, won't he? Wal, there's only one thing for it then, and that's for me and Daise to drive up to Jerusalem some weekend and let him look me over."

Ada had never met a fellow like this. Tall and dark. With the rangy grace of a race horse. Aristocratic even. Full of music. That Congregationalist George Pullman couldn't be such a bad worldling boss for him after all.

"I'll bring you straight home here."

"I don't know what to say."

"Tell you what. I'll tell your dad myself what we did. Flat out."

"You don't have to do that, for goodness gracious sakes."

"Then you'll come along with me and Daise?"

A sigh lifted her chest. Alvin Ravenhorse was lost to her forever. What he'd been to her would be caught in her brain like the hint of a perfume still lingering in an old dress put away in a hope chest. She wanted to be loyal to that scent, at the same time that she was intrigued by this Alfred.

Alfred stepped closer. "Wal, it's about time to go."

"Oh, all right." It was wrung out of her.

"Good. I'll get up Daise."

"You'll stick close to the bunch? I can trust you?"

"Lady, with me a promise is a promise. I ain't never fudged on one yet."

All went well. The weather wasn't too bad, not much wind, and no snow. The road, iron hard with frost, was as smooth as a floor.

Fat John let out the trotters a little near the Tamming lane to see if he could pass Alfred. But the trotters hitched to the carriage were no match for Daise hitched to a buggy. Alfred had only to say, "Daise!" and Daise took off. Alfred didn't even have to wiggle his whip. The cousins in the carriage cried in high glee at the fun.

Catechism in Bonnie wasn't much different from catechism back home. The same sort of boys talked rough in the barn. The same kind of girls giggled behind muffs inside the church. And Reverend Graves, a muscular man who reminded Ada of Luther, hearty, with a twinkle in his eye, asked the same sort of questions Reverend Carpenter asked and then shaped the dialogue around the affirmation of Christ.

One sad thing happened. As most of the girls started walking up the street in groups of twos and threes toward the bright lights uptown, Allie decided to wait for Willie Alfredson on the steps outside the south door. When Willie finally did hitch up his horse, he didn't whirl up to get Allie, but instead set sail after one of the fast Tillman girls already some ways up the street. And Allie, dejected, had to climb into the carriage with her brothers and ride home with them.

Alfred and Ada whirred along behind the carriage.

Pretty soon Alfred said, "Allie is better off without him anyway."

"If she can forget him."

Alfred adjusted the buffalo robe over their laps. "Willie is my cousin but I have to say it. He's woman-crazy. Always was."

"He holds her cheap then."

"You should hear him talk about her in the church barn. What he done to her up in her old man's haymow when everybody was to church."

"He was probably only bragging."

"No, he was telling the truth all right. He could never have made up all them things he said he done to her."

"I don't believe it."

"Wal, Allie is a little loose, you know."

Poor Allie. Now she'd probably have an awful time getting a man. Her only chance would be if some boy from some other town came courting her and nobody happened to tell him the gossip about her.

Alfred spoke more to himself than to Ada. "It's in the Engleking blood. They've all got that hot hair. Every last one of 'em."

"Mister Alfredson. Please."

"Wal, they ain't called the trembling Englekings for nothing, you know. With their white-gold hair in their eye."

"Alfred, I prefer to think we're all covenant children and that a covenant child behaves himself."

"Mabbe so. But Allie's still loose."

Daise had been waiting for Alfred to ease up on the lines a little so she could pass the Engleking carriage. Daise liked having a clear view. Finally, when Alfred didn't give her the rein, she took off on her own. She whistled past the carriage.

"Your horse likes to chase," Ada remarked.

"She can't stand to have anybody ahead of her. Gotta be first."

"Like horse like master?"

"Wal, I don't always like to suck the hind tit."

"Mister Alfred Alfredson. Really. Such language."

A train whistled south of them. It could be heard distinctly over the patter of Daise's hooves and the crinching of the wheels on the frozen ground. The whistle rose and fell several times, moaning, wailing.

Alfred cocked an ear. "Listen to that engineer. He sure knows how to play that steam engine whistle. Like it was a mouth harp."

"That must be the same train I came on."

"The 9:07 and right on time."

"Oh. That means it's after nine then."

"I get it. Your pa wants you home by nine, doesn't he?"

"I'm afraid so."

"When I see him I'll tell him it was my fault. He can blame me."

"That's nice of you, Alfred. But Pa will not hold me guiltless, especially after I agreed to go along with you in the first place."

Alfred shook his head. "For the life of me, I just simply can't see that it's such a sin to ride in a buggy with me."

Ada took her hand out of her muff and touched Alfred's arm. "Alfred, please." She liked touching him.

"Wal, I'll look him in the eye and tell him what I think."

"Before you drive up to see me in Jerusalem, Alfred, you'd better think about a couple of things first."

"Can't I see you again next Sunday at the Englekings here?"

"I'm going home Wednesday."

"Oh."

"I don't think you should plan on seeing my pa about me until you've made a few changes in your life."

"Name them. Fire away."

"Well, I can't marry a man who fiddles at squareskip things."

"Anything else?"

"And the way I believe, I can't very well marry anybody from another church. It has to be somebody from my church. It's better that way."

"Anything else?"

"Do you chew tobacco?"

"Once in a while."

"That's a filthy habit."

"Your uncle chews."

"I know it. And I think it's just awful of him."

"And my boss George Pullman chews. And he's the high nuts around here."

Ada shuddered. "And, I can't abide rough language. Shame on you. You had better wash out your mouth with soap tonight when you get home."

Alfred laughed. "Why wait that long? I'll let you wash it out when we get to the Englekings now."

"Alfred, I'm serious." This man didn't date girls much? Where did he get all that self-confidence around girls then?

"I'll talk to Daise about it on the way home after I drop you off. See what she says."

"A horse?"

"In a manner of speaking. I like to talk to myself when I ride alone. And Daise hears me."

"Oh." Ada smiled to herself. What a singular fellow this Alfred was.

The Engleking gang invited Alfred in for a cup of hot chocolate. "A warm cup for the road."

"Wal," Alfred said with a smile up one side of his face, "we better ask Ada here for her permission. She's pretty strict."

All the Englekings chuckled.

"Wal, Ada?"

"Fine with me."

Alfred helped Ada down. Then he got out a cooling blanket and threw it over Daise. He buckled up the surcingles snug. Daise let him fuss over her like a child being given its favorite blanket.

They were all sitting around the table, joking, sipping the last of the hot chocolate, when Allie, having recovered from the snub given her at church, remembered they had an old fiddle upstairs in the attic.

Fat John woke up from what appeared to be a little nap between swallows. "Say, get it, and let's have Alfred play us a few tunes."

"But on Sunday?" Aunt Josephine wondered.

Uncle Big John let the spring of his armchair bring him forward, wide beard and big belly and all. "Get it, Wilmer."

Wilmer got to his feet. "For once I don't mind being picked on."

"No dancing though," Aunt Josephine warned.

"The children can't 'praise him with the timbrel and dance'?"

"No dancing," Aunt Josephine said in her flat-out Frisian manner. "I'm setting my foot down on that."

Ada was relieved. It would have been awful to have to report to Pa that her cousins danced on Sunday in their own home.

Alfred examined the varnished surface of the old fiddle, its fragile bridge, its tight black pegs, and with a pleased look announced that it was still a pretty good one. The strings were slack and he carefully brought them up to pitch, critically, according to some inner tuning fork in his head. The horsehair on the bow was slippery and he rubbed on some rosin.

Alfred fitted the violin rest under his strong chin and began sweeping the bow back and forth with some practice runs. He paused a moment, eyes rolling behind closed lids. Then smiling a little to himself, with a swift look at Ada, he brought forth a lovely tune.

Ada smiled too. He was playing "Ninety and Nine."

Everybody fell silent, listening intently, caught up in the sweet wailing sound.

Alfred paused. He adjusted the peg on the A string.

With another swift glance at Ada, Alfred began a new song. The fingertips of his left hand, especially his pinky, pinned down the notes with precision, vibrating slowly.

Ada knew the song. She thought the words to herself:

"Aura Lea, Aura Lea,
Maid of golden hair."

Ada found herself admiring the way his fingertips danced on the fingerboard. For a big man he had a wonderful touch. She could picture him touching her. He would make a kind lover. The orange light from the pulldown lamp fell on his fingers just right for her to see that his nails were neatly clipped and clean. All the other fingernails around the table—Fat Sherm's, Fat John's, all of them—had dark funeral rings from milking. Filthy. Alfred must have taken particular pains to scrape out the milking marks with a pocket knife.

He played "Beautiful Ohio" next.

Ada knew the words for that too. She couldn't resist singing them aloud. She blushed a little as she went along:

"Seeming in a paradise of love divine,
Dreaming of a pair of eyes that looked in mine."

When the song was finished, Alfred let his bow fall. He gave Ada a look. It was as if he'd shot a needle through her. "Lady, you can sing."

Cousin Ada's eyes licked at Ada with green jealousy. "Well! Ada had better have something to make up for her big feet."

Alfred put the violin and bow back into the case. "Wal, Mrs. Simmons that was, her feet ain't too big for me. They're just right." He stood up, and stretched. "Wal, Daise will be crabby if I don't soon head her for her warm bed of straw. Good night, everybody. And Tante, thanks for the hot chocolary. It hit the spot."

"Come again."

Ada ❦ 5

ONE EVENING EARLY in April, Minnie Alfredson came over all excited. Her green eyes were seething with great news. "Ada, guess what."

"What?" Ever since Ada had discovered that Minnie was Alfred's cousin, she'd felt especially warm toward her.

"Mr. Badger wants me to come in tomorrow and take some pictures. And he's going to take them of me all for free too."

"He is?"

"Yes. It's for the Pretty Girls' Photo Contest in Chicago."

Ada wasn't surprised. Minnie was a smart little thing. She was known as "the Jerusalem doll." Ada said, "How wonderful."

"Oh, Ada, I just had to tell somebody."

"It's nice of you to come over."

"Ada, I want you to come along. I'll be in the studio with him alone and all, you know, and I hear he sometimes likes to touch the girls when he shows them how to pose."

Ada thought maybe that would be all right. "What do you think, Pa?"

Pa looked up from reading Calvin's *Institutes*. Pa still held Minnie responsible for having lured Ada out to the roller-skating rink that one time, thus getting her involved with Alvin Ravenhorse. Pa meant to say no. But a second look at Minnie's eager face and he melted. "I suppose it'll be all right."

"Can she really?" Minnie cried. Then Minnie flourished over in her glancing purple dress and kissed Pa fulsomely on the cheek, a good loud smack. "Oh, thank you, Mr. Engleking. I didn't know what you'd say."

Ada was surprised to see Pa pinken a little over his cheekbones. He looked young for a moment.

Ma came in at that moment. While hustling the young children off to bed, she'd heard a suspicious sound out in the parlor. When she saw there was only a girl there with Ada, Minnie, and not a boy, she looked puzzled. She'd fully expected to see that some boy had come in and kissed Ada. When the two girls smiled at her puzzlement, she grumped, and settled prutish in her chair across from Pa. "Mrmm."

"Oh, Ada, I'm so glad you can come along."

Pa returned to the reading of his *Institutes*.

The next morning Ada put on her blue dress with the black velvet crossbars over the bosom. It would help Minnie show off to better advantage if she came in a quiet dress. Ada put up her gold-red hair combed back and piled on top. She wore a lace choker with a gold pin at the throat. She also slipped on her heart-shaped locket with its gold chain.

They met on the courthouse steps.

Minnie looked like a peony. She'd put on her prettiest pink dress and wore a pink ribbon in her yellow hair.

"I hope Mr. Badger will like me this way."

"He will."

"I put on pink because in his ad Mr. Badger says he gives special attention to crayons."

"In a colored photograph you're sure to win."

"Wouldn't it be something if I really did win the contest? That ad says I'll get a free trip to Chicago. But I suppose it'll be just my luck not to win."

"Sufficient unto the day."

Minnie looked Ada up and down, critically. "It's too bad you're so tall, Ada. Being tall don't go over so good in a beauty contest."

"Don't speak of it."

Badger's Art Photography Shop stood next to the pink brick First National Bank. Its window was full of photographs of prominent local people.

The girls entered with a wondering look. There was a smell in the long narrow shop of an old fruit jar in which vinegar had been kept too long. As the front door closed behind them a bell rang.

Mr. Badger emerged from the back, brown eyes blinking. He was a gaunt man and wore a brown smock.

"Well, here I am, I guess," Minnie cried.

"So I see."

"I hope I put on the right dress." Minnie did a little whirl and a flounce. "I hope this is what you wanted."

Mr. Badger surveyed her briefly. "Looks all right to me."

"This is my friend Ada Engleking. Isn't she the tall one though?"

"That she is. But on her it looks good." Mr. Badger folded his gartered arms over his chest. He looked Ada up and down with interest. "How come I've never seen you around before?"

Ada looked down at her hands.

Minnie said, "Her pa is pretty strict."

Ada said, "Minnie! Pa isn't that strict."

Mr. Badger continued to look at Ada with lively eyes.

Minnie was eager to get on with the picture taking. "Well, I'm ready, Mr. Badger."

"Yes-s."

Ada thought that Minnie for her own good should hold herself in more.

Mr. Badger let his gartered arms fall. He was at least a half-foot shorter than Ada. "Have you ever had your picture taken, Miss Engleking?"

"No."

"Never?"

"Well, a snapshot maybe."

Mr. Badger stood in thought.

Minnie didn't like what was happening. She placed her hands on her wasp waist and flicked an angry look at Ada. "Maybe you don't want to take my picture after all, Mr. Badger."

Mr. Badger came to. "Don't worry. I'm going to take your picture. But I'm thinking I should also have one of your friend here. Then I'd have two chances to win."

Ada backed away. "Oh, but I'm not having my picture taken."

"Why not?" Mr. Badger said.

Ada shook her head. Adelheid Engleking in a pretty girls' contest? God had not created her for such things.

"Tell you what, Miss Engleking. I'll make you the same offer I made Miss

Alfredson. Three dozen copies free. Whether you win or not."

Minnie squeaked. "Do you think she's pretty enough?"

Ada could understand Minnie's distress. It meant so much to her to be thought a pretty doll. Ada said, "No, I don't want to."

"Come now, Miss Engleking," a coaxing tone entered Mr. Badger's voice, "taking a picture won't really hurt you."

"But—"

"—and I'm sure that if I take a good one your parents will be glad to have a good likeness of you. A record of how beautiful you looked at this stage in your life. Young innocent girlhood."

"They wouldn't want it entered in a contest though."

Mr. Badger smiled brown eyes at her. "Where did you get such a wonderful complexion? Do you use some kind of special preparation?"

"I just wash my face with cold rain water in the morning when I get up."

"Amazing."

"That's all."

"Well, whatever it is, keep it up. You'll be beautiful for the rest of your life."

Ada began to edge toward the door.

"Hey, where you going?"

"I'm sorry, Mr. Badger, but I can't have you taking my picture." Ada threw Minnie a look which she hoped she'd understand. "Minnie, I'll meet you later in the bank next door."

Mr. Badger moved quickly to block the door. "Tell you what. I won't enter your picture in the contest then. I'll just take it because it'll be my pleasure to have it. Because I've got to have a picture of you."

"No-o."

"Please. Surely your mother will be happy to have one."

"Mother, yes, Father, no."

"Oh come now. Doesn't your father like having his daughter considered beautiful?"

Ada laughed self-consciously. "I'm too tall. And my feet are too big. And I have too many freckles. Everything is wrong for me to be considered beautiful. Ask Minnie here."

"Perhaps I'm the best judge of that."

"No, Mr. Badger."

"Are you ashamed of what you are?"

"I'm not ashamed of how the Lord made me, no. It's just that I know the mail-order catalog doesn't carry my size shoe."

"You're a tall person and you have feet according."

Ada shook her head nevertheless.

"Your boyfriend tell you this?"

"I don't have a boyfriend."

"You date though, don't you?"

"I did once."

"Did he think you were too tall?"

"No."

"Come." Mr. Badger had gradually, imperceptibly lessened the distance between himself and Ada, and swiftly though smoothly took her by the elbow. "Young lady, you're coming with me to my studio in back and I'm taking your picture."

"Mr. Badger." Ada always turned to putty when someone touched her.

"Come. We're taking your picture."

"But . . . "

"Come."

"If you'll promise not to enter it in a contest."

"I promise."

Minnie was outraged. "But what about me?"

"You come too, Miss Alfredson. And your picture I'll enter in the contest. There, that make you happy?"

"Well! I was going to say."

Ada ❦ 6

TWO WEEKS LATER on a Monday, Ada got a penny postcard in the mail. It was the first mail she'd ever received. It was written in a woman's hand and postmarked in Bonnie.

> Dear Ada—My boss says he'll give me two days off next weekend so Daise and I can drive up to see you. Will you be home? I want to meet your pa and ma too.
>
> Alfred Alfredson

Ada's heart began to beat light and high. Alfred would be coming the next Saturday. She looked at the card again. What a funny handwriting for a man. He must have asked Mrs. Pullman to write the card for him.

Ada had just taken a part-time job at Reverend Carpenter's, Wednesday through Sunday, to help Mrs. Carpenter care for a little baby boy they'd adopted. Mrs. Carpenter suffered from occasional fits of melancholia and the good reverend, because they were not able to have children of their own, had thought that the care of a child might help give her some purpose in life and so lighten the darkness in her mind. Ada would have to ask Lady Carpenter if she couldn't move up her five days.

That night after the younger children were in bed Ada told her pa and ma about Alfred.

Ma wasn't too sure she was going to like this Alfred from Bonnie. He sounded a little like her own Alfred.

Pa surprised Ada. After Pa heard her account of meeting Alfred at the shindig, and then at Uncle Big John's house, of how this Alfred was frank and forthright, that he too was of Frisian descent albeit from West Fryslân, he sat in thought a while, behind a hand over his brown moustache. Then he finally said, "Write and tell him to come if that is his mind. Perhaps, given time, you can persuade him to join our church, and then you will be the instrument for the salvation of yet another lost soul. Sometimes people coming from another denomination make the best Christians. As witness our own Reverend Carpenter, who was once a Lutheran."

Dear Pa. Ada went over and kissed his gaunt face. As she did so she noticed that several stubbles in his brown beard, grown since his morning shave, were a whitish gray. Pa turning gray? When he was still so handsome?

Pa got Ada a penny postcard. The postcard had a picture of the county courthouse on the front of it.

Every few words Ada had to wet the point of her pencil with the tip of her tongue.

> Dear Alfred—Pa says it will be fine if you want to come up this weekend. We'll put up a cot for you in the hall where the boys sleep. I will pray for nice weather and for your safe arrival. Give our greetings to Mr. and Mrs. Pullman. And thank them for me for giving you the weekend off. May God bless you.
>
> Ada Engleking

Alfred ❦ 7

WHEN ALFRED CAME in from the field at noon, he took off his shoes on the porch, washed himself with tar soap, parted his black hair neatly, and ambled easy into the dining room.

Mrs. Pullman had a smile for him. Mrs. Pullman was a slim woman with a large bosom and a strong chin. She had very white hair, a real snowball. Her mouth was the woman in her and when she smiled it was always like a rose.

Alfred saw the postcard on his plate as he drew up his chair. He spotted his name immediately. He had learned to recognize his own name, but more he couldn't read. That sinking lost feeling, like when a plow hit a submerged boulder in a field, came over him again. Darn. The little bit of schooling he'd had as a boy had been lost on him. Pa had moved around too much. Each time just as he'd started to learn to read, Pa'd moved again. Then Ma died and he'd been kicked out of the nest and had had to go to work to help support the family. And had to do it too until he was twenty-one. He was now twenty-four. If one raised a boy to be a workhorse, it was pretty strong to expect him to win sulky races at the county fair. Mrs. Pullman had several times offered to teach him to read in the winter months, when he had a little free time, but he had said, no, it was too late now, he'd marry a woman who could do the reading and writing for him. To just sit and stare at those little hen tracks on a page for a couple of hours a day would only give him a headache.

Charlie Pullman came in and took his seat at the head of the table. "Well, Alfred, what did she write you?" Charlie was a jolly man with a red English face. He always wore a red vest, whether he had on overalls or a dress suit, and always combed the tuft of hair on the front of his balding head straight up which made him look like a cardinal.

Alfred handed the card to Mrs. Pullman. "Read it for me, please."

Mrs. Pullman sat down across from Charlie Pullman. She read the card slowly.

Alfred pinkened.

Charlie Pullman laughed. "Well, Alfred, you're free to go like I said. We're way ahead of the neighbors in our field work, thanks to you."

"Much obliged." Alfred reached for the card from Mrs. Pullman. He stared at the handwriting again. It was like looking at those funny Indian scratches on those stones sticking out of the hills overlooking the Big Rock River west of the farm. He turned the card over and stared at the picture of the courthouse. After a bit he cleared his throat and put the card in his shirt pocket. The card was his very first mail.

On the first ding of the alarm clock, Alfred bounced out of bed. He lit the lamp. It was five.

He stretched. "Wal, this is gonna be my red letter day."

He went over to the crock basin and washed up. He peeled off his nightshirt and for the first time that spring climbed into a new set of summer underwear, ribbed shirt and drawers.

He dressed in a stiff white shirt, new black suit, black tie, and black hat. He'd have to sit like a bishop all day long.

Daise didn't like getting up from her straw bed. It was one of the few times Alfred caught her down. But when Alfred slipped a sugar cube between her lips, she scrambled to her feet. And when he gave her a couple of ears of red corn, which she dearly craved, she was willing to accept the harness. Her freckled muzzle working on the red corn in the yellow lantern light was a pretty thing to see.

Daise groaned as Alfred backed her into the buggy shafts. She groaned when Alfred hooked up her traces.

"Now, Daise. It's only six looks to Ada's."

Daise fluttered her nostrils when Alfred pulled her checkrein up tight.

Gathering up the lines, Alfred stepped into the black buggy. "All right, Girl, let's get high behind."

Daise hardened her belly and leaned into the traces. In a moment she was whirling down the road.

Alfred had the eyes of a cat. He could make out the grass edges of the road. But Daise could see even better in the dark. She took the rutted track on the right unerringly.

They took the shortcut down Big John Engleking's back road and shot through his yard. It was still pitch dark out and the windows in the Engleking country house had the eyes of a stone-blind man.

Every now and then, when one of the wheels cambered tight in a rut, Alfred could hear grease frying in the axle. Sometimes, when Daise lifted her black tail, he got a whiff of piss-soaked breeching.

That time after catechism, when he'd helped Ada down out of the buggy, he got a feel of her slim waist. It was like taking hold of a well-made bundle of oats, where the twine pinched the middle in.

As the buggy wheeled along, watchdogs awoke every half mile at the various farmyards. From the pitch of the bark Alfred could tell what kind of a dog it was: terrier, collie, shepherd, bulldog. It was like listening to a full choir: soprano, alto, tenor, bass. Sometimes the dogs for three miles went at it in concert. In those farm homes nobody knew that a young man by the name of Alfred Alfredson VI from Bonnie was driving up to see a lovely woman named Ada Engleking in Jerusalem. It was a sweet secret.

When they hit Chokecherry Corner, the sky began to lighten.

"Well, Daise, old gal, it's gonna be a high sky today."

Every now and then he let Daise catch her breath, walking her a quarter of a mile for every two miles run.

Once he let her walk too long and she wried her neck around under the checkrein and reached down to crop some choice grass alongside the road. She was devilish clever at the contortion. Alfred dropped a line on her butt. Daise made a last snap at the grass and started up again.

When Daise rat-a-tat-tatted down the main drag of Sioux Center, lamps in various kitchens were just being lighted. The street was as smooth as a pool table. Those Sioux Center hotshots were sure quick to get out their road drags.

He slowed Daise down to a walk twice more before he reached Ada's town, once after he'd crossed the Floyd River bridge in a long low swale, and once on the western heights overlooking the town. The sun was up and it shimmered on the white and red celluloid rings in Daise's checkrein. Dew in the grass along the road glittered with the fire of diamonds.

He became hungry. He could stick both fists inside his trouser band. "Stomach's hardly bigger than a walnut."

On the northwest edge of town he spotted a man working in a cemetery. He pulled up. "Say, I'm looking for the Alfred Engleking home. Could you show me the way?"

The man removed a pipe from between his yellow teeth. "See that water tower over there?" The man pointed with his pipe. The nickel band on the pipestem gleamed in the sun.

"Yeh?"

"Engleking lives a block and a half south of that. On the east side of the street. It's a white house with a green trim. And it's got a kind of white decoration on the porch. Like a woman's tatting."

"Thanks."

Alfred drove on. Some of the homes had a cow in back. A few had chickens penned up in a tight little yard. Children ran down the center of the street ahead of him rolling hoops. Women weeding in gardens straightened up to stare at him rolling past.

Alfred drove through the shadow of the water tower where it lay across the street. Immediately after he spotted the house with the white decoration like a woman's tatting.

He needed to give the left line only the littlest touch and Daise headed straight for the hitching post in front of the Engleking house. Daise pulled up so suddenly Alfred found himself becking involuntarily. Daise fluttered her nose, once, and then looked over her shoulder at him already in a hurry to have her checkrein loosened so she could crop the grass underfoot.

It made Alfred laugh. He flipped back the yellow duster and hopped out. In two motions he'd loosened her checkrein and tied her to the post.

He mounted the front porch. He felt his tie into place.

A white curtain moved in the near window. A pair of stern gray eyes peered at him. They examined him from head to foot. Wrong house?

Alfred looked up and down the street, saw no other white house trimmed in green with the tatted decoration. Right house. The witch in the window was probably only the housekeeper.

He rapped.

There were womens's voices in the house, one scolding, one sweet. The scolding one was angry that they had company so early in the moring; the sweet one acted surprised.

The door opened and Ada in a white apron and a white dusting cap stood before him. "Alfred! I didn't expect you so early." Her eyes turned very blue. "You must've driven all night."

Alfred doffed his black hat. "Wal, if you don't want me around till later, I can easy take a walk up town and have a look at the sights."

"No, no. Come in. We're glad to see you."

Alfred ambled in.

Across the parlor from him, also in an apron and a dusting cap, erect beside a plush chair, stood the witch with the stern gray eyes.

"Alfred, this is my mother. Ma, Alfred Alfredson."

"How do, mam." So that was Ada's mother. Alfred couldn't remember his own mother very well—he was only a boy when she died—but what he did remember was that, though sad, her eyes were always tender.

Mrs. Engleking continued to stand like a burgomaster. She stared gray mad at him, trying to eye him down.

Wal, like he'd told Ada, there wasn't a woman in the world he couldn't look in the eye. So he glared right back at her.

Ada blushed for her mother. "Ma. Please."

Mrs. Engleking lifted her chin a couple of inches. She had on her gold-rim spectacles and the small clear lenses caught the light from the bay window.

Ada said, "Oh, Ma, can't you just say hello? Please?"

"Hello."

Alfred nodded ever so briefly, still staring back at Mrs. Engleking.

A little girl appeared in the opening to the parlor. Wonderingly she gave him a little flirty smile. "Are you bigger than my pa?" The question came out of her like taffy.

"What a question to ask Mr. Alfredson," Ada scolded

Alfred kept up his staredown with Mrs. Engleking. Out of the side of his mouth, he said, "Wal, little girl, I ain't seen your daddy yet."

Mrs. Engleking also kept up her end of the staredown. "Joan, wait until you're spoken to before you're heard from."

"Ya, Ma."

Ada said, "This is my little sister Joan."

"Hi."

Alfred's eyes began to smoke at Mrs. Engleking. It was best to let the old lady know right off the bat who was going to be boss in his house. No mother-in-law was going to be laying down the law to him.

"Well," Ada said, "come, sit down, Alfred. Have a chair."

Alfred said, "Ada, I came too early. Why don't I wait outside until you get your house in order."

Mrs. Engleking broke first. Her eyes jerked to one side. "Our house is always in order, Mr. Alfredson. Even without servants."

Alfred let down then too. "I didn't mean it that way, Mrs. Engleking, begging your pardon."

"What did you mean then?"

That old witch. Maybe she'd broken off first but she still was a tough one. "Wal, when I come to the door it sounded like I'd come too early. I should've let Ada know when I was coming."

Mrs. Engleking nodded, once. "If you could just give us one hour." She turned, her gray dress and white apron moving all in one block. "Joan, you know where Pa and John are, don't you? By the courthouse there?"

"Ya, Ma."

"Show this gentleman where he can put his horse in the barn, and then take him to where Pa and John are working."

"Ya, Ma."

"My husband is laying the walks for the county courthouse this year," Mrs. Engleking explained. "A special job."

Ada said, "I can take Alfred there, Ma."

"No, I want you to help me straighten up the house. Besides, I want to talk to you."

With Joan helping him, Alfred drove his buggy up beside the house, unhitched Daise, and led her into the single stall of the barn. He got out a sack of corn from the back of his buggy and gave Daise a half dozen ears to eat. He took off her harness and gave her a quick currying. He was careful to stand far enough away from her to keep floating hair from catching on his dress clothes.

Across the manger was a workshop of some kind. A strong smell of leather and freshly cut wood hung in the air. Several iron shoe lasts stood on a low workbench. The largest last was the most used. Hands had worn it down to its natural color of iron gray. Beside it lay a neat pile of sides of leather and a stack of wood blocks. Up on a shelf under the south window stood a row of freshly made leather workshoes as well as freshly whittled wooden shoes.

"All right, Joanie, lead the way to your pa."

They took the shortcut through the alley. They went past one of the tallest cottonwoods Alfred had ever seen. It hurt him in the back of the neck to look all the way up to its top. A breeze was moving through its upper reaches, making the glittering leaves sparkle like glass pendants.

Joan asked, "Have you got a little brother?"

"Sure have. Two of 'em. Why?"

"Maybe one of 'em can be my boyfriend. I need one too. If Ada can."

Joan was like a kitten who couldn't resist rubbing itself against a person's legs.

The courthouse stood on a rise of land in the center of a block, fronting to the east. It was made of sandstone, ranch rose in color, with white stone for door and window trim. A cinder drive curved around through green grass to its delivery service entrance in the rear. Two walks also curved around to the back door. The copper roof on the cupola shone a dull green in the sun.

Mr. Engleking and his slim son were working near a row of trees along the west side.

Joan ran up to her father and took hold of his hand. "Pa, Ada's boyfriend came early."

Mr. Engleking looked down at his daughter a moment. "Out of the mouth of babes." He turned and smiled at Alfred.

The two men shook hands firmly.

"Nah, and this is my oldest boy," Mr. Engleking said. "John."

Alfred and John shook hands too.

John gave Alfred a boy's clear look. Alfred wasn't sure what it meant.

"I'm sorry I'm too early," Alfred said. "But Daise is a pretty good stepper."

Mr. Engleking smiled some more. "It's fine."

"Wal, your womenfolk didn't seem to think it was fine."

"You mean, the Missus."

"Yes. Not Ada, of course."

Mr. Engleking got out his pipe and silver tobacco box and lit up.

Alfred got out his tobacco then too and had himself a pipe.

"We could use a little rain, " Mr. Engleking said.

"That we could," Alfred agreed.

"Where we're digging here it's cork dry an inch under the sod."

"That dry, huh."

Joan spoke up. "Pa, is Mr. Alfredson bigger than you?"

Mr. Engleking smiled down at her. "I guess he is a little."

"But there can't be anybody bigger than you, Pa."

"Why not, daughter?"

"But how can he be? Ain't you my pa?"

"Shh now, Joanie. Run along to mother now."

Joan went back to the house reluctantly. She wanted to stay with the men.

Mr. Engleking said to John, "We'll pour this batch and then quit for the day."

"No, no, don't quit because of me, please," Alfred said. "I don't mind hanging around until noon. We can visit while you work."

"Shucks," John said, "and here I was about ready to kiss you for coming so early. So I could have Saturday off after all."

Alfred smiled.

Pipe finished, Mr. Engleking and son went back to work

Alfred helped John carry water from the courthouse pump, careful not to spill any on his clothes. Alfred observed that John, for all his slim boyish frame, had muscles inside that blue denim jacket of his as strong as tugs. "You're fifteen, ain't you?"

John gave him a faintly mocking look. "Eighty subtract sixty-five, yep."

"That's kind of a long way round to say fifteen."

"Well, you see, I'm going for eighty years and I always figure back from that."

Alfred smiled. This John was kind of a friendly smart one like his cousin Fat John back in Bonnie. "The way you talk, a man'd almost be afraid to ask how much you weigh."

Again John gave Alfred a mocking look. "Well, with a hard-on I can sometimes manage a hundred forty and a half pounds."

Alfred let go with a hearty laugh. That half pound.

"John," Mr. Engleking said with a quiet side look. His brown moustache quivered, once.

The walk they were laying ran along the west side of the courthouse grounds. What they'd laid earlier that morning glistened a greenish wet gray. Ahead lay an empty trench six feet wide and some four inches deep, cut into the green turf. Coarse gravel lay in the bottom of the trench.

Mr. Engleking wielded the trowel and the edger with all the finesse of an expert flesher.

Alfred said, "That's a pretty thick walk you're making, not?"

Mr. Engleking nodded. "I learnt that from Pete Waxer. We used to lay them two inches thick. But we soon learned that the frost broke up those walks. Too thin. So we tried four inches. And that worked better."

"But, Pa," John protested, "you invented that, not Pete."

"No, son, give credit where credit is due."

"Pa, if anything, you and Pete invented it together then. Just like you invented putting that contraction gap in the walk every four feet. With the edger. To control the cracking if the frost's gonna crack it."

Mr. Engleking smiled that his son spoke up for him.

As the three strolled home for dinner at twelve, John asked, "You play ball, Alf?"

"I pitch sometimes for the Lakewood nine."

"Say, maybe we can knock up some flies after dinner. While Pa takes his nap. I got a bat and ball and glove."

"Okay by me."

Mr. Engleking frowned. "That's not a game for grown men, son."

"But it's fun though, Pa."

"I'm sure the good Lord considers it foolishness, John."

"Don't the Lord ever have any fun, Pa?"

Mr. Engleking mused over his pipe. "Well, all right, if Alfred will play with you. But mind, no playing tomorrow. That's the Lord's day."

"Yeh, I know. On Sunday we're not supposed to have any fun."

Mr. Engleking and John took off their shoes on the back porch and entered the kitchen. Alfred followed them in. All three looked to see what mood the missus was in.

Mrs. Engleking stood by the stove stirring a big pot of green pea soup. She had put up her hair into two severe knots at the back of her head. The table was set with company plates, mostly delft blue.

"Dinner ready, Ma?" John asked.

"No ball-playing before dinner."

John shrugged. "Just asked, is all."

The men washed up, combed their hair, drew up their chairs to the table. Alfred was given Joan's place beside John and across the corner from Ada. Joan sat between her father and the baby.

They were well into the meal, about to have rice pap with sugar and cinnamon, when Baby Sherman noticed that the shadow of a cloud had passed over the house. Bright sunshine vanished from the grass outside the window. "Baby beddy, no no."

Mrs. Engleking thought what the baby said so cute she began to cry to herself.

Everyone at the table fell silent. Spoons clicked.

Mrs. Engleking finally couldn't hold it back. "Yes, and no one knows the grief of a mother who remembers a favored child lost to that awful pneumony. My poor Shermie One, lying dead and cold in his grave there, where it's always wet along the low side of the cemetery there . . . you were so smart, so sweet, taking after my smart father and my smart brother, who knew everything—"

Mr. Engleking said quietly, "Still now, wife."

Mrs. Engleking turned to Alfred. "That was my other baby Sherman, the one who'll be dead now next October four years, after whom this Sherman Two was named, who's a good smart baby too of course, but not as—"

"Wife."

"Oh, I know you, Alfred Engleking, you wretch without a heart. Why, you never shed a tear when we lowered him away to the worms—"

"Wife!" All in one motion Mr. Engleking pushed back his swivel chair and came to his feet. White moved over his cheeks. He blazed down at her. "Wife, who can ever measure grief? I've got it so hollow here in my stomach. . . . Enough of this now."

Mrs. Engleking knuckled under. And shut up.

John looked up at the clock. He still wanted to play some catch.

Alfred caught movement in the weather clock. The old couple had just then begun to switch positions, the old lady with her bad weather clothes coming out and the old man with his good weather clothes retreating.

After dinner Alfred and John went across the street to the grammar schoolyard and played ball while the old man took a nap on the parlor sofa. They took turns hitting each other towering flies.

John let Alfred know he thought him a pretty good skate.

A little after one John and Mr. Engleking went back to laying sidewalks.

Ada took Alfred for a walk. They visited Reverend and Lady Carpenter in the parsonage. Ada wore a flowered straw hat and a green coat and carried a purple parasol. Both were tall and made a handsome couple.

When they stepped outside again, they discovered a soft wind had risen. It was a surprisingly warm wind.

Alfred nodded toward the southeast. "I don't like the wind in that corner."

Ada looked out over the trees to the west. "The sky is working up all right. Maybe we'll get our first rain of the year."

Ada next took him downtown and showed him the bakery, the grocer, the bank, the blacksmith shop.

At four o'clock a line storm suddenly appeared along the horizon to the west. They had to hurry to beat it home. Mr. Engleking and John came clattering along behind them.

Mrs. Engleking held the door open for them. "Nah, I was beginning to wonder if you was gonna stay out in the rain with the horses."

Mr. Engleking hung up his cap and jacket, kicked off his shoes by the heel, and without a word strode directly through the house and took up a position in front of the parlor window facing west.

Mrs. Engleking nodded toward her husband. "There stands my brave man again. The least cloud and he begins to tremble like a rabbit."

Ada explained, eyes down, "Pa was almost killed by lightning once. He was working in the barn out in back, when lightning hit our big cottonwood by the alley and then jumped across into the barn. When we ran out there to see what'd happened, we found him on the floor. He was half-paralyzed for a week."

"Yes," Mrs. Engleking added, "he lay there as stiff as an ironing board."

Alfred nodded. "My boss always gave me orders to get in under a roof the minute I spotted a thunderhead coming."

Mrs. Engleking lighted the lamps. The orange lights coming on one by one made the house feel cozy.

Thunder boomed west of town.

Mr. Engleking's eyes widened to a very light blue. "Wife, is the cellar door open? In case we have to make a run for it?"

Mrs. Engleking headed for the kitchen, ignoring her husband. "Ada, come help me make supper. You can slice the potatoes."

Mr. Engleking called after Mrs. Engleking sternly. "The cellar door, wife."

"Yes, yes, my lord, the door to hell shall be opened for you."

John smiled at Alfred. "Sit down. You and me don't have to make a run for the basement just yet."

From his rocker, Alfred could see the sky darkening up rapidly over the roof of the grammar school across the street.

Mr. Engleking watched. "I don't like it when it don't lightning much to begin with and it's so pitch black out. It's God's wrath in the form of lightning that I worry about."

Alfred thought: "Does he think God's out to get him personal?"

A great crack of thunder exploded behind the treetops across the school grounds.

The earth shuddered. The basement under the house boomed.

Mr. Engleking backed a step from the window. For a second his face resembled a galvanized pail. He swallowed. Then he began to sing in a deep baritone voice:

"My soul thirsts for God, for the living God:
When shall I come and appear before God?"

Ada and Mrs. Engleking appeared in the doorway drying their hands in their aprons.

Alfred was astounded at Mr. Engleking's behavior. It was all kind of crazy.

Mr. Engleking's voice deepened into the old psalm:

"Why art thou cast down, O my soul?
And why art thou disquieted in me?"

The long dark loaf of cloud zoomed low over the trees. Thunder boomed again. And suddenly water dropped in lashing sheets, on the roof, against the window panes.

Joan ducked under the dining room table. Baby Sherman began to cry.

Mrs. Engleking knicked down, closing her eyes a second. "Domeny on the roof. Listen to him up there jumping up and down, warning us to be good now."

Mr. Engleking's voice deepened an octave. It could be heard over all the tumult, a strong crackling basso:

"Deep calls unto deep as the voice of Thy waterspouts.
All Thy waves and Thy billows roll over me."

John winked. "We're okay so long's Pa's singing. It's when he starts to pray you gotta worry. Because it's the basement next after that."

Again a vast thunder rumpled the roof. Dishes rattled in the show cabinet. Windows whammed.

Mr. Engleking folded his hands and began to pray slow and clear. "Lord God in heaven! Powerful Thou art! Yet have mercy on us, miserable creatures that we are!"

A hard wind came up. Water began to squirt through the window sills.

"Forgive us all our trepasses! Keep us from harm! Thy will—"

Whack! A branch hit the bay window. The glass held.

John leaped to his feet. "Wow!"

"To the basement!" Mr. Engleking cried, arm pointed like a semaphore. "Hurry! The Lord's will."

"See?" John said with a look at Alfred.

Everyone scurried for the cellar door. John grabbed up his crying little brother. Ada remembered to grab a lamp so they could see their way. The steps were so steep they all had to step down backwards. Mr. Engleking was the last to clatter down the wooden stairs. All gathered around the ice-cream freezer.

In the weak lamplight all eyes were like egg yolks.
Last year's potatoes smelled like vinegar.
Ada decided to take up the singing for her father:

> "O God, our help in ages past,
> Our hope for years to come,
> Our shelter from the stormy blast,
> And our eternal home."

Ada moved the lamp with the rise and fall of the melody.

Again Alfred liked her voice. It was as true as a tuning fork. Her golden freckles went well with her golden voice.

The rain let up on the roof. The thunders receded into the east. Baby Sherman quit crying. The silence of spaces fell on the house.

They stood wondering in the shadowy cellar.

Mr. Engleking gave Ada a look. "I guess we can all go upstairs again."

Mrs. Engleking sighed. "God be praised."

The next afternoon at four Ada went along with Alfred when he went to get Daise from the barn. As he threw on the harness and buckled up the belly band, he said, "That surely was a good sermon your domeny preached today. That we should be patient with each other."

"Do you think then you could get used to our church?"

He took down Daise's bridle from a peg. "Sure."

"You wouldn't feel bad about leaving the Congregational Church then?"

"So long as I had someone like you to live for, no."

"Alfred, you must not change church for me, you know. You must do it because it's the right thing to do."

"I know."

"And you can abide my strange family?"

"Ha. Wait'll you see my pa. A wild mad Frisian."

"You can accept my mother?"

"She isn't going to live with us, is she?"

"Of course not."

Alfred opened Daise's mouth with his fingers and slipped in the bit of the bridle and then buckled up the throat strap. "Though I do have to say this, Ada, begging your pardon. I want to respect your mother and all, but the truth is, when it comes to your father, your mother is a mean witch. I say this flat out because it's the truth."

Ada's blue eyes closed slowly, as though she were swallowing something not very nice to eat. "I know, Alfred. And it is a matter I've prayed over many a time."

Alfred put his arm around her slim waist. "Listen, love, the main thing is, you're the sweet one. Now, let's have a kiss, and then Daise and me will roll for home. Tomorrow's another day of work."

Ada lifted her pink mouth.

Alfred looked deep into her eyes a moment, until he saw mayflowers coming out, and then he gave her a firm dry-lipped kiss. He also gave her a quick hard hug. Then he led Daise out of the barn.

Ada followed him. She held up the buggy shafts while Alfred backed Daise into them. She hooked on the leather tug on her side.

Then, holding the lines in one hand, Alfred hopped into the buggy. And was off. Daise had a habit of leaning into a hard ears-down run the moment Alfred mounted into the buggy.

"Bye!"

"Bye!"

Alfred also waved to John and Joan and Mr. Engleking standing on the front porch and to Mrs. Engleking watching from the parlor window.

Ada ❦ 8

THE WEDDING WAS set for January twenty-second on a Sunday evening. Once Ada made up her mind to it, it wasn't so hard after all to put aside further thought of Alvin Ravenhorse. That was done now.

Ma tried to talk her out of it though. "That my daughter, my very own daughter, issue of noble blood, should marry an ignorant farm hand. Ugh!"

Ada counseled herself to be patient with her mother. "I haven't told you this before, Ma, because I don't think Alfred wants me to mention it. But he is Alfred VI in a straight line of Alfredsons."

Ma stood stiff by her stove. "His father is then Alfred Alfredson V?"

"Yes." Ada sat down by the table to peel some potatoes.

"And where is this father?"

"Out in the Dakotas somewhere."

"Will he come to his son's wedding?"

"I don't think so." Ada picked out a deep eye of a fat potato.

"Because he's too poor to come? Or because his son is too dumb to write him?"

"It's too far away."

"Hmf. The conceit of poor peasants who give themsleves titles. VI. V. Imagine. Phaa! Just some sweepings out of the Old Country."

"They were rich once, Mother. They lost everying in a pestilence. Horses, cows, pigs. Like Job, Alfred's forefathers fell on evil days."

"Hah. Another one like your father. Poor as a church mouse, yet still hanging onto a fable, that his people once were somebodies."

John was sitting in Pa's swivel chair studying his catechism lesson. When Pa wasn't around he liked to sit in it.

Ada asked, "John, what do you think of Alfred?"

"He's all right."

''Are you ready to accept him as your brother-in-law?''

''I guess so. He ain't book smart, but he sure can smell out what to do with that strong nose of his. And, man, can he throw a curve!''

''That last part there I'm not sure is a compliment.''

''You're a woman, Ada, and there's some things a woman'll never understand. Once in a while a man's just gotta have a little fun.''

"Why?"

John gave her a faintly mocking smile. "It's the dog in a man."

Ma jumped on John before Ada could. "What? For landsakes! That's scandalous, to compare people with dogs."

"That's the prone-to-evil part, Ma, that Domeny always talks about."

"Well!" Ma grabbed hold of her corset through her gray dress and gave it a jerk down, hard. "Well, I'm not a bitch, I'll have you know."

Ada and John laughed at the way Ma clutched at her corset.

Ma resented their laughter. She pointed a finger at Ada. "Yes, and I once had a girl's waist too, you know. It was as small around as a weasel's. But just wait until you've had as many babies as I've had—"

"Ma!" John broke in. "We've heard that already. Many times."

"Yes, and you're going to hear it again too. Many times."

Ada finished peeling the last potato. She lifted the pan with its peelings and set it with a light thump on the table. "Alfred will run the farm, I will run the house."

Ma still pruttled about. ''And then to be a farmer's wife.''

"What's wrong with being a farmer?" John challenged "That's what I'm going to be. America gives you one chance to make it big, and that's on a farm. That's what's so wonderful about this country."

"As a renter?"

"Yessiree. Some farms you can rent with the agreement that the rent applies against the principal. By hard work you can at last own your own farm."

"I had it far better in the Old Country," said Ma.

"Besides being free. Nobody to tell you when to get up. Nobody to tell you when to go to bed. That's for me."

"Then there's no chance you'll ever go back to the Old Country?"

"Never."

Ma began to cry. "Then all my grieving is for nothing."

Over the days, Pa had come to like Alfred and looked forward to the weekends when Alfred would come up from Bonnie. Pa liked it that once Alfred had been convinced that he'd been wrong about something and should change his mind, he changed it. Alfred joined Ada's church in Bonnie, and no regrets. Alfred had occasionally taken a chew of tobacco, but when asked by Ada to quit, he quit. Alfred also quit playing for the square skips around Bonnie, and turned his musical talents to playing hymns and psalms. No ifs, ands, or buts.

Two days before the wedding Alfred came up on the train to help Ada with some last-minute errands. He slept, as he had on his last several visits, on a cot in the hall upstairs. John for a joke offered to stand guard at Ada's door those last two nights, but Ada with a quiet laugh declined the offer.

Ada had never seen Alfred look so handsome. His wavy black hair shone like the crown of a redwing, with glancing green lights in it, sometimes even with a glossy violet. Every now and then when Alfred looked at her his light gray eyes burned like coals in a base burner.

Somehow Ada still couldn't get excited. Wedding time came at her like it might have been some church service. She was sure she loved Alfred. But she loved him quietly.

Ada made up with Minnie Alfredson, Alfred's cousin, and persuaded her to be the bridesmaid. At first Minnie crabbed about that affair at the photographer's, but at last agreed. Minnie had found a boyfriend named Lemuel Longwood, who, as it turned out, was a friend of Alfred's, and who, in the old days, used to skip to Alfred's fiddling.

Pa got wind of it that some of the young people were planning to have some fun with the newlyweds after the wedding. So Pa told Reverend Carpenter to announce in church that Sunday that under no circumstances was there to be a chivaree or he would call the marshal. Absolute.

At seven-thirty Sunday evening, Alfred and John went ahead and waited in the consistory room with Domeny. John said he'd be glad to serve as best man and was only sorry that he couldn't have the first-night rights.

The church was full at eight. The young people thought it a wonderful lark that there should be a wedding instead of the usual catechism. For once on a Sunday night they could relax and enjoy themselves. The old people came in bunches. They could go to a social event instead of having to sit at home twirling their thumbs.

It all went as though part of a dream. At quarter to eight, Ma and John and little Sherman were ushered to their seats on the front bench. Alfred, dressed in a new black suit and silver tie with a small diamond stickpin and black patent leather shoes, and John, also dressed in black, took up their positions just under the pulpit up front. Minnie, in white, took up her position across from Alfred and John. When the organist started playing, "Here Comes the Bride," Pa held out his arm for Ada and she took it, and together they marched up the aisle toward where Reverend Carpenter and Alfred and John waited. Pa too was dressed in black. Pa looked young. He'd had a stomachache earlier in the evening, but a couple of glasses of warm water had quieted it down. Ada and Pa walked in perfect step to the music. They made a handsome couple. Ada had put on a touch of eau de cologne here and there. But as she walked with her father toward the front of the church, she could smell stronger waves of it coming from the women sitting on either side of the aisle. The lingering traces of cigars that some of the men had smoked earlier also came to her.

The organ stopped. Pa left Ada standing beside Alfred and retired to a seat directly behind her on the aisle.

Ma let out a tragic sigh.

Ada was numb to it all. Her corset was too tight. Walking down the aisle, she had the feeling she was sitting in a swaying swing.

"Just so I don't faint," Ada thought. "Lying flat on the floor with my legs apart at my own wedding, what a disgrace that would be."

Domeny began. "Beloved congregation. We are gathered here this evening to witness the merging in holy matrimony of two souls into one."

The whole church fell silent, intent on the tableau up front.

Domeny was into the ceremony a ways before Ada's mind began to fix on what he was saying. She liked to savor the full meaning of things read.

Alfred loomed silent and warm beside her. John rubbed his nose.

Domeny read on. The ritual dreamed on.

Again Ada had to work to be part of it.

Presently Domeny addressed them personally. That was the part the audience liked best. Domeny sometimes came very close to mentioning the intimate business of marriage. The rest the audience could easily fill in for themselves. "A three-strand rope is not easily broken. A marriage in which God, husband, and wife are the strands is not easily broken either. Firstly, God. God we all know lives in heaven. He is our Maker. He is our beginning and our end. We cannot escape being in Him and being a part of Him even if we wanted to. To remove ourselves out of Him is an utter impossibility. The one cannot be true without the other. All things begin, and have their being, and end, in that truth. That is God. Secondly, the husband. Him we expect to be the inventive provider, the worthy sire, the strong protector of the castle. He is the seminary from whom ideas for a happy life spring forth. In a word, he is the father. Thirdly, the wife. Her we expect to be the loving mate, the buttress to help take up the shocks of adversity, the support who helps her husband ride out the storms of life. She is the cup that overflows with love, the holder in whose flesh and from whose flesh we have issue, the vessel from whose bosom the helpless receive nourishment. In a word, she is the mother."

Ada trembled. When she'd come down the aisle with Pa, she hadn't seen Alvin Ravenhorse anywhere. "But I must not think of him." She tried to smile. She remembered a funny thing John had said, that in buying her a wedding gift he knew for a fact he wouldn't have to buy his sister a Princess bust-developer. That John. He sure had a busy funny bone. Maybe if Pa had been married to a more companionable woman he too might have had a funny bone. But then of course in that case neither she nor John would've been there. It would have been somebody else thinking odd thoughts at her wedding. Well, she would be a good wife to Alfred. She would help him be a fine man somehow.

"Do you, Adelheid Engleking, take this man''—a baby bawled just behind them and the domeny's next words were lost—"so help you God?"

All of a sudden Ada stood on the edge of a wide pond. She found she had all kinds of time to sail across it. Should she change her course? "I want babies, yes. Oh, I want them very much. But they've got to have the right father." Her boat came to rest halfway across the pond. ''Alvin Ravenhorse wouldn't have been the right father.

Though with him I could smell crazy perfumes." Then she saw a tall cottonwood tree across the pond. It was scattering soft fluffy seeds by the millions all across the prairie. She'd always loved the great cottonwood by their alley. The cottonwood across the pond was Alfred. It would always be a tree to sit under on a hot day. Its shelter and its shade would always be a blessing for her, weary and overworked. It would withstand even the hardest winds. The sun glinting on its shiny leaves would always be a joy to behold. Scattering seeds upon the earth. She would. "I do."

Of a sudden there was behind Ada the sound as if a cistern were being primed, uhk, uhk, the water not quite coming. Then silence. Then right after, a loud thump on the floor. A brush of air touched the bottom of Ada's dress.

Ma had fainted. Poor Ma. She had a heart that, when she got excited, would sometimes skip a half dozen beats in a row. Then beat real fast for a few seconds. Then skip some more. So that she'd turn white, then purple, then white. Ma would sometimes even faint during a sermon. She always complained afterwards that just before she passed out she felt as if someone had locked her in a close room. Poor Ma. She was like a wild sea in a tub.

John and Pa knew what to do. With old stoic faces, John left Alfred's side and Pa got up from his end of the bench, and together they carried Ma out, John holding her heavy legs one on each side of his hips and Pa with his arms under her shoulders. All around them heads turned, necks made ruffing noises inside stiff collars, busts rustled under silk waists. John and Pa pushed through the double doors of the consistory room and disappeared.

Reverend Carpenter hardly paused. "Do you, Alfred Alfredson, take this woman to be your lawful wedded wife, so help you God?"

"I do."

"Adelheid and Alfred Alfredson, I now pronounce you man and wife."

The congregation breathed a slow breath.

The organist touched the white and black keys up in the console of the great organ. Joyous music purled past the domeny and then around the black and white couple and then over the whole outspread of lifted faces.

Alfred took Ada by the arm and led her down the aisle and then into the consistory room.

They found Ma sitting on the edge of a table where Pa and John had first laid her out. Ma was pale, still sucking for air, weeping. She was lamenting that oh dear God why was it that a heart attack had been visited upon her at just the very moment when her daughter had reached the high point of her life, the act of marriage?

"You're all right though now, Ma?" Ada asked.

"Och, ya. But I missed the greatest moment of your life."

Ada kissed her. "You were with us in spirit and that's what counts."

John let out a deep breath. "I'll say she was. For a minute there I was positive that this time she was gone for sure."

Ma bristled. "I'll have no mockery now."

Alfred asked Pa, quietly, off to one side, "Does Ma often get that way?"

Pa nodded. "Often. She gets nervous in a crowd. It's a nervous condition."

"Nothing you can do for it? Pills or something?"

"Pills, no. But we have noticed that when you keep her hands open she seems to come out of it faster."

John couldn't resist having his fun. "Pa, someday, when you've got her hands open like that, quick pour in a little warm water and see what happens."

Alfred put a hand to his lips and laughed behind it.

Pa stood quietly patient beside Ma. "For a minute there she looked like that time when they operated on her for gallstones," Pa explained. "Those days they didn't have ether when they operated. You just had to lay there and let them cut you open with the knife when you were raw wide awake."

Guests began to pour into the consistory room.

Ada and Alfred, Minnie and John, and Pa, and Joan and little Sherman, and at last even a sighing, beaming Ma formed a line. Everyone wanted to congratulate the happy couple. Cigar smoke swirled overhead.

Later as they were leaving church together, John stuffed a small package into Alfred's overcoat pocket.

"What's that?"

"When Pa said no chivareeing, that meant no fun for me either."

"How so?"

"Oh, I was going to throw a handful of seeds over you two to make sure you'd bring me some uncle-sayers."

Alfred felt of the compact package. "Rice, you mean."

"Yeh. Tell you what. Why don't you two make your first meal together out of it? That'll be one way of getting it into you."

Alfred again put a hand to his lips and laughed behind it.

Ada and Alfred walked home together. Corner lamps lighted their way.

Ada knew who she was down to her corset but from there on her legs moved of themselves.

Alfred's hand on her elbow was shy and firm by turns. "That man can surely play that organ. I almost forgot I was getting married."

"Alfred."

"It must be a lot more complicated than playing an accordion."

Ada thought: "I wonder what comes next?" Ada thought: "Just so it doesn't turn out to be something mean and low like that time Alvin tried." Ada thought: "If one has the begetting of children in mind, I suppose then it's a holy thing."

They entered the house together.

Surprise! Her folks had spirited a wedding cake into the house after all. It stood three tiers high on the living room table. There was also the wonderful smell of coffee in the house. How nice.

Standing off to one side was another surprise. Mr. and Mrs. Garland Ault. Gar Ault was the principal of the parochial grammar school across the street. He'd once been Ada's teacher. He was a trim man, always dressed dapper. His wife was a wispy little thing with veils about her face and frills at her wrists. "Congratulations and many happy returns," both cried.

Ada and Alfred beamed. Principal Gar Ault, like the domeny, was an important personage in the community and for him to drop by was a compliment. Ada said, "How very thoughtful of you."

"Not at all," Mrs. Ault said.

Gar Ault was holding something behind his back and he now held it out to them. It was a book. He gave it to Ada. "For you both."

Ada stroked the book. It was bound in cream-colored cloth. Its gold lettering gleamed in the light: *Our Marriage Formulary* by Dr. B. Wieland.

Ada thought: "Dr. Wieland is of our faith and what he'll have to say about marriage will be uplifting." Ada could feel herself pinkening over her cheeks. It struck her that Gar Ault was maybe being just a little bit of a busybody in giving them such a book. She had often caught him looking at her in a peculiar way. Still Ada respected him.

Ada looked up at Alfred. "Isn't it nice of my old teacher to give us this book?"

Alfred stared down at the gold letters. "Some kind of doctor book?"

"No." She read the title aloud for him.

John laughed. "You won't find any bare naked pictures of people in there, Alf, if that's what you're thinking. Only just a bunch of rules on how not to have too much fun."

Garland Ault reddened. After a moment he hooked his thumbs in his vest pockets.

Ma sputtered. "Now, John, we'll have no mockery about holy matrimony."

It was Pa's turn to give something. He took an envelope from the inside pocket of his jacket and handed it to Ada. "Now that you're going to set up a new home, we have this for you."

Ada took the envelope with wondering fingers. She turned it over several times. An odd soft smile moved along her lips.

"Well, Ade, are you afraid to open it?" John wanted to know.

"Why should I be afraid?"

John shrugged. "For all I know maybe you came home with your pants on over your head after all. I can't watch everything around here."

"John!"

Alfred reddened. He was more angry than embarrassed.

"Open it," Ma said.

Ada opened the flap with a finger and looked inside. "Oh!" She counted them. Ten fresh bills. Ten dollars each. She showed them to Alfred. "That'll go nice with the two hundred dollars you've saved up."

Ma came alert. She shot Alfred a direct look. "You've saved up that much? Two hundred dollars?"

"Yup. And I've also got my horse and buggy paid for. Plus of course all my clothes."

Ma thought that over. "Why, you two are rich then." It began to sink in on her that this was a good match after all. She turned to Pa. "Why, they're starting out married life better than we did. When here I came from higher issue."

Pa turned pale under his lean jowl.

Ada quickly asked, "Where's the cake knife?"

Ma came to with a forced blink of eyes. "Ah. And now it's my turn to give you something." She picked up a slender package from behind the tall cake and handed it to Ada. "This came in the mail last week."

Ada looked at the postmark. It was from the Old Country.

"It's from my brother," Ma said. "Uncle Alfred. The one that's in the foreign ministry. Taking orders directly from the Queen herself. I wrote him that you were getting married."

"Well, are you afraid to open that too?" John asked.

"Of course not." Ada handed the package to Alfred. "Here, it's your turn to open something."

Ma didn't like that, but she managed somehow to bite her tongue.

Alfred removed the strange waxy wrapping paper. A black leather case came to view. Alfred opened the case. There on silver satin lay a carving set, knife, fork, and steel.

Ma beamed tears. "It's not a cake knife, but I thought it would be nice to cut the cake with it anyway."

"Of course, Ma," Ada said.

Alfred picked up the gleaming knife and ran its cutting edge along the side of his thumbnail. "Sharp enough to cut a hair."

"And it's long enough," John said, "to cut me a big piece of cake. Mmm."

"It's a beauty," Garland Ault pronounced. "Those ivory handles."

Alfred handed the knife to Ada. "Here, you cut the cake. That's something I don't usually do."

Ada pushed it back, gently, a yielding smile on her lips. "No, that's for the man to do."

Pa stood by smiling. "For the man to do, yes, but you're to help him, Ada."

Alfred touched the knife onto the thick white frosting of the first tier. "Here?"

"Yes, there. Just past that pink rosebud." Ada placed her hand on Alfred's hand and helped him press the knife down into the cake. The sharp knife cut cleanly, down to the bottom.

Ada then finished cutting the cake. She cut more than enough pieces to go around.

Ada noticed that Pa took only one bite of the cake and then quietly set it aside. He gestured for John to finish it for him. Ada thought: "Something's wrong with Pa's stomach."

Every now and then John got up to look outside.

Pa finally asked, "Son, what are you looking for?"

"I thought maybe some chivareers might come anyway."

"Then I get the marshal."

"Aw, Pa, the young people don't mean any harm by it."

"Son, marriage is not a moment for sport and jest."

Principal Ault nodded. "Those are my thoughts exactly."

John gave Principal Ault a sour look.

Presently Garland Ault and his wife got to their feet. It was time to go home. As they stood in the doorway, Principal Ault couldn't resist it. At the last second he had to quick try and give Ada a kiss. It was almost sneaky the way he went about it. And he missed giving Ada a full kiss on the lips because she saw it coming and in turn quick gave him her cheek instead.

Mrs. Ault trilled out of her veils. "A kiss for the bride, aha. Why, Gar, I didn't know you had any romance left in you."

Principal Ault ran a forefinger over the spot where Ada's lips had touched. "Good night, everyone. God bless."

"Thank you for the book," Ada called after them.

"You're more than welcome."

Ma closed the door behind the company. "Nah. At last."

"Yeh, Ma," John said, "what was all that about in church there tonight? The way you put on, it was like you was getting married instead of Ada."

Ma bristled. "I guess a mother has a right to grieve some when she loses a daughter. I've already lost a favorite son."

"John," Pa said, "that's enough now." Pa then gave Alfred a kind smile. "What we really should say is that tonight we've gained a son."

Alfred allowed himself a smile.

Ma didn't like the way the subject had been changed. With a knick of her gray head she indicated that Ada and her man should now go to bed. The newly married couple were to sleep in Ada's room upstairs. She informed Ada in a conspiratorial whisper, "I left the big chamber pot under the bed."

John heard the whisper. "What? Is Alfred a bed wetter like our Joan?"

"I ain't either a bed wetter," Joan cried. "Always."

"Still!" Ma hissed. "And you, John, with your mockery . . . "

Joan pouted. "I don't wanna sleep downstairs on the sofa."

"Shh."

"Maybe I'll wet the sofa."

"Ssst. If you dare."

"Why does our new son Alfred have to sleep in my place? Sons ain't supposed to sleep with daughters, are they?"

"It's only for one night, child."

Joan's eyes slowly opened. "You mean, then Ada will be gone?"

"Yes, child."

"For good?"

"Yes. Now get into your nightgown. I'll get the rubber sheet for you."

"Goodie goodie. Now it's my turn to be papa's big girl."

Pa gave Joan a wan smile. "Yes, little daughter, tomorrow it'll be your turn."

Ada led the way with a night lamp, Alfred following. The stairs creaked. Both had to duck as they entered her bedroom. There was just enough headroom in the center for Alfred to stand erect. It was chilly in the room. The only heat came through the grill around the stovepipe.

"Boy," Alfred said, "this is gonna be one night when we'll have to be bed warmers for each other."

Ada smiled, nervous. "Well, it's only for one night."

The clothes closet was too small for either of them to undress in. Ada thought maybe they should take turns undressing out in the hallway. Then she thought: "Though now that we're married I can hardly ask Alfred to leave the room."

She turned her back on Alfred.

He followed suit.

She undid her knotted sash and then reached around to undo the hooks down the back of her white dress. She couldn't quite reach the top hook and eye, and after several tries, sighed and said, "Alfred, will you undo me?"

"Be glad to." Alfred already had his suit off and stood in his shirttails. He undid the top hook.

"And I guess my corset too."

Alfred tugged at the top of her corset several times. "Who the heck tied this knot for you?"

"Oh." Ada had to laugh. "That John. He did that on purpose."

Alfred worked and tugged at the knot. Finally he said, "I'm sorry, but I'm going to have to go at this with one of my eyeteeth. It's the only sharp thing I got on me." Alfred leaned down and bit into the knot.

Ada could feet his shaven cheek against her skin above the corset. For a fleeting moment she smelled a crazy perfume.

"There," Alfred said. "I think she'll come now." He gave the knot several deft little tugs and it came apart. "There you are, love."

"Thanks, Alfred."

Ada finished removing her corset. Her belly, released, gave two little humping motions of its own, as though not connected to her. Ada drew in a deep breath. "What a relief to get out of that torture rack."

"Why do you wear it then? You're slender to begin with."

"You're right. It is a foolish custom. It's just something to help a girl catch a man with. I'll be glad when that style changes."

"Ain't you caught your man now?"

"Alfred, I don't like to think I caught you."

"Wal, I guess I don't like to think you did either."

"We girls should use common sense more in the way we dress."

"When the babies start coming you won't need to wear it then."

Ada thought: "My, how frank this man can be. But it's good. Good."

They continued undressing back to back. When Ada got to where she could take everything off by the bottom route, she slipped her nightgown over her head, and then finished by pulling her petticoat and stockings out from under it.

They turned sideways to each other, gave each other covert looks.

Ada hated the look. "What side would you like to sleep on?" The head end of the bed was near the window. "I've always slept against the wall so Joan wouldn't have to crawl over me to get at the white owl."

"I'll take the outside then. Besides, if a woman can stand on a man's right while they're getting married, she surely should be able to sleep on a man's right in bed."

"That's the way it'll be then, Alfred."

Ada was quite surprised to find she was in good control of herself the first night she was to lie with a man. She thought of Ruth the Moabitess, who quite calmly lay herself down at the foot of Boaz. "For all the city of my people doth know that thou art a virtuous woman. . . . And she lay at his feet until the morning; and she rose up before one could know the other."

Ada knelt on the floor beside the bed. "I don't know how it is with you, Alfred, but I'm accustomed to praying before I go to sleep at night."

Alfred stood stock still. His bare legs showed through the split down the sides of his white nightshirt.

"Alfred?"

"Wal." Then he settled down beside her. His kneecaps made two distinct little knocks on the floor. "Maybe it'll be a good thing at that."

"If you want, we can pray silent together."

"All right."

Ada prayed to herself. She asked her Father in heaven her soul to keep. She promised that in all she did she would always have Him in mind, that her soul was first of all His even before it was her husband's, that when the time came for her to accept her husband's fatherstuff she would be loving and tender with him at the same time that she would always be remindful of Him. In Jesus' name, Amen.

Ada didn't know what Alfred prayed, but as they stood up together she could see in the soft orange lamplight that his face had set into quiet male resignation. He didn't really like everything that was going on, but he loved her and would go along with what she wanted.

Ada kneed herself into bed and slid under the covers to the wall side. "My, but the bed's cold."

Alfred went over to the lamp and held his hand cupped over the glass chimney. "All set?"

Ada remembered something. "I forgot to visit the white owl." She was a little nervous after all. In going to bed with Joan a visit to the white throne was always uppermost in their minds, almost more even than the bedside prayer. "Why don't you . . . " She blushed. The animal side would have to be dealt with after all.

Alfred caught on. "I tell you what. Why don't I just step out in the hall a minute this first time?"

How considerate of him. "All right, Alfred, that'll be fine."

Later it was Alfred's turn. The chamber pot now held their mingled waters.

Alfred blew out the light and got in beside her.

They lay side by side. His right elbow barely touched her left elbow. Both worked their big toes several times against the upper sheet.

Ada sighed. "What a relief I don't have to worry about Joan tonight."

They could hear Ma storming around downstairs getting everybody off to bed.

Ada said up into the dark, "It was a lovely wedding despite all."

"That it was. Though your ma sure threw a scare to me there for a minute."

Ada sighed some more. "Poor Ma."

"Yes. But don't forget your poor pa."

"Yes, him too, of course."

Alfred slipped his arm under her and gave her a light hug.

Ada decided to permit it.

Their bodies slowly warmed each other in the cold sheets.

Alfred turned a little on his side and touched his chest against hers and gently let the flat of his hand fall on her belly.

Ada took his hand in both her hands. What wonderful fingers he had, long and strong. And always clean. "Alfred?" she whispered.

"Yes, love."

In turning toward her he lay in such a way that she could make out what felt like a third hand. "I had it in mind"—her heart began to beat very funny—"I had it in mind that we shouldn't do it right away. That we should wait until we mean to have children."

"Love."

"I know that a good wife should submit to her husband and that she should not deny him his conjugal rights, but I don't want the baby to arrive until after we're married at least a year."

Alfred thought that over. "Wal, I guess there is a chance of it the first time all right. Once is all a stallion needs to make it stick."

How could a man with such clean gentlemanly hands be so blunt.

"But you shouldn't worry about people pointing fingers, Ada. We know what we know, private, and what we know is none of anybody's business. Including your ma's."

"I know, Alfred. It's just that I want to get used to living with you first before I begin carrying a baby. Really get to know you. I don't want to be like Ma. Have a baby I'm not ready for."

"Is that what Ma says about her children?"

"Hush now, Alfred. Judge not that ye be not judged.'

"Wal, me, I wouldn't feel that way, you can bet your sweet life on that."

"That's because you're a man and don't have to bear them."

"I have to support them though, don't I? Feed and protect them? And instruct them if they're boys?"

"Yes, Alfred, that you do. But I still don't want a baby right away." Ada went on. "I thought maybe that when our first child did come, it could arrive on my birthday. Or else on Ma's."

Alfred subtracted in the dark. "You mean, we gotta wait until the third of April? Three whole months?"

"Thereabouts."

Alfred heaved a sigh that came out of his toes. "I don't like it. But . . . Wal, if that's your mind, that's what we'll do. Because I like to please you. And because I promised to be good to you. I've waited this long all these years, so I guess I can wait three more months."

It wasn't long before it felt as if Alfred had only two hands.

Gradually they fell asleep.

Ada ❦ 9

As a sort of honeymoon they visited some relatives on her father's side in East Siouxland.

Ada was disappointed in the relatives. A cousin Henry Engleking had married a Thila Rook and Thila had especially shocked Ada when they went to the privy together one evening just before going to bed. Thila said laughingly that if her husband Henry soon didn't show more ambition in bed she knew of a neighbor who did. Ada could see that Thila was going to come to a bad end.

Ada and Alfred next stayed with Pa and Ma for a week. It was that time of the month for Ada. Ada was pleased to see how considerate Alfred was about her red flowers. It made her all the more fond of him.

Both began to feel how unnatural it was to be always visiting somebody else, eating from another's board, always having to be polite.

Late one February afternoon, on a Monday, they took the train for Bonnie. They stayed at the Bonnie Hotel overnight.

The next morning while Ada bought their first groceries, Alfred got Daise and buggy from the livery stable. Alfred tied Ada's trunk, hope chest, and their suitcases, onto the turtle of the buggy. Then they drove to a farm sale in progress two miles north of town. By careful bidding they bought a small kitchen range, a base burner, a couple dozen lengths of stovepipe, a double bed with mattress, a small kitchen table with two chairs, a kitchen cabinet, a washtub, a Sears cream separator, and a bushel basket, all in fairly good condition. The whole lot cost them $31.50. They arranged with Fat John to bring the stuff over in a sled that very afternoon. Fat John also had just got married and lived over on the Canton road north out of Bonnie, not too far out of the way. By three they were on their way to the farm Alfred had rented. It was on the Rock Falls road five and a half miles north of Bonnie.

The day was clear. They had to ride straight into a busy north wind. It wasn't long before both their noses were red. After a while even Daise had to snuffle, and then got it into her head that she should turn around and go back to town to the warm stall in the livery stable. Alfred's steady hand on the ribbons and a firm, "Daise," kept her going.

They rolled past a country school and then up a slow hill. A row of ash trees lined the west side of the road.

Alfred pointed. "There it is, love. The red barn on the left."

Alfred hadn't said much about their new home, only that the soil was rich and that the barn had just been painted red. From a distance she could see that the house needed paint.

Alfred gave the left line a slight pull, and Daise, after a moment's resistance, rolled onto the farmyard. Daise pulled up in front of the house gate.

"Why, Alfred, this is nice. A real nice grove. And it's all up on high land so you can see a long ways."

"Yeh, but the other renters left the yard a mess. Let it get all run-down." Alfred pointed at piles of rotting cobs, tin cans, and chicken feathers everywhere, and gates hanging on one hinge. "Them Windmillers was a lazy lot. The only reason we got it was that Mrs. Windmiller's mother, Old Lady Gately, who owns the place, finally got mad and told them they had to get off. Some days Windmiller hardly did a tap of work. A good-time Charlie."

"Where did these Windmillers go?"

"He took a job as drayman in Rock Falls. That was about his speed."

"What kind of a woman is this Mrs. Gately?"

"She's sort of soft-hearted. Everybody was surprised when she kicked off her own daughter."

"It sounds like she's a good woman."

"She is. She's letting us rent the place for two-fifths of the crops and four dollars an acre for pasture and hay land."

Ada studied the small story-and-a-half house. "Before you put Daise away, let's go have a look at the house together. It's scary to go into an empty house alone."

"All right."

They stepped down. Alfred set the broken gate ajar so they could get through. Short broad planks, crudely set as a boardwalk, were half-rotted away. The wooden step into the lean-to was cracked, with the nails half-popped by frost.

Inside the house it was better. The rods for the curtains were still in place. In the kitchen the blue linoleum, except for a spot where the stove had stood, was also in good shape. The wallpaper, of yellow imitation scrollwork, was fairly decent. The smell of lye soap intermingled with rancid lard lingered in the air. They also inspected the living room, parlor, and single bedroom. Ada rolled up the buff blinds to let in the light. The rolls all worked. All of it was neatly swept up. The wallpaper in most rooms wasn't too bad.

"The mister may have been a slouch," Ada mused aloud. "But Mrs. Gately's daughter seems to have had some pride left."

"Tell you the truth I'm surprised," Alfred said. "Just after Christmas the house looked awful. Dirty diapers everywhere."

"A woman, no matter how degraded, will always clean up after herself when she leaves a place, if only because she doesn't want the next woman to gossip about her."

"Where'd you learn all that?"

"It's the way a woman is." Ada went back to what was to be their bedroom. "Just the same, I'm gonna scrub this house from top to bottom. Then I'm going to wallpaper every room."

"But why, when it don't look too bad?"

"That's also the way a woman is. I want to start out with a complete new lining in our nest."

"All right. But you're going to have to do most of it alone. I've got my work cut out for me on the yard. And then later in the fields."

"I know."

Ada had a vision of how it must've been for the other woman, who'd submitted herself to her man and had her babies in that very room, the arguments, the kisses, the perfumes, the tears, where the furniture stood and the way it looked, the color of the rugs, the way the curtains hung. What an awful decision for the mother, Mrs. Gately, to make, asking her very own daughter to leave the old homestead.

Alfred shivered. "Sure hope Fat John gets here soon with them stoves. Because it's gonna take a while to drive the chill out of these walls."

"Let's see what the upstairs looks like. You can always tell if the roof leaks by looking at the ceilings in the upstairs rooms."

They climbed a narrow steep stairs, Ada leading the way. On the second floor there were only two tight rooms with dormer windows and peaked ceilings. One look was enough. The roof did leak. There were all sorts of brown rings on the overhead wallpaper. It was as though a Windmiller bed wetter had been in the habit of sleeping on the roof.

"Looks like the landlady is going to have to shell out for some shingles," Alfred said. "Besides the paint and fencing."

Daise whinnied outside.

"Ah," Alfred said, "here comes Fat John. Now to quick get things unloaded and into the house."

They hurried downstairs to greet Fat John.

Ada held the door open for the two men as they carried the furniture into the house. Fat John also helped Alfred carry in Ada's trunk, hope chest, their suitcases, and the groceries. By the time they finished, a lilac dusk lay over the snow-brushed land.

Fat John smiled out of his sheepskin collar. "That it?"

"You bet." Alfred held out a hand. "Next time it's my turn."

Fat John looked at Alfred's hand, after a moment shook it.

Ada said, "I'm sorry we don't have the coffee on."

"That's all right. I've got to get going anyway. Wife Etta still hasn't learned how to milk the two cows we got."

Alfred looked east. "You'll have a full moon in a minute."

"Flick and Fly would know the way back even if it was as dark as the inside of an old maid's bloomers."

"Wal then, easy does it."

"Yeh, and the longer the harder." With a sly smile Fat John climbed into his sled, unhooked the lines, flipped them once, and with a crunch of sled runners his black horses took off.

Alfred quick scratched through the flattened cob pile for a basket of dry cobs and brought them into the kitchen. He and Ada set the kitchen range on the same spot Mrs. Windmiller had hers standing. Despite cold fingers they fitted the stovepipes in place and secured them at the elbows with a piece of wire hooked to a screw in the ceiling.

Ada balled up some loose paper and stuffed it into the stove.

Alfred touched off the paper with a match and then loaded in several handfuls of cobs. "Now we'll see if this chimney draws." Alfred clapped dust off his mittens.

After a moment flames began to lick up the chimney.

"She draws," Alfred pronounced.

Ada felt good about the roaring stove. "I'll quick make us some supper while you put Daise away."

It was just six when Ada and Alfred sat down to their first meal in their own house.

Ada sat on the stove side; Alfred sat where he could see out over the yard through both the west and south windows. Ada's old night lamp in the center of the little kitchen table was their only light. The yellow walls of the kitchen and the blue floor took on the warm colors of a home. Soft silver steam plumed off the boiled potatoes and cabbage and sausage where Ada had set them in front of her husband. The coffee pot murmured on the stove.

"Wal," Alfred said, "tonight we don't have to wait for some other head of the house to ask the blessing."

Ada smiled across the table. "That's right. Now at last you can lead in prayer at your own board."

At that Alfred turned shy.

"Is there something the matter, Alfred?"

"Wal, Ada, come to think about it, I ain't never prayed out loud before. In front of anybody."

Ada folded her hands in her lap. "Alfred, I grew up used to having the head of the house, the man, lead in prayer."

"I know."

"And I'd surely like it if you would lead in prayer in our house."

"Must I?"

"Yes. Go ahead. The words'll come. Just take those words you find in your heart. Those are the only ones the Lord is interested in anyway."

Alfred folded his hands and closed his eyes. His high nose shone in the mellow light. The alarm clock ticked on top of the stove. Alfred's face slowly swelled up red.

"Come, Alfred. Look for those words in your heart and use them."

Alfred shook his head. "All I have there is feelings."

"Speak those feelings then."

"Trouble is, my feelings are mostly rich cream and haven't been made into butter yet."

"You're using words to tell me about it."

Alfred sat a while longer, eyes closed, lips quivering.

"Come, I'll help you." Ada closed her eyes. "You say after me: Bountiful Father in heaven."

"Bountiful Father in heaven."

"It is fitting and proper in the evening of this day, at the end of our cares and labors, that we draw nigh unto Thee. . ."

Alfred repeated the words after her, tongue aping her intonation exactly.

" . . . to ask Thee to bless this food that Thou hast given us and which we have prepared here for ourselves."

"That's not the same as your pa's."

Ada, startled, opened her eyes. Alfred had also opened his eyes and was staring at her. "Shh, Alfred, close your eyes. We're in the Lord's presence. Of course I know it's not the same as Pa's. I thought we should have our own prayer. That people will think of as belonging to us."

"Then you've thought about this before? To help me?"

"Shh, Alfred. I meant no harm by it. I was only thinking of both our welfares. And how we should live our own kind of family life." She closed her eyes again. "Go on."

Alfred went on.

"May it nourish our bodies and give us strength to do our work and to fight the good fight against the evil one. Bless our humble home. Bless all our work. Bless those near and dear to us wherever they may be."

Alfred followed her word for word, perfect.

"Forgive us all our sins. In His name we ask it. Amen."

When he finished after her, Alfred slowly looked up. There was a look of surprise in his eyes.

"What's the matter, Alfred?"

The look of surprise became a soft smile. "Them words fit my feelings exactly. Rich cream and all."

Tears entered the corners of Ada's eyes. She thought of getting up and kissing him but decided against it, not wanting to arouse him.

Alfred helped himself to the potatoes and cabbage and sausage. He spilled a liberal helping of flour gravy over it all. "Mmm. Looks good. After the day we put in."

Ada helped herself too.

Alfred chewed absorbed to himself. "Tastes great too." He buttered himself a slice of bread. "You're a good cook all right."

"Anybody can be a cook, Alfred."

"Not a good one they can't. Just make the rounds of a threshing ring once and you'll know for a fact that just anybody can't. Them kind of brains ain't handed out every day."

"It doesn't take brains to be a cook. It only takes a tongue."

"Ada, I tell you, until I met you, I'd just about decided to remain a bachelor because of all the bad cookin' I'd run into."

"Now, Alfred."

"It's the truth." He dabbed a corner of bread into the gravy and lifted it into his mouth. "Mmm. But, thank God, I can see now that it was a good thing I didn't take up that trade."

Ada laughed out loud, merrily. "Oh, Alfred, sometimes you can be such a card."

For dessert Ada opened a can of peaches. "Next summer I'll can our own. I really don't care much for store peaches."

Alfred gave her the smile of a husband with a full stomach. "All I ask now is for the coffee to be good."

Ada began to feel sweet and warm about sitting with Alfred alone far out in the country. They were going to have a happy life together. She could smell the faint whiff of wild roses in the kitchen.

The coffee with the canned milk and sugar was good. Alfred leaned back in his chair, sipping and savoring the brew, slowly.

Ada got up and put some more cobs in the stove. The kitchen walls, slowly warming up, began to crack lightly here and there. She reached up and set the damper to hold the fire better.

Alfred found his pipe. "Wonder where we put that pail of tobacco."

"I think we should finish first, don't you think?"

"Yeh, I suppose we should." Alfred lay his pipe beside his plate. He sat a moment looking troubled at his hands.

"What now, Alfred?"

"Tell you." Gradually the troubled smile was replaced by a sly country look. "I suppose according to your lights, the head of the house should also read from the Scripture in family worship."

"Not necessarily, Alfred."

"You know I can't read American worth sour apples."

"Shh, Alfred."

"Not that there ain't any languages I can't read. I can read a horse's ears, and a dog licking dew off the grass, and a cat laughing, and a nicker of a horse a mile off."

"Oh, Alfred, maybe those are the hardest languages of all to learn."

"Wal, I just thought I'd mention it."

Ada went over and opened her suitcase where it stood near the door to the living room. She got out a new family Bible. Reverend and Lady Carpenter had given it to them as a wedding present. Ada came back and settled thoughtfully in her chair. She stroked the black cloth binding, traced out the five gold letters, B I B L E, with a fingertip, and then, tipping the book up, sought out the gold silk ribbon where she'd placed it. "I thought that on our first meal alone we'd start with the very first chapter of the Bible."

"Good. I approve."

Ada turned her chair a little to catch the light. The print on the fresh new page was clear. "In the beginning God created the heaven and the earth. And the earth was without form, and void; and darkness was upon the face of the deep. And the Spirit of God moved upon the face of the waters. And God said, Let there be light; and there was light. And God saw the light, that it was good: and God divided the light from the darkness. And God called the light Day, and the darkness He called Night. And the evening and the morning were the first day."

Ada read with the clear voice of a soprano. Out of the corner of her eye she could see that Alfred was listening intently.

"And to every beast of the earth, and to every fowl of the air, and to every thing that creepeth upon the earth, wherein there is life, I have given every green herb for meat: and it was so. And God saw every thing that He had made, and, behold, it was very good."

When she finished the chapter, Ada replaced the silk marker. She closed the good book softly.

Alfred's eyes opened high and grave. "That's the first time I ever heard some of them things read in there, you read so clear."

Ada smiled at her dear man. She thought to herself: "The head of the house should also give thanks. But maybe it's too much to ask him to memorize two prayers in one day." Aloud she said, "Shall we close with silent prayer? Later on we can make up a good prayer of thanks for us to use."

"If you say so."

They bowed their heads.

The clock on the stove ticked a full minute before both raised their heads again, first one slowly, then the other slowly, eyes volving open to see if the other had finished.

Alfred picked up his pipe. "Now, lady of the house, can I smoke?"

"You may. I'll get your tobacco pail. I know just where I put it."

They washed dishes together, chattering about all the things they'd done that day. Then, carrying the little night lamp with them, they put up the iron bed in the bedroom off the kitchen. When they had it stuck together, they found it wouldn't stand level. Alfred had to get a crowbar and bend one corner down.

"Someday I want a new brass bed," Ada said. "When we can afford it."

"We'll get it."

Ada made the bed with sheets, blankets, and a thick quilted comforter. She fluffed up the pillows and slipped them into fresh white cases. She put their nightgowns under their pillows. Alfred got the thunder mug and set it under the foot of the bed.

Alfred stretched mightily. "I don't know about you, lady, but I'm ready for bed. I'm whoofed."

"So am I."

Alfred went outside to see if the stars were still in place.

Ada carried the little lamp into the kitchen to the washstand behind the door. She splashed some rainwater into the washbasin. There were ice crystals in the water and the washrag felt marvelous cool on her face. She enjoyed washing her face and neck the last thing at night and the first thing in the morning.

Alfred came back in carrying an armload of wood he'd picked up in the yard. "Almost break your neck walking across the yard at night." Alfred filled the stove and set the damper for the night. He picked up the clock, wound it, and carried it into the half dark bedroom.

Ada was so tired she felt languorous. She carried the lamp into the bedroom again. As she set the lamp on a chair, she felt a soft little cloud of sleep coming over her. The little cloud began to swirl in her head and she slowly drooped to the floor.

Alfred, half-undressed on his side of the bed, hurried around to her side. "Hey, Ada."

After a moment Ada could feel Alfred shaking her by the shoulders.

"What happened?"

"I don't know," she whispered. "All of a sudden I just started falling. It seemed like I was never going to reach the floor. Like I was more floating than falling." She could feel that her face was white. "It was like I was going to smile and fly at the same time." She noted that she'd fallen with her legs apart. It was pleasant lying that way.

Alfred gathered her up and set her on his lap.

"Now I know how a swallow feels when it dips around in the air."

"You didn't hurt yourself?"

"No. I had plenty of time to land just where I wanted to."

"Gotske, lovely, you scared the dickens out of me." He soothed her over the arms and shoulders. "Mmm, you smell good. Like ripe milkweed."

Ada lay dreaming in his arms. She herself had noticed several times that her skin smelled best some eight days after her flowers.

"Are you all right now?"

"Yes." She made a feeble gesture to unbutton her dress in back. She spoke in a haze. "I've sometimes come close to fainting when I wear that dratted corset. But I wasn't wearing it today. I dunno."

"Let me help you." Alfred's sure fingers quickly unbuttoned her dress down in back. "Maybe this'll make you feel better."

"Yes."

He slipped her dress off, then her petticoat, pleasantly wrestling her around a little as he did so.

"Alfred." Before he got down to bare skin she tried to reach for her nightgown under the pillow. Neither one had as yet seen the other naked. She couldn't quite manage it.

He read her thought and got the nightgown for her. He tried to slip it on over her head.

"Alfred." She finally managed to reach up an arm to help him. There was an awful lot of her lying naked in his lap.

He cradled her up lovingly. Her breast filled his hand, with only the nipple showing between thumb and forefinger. "Love."

"Alfred. We agreed. It's not April yet. I don't want a Thanksgiving Day baby. Nor for that matter a December baby. That's Christ's month."

"Love." His hand wouldn't move. "Love."

She could feel him rising under her. "Alfred."

He swung her onto her side of the bed, and then, letting go of her, with one hand swept the blankets up over her and tucked her in.

"Thank you, husband."

He went around to his side, finished undressing himself, slipped into his nightshirt, blew out the little lamp, and got in beside her.

She lay dreamy, limbs open.

"Feel better now, love?"

"I don't know." That was a mistake.

He slipped an arm under her head and cuddled her close. "What happened to make you feel so dizzy?"

"I wish I knew." She could feel that third hand of his again. It was pressing warmly through their nightclothes. She looked around inside herself for some kind of argument to resist him.

"Love." There was a sound of a groan in his whisper.

Poor man. She felt sorry for him. To be denied so long. Cousin Ada hadn't denied her man that long. While Cousin Allie hadn't denied her lover Willie Alfredson at all.

He slipped her gown up past her hips.

It was pleasant. What harm if the baby was born a month or two early. Maybe it would be nice to have a child born sometime before Christmas. Have it as a Christmas gift. So what if the baby was born before their first year of marriage was up? Her belly made an odd humping motion, once, folding up a little at the navel. Almost immediately she felt herself melting, all through her innards, so that there was no resistance in her, no chance to close her limbs.

His breath began to whistle in her ear. His hand seemed to be everywhere at once. At last a fingertip found where she was melting. Too late. He managed to come upon her. There was some fumbling.

Her eyes rolled up into her head. "Ouch."

"Hurt you?"

She embraced him. "It's all right."

The moment of entrance was upon her. He moved slowly into her. Holy union. It was happening at last. So this is what it meant. He trembled upon her. Lord bless. He began to rock upon her. Except for where it had hurt her for a second it was pleasant. The hurt felt like a skinned finger smarting. He rocked a little faster. He clutched her in his arms and held her very tight. After a moment he crushed her to him, several hard times, straining up into her, reaching, reaching. A wondrous groan escaped him. Just so he wasn't using her for his own pleasure but was doing it as part of the Lord's wish for them to be fruitful and multiply and replenish the earth.

He became limp upon her.

For the man it meant a whole lot more than it did for the woman. Maybe, though, that would be made up for when she breastfed her babies.

He slid off and lay beside her. He seemed to retreat from her, to draw off into the distance.

The aftereffects of the swooning slowly left her. She could feel where a part of him still touched her. There was hardly enough room in the bed for their two lanky bodies. Yet she managed to withdraw from him. She began to feel like she sometimes did when she was about to get a headache. Like her whole body was swollen.

He turned on his side away from her. He fell asleep.

She slept fitfully. Toward morning the overall swollen feeling went away. And thank God, she didn't get a headache.

Once when she jerked awake she heard him murmuring. She could make out some of the words.

" . . . that we draw nigh unto Thee . . . Bless our humble home . . . Bless those near and dear unto us. . . ."

Poor man. Even in dreamland he was busy learning the prayer she'd taught him.

Alfred ❦ 10

A SIGH AWOKE Alfred. He blinked his eyes in the dark. He listened. Ada was still slumbering in slow falls of flesh beside him.

The first time was always the best time. That first horseback ride across the pasture. Of course that first time ever with a lovey woman was the best of all. It felt more to home and warmer than a tongue did in one's mouth.

Now when he went to town he could look other married men in the eye and think, "I know what you know." He also knew now what Ada's father knew. It surely was good to be a man and the head of a house at last.

He turned slightly and placed a hand on her slim belly.

Her hands began to fight off a haunt. A sound bubbled in her throat. Then she turned away from him, still sound asleep.

Wal, he could think about it all day and wait until tonight.

He reached down a hand to his overalls where they lay on the floor and searched a match out of the bib pocket. He snicked the head of the match with his thumbnail and it instantly fizzed up into a blue light. Yep, it was six on the dot. He swung his feet out of bed, reached for the clock, and clicked off the alarm before it could ring. He leaned forward and with what was left of the match lit the little lamp. The chimney made a crinching sound when he pinched it back into place.

Ada awoke and came up with scratching fingers. Her blue pupils were almost lost in balls of white. "In God's name, where am I?"

Alfred smiled over his shoulder at her. "Right where you're supposed to be, love. With your hardworking husband in your own bedroom."

Her eyes blued over and she arrived from wherever it was she'd been. "Oh, Alfred, what an awful dream."

"It was, huh."

She shook her head. She rubbed her eyes. "There was this gas smell of milkweeds. Then my hips, I couldn't move them. Then my father came and whispered something in my eye and then I began to fall. Then a girl named Grace called my name. Then a strange man placed a sword on my hip like my hip was a cake and it was when he was going to cut me up in slices I woke up."

Alfred didn't know what to say.

"Such an awful dream, Alfred."

"That'll happen sometimes I guess." He ran a hand over his face. He could still smell the sweetness of her on his fingers.

"What time is it?"

"Six. And time to be up and at 'em."

"That's right. There's the house to red up. And then later that public auction."

Alfred was glad to see she didn't seem to feel bad about what they'd done the night before. "I'll make us some coffee."

"It's funny that the girl's name should be Grace. I don't remember a girl named Grace."

They went at it right after breakfast.

Alfred put up the base burner in the living room for Ada. Then he checked the barnyard fences to make sure they were tight. He also cleaned up the main yard, tin cans, scraps of wire, broken boards. The wood he chopped up for fuel and brought into the house.

When he went up into the mow to see if there might be some little hay left for Daise, he spotted a dozen empty whiskey bottles scattered around in the loose chaff.

"Why, the poor devil. Mister Windmiller drank by himself. A sop rag." Alfred turned over one of the bottles. The label had a picture of an old crow sitting on a fence post. "So that was the real reason why Old Lady Gately chased him off the place."

Alfred got an old gunnysack and gathered up all the empty bottles.

Just as he was descending the ladder, his eye caught a glint of glass high up on a sill next to the big hay door. Yet another bottle?

He lowered the sack of bottles to the alley below and then climbed up to the high sill. Sure enough. Another one. But this one was full. The seal was unbroken. "What do you know."

Alfred stuck the full bottle in his mackinaw pocket. Clucking to himself, he went down and picked up the sack of clinking empties and dumped them on the junk pile in the grove.

He stuck his head into the kitchen a minute. "Hey, look what I found." He held up the full bottle. "The haymow was full of empties."

Ada looked up from where she was washing dishes. "Is that . . . ?"

"Yep. Whiskey. Must've forgot where he hid this one."

She wiped her hands in a towel and came over and took the bottle from him. "Old Crow," she read. "What are you going to do with it?"

"Wal, at first I thought I'd throw it away with the empties on the junk pile. But then I thought, no, one of these days one of us'll have a cold and then this'll be the clear dope for it. Medicine."

Ada frowned. "Liquor in our house?"

"Old George Pullman always a kept a bottle handy for colds."

Ada gave way grudgingly. "All right. For medicinal purposes then." She turned and headed for the bedroom. "The poor poor woman."

"Hey, where you going with that?"

"It's going into my clothes closet and there it's going to stay."

"All right, if you say so, lady."

By nine they were on the road heading for Mrs. Bernie Moss's place two miles south and three east. Bernie Moss had been killed by a mad bull and Mrs. Moss had decided to move to town. She was holding a public auction of all their farm property as well as some of the household goods.

The junk was sold first. Junk was always hard to get rid of and if it was sold at the end of the sale, after the best stuff had been put on the block, it went for nothing. For a couple of dollars Alfred bought an odd lot of tools in an old bushel basket: hammer, pliers, pincers, wrenches, brace and bit set, screwdriver, chisels, plane, saw, awl, punch, curry comb, and horse brush. For two bits he bought a pail of nails and staples and copper rivets.

Alfred helped Ada bid on a washing machine and got it for three dollars. He bid on two oak rocking chairs and got them for a dollar each.

He bought a lumber wagon that was still in good condition, plus a set of sled runners to go with it, a half ton of hard coal, and nine bushels of sacked grain, all for ten dollars.

After the free lunch at noon, the sale of the livestock began. Alfred spotted a three-titted cow, just fresh, that looked like she might be a good milker despite the defect. She went cheap, only ten dollars, and Alfred and Ada had their first cow. A little later Alfred bid on a poorly matched team, a sorrel mare three years old and a black gelding nine years old, fifty dollars, harnesses included, and they had their first team of horses. The mare was a heavy raw horse and the gelding a skinny fellow.

Ada wondered a little about Alfred's last purchase.

"Just wait, I'll find matches for them at another sale sometime and then I'll have two good-looking pairs. And that mare I can breed for colts."

At the end of the sale, when everybody was leaving, Ada noticed a farm couple arguing with the clerk from the First National Bank about a sewing machine they'd bid on. The sewing machine was a Singer and almost new. The couple couldn't pay cash for it and their credit wasn't any good. The woman was crying. She wanted that sewing machine so bad. The man was red-faced, embarrassed.

"Alfred," Ada said, "look."

"Yeh, I been watching 'em," Alfred said. "It's the Rileys. They live east of us along the Big Rock. It's all sport and no work with him too."

The bank clerk, Chauncey Mack, spotted Alfred and Ada. "Say, Alfred, maybe you'd like to buy this for your bride."

"How much?"

"Seven dollars and fifty cents." Chauncey had a lot of smiling teeth.

"That's pretty steep."

"Not for what's practically a new Singer."

Alfred turned to Ada. "Wal, do you want it?"

Ada's heart went out to the crying woman. "Maybe this lady here can figure out some way to pay for it."

Chauncey pursed his lips. He had the eyes of the true banker, quick to size up people. He knew when a silver dollar and a golden conscience rang true.

Ada turned to Mrs. Riley. "Can't you really figure out some kind of way to raise the money?"

Mrs. Riley was a short fat woman. The only thing left of her one-time beauty was her slim ankles. "Them little tykes, cold, running around in their rags. I can put the Singer to good use."

Chauncey pinched a question at Ada. "But you need a sewing machine too though, don't you?"

Ada slowly shook her head. "Right now we can do without."

Chauncey nibbled at his lips. Then he shot a hard look at the Rileys. "All right. Take it home. But if you don't somehow raise the money within sixty days, then I'll repossess it."

Mrs. Riley let up crying. She gave Ada a shy look. "I won't forget this."

"That's all right, Mrs. Riley."

Riley offered to help Alfred load up his goods in his new-bought wagon. Riley, for all his haggard eyes, was a well-set-up man.

Ada drove Daise and the buggy home while Alfred drove the new team and the loaded wagon. Before it got dark Alfred drove over to the Murrays and got a load of ear corn. That night Daise had a dozen ears of her favorite dish.

Alfred and Ada sat down to a simple supper of potatoes and cabbage and rice pap. Alfred didn't wait for Ada to prompt him. He plunged right in. "Bountiful Father in heaven, it is fitting and proper in the evening of this day, at the end of all our cares and labors, that we draw nigh unto Thee. . . ." The right words kept coming up out of a misty red place in his head and the next thing he knew he was finishing it. "In His name we ask it. Amen." He opened his eyes.

"Why, Alfred, you know it already."

"Sure. I don't need to be told twice. Mostly."

She looked at him.

He smiled a high nose smile. "I'm not as dumb as your ma thought at that, am I?"

"Alfred, if you'd have had schooling, it's hard telling what you might've become."

Alfred helped himself to the steaming potatoes. "I like it just the way it is."

"You've never had any ambition to be something else? Something high in the church, say?"

"Nope." He paused over a chunk of potato. "Wal, now that I've heard your organist play, a church organist maybe. To be able to play the pipe organ like him, that would be great."

"But otherwise nothing else?"

"Nope. I like the outdoors."

After a moment, Ada said, "Yes, in the eyes of the Lord a laborer tilling His fields is a good thing to see."

After she'd read Chapter Two from Genesis, Alfred wondered out loud if she shouldn't teach him the prayer for thanks next.

"Why, Alfred, of course. Nothing would please me more.'

He followed her phrase for phrase: "Merciful Father in heaven, we are humbly thankful for the food and health given us this day. We thank Thee for the Revealed Word from which we have been given moral guidance. We thank Thee for all the many good things given us this day. Guard and protect us from evil in the night yet to come. Help us to be kind to the unfortunate. Bring us light and open our minds, O Lord, that we may see ever farther into the lengths and depths of this world that Thou hast created for us. Forgive us all our sins. In His name we ask it. Amen."

As they were going to bed, Alfred found a fresh nightshirt under his pillow. "Girl, you don't need to give me a fresh nightshirt every night."

Ada unbuttoned her shoes, smiling quietly to herself.

"What's wrong with me wearing the one I had on last night?"

Ada pulled her dress up over her head.

"I don't get it." Alfred slipped on the fresh nightshirt and opened up the bed on his side. "But, if it's your mind to make a mystery of it, far be it from me not to let you have your pleasure."

Ada also had a fresh nightgown under her pillow.

Alfred's eyes opened in wonderment. "You a fresh one too?"

"Shall we pray?"

They got down on their knees each on their side of the bed and prayed silently to themselves.

Alfred had barely nuzzled his nose in his pillow when he noticed she'd also put fresh sheets on the bed. "Say, and clean straw too."

"Well, Alfred, if you must know, when I went to make the bed this morning, there were some pink spots on everything."

"Oh."

"It's all right. We can both be proud of it."

Alfred lay in thought for a while. Blood put a different light on things all right. It probably meant she wouldn't be of a mind to let him touch her that night. Shucks. Wal, it was maybe just as well. Ada believed you shouldn't do it unless you had children in mind. Also she wanted to wait until the child could be born in January.

Alfred leaned up on an elbow and holding his other hand over the lamp chimney blew out the light.

Ada rustled at ease beside him. "Good night, my husband."

"Night, love."

Ada ❦ 11

ALFRED FINISHED CLEANING up the entire yard, both around the house and around the other buildings. He trimmed out the dead branches in the grove of walnuts north of the house. The dead wood made for a considerable pile of fuel for the stove. He replaced the broken panes in the barn and the outbuildings. He fixed the barn-door hinges and reset the door hooks so all could be shut snug at night. A door was a door only when it could be closed tight. He put new rope where needed in the hay slings and sharpened the prongs of the hayfork. He fixed the fence in the little night pasture as well as in the big pasture. Luckily most of the cedar posts were in good shape, so all he had to do was tighten the barbed wire. He repaired the storm windows of the house as well as the storm doors, making every one fit wind tight.

Inside the house Ada scrubbed the walls and floors. She repapered every room with a color and a design of her own liking, light blues and greens. She put down new linoleum where needed. She cleaned tan blinds, put up new rods, hung clean white curtains. The inside cistern pump on the washstand sucked up more air than it did water, sometimes sounding very much like a just-stuck hog, a most disagreeable sound, so Ada took it apart and put in new leathers. The cellar door in the lean-to off the kitchen had one corner that sometimes got stuck. She got Alfred's plane from the tool shed and neatly trimmed it down until the door fit perfectly.

When they could, Ada and Alfred attended public auctions held in the area, and gradually they managed to get all the basic equipment needed to start farming: disc, harrow, grain seeder, corn planter, walking cultivator, mower.

To make it simple for them to pay for the things they bought at public auction, Chauncey Mack suggested that they open a checking account at the First National, since Alfred was already a depositor. Writing checks against a balance in the bank was getting to be a common thing, Chauncey said.

Alfred had to learn how to write his name. Ada helped him in the evenings after supper. She first made him fill a lined page from her linen tablet with capital A's, then the letter l, and so on. Since his last name was Alfredson, all he had to learn for that was the last three letters. Once he had them down, she taught him how to put all the letters together, *Alfred Alfredson*. For some time no matter how he concentrated, his script was always a little shaky where one letter joined another. He had to think it out from letter to letter.

Ada thought: "What a funny brain that man has. He can learn a whole prayer by heart just hearing it, but when it comes to looking at black letters on white paper he can't."

Ada suggested that when it came time for him to write a check he should ask the seller to fill in the check and then casually sign it. That way no one would catch on he couldn't write.

A curious thing happened when she taught him how to write numbers. He caught on right away. When she taught him some simple arithmetic, he also did well at that. Though again he did better adding and subtracting in his head than on a piece of paper. He seemed to pick up arithmetic just like he picked up a tune just hearing it once.

"It's the way God made him," Ada thought, "not like the rest of us. Though it's going to be hard to explain to people that because he can't read or write he's not dumb."

In middle March, Alfred came across another odd-matched team of horses, a sorrel gelding four years old and a dark brown gelding eight years old. He bought them for forty dollars, harnesses included. That gave him two fairly good matched teams, a pair of young sorrels and a pair of steady old boys. Even their names were good matches. The sorrels were called Beaut and Bob and the dark pair Duke and Dan.

The first week Daise wasn't too sure she liked having the four new horses around. She sometimes kicked at them when they came near her, and flounced her long black tail in their eyes. But then one morning at the water tank, when Duke shouldered her out of the way and drank first to his heart's content, she changed her mind. Duke was her king. After that she let the other horses alone, provided that first Duke and then she had their fill. When she and Duke had to separate upon entering their stalls inside the barn, she reluctantly let him go, always with a little whinny.

When the frost went out of the ground on the twenty-first of March, Ada wondered if Alfred shouldn't dig a new vault for their two-holer privy before he began his field work.

"What's the matter with where it stands now? It's kind of protected there behind them lilacs."

"I don't like to sit on top of where I can smell someone else's waste."

"It won't jump up and bite you."

"Alfred."

"All right. I don't use the place myself, so it don't make any difference to me where it sets."

Alfred dug a new vault as close to the old one as possible, six feet down. He set the privy up on a single row of cement blocks. He tar papered the lower part of the privy and threw dirt up around the sides to keep out the wind on a cold day in January.

"There you are, lady. All you need to do now is paint it and it'll be fit for the queen herself."

The next day Alfred began disking in the field and then for two weeks Ada hardly saw him during the light hours. He was in a rush to keep up with his neighbors. That first year everybody would be watching to see if he really could run a farm.

One morning on the third day of April, Ada walked south a mile to pay Mrs. Alan Weatherly a visit. Alfred had visited with Alan Weatherly across the fence the day before and over a pipe Alan mentioned that his wife Alta was having great luck with their new chicken brooder that spring. His wife had more chickens than she knew what to do with. Would Mrs. Alfredson want a few? Ada would.

At the mile corner, Ada stopped a moment to watch the school children playing under the ash trees. It was recess time and the children were playing wink. Their cries as one or another of them was caught winking at a hidden player filled the air like birdsong. The teacher, wearing a blue dress, stood on the cement stoop facing the morning sun. The teacher held a hand over her eyes. When Ada smiled, she waved her hand a little.

"Someday soon our child will be going to school there."

A farmstead lay catercorner across from the schoolyard. The shadow of its near row of box elders lay all the way to the shoulder of the road. Alfred had come home with the story one day that there'd been some kind of family quarrel there, such crazy mad ruckus that they'd deserted the place, with the result that it had gone all to weeds and moss. With spring growth only now just beginning to poke out of the earth, the place looked its worst. Meanwhile the birds and squirrels and skinks had taken over.

A meadowlark called nearby. "This *here* is *my* place."

She couldn't locate the bird at first. She kept moving her eyes back and forth like she often did looking through a screen door trying to find movement farther away. Finally she caught sight of it. On a fallen post. There was a little spot of yellow that at first glance appeared to be a single dandelion. Behind the yellow spot was a twitching rusty scissors, the tail, incessantly opening and closing.

Another meadowlark farther down the draw, in a gray slough, spoke up. "This *here* is *my* place."

Ada spotted the second bird after a moment too. It was sitting on a dry stalk of ragweed. When it let go with its wild pure pealing cry, it made the single weed rock back and forth.

The two birds began to vie with each other to see who could claim that his place was the most his place. They were both being bossy about it as well as happy about it. They were also courteous about it, the one always waiting for the other to finish his announcement.

Such rich liquid ringing warblings Ada had never heard before. Again she smelled a heavenly gaseous perfume. Her limbs felt loose. She wished someone, Alfred, Pa, even Ma, were around so she could throw her arms around them and kiss them.

"This *here* is *my* place."

"Such a funny feeling. Because I also want the Holy Ghost to enter my soul."

A third meadowlark across the road and nearer the Weatherly grove, let fly with his clear proud cry of possession. He sang it a little differently. "Peent. Peent. It's the spring of the year."

"Another country heard from. Oh Lord, how marvelous are all Thy works."

"Where, where, where," went the meadowlark, until, upon the last note, the effort to sing lifted it up into the air, some twenty feet, so that it cried a hurried, ecstatic, "Glad you see the light at last!"

The Weatherly yard behind its evergreen windbreak was quiet. The maples overhead had just begun to thicken out with fat buds. White chickens were everywhere, picking up bits of lost grain.

Ada strolled slowly up to the white house gate.

"You're the new neighbors, aren't you?" a voice suddenly said from a plot of black earth between the house and the road.

Ada blinked. What she'd mistaken for some clothes drying over a sawhorse turned out to be a woman bent over planting something. Even more startling was the voice. It was as deep as a man's.

"Yes, I'm Ada Alfredson."

The woman doffed her canvas gloves. "I'm Alta Weatherly."

Ada stepped through the house gate. "I see you're planting your garden already."

"Some lettuce." Alta stepped toward her. She had shambling legs and was extraordinarily tall, taller than Ada. "Lettuce likes to get into the ground early to catch those soft April showers."

"You're not afraid of a late frost?"

"Lettuce handles the frost pretty well. It has ruffled leaves." Alta smiled, curiously laconic, a little like Uncle Sam on those posters in the post office. "I suppose you're come to ask about the chicks?"

"Yes."

"Come." Alta led the way to a small white building. When she opened the door, a wonderful flutter of fuzzy golden wings exploded before them. Hundreds of shrill cheeps in unison cracked in the ear like a toothpick poked in too far. The smell of sweet chick manure hung in the air.

"Goodness gracious!" Ada exclaimed.

"Yes, there's about six hundred in here. Every egg seemed to hatch."

"How many did you expect?"

"About four hundred. That's plenty for us."

"Then you've got about two hundred for sale?"

"Yes. And all of them white Plymouth Rocks."

Ada stared down at them. It was as though the floor was covered with a great flock of tiny hairy cupids, all of them golden. God could not have made them more beautiful. "How much?"

"Oh, five cents apiece."

"I'll talk to Alfred this noon."

"Good." Alta looked at Ada kindly. "One word of advice."

"Yes?" Ada couldn't get over it that there should be a woman taller than she, by at least a couple of inches.

"Don't use the old Windmiller chicken house on your place. It's loaded with lice and disease."

"Can't one fumigate it?"

"You're better off starting with a new one."

"Oh, dear."

"It won't take your husband long to make one." Alta nodded. "And now that we've settled that part of your visit, how about a cup of tea?"

Keeping their toes down to avoid stepping on the fluttering chicks, they shuffled out of the brooder.

Ada asked Alfred to inspect the chicken house. One look was enough for him. "We'll burn it, nits and all." He wrung his right ear, the one he usually slept on. "The dang thing is almost rotted through anyway. Maybe we can get the landlady to get us some wood and roofing for a new one." He wrung his ear again. "In the meantime, since the corncrib is empty, you can use that for your chicks for a while."

They were walking back to the house, when Alfred's keen ear caught something. He stopped. He stood as still as a tree.

"What's the matter?"

"Puppy. Over in the ditch alongside the road there."

Alfred stalked down their short lane, Ada following him.

"Sure enough. No wonder my ear was ringing."

Alfred picked up a little curl of gold fur out of the grass. The moment he touched it the little thing whimpered. It wasn't much bigger than a ring of sausage.

"A collie pup. Well well." Alfred stroked it. "Somebody must've threw it out here to get rid of it."

Ada clapped a hand to her forehead. "Now I remember. I heard a little yelp just before dinner. But when I looked outside, all I saw was a buggy going down the road. Real fast."

"That's it then. Somebody dumped him by our lane figuring we'd find him and give him a good home, being as we're just started farming and would pretty soon want a dog."

"They must've felt guilty about getting rid of it."

"Maybe it was some kid with his mother doing it before the old man stuffed 'em in a sack and drowned them in the river."

"How awful." Ada reached out a hand and softly stroked the humped back of the pup. "Why," she said, "it can't see yet."

"That's what I was noticing. Probably about a week old." Alfred looked under it. "Yep, it's a him all right."

"Poor thing."

Alfred placed the pup gently in Ada's hands. "Here, you take him. He better get used to you more than me. Because I won't be around as much to fuss with feeding him."

The pup had small ears, a round head, and a pugged nose. Ada could feel its heart beating against her fingers. "Well, you little rover boy you, you've already had a pretty wild time of it, haven't you?"

"That's a good name for him. Rover."

Ada nodded. "Yes. Rover. Rover."

"When we get our boy, he'll make a great playmate for him. As well as a watchdog."

That evening Ada lined an old shoe box with a piece of old flannel for the pup to sleep in under the stove. The little pup had supped well on cow's milk. Alfred had improvised a nipple out of the finger of an old rubber glove.

"Wal," Alfred said, "I don't know about you, but I'm going to bed."

Ada gave the pup one more soothing touch over its soft round head, made sure it was tucked in warmly, then made moves to go to bed herself. It had been a long day.

She pumped herself some cold rainwater from the cistern. She washed herself. Her skin seemed more golden than usual. She had the look of a ripe peach. It was probably because of the walk in the sun that morning. Of course it could also be that just a week ago she'd put aside her Venus protector.

She looked closer. The sun had also brought out the freckles over her nose. Ma'd once said that there was a way to get rid of them. Let a washcloth out overnight so the dew could set in it, and then the next morning wash off the freckles with the dew. Ada leaned over the white basin and luxuriated in bathing her cheeks with handfuls of water.

Accidentally she happened to sniff a couple drops of water up into her nose, high. She had to snort sharply to blow them out. She could smell clouds in the water and some kind of wildflower.

She wrung out the washcloth. She dried her face. She emptied the basin. She blew out the kitchen light.

She found Alfred sound asleep lying on his back. In the muted light his face lay in handsome repose against the white pillowcase. The high nose suggested a strong and manly husband. She liked it.

With him sound asleep she didn't have to put on her nightgown first and then undress under it. She had a glimpse of her own naked body just as she lifted the nightgown over her head. The nightgown fell around her with a sensuous rush of soft flannel.

She blew out the light and slid quietly in beside her husband. She tucked the quilt in under the edge of the mattress on her side.

She lay breathing softly. She thought over the events of the day: the buying of the golden cupid chicks, the finding of the golden curl of a collie.

"How tender and understanding Alfred has been all these weeks since that time we did it in February," she thought. "He hasn't bothered me since. When he could easily have been a pest. Etta of Cousin Fat and Minnie of Lemuel Longwood say their men bother them at least a couple of times a week. What must those men be thinking of, when the only time you're supposed to do it is when you're planning to have children? And not for the fun of it."

Ada thought: "It's about three months since we got married." She calculated in the dark. "Nine months from now it'll be my birthday. The third of January. It'd be something, wouldn't it, to have the baby on my birthday. Yes, and have Alfred father it just three days after his birthday."

She pushed her nightgown down and then caught the hem of it with her toes. She liked to make her toes snug inside her nightgown. It always took a while for her feet to warm up at night.

The motion disturbed Alfred. He rolled away from her. He muttered something, breathed deep several times, then said, very clearly, "Finished getting in the oats today."

Ada smiled to herself in the dark.

Pause. Then he added, still in sleep, "That'll show those Englekings I'm not so dumb." He took a sudden snort of breath. And woke up. "Huh? What?"

Ada's smile tickled up into her cheeks.

"Did you say something?"

"No, Alfred. But you did."

"Oh."

"You said you finished getting in the oats today."

"Oh. Well. I'm the first in the valley too."

Ada heard male pride in his voice. It was good to hear. It was just like the pride of those meadowlarks she'd heard that morning.

"That'll show 'em there ain't no flies on me."

That curious wonderful smell of heavenly gas was in her nose again. There was a feeling in her that her innards had turned to warm honey. She turned and put her arms around him. She wanted to be part of his sense of triumph. It was a good and noble thing to have planted seed in the earth in their proper season. She wanted to catch him in her arms at the very peak of his best moment as a husbandman of the fields. "My husband," she said, "is it not time for our planting too?"

"Hum?"

She opened her thighs and drew him against her and with her arm around his hips pressed him close in love.

He awoke as a man. In a few moments he was upon her, and with several deft motions thrust his hard silken stalk deep into her.

All too soon it was over. But it had been pleasurable like the other time. And both man and wife at the same time had wanted to engender a child in the April of their first year of married life. The Lord could not help but bless them. She would conceive. She could feel his seed lie in her belly in slow lazy curls.

"Good night, my love."

Later in the night she was awakened by his hand moving on her belly. His hand was urgent.

"Again, Alfred?" she whispered, not resisting him.

"Oh, love, the last time we did it only once and there was no baby. I was thinking that if we did it again, we should do it several times in a stretch. Like the creatures of the field do."

"Is that what they do?"

From her tone he caught on that she wouldn't mind. He was soon upon her.

Twice more during the night he awakened her. Each time she whispered with sweet acceptance, "Again, my husband?"

It was all pleasurable. It was like the taste of honey. She knew she wasn't getting out of it what he was, that strange hinnying cry of intense pleasure. But she took comfort in the thought that all those sweetly streaming seeds were now trying to find a home in her womb.

She let him be a king for a week.

Ada ❦ 12

BY EARLY SUMMER Ada's nipples began to feel touchy.

It was Wednesday morning. Through the open window drifted the faint perfume of the last of the lilac blooms. Rover lay on his belly in front of the screen door on the foot-wide carpet, looking out at the white pullets pecking in the grass beyond the house gate.

It was time to feed the chicks, always a pleasant task. Ada wiped her hands on the towel above the sink, then buttoned on her yard shoes. She looked down at the pup. "Ready?"

Rover knew the word. He got to his feet and leaned ready to go. Rover had grown into a sharp young dog with a flowing golden tail.

"Good dog." Ada pushed open the door and went to the granary, with the pup padding at her heels. She scooped up a pail of ground corn from a bin and headed for a clean spot in the center of the yard where there still wasn't too much chicken dung.

"Chick! chick! chick!" she called.

In an instant gawky white pullets converged on her from all points of the farmyard. Those farthest away raced fastest, running as hard as they could go on their yellow legs, using their half-formed wings to build up speed.

Ada waited until all two hundred had gathered at her feet. They fluttered up against her legs in waves of cresting white. Sometimes their surges buried the pup at her heels. Rover had learned to suffer their fooster of fledgling wings. Their beaks were open as wide as they could get them, pink with yellow edges, red tongue belling like the anther of a tiger lily.

She began spraying out handfuls of cracked corn like a sower seeding a field. The chicks followed the sprays to either side behind her in sudsing wavelets. By the time she'd emptied the pail the two hundred chicks were scattered out over the yard in even ranks. Their rapid pecking was like the sound of falling drops of rain.

Rover continued to sit. He looked mildly around him at the busy peckers. His golden tail plumed up in pleasure.

Ada strolled back through the working chicks. She had to shoo a path for herself. She moved leisurely, the hem of her long green dress flowing across some of the wigging white tails. When she reached the center of the feeding chickens, Ada upended the pail and sat down on it.

She studied her flock in loving reverie. How lovely to be raising her own live creatures. So far she'd lost only four. The pullets were all in the half-fuzz and half-feather stage. Though endearing. Soon some of them would be ready for eating and then would come that awful time of having to kill them.

"Alfred can do it," she thought. "I know I'm not."

A robin called in the walnuts behind the house.

Rover came over and licked the back of her hand once.

One of the gawky pullets stepped up to Ada's left shoe and picked sharply at the bottom button. The black button was shiny and it bobbled about upon each peck. The pullet pecked at it a dozen times. It wouldn't come loose. Finally when the pullet made out that the shiny pellet wouldn't come free, it cocked its head sidewise up at Ada and gave her an angry yellow-rimmed eye. "Keck," it went, and went off looking for another pebble.

Ada smiled. She petted the collie beside her. She sat in the midst of her chickens for a long morning minute.

When the sun began to warm the backs of her hands, she got to her feet, reluctantly, and put the pail away.

She picked up a packet of lettuce seeds, got the hoe and rake, and headed for the small kitchen garden east of the house. In late April, Alfred had turned over a small plot of black dirt for her with his walking plow. It was some twenty feet square. She'd already planted peas, beets, beans, cucumbers, lettuce, and radishes. The radish crop was about gone but there was still time to plant another lettuce crop in its place so they'd have fresh greens in August. She pulled up the remaining radishes, most of them spindly and bitter. She snapped off their heads anyway and carefully piled them red in the grass, white roots spread out like the tails of dead mice. She'd use them in the soup that night. One couldn't afford to waste a thing.

She hoed the little patch, four feet by four feet, raked it level, then sprinkled several pinches of lettuce seed over it. The seeding motion reminded her of a fairy tale. All she had to do was wave her hand over the earth like some magician, and the black soil, with all its wonderful pink angleworms, would burst into a green garden.

A few of the seeds stuck to the palm of her hand. They resembled tiny needles. They stuck together as though magnetized. She wondered if human fatherstuff looked like them.

She raked the patch thoroughly, then sat down on her heels and patted the dirt down firmly. Husband Alfred had taught her that. To show her how important it was to firm down the soil, he'd deliberately stepped across the radish patch early in May and a week later the first radishes to show were those growing in his footprints.

She slapped her hands free of earth and dust. She brought the garden tools back to the tool shed.

She made Alfred four dried-beef sandwiches and put them in a paper sack. She filled a small pail with coffee, cream and sugar added. She called up Rover and with him at her heels headed through the walnut grove and then north along the end of the field. She looked across the neatly checked rows of corn to see where Alfred might be. After a bit she spotted a little plume of dust rising beyond the last soft lift in the land. Soon black horse ears perked over the thin shimmer of green corn. It was Duke and Dan and they were coming toward her. Good. It meant Alfred was on the back round and would reach her end of the field in a couple of minutes. She walked to the last row he'd cultivated and sat down against a fence post. Rover lay down in the grass beside her.

There wasn't a breath of wind out. The sky was as blue as a field of flower flax. The sun shone gold on a rolling green land. The perfume of wild roses came to her from the ditch behind her. There were so many meadowlarks calling around her, up and down the road and across the fields to all sides, that they reminded her of a passage in the Gospel. "And suddenly there was with the angel a multitude of heavenly host, praising God."

The longer she sat the stronger the aroma of the wild pasture roses became. Sometimes the scent was so fresh, so sweet, it was as if someone were whispering in her nose. She leaned around the fence post to get a better look at the flowers. Not a foot away hung a single perfect wild rose. It had just bloomed; some of the sticky rosin of the bud was still on the tips of the sepals. Scent arose from the pale pink petals like heat waves.

A red ant appeared between two of the petals. It was as though an actor had stepped out between pink curtains for a final bow. The red ant ran angularly over the short hairy anthers. The ant's legs picked up pollen. After a moment its legs looked as if they'd been dusted with yellow sulphur. Just as the red ant stuck its nose down into the hairy bed of anthers, a huge black-and-yellow bumblebee buzzed down out of nowhere and landed beside the red ant.

"Oh," Ada breathed. She was deathly afraid of bumblebees.

The red ant didn't like having the bumblebee around either. It started; lifted its nose; then darted off the yellow stage, disappearing behind the pink curtains.

The cumbering bumblebee, self-absorbed in its bee brain, hardly noticed the red ant. It tottered about on the dipping bloom. Finally it found what it was looking for, a drop of rose nectar. Hugely it lowered its tail and began sucking.

"Boss," Ada scolded.

"That's me."

"What!" Ada jerked around. She cleared her eyes with a blue blink and looked up at her husband. "You scared me. I didn't hear you coming." Alfred had left the horses standing facing the road into the wind.

"So I noticed. You were so busy with that flying grizzly bear." Alfred leaned down and petted the top of Rover's head. "And I see you had to come along, hey?"

"What an odd thing to call a bumblebee."

"That's what a bumblebee is in the bee world."

Again Ada was struck by how apt her husband's talk could be.

In a moment the bumblebee buzzed off.

Ada gave Rover a playful scolding look. "You're some watchdog, you are, not to warn me my husband was coming."

Rover looked at her, worrying about the tone of her voice.

"A well-trained dog never barks at the master." Alfred settled on the grass beside Ada. He opened the paper sack and smelled into it. "Mmm, dried beef and fresh butter." With his jackknife he pried at the lid of the little pail. It came open with a little poof and coffee steam rose to his face. "Ahh. Bull's-eye. You've cotched me right in the middle of my stomach." He held out the pail to her. "First sip?"

"No. Not this morning."

"Well then, begging your pardon, here's to you." He took a good long drink, his Adam's apple uggling up and down.

Ada observed that Alfred's clothes were splotched with sweat, under the shoulder straps of his overalls, under his arms, over the tops of his lean legs. The wet spots in the folds of his overall were crusted over with gray dust. His sweat had the smell of a hearty man's sweat, not at all boarish sour like some men's sweat.

A shiny black carriage with two dappled grays came down the highway from the north. A stranger was handling the ribbons. He tipped his gray hat in greeting as he whizzed by.

Ada remarked, "Our road's getting busier lately."

"Sure. Haven't you heard?" Alfred said. "The map makers made our road here the main highway between Sioux City and Winnipeg."

"That far."

"They're going to call it the King's Trail."

"Say now, that'll mean we won't be living in such an out of the way place after all, will it?"

"Nosirree. And the best news is, they're going to grade up our road. Make it higher and broader. Maybe even gravel it."

"Then we can go to town any time, can't we? Not have to worry about muddy roads after a rain."

"That's right." Alfred selected a sandwich. With a walking cultivator he had to hold down the shovels and guide the horses with the lines over his shoulder all at the same time. The brutal work always gave him a tremendous appetite. Yet he took modest bites of his dried-beef sandwich.

"Maybe now the folks will come and visit us sometime."

Alfred chewed silently for a few moments. "Still lonesome for them once in a while?"

"Aren't you for your family?"

"For Pa, no."

"Have you heard from your pa lately?"

"You know I haven't. He's out in the Dakotas somewhere."

"Someday I'd like to meet your people."

"You will. The Dakotas are dry and Pa'll get burned out. And then he'll remember how good he had it back here in Bonnie." Alfred finished the last of his sandwiches and then drank up his coffee. "Man, that was good." He smacked his lips. "Yeh, Pa will be back before the year is out. It takes about that long to lose everything in the desert."

Ada picked a single wild clover and held it to her nose. Its red-brown cylinder smelled like a sleepy puppy. "Do you think your pa would hurry home if he knew he was soon going to be a grandpa?"

Alfred's high nose thought her question over. "You mean, we're going to have a grandson for him pretty soon?"

She looked him full in the eye. "Yes."

He slipped an arm around her waist. "You're sure?"

"As sure as a woman can be."

"Love." He put both arms around her and kissed her. He kissed her several times, warmly, soundly.

She let herself lean against him. She felt so very strange to be thinking of herself as a mother-to-be. It was hardly what she'd once believed as a little girl, that the mother swallowed some special yeast, and the yeast baked a baby in her belly. So this was how the world really kept going. The women kept dividing in two.

Alfred cupped her breast in his brown hand. His arm tightened around her and he began to heat up.

"No, Alfred. Not out in the open like some animal of the field."

"But I'm a human being of the field."

"No, Alfred. I have other kinds of loving thoughts. Not those. I'm not in the mood for that."

"Not in the mood? Wal, now, that I'll listen to. That's different." He gave her a loud smack on her cheek and let her go. Then he dug his curved stem pipe out of his bib pocket and lit up.

Ada liked the smell of his tobacco.

A half hour later, as she walked home along the fence, she was startled to see a gopher slink through the deep grass with the motion of a snake. She watched the gopher duck down into its hole.

Her eyes next caught sight of a hummingbird flitting by. The hummingbird darted straight for some ragged lavender flowers growing in a wet spot in the ditch. The ruby throat and the green body went well with the pinkish blue bracts and the paired winglike green leaves. The bird could have been the flower or the flower the bird.

Then she recognized the flowers. "Say, that's a patch of wild bergamot. A kind of mint. That'll make good country tea if I dry its leaves."

She slipped through the fence, careful not to catch her dress on the barbs, and gathered up an apronful of the long square stems.

Ada ❦ 13

EARLY ONE MORNING in August a rooster crowed in the doorway.

"That sounds like company's coming," Ada remarked to herself.

Around ten she put away her dust cap and slipped into her yard shoes.

She was about to pass through the house-yard gate, when she saw the mailman, Slim Lehr, coming up the highway in his oblong box buggy. She stood a moment to see if Slim would stop at their mailbox.

"It's Thursday. The paper should at least be there." Ada didn't think much of *The Bonnie Review*. It was mostly full of silly gossip about local people and canned news about faraway places. Of more value to her was the other weekly, *The Watchman*, the church paper, but that wasn't due until Saturday.

Slim Lehr did stop. But not beside the mailbox. He rolled past it a few feet and then pulled up. He stepped out, and then helped a young lady down. He lifted out a brown suitcase and set it beside her. Next he handed the young lady a rolled-up newspaper. Then tipping his hat, nodding, he got back in and drove off.

"That rooster was right. We are getting company today."

The young lady looked around wonderingly, at the trees in the grove, at the red barn. Then her eyes fell on Ada standing in the house-yard gate. Her face brightened and she picked up her suitcase and started toward Ada. The young lady was tall and slender. She had on a broad white hat, a white dress, and white shoes. As the young lady came closer, Ada saw she had red-brown hair and green eyes. Her tall way of walking was vaguely familiar.

"Are you Ada?"

"Yes."

"Good. Then I'm at the right place." The young lady smiled. The smile opened up what was otherwise a firm, even refined, face. "I'm Karen Alfredson, Alfred's sister. You've maybe heard of me."

"My goodness. Yes, of course. You're tall like he is."

"Yes. And like you are."

As they sized each other up both had large smiles for each other. The sun was bright out and both cast slim shadows on the grass.

Ada held out both her hands. "Karen. It's good to meet you at last."

Karen set down her suitcase and took both of Ada's hands in hers. "Well, and it's good to arrive safely at last." With a little laugh Karen added, "I hope Alfred didn't tell any tales out of school on me."

"No." Alfred actually had been pretty silent about his sister, as well as the rest of his kin. There was some dark thing at work in the Alfredson family.

"That's good." It was easy to see Karen was quite surprised to find that her brother had married a decent-looking woman at that. "Well, I suppose I had better tell you how come I arrived a day late."

"A day late?"

"Yes. Didn't you get my letter?"

"No."

"That's funny. I wrote you from Sioux City a week ago. You see, I finished taking normal school training at Morningside College, and I wrote to ask if it was all right if I stayed with you people until school started. Then come September first I'd go back to boarding at the Murrays'."

"You teach?"

"Yes." Karen pointed down at the country school on the corner below. "Rock Township No. 3. I've been gone from that school for a year."

"We never got any letter from you."

"Then the mails must be slow again. Like they were last year." Karen looked down at the rolled up newspaper in her hand. "Maybe it's . . . " She opened the newspaper. "Why, here it is. My letter to you folks." Laughing, she handed it to Ada. "Personal delivery. Maybe you better read it to see if I really am welcome after all."

"Why? Is there something in it we should know?"

"No. I was just saying."

At that moment Rover appeared from behind Ada's long dress and began barking furiously at Karen. He set up such a clamor, sudden and loud, and showed such fierce teeth with his head held low, that both women retreated several steps.

"Here, here," Ada scolded. "Why, you naughty dog you. This is company. You be nice to our company now. She's a nice lady."

Rover barked harder. The hairs on his golden tail stood out like quills.

"Rover! Now you keep quiet."

Karen's face fell inward, resigned. "It's all right, Ada. Animals have never liked me. For some strange reason."

"But Rover usually has such a good disposition."

"No animal has ever liked me. When I've always so wanted a pet."

Ada stooped over to pet Rover. "Now you see here, you— "

Rover drew back his head like a snake; snapped at Ada.

"Why!" Ada gasped. "That dog! Whatever has got into him." Ada stamped her foot at Rover. "You bad dog!"

On the sound of the word "bad" Rover did quiet down. He backed off several steps. Though he couldn't quite suppress an inward moaning fury.

"Well," Ada said, "at least we got him to quit that awful racket barking." She gave Karen an apologetic smile. "Come, let's go in the house. There we can talk in peace."

"Then I can stay?"

"Of course you can stay, Karen. My goodness, what else?" Ada glared at Rover once more to make sure he wouldn't start up barking again. "Alfred isn't home today. He's out threshing at the Stoefens'." Ada picked up Karen's thin suitcase. "Come." Ada led the way into the house. Ada was careful to leave Rover outdoors.

Karen wiped her feet on the rag rug just inside the door. She surveyed everything with a kindly smile that at the same time was a little critical. "Why, Ada, what a neat homey little kitchen."

"Oh, I try to do the best I can with what little we have. That first year one really has to skimp, you know."

"Oh, but you know how to dress things up tastefully."

"Well, I try to make do." What had Alfred's sister really expected? And that Alfred, why hadn't he ever told her that his sister was an educated woman? "Would you like to see the rest of the house? And at the same time I can show you to what we call the guest room."

"All right. But really, Ada, this is darling. And I know how this house looked before. I visited the Windmillers here once when their daughter Tessie got herself into a mess."

"Their daughter Tessie? I never heard about that."

"Yes, one of those Horsberg boys. They live just north of here. Adolph got her in a family way. And right under my nose too. They were pupils of mine." Karen rolled her green eyes.

"I didn't know that."

"Aaarch. I didn't know people could be such animals. Like pigs."

Ada thought: "Now it comes out. Maybe there was more to it than just Mister Windmiller's drinking." Ada said, "I'm sorry to hear that." Their talk was bordering on mean gossip. "Come, let me show you the house. Then I'll make us some coffee."

"No coffee for me," Karen said, flat. "That's poison."

"Tea, then?" Karen, for all her education and manners, had a way of being awfully blunt.

After they toured the little house, and Karen's suitcase was brought upstairs to the guest room, they sat down to tea.

As the day progressed, with both of them beginning to like each other more and more, they began to share each other's family histories.

Ada's notion of Alfred's family was pretty hazy. Alfred she knew a little about, that he was taken out of school when his mother died and was put out for hire at the Charlie Pullmans' while still only a boy. But Ada was surprised to learn that Karen, upon their mother's death, had been placed with foster parents, the Gordon Hamiltons. It accounted for Karen's fine airs, since the Hamiltons had come from England by way of Vermont. Alfred's father, Alfred Alfredson V, had kept the four younger children, Janet, Richard, Abbott, and Gerda, and had promptly left town. It appeared that Alfred V was a restless man. Some years later Alfred V returned to Bonnie. He got married a second time to a widow from Massachusetts named Bettie Mercer. She was a mail-order bride. To eliminate family argument Alfred V put Janet out to work for a neighbor named Herman Johnson and Richard out with the family of Bob Crout.

"Alfred tells me that your father's out in the Dakotas now," Ada said. By that time it was mid-afternoon and they'd once again sat down for a refreshment, a glass of lemonade.

"Yes, Dad continued to be unhappy here in Bonnie. He never found what he wanted to do in life. He made storm cellars here. Why, he and Billy Mather laid most if not all the walks in Bonnie. Sometime when you're in town and you get a chance, take a look and you'll see their initials in all the sidewalks."

Ada's eyes opened. "That's like my father. He and brother John laid most of the walks in my hometown."

"Isn't that odd."

"Yes."

Karen's eyes half closed. "I once walked with Dad to a country school northwest of town where he was working on a cyclone cellar. I must have been about eight years old." Karen shook her head in memory. "But that walk was too much for me. I never went again. Yes, Dad was a hard honest worker."

"So then Alfred's father is out in the Dakotas somewhere with Gerda and Abbott and the new Mrs. Alfredson?"

Karen's green eyes fluttered. "Well, no, the truth is his new wife Bettie is here in town."

"What? They've separated?"

"Only temporarily. She went out there with Dad all right. But after a month of it she came back. She said she couldn't stand the desolation out there."

"Why, Alfred's never mentioned that his stepmother was here in town. I wonder why he never told me."

"Alfred and his father had a falling out."

Ada felt hurt that Alfred hadn't told her about his stepmother living in town. A fly came whizzing from nowhere and landed beside her glass of lemonade. Ada stealthily picked up the flyswatter, and with a sudden pounce, got it. "Is Mrs. Alfredson living alone in town here then? Or what?"

"She's a housekeeper. For Chauncey Mack."

Ada gasped. "No wonder Chauncey looks so funny at us sometimes. No wonder."

"Yes, poor woman. As Dad says, a setting hen gets nowhere."

"Don't you like her?"

"She's all right. She's a little mad right now that Dad traded his home here in Bonnie for a section of land out in the Dakota desert." Karen fixed Ada with an anxious look. "Please don't get after Alfred for his not telling you. I don't want to cause trouble."

"Oh, Karen, of course I won't."

There was a flash of morbid curiosity in Karen's green eyes. "Too many husbands and wives don't get along as it is."

Ada gave her a soft smile. "You don't have to worry about us. Alfred and I get along real good. He works hard. He's full of fun. In fact, he's so full of fun I'm sometimes afraid poor Alfred is getting cheated out of his husband's rights. I know he'd like to bother me more than he does. But he doesn't because he thinks of me and my wants."

"That's the way to handle those men. Don't give them an inch. Make them behave." There was a sound of angry wasps in Karen's voice. "If you're not careful, they'll just use you for their own selfish pleasures, and then throw you aside like some used dishrag. Men only think of one thing." Karen took a sip of lemonade. "Always."

"Well, Alfred is a good husband and I like to be nice to him once in a while. Just to please him. Though now with a baby coming I'm afraid he's going to have to deny himself for a while."

Karen more dropped than set her glass on the table. She snapped a look at Ada's belly. "You don't look like you're with child."

"I am though."

"You're really going to have a baby?"

"Yes."

Jealousy crinkled at the corners of Karen's eyes. Some kind of dark knowledge stirred in the depths of them, far back. "Aren't you afraid?"

"Of what? I think of it as a coming joy, I'm so happy about it."

Karen swallowed with difficulty. "Well, that means . . . when do you expect it?"

"In January. About the time of my birthday."

"Did you plan it that way?"

"Sort of. I was also thinking of my mother's birthday. Mine comes the third of January and hers the fifth."

"That's different. Hmm, that means I'll soon be an aunt." Karen laughed suddenly. It was the laugh of a child coming upon something good when it hadn't expected it. "Aunt Karen. Won't that be something."

"Yes, it will."

"Aunt Karen. I hope it's a little girl. Boys are always so nasty."

Ada had to smile. Karen's father had once been a boy, hadn't he? "Alfred, of course, wants a boy. To carry on the Alfredson line with. If we have a boy, he'll be Alfred VII."

"Och! Those men with their blood lines. As though we women count for nothing. Why can't there be a family line by way of women? The truth is, the Andringham line by way of my mother is every bit as important as the Alfredson line." Karen touched her lips with a white handkerchief. "Those men think us cows that we have to be bred with the best gentleman cow around."

Again Ada had to smile to herself how Karen, for all her college education, could occasionally be so uncouth. Alfred had that same trait.

"That reminds me. I forgot to tell you why I was a day late."

"Oh, that's all right, Karen. I'm glad you're here now."

"No, I want to tell you. You see, I've got some kind of female trouble." Karen blushed. "You see, I didn't get my flowers until late, until I was eighteen. You know, friends come to stay? One's period? Well, it still misses sometimes. For whole months at a time. So I decided to see a doctor in Sioux City who specializes in female trouble."

"I see."

"You'd almost think I was getting a baby, it skips so." Karen laughed, with broken gusts of breath. "But of course that's ridiculous. Since I haven't even let anybody kiss me. I'm still like a little girl, sweet and innocent."

Ada happened to catch sight of the clock on the stove. "Oh, I've got to get supper started. Alfred will be so hungry when he gets home."

Karen shot a pinched look at Ada. "And he'll come home real tired too, won't he?"

"Not Alfred."

"You mean, he's got that much pep?"

"Alfred's never down. He's as tough as an ash tree."

"Hmp. That's because he . . . Well, Dad's that way too. Men!"

Alfred ❦ 14

ALFRED GOT HOME early. The threshing crew finished up at the Stoefen place around five, too late to start the next job at the Horsbergs before dark. He went into the house with his man's smile to give his Ada a kiss and a hug and to let her know they could have supper early—only to find Karen sitting in his chair in his favorite corner. He stared speechless at his sister.

Both women smiled up at him, Ada warmly and Karen coolly.

In his sweat-ringed overalls and his dust-dirty face and arms, Alfred right away felt ill at ease. He rasped his bristly chin with a calloused hand. "Gotske," he finally muttered.

"Why, Alfred," Ada said, "is that a way to greet your sister?"

Alfred knew he should say something nice to his sister but part of him had set its shoulder against her.

"Alfred?"

Alfred's mind sparked rapidly. He thought: "I'll betcha she's filled Ada with a lot of guff about us Alfredsons. I can tell. Ada has that forgiving look in her eyes."

Karen got to her feet. "I can take a hint. I'm not welcome in my brother's house."

Alfred snapped his hand down. "Sit. Sure you're welcome. Though that's my place you're sitting in."

Ada frowned. "Alfred, can't you at least say hello first?"

"Hello, Sis."

"Well," Karen expostulated, "I declare. Hello."

"Karen says she can visit us a couple of weeks," Ada said.

"If that's what she wants."

Karen didn't like giving up Alfred's chair. "When school starts down at the corner, I'll board at the Murrays' again."

Alfred retreated a step. "You're going to teach that close by?"

"Yes." Karen got herself another chair. "Alan Weatherly promised me my job back after I finished normal school ."

Alfred thought: "Karen just maybe might be good for Ada. Be woman company for her in the winter months ahead." He clapped his hands together. He said aloud, "All right." He got up a warm smile for Ada. "I just came in to tell you I can be through with chores in about a half hour." With a further smile, Alfred left for the barn.

He was carrying milk to the house, a pailful from their only cow, when he noticed both Ada and Karen staring out of the screen door at something down at the corner below. He entered the lean-to. As he poured the milk into the separator tank, he called into the kitchen, "What's louse?"

"There's some gypsies down at the schoolyard below," Ada said. "With a covered wagon."

Alfred had a look for himself. Sure enough, there stood a covered wagon under the trees, with a couple of little tykes running around it and a little fire burning at the edge of the roadside ditch. "Son of a gun. Wal, no use for them to come up here. We haven't got much for 'em to steal. Yet."

"Alfred," Ada scolded, "not all people steal."

"All gypsies do."

Alfred began to turn the handle of the separator. Soon he had the proper speed and he opened the spigot on the tank. In a moment skim milk came out of the bottom nickel spout, splashing into the milk pail, and cream out of the top spout, purling into a small stone crock.

When he finished separating, Alfred took off his sweaty clothes and put on fresh overalls and shirt. He next gave his face a good scrubbing in the kitchen sink. It felt good to be done with the day's work and cleaned up. Better yet there was a good supper coming up by the best cook in Leonhard County. He combed his black hair meticulously and sat down in his favorite corner.

The womenfolk set the table, all the while still speculating about the covered wagon below, telling each other various stories they'd heard about gypsies, Karen about their kidnapping of little children and Ada about their talent for music.

Finally all three drew up to the table for supper.

Alfred asked the blessing. About halfway into the prayer, Alfred thought it might be nice after all to let his sister know that, really, he was glad to see her, so he cleverly inserted an item about her. "We thank Thee for the safe arrival of our sister. Bless us together in the next couple of weeks. May we once again feel warm toward each other like in the old days. Bless her work in the coming school year." That ought to show her, and at the same time it ought to please her. "Forgive us all our sins. In His name we ask it. Amen."

Alfred opened his eyes, curious to see what his two women had to say about that.

Ada had a quick smile of admiration for him.

Karen was dumbstruck. It was plain to see she hadn't expected Alfred to be able to rattle off a prayer at all, let alone one as good as that. That little item he'd put in for her benefit had thrown her for a loop. Karen said slowly, "I thought maybe you folks might practice silent prayer."

Alfred didn't even bother to smile. He looked for the potatoes.

Ada said, "I've always believed that the head of the house, the man, should lead in family worship."

Karen said, sadly, "I wish Dad would have done that."

Alfred said, "Yeh, he didn't even believe in silent prayer. And he can read."

Karen fired up. "Dad is not an atheist."

Alfred said, "I didn't say he was. All I know is he acts godless."

"Then you think our father is going straight to hell?"

Ada's blue eyes flicked from one face to the other. "Shh now, you two. And that right after we've prayed. When we were just in His presence." Ada shook her head at Alfred. "Is that a way to talk about your own father?"

Alfred blinked. The truth was the truth. "Wait'll you meet him. Then you can see for yourself."

Karen was almost in tears. "I love my father, I'll have you know."

For a little while there was only the sound of an occasional click of a fork on a plate and the clock ticking on the stove.

They were into the dessert, some canned crab apples which Alfred dearly craved, when Karen, looking through the screen door, suddenly exclaimed, "Look, there's those gypsy children coming onto your yard."

Alfred looked. By golly. Abruptly he stood up. "They're after out pullets, I betcha."

Ada put down her fork precisely across the top of her plate. "I wonder. They wouldn't steal chickens in broad daylight, now would they?"

"A nice juicy pullet roasted can taste mighty good."

It was a boy and a girl. The boy was carrying a small tin pail. Their clothes were patched. Both were bareheaded and their brown hair was sunburnt over the top. Their bare feet were so tanned that even from where Alfred stood he could make out their pale toenails.

"Where's the dog?" Alfred asked. "I'll sic him after them."

"Wait," Ada said.

The boy and girl headed straight for the well outside the gate, completely ignoring the chickens prinking about in the grass.

"See," Ada said, "all they want is a little water for cooking."

Karen put a hand to her throat. "Why, they look familiar, those two."

"Gypsies?" Alfred snorted.

"But they do," Karen insisted. "They're about Abbott's and Gerda's ages. Oh, how I miss my darling brother Abbott."

"It's all in your head."

Rover emerged from under the stoop. He didn't bark. He ran out through the gate and advanced to within a dozen steps of the boy and girl, then sat down.

The girl spotted the dog first. She said something to the boy. The boy stopped in his tracks. When he saw the dog meant no harm, he settled down on his heels and began to make a coaxing sound with his lips.

Rover cocked his head to one side, waved his long pluming golden tail; advanced a few short steps; sat down again.

The boy in turn advanced a few steps, settled to his heels again. He gave the dog his most winning smile.

Suddenly the boy lunged forward and tried to catch Rover. He got his arms around him but couldn't quite hold him. The dog squirted away.

Something in what the boy did, or said, seemed to reassure the golden collie nevertheless, and he laughed a long pink tongue at the boy, and playfully began to skirl in circles around him.

"Yere puppy, yere puppy," the boy called.

Rover was deliriously happy. Here at last was a playmate his own age. He began to leap on two legs at the end of his circling eights.

The boy yearned to touch the dog. He sprang for him again. Missed.

Then the boy began to run after the dog. He moved out after the dog like a sprinter. His legs flashed past each other.

The dog dug in, butt settling low, tail pluming straight out.

Incredibly the boy didn't lose ground to the dog.

"Look at that kid run!" Alfred marveled. "Just like Abbott used to run in them footraces. To a T."

The boy's legs flickered even faster. He gained on the dog. The two were almost past the red corncrib. Then the boy made a headlong dive. And caught the dog.

"It is Abbott!" Alfred cried. "Nobody in the world can run like that except Abbott hisself."

There was a gasp from Karen. She too stood up. "Are you sure?"

"Yip. And that's little Gerda with him."

Ada got to her feet then too. "You mean . . . ?"

"I don't mean nothin' but."

Ada said, "Then that old man down there by the roadside fire there, that must be your father."

"Pots and damnation."

Karen pinkened with joy. "My own little brother Abbott." Gathering up her long dress Karen darted out of the door. "Abbott! It's me. Your sister Karen." Karen ran to where Abbott was cuddling the pup. Rover had accepted capture in good grace and was kissing Abbott's face ardently with a long pink tongue.

Gerda, bewildered, watched her sister race past her.

"Abbott, Abbott, my own little darling brother." Karen fell on Abbott's neck and began kissing him too. Abbott's brown head disappeared beneath the gold fur of the dog and the tumbled red-brown hair of Karen.

After a moment Rover erupted out of the heap of arms and legs and backed off. He recognized Karen and began to bark furiously at her.

Ada said, "Alfred, I think you better go out there."

Alfred's voice fell a whole octave. "Yeh. If that don't burn the salt."

"Oh, Alfred, really, I didn't know you could carry such a grudge."

"Wal, the old man did some pretty mean things to me in his day."

"Think of your mother then and what the whole family meant to her."

"I suppose you're right." Alfred pushed through the screen door. "Wal, wal, look what blew in with the tumbleweeds."

Abbott broke out of Karen's hug. When he saw who it was he jumped to his feet with a shout of joy. "Do you live here too, Alfred?" Abbott had to speak up to make himself heard over the barking of the dog.

Alfred grinned down at his young brother. "I better live here."

"Really, Alfred?"

"Yip. This is my place all right. I live here with my wife. Karen just happened to come along today."

Abbott gave him a boy's wondering look. His dark cheeks gave his blue eyes the high look of a haunt. "You mean, I now have another sister?"

"That's right." Alfred turned on the dog. "You shut up! Hear? Now!"

Rover instantly slunk down.

Abbott looked toward the house. "Is that her?"

"You bet."

Ada moved through the gate toward them. She smiled. "Hello."

Abbott smiled too, shyly. "Hello, Sis."

Alfred looked Abbott up and down. "Grutnicks, boy, but you've grown."

Abbott's smile widened. "You think so?"

"Why, you've put on at least four inches."

"I hope so. Because I want to be as big as you."

Ada touched Alfred's arm. "What about Gerda?"

A tiny frown quirked Alfred's dark brows, then passed. Gerda. Yes. The one he'd fooled with a long time ago, when he didn't know any better, about which Karen had reported to his father that "Alfred laid on Gerda for a minute or so." Alfred said, somewhat shyly, "Hi Gerda."

"Hi." Gerda didn't quite smile. She had very light blue eyes like her two brothers, and a slender body. She was just beginning to bud out.

Ada stepped forward. "And I'm Ada, your new sister."

"Hi." Gerda gave Ada a quick smile.

Karen stood up. With both hands she pinned back her hair. "Gerda. It's good to see you again." Hair in place, Karen held out her two hands and took hold of both of Gerda's. "Why, you look like Indians, you two."

Abbott laughed his wide boy smile. "We should. We've been living with real Indians for almost a year."

"Real Indians?"

"Yep. Oglala Sioux. Our land was right next to their reservation."

"But real wild scalping Indians?"

"Sure. Only they don't scalp anymore," Abbott said.

Alfred almost sneered. "So that's what Dad lucked out West for. To live like an Indian."

"But Alfred," Abbott protested, "it was fun being out there. No school. And we could run in any direction and never have to worry about a fence."

Karen was so happy to see her little brother and sister she was almost weak with it. "To think that my little Abbott and Gerda lived with savages and survived."

"No, no," Abbott cried, "you've got it all wrong. It was great sport. I never had so much fun in my life. There never was no danger and I made the best friends there."

Karen kept wanting to touch Abbott. "My, but you've grown tall."

Ada placed a hand on Alfred's elbow. "Alfred, don't you think you ought to go down there and invite your father up? You mustn't let your own father stay out overnight along a roadside ditch."

"No, I guess not."

"And tell him we have plenty to eat if he doesn't mind simple food."

"All right." Alfred looked at Abbott and Gerda. "You two might as well stay here. I can get him alone."

"Come, you two," Ada said.

Alfred strode down the road. He wondered what he should say to the old man. The more he thought about it, the more he was sure Dad had planned it that way. Dad must have found out from someone where his oldest son lived. And in his sly way he'd sent his two youngest kids up for water in the hope that his oldest son would recognize them and so invite them all in for supper and the night. There was a well lower down the hill, just across the fence from the school grounds, and Dad could just as well have sent Abbott and Gerda there to fetch the water.

Alfred stepped around the dusty covered wagon and came upon his father seated on a box in front of a little crackling bonfire. Dad was smoking a corncob pipe. He always smoked his pipe with the bowl upside down. Alfred half expected his father to be wearing Western-style clothes. But Dad wasn't. He was wearing railroad clothes—gray engineer's cap, gray hip overalls, gray shirt, and boot-type shoes. He was neatly shaven.

Alfred stared down at his father. "So you've decided to come back to good country, eh?"

Dad Alfredson slowly looked up. He wasn't wearing his usual big dark glasses. His light gray eyes were sensitive to light and on bright sunny days he was careful to protect them. He'd almost ruined them those years he'd sailed the seven seas. His well-trimmed brown moustache twitched at the corners.

Alfred could feel the old piercing power of his father's look taking over again. When the old man wanted to, he could stare holes right through one with his light gray moon-touched eyes. "Wal, you better hitch up your plugs again and bring your rig up to my yard. Here, I'll help you."

Dad stood up. He was almost a foot shorter than his son. Yet with his broad slab of a body he appeared to be every bit as powerful. "B-b-but what does the cook say, son?" Dad sometimes stuttered.

"Ada says if you don't mind simple grub you can have supper with us."

"Abbott? Gerda?"

"By now they're already scrubbed up."

Dad considered his corncob pipe a moment. "That's that then." He clapped out his pipe in his hand and threw the ashes into the fire. Then he kicked dirt over the little fire until he'd smothered it. A last rope of smoke wisped up past his face and was gone. He put his pipe away.

The two men hitched the horses to the covered wagon without any waste motion. The horses were small red pintos with a brand, Flying V, on their right flanks. They'd been cropping deep green grass lustily in the ditch and were sullen about having to go to work again.

Alfred gave the near horse a light whack over the shoulder. "Don't worry. In a couple of minutes you can be eating fresh oats."

Dad glanced at the oats field west of them where shocks of grain stood in neat rows. He said nothing.

Both climbed onto the spring seat up front. Dad picked up the lines and drove. An old silence grew between them.

They pulled up a dozen paces past the house gate. They unhitched the pintos and brought them into the barn, Alfred ushering them one by one into Daise's stall. The pintos snuffled at the strange surroundings, and hung back, but when Alfred threw them each a couple of bundles of oats, they forgot their fears and soon were munching contentedly.

"When they get through eating," Alfred said, "we'll let them out with the other horses. That is, providing Daise and Duke agree. They sort of run the night pasture for me."

"The p-p-pintos won't fight. They've been gelded."

"Good. They could use a good roll in the dust."

Dad was quietly sizing things up: the well-kept harnesses, the manured-out stalls. "I see George P-P-Pullman made a good farmer out of you, son."

"I should hope so."

"That was at least one good thing I done. Put you out with him."

Alfred held his tongue.

They stepped outside and headed for the house. Dad walked with the jaunty swagger of a sailor on the rolling deck of a ship. It enabled him to keep up with Alfred's long-legged gandering stride, step for step.

Dad appeared to approve of the neat yard too. Then his glowing eyes fell on the chicken house. "What's that boarded up for?"

"It's full of lice and disease. I'm gonna burn it down."

"You expect to be butchering soon, don't you?"

"Yes."

"And you'll be smoking beef and sausage?"

"I guess so."

"Use it for a smokehouse for a year. That'll take care of the vermin. Specially if you use old cedar posts for fuel."

Alfred wished he'd thought of that first. Making a smokehouse out of it would save him the time of having to build a new one.

"Usually when people fumigate they don't do it long enough."

Alfred held the door open for his father and they entered the little kitchen together. Alfred glanced around surprised. Ada and Karen had moved the supper out into the living room onto the big round oak table. The kitchen was too small to seat more than three. "Wal, Dad, it looks like somebody here thinks you're special company. This'll be the first time we'll have eaten out there."

Ada came out, beaming, eager to meet her husband's father.

Alfred tipped his head in his father's direction. "Wal, here he is, wife. My old prodigal father."

Ada took Dad's blunt hand in her two slim hands. "Well, Pa, at last." Dad's hand was burnt dark by the Dakota sun, hers were a house pink. Ada was a hand taller than her father-in-law.

Dad's eyes turned to glowing opals. His moustache moved. "Thanks, daughter."

Karen stood crying in the door to the dining room. Her eyes resembled rain-sprinkled pools of water. "Hello, Father." She advanced a step, began to cry even more, then fell on her father's neck, wresting his hand out of Ada's hands. Karen was also taller than Dad.

The old man stood stiffly patient.

"Oh, Dad, it's so good to have you home again," Karen wept. "Does stepmother know you're back?"

"Hardly. We drove in from Canton today. Bettie will be told in due course." Gently Dad separated himself from Karen.

"Well, Dad," Ada said. "I suppose you're hungry. Here's a towel for you. And after you've washed up, we can all sit down. The three of us still have our dessert to eat. And we can take our time with that. As well as sip tea to keep you company."

"Tea?" Dad smiled. "Ah, that will be a treat. A true lust."

"It's tea I made from some wild bergamot I found."

"That's even better. Especially if you use Siouxland well water. Oh, how I've missed that good water."

Ada arranged the seating. She placed Alfred at the head, with Dad across from him, then Abbott and Gerda on Alfred's right, and Karen and herself on the kitchen side.

Abbott ate with the hunger of a racing horse. Gerda, who usually picked at her plate like her sister Karen, for once fairly gobbled down the food. While Dad ate with sure measured gestures—he'd learned to appreciate good food for what it was, and to savor it, mouthful by mouthful, no matter how hungry he might be.

When all had finished eating, and Ada had read from Isaiah, the first chapter, "Your country is desolate," and Alfred had offered thanks, with a well-inserted item about his father's return, everyone pushed away from the table and sat back feeling wonderfully full.

Dad asked the lady of the house for permission to smoke. Ada gave it, and Dad filled his corncob pipe with several pinches of Corn Cake tobacco. He lighted up with the bowl turned over as before.

Ada was intrigued. "May I please ask why you should smoke with your pipe upside down?"

Dad smiled under his moustache. "I hate to waste smoke. And the pipe is less apt to go out that way. The hot coals work upward with the draft."

"But won't the ashes fall out and burn holes in your clothes?"

"There is some danger of that. But I usually make it a point to smoke over bare ground. Or an empty plate."

"It's a filthy habit," Karen sniped. Then she quickly added, "I'm sorry, Dad. But that's what I think."

Dad smiled some more.

Alfred filled his pipe too, with Long Distance tobacco. "Wal, Dad, now that you're returned, tell us how it was out there in the wild Dakotas, and what you all did, and did you have any close shaves with the redskins?"

"Yes," Ada joined in, "we've heard so much about the wild Dakotas, just how was it out there?"

Dad spoke past his yellow pipestem. "Rough-ty."

Alfred was disappointed. "Is that all you got to say about it?"

"Son, for once your Bible is right. It is a desolate country. And besides that, it's hotter than hell."

Abbott had to laugh. "Tell 'em what you did one day, Dad. When you went to see how hot it really was. What you did with that egg."

Dad laughed too. "It got so hot around two o'clock one day that just to show That Fellow Up There that He'd let things get out of hand, I fried an egg on our sidewalk. It took a while, but it fried."

"Not really now," Ada said.

Dad sucked ruminatively on his corncob. "Yes. I hated to admit I'd made a mistake going out there. I hated to give up our claim. But I finally just had to. When you start singing songs to yourself, it's time to pull up stakes." Dad reached for his glass of water and took a slow loving sip of it. "You don't realize how good you've got it here with this good water to drink." He deftly wiped a few drops from the draggled ends of his moustache. "Out there water's got alkali in it. Yet to survive you've got to drink it. Until at last you become so full of alkali that you start calling coyotes by their first names."

All laughed.

"The only green I saw out there was the green I took into the country. In my pocket. The good old dollar bill."

Abbott said, "Tell 'em about what our pet calf did once, Dad."

"Ha. In nosing me over one morning looking for tag end to suck, our pet yearling spied some green in my vest pocket, and he licked it out, bill by bill, and I turned around just in time to see the last of my bankroll going down his throat."

"Goodness," Ada exclaimed. "Then what?"

Dad smiled. "We were a little short of meat at the time."

"You butchered the calf?"

Dad nodded.

Abbott had to laugh some more. "Funny thing was, when we opened up the calf's stomach, we found the bills all neatly rolled up into a bankroll again."

"Oh come on now," Alfred snorted. "That's going too far."

"No, it's a fact." Abbott almost fell off his chair laughing. "The one dollar bills first, then the fives, then the tens."

Alfred leaned back on two legs of his chair. "Now you're just plain lying."

"Dad?" Abbott appealed, still laughing.

"That's right." Dad tongued up several smoke rings. "Just like a cow over a period of time will slowly roll up hair into a ball in her stomach. You know, hair she's cropped from a horse's tail for the salt that's in it?"

Ada had been laughing along with Abbott, but now she began to wonder herself. "But ones and fives and tens in just that order?"

Dad pursed up another boiling smoke ring. "Well, the calf licked them off that way."

"Aha!" Alfred let his chair come down on all fours again. "I gotcha now. In the calf's stomach the ones would've been on the inside and the tens on the outside. They'd be rolled up backwards because of the way they went in."

All laughed again.

"But serious now, Dad," Alfred said, "what did you really get out of going to the wild Dakotas? When you left there now, did you sell your section of land to somebody else?"

Dad clapped out his pipe in the palm of his hand. "That's the sad part of it." He carefully dropped the ashes into the folded cuff of his gray overalls.

"How so?"

"The man I traded with never did own that land. His deed was false. The government still owns it. In fact, the government all along had plans to make a park out of it. They're going to call it The Badlands." Dad stroked his brown moustache meditatively. "Yes, all I got out of it was some cactus and a bad case of diarrhea."

Alfred's eyes rose over his high nose. "That's all you've got to show for that whole year?"

"Yes. Except of course I still have the wagon and the horses."

"Horses? Your call them things horses?"

"Don't belittle those Indian ponies. They may not pull with your big farm horses, but they're awfully tough. They've got the hot blood. They'll work in heat where your horses will drop dead."

"Don't tell me you traded the horses you went out there with even up for them things out there in the barn?"

"Yes, I did."

"But they're just wild broncs, Dad."

"All the more reason they're tough."

"Cactus and diarrhea." Karen laughed in a silly way. "What a combination."

Dad tried to cross his legs at the knee; couldn't quite make it. His legs were too stumpy. "Well, Karen, actually, there's some nourishment in cactus. In a pinch you can brush off the stickers and make a masty soup out of 'em."

Abbott said, "You forgot to mention another thing, Dad."

"What's that son?"

"Don't you remember? That six-shooter you got out there in the wagon and how you learned to shoot it?"

"What!" Alfred cried. "Dad learned to shoot like a cowboy?"

Dad tried to hide a fleeting smile. "Had to. The Flying V boys liked to ride across my claim and throw a rope around our privy. I kept warning them to stay away. But then one day one of the cowboys threw down on me and that was enough. I don't like looking into the barrel of a gun. It makes for an awful narrow point of view. So I drove to town and bought me a .45 Colt and taught myself to shoot."

Abbott said, "Dad trained himself by shooting at flies sitting on the swill pail."

"Hoh," Alfred said, "I bet that swill pail soon had more than one leak."

Dad smiled. "I shot at the flies as they showed up over the edge of the rim."

"Some more plain lying."

"No," Abbott said, "Dad did. Didn't he, Gerda?"

Gerda nodded. She kept looking at her brother Alfred with cowed eyes.

Abbott said, "Dad once even shot the buttons off Gerda's blouse."

"You mean, while she had it on?" Karen cried astounded. In empathy Karen covered her own fried-egg breasts with her hands.

"Of course not," Abbott said scornfully. "It was hanging on the clothesline."

Ada had a question. "Dad, you say you came out of it with some cactus. Does that mean you took some with you?"

"Yes, daughter. I have a few prickly ears in the wagon."

"Could I have a slip of one?"

"Daughter, you may. And you plant it in the ground with only one-third of the ear showing. It'll take root of itself."

Alfred changed the subject. "What are you going to do now, Dad?"

"Hunt up B-B-Bettie and start over." The stammering meant Dad had been touched in the quick again.

"What about living in the meantime?"

"B-B-Billy Mather wrote to say he needs me to lay more sidewalks. And the railroad says they'll hire me any time I show up."

Later that evening, after the dishes were washed, and the young Alfredsons had gone to sleep in the covered wagon, the grown-ups sat outdoors on the stoop in the cool of the evening.

Dad didn't have much to say. He smoked his pipe. But Karen was full of talk, and she furnished Dad with all the latest news.

Karen in particular went into the case of Lennie Meadows, with whom Dad used to work. One dark night Lennie decided to take a shortcut across the switchyards in Sioux City and got run over by a boxcar that'd just been broken out by a switch engine. Lennie apparently in all the city noise around hadn't heard it coming down the tracks, and got run over.

Alfred said, "They had to pick up his remains in a washtub."

"How awful," Ada said.

"Yeh." Alfred said, "that's what you get for taking a shortcut."

Dad removed his pipe from under his moustache. "I wonder how many lives have been saved taking the long cut?"

Alfred gave Dad a queer look, and fell silent.

Ada had a smile for her father-in-law. "Dad, you sure pick things up in an odd way sometimes."

Dad refilled his pipe with more Corn Cake. He lighted a match, its flame a glowing orange in the rusty dark. He held it under the upside down bowl until he had the tobacco crackling good.

"Dad," Ada said, "I didn't mean to embarrass you."

"It's a good question though, daughter. It's one I think about nights when I can't go to sleep. Why I was born so contrary."

"Is that the reason you don't go to church?" Ada wondered.

Dad blew a smoke ring up into the dusk. As the smoke ring rose it took on an opalescent color. It fanned out slowly, and disappeared. "Daughter, I never was much for going to church. Even when I was a little boy in the Old Country. You know how it is when you're a child. You see through people pretty quick. That they're all false fronts. And the ones with the most false front of all are the ministers. How else, when they have to repeat the same sermon over and over again, and try to act like it's the first time they've ever said it?"

"But how can one ever tire hearing of the Lord?"

"Daughter, it's been my experience that when you've heard one sermon, you've heard them all." Dad spoke with some asperity. "For myself, I don't like to chew my cabbage twice."

"What about the joy of fellowship one experiences with fellow covenant children?"

An even row of teeth appeared beneath Dad's brown moustache. "Hyp-p-p-ocrites.

As false as that false front up on the p-p-pulpit."

"Well, then let's forget about fellow covenant children," Ada said, "and think of only you and God."

"Exactly," Dad snapped. "And I don't p-p-propose to help p-p-pay for an enormous edifice, a church building, for just me and God to sit in. Too expensive for me. When besides, God p-probably p-prefers to be in the one He built for Himself, nature, and when I for a fact prefer to sit under a cottonwood and smoke my pipe and think my thoughts about the wonders I see around me." Dad clapped out his pipe against the side of his boot shoe. The ashes scattered over the walk. "Sorry to lose my temper a little, daughter, but don't talk to me about ministers and churches. They're not for me. I p-prefer the smell of p-plain fresh bullshit under my own cottonwood to what I can smell inside a church. And I say this even though I'm about as broke as a man can be and still be considered a citizen. I'm ragged, true. B-but I'm right." Dad stood up. "And now, if you'll excuse me, it's time to go to bed." Dad placed his hand over his belly. "But first a trip to your privy. To humor my new friend Mister Johnny Diarrhea." Dad leaned into a run and disappeared around the corner of the house.

Silence.

Finally Karen said, "Poor Dad and his troubled belly. Too bad the cactus he brought with him can't stanch the trots."

"Wal," Alfred said, "he brought it on himself, is all I can say. He always knew best. You could never tell him a thing."

Later, lying beside Ada, Alfred had trouble finding sleep. Alfred could hear Karen upstairs stirring around getting ready for bed. There were no sounds from the covered wagon outside where Dad had retired with Abbott and Gerda for the night.

Alfred felt funny in his chest. He wondered if his heart was going bad on him. He felt of his pulse. No, his heart seemed to bump along all right. It just felt uneasy.

"Wal," he thought to himself, "now that Dad's back, I suppose we'll have to drop in and see him now and then. And Ada will see to it that we do too, with her forgiving Christian heart." He thought further, "Good thing I never once came close to hinting to Ada what I nearly done to Gerda. That time when I laid on her. Of course I was only a little kid then and didn't know no better."

It was as if Ada heard him thinking in her sleep because at that moment she cleared her throat, softly. "Poor Gerda."

Gotske, that Ada, she sure had a way of knowing a man's mind.

"And poor Dad, kicking against the pricks."

Alfred thought: "Poor Dad nothing." The idea of Ada sympathizing with Dad made Alfred so mad he kicked his legs straight out.

"Alfred?" The little bedroom made Ada's voice sound warm and close.

Alfred raised one knee. The sheet fell off farther. "Yeh?"

"I can't sleep either, thinking about your family. And how strange it was to meet them at last. And how they surprised me."

"They surprised you?"

"Yes. They turned out to be a whole lot better than you let on."

"Better? How can you say that?"

Ada turned her head. "Oh, Alfred."

"Wal, here my old man comes out of the wilderness all haired over like a curly wolf, and by golly you almost have more time for him than you have for me."

"Why, Alfred, isn't that the Lord's way? To be more concerned about the one sheep that is lost than the ninety and nine that are safely within the fold?"

"Providing that one sheep ain't an old goat."

"Oh, Alfred, your father is not an old goat. I like your father."

"Hoh. Did you ever stop and think that maybe Dad's right that the other ninety and nine are the hypocrites?"

"I've thought about that. But the ninety and nine have a better chance to gain heaven within the bosom of the church than outside it."

Alfred crossed his legs. His skin prickled all over. "I know I should show respect for Dad, and all that, but I tell you, Ada, after seeing him today, I still can't help but think again he's going up the wrong road. And that's hard to respect."

"Don't you love your father, Alfred?"

"Sure I do. But that don't keep me from seeing that he's turned bad."

"Oh, now, Alfred. Your own father?"

The next day after breakfast, Dad pulled out for Bonnie to start over with his second wife, Bettie.

Alfred ❦ 15

THAT FIRST YEAR Alfred had a good harvest. The oats went forty bushels to the acre. After he'd filled the granary, he sold twelve hundred bushels to the Farmer's Grain Elevator in Bonnie for thirty-six cents a bushel. He deposited a check of $532.00 in Chauncey's bank. He also got three crops of hay from his alfalfa field and put it all up in the haymow.

But the best was the corn crop. When he was about half done picking in early November, Alfred saw it was going to come in at a good fifty bushels to the acre. In all, it would probably total three thousand bushels. Corn was bringing fifty cents a bushel for the best grade that fall. Half of that corn check would cover the rent for the year, two-fifths of all the crops, plus four dollars an acre for pasture and hay land. The rest he and Ada could keep for themselves. They were going to get a good leg up even before their first year was out.

"Now let the good wife have an easy time of it with the boy and the whole harvest will be in complete."

Alfred wondered if their boy would be born the way a calf was born. With a cow it was like watching someone shake a fat pumpkin out of the neck of burlap sack. A female sure had the stretchingest flesh.

It was almost three o'clock on a warm day in November. Alfred had a couple of rods more to go to reach the end of the field. The sun struck him in the face in a deep slant. He had to pull his cap down over his eyes to make sure he didn't miss any corn ears, especially occasional fallen ears. Field spiders were a nuisance. Alfred had to wipe an occasional trailing spider thread from his face. Spider threads tickled so. It had warmed enough that day to release what little frost was in the ground, and for a little while the black dirt stuck to the wagon wheels, matting up with pigeon grass as it thickened. Later the dirt dried some, and then the mud slowly flaked off and the iron rims became clean again.

Every now and then Alfred threw a look at the neighboring cornfields. Frank Murray was picking his high forty. The Horsbergs were out with three wagons on their low sixty. Weatherly was alone in his rolling field.

Alfred had only a rod more to go, when Frank Murray across the line fence suddenly began to cuss out his horses. It was a still day and Alfred could hear him clearly.

"Whoa there. Stop, you sonsabitches. Stop! Oh for chrissakes, now I got to run a mile to deliver one ear of corn to my own wagon. Whoa! By God, I'll show you. Back up or I'll beat the bejabbers out of you front and back both, come vomit or come diarrhea. Back. Back up, you brown-assed bastards. Oh for jesuschrissake, not that way. Oh God, I think I'll just quit. Yes, I think I will. It's no use, goddammit. Giddap you lazy shitasses. Move. Get. By God, I'll fix you. Get! Get! So you've decided to wake up, have you? Good. All right, now, whoa! Whoa! For chrissakes, that's too far. Once again I've gotta run a mile to deliver one ear of corn to my own wagon. Now I'm quitting for sure. Yes I am. Yes I am."

Alfred found himself smiling as he stood perfectly still listening to it all. Then, remembering he was picking corn and not attending a sideshow, he went back to picking.

When he got to the end near the line fence, he took off his left mitten and relieved himself. He was proud of his waterfall of a stream. It made a fine rushing sound in the pigeon grass. He was also proud of his tool. Even soft it was like a long pale potato with a single eye at the end. Finishing, he flipped it a couple of times to get rid of the last couple of drops, only to have one of the drops come sailing up past his nose and catch the sun just right so that for a second the drop looked like a flying firefly. The drop missed the bill of his cap and arched out over a crumpled cornstalk. With a retreating motion of his buttocks he drew his tool back inside his overalls.

"Now for a bite of dried beef and a swallow of tea."

From the toolbox on the boot of the wagon, which he humorously dubbed his jewelry chest, he got out the lunch, then climbed up into the wagon itself to sit on the corn. The wagon was about half full, a mound of golden ears lying in a slanting pile part way up the bangboard.

He munched the sandwiches with relish.

He threw a glance at his pasture to see if the new brockled heifer, Belle, bought in July, was getting along with Three-tit. She was. They were grazing together near the road where the grass was still a deep horehound green. Birds were following the two cows around, sucking up the last fat flies of the season. The flies were slow because of the chill in the air and the birds caught them on their first pass.

A half mile to the southwest a plume of tan dust chased down Curvy Road. That had to be the mailman, Slim Lehr, on the last leg of his route.

Alfred rinsed the crumbs from between his teeth with the last of the tea and put the little pail away.

He leaned back on the bumpy corn. The sky was so blue it had gold specks in it. The air was as cool and sweet as unfermented cider.

In one way it was too bad Ada was so far along with child. Because now she wouldn't let him have his husband's rights. Wouldn't even think of it.

"Wal, all I can say is that King Solomon sure was lucky in the Bible that they allowed him to have a thousand wives."

It would be a sweet lust. Especially today with the sky so warm and lazy and the corn smelling like warm syrup. Yes, it surely would be nice to peel a potato with Ada again.

He noticed an ear with much of the shuck still on. He stripped the husks back from the hairy point and broke them off at the base. The ear came out gleaming, some ten inches long, a good two inches thick. It fit well to his two hands. Corn was prime that year, with fine ridges running straight back. He found a red ear, also with some of its husks still on, a little thicker than the other ear. He cleaned it off, including the hair at the end, handling it as though it were part of himself, an old private familiar gesture. He let the red ear fall from his hand.

A twirling corn leaf caught his eye. It was some ten rows down in the still unpicked corn. It was odd for a leaf to be whirling around and around like a toy weathervane. Especially with no wind out.

He narrowed his eyes; stared intently at it.

Yes, there it was all right. Standing absolutely still. Both its coat of hair and the dried corn leaves around it had the color of slightly weathered lumber.

A panther. A real live panther. Its tuft of a tail was switching around a little and it had been that switching that had caught Alfred's eye. The panther's golden eyes in its great box of a head were lit up by the sun from the side and looked more like shining hollows than eyes.

Then Duke and Dan became aware of danger. Their ears began to flop back and forth and their nostrils fluttered like stove dampers.

A painter, as Dad would say. Or a cougar, as Chauncey called them.

But here? On his farm?

Trapper Bill Steyne had talked about seeing panthers around the river bottoms in the old days. But not lately. This wasn't a wilderness anymore. All the deer were gone.

Fear went through him like a spasm of rheumatism. Sweat broke out over his cheeks and nose. He thought: "Don't move. Don't even blink your eyes."

Duke and Dan were trying to stare past their blinders, pulling their jaws askew against the lines. The lines were wound around a peg up front on the wagon box.

"By God, I'm a coward."

He could feel the point of each corn ear prodding him in the rump.

A little breath of a breeze moved over him. It came from where the panther stood. Then the breath rustled the leaves just to the rear of the horses. Next it ruffled the black manes of the horses.

The horses let go with a snort and popped their tails tight. They sprang into a gathering run, taking the heavy wagon with them, pulling it with difficulty, slowly going faster, veering off to the right, away from the panther, avoiding the line fence ahead.

Alfred, caught off balance, fell sideways on the pile of corn. "Whoa!" He scrabbled to get his balance. The pile under him began to cascade down. He slid to the rear of the box and banged his head against the endgate. He landed with his feet higher than his head. His cap fell off.

"Gotske."

With great effort he gathered himself against the increasing momentum; and at last, gaining on it, hurled himself forward to the front of the wagon. The wheels bounced across the hilled rows. The wagon shook so much he had trouble unwinding the lines from the peg up front. Finally the lines were free, and winding his hands around into them, he hauled back, so hard the horses reared up, running up into the air. "Whoa!!" He put his whole rough voice into it. "Whoa!!" His stud roar was loud enough to make the horses stop dead in their tracks.

Alfred looked back.

Out of the corner of his eye he saw the big cat leap over the line fence and disappear into Frank Murray's cornfield.

"Unpossible." Alfred's breath whistled in his nose. "If that wasn't something."

He looked to see where Frank Murray was with his team and wagon. Standing carefully up on his load, Alfred could just make out the gray edge of Frank's bangboard going the other way. If the cat kept going down the same rod it'd almost be on Frank's tail in another minute.

"Frank's too far away for me to call him. Let's hope the big cat turns south and heads down the creek along Curvy Road. That route will take him into the river bottoms."

Alfred held the horses steady. He could feel the horses' heavy breathing in the lines.

"Funny that big cat should show up here in farming country. It must've followed something up here. A family of coons maybe."

Gradually the horses quieted down under his powerful control.

"When Dad was working on the section, he says he sometimes saw some wonderful things along the river. He'd come on 'em all of a sudden and there they'd be. Coyotes. Wolves. Once even in the old days a gray grizzly below Lakewood there. Dad used to say that the young folks weren't the only ones having a night life."

Alfred listened to see if Frank Murray's horses might smell the cat. But after a few minutes when he didn't hear a commotion in that direction he decided the cat had headed along Curvy Road all right.

He heaved several big sighs to get on top of himself.

"Wal, I guess I better get back to work. Duke, Dan, giddap."

He completed the turn the horses had started and swung them into the next two rows going back down the other side of the standing corn. He tied up the lines at just the right tension on the peg up front. He stepped down, stretched himself, slipped his left mitten back on, and went back to picking. Grab, hook, gather, pull. Bang.

"Better not tell Ada about this. We don't want her to throw that kid."

That night in bed, in the dark, Ada suddenly took his hand and placed it on her swollen stomach. "Feel that, Alfred. Quick."

There was a considerable commotion in her belly all right.

"Isn't that something?" Ada whispered, love in her voice. "He's been so active today. Why, I've had to sit down several times, he acts up so."

"Feels like a catfight going on in there."

"I think he's going to be a runner the way he kicks his legs so."

"What makes you think it's a him?"

"Because he's so active. Ma said that both Joan and me were fairly quiet. But that John and both the Shermans were busy in her stomach."

Alfred could feel the baby struggling under his hand quite clearly. "Good thing he's going to be a runner, like you say, after what I saw today." Too late Alfred bit on his lip. Now Ada wouldn't be satisfied until he'd told her. He'd let too much of what he'd seen into his voice.

"What was that?"

"Oh . . . nothing."

"Tell me."

"No."

"Alfred. There was something though, wasn't there? Alfred?"

"Wal, it probably don't mean much. The critter just got lost. By now it's way down along the river bottoms somewhere."

Her stomach muscles stiffened under his hand. "What was it, Alfred?"

He told her.

"A lion? Out here?"

"I saw him all right. But I think he was as scared of me as I was of him."

Ada sucked in a breath. "But will he be afraid of little babies?"

"Darn it, I shouldna mentioned it. Me and my big mouth."

Ada said nothing.

"Don't worry, love. There hasn't been a big kitty around here in years." Alfred put his arms around Ada. "And anyway, they don't like human being flesh. Tastes too much like their own."

Ada ❦ 16

ADA BOUGHT A block calendar for their family worship, a leaf for each day of the year, and on each leaf a text from Scripture with a short meditation. They read a leaf each morning at breakfast, instead of the usual chapter from the Bible. Each leaf could be a sort of daily manna. The calendar was tacked up on the wall over the table within easy reach.

On the morning when Ada tore off the fifth leaf, a blue whistler of a snowstorm was howling outdoors. It had blown in from the north during the night.

Of course Ma Engleking had to be on hand when her first grandchild was to come into the world. She'd come down on the train the week before because she was sure the boy would be born on her birthday, the fifth of January. Ada had already lost out on her hope that the child would be born on her birthday, the third. But the way Ada felt that morning she was sure it wasn't going to be born on the fifth either.

Ada read the text first: "And when her days to be delivered where fulfilled, behold, there were twins in her womb. And the first came out red, all over like an hairy garment, and they called his name Esau. And after that came his brother out, and his hand took hold on Esau's heel, and his name was called Jacob. And the boys grew, and Esau was a cunning hunter, a man of the field, and Jacob was a plain man dwelling in tents. And Isaac loved Esau, because he did eat of his venison. But Rebekah loved Jacob."

Ada paused before reading the meditation. She liked to think her own thoughts about a text before hearing what someone else might have to say about it.

Ma heaved a sigh at her end of the table as she too brooded within her voluminous flesh on what had just been read.

Alfred sat quietly with his head back and his eyes closed.

After a moment Ada read the meditation. "God in His infinite wisdom decided that there should be more than one issue from the seed of Abraham and Isaac at this point in history: one issue to take the route of the heathen, who worshiped nature, the other issue to take the route of the covenant child, who worshiped God." Ada thought the meditation was somewhat flat compared to the lively text of God's word. "God in His infinite wisdom had something in mind when He made this arrangement in those ancient times. We see the results today—on the one hand, the scoffer and the man of the world, and on the other hand, the devout Christian and the man of God."

Finished, Ada murmured, more to herself than to the others, "Strange that we should be reading this particular text today."

Alfred had a smile for Ada. "Maybe we're gonna have twins. A hired man for me and a hired girl for you."

"Twins? Oh no."

Ma said, "Storming like this can only mean one thing. The baby's going to be a great man."

"Pah," Alfred said, "if the baby is going to arrive today, storming like this can only mean one thing—that I'm gonna have a heckuva time getting the doctor out from town."

"Too bad we don't have the telephone," Ada said.

Ma folded her hands in her thick lap. "Pray God that when and if the boy does come, he doesn't come with a full set of teeth. Those kind always turn out bad. Werewolves."

Alfred reared up. "A full set of teeth, woman? What are you trying to do, scare my wife?"

Ma rolled her eyes up at the ceiling with an air of superior knowledge. "I know of a case where it happened."

"Did it ever happen to any of your relations?"

"No, of course not."

"Wal, it sure as the dickens didn't happen to any of my relations. So what kind of talk is that."

Ada said, "I wish now I'd have been a nurse in a doctor's office for a while. Then I would've known how it goes."

"You should have been around when our new brockled heifer, Belle, had her first calf this fall."

Ma sniffed. "Well, if it turns out to be a girl instead, there'll be one consolation at least."

Ada wished Ma would hold her tongue. It had been like a stickly barley beard in Ma's throat that her husband, her son-in-law, and her son-in-law's father were all named Alfred, and that if the baby did turn out to be a boy, it probably would be named after them. For herself, Ada had already resigned herself to the fact the boy would be named Alfred Alfredson VII.

The stove damper fluttered. Twice the wind came blasting down the short black stovepipe, backing up the smoke, making it puff out around the stove lids. There was a smell of burning cobs in the tight kitchen.

"Nah," Alfred said, folding his hands, "let's give thanks. I better get up some hay in case this storm lasts a couple of days."

Finished, Alfred put on his red six-buckle boots, blue storm cap and black-and-blue checkered mackinaw. "I'll be in for a cup of coffee around ten or so," he promised, and disappeared into the storm.

Ma did the dishes. When she hung up the dishcloth, she had something to say. "Your husband has his nerve comparing you to his new brockled heifer."

Ada was going over some used diapers Ma'd brought along. They were brother Sherman's diapers. "Well, Ma, the truth is, maybe I would've learned something watching that calf being born."

"Nor does he think much of his wife's mother and what she might know about having babies, she who's suffered through having had five of them."

Ada came upon a threadbare diaper and put it to one side. "God's animals don't seem to suffer much. Maybe that's at least one thing we could learn from them."

"Daughter, we're supposed to suffer. Because we're sinners. While the animals don't know any better."

"But isn't it natural to have babies?"

"God ordained that we should have them in pain."

Ada comforted her big belly with her hands. "Let's go into the other room, Ma, if you're done here."

"First some more cobs in the stove."

The two women sat huddled near the nickel base burner. Their faces slowly warmed in its radiating heat. When the wind sucked at the chimney, the live coals in the base burner for a moment resembled a pile of little oranges. The little panes of isinglass clicked and blinkered in and out. Ma sat sideways to the south window so that she could see to knit. She was making a soaker out of blue woolen yarn. Ada sat across from her, darning some heavy work socks for Alfred. She used strong store cord for the holes.

"One thing has been a gain, being with child all these months," Ada said.

"What can that be, for goodness sakes?"

"It's such a relief not to have to use those draining cloths every month."

Ma shook her head reprovingly. "Now you're complaining about God's handiwork. You know He placed that curse upon the woman to remind her that she was born in sin and that she gives birth in sin."

"I don't believe God intended it as a curse."

"Not?"

"No. God is also a god of love and He can't mean us bad all the time."

"Well! If God were a woman instead of a man, maybe so. But so long as He's a man, you can depend on it that He'll have it in for us a little."

"Ma! Now you're the one that's complaining about God."

The little house stood solid against the storm. Only the windows made cracking noises. Sometimes the two chimneys hooted like power station whistles.

Ada looked through a little spot in the window where it still hadn't frosted over. The storm had thickened and she could no longer make out the house gate.

"I hope Alfred can find his way back to the house. It'd be awful if he got lost on his own yard."

Ma clicked her needles. "Don't you feel anything? No cramps?"

"Not yet. It just feels like I'm slowly dividing in half, is all."

Ma shook her head. "I don't know what to say."

"I'm not afraid. It is God's will, whatever happens. I am ready to do what He asks of me."

"Maybe you should get the doctor anyway, now, and have him on hand just to be sure."

"Oh, Ma, we can't ask the doctor to do that. Suppose the child decides not to come for a week? In a week's time a lot of people can get sick."

"Hmp."

There was a noise at the kitchen door and a second later Alfred stomped in. He was covered with snow. His face was squared in blue outrage at the whole idea of the storm. He gave himself a great shake, spilling flowery snow all over like a hairy dog shaking off drops of water after a swim. He removed his winter cap and gave it several whacks over his knee. "It's umpossible out there, love. I don't know what Satan has in mind for us today, but whatever it is, it ain't good."

Ma humphed to herself. "If Satan was responsible for this storm, you can be sure it'd be snowing hot ashes by now, not snowflakes."

Ada smiled at Alfred. "You made it back safe to the house."

"Sure. On the way out I took and tied your clothesline from the porch door to the barn." Alfred took off his mackinaw, then his buckle boots. He eyed the stove. "Good, there's still some coffee on."

Ada saw he was going to drink from the spout. "Take a fresh cup, Alfred. And it's not good for your stomach to drink it black. Get yourself some cream and sugar and come here and sit with us."

Alfred helped himself to coffee, cream, and sugar. "Wish you had some bear sign."

"The doughnuts are in their usual place."

Alfred sat down beside them and put his feet up on the nickel railing. The chimney hooted above them. "Wal, I got in enough hay for two days. Now all I have to worry about is the chickens. It felt pretty cold in there when I checked them a minute ago." He took a sip of coffee, then bit hungrily into the doughnut. "Lucky I installed that burner in there when I smoked our baloney and meat this fall."

Ada could hardly bear to see Alfred eating.

Alfred set his cup down. "Whough! I'm only just now catching my breath. Out in that wind it's like there's a hand over your mouth. Out to choke you."

Ma held up the blue soaker to see how far she'd come. "Ada, do you think I've got this big enough now?"

"I think so."

Cast iron cracked in the kitchen.

Alfred dropped his feet to the floor, his cup rattling in its saucer. "The stove in there is cooling off. I knew I should've filled it when I was out there." He hurried into the kitchen.

Ma said, "Or shall I make it still bigger?"

Ada considered. "Maybe you better. Soakers always shrink a little. And if it's still too big, we can take in a tuck or two."

Ma nodded. "I'll hurry and get this done and then I'll peel the potatoes for dinner."

Alfred returned to his chair. "You know, I could easy go to sleep sitting here."

"Why don't you?" Ada said. "Go lay down on the couch there. You may be up all night getting the doctor."

Alfred ran a hand over his red face. "You know, I think I will. Wake me up when the potatoes are ready."

Ma asked, "Is the cob pile outdoors handy?"

"I knew there was something I forgot." Alfred managed a smile for Ada. "This is our first blizzard together and we haven't had much practice at it yet." He got up to get the extra fuel.

Ada gave a start. "You won't get lost now just to get a few cobs?"

"I'll get some from the new pile. The clothesline I strung to the barn goes right by it." Alfred put on his heavy clothes again and went outside.

From her chair, through the little clear spot left in the south window, Ada saw him pick up the basket. A couple of steps and he disappeared into the flying snow. "All for a few cobs," Ada murmured.

Ma kept at her knitting with remorseless fingers. "The baby has to be born in a warm place. Even the Christ Child had a warm manger."

Alfred didn't return right away. A half hour passed. Then an hour.

Ada got up and began to pace heavily around the base burner. "Where could that man have gone?"

Ma finished the soaker. She got out a dishpan, put in some potatoes and water, and sat down by the stove to peel them.

"He must've found something else wrong out there."

"Sit down, child."

At exactly twelve noon Ada saw him loom up suddenly in the snow. He was not only carrying a basket full of cobs but also had several gunny sacks full of cobs slung over his shoulders. He looked enormous carrying it all. Ada hurried, heavily, to open the door for him.

"Wouff!" he exploded as he stumbled into the kitchen. "That was something. But I made it."

"What took you so long?"

"Stove in the water tank went out. Come to find out it'd sprung a leak. So I quick had to solder it."

"Well, I was afraid for you. Now I wish we could have waited a month to have this child."

"Ho. We could have a worse blizzard the fifth of February."

Ada looked at all the cobs. "That should be enough until tomorrow."

"I should hope so." Alfred shed his heavy clothes and boots, and Ada took the broom to him and brushed the rest of him off. Alfred said, "This is worse than . . . why, it's like standing with your nose head on into the blower of a threshing machine, it's coming at you so hard and fast."

By a quarter after twelve they sat down to eat. The bowl of potatoes steamed like a smokestack.

Ada sat with the other two mostly to read the Bible afterwards. She watched Alfred pitch in. Poor man. He ate like a starved dog. "How is our Rover boy doing out there in the barn?"

"Ha. He knows what to do in a storm. He's dug himself a hole into the hay and all you can see of him is his nose sticking out."

They were having canned crab apples for dessert when the three windows in the kitchen slowly lit up.

Alfred looked up. "Hey, maybe the storm is letting up a little."

Ada excused herself from the table. She went to their small bedroom, got the pot from under the bed, and gathering up her dress relieved herself. When she stood up again, she whispered to herself, "That was strange. It dropped out like you empty out a glass of water." As she started for the kitchen again she discovered she had to walk with her feet wide apart. "I think it's close now. Funny there haven't been any cramps yet."

Back at the table, Ada read the Twenty-third Psalm. "Goodness and mercy shall follow me all the days of my life."

Alfred gave thanks. Then he filled both stoves and lay down on the couch for a nap.

Ada saw that he'd lain down without covering himself. She got a blue comforter and spread it over him. He didn't notice. He'd already fallen asleep. She could smell the male vigor of Alfred rising out of his clothes. His breath was as mellow as meadow hay. She even got a whiff of his ear wax, a scent like burnt brown sugar.

Ada stood smiling at him. He would soon be the wise father. "Now I am glad that this man's seed, not poor Alvin's, quickened me. He never gives up. Even in the midst of storms he's cheerful. I shall give my all for him. Open my belly, freely, so that issue of his blood shall be born easily and swiftly, Ma notwithstanding."

Ada held her belly lovingly. "What is also very strange is that lately I haven't had that odd heart feeling. As if my heart is very strong again, like it was when I was a little girl, before I had those sore knees. It's like I swallowed some kind of magic drink."

She eased herself down into her rocker. She rocked slowly. The left runner creaked rhythmically, like a cricket with a cold. She smiled at the pleasant sound of Ma talking to herself as she washed dishes in the kitchen.

"I sit so wide," Ada murmured to herself.

Presently Ma joined Ada in front of the base burner.

"It's like waiting for the first rose of summer to open," Ada murmured. "It takes forever when you sit and watch it."

"God's will."

They'd finished supper. But between swooping gusts of wind one could occasionally make out a light in the Weatherly house a half a mile away.

The stove behind Ada talked. Ashes were settling in the grate below.

After a while, pipe finished, Alfred reached for his harmonica from the shelf over the table and began to play "Ninety and Nine."

Ada smiled. Her thickened lips fanned back into her pale cheeks. How loving of Alfred to cheer her up with her favorite tune.

Soon Alfred became lost in his silver playing. Tune after tune floated up from his gently whumpfing hands. "Sunshine in thy face was seen, kissing lips of rose." "As I went walking one morning for pleasure." "Dreaming of a pair of eyes that looked in mine."

Suddenly wild roses seemed to have bloomed in the kitchen. And then, a moment later, the baby gave a great kick in Ada's belly, with both its feet, hard up against her lungs. Her stomach compressed on itself, trying to squeeze out the child.

"Ahhh," Ada cried. "There." At last a birthing pain. So that was the way it felt.

Alfred knew right away what was happening. He put his harmonica away and got up to go.

Ma sat down and began to run yellow tears. "Ya, ya, I'm going to be a gramma on my birthday after all."

The powerful squeezing let up for a moment. Ada held out a hand to Alfred. "Do you think it's safe for you to go?"

"You want Doc Drury, don't you?"

"I think so. Though if I had to I think I could manage with Ma."

"I'll take Duke and Dan on the bobsled."

"The road won't be blocked?"

"I'll take the high ground if I have to. I'll cut my way through the fences with a pair of pincers on the way to town, and on the way back I'll patch 'em up again."

Alfred put on a pair of thick felt shoes and then his red six-bucklers. He bundled himself up in his coonskin coat, carefully fastening the frogs all up and down the front. He topped it out with a big fluffy fur cap. Then lighting a storm lantern, slipping on a pair of fur gloves, and giving Ada a smiling kiss, he leaned into the darkness and was gone.

"Ochh," Ma cried, "would that my husband could've kissed me once like that."

Ada was furious with her mother. "Ma, Pa will never kiss you that way so long as you complain about your lot in life. Always throwing it in his face that you are of higher issue."

Ma began to weep. Her eyes became blurs of water and her face a mottled red. She wept in an Old Country manner. Only the uprooted understood. The young people born in this new country wanted a happy song from her, when what she felt in it was only grief.

Ada relented. "Let's go into the other room, Ma. I want to be in my rocker when the next one comes."

Ma sniffed a couple more times, then immediately became all brood hen. "You get into your nightgown and then into bed. Instead of sitting out here. I'll set on the hot water and get out the crock basin."

"There's always plenty of warm water in the reservoir, Ma."

"Daughter, lay down. I know my business."

Ada put on a pink flannel nightgown. But she didn't lay down. She put on a blue robe and woolen scuffs and returned to her rocker.

An hour passed before the baby kicked down again. Ada's belly followed with a hard squeezing motion. It lasted a couple of seconds.

Ma didn't like it. "At that rate it won't be born until tomorrow."

Ada laughed, "Why, Ma, that's up to the child, isn't it?"

Ma fell into a watchful silence.

The third pain came at a quarter of eight.

Ma shook her head. "No, it's not going to be born in time to make it on the fifth."

Ada tried to look out through the peephole in the window. She couldn't make out much. The pulldown lamp behind her cast a mild orange light. "I think the wind's getting stronger again."

Ma refixed her glasses on the end of her nose. Such matters as wind and weather were for men to worry about.

In the next three hours Ada had five more labor surges. Some were as strong as the first one, some weaker. They were spaced about a half hour apart, neither speeding up nor slowing down.

At eleven Ada placed a rubber sheet over the bottom of the bed, turned the night lamp down a little, and crawled into bed. Ma lay down on a cot near the hard-coal burner. The bedroom got its heat through the door, which had to be kept open during cold weather. Ada wondered if maybe the tight little bedroom on the north side of the house wasn't too cold a place for a child to be born in.

Ada folded a towel under her bottom and explored herself with gentle fingertips.

Great stars alive. She really was spreading open down there all right. Her bottom was parting like a drying rack.

Midnight came.

Ada thought: "But where is my husband? And poor Doctor Drury? Out there in that freezing wind and blizzard they may be dying this very minute. Or the horses could've fallen into a hole somewhere."

Ada napped between pains. From her girl cousins she'd heard that birthing was a woman's hell on earth. But Alfred appeared to be right that it was a natural thing just as it was with all of God's other creatures.

Once as she napped Ada dreamt she was in a garden of flowers. Green paths intersected the various plots. As she strolled along, lungs expanding with rose perfumes, she became aware something was burrowing under the path she'd taken. It was a mole. It was trying to sneak unnoticed from a plot of tame roses across to a plot of wild roses. As she watched, the humped-up runnel enlarged. So did the mole inside it. The mole sensed her watching it. It gathered itself up into a ball to make one last quick push through the sod. Once it got over into the loose dirt of the wild roses it would be safe. Ada drew in a deep breath. She coughed at the same time that the mole, nose hard, surged through the sod. "Oww!" she screamed.

Waking, Ada clapped her hands to her bottom between her open legs. My God. "Ma? Come quick. I'm sticky all over."

Ma came tumbling into the bedroom. "What is it, daughter?" She turned up the lamp. She fitted on her glasses to see better. She peered. "In God's name. Ahh. Quick now, I'll get the hot water."

"Akkk," Ada cried as the mole child made another surge.

Ma came flying back with the hot water, a bar of soap, a bundle of white rags, and scissors. Trembling, she splashed water too fast into the crock bowl and some of it spilled over the rug.

"What a strange wonderful thing," Ada cried. "It hurts awful but it is so wonderfully fulfilling. Akkk. They're coming fast now."

Ma looked at the alarm clock. "Why, it's four in the morning." Ma shook her head grudgingly. "The child will have a birthday all to itself."

"Hakk-k. Oww. There it is I think."

Some kind of creature let go with a wet bawl.

"A little more," Ma urged. "Push, child."

"Isn't it born yet?"

"Only the head. There's still the shoulders."

"They must be awfully bro . . . owh! There. Dear Lord Jesus, at last." Ada felt as if a big hand, the Lord's, had scooped out her innards with one motion, relieved her of a blessed burden.

Ma refixed her glasses on her nose. She was sweating. She caught up the bawling child and turned it over. "A little apricot. And good Grutkins! A little hard carrot with it. Born naughty. Just like a man."

Ada rose up on her elbows. She stared. "A real boy all right. And he has dark blond hair."

Ma was smiling her best. "Yes, a lot of hair." Ma lay the baby over Ada's belly. Quickly Ma tied up the cords in two places with white bandages. Ma picked up the scissors. There was a sound of snipping wiry silk. "There, my grandson, you are free."

Ada rested on her elbows. "Strange that his hair should come down to his eyebrow so. On the part side. And so far down over on the back of his head too. All the way to his shoulders."

"Ya, ya. There's always a special mark on them when they're going to be important people." Ma picked the baby up with a hand under its chest and began to wash it with warm water.

Water on the back of its head made the baby howl.

"That's it, you rascal, roar your heart out. And while you're at it, cry for me too. Because now suddenly I'm an old woman. A gramma."

Ada saw that her breasts had leaked a little into her nightgown, a faint pink. They were full to bursting with milk.

"There, there, little one," Ma clucked. "My, what a strange one this one is. He has a neck as strong as a fish."

Ada could feel her face smiling. It was like it was happening twice at the same time. "Well, Gramma, when can I hold my first child at last and give him titty?"

"After I give him his first diaper. And cover his shame."

An hour later Ada had her legs together again. The baby, after being wrapped in warm flannels, had fallen asleep. Gramma had finished cleaning up. And the afterbirth was safely in the chamber pot under the bed, the lid firmly on.

Presently, as if it were being revealed as part of a dream, there came a plunging sound outside.

Ada listened intently. There it was again, loud enough to be heard over the rushing wind. "That must be Alfred. Thank God he's made it safely."

"A little late," Gramma said with a self-satisfied smirk.

"We were so busy here, I forgot to worry much about Alfred in the storm outside."

The door to the kitchen burst inward. Boot buckles jingled.

"Alfred?"

"Love? Are you still all right?"

"Yes. What about you?"

"I'm fine." Alfred loomed into the doorway of the bedroom, coonskin coat plakked with ice and snow. His fur cap appeared to have enlarged. He entered with an atmosphere around him, so cold Ada could feel it where she lay. Instinctively she drew up the bedcover a little to keep the chilled air from touching the child.

Alfred caught the motion. "Gotske!" Then he called over his shoulder. "Doc, come on in here. Don't bother to take off your boots."

Measured footsteps sounded through the living room, and then another heavily furred man stood in the doorway. Dr. Thomas Drury, though not as tall as Alfred, was still a big man, with massive shoulders. He had a very full face, thick brows, and quick warm black eyes. His glance went directly to the bundle in Ada's arms. "Too late, I see. Good." He spoke with broad round accents.

Ada had to restrain a laugh, it hurt her so between her legs. "Yes, the Lord has favored us."

Dr. Drury looked at Ada's cheeks. "Your color is good. All went well then, I take it."

"It did. I was surprised myself it went so easy."

"For the first one, yes."

Alfred asked, "What is it?"

Ada partly uncovered the baby's dark red face. Its eyes were closed, its mouth puckered. It resembled a hairy cub dreaming to itself. "It's a boy. And to make sure we saw that, he was born naughty."

"Wow." Alfred took off his fur cap. He looked at Dr. Drury with pride. "Wal, Doc, that's my girl for you, every time."

"Did you get lost, Alfred," Ada asked, "that it took you so long?"

"No. I went right along. But I had to zigzag so, back and forth across the fields, taking the high ground above the snow, that I just couldn't seem to make time. The worst was, Doc here was on a call in Amen, and I had to go all the way out there and get him."

"Oh, that explains it. I worried so."

"I thought you might. But you can rest easy now. The storm's at last really letting up. The wind's still about as strong as it was, but the sky is clearing off. You can see stars overhead."

"God be thanked."

"Get into the kitchen you two," Gramma scolded. "Bringing in the North Pole like this. And take off your duds."

Alfred held up his hand. "Wait. Ada, where did we put that bottle of Old Crow I found up in the haymow? When we first moved onto this place?"

Ada frowned. "What do you want it for?"

"I think this calls for a swallow."

"I thought we were going to use it only for medicinal purposes?"

"Wal, that's what I'm going to use it for. When I give this medicine man a snort to keep him from catching a cold."

Ada allowed him a smile. "It's in the clothes closet. And when you get through with it, be sure and put it right back there."

"Don't worry." Alfred smacked his red chapped lips. "Come on, Doc, before Gramma here takes a bite out of our behinds."

Later, Dr. Drury examined and weighed the baby. He announced that the son and heir was in perfect health, that he was a skinny twenty-four inches long and weighed ten pounds.

Alfred exulted in it all. "Ain't he a champ though, Doc?"

"He sure is."

"He's our new white hope. The one who'll finally take on the great Jack Johnson himself."

A wondering look had entered Gramma's eyes. "It's funny, but the baby doesn't look like either one of you. Neither Ada nor you."

"Who does he look like then, for godsakes?" Alfred exclaimed.

"His grandfathers."

"Wal, suppose he does, what's wrong with that?"

"They're too much like giants. And I've had enough of one giant."

"My dad is a giant at five foot six?"

"You know what I mean."

"Wal, whoever he takes after, even if it's The President, I still say he's an A-number-one champ."

The baby began to squall.

Alfred beamed. His face had slowly turned red in the warm house. "Listen to him, will you? He's got the voice of an auctioneer."

Ada smiled. "I think he's maybe a little hungry by now."

Alfred gave Dr. Drury a sliding smile. "Might be a good idee to clear the rust out of his boiler pipes with a little bumblebee juice too, not, Doc?"

Gramma bulged up like she might have man muscles. "That's scandalous, to think of giving a baby what's still wet from the other side some whiskey."

Dr. Drury had a sliding smile in turn. "Alfred, I'll take his share, if you don't mind. For the road. And then we better hightail it back. The Lord only knows what's been happening in Bonnie while I've been away."

Alfred held up his hand. "Okay. But first I better pail my two cows. Or their udders'll have burst by the time I get back."

Then, with Alfred laughing his happy man's laugh, the men left.

Ada turned her full attention to the bawling baby. She cradled him in her right arm. "There, there, little one." She opened her maternity nightgown and lifted out her breast. Her breast was so full it was rigid. It hurt to even touch it. Milk was filming into pink drops on the teat. "Now, now, little one." The baby made crude clawing motions with its hands and feet. Ada held the baby up so that her running nipple entered its wide red mouth. "Here you are." The moment milk touched the baby's ululating tongue, the baby took up the teat, full mouth, and immediately began sucking. Her milk, at last released, began to squirt into the baby's mouth. The baby managed to swallow fast enough to keep up.

Ada couldn't get over how delicately sweet it was for those baby lips to be closed over her nipple, working it, while its pink fingers twitched involuntarily on her breast, indenting it, making the breast part of itself. Those sweet pink lips were helping themselves to the juice of life. It even felt as if the juice of her brains was draining out through her breast.

"O Lord, how marvelous are all Thy works. My breasts declare it."

Ada ❦ 17

THEY NAMED THE baby Alfred, as was expected. Alfred Alfredson VII.

Ada had several pet names for him. First it was simply Baby. Later she called him Free.

Alfred's brows came up the first time Ada used the nickname Free. It was April. Gramma had left for home again. They'd just finished having a cozy supper together. The baby was suckling lustily as Ada sipped at a cup of green tea. "Free?"

"Yes. I've never seen a baby so free with his hands. He's always waving them around. It's like his hands were meant to be wings."

"Free." Alfred lit his pipe. "Wal, just so it don't mean he's gonna be free and easy around women."

Ada looked down in love at her suckling baby. The silk edge of its blue blanket shielded the side of its pink face. Each time she breathed her pear breast touched gently against his cheek. The little fellow's mouth was just big enough to hold her brown nipple. "I don't think we're gonna have to worry about that with him. He's going to be a good boy." She shook the baby a little in love. "Aren't you, Free, my love?"

Alfred stole a look at where her breast with its net of fine blue veins lay exposed. He was beginning to have ideas again. A couple of nights ago her nursing the baby at two in the morning had awakened Alfred and the soft sound of the baby's lips on her nipple had given him a considerable bump in his nightshirt.

Ada brushed down the baby's dark red hair, stroking gently. "Strange that he should have two cowlicks, one on each corner in back here." She touched a forefinger into the two centers of where his hair stuck up. "Two little moons." Free had a long head, wide and high in back and narrow and slanting in front. "Well, I don't mind the two cowlicks. Those we can train. But I surely hope in time he loses this strip of hair here where it comes down to his left eyebrow. I want him to have some kind of forehead." Ada smiled down at the baby. The morning light was kind to her. Her freckles appeared to be golden. "And I don't mind either his hair running down so far in back. That we can hide under his shirt."

Free's suckling gradually slowed as sleep overcame him. Her nipple slipped from between his puppy lips.

"Titty time is rest time for the mother all right."

Alfred said, "Maybe he inherited those cowlicks one from each side of the family. One from your side and one from my side."

"Just so he's not going to be a man divided against himself."

"In fact," Alfred went on, "I claim the one on the left corner for my family. Because that's where I got mine."

Ada laughed. "That leaves me with the other one."

"Wal, you womenfolk generally have it on the other side."

Ada fell into a smiling silence. Baby Alfred had worked up a little sweat with his hungry nursing. Ada took the silk corner of his blue blanket and gently wiped away the beads of perspiration from the right side of his forehead. The arrow of blond hair coming down to his left brow appeared to be dry.

The beads of sweat reminded her of the drops of water Reverend Graves had sprinkled on the baby's face during baptism.

. . . . In late January she and Alfred, both tall, stood up in church and had their baby made a covenant child of God. The low January sun struck sharply through the circular colored window high in the south wall of the transept, casting a sacral glow over them.

Reverend Graves read the formula for baptism from the pulpit in his firm muscular manner. He reminded Alfred the father and Ada the mother, both now confessed members of the Bonnie Christian Church, that the child was born in sin and could not enter the kingdom of God just as it was. The child needed to be baptized at the hands of a minister of God so that its uncleanness might be washed away and it could be reborn again. God wanted clean souls in a pure heaven. After Alfred and Ada had responded to the several questions directed at them, Alfred's voice a strong baritone, Ada's voice a clear soprano, and after they'd agreed to bring up the child in the paths of righteousness, Reverend Graves stepped down off the pulpit and approached Alfred and Ada where they stood in front of the first bench. Elder Etten came up sleepily to hold the silver baptismal font.

Alfred handed Reverend Graves a slip of paper on which Ada had written the name of the baby. While Reverend Graves studied the handwriting, Ada handed the baby over to Alfred for the head of the house to hold it. Ada next placed a soft washcloth around the baby's face.

Reverend Graves beckoned for Elder Etten to hold the silver beaker a little closer, then dropped his whole hand into the water, withdrew it and gave it a little wringing shake to shed some of the water, and then, reading the name from the piece of paper, proceeded to shower the baby's blond face with a sprinkle of water each time he pronounced a key word: "*Alfred Alfredson*, I *baptize* you in the name of the *Father*, and the *Son*, and the *Holy Ghost*. Ah-*men*." Then Reverend Graves drew a handkerchief out of his sleeve and dried his hand.

The several little showers of cold water on Alfred Alfredson VII's face woke him out of a sweet sleep. Alfred VII let go with a bellow to let his titty-ma know that a catastrophe was at hand. He bawled so loud that the whole church, already silent so as to be sure to catch the name of the child, became even more silent.

Ada blushed. She'd so hoped the baby would've accepted the baptism quietly. She hated it when babies fussed at their baptisms. It broke up the holy mood of the occasion. Alfred the father raised his high nose at all the noise coming from the crook of his arm. He didn't like it either. Reverend Graves's eyes twinkled as he pocketed the child's name for later recording. Ada then reached for the baby.

As Alfred VII passed from his father's arms to his mother's arm, he bawled in an even louder key. And he further made his point by letting go with some small thunderclaps deep in the cocoon of his blankets. They were followed by a maffled sound emphatically expressed.

Ada glanced furtively to either side to make sure no one but the four of them had heard it. Ada wiped the trickling drops from the baby's face. She managed to do it with a deft circling motion, ending up at the child's roaring mouth.

"Shh, shhh, quiet now, baby, please."

Muscular Reverend Graves reascended the pulpit and concluded the baptism with prayer. "O Father in heaven, this covenant child has been received in the bosom of

Thy church." Then the congregation rose and sang a psalm. "When I remember those things, I pour out my soul in me; I went with them to the house of God, with the voice of joy and praise, with a multitude that kept holy day."

Ada raised her voice in song with them. And by the time she came to the words "holy day," baby Free had fallen silent, soothed by the voice that came with titty. . . .

The stove made a contracting noise.

Alfred emptied his pipe in the palm of his hand, and lifting a stove lid, deposited the ashes into the stove. "You know, I can't help but think that the reason Widow Bettie came all the way out here from Massachusetts to marry my dad was that she needed her weeds plowed."

Ada came back into the kitchen. She stared at her husband. "Where on earth did you ever get that idea?"

"It just now come to me."

Ada was again dumbfounded by the difference between the man's world outdoors and the woman's world indoors. It was almost as if there were two different races living side by side. "Her weeds. The idea. When widow's weeds means a woman's still grieving."

Alfred poured himself a cup of coffee. He dropped in a spoon of sugar, then looked for the cream. He spotted it behind the potato bowl. "Chase the cow my way, would you please, my lady?"

"What?"

"Never mind. You're busy." He reached across the table and helped himself to a liberal spurt of cream.

"Ow." Baby occasionally gave her breast a spasmodic pinch with his fat fingers. "Say, you, it's about time I gave you your first manicure."

Alfred sipped his coffee with another covert look at where her breast lay exposed.

"Alfred, you shouldn't talk that way about your father's chosen wife."

"I suppose not."

"It's not the Christian way."

"No, I guess it ain't."

"She has her side of it too."

"Maybe she has. But her side of it sure ain't helping my dad any. With her talk of property. Property property! As if that was the be-all in life. Telling him last summer after he came back from the Dakotas that if he didn't build her a house pronto, and make them a little barn so they could have a cow, she was gonna pull up stakes and head back for Massachusetts. Hoh. Wal, let her go, I say."

"But maybe that's what your restless father needed. Someone to make him settle down. Be practical."

"Have a cow in town. I can just see my dad. Chambermaid to a cow."

The next Sunday, Ada persuaded Alfred to stop at his father's house after church. It bothered Ada that her husband's father should be so anti-church. She thought that by their example they might get him to go once in a while. Bettie had said that though she was a Congregationalist she wouldn't mind trying the Christian Church a few times.

Ada wasn't too taken with stepmother Bettie either, but she did like Alfred's father. That short block of a man was a real power. He'd built his present house out of his own homemade cement blocks in the short space of three months with only young Richard to help him.

At three-thirty the sun was still high in the sky when Alfred pulled up in front of Dad's new house. Alfred stepped down from the buggy first and took the baby from Ada. After she stepped down, he handed the baby back to her. He deftly tied Daise to the hitching post and then walked up to the front door with Ada.

Ada noted immediately how neat the yard was.

Stepmother Bettie, face in the front window, spotted them coming and quickly hurried around to the south door of the kitchen. "This way, folks. We've still got the front door closed for the winter."

As they took the walk around, Ada saw how all the windows on the sunny side of the house were full of potted flowers. "Look at that," Ada exclaimed. "I didn't know she liked flowers that well." There were geraniums, begonias, African violets, and finally even the cactus Dad had brought home with him from the wild Dakotas.

Baby began to squirm inside its fat roll of blankets. The cold air was getting in under the tip of his outer brown blanket. His eyes volved under his eyelids.

Stepmother Bettie stood looking down at them from the doorway. She was a plump woman, auburn hair touched with gray, eyes a light blue, and a strong chin. Her slow smile seemed to enlarge her chin. The skin over her cheeks was mottled as though she might have a fever. Her nose was red. "Oh, you brought the baby. Good. Come in, come in."

The smell inside was like that of a greenhouse, of green air almost too rich to breathe.

Dad was sitting by the stove, feet in the oven door, reading a book in the light of the north window. He had on freshly washed work clothes, blue jeans and blue shirt. Seeing the company, he put his book aside. "Well, it's my son and his lovely wife Ada." He stood up. His moon-touched eyes steadied on them. A guarded smile formed under his moustache. It was obvious that Dad and Bettie had had words. They weren't looking at each other.

Alfred decided to be of good cheer. "Wal, Dad, throw another cob on the fire and we'll help you drink your tea."

"Done."

Bettie whispered in a ratchy voice, "Is he asleep?"

"I think so." Ada opened the silk-edged inner white blanket.

Baby had quit his squirming. His eyelids lay closed and untroubled.

Bettie breathed thickly. "He's sweet." A drop formed at the end of her red nose. "I never had one, you know."

Ada didn't know what to say.

"Oh, it's all right. The Lord's"—before Bettie could cover her mouth a cough exploded out of her and a little flag of phlegm the color of tapioca landed on the baby's pink cheek—"will. Oh, pardon me." Bettie turned a deep red. She dug a handkerchief out of her gray apron and quickly dabbed up the sputum.

"You've got kind of a cold there."

"Yes, I can't seem to shake it."

Dad stared holes right through Bettie. "Bettie's always got a cold. The whole winter long."

"I've got a kind of an asthma," Bettie said.

"Then why do you keep all them flowers around?" Dad demanded. "Every time one of them blooms you start wheezing."

Ada had a smile for Dad. "I thought you liked flowers."

"Only those yellow cactus blooms. I came by them the hard way."

"I like to think flowers are the whispers of God."

Dad sat down again. He gestured for Alfred to sit across from him at the oven door. Dad filled and lighted his pipe. "That's bullshit, daughter, and you know it, b-begging your pardon."

Ada didn't even blink. Usually she'd straighten up very ladylike when she heard bad language. Apparently far back in her head a part of her thought it was all right for Dad to use rough language. "Where's Abbott? And Gerda? I was hoping to see them."

Dad said shortly, "Out playing with the neighbor kits somewhere."

Alfred got out his pipe too. "Wal, Dad, it looks like you got out of bed on the wrong side this morning."

"B-Bullshit."

Ada decided to change the subject. "I didn't know you liked flowers that much, Mom. The last time we dropped in I think you just had a few around."

"I had them stored at the Meads' until the house here was done." Bettie liked being called "Mom." "Why don't you put the baby down on the leather couch. I don't think he'll roll off there."

Ada put the baby down.

"Come, I'll show them to you." Bettie led the way.

As Bettie and Ada entered the living room the fronds of two maidenhair ferns stirred a little. It was almost as if the ferns knew friends had come to visit them.

Plants had been set to catch every possible bit of sunlight, on shelves, on pedestals, on swing-arm supports. The air was an even richer green in the living room. The plants loved Bettie.

Ada leaned over a trailing vine. She didn't quite touch it. "Wandering Jew. That's the first one I've seen since I worked for Reverend Carpenter." Ada gave Bettie a smile. "He married us."

"Is that so."

"It's a strange plant."

"I took it with me from Massachusetts." Bettie smiled wryly. "It's curious that you should have seen one in a reverend's house."

"You mean, because it's named after the man who mocked Jesus on the way to His crucifixion? And ever since has had to wander over the face of the earth?"

"Yes."

That was a sad legend all right. Ada next leaned over a rare plant with a dozen dainty pink flowers. "Baby's toes."

"We call that baby's feet where I came from."

Sunlight streamed through the green leaves. It gave the faces of the two women a bluish-yellow cast. It gave the whitewashed cement walls a light green tint. The green air made Ada's heart beat harder.

Dad called from the kitchen. "Where do you keep the tea leaves, Bettie?"

"Coming." With a tired step Bettie headed back to the kitchen.

Ada followed her.

Bettie reached for a spread-out newspaper on the top of the stove. It was covered with drying leaves and a few rose hips. She crumbled a handful of the dried leaves into a little sack, along with a crushed rose hip, and hung it in a large blue teapot. She gestured for Ada to sit down at the kitchen table. She set the table, now and then dabbing at her nose with a soggy handkerchief.

Ada's glance fell on the red book Dad had put aside when they came in. "What are you reading there, Dad?"

"Engels."

"What's it about?"

"Well, daughter, Engels writes about the other side of this Christianity you admire so much."

Ada waited for him to explain.

"Engels was a rich man's son who took pity on the men who worked for his father. The working class. He fought to improve their lot. And he knew more about how to get socialism off the ground than Marx did."

Alfred reared back on two legs of his chair. "Socialism?"

"Why not?"

Ada was sorry she'd asked. The idea that Dad should be reading about socialism, when Alfred still couldn't read at all, would only further set son against father.

The teakettle on the stove began to shoot steam. Bettie poured some hot water into the teapot. She was careful to hold onto the end of the little sack of leaves so it wouldn't fall in.

Alfred looked at his father. "What does your friend C. Rexroth say about you reading socialism?"

Dad clapped out his pipe. "He gave me the book in the first place."

"You mean, he reads such stuff too?"

"Sure. Why not?"

Alfred came down on all four. "You know, I can hardly believe that Old Cee would want to read about such bullshit."

"Alfred," Ada warned, "your language please."

"Hey," Alfred said, "How come Dad can say 'bullshit' and not me?"

Dad allowed himself a large smile. "Because you don't have the right tune, son. You've got to say it like Teddy Roosevelt."

"B-B-Bull . . . shit!"

Dad laughed. "Well now, that's some better."

From then on the visit went tolerably smooth. When Ada exclaimed over the taste of the tea, Stepmom Bettie said it was probably the crushed rose hip that gave it that special tang. Dad surprisingly agreed, and asked for another cup of it.

Four days later, at night, Ada was awakened by a funny noise coming from the baby's cradle. The baby made a sound like a hurt puppy.

Ada hated to get up. She'd been busy with spring housecleaning that day. And Alfred beside her was sleeping the sleep of one who was also dead tired. He'd been out disking all day in a raw wind.

Baby coughed. Deep and moist.

Ada stole out of bed and turned up the night lamp a little. She had a look at the baby in its cradle by the door. She placed her hand on his forehead. Why, the baby had a raging fever. It was hot. She turned the night lamp way up. "Alfred!"

"Mmm."

"Alfred, wake up, our baby's quite sick."

Alfred slowly rolled over and sat up.

"He's breathing funny. He's so sick he's hot."

Alfred's eyes opened wide. He glanced at the alarm clock. "One in the morning. Think I ought to go get Doc?"

"I don't know. You worked so hard today I hate to ask you to do it."

"Wal, we can't lose our crown prince either, you know."

"What a thing to say." Ada reached in under the baby's blanket. "Why! he's soaking wet." She withdrew her hand and sniffed her fingers. "And it's not from number one either."

A deep cough ratched in the baby. The baby rolled its head from side to side. Phlegm slid stringy out of one side of its mouth. The baby's nose was completely stopped up.

"When'd you first notice he had a cold?" Alfred asked.

"Yesterday. His nose was a little red. And he didn't nurse too good." Ada's breasts were still full and stung a little. "It's just about num-num time again."

"Ain't he about ready to quit that two-o'clocker?"

"Well, he's always still so hungry at two."

Alfred swung out of bed and came over and placed his hand on the baby's forehead. "Gotske! He is hot. That settles it. I'm getting Doc."

"Good, Alfred. Good. And I'll hold the baby and pray until you come back with him."

Alfred climbed into his clothes.

"At least this time there's no blizzard," Ada said.

Alfred snapped on his overalls suspender. "Stepmom and her coughing like that right in his face."

"God's will, Alfred."

"Not when people should know better."

Daise went like the wind, and Alfred was backwith Dr. Drury by three.

Dr. Drury placed the baby on the living room table under the pulldown lamp. His dark-haired hands moved tenderly over the baby's body. He took the baby's temperature: 103°. The pulse: 150. He bared the baby's chest and listened to it with his stethoscope. He placed the flat of his left hand on the baby's chest and tapped it with the forefinger of his right hand. Gradually his warm dark eyes became grave dark eyes.

Ada and Alfred stood to one side of him. They waited.

"When did his bowels move last?"

"Let's see." Ada closed her eyes to remember the better. "Why, that's right. Not since yesterday morning."

Dr. Drury bundled up the baby and handed him over to Ada.

Ada clutched the baby to her breast. She could feel its little heart beating desperately. She trembled. "Well?"

"It's pneumonia all right."

Pneumonia? Ada almost fell over.

Dr. Drury ran a hand over his face. "Yes."

"Can't you give him something for it?"

"I can. But it won't do much good."

"Ain't there no medicine for pneumonia?"

"Not really."

"I can't lose my baby, doctor."

"Nor can I."

Alfred sat down with a thump. His face was like milk crystals. "What about a poultice?"

Dr. Drury shook his head. "Bundling him close with flannel is about as good."

"Wouldn't a mustard plaster draw it out though?"

"Can't draw pneumonia through a ribcase." Dr. Drury held his chin in hand. "First we've got to bring down that temperature. Before he burns up. Let's bring his cradle in here where the heat's apt to be more even."

Alfred got the cradle.

"And, Ada, you take off some of those covers."

Ada laid the baby gently in the cradle and removed several blankets.

"Now, can you get me some washcloths and some cool water?"

Ada scurried to do it.

Very gently, as if he were handling a shell-less egg, Dr. Drury began laving the baby's face with a series of cool washcloths. Gradually the pan of water warmed up. Ada, hovering by, replaced it with fresh cool water from the cistern pump.

Alfred sat still in his chair, watching, brows drawn.

An hour ticked by. After baby's heat had warmed up a half dozen pans of water, Dr. Drury took its temperature. Still 103°.

Alfred ground his hands together. "Too bad this ain't the hailstorm season."

"You mean, pack the baby in hailstones?"

"No, feed 'em to him like candy. They say that makes for a good medicine."

"Might bring down the temperature. But that's about all."

Ada reached in under the baby's shirt a moment. "His skin's turned dry."

The baby shook as if it had the ague. Its cheeks burned a brilliant scarlet. Its little hands worked like the claws of a dying hawk.

"Shouldn't I try to feed him?" Ada asked. "It's long past his feeding time."

"Try it. Feeding him just might bring him to a sweat again."

Ada offered the baby titty. Baby didn't seem to recognize what was being offered. It rolled its head from side to side. "His nose is too stuffed to smell food, Doctor."

At six, Dr. Drury decided to quit the cool washcloth treatment. "Let's bundle him up again. We'll risk his running too high a temperature. We've got to get him to sweat."

By the time the sun came up at seven, little Free's temperature had climbed to 104°.

Dr. Drury nodded to himself suddenly. "Get me the mustard and some flour."

Ada hurried to get them.

Dr. Drury mixed up a fine paste and applied it to the baby's chest an inch thick.

"Wow!" Alfred exclaimed. "That stuff sure smells ferocious. Worse than a horse barn on a hot day."

Little Free's nose thought so too. It began to twitch.

At eight o'clock Alfred put on his outdoors jacket.

Ada looked up wonderingly.

"Lady, I got to pail them cows. Can't let them be thrown off schedule too much or they'll dry up on me."

"That's right." The thought of those two poor cows out there patiently waiting made Ada all the more aware of her own swollen breasts. She stroked the sides of her bosom. "What am I going to do if he doesn't eat in a couple of days?"

Dr. Drury held his head to one side. "You may have to express them yourself, Ada. To avoid clotting. When his appetite returns he won't like the clotting."

Ada prayed to herself. "Oh Lord, let this thing pass us by. But Thy will be done, O Lord, not ours."

"Call me if you need me." Alfred gave Ada a swift scratch kiss on her brow, then went off to do his chores.

The mustard plaster plus the bundling didn't help either. The baby's temperature rose to 104.4°.

"You don't have some other kind of medicine in town?"

"No. With pneumonia you've got to make it on your own."

"Then he's got to be a strong baby?"

"Yes.

"Well . . . God's will."

"Ada, I fear He intends that only the strong shall survive."

"And here it was always my thought that God was surely on the side of the weak."

Dr. Drury took the baby's pulse yet once again. He shook his head slowly.

"Would you like some breakfast, Doctor? I know Alfred will want some nourishment when he comes in."

"Yes, that will be fine."

Ada made oatmeal porridge, eggs and bacon, sliced bread toasted in the oven, and a batch of fresh coffee.

When Alfred came in both men ate with relish. She herself couldn't eat.

Toward noon Dr. Drury decided to put on more blankets and raise the heat in the living room.

"The kid don't cry much," Alfred noted.

"Yes, I noticed that," Dr. Drury said. "Probably because his mother is calm around him."

By two o'clock, the baby's temperature was up to 104.7°.

"My God, Doc," Alfred said, "that little fellow's gonna burn up."

Dr. Drury said nothing.

"He'll never have much gaff if this keeps up."

Ada got up and went over to the bay window and looked out over the yard. Her heart beat high and very fast in her throat. The purple buds on the maples along the road were already thick. It was as if a colony of bumblebees had swarmed into the trees. It appeared the buds were going to be open too early and a late spring would surely kill them.

For two days little Free sucked for his life through flags of greenish-yellow phlegm. Dr. Drury muttered to himself a half dozen times that he couldn't understand what kept the little fellow alive. He should've long ago drowned in his own chest. The fever varied. At night it sank to 101°; during the day it climbed to 104° plus.

Ada went to her bedroom several times to milk herself in a little pan. It took her a while to learn how to do it. A woman's nipple as compared to a cow's teat was quite a different thing. One couldn't get much of a hold on a woman's nipple. And it didn't do any good to squeeze the whole breast either any more than it did to squeeze the cow's whole udder. Also the milk came out quite clotted. But she managed somehow. "It sure makes a person feel funny."

Outside the sun shone warm both days. The purple buds began to show wings.

Ada saw that Alfred was itching to get his oats planted.

On the evening of the third day, the color of the baby's spit changed from a greenish-yellow to a plain dull yellow, while the baby's cheeks changed from a bright red to a sick white. Its breath came like steam pushing up through boiling porridge.

Dr. Drury took the baby's temperature. 105°. The pulse was up to 170. "Well, here it is."

Ada's heart began to beat so swift she had to go open a window a crack. "Dearly beloved Jesus," she whispered, "let this cup pass us by."

Alfred stood behind Dr. Drury. "If he don't break out into a sweat pretty soon . . . "

Ada agonized. "God's will."

Presently the baby's breathing slowed down.

"Ah." Dr. Drury leaned his big shoulders into the baby's cradle. He took its temperature again: 102.4°. The pulse: 120. "That's better. The fever is broken."

Alfred cracked his knuckles. "Either that, or he's dying."

Ada placed a hand on Alfred's arm. His muscles were all knots. "Please, Alfred."

In another minute the baby began to breathe rapidly again, faster than before. It's sick-white face turned a choleric purple.

Dr. Drury took its temperature: 105.2°. The pulse: 174.
Baby's breath whistled.
All three leaned over the cradle, intent on the little swollen face.
As they watched, tiny, very tiny, beads of sweat broke out on the baby's forehead. It was like watching the world roll over.
"Look at that, would you!" Alfred cried. "He's turning the corner."
The little beads of sweat rapidly became large drops of sweat.
Ada took a dry washcloth and gently wiped off the moisture.
Alfred reached under the blankets. "He's sopping wet too, Doc."
Dr. Drury took little Free's temperature once more: 101.4°. The pulse was 110. "He's broken the back of it all right."
"Then the crisis is really past?" Ada asked.
"He's made it, Ada."

Alfred ❦ 18

SOON BABY FREE could sit up in a chair. Sunshine put roses in his cheeks.
The moment Alfred thought the boy was strong enough he began to play stunts with him. Alfred liked to pick him up by his wrists and ankles and swing him around and around in rising and falling circles. Free loved the impromptu flights. He squealed in delight every time he soared up near the ceiling. As Alfred swung the baby around and up and down, he pirouetted neatly on his toes. The two little wrists fit exactly in Alfred's right hand while the two little ankles fit in his left hand.
Light from the pulldown lamp flashed in Ada's gold hair. "Alfred, I'm not sure it's good for the child to laugh like that."
Alfred gave Free an especially daring swoop up in the air, and then, at the very top of it, held him against the ceiling for a second.
Free let go with another wonderful baby laugh.
Alfred let the baby swoop down to the floor, then tossed him up in the air for a short free ride, and then, just in time, playfully, caught him before he fell.
Free let go with a peal of joy.
Ada smiled at Free. "So you like being a swallow, do you?"
"An eagle, you mean," Alfred said.
Free kicked his feet asking for more.
Alfred had begun to puff. "No, boy, that's enough for today."

Three months later, one evening after supper in early October, Free once again got up off the floor and stood beside a chair.
Alfred saw it. "Now to get him to take his first step."
"Now, now. Let him do it in his own time."
Alfred held out both hands to the boy anyway.
Free smiled a baby's shrewd smile to himself.
"Come. Come now," Alfred coaxed softly.
Free waved one hand while he held on with the other hand.

''Ada, love, I betcha if you was to hold out titty to him he'd take that first step quick enough.''

Ada shook her head, smiling. ''There's no rush.''

''But of that bunch born in January I want him to be the first to walk. You know, Fat John's boy. Hal Haber's boy. And that Catherine of Bill Haber. All of them.''

''No, Alfred. If the boy walks too soon he may have trouble with his joints later on. Like I did.''

''I didn't know you walked too soon.''

''At nine months. And I sure had sore knees when I was twelve.''

''Them was only growing pains.'' Alfred got down on his knees and put out his hands until they were within a couple of inches of the boy. ''Come.''

But Free wouldn't take that step.

''I know what'll make you come, boy.'' Alfred got out his watch and dangled it by its gold chain in front of the boy.

Free's little tongue lolled out round and his face turned serious. Then, after a moment, he reached for it.

''Hey, not so fast there,'' Alfred laughed as he jerked the watch out of reach.

Free continued to stare raptly at the swinging watch.

Alfred held the watch against the baby's ear a moment. ''What do you think of that, huh?''

Free's blue eyes closed over with a milky distant look.

Again Alfred dangled the watch just out of reach. ''See?''

Free stared at the swinging watch. All of a sudden he took two steps and reached up and grabbed the watch in his tiny fist.

''Wow!''

''Alfred, not really.''

Alfred was overjoyed. ''Look at that, would you? He's done it. Took his first step as a man.''

Ada's eyes turned moist.

Alfred picked the boy up and gave him a big hug. Then Alfred settled in his rocker with the boy on his lap and let him play with the watch a while.

Baby Free held the watch to his ear, turned it over, listened some more, finally decided that the best way to possess it was to swallow it.

''Hey, that we can't have. Or we'll have an awful bellyache.'' Alfred had to force the watch from the baby's hands he held on to it so tight. ''The little son of a gun has got a pretty good grip already.'' Alfred put the watch away.

Free studied to himself a few moments; then let go with a bellow.

''Nope, no more. That's done for tonight.''

Free bawled louder.

Alfred frowned at the same time that he had to laugh a little. ''Man, when he gets his mind set on something, he's got it set, hasn't he?''

Ada held out her arms. ''Here, let me take him. It's about titty time anyway.''

Free liked that even less. When Ada lifted her breast into his mouth he bbbt it out with his tongue.

''What a temper,'' Alfred marveled.

Ada laughed. ''Why don't you go outside a while and let me alone with him. Out of sight.''

Shaking his head, Alfred got his cap and jacket and went outside.

Alfred heard that the orphanage in the valley below, the Siouxland Home For Little Boys, had some prize young Shorthorn bulls for sale. The bulls were two years old, had been dehorned, and were ready to breed stock. Alfred fancied the Shorthorn cow for its beef and milk both and wanted to breed his cows to a good Shorthorn bull. His two cows, Three-tit and Belle, were mostly Shorthorn, as were Reddy and Spot, the two heifers he'd bought on a farm sale that fall.

Adam Erdman, owner of the orphanage, brought the young bull over one sunny day. Adam rode a small compact bay who kept snaking after the bull no matter how the bull doubled on itself.

Alfred spotted them coming up the road. He ran to open the gate near the barn. He made sure the cows were some distance down the pasture, locked Rover in the barn, and then hurried out onto the road to help turn the critter into his yard.

The bull was a beauty. He had a broad white shield of a head and high chunky red shoulders with short powerful legs. But he was so young he didn't quite know his mind. He'd been raised with other young bulls, hadn't been around female cattle since he'd been weaned, and was confused by all the smells he ran into along the road. One moment he'd be in the ditch cropping at succulent grass, the next moment bumping into the fence, the next be trying to get past the horseman to go back home.

Adam's horse kept chousing the bull forward.

When the young bull got to the lane, Alfred began to wave his hands up and down to turn him. ''Shuh. Huh. Soo-ah!''

The young bull stared at Alfred with lowered head, studied to himself a moment, then shot to his left onto the yard.

''Good,'' Alfred cried.

The young bull ran straight for the barn, until out of the corner of his eye he spotted the water tank. He stopped. He sniffed the air with a leering upper lip, liked what he smelled, and trotted over and had himself a drink.

Adam reined in his horse a couple dozen steps behind the bull. Adam was a small blond man about thirty years old. He had a natural twinkle in his blue eyes. He was known to be one of those godless atheists, and yet, at the same time, was also known, somehow, to be a kind good-hearted man. The orphans left in his care loved him.

Alfred noted there was a light wind out of the south. ''When our young tom gets a whiff of that she-stuff below there he may head through that gate on his own.''

''Got one bulling down there?''

''Yep. Reddy, a heifer.''

"If he knows what that means." Adam looked down to where the cattle were grazing. He leaned an elbow on the pommel of his saddle. The bay under him switched a lazy tail at the last few flies of the year. ''Is it that red heifer?''

''Yeh. The one with the tail up a little.''

Adam smiled. ''This is going to be fun to watch.''

After a while the young bull had enough to drink. His head came up. Glistening drops of water ran off his rubbery nose. Flexing motions moved under his red-and-white pelt.

The two men waited.

Then the young bull picked up the strange new scent. His white snout lifted. He sniffed until his upper lip curled up off his teeth. He took one more sniff, then shied away from the tank and ran through the open gate. He set off at a fast trot straight for the two cows and the two heifers below.

The four critters looked up from their grazing. The nearest one was Reddy the heifer, hardly more than two years old herself. Her red tail, arched up a couple of inches, switched indolently at some flies riding on her shoulders.

Alfred couldn't see the action quite as well as Adam up on his horse, so he jumped up on the cover of the water tank.

The young bull's first thought was that the she-stuff was the enemy and therefore something to be butted and knocked down. He bellowed as he ran toward them, lowered his broad head straight for Reddy.

Reddy pricked up her flop ears.

About a dozen steps away the young bull got the full benefit of Reddy's peculiar and wonderful scent. He came to a stiff-legged stop within a few feet of her.

"Watch now."

An electric charge snapped on in the young bull. It was strong enough to make him shudder. His butt arched up and down a couple of times in involuntary practice thrusts.

Reddy shied half around, and in so doing presented her buttocks to him.

As if on signal, the young bull broke out of his stance, charged and mounted her, and eyes closing drove his gleaming pink rapier home—at the same time letting go with a surprised strangled bellow. He slid off Reddy and fell to earth in a dead faint, hitting the ground with a heavy thump. He lay as though stunned by the blow of an axe.

"For godsakes," Alfred exclaimed.

"Yeh, now he knows what it means to be a man," Adam laughed.

Alfred had to laugh then too. He jumped down off the water tank.

The young bull began to kick. After a couple of seconds he came to, immediately scrambled to his feet and looked around. The first thing he saw was the heifer Reddy, tail lifted a little higher. He stared at her. He went over and sniffed her. Slowly his upper lip curled up in a great leer again, as though caught in a twitch. His rump arched up a couple of times. Then, with another surge, he mounted her and once more drove his limber rapier home. This time he didn't faint. Instead he slid off her back with a thoughtful air.

"Well, Alfred, you've got you a good tom bull there."

"I guess so."

That evening when Alfred told Ada about the affair she didn't laugh one bit.

"You don't think that's funny?"

"No."
"Not even a little bit funny?"
"No."
"Women!"

One night early in November, after both were in bed and the light was out, Ada told Alfred that sometime next July they could expect another little visitor.

Alfred was exhausted from picking corn all day, and had hardly been able to stay awake, but her news made him sit up in bed. "Another baby?"

"Yes, my husband." She placed a hand on his arm in a loving manner. "And I pray God that this time it may be a girl."

"Yeh. A little hired girl for you in the house."

"But now we've got a problem. With the next baby on the way I better start weaning Free. And soon, too, or it'll take something away from the second one while I'm carrying it."

"Yeh, that's true. I do the same thing with the cows. Dry 'em up if the bull happens to hit them too early."

"But Free isn't going to like it. He still drinks a full share besides the corn mush and oatmeal I give him. So hungry."

"Mix in a little cow's milk with a little more corn mush each day until you've picked up the slack."

"That's a good idea, my husband."

Little Free liked the extra portions of corn mush and oatmeal and ate them all right. But the more Ada cut down on titty the crankier he became. He knew the difference between cow's milk and titty milk. He began to fuss a lot and cried a good part of the day.

When he cried at night, Ada had to get up and pacify him. Alfred was working very hard and needed all the rest he could get. When little Free wouldn't quiet down, she at last had to nurse him.

A couple of weeks went by. Again Alfred and Ada were in bed and little Free commenced to fuss and whine in his crib.

"Darn kid," Alfred murmured under his high nose.

Ada sighed. "He surely fancies feeding time all right."

"Did you try the pacifier we bought?"

"He spits that out like it was poison."

"Maybe it's time for his first licking."

Little Free gave a violent kick in his crib.

"Shh," Ada hissed at the crib in the dark.

Then little Free said quite distinctly, "Num num."

Ada sat up. "Did you hear that?"

Alfred grunted.

"That was his first word."

"Naw. It's the sound he makes for titty."

"It sound to me like he said, mom mom."

"Naw. It's all in your head. He ain't old enough to talk yet."

"I dunno." Ada called softly over to the crib." "Baby want mommy?"

"Num num."

"Ma ma? Baby say ma ma?"

"Ma-ma."

Ada gave Alfred a push. "See? He did so say mom mom." Ada threw back the quilt.

Alfred opened his eyes. "What're you going to do?"

"Feed him, of course."

"Nosiree you don't." Alfred sat up. "In fact, I want you to quit giving him titty starting right now."

Ada sat very still, suddenly a stubborn mother.

"Ada, you've got to draw the line somewhere."

"But you need your sleep."

"I'll have the corn out tomorrow and after that I can go without sleep for a week if I have to. If only to train that boy right. We can't let him be the head stud here. He's still only a little button of a thing."

"Then we're just going to let him cry now then?"

"Yep. Till he gets sick of it."

"That's cruel, Alfred."

"Not in the long run, it ain't."

Free's gramma came down for a week at Thanksgiving.

Little Free still hadn't given up his crying. In the morning he was satisfied with the food given him out of his little plate. But around noon, near dinner, he began to whine after Ada, tagging along behind her as she set the table, hanging onto her apron and crying for num num.

"Until now he's always been such a good baby," Ada lamented. "We've never had any trouble with him."

Alfred said over his pipestem, "That's because you've spoiled him."

Gramma gave Alfred a throw of hen eyes. "My daughter's too wise to spoil her child."

Alfred laughed. He thought Gramma's mads somewhat hilarious.

"Why don't you play with him more?" Gramma pursued. "Ya, I mean you, his father."

Alfred put his pipe aside. "Lady, I have. But the only thing that'll shut him up is acrobat rides. And Ada ain't exactly crazy about that for him either. Afraid it'll wake up a wild streak in him."

Gramma tried a white peppermint caught in the corner of a handkerchief. But that really wasn't what Free wanted either and by the time the three grown-ups were into their potatoes and meat, he was crying again. Finally Ada had to pick him up and hold him in her lap.

Alfred helped himself to a second plate of meat and cabbage. "We still got that whiskey left, ain't we?"

"What do you want that for?" Gramma challenged.

"Make him a whiskey tit. That'll put him to sleep."

"And make a drunkard out of him?"

Little Free pulled at his mother's blouse.

Alfred next helped himself to a bowl of hot rice. He dropped a couple of dabs of butter on it which melted immediately into little gold islands. He next sprinkled on some cinnamon and sugar. It made for a great dish. "I agree about the whiskey. But if you women are going to be stubborn about spoiling him . . . "

Gramma spoke grimly over her bowl. "You forget that part of that boy is of my blood. Of the Alderling blood. Which is of higher issue."

Alfred snorted. "Now you sound like my gramma in Sioux Center. She was always talking about her blood being of higher issue too. When the Alfredson blood is already pretty good."

Ada shook her head. "I wish there was some way I could remove that knife between you two." Tears showed in her eyes. "The way you two talk about your blood, you sound like a couple of Sioux City livestock commissioners."

Alfred's nose came up. "I'd never mention my side of it if it wasn't for her."

Little Free cried and cried in Ada's lap.

Alfred helped himself to some coffee. "Ada, I feel sorry for your dad. If I had to live every day like this with your mother, believe you me, I'd do something about it."

Gramma snorted. "Just what would you do."

Alfred set his cup down in its saucer with a light clap of sound. "I'd take you over my knee, pull up your petticoat, and give you the licking of your life on your bare behind. Because you don't guy me, Missus."

Gramma turned beet red. "You would not!"

Ada burst out laughing. "What a sight that'd be."

"Here, let me hold that kid a while," Alfred said. He took the boy from Ada. He set him firmly down on his left leg close to his chest. He reached for the boy's bowl of mush and set it in his own bowl. He took the boy's little silver spoon and dipped up a mouthful. "Now, young man, let's see you eat what's good for you."

Little Free instantly shut up. He looked up at his father with wide blue eyes. After a moment he opened his mouth and accepted a spoonful.

"You see?" Alfred said.

Gramma was jealous. "He's afraid of you, that's why he behaves for you."

"No. He just knows he can't get away with being cranky around me. Because he knows who's boss."

Ada was relieved. She hurried to eat her food before it got any colder.

Alfred fed the boy the rest of the mush without any trouble. "Slick and clean. That's it, boy."

Little Free continued to be quiet while Ada read from the Bible and Alfred gave thanks.

There was a look about Gramma as if she wished she could stoke the boy into crying again.

After Alfred had filled the stove, he took the boy with him to his rocker and played some tunes for him on his harmonica.

The boy became very quiet. His eyes fastened on the gleaming instrument in Alfred's supple hands.

At eight o'clock it was time for the boy to go to bed. Alfred gave him up to Ada and she changed him for the last time, put on his soaker, and slipped on his nightgown. She brushed down his now white-blond hair. The boy liked all the handling and had a soft smile for Ada.

But the minute she put him down in his crib and before she'd even tucked him in, he was back to bawling again, louder than ever.

Ada rocked his crib for a while. It didn't help.

"Get out of there," Alfred called from his rocker. "Get away from him. Close the door and let him bawl."

"My daughter will know when it's time to quit rocking him," Gramma said from the other side of the glowing hard-coal burner.

Ada whispered urgently, "You naughty little boy, you better go to sleep or Papa will get after you!"

Alfred loved to watch the softly glowing orange coals while he mused over the events of the day. It was a joy to think about the good work done. His stomach always churned especially well then. A bright blue coal rolled down the side of the glowing orange pile inside the base burner. It ticked lightly against the near pane of isinglass.

"Shh, baby," Ada murmured. "You've got to be quiet. Please."

Little Free was mad that they dared thwart him. He wanted titty and he wanted it right now. He bellowed.

Alfred dropped his feet to the floor. "That's enough." He strode into the small bedroom, blew out the night lamp, and taking Ada by the shoulders pushed her out into the living room. He closed the door behind them. "Now. You stay out of there, hear?"

"He'll yell his head off until we do something."

"Of course he'll yell. Let him."

The dousing of the light and the clicking door silenced little Free for the moment. That hadn't been at all what he'd expected.

"See?" Alfred said.

"But that's only for a couple of minutes. When he starts up again he'll yell until he hurts himself."

"Well, if he does, we'll just sit out here until he finally gets tired of it and quits. And once he learns that when the light goes out and the door closes he might just as well quit crying for all the good it's going to do him, he'll quit."

"But that's mean," Gramma said.

"It's even meaner if we don't train him right. Now. Before he gets spoiled rotten. And I don't want a rotten son." Alfred pointed to Ada's rocker. "Sit down there, lady. Take it easy. You're not going anywhere. At least not in the direction of the bedroom."

Reluctantly, yet sighing in some relief, Ada finally did sit down.

Alfred sat down too.

All three rockers creaked.

The stove crackled quietly.

Five minutes passed.

Then of a sudden there was a true outraged baby roar from behind the bedroom door.

"See!" Gramma said over her clicking needles.

"Just sit tight," Alfred ordered.

Ten minutes went by. The boy cried in a series of high rages and low subsidings. Now and then he fell completely silent as if sure that now they were about to relent and would come and get him and give him some beloved num num titty. Then he picked it up again.

Alfred filled and lighted his pipe. He was beginning to feel hot inside. Alfred thought: "That damned kid. Thinks he's the boss here. Well, he's got another think or two coming on that. And right on his soft pink little ass too."

Gramma got up abruptly. "That's enough of that crying. I'm not going to let my only grandchild hurt himself crying just because he has a bully of a father." She started heavily for the bedroom.

Alfred was too quick for her. He blocked the way. "Oh no you don't."

Gramma refixed her gold-rim glasses on her nose and glared up at him. "Get out of my way, monster."

Alfred gave her his best stare-down look.

A funny smile to one side began to twist Ada's lips.

"Beast! Out of my way. I mean to save my grandson from your cruelty. He's only a tiny little baby." Gramma charged Alfred. She surged up against him like a fat feather bed folding up around a bedpost.

Alfred stumbled; then, bracing himself, held his ground.

Gramma once more refixed her glasses on her nose. "Why don't you hit me, you beast? Knock me down? Instead of just standing there. It's what you'd like to do, you know that, so why don't you?"

Alfred smiled grimly down at her.

"He's dying in there. Let me in!" Gramma surged into Alfred again.

Alfred, really hot now, gave Gramma a little shove back.

Gramma hadn't expected that, and she tottered backways a few steps.

Ada stood up. "Say," she said, "don't you push Ma around."

"Tell her to behave herself then," Alfred snapped. "Tell her to remember she is a guest in my house."

Ada got hot. She sailed over and surged into Alfred too.

Gramma saw her chance. While Ada was pushing against Alfred, she quick tried to sneak past them on the other side. She managed to grab hold of the doorknob before Alfred saw her.

"Hey you!" Alfred cried. "So now it's two against one, is it?" Then Alfred had to laugh. All that soft flesh against him . . . it was like fighting a couple of soft haycocks, one a fat one and one a high one. He put an arm around each of them and with a grunt rushed them across the room, sending them staggering. And, before they could recover, he grabbed his rocker and planted it in front of the bedroom door and sat down. "Now," he said, "we'll see who's boss around here."

All of a sudden the boy fell silent on the other side of the door.

"See," Alfred said, "he's finally quit. He's cried himself to sleep."

Looking a little like baffled brood hens, they slowly went back to their rockers and resettled themselves.

Presently Alfred, leaning back, heard the boy heave a sigh, then another one, and then settle down into a light baby snore.

Alfred smiled. "Now, you two. After this you tuck him in, blow out the light, say good night firmly but warmly, and get out of there. Do that a couple of times, and you'll never hear a peep out of him again after you put him to bed. Hear?"

Gramma sniffed. "You won't be able to blow out the sun in the summer."

Free fussed a little the next night when they put him to bed. But it didn't take long before he was sound asleep. After that he was a real good boy.

A week later, Gramma gone, Alfred came home from town with two presents for the boy, a high chair and a teddy bear. The high chair was a fine-looking affair. It was made of golden oak and had a large drop table. The teddy bear was a darling thing. It had cinnamon fur, a blue ribbon under its chin, and black-and-white button eyes.

"How come you did that?" Ada wondered, smiling at the gifts. "Isn't that all pretty expensive?"

"It is. But I think it's worth it."

Free was standing in the middle of the kitchen when the presents were unwrapped. He was fat with winter bundling.

Ada knelt beside him. "Isn't that nice of your daddy? Getting you your Christmas and your birthday presents so early?"

Free stared at the glinting chair and the teddy bear.

Alfred said, "Come supper time, you put that high chair beside my chair. I'll feed him from now on."

"That's all right by me, Alfred."

"And that teddy bear is for him to play with in the house in the wintertime. In the summer he can play with Rover under the trees."

"Whatever made you think of a teddy bear?"

"Wal, the boy needs somebody to play with. And I wasn't about to get him a doll and put the hex on him."

Free soon made up his mind which he liked best. He toddled over to the table and reached for the teddy bear. He took it in his arms. It was almost as big as he was. He examined it carefully, the eyes, the ribbon, the belly, its bottom to see if it had one, and then, smelling it, hugged it.

After that he wouldn't go to sleep unless he had his buddy bear in bed with him.

Ada & 19

ADA WAS HOME alone when the labor pains came on the sixth of July. Husband Alfred was helping a sick neighbor get his corn cultivated for the last time. Free was out in the grove with Rover.

She had forebodings about their second baby. She wasn't ready to have it quite that soon. But Alfred had been so ardent, and so very gentle, last October, and there had been so many nights when in turning over in sleep she'd bumped against his hard stalk, and she'd heard him groan in hurt, that at last when he'd clutched her firmly by the thigh she'd divided for him. She hadn't been able to erase from her mind the picture of his stalk sticking up past his nightshirt that time she'd had to put on the night lamp a minute to see why Free was fussing. In the soft gold light the head of it had a wonderful healthy glow, pink and shining bright. It made her think of that passage in the Bible where it told about the Israelites being led by a column of fire at night. No, the Lord had not been in this one. Sometimes it was wrong to feel sorry for a husband. So she'd dragged through the winter months carrying the second baby.

It was around nine when the first cramp grabbed her. It came more as a dull push than a happy kick. Nor was there any smell of wild roses around. The second cramp came an hour later. It was going to be one of those slow labors, a bad one.

The first thing to do was to get the house in order so things would run pretty much by themselves while she lay abed. Gramma couldn't come down because Grampa wasn't feeling well. After the doctor finished with her, she and Alfred would have to make do by themselves for a while.

She had her third pain around ten forty-five. Her fourth pain came at eleven-thirty.

She pretty well had things organized by twelve when it struck her that she had seen neither hide nor hair of the boy and the dog for a while.

"They've been awful quiet out there."

She went to the little bedroom window in back and looked north into the grove where the two usually played. No sign of them there. She went to the front screen door and with a hand over her eyes looked out over the yard. No sign of them there either.

She stared out over the yard, thinking desperate thoughts, scared, her heart beating funny. Holding her belly with one hand and her heart with the other, she stepped outside and called loud and clear, "Free? Where are you, boy?" It hurt her under the ribs to call. "Free?"

No answer.

She walked around behind the house and out under the walnuts a ways. "Free, it's time for you to eat, boy. Num num."

No answer.

"Now where in the world could that dratted kid have gone to?" She looked out over the field of waving light green oats to the north. No sign of his white head or the dog's golden tail that way.

She next walked behind the corncrib and looked out across the rows of waving dark green corn to the west. The corn was about to tassel out. If they'd wandered in that direction she'd never find them.

"Maybe I can get the dog to come and then Free'll follow." She called as loud as her heavy belly would allow. "Yuh Rover! Yuh Rover!" She suck-whistled sharply several times. "Rover?"

No sign of a waving golden tail.

She said to herself, "I need help."

As she headed for the barn, she was seized by the next labor cramp. This one grabbed her so forcibly and made her so weak in the knees she had to sink to the ground on all fours. "Oh Goddd."

When the pain passed, she got up and hurried into the barn. She swished down the feeding alley. "Free? Rover? Where the dickens are you two rascals?"

Only pigeons cooing in the haymow ruffled the silence. The dim light in the barn was scary.

She hurried out into the bright sun again. "It's as though I'm about to die." She pushed up her milk-heavy breasts with both hands and held her heart. "But I can't die yet. There's so much to do yet. Have this baby born. Raise my willful Free." She was afraid she was going to suffocate right there on the open yard on a nice bright sunny day in July.

The windmill by the water tank began to turn. There was just enough breeze out to make the glittering blades go. The gears made a squeaking sound. It was like a mouse was being squeezed to death.

Another cramp grabbed her. As it set in she could feel her heart under her hands gradually settle down and begin to beat solidly and steadily. A fidgety horse was at last being called upon to get to work and gallop steady. After a few moments her breath also fell back to normal. How odd that as soon as her bottom half went into convulsion her top half became calm. It was like a team of horses that hadn't yet learned to pull together. First one horse was ahead, then the other.

"If only my strong husband was here, he'd steady them both."

The cramp passed away.

Where could that dratted boy and dog have gone? "Free? Rover?"

She recalled that the day before she'd caught the boy by the water tank looking down at the bullheads. Alfred had earlier seined fish in the river and when he came home had tossed the smallest bullheads into the tank. Fish tended to keep the tank clean of moss. She caught her breath in terror. The boy couldn't have fallen in? Drowned? But then where was the dog? A dog would hardly drown in a tank. Though the dog, scared, might run away.

She went over to have a look. She could just barely make out the bullheads wiggling their dark tails lazily in the darkest green shadows. She saw no sign of the boy on the bottom.

Another pain. It grabbed her so fiercely she let go with a howl of pain. The cows out in the barnyard looked her way. One of them, Three-tit, lowed, and then came over to the fence and stared at her wide-eyed. Three-tit lowed several more times.

"Free, you darn little kid you, where are you, for godsakes!"

A laying hen came walking from behind the hoghouse. There were a lot of deep weeds there near the ditch. "Ech, ech, ech," the laying hen complained, "how my behind hurts."

"Ohh," Ada said, "another one of you pesky hens hiding your eggs again."

"Yech, yech, yech, how my behind hurts."

"From all that noise you're making"—Ada couldn't resist a smile at herself—"I can't figure out if you're laying babies or just plain eggs."

By four o'clock she was wild. She'd twice more searched the yard and the outbuildings; still couldn't find the boy and dog. She'd also had a half dozen more labor pains; still wasn't much closer to having the baby.

Then she heard a motor. She looked under the trees. Yes, it was an automobile, just coming over the Weatherly hill, a plume of tan dust following behind it. She hurried out to the road to stop it.

It turned out to be Dr. Drury.

"Of all things," Ada gasped, as she stepped up to Dr. Drury on the driver's side, waving the dust out of her eyes, "you, Doctor!"

Dr. Drury raised his dust goggles.

"Doctor, you're just the man I need. I can't"—she had to hold her heart again—"find Free and the dog, Doctor. And Alfred's helping the Raths today. And now on top of all that, I'm having labor pains."

Dr. Drury removed his right glove and took her left wrist. While he took her pulse, the motor of the car, a Maxwell, tumbled serenely under its copper-trimmed hood. "Hmm. A little fast." He looked directly into her eyes. "I'm headed in Rath's direction. To check out old Jake Priester. I'll stop in at the Raths' first and tell Alfred to hurry home to help you find the boy. Meanwhile, you get to bed and when I get through with old Jake, I'll be right over."

"All right, Doctor. But I better tell you this one is not going so good."

"What seems to be the trouble?"

Ada could feel the regular tumble of the motor through his hand. "I don't seem to be making much room for it to be born through."

Dr. Drury's black eyes closed. Then, after a moment, his eyes opened warm upon her. "Listen, this is what I want you to do. Instead of going to bed, keep walking as you can, back and forth over the yard. Right through each one of your labor pains, you hear?"

"All right, if you say so. In a way it's already helped a little that I've been chasing everywhere looking for that boy."

"Exactly. Now, if you'll excuse me, I'll get on to the Raths and then old Jake Priester." Letting out the brake and pulling down the gas lever, Dr. Drury took off with a gathering rush and flying gravel.

Ten minutes later Rover came pattering up behind her where she stood bent over having another labor pain. She had been unable to walk through the next pain. She spotted Rover too late to see from what direction he'd come. His golden tail was down, his back humped. He panted slowly, red tongue out.

When she could straighten up again, she reached out to pet the dog. "Where's Free, Rover? Huh? You show me where Free is."

Rover's gold-brown head sank even lower.

"Dear God, the boy's dead, or Rover would never have left him."

Alfred came galloping onto the yard, cultivator shovels clattering. Duke and Dan were lathered over with sweat. Alfred stood up on the tongue lashing the horses. He looked exactly like that painting of Ben-Hur the charioteer. He hauled up hard on the lines— "Whoa!"—and stopped beside her in the middle of the yard. "Found him yet?"

"No, Alfred."

Alfred spotted the dog lying in the shade of the corncrib. Alfred was sopping wet with sweat too. "Hey, what's he doing here? Doc said he was gone with the boy."

"Yes, Alfred. Rover all of a sudden showed up alone right after I talked to Doctor."

"Gol darn."

"Yes. When the dog came home alone I really began to go crazy with worry."

Alfred hooked the lines onto a lever of the cultivator and jumped down. "What about you?"

"I'm all right. It's the boy being lost that we got to worry about now." Something in Alfred's manner reminded her of the time he'd seen a panther while picking corn two years before. "That panther couldn't have gotten him? Scaring off the dog first?"

"Naw." But Alfred began to shake too. "Nobody's talked about seeing a big cat around lately. At least not that I know of."

"Alfred, I'll never forgive myself if that boy is found dead."

"Now now." Alfred's tan face became solemn. "Tell you what. I'll go make a circle of the yard and look for a sign. To see which direction the boy went. You go tie the horses there to that hitching post."

Ada hurried to tie up the horses. She saw Alfred go over the fence beside the water tank and examine the ground below it. There was a hole in the fence at that point. "Dear God, I forgot all about that hole. That's where the dog and the boy always sneak through when they want to play on the strawpile."

Then Alfred saw something. He nodded to himself. He leaped over the fence, not even bothering to open the gate. Still looking closely at the ground he began to take long slinging steps down the pasture toward the corner schoolhouse. Their four red-and-white cows and the young Shorthorn bull were grazing near the well below.

Ada thought: "The bull's got him. That's why the dog came home. The dog's always been afraid of the bull."

Ada had to see. She opened the gate, passed through, hooked it behind her. She picked a path around mounds of horseballs. Lifting her skirt, trying to keep her heavy belly from bobbing too much, she hurried after Alfred. Cowplotches dotted the green grass. The blue air of the afternoon had the smell of fermenting barley.

Two-thirds of the way down the hill Alfred stopped. He heard Ada coming behind him and held up a hand for her to be quiet. He nodded toward the cattle below.

Ada moved up silently beside him. "What's the matter?" she whispered.

"Shh. Just look."

"Where? I don't see anything."

"On the ground behind the bull. See where he's laying flat on his back there?" There was a smile in Alfred's whisper. "With his legs up in the air?"

The curly-haired young bull grazed forward a few steps.

Then Ada saw the boy, little legs up and slightly crooked at the knee, bare heels shining in the sun. "Dead?"

"Shh. Look. Watch."

Free lay with his hands caught under his white blond head, elbows out. He was looking straight up at the sky and his blue eyes were mooned over with drifting private thought.

As Ada watched, Free let his knees sag to his chest a moment, then kicked them straight out.

"Free!" Ada cried. Then she ran to pick him up.

Afterwards Alfred had to shake his head, marveling. "There he was, laying flat on his back right near the bull, feet up in the air like a goose trussed up for Thanksgiving not a worry in the world. Even after the bull must've chased the dog off."

"He could've been killed," Ada said.

"Wal, truth to tell, if the bull was to attack, the boy was doing exactly the right thing, laying on his back close to the ground. There ain't much a dehorned bull can do to you that way. Except maybe to step on you."

"Ohh."

"That's why I always like to dehorn the bull."

Ada let down. Slowly she could feel herself opening up below.

By midnight another baby was born. It was a boy and they named him Everett.

BOOK TWO

Lords of the Barnyard

To
EDWARD JOHN,
FLOYD,
JOHN GARRET,
ABBEN CLARENCE,
HENRY HERMAN
brothers

Free ❦ 1

A YEAR LATER.

"Have you had enough to eat, Free?"

Free nodded.

"All right, then go out under the trees and play."

Free didn't move.

Ma picked up the baby and sat down in her rocker. She opened her dress and lifted out some wonderful titty and gave it to the baby.

Free waited.

Ma saw Free looking. She smiled. "Don't tell me you still want some. Not a great big boy like you." Ma smiled. "Titty is bah-bah for big boys like you."

Baby looked around with its mouth and at last found it. Yum.

Ma scolded Free with her eyes. "Go on, go play with Rover. In a minute baby will be asleep and then Mama wants to go take a nap herself. Hear?"

Free didn't want to play in the grove. The grove was all played out.

"Well, well, look whose lip is hanging all the way down to the third button."

Free wished his baby brother was a wienie. Then he could eat him.

"Go, boy, before Mama gets angry."

Rover, lying outside the screen door, got up. His tail was down. Rover knew when Ma was mad.

Free dragged his bare feet across to the door. The slick floor felt cool. If only Teddy Bear could walk like Rover, what fun they'd have then. Free loved Teddy Bear the best because he didn't wiggle around in bed at night. But Teddy Bear couldn't lick him like Rover could. "Ma?"

"Yes, boy."

"When can baby play with me?"

"I'm afraid that's going to be a while yet, boy. For some reason which only God can explain, your baby brother is not going to be as quick to walk as you did."

Free glared at his suckling brother. If only his brother could play. He'd put him in the ground like a potato and hide him. Then he could have that yum yum for himself again.

"Maybe we ought to get you a little kitty to play with. Because a person can see you're tiring of that dog."

Free wanted a big kitty, not a little kitty. Pa said that he'd once seen a great big kitty out in the cornfield. A big one was better than a little one. A big kitty a boy could fight with. Roll him around. Rover didn't like rolling around any more. Rover got mad and bited. Free sucked his tongue against the roof of his mouth. He'd go find that big kitty. "Bye, Ma."

"Bye, boy. And play nice now."

Free footed it down the privy path. He entered the shade of the trees. He scuffed out to the cornfield fence. Rover followed him step for step. Rover's tongue was hanging out already.

Free leaned on the lowest barbed wire and looked into the cornfield. The corn was like little trees. There were whole bunches of them so that there were lots of hallways. He stared down the hallways trying to see if he could spot the big kitty.

Free dropped down on all fours and scooted under the fence. Rover scooted with him. If only Rover could walk on two legs too. Then they could be brothers. Rover could talk then too, instead of just bark and whine. Pa was too big to be friends with.

The cornfield hallways were awfully long. There were so many. "Big Kitty, I betcha, is on the other side." Maybe he and Rover ought to take the road and go around and try to find him on the Horsberg side.

Free stepped toward the road. Rover let his head down and followed him. They went a long ways.

Free stopped when he got to the highway fence. He remembered something. Pa said for him never to go out on the road because the Indian gypsies would catch him and take him along with them and hide him from Pa and Ma. The Indian gypsies might even eat him, Pa said.

Rover smelled something on the side of the fence post. His tail went straight up. Then Rover turned sideways and lifted his hind leg and peed against the post.

That was fun. Free opened the fly of his blue overalls and dug through the slit of his underwear and pulled out his pisser. His pisser was asleep like a baby mouse. He pinched it a couple of times to wake it up. Yep, it could pee too. He went over to the fence post and lifted his leg and peed in the same place where Rover peed. Once his pisser got started it had to pee quite a bit. Slowly he got dizzy standing on one leg. At last he tipped over and landed with a bump. There was a loud bang inside his head. His pisser quit and hid back in his pants.

Free got up and brushed off his overalls and checkered gray shirt. He buttoned up.

Rover smelled something else. It was in the cornfield somewhere. He looked back over his high tail for Free to follow him. There was a cocklebur caught in the dog's tail and it looked funny. Rover trotted slowly.

Free trudged along slowly. Free began to sweat. Corn leaves touched his nose. The cornfield smelled like milk from a cow. Rover stopped sometimes to let Free catch up.

A rabbit jumped up. Rover jumped up surprised too. Then Rover ran after the rabbit and was lost. Rover was gone.

Free stood as still as a cornstalk. He didn't move. The dog was lost.

"Yere, Rover."

Rover didn't come.

"Yere, Rover."

Pretty soon Rover found himself again and came running back. His tongue was hanging out real tired.

"You better rest, Rover."

Rover lay down on the ground. He puffed.

Free liked that. He lay down too. He nuzzled his head on the dog's back. The ground under them was warm. Free took a little nap.

Rover got up. Free's head slid off and he woke up and then he got up too. Rover went first and they walked some more.

Pretty soon they came to a fence. It was the Horsberg pasture. On the other side of the fence were some red cows. One of the cows was laying down. The red cow made a funny noise like she had to go to the toidy real bad. The red cow's tail was pushed over. She moaned a couple more times, pretty bad too, and all of a sudden something like a wet teddy bear jumped out of the cow. It slid out across the ground.

Rover wanted to go and look at the wet thing, but the red cow saw him and bawled at Rover and then got up. The red cow ran at Rover. Rover had to quick slink back under the fence. The red cow looked at Rover a long time. Rover just looked back, and his red tongue hung out and sometimes curled up at the end a little.

Pretty soon the red cow went back to the wet teddy bear and began to lick it. Where it was licked the funny teddy bear had red hair that stuck out. The cow kept licking. Slowly the wet teddy bear changed. It had a real mouth and eyes. The cow licked the teddy bear's head some more, and then two ears flopped up. It was a calf. After a while the calf began to shiver and wiggle. It sure liked all that licking. That's why it was fun when Rover licked your face.

The red calf got up and stood a minute and then it fell down. It opened its mouth and bellered. Then it got up once again and stood a minute and again it fell down. It bellered.

Once more the red calf got up. This time it didn't fall down. It rocked like a rocking chair by itself. Then it went over and began to bump its nose under the cow's belly. After a while it found a titty. The cow had a lot of them. They were all dripping. That calf sure was lucky.

Rover was sick of the red cow. He went into the cornfield again. He kept looking ahead. His tail was still.

Free followed Rover. The ground turned cooler. The tassels high up began to shine sideways.

Free was real hungry. The corn ears hung over him. One of the corn ears had hair parted open at the end. He wished the corn ear was a titty. It sure looked good.

The dog kept on going.

Free didn't care. He touched the corn ear. The hair on it was as slick as the corner of his blue blanket. He stroked it with his fingers. He stroked it once with his nose. The corn hair was slick.

Rover came back. He was panting.

Free stood on his toes and sucked at the end of the corn ear. Hey. There was milk in the corn ear. And good milk too. Yum. Better milk than cow's milk.

Free sucked all around the end of the ear. He stripped back the hair and the husk and sucked higher. And he bit into it. Then he got even more milk. He couldn't do that with Ma.

Free found three more open corn ears. They were all good. Pretty soon he was full up to his chin.

Free felt sleepy. He looked for a soft place. It was all clods around.

Rover began to growl. His tail poked straight back. Rover was mad at something.

Free looked where Rover was looking. Free hoped it was Big Kitty. He would like to stroke it.

Rover barked. It hurt the ears the way Rover barked. There was something in the corn. Then Rover began to bark like he was scared too.

A tassel began to wiggle a little ways down the row. It turned slowly like a windmill.

Rover barked and barked.

Free looked harder. Then he saw it. Big Kitty. It looked just like the corn. It had eyes as big as two burning cobs. Boy, but Big Kitty had a big head. It was as big as Ma's coffee grinder.

Rover barked real scared. Rover backed up until he was backed up tight against Free.

Big Kitty's tail sagged down and he came toward them. What a big tail. It was longer than a bull's tail.

Rover went crazy. He backed up so hard against Free that Free had to back up too. Rover yelped crazy. Then Rover's ears snuck down and all of a sudden he went after Big Kitty.

Big Kitty growled. Big Kitty snapped his tail. Big Kitty opened his mouth big and red and full of long white teeth.

Rover jumped at Big Kitty and bited him in his behind. Big Kitty hit Rover with a paw. Rover rolled over and yowled. Rover jumped up again. Rover was so mad he swelled up big and sicced after Big Kitty again and bited him on the top of his neck, growling and trying to shake him.

At last Big Kitty had enough. Big Kitty turned around and galloped away.

Rover chased him. Rover barked hard after him.

Free stood waiting.

Then Rover came back. Rover was real happy. He laughed with his long red tongue hanging out.

Free put his arms around Rover. He loved Rover. He hugged Rover and Rover licked him back.

It got dark. Free walked beside Rover with his arm around his neck.

Pretty soon Rover was lost in the dark. Free wished Ma would call them so they could know where they was.

When it got black out, Free didn't want to walk any more. He pushed the dog down to the ground and then lay on him. He made a pillow of Rover's belly. He could feel Rover panting under him.

Free held Rover in his arms. He pretended Rover was Teddy Bear. Rover was a good dog. Pretty soon Free fell asleep.

Free's pillow began to wiggle. Then the pillow got up and Free's head hit the ground. Then Free woke up. Hey. There was corn all around. Free rubbed his eyes and looked again. Yup. He was in a cornfield and not in his bed. The sun was shining sideways on the tassels.

Rover licked him in the face. Rover whined and ran a little ways down the row and then came back and licked him in the face again.

Free got up. He knuckled out the corners of his eyes. The meadowlarks were singing. They sounded like Pa blowing on his harmonica.

Rover smelled something again. His tail poked straight out. Only this time Rover wasn't mad. Then Rover took off and was gone.

Free stood still. The meadowlarks kept singing. All around in the cornfield they were crying, "Here-we-are."

A grasshopper jumped from a leaf to a corn ear.

Free stood very still. Yup, Rover was lost again.

A gopher popped out of the ground down the corn row a ways. It sat like a little Teddy Bear. It sat listening for Rover too.

Ma was surely going to scold him. But it wasn't his fault. Rover was lost.

After a while Rover came running back. He was carrying a bunny. The bunny's head was hanging down like Teddy Bear's did sometimes. The bunny was all tore up on one side and his blue insides showed. Rover laid the bunny down on Free's bare toes.

Free touched the bunny. The bunny was warm. Teddy Bear was always just hair and cool. Rover began to whine. He looked at him with his brown eyes. Then Rover took the bunny a little ways down the row and scootched down on his belly and began to eat him. Rover's big yellow tail waved around and around like Big Kitty's did. When Free looked at Rover, Rover growled at him.

The meadowlarks kept singing, "Here-we-are, here-we-are."

Rover chewed and slupped blood. He broke bones. He bited the hairy legs in two. He spit out the rabbit's tail.

Free wished he had some corn mush with milk and sugar. He saw some more corn ears with a titty end showing. He bent them down and sucked them and bited them until he was full.

Rover got up and started walking down a row. Free followed him.

Rover lifted his leg and wetted a black clod. The clod slowly wore away. Free was going to do number one too but then he had to do number two, so he unhooked a suspender and sat down. There was no catalog wipe like Ma used in the privy. Free saw an old cornstalk sticking out of the ground. It was crinky soft. He used that. It hurt a little but it was all right.

Rover walked ahead again.

They hit a patch of cockleburs. Free wanted to go around the cockleburs, but was afraid Rover would get lost again. He followed Rover through them. Rover's tail got thick full with them.

The sun started shining straight down into their eyes. It was hot. Free sweated. Rover let his tongue lap out.

Pretty soon Rover heard something and he stopped. Free stopped and listened too.

Rover looked like he was going to back up. But then he didn't.

Then Free heard people talking. It was somewheres nearby. One of them was Pa. Hey.

Pa said, "What I can't understand is that Rover should get lost. That fetch-stickin' dog should know better."

Neighbor Weatherly said, "The dog is probably just being loyal to the boy. When we find the boy we'll see the dog."

Pa said, "Wal, he's just got to be in this cornfield. I made a cast around the whole field and I found his barefoot tracks going into it, back by the grove there, but not out of it anywhere."

Neighbor Murray said. "He better be. We've looked everywhere else."

Pa said, "Yeh, Ada was pretty wild mad at me last night when I wouldn't look for him in the dark with a lantern. I told her that so long as the dog hadn't come home yet, the kid was safe somewhere."

Neighbor Rath said, "If that big cat didn't get the both of them."

Pa said, "Naw. Panthers don't care for human meat. Too sweet."

Neighbor Murray said, "Well, if it was my wife, the big cat wouldn't think her very sweet." When neighbor Murray talked he always looked like he was snapping at food like Rover snapped at that bunny.

Pa said, "Keep looking careful to both sides as we sweep through now, you guys. It's easy to miss 'em when you're covering four rows. The kid's got hair about the same color as the tossel. If we don't find him this time through, I'm gonna get the sheriff and ask him to call out a posse."

Neighbor Murray said, "Another expense for the taxpayer, goddam."

Free called out, "Here I am, Pa."

Silence.

Neighbor Weatherly said, "I think I heard the boy."

Pa said, "Where?"

Neighbor Weatherly said, "Over toward the road."

Pa called out, "Free? Where are you, boy?" Pa didn't sound mad.

Free saw Pa standing as high as the corn tassels. "Here I am, Pa." Free started to run across the corn rows toward him.

Pa's eyes were like surprised horse eyes. "Free! Son!" Pa picked him up. Pa hugged him like Ma sometimes did.

The neighbors came breaking across the corn rows.

Rover came slinking up behind Free.

Pa held Free tight in his arms. "You little dickens you." Pa laughed and shivered at the same time. "Lookit him, would you? He's got sweet corn all over his mug."

Neighbor Weatherly smiled. "Yes. And the dog's got rabbit fur along his lip there. They knew how to live off the land all right."

Pa said, "I better let Ada know we've found him." Pa put thumb and finger between his teeth and blew out a toot like a steam engine. He whistled four times. It was so fierce Free had to cover his ears. Rover didn't like it so loud either. He lifted his nose and yowled.

They all walked toward the yard. Pa carried Free.

When they hit the grove, there was Ma.

Pa lifted Free over the fence. "Are your other ninety-and-nine safe? Because here's your lost son, lady."

Ma grabbed Free. She didn't say anything. She hugged her son even worse than Gramma did.

Pa stepped over the fence. Pa said with a laugh, "I guess my boy's got the runaway fever all right. Like my dad always had."

Neighbor Weatherly said, "I've heard tell about your dad."

Pa shook his head. "They tell some strong stories about him when he was a boy. Gramma in Sioux Center says that in the Old Country they had to tie him to a tree with a rope or he'd run off somewhere. She says tying him to the tree hardly fazed him though. He'd just back up as far as the rope would allow, and then he'd run lickety-split the other way to the end of the rope until it snapped, dive into the canal and swim across it and so get away. Later, when Dad grew up, he sailed before the mast."

"Is that so?"

"Yeh. He thought he had a right to see the world, I guess."

Free ❦ 2

LANDLADY GATELY FELT sorry for her daughter after a while and told her she could go back to living on the farm again provided her husband would sign a pledge not to drink anymore. Son-in-law Windmiller was glad to promise. He hated the dray business. That meant of course the Alfredsons had to move.

Pa found them a farm closer to town. It was on the Canton road north out of Bonnie. Fat John lived on that road too. So it wasn't so bad. The only thing lost was all that work cleaning up the Windmiller mess when the Alfredsons first moved onto the place.

The new place was Mr. Alvord's farm. Mr. Alvord was strict with his renters. Years ago he'd planted a grove of mulberry trees and every weekend he came out to see how the trees were doing. He didn't like it if little boys climbed those trees, so Free was afraid to play in the grove. There were only five trees Free could play with, Mr. Alvord said. One was the big cottonwood on the northwest corner of the grove and the others were box elders along the lane by the house. There was a rig fixed up in the four box elders to hold Pa's hayrack off the ground so the hayrack wouldn't rot. The box elder was a nuisance tree, Mr. Alvord said, and what the children did to them wasn't going to worry him. In the summertime the mulberry trees would be full of mulberries. But Free couldn't have any, even if some fell to the ground. Mr. Alvord would pick them up himself.

Ma complained for a while that she was awful tired by suppertime. She was repapering the whole house even though the house was neat and clean. She said she couldn't live with other people's colors.

Pa was too busy out on the yard and in the field to be worrying about color schemes.

His scheme was to get the crop in as quick as possible. He hadn't been able to get all the plowing done the fall before so he had to work double hard. But Pa wasn't tired. He was full of pep.

Ma said, "If only Everett was housebroke, that would help. Every time I turn around I find him with his pants full. Or wet down one leg."

Pa said, "The pantsful part I can't help you much with. But the wet leg part I can."

"Well, if you can, I wish you would," Ma said.

"I'll do with him like I did with Free." Pa took Everett by the hand. "Come with me, boy." Everett could just walk. Pa took him outside on the back porch where the sun was going down.

Free went along to watch.

Pa took out his own pisser to show Everett. Pa's pisser looked like a toy balloon with the air let out of it. Pa pushed inside himself a couple of times and pretty soon he began to pee. "See, Everett, this is the way you do it. Peepee on the grass and not down your pants leg."

Everett looked up sideways at Pa's pisser.

"See?" Pa said. "Now let's see you do it."

Everett looked up sideways some more.

"C'mon, boy," Pa said. "Hurry. Or the first thing you know I'll run out."

Everett kept looking up sideways.

Pa said, "Free, you show him how you do it too."

Free said, "I don't need to go just yet, Pa."

Pa said, "Go anyway. You can. Because I've run out." Pa backed his pisser into his overalls.

Free got out his pisser too. He pushed inside himself. Pretty soon it came.

"See, Everett?" Pa said, buttoning up. "Even Free does it off the porch on the grass. Now you do it. C'mon."

Everett got out his pisser then. He pushed. Pretty soon he was pissing off the porch too. The red sun made both streams look like strawberry pop pouring out of two straws.

When it was over, and Pa'd told Ma, Ma said, "Well, that's fine. Now if we could only get Everett to quit wetting his bed every night. Always having to change his bed every morning is a nuisance."

It was true. Free slept with Everett, and Everett always wet the bed. And he always managed to wet the bed even on Free's side.

Pa said, "Wal, maybe we can fix that too."

That night, just as Free was dreaming that he and Rover had found a new foxhole and they were going to dig it deeper so they could crawl down into it, Pa was shaking him awake.

"Come, boy, I want you to be an example to Everett, show him how to peepee in the pot. So he won't wet the bed tonight."

Free felt of himself inside. He didn't need to go yet. "I can't, Pa."

"Come, try a little bit anyway. So Everett will get the idee not to go in bed. You don't always want to wake up in a stinking bed, do you?"

Free was sleepy but he agreed with Pa. He rolled out of bed and got down on his knees. He reached under the bed and pulled out the white owl and took off the cover. He aimed his pisser and pushed. It was about midnight and his pisser was awful small.

Pa pulled Everett out of bed and made him watch. "See?"

Everett looked sideways down at the chamber pot. He watched Free push. There was a brown curl like a gopher sitting on Everett's curly head.

Finally Free made a prinkly noise on the bottom of the white owl.

"See, Everett? Peepee in the white owl and not in the bed. See?"

Everett got down on his knees then too. He peed a little bit in the pot.

"More," Pa said. "Can't you do a little bit more, Everett?"

Everett pushed hard. Then he peed a whole lot. Pretty soon it sounded like milk streaming into a pail half full with foam.

"That's a good boy, Everett," Pa said. "A real good boy. Now you two boys can both go back to sleep. "

When Free was back in bed, in his own warm spot, he said, "Pa?"

"Yes, boy?"

"Who did I wet the bed for when I was a little boy like Everett?"

"What?" Pa stared at him. "What a question. Go to sleep, boy."

After that just before Pa and Ma went to bed, Pa always got Free and Everett out of bed a minute. And in the morning the bed was dry and sweet. What a relief that was.

When Free saw how little the shadow was beside the back porch, he knew it was time for Pa to come home. Free ran behind the barn and looked out toward the back forty where Pa was cultivating the corn. Yessir, there came the horses' heads, two fiddles with bridles on, with Pa walking behind. They were coming along the edge of the field.

Free opened the iron gate for Pa.

Pa was covered with dust and his smile was red. "Boy, you're slowly but surely turning out to be my favorite hired hand." Pa drove the horses onto the yard. Duke and Dan had dust all over themselves too, but their smiles were all white slobber. Pa unhitched Duke and Dan in his usual slick way. "I think you better let me lead them to the tank today, boy. We turned over a nest of bumblebees this morning and that's raised the bronco in 'em a little."

Free looked ahead toward the water tank. Pa had big bullheads in it to eat the moss. Bullheads needed little wings to move in the water like hawks needed big wings to move in the air. They had ticklers like a cat. They'd whip their tails and then, flip, would be gone into the dark side of the tank.

"Pa, can I run ahead and look at the bullheads? Everett's by the house with Rover, so we don't have to worry about him falling in."

"Sure, go ahead, boy. But be careful."

"I will, Pa."

Free ran down the lane. Pa was a great pa to let him do some things. Free stepped around a mud puddle and leaned over the rim of the wooden tank. Look as he would, he couldn't find the bullheads. The sun got into his eyes where he stood, so he crawled on top. With his head hanging over the edge of the wooden cover, he looked all around. It was fun to hang down headfirst. There were little islands of green moss floating around with shadows under them. The water was green like the fish were and it was hard to see them. Free leaned farther over, trying to see through into the deepest green shadow. He still couldn't see the bullheads. He leaned still farther over the edge. His suspender caught on the edge of the tank cover, then, snap, came free. Free felt himself teetering on the edge. The edge was wet and slippery. In a minute by golly he was gonna fall in. And drown. Pa would surely lick him for that. Free hung on. Then his fingers, then the bib of his overalls slipped farther, and then—kerplunk!—in he fell. Wowie. Man. Water in the nose. Choking. Somewhere in the water bullheads with sharp ticklers were sailing around all stirred up. Nose cracking green. Then before he knew it he was exploding out of the water. He landed on the ground just on the other side of the mud puddle he flew so far. It was like his throat was stuck. He sucked and sucked for air. "Uhk. Uhk! Uhk!!" Boy, was that water ever cold. Man. He got to his feet. He looked around for Pa. He saw Pa through what was like Gramma's wavery glasses. He staggered toward Pa, legs wide apart, arms stuck straight out to either side like a scarecrow. His pants legs stuck to his legs and made a funny slucking noise. "Uhk!" Oh boy his nice new blue shirt was wet too. "Uhk."

"Hey," Pa cried, "what's the matter with you, boy?"

"Pa . . . I fell in."

"Yeh, I can see that. What happened?"

"I leaned over . . . too far."

"You look like a drowned-out gopher, boy." Pa didn't mean to laugh at his own boy. But he couldn't help it. "Boy, boy, next time be more careful."

"Ya, Pa."

"Wal, you better run to your ma now and ask for dry clothes."

"I'm so cold."

When bindering time came Pa had to have help for a few days. From church one Sunday Pa took along a hired man named Lew Westraw. Lew was a smiling fellow and was full of jokes. He liked little boys.

It was a very hot July. Pa said it was a scorcher. Everybody was sweating, Pa, Ma, Lew, horses, pumps, the lemonade pitcher. Dogs and chickens dragged around with their tongues hanging out. Free and Everett played under the trees. Ma said for them to be sure and keep their little straw hats on even under the shade trees.

The best place to play was under the big cottonwood on the northwest corner of the grove. It was about the highest tree in the world and it had the coolest shade. From its shade they could see Pa bindering in the field and Lew setting up shocks behind him. Free played he was bindering the grass and Everett shocked behind him.

Pretty soon Lew yelled over to them. "Free?"

Free got to his feet and looked.

"Free, can you go get me some water to drink?"

Free stared at Lew.

"Your dad's broke down on the other side of the field and he's got the water jug with him under the seat there. Will you, huh?"

Free looked across the stubbles and all the shocks. He could see mist rising out of the ground like the whole country was a steam kettle.

"Hurry, boy. I'm real thirsty and I'm about to keel over."

"All right."

Free and Everett ran to the house to tell Ma that Lew needed water to drink. But they couldn't find her. Free saw an empty pail on the front porch. It was the one Ma got the eggs in. Free dumped the straw out of the bottom of it and went to the cistern pump in the kitchen. But the pump wouldn't work. It made sucking noises like it had a bad sore throat. It had to be primed first. Well, the next best place to get water was from the water tank.

When Free and Everett got to the gate by the barn, Free said, "Everett, you stay here till I come back, hear?"

Everett looked sideways. Everett could never say yes. Free gave Everett a mad look. Then Everett stayed by the gate.

Free ran to the tank. Free didn't dare look for the bullheads. He quick dipped the pail into the water and came up with it full. He hurried back.

Free took the shortcut along the path north of the grove. The hard path burned. Free walked on his toes a ways, then walked on his heels with the toes up. Everett did the same, following the leader.

After a while Free came across a grassy spot. He stopped a minute to cool his hot feet.

Free wondered to himself a while. If only a rain would come along to cool the ground. Free looked up at the sky. No clouds. Well, then the next best thing to do was to splash a little water on the spot where his foot was to land next. He poured out a little splash a little ways ahead of him. He stepped on the wet spot. That was much better. Free poured a splash ahead for the other foot and stepped on that. Better too. Free kept pouring little splashes where his feet would land next all the way up the hard hot lane. Everett followed him, stepping carefully in Free's footsteps, still following the leader.

Free and Everett were so busy making cool spots to walk in they didn't notice Lew had come part way to meet them. They almost bumped into him.

"What in the world—" Lew said.

Legs apart, Free stared up at Lew. Behind him Everett stared up at Lew too.

"Ain't that supposed to be my water you're pouring there?"

"I guess so."

"How much water you got left in that pail there?"

Free handed up the pail.

Lew looked. "My God, about an inch left. Hardly enough for a field mouse." Then Lew looked into the pail again, and started to laugh. "Is this fresh water?"

"I guess so."

Lew dipped a finger in the pail and came up with some green stuff on it. "Moss, for godsakes. Did you dip this out of the horse tank?"

"I guess so."

Lew stared down at Free. He pushed back his straw hat. Sweat dripped off the end of his nose. Lew's eyes became as big as an owl's. "That's what you get when you send a boy out to do man's work." Lew stared into the pail again. "You know, I'm so dumbed thirsty I've got to drink it." Lew drank up.

Free still stood with legs apart on the last two wet spots. Free watched Lew's Adam's apple go up and down like a pump handle.

Lew handed the pail back to Free. "Sorry I had to take all your water." Lew gave him a straight smile. "I suppose now you won't be able to walk home."

Free looked back. So did Everett. The spots behind them had already dried up.

"Well, you can't stand there like a couple of statues all day."

Free stared at the hot ground.

"Why don't you just run real fast?" Lew said. "That way your feet won't touch the ground long enough for you to get burnt."

Free felt nervous around Lew and his jokey face. Free broke into a run and headed hell-a-kiting for the shade under the high cottonwood tree, empty pail bumping against his leg. Everett followed him.

Lew began to laugh. Free could hear Lew going at it, slapping his knees, as Lew walked back to his shocks.

When Lew left after threshing, Pa came home one day with a wonderful surprise. Pa'd caught a ride to town with neighbor Stickney and Free was wondering already how Pa would get home because Stickney came back early without Pa. Pretty soon Free heard a purring on the yard. Then he heard a car horn. The horn sounded like a hungry calf bawling. Free looked. It was a brand-new car and it had chains to turn the wheels. And by jiminy there was Pa driving it.

Free and Everett ran outside. Ma followed, wiping her hands in her apron. Rover barked real loud, and then ran scared into the barn.

Pa circled the yard a couple of times to show off. With a high smile he pinched the bulb horn again. His chin was shaved and it shone in the sun. Finally Pa stopped by the house gate.

Pa said, "How do you like our new Overland? Pretty nifty, ain't she?"

Ma kept wiping her hands in her apron. She was afraid of the car.

Pa said, "Get in and I'll take you out for a little spin."

"Oh, Alfred, I'm not dressed for it."

"C'mon, I'll drive you around the section. Nobody'll see you."

"No, Alfred."

"C'mon. You're gonna have to take your first ride sometime. Because cars are the coming thing, you know." Pa pulled down a little lever under the steering wheel and the motor purred up real loud. "C'mon. You kids get in the back seat."

Free and Everett quick climbed in back.

"C'mon, Ada," Pa said, coaxing her.

At last Ma got in front.

"Ready? Go?"

Ma smiled a little sick.

Pa pushed a lever and the chain drive in back began to make an urring noise and they took off. Pa headed the Overland up the lane. He turned the steering wheel and they curved onto the road.

Free watched carefully to see how Pa did it.

"Now watch our speed," Pa said. Pa pulled down the little lever under the steering wheel again and the motor began to roar and the chain drive began to sound like Aunt Karen singing. The wind blew in their faces and tore at their hair something fierce.

Ma grabbed hold of the door with one hand and her heart with the other. "Not so fast."

"Ho," Pa said. "This ain't fast. Wait'll I really pull her ears down."

"Alfred, you go any faster and I'll jump out."

"Hoch."

"I will. I don't like to go fast. I never did."

Free and Everett had a lot of fun going fast in back.

"Alfred!"

"Oh, all right." Pa slowed down then. "But I was a long ways from having her wide open."

When they came to the Stickney place, white chickens were all over the road and in the ditch. Pa pinched the bulb horn and it bawled at the chickens. The chickens all cackled up and sailed into the cornfields on both sides.

"Wal," Pa said, "I almost gave the Stickneys chicken dinner tonight."

Ma kept gripping the door with her one hand and her heart with the other. "Don't go so fast."

Pa looked at Ma a couple of times. Then he felt sorry for her and slowed down some more. The wind died down then too.

Pretty soon they were back on their own yard. Pa pulled on a lever and the car squeaked under them and it stopped in front of the gate.

"Wal, lady of the house, now wasn't that a slick ride?" Pa said.

"I prefer Daise and the buggy even though she goes too fast too sometimes." Ma shot out of the car like she had to go to the privy real bad right away.

"Wal, I declare," Pa said.

One day Pa came home with a new coaster wagon. Pa said he'd bought it so Free could do chores with it, like, get cobs in it for Ma, bring the milk pails out to the barn for Pa, feed the chickens.

Free and Everett played horse and buggy with it and took turns pulling each other. First Free was Pa and Everett was Daise. Then Free was Daise and Everett was Pa. Everett wasn't a very good Daise.

Free noticed that the letters on his coaster looked like the letters on Pa's new car. So Free asked Ma about it.

"Why, yes," Ma said, surprised. "They are the same. O V E R L A N D. Isn't that nice."

Oh boy.

Free decided to drive his Overland. He knelt his right knee in it, held the steering tongue with his right hand, and rolled the coaster ahead by pushing his left bare foot on the ground. "Bbbpt," Free purred. "Boy, listen to that motor. Bbbpt-n-bbbpt-n-bbbpt."

Ma wasn't sure she liked Free's new Overland either. She thought Pa went too fast with his and she didn't like it that Free always went bbbpt-n-bbbpt with his. Ma said, "Free, why do you always have to make that funny noise all the time?"

"That's to show it's going, Ma. It's the motor doing that."

Ma shook her head. "That bbbpt-bbbpt is going to give you thick lips. If you keep that up within a year you'll look like a Ubangi." They'd seen a Ubangi a missionary had brought to their church once. The missionary wanted the people in the Christian Church to know where their collection money went. "And you wouldn't want to look like that, would you?" Ma pushed her lips out real thick and for a second she looked worse than a Ubangi.

"Ma, my dandy Overland is a car and the motor's got to run or otherwise it won't go anyplace."

"Just the same, I don't want you to get thick lips. Later on, when you grow up, people'll think you're a beast around the women."

"All right, Ma."

"Try and remember now, will you?"

"Yes, Ma." Free pushed off in his fast Overland. "Watch my speed now, Ma. Bbbbpt . . . oop."

Ma shook her head. "What's the use."

A week later Free suddenly had a friend. Ma's younger brother Sherman came to play with him for a couple of weeks. It was because Grampa Engleking was sick.

Sherm was three years older than Free. Sherm had white hair like Free but his hands were slimmer and his feet smaller. Sherm took the lead most times when they played, just as Free took the lead with Everett. Sherm sometimes favored Everett to help him catch up to Free. Sherm really was a lot of fun because he could think of lots of new ways to play. He liked to play bat-and-ball the best. He made a bat out of a fork handle and they used Everett's red rubber ball. Sherm could hit the red ball over the chicken fence. Free could only make it roll up against the fence. It always scared the chickens and made them fly up.

By the time Sunday came Free knew he liked Sherm better than anybody in the whole world, better even than Ma. Free asked if Sherm could sit by him in church, and Ma said, yes, he could, if they were all good boys. Free was wearing his new sailor outfit and Sherm said he looked good in it. After church all of

Sherm's cousins, kids of Uncle Big John, came around and shook hands with Sherm, and talked jokes and smiled. Free was a little jealous of them, but he knew that pretty soon Sherm would be riding home with him and then he'd have him all to himself again. And when they got home Free felt even better because he heard Sherm say to Ma that that Bonnie branch of the Engleking family all shook hands like they'd just wiped themselves and was ashamed of the hand they'd just wiped with.

"Foo," Ma said. "Don't talk like that about your own cousins."

Pa spoke up. "Wal, your little brother speaks the truth." Pa began to like Sherm then too.

Ma shook her head. "One should always love your cousins."

"That's sweet and kind of you," Pa said. "But then you always had a soft side for floaters."

The next day Sherm decided to play up-in-heaven. Pa'd hung the hayrack up in those four box elders by the lane again, and Sherm showed Free how to shinny up one of the box elders and then drop down onto the hayrack. Sherm called the box elder Jacob's ladder. They had to help Everett up. It was a good place to play up-in-heaven because the floor of the hayrack was as slick as glass. Sherm played that the hayrack floor was a street of pure gold. The sides of the rack were the walls of a schoolyard in heaven. Sherm had gone to school already one year. Sherm and Free and Everett played they were saved in heaven, that it was all a wonderful place and a fitting climax to their life here on earth, and they sang His praises and psalms, and they prayed that God might smite the heathen and the mosquito.

The day after that they got tired of it. There wasn't much to do in heaven. So after dinner at noon, when Everett had to lie down for his nap in the boys' bedroom upstairs, Sherm said he and Free probably should take a nap too in their hayrack heaven.

They napped a while.

When Free woke up he saw that Sherm had taken out his pisser and was playing with it. It looked like a fresh toadstool.

Sherm caught him looking. "Why don't you take yours out too and play with it."

"Ma'll get after me."

"She can't see us from here. Just look and you can see she can't."

Free looked. Ma couldn't see them all right.

"C'mon. It's fun."

Free began to feel like he wanted to but he was afraid.

Sherm rolled over on his stomach and peed through a crack and sprayed the grass below.

Free felt he had to go then too, so he turned on his stomach and peed through his own crack. He watched it splash below. He could see where his water kept hitting a weed and making it bend over.

They laughed about that. It was naughty but it was fun.

Sherm rolled over on his back again. He kept playing with himself. Pretty soon his pisser stood straight up like a stalk of asparagus with a red radish at the end.

Free played with his then too. It felt good. Pretty soon it began to stick up. It was the first time. Free was surprised. He'd always thought he had a small one, no bigger than his pinkie.

"This'll put hair in the palm of your hand," Sherm said.

"Yeh," Free said dreamily.

"Strip it back," Sherm said.

"How?"

"Like you skin an onion."

Free skinned it back. "Say, that hurts."

"That's when your petcock feels real good."

"It don't me. Man. Oooh, it's really beginning to hurt."

Sherm kept playing with his. "It'll feel better pretty soon. Just keep doing it." Sherm began to look dreamy too. "It's really beginning to feel like heaven up here."

"Now I wisht I hadn't started. Oooh."

"Spit on it. Make it slippery."

Free groaned. "Now what am I going to do? Oooh."

Sherm lifted himself up on an elbow for a closer look. "Say, the head's turning black and blue."

"What am I going to do, Sherm? I'm going crazy with the pain of it. Man-oh-man." The head was turning slick and blue. And big. It was like he'd tied a string too tight around a thumb. "Sherm, I can hardly see any more."

Sherm jerked his petcock back in and buttoned up his fly. "I better go call Ade."

"Nooo." Free banged his head hard on the slick boards. It shook the whole hayrack. "She'll be ashamed of me."

Sherm stood up. "Then I better go get your dad."

"Nooo. He'll lick me."

"Well, we can't have you die on us." Sherm jumped down to the ground and ran for the house.

Free didn't know what was the worst, that awful ring of pain or the way Ma was gonna look.

Ma came swishing toward the hayrack. Sherm came trotting after her, eyes wide. Ma was mad. "Free, what are you doing up there?"

"Oooh."

Ma stood on her toes and tried to look into the hayrack. She couldn't quite make it. "Free, get down out of there right away. Right now." Ma grabbed the side of the hayrack and shook it. "You hear?"

Free began to bawl. "Oh, Ma, I can't move it hurts so."

"Then Sherm you get up there and help him down." Ma had never sounded madder. "Hurry." Ma shook the rack again. "Whatever were you boys up to, for landsakes?"

"Nothing," Sherm said.

"Sherm, you're probably at the bottom of all this."

Sherm shinnied up the tree and dropped into the hay rack. "Here, Free, let me help you down."

Free didn't even dare to pull his pisser back into his overalls it was so swole up. He let Sherm help him to his feet. "I can't shinny down that tree with this."

Ma rose on her toes again and looked through the crack. She saw it. "In God's name! What did you do to yourself?"

"We was only playing when this happened, Ma."

"Playing?"

Sherm held Free up. "Yeh, Ade."

"Och! May God save us from the fate of Sodom and Gomorrah! Free, get down off that rack right now." She held up her arms to catch Free. "Climb over the side and I'll help you down. Hurry."

Free finally did manage to climb over the side, his back to Ma.

Ma caught him from behind and lowered him to the ground. "Now, let me have a look at that."

Free closed his eyes. He whimpered both in shame and in agony.

"How did this happen, for godsakes? Did you fall on it?"

Free shivered.

"Sherman, just what were you two doing up there?"

"We were just skinning our onions."

"What's that, in God's name?"

"Stripping her back. All the guys do that in Jerusalem."

Ma shook her head. "Teaching my boy bad habits so early in life, shame on you, Sherman." Ma looked at it again. "Well, he's gonna burst there if we don't quick get help. Sherm, you run and get Alfred. March!"

Sherm ran.

Ma picked Free up and carried him into the house. She took him into the bedroom and put him down on Pa and Ma's bed. Very carefully Ma slipped off his overalls and underwear.

Pretty quick Pa came banging into the bedroom. "What's the matter here?" Pa took one look. "Oho. I know what that is. I had the same thing happen to me once."

"You did, Alfred?"

"Yeh. My dad said he had the same thing happen to him. It's in the family."

"It's in the family to play with it?"

"No no. I mean, it's in the family to have a tight foreskin. Shucks, as for playing with it, all boys get around to being a little curious about themselves." Pa stared down at Free. "I better go take him to the doctor."

"Wait," Ma said, "Dr. Drury is on vacation."

"What a heck of a note that is at a time like this."

"Wait," Ma said, "the Stickneys just got one of them new things put in their house, a telephone. Maybe from there you can call that doctor over in Wodan."

"Yeh. What's that doc's name?"

"Uhh . . . Dr. Barber. I remember his name because he's the one that's part Indian."

"What's his being an Indian got to do with it?"

"He's part barbarian. It goes with his name Barber."

"Oh." Pa leaned over Free for a closer look. "I'll go and call him."

Free fainted twice before the doctor from Wodan purred onto the yard with his chain-drive car.

Dr. Barber came slow and easy into the bedroom. He had a black vest with a silver watch chain. "Well, what have we got here?" He set his little black suitcase on the end of the bed. He bent down for a look. "Well well, a slight case of phimosis."

Ma was rubbing her hands. "Is that bad, doctor?"

"No." Dr. Barber had a jolly voice. He smiled nice and had a silver tooth. "No, phimosis means a tightness of the orifice of the prepuce so that it cannot be retracted over the glans. The boy was probably able to retract it when the glans was in a flaccid state, but he couldn't slip it back when the glans became engorged. The blood could flow into the glans but couldn't flow out of it. It's a congenital anomaly seen occasionally."

Free caught on it wasn't so bad after all. He groaned a little bit easier.

"And now," Dr. Barber said, "I think I'll have to ask that everybody leave this room except the father. I want him to help me."

"Ma?" Free cried.

"Now now," Dr. Barber said. "Everything's going to be all right, sonny." Dr. Barber took a piece of white cotton, poured something into it, and placed it over Free's nose. It smelled like sweet gasoline. And then Free was gone.

When Free woke up, there were heads leaning all around the bed looking down at him, Ma, Pa, Dr. Barber, Sherm, Everett. Free felt funny in a sleepy way.

Sherm looked at something between Free's legs. "What happened, Ade? Did the doctor cut off Free's pisser?"

Pa and Dr. Barber smiled.

Everett held his hand to his nose. He was smelling that sweet gasoline stuff in the room.

Ma smiled too. But it was a ma smile. "It's nothing to laugh about, Sherman. And if I was you, I wouldn't have too much to say around here."

Dr. Barber said, "Free's going to be all right."

Ma asked. "How long must he wear that bandage?"

"Oh, about a week. He's a healthy boy and he'll heal fast. Here's some salve for it."

Pretty soon the doctor left in his purring chain-drive car.

After that, when Free had to do number one, he always had to run to Ma to ask her to undo the bandage a minute. They'd go around the corner of the white house together so nobody would see them do it from the road.

Free didn't play with himself again for quite a while after that. And Ma and Pa never talked about it.

Free ❦ 3

ONE EVENING WHILE Pa was milking cows in the barn, Ma got disgusted with Everett. Everett kept climbing up on a chair trying to sneak some butter out of the butter dish with his finger. Ma had already set the table for supper.

"Free, I've got to finish this mopping here in the kitchen before your father comes in from milking. Will you keep him from getting at the table? For mother?"

"Sure, Ma." Free left off playing with his blocks and placed himself between Everett and the table.

It didn't take Everett long to figure something out. Free had been building a city with the blocks and didn't like it if Everett helped him. So Everett went over and tore down some of the houses along one side of the city.

Free got mad. He went over and blew up his cheeks at Everett.

Everett backed away.

"Now you keep away from my town," Free said. Free fixed up the houses of his city again. It took him a while because the light wasn't very good where he was building. Ma had the lamp reflector aimed more at where she was mopping.

"Free! I thought I told you to keep Everett from climbing onto that table."

Sure enough, there was that darn Everett up on the chair again and about ready to get another finger of butter. Free hurried over and pulled Everett off the chair. Everett hit the floor hard.

"That's better," Ma said.

Tears showed in the corners of Everett's eyes. Then he too got mad and ran for Free's block city to kick it down.

Free beat him there. He pushed Everett away so he couldn't quite kick down the houses.

Everett then ran for the table.

Free quick beat him there too.

"That's the good boy, Free," Ma said. "But don't hurt him." Ma poured the dirty water out of the mop pan into the slop pail. Sighing, she reached up for the kettle on the stove and began to pour fresh hot water into the mop pan.

Again Everett ran for Free's city.

Free grabbed him and shoved him away.

Everett ran for the table.

"Free!" Ma warned as she poured. "Watch him."

"Coming." Free got there just as Everett was part way onto the chair. Free gave him a hard push. "That'll teach you."

Everett lost his balance and fell backwards off the chair. He landed in the mop pan where Ma was pouring hot water. Some of the hot water went down inside the back of his red checkered shirt.

"Everett!" Ma shrieked. With one hand she pushed Everett out of the pan and with the other hand she threw the kettle up on the reservoir of the stove. "Everett!"

Everett's eyes sank in close to his nose.

Ma jumped to her feet. She thought of something. There was a red can of Calumet Baking Powder standing on the cabinet shelf. She grabbed it, and pulling Everett's shirt open at the collar in back, poured the whole can down the inside of his shirt. Then she jumped to the door and yelled. "Alfred! Quick! Something awful's happened to Everett!" Then Ma grabbed Free by his collar and shoved him on the run outdoors into the cold without any coat on and yelled after him, "Hurry get your father from the barn!"

Free ran like the dickens.

Just as he came to the cow door, Pa popped out. "What's the matter now, son?"

"Ma poured some boiling water over Everett."

"Gotske. If that don't frost the devil himself. You kids." Pa leaned into a run for the house. Against the light of the kitchen window Pa's legs flickered through each other like black scissors cutting real fast.

When they got in the house, Ma had already torn the clothes off Everett and he lay naked on his belly on a rag rug. Ma had aimed the reflector on the lamp at Everett. There was an awful big blister on his back. It lay on him like a water bag. There was baking powder and flour all over it.

Pa stood chewing his teeth.

Ma's breath shot out like steam. "Yah!"

"I won't ask how this happened," Pa said. "At least not right now. But I will ask, what next?"

"I already threw baking powder and flour over it. I read about what to do with burns in that *Farm and Fireside* we get. Flour absorbs the heat. And shuts off the air."

Pa wrung his ear. "We dassent move him."

"Oh, Alfred, this is awful."

"Wal, there's nothing for it but to get the doctor again."

"Just so the boy doesn't die in the meantime."

Pa looked around at Free. "Where were you when this happened?"

Tears bubbled into the corners of Free's eyes. "I couldn't help it, Pa." Free put up an arm in case Pa hit him a crack over the ear. "Everett kept trying to lick the butter and I just kept pushing him away from the table."

Ma said. "I thought you weren't going to ask how this happened?"

"I know. But somebody ought to get licked for this."

"Wait. It wasn't the boy's fault." Ma quick told what had happened. "If it was anybody's fault it was mine."

Pa pulled his cap low over his eyes. "Wal, all right, I'll lick everybody later. But right now I better hightail it to Bonnie and get Doctor Tom."

Everett didn't cry. His eyes had turned cross-eyed against his nose.

Dr. Drury finally came. He examined Everett carefully. He didn't look too worried. "Ada, you probably saved the boy's life with your quick thinking, emptying that can of baking powder into his shirt. That kept it from being a third-degree burn."

"Then he isn't going to die?"

Dr. Drury shook his big round head. "No. But he won't be able to move around much for a couple of weeks. Eventually it should all heal over fine."

"How will you be able to bandage it?"

"We won't. We're going to leave it just as it is."

"You ain't gonna prick the water out of that blister then?" Pa asked. "Sneak up on it from a little ways off to one side under the skin?"

"No. The tissues beneath it need that moisture, and they'll reabsorb most of it. Besides, if we can keep the blister from breaking we'll keep the germs out." Dr. Drury smiled down at Everett. "Think you can sleep on your tummy for a while?"

Everett was still lying on his belly and he had to twist his head around to nod. Two tears finally ran down out of his crossed eyes.

"Good boy. Do that and you'll be fine."

A week later Everett couldn't raise his left hand. Pa and Ma took him to Dr. Drury right away. Free went along.

This time Dr. Drury did look worried. He looked Everett over for a long time. He asked Everett to do this and that with his left arm and then to do this and that with his left leg. Everett could move his leg a little but not his arm.

"It has to do with that whole side of him, doesn't it?" Ma said.

Dr. Drury asked, "Your other boy here, has he had any trouble moving his limbs?"

"No," Ma said, "no, he appears to be as active as ever. Why?"

Dr. Drury thought to himself some more.

"What is it, Doctor?"

"I'm afraid it's infantile paralysis."

Ma had tears. "Oh, if only I'd have sent those children into the living room while I mopped that floor."

"Ada, that burn over his back had little to do with it."

"You're sure?"

"Positive." Dr. Drury turned Everett around and examined the long red scar down Everett's back. "At least this seems to be healing pretty good. Except for some proud flesh here over the shoulder blade."

"Proud flesh?" Ma cried.

"Yes. But that's not serious. Proud flesh is just some tissue growing too fast and it takes on a granular appearance."

"But doesn't proud flesh always leave an ugly scar?"

"It may. But the main thing is, the boy heals fast. And because he does he may also very well recover the use of his arm. You have tough children, Ada."

Ma's face was white.

"Now," Dr. Drury said, "I think what I'll do is this. Prescribe some exercise for the boy's arm. And his left leg too." Dr. Drury wrote on a piece of paper. "Twice a day. If you keep at it faithfully, I think he'll come around."

It was a whole month before they saw a sign that Everett's arm was coming around. They were having supper when Everett moved it. The butter dish stood close to his plate and he moved his left hand toward it. His eyes looked straight at the butter. He wasn't cross-eyed anymore either.

Free ❦ 4

FREE GOT THE mail from the mailbox for Ma. There was a letter in it from Gramma. Free could always tell when it was Gramma's letter because she liked to tack mousetails onto the name here and there.

Ma read the letter aloud to Pa at the dinner table at noon. The letter said Grampa was failing and before he looked much worse the whole family ought to get together and have a family picture taken. It would be nice to have one for the future.

Ma turned the letter over and then she turned white.

"Wal, now what?" Pa had his feet up on a rung of Everett's high chair.

"Doctor says Pa has a tumor in his stomach."

"Humm."

Ma looked past Pa. "It's cancer."

"Does it say that for sure there?"

"No. But I can read between the lines." There was a look on Ma's face like she was expecting a cyclone. "Poor Pa. He's never had it very good here in America."

Pa snorted. "With that mother of yours for a wife it's no wonder."

"Now, Alfred, I will not hear my mother blacked."

"Ada, you know yourself she has a real mean streak in her. She's always had it in for your dad."

Ma looked at the letter some more. Her face, especially over the cheeks, looked like a snowdrift.

Pa dropped his feet to the floor. "Ade, then I guess what we better do is get that Lew Westraw to do our chores for us for a couple of days and right away push off for Jerusalem."

Free's eyes opened wide. "Take a long trip in our new Overland, Pa?"

Pa roughed up Free's hair. "Yup. We'll wind up her tail and see the sights."

"Whoopee!" Free cried. He leaped off his chair and gave Pa a big hug. "We're going to go on a long trip to Gramma's town. And see Sherm."

Pa had to laugh. "Yeh, I suppose for you that's going to be a great lark." Pa's eyes closed a little. "I remember the first time I drove to Gramma's town with old Daise." Pa gave Ma his moon look. "I went there to spoon with your mother, son."

"You did no such thing," Ma said. But Ma smiled a little.

Pa said, "Well, Ade, shall we do her? I've just got time before corn-picking."

"I suppose we should. But promise me you won't drive fast. My heart's heavy enough as it is."

"Love, I won't even coast downhill fast."

They went on Friday. It took just about half a day to make it. The Overland got hot twice and they had to stop for water, once at Chokecherry Corner, and once at Sioux Center. There was dust all over everything. Their eyes had big brown boogers in the corners. Free had a stomachache. He felt like he had to go to the toilet all the time, when he couldn't.

Sherm saw them coming around the water tower corner. He quick ran across the road and pointed to where they should park the car, on the north side of the barn where they could turn in by the alley. Sherm was waving his hands so hard he almost mixed Pa up. But Pa drove around under a big yellow cottonwood tree and stopped the car in the right place.

The cottonwood tree they stopped under was a giant one. Free couldn't believe a cottonwood could be so big. Free forgot about his stomachache and climbed out of the car and the first thing went up to the cottonwood. It was twice as big as their own cottonwood back home. He stared at the big bottom of it where it curved down into big roots. It was bigger around even than Ma's dining room table. The roots looked like sows sleeping in mud. Then Free looked up. Up and up. The yellow leaves at the top were so high they appeared to be a cloud of yellow wasps circling around themselves.

Pa and Ma got out of the car behind him.

Sherm touched free on the elbow. "Hey, ain't you gonna say hello?"

"Sure."

"Well, you better. I'm your uncle and I can make you say it."

Gramma came big and wide out of the kitchen door. Her glasses flashed in the light. "So. You came after all. Well well." She rolled her hands around in her apron. "And my little grandsons came too." She held out her arms for Free. "Come, give your old Gramma a great big hug and a kiss."

Free liked Gramma when she came to visit them, but he didn't like all that mushy fuss she made over him. Free smiled a little and let Gramma give him a wet kiss.

Gramma kissed Ma next, Gramma crying. Then Pa shook hands with Gramma and nodded down at her.

Gramma saw Everett sitting alone in back of the car and she reached in for him and gave him a big crying kiss. "Poor little fellow, and how are you after your accident, hah?" Then Gramma smelled Everett's pants. "Fooey!" she said.

Ma hung her head a little. "Yes, I know. I think he did that on this side of Sioux Center."

"I thought he'd be housebroke by now."

"He was. But that bad burn set him back."

"Poor little beggar."

Pa said, "Where's John?"

Sherm said, "He's laying cement walks for the city."

"Wal, after I say hello to your dad, I'll go look him up."

Free could see an old man sitting at a table through the kitchen window. The man had a brown moustache and he was leaning ahead the better to see them. He looked like he was tired. Free didn't remember him.

Ma saw the man in the window too. "Oh, how Pa has changed."

Gramma began to cry all over again. "Yes, poor man, he wanted to walk out here to greet you but I wouldn't let him."

"It wouldn't have hurt him to come out," Sherm said. "Some sun would've done him good.".

"Sherm, still you," Gramma snapped. Gramma swallowed her tears. "What do you know about what he can do, boss?"

They went into the house. Ma carried the diaper bag. A slop pail smelled on the porch. Onions frying in beef suet smelled in the kitchen. The smells weren't very nice.

Ma herded Free and Everett toward the old man by the window. "Come and say hello to your other grampa, boys."

The old man's brown moustache was a big one. He had white eyebrows. He looked gray holes right through one. His armchair was bigger than Pa's. He was awful sad about that tumor in his stomach. He looked at Free's nose, then at his hands, then at his shoes. "So," he said, "my namesake is really growing up, isn't he?"

"Shake hands with Grampa," Ma said.

Free held out his hand.

Grampa took Free's hand in both his hands. He had big hands. He was like Pa.

Free took back his hand.

Gramma started to spill tears again and got her glasses wet. "Yes, little Alfred, there he sits now, this once great strong man, too weak to stand up and greet his grandsons."

"He can get up if he wants to," Sherm said.

Ma leaned down and gave Grampa a kiss on one cheek. Then she pushed Everett forward. "Everett, you too, shake hands with Grampa."

Everett held out his hand. He looked sideways at Grampa.

Pa next shook hands with Grampa. "Well, Pa, it's been a while."

"Yes, Alfred. Too long." Grampa had a bad sore throat.

Pa took a chair by the window across the table from Grampa. "Nice weather we're having this time of the year."

Grampa leaned on the table with both arms. The armchair made a cracking noise. "Yes. Good weather to lay cement." Grampa looked holes through Pa too. "And how are you getting along with your fieldwork?"

"Fine. Got the last plowing done. Ready to start picking corn the minute we get a good frost."

Ma took Everett by the hand and with the diaper bag went into the other room to change him.

Sherm winked at Free. "Let's go outdoors and play. It'll be an hour yet before supper is ready."

Free followed him outside.

"Don't get your clothes dirty now," Ma called after them.

Free couldn't get that big cottonwood out of his head. "Did you ever try to shinny up that tree, Sherm?"

"Naa. Too fat for you to get your arms around it. Besides, cottonwood branches are mostly too dangerous to step on."

"Why's that?"

"They snap off too easy."

"Hain't your grampa got a ladder to climb it?"

"That's your grampa, buster, and my dad."

"Your dad then. Hain't he got a ladder?"

"What good would that do? 'Twouldn't be nearly long enough to reach up to the first fat limb to step on. Besides, Ma wouldn't let me do it."

"You mean Gramma."

"Your gramma, buster, and my ma."

Free stared up at the great tree. Some blackbirds were sitting on a branch halfway up. The wind was giving them a nice seesaw ride. They were singing their pink tongues out. "Man."

"You better have a good look at it while you can."

"Why?"

"The city says we gotta cut it down this winter."

Cut down such a great big wonderful tree? "Why?"

"It's dying where the lightning hit it last summer. Look." Sherm led Free around to the neighbor's side of the tree and pointed to where the bark was peeled off. Rotten wood showed at the bottom of the white scar. Sherm gave the rotten wood a kick and his toe sank an inch into it. It was punk already. "The city's afraid a strong northwest wind'll blow it over someday and land it on those privies and barns and smash 'em." Sherm gave the tree another sharp kick with his shoe. "Yep, this old boy is done for. This winter Pa and John are going to saw him up for stovewood."

"Ain't Grampa too sick to work now?"

"Pa ain't all that sick. It's all in Ma's head."

Free wondered what that tumor in Grampa's stomach looked like. "Is Grampa going to have an operation?"

Sherm got mad. "No, he's not going to have an operation."

Free was glad then. Operations were terrible. Pa once told Ma about the operation they gave Mrs. Liveright and how they had all her bowels out lying on her chest while they looked for a tumor in them. Mrs. Liveright died.

"Let's go and play on the schoolyard," Sherm said again.

They ran across the street.

Sherm said, "Let's go look on the other side of the schoolhouse where they're building a new wing. C'mon, you can see where they've cut a big hole for a new door right through the old wall."

They ran around behind the schoolhouse. The carpenters had gone home for the day and Free and Sherm could go where they wanted to. There were new boards sticking out everywhere, and like Sherm said they'd cut a big square hole right through the gray stucco wall of the school. It was a lot like butchering. Sherm led the way through the new hole into the old school.

"Wanna see where I sit?" Sherm asked.

Free nodded. So this is what a school looked like inside.

Sherm led the way into a room full of small desks. Sherm pointed to a desk in back. "Teacher put me in the back because I always got my hand up."

Free stared at the desk. "Why do you do that, hold your hand up?"

"If you know the answer you always raise your hand, you dumbbell. And if you have to go to the toilet."

"Oh."

"Sit in my seat once," Sherm said. "See if it fits you."

Free slid into the slick seat. He held onto the sides. It fit him just fine.

"Open up the desk," Sherm said. "Lift up the top."

Free looked inside. There was a book in it and a pencil box and a tablet and a little slate with chalk and a box of colors. Free wished he could have a double-row box of colors too.

Sherm tore a sheet out of the tablet. "Let's see how good you can color. That's what we had to do first."

Free had to do number two. It felt like it was almost there. Maybe he was now getting the trots from that stomachache he had on the way over from Bonnie. He pinched it back because he was too busy just then.

"Go on, color it."

Free took a brown color and drew a picture of Rover. He took a yellow color and colored it like Rover looked.

"Say, maybe you won't need to go to school. You color pretty good already."

Free couldn't help but laugh at that. And in so doing he let a little slip out. His pants were going to be a little bit aacky.

Pretty soon Sherm said, "Peuu! Did you let one?"

"No."

Sherm started to go up some stairs, when there was a call from across the street.

"Sherman, it's supper time. Sherman?"

"Shucks," Sherm said. "Well, I suppose we better go eat."

When they got in the house, Gramma was setting the table with company dishes, and Grampa was still sitting by the window. Pa was outside somewhere and Ma was holding Everett on her lap. Gramma put her hand on Free's shoulder. "I'll bet you're hungry."

"A little bit." Then Free said, "Ma, I saw where Sherm sits in school."

"In school?" Ma said. "How did you get in there?"

"Sherm showed me. They're fixin' up the school and you can get in there through a new door hole."

Sherm smiled. "Yeh, I let him sit in my seat. Say, Ade, he's gonna be good in school."

"How would you know that?" Ma asked.

"He can color pretty good already."

Gramma drew up her nose. "Did somebody wind around here?"

"Maybe it's Everett again," Ma said. "The trip's upset him a little I think." Ma smelled Everett over. "No, he's all right. Is it you then, Free?"

Free drew back.

Gramma came after Free. She caught him by his navy blue collar. She sniffed him up close. "I thought so. You come with me. Into the bedroom." Gramma waved Ma away. "I'll take care of him. He's my grandchild and we're good friends. Come."

Free let Gramma push him into Sherm's bedroom. Gramma pulled down his pants. "Oho. It was more than just a bang in your pants at that, wasn't it? Lucky it wasn't much. Didn't quite stain through to your blue trousers. Here, we'll take off your underpants and I'll quick wash it. You can run around in just your navy blue trousers until your underpants dries."

Ma came into the bedroom. "Shame on you, Free."

Gramma smoothed things over. "Accidents will happen, Ada. Now, boy, run along. And ask Sherm to show you where our privy is."

Sherm was outside under the apple tree in front of the kitchen door. He was kicking through the tree leaves.

"What are you doing?" Free asked.

"I was sure I saw an apple in the grass here this morning. There was one left. Hmm. John must've seen it and beat me to it."

Free wished Ma had an apple tree that close by the kitchen door. Then they could just climb up in the tree and pick all the apples they wanted any old time.

"There comes your Uncle John," Sherm said.

Around the corner of the barn came Pa with another fellow. The other fellow looked like Sherm, only bigger. He had the same eyebrows, white. Though where Sherm had gold hair the other fellow had brown hair. Pa and Uncle John stopped to look at Pa's car. Uncle John unbuckled two snaps on one side and opened up the engine hood. Uncle John looked inside. He liked the Overland too.

"She got a lot of jazz?" Uncle John asked.

"Hardly have to shift her to intermediate up a hill," Pa said.

Uncle John spotted Free. He closed the hood of the Overland. "Well, well, my first uncle-sayer." Uncle John was almost as tall as Pa. He was wearing overalls and a jacket all splashed over with cement. There was a smile on his lips like he was going to wink. "Can he milk a cow yet, Alfred?"

Pa smiled. "Not quite. But you ought to see him dive after bullheads." Pa told Uncle John about the time Free fell into the water tank.

Free got mad at Pa. Now Uncle John would always have something to tease him about.

Sherm asked, "Are you too tired to play catch tonight, John?"

"What? I'm never too tired to play baseball. Think we still got time before supper?"

"Sure," Sherm said. "Ma ain't started the potatoes yet."

"Funny they called us so early then," Free said.

"Oh," Sherm said, "the womenfolks always want you handy just before supper."

Uncle John rubbed his hands together. His hands sounded like sandpaper. It made Free shiver. "Go and get the gloves then. Alfred, you still play, don't you?"

"I quit the Congregational team when I got married," Pa said.

"Well, but you can still play a little catch, can't you?"

"I guess so. Ada won't mind too much."

"The heck with Ada. Never let the women tell you what sports you can't play." Uncle John rubbed his hands some more. "And Sherm, bring a glove for my little uncle-sayer too."

"Wal, now I dunno," Pa said. "The boy ain't played much yet. Just with a rubber ball with Sherm."

"What?" Uncle John rolled his blue eyes like it was the worst news he'd ever heard. He pushed back his blue cap so far his brown hair boiled out in front. "What, you've never stopped to play catch with your own little boy? When he's got such wonderful big hands?"

"Ada don't like for me to teach him baseball."

Uncle John waggled his big finger up and down at Pa. "Listen. Ade's a great gal. You know. But there's one thing where she's plain flat-out wrong. She gets that from Pa, who doesn't like baseball either."

Sherm showed up with four gloves. One of them was a little boy's glove and Sherm gave that to Free.

Free put it on. Then Free felt that number two was almost there again. "Say, Sherm, where's the privy? I've gotta go quick."

Sherm pointed. "Under those grapevines."

When Free came back, Pa and Free's two uncles were already playing catch. They were playing burnout and laughing when they made the other fellow drop the ball. Free stood watching them until Uncle John noticed him.

"Hey, boy, here's one for you. Put your glove on." Uncle John lobbed him the ball. "Be careful. It's hard. Don't let it hit you on the nose."

Free stuck up both hands and caught the hard brown ball. With a glove on, the hard ball was easier to catch than a rubber ball barehanded.

The four of them made up a square and threw the ball around the corners. It slowly got dark out and pretty soon it was hard to see the ball.

"Say," Uncle John said, "that kid catches good."

Pa was smiling a big smile. "He does at that."

After a while there was a knock on the kitchen window behind Uncle John. It was Grampa and he was wiggling a finger at them.

"Guess it's time to put on the feedbag," Uncle John said.

"Shucks," Sherm said, "just when we was having fun."

They threw their gloves on the porch and marched inside. In the kitchen it stunk of more onions frying in cow fat. Free hoped the potatoes weren't going to be fried that way. The four of them washed up in turn.

"Now," Gramma said, "where shall we put everybody at the table?"

Free put his hand in Uncle John's big hand. "Can I sit by you?"

"Sure," Uncle John said. "That's all right by you, ain't it, Ade?"

Ma smiled a little pinched. "Provided Alfred sits on the other side of Free. That boy can be so self-wise sometimes."

They all sat down, Uncle John and Free and Pa on the sink side, Sherm and Ma and Everett on the living-room side, and Gramma and Grampa on the stove side. The time clock and the Bible on the shelf and the weather clock above them had the fourth side.

"Nah," Grampa said, and he looked each one in the eye, "let us say grace." Grampa rested his elbows on the table, folded his hands in front of his face, and closed his eyes. "Oh, Lord, who art our refuge in a world beset by violence, we come to Thee in the evening hour of this day. . . . "

Free folded his hands in front of his face too. He opened his fingers a little and peeked through. Gramma was rolling her eyes around behind her shut lids. Ma sat quiet with one hand on Everett's arm. Sherm was quiet too. Pa on Free's left was breathing slowly. When Free sneaked a look up at Uncle John he had a surprise. Uncle John was peeking through his fingers too, and right at him. Before Free could quick close his fingers, Uncle John gave him a big slow wink, and then made a little motion with his head that he'd better quit peeking or somebody'd catch him. Free pinched his eyes shut. He loved his Uncle John.

" . . . thank Thee for bringing these our loved ones safely to our family board. In Jesus' name. Amen."

Pa whispered down at Free. "Go ahead."

Free recited his little after-prayer. "Lord, bless this food, for Jesus' sake. Amen." Then he opened his eyes.

Grampa looked at Everett for his turn.

Ma said, "Everett doesn't say his just now, Pa. After that accident he lost everything he'd gained."

Uncle John poked fun at Everett. "A backslider, I see."

"Now now," Gramma said, severe, "let's have no mocking of little innocents."

Grampa began to pass the food. He didn't take anything himself. The blue bowls of food came around the table to Pa. Pa first helped Free and then himself and then passed them on to Uncle John. Free got fried potatoes with onions, a piece of boiled sausage, one little round red beet, and a heaping mound of sauerkraut. Pa sprinkled on some salt and pepper and told him to pitch in.

The little red beet was good. The sausage had just enough salt in it. The kraut was pretty good with pepper on. But the fried potatoes with onions in 'em were awful. The fat in them made Free's lips feel waxed. Free wished Rover was under the table. At home Rover on the sly always helped him eat things he didn't like.

Gramma was looking mad at Grampa's plate. "Nah, here I go out of my way to make a special meal for my husband and now look at that. He doesn't eat any of it."

Grampa said, "I can't have any fried foods." Grampa was almost too tired to talk. "You know how fried potatoes lay heavy on my stomach."

"It isn't that at all. It's more that you're being stubborn and won't eat anything I make."

Grampa talked slow. "Wife, all I asked for was some thin broth. And that shouldn't have given you too much trouble to make."

Gramma humphed. "Thin broth can't fatten you up."

Grampa closed his eyes and rested them on his knuckles. "All I asked for was some thin broth. In my own house."

Everybody at the table looked at their plates. Free dug into his waxy potatoes even though he hated them.

Gramma stood up so quick she almost tipped the milk pitcher over. "All right then, if soup you must have, I'll make you some pea soup. Special for my lord and master who dares to think that someone of higher issue should be his slave."

Grampa leaned harder on his knuckles. "Wife, please. It's only thin broth I want. Not thick pea soup."

Uncle John slammed down his knife and fork. "Ma, dar-gonit, why can't you give the man what he asks for? Once?"

Gramma swelled up. "What! One of my own children dares to take the part of a tyrant father?"

"Yeh," Uncle John said, "I do take the part of my dying father."

"What!!"

Uncle John wried his head around like he was at the same time just a little bit afraid of Gramma. "Well, Ma, Pa feels real sick to his stomach and he can't stand to have heavy food on it."

Gramma glared like a mad rooster.

"Well, isn't that why Ade and her family came up? Because Pa is so sick we thought we better quick get a picture of the whole family before it was too late?"

Tears almost squirted out of Gramma. "Ohch! Everybody is against me, when what I had, taking those gallstones out of my belly with a knife and no ether, was much worse."

Ma got up and put a hand on Gramma's shoulder to calm her down. "I know where you keep things and I'll quick make Pa some thin broth. After all, I don't often get a chance to cook for my father any more."

Gramma sat down. After a while she began to pick at her food.

Everybody ate quiet while Ma fixed the broth.

Free ate some more of his awful potatoes. He decided to look at other things while he was eating so he wouldn't know what he was putting into his mouth.

Up beside the clock was a clay plaque with some letters cut into it. Free pointed with his fork. "What does that say, Uncle John?"

Uncle John gave him a funny wink. "Ask Grampa. He took it along with him from the Old Country."

"Grampa?"

Grampa smiled, sad. He read the letters with whispery lips. "Sjuch, God is great en wy bigripe Him net."

"What does that mean, Grampa?"

"It means, 'See, God is great and we understand him not'."

"Why can't God talk American?"

Grampa's eyes almost closed. "Out of the mouth of babes. . . . Well, grandson, God can. It's just that that's the way He once talked to my grampa. A very long time ago. In Frisian."

"Oh."

The weather clock next caught Free's eye. He noticed that the old lady wearing bad weather clothes had moved out of her door a little ways, while the old man wearing good weather clothes had snuck under the roof some so he wouldn't get wet.

Pa saw where Free was looking. "Let's hope this weather holds until we get home. I still haven't bought tire chains for the Overland."

Uncle John nodded. "Especially around here. When gumbo gets wet you can roll up the whole county on your wheels."

Everett tried to sneak a finger of butter but got caught at it by Sherm. Sherm hit his finger hard enough so that the butter flew up and landed on the bridge of Gramma's glasses. Gramma jerked back, crossing her eyes. She removed the finger of butter. Uncle John had to laugh.

"Is Joan happy working for the Waxer family?" Ma wanted to know.

Gramma muttered a little. "So long as it lasts."

Uncle John said, "I think Joan's come home from there with her pants on over her head a couple of times. With young Pete Waxer."

Someone coming home with her pants on over her head? Free had to laugh, until he remembered that his own underwear was drying somewhere in the house.

"Yes, yes," Gramma said, "and that wild friend of hers, that Genevieve Hass, she isn't helping much either."

"What's the matter with her?"

Gramma wouldn't say.

Uncle John laughed. "Nothing's really the matter with Genevieve . . . excepting she's so pretty it'd be well worth the sin of helping her take off her pants."

Grampa raised his blue eyes. "John."

Uncle John laughed some more. "Pa, you know as well as I do that so long as the good Lord makes them two machines different, young people are gonna put 'em together to see what'll happen."

"Nevertheless, John."

"Yes," Ma said, "and all pitchers have ears."

"Is that Joan our Aunt Joan, Ma?" Free asked.

"Yes, that's your aunt," Ma said. "You'll see her tomorrow when we take the family picture."

The broth was finally warm and Ma served it to Grampa in a blue bowl.

Grampa sipped it slowly. "Ahh. That's choice. Bliss for my stomach at last." Grampa began to perk up a little.

Next came the rice. With brown sugar it was wonderful. Uncle John smeared Free a slice of dark rye bread. The slice was as thick as a little psalmbook. With butter and sugar sprinkled on it was wonderful too.

When everybody was just about done eating, Gramma looked at Free with a beaming smile. "Well, little son, are you full?"

"Way up to here." Free held his hand level with his Adam's apple.

After supper it was too dark out to play catch. So Sherm got out his tin soldiers and cannon and they played under the round living room table. Sherm took the blue soldiers and played he was the North. Free had to take the gray soldiers and play he was the South. Free didn't know how to play war very well, so he let Sherm show him. The soldiers had to march this way and then that way. The generals had to move the soldiers around a lot. And you couldn't shoot a general. Sherm let Free win a couple of battles. Sherm always won the war though. There were more blue soldiers than gray soldiers, and more cannons on Sherm's side, so if one shot down the soldiers one for one even steven, Sherm was bound to win.

Free noticed a big picture on the wall next to the breakfront. It showed some soldiers marching around, and a general with a lot of medals on his chest. The soldiers were in blue just like Sherm's soldiers. "Are they from the same country as your North, Sherm?"

"Nope."

"What country is that up there then?"

"The Old Country."

"And where's that?"

"Far across the sea."

"Where is the sea?"

"Cripey, Free, don't you know anything?"

"Not that much."

On the other side of the breakfront hung another picture. It showed sharp hills and some heavy hanging clouds with rain falling under them, and a wide river with a boat on it.

"What's a sea?" Free asked.

"A place where there is so much water you can't even build a bridge across it."

"Like up in that picture?"

"C'mon, keep playing. It's your turn to retreat."

It was no fun losing wars. But Free liked the way the soldiers were made. They had noses. And some of them were smiling.

Soon it was time to go to bed. Free saw Gramma reach into her mouth and pull out her teeth. She put her teeth in a glass of water. The teeth smiled in the water. When Gramma closed her lips she looked like a goat.

Gramma had to laugh at the way Free stared at her. "Yes, sonny boy, my teeth are like the stars, they come out every night."

Ma caught hold of Everett and took him into Sherm's bedroom. She made him get down on his knees beside the pot. But he wouldn't pee until Free and then Sherm did it in the pot a little bit first.

Gramma went over and felt of Free's underwear where it was drying over a chair. "Aha. Dry enough for you to wear in bed tonight."

"Just a minute," Ma said. "I brought along his nightgown."

Sherm and Everett and Free got down on their knees beside the bed. Sherm prayed and then Everett prayed.

"Well, Free, how about you?"

"Ma, is Grampa the same thing as God the Father?"

"Why, for heavensakes, no. Whatever made you ask that?"

"Well, he looks like Him in those pictures we got at home."

"No, God is above Grampa, and much stronger."

"Then God never gets a tumor in his stomach?"

"Boy, what kind of a question is that?"

Sherm got up off the floor. "Yeh, he asks you the shirt off your behind if you ain't careful."

"Pray, Free."

Free folded his hands on the bed and closed his eyes. "Now I lay me down to sleep, pray the Lord my soul to keep. And Father God, tonight go into Grampa's room and take his tumor away while he's sound asleep and throw it into hell. Then tomorrow Grampa can get up and play ball with us and be just fine. For Jesus' sake. Amen."

"Good gracious," Ma said.

Gramma, standing behind them, started to cry.

Ma shook her head. "All right, Free, get in bed. Such a prayer."

"God might just listen to that one," Sherm said. "And that'd be all right by me."

Ma shook her head some more as she tucked them in. Then she picked up the night lamp and shooing Gramma out ahead of her left them in the dark.

Free could hear the grown-ups going to bed. Grampa and Gramma were in the next room. Gramma kept grumbling around for a long time, and was bouncing kind of mad on the bedsprings, until Grampa finally roared up hoarse. "Woman, forbear. Please!"

Sherm began to play tricks in the dark, so Free had to keep his eyes open. Once Sherm let a little one, real soft in his hand, then quick closed his hand over it and in the dark put his hand over Free's nose.

"Peuu!" Free exploded. "Your insides smell like an old haymow."

Sherm laughed. "That's how you smelled coming out of that schoolhouse this afternoon."

"He who first notices dirt has it himself in his shirt."

"Say, that's a pretty good comeback. I'm gonna use that on John sometime. He's always claiming I'm the first to let one."

Free's eyes got used to the dark. Pretty soon he made out a picture of a train on a calendar hanging on the closet door. The engine was coming fast, smoke pouring out. Sometimes when Free let his eyes close a little bit, the boiling smoke looked like the pompadour of a lady. The headlight of the steamer became her nose. The picture went back and forth in his eyes, first being a flying train and then a dressed-up lady.

Everett began to snore like a fat little pig. Sherm snored some too.

Free saw the dressed-up lady more times than he saw the flying train. He began to make up stories about the lady. As he fell asleep she changed back into a train.

The next morning, right in the middle of all the bustling around to get ready to go to the photographer, Aunt Joan showed up. Ma and Aunt Joan hugged each other. Pa smacked Aunt Joan on the neck. Aunt Joan was kissing all over the place.

Everett kept looking at Aunt Joan's head in a funny way. Pretty soon he got down on his hands and knees and looked under her dress.

"God goodness gracious sakes," Aunt Joan cried, catching up her dress tight around her behind, "what's that boy of yours up to, Ada?"

Ma didn't know. She shooed Everett away.

Free knew. "He's looking to see if Aunt Joan's still got her pants on."

"Me got my pants on?" Aunt Joan cried. "Whatever . . . oh." Aunt Joan turned red. She looked like a great big radish.

Uncle John laughed right out loud. Gramma threw her apron up over her eyes. Grampa just looked. He didn't say anything.

At ten o'clock Pa and Uncle John carried Grampa out to Pa's car. They carried him like they were firemen. He hardly weighed more than a pheasant, Uncle John said. They all got in, everybody sitting on everybody's lap. Aunt Joan kept squealing all the time.

Pa drove over to the Badger's Art Photography Shop, and then once again Pa and Uncle John carried Grampa. They set him down inside on a leather bench.

Grampa puffed from all the commotion. The collar of his fried shirt hung loose on him and his bow tie wouldn't stay level. Grampa's moustache was combed just like his hair. He had the same hair growing under his chin down to his neck.

Mr. Badger wore garters around his arms above the elbows instead of around his legs above the knees. He ordered everybody in place.

"Why do we have to take this picture?" Sherm kept saying. "I don't think Pa is that sick."

Free began to wonder what it was that made people die when somebody was going to take their picture.

Mr. Badger hid his head under a black rag. He held up a toy bird in one hand and a rubber pinch bulb in the other hand. "Look at the birdie, folks. Please settle down now and look at the birdie." Mr. Badger waited a second. "And you there, Sherman, smile, will you please?"

Sherm gave him a look. "Maybe if your birdie could fly I might smile."

Free hated it too when people tried to get him to smile when he didn't feel like it. Free didn't like the place.

Finally the family settled down and Mr. Badger took a lot of pictures. Grampa sat in all of them. He sat with his hands together like he'd just got through clapping.

Then it was Free's and Everett's turn.

"Me?" Free cried. "And Everett?"

"Sure. We won't get another chance like this again," Pa said.

Free got scared. "But I don't wanna die."

Ma laughed. She put her arms around Free and then pushed him along. "Go on, stand over there where Mr. Badger wants you."

Free leaned back. "But I don't wanna."

"Free," Pa barked. "Get over there. March!"

Ma said, "Look, Everett is willing."

"Yeh," Free said, "he don't know no better."

Pa stomped his foot. "Get!"

Free went over and stood beside Everett. So that was why Ma'd taken his new blue suit along and had him put it on that morning. Everett had put on his new black velveteen outfit with pearl button shoes. Free looked mad.

Pa stomped his foot again. "Don't you get your bristles up now."

Ma shook her head. "Free is bound not to smile. See what a face he pulls."

Mr. Badger finally couldn't wait any longer for Free to smile, so he pinched the bulb in his hand. Click. He came out from under his black rag. "Well, folks, that's it. I'll send you the proofs as soon as they're done."

They all rode back to Grampa's house in Pa's car. Pa parked the Overland under Grampa's giant cottonwood. The giant's yellow leaves were falling down like gold money on the lawn everywhere. Grampa held both his hands over his belly when Pa and Uncle John carried him inside. Aunt Joan bawled to see the sight. Ma watched and only looked sad.

Gramma quick threw together a meal so Pa and Ma and kids could have a bite before they started for home. The womenfolk got the table set so quick Free and Sherm didn't get a chance to play some more catch.

This time the fried potatoes were awful. Free pushed the suet-stiff potatoes to one corner of his plate.

"Ma," Free asked, "can I have a slice of rye bread with butter and some sugar sprinkled on it?"

Pa took a look at Free's plate. "You better finish your potatoes first, boy. So long as there's a single starving heathen somewhere on earth we don't like to see food left on a plate."

"No."

"Eat your potatoes and then you'll get your rye bread."

"No." Free could feel everybody looking at him, even Grampa. "They're liable to give me a tumor too."

"What!"

Ma gave Free one of her better-do-it smiles. "Free, you can easy eat that. The rest of us did."

"No."

"What!" Pa cried again. Free could tell that if they hadn't been with company Pa would have given him a crack over the ears by then.

Gramma shamed a finger at Free. "What? You won't eat the potatoes that your Gramma's specially made for you?"

"No."

"Now, Free," Ma said, "you better hurry and eat them or Grampa will get after you."

Free looked at Grampa. Grampa was beginning to look a little mad all right. Grampa was sipping slow at his broth.

Ma said, "Look at Everett. He's eaten all of his. And now he can have his slice of rye bread with butter and sugar on it."

"Huh. Everett don't know no better."

Pa took Free by the ear and began to twist it. "H-a-a? Will you eat your potatoes now or not? H-a-a?"

So his ear wouldn't come off Free had to raise up off his chair and tip back his head as far as he could.

Uncle John had to laugh. He was kind of laughing at Pa. "Say, that little uncle-sayer of mine has sure got a lot of gravel in his gizzard."

"Yeh," Pa said, "and he's also going to have some greasy potatoes in his gizzard if he knows what's good for him."

Gramma gave Pa a brooder hen look. "Alfred, that's mean, twisting his ear like that. First thing you know, you'll make him deaf."

Pa let up then. They were with company.

Ma tried her special smile again. "Be a good boy and eat up your potatoes."

"No."

"What!"

This time it was Grampa who'd let out a warning sound with his hoarse voice. He put both hands on the table and slowly got up. He got taller and taller. Standing up made him puff. Everybody ducked down a little. Even Pa. Grampa stared at Free to eye him down.

Free stared back at Grampa.

The clock ticked loud. The kettle on the stove cracked.

Free began to feel sorry for Grampa. Grampa was going to die. So Free decided to uncle under. He looked down at his plate. He forked up one of the suet-stiff potatoes. Bllillick.

"That's better," Grampa said, and slowly sat down again.

Free ate his potatoes. Every last bit of them. They all went down crossways. He could feel them sitting there plugging up the works.

As soon as Free had cleaned his plate, Pa smeared him a slice of rye bread with butter and sugar on it.

At three o'clock they were all loaded in the car, Pa and Ma up front, and Free and Everett and a pailful of diapers in back.

"Sorry we got to hurry," Pa said. "But we got a long way to go and I don't like to drive after dark. And the law won't let us drive faster than eight miles an hour through towns either."

"What's the fastest you've ever gone with her?" Uncle John wanted to know.

"Twenty-five once."

"Yes, and that was way too fast for me," Ma said.

Pa laughed. "Yeh, between the law and Ada here, we don't drive very fast."

Pa let out the clutch and they backed past the giant cottonwood tree. They waved good-bye to Grampa looking out of the window. Gramma had come out to the car and she was crying worse than Aunt Joan. Sherm looked cocky tough and hardly waved good-bye. Uncle John pretended he was going to stand on his head, then pretended he couldn't quite make it. Pa shifted gears, and waving once more they rolled down the alley.

They rattled past the cemetery.

Ma looked at all the gravestones shining in the low sun. She shook her head. "I'm afraid I won't see my father alive again."

Pa said, "Yeh, he's getting pretty long in the tooth all right."

The rest of the way home Free and Everett huddled together under the buffalo robe on the back seat. Soon they fell asleep. The diaper pail didn't tip over once.

Ada ❦ 5

JUST BEFORE THANKSGIVING DAY, Neighbor Stickney dropped by to say that they'd had a telephone call from Gramma's town. Grampa was failing fast now and could Ada please come? Grampa wanted to see his daughter yet one last time.

Ada took the Cannonball at 4:14 in the afternoon. It was a lonely ride. The passenger car kept bumping and jerking along. The brown varnished interior smelled of old sour cigars. The windows were streaked with soot and cinders.

Pa'd had so little pleasure from Ma. Poor peevish Ma. Couldn't she see that she was driving Pa into an early grave with all her balky behavior, begrudging him even light broth? As if Ma could decide in her mouth what he liked.

"If I wasn't a Christian," Ada sighed, "I'd hate her to death."

Brother John was at the depot when she arrived.

Ada stepped down off the train. "How's Pa?"
"Just barely alive. He says he's gonna hang on until you get there."
"Poor Pa."
"Yeh."
They walked home in silence. They walked close together.
The moment Ada entered the kitchen she again became aware of Ma's sorry cooking. The smell of Ma's fried foods was enough to make anyone short of breath. It was as though, mad because she couldn't be a queen somewhere on earth, she'd then taken it out on her family through her cooking.
"Where's Ma?" Ada asked.
"Probably out in the privy," John said. "She spends a lot of time there when things get tight around here."
Ada took off her hat and went directly to the folks' bedroom.
She found Pa awake. His head lay slack on his pillow. A good heartbeat pulsed up regularly past his Adam's apple.
"Pa?"
"Thank God," Pa whispered. His eyes fastened on her. "One last time. The only one who ever appreciated all I had to go through."
Ada fell on her knees beside his bed. "Pa." She saw that his once strong body was now hardly more than a gunnysack of bones.
Pa's bone hand found the top of her head. "Now I can die in peace."
Suddenly there was an angry screeching behind Ada. It was Ma, mad. "Yes, look at him, look at him, there he lies now, Baron Engleking, the great man, emptier of privies, who's going to desert us now by escaping off to heaven. He thinks. Hah. God may have other ideas about that!"
Ada came up off her knees in one motion. Her heart beat violently at the root of her tongue. "What an awful thing to say of your dying husband." It struck Ada, much as she hated to think it, that Ma was jealous of how much Pa liked his daughter. How many times in the past hadn't Ma criticized her for the way she walked, when Pa already thought she walked like a lady. Pa had once said that his daughter's bearing was that of a true Frisian woman.
Ma made a funny sound, then tipped sideways and fell with an awful thump on the floor.
John came running in. "In God's name . . . Oh. I thought maybe Pa'd fallen out of bed." John sighed relieved. Then he reached down and rolled Ma over on her back. "One of her fainting spells again I see."
Pa gasped up out of his pillow. "Keep her hands open. She comes out of it faster that way."
"Pa," Ada said with a sob, "that you should still think of Ma's welfare."
"I always meant to be a loving Christian husband," Pa said. "Though she sometimes made it hard for me to be that."
There was a shudder in Ma's huge body. She came to as suddenly as she'd passed out. With John helping her, she got to her feet. She pulled her dress and corset down. "No one will ever know what I've had to suffer all these years liv-

ing in a crazy wilderness with a husband who didn't have a red cent to his name."

Pa said nothing.

Ada thought to herself: "Pa's face is so pale. How can a man become so thin and yellow, and still be alive?" Ada thought: "My darling father, how I love thee, how I love thee. Yet, God's will be done. I rest assured that our Father in heaven wants you with him in salvation because you are as precious to Him as you are to us."

Sherm entered in his nightshirt. His young boy legs shone pale. "Free didn't come?"

Ada loved her youngest brother very much for the doughty way he resisted the bad. She said gently, "Everett needs somebody to play with too, Sherman."

"Can Everett use his left arm much?"

"A little. As that burn scar gets smaller his arm seems to get freer."

"Good. Because otherwise it wouldn't be much fun playing with a one-armed brother."

Ada looked at Pa again. His blue eyes sucked at her as though to take her very face with him into glory. "Are you able to keep any food down at all, Pa?"

John said, "Pa can't even stand the mention of food around him."

"When's the last time Pa had anything to eat then?"

"He had some of my special soup two days ago," Ma said defiantly.

Ada took Pa's hand. His bony fingers were cold, as if he'd been outdoors without his mittens on. "Would you eat some light broth if I made it for you?"

Ma's bosom heaved in a rage. "What's wrong with my making him some?"

Pa let his eyes close. His eyebrows stuck out like puffs of cotton.

Ada stood up. "Well then, if Pa won't take any nourishment, I don't think we should all be in his room at the same time. It's too close in here already. Even I have trouble breathing. Out, everybody." She waved her hands shooing them ahead of her. "And, now that I am here, I'll sit by him the first part of the night."

Ma drew herself up in billowy majesty against Ada. "And where do you propose his wife should sleep?"

Ada was furious. "Do you mean to say you've been sleeping in here every night with this dying man, you with all your grumbling and your growling around all the time?"

"Yeh," Sherm said, "what about that, Ma?"

"Where else but by the side of my husband, who needs me most now in the hour of his greatest need?"

Ada shook her head. "Ma, Ma, you should've got that cot down from upstairs and slept on that in the living room there. And not in here bothering this poor man with all your . . . your getting in and out of bed."

"Yeh," John said, "that's what I say too. In fact, I'm going to get that cot down right now." John, with Sherm helping, immediately went upstairs and brought the cot down.

The house finally settled down. Ma, pruttling, did lie down on the cot just outside the door. John and Sherm went to bed in their own room, leaving the door open so Ada could quick call them if need be.

Ada turned down the night lamp. She sat facing her father.

A wind roughed up the trees outside.

Pa drifted off. It wasn't really sleep. He was mostly just a heart beating and a pair of lungs sucking air.

After a while Ada's eye was caught by a black-trimmed print hanging on the wall above Pa's bed. It pictured the persecution of Christians in the ancient Roman Colosseum. She recalled it was one of Pa's favorites. It was called *The Last Prayer* and it showed some hundred kneeling Christian martyrs about to be devoured by starved lions. One Christian was standing at the edge of the huddled group, face lifted to heaven, praying while thousands of spectators up in the stands jeered and mocked him. Ada thought she knew why Pa liked that picture.

Pa awoke at midnight. His long gray eyelashes opened wide under sharp white brows. His eyes slowly centered into small dark blue dots. "Well well," he whispered, surprised, "I see I'm still here."

Ada gave him an angel's smile.

"Such strange dreams I had," he whispered. "Thoughts. I dreamt about that old cottonwood I planned to cut down this winter. For firewood. But now of course I can't. And then I dreamt about a wild boat ride across the Dollart. With my pa and ma. And my two brothers and a sister. Oh, such a storm it was. Waves, oh! With soldiers chasing after us in another boat and shouting and shooting at us. Those dreams were like real tastes in my mouth."

"Yes, Pa."

"It was all so true-like."

"Shh now, Pa. Go to sleep."

John took up the watch at one.

Pa was still alive the next morning when Ada awoke. Despite black looks from Ma, Ada made some beef broth and brought it to Pa.

At the smell of the steaming broth Pa gave Ada a wonderful look. His thin nostrils moved a little. The yellow in his cheeks pinkened some. He even managed to slide up on his pillow a couple of inches.

But when she held the silver spoon to his lips as she might to a baby, he drew back. "Not with a spoon," he whispered. "I can't stand the touch of silver on my lips anymore."

"You mean on your teeth, don't you?"

"No, daughter, my lips. Anything metal makes my lips feel like a raw nerve." His breathing almost stopped. "The pain of that thing in my stomach reaches all the way up to my lips."

"But how will we get you to take it then?"

His eyes fell shut. It was as though the catch to a window blind had let go for a moment. The cracked lips under his brown moustache mused to themselves. Then he opened his eyes. "With a feather."

"A feather?"

"Get a goose feather. I should love to have broth put on my lips with a goose feather."

Ma stood listening in the doorway. "And where does the baron of the Engle-king kingdom think he may find such a luxury?"

"There's an extra sack of goose feathers up in the attic," Pa said. "For tick-ing. Get one."

Ma set her hands on her hips. "Those are chicken feathers. I used up all the goose feathers."

"Get a chicken feather then," Pa whispered, resigned.

Ada remembered where Ma kept the sack. She selected one of the larger chick-en feathers. She rinsed it in warm water. Again she sat beside Pa and took up the bowl of broth.

She feathered up a drop of the dark broth and deftly reached it under his brown moustache and wetted his lips with it.

Pa's yellow-coated tongue came out and licked it up. "Ah."

Slowly, patiently, Ada feathered up drop after drop of the broth.

There was a sound of someone sawing wood outdoors. Pa heard it. "Is that John cutting down the cottonwood?"

Ada went to look. "Yes. And Sherman's helping him."

Pa sighed out of his flat body. "John and I were going to do that together."

"Yes, Father."

Pa took a few more feathers of nourishment.

Later, Ada remarked to Ma, "I find it strange that Reverend Carpenter hasn't called on Pa in his last extremity."

"Oh, Domeny's been here," Ma said. "But he comes reluctantly, I fear."

"But why?"

"I think it's because he's a little afraid of this man of mine. Because this man of mine will make no complaint to him about his lot in life. His pain. Just as Job's friends were afraid of him."

"Oh, Ma, I find that hard to believe."

"No, Ada, I think Domeny is afraid of Pa's willpower." Ma spoke with some pride. pride.

Ada shook her head. Ma was sure a ball of stubborn contrary knots.

Ma went on. "That it is not of this earth."

"Well, and there's another thing," Ada said. "I can't help wondering why on earth the doctor didn't operate."

"It was already too late when the doctor decided it was cancer."

"They operated on you once for gallstones."

"Yes, and without ether too. Which they didn't have then." Ma began to weep that old pain all over again. "What I've suffered through, oh, oh."

Ada was sorry she'd brought it up.

"Yes, yes," Ma lamented, "but nobody wants to remember that."

Ada got up and gently pushed her mother out of the bedroom.

Pa napped. After a while more color returned to his cheeks.

At noon John and Sherm came in with big rosy cheeks, hungry as wolves. They peeked in to see how Pa was.

John said, "Say, Pa, you're looking better."

"That's what I think too," Ada said.

Pa's brown moustache moved. "How's the tree coming?"

"She's about ready to drop, Pa. I've got the undercut just about right to drop her down the alley past the barn."

"Good boy."

"So if you hear a big crack sometime this afternoon, and the house shakes, you'll know what it is."

A sly smile curved at the corners of Sherm's lips. "And if you hear a scream it'll be Old Lady Kolder caught under it in her privy."

The rosy vigor of his sons sharpened Pa. His eyes brightened. "Sorry I'm not of much help, boys."

"Oh, that's all right," John said. "We're lucky it's vacation time so Sherm can help me."

As the boys talked the thought shot through Ada's mind that when the old cottonwood tree finally dropped Pa's heart would stop too.

While the boys ate a lusty dinner, Ada fed Pa some more beef broth with the chicken feather. Afterwards John read a chapter from the Bible, the first chapter from Revelations, and then gave a short prayer of thanks. Pa followed the family worship from the bedroom, door open.

It was exactly three o'clock when there was first a vast rushing sound, and then the great cottonwood tree hit the earth with a crushing smash, followed by little cracking sounds as branches flew everywhere.

Ada first made sure Pa's heart hadn't stopped. Then she went to look. From the kitchen window she could see the cottonwood lying directly south down the alley. It had just missed the barn on one side and Mrs. Kolder's privy on the other. The fallen tree lay all sprawled out like some calamity in a nightmare.

"Well," she thought to herself, "at least that premonition was wrong."

After supper, John was full of glee. The cottonwood had dropped exactly where he'd wanted it to land. "To within the inch," he told Pa.

Pa smiled. "Yes, John, you will do."

The next day Pa looked so much better that it was decided Ada could go home again for a short while. She was needed at home too.

Ada sorrowed for her father all through that winter. Blizzards came. Sometimes she and Alfred were cut off from news for days. Ada worried that Pa might die during one of those storms he'd feared so much. She could hardly go to his funeral if they were snowbound.

Twice she caught a ride in a neighbor's bobsled to Bonnie and called Reverend Carpenter long distance and asked him to go get John to the phone. Pa wouldn't have a contraption like a telephone in the house. John told her that Pa hadn't gotten any worse, that he was hanging on, that the doctor couldn't understand how he could stay alive on so little nourishment.

"Reverend Carpenter visits him regularly now," John said.

"That's good."

"Domeny says it's one of the miracles of God, that he now knows he must be a witness to it."

On the ninth of March, at noon, the call came. Stickney came riding over to tell Ada. "Your pa has only hours left."

Ada caught the 4:14.

But it was too late. Pa died while she was changing trains in Maurice.

Ada had to hold her chest as John told her about it. She was standing in Ma's kitchen. She was sure for a couple of minutes she was going to drop dead herself and join Pa on his long flight to heaven, to salvation.

John himself had to hold his face in a hard square set to keep from breaking down. "Ade, he absolutely refused to use morphine at the end there. Just wouldn't take that pain-killer. Said that God intended for him to endure it naturally, that he was not going to shirk the burden God had placed upon him. Fact is, Ade, I think that the pain got to be so great at the end there that his nerves burnt out and he couldn't feel it anymore."

Sherm spoke up. He'd come silently upon them as they talked in whispers. His lips were drawn back in a boy's white snarl. "Yeh, we pop out of the womb, we eat, we shit, sometimes fart, we cut down a tree, we pop back into the womb."

Ada was scandalized. "Sherman! That's blasphemy. God will strike you dead for saying things like that."

Free ❦ 6

PA GOT THEM out of bed at six in the morning, had breakfast with them, lighted the Overland's carbide lights, and with his eyes blazing in the dark like an extra pair of carbide lights, drove like the wind all the way to Gramma's so as to be on time for the funeral. Free and Everett sat in front.

As they entered the alley, Free right away noticed that the morning sky around Grampa's place looked funny. It was like the top of an egg had been sliced off. The giant cottonwood tree was gone. Grampa and the tree had both died of the rot cancer.

Pa turned in beside Grampa's barn and then Free knew what Uncle John had done with the cottonwood. There was a pile of wood near the barn as high as a hill. When Free looked at where the tree had stood he saw the flat top of a stump that was wider than Ma's dining room table.

Pa shut off the motor. He looked at his watch. Just as he did so, the big courthouse clock struck nine. Pa nodded. "Right on the dot." He put his watch away. "All right, kids, out with you."

Gramma sat by the window where Grampa was supposed to sit. She saw them. She started to cry.

Ma opened the door for them. She picked Free up and gave him a tight hug and kissed him. She wasn't crying. She next picked up Everett. "Why, Everett, you're dry. What a good boy you've become."

Pa said, "Yep, I laid down the law to him. Told him I was too busy to be cleaning him up all the time. That he just better run around with wet pants if that was his mind."

Gramma got up out of Grampa's chair. She swallowed a couple of times in the middle of her crying. She was getting mad at Pa again for being mean to her grandchildren.

Uncle John and Uncle Sherm were all dressed up in their Sunday suits. Their eyebrows looked extra white. They sat in their chairs and didn't say a thing. Uncle John had a big red bump on the back of his neck just above his collar. When Free asked him what it was, Uncle John said it was a dried-up carbuncle. It had a lot of holes in it where the boils had popped out.

Aunt Joan was busy polishing the stove black. She kept dropping tears on the still warm stove lids and then they fried up into little puffs of steam. The tears made little spots on the stove and she had to black them over again.

"Come," Ma said, "we've laid him out in the parlor." Ma took Free by the hand. Pa took Everett. Gramma followed them.

There was a long black-and-silver box in the parlor. The lid was open. The lid was thick with puffed-out silver silk. Free had to stand on Grampa's footstool to look in. Pa took Everett up on his hip.

Grampa lay sound asleep on some more puffed-out silver silk.

"Take a good long look, Free," Ma said, soft. "Because once the company comes you won't get a chance to see him again."

Grampa's hands were folded. His fingers were so thin they looked like they'd been left in water overnight. Grampa had on his serge suit and black bow tie just like that time they took his picture. His neck was even thinner. His moustache was better trimmed. His eyelids were like they'd been stuck together with flour paste. His eyebrows looked like white cotton. His cheeks were painted red a little like Pa said a woman's shouldn't be. Grampa didn't move an inch.

Gramma couldn't stand them looking at Grampa. "Yes, yes, my grandsons, there he lies now, the mortal remains of your noble grandfather, while his immortal soul has flown off to heaven, where he lives with his Maker in salvation forever."

Pa's eyes half closed. "Yes, he was a great man. I'll miss him. As someone to look up to."

Gramma cried. "Och, no one will ever understand the life I had with that man. So deep, he could write Domeny's sermons for him. Och, och, to think he's gone forever." Gramma shook to herself. "But then, all his troubles are over. By now he's already singing psalms in heaven with all the rest of God's angels."

Free could see that Gramma was one of those grammas who had to fight with you while you were alive and cry over you when you were dead. But Gramma was all right with little children.

Everett asked, "When Grampa gets through singing his psalms in heaven, can he have ice cream then?"

Gramma almost fainted. "What a rare question."

Pa and Ma looked at each other and smiled a little bit.

Pretty soon the people came. Free and Everett sat with Pa and Ma in the back of Gramma's bedroom, where they couldn't see anything. There were so many people there that many had to stand outside on the frozen lawn.

Free could just barely hear the domeny. Reverend Carpenter said Grampa's life was an open book of Christian example. It was a book that all could read. Pretty soon the domeny read from the Bible. Job didn't complain either, even when his friends said he should. Then Domeny prayed Grampa into heaven.

The grown-ups took Grampa in his coffin to church. There the domeny said the same thing over again to the same people, only it took him a lot longer. Church was plumb full.

Then the grown-ups closed the coffin and took Grampa out to the cemetery. They put the coffin on some straps over a deep grave. The grave was wide enough for a four-holer privy. There Domeny talked and prayed a little, just a few words in farewell. Four men turned little crank handles and the coffin with Grampa in it sank into the grave. Domeny grabbed up a handful of dirt and threw it in after the coffin. Then Pa led them all back to the Overland.

A lot of people stopped by Gramma's house again and had coffee and cake and celebrated. Gramma was excited. Sometimes she laughed and sometimes she cried. She let some people kiss her.

Ma and Pa, and Uncle John and Aunt Joan, didn't say much. Sherm sat mad behind the stove through it all.

Free helped himself to seconds on the dark cake. Nobody was watching, so he could. Cake was the only thing Gramma made that was any good. She knew how to do that. She put in a lot of raisins and prunes and brown sugar and some kind of slippery stuff the color of dark cistern water that you could just see through. Everett kept sneaking a finger of butter and putting it on a corner of his piece of cake and then biting off the corner. Free finally decided to try a little butter too. It was good. Free and Everett ate cake until their bellies were about to bust.

At four o'clock Ma at last had to say good-bye. Gramma gave Ma a little package to take home. Pa shook hands all around Free and Everett had to kiss Gramma four times. They all climbed into the car and Uncle John cranked the car and then Pa backed into the alley and they took off.

When they got home Ma opened the little package Gramma gave her. It had two things in it: a picture of lions ready to eat Christians and Grampa's silver tobacco box.

Ma right away got a hammer and nail and hung the picture of the lions and the Christians over Pa and Ma's bed.

The tobacco box was for Pa. Pa played around with the silver box in his hands for a while. He smelled in it a couple of times. It was all gold inside.

"Tell you what, Ada," Pa said. "This tobacco box is too good to carry around on the yard. I can easy lose it bending over. I'll use it only to church."

Ma liked that. She gave Pa a kiss on the nose.

Free ❦ 7

AUNT KAREN VISITED in August. She was going to teach school on the corner. She arrived early to clean up the school before the pupils came. Later she was going to room and board with the neighbors.

Ma didn't feel well about then, and to get Free out of the house Aunt Karen took him with her to the big cottonwood on the northwest corner of the grove. It was cool under the high green leaves.

Aunt Karen found a nice spot of short grass by the fence. Like Rover sometimes did, she turned around twice before settling down. She got out her tatting and began to make doilies.

Free walked around the cottonwood a couple of times. He measured it with his arms. It wasn't nearly as big as Grampa's giant tree. He examined it on the north side to see if it had the rot cancer. He even poked in between the cracks in the rough bark with a piece of rusty barbed wire. But so far as he could tell the cottonwood was all right. Good.

Free spotted some red ants running up the cottonwood trunk. He watched where they ran. They went out of sight up into the green leaves. He wondered what they were looking for up there. Pretty soon he spotted some of the red ants coming down again. They were all carrying what looked like a tiny drop of white syrup. Free wondered if it was sweet. But he didn't dare rob the red ants because of their stingers. Free followed the ants carrying their white drops into the grass. They ran along a kind of a road. The road went through some tall grass and then across a bare spot of dirt and then over some twigs and finally, there near the fence post, right behind Aunt Karen's sitter, was a heaved-up piece of ground that was full of boil holes. The red ants went in and out of the holes. Some of the ants in the anthill came out to help the other ants carry in their little drops of white syrup.

"What are you doing there?"

Free had forgotten all about Aunt Karen. She was looking at him over her tatting. "Nothing."

"Crawling around on your hands and knees like that. It's no wonder your overalls are always worn out at the knee." Aunt Karen held her head over to one side so that her red hair hung down a little. Her eyes were like green glass and blinked a couple of times. "What were you following there in the grass?"

"Just a red ant."

Aunt Karen began to smile pretty. "What was the ant doing?"

"He came down out of that tree carrying a drop of white syrup."

"Tree sap. Gathered from a tree tip. Food for next winter."

"You mean he got that from way up there at the tippy top of the tree?" Free leaned back in the grass and stared up at the top of the tree. "That high up?"

"Yes, Free. The ant is a wise creature. It knows enough to get in its food when the weather's warm. Because when it gets cold it can't move on the snow. In the winter it lives deep in its home there under that anthill, where it's warm, and lives off the food it has stored in its underground pantries."

Free stared at the anthill a while. So that was it. They lived like people did.

Still smiling pretty, Aunt Karen went back to her tatting.

Free lay on his back in the grass looking up at the tree. He lay with his head cupped in his hands, legs crossed at the knee. The treetop moved back and forth in the light breeze. The leaves rattled against each other like a lot of little leather mittens. The top leaves were so high they were almost blue. "Aunt Karen, if I was to climb that cottonwood way to the top, like Jack did that beanstalk, could I see the angel country?"

Aunt Karen breathed funny. "Why, whatever made you think of that?"

"Well, Ma says Grampa is up in heaven now with the angels, and I'd like to see what he's doing there."

Aunt Karen didn't say anything for a while. She just sat there in the grass and tatted.

Free dreamed that he could easy fly up there. There had to be some way of doing it like he sometimes flew around in his dreams.

"What a strange boy you are."

Free crossed his legs the other way.

"Whatever is to become of you, Free?"

"I dunno."

"Farmer like your father? Teacher like me? Or a preacher like your domeny?"

"Pa says he wants to be the best there is."

Aunt Karen tatted a while. "Well, me, I wish I could have been a really good poet. Not just a rhymer of pretty words." Aunt Karen had written a little green book full of poems. Free had heard her read some of them to Pa and Ma one evening. Ma thought the green poems were sweet. Pa didn't have much to say, except that once, when Aunt Karen read about Grampa Alfredson in one of the poems, he took his pipe out of his mouth and said, "Pah." Aunt Karen tatted some more. She waved a fly away. "Yes, like Elizabeth Barrett."

"What's the best thing to be?"

"Why, a poet, of course."

"Better than being a general?"

"Yes. Nobler even than being a President."

"Then that's what I'll be someday. A poet. Because I want to be like my pa. Be the best there is."

That winter Free and Everett got a toy train for Christmas, a black engine and a coal car, four green passenger cars, with tracks, a green depot, and a brown grain elevator. You had to wind up the engine like a clock and then it would go around the track just about four times by itself. Pa bought it as a surprise. It was a real train, not just a block train.

Pa played train so much with his boys that Ma had to laugh. "I think you bought it as much for yourself as for them," Ma said.

Free ❦ 8

THE NEXT WINTER Mr. Alvord, the landlord, told Pa that his daughter was getting married and that she wanted the farm. So Pa had to look for a new place to rent.

Pa finally found a farm in the same section where he and Ma had first lived. It was kitty-corner across from the Windmillers. People called it the Bowman farm and Pa said it had good buildings and tight fences. The house was fairly neat, Pa said, but since Ma would want to repaper it anyway he hadn't looked too close at that.

Ma was real tired because she had a heavy belly. She wished she didn't have to move again. She'd just got the Alvord house fixed up the way she wanted it, and now all of a sudden all that work was for nothing. But, the Lord's will.

Uncle John got married to Aunt Matilda about that time. They couldn't move onto their own new place until the middle of March, so they helped Pa and Ma move. Aunt Matilda was the sister of that Lew Westraw who'd shocked grain for Pa. Aunt Matilda wasn't jokey like her brother Lew was, but she sure knew how to laugh. She'd always pretend to be mad at first and then would give up and laugh and laugh.

Pa and Uncle John first moved the machinery and the barnyard stuff, all in one day. The next day they moved the household goods and the kids. On the last load Pa drove the Overland over on the frozen rutted roads.

Just in time too. That weekend a blizzard came whistling in from the northwest and in two days changed the whole world. While the storm lasted, all Pa and Uncle John could do was milk the cows and sit by the stove and wait. They all mostly sat in the kitchen because Pa decided it was no use putting up the hard-coal burner anymore that year.

Sometimes Uncle John had to be alone with Aunt Matilda. He took her into the cold parlor where the furniture was standing any which way. That was all right because sometimes Pa had to be alone with Ma in the bedroom too. But what Free didn't like was the way Aunt Matilda would squeal in the parlor. She'd yell, "You cut that out, John!" Then Free would get mad at Uncle John. He felt sorry for Aunt Matilda and he wanted to help her. Free would try to get into the parlor. But Uncle John was too clever for him. Uncle John would lock the door by hooking the top of a chair under the knob on the other side. When Uncle John heard Free jiggling the doorknob and bumping against the door with his hip, he would tease Aunt Matilda all the harder and she would holler like anything.

Free banged some more on the door. "You leave Aunt Matilda alone in there or I'll get you, you hear?"

Pa had to laugh in his armchair by the stove reservoir. "Look at that kid, would you? At his age he's already acting like a boss stud."

Ma said, "Please, such talk I don't like in my house."

All of a sudden Uncle John jerked open the door and leaned mad down at Free. "Will you quit banging on our door and keeping us awake?"

Free ducked down.

Uncle John had to laugh. "Man, man, what a rare uncle-sayer you are." Then he picked Free up and gave him a big hug.

Free didn't like being mocked. He broke out of Uncle John's hug.

Aunt Matilda came to the door. She had a red smile.

When Uncle John saw that Free didn't take to his hugging, he started to pinch Aunt Matilda on her behind. "Ha? ha? How do you like that, ha, wife?" All the while he kept one eye on Free.

Free hit Uncle John a hard one in the belly.

"Hey, kid, why always hit me when I tease my wife? Why not hit your dad? He likes to tease your ma too sometimes."

"Because Pa don't pinch Ma in the behind like you do. All he does is kiss her once in a while."

"Kiss her once in a while? Why, that's even worse. That's one of the worst sins there is, according to our church."

Free didn't like it that Uncle John used domeny talk on him.

Then Aunt Matilda felt sorry for Free and she reached down and hugged him too. Free let her. She smelled a little like new yeast.

The storm went on and on. Pretty soon the grown-ups got around to playing games with the kids. The storm was like a long picnic.

Pa first played shot-out-of-a-canon with Free. Pa lay down on the rag rug by the stove and doubled his feet against his chest and held his hands flat open by his shoulders. Pa told Free to set his feet in his open hands and to lean his belly on the soles of his shoes.

"Ready?"

Laughter spilled out of Free. "Ready."

"You ready over there, John, to catch him?"

Uncle John quick sat down on the floor a little ways over. "Fire!"

Pa gave Free a tremendous push up with both his feet and his hands.

Free sailed across the kitchen. High. He shrilled. Ma and Aunt Matilda cried, "Goodness gracious me," at the same time. Then Free came down and Uncle John caught him by the chest.

"Do it again, Pa," Free cried, breaking out of Uncle John's hug and running back to Pa.

"Okay, boy. Climb onto the cannon again."

Laughing, almost fainting from the sheer joy of it, Free set his feet in Pa's big hands again and lay his belly on the soles of Pa's shoes.

"Ready? Go?"

"Fire!" Uncle John said.

With a hard grunt, Pa shot Free up in the air. Free almost hit the ceiling the second time. And when he came down Uncle John caught him by the chest again. What fun.

Everett ran over to Pa. "Me, too. Can I, Pa?"

"Sure, son."

"Did you hear that?" Ma said. "How clear Everett asked that?"

"I sure did," Pa said. "When he gets excited he seems to be more all there."

Pa shot Everett up in the air then too. Pa didn't shoot him up as high though. Everett didn't laugh wild like Free did either.

Pretty soon Pa and Uncle John got tired of playing shot-out-of-a-cannon. It made them puff.

Free said, "Don't you know any easier games then, Pa?"

"Boy, boy, when you get started, there's no end to it for you, is there?"

Uncle John said, "Free, did you ever see the dolls of Ingelân dance?"

"No." Free began to laugh already at what was coming next.

"Ade, you got an old underpants I can use?" Uncle John asked Ma. "In one of your old rag bags?"

Aunt Matilda didn't know if she was going to like that game. "You're not going to pretend to be a woman now, are you? I hope."

Free said, "I know where the rag bag is." He ran to get it.

Uncle John took the bag and emptied it out on the kitchen floor.

Ma shrieked when she saw all the stuff that came out. "Oh no."

Uncle John sorted through the tangle until he found what he wanted. He dressed up his left leg with a torn dusting cap on the foot, a ragged scarf around the ankle, and a ruptured corset down the calf and thigh. He dressed his right leg with a half-unraveled stocking cap on the foot, another ragged scarf around the ankle, and below that a holey little mackinaw that Free once wore.

"Now," Uncle John said, "watch."

Uncle John lay down on the floor and stuck his feet straight up in the air. His two legs looked exactly like a couple of beggars, a bum about to go out for a walk with his wife. Uncle John knicked his legs at the knee a little, and wiggled his feet, and then wiggled his toes. It really was a true couple.

"By golly," Pa said, "wife, now don't you go and give them two a handout."

Ma laughed. For once she enjoyed Pa's dig about her being too good-hearted.

Free and Everett took a seat on the floor in front of the dolls of Ingelân. Uncle John made the dolls bow to the audience, slow and extra solemn.

"Oh boy," Free cried, "this is going to be real comical."

Uncle John put the dolls through a pantomime of trying to kiss each other. They always just kept missing the mark.

Free laughed.

Next the dolls of Ingelân had a fight. They tusseled around with each other.

"Now let them make up."

The dolls fell over each other trying to give each other a kiss again.

"Now make the old man give her a pinch on her behind."

The man doll leaned way over and nibbled at her behind.

"Now make the old lady yell her head off."

The woman doll jerked up like she'd been jabbed by a fork.

"Now make the old man give her another smootchie."

Uncle John wiggled the toes of his right foot so as to make the man doll push his nose in under the woman doll's dusting cap.

Free rolled on the floor he laughed so hard.

"You better not let that boy laugh too much," Aunt Matilda warned, "or he'll go into hysterics."

Ma herself had to hold down her big stomach to keep from laughing too much. Pa had a smile as big as half a pan of pie.

When they'd all tired of the dolls of Ingelân, Uncle John thought of a game especially for Everett. After making sure Everett was dry, he lifted him up on his lap. "Close your eyes, boy."

Everett closed his eyes.

Uncle John tapped Everett gently on the forehead with a knuckle, "Knock on the door." Then he opened one of Everett's eyes with a finger and thumb, "Peek in." Then he twisted Everett's nose, "Turn the knob." Then he pried open Everett's mouth with two fingers and stepped inside with them. "Walk in." Then he took Everett by the chin and shook it, "Hello, Mr. Chinny Chin-Chin."

Everett smiled.

"Do it again," Free said.

"Hey," Uncle John said, "why for you?"

"Because it's fun for Everett."

"Good boy. That's the way to make the world go around."

When it was time to go to bed, Pa had one more thing to show them. He picked Everett up and set him on his lap. He took hold of Everett's hand and ticked off the fingers one by one:

" 'To bed, to bed,' says Thumb-a-ling.
'But first something to eat,' says Lick-the-pot.
'But where shall we get it?' says Long-a-ling.
'Out of Gramma's pantry,' says Ring-a-ling.
'That I'm gonna tell on,' says Little Thing."

Everett smiled better.

"There's another one for the foot," Ma said, reaching for Everett's pink toes where they peeked out from under his nightgown. She leaned over her big stomach and smiled as she sang a little song:

"Little toe tight,
Little penny white,
Little toe thistle,
Little penny whistle,
Winkum boy."

Everett laughed. Just a little bit.

Free hopped onto a chair and stuck out his toes for Ma to tick them off too.

Ma never finished. Free was so ticklish that Ma'd hardly touched his little toe and he stiffened and leaped off the chair. He looked exactly like he was going to get the fits.

Uncle John gave Ma a look. "Better not tickle that one too much."

"I guess not."

"Why not?" Pa asked.

"You can throw his nerves out of kilter," Uncle John said. "I seen it happen once. There was one like that back home. Everybody knew he was ticklish, and by golly, just to have a little selfish fun at his expense, if they didn't tickle him into insanity."

"Oh," Pa said.

Off to bed the kids went.

By the third morning the wind died down and the sun came up like a big gold watch. The sun shone into the kitchen so sharp it hurt the eyes. It was pretty outside. The trees were covered with thick hoarfrost. Pa and everybody felt a lot better at breakfast.

When Pa looked out of the pantry window on the north side he saw a big curving snowbank. The snowbank was level with the upstairs window and it had buried the privy. Pa said, "Wal, John, it looks like the womenfolks are gonna have to use the barn for their privy."

"Nosiree," Aunt Matilda said, sharp.

"Yes," Ma said, "and what are we going to do with all them full white owls."

"My pot runneth over," Uncle John said. "Surely, as I sit in the snowbank, a cold hind end shall follow me all the days of my life."

Aunt Matilda slapped Uncle John across the mouth. She did it before Ma could scold him. "That'll teach you not to blaspheme."

Uncle John turned red around the mouth. Still he could smile. He said to Free, "You see, it was really me that was always squealing in the parlor there, not her. You got after the wrong one. She was hurting me."

Pa said, "What we can do is dig us a temporary privy in the snowbank there, place a board in it, and go off from the board."

"Goodness gracious," Aunt Matilda said, "now I've heard everything."

Ma said, "But you still haven't told me what to do with my full white owls."

Pa said, "Wal, we'll just have to dig us another privy a little ways farther down for you to empty your waste in."

Free said, "Pa, can I go play outside on that snowbank?"

"Okay. But you better bundle up good. It's four below out there."

Soon the men were busy at it. Pa dug out the temporary room for their privy, Uncle John dug out the little room for the waste. The snowbank was as hard as ground. The men had to grunt to get out the big chunks of snow. It was so hard Free could walk over the snowbank without leaving any tracks. Pa got a two-by-twelve plank and fitted it into his little privy room. Then he tested it to make sure it wouldn't tip over on him. Free squatted on it too to try it. Without taking his pants down he knew it was going to be too cold for him to do number two out there. He would do that number in the barn with the men. But the poor women, they'd have to suffer through it. Just be quick about it, is all.

Uncle John helped Ma by emptying all the white owls for her.

Free helped him with their little pot. Free couldn't get over the awful color the mess left in the snow after it had soaked down into it.

"Yeh, boy," Uncle John said, "this is one time you really can say that though your sins be as scarlet throwing them in a snowbank ain't gonna make 'em white."

While Pa and Uncle John slopped the hogs and fed the fatteners hay by the cattle barn and spilled grain for Ma's white chickens, Free explored the strange new hills on the yard. The great snowbank had made the whole yard over. Some of the littler snowbanks had hoarfrost on them, and it made them so slippery he could slide down them like they'd been greased. He yelled and showed off in front of the kitchen window so Everett could see him.

Free's tumbling down the snowbanks finally brought him near the pump in front of the chicken house.

The black iron pump handle was covered with hoarfrost too. It looked like a sugar-coated stick of licorice.

Free couldn't resist it. He pulled down his shawl and leaned down to lick the frosted pumphandle.

His tongue stuck to the pump handle. He was tied to it.

He tried to pull free. He pulled hard enough to feel his tongue all the way back to its root. Yow. He eased up a little, only to find that more of his wet tongue became stuck to the frosted iron. Now what.

He stood absolutely still. He didn't dare shift his feet. He looked past his nose to see if he could make out the edge of where his tongue was stuck to the iron, crossing his eyes until they hurt in the corners.

"Ulll!" he uttered as loud as he could.

Silence on the yard. The men and the dog were in the barn.

Free peered sideways across the yard to the kitchen window to see if Ma or Aunt Matilda might not be looking out. But there was no pale face at the window. Not even Everett.

"Ulll." It hurt to call. The surface of his tongue tore a little along the edge.

He could feel his tongue beginning to freeze. If someone didn't come quick his tongue would freeze into a solid lump. Suppose they had to cut it off to get him free? He'd never be able to taste dark rye bread with sugar sprinkled on.

"Ulll!"

Suppose nobody saw him in time. Why the whole of him could freeze into an icicle, not just his tongue. Into a statue like the one in the courthouse in Rock Falls.

"Ulll!"

Then his lower lip became stuck, just a tiny edge of it. With an effort, trembling, he managed to draw the lip in enough to free it. Wow. If his whole mouth got stuck they'd have to cut off half of his face to free him.

A barn door cracked open.

"Ulll!"

"Hey, what's the matter there, boy?"

Thank God. Free couldn't see Pa because he didn't dare swivel his eyes that way. He didn't even dare wave for fear of ripping his tongue.

Pa came stepping over. Behind him came Uncle John. Both stopped.

Free could feel them staring.

"Gotske."

"Yeh," Uncle John said, "here's one time you won't have to tell him to freeze to it and not let go."

"Yeh." Pa leaned down for a closer look. "Man, he's really stuck to it all right. Below zero like it is, he's going to have a frozen tongue in a minute."

Uncle John couldn't resist being jokey some more. "Maybe we should tickle him and then he'll jerk himself free. Ha, Free?"

Free waited, bent over. He didn't even dare shiver. If Pa wanted to give him a licking now there was nothing he could do about it. Couldn't dodge or anything. Certainly couldn't quick put a board in his pants.

Pa said, "Wal, the only thing for it is to disconnect the handle from the pump and carry both him and it to the stove in the kitchen. Got a plier handy in that plier pocket of yours?"

"You bet. Coming up," Uncle John said.

Pa took the plier, pulled out the cotter pin, and removed the bolt. Carefully he lifted the handle away from the pump.

"Ulll."

Uncle John said, "Better let the kid hold the handle. He'll know just how much stretching his tongue can take. He can hold it to the rhythm of his own step too."

"Good idee," Pa said. "Think you're strong enough to carry it yourself, boy?"

Free carefully took hold of the frosted handle, a hand to either end.

"Okay. Now walk slowly toward the house. One easy step at a time. Uncle John will walk on one side of you and I'll walk on the other side, in case you stumble."

Free walked very carefully. He could see past the pump handle just enough to make out where he should step next. The frosted handle was so bitter cold he could feel it through his wool-lined leather mittens. As he approached the stoop of the kitchen, he could see out of the corner of his eye that the womenfolk were staring at him through the kitchen window.

Pa opened the door.

Free edged the handle in sideways.

"Over to the stove now, boy. I'll open the oven."

Free headed carefully for the hot oven.

Ma said, "What in God's name . . . ?"

"Yeh," Pa said, "some people's kids stick their fingers into things and some stick their tongues onto it."

"Better call the doctor."

"What for? It'll thaw off in a minute."

"How do you know?"

"I did this too once when I was a kid."

"The things you men don't get into as kids."

Pa and Uncle John helped Free hold the heavy pump handle, each at an end and Free in the middle. The frost got thicker at first. But pretty soon it began to melt off. Then all of a sudden Free's tongue came free.

"What do you have to say for yourself now?" Uncle John asked.

"Mmm." Free's tongue felt like it had been starched. He couldn't form words right away.

Later in the week, when the road was scooped out, Uncle John and Aunt Matilda went to live on their own place.

Free ❦ 9

ONE NIGHT LATE the next month Free woke up and heard Ma yelling her head off. He and Everett were sleeping in the same room with Pa and Ma because it was still too cold upstairs. Pa had tied down the blankets at the corners the night before because Everett was hoggish and liked to roll up in them on his side. So Free couldn't sit up and see what was the matter.

Free slid up in the bed a couple of inches until his head hit the white iron end and then took a peek. The lamp reflector was shining straight at Ma's high stomach. Also in the room was a new doctor with a black moustache and a gold watch chain. The doctor and Pa were whispering together. Ma let out another yell and then Pa came over to look at Free and Everett.

Free quick closed his eyes.

"I don't think they heard a thing," Pa said.

"I still recommend they be moved out of here," Doctor said.

"They're both dead to the world," Pa said. "They'll be all right."

"Well, if your wife doesn't object, okay."

There was some more whispering. There was a smell of a medicine just like the one Ma had put on his pisser that time he'd skinned his onion.

Ma said, plain, "I wonder if it's worth it all."

"Now, Ada," Pa said.

"Dr. Halmers," Ma said, "isn't there some way this cup can pass me by? By cutting me open a little more?"

"There's less risk of infection taking the natural birth route."

"Mercy," Ma whispered.

Free soon was too sleepy to stay awake. Slowly he withdrew his head under the blanket again. And was gone.

Much later Free felt Pa untying the upper corners of the blankets.

Free looked around. The sun was up. It was morning.

''Well, son,'' Ma said from her bed, ''good morning.'' She was sitting up against her pillows.

Free sat up. ''Morn'n.''

Ma was holding a bundle in her arms. Some baby hair stuck out of the open end of it. There was a smell in the room like Pa might've just butchered a chicken and hadn't thrown the insides outdoors yet.

Free wasn't sure he liked seeing the new baby. Another bed wetter? No thank you.

Pa was smiling like he'd pitched and won a ball game. ''Yes, son, you've got a brand-new baby brother named Albert.''

Free was surprised. ''Can the baby talk already?''

''Why, no, son. What makes you ask?''

''Well, if he can't talk, how do you know his name?''

Pa laughed and shook his head. ''Boy, boy, sometimes you're worse than a lawyer the way you trip up a fella.''

Ma put on a smile she sometimes used when she wanted Free to do something he didn't want to do. ''Free, my son, aren't you going to come over here and looked at your new little brother?''

Free gave Everett a kick. ''Wake up, you. Ma wants you to go over and see Albert.''

Everett first smiled and then woke up with his blue eyes. He had been playing he was asleep. ''Where?''

''Over here, Everett,'' Ma said. ''Come on over, the both of you.''

Free and Everett climbed out of bed and went over to Ma's bed. The floor was cold on their bare feet.

Ma folded back a new blue blanket and there was a baby sucking on Ma. The baby looked like a big baby mouse. Its eyes were closed.

Free remembered something. Everett used to suck on Ma too. Ugh. Look at the pink milk running out of the corner of the baby's mouth.

"Don't you like the new baby, Free?"

"I do," Everett said. "Can I play with him, Ma?"

"Yes, you may when he grows up a little."

''Will it be my turn now to be boss of him?'' Everett asked.

Ma laughed. She puffed. She had a red face and was tired from something. ''If he'll let you boss him.''

Everett smiled at Albert.

Ma said, ''But of course we mustn't play boss just so we can be the boss. We're all God's children and we are all equal under His eye.''

Pa rumpled up their hair. ''Now, pick up your clothes and take them out into the kitchen and I'll help you dress by the stove. March, get, go.''

''I can dress by myself," Free said.

''So can I,'' Everett said.

''Wal, good. Maybe things will be a little easier around here now that we've got a new baby in the house.''

Ma said, ''Free, don't you like your new brother?''

''I guess so.''

Pa steered Free and Everett ahead of him into the kitchen. ''Wal, Ade, what would you like for breakfast this morning?''

''Do I get it in bed?'' Ma asked smiling.

''Love, whatever your heart desires.''

''Then I'll have some warm oatmeal and milk.''

Pa brought Ma her food on a tray, and then came back to sit at the table with his two boys. Pa left the door open so Ma could hear him ask the blessing. After the amen, Pa poured a puddle of steaming oatmeal into Free's bowl, into Everett's bowl, and last into his own. Pa was about to add milk and sugar, when Free covered his bowl with his hands.

''Hey,'' Pa said surprised, ''don't you want any milk?''

''Can I have some butter instead?''

''Why, if you like it that way, I guess so. But what's wrong with milk?''

Free could still see the pink milk running out of Ma's breast.

Pa fixed his eyes sideways on Free. ''Because this is a special morning you get the butter this one time. You hear?''

''Why can't I always have it, Pa?''

''Because skim milk is both better for you and cheaper for me.''

Free watched Pa drop a couple dabs of butter on his hot oatmeal, watched the dabs melt into little yellow lakes, then watched the sugar melt into that as Pa sprinkled on a spoonful.

''Me too,'' Everett said, holding out his steaming bowl.

''You see? There you go,'' Pa said. ''What you want he wants.'' Pa shook a finger at Free. ''Always remember that. You're the oldest and you've got to set the example for the rest.''

''What's going on out there?'' Ma called from the bedroom.

''Nothing,'' Pa said. ''I'm making some exceptions and also laying down a few laws.''

Pa had to make the noon dinner. Free and Everett watched him to see if he did it right. When Pa was about done, Pa poured out a glass of skim milk for both Free and Everett.

''I don't want any,'' Free said.

''What, no milk? It'll give you wonderful white teeth like this.'' Pa showed his teeth like a wolf.

Free shook his head.

''Why not?''

Free wouldn't say.

''What's going on out there?'' Ma called from the bedroom.

''The kid don't want his milk. I don't know what's got into him.''

''Oh.'' Ma sighed. ''Well, let it go for a couple of days. Until I can sit at the table again.''

That evening Free tried to be a good hired man. He fed the chickens for Pa. He got the eggs. He got the cobs.

While Pa was milking, Free fed Rover some milk in his pie tin. When Free saw how Rover lapped up the fresh milk, he wondered if maybe that wasn't the way to drink milk. Maybe when it was fresh it would taste all right. Pa would scold him of course for drinking out of the same tin with the dog. Waiting until Pa had settled down beside his third cow and had started a noisy pingpanging in the bottom of his pail, Free poured some extra milk into Rover's pie tin. Rover leaned away so Free wouldn't spill over his nose. When the tin was full to the brim, Free got down on his knees and took a sip. Warmth from the milk smoked up around his face. His stomach went yuk. Free wiped his lips on the sleeve of his mackinaw, hard.

Rover growled for Free to get away from his tin of milk.

Without turning his head Pa said, ''Don't go near that dog when he's drinking or eating.''

That night for supper Free again wouldn't drink his milk. Pa humored him once more by drinking the whole glassful himself just to show how tasty it was.

The next morning Free wanted butter and sugar on his oat porridge again, not skim milk and sugar.

Then Pa laid down the law. ''All right, son. You're not going to get anything to eat, not a thing, no potatoes, no baloney, no rice, until you first eat that bowl of oatmeal and milk. Hear?''

Free looked back at Pa, stubborn.

''No bread with butter and jelly on it either. Nothing."

Free was mad. He reached under the table and gave Everett a pinch because he was eating his bowl of milk and porridge.

At noon when Pa set the table, he placed Free's breakfast bowl in front of him still with the milk and oatmeal in it.

Free gave it a black look.

Pa shook a finger at him. ''You eat that first and then you can have meat like the rest of us.''

"What is going on out there?" Ma asked from the bedroom.

''Your oldest kid won't take anything with milk in it,'' Pa said. ''So I'm gonna break him of what's getting to be a bad habit.''

''What are you doing?''

''I've set his bowl of milk and oatmeal in front of him again. The one he wouldn't eat this morning.''

''Oh, Alfred.''

''I'm sorry, but that's the law. He needs the milk. And I just won't be bothered setting out special food for him.'' Pa glared at Free.

Free asked, ''Can I pour the milk off and then eat it?''

''No.''

"Then I don't want it."

"Okay, boy, starve then."

"Alfred," Ma scolded from the bedroom.

"Never mind, Ada. I'm running this shebang. When he gets hungry enough he'll eat it, you can bet your boots on that."

Free watched Pa and Everett eat their meat and potatoes. They smacked their lips to show him what he was missing.

That night Pa set out that same bowl of milk and oatmeal for Free's supper. The oatmeal where it showed above the milk was beginning to look a little like a dry island.

Free wondered if he couldn't get the milk down somehow by sprinkling on a lot of sugar. He played with that idea until he remembered that Pa always handled the sugar spoon. Looking black, feeling hollow, he again had nothing to eat.

Later on, just before Pa washed the dishes, Pa surprised Free by giving the dog his bowl of old milk and old oatmeal.

Free thought: "Hey."

Pa caught his look. "It don't mean what you think it does, kid. Tomorrow the first thing you get some milk again."

Sure enough, at breakfast, there it stood, a glass of that darn blue skim milk.

"Sonny, you're gonna have to drink that milk, or starve. I'm going to break you of that."

That afternoon when Free went outdoors to play he looked around for things to eat. He remembered Pa had ground some corn for chicken feed. If the chickens liked it maybe it was good to eat. He went to the feed bin and tried a handful of it. But after chewing on it a while he decided it was too dry and cracky. Next he remembered cows like alfalfa hay, expecially the tiny green leaves. So he went up in the haymow and tried that. Ffft. It was worse than eating dry tea leaves.

Free had seen Uncle John take a shortcut down out of the haymow, the opening above the alley of the calf pen. There was no wooden ladder on that end of the haymow. He'd admired the way Uncle John had let himself hang from the ledge for a second before dropping down to the alley floor below. It had to be fun.

Free swung himself over the ledge and let himself hang down by the fingertips a second too. Hey. It was fun. Free let his feet swing back and forth a couple of times.

On about the tenth swing, the fingers of his left hand slipped a little on the ledge. Hey. He'd almost lost his grip. He might have landed on the feed bunk and not on the hay below.

He glanced past his black overshoes. There was no thick mound of hay below in the alley. He'd forgotten to pitch some down first. Now he was in for it. He had to drop down on hard cement.

Scared, he yelled out, "Hey, Pa, help!"

Then Free remembered Pa was out in the field somewhere, too far away to hear him. Free's next thought was to call Ma. But then he remembered Ma was still in bed with that new baby, Albert.

He looked past his nose, past the buttons on the front of his mackinaw, trying to see just how far down it was to the hard cement below. When he finally got a good look at the floor, he became even more scared. Man, was that ever a long ways down.

He was going to break his neck and die.

His fingers began to get jumpy. The fingers of his left hand were the worst. If his left hand gave out he could hardly hold on with only his right hand. What was worse, he was beginning to have trouble getting his breath. It was like a clamp was slowly closing around his chest.

"Dear Lord Jesus, please, this is the worst fix I've ever been in. Help save me. For Jesus' sake. Amen."

Nothing happened. The Lord Jesus was probably too busy with other work to hear him. In a minute he was going to fall.

He wondered if maybe he couldn't get a leg up over the ledge, and so make it back up into the haymow. He tried it. Up. Up. The muscles of his arms trembled and jerked. He got one knee up. Then knew he couldn't do it. His arms weren't strong enough.

"Help!!"

"Free?"

He held his breath. He listened.

"Free?"

It was Ma. Ma was up again. Jesus had heard him and sent her.

"Ma! I'm here in the barn and I can't get down. Ma?"

"Where?"

"Here in the calf pen."

"For heaven's sake. That boy. What next?" It took Ma but a moment to show up in the door. She had on Pa's overcoat and his six-buckle red boots. "Free!"

"I'm sorry, Ma. I was gonna do what Uncle John once did."

Ma came over and caught Free by his ankles. "All right, let go. I've got you."

Free let go and settled in Ma's arms. He turned and hugged her head.

Ma hugged him back and lowered him to the floor. "Boy, boy, what are we going to do with you, the way you always get yourself into a fix."

Free looked at his fingers. They were deep blue at the tips and white all the way back to the second knuckle. It hurt something awful to rub them. It was like someone had pounded a shingle nail through the fingernails.

"Ochh. Well, you might as well come in for a piece of cake I made."

Oh boy. Ma wasn't going to make him drink that darn milk first then. "All right, Mama." He looked up at her full of love. "Are you better now, Ma?"

"Much better, son. Go." Ma gave him a push and started him toward the house. She walked stiff behind him.

But when he sat in his place by the table, awaiting the treat, he got the dumps again when he heard what Ma said next.

"That's right. I almost forgot. Pa said you had to drink your milk first before you could have anything else."

"But, Ma, this is lunchtime. Not the regular meal."

"I'm sorry, boy. But when your father lays down the law, we've got to obey."

"God-darn that Pa. Always laying down the law."

Ma was shocked. "Free! Did I hear you swear?"

"I guess so."

"Well, don't you ever let me hear anything like that again. Especially not about your pa. Your pa's been the sweetest man alive while I was having this baby. He was anxious to get out into the field, yet took the time to do all the housework for me while I was in bed. He's a great man, son."

Free said nothing.

Ma set out a slice of fresh-baked chocolate cake. It had raisins in it and brown sugar frosting on top. Ma also set out a glass of blue skim milk. "Well, here's your milk. Drink that, and the cake's yours."

The cake looked good.

"Come now, Free, don't be so balky."

"Is the milk cold? I can't drink it if it's still warm."

"Yes, it's cold."

Sighing, hating to give in, but loving his raisin cake more, and Ma too a little bit, Free pulled an awful face and then, quickly as he could, gulped down the glass of blue poison.

"Thank God," Ma said. "That's over with."

Free ❦ 10

UNCLE ABBOTT, PA'S brother, came for a week.

Free liked Uncle Abbott right away. Uncle Abbott wasn't jokey like Uncle John, but Uncle Abbott was a real foot racer. Pa said Uncle Abbott always won all the footraces at the county fair. Uncle Abbott had black hair like Pa, except that his wasn't turning white like Pa's. He had kind blue eyes, though Pa was taller.

Sunday after church Pa said for everybody to come along and see some holes in the back of the pasture. Pa said he couldn't figure out what was digging them, the holes were so big and deep. It was a sunny day and the grass was just green. Ma came along too after first making sure that Everett and Albert were taking their naps. Pa, Ma, Uncle Abbott, Rover, and Free walked in an even line. Ma sometimes stopped to look at a spring flower.

Soon Free and Uncle Abbott were running some short races on the way out, to see who could get to an old bull thistle stalk first, then to a gully first, and then to an old cowplop first. Uncle Abbott had on new white tennis shoes and Free had on brown tennis shoes. Free won every time. But Free could tell Uncle Abbott let him win because he liked him so much. Ma had a wide smile for Uncle Abbott because he was good to little boys. Ma liked Uncle Abbott about as much as she liked Pa.

Free took Uncle Abbott's hand and gave it a pull. "I betcha you can't beat Rover."

"I can't, huh? Well, we'll just have to see about that." Uncle Abbott's blue eyes twinkled. He snapped his fingers at Rover. "Come on, let's you and me race. Huh? huh?"

Rover liked games too. His tongue came out and laughed. His gold tail waved back and forth. He looked around for something to chase.

Uncle Abbott winked at Free and started to run for the hill ahead. Right away Rover caught on. He passed Uncle Abbott. Then Uncle Abbott went faster and passed Rover. Then Rover speeded up and passed Uncle Abbott. First the two white tennis shoes were flickering ahead and then the four white paws were galloping ahead. They passed each other four times.

"Look at that Abbott run," Pa laughed as he watched them go. "Nobody in the world can run like that."

Ma was laughing too.

Free ran up the slope after Uncle Abbott and Rover to see who would win at the end of the pasture on the other side of the hill. When Free got to the top of the hill, puffing, he saw that Rover was ahead again.

All of a sudden Rover saw something to one side. He left off racing and headed straight for the new holes in the pasture Pa had talked about. There was a furry gray animal running across the grass and heading for the new holes too. It had a black belly. Rover was too quick for the animal and got between the animal and the holes.

Uncle Abbott slackened down; then stopped to watch.

Free stopped too. His belly suddenly hurt from all the running. It was a side ache.

The gray animal looked at Rover a minute and then ran straight for him. It snapped at Rover. Rover tried to jump sideways but couldn't quite make it. The gray animal bit Rover in the leg. Rover yelped. Rover dropped his tail and started to run for home. The gray animal chased after him. Rover speeded up like he did when he was racing with Uncle Abbott. The gray animal couldn't keep up.

But then the gray animal spotted Uncle Abbott. It went after him next. It was moaning like it was real mad at everybody. It was twice as wide as it was high.

Uncle Abbott wasn't laughing any more. He waited until the gray animal almost had him, then jumped straight up and the animal sailed under him, missing him. Yow.

Uncle Abbott yelled. "Get back!"

Free looked around. There were Pa and Ma standing behind him.

"Pots and kettles," Pa said, "it's a mad badger."

The badger went after Uncle Abbott again. Once more Uncle Abbott dodged him by jumping over him.

Pa looked around. He saw where a fence post was broken off. He ran over and with both hands gave it a rip. The staples in the post went flying around like bullets and the post came free of the barbed wires. Pa grabbed it by the top end and ran down to help Uncle Abbott.

The badger heard Pa coming. It whirled around in its tracks. It could turn around as quick as a swivel chair. It had a small head but it was so mad it made its mouth big by showing its teeth. It moaned. Foam boiled in the corners of its mouth. It looked this way, that way, then didn't care about the big stick Pa had. It ran straight for Pa's legs.

"Billy Blitchers! That dang thing means business." Pa got set with his club. When the mad badger almost had him, Pa jumped to one side and hit the badger an awful whack over the top of its neck. The badger flipped up into a ball and rolled over on its back. Its black belly shivered.

Uncle Abbott and Ma came over. They stared down at its black belly. Ma held her arms crossed over her stomach. Uncle Abbott stood with his hands on his hips.

Pa said, "The dang thing had to be crazy to go after us like that."

Uncle Abbott nodded. "They're known as stubborn fighters when cornered. But they've never been known to attack people."

Pa said, "You know what proves it to me that it was crazy?"

"What?"

"It was out in broad daylight."

"That's right. They're mostly a night creature."

Ma slowly shook her head. "I wonder why God made such a creature? All it seems to do is ruin pastures. Of what earthly good is it?"

Uncle Abbott said, "They're death on gophers though."

Free looked at where Rover was licking his right front leg. "Pa."

Pa went over and had a look at Rover. "He got bit all right. But not deep."

"Then he won't die, Pa?"

"Naw."

Then Pa went over to make sure that the mad badger was dead. He hit it a couple more times on its head with the post.

Uncle Abbott had to go back to work. Everybody missed him.

Soon warmer days came along and Free and Everett could play in their sandpile near the sack swing. They played they had two cities.

Rover lay on the grass by the hog fence. His right front leg was hurting him and every now and then he gave it a good bite. Once he barked at it.

Pretty soon Everett felt sorry for his friend Rover. He went over to pet him.

Rover didn't want to be petted. He whirled around like a swivel chair and showed his teeth. He wanted to bite Everett and then remembered he liked Everett and so didn't. He was mixed up.

Free got to his feet. He looked around for a club. He couldn't find a loose fence post like Pa did, but there was an iron rod stuck in the ground where Ma had planted some flowers. Free went over, unhooked the store string tied on it, jerked the rod out of the ground and hurried over to help Everett in case Rover should bite him.

Rover saw Free coming. He didn't like to bite Free either.

"Get away from him," Free told Everett.

Then Rover snuck his head along the ground and tried to bite Everett's shoe.

Free jumped in between them and stuck the wagon rod into Rover's belly to hold him off.

Rover snapped at the iron rod. His teeth clicked on it. It was like sparks flew out of his mouth, only it was mostly foam. Then Rover got past Free and gave Everett's button shoe a good bite.

Free got mad then too. "You darn dog . . . you leave my brother alone." Free hit Rover a whack over his gold shoulder.

Rover felt sorry then. He slunk away and hid under the corncrib.

Everett looked down at the tooth marks in the toe of his black shoe and began to cry.

"What's going on out there?" Ma asked from the porch door. "And you put that iron rod back where you got it."

"But Ma, I had to have a club. Like Pa did."

"What for?"

"Because Rover wants to bite Everett."

"Och. That I'll believe when I see it." Ma came down the walk. "And why is Everett crying? Did you hurt him?"

"No. The dog did."

"Och."

"Well, Ma, those sure ain't my tooth marks on Everett's shoe." Free pointed at Everett's black shoe. Rover had bit deep enough into it for the gray insides to show through.

"Good grit." Ma settled down on her knees for a closer look. "Why, Rover did bite him." Ma waved back some gold hair from her eyes. "What did you kids do to Rover?"

"Nothing."

"Yes, yes, it's always nothing. I know."

"But Ma, we were just playing cities and then Everett went over to pet Rover because Rover was biting his leg because it hurt him."

"Biting his leg?"

"Yes, Ma."

"Where's Rover now?"

"He hid under the corncrib."

"Oh." Ma put her arms around Everett. "It's all right. Rover really didn't mean it." Ma unbuttoned Everett's shoe and took it off along with his stocking. "At least the bite didn't go through to the skin." Ma looked like she was scared of something. She put Everett's stocking and shoe back on. She stood up slowly. "Come, you kids. It's almost dinner time. You better go wash up ahead of your father. He'll be home from the field any minute now."

"But Ma," Free said, "Pa always lets me lead the horses—"

"Into the house with you. No more talk about it."

That noon Ma told Pa about what the dog did to Everett.

"Hum," Pa said. He looked at the tooth marks in Everett's shoe. "Did it go through to the skin?"

"No. There were no marks on the boy."

"So."

"Yes," Ma said. "It's probably that rabies we heard about."

"Sure is funny that a badger should have the rabies. When usually it's skunks."
"Maybe a skunk bit the badger."
"Instead of spraying him. That sure would've surprised the badger."
Ma sighed. "Daily we are surrounded by a thousand dangers."
"Pah," Pa said. "That's true of any place."
"I meant on this earth, Alfred, as compared to heaven. Where, God willing, I hope to go someday. That's what I'm living for anyway."
After Pa finished his pipe, and had a short snooze, he got down his .44 from its nail over the door to the pantry. He opened the gun and looked into the barrel. "Say, that's right. I used the last of my shells over on the Alvord place. On those rabbits eating up your garden."
Free stared at the shiny blue barrel. Someday he would have a gun of his own too and then he'd shoot up the Huns and win the world.
Pa put the gun back. "Where's my leather mitts?"
"Be careful, Alfred, that you don't get bit."
"You kids stay put here until it's over with."
Pa went out to the corncrib. Free and Ma watched him through the kitchen window. Pa sat down on his heels and tried to coax Rover to come out from under the corncrib.
Finally Rover came. Rover showed his teeth though. Pa smiled back and coaxed Rover some more. Then all of a sudden Pa's hand shot out and he grabbed Rover by the back of his gold neck. Rover couldn't do nothing. Rover wriggled and jerked and tried to get at Pa, but Pa had him tight. Pa held Rover away from him.
"Merciful heavens," Ma said.
Pa walked over to the sack swing and with one hand tied the rope of the swing in a knot around Rover's neck. He gave the knot a good jerk so Rover couldn't jump out of it. The sack full of straw hung against Rover's back. It was like there was two dogs hanging there, one with a tail and one without. Rover jerked and jerked, and the sack flopped with him.
Free stared wild-eyed. "Will Rover die now, Ma? Like Grampa?"
Ma put her hand over her heart. "Yes, dear boy. And how sad it all is. I remember when I found Rover in the ditch by our first place."
"I don't remember that."
"It was before you were born, boy."
"Was I dead then yet?"
"No, you weren't here then yet."
Rover kept jerking. It was awful.
Finally Pa walked over to the corncrib and got a neck yoke. He came back and hit Rover a hard crack over the head. Rover quit jerking.
After a while Pa brought his leather mittens into the house.
Free was mad. "Why did you have to hit him, Pa?"
"Because I couldn't stand to see him suffering." Pa cried a couple of big tears. "He was such a great dog. The best I ever knew."
Free was upset. He didn't know Pa could cry.

Free 11

THE LITTLE PIGS didn't need their mothers any more. They could drink Pa's skim milk. As soon as the sow mothers got lazy fat, Pa had them loaded on the Cannonball freight. Pa went along with the sows to the Sioux City stockyards to get the money.

For two days Free and Ma did the chores for Pa. Everett got the cobs for the stove. Everybody worked except Albert, the new baby.

The third day about noon Old Horsberg drove onto the yard in his new copper-trim Ford. When Old Horsberg stepped on the brake, the new Ford stopped and stood shaking.

A tall man stepped out. The tall man had on a new gray hat with a black band and a new overcoat with a small velvet collar. He also had on new black gloves and black shoes.

Free didn't know why but he was afraid to say hello.

Old Horsberg goosed the motor and the copper-trim Ford shook and then it slowly turned short and rattled off the yard.

"Wal," the tall man said, "ain't you kids gonna greet your pa with a tight hug?" The tall man had a smile like Pa's.

Everett walked up and gave the tall man's leg a tight hug.

Free smiled a little but hung back.

Ma came to the doorway. The doorway was around her like a picture frame. "Why, Alfred, you're all feathered out like a new rooster."

"Yip," the tall man with Pa's smile said. "How do you like your new husband?"

It was a new Pa then.

Ma had to laugh. "As brother John would say, you're all dressed up like a sore toe."

The new Pa's smile became bigger, like a half-moon. He was carrying two packages. The new Pa walked into the house. "I thought it was about time I looked the part of the husband of the queen of Leonhard County."

"I'm no queen."

"You are to me." The new Pa set down the packages and threw his arms around Ma and gave her a squeeze so hard she groaned. "And how did all my loveys get along while I was gone?"

"Just fine," Ma said.

"I got the cobs," Everett said.

Free didn't know if he dared to brag to the new Pa. Everett sure was free with the new Pa. But then Everett never knew any better.

Ma said, "We had no bad weather. Nothing but sun every day. And the boys were both so busy they didn't have time to get into trouble."

The new Pa paraded up and down in the kitchen in his new clothes. "Wal, it looks like you were all good peoples while I was gone. Come, let's see you open this package once. This one here."

"I hope you didn't buy us anything foolish now," Ma said.

"Open it up," the new Pa said.

Ma felt of the new Pa's coat sleeve first. "That's good material. I'll bet it cost you a pretty penny."

"Seventeen dollars on a sale. Gray kersey."

"I like that Chesterfield collar. It becomes you, Alfred. But weren't you afraid it'd get covered with soot on the train?"

"Truth to tell, I had all these new things of mine in this other package here until I hit Bonnie. Then I just had to put'em on so I could show off a little when I hit the yard."

Ma untied the strings of her new package. "Did the sows bring a good price?"

"I got the top market. The right weight on the right day."

Ma lifted a new purple dress out of the package. "Alfred, you shouldn't have."

"Why not? If I can wear a Chesterfield overcoat, you can surely wear a queen's dress."

Ma was smiling as big and as wide as the new Pa.

"Try it on. See if it fits."

"How would you know my size?"

"Now wouldn't that be a pretty how-do-you-do if I didn't know that. When I hold your middle in my arms every night."

It really was their Pa then except that he was also a little new.

Ma looked at her boys. "You do not."

"Put it on."

Ma went to their bedroom to try it on.

Free asked, "Did you bring us a present too?"

"You betcha life I did. Here." Pa opened the package deeper and lifted out some new leather mittens, one pair for Free, one for Everett. They were lamb-lined. "For next fall. I got 'em cheap on a sale."

"We can't wear them now then?"

"No. They're for when you start school next fall. When it gets cold. Won't that be nice? You can carry your lunch bucket without getting your hands cold. They're much warmer than just wool-lined mittens."

Free and Everett put them on to see if they fit. They were a little big.

"Just right," Pa said, "by next winter you'll have grown into 'em."

Ma came back in, wearing her purple dress. She'd piled her gold hair on top of her head.

"Wow!" Pa said. "Now I'm glad I did come back." He put his arm around Ma's middle and made her bow to the kitchen stove with him. "Your majesty," he said to the black stove, "the Duke and Duchess of Siouxland."

Ma and Pa looked better than a picture in a book.

Pa made Ma take a couple of fancy dancing steps with him and then he gave her a little airplane ride.

"Eee! Alfred, put me down."

Free liked the new part of Pa. Maybe this new part of Pa would let him have two spoons of sugar on his oatmeal for breakfast. Maybe he'd even let him have some raisins and some shredded coconut on his rice for dinner.

That noon, after they'd all had meat and potatoes and vegetables, Ma set a big bowl of steaming rice on the table. The rice kernels were so swelled up they looked like hailstones. Pa gave the boys each a good plate plumb full. Pa sprinkled on a spoon of sugar.

Free touched Pa on the elbow. "Can I have two spoonsful, please? And some raisins and coconut on top?"

Pa almost fell out of his swivel chair. "What!" Pa looked over at Ma. "If that don't put the cap on it. Have you been spoilin' my boys while I was gone?"

"No."

Pa looked down at Free. "Where'd you ever get the idee that you could have double the usual amount of sugar? Including raisins and coconut?"

"I thought maybe the new part of you would let me."

It hurt Pa to hear that. "No, son, your Pa hain't got a new part to him. It was just the clothes that was new." Pa tried to smile like Uncle John. "I'm your same old Pa. I hope that's all right by you."

Free looked down at where the one spoon of sugar had been sprinkled on his rice. He watched the little islands of sugar slowly sink away. Finally he picked up his spoon and began eating before all the sugar had disappeared. It was the same old Pa all right.

Free ❦ 12

A COUPLE OF months later Ma got Free up early and gave him a whole new set of clothes to put on, black stockings, blue overalls, brown Wear-U-Well shoes, a blue-and-green checkered shirt, and a blue-and-black stocking cap.

"Where are we going, Ma?"

"You're going to school, son. Don't you remember my telling you yesterday?"

That's right. Ma and Pa had talked about it.

Free liked the new stocking cap. "But, Ma, ain't it too hot for that yet?"

"I want you to wear it to help keep your wild hair in place."

Free said, "What do I have to go to school for?"

"To learn how to read."

"But, Ma, I can read 'cat' and 'dog' already."

"Boy, someday we want you to be able to read the Bible."

"Must I go?"

"Yes, you must."

Free's lower lip thickened.

Pa clapped out his pipe in the stove. "Nah. Are you almost ready? I'll take you in the Overland. The road's dry today."

"But—"

"No buts about it," Ma said. "To school you go. It's going to be a lot of fun. And here's your dinner bucket. I've put in your favorite sandwich. Rye bread with sugar."

Free scowled at Everett.

"Boy, someday you're going to look back to this morning as being the happiest day of your life," Ma said. "I wish I could go to school again."

Free took the dinner bucket. It was a syrup pail they'd just finished emptying. Ma had washed it the night before and had scratched off the Karo label.

Ma said, "Now tonight, when school is over, I want you to walk home with the Horsberg children. There's Peter and Paul. And little Alvina. They're about your age. And there's Louise. She's older and she can watch over you all."

"Did you hear your ma now?" Pa asked.

"Yes."

"You'll have to walk home alone from the Horsbergs to here, so be careful of talking to strangers. Watch out especially for gypsies and Indians. The gypsies like to steal kids and then hold them for ransom. And the Indians like to steal white children so as to replace their own children that they've lost to sickness."

Free lighted up inside. Indians? Hey.

"Once you're over the hill here, I can keep an eye on you from our kitchen window. Do you hear?"

"Ya, Ma."

"And your teacher's name is Vera Fenster. You're to call her Teacher or Miss Fenster."

"Will she be the boss?"

"She'll be the boss."

Free followed Pa outdoors. Pa cranked the Overland, then got in on the driver's side, while Free got in on Ma's side.

Ma waved from the doorway of the kitchen. Everett stood beside her and waved too.

When they turned the corner past the Horsbergs', Pa said, "Boy, I want you to like school. You want to remember your pa couldn't go much. That was because his ma died when he was only a kid, and the family got busted up, and he had to go out and work. But your ma is alive and well, and your family is still all in one piece, and so you'll have a chance to go all the way through the eighth grade."

The Overland ground slowly up a hill. When they rolled past the Windmiller place, two little girls were just coming out of the house to go to school too.

Pa turned into the schoolyard. A lot of wild kids were running around under the trees.

Pa placed his hand on Free's shoulder. "Come. I'll take you in to meet the teacher first. Pick up your pail."

There was a strong smell of oily paint in the school. The walls were brown below and white above. A wind was blowing white curtains around. Some old men were staring out of pictures on the wall. There were rows of seats just like Sherm had in his school in Gramma's town.

A lady like Aunt Karen, only fatter and more jolly, sat behind a big desk. "Hello, there."

"Hum," Pa said. He walked up to her with Free. "Miss Fenster? I thought I'd bring over my boy on his first day of school." Pa fumbled a piece of paper out of his bib pocket. "My wife wrote down the boy's name on this. Here you are."

The teacher stood up. She had on a green dress. Her hair and her eyes were brown.

She read from the piece of paper. "Alfred Alfredson. Good. Welcome to Rock No. 3, Alfred."

"Hum," Pa said. He smiled at the teacher like he wanted to go to school too. "We mostly call him Free."

"Free. How lovely." The teacher smiled like a handful of flowers.

"Yum. Wal, I better get on home. Still have some plowing to do."

"Yes, Mr. Alfredson. Thank you for bringing your son. It's good to see parents taking the time to start their children off on the right foot."

Pa left.

"Well, Free, I suppose you'd like to know where you're going to sit." Teacher went over to the last row of desks on the sunny side of the schoolroom. "Right here in the front seat. That all right with you?"

Free stared at the desk. The sloping top had the color of a ripe apple. Somebody had cut letters into it with a hard-lead pencil.

"Do you like your desk?"

Free nodded. In Gramma's town Sherm had a seat in the back of the room.

"Come. I'll show you where to put your dinner pail." Teacher led the way out into the hall. A row of dinner buckets was lined up under some coat hooks. "Here you are. Your place is at the end here. Under this coat hook. Later on, when it gets cold, you're to hang your mackinaw above your dinner pail. As well as that stocking cap, which you can hang there now. Let's see if you can reach that high."

"Ma said I should wear it to help keep my wild hair in place."

Teacher laughed. "She's right, of course. But today it's pretty warm out, so why don't you just hang it up here? And if your hair gets too wild you can always comb your hair over by this mirror here."

"Yes, Teacher."

"Now. Would you like to go out and make friends with your new playmates?"

"Do I have to?"

"No." Teacher gave him a smile like Ma did when she wanted something out of him. "But right now I can't play with you because I'm too busy. Come." She put her hand on the top of his head and steered him outside.

The sun shone on them. It made the beads on the front of the teacher's green dress shine like dew on grass.

A little girl came running up. "Teacher, can that new little boy play pom-pom-pullaway with us?"

"Yes. Free, go ahead and play with her. That's Alvina Horsberg. Your neighbor." Teacher gave Free a loving push.

Free ran with Alvina under the trees.

"Do you know how to play pom-pom-pullaway?" Alvina asked.

"Sure. My Uncle Sherm taught me how."

"Good then. Let's line up on this base. We're safe here by this big tree. And we're safe over there by the fence. But in between the It kids can catch you." Alvina had eyes like a pet mouse. She was so excited she was shivering. "Now!" she cried. "Go! They ain't looking." She took off. The wind lifted her dress.

Free took off then too. His new shoes helped him run. Some of the It kids saw him go. They tried to catch him. He ran like the wind. They couldn't quite tag him. He hit the fence across the schoolyard and bounced back. He grabbed the fence again just in time not to get caught.

Hey. This was fun. He could run fast. Those It kids couldn't catch him.

Some It kid hollered, "Pom-pom-pullaway. If you don't come, I'll pull you away."

Again everybody ran, breathing like steam engines.

Pretty soon Teacher came out on the stoop with a brass bell and rang it. A-cleng, a-clang. Loud and clear. A-cling, a-clang.

All the children ran into the school. They crushed through the door like little pigs all trying to get into the hog house at the same time.

"Now now, children." Teacher stood just inside the door. "One at a time, please. In an orderly manner. Like little ladies and gentlemen." Teacher could smile nice at the same time that her voice was strict.

Everybody marched to their places and sat down.

Free headed for his seat. The seat part was slick and it fit him good. He lifted the lid and looked inside. The desk was empty. It smelled like a mouse nest, only sweet.

Teacher marched to the head of the schoolroom. She stood by her desk. There was some writing on the blackboard behind her. "Come to attention, children." She smoothed her green dress down over her hips. "What a nice sunny day we're having for our very first day of school. A lovely way to begin the school year."

"It's way too nice," a voice growled in back. "I'd rather be out in the field plowing."

Teacher didn't like to hear that, but she smiled anyway. "That's enough out of you now, Tom Robson."

Some of the kids snickered.

"To start the morning off right, let's sing our national anthem, 'The Star-Spangled Banner.' As you can see, I've written the words of the first stanza on the blackboard. For those of you who may have forgotten the words." She smiled with her brown eyes. "For shame, if you have."

Alvina, sitting just across from Free, raised her hand. "I still know it good, Teacher."

"That's fine, Alvina." Teacher smiled. "And now I have a nice surprise. You've probably noticed it already. During the past summer our school acquired an old parlor organ." Teacher walked to the wall near Free and touched an organ. It was just like Ma's. "The Acme Queen." Teacher pumped a pedal with her foot and pushed down a white key to make it give a little toot. "I'm sure that during the coming year we'll find that our singing will greatly improve." Teacher sat down on the organ stool and began to pump both pedals. The old organ began to wheeze. "Everybody please stand. We always stand when we sing our national anthem. Out of respect for our flag and our country." Teacher pointed to a red and white and blue flag draped on the wall over the blackboard.

Knees hit the iron sides of desks and everybody stood up. Shoes scuffed the oiled floor.

Teacher touched the keys and then, nodding her head to get them all started at the same time, began to sing. "Oh, say, can you see by the dawn's early light."

By the fifth word most of the pupils were singing. Free could see that they were all following the words on the blackboard. He knew the littlest words all right, but didn't need them. He already knew the song by heart. Uncle Sherm used to sing it for the fun of it. Free joined in. "What so proudly we hailed."

Teacher heard him. She gave him a quick little smile.

At that Free tipped back his head and let go like a robin in a tree.

Teacher played the organ louder; everybody sang louder.

For the last line Free took a deep breath. Carefully he fitted his voice in with Alvina's next to him and roared it out: "Our flag was still there yet."

For one long lingering second Free heard himself singing solo before the whole school—"yett!"—at exactly the moment that Teacher lifted her hands from the keys. The school kids couldn't help but let out a quick funny blat of laughter.

Teacher held her hands above the keys another second, then called out quick and loud, "Continue! continue!" and jumped her hands on the next notes: "Oh, say, does that star-spangled banner still wave. . . ."

Free could feel his cheeks burn.

When they finished the anthem all the kids looked at Free like he might have wet his pants.

Teacher got up from the organ stool and came over and placed her hand on Free's head. "It's all right, Free. We all make mistakes." Then she looked stern at all the kids. "Free added that one word, 'yet,' because, like a good American citizen, he wanted to make sure you knew that our flag really was still there. Yet."

The little kids shut up. But the older kids still laughed.

Teacher next passed out the books. Two boys helped her.

Free got a book that was mostly full of pictures. The ABC's were in front. He knew them pretty well. He found the cat and dog page.

Teacher asked the older children to read a poem with her. It was about a blacksmith who worked under a tree. He was not like the one in Bonnie who worked in a black smoky shop. The blacksmith in the poem rolled up his sleeves and washed his arms so they could see his mighty muscles, while the one in Bonnie had dirty black sleeves that he never rolled up. The other children had to learn the poem by heart.

Teacher soon turned to the primary graders. They had to look at the ABC's in their primer. "I wonder," said Teacher, "does anybody in the primary grade already know his ABC's?" Teacher looked at the three primary-graders in Free's row.

A girl behind Free raised her hand.

"Catherine Haber? Do you know them? Let's hear you then."

Catherine started out pretty good, but when she reached O she got stuck. She couldn't think of what came next.

Free smiled. Catherine had got stuck in the easy part. It was always easy to remember the K-L-M-N-O-P part. It was harder right after T-U.

"Anybody else?"

Free hesitated. Should he raise his hand?

Teacher saw him wiggling. "Free?"

Free turned red.

"Do you know them from the beginning, Free?"

Free squirted a look at Alvina. She was watching out of the corner of her mouse eye all right.

"Go ahead, Free. Pay no attention to anyone else."

Free started in. He recited them in clusters: "A-B-C; D-E-F-G; H-I-J; K-L-M-N-O-P; Q-R-S"—he took a breath and, knowing the next letters were the hardest to do, let them all come in one burst—" T-U-V-W-X-Y-Z."

"Wonderful, Free. Who taught you to say them that way?"

"Aunt Karen. She's a schoolteacher too."

Teacher played with a piece of chalk in her hand. Her fingertips were white with it and her green dress had a white smudge over the hip. "Do you know how to write them, Free?"

Free shook his head.

"All right then, we'll begin by writing the letter A today. Both the big A and the little a. Come to the board here, you three, and we'll all try it together."

At ten-thirty, Teacher declared it was recess time. "Fifteen minutes, children. Turn. Rise. Now the little children in the first row there, pass. One by one. Let's please be little ladies and gentlemen. In an orderly manner now."

Free followed his row outside. The sun was higher in the sky.

Alvina invited him to play pom-pom-pullaway again. Free ran and ran, first to the trees, then to the fence, then back again. Nobody appeared to be able to catch him. He always managed to dodge through the line of Its. It was better than being a bird.

Tom Robson was mad when he couldn't catch Free. "That darn little Alfredson kid is like a wild animal he runs so fast."

All too soon Teacher rang the bell.

Teacher next wrote some numbers on the blackboard for the eighth-graders to do. The white chalk had too hard a point and it squeaked.

Free shivered. It was like when Ma scraped out the bottom of a saucepan.

Teacher saw him squirming. "What's the matter, Free?"

Free felt everybody looking at him again. He said nothing.

Teacher smiled a ma smile. "It's all right, Free. It gets on my nerves too sometimes. Every now and then the chalk will have a grain of sand in it. Let's see if we can find a softer piece." She looked in a chalk box by the stove. "Here's one that looks soft." She wrote with it some. "Yes, that's much better. Isn't it now, Free?"

Free nodded, hoping that everyone would quit looking at him.

After a while Teacher wanted to know if any of the primary-graders could count.

Free could count a little but he didn't want to raise his hand. He remembered Sherm telling him that Sherm's teacher had moved him to the back row because he always had his hand up. Free liked Miss Vera Fenster and wanted to keep his front seat so he could be close to her.

"Free?"

Again Free recited in clusters: "1-2-3-4; 5-6-7-8; 9-10; 11-12; 13-14-15; 16-17-18-19. . . ." Free frowned at the ceiling.

"Is that all the farther you can count?"

Free nodded.

"Do you know how to write those numbers so far?"

Free shook his head.

"Well, maybe if I were to tell you a little story about each one of our numbers it would help us." As Teacher wrote the numbers on the blackboard, she told something about each one:

"1 is always very straight.
2 is crooked.
3 is curly.
4 is burly.
5 is always hard to make.
6 is never hard to make.
7 has one leg.
8 is double.
9 is no trouble.
0 is like an egg."

Hey. That was pretty slick.

Teacher saw the look on Free's face. She smiled. "Now. Let's all recite the little stories about our numbers together."

They sang them out together four times.

"Good," Teacher said. "Come to the board now, you three, and we'll all try writing our very first number. Mister One."

At twelve o'clock, Teacher dismissed school for noon hour recess. They all picked up their dinner buckets as they passed outside. They scattered out over the school ground in little groups.

Free went over to a fat tree and sat down at the foot of it.

Pretty soon Alvina and Catherine came and sat down at the foot of the tree too, one on each side of him.

Free's sandwiches tasted dry and cold. The bread with plum jelly had a red stain soaked all through it. It made him think of a blood-soaked rag around a toe. The black rye bread with sugar on, though, was better.

Alvina said to Catherine, "I know why you couldn't think of P next."

"Why?"

"Spell 'pig' backwards and then quick add 'funny'."

Free said, "She can't even spell it forwards yet."

"Oh ya, I forgot," Alvina said. "Well, here, I'll help you. G."

"G," Catherine said, not wanting to.

"I."

"I."

"P."

"P."

"Funny."

Catherine blushed, and wouldn't repeat it.

"That's a dirty trick," Free said.

"It's only a joke," Alvina said.

Catherine was so ashamed she hid her face.

Peter Horsberg and Gladys Windmiller were the first to finish eating. They hurried toward the schoolhouse. Right behind them came Paul Horsberg and Hesta Windmiller. All four put their dinner buckets back in the hall.

"Where you kids going so fast?" Alvina called after them.

Peter whispered something to Gladys, then started to lead her by her belt around to the back of the school. Gladys was a thin-legged thing like Catherine.

Alvina said with her mouth full of food, "I'll betcha they're going into the coal shed. Like they do at home in the grain bin." Alvina gulped down the last bite and got up. "Come on, let's quick play pom-pom-pullaway."

Louise Horsberg saw what Peter wanted to do too. When Paul and his girl Hesta started to follow Peter and Gladys, she got up. She was almost as big as teacher. She called out real loud, "Peter, Paul, we're all going to play pom-pom-pullaway. So don't you run off."

Free didn't understand what was going on.

"Aw, shucks," Peter said. "Well, I sure ain't gonna be It first then."

"I'll be It," Louise said.

Once again pom-pom-pullaway was a lot of fun.

Before Teacher rang the bell, Louise was the one to catch Free. Alvina, who had been made It too, helped corner him. All three fell down in a heap on the grass. They laughed together.

In the afternoon Teacher passed out some paper and a few old stubby crayons to the primary kids and told them to color.

Free's paper had a skinny dog and a rabbit traced on it. They didn't have any hair. He colored the dog yellow and the rabbit blue and gave them both some hair.

The older kids had to do things like grammar and history and spelling. The older kids hated their schoolwork. They groaned all afternoon.

At three-thirty Teacher tapped her desk for attention. "Now, children, I want you to listen carefully. We're all going to need a few extra supplies, things which the school board couldn't furnish us. I've written down what you need on a slip of paper." Teacher passed out the slips. "When you get home tonight, would you please hand them to your mothers? Hear?"

Free stuffed his slip of paper in the bib pocket of his overalls and buttoned it down good so he wouldn't lose it.

The older kids opened their slips and read them. They said nothing.

"All right. Turn. Rise. Pass. Until tomorrow then."

Free picked up his dinner bucket, set his stocking cap on one corner of his head, and started walking home with Alvina and Louise.

Peter and Paul walked to the Windmillers' with Gladys and Hesta. When they got to the Windmiller lane, Peter and Paul wanted to go play in the Windmiller grain bin with Gladys and Hesta a while.

Louise hollered them a warning and made them come along with her.

"All right then," Paul said, "since I'll have to get the cows the first thing when I get home, I'm gonna cut across the field from here then."

Louise said that was all right.

The other four walked on, Alvina with Free and Louise with Peter. Peter was balky all the way. He kept kicking dust at Louise. He said she was always spoiling his fun with Gladys. He said it was no fairs. Louise had plenty of fun playing with Tom Robson sometimes in that deserted farm kitty-corner across the road from the schoolhouse, like Adolph always did with Tessie Windmiller.

"Shut up," Louise said.

When they got near the culvert by the Horsberg windmill, Peter all of a sudden grabbed Free's stocking cap and jumped down into the ditch and threw it into the culvert, way under the road.

"Hey you," Free cried. "That's a dirty trick."

Peter showed his teeth. "Ha ha." He had long teeth like a wolf.

Free tried to hit Peter with his dinner bucket, but missed when Peter skipped back.

"Hey, there," Alvina said, "don't you hit my brother, Mister Free." Alvina had long teeth too. It was funny but Free hadn't noticed them on her before. Free looked to see if Louise had them. Louise was looking funny at him, and her mouth was open, but she didn't have them.

Free went after Peter with his dinner bucket again.

Alvina let out a warning yell; then went after Free with her dinner bucket. She missed his head and hit him on the shoulder.

"Here here," Louise said.

Free got down on his hands and knees and looked into the culvert. It was almost dark inside the culvert. He could just barely make out his blue-and-black stocking cap. The culvert was too narrow for him to crawl into. Free began to cry he was so mad.

Louise went over to the other end of the culvert and looked in too. Free could make out her face so long as she didn't get too close to the opening. "That darn Peter," she said. She stood up. "Peter, you get Free's stocking cap out of that culvert right this minute."

"Do it yourself." Peter showed his teeth once more and ran on home.

Alvina hooked her thumbs in the corners of her mouth and pulled her teeth real wide at Free. "So there," she said, and ran on home after Peter.

Free cried. "Boy, will I get it when I come home."

Louise put her arm around Free. "Shh, now. We'll think of something."

Free pushed her off. "I knew I shouldna wore my stocking cap to school this morning. I told Ma so too."

"Don't worry, Free, we'll think of something."

"You gotta get a stick to get it out of there." He could feel his tears drying on his cheeks.

"Wait here and I'll go get us a long stick from our grove."

Free spotted a willow tree growing in some slough grass east of the road. "Wait. I know what."

Free crawled under a barbed wire fence. The willow was an old fat tree. He hunted through its branches looking for the right one. Most of the branches were too thick. They grew out of the bottom of the tree like leaves of an artichoke. Finally he saw one. It was thin, mostly dead, and when he gave it a pull it broke off cleanly at the bottom. Free threw the branch over the fence and crawled under after it.

Louise picked up the branch. She broke off most of the little twigs. "You're pretty smart at that, Free. Saved me walking home and back." Louise lay down on her stomach and pushed the branch into the culvert.

"Can you reach it?"

"It's long enough all right. But somehow . . ."

Free got down on his belly on the other end of the culvert. He watched Louise scratch at the stocking cap with the stick. The stick was too smooth to catch it. "Wait. I know what'll hook into it." He got up and went over to Louise's side. "Take it out once."

Louise drew out the branch and gave it to Free.

Free carefully bent back the last few inches of the tip of the branch, until it cracked. He carefully set the cracked edge apart so that the bent end stuck out. "Now try it."

Louise shoved the branch into the culvert again and reached in as far as she could. She lowered it onto the stocking cap. "There."

"Is it coming?"

Louise started to pull it out. "Yes, it is." She talked into the ground. She was like a deacon handling a collection pole in church. And there was his blue-black stocking cap. Louise grunted and stood up. "I told you we'd think of something, Free."

Free picked up his stocking cap. Some old grass was caught in it, and the black tassel was a little muddy, but at least it wasn't lost. He brushed it off and put it on.

"What do you say now, Free?"

Free gave Louise a grudging smile. "I like your teeth."

"My teeth?"

"Well, your mouth then."

"Oh, Free, what a contrary one you are." Louise took his face between her hands and kissed him. Louise had nice thick lips like Ma. "But you're a darling too."

When Free entered the house Pa was having a cup of coffee and Ma was stitching up a rip in Everett's overalls.

Free had trouble being the first to say hello.

"Wal," Pa said, "you made it home alive, I see."

"Here comes our scholar," Ma said, smiling.

"Wal, what did you learn today?"

Free dug out the slip of paper Teacher had given him and handed it to Ma.

"What's this?" Ma said. Then she read it aloud. " 'Your child will need a box of colored crayons and a small slate. White chalk will be furnished by the school. Thank you. Vera Fenster.' "

Pa set his cup down. "What, the school ain't gonna furnish 'em?"

Ma wasn't sure she liked it either. But she finally said, "Well, crayons and a slate shouldn't cost too much."

"But it's the principle of the thing," Pa said. "A public school ain't supposed to be like a church school."

"Free, change into your old clothes now before you do your chores."

"Ya, Ma." Free wasn't sure he liked getting a slate either. If the chalk had a grain of sand in it like the one Teacher had that morning, the screaky noise was going to drive him crazy. But a new box of colors, now that was something else. He could just see them, glossy brand-new, with sharp points, all in a stiff row in their box.

School was going to be all right.

Free ❦ 13

THE NEXT FIRST of March, Old George Bowman, the landlord, told Pa that George Junior wanted to farm instead of run a store, so Pa and Ma had to move again. Luckily, a Mr. Haines had a farm for them across the road and a little closer to school.

"We're always moving," Ma said. Ma looked disgusted out of the kitchen window. "Just when I get the house all fixed up neat, the way I want it, then, sure enough, we got to move again."

"Yeh," Pa said, "and I always got to dig a new hole for the privy. Let alone fix up all the fences."

"Someday I hope we can move onto a farm of our own." The sun danced on Ma's gold hair. "If we could just have that, along with a daughter, well, that surely would be heaven on earth at last."

Free asked, "Is Uncle John going to help us again?"

"Yep. And your Uncle Sherm is coming too. With Gramma, who's gonna help your ma."

"Ain't Sherm got school?"

"No, they've got spring vacation there."

Hey. Sherm was coming. Golly. Then another thought hit Free. "Is Ma going to have another baby then?"

Pa's mouth fell open. So did Ma's.

Pa said, "Where did you ever get that notion, boy?"

"Well, every time we move there's a new baby. And Ma just said she wished she had a daughter."

Ma didn't know if she should smile or not.

Free said, "Well, anyways, maybe I can stay home when Sherm comes, ha Pa, please?"

"No," Pa said. "And that's final."

Free turned to Ma. "But can I though anyway?"

"Hey," Pa said, "I just said no."

Free could tell that Ma kind of thought it would be all right if he could play with Sherm. "Ma?"

Pa's eyes turned sharp. "No! Now get to bed."

Ma said, "Besides, Free, you don't want to break your perfect attendance record now, do you? So far you haven't been absent or tardy yet."

Free got mad. "I don't like that old school. Peter is always wanting to do funny things to Gladys."

Pa and Ma looked at him, then looked at each other.

Free knew he'd made a slip. He decided to clam up about those naughty Horsberg boys. Nobody was going to catch him being a tattletale.

"Funny things, Free? Like what?" Ma asked.

"Nothing. He just teases her."

Pa wouldn't let go of it. "How does he tease her?"

Free almost let it slip out. "That deserted house across from school. The kids sometimes sneak over there and look around in it."

Ma said, "Let sleeping dogs lie, Alfred."

"Yeh," Pa said, "I guess I better."

Free thought: "I wish I could just catch 'em at it once and see what it is they do."

The next morning very early Uncle John came rattling onto the yard in his wagon driving his favorite bay trotters. It was pitch dark. He and Pa wanted to finish the moving all in one day. Gramma and Sherm came with him. They were standing in straw in the bottom of the wagon to keep their feet warm. Pa already had the chores done, and Ma had the breakfast ready, a lot of pancakes and syrup and fried eggs.

Pa and Uncle John helped Gramma down out of the wagon. It was like they were unloading a barrel of salt. Gramma began to cry again when she saw her only grandchildren. Her kisses were wetter than ever. It took Ma a while to cool Gramma down.

When they were about done eating, sitting warm around the table, Sherm said, "I was hoping you'd have spring vacation too, Free."

"We don't have any in our country." Free was almost in tears.

Uncle John said, "It's probably just as well. Sherm's going to herd the cattle over. So he won't have much time to play with you anyway."

"I could help him," Free said. "I'm good with cows."

Pa leaned his big nose into Free's eyes. "You won't give up, will you? You're worse than your muleheaded grandfather."

Gramma got mad where she sat holding baby Albert in her lap. "My husband Alfred may have been stubborn," she said, "but he was not a mule."

Pa swung around to Gramma. "You keep out of this, Missus. I was talking about my own father."

Gramma let up her lid a little and cooled off.

Ma said, "Now, now, let's not have any bad words on the day we move."

Uncle John agreed. "Free, maybe we'll be all done moving by the time you get home from school. Then you and Sherm can go exploring all you want to on the new place."

"Yeh," Sherm said, "maybe we can even have a corncob war up in the haymow."

"See," Ma said, "you're still going to have a lot of fun with Sherm. Now. I'll read this daily meditation and then Alfred you finish, and we can all go about our appointed tasks."

A half hour later Free put on his stocking cap and mackinaw, slipped into his buckle boots, picked up his dinner bucket, and started off for school. Everybody said good-bye to him but he wouldn't say it back.

The road man had dragged the ruts flat the day before. Clods the size of eggs lay along the edges. As Free trudged along he kicked at the larger clods, demolishing them as though they were puffballs.

He paused at the mailbox of the new place they were going to move to. It was halfway up the long hill. The barn doors on the new yard were all open. So was the sliding door of the granary. He wished he and Sherm could go exploring on the new yard right that minute.

When he came to the top of the hill he looked back. Pa and Uncle John were just coming out of the Bowman lane with a wagonful of shiny furniture. He looked a minute longer, until he saw Pa waving a fist at him to get going to school, then hurried on.

Free stopped by the mailboxes on the corner. Looking over at the Horsberg place, he saw Louise and Peter and Alvina and Paul just then leaving their house. Free quick ducked down in the ditch behind the mailboxes. If they saw him they'd wait for him. He was still somehow hoping he could stay home from school and play with Sherm. Over the edge of the tall grass he could see Louise looking his way to see if he was coming. Louise still liked him and always waited for him if she spotted him coming. Peter and Alvina and Paul of course didn't care a snap if he came or not.

He stayed sitting there. He watched the Horsbergs out of sight beyond the row of trees near the Windmiller gate.

He knew that if he waited much longer he'd be late for school, and there would go his perfect record of never being tardy. Worse yet, if he played hooky all day, he'd also be marked absent. Teacher might even send the truant officer after him.

The sun rose. It became cozy in the deep dead grass under the mailboxes. It was where the road man hadn't been able to cut the grass with his mower because of the posts. Old wild roses lay bent under the Horsberg mailbox. Free picked several of the hips and chewed them. They tasted like strong tea.

It was hard work waiting for the day to hurry up and pass by. He picked another rose hip and bit into it.

Sherm was probably done now herding the cows and horses over.

He got up and walked back up the slope. Near the crest of the hill he crouched down. He peered over cautiously.

Yep. There was Sherm. He was just then waving the cows up the lane of the new place. Ma was standing with her back to Free waving her arms too. She was helping Sherm turn the last couple of calves into the lane. And there down the road came Pa and Uncle John in their wagon, with Gramma holding the baby and Everett peeking over the edge to see how things were going. Lucky Everett.

Sherm and Ma drove the livestock into the barnyard and closed the gate. The cows bawled for their old stanchions. The horses sported around in the new barnyard. Some of their tails went off like Fourth of July firecrackers. Ma and Sherm walked back to the house and got there just as Pa and Uncle John unloaded Gramma again. They all went into the new house. Pretty soon some smoke started to come out of the kitchen chimney. Everett was seeing the insides of the new house first.

Pa and Uncle John came outside again. They were wiping their mouths. They'd had a cup of coffee and some cake then. They climbed into their wagon and rattled off for the Bowman place to get some more things. Sherm could play for the rest of the day. It wasn't fair.

Free climbed through the fence and entered an old cornfield and then took a row that ran straight down to the cobshed by the house. He climbed through a fence and snuck behind the cobshed, making sure no one could see him from the kitchen windows.

Just in time. He heard someone come out of the house and take the walk a ways and enter the cobshed.

There was a hole in the backside of the cobshed. The edges of the hole were singed a little. It was where the exhaust of a gas engine had come through. He set down his dinner bucket and sagged down and put one eye to the hole and peered inside.

On the other side of the cobshed the sun was shining like a gold lamp through the open door. He could see everything inside very clearly. Ma was shoveling up some cobs into a basket. Ma's washing machine had been set inside already and close by stood Pa's cream separator.

He must have made some kind of noise because Ma looked around. She right away spotted an eye at the exhaust hole. She scared up. "Free!"

Free slowly drew back an inch.

"Oh, I see you there all right, boy. I'd never mistake that blue eye of yours." Ma shook her head. "You better not let your father catch you around here when he comes back with the next load. He's been muttering to himself all morning about you."

Free drew back another inch.

"Playing hooky from school, fooey! And you my son. I never thought you'd pull off a stunt like that." Ma again acted like she herself wouldn't have minded so much if he'd have stayed home to play with Sherm. But rules were rules. "What you forget, boy, is that you'll be marked absent on your report card today and that your pa will see."

Free picked up his dinner bucket and snuck back into the cornfield. Sadly he trudged up the same row he'd taken down. He was just going over the rise when he heard Pa and Uncle John come rattling out of the Bowman place once more. Pa'd missed seeing him by a hair.

When he got to the mailboxes, he turned stubborn once more. He hated to give up the idea of playing with Sherm that day. It wasn't fair. He sat down in the grass.

Besides, he was in trouble no matter what he did now.

He was hungry. He opened his dinner bucket and peeked in. Hey. Ma had made him a special lunch. Sliced beef with mustard. Black rye bread with lots of butter and brown sugar. And a big red apple.

He decided it wouldn't hurt to eat one of the sandwiches. He tackled the one with the sliced beef and mustard. One side of the sandwich had a lot of butter on and when his tongue hit that, yummy.

There was a rattling on the road, and looking up he was surprised to see their mailman, Slim Lehr, curve toward him and pull up beside the first mailbox. Slim Lehr had one of those new Model T Fords and he sat on the wrong side so he could reach the mail into the boxes. He looked at Free a second and then went on filling the four shiny mailboxes, the Horsbergs', the Johnsons', the Windmillers', and the Stoefens'. When he had them all full, he looked down at Free. "Ain't you supposed to be in school today, boy?"

Free sat with his mouth full of sliced beef and mustard.

"Ain't you the Alfredson boy?"

Free chewed once.

"Well, if you don't want to talk, it's no skin off my nose." Slim Lehr goosed up his motor and rolled on.

The beef sandwich made him really hungry. He looked up at the sun. It was near noon. Close enough anyway so it wouldn't hurt if he ate a little more. He broke the rye bread sandwich in half and ate that. Crumbles of brown sugar sprinkled down the front of his mackinaw. When he finished the half sandwich he brushed off his front.

The telephone wire above him hummed. It sure was loud that morning. He could hear it over everything. He wondered what it was saying. Finally, curious, he went over and placed his ear against the corner telephone post. Say. Through the post the wire sure hummed loud. But there were no voices. Just the music of the humming, slowly up and slowly down, like waves on a very wide pond.

He went back to his spot in the grass under the mailboxes.

Footsteps on the gravel road came toward him. He looked up. It was Mrs. Horsberg coming to get her mail. She had a wrinkly look around her mouth and her eyes were like a domeny's. She had her hair pulled up into a knot on top so that her head looked like a big gray cabbage. Mrs. Horsberg was wearing a long gray apron and she had her hands in the pockets.

"Aren't you supposed to be in school, boy?"

Free couldn't hold up to her eyes.

"Did you hurt yourself that you can't walk any farther?"

Free wished she'd just mind her own business. Get her mail and go on home. If Sherm had been there he would've known what to say to her.

Mrs. Horsberg stared stern at him some more. Then she got her mail and went on home. She looked back twice.

He looked at the half sandwich that was left. No use in saving the rest of the lunch for later. He emptied the dinner bucket.

He'd just thrown away the apple core, and had pressed the lid back onto his dinner bucket, when he heard rattling wagon wheels coming up the other side of the hill. It sounded like Uncle John's wagon. It was coming awful fast. Then he saw dust, then two horses' heads, then two people heads coming over the top of the hill. It was Uncle John's bay trotters all right. And galloping galley-west. The wagon was swinging from side to side it was coming so fast. The wheels hit ruts in the road and bounced around. Pa was driving and he was whipping up the trotters with the ends of the leather lines, so hard the lines popped on the butts of the horses. They were on top of Free before he could move.

"Whoa!" Pa roared as he hauled back on the lines. The pair of bays went up on two feet pawing. Dust flew up all around. Pa reached down to pick something up and then jumped down out of the wagon and came walking long steps straight for Free. Pa was swishing the something back and forth behind his back. A black horsewhip. The horsewhip made jerks like the tail of an angry cat. "So you thought you could play hooky today, ha?"

Free tried to get up but couldn't.

"Thought you could hide on this side of the hill where I couldn't see you, ha?"

"But, Pa—"

"But you forgot though there's people living on this side of the hill too, ha? And you forgot the new house has a telephone, ha?"

So that's how Pa found out. That darn Mrs. Horsberg.

"Get up off that one-spot of yours and start running for school. Right now! You little tramp. March. Walk chalk."

Again Free tried to get up but couldn't. His sitter was already stinging where in a second the horsewhip was going to get him.

"B-but, P-Pa—"

"Get!" Pa's hand came around with the horsewhip. He laid it across Free's shoulders.

"Ow." Free yelled. Though the thick mackinaw helped.

"Alfred, for godsakes, man," Uncle John cried from the wagon, "that's going pretty far." Uncle John picked up the lines Pa'd dropped.

Pa snapped around at Uncle John. "This is my kid, not yours, and goddam it, just you keep out of it if you know what's good for you."

Uncle John couldn't do anything but shrug his shoulders then. He gave Free a sad face.

Sherm was in the wagon too. Free hadn't noticed him before. "Alfred, you know what you're doing, don't you? You're horsewhipping your own flesh and blood."

Pa got so hot hearing Sherm talk that he leaped up, then came down with a thump. "Arrr!"

Free knew he'd better move or he'd just get it worse. He turned over on his hands and knees, then quick snuck-rolled onto his feet and so got out of reach of that horsewhip. He wondered if he could outrun Pa.

"Come back here and pick up your dinner bucket."

"It's empty already. I can pick it up on the way home tonight."

"Come back here and pick it up."

Free had to do it. He stepped over and picked up his dinner bucket. He kept his quivering butt turned well away from Pa.

"Run for your life, Free!" Sherm yelled.

Free took a couple of trembling steps toward school—then suddenly broke into a run.

Sherm's yell made Pa mad again. Four long steps and Pa caught up with Free and let him have the horsewhip around the butt.

Free yelped like a shot dog. "Ow!" He jumped into hopping runs like a jackrabbit. His empty dinner bucket banged against his leg. "Ow!"

"So you still played hooky even after the warning I gave you this morning, did you, ha? Wal, goddam your hide, I'm going to whip you until I bring the blood." Flish went the horsewhip.

"Ow!"

"So you and I are going to have a showdown to see who's the head stud around here, are we?" Whish went the horsewhip.

"Ow!"

"Wal, by God, after today there ain't never going to be any doubt about it." Whosh went the horsewhip.

"Ow! Ow!"

Free ran for his life. The popper on the horsewhip burned him worse on his behind than that frosted pump handle on Bowman's place had burned his tongue. He cried. He ran. He cried so hard sobs came out of the bottom of his lungs like they were vomits.

Pa let up on the whipping only after Free had crossed the culvert, the same culvert into which Peter had once thrown his stocking cap.

Free ran and ran. He crippled up the hill as fast as he could go.

Pa stood watching him another minute, then finally turned around and went back to the wagon.

Free sobbed all the way to school.

The kids were all outdoors playing on the schoolyard. It was noon recess.

Teacher saw him coming. She saw something was the matter with him. She opened the door for him. He went straight for his seat. His behind burned him but he sat on it anyway.

Teacher didn't say anything for a while.

He wouldn't look at her. Big sobs kept coming.

Pretty soon she came over and sat on top of the desk next to his. "Aren't you going to eat your dinner with the other children outdoors, Free?"

He couldn't talk. He shook his pail to show her it was empty.

Slowly his big sobs broke up into little dry sobs.

"Take off your cap and coat and boots then, Free, and put them out in the hall. And take your dinner bucket too."

Free numbly did as he was told. Then he shuffled back inside.

Teacher stared at the seat of his overalls. "Blood," she whispered. "You poor dear boy. What happened? May I know?"

"Pa horsewhipped me."

"Not really."

"Pa horsewhipped me."

"But why?"

"Because I wanted to stay home and play with Sherm. Sherm's from Gramma's town and they've got vacation there for little children." Free began to cry out of the bottom of his lungs again. "And that ain't fair, Teacher."

"Oh, Free. Free."

Teacher didn't ring the bell at one that noon. She waited until Free quit crying.

Teacher was fine.

Double sobs kept breaking out of him like hiccups all afternoon.

Alfred ❦ 14

ALFRED CLIMBED BACK into the wagon. He reached for the lines. "Here, I'll drive home."

"They're my horses," John said. "I think I can still handle 'em."

Alfred threw John a sharp look. That John could be a hard one too. "All right, drive then."

The three rode onto the yard in silence. Alfred and John unhitched the horses together and took them into the barn. Sherm went on ahead to feed them, taking his time.

The silence continued as the men walked into the kitchen and washed up. Alfred's nose was still so thick with anger he almost missed noticing they were having his favorite dish that noon, fried sausage.

"What happened?" Ada asked. She was sweeping up some of the litter from the moving so they could sit down in at least one clean corner of the strange kitchen.

"Nothing," Alfred said. The mirror still wasn't up so he had to comb his hair by making a guess as to where the part was.

"That true, John?"

John buried his face in water and suds.

"Say now, what did go on?"

Alfred sat down with a thump at the head of the table.

Sherm stood leaning in the doorway waiting his turn to wash up. "Well," he said, "if you two older nuts won't talk up, then I guess I better. Ade, your husband horsewhipped your child down the road."

"What?" Ada cried.

Gramma had been listening in the living room where she'd been minding the baby and keeping Everett from getting underfoot. She got up with a cracking noise and steamed into the kitchen. "Did I hear right, that you horsewhipped your own boy?"

"Yes, I did," Alfred said flat out. "I tanned him all the way to the Horsberg culvert. And if he ever plays hooky again, I'll tromp him into the earth if I have to, in order to make him behave."

Sherm stared Alfred in the eye. "Yeh, I hear that when your kids are only a little bit naughty, you like to kick them in the ass like they was footballs."

Gramma swelled up even more. "What! He kicks my boy grandchildren in the clots?"

"They're my kids, not yours," Alfred said.

Gramma threw a look up at God in heaven. "Why don't you just kill my grandson while you're at it? Get rid of him?"

Alfred sneered. "Like you got rid of Ada's pa by driving him into cancer?"

Gramma took a couple of steps toward Alfred as if she meant to hammer him with her fat fists.

From his armchair Alfred reached up and gave her a shove backwards against the stove.

Gramma bounced off the warm nickel railing of the stove. She was outraged. She came back at him with a waggling trembling finger. "Oh, you big brave man you! It's pretty wonderful for you, isn't it, to have the strength of a giant, ha?" A drop of sweat flipped off the end of her red nose. "But let me tell you something. It's the work of an evil tyrant when strength is used to destroy little ones like your own son. The poor little fellow."

John finished combing his hair. He quick stepped in between Alfred and Gramma. From somewhere he managed to come up with the wry smile of the peacemaker. "You know, most times I'd be scared to death of the way you two roar at each other . . . except that right now I'm more worried about what a close friend of mine is thinking."

"What friend?" Gramma demanded, checked.

"Friend Tapeworm. He's just told me that he's going to eat a hole right through the bottom of my stomach if I don't hurry and eat for him."

It didn't raise a laugh but it did cool things off.

Ada put aside her broom. "Well, maybe we're all a little jumpy and tired from working so hard."

Sherm next finished washing up. He took a chair across from Alfred.

Alfred placed his elbows on the table. "Where are the children?"

"I just rocked the baby asleep," Gramma said, short.

"And Everett?"

Ada called into the other room. "Everett? We're ready to eat."

Everett came in with a sidelong glance at everyone, not sure it was safe for him to come. He climbed into his chair.

"Now," Alfred said. And closing his eyes and folding his hands over his face, he asked the blessing. He had the presence of mind as he went along to insert a couple of remarks about the present company and why they were there. "And bless all our loved ones, wherever they may be, those near and dear unto us, both at home and in far distant lands. In Jesus' name we ask it. Amen."

As Gramma opened her eyes, she made a superior sniffing sound. "I have a question to ask of the head of this house."

"Shoot," Alfred said.

"When you just now prayed that God should 'bless all our loved ones, wherever they may be,' I hope that included your own son just a mile and a half away from here, where he sits in school with a broken heart?"

"Ma!" John exclaimed. "My goodness, you surely do like to make argument, don't you? Always."

"I don't either like to make argument," Gramma snapped. "But I do like to discuss things."

"Ma, the way you discuss things you pretty near always argue."

Ada let go with a merry laugh.

Alfred had to smile then too. "Ma, when I pray as the head of this house, I pray for everybody, my wife, my son, you, my company. And now, Ma, and I have to say it, it's been a great help to have you here. We properly appreciate it."

John gave Alfred an appreciative smile. "Well, now that we got that off our minds, maybe me and Friend Tapeworm can eat."

The canned sausage fried to a crisp brown never tasted better. As he ate, Alfred mulled over his thoughts one by one.

. . . . Things had not gone well lately. Both of his brothers, Abbott and Richard, had been drafted to help beat the Kaiser, and the way the soldiers were dying in France, both might be killed before the war was over. Dad Alfredson had been so bitter about the entry of the United States of America into the war, to help save the nuts of those damned English, that he refused to see his two sons off on the train, and had announced downtown one day that if his two boys came home on a furlough, he was not going to let them into his house if they wore their uniforms.

What happened shortly after had been very upsetting. Someone had figured out that Peter Hooks, Dad Alfredson's neighbor, was taking in more food than he and his wife could possibly eat, more even than hoarding might account for, and had reported the fact to the sheriff. Sure enough, upstairs in the attic, the sheriff had found son John Hooks hiding from the draft board, as fat as a white grub. Old Peter Hooks had built a small dumbwaiter in his house, with which they could elevate son John's food up to him each day as well as lower down his slop. The whole town went into an uproar over the discovery, and some of the young punks, not yet old enough to go to war themselves, painted Old Peter Hooks's house yellow.

Dad Alfredson had watched the young punks with their wild yallooing and their flaming torches and their yellow paintbrushes at work, and when they came to the gate of his yard next to paint his house yellow, he stepped out onto the stoop armed with his six-shooter, took dead aim at one of the flaming torches they were carrying, and shot it out, and announced, "The first man through that gate gets it in the belly button next!" That'd backed them off, but the scandal of it went all over town. It wasn't pleasant for Alfred to hear people gossip about his father being a Hun-lover that spring of 1918.

And then there was poor Ada herself, expecting again in October, with baby Albert barely weaned and her always grabbing her chest where her heart was. On top of all that Ada would no longer pleasure him nights, like she'd sometimes done while carrying the other boys those first months. He and Ada were usually friendly all day long, but after the sun set, about bedtime, she'd become as silent and as strict with him as a grape-juice Baptist, and so naturally this in turn made him as charged up as a penned-up bull. And now they'd had to move. . . .

"Alfred?"

"Yes?"

"I suppose the ground's too frozen yet to move the privy?"

There it was again. Work, work. Savagely he cut his sausage into a dozen red dollars. Just barely he managed to keep his temper. "Love, I'll get at digging that new privy hole as soon as I can. Though why old Haines had the carpenter build a three-holer here for this place is beyond me. He must've intended for his renters to hold some kind of a brass band concert in it, it's so roomy. It'll call for a hole in the ground twice as wide as the one on the Bowmans' place. Mother and child going to the privy together is one thing, for training's sake, a big hole and a little hole, but three holes, with a great big hole, a middle-sized hole, and a little hole . . . what's it all for?"

John said with a straight face, "Well, Alfred, you know what they say—in the whole world there ain't two butts alike, and having three holes of different sizes, it at least gives a man a choice as to whatever seat comes closest to fitting him."

"A man can adjust to one of two just as easy," Alfred said. "I know I can. Why, I can even adjust to the little hole, if I have to."

"Well, I can't," Gramma said.

A wonderful astonished look came over the faces of her two sons John and Sherm. After a moment they exploded into laughter.

Neither Gramma nor Ada thought it very funny.

They finished dinner with Ada reading a short passage from Job, and Alfred giving thanks. And then all hands went hard at it again.

It was three o'clock when the men hauled over the last load of goods. After a quick cup of coffee and a slice of bread with butter and jelly, John headed for home.

Alfred didn't see Free come home. He'd been too busy getting his barn in order. But around five he saw the boy getting the eggs from the chicken coop and a bit later saw him hauling in the cobs with Sherm.

Alfred felt guilty about the tanning he'd given the boy. He'd whipped the boy in anger, and that was wrong. Yet, doggone it, the boy had to learn that most times duty came first, not fun.

When it got dark Alfred got the lantern from the porch. He shook it to see how much kerosene there was left in it. The splashing inside told him there was enough for that night. He eased up the globe with his thumb, lighted the wick, and let the globe down gently. Going back to the barn, carrying the milk can and pail in the other hand, he watched the shadows of his legs go scissoring into the grove like the legs of a giant. Just as he was about to step into the barn, he looked back at the house. The lamp was on in the kitchen, shining a warm yellow in the west window. He saw Ada move across the light, going to the pantry under the stairs. His heart thumped hard in his chest. Already with the lit lantern in his hand, and the lamp in the kitchen, it was as if they'd lived on the new place for years.

"Someday we've got to have a place of our own. With no debts."

He hung the lantern on a hook above his four cows. He picked up his stool, sat down under Belle with the pail caught between his knees, began pinching tits. After a while he settled his head into the hollow between her rear leg and belly. The musk smell in her red hair was comforting.

It took him a half hour to do the milking and separating.

When he entered the house, he was pleased to see Free playing with Sherm and Everett under the table. Free's laughter was as merry and as pure as ever. Good. He didn't want to lose the love of that little fellow. They had to be friends if they were going to do great things ahead.

"Supper ready?" he asked with a smile.

"Just about."

Free glanced at him from under the table. Free first gave him a cautious look; then, seeing his smile, gave him a wide grin of his own.

After supper, as Alfred filled his pipe and put his feet in the fuel box by the stove, he asked Free to get him a lucifer.

Free ran to the little box hanging over the stove and dug out a wooden match. "Can I light it, Pa?"

"Sure. But don't scratch it on the stove top there, or you'll get Hail Columbia from the lady of the house."

"Pa, how do you do it on your pants leg?" Free tried to light the blue-and-red tipped match along his raised leg. It didn't work.

"Hold your pants leg tight, boy. Like so." Alfred took the match, raised his knee until his overalls were taut from hip to knee, then gave the match a vigorous fluid swipe along it. The match flamed up.

Free laughed. "Someday I'm gonna do that. When I'm big like you."

Alfred moved the flaming match back and forth over the bowl of his pipe as he sucked, until the knots in the tobacco began to crackle.

"Can I blow it out, Pa?"

"Sure, son." Alfred handed the end of the match to him.

Free watched the flame a moment, until it almost touched his thumb and fingertip, then snapped it out and threw it into the stove.

Ada handed Alfred an envelope. "You better have a look at this while you're in a good mood."

Alfred opened the flap and drew out a folded blue card. "Oho, your report card, huh, boy?"

Free's face sobered over.

Alfred had learned from Ada what the different sets of hen tracks meant. Quickly he ran his finger down the new entries made in ink. He compared them with the marks of the previous month. "Wal, this looks all right to me. In fact, it's mostly better than before."

Free didn't smile. He waited.

"Is there something I missed?" Alfred started at the top again. He had learned what the various categories meant by their position on the card. "Deportment. Oho. I did miss that one. You fell from 90 to 80, boy. What happened?"

"I dunno."

Alfred read further down the line. "Say, you should've been marked tardy as well as a half-day absent today. How come?"

Free dared to look him in the eye. "Maybe because the teacher thought I had a good excuse."

There was that strong head again. "By golly, boy, after what happened today, I should think you'd just about run out of smart answers for a while."

Before Free could get into more trouble, Ada broke in. "Teacher sent along a note."

"She did, eh? What does it say?"

Ada took a piece of paper from her apron pocket and read it aloud: "Dear Mrs. Alfredson, I thought perhaps you'd like to know that I've entered the following remarks about your boy in the monthly record which I'm required to send to the school superintendent's office: 'No. 17. Good. He has read his primer thru 3 times and has read several other books.' No. 17 is your son. Miss Vera Fenster."

Alfred didn't know what to say for a moment. This boy of his could read that well? And still only in the primary grade? Gotske. The boy was already ahead of him. No wonder he had such a strong head.

There was a sob from Gramma where she was washing dishes in the sink. "Oh, Free, how you bring to mind my first Shermie again. That angel, who is surely in heaven, sitting at the right hand of the Father—"

"Ma!" Sherm cried from under the table. "Please! Before you drive this Shermie into his early grave."

Gramma jerked erect. "Sherman!"

"Well, I don't care." Sherm knocked over the tower he'd been building, the blocks flying every which way, even under the stove. "I wish to God you'd never named me after him. I would much rather have had a simple name like Pete or Sam. Even Poop would have been better. Now I can never do anything but what I've always first got to worry what Sherman One might have done, and not what Sherman Two"—Sherm gave his chest a resounding whack—"should do."

Gramma wept. "Boy, boy, you don't know what you're saying. But I forgive you." Gramma turned her tears on Free. "Yes, my darling grandson, my Shermie One could read and write before he started school. He knew that naturally from birth. Sometimes when my husband . . . that's your grandfather . . . you remember him, don't you? Sure you do. When my husband couldn't go to church, little Shermie One would repeat the whole service for him when he got home, word for word, including the psalms and the prayers. Ach! And then he had to die of scarlet fever. Och! If only—"

"Ma," Sherm said, "you're running things together again and getting them all mixed up."

"—if only he could've lived, Free, what a joy it would have been for you to have known him. But now he lies there in his new grave with his head twisted to one side and his white-gold hair still growing—"

"New grave?" Alfred exclaimed.

"Yes, new grave," Gramma sobbed. "His bones were drowning in the old Engleking plot, so John and the cemetery caretaker dug him up and moved him and my husband to the new plot I bought on higher ground."

"I didn't know about that. Did you, Ada?"

"Ma told me this morning," Ada said.

Gramma rambled on. "John thought of digging up his grandparents too, Great

John and his wife Adelheid, and moving them to higher ground. But the caretaker didn't know where they lay any more."

"What?" Ada cried. "Now that I didn't hear about. You say he couldn't find them? Have there been grave robbers around here then too?"

"I don't know," Gramma said. "There well might be."

"There better not be," Ada said. "Gramma Ada was wearing the family golden casque when she was buried."

"By the way, I better . . ." Gramma hesitated. After a moment she shook her head. "I was going to ask you something, but now I've forgotten what it was. Shucks." Gramma smiled at her forgetfulness. "Well, it must've been a lie if I can't think of it again."

"Anyway," Alfred said, "getting back to our boy here . . . son, what did you do in deportment that it's so low?"

"Nothing." Free started to help Sherm pick up the scattered blocks. "Except Peter was hurting Gladys and I kicked him off her."

That again. Alfred bit on his tongue.

Gramma raised a hand out of the dishwater and touched her forehead. "Now I remember what it was. Can you raise Jerusalem from here long distance?"

"You bet," Alfred said.

"Good." Gramma dried her hands in her apron. "I better do it right now then before I forget again. When I left home I forgot to tell our church janitor, Garland Stanhorse, something. Only he doesn't have a phone so I've got to call our new minister Domeny deCockcock and have him go over and tell him. What's Central's ring here?"

"One long."

Gramma walked heavily to the phone in the living room. The night lamp was on and its orange light made the two nickel bells on the dark walnut phone box gleam like cat eyes. Gramma cranked the handle a dozen times, then held the black receiver to her ear. She stood waiting, eyes rolling around under her closed lids. "Central? I want to talk to Domeny deCockcock in Jerusalem. . . . Ah. Hello, Domeny . . . What?" Gramma backed a foot away from the phone and began to shout at it. "You're going to have to talk louder, Domeny . . . What? What? . . . Just a minute." Gramma turned to Ada. "Maybe you know how to run this thing. I can't hear a blessed thing over it. Just some squeaking on the other end."

Ada took over the receiver. "What shall I tell Domeny deCockcock to tell the janitor?"

Gramma turned pink. "Well, Gar offered to water my flowers for me while I was gone, but I forgot to tell him where I hid the key."

"Gar? You call him Gar?"

"What's wrong with that?" Gramma sputtered. "After all, we're Christian friends. Decent."

"In that case you better talk to Domeny deCockcock yourself." Smiling, Ada turned to the mouthpiece. "Central? Give us a better connection and then let my mother try again."

Gramma took the receiver reluctantly.

Alfred spoke up from his armchair in the kitchen. "Stand closer to the mouthpiece, Ma. It won't bite you."

"Too many bosses I got," Gramma complained. "Central, have you still got hold of Domeny deCockcock? . . . All right . . . Domeny? Yes, this is Mrs. Engleking . . . Yes, yes, I'm all right. What I want to know is . . . What? What? . . . Shucks, I still can't hear him good. And it sounds like he can't hear me at all. Hello? Hello?" Gramma got mad, and abruptly slipped into Frisian, her mother tongue, speaking rapidly for about a minute. "What was that, Central? I mayn't talk in German? But I'm talking in Frisian . . . You never heard of it? Why, the Frisians hate the Germans worse than the Americans do . . . Och!" Gramma turned to Ada again. "Central says I'm pro-German. Can you imagine? And she says that they can't have any pro-German talk on the telephone because I could be a spy. Me, a spy?" Gramma rolled her eyes to heaven.

"Well, Ma, talk American then."

"But it looks like this phone only understands Frisian. Domeny could understand me perfectly well when I spoke Frisian."

"Here, let me." Ada took the receiver. "Central? Central?" Ada waited, eyes closed. "And now I can't hear anything."

"See?" Gramma said. "See?"

Alfred had enough. He got up and went into the living room. "Give me that phone." He took the receiver from Ada. "I know what's wrong. Too many listening in on the line at the same time weakens the juice." Alfred adjusted the mouthpiece for his height and spoke firmly and clearly into it. "Listen, all you coffee gossips, let me read the Scripture to you. Rubbernecking, butting in, whistling, or making other noises is cause for removal of your telephone, did you know that? . . ." He listened a moment to the humming wire. "I ain't heard any clicks. That means you're all still on the line. Get off this line!" He listened some more, then said to Ada over his shoulder, "I know how to rattle their hocks, by God." Alfred adjusted the mouthpiece again so he could speak even more directly into it. "Listen, Mrs. Dingleberry, I know you're still there, hanging on. Because I can smell you. . . . What! What!" Alfred's face contorted, he was so surprised by what he heard next. Someone, a woman, had dared to speak up on the wire. "Ha, Mrs. Murray, better that you should say that the fart calls the kettle black—"

"Alfred!" Ada scolded behind him. "Such talk." Though she had to laugh too.

"It's only that poor nervous Mrs. Murray," Alfred said. "Raised on prunes and proverbs." Alfred sneered down at the mouthpiece, deliberately leaving it uncovered. "I know what her husband Frank Murray ought to do with her too. Upend her, pour in a little kerosene, and shake well. And if that don't liven her up, put a match to it."

Gramma was going wild. "Can Domeny deCockcock hear all this?"

"I dunno. I guess so."

"Oh, good grutkins, then I'm disgraced forever."

"What, Central? What?" Alfred spoke into the phone again. "It's against the law to talk like that over the telephone? Wal now, what about all them rubberneckers on the line spoiling our long distance call? . . . All right, tell 'em to get off then. . . . Ah, that's better. Did you hear them five clicks? I told you there was rubberneckers on this line . . . . All right, Ma, here, talk into this phone and finish your call with Domeny deCockcock."

Afterwards, when all had quieted down, Ada asked Sherm, "Who is this Garland Stanhorse fellow, this janitor Ma knows? What's he like?"

Sherm was still smiling about all the commotion they'd had over that phone call. "Well, Domeny says he's the best janitor we've ever had. But better yet, Gar's got an important nose."

"He hasn't either got a big nose," Gramma snapped.

"Well, Ma," Sherm said, "from where I sit on Sunday, when Gar brings that glass of fresh water down the aisle just before Domeny ascends the pulpit, you'd say his nose looked important too."

Gramma turned pink again. "Important. Fooey."

In bed an hour later, Alfred could feel Ada still laughing beside him. "What's so funny, love?"

"Nothing." Ada put an arm around him and kissed him. "For all the crazy things you sometimes do, Alfred, you're still a dear husband. Do you know that?"

Alfred held still. What was this?

Ada kissed him again. "In some ways," she whispered, "in some ways, I hope Ma has fallen in love with this Gar. She's been so lonesome these last years. And it'd be even better for Sherman. Poor boy. He needs a father bad."

"Yeh," Alfred said, "I guess so." Then he turned on his side and kissed Ada back.

After a while Ada permitted him his pleasure. He could feel the little baby in her belly between them quite plainly. It was like he'd draped himself over a long pillow with a hard rubber ball in the middle of it.

Ada ❦ 15

ADA WASN'T SURE she was going to make it this time. Baby was due at any moment and here her heart was bobbling around like a lid on a boiling kettle. Twice she and Alfred had driven in to see Dr. Halmers about the faint feeling she had in her chest. Each time Dr. Halmers had smiled warm under his black moustache and told her it was only a case of a nervous heart and not a bad heart.

"It's all in your head, Ada. The day you decide you've got a good heart that day your heart trouble will disappear."

Ada always felt reassured after seeing Dr. Halmers. At least for a couple of days. The trouble was that after a week that odd faint feeling would come back again. Secretly she knew the doctor was wrong.

A couple of times she'd noticed the smell of liquor on Dr. Halmers. That had bothered her. She liked him, trusted him, wanted to like him even more. But to think of him as a drinker was to think of him as a sinner.

She mentioned it to Alfred one night just as they went to bed. "I hope doctor isn't drinking when I'm having this baby."

"Don't worry. Doc only drinks after office hours."

"But suppose the baby's born at night?"

"Don't worry. A doctor'll know how to sober up fast."

Ada shook her head in the dark. "It's always such a puzzle to me why good men so often have to drink."

"Love, it probably comes with the kind of work they do."

"But why?"

"Because they see too much. Just imagine if you had to treat Mrs. Frank Murray for the piles. The sight of that would be enough to give a man gray hairs all the way down to his armpits."

"Ugh."

"I'll bet that woman's got more dingleberries than our pasture has wolfberries."

"For goodness sakes, what makes you say that?"

"Wal, Frank says she's so shy she takes a bath in the dark."

"That's enough of that now, Alfred."

The next afternoon Ada heard their ring, two shorts and a long. It was Stepmother Bettie calling from Bonnie.

"Oh, Ada, I don't know how to tell you."

"What now?"

"We just this morning received a telegram from Camp Forest, Georgia."

"Abbott?"

"Yes. Alfred had better get set for the worst."

"Not . . . ?"

"Yes. Abbott died of the flu. You know that great flu epidemic that's been running wild through the country? Well, our men in the Army camps have been dying like flies."

"Not Abbott."

Stepmother Bettie sobbed on her end of the line. "The Army wants to know if we wish to have his body sent home."

"What does Dad say?"

"Dad says he'll have nothing to do with it."

Ada could see again Abbott jumping over that badger.

"Besides Dad says the Army seals the coffin and the people back home never know if they got the right body back."

"Oh."

"Karen is boarding with you people now, isn't she?"

"Yes. She's teaching again at Rock No. 3. Where Free goes to school. But she won't be home for another hour yet." Ada checked her heart. It was still beating steady and true. Good. She was really needed by her family now. "Mother?"

"Yes?"

"Listen. I'll talk to both Karen and Alfred tonight and then I'll call you back. I'm sure they'll want Abbott brought home if at all possible."

"That's what I thought. I'm sorry I had to be the one to tell you the sad news."

Two hours later, she told Karen and Alfred.

Karen wept. "My beautiful brother Abbott."

Alfred sagged in his armchair. "Wal, there goes the fastest foot racer what ever lived. And no kids left behind that he might have passed it on to."

Ada asked, "Well, what shall I tell Stepmother?"

Karen sobbed. "Of course we want him back."

Alfred said, "But what if they send the wrong coffin?"

Karen gasped, "The government wouldn't dare do that, would they?"

"The government can pretty darn well do what it wants to. Look what they did last spring, accusing Ada's ma of being pro-German and a spy."

All three sat in black silence.

At last Alfred got up and helped himself to some black coffee from the pot on the back of the stove. He drank directly from the spout. "All right, I'll go to Sioux City. I'll have the officer there break the seal and make sure the right body is in the right coffin."

"But by the time Abbott's body gets here it'll be so deteriorated you won't know if it's him," Karen said.

Alfred wiggled his nose. "Remember that silver plate they put in Abbott's left arm? To help mend that broken bone? I'll look for that."

"How awful," Ada murmured.

"Yeh," Alfred said, helping himself to some more cold coffee from the spout, "yeh, but some things you've just got to do."

At supper that night no one had much to say. The children had been told that their Uncle Abbott had gone to heaven and they too ate in silence.

Ada wasn't very hungry.

Alfred, however, ate like always, heartily. He finished his potatoes and sausage and cabbage, and then reached for a slice of bread. He dearly loved thick slices of fresh baked bread, with butter and plum preserve. But Karen had cut the bread that night to be helpful and that had been a mistake. Karen always cut the bread too thin. Alfred paused. He held the slice he'd picked up between thumb and forefinger, pinkie lifted, and fixed Karen with an utterly disgusted look.

"What's the matter?" Karen said.

"I see you're still being tight with my bread."

Karen gave him a hurt look.

"Sis, I don't care how thin you cut your bread in your own house. But in my house I want you to cut it so it'll have some heft to it."

"Only ignorant people like it cut that thick." Karen picked up a corner of bread from her plate and held it up between her slender lady fingers as if it were a wafer. She nibbled off a dainty bite. "Alfred, remember, you have some little imitators sitting at your table."

"Pah!" Alfred exploded. "I'm not asking you to cut the slices two inches thick. I'm not even asking you to cut them an inch thick. All I want is just enough thickness to them so they won't fall apart in my hand."

"Break the slice into smaller portions then. Like so."

"Too thin." Alfred held up the fragile slice of bread again. "Look. I can actually see through it like it was a piece of cheesecloth. Why, there ain't enough gaff in this miserable thin slice to keep a sparrow alive for one day." Alfred got more and more worked up. "Why, it's so light I don't dare breathe hard on it for fear it'll blow away. Why, if I was of a mind to, I could blow it from here to you with one breath. In fact, I'll prove it to you." Alfred filled his lungs, and holding up the thin slice, let go with a blast of air. The slice of bread took off and sailed completely over Karen's head and landed on the rag rug in front of the sink behind her. Even Alfred was startled to see it sail that far. "You see," he cried in triumph.

Ada frowned, "Alfred, please now. I'll cut a slice of bread for you just the way you want it." She pushed back her chair to get up.

"No, skip it," Alfred said "I don't want any bread now."

"Alfred."

Alfred studied to himself a moment; then let down. "Wal, I guess we're all on edge a little, what with everything. But I will have some coffee."

Karen, aroused, wasn't done with it. "Don't pour any for me, Ada." Karen picked at her food here and there, as if eating were beneath her, a kind of unfortunate carnal necessity that mankind had been cursed with. And wasn't it a pity that some of the food became waste. "Not after the way Alfred drank out of the spout this afternoon."

Ada had something to say about that too. "Yes, Alfred, I think that is a very bad habit."

"Never mind now," Alfred said. "I'm in my own house and I guess I can drink coffee any way I see fit."

Karen swallowed her bird bite with a light throat sound. "I can see now where Free gets his bold nose."

"Sis, if you think the boy is naughty in school, lick him."

"While his brother is like a mouse beside him. Poor Everett."

"What do you mean poor Everett?"

"Well, to keep him from going under in school, I've been holding Free back and pushing Everett ahead."

"That I approve of. I do the same thing here on the yard."

"But you don't help it any by the example you set at your table."

Alfred dropped his fork on his plate. It landed with a little clang. "I wish to God you'd get married one of these days, you old maid."

Karen's head made a slow high motion. Then, after a moment, with a pinched laugh at herself, she said, "Well, you know what they always say, 'An old maid is an unclaimed treasure.' "

"An antique virgin would be more like it."

Baby Albert, sitting between Ada and Alfred, began to bawl.

"Now see what you've done with all that loud talk," Ada said.

Alfred listened to the baby crying a moment; then softened. "You poor little starving thing you, so papa's forgot all about you, eh?" Alfred filled the boy's little plate with some rice pap and began to feed him.

Ada didn't know whether to smile or to frown. Fact was, she was a little jealous of the way Alfred and Karen could sometimes talk about the old days, back when their mother was still alive. Ada had felt especially jealous the last weeks when she'd elected to stay in bed mornings with her heavy belly, to get in a little extra rest, while those two got up early and full of morning cheer drank coffee together. Ada could hear them clearly from where she lay in bed. For all their squabbling they shared some kind of secret together.

Ada remembered how about a month ago, when she'd begun to tell Karen a little about her private life with Alfred, complaining a little that Alfred wouldn't let her alone in bed, that to her surprise Karen suddenly began to suck air as if she were about to faint, and that Karen had shown teeth, and said, "Those men! Beasts, every one of them. And it's all in their heads. They can control themselves if they really want to. If they'd just pray hard. Besides, it's a mortal sin. So you just get after Alfred, Ada. You got to begin by saying no first, real loud, as if you really meant it. So he won't get a chance to build up any ideas to begin with."

Yes, Karen both hated and loved her brother, hated him for whatever memory it was she shared with him, at the same time she loved him because of it. It had to be a memory like the one she herself shared with Alvin Ravenhorse.

The baby in her belly suddenly gave a kick. "Oe."

Alfred looked up.

"It's nothing." Ada felt nauseated. She had so little room. "It's nothing." Ada turned to Karen. "I wonder . . . would you read a passage from the Scriptures for us tonight? Pick your own text in memory of Abbott?"

"I'll be happy to." Karen turned to smile at Free. "Will you please get me the Bible then?"

"Sure." Free reached under the table and got the Bible from where it lay on a crosspiece. The crosspiece held the table together when an extra board had been added.

The spoons around the table fell silent.

Karen read with a gentlewoman's eloquence. "The Lord is my shepherd; I shall not want. He maketh me to lie down in green pastures: He leadeth me beside still waters."

At eleven o'clock a great fist grabbed Ada by the belly and woke her. It made her heart jump. Ahh. The baby was on the way.

Ada reached over in the dark and placed her hand on her husband's shoulder. "Alfred?"

Alfred sat up as though he'd been awake all along. "What's up?"

"You better call Dr. Halmers."

Alfred ran a hand through his hair. "All right." He slid out of bed and applied a match to the night lamp.

"And let's hope this is one night our good doctor hasn't indulged."

"Doc'll be all right." Alfred pulled on his clothes in one continuous flow of motion. He stomped out into the living room and lit the lamp on the table. Then he rang up Dr. Halmers.

Ada listened to Alfred's end of the call. When he'd finished, she asked, "How did he sound?"

"As sober as a judge. He said I woke him out of a sound sleep."

"Good. Now I'll get ready for him."

Ada got out the tub and gave herself a good scrubbing in the kitchen. She got out the towels and placed them on a chair near the bed. She put some rubber sheeting under the bottom sheet. She checked the children upstairs. They were sound asleep. So too was Karen in the east room upstairs. Good.

"Now if I can manage not to yell too loud."

She went to the kitchen and filled the kettles with water to heat.

Alfred watched her as he sipped at a cup of lukewarm coffee. "Golly, woman, you're as bad as a mother cat getting ready."

"It's something all mothers have done since Eve."

By the time Dr. Halmers arrived she had had two more pains.

Dr. Halmers examined her immediately. "You're doing very well, Ada. It won't be long."

"Does my heart seem to be all right?"

"How does it feel to you?"

"Well, it hasn't been behaving funny lately."

"There's your answer." A warm smile moved under his black moustache.

The clock in the living room struck its cathedral gong twice.

Alfred peered around the corner of the doorway. "I'll be in the kitchen, you two, if you need me." He smiled at Ada. "Somebody's got to baby the coffee pot along and keep it fresh."

Ada gave him a crinkled smile in return.

A dozen pains later, the head slid out. There was a good loud bawl.

"Ah," Dr. Halmers whispered softly, "one more good push, Ada, and then the shoulders'll be through."

She coughed as she pushed, and that did it.

"Ah. Very good." Dr. Halmers's lower lip pushed out in absorbed thought. There was a snipping sound. "Now to tie him up."

"Oh, dear," Ada cried, "it's a boy after all."

"Yes. A fine-looking little fellow."

"I'd so set my heart on a girl. For me in the house here. To pass on what I know. What it means to be a woman. That's important too."

Her heart gave a series of cricket leaps. Then, as she watched, everything slowly faded away, until all she saw was Dr. Halmers's lower red lip pursed in thought. And then that too was gone.

A long silence as sweet as snow.

Slowly she came to. There was a feeling that she'd been on a long trip somewhere. There'd been talk about her duty to her family and that perhaps it would be best for her to return home. Her eyes were open for several moments before she began to make out people moving fast around her. Quick motions. Even violent gestures. One moment Dr. Halmers was hunching up her chest as though to help her breathe, the next moment he was doing something to a baby that lay at her feet.

There was a strong smell of carbolic acid in the bedroom.

"Alfred, quick find me some table salt. Hurry!" Dr. Halmers's voice had the power of God.

"Coming up, Doc."

"And get me a pan of lukewarm water too."

She heard Alfred go bounding away; heard him come bounding back.

"Water bottle."

Alfred opened a dresser drawer. "Here."

Dr. Halmers swung over her again. He was like a big dog standing over her. "Ada? Are you all right? Ada?"

What was all the fuss about?

"Ada? Are you here, Ada?"

"I guess so."

He took her pulse. "Well! at least that's back to normal. Ada, can you hear me?"

"Yes."

"Work at your breathing, you hear? It's terribly important that you work at your breathing."

She smiled. "Why, doctor, when was it not important to keep breathing?"

"Keep breathing while I take care of the baby a minute."

That sharpened her up. She drew herself up on her pillow. She looked at where her baby lay at the foot of the bed. It lay limp, head loose, like a baby doll tossed to one side.

Lower lip protruding, Dr. Halmers first poured some warm water into the red water bottle, then threw in several pinches of salt, then screwed in the plug. He shook the water bottle vigorously, up and down, sideways, making wobbling liquid sounds. Then he removed the plug and screwed in the end of a rubber tube in place of it.

Dr. Halmers threw a quick look at Ada. "You still here?"

"Yes."

"Good. Don't slip away on me again."

Dr. Halmers slipped the end of the rubber tube into what was left of the cut cord of the baby. "Now, Alfred, hold up the bottle. Higher. So the salt water will flow into the baby. By gravity."

"Doctor, what happened here?" Ada asked.

"While I was trying to save you . . . look."

Ada looked where he pointed. The reddest blood she'd ever seen in her life lay in a puddle near her hip. "Oh dear God."

"Yes, a just born baby can bleed to death the first few minutes. Before the natural shutdown occurs." Dr. Halmers fitted a stethoscope to his ears and listened to the pheasant chest of the infant. "Come, little fellow, come on now. Let go with that beller again."

The baby was breathing a little, very shallow, reminding her of the movements of a curtain in an open window on a calm day.

"Water bottle feel any lighter, Alfred?"

"Some."

Ada stared. "What in the world are you doing, Doctor?"

"I'm replacing the blood he lost with some salt water. A salt transfusion. He almost bled to death."

"But, salt water?"

"Sure. Replace the little bit of ocean he lost."

"I don't understand."

"That's where we all came from originally. The ocean."

"Now you've completely lost me, Doctor."

"The salt water that's in our blood, Ada, it's all that's left of the ocean in us."

"You mean, that's why our blood always tastes salty?"

"Yes. The sea is deep in us, Ada."

It was some more of the good doctor's atheistic thinking. "I prefer to think we came from mother Eve."

"And from Adam. Don't forget him."

Alfred said, "The water bottle feels considerable lighter, Doc."

Dr. Halmers gently chafed the baby's ribcase. "And I think the baby feels warmer."

Ada folded her hands. Lord, was she tired. "I feel so light-headed."

Dr. Halmers reached for an open safety pin from the top of the dresser. He dipped the safety pin in a pan of carbolic acid. He picked up one of the baby's little wrinkled feet and pricked it several times.

"Now what are you doing to my baby?"

"Trying to get him mad."

"But why?"

"I want him to beller at me." Dr. Halmers pricked the baby again.

At last baby jerked and opened its mouth and let go. "Aaaa!"

Dr. Halmers's eyes closed for a moment. "We got him back." With a swift jerk Dr. Halmers pulled the rubber tube out of the baby's cord. "You can put that water bottle aside now, Alfred." Dr. Halmers quickly tied the baby's cord. He wrapped up the baby warmly, then handed it over to Ada. "Whenever you feel ready to nurse him."

Later, Alfred dug out the bottle of Old Crow. "How about a snort?"

An unholy gleam appeared in Dr. Halmers's eyes. "That would be just dandy."

Ada held her tongue.

Alfred filled two shot glasses and gave one to Dr. Halmers. "Welbecomen."

"Skoal."

Both men licked their lips.

Alfred held the bottle up to the light. "Still have this left over from when we had our first baby."

Dr. Halmers was astounded. "You mean, the only time you tap this bottle is when you have a baby?"

"That's right."

"Then that's the same bottle you dragged out when your last baby was born on the Bowman place."

Alfred beamed proudly. "Yes."

Dr. Halmers turned his head sideways and spoke to the darkest corner of the room. "Lord."

Just then the baby began to nuzzle around looking for a nipple.

Dr. Halmers nodded approvingly.

They named the baby Jonathan, after Ada's brother John.

Two weeks later, Alfred took the train to Sioux City to meet the body of his brother Abbott. The body turned out to be the right one. There was a silver plate in the left arm. Alfred rode in the baggage car with the body.

On the day of the funeral, Dad Alfredson still refused to have anything to do with the remains of his son Abbott. He stayed home and smoked his pipe.

Karen cried for days. "Poor Abbott. He was my silver brother, with a soul as pure as snow."

Two months later, Alfred came home from town with a sad face. Ada was looking out over the yard through the kitchen window and spotted it right away.

Presently Alfred came in carrying the groceries.

"What's the matter, Alfred?"

"Dr. Halmers committed suicide."

"Dear God, no."

"Yeh. Hung himself in the back of his office."

Ada had to hang on to the edge of the table for a moment.

Alfred stared down at his hands. "And now I'm wondering if I did the right thing giving him that snort of Old Crow."

Ada continued to hang onto the table. "And I so wanted to meet him in heaven someday," she whispered. In heaven there'd be no fear of carnal sin if she showed she liked the good doctor a lot.

Free & 16

FREE AND EVERETT hurried up the lane for school.

Across the highway the blue hill in the Horsberg pasture was covered with purple flowers.

"Hey, look," Free said. "Ma'd like to know about that."

"What are you going to do?" Everett said.

Free bossed Everett with a look. "I'm gonna run back and tell Ma about them flowers a minute. But you keep on going walkin' to school, you hear? You're so slow I can easy catch up with you."

Everett held his head sideways.

"Hurry now," Free called over his shoulder as he started to run back to the house. "Or I'll beat you up."

Everett swung his dinner bucket around a couple times, then began trudging on alone.

Ma acted surprised. "Really? Where did you say?"

"In the Horsberg pasture across the road there."

Ma followed him outdoors. She first looked up at the new purple leaves of the maple in front of the porch, then leaned down to look under the apple trees toward the Horsberg pasture. "Why, you're right, Free. The mayflowers are out."

"Is that what they are?"

"Yes. The first flowers of the year. It means spring is at last here."

"Hey, I'll pick you some when I come home from school tonight then."

"Well, now, son, the mayflower is the one flower you shouldn't pick. It's wild and shy, and it dies almost on your picking it." Ma gave Free a smile. "You're a sweet boy to tell me about the mayflowers though, son. Now, you better mosey on to school."

Free easy caught up with Everett by the mailboxes. It was where Pa had licked him. The morning sun glanced sharp off the tin fronts. "See, I told you you walk so slow. Now, c'mon, hurry or I'll take a willow stick to you and whip you all the way to school."

They got there plenty early. Most of the kids were playing around the flagpole. Free and Everett quick put their dinner buckets in the hall and then ran out to join the other kids.

"What're you playing?" Free asked.

"Maypole," Alvina Horsberg said. "You boys are s'posed to stand under the flagpole and then we're s'posed to throw a flower at you. If we hit you, you've got to go where we say." Alvina already had picked a handful of dandelions. She took one and threw it at Free. Free ducked and it hit Everett instead.

"Ha ha ha, you hit Everett, not me." Free pushed in amongst the other boys packed around the foot of the flagpole.

"Everett don't count," Alvina said.

The girls began to dance in a circle around the boys. The girls sang a carol:

"We've been wandering all night,
And rambling all day,
We've picked us each a dandelion,
Come with us and play."

Each girl, big Louise included, threw a dandelion at the boy of her choice. Alvina again threw a dandelion at Free and missed.

When Gladys Windmiller threw her dandelion, Peter jumped in such a way as to make sure it hit him.

Louise didn't like that. "You're s'pose to try and dodge."

"But I was dodging yours," Peter protested, "when hers hit me."

"I know what you got in mind," Louise said.

"Come on," the kids cried, "before Teacher rings the bell."

Again the girls tripped around the boys, singing:

"Ring around the rosy,
Pockets full of posy,
Ashes, ashes,
All fall down."

On the last word the girls all squatted down, while the boys fell down all in a bunch. From their squatting position the girls again threw dandelions at the boys.

This time Gladys's dandelion hit Peter. She jumped up and claimed him. Her open mouth trembled like a new lily.

Louise got mad. "I'm quitting. You're s'posed to just hit anybody and have fun. Not do it with a plan you had in mind beforehand."

Peter sneered. "I suppose when you do this with Tom Robson"—Peter ran one forefinger naughty back and forth between the other forefinger and thumb—"you ain't having fun."

"Now I am quitting," Louise said.

"Oh, don't quit, Louise," the kids cried.

"Hey, look," Alvina said, "Tom Robson's caught something behind the girl's privy there."

Everybody looked. Tom was holding up something that was wriggling. He and Tim were laughing big white teeth. Tom and Tim had refused to play maypole. They said it was an old-timer's game.

The whole bunch of kids swooped across the schoolyard like a flock of crows.

Tom had a gray field mouse by the tail. Head hanging down, the mouse kept closing its tiny eyes.

"Can I hold it?" Alvina cried.

Tom shook his head. "You don't know how to hold it so it can't climb up on its own tail."

The mouse tried to climb up on itself by curling up over its belly.

"See," Tom said, giving it a little shake so it hung head down again.

Louise had a sour look in her eyes, but her mouth was smiling. "Let it go, Tom. The poor little thing."

Tom laughed at her. The devil was in his black eyes. "No, I got other plans for Mister Mouse." Tom looked down at his brother Tim. "Tim, dig out my sack of Bull Durham."

The devil was in Tim's black eyes too. He dug out the little sack of tobacco from Tom's bib pocket.

The girls were all standing on their toes, squeaking.

"Don't be scared," Free said to Alvina. "It's only a mouse."

"Yeh," Alvina shrilled, "how would you like to have that mouse climb into your bloomers if you was a girl?"

"Let it go, Tom," Louise pleaded.

"Tim, empty the rest of what tobacco is left into this front pocket of mine." With his free hand Tom held open his left front pocket.

Tim shook the tobacco into the pocket.

"Now open the little sack as wide as you can. Like we was gonna sack potatoes in it." The morning sun shone glossy on Tom's slick black hair. With a quick look at Louise he dropped the mouse into the sack. He tucked the tail in too. It all just fit. He quick jerked the pullstrings shut and the mouse couldn't get out.

The girls right away felt better.

Catherine Haber said, "I'm gonna tell Teacher that you smoke tobacco, Tom Robson. Because you're mean to little mices. So there." Catherine had the eyes of a pure tattletale.

"Poh!" Tom snorted. "Teacher is a ninnypisser. You should hear what my dad says about her. He says she's such a prune she separates the women books from the men books and puts them on different shelves."

"For shame, Tom," Louise scolded. "You shouldn't talk that way to Catherine. She's only a little girl."

Tom said, "You know what would be fun?" He had that devil smile again.

"What?"

"Take the mouse into school and then when Teacher starts to play the organ, let the mouse out and see what it'll do."

"Hey," the kids cried.

Tom looked the bunch over. "Who'll let the mouse out when Teacher starts to play?"

"Why don't you do it yourself?" Alvina asked.

"Well, I caught the mouse. That's my share of the work. Someone else can let him out."

Free smiled to himself. Their new dog Tricks sometimes howled when Pa played the harmonica. The mouse would probably run around funny when it heard the organ play. Free said, "I'll do it."

"But Teacher is your aunt," Tom sneered. "You'll snitch on me."

"Oh no, I won't. Honest."

"But you won't know when to let it out."

"Oh yes, I will. When Teacher starts to play 'The Star-Spangled Banner,' I'll open the sack."

"Well, it sounds like you'll do it all right. Now listen close. When Teacher rings the bell, carry it into school in your pocket. Don't say a thing. It can't bite you inside this sack."

Alvina said, "I suppose Free'll let it out when he sings, 'Our flag is still there yet.' "

Free gave Alvina a black look. If she didn't shut up pretty soon he'd hit her one in the belly. "A big mouth looks better when shut."

Aunt Karen rang the bell and looked around the corner for them.

All the kids shut up. Free quick stuffed the mouse in his pocket and walked easy into the schoolhouse. The mouse was quiet in his pocket. Free took his seat in the second row. Aunt Karen had moved him up to the second grade, skipping the first, and he could sit there.

Aunt Karen checked the attendance. "All here. And on time too. Good." Aunt Karen got up from her desk and went over to the organ. "All right, everyone, let's all start singing on time this morning. Let's have no stragglers today. And you too, Tom." She sat down on the organ stool and began to play the first notes of "The Star-Spangled Banner."

Everybody flicked a look at Free's pocket. Tom didn't.

Free carefully pulled the little sack out of his pocket. The mouse inside got scared and balled itself up tight. Free pried the pullstrings apart. Then he leaned over and shook the mouse out. A funny dried-milk smell came out of the sack along with the mouse. The gray mouse landed on the oiled floor and rolled over. Then it sat up. It had white whiskers on its nose. The whiskers wiggled slow like the legs of a daddy longlegs. All the girls lifted up their legs and sat on them. Aunt Karen started to sing. Everybody quick joined in on the second note so she wouldn't look around at them. Aunt Karen tipped back her head and sang, "O say can you see." The mouse couldn't stand the sour sound. It shook its head; then ran under the seats straight for the organ music. The girls shrieked and the boys suddenly sang very high. Aunt Karen, still playing, turned around to see what the commotion was all about. The bottom of her eye caught sight of the mouse. She squeaked then too, and in one jump climbed onto the organ stool. The music quit and the mouse disappeared.

Aunt Karen hugged herself. Her long legs were so clamped shut they looked like a couple of fishing poles nailed together. "Boys! Boys! Quick catch that mouse. And you girls stay where you are."

Tom and Tim gave each other a sly black wink, then tumbled out of their seats and began looking for the mouse. The other boys helped. There was a lot of running around, and yelling, and banging against the desks.

Free thought he better help too or Aunt Karen would wonder.

The girls kept shrieking and sitting on their legs.

Tom Robson was the strongest in school and he pushed the organ away from the wall. As he did so the organ bumped the stool on which Aunt Karen stood. She shrieked, and teetered, and waved her arms around like a depot agent trying to flag down a through train. Finally she got her balance back.

Free could just slip in behind the organ. He got down on his hands and knees. He looked quick everywhere. There, under the pedal, he spotted the mouse's tail. He took a breath, held his thumb and finger ready like a cat, then snapped up the mouse by its tail. The mouse came out of its hiding place with a squeak. "I got'm," Free cried.

"Are you sure?" Aunt Karen cried.

"Look." Free came out from behind the organ and held the mouse up. He held it the way Tom had held it outdoors. He felt like a hero.

The girls fell silent. They stared at Free and the mouse.

"Shall I kill him?" Free said.

"Gracious no," Aunt Karen said. "I don't want that on my conscience too. No, just carry him outside and let him go free in the grass."

Free carefully carried the gray mouse down the aisle. Twice the mouse tried to climb up on its own tail and twice Free had to give it a little shake to make it stay hanging down. Free opened the door with his left hand and outside let the mouse down into the grass. There was a scaly feeling on his fingertips where he'd held the mouse's tail. He rubbed it off on his pants leg. Then he went inside to his seat.

Aunt Karen gave him a big smile. "Thank you very much, Free." She climbed down off the organ stool. "Mercy, wasn't it strange for that mouse to come into the schoolhouse when it's spring and warm out?"

Everybody sat quiet.

Alvina sat in the third-grade row. She twitched in her seat a couple of times. Then out of the corner of his eye Free saw her hand go up.

"Yes, Alvina, what is it?"

"I know who let the mouse out."

"Why, Alvina, we all know Free took it out. . . . Oh, you mean, somebody brought him inside here and then let him go?"

Alvina nodded, slowly.

Aunt Karen stood very stiff. "Who?"

Alvina slowly pointed a finger. "Him. Free."

"Oh, come now. He was our hero in removing the mouse."

"But Free did. I saw him."

Aunt Karen said, "You know I don't like mischief-makers."

"But he did."

"Maybe," Aunt Karen said, "it's more simply done if we just ask Free himself. Free?"

Free gradually let his eyes curve down.

"Free? Look at me."

Somehow Free got himself to look up again. Then, miserably, he nodded his head.

The whole school waited to see what would happen next. All eyes flicked from Aunt Karen to Free, and back again.

Aunt Karen could scarcely believe it about her nephew. Her eyes began to look like hard water.

Louise raised her hands.

"Yes, Louise?"

"It was Tom who talked Free into it. Tom caught the mouse in the grass and put it in his tobacco sack. Then he gave it to Free for him to let out when you started to play the organ."

"Ohh." Aunt Karen slowly turned to look over at where Tom sat.

Tom gave Louise a devil's mean look. He'd get her at recess.

Louise stuck her tongue out at him. She still had it in for him because of what he'd done to her a couple of times in the deserted farmhouse kitty-corner across the road from the schoolhouse.

"Is that true, Tom Robson?"

Tom looked Aunt Karen square in the eye. "Sure it's true."

"You placed it in a tobacco sack?"

"Yessiree. In a gen-u-wine Bull Durham sack."

"Then you smoke, Tom?"

"I sure do."

"Do you smoke on the school grounds?"

"Sure. Why not. This is a free country, ain't it?"

"All right, Master Tom. I want you to sit over here on the dunce stool a while."

"No."

"No? You mean you won't do it?"

"No. I don't have to."

"Well, we'll see about that, Master Tom." Aunt Karen came down the aisle and took hold of Tom by the shoulders and gave him a pull.

Tom quick grabbed hold of the sides of his seat.

"Let go of that seat."

"No."

Aunt Karen spotted a ruler on Tom's desk. She snatched it up and began to whack him over the knuckles with it to make him let go of the seat. She pulled at his collar with the other hand.

Tom laughed at her.

Aunt Karen got mad. She whacked wild at his hands. When he still wouldn't let go of the seat, she turned the ruler on its side and began cutting at his bare knuckles with the metal edge.

"Ow!" Tom roared. "That ain't fair."

"Let go then!" Aunt Karen cut away at his hands.

Blood began to show on Tom's knuckles. At last he had to let go.

Aunt Karen gave Tom a jerk and he fell out of his seat to the floor. She began to kick him. She had toes as pointy as a pickaxe.

That hurt Tom even worse. He began to bawl like a small boy. Finally he got up and ran to the dunce chair and sat down.

Free felt ashamed for Tom. Free also felt ashamed of Aunt Karen.

"There," Aunt Karen said. "I guess now we know who's boss in my school." Aunt Karen pointed a finger at Free. "And as for you, young man, when I get home tonight I'm having a talk with your father."

Free's belly began to feel like a tobacco sack pulled up tight.

All sang "The Star-Spangled Banner" then, loud and clear.

Reading came first. Free went up to the recitation bench with his Baldwin & Beader Reader. He had read a page when Aunt Karen stopped him. "By the way, Free, don't look now, but how do we spell 'believe' again?"

Free had trouble with ie and ei. He'd skipped the first grade where they studied that. Free looked around, desperate. After what happened that morning he was anxious to please his aunt. "B—e—l . . . "

"Go on."

Everett in his front seat was trying to catch Free's eye.

"Go on, Free."

"B—e—l . . . "

"Free," Everett whispered from behind his hand, " . . . i—e—v—e."

"Here, here," Aunt Karen said. She looked puzzled at Everett. "How come you know how to spell that word?"

"I heard Free spell it at home last night."

Aunt Karen chewed on her lip. "Oh."

"I like to help my brother. He saves me from the gypsies."

All the kids in school laughed. Tom on the dunce stool laughed the loudest.

Aunt Karen had to laugh then too. "All right, Everett. We thank you very much for your help. But Free has to learn how to spell it by himself. Now you tend to your own reader. You hear?"

Everett ducked down behind his book.

"Free, what was that little rhyme I once taught you about i and e?"

That's right. "I before e except after c, and when spoken as a as in *neighbor* and *weigh*."

"And how do you spell it now?"

"B—e—l—i—e—v—e."

"Correct. Go on with reading."

It was hot out during noon recess. The kids ate their lunch under the trees. But Peter and Gladys crawled into a little lean-to on the north side of the coal shed and ate lunch by themselves. It was where the kids' dogs could go while the kids were taking school.

Pretty soon Paul and Hesta went over to see what Peter and Gladys were doing in the lean-to because it was so still in there. They had to be done with lunch by now. The next thing the rest of the kids knew those two had also crawled into the lean-to.

Tim liked Hesta almost as much as Paul did. He went over and looked in. What he saw made him mad. He was bawling he was so mad.

Free went over to have a look. At first he couldn't make anything out it was so dark in the lean-to. After a while his eyes opened up and he could see them. Right away Free began to feel hot.

Tim looked in some more. Then he kicked the side of the lean-to. "I'm going in and tell Teacher, you kids."

Paul talked up. "You're not getting a turn at my girl. Because I love Hesta."

Catherine Haber snuck up on the other side of the lean-to. She suddenly stood up and sucked in a big breath. "You bad boys. What you're doing. Shame, shame, double shame, everybody knows your name."

Hesta was busy, but she knew she'd better speak up or Tim would get her in trouble. "Please wait a little," she said betweentimes, "won't you, Tim? Pretty please?" She talked very sweet. "When he's done with me."

"Well, if you want me to, Hesta."

Free felt so hot all over he could hardly stand up. "Can I have a turn too?"

"No," Paul said. He talked mad. "Can he have a turn, Hesta?"

"Oh," Hesta said, "can't he just once? I don't mind."

Tim stuck a fist under Free's chin. "Hesta don't have to share three boys, does she?" Tim's black eyes rolled around like the eyes of a crazy pig. "It's not fair to her."

"Say, you," Free said, glaring back.

Peter and Paul began to make funny bouncing noises on their girls. The girls' bellies sounded like a couple of water bags.

Pretty soon Free had to do number one bad. He started to run for the boys' privy. One of his legs ran stiff.

"Where you going?" Tim called after him. "Wait. I gotta go too."

Free took the first hole in the privy. But he had trouble aiming straight. Tim took the second hole. He couldn't hit the mark either. Free leaned way over and then finally made it go in right. A barn smell came up through the two holes.

Tim looked over to see what Free had and then looked down at what he had. He started to laugh. His black eyes turned brown. "Boy, I bet with these hard ones we could win any peeing contest in the world."

"Not in here we couldn't though."

"Let's go behind the privy and see who can pee the farthest."

"Okay."

Both boys shut off their streams, then pushed their tools back in their pants and held them in place from inside their pants pockets in case anybody should be looking from under the trees. But no one saw them.

Tim scratched a mark in the grass with his toe. "We'll stand in line and shoot from here."

Tim got out his tool again and aimed. He hit a wild rose about halfway to the fence. The wild rose bobbed up and down under the stream.

Free in turn let fly. He splattered the same wild rose.

Both burst out laughing, clear and merry. What a lot of fun. Their tools fell slack.

Tim pinched his off a minute; then, pushing, let it go again. This time he hit a milkweed a couple of steps beyond the wild rose.

Free did the same thing and hit the same milkweed.

"Still tie," Tim said. "Shucks, and here I ain't got any more water to fight with."

"I still got a bit left."

"Hey, what are you two kids doing?"

Both started guiltily, and looked around. It was Tom.

"What're you doing?"

"Nothing."

"A peeing contest, hah?"

"Aw, we was just having some fun, Tom," Tim said.

"Ha! So you two little pigtails think you can pee far, huh? Wait'll you see the champ in action." Tom got out his tool. It was bigger soft than theirs were hard. "Watch me."

Louise came over, but when she saw what he was going to do, she turned right around and headed for the trees.

Tom held his tool pinched, and pushed inside himself a couple of times like he was priming it, until his face got red, then let go. Out sprayed a long yellow stream. It hit the nearest post in the fence.

"Wow!" Free cried. "What a pisser. Man alive."

Tim let go of his tool and withdrew from the contest. He buttoned up.

"Man," Free said, and withdrew from the contest too.

A bell began to ring on the other side of the schoolhouse.

"Well, I guess recess is over," Tom said, and buttoned up too. Tom smiled the cat smile of the great champ.

All three hurried for the front door. Peter and Gladys, Paul and Hesta crawled out of the lean-to and filed in behind them. Everybody looked like they'd played pom-pom-pullaway hard that noon.

Aunt Karen closed the grammar book she was holding. It was three o'clock. "All right, that's enough for this week. It's Friday afternoon and story time. That is, if you've all been good." Aunt Karen sighed. "Actually, this hasn't been such a good day for us, has it? And I don't understand it either. For four days this week you were all perfect little angels. And then all of a sudden today . . . well, it was as if you all went berserk or something. But, oh, I'm too tired to punish you with more schoolwork. It's easier to read to you. Besides"—Aunt Karen gave them all a little forgiving smile—"I'm kind of curious as to what is going to happen next in our story. Aren't you?"

"Yes, Teacher," everybody said. Everybody was happy to be let off so easy. They all quick cleaned up their desks and sat up straight. Those were Teacher's rules before she'd begin to read to them.

Aunt Karen picked up a big red book from her desk and opened it at the blue silk marker. "Let's see. Who can tell us what has happened so far? Quickly now."

A scattering of hands went up.

"Free?"

Free looked up at the ceiling to see it clearly. "A long time ago there was this Eurytion who was part man and part horse. From his hips up he was like a man and from his hips down he was like a horse. He had two arms and four legs. Well, this Eurytion, he once tried to run off with the bride. Her name was Hippodamia. This made Pirithous, the groom, mad, and he chased Eurytion out of the wedding hall. It was a big fight."

"What did they call these creatures who were half man and half horse?"

"Centaurs."

"Good, Free. You remembered."

"Are there any centaurs around anymore?"

"No, Free. What we've been reading here is really just a story. You know, make-believe, pretend."

"Then there never was any centaurs ever? Truly?"

"Well, in this story there was one."

"Oh. Then there could have been some?"

Aunt Karen smiled. "Let's just say there once were some centaurs and get on with the story. Shall we?"

Free raised his hand a little ways. "Suppose we had some of these centaurs around today, where would they come from?"

Aunt Karen laughed. "Well, maybe the mother could have been a mare like your Daise at home and the father could have been a man like your . . . " Then Aunt Karen stopped. She scowled herself. "Let's get on with the story itself." Aunt Karen sat on the edge of her desk and began to read.

Free listened as he looked out of the window. He always had to look out at the sky if he wanted to get it all. The story said not all centaurs were wild like Eurytion. Chiron was a good centaur. He was a great hunter. He was a good doctor. He could play the harp. He could prophesy. And he was a good teacher. Some of his pupils became generals. His best pupil turned out to be a famous doctor, Asclepius, who was so good he could make the dead come alive. Chiron, in fact, became known as such a great teacher that when he died, Zeus, that is, God, placed him among the stars. He became the constellation Sagittarius. The end.

Once more Free raised his hand.

"Yes, Free?"

"Supposing there was such a thing as a centaur, and you had two of them, could they hitch themselves up to a plow by theirselves, and then go out and plow in the field by theirselves too, without having anybody around to drive them with lines?"

Aunt Karen's light blue eyes opened up as big as Pa's eyes sometimes did when he was surprised. Then she really had to laugh. She laughed until she began to act silly. "Oh, Free, my dear boy, you have the wildest imagination sometimes."

Free could feel all the kids laughing at him. He turned hot.

"Free, you're so . . . I'm almost inclined to forgive you for letting that little gray mouse out this morning.

When Free got home that night, he did his chores perfect. He got the cobs making sure to pick nothing but dry ones from the hog feed lot and no wet ones.

When he got the eggs, he went out of his way to look for new nests, since in the spring the brood hens tried to hide their eggs from people, under the corncrib, up in the haymow, up on top of the straw pile where the sparrows liked to hide their nests.

Just the same at supper table that darn Aunt Karen still told Pa and Ma about that mouse in the tobacco sack.

At first Pa looked like he was going to get the razor strop and lick Free. But after a minute Pa burst out laughing. He slapped his leg and almost fell out of his armchair.

Aunt Karen got mad. "Then you aren't going to punish the boy?"

Pa waved at her. "When I done the same thing myself? Naw."

Aunt Karen's lips crimped up real thin. "Then I wish I might have punished him myself this morning."

It was a good thing Aunt Karen didn't know about that long-distance number-one contest behind the privies.

Free ❦ 17

AUNT KAREN'S RED book didn't have any pictures of those centaurs, so Free was quite puzzled as to just how the two parts, man and horse, were joined together. Did the human fuzz around the belly button shade off into the horse hair below? When the centaur did number one, did he just let it go in the grass. And if the centaur had a man's head, didn't he feel ashamed when he did number one and number two out there in plain sight in the pasture?

A couple of Saturdays later Fat John drove on the yard with his horse and buggy. He was leading another horse and it followed along behind the buggy. The other horse was a big black fellow. He kept running sideways, flopping his tail, rolling his eyes, and humming hoarse to himself. He was a monster he was so big.

Free was in the barn and at first couldn't hear what Pa and Fat John were talking about. Ma had come out on the front walk a second to say hello, but when she saw the big black horse she went back into the house. A minute later she and Aunt Karen showed up in the kitchen window as though looking for someone. Free knew who they were looking for—him. So he carefully went over into the calf-pen side of the barn to stay out of sight. Something was going to happen on the yard that was not for little kids to see.

Free watched Pa and Fat John lead the great horse behind the barn. It was where men did things out of sight of the kitchen window.

Pa said, "I don't know where that kid of mine went."

Fat John waddled along. The only way Fat John could move forward was to swing his big belly from side to side. "Twon't hurt him none if he sees it. And a good thing too."

"You think so?"

"Sure. I knew about breeding stock ever since I can remember."

Pa laughed. "Ha. It's you who's the prick peddler today, not me."

Fat John smiled with his fat lips.

"Just the same," Pa said, "I want that boy to wait a year." Pa raised his head and called out. "Free?"

Free made sure he was well hidden behind a big spider web spread across the calf-pen window. This was one time he wasn't going to answer Pa.

"He must be in the grove playing," Pa said finally.

Fat John said, "Well, where's that Fan of yours?"

Free's eyes opened. So that was why Pa had kept Fan alone in the barn that morning.

Pa got Fan. He led her outdoors behind the barn. Pa had just bought Fan at a sale. She was a young horse and had a red coat. Her tail and mane were as black as the black coat of Fat John's fat horse. Fan walked with her tail up a little, like a mopstick stood out to dry.

The minute the big black horse smelled Fan he started to act crazy. Fat John had all he could do to hold him. The black horse slobbered all over Fat John's hand where Fat John held him by the bit.

Pa laughed nervous. "You're right, Fat. That stud of yours is chuck-full of ambition." Pa led Fan up to the stud.

Fan wasn't sure she liked the stud. Her tail clapped down tight.

The stud wanted to bump her over. Then he bit her.

"Mind your pasture manners now," Fat John said.

A big black club showed up under the stud. When the stud turned Free saw it clear. What a tool. Compared to it Tom Robson had nothing.

The stud bit Fan a couple more times. Fan began to like it. She whinnied, then held her head down, and quit sashaying away from him. All of a sudden, like a steam engine charging up a hill, the stud stood up on his hind legs and ran himself on top of Fan. At the same time his tool disappeared under Fan's tail. Fat John reached up a hand to help the stud but the stud did it himself. Then the stud began to bounce on Fan like Peter bounced on Gladys that time in the lean-to at school.

Pa and Fat John watched. Pa and Fat John each stood on one leg with a hand in their pockets.

Pretty soon the stud shook all over and then his head hung down. Fan staggered around under him to hold him up.

"Well," Fat John said, "your new colt's well on the way."

"You guarantee it?"

"Black Charlie's service calls always stick."

Free's eyes closed to slits. Hey. This was what the rooster did to the hens, and the boar to the sows, and their dog Tricks tried to do to neighbor Bowman's dog every time it came over. It had to be fun or the animals wouldn't be doing it so often. But Free for the life of him couldn't imagine what kind of fun it was.

The stud slid down. He shook his head. He saw the water tank and pulled on the hitching strap to let Fat John know he needed a drink. Fat John let him pull him along.

The stud drank a lot. After a while the stud peed on the ground, straight down, like a water hose. It was probably the way the centaur would do it.

Pa led Fan through the pasture gate, took off her halter, and let her go free for the day. She walked like she had the gout.

A week later Pa came home with a hired man. His name was Guy Baker. Guy had just arrived from the Old Country and he had different clothes. His shoes were especially strange; they had big hard round toes. A man could drop a sledge hammer on them without hurting the toes inside.

Pa got the hired man because they couldn't get help for Ma in the house. Aunt Karen had to go to summer school in Sioux City to be a better teacher or else she could have helped Ma. So Pa had to help Ma, washing the clothes, doing the dishes at night, while the hired hand picked up the slack on the yard.

It rained one day. Pa couldn't think of any rainy-day jobs, so Guy found himself with some free time on his hands.

Guy said, "It's a good day to lay up in the haymow and snooze," and went off to the barn.

Free got that red book from Aunt Karen's room upstairs and crawled into the storeroom. He read with his own eyes the story about the centaurs again, at the same he took an occasional lick from the bottom of the new sack of sugar where the stitching had unraveled a little.

Showers kept spilling against the window panes with a dim sprinkling sound.

After a while, tiring of reading the same stories again, tiring of nothing but straight sugar to eat, Free began to wonder what hired hand Guy might be up to in the haymow. He put the red book where he'd got it, in Aunt Karen's room, and finding an old denim jacket of Pa's, draped it over his head and barefoot ran to the barn.

Free thought it might be fun to play a trick on Guy while he was asleep in the haymow. He'd sneak up the ladder and get close enough to tickle Guy's nose with a straw, make him think a spider was running around on his face.

Cautiously Free poked his head up through the haymow hole and looked around. He didn't see Guy at first. The haymow was pretty dark on a rainy day.

Up in the cupola some pigeons were strutting around. They cooed. Sometimes they mocked each other's cooings. The grampa pigeon, a red-purple fellow two feet long, didn't coo at all. Nobody mocked him.

Free heard a rustling noise. Again he looked around cautiously, making sure the soles of his bare feet didn't make a squinching noise on the smooth wooden rungs of the ladder.

Guy was half-sitting up on some hay directly under the cupola. A shaft of soft light from the cupola lay on him.

Free stared.

Guy was playing with his tool. It was way bigger than Tom Robson's. And Guy was staring at it like he couldn't believe what he was looking at. And the more he played with it the more his eyes couldn't seem to believe it. All of a sudden Guy had to quick roll on his side so as not to get some stuff over the front of his overalls.

What in the world?

Gradually Guy's eyes cleared up and he could see again. He buttoned up. Then he saw Free looking at him. "How long you been there?"

"What're you doing there?"

It was easy to see Guy was worried that Free might tell Pa what he'd seen. "C'mere and I'll show you how to have a lot of fun too."

It was connected with what the stud did to Fan. "What was that stuff that came out of you?"

Guy tried to be jokey. "Buttermilk."

"What was it really?"

"Human seed."

"Like lettuce seed?"

"Yes."

"Will human seed work in the ground?"

"I'm afraid not. It has to be planted in a woman."

"Like a stud in a mare?"

"Right. Now you're getting it."

"Why don't you put your seed in a woman instead of in the hay?"

"Because I'm not married yet." Guy sat up, elbows on his knees.

The aroma of dried hay was like the smell of hardened honey on the lid of a honey pail.

Another shower passed over the barn. It made a homey sound on the roof.

The pigeons didn't like being cooped up in the cupola. Rain was no fun to fly around in. They sassed each other with their beaks. Finally one of the dark blue pigeons pecked at the red-purple grampa pigeon. Grampa pigeon flared up and clattered his big wings around and cooed up a low bellow like a bull, scaring all the other pigeons. After that the other pigeons sat quiet for a while.

"Boy, you married your right hand yet? Madam Palmer?"

Free backed down the ladder a few rungs, withdrawing his head.

"I suppose now you're going to run off and tell your pa?"

Free pushed his head up through the opening again. "Will you do me a favor?"

"Yeh. Sure. Name it."

"Help me make a centaur?"

"A . . . what?"

"A centaur. They're half horse and half man. The bottom half is a horse and the top half is a man. From the belly button up."

Guy's eyes opened in memory. "Hey, that's right. I saw a picture of them once. I remember thinking at the time that a farmer could just give them orders in the morning, what to do for the day, and then go back to bed."

"That's what I thought," Free said, excited, glad that Guy understood. It was all to help Pa. And then too it would be fun just to look at the centaurs.

"What did you have in mind, kid?"

"We could take a fork handle and auger a little hole in the end there, then put in a penny firecracker with a long fuse, then add in some of your seed there, then push it into Fan like the stud done with his tool, then light the long fuse and have the firecracker explode in her."

Guy whistled. "What an imagination."

"Well, you've got to shoot the seed into her somehow."

"Your Fan is going to think that fork handle pretty darn cold compared to the stud's tool."

"Well, couldn't we warm up the handle a little first?"

"Also I don't think Fan is going to like that kind of explosion."

"Then it won't work?"

"Not a chance, kid."

Free withdrew his head.

"Where you going, kid?"

Free didn't answer.

Another shower passed over the roof of the barn. It sounded like a hundred million mice were crossing a bridge.

Free went back to the house in the rain.

The red book didn't appeal to Free anymore. Instead he got the Bible from its little shelf under the table and looked for the chapters where it told about all the battles David had to fight before he could become king.

That night, as he was feeding the calves skim milk, Free overheard Guy telling Pa about Free wanting to have Guy make centaurs.

Pa laughed. "That's been tried before. And with no success that I know of."

Free could tell that Guy was fishing Pa to see if Free had told him. Guy hadn't told Pa all there was to tell.

Free ❦ 18

GUY BAKER HAD to go. Ma began to feel a lot better and Pa got caught up with his work. Also Free was helping a little on the yard. Pa felt sorry for Guy and got him a job with a farmer closer to Bonnie.

The first night after Guy was gone Pa told Free to get the cows. "It's high time them cows was pailed."

Free dragged his feet. "Old Tom don't like me very well, Pa."

"G'wan, get 'em. None of the milk cows are bulling just now so Old Tom won't bother you."

Free had to do it. He took the shortcut through the grove and came out on the pasture just where the cows were grazing.

Old Tom was the closest to the yard. It meant that after Free had picked out the six cows they were milking, he'd then have to drive them past where Old Tom was being bossy over a red heifer.

Free moved quietly through the herd of cows. Gently he shooed up those he wanted and started them for home. His bare feet hardly made any noise in the short grass. His toes knew how to miss the cowplops while his eyes were busy watching the bull.

Old Tom looked around a couple of times, swinging his big white head around to chase off the flies from his shoulder. His short tail was as busy as a windmill at the other end. He kept close watch over the red heifer. If she took a step ahead, he took a step ahead.

Free drove the six milkers along easy. Old Belle had a bag so heavy that on every step milk squirted out of it. Pa was right that it was high time they were pailed.

All of a sudden the cow named Spot decided she had a wild hair. She was jealous of the red heifer. She turned and ran right past Free's waving arms and then chased between Old Tom and the red heifer.

Free swore at her. Then mad, he went after her.

Old Tom didn't like the interruption very well. He swung his head at Spot. He missed.

Spot threw up her white tail, then curved around and headed back to rejoin the other five milkers.

It was then that Old Tom finally took a good look at Free.

Free froze into a post. He didn't even dare throw back his head to get the white hair out of his eyes.

Old Tom wasn't fooled that Free was only a post with overalls on. He pawed the earth, lowered his great white forehead, and charged.

Free broke. His eyes picked out a low spot in the grass under the barbwire fence. If he could just make that he'd be safe. It felt like his legs were already running before he moved. Old Tom thundered behind him. That big white forehead was only inches from his butt. Thank God that Pa'd had the bull dehorned. Free speeded up. He worked his arms like a fast scissors. That helped. He dove for the low spot, skidded on his chest, bounced up onto his feet on the other side of the fence, and all in one motion kept right on running along the end of the field for home. The six cows could wait.

Old Tom behind Free hit the fence with an awful bounce. The barbwires screamed in the staples all up and down the line. And toppling, Old Tom piled on over the top of the fence and landed on Free's side of it. One of his legs was hooked in the wire, but Old Tom, bellowing, gave his leg a mighty jerk and was free. Then, lowering his head, Old Tom set out after Free again, on the cornfield side of the fence.

Free quick looked ahead. Ah. Another low spot in the grass under the fence. Free angled for it, then dove under the fence, skidding on his chest. He made it on the pasture side of the fence. Old Tom hit the fence just behind him with another awful wrenching sound.

"Pa!" Free yelled toward the yard as loud as he could.

This time the bull augered his way through the fence and in a couple of seconds was after Free again. The bull came after him in faster and faster gallops, snorting, bellering.

Looking ahead he made out there weren't any more low places. He would have to take his chances through the thick high grass.

"Paa!"

"Bororr!" The bull was almost on top of him.

Free decided to dive under the fence anyway. He pitched himself headlong, made himself as slim as he could, slid under the fence, hooking his shirt a little on a barb.

The bull hit the fence above him a great whanging sound. That really made the four barbwires slack. For a second it sounded like the bull had got hung up in the barbwires. His bellow came choked.

Free scrambled to his feet. "Pa!" he squeaked.

He'd run some twenty steps when the bull worked himself free of the slack fence and was hot after him once more.

Free looked at the fence ahead. Two more bounces under and he'd have it made to the safety of the barn.

"Bororr!"

All of a sudden Pa showed up at the edge of the grove. He was carrying his .410. Pa ran a little ways toward them; stopped, aimed, fired.

Birdshot whistled past Free; smacked into the bull behind him. The blast was only some bees flying real hard at the bull. It didn't faze the bull in the least.

Free kept running. About then a powerful ache caught him in his left side. It was like someone had jabbed him with a fork.

Pa fumbled for another shell, couldn't seem to find it, then dropped his gun. He picked off his straw hat and began to wave it at the bull. He jumped wild up and down. He yelled.

The side ache got so bad Free had to double over and grab for his side as he ran. A couple of dozen steps more, and he stumbled, pitching headlong on his face.

Pa's eyes opened a wide gray. Then Pa thought of something. He stuck his finger and thumb into his mouth, took a deep breath, and blasted. The whistle came out so sharp Free thought his ears would crack.

It scared the hell out of the bull. Old Tom suddenly veered off, curving around so short his hooves threw up dirt and corn plants all over Free.

Then Pa remembered where he'd stuck the other bullet. He dug it out; shoved it into the .410; aimed a shot at the rear of the flying bull. He hit him. It must have been a tender spot because the bull let out a great howling bellow and really speeded up toward his red heifer.

Free ❦ 19

FREE LAY in the hammock under the maple trees. By making a motion with his knees he could get the hammock to sway back and forth almost by itself. The only trouble was that if you swung a hammock too far it could easy flip over and dump you on the ground.

It was past lunchtime. When the wind blew a little, pieces of sun skittered around under the maple leaves.

There was nothing to do.

The fun they'd had Decoration Day at the church picnic happened so long ago that Free had trouble remembering it. Some of it he couldn't even remember at all. And the fun they were going to have at the next church picnic, on the Fourth of July in Bosch's grove near Chokecherry Corner, was so far off there was no use even thinking about it. It would take at least two more whole long weeks before Ma would even begin to wonder if she shouldn't make some pies and potato salad for it.

When a fellow went to bed at night a fellow had nothing to dream about for the next day, about what fun they might have tomorrow. Why, the crab apples weren't even ripe.

Free heard the sows squabbling out in the hog feedlot. A chicken cackled up a storm. A fat old sow had probably just missed catching it. Pa said now and then an old sow liked to eat a chicken.

The chicken squawked again.

Free slowed his swinging and looked through the ropes at the end of the hammock. Yep, it was a chicken all right. It was sailing out of the feedlot with its tail hanging crooked. Some feathers were falling out as it sailed.

Free also spotted Albert. That darn kid. There he was toddling over to the feedlot. Free watched Albert until he got to the wooden fence. Then sure that Albert was only going to look through the fence, Free went back to swinging.

Free wished it would rain a cloudburst. Then he and Everett could get out their new boots and go wading in the flooded pasture again. The last time there'd been a real soaker, they'd gone wading down by the culvert. But they couldn't find any holes to test how deep they could go in their Red Ball Brand boots. What fun that'd been. The crabs didn't like it that he and Everett could go wading around in their play places. But the crabs couldn't do anything about it. Toes were safe inside the black rubber boots.

The redwings didn't like for them to be wading around in their pasture either. Some of the redwings had big red shoulder pads. Free could always tell when he got close to a nest along the creek. The redwings would start flying low around them, scolding them, crying, "Ok-kaa-lee, you!" By looking carefully in the grassy tussocks, a fellow could find them, three or four eggs, bluish-white with a lot of brown dots on one end. "Uck, uck," the boots would go in the mud. "Ok-kaa-lee, you. Ok-kaa-lee, you," the redwings would cry.

But just now though, compared to the fun Uncle Sherm was having in Gramma's town, the country was dead.

There was a shriek out in the hog yard. Hey. That was not the squawk of a chicken. Then the old fat sows roared up too, snorking like Pa's four-horse engine, "Snew-akk-ooo-chew!"

Albert.

Free sat up and rolled out of the hammock all in one motion. He darted past the garden gate, climbed the board stile by the windmill, shot across the barnyard, leaped up onto the plank fence around the feedlot.

Yow! Albert was down and the fat sows were eating him. The sows were fighting over the first good bite of him. Albert, on his back, was crying so hard his tongue was flittering in and out of his mouth. His eyes were crossed almost out of sight under his nose.

Wild, Free quick looked around. He spotted a wagon rod stuck in the ground near the fence. With both hands he jerked the rod out, then surged up over the plank fence, landed right in the middle of the biting sows, began flailing away at their humped-over dipping necks. At the same time he began kicking at their snouts with his bare feet.

"Albert!" he yelled. "Get up! Get up!"

The old fat sows left off biting Albert and charged Free. Their snouts came yukking straight for him.

Free got mad. What! Pigs dared to tackle him? He was Free Alfredson. A wild shout came out of him. He whaled at their flat snouts with his iron rod so hard and so fast he looked like an eggbeater.

"Get up, Albert! Get out of here, you dumb bastard! While I fight 'em off."

But Albert just kept laying there in the hog turds and dirty corncobs. His crossed eyes were stuck under his nose.

There was nothing for it but to drop the rod, grab Albert, and throw him over the plank fence.

"Yuk ugg! Yuk ugg!" The round snouts of the mad sows came after Free like a bunch of sink drains. One hog got in a good bite just above Free's knee. She ripped open his overalls.

"Yousonsabitchesbitingme!"

In one great leap Free jumped clear over to where Albert lay; grabbed him by the pants and belly; threw him way over the fence. Then, before the sows could wheel around and grab him, Free sprang way up over the top of them, coming up off the ground like a grasshopper, lifting himself sailing over the fence, and landed on his belly beside Albert. Ugggh. Both were safe.

The fat sows ruckled up against the plank fence mad at them.

Ma's voice was suddenly crying above Free. "Boy! Oh my boy."

Free rolled over.

There stood Ma in her long green dress. Both her hands were holding up her gold hair.

"Free, Free. What a brave boy you are."

Free ❦ 20

PA BOUGHT FREE a baseball, a bat, and a glove at a farm sale. And Sherm came for a week with his glove. Free and Sherm and Everett played ball for hours using the corncrib as a backstop. Over the fence onto the manure pile was a home run. Sherm once had six home runs in one day. Afterwards Free always had to pitch the dirty ball. Free didn't get any home runs. Everett got one though, a lucky bounce over the gate. In the evening Pa sometimes played too and then they really had fun. Pa could throw a curve and Sherm couldn't hit that for a home run. A curve was a magic thing. Free tried to throw one, but just couldn't get the ball to bend.

Then Free and Sherm got to wondering who could climb the highest. They climbed an elm tree near the house. Everett fell on his first try, so Sherm told him he could watch them from the ground, but no more climbing, you hear?

The row of giant cottonwoods in back of the grove caught their eye next. But the cottonwood was also the most dangerous to climb. It was hard to tell when a cottonwood branch was solid or had secret rot in it. The safest tree was the ash but the ashes didn't grow very tall. The box elder was just a dirty old tree. And the maple was tricky. Though the maple had one thing in its favor. It had big smooth limbs that swung out level and a fellow could lie down on one and take a nap.

The tallest cottonwood stood near the pasture creek. It sure speared up. Sherm led the way. He tested each branch above him before he let go of the one below. Free watched carefully and then followed the leader, taking the same ones Sherm took.

Near the top Sherm said he didn't know if he cared to go any farther. He said he had trouble getting his breath, they'd climbed so high. His blue eyes were black in the corners.

Free said he'd try it then.

"But why? I'm the oldest and the one with the most sense," Sherm said, "and I say no."

Free looked up. The tippy top was about the length of a stepladder above him. The green leaves up there made a soft leathery noise.

"Are you going to try anyway?"

"Yip,"

"Okay. It'll be your own fault if you break your neck."

Free worked himself carefully past Sherm. He had to place his bare toes on the outside part of the two twigs Sherm was standing on.

"Careful now."

"Don't worry."

"You sure now you can do it?"

"Is this cottonwood higher than the one Uncle John cut down when Grampa died?"

"I wouldn't know. And I couldn't care less."

The last few feet Free could find only three twigs he dared to trust. Higher than that they'd break off. The wind brushed through the green leaves. Sometimes the wind blew his white-gold hair in his eyes. Free hugged the thin trunk of the tree. It was like sitting on the back of a weak dog. Free looked around at the country on all sides. "Yow."

"What's the matter?" Sherm called up below him.

"Nothing." Free wried his head around some more, back and forth. "I can see John Westing's cupola. And I can see the gold ball on top of the flagpole by our schoolhouse."

"Oh, come on now. That's got to be a mote in your eye."

"And there's our neighbor Mr. Rath bindering already. His binder looks like a great big white butterfly eating through his field."

"You better get down from there. You're beginning to sound like you're out of your head."

"And I think I can see the water tower in Bonnie."

"Free, the tip is slowly beginning to bend over more and more. The next thing you know it'll break off."

"But I can't find where Pa is. He and the landlord was supposed to be salting out the Canady thistle in the back of the pasture this morning." Pa had said at breakfast that Mr. Haines was coming with his spade and sack of salt. Mr. Haines hated the Canady thistle with all his soul. When he'd spot a thistle, he'd stick his spade in under it, pry it up a little, throw in a handful of salt, and so kill the thistle. "They must be behind that hill there."

"Get down. I just heard the tip crack."

"But, Sherm, this is fun. Wow."

"Well, you do what you wanna. But me, I'm climbing down."

"I feel like I'm about to fly, Sherm."

Sherm began to work his way down the trunk. "You better make sure you've grown some wings first." Sherm's voice gradually became fainter as he went down.

Free hung on a while longer. The tree top swayed back and forth. It was much more springy than a hammock. And ever so much more fun. It was as wiggly as a buggy whip. It went up, then down, instead of down and then up. Man, this really was fun. This was better than eating pure sugar.

Sherm called up from the ground. He'd made it. "C'mon! Are you coming? Me and Everett are hungry."

Free took one last look around at all the great sights. Then, sighing, he both slid and climbed down. He lost one button, the one on the right suspender snap.

When they got to the house, Ma said, "Where in the world have you kids been? I've been calling and calling you for dinner."

"We didn't hear you."

"Well, it's too bad, because it's too late now. I've got the food all put away. Why, Pa's even had his nap already and has left for the neighbors to help them. Mr. Haines already left too."

"You mean you're not going to feed us dinner?" Sherm cried.

"That's right. I've told you kids before that if you ain't here on time for your meals—no food. I'm much too busy to be setting out two dinners."

"Oh, Ma," Free said, sad, trying to shame her with a look.

"I'm sorry. Look at all that patching I have to do. And now I see you've lost another button. When will my labors ever end?"

"Ma, you're not being fair," Free said.

Ma grabbed Free by the overalls and with the other hand picked up the sewing kit. "Here. Stand still a minute, you wild horse, and I'll at least put on this button for you." Ma shook her head. "Someday, when I'm cold and dead and lying in the grave, then you'll think about me and appreciate all the things I've done for you. But," she sighed, "by then it'll be too late."

Sherm twitched by the door. "So we better be nice to you while we can, hah, Ade?"

Ma looked at Sherm, sharp. "No smart talk now, little brother." Ma had a way of biting her tongue as she sewed that made it look like she had three lips. She glanced over at where Jonathan, the baby, lay in his basket. "Sherm, will you adjust the gauze over the baby's face? So the flies can't get at him?"

Sherm dragged his feet. But he did it. He liked babies, especially if they were nephew babies.

"Now, where's the scissors? I suppose I've mislaid them again. Oh dear. Well, I'll just have to do without." Ma leaned down to bite off the thread with her teeth. She had a little catch on her eyetooth in which she could snip the thread. She didn't quite bite it through the first time. When she failed a second time, she got mad and went after the thread like a bulldog. And accidentally bit her tongue. That put her in a rage, so she got the butcher knife and chopped the thread off. Free was scared to death of the knife. So was Sherm. "Now," Ma said, "under the trees with you. Both of you." Ma was about to cry. "Everett, you too."

Free and Sherm and Everett ran outdoors. It didn't pay to be around Ma when she got that way. They sat in the hammock under the maples thinking things over, feeling sorry for Ma.

Pretty soon Sherm said he felt awful hungry. "Too bad the crabs in the orchard ain't ripe yet."

"Can't we eat them anyway?" Everett asked.

"Not if you don't want the royal roaring diarrhee," Sherm said.

"If we put some salt on 'em," Free said, "from Pa's barrel of rough salt for the cattle, we maybe could."

"No," Sherm said. "But I tell you what. Let's instead play we're fasting. Like they sometimes do in the Bible. That way the next time we'll have the better sense and think of when it's dinner time."

They sat in silence, swinging slowly back and forth in the hammock.

Sherm sighed. "But I sure do miss those boiled beets."

Free loved fresh boiled beets himself. When a person played with one just right in his mouth before he bit into it, it almost felt like he had two red tongues.

"Yeh," Sherm said, "too bad."

"Hey," Free said, "I got an idea."

"What?"

"I know where the beets grow in the garden. Why don't we go and just pull up a half dozen, slice 'em up, fry 'em ourselves, and that way we have our noon dinner anyway? The most important part of it?"

"Now you're talking like a good hired hand. Show me."

"What about some onions too?" Everett asked.

"Who wants skunk eggs when he's got beets to eat?" Sherm said.

They pulled up a dozen red beets. They wrung off the tops and washed them in the cattle tank. Sherm got out his jackknife and sliced them up. Free meantime went to the junk pile back in the grove and found an old milk can cover. Sherm spread the sliced beets in the tin cover.

"Now," Sherm said, "to make a fire to fry them on. A hot one." Sherm cocked his head to one side. "Uh-huh. I know what we'll do. C'mon." He led them to the hundred-gallon gas tank behind the corncrib just into the edge of the grove. Pa'd set the the big red tank in the shade so the sun wouldn't make the gas too hot. Sherm and Free scratched up a couple of handfuls of dry twigs and piled them under the nozzle of the tank. Sherm opened the nozzle sideways a quarter inch and let some gas spill over the twigs, then shut it off. Some drops kept dripping off. "Now," he said, "what we need next is a lucifer."

"I know where one is," Everett said. "Pa left two matches inside the smokehouse. Above the door there."

"Ah. That's being my good hired hand. Get 'em."

Sherm needed only one match. The pile of twigs almost exploded because he'd let so much gas spill over them. The gas kept dripping on them a little too, and each drop went off like a mizzling firecracker.

Soon the beets bagan to fry.

"Can I turn 'em over?" Free asked.

"Now you're really being my favorite hired hand. Knowing what to do next without being told."

Free turned the sliced beets over with a green twig.

Everett rubbed his stomach. "Sure makes me hungry smellin' 'em."

Soon the flames were as red as the beets. When the twigs began to burn the smoke turned gray. The flames reached up around the nozzle of the big red tank. The fire got so hot Free had to hold up a hand to protect his face.

Ma spotted them through the kitchen window. Then she stepped outside. She yahooed, "Are you kids playing with fire?"

Sherm was going to say something smart, but just then saw Pa coming down the lane in the old grinding Overland. "Oh oh."

Pa pulled up beside the walk near the cobshed. He stared at their little fire. Then he moved. He rose out of the car like a dog leaping over a fence. He came straight for them.

All three kids scattered to get out of Pa's way.

Pa shot for the frying beets. With one great kick he sent the fire and the pan of beets sailing into the grove. He kicked it all so accurate that not one single twig was left burning on the ground under the nozzle of the red tank. Then, cussing a blue streak, Pa went over and stomped out all the burning twigs in the grove one by one.

Free stood absolutely astounded. He'd never seen Pa look so mighty.

Pa went over and touched the sides of the big red gas tank. He jerked his hand back. "Gotske!"

Ma came sailing up in her long green dress. "Alfred?"

"Them kids! In another minute if I hadn't've driv onto the yard, they'd all have been blown to kingdom come."

"They . . . would?"

"Sure! You heat up . . . God! one hundred gallons of gas!!"

Ma held up her gold hair.

Pa snapped at her. "Didn't you see what they was doing? You're always looking out of the kitchen window otherwise?"

Ma let her hands fall to her side.

Pa next snarled around at Sherm. "And you, you were the oldest on the yard. Where in the hell was your brains, for godsakes?"

"Your wife here wouldn't feed us this noon," Sherm said. "Because we came in late. So we thought we'd cook our own dinner."

"Do you know you almost cooked yourself right straight into hell?" Pa sucked air like he was going to bawl. Then, crumpling up a little, he picked Free off the ground and gave him a great big hug. "Boy, boy, please, for godsakes, after this have the better sense and always ask me first where you can strike a match. And never strike one near a gas tank. No matter what. You hear?"

"Ya, Pa."

Pa let Free down then and gave Everett a hug too.

But Ma didn't cool down quite as fast. She kept muttering to herself that they ought to put all three rascals in the closet under the steps for a while. "In the black hole."

"One hundred gallons of gas."

Free ❦ 21

A COUPLE OF WEEKS later Aunt Karen came home from summer school.

It was also time for Sherm to go home. Aunt Karen offered to take him to the depot. She said she wanted to make herself useful.

Pa wasn't sure he should let Aunt Karen drive Daise. Daise was choosy about who held the ribbons. You could tell that, Pa said, by the way Daise wore her ears. If one ear was down, it was a signal Daise meant no.

"What if both ears are down?" Aunt Karen asked.

"That means, look out, she's gonna kick the door down."

Aunt Karen was pretty perky. "I'm not afraid of a simple creature like a horse."

"Ha," Pa snorted, "she's got more brains than you might think."

Pa hitched Daise to the buggy and brought her up to the house. Aunt Karen got in while Pa held Daise by the bridle. Pa said, "Take them ribbons in your hands like there's no question about who's the boss. You know, the way you run a school. March. Get. Walk chalk. As long as she knows you know what you're doing, she'll leave you alone."

Free and Sherm climbed in. Free sat in the middle. Sherm carefully spread the yellow silk duster across their knees.

Aunt Karen held onto the lines like they were sticks.

Free had a question. "Pa?"

"Ya, boy?"

"Can we have two nickels?"

"What for?"

"To buy us each an ice-cream cone. A going-away present for Sherm."

"Boy, I'm so poor I can count my entire wealth without removing my hand from my pocket."

"Oh."

"I'll buy you each a cone," Aunt Karen said. "If you behave."

"Good," Pa said. "All right, ready?"

"Ready." Aunt Karen's lips made a line like a knife scar.

Pa let Daise's bridle go. And Daise took off full speed. It was like Daise had no low gear in her. They sailed around the corner of the cobhouse. Ma stood waving in the door watching them go.

The first few miles everything went fine. The sky was clear. There wasn't much dust. Daise ran down her side of the road at a steady fast pace.

Aunt Karen began to feel good. She was driving that dratted headstrong Daise. Wasn't it wonderful? At last she'd come across an animal that didn't mind her.

What they hadn't seen though back home was that a bank of clouds had been building up over Bonnie. The trees on the yard had been in the way. But when they came over the Alan Weatherly hill, they saw the anvil cloud. They headed south down the hill toward it.

It was very still out.

Daise dropped four golden apples at the next crossroad. Aunt Karen looked the other way.

The shadow of the cloud reached them just as they rolled past the lane of the Siouxland Home for Little Boys.

Daise looked up at the cloud, looked around at Aunt Karen, then went back to digging down the road.

Aunt Karen got nervous. "What did Daise mean by that look?"

Neither Free nor Sherm said a thing. They sat up a little straighter and waited.

Aunt Karen studied Daise's ears. The ears were still straight up. Aunt Karen sawed the lines back and forth a little to let Daise know who was the boss. Then Aunt Karen settled back and held onto the lines some more like they were sticks.

They crossed the Big Rock River bridge. Rattledy-rumbledy-rumm.

It got dark fast above them. Though the earth was still light.

Daise coughed once.

Lightning snapped in front of them. It struck a willow tree beside a pond and pulverized it to toothpicks.

Daise took another look at the sky above her, then made up her mind. She turned right around in the road, veering the buggy around behind her like it was a slingshot, up on two wheels, everybody almost falling out.

"Here you!" Aunt Karen cried.

Daise straightened out heading straight north, and the buggy came down on all four wheels again, and everybody fell back into place.

"Daise, you!" Aunt Karen pulled on the lines. "It was my thought we could drive onto the next yard there and take shelter in a corncrib alley. Until this little shower passed over."

Daise put the socks into it. As Daise went faster and faster her rear gradually lowered. Her buttocks began to rotate like the universal couplings on Pa's elevator.

"Here, you darn fool you. Don't you know I'm the boss?" Aunt Karen sawed on the lines like she was trying to close the drawstrings of a sack of potatoes. She placed her pointy toes on the dashboard to get better leverage. "Daise!"

Daise just kept on digging. They shot across the bridge so fast the black trusses on either side looked like a tight picket fence. Brrupt! and they were across.

The brrupt made the two boys laugh. They looked at each other, then began to imitate the sound. "Brrupt!" one would say; "brrupt!" the other would echo. Then they'd laugh like fools. Finally they got to laughing so hard they almost slopped out of the buggy. Even when the first big drops of rain hit the buggy top they kept on laughing.

"Oh, well, pshaw," Aunt Karen finally said, "all right, have it your way then, Daise, you darn stubborn horse's patoot you. But I'll be switched if I hold onto the lines anymore under the pretense I'm still boss, when I'm not." She wrapped the lines around the whip holder.

By the time they arrived on the yard, it was dry out and the sun was shining on the apple orchard. Daise stopped by herself.

Ma came out of the house and Pa out of the barn. "What happened?"

Aunt Karen cried and laughed both. "We had a near collision with a little shower and Daise decided she didn't like the lightning."

Pa looked east over the hill. "You mean that little cloud?"

"Well, it was pretty big when we met it by the bridge," Aunt Karen said. She stepped down out of the buggy. "And that's the last time I'm ever going to have anything to do with that animal again. Fawh."

Pa took Daise by the bridle. "Wal, if Daise decided you should turn around and come home, it was probably the best thing to do. She usually has the better sense."

Ma put her arms around Aunt Karen. "It's all right, dear. That horse is enough to drive anyone to distraction. Alfred had her before we got married and I think he spoiled her."

Pa said, "All right, you kids, get out."

"Can Sherm stay another week then, Pa?"

"It sure looks like he's going to, don't it?"

Free was feeding the calves skim milk after supper when he heard someone coughing in the barn. Daise. Pa had let her stay in that night.

After rinsing out the calf pails, Free went to look.

Daise was lying down. Her belly had fallen in, pus was foaming in her nose, and when she coughed her legs kicked out stiff.

Free had never seen a horse lying down. Pa'd said that one never caught a horse lying down because a horse slept on its feet, that if you did catch a horse down it was a bad sign.

When Free burst into the kitchen he found Pa smoking his pipe. "Pa, Daise's down. And she's coughing."

Pa clapped out his pipe in the stove. "You say she's down?"

"Yes."

Pa put on his shoes and straw hat and hurried to the barn.

Free ran beside him. "Daise coughed a couple times when we was going to town with Aunt Karen."

"Hum." Pa took one look at Daise then sat down on his heels beside her. "Gotske. She was still up when we was milking."

Free sat down on his heels too. He watched his father. "Is coughing bad for a horse, Pa?"

"Shut up. And let me think a minute."

"Ya, Pa."

Free hoped Daise wasn't going to be mortal sick.

"Daise," Pa said.

Daise flopped one ear. It raised dust out of the straw.

"What's the matter, girl?"

Daise flopped her ear again.

Pa scratched her between the ears.

As Pa and Free sat in the deepening evening dusk, Daise's breath slowly began to rattle more and more, until at last she broke into a hoarse cough.

Pa bit his lips in. He stood up and got a horse blanket and threw it over Daise. He gave Daise another father look, then hurried for the house.

Free ran beside him. He didn't dare say a thing.

Pa went straight for the telephone. He rang for Central, one long hard ring.

Ma was changing the baby's diaper in the living room. She looked at Pa with big blue eyes. There was a row of safety pins between her lips.

"Central? Get me Dr. Overslough. The veterinarian in Hello."

Ma took the last safety pin out of her lips and fixed it in place. "Is he the nearest vet, Alfred?"

"No, we got one in Bonnie. Dr. Hopp. But he don't know sic'em about horses. I wouldn't even trust your mother with him."

"Oh."

"Your brother John tells me he castrates with a dirty knife. Didn't even have the decency to clean it in some distillate that was handy."

"Isn't it going to be expensive to get a vet all the way from Hello?"

Pa whirled around. "My God, woman, that's Daise that's sick. My Daise! You know, the horse that's been with me all these years. Who even took me to Jerusalem to see you that first time."

Ma put the baby in its crib. "Maybe Daise is just getting old."

"She's got pneumonia."

"Oh, Alfred, maybe it's just a cold."

"There ain't no such thing as a cold for a horse. When a horse begins to cough, it's already got pneumonia." Pa listened to the black receiver. "What's that, Central? . . . What? . . . You say he's on vacation? . . . When my pet horse is dying? . . . No, I didn't say my pet wife. I said, my pet horse . . . All right." Pa hung up. "What's that Overslough taking a vacation for in the summer, the very time when animals are most apt to get into trouble? The piker. Vacation. I wisht I could have a vacation once."

"Well, so far as that goes I wish I could have one too," Ma said softly.

Pa went to the pantry. "Got any medicine in here?"

"No, I don't think so."

"No liniment?"

"We used the last of that when you picked corn last fall."

"Then where's that bottle of Old Crow? There's still some left in that, ain't there?"

Ma had a little smile. "Now that's something I want to see. A horse drinking whiskey. Especially Daise."

"Please," Pa said. He was almost crying.

Ma dug out the old whiskey bottle and with another little smile handed it to Pa.

Pa stuck it in his back pocket.

Back in the barn Pa lit a lantern. He hung it on a nail on a crossbeam. He turned up the wick. Webs hung everywhere.

Pa stared. "Daise, old girl."

"What's the matter, Pa?"

"It's worse than I thought. She's got the galloping pneumonia."

Free hardly dared to think what was going to happen next.

"It's like Old Charlie Pullman said. Once a horse is down, you might as well start digging her grave."

"Isn't there anything you can do, Pa?"

"Too late."

Their Daise, the pretty gray roan, always so peppy and ornery, she was going to turn into a pile of bones? While Aunt Karen, who couldn't handle her, was going to continue being a schoolteacher?

Pa sat down on his heels again. He ran his hand up each of Daise's ears, like he was milking them, gently. "Why must you jump the fence just now? You were getting to be tame enough for my boy here to handle you."

Free stood with his legs crossed.

Daise breathed slow, hoarse, rough. Matter bubbled out of her nose and ran into the straw.

"Daise? Girl?"

Her lungs blasted out a great cough. She took breath for yet anouther cough. And then, before she could get the cough out, she died. Slowly breath oozed out of her. Her mouth made a sound like a just punctured rubber tire. Her belly gradually collapsed away from her ribs, sinking inward, leaving a hollow big enough to put a bushel basket in.

The next day Pa wouldn't call the rendering plant. "I'm burying her myself in the pasture," Pa told Ma. "Where she had her most fun. And I'll do it even if it takes me all day to dig a hole big enough."

For a week after that, Free had nightmares about Daise. In one nightmare

Daise was chasing Aunt Karen across the yard biting her in the behind. In another nightmare a great big red ant with Pa eyes was carrying Daise around on its back. All that was left of Daise was a husk. She looked like a dead beetle. She really was dead.

Free ❦ 22

PA GOT BEHIND in his bindering. The oats east of the house were dead ripe and had to be cut pronto. One good windstorm could flatten them in a minute and then all that wonderful grain would be lost.

Grampa Alfredson heard about Pa's troubles and offered to help him out. Wife Bettie had died the past February from apoplexy, and he was lonesome living alone in his house. The railroad had laid him off his section job for the summer and the people in the area weren't building cyclone cellars anymore.

Pa asked Ma about it.

"I think your father is entitled to a warm corner in his son's house," Ma said.

"He's got funny manners. I can see where you might not be able to tolerate them. Like I can't some of your mother's."

"Alfred, I've always liked your father. And now that Karen's left us, he can sleep in her room."

"Okay, that's settled then."

Pa thought Grampa should run the binder, have a sitting job, while Pa did the shocking. But Grampa quietly told Pa he was still tough enough to shock. "I've got only one thing wrong with me and that's that darn diarrhea I still have from Dakota. Thank God your wife bakes great bread. That'll help slow it down some."

Free liked this Grampa. This Grampa sometimes told stories about when he was a sailor on the seven seas and had a girl friend in every port.

Free got a bad shock, though, the second night Grampa was there. The Underhills had dropped by to see the baby, and with them came a boy named Edward. Edward was six years older than Free, but he wasn't much bigger, and he wasn't any smarter. Free had talked to him a couple of times while getting the cows. The Underhill pasture was across the fence from their own. Edward had shown him a fat bull snake which had just swallowed a baby rabbit whole. The snake looked like a tangled rope with a fat knot at the front end, with one baby rabbit leg still sticking out.

The Underhills came just as Free was about to feed the calves. In his joy at seeing a play pal come on the yard, Free forgot about the calves. Edward had a soft smile.

Free showed Edward a set of play hay slings he'd made. They fit exactly in his coaster wagon and he and Everett had already hauled in several loads of loose grass for play hay and had put it up in the little smokehouse, just like Pa did his hay in the big red barn.

"Free!"

Free jumped. He hadn't expected to hear his name called that curt and short. He looked toward the house.

There sat Grampa on the cistern head smoking his corncob pipe upside down. His engineer's cap was pulled down over his eyes. It was hard to make out if he was thinking mad at Free or what. His lower lip stuck out from under his rainbow moustache.

"Yes, Grampa?"

"C'mere a minute."

"But I'm playing with Edward and—"

"C'mere!"

Free had never heard Grampa talk hard. He didn't know what to make of it. Free approached Grampa warily.

Grampa puffed on his pipe until Free was within a couple of steps of him. Then Grampa removed his pipe from his lips. "Haven't you forgot something?"

"Not that I know of, Grampa."

All of a sudden Grampa jumped at him and hit him one over the head.

Free staggered and fell down. "Hey, you ain't got the right to do that."

Grampa pointed his pipestem at the two pails of skim milk standing by the cobhouse. "What about the calves tonight?"

Free scrambled to his feet. "Oh, that's right. I forgot."

"Did your mother forget to feed you tonight?"

"No, but—"

"Then you mustn't forget to feed your calves. Those calves are your responsibility, just like you and your brothers are your mother's responsibility." Grampa gave his pipe a deep suck. "You want to always remember, boy, that the mothers of those calves are the foster mothers of mankind. Your foster mother. And in time those calves will become the foster mothers of your children. So treat them well."

"Ya, Grampa."

"Duty first, pleasure after."

"Just the same, though, Grampa, you ain't got the right to hit me. That's only for my pa and ma to do."

"I'm your father's pa. And that gives me the right to punish a grandson as if he were my own son. When I think he needs it."

Free didn't know what to say to that. He was also ashamed that his new friend Edward had seen him get the dickens. Eyes on the ground, Free said to Edward, "I guess I better feed the calves first then. Afters I can show you how we use the dog Tricks to pull the hay up into the smokehouse. You wanna help me?"

Grampa raised his arm and pointed toward the barn. "You feed those calves alone. Company will only disturb them."

"But Edward feeds the calves at his place."

"Alone, I said. Now get."

Free got.

It was Free's job to bring the men lunch at ten o'clock and at three o'clock. Ma made it ready and then he carried it out to them in two little pails.

It was sometimes a problem to find where Grampa was shocking, on the east side of the field, or the north side. Wherever it was, Pa wanted the lunch brought to that spot so he and Grampa could eat at the same time and then afterwards have a pipe together. That of course meant Free sometimes had to go a long ways across the stubble field. It was tough walking through the stubbles barefoot. There were the prickles of wild roses to watch out for, and the cut-off stubs of bull thistles, and the stickery roots of old cornstalks.

As he walked along the south side of the field, then the east side, looking for Grampa, carefully following the flattened track made by the binder bull wheel, it struck Free that Pa's oatsfield looked awfully neat. That had to be Grampa's doing. Every shock of six bundles was set exactly north and south and shaped like a sharp long tepee, with the oatheads tusseling out on top like jumping jets of amber water. Free had asked Pa once why straight north and south, and Pa had said, "So the sun can get at the bundles better. All morning long on one side and then all afternoon long on the other. Oats needs curing, boy." Every shock was also set in line with the one behind it, so that the field looked like a battleground with neat lines of armies marching across it. Grampa was always tidy.

Free spotted the white reels of Pa's binder in a little hollow across the road from the Rath place. Pa had stopped to rethread the needle of the binder and Grampa just happened to be there too. Both Pa and Grampa had a big welcome smile for him.

Pa said, "Set the lunch over in the shade of the binder there, boy. And then shag up some bundles for us to sit on."

Grampa needed only two bundles to sit on. He leaned against the canvas shield of the platform and let go with a big sigh. His face was streaming with sweat. Drops of it hung in the tips of his moustache. His lower lip was burned red by the sun. His shirt was sopping wet.

"One more hole to thread and I'll be right with you," Pa said. Pa mouthed the end of the yellow twine string he was holding to form it into a wet point, then leaned down into the back of the machine and carefully inserted the wet point into the hole of a long curved shiny needle. When the machine was going the long needle worked like a woodpecker trying to pull a worm out of the lawn. "There," Pa said, "got her." The machine was covered with chaff and dust. Some of it had got on Pa's hairy arms and the side of his face. Pa brushed himself off. He flaffed off his sweaty overalls too. "Actually that's pretty good twine them jailbirds made this year. Last year I had to climb down off this fetchsticking machine almost every other round and rethread her."

Free pointed at the big wheel under the binder. "Why do they call that the bull wheel?"

Pa selected four bundles and sat down. He had long legs. Like Grampa he sagged against the canvas shield of the platform and let go with a big sigh. He took off his straw hat and wiped his face on his rolled-up sleeves. "Because it's the main driving wheel. The big wheel that turns all the gears and chains of the machine. And with a bull being bigger than a cow, they call it a bull wheel instead of a cow wheel. I guess."

Free picked up two bundles for himself and sat down. The smell of fresh oil, just squirted juicy and running into all the moving parts of the machine, mixed in sweetly with the smell of mown oat stalks. Ma had also put in a sandwich for Free, as a reward for bringing the lunch, dried beef with a thick layer of homechurned butter, and the smell of that was good too. It was great fun to be biting off a big chunk of bread like Pa and Grampa.

The Rath dog, a long yellow critter, half hound and half collie, came across the road and ran slinking toward a shock near the fence. He'd smelled something. Sure enough, just as he started to sniff into the little dark alley under the six bundles, a rabbit shot out of the other end and began running across the open stubble field. The yellow dog took out after it. The dog gained rapidly on it. At the last second the rabbit dodged into the still uncut grain, and the dog lost it. Then the dog began to make great leaps in the grain, soaring up and then coming down with a pouncing fall, going higher and higher each time, trying to locate the rabbit at the top of its jump. At last the dog landed right next to the rabbit. There was a squeak and the rabbit darted out of the grain across the open stubbles again. The dog stretched out after it in a dead run, with long dolloping throws of its slender legs. The rabbit darted behind this shock, then that shock; doubled back, darted forward. Once the rabbit shot under a shock. The rabbit didn't disturb the shock. But the dog did. The dog sent the bundles flying, three to a side.

Free, Grampa, and Pa stopped chewing to watch the desperate chase.

The rabbit once again headed for the standing oats. Again just made it. This time, no matter how the dog pounced around in the tall oats, the dog couldn't find the rabbit. The dog leaping up out of the golden grain looked like a great goldfish surfacing over and over again in a pond of yellow water.

"Wasn't that funny?" Free said. "He let her get away twice."

Grampa finished off his last sandwich with a swig of tea. "Not so funny, really, when you consider that the dog was only running for its breakfast while the rabbit was running for its life."

Free had himself a swig too. "Still and all, that yellow dog's got to be pretty dumb to let a rabbit get away."

Grampa's moustache moved like he might be smiling under it.

"Just like our dog Tricks. He can be so dumb sometimes."

"Our Tricks?" Pa said. "Naw."

"Oh, yes, Pa. You know how when Tricks gets a bone from Ma and goes out on the grass and chews on it a while, and then, looking suspicious all around, goes and buries it in the grove? Well, afters, the next week or so, when he goes looking for it again, he can never find it. He looks all over for it, smelling and smelling, digging here and there, so that finally, I gotta go and show him where he's buried it."

Both Grampa and Pa laughed out loud at that. "You mean, you help the dog find his bones?"

"Sure. He can't remember."

Finished with their lunch, Pa pressed the lids back on the gallon pails.

Grampa gave Pa a look. "Can we smoke here?"

"I know I am." Pa muttered a little to himself. "Ever since the good wife put her foot down about me chewing Climax, I've had to smoke a pipe. When chewing is ever so much safer in a tinder-dry field."

Grampa tamped his corncob pipe full with his favorite Corn Cake tobacco, then turned the pipe over and lit it. The match flame leaped up into the pipe on each draw.

Free saw Grampa hold the palm of his hand under his pipe to be extra safe. "What if you two should happen to start a fire here, Pa?"

"Not likely. No wind. And we could quick stomp out what little got started."

"But supposin' a dust devil came up just then?"

"Got your supposin' cap on again today, hah?"

"But what would you do?"

"Wal, we'd have to get up and pee on it. With all that tea we just drank, a whole gallon of it, the three of us would make a pretty good fire brigade. When you got three fire engines working together, a fire ain't got much of a chance."

Free smiled to himself at the picture. He himself would go after the little flames along the edges, Pa could go after the highest flames, and Grampa could go after the middle ones.

Then Pa and Grampa began talking about some things Free had little interest in, and he dreamed off by himself.

His attention was drawn to a big red ant trying to cross the top of his tanned foot. It was dragging a single oat kernel. Both the legs of the red ant and the sharp point of the oat tickled. His foot wanted to jerk itself to get rid of the itching, but, willing it, Free managed to keep it rigid. He wanted the red ant to make it to wherever it was going. To help it along he very slowly turned his foot over until the red ant with its heavy load began to go the other way. Relieved that the going was suddenly easier, the red ant hurried into the pigeon grass undergrowth.

Then Grampa said something that made Free listen again.

"Alfred, there are times when I don't think you deserve Ada."

"But you do, hah?"

"That's not the point. You don't seem to understand that smart women usually turn bullheaded as they get older. But Ada hasn't."

"Now I just wonder," Pa said, "if my own ma would have turned bullheaded if she'd have lived."

"I've thought about that." Grampa's eyes closed upon his pipe. "And it's my conclusion that I don't think she would have. She too was of the patient type. And because I lived with one like that, I think I'm in a good position to be a judge of your wife."

Pa's pipe began to crackle. "And I suppose you deserved my ma, but I don't Ada, hah?"

Grampa didn't say anything.

"I know about you," Pa said. "Your brothers told me. About how you once got caught on the kitchen floor with a girl. By a soldier. Was that before or after you married my ma?"

Grampa got excited. "B-brothers of mine? Sons of bitches."

"Nicholas. Andrew. They tell about it laughing, of course."

Grampa clapped out his pipe. He dug a little hole in the ground, dropped the dottle into the hole, and covered it.

"Now me," Pa said, "there ain't a woman in the world I couldn't look in the eye. Both before and after I got married."

Grampa's lower lip slowly curled up.

"There's a lot of things you did I never could understand."

"Like what?"

"You bragging once that you sent Abbott and Gerda out to steal chickens on the way home from the Dakotas."

Grampa let out a growl like he thought Pa was pretty dumb not to understand that they'd had to take them chickens.

"Oh, I wouldn't put it past you, Pa. Because I can remember how when we lived in Missouri, t' Lebanon, how you sent Karen and me out each morning with a gunnysack to beg for old bread anybody might have left over, at the back doors in town."

"That's all past now, Alfred."

"Not in my head it ain't. That was burned into me so it's like it's alive in there yet today. Yeh, you sitting like a great Lord in your chair there, smoking your pipe upside down, complaining we didn't know how to beg."

"It had to be done that way, Alfred, b-because p-people tend to feel more sorry for children than f-for grown-ups."

"And how I had to go through the woods to bring you lunch when you were cutting railroad ties, and how I once ran into a hoop snake and was scared out of my wits, and you bawling me out for being late because I then went the long way around by the tracks." Pa put his pipe away in the bib pocket of his overalls. Pa was almost crying. "But it all fits. Any kid who has to be tied to a tree by his parents for fear he'll run away, and then who still goes and breaks the rope and runs away to sea, is, to my way of thinking, bound to have some mighty high notions of hisself."

Free broke in. "Grampa?"

"Yes, boy?" Grampa spoke tenderly.

"What did that soldier do when he caught you on the floor?"

"So, that didn't get by you, did it?"

"Grampa?"

"I took his gun away from him."

"Didn't he fight you back?"

"I was too quick for him." Grampa remembered to himself for a moment; then let go with a snort. "I tied him to a chair and made him watch. Ha, and the girl was hot for the play, too."

"Watch what, Grampa?"

"Oh, never mind. You're too young to know about such things."

Pa said, "Ho, maybe I am too."

Free said, "Like what a stud does to a mare?"

Grampa looked at Pa. "Have you let him watch that?"

"No, I haven't. But he's got a nose like a witching stick for such things. He's into everything and always way ahead of you."

Grampa's eyes closed behind his dark glasses. "Yes, well, we're apt to forget how much we already knew when we were seven."

Pa let down a little. "Yeh, and it's the women and their ministers who keep trying to make us forget what we knew."

Grampa looked down at the ground.

Pa decided that the bull wheel needed some extra greasing. He got out a pail of grease. With his finger he packed the grease cups on either side of the bull wheel. As he screwed the cups down grease slowly mattered out around the bearings below.

Pa wiped his finger on the leg of his overalls. "Wal, time to roll again. No rest for the wicked."

"Hah," Grampa snorted, "nor rest for the poor, you mean. The wicked usually have an easy time of it."

Pa climbed into the spring seat on top of the binder. "Pa, you're as bad as that kid of mine there. No matter what I say he's always coming up with a contrary idee too. It's enough to make a man go out and beat up on bulls."

Grampa all of a sudden turned around and walked away. He went to the end of a row of bundles and began setting up shocks.

Pa watched Grampa go. He thought to himself a minute, then flipped the lines. "All right, Fan, Prince, get, go."

The horses groaned. Their great butt muscles flexed as they leaned into their collars. The bull wheel began to roll and all the chain drives and sprocket wheels rattled up merrily. The white reel gobbled into the standing grain.

The next day was Sunday. Free was glad. Pa had traded the old Maxwell in for a brand-new Flying Cloud Reo at Roy Wickett's garage and Pa would be driving it to church. Pa had no trouble getting him and Everett to hurry and dress up in their Sunday clothes. Both thought it took Ma an awful long time to get ready.

At quarter to nine Pa finally went out to the corncrib and backed the Reo out of the alley. The long black car shone like a great polished shoe. It had a radiator like the snout of a hog. A spare tire set into the running board on the driver's side. The best part was the wide brown steering wheel. The way Pa rolled the big wheel around, back and forth, he looked like the captain of a ship.

Pa pulled up beside the walk by the cobhouse with a big smile. "All right, you little shitepokes, in you go." He leaned across and opened the back door. "Easy does it now. Let's not bark up the car on its first run."

Free and Everett sat in back like a couple of wondering squirrels. Free sat behind where Ma would sit so he could watch across and see how Pa would drive the Reo.

Pa went into the house. The idling motor shook the car like a sewing machine working on overalls. Pretty soon Pa came out of the house carrying Albert, and Ma came out carrying baby Jonathan. Pa set Albert between Free and Everett in back and then got in behind the wheel. Ma got in beside Pa and held the baby on her lap. Ma looked the dashboard over with sharp eyes. Finally she located the speedometer. That meant Pa wouldn't dare to drive fast.

Free waved at Grampa where he sat smoking his pipe on the cistern lid. "Bye, Grampa." Everett and Albert waved too.

Grampa just stared. With his dark glasses he looked like a big horsefly with large round eyes.

Pa shifted into low. The gears made a crashing noise. "Still haven't quite got the hang of shifting this make yet," Pa said. The Reo rolled forward. Then Pa speeded up a little and shifted into second, again with a crashing sound. "Roy Wickett did it as smooth as silk." After Pa turned up the highway, he shifted into high, and that time did it smoothly. "Aha, so that's how you do it."

Ma held the baby tight. With her other hand she made sure the hatpin in her white shepherdess hat was in good and deep. Her blue eyes were on the speedometer. The jiggling arrow pointed mostly at twenty.

The motor pounded up the hill. The redheaded woodpeckers climbing the telephone poles got scared and flew off.

Pa drove a steady twenty until he got to the Windmiller lane. There the Reo began to pick up speed downhill. Pa liked the way the big new Reo rolled.

"Haven't driven her five hundred miles yet," Pa said, "but it won't hurt to open her up a little."

"Don't you go over thirty," Ma said.

"Aw, love, come on now."

The wax flowers in Ma's white shepherdess hat began to rattle. Ma let go of the baby in her lap and held onto the hat with both hands. "When you hit thirty per I'm jumping out."

Pa smiled his strong chin smile. "Don't be so skittish. Let me show you a little speed with this Flying Cloud." And Pa pulled down the gas lever anyway.

The Reo motor rumbled up, firing like a long string of firecrackers, and away they went. Fence posts flew by.

Free and Everett looked at each other. They laughed. What sport to be flying across the ground so fast. Speed was like being a bird.

Ma saw the needle jiggling on twenty-nine. "Alfred."

"Aw, c'mon, Ada, this road is as smooth as a race track."

"Alfred, I love you and all that, but speed and my heart don't go together."

"Love, I got a three-month guarantee on this car. It's perfectly safe. Nothing can go wrong with it."

"The Lord will decide that."

They flashed by schoolhouse No. 3. And then, just as they passed the deserted farm kitty-corner across the road, a funny kettering noise rose in the motor. It sounded like Tom Thumb hammering away very fast on a little anvil. And then, bom! bang! krang! a piston the size of a syrup pail came flying up through the black hood. And the engine went dead.

"Gotske!" Pa cried. "She's thrown a piston."

"Ya," Ma said, "there you go with your Flying Cloud."

Pa quick pulled on the brake.

The Reo finally stopped at the bottom of the hill.

"You see?" Ma said. She opened the door, and with the baby stepped down to the ground. Ma gave Free and Everett a white look. "C'mon, boys. We may as well start walking home."

After a minute Pa got out of the car too and went back and picked up the thrown piston. He looked at it; then with a shake of his head dropped it in the back of the car.

"Now what will you do?" Ma asked as they all walked home in the dusty gravel. "All that money lost."

"I'm going to trade the three-month guarantee I got on it for a new Buick. A Buick is bound to be a good car."

"You poor man," Ma said.

"Meantime, Roy Wickett can come get what's left of his great Flying Cloud. I know I'm not going to touch it again."

A few minutes later Rath's hired man came along in his jitney Ford. He gave them all a ride home.

Ma decided to hold church anyway. It would be with just their own family and they'd have it in the parlor. The parlor was for Sundays and what better time than now what with everybody all dressed up.

Ma went out to where Grampa sat on the cistern head. "We should be very pleased if you'd join us in worship, Pa." Ma gave Grampa one of those smiles that was hard to turn down.

Grampa shook his head. "Enter your parlor in these duds?"

"I'm sure the Lord won't mind your clothes if I don't, Pa."

"Now, Ada, you know I don't hold much with that autocratic institution, the church, where one man does all the ordering around and the rest of us have to just sit there and take it."

"I know you don't. But this will be a family service in which all members of the family can participate."

"I can't stand hypocrite sin-busters."

Pa just stood in the doorway with a funny smile.

Grampa gave his pipe a great suck. "Daughter, I'm a socialist. The exact opposite of what your minister believes in."

"Why don't we discuss this in our service in the parlor?"

Grampa slashed his short right arm this way and that way. "Your church believes in a government run by ministers who act on what they suppose are God's instructions . . . were He there. And that kind of government can lead to a tyranny worse even than Bismarck's. Or Cromwell's. Or that goddam John Calvin's in Switzerland."

"Careful what you say there about John Calvin there," Pa said.

Ma said, "Don't you believe there is a God?"

Grampa clapped out his pipe and slipped it into his bib pocket. "All right, daughter, I'll give in a little, seeing it's Sunday. Let's go into your parlor if talk religion we must."

"Good," Ma said. She smiled to herself as she led the way inside.

Grampa took off his shoes on the porch and went into the parlor in his socks. He took a high-back chair next to the maidenhair fern. He hooked his engineer's cap over his knee.

Ma let up the shades and everybody could finally see what there was in the parlor. The shaded room suddenly became a gold room.

Ma sat on the round organ stool, Bible in hand, while Pa took the big oak rocker and Free and Everett and Albert sat down in a row on the leather seat chairs along the wall. Jonathan the baby was placed on his belly on the floor. The rug under him was brown with a picture of a gold lion in it.

"Now," Ma said, "it happens I believe that the man should conduct the service, but since Alfred has trouble reading I think that in this case the woman can be forgiven for reading a short passage from the Bible." Ma opened the good book and lay the blue silk marker to one side. "I shall read Psalm 100, one of my favorites. 'Make a joyful noise unto the Lord all ye lands. Know ye that the Lord He is God. It is He that hath made us and not we ourselves. We are His people and the sheep of His pasture. Be thankful unto Him and bless His name. For the Lord is good. His mercy is everlasting, and His truth endureth to all generations.' "

By the time Ma finished, the parlor was very silent. Pa was studying his crossed legs and Grampa's lip was stuck out like he was trying to pry a piece of food from between his teeth with his tongue.

"What was the last word read, Free?"

"Generations."

Everett gave Albert a sly pinch in the sitter. Albert cried.

Ma looked severe at the little kids. "Still, you. This is church." Ma then gave Pa a look that meant he should lead in prayer.

Pa folded his hands over his crossed knees. He closed his eyes slowly. "Forgiving Father in heaven, we come to Thee at the midpoint—"

Ma broke in, eyes closed. "This is not at the table, Alfred."

"—of this day in humble family worship out in the country instead of church in town. We are sorry we can not foregather with Thy beloved congregation. Our old Reo went on the blink—"

"Alfred," Ma whispered sharply.

"—but maybe in the long run it'll be for the best, since I can get a better guarantee on a new Buick—"

"Alfred."

Free snuck a look at Pa.

Pa opened his eyes a second. "But, wife, Domeny goes into pa'ticulars in his long prayers on Sunday. He talks to God personal, about the weather, the crops, about the rowdy boys in the back seats, the laggards not paying their share of his salary, and all such like other things no different from our brokedown Reo."

"Alfred, I fear the head of this church in this parlor here serves without salary."

Grampa hadn't closed his eyes. He was smiling.

"Yeh, well . . . " Pa closed his eyes again. "Bless the Word read and may it touch our hearts and minds so that we'll be better citizens of Thy kingdom."

Everett gave Albert another pinch.

Albert was going to bawl, he opened his mouth for it, but when he saw that neither Pa nor Ma had seen Everett do it, he decided it was no use to bawl. So instead he gave Everett an elbow in the belly.

Pa finished up the long prayer with a brand-new ending. "And lastly, we have a scoffer in our midst who is also a loved one. In Thy infinite mercy, an it please Thee, show him the right way. Let him know that him being stubborn will get him nowhere. Also, being that all pots have ears, his being that way sets a bad example for the little ones, one of whom already shows signs of being another Bolshevik."

Free quick closed his eyes tight. Bolshevik meant him.

"In His name we ask it. Amen."

Ma wasn't sure she liked that Bolshevik part. There was the start of a black look around her eyes. But at last she decided not to pick at Pa about it and instead got up a sweet church smile. "Let's all sing a psalm together." She swiveled around on her stool and opened up a songbook on the music rack of the organ. "Psalm 84." Ma pumped up the organ and played the prelude. The red silk in the sound holes vibrated. Ma sang the first few notes alone. "How amiable are Thy tabernacles, O Lord of Hosts." Then Pa joined in, and then Everett. Pa sang a little behind like he didn't know the words quite and had to wait for Ma to mouth them first. "The sparrow hath found an house, and the swallow a nest for herself, where she may lay her young."

Grampa didn't sing. He just stared at the sleeping lion in the rug. He was still smiling.

Ma sang clear above them all. "Showers passing through the valley make it a well." Sunbeams shining through the colored glass above the bay window picked up some motes and made them fly around like fireflies. "A day in Thy court is better than a thousand in a desert. Rather would I be a doorkeeper in the house of God than a dweller in the tent of wickedness."

When the song was done, Ma thought to herself a second. "Who would like to expound on the word read?" Ma fixed on Pa.

Pa thought hard. Pa liked for the domeny to pound on the pulpit a little, to make the dust fly out of the big brown Bible. Free thought that was what Ma meant by expound. Too bad Pa wasn't a preacher. If Pa was to pound the Bible, he'd surely make those sleepers in the back of the church sit up and take notice.

"Nothing?" Ma said.

Pa didn't have a single idea.

"Grampa?"

Grampa harumphed. The last couple of days he sounded like he had a bit of a cold. "Daughter, I have no comment to make on Psalm 100. The way you read it, it's meaning is perfectly clear." Grampa looked Ma in the eye. "But I wonder if you'd read my favorite psalm?"

"Of course. Which one?"

"Psalm 137."

Ma looked up the psalm. She gave the children each a look to make sure they'd keep quiet, then read it aloud. "By the rivers of Babylon, there we sat down. Yea, we wept when we remembered Zion. We hanged our harps upon the willows in the midst thereof. For there they that carried us away required of us a song, and they that wasted us required of us mirth, saying, Sing us one of the songs of Zion. How shall we sing the Lord's song in a strange land? If I forget thee, O Jerusalem, let my right hand forget her cunning. If I do not remember thee let my tongue cleave to the roof of my mouth; if I prefer not Jerusalem above my chief joy. Remember, O Lord, the children of Edom in the day of Jerusalem, who said, Raze it, raze it, even to the foundations thereof. O daughter of Babylon, who art to be destroyed, happy shall he be that rewardeth thee as thou hast served us. Happy shall he be that taketh and dasheth thy little ones against the stones."

The motes in the sunbeams slowed down.

"What a strange way for a psalm to end." Ma closed the Bible slowly. "It's almost a hymn of hate."

Grampa was surprised. "You never read it before?"

"It really belongs in the Devil's Bible."

"Now there's a thought," Grampa said. "If God would allow the Devil to have a Bible of his own. To give his side of it."

Ma's blue eyes opened wide. "Well, true. Since God is supposed to love all creatures, that must also include the Devil."

Grampa's eyes shone at Ma like he thought her an angel.

Ma said, "Yes, I wonder if anybody ever speaks up for the Devil."

Pa said, "Say, you two better remember who's on our side."

Ma said, "Grampa, tell us why you like that psalm?"

Grampa made a motion as if he still had his pipe in his mouth, then when he saw he didn't, stuffed his hand in his pocket. "The older I get the more I remember the days when I was young. In the Old Country. And those memories have absolutely nothing to do with what I see around me here. As if I am utterly cut off and alone. And the more I live the more lonesome I feel."

Ma sat up straight. "Why, Grampa, you're with us. You know that. We all love you."

"Yes, my daughter, I know you do. And I love you for it too." Some yellow tears ran out from under Grampa's dark glasses. "But you didn't have your youth with me. We have no memories together of the Old Country that we might share."

Free couldn't stand to see older people cry.

Pa couldn't stand to look at his dad crying either.

Ma's face became all worked up. "I didn't realize . . . "

Grampa wiped his tears on his shirt sleeve. He tried to smile. "But I have to say one thing for America. I've gradually come to learn it's a place where you just naturally look ahead to the future. Everything's done here with an eye on what it's going to be like tomorrow. While in the Old Country they're always looking back over their shoulder."

The sun moved across the carpet. It shone on the lion's tail and then on the shiny buttons of Albert's new black shoes.

"Well," Ma said, "this has turned out to be quite a rewarding service after all. We all learned something about each other, something we didn't know before. The Lord is right when He says that it's good for the soul to bring private thoughts out into the open. There's nothing like confession."

The sun next reached the golden oak floor. It reflected up at Ma, making the beads on her purple dress shine like the eyes of ladybugs. Each time she breathed the chatelaine ladies' watch pinned on the bosom of her dress shone like a little gold sun.

Sight of Ma's watch reminded Free of something he'd done. If he were to confess about that pretty watch . . . wow, church in the parlor would turn into something really lively. He hadn't meant to take the watch to school.

. . . . It was Saturday and Ma and Pa and Aunt Karen had gone to Grampa's wife's funeral. Free had to stay home and keep an eye on the kids. Ma'd put baby Jonathan to bed for his nap so Free and Everett and Albert could play out in the sandpile.

Shortly after the folks left Jonathan began to cry.

Free waited a while to see if the baby would quit crying of itself, but when it didn't he went in to see what was up.

The baby was wet. If he wasn't changed he'd bawl all afternoon long. Jonathan already was a peaked baby and cried a lot.

Free took off the wet diaper, catching the safety pins in his lips like Ma did, threw the soppy diaper into the pail under the crib, folded a dry diaper into three points, slid it under the baby's bottom, and pinned it on. Baby seemed to like the dry diaper, and the minute he was covered up with a silk comforter went sound to sleep. Relieved, and thinking that Ma would be proud of him, Free turned to go.

Just as he stepped past the bureau, something gold caught his eye. Ma's watch. Ma was very proud of that watch.

Free went over for a closer look. Two little cupids were hugging each other on the cover of the watch. The cupids looked like they were happy and wanted to tell everybody about it.

Pa and Ma's bedroom was always a wonderful place to go sneaking into when they were gone and a fellow could be sure no one would catch him at it. It was full of secrets that Pa and Ma had together, things they would catch each other's eye about but never talk about in front of the kids, things like how to make babies, and how the fathers and mothers decided to name the baby. Pa and Ma's bedroom was full of whispers that they told each other in the dark, while the kids were upstairs sleeping.

Free pushed down the stem of the watch and the case popped open. It was three minutes to two. The second hand moved in smooth even jerks, first to 10, then to 20. The inside of the face was made of such slick gold it shone even in the dusky room. Free watched the second hand make two full turns, then, glowing with love for the watch, pinched it shut.

"If I had a watch like this, the kids in school sure would be jealous of how good my pa and ma was to me."

Free wondered if he couldn't sneak it out of the house for a day and take it to school.

Well, if he did, he'd have to be awful careful where he carried it on him, in what pocket, as long as he was still in the house with Ma or Pa. Once he was on the road, though, he was all right.

"I know what. I'll hide it in a little sack in the culvert at the end of the lane and then on the way to school I can pick it up."

He took the watch. He went to the black hole under the stairs, and searching through Ma's bag of rags found a used salt sack. He carefully wound the watch and then slipped it into the sack. Then, making sure the kids were still playing under the trees, he slid out the back door and ran to hide the watch in the culvert.

The next Monday everything worked to perfection. Nobody was looking when he fished the salt sack out of the culvert.

Free decided not to show the watch until the noon hour recess. Aunt Karen usually left the kids alone then. The kids ate under lunch under the trees.

Free finished his lunch first, and then importantly pulled out his watch to see what time it was. He pushed down the stem and the face popped open. "Twenty after twelve," he announced, "so I guess there's still plenty of time left to play."

All the kids were shocked. "Where'd you get such a nice gold watch?" Catherine Haber demanded.

"Ma and Pa gave it to me."

"I betcha you stole that watch," Alvina said.

"I didn't either."

But he had, and after a while the sandwiches he'd just eaten began to sit heavy on his stomach. He put the watch away into its little salt sack and then into his pocket.

At one o'clock Teacher rang the bell and everybody filed in.

And the minute everybody was in their seat, up went Alvina's hand.

"Yes, Alvina?"

"Free's got a gold ladies' watch in his pocket."

Aunt Karen looked at Free. "Is that true?"

Free wanted to go over and hit Alvina. Now for sure Ma would find out. Worse yet, Pa. Oh boy.

"Free?"

Free wanted to say no. But at last, turning so red it stung him over the cheeks, he hauled out the little salt sack and held it up. He gave Alvina a mad look to let her know he was going to kill her.

Alvina stuck out her tongue, just the tip of it, enough for him to see but not Teacher.

Aunt Karen took the sack and looked in it. Her eyes turned dark. She closed the sack. "Thank you. I'll see you about this during the next recess." She went back to her desk, placed the little sack on it, and began teaching the kids.

At recess, after all the kids had gone outdoors, Aunt Karen called him to her desk. She made him stand beside her. He never liked it when she sometimes put her hand on him, but it looked like he was going to have to let her do it this time.

"Free, what are you doing with your mother's watch?"

Free decided the best thing to do was just to tell the truth. That was a lot better than lying and then getting bawled out for two things. He told her everything.

Aunt Karen liked it that he looked her in the eye as he told her. "Why did you take it?"

"I guess I just wanted to show those Horsbergs that I had nice folks too."

"Do they think you've got bad folks?"

"They think Pa and Ma are awful strict."

Aunt Karen thought about that a while. Finally she said, "Free, when I was a little girl, I once pulled off a foolish stunt like this too. It was about my father. Your Grampa. I wanted people to think he was the best father there was too."

Free held his eyes steady on her.

"Free, look, I'll make a bargain with you. If you'll be a good boy in school for me for the rest of this spring, I won't tell your mother. Or your father. And I'll see to it that this watch gets back safely on your mother's bureau without her knowing it. Somehow. All right?"

After that, for a little while, Free didn't mind if Aunt Karen placed a hand on his shoulder. Or his head. . . .

Back in the parlor, Ma was shaking her head in that way she had of reproving one and yet of being nice about it. "You surely do have it in for the storekeeper, don't you, Grampa?"

Grampa had his chin out. "Yes, I do."

"Have you ever thought of running a store? It seems to me with your sharp mind you'd run a good business."

"Never. It's either king or peasant for me. Nothing in between. Either a Pierce Arrow or my little speeder on the section."

"What do all your IWW tramp friends think of your Pierce Arrow idee?" Pa wanted to know.

"What's wrong with a railroad stiff owning a Pierce Arrow? If he works hard?" Grampa asked. "He'll probably know how to take care of it better than the rich man."

"Pah! Hoboes can't work worth a lick."

"Why should that pinchpenny Rockefeller deserve more than Joe Hill?"

"Just don't invite any of your 'I Won't Work friends' here for a handout. We hardly have enough to eat for ourselves as it is."

"Alfred," Ma said, "the Lord and I will share our crust with the poor."

"What I can't figure out," Pa said, "is how you, a socialist, can be such good friends with Rexroth, a rich man."

"Rexroth has a heart for the poor. And an open mind for new ideas. He doesn't get upset when he hears things ag'in him. And, he can laugh. When I told him once I thought that the farmer was the red corpuscle of our country, while the city fellow was the white corpuscle, Rexroth laughed all day. You see, he can laugh at himself. He realized he had a pasty face from being inside all the time, while I had a red face from being outside on the section."

"And there's another thing I can't figure out," Pa said, "and that's how come a proud man like you can be content to work on the section?"

"Son, the world is like an orange. And my section is railroading."

Ma asked, "Doesn't your conscience ever bother you that you've never really lived up to your talent?"

Grampa said, "When I go to bed I leave my troubles in my clothes."

Free looked up. That wasn't really quite true. He'd often heard Grampa pacing back and forth in Aunt Karen's room after everybody had gone to bed.

Ma shook her head at the way Grampa had of being so strange and wonderful. "Well, anyway, this little family worship has surely served to make me better acquainted with you. It helps me feel for you even if I don't always understand you."

"Thanks be to you, daughter. And believe me when I say that I think you're an angel."

Pa didn't like the way Grampa and Ma smiled at each other.

Then Ma folded her hands and closed her eyes and prayed. "May the Lord cause His countenance to shine upon us, and give us peace, in this our humble home. Amen."

Grampa got up, clapped his cap on, and went out and sat on the cistern lid again. He lit his corncob pipe. He sat and thought to himself a long time. A couple of times he coughed.

Pa finished bindering early the next week. He'd got all the dead ripe oats safely cut. Better yet, Grampa had it all shocked up right behind Pa. Grampa picked the last bundle off the binder and set it butt-down against the last shock before the chains on the binder quit rattling.

Pa said that he'd never had a hired man to match what Grampa had done. Grampa's short strong body just went on stomping and stancing along from morning to night until the bundles had flown into shocks.

At six o'clock they couldn't find Grampa for supper. Ma called upstairs for him and Pa and the kids looked everywhere on the yard.

"I wonder where that strange one could've gone," Pa said.

Free said, "He heard you when Ma wondered if you shouldn't go get some table salt for her and you said you couldn't go to town today because Roy Wickett still hadn't brought out the new Buick. And now that Daise was dead you didn't want to use the workhorses because it was too hot for them to go that far."

"He didn't hear that. He was sitting on the cistern outside when your Ma and I talked about that."

"But he did though. I saw him. He held his head sideways to hear you better."

Pa's eyes opened. "Now a light goes up. Why, that stubborn independent cuss. That's just like him."

Ma said, "You mean, he walked to town?"

"That's just what he done."

"That poor man, walking all the way to town after shocking all day. Because he didn't want to be a bother." Ma shook her head. "Just so the heat doesn't get him."

"Oh, you needn't worry about him. He's tough. I wish I was as tough."

"Just the same he was sixty last February."

"Wal, what do you want me to do, get out the old plugs after all and see if he made it?"

Ma said, "Too bad he won't have a telephone."

"Wal, so far as that goes we could call the Shatwells. They live next door to him. They could send their grandson Dale over to see if he made it."

"All right, I'll call there," Ma said. "Meanwhile, you kids wash up and comb your hair."

By the time the kids sat down, Ma had finished phoning.

"Wal?" Pa asked.

"He's home. They looked out the window and saw him weeding his Dakota cactus."

Pa turned his swivel chair to face the table. "Good. Then that's a worry off our mind."

The next evening the phone rang. Ma answered. After a minute she came back with a hand to her throat.

"Wal?"

"That was Mrs. Shatswell. She says their grandson Dale went over to visit Pa just before supper. He found him sick in bed."

Pa stared.

"I just wonder. . . . " Ma said. "Maybe we better call Karen over at the Harmers' and tell her about it. I know she'll want to go in and take care of him a couple of days."

"Good idee. I'm riding into town with Weatherly in the morning to get the new Buick. I can look in on Pa then."

Later at supper, Pa prayed for Grampa.

The next day around noon a new horn blew coming down the lane. The kids right away knew who it was. They jumped up from their play and ran to the end of the sidewalk where Pa would stop.

"Ma? Hurry. Here's Pa with the new Buick."

In a moment it came flashing around the cobhouse, running smoother than a sewing machine. It rolled to a stop beside them, with Pa, smiling, making the front wheel just miss their bare toes. The top was down and folded up like a woman's bun in back.

Free, Everett, and Albert stared at it.

The screen door slammed behind them. Ma came slowly down the walk.

Pa gave Ma his strong chin smile. "How do you like her?"

Ma rubbed her arms at the elbows.

"Wal, I declare, is that all you got to say?"

Ma looked the new car over carefully from front to back. "I was hoping it was going to be a sedan. Touring models can be so cold and drafty in the winter."

"That's coming. I ordered a sedan top. Meantime, if it rains we can just put up the top and quick snap on the curtains."

Ma leaned in and looked at the dashboard. "Oh, dear, this one can go up to eighty."

"Yeh, wal, that's what it says there. But they always put a higher figure there than it can really go."

"That's good." Ma touched the blue-brown finish. "My, it's shiny. They must've waxed it in the factory."

"Roy waxed it for me. Oh, I tell you, that Roy, he's a great one for cars."

"And how was Pa?"

Pa's face fell. "I just didn't get time to run over there. But I heard Karen made it and is there. So I thought we could all go for a spin this afternoon and see him."

Ma thought this over. "Maybe that's a good idea. Besides salt I need some fruit-jar rubbers for canning."

The kids began to jump for joy. "We're going for a ride in the new Buick! Can we have an ice-cream cone too, Ma?"

"Well, I don't know now," Ma said. "Buying this new car could mean we may have to give up some things."

"But we didn't go anywhere on the Fourth, Ma. We missed out on our twenty-five cents a year to spend then."

Pa laughed. "Wow, those kids don't forget a thing, do they?"

They were having buttermilk-and-barley soup when the phone rang. This time Pa went to answer it. When he sat down again he looked old.

Ma waited for his to say what it was.

"Wal, now we got to go. He's worse. He's out of his head."

Ma turned white.

"Yeh. He's got pneumonia."

Free loved buttermilk-and-barley soup, especially the taste of the puddle of syrup poured in the middle of it. He liked to catch up a little corner of the syrup with each spoonful. But hearing about Grampa being sick, he didn't care if he never saw syrup-colored soup again. Pa's grampa was going to die like Ma's grampa did.

The new Buick rode a lot smoother than the old Reo. The smell of the shiny black leather seats made Free think of holidays. But riding to town that day wasn't much fun.

They drove straight to Grampa's cement house. They found Aunt Karen crying by the yellow roses.

Karen, crying, led Pa and Ma into the back bedroom. The kids had to stay in the kitchen.

Free had to know. He told Everett and Albert to watch the baby and see to it that he didn't roll off the sofa. Free stepped outside.

But Everett and Albert were scared of Grampa's house. After a minute they followed Free outdoors.

Free tiptoed around the north side of the house. Everett and Albert followed the leader. When Free reached the open window of Grampa's bedroom, he could hear him. Grampa's breathing sounded awful, like when Ma sometimes let the oatmeal boil and bubbles of steam burped up through the thick stuff. Free crouched below the window, making sure nobody inside could see him.

Everybody was breathing hard in the bedroom, Pa, Ma, Aunt Karen. But Grampa was the loudest. He was getting hoarser by the minute.

"Poor man," Ma whispered.

Grampa began to mutter. "Close in here." Grampa coughed so that he almost choked in it. "Hot."

"Does this fan help any, Dad?" Aunt Karen asked.

Then Grampa spoke loud and clear. "When you bury me, make sure I'm dead, you hear? Promise now."

Aunt Karen gasped. "Why! he's thinking about Bettie. How her body remained limp in the coffin. With her face flushed. Doctor said she died of apoplexy, but Dad always claimed she'd only fallen into a deep fit. That they buried her still warm."

"Sis," Pa whispered, "you mustn't pay too much attention to what a man says when he's out of his head."

"He's said this before. That under no circumstances were we to have his body embalmed. Because he still might be alive."

"You can throw the lines away," Grampa said, short.

"What, Dad?"

"Get ready for the big jump."

"Dad?"

"All my life I tried to live as straight as a wagon tongue."

Silence.

"But when you start out with a warp in you to begin with, you've got to work at it every day to keep it straight."

Aunt Karen began to wave the fan so hard Free could hear it go whuff whuff. "We promise, Dad."

Grampa's throat worked like he was priming a pump in his chest. At last he blasted it open.

The sound of heavy spit ripping apart made Free sick to his stomach. He almost threw up in the grass. A little bit did break up into his throat. He could taste buttermilk with soured syrup on his tongue. He had enough. With a sharp gesture at his two brothers, he led the way back into the kitchen.

Everett whispered, "Is Grampa going to be dead like Daise?"

Free put a finger to his lips to shush him.

"And be put in a hole in the ground in the pasture?"

Free quick went over to the window and looked outside.

Pretty soon Aunt Karen and Ma came back in the kitchen. Pa's said he'd sit by his father and watch over him for a while.

"This will delay your wedding, won't it?" Ma was saying.

"Yes," Aunt Karen said. "But my father comes first."

"I feel awful that we let him walk to town."

"But you couldn't help it. He's always walked out and back to those cyclone-cellar jobs in the country, you know."

"Just the same Alfred should never have let him shock all that grain."

Aunt Karen stood looking down at where the baby slept on the sofa. Then she laughed kind of silly. "Ada, at least you won't have to worry about us not having children. I've decided."

"Why, Karen, whatever makes you say that," Ma cried, "just now?"

"I don't know much about such things yet, but we'll work it out some way. Kon is mine for good now."

Ma bit on her lips for some reason.

"Can you imagine? And here last winter I was worried Kon wasn't going to give me back my promise."

It was Aunt Karen who was out of her head, not Grampa.

Someone knocked on the door. It was Dr. Fairlamb come to check up on

Grampa again. Dr. Fairlamb was a square-set man with a growly look. His dark hair was cut close like hog hair. "Sorry to be a little late." He gave Ma a look. "One of your Engleking relatives had another baby and the delivery was difficult."

"Oh?" Ma said, with a wondering look. "Who was that?"

"Fat John."

"That's right. I'd heard that Etta was expecting again."

Dr. Fairlamb's short fingers tiddlytapped on his black case. "Well, I better go in and have another look."

Aunt Karen made tea.

It was ready when Dr. Fairlamb returned from Grampa's bedroom.

"Won't you have a cup, Doctor?"

"No, thanks."

"How is my father?"

Dr. Fairlamb's fingers turned quiet. His black eyes knew something. "I told Alfred to pile on the comforters to make him break out in a sweat."

Ada said, "That's just what our old doctor advised when little Free here had the pneumonia. To bring on the crisis."

"I don't expect the congestion to break until your father's temperature hits 106°. That's why I recommended more comforters."

Aunt Karen saw the doctor out to his car.

After the grown-ups had their tea, and the kids each had a piece of Aunt Karen's devil's food cake, Ma walked downtown to get the salt and fruit-jar rubbers. The kids went along for the sights. The whole town looked sad. There was hardly anybody along main street. Even the pool hall was empty. All the town loafers were out shocking grain somewhere.

On the way back Free picked up something in the air. When they were even with the Shatswell house, there came Aunt Karen sailing out of Grampa's front door.

Ma started to hurry then.

Aunt Karen came running up, out of breath. "It's come!" she cried. She looked at them wild, then went on legging it past them and into the Shatswell house.

"Dear me," Ma cried, "she's calling the doctor again."

They hurried into Grampa's house. Ma ordered the kids to stay in the kitchen, then sailed into the bedroom where Pa was with Grampa. "Alfred?" The door closed behind her.

Free listened and listened, but couldn't hear a thing.

Free, Everett, and Albert sat around the kitchen table. There was nothing to do. The tablecloth was a plain slick yellow. It didn't have any pictures on it to trace your finger on.

"It just can't be Grampa is that sick," Free thought. "Just can't."

Pretty soon Everett leaned over and put a hand to his sitter.

"You gotta do number two?"

Everett nodded.

"You don't want to fill your pants on a day like this, do you?"

Everett rolled his eyes sideways. Then he got up and slowly went outdoors to the privy. He walked as if he was riding a stick horse.

Free heard Aunt Karen come crying in through the door on the other side of the house. She hurried into Grampa's bedroom. The grown-ups were all talking at once, and then the bedroom door closed again.

The tea kettle sang on the stove.

The bedroom door opened and everybody came out crying. Pa was almost the worst. It was hard to see Pa cry. Pa had an arm around Karen and she was weeping against him. Ma cried without making a sound and kept rubbing her elbows.

They cried and talked broken for about a half hour. They didn't do anything for Grampa back there.

Finally Aunt Karen said, "I know you want to go home and do your chores, Alfred. So you better go."

Ma said, "Don't you want one of us to stay with you tonight?"

"Young Dale Shatswell said he'd come if I asked him."

Pa said, "I'll come back after chores."

"If you would, Alfred," Aunt Karen said.

"Since Pa didn't want us to have him embalmed, somebody's going to have to keep cold towels on his face," Pa said. "To prevent discoloration."

"Yes. Dale and I can start doing that. Until you come."

Ma said, "And I'll get on the telephone the minute we get home and let the other children know. Janet and Gerda. And Richard."

Aunt Karen sighed. "Well, by now Dad is having a good talk with Abbott up in heaven."

"Yes, let us pray so," Ma said.

"Oh, and don't forget to call Kon," Aunt Karen said. "I'll need him more than ever now."

"I will," Ma said. "I'll be happy to."

That was because Ma liked Kon a lot.

Dr. Fairlamb came just as they were all getting into the new Buick. He couldn't come any sooner. He went inside and certified that Grampa was dead.

Free ❦ 23

NOW THAT THEY'D moved across the road and lived in the Rock No. 4 school district, it was decided Free and Everett had better go to the No.4 school that fall. Besides, Ma had at last come to the thought that those Horsbergs had dirty minds.

Free didn't know anybody at the new school and wasn't sure he was going to like it. But the teacher was kind. Her name was Miss Olden and she was jolly all the time.

Two days after school started, some of the kids from Rock No.3 showed up, Peter and Paul Horsberg, and Gladys and Hesta Windmiller. Their teacher was sick and until she recovered they had to go elsewhere. Alvina was sick too. They came in a carriage with Peter driving an old bay plug named Gip.

Free didn't care to be close friends with Peter and Paul. Yet he asked Peter if he could ride along with them, but Peter said no. When he and Everett tagged along behind the carriage a ways, Peter got mad and shook his fists at them. After that Free and Everett cut across the cornfield home.

About that time Uncle Richard came to help Pa pick corn. Uncle Richard had come back from the war safe. While he was in France he had to cook for the Army and became famous for his pancakes. He could make pancakes an inch thick, without even using milk, just water. It was in the way he mixed up the batch.

Soon something wasn't going right for Peter and Paul with their horse and carriage. One day in October Peter said Free and Everett could ride along after school if they wanted to.

They all piled in. It was a sunny day. Free and Everett sat in front with Peter, and Gladys and Hesta sat in back with Paul. Free thought it a lark to be riding home from school in a carriage instead of always walking. They rolled on past Rath's place. A redheaded woodpecker kept flying up ahead of them from telephone pole to telephone pole. Each time they came up even with it, almost, it'd fly off and swoop up to the top of the next pole.

Uncle Richard was picking corn in the field along the road. Free could see his bangboard moving across the yellow cornfield like a sail on a golden lake.

When they came to a little draw, Peter pulled up. "Whoa, there, Gip." Peter looked around to all sides. The low spot in the road was exactly where no one could see them from any yard around.

Peter handed Free the lines. "Now you make sure Gip doesn't run home. Just hold him until we get back."

Free handled the lines. "Where you going?"

"In the cornfield. To do it to our girls a while. Like always."

Free felt sick. He wanted to get out and cut across the field home. "Why don't you just tie the horse to a post if that's all you want of me?"

"Gip's learned how to break the hitching strap. He pulls on it until it snaps and then he starts to eat grass down the road. The last time he almost ate his way to the corner before we caught up with him."

Free saw that he was only a hired hand for the Horsbergs.

Peter and Gladys, and Paul and Hesta, crawled under the fence and disappeared into the cornfield. They were in there a long time.

Free and Everett sat waiting, twiddling their thumbs.

At last the four came back. The girls were smiling down at their belts and they had dust and pigeon grass seeds on their backs. The boys looked important and had tracks on their flies.

It made Free mad. He gave the lines back to Peter.

When they got to the corner, Peter stopped Gip to let Free and Everett off. "See you tomorrow after school then."

Free waited until he was past the mailboxes. Then he turned and said, "Nosiree, I ain't your hired man."

That night at supper, Uncle Richard looked up from eating johnnycake. "Say,

Free, what were you kids doing in the draw there after school?" Uncle Richard held his face to one side a little.

Free let his hair slide down over his eyes.

"What were those Horsberg kids doing?"

Ma picked it up. "Are those Horsbergs at it again, Free?"

Free wouldn't tattle. He threw Everett a look to keep still too.

Ma sighed. "I'll be glad when those Horsbergs can go back to their own school."

One Monday morning the Horsbergs and the Windmillers didn't show up. Their teacher had come back over the weekend.

"Good riddance," Ma said.

Edward Underhill went to No. 4 too. He was dumb like Everett except that he was older.

One day after school Edward smiled at Free as they all put on their overshoes and coats and stocking caps. "Free, why don't you walk kitty-corner home with me through the Walker pasture? That creek goes through your pasture too."

Free snapped his last buckle shut. "Ma wants us to take the long way home around by the road so as not to tear our coats going through fences."

"I know a safe way. Otherwise my ma wouldn't let me either."

"How you gonna get through the fence?"

Edward smiled with his eyes closed. "Follow me."

Free decided to take the shortcut. "C'mon, Everett, let's go with Edward. Hurry, you're always late."

Edward knew of a good way to go home all right. At the edge of the school grounds he showed them where the creek had washed out the bank under the fence. It was where they could easy stoop through. From there they followed the creek down the Walker pasture.

Edward showed them the things to see. Some water bugs were rowing themselves across the pond near the bridge. Two of the biggest woodpeckers Free had ever seen had their home in a long row of tremendous cottonwoods. The woodpeckers were so big they looked like Pa's arm with a hammer in it pounding a nail in. Under the two logs crossing the creek lived a bossy mink. In an old well the wooden walls were rotting and caving in.

When they hit the corner of the line fence between their farms, Edward smiled. All the Underhills smiled with loose lips. "See that corner post there? I fixed some cleats on it. On both sides. So you can climb up one side and then down the other."

Free thought that was pretty slick.

Edward climbed over first and came down on the Underhill side. Free went next and landed on the Alfredson side. It was safe all right.

"C'mon, Everett."

Everett climbed over and even he did it easy. No torn clothes.

"Well," Edward said, "I better hustle on home and do my chores. See you here tomorrow morning."

"See you."

Ma was plumpfing up the bread dough on the kitchen table. She was having fun doing it. She picked up the dough with both hands, tossing it all the way to the ceiling, and then let it plop into the bread pan. When the dough hit it puffed up a little smoke.

Everett laughed. "Do it again, Ma."

Ma smiled. She boxed the dough a couple of times like she was a Jack Johnson; then, picking it up again and holding it up against the ceiling, let it whumpf down into the bread pan.

"Do it again, Ma."

Free noticed Ma had thirteen bread tins set out on the back of the stove, all greased and ready to go. "Who's the extra bread going to be for, Ma?"

"Well," Ma said, "it's not going to be for the ninety-and-nine."

Pa looked up from where he was sitting with his feet in the cob box. "Your mom's taking up with the tramps again."

Free looked at Ma wonderingly.

"Yeh," Pa went on, "ever since your grampa died, she's been giving handouts to the railroad bums that drop by. And I now know for a fact that this place is marked to show that the lady of the house here is an easy mark."

"Oh, Alfred, now you're stretching it a little."

"No, it's a God's fact." Pa gave his pipe a deep suck. "Them IWW's have got the corner post up by the mailboxes marked with a sign."

"Oh, come now, Alfred. Christ always had time for the hungry."

"For Bolsheviks? I don't hardly think he did."

"Somebody's got to speak up for them too."

"Look, good wife. Suppose sometime a Bolshevik comes down our K T Highway, and sees that arrow on the corner there, and then comes and knocks on the door here, and proceeds to do some dirty work, while I'm in the field on the other side of the farm, hah? Then what?"

"I'll just appeal to his better nature."

Pa snorted. "I suppose you'll even turn the other cheek?"

Everett didn't care to hear about the IWW Bolsheviks. "Can I have the first new heel, Ma? With lots of melting butter on it?"

"Sure, son. Eat the end and you get curly hair."

Free knew it really was his turn to have the first end of bread, but decided not to argue about it. He was more interested in something else. He put on his yard clothes.

Pa caught him just as he was going out the door. "Just a minute there, you. There ain't many of those fresh shelled cobs left, so I guess you better go back to gathering up those cobs in the hog yard. One basket of good cobs and one basket of hog cobs."

Free hated to get hog-yard cobs. In the evening dusk it was sometimes hard to tell a cob apart from a frozen hog turd. The cobs had to be practically picked up one by one.

First though he went up the road to the neighbor mailboxes to see if there really was a sign for tramps on the corner post.

It was almost too dark to find at first. But when he took off his mitten and ran a finger up and down the cedar post, he found it. It was a stick figure: ♀. It had been cut into the post with a jackknife. To the right of the circle was the number 1 and the letter R. He guessed that the 1 and the R meant first place on the right. Pa as usual was correct.

He went back to the yard. He got the eggs. He got the hard coal for the base burner. He got the fresh shelled cobs.

Last he got the cobs from the feedlot in the hog yard. Most of the cobs were trampled into the ground and frozen into it. It took a while to collect a handful and when he finally threw it in the tin basket it hardly covered the bottom.

"Pa ought to get hog cobs once," Free muttered. "Then he'd know how tough it is."

Bent over, he threw in several more handfuls. Still didn't cover the bottom.

"This is going to take a terrible long time." His lips curled in boy rage. "There won't be any time left to play before milking."

With his mittens pulled on tight, he could hold just about ten cobs at a time.

Ten at a time. Say, maybe if he were to make a game of it it wouldn't take so long. Ten times ten made a hundred. A hundred could just about fill the basket. It shouldn't take too long to hustle up a hundred cobs.

He counted the handfuls. First ten. Second ten. He made up his mind not to look into the basket until he had the whole hundred cobs in. Fifth ten. Seventh ten. Ninth ten. "Ugh, a hog turd!" Ninth ten again. Tenth ten.

He looked in the basket. When he saw how little a pile the hundred really made, he sagged on his heels. "That dummed basket must hold a thousand cobs then."

"What's a matter, boy?"

Free looked up. Pa.

Pa was smiling. "Having troubles, are you?" Pa bent over and began to help him. Pa was wearing his black-and-blue mackinaw and every time he bent over it slid up around his neck a little. "There sure ain't many loose dry ones, is there?"

"There sure ain't." Free wanted to hug his father for coming to help him.

"Tell you what. Just a minute." Pa went over to the crib and got the potato fork. "Now let's have a try at it." Pa set the fork into the frozen layer of cobs and manure and shoved. Up came the cobs, most of them loose. Pa ripped out four paths through the mixture. Then he set the fork to one side and helped Free gather up the drier cobs. Together it took them but a minute to fill the basket.

Sometimes Pa could sure be a good father.

Larry Grey became Free's friend next. Larry was in the same class with Free and was just as smart. It was too bad Larry lived in a different direction or they could have walked home from school together. His folks were Lutheran.

As spring set in, Free and Larry played on the same team in baseball. They told each other about their fathers and mothers. Both Free and Larry hated to get hog cobs. Both hated to reach under a pecky brood hen for her eggs. Both thought long prayers in church were way too long. Of all the school books both liked the reader the best.

By April Fool's Day, Free decided he loved Larry better than anybody in the whole world. They never had to work on each other, or act hurt, to get their way.

Sometimes he couldn't help but put his arm around Larry's shoulder. Sometimes Larry couldn't help putting his arm around Free's middle. Free was taller and they liked it just the way it was.

Edward tried to get Free back as friends, but Free wouldn't go for it. That made Edward mad and he began to bully Larry around. He snatched Larry's stocking cap off and threw it in the boys' privy, then laughed when Larry had to fish it out with a stick. He said Larry's stocking cap had the right color so a person couldn't tell where it had been. When Miss Olden and all the kids were out on the schoolyard during noon hour recess, Edward pretended he had to go to the toilet and then snuck around the other side of school and went inside and tipped Larry's ink bottle over on Larry's desk. He did that so Larry would get a "poor" in deportment.

Free wanted Larry to get a club and beat Edward up. Larry's sister Elsie wanted Larry to fix Edward too.

Larry only smiled and said he couldn't be bothered with a guy whose real name was Mister Eddie Underwear.

Everybody laughed hearing how Larry took care of Edward Underhill with just a couple of words.

Edward went off by himself and sulked behind the willows.

By last recess time Edward was so mad he tripped Larry as he ran around second base for a triple. Larry fell with an awful whumpf on his belly right on third base. Third base was a gray stone sticking up out of the grass. Larry turned white and passed out.

Free saw black. Free was so mad he didn't even stop to think that Larry might be dead. "You bastard!" Free ran over to the willows and picked up a club with a knob on the end of it. He came roaring back.

Edward took one look, then ran straight for home. He jumped over the fence and galloped down the pasture like a coward.

Free bounced himself under the fence and chased Edward all the way past the cottonwoods where the big woodpeckers lived.

Miss Olden called after them. "Here, you boys! Free? Edward? You come back here right this instant. Both of you."

Edward kept running.

"Right this instant!"

Free finally stopped. But he was still mad. When he crawled under the fence onto the schoolyard again, he didn't want to give up the club at first.

"Free!" Then Miss Olden grabbed for the club and gave it a jerk. "Let go of it. Right now."

Elsie was trying to help Larry get his breath back. The other kids stood watching in a bunch.

"Let go of it!" Miss Olden gave the club another hard jerk.

"Edward didn't have to hurt Larry."

"Never mind about that now," Miss Olden said. "Just you give me that. We can't be having you run around here like a wild cave man. Give me that." Miss Olden gave the club still another hard jerk.

Free finally gave it up.

"I can't be having my pupils carrying clubs to their seats." Then Miss Olden put her arm around Free to let him know she was on his side. "My goodness, Free, you mustn't let yourself get so worked up. It isn't good for you. Look at you. Why, you're flushed red all the way down to your neck." Miss Olden threw the club toward the woodshed.

"Somebody ought to give him a good licking though. He's a d-dirty kid who plays mean."

"Why, Free, you're so worked up you're stammering."

"But he is. You should hear what he says sometimes in the b-b . . . "

"Sing it if you can't say it, Free. Best way to get over stammering is to sing what you've got in mind."

"B-but I got it from Grampa and he n-n . . . "

"Sing it out, Free."

Free finally sang it. "Never got over it when he got excited."

"That's better. Now, what does Edward say in the b-b?"

"Boys' toilet. That the best time to polish brown shoes is when you do number two. Then nobody can tell the difference on your fingers."

Then Miss Olden got mad. She got the bell and rang it. Everybody had to get to their seats in a hurry.

Elsie and Free helped Larry to his feet. Larry could get his breath again by coughing a little first.

For that day Miss Olden marked Edward Underhill a half day absent and Free Alfredson "poor" in deportment.

Ada ❦ 24

THE PHONE RANG one evening in the middle of April. Ada answered it.

It was her cousin Garrett Engleking. Ada liked Garrett. He had warm blue eyes and a handsome blond pompadour. "I thought maybe I better call and tell you, Ada, that Dad is worse."

"I didn't know he was sick."

"He hasn't really felt right for about a month. Doc thinks he's had a light stroke. And now he's got the hiccups."

Ada fixed her eyes on the pair of nickel bells on the telephone box. Hiccups? That could be serious.

"The real reason I called, Ada, is that Dad asked to see you."

"He did? And here I thought he didn't like it that I'd sometimes been a little critical of him."

"Dad admired your spunk, Ada."

"I'll try and come."

It rained the next day. Alfred said it was too muddy to take the car. He suggested she take the horse and buggy. "The gray, Nell, is pretty fast."

"That I'll do. It's Saturday and I should get some groceries too."

Ada took Free along. It was time the boy learned about such things. It rained all the way to town. By the time they drove down Big John's lane, Nell of herself had slowed to a walk. Mud was splattered all over the front of the dashboard. The lane had been graded, high in the center, and Nell had trouble keeping her footing, sliding from one side of the center ridge to the other. The buggy left a wriggling trail in the mud.

Garrett saw them coming and met them in front of the house. He had a subdued smile for them both. Rain ran off his yellow slicker and red boots. He tied Nell's hitching strap to a post.

Ada stepped down, then helped Free down. "Good weather for ducks."

"Even better for pigs." Garrett nodded toward some sows wallowing in mudholes near the milk shed.

Aunt Josephine opened the kitchen door for Ada and Free. Aunt Josephine was red from crying. "Och, Ada, how good of you to come."

"How is Uncle?"

"Come. See for yourself."

The girl cousins were crying in the kitchen. They barely managed to return Ada's greeting.

Ada took Free by the shoulder and steered him ahead of her as Aunt Josephine led the way into the bedroom.

The bedroom was gloomy. Dark portraits of Grampa Great John and Gramma Adelheid hung on the far wall. The portraits were like those her father Alfred once had. A chest of drawers and a bureau, made of black mahogany, stood dark along the near wall. A thick Persian rug, purple with a gold outline of a lion on it, lay beside the bed.

The huge four-poster bed with its brass pillars stood in the southwest corner of the room. A weak light from the two windows fell across the foot of it. What helped the eye make out the man lying against a pile of pillows was the hiccups. The hiccups rocked him and the bed so that he looked like he was in the grip of a relentless thrashing machine. The slags of loose flesh of the once great bulk of a man rippled each time like water under a wind.

The smell in the room was the one smell Ada couldn't stand. Yeasty boar. She'd once entered the hog house looking for eggs just as a boar had finished with a sow. The smell of that boar she'd never been able to get out of her head. She sometimes smelled it on Alfred. It was the kind of smell one sometimes got when butchering a rooster, when one accidentally cut through seed glands, except that it was much stronger. A woman who hated being pregnant all the time loathed it with all her soul.

"Uncle John." Ada stared at the shrunken shell of the man. He looked more like the bled carcass of an old boar than a human being. He even resembled her own shrunken father when he lay dying.

"Sit"—hckk—"down."

Aunt Josephine pushed up a chair for Ada. Free stood nearby.

Uncle Big John stared in thought at Free. His red beard, faded to pepper, lay spread across his sunken chest like a hairnet. "Your son resembles"—hckk—"the Engleking side all right."

"Yes, that he does." Ada ran a hand over Free's blond hair. With her fingertips she tried to wet down Free's two cowlicks. "Free, this man is your great-uncle. It isn't often you get to see one of those, is it?"

Free gave Uncle Big John an intent look. "Hello."

Uncle Big John's hiccups sometimes shook the bed so hard they made the brass vases wobble on the corner posts.

"Ada, I wanted to see you. . . . " Uncle Big John paused, then flicked a look at Free. "I wonder . . . ?"

"Yes." Ada put a hand on her boy's shoulder. "Free, why don't you go out in the kitchen for a while and see what the girls are up to?"

Free gave his great-uncle another look and left.

Aunt Josephine moved to the foot of the bed and stood looking down at her husband, crying silently.

The dark bags under Uncle Big John's eyes hung sagged, pulling his lower lids open and red. "Ada, my brother Alfred is dead, so I can't tell him now how sorry I am for all those mean things I did to him in the past."

"Uncle, I'm sure that where my father now is he has long ago forgiven you. If forgiveness was needed."

"Yes, I suppose he has. But the trouble is, Ada, it's this me here"—he gave himself a whack on the chest, the thump shaking him almost as much as a hiccup—"that still feels guilty. So guilty. At the time I thought him a fool not to be enjoying some of the lusts of the flesh a little. But now that I'm near the end . . . I don't know . . . maybe he was right after all. Because"—hckk—"what has it availed me? If this is the way it's going to end . . . "

"Oh, Uncle, you may live for a long time yet."

Hckk. "No, the end is near." Tears dripped out of his red-bleared eyes. "Oh, Ada, I'm so afraid that I'm not going to be saved."

Aunt Josephine began to keen. She sounded like a dog whining outside a door desperately wanting to get in.

"Has Domeny been here?"

"Every day. He appreciates my having been an elder in his church."

"Has he prayed with you to ask for His grace and forgiveness?"

"Yes. But nights, after he's gone, I'm back to where I was before. Afraid for my soul. That I may have been already utterly condemned to hell."

"Isn't the doctor giving you anything for those hiccups?"

"We've tried everything." Hckk. "Holding my breath. Having someone come in and scare me when I least expect it. Drinking a gallon of ice-cold water real slow. Lying down with my feet higher than my head. Breathing in and out of a paper bag until I faint. Doctor even tried to get me to vomit just as I was about to hiccup."

"Why that?"

"He said a hiccup was really" —hckk— "only a half-hearted attempt to vomit, and that by making a real try at vomiting it might finally satisfy that impulse."

Ada felt curiously strong. She wanted to go over and put her arms around her uncle and comfort him with kisses in his last moments. How the mighty had fallen. This once powerful king of the Englekings lay on his deathbed a whispery husk.

"I never became that simple honest man out in the country." The threshing rack of his hiccups rocked him as if it meant to shake every ounce of flesh out of the sack of his skin before it was through with him. "And now the Lord has struck me down with this awful affliction."

Aunt Josephine continued to stand as stiff as a broomstick, crying her heart out. Tears dropped, spotting her gray dress. She gripped the brass end of the bed so hard the palms of her hands made squinching noises. "Such a great man. That he should have to leave us now in the prime of his life." Her voice broke. "Tragic. When I wanted so to bear him yet another child."

"Why, Tante," Ada exclaimed, "you've already had a dozen by him."

"Not so. I've only had ten by John."

"Well, yes, I guess I was thinking of those four Uncle John had with his first wife, that you raised as your own."

"I wanted another child from his loins. The seed of a noble man is precious when a new people are filling up a new land."

A thought occurred to Ada. She turned to Uncle Big John. "You've made your peace with stepson Wilmer Youngman? Tante's child with her first husband?"

"He and I prayed together yesterday."

"Then what you want of me is for me to stand in my father's shoes and forgive you?"

"Yes." Hckk. "If you would, daughter."

Ada's heart flowed out to her uncle. She slipped off her chair and knelt beside his bed. She placed her folded hands where he could reach them. She waited until she felt his hand, gnarled, almost cold, cover hers. Then she began: "Our heavenly Father, we approach Thee on bended knee, beside the sick bed of a loved one whose heart is tormented with guilt, with old remembered slights given others, and we ask Thee now to incline Thy ear and hear our prayer. Oh Father, forgive this Thy humble servant. Oh Lord, give him grace more than strength, so that he may look forward with joy to the new and wonderful life ahead that awaits him in heaven. Bravery is not enough at death. Only the consolation that one is saved will help. At the same time, oh Father, if his life is to be spared for yet a little time, yes, then give his body strength to overcome this strange affliction. Give back to this poor humble sinner at least a small portion of his once mighty strength. Comfort him with the thought that in any case he shall some day, sooner or later, not only meet his Maker, but also his beloved brother, and his beloved father and mother, on that other shore. Forgive us all our sins, we ask it all in Jesus' name. Amen."

Then Ada got to her feet and leaned down and gave her uncle a kiss. As her lips touched his lips she felt them quickly purse up and kiss her back. It was the way Free kissed her when he specially wanted her love and affection.

Free ❦ 25

FREE COULDN'T STAND to see Ma's cousins crying in the kitchen. He liked the littlest one, Fredrika, with her freckles and long gold pigtail, but she was crying the hardest, like she was the one who really knew her daddy wasn't going to get better.

Free wandered out onto the small porch. The porch had but one window and it overlooked the milkshed and the hog yard beyond.

Free couldn't get Uncle Big John's eyes out of his mind. With those blue sacks under them, and that watery red flesh showing, they reminded him of hog eyes.

Free's eye caught something. Those sows down there in the rain, by that mudhole . . . why . . . there was one dead. And . . . gotske! she was being eaten up by the others. Her head was almost buried in the mud. Only one pointed ear showed. A dozen or so black sows were tearing off slabs of her fat and meat, and then with the motion of a bull snake were swallowing them. The fat sows ringing their victim were in a rush to see who could eat the most. Like real hogs.

Free had to work to get his breath. The thought shot through him that if he hadn't jumped into the hog feedlot back home that time to save Albert this is what would have happened to Albert.

Free ran out into the rain. He saw Garrett greasing the wheel of a wagon near the corncrib. "Look, Garrett," Free cried, "them hogs're eating each other."

Garrett glanced over at where Free pointed. Then, after a second, he dropped his wagon wrench and in his red boots stomped down to the fence by the milkshed. He stared at what was left of the dead hog. "It's the cripple sow. She was down yesterday and must've drowned in the rain during the night."

"Can't you do something?"

"Too late now."

Free knew that if Pa had been around he'd have been in there with a club.

"I'd save what meat was left," Garrett said, "except that she was too diseased to butcher in the first place."

"But won't the other ones get sick eating her?"

"No. They eat slop, you know. And all other kinds of spoiled crap out of the kitchen."

The sound of the great sows slugging down big hunks of raw meat was too much for Free. His stomach erupted, trying to vomit.

Garrett looked around at him. "Say, boy, don't do that too often or you'll get the hiccups like Pa."

Free had enough of what was going on out on Uncle Big John's terrible yard. He went back into the kitchen. He asked one of Ma's crying cousins for a glass of water. Sweet-looking Sadie gave him one.

Free ❦ 26

THAT SUMMER THEY had a bumper crop of apples. While the apples were still green,

Ma had an awful time keeping the kids out of the orchard. Free got into them once and had the trots so bad Ma wondered if they shouldn't call the doctor.

When the Duchess apples were ripe, Ma let them each have a white mushy apple at ten, another one after the meal at noon, another again at three, and then a last one when they went to bed. Later when the littler crabs turned pink, they were allowed to have two apples each time.

Twice they sneaked into the orchard anyway, once by way of the tall weeds in the hog yard and once by way of the tall corn across the lane, and got caught both times. Pa gave Free a licking first, then Everett. When Pa turned around to give Albert his licking, Albert had disappeared. Albert was always quick to see trouble coming and would slide away and hide. Pa would sometimes laugh about how clever it was of Albert.

One day Aunt Karen came over with her husband, Konstant Harmer. The kids liked Aunt Karen all right, but they really liked Uncle Kon. Uncle Kon always had a little something for them, a campaign button, a new kind of pencil, or a new ruler for school. Also, when they went to visit him at the Harmer house, Uncle Kon would always turn on Old Man Harmer's Atwater Kent radio so they could hear music all the way from Pittsburgh. Without wires. Straight across the country through the air.

The minute Aunt Karen and Uncle Kon, and Pa and Ma, disappeared into the house to sit and talk a while, the three kids looked at each other, smiled a little, and knew what to do. With company present, Pa wouldn't be so hard on them. They ran out to the tree where the harvest apples were ripe. Free climbed to the top where the reddest apples were hanging, and picking them, threw them down to his two brothers. Then they sat on the grass and ate the honey-centered apples, until their stomachs began to squeak like dry wagon wheels.

Pa happened to look out through the screen door and spotted them. "Pots before kettles," he cried out, and jumped up and ran outside.

Uncle Kon hurried after Pa. "You're not going to punish them?"

"I'm sure thinking of it."

Ma came outside then too. She shook her head at Free. "When I told you kids to go out under the trees and play, I didn't mean these trees."

Aunt Karen watched from the doorway. She was laughing. "They're so cute. Their faces all smudged over with apple juice and looking guilty. Kon, you ought to take their picture."

"Hey, wait a minute here," Pa said, "you ain't rewarding them for stealing apples now, are you?"

"Oh, Alfred," Uncle Kon said, "we've all stolen apples in our day, haven't we?"

Pa gave up. "Wal . . . have it your way. But I don't want to hear any complaints out in that privy tonight."

For the snapshot Uncle Kon made them get into the hammock. They sat in a row. Everett held his nose. Albert looked like he was plumb full. Free smiled to himself under his beat-up straw hat. Behind them in the grass, a hen called to her brood of chickens to help her eat all the windfalls.

Later that week, Pa picked all the harvest apples and wrapped them in paper torn from the Sears Roebuck catalog. He stored them in a barrel in the cellar.

"Now. Them apples are for this coming winter," Pa announced. "When we'll eat them one a day. You kids hear me?"

"Ya, Pa."

"That way we can spread 'em over the year a little."

One evening just before supper, Ma asked Free to get a can of pickles out of the cellar for her. She felt they should have something green to go with the meat. To get the pickles Free had to use the outside cellar door.

Once he was in the cellar, he couldn't resist it. He dug out a couple of wrapped apples, rearranged and fluffed up the remaining apples so as to make the barrel look as full as before, then going halfway up the steps threw the apples out into the deep grass toward the hammock. Later after supper when nobody was around he'd go outdoors and eat them.

But Pa had been sitting smoking his pipe in the living room as he waited for supper, and he saw the apples fly past the bay window. With their paper wrappings fluttering, they looked like low-flying fall birds.

Pa didn't say anything right away. He just had a peculiar look all through supper. When the dessert, a pear preserve, was being dished out, Pa held up his hand. "Hold on here. No pears for that fellow. His dessert is laying out in the grass."

"What?" Ma cried.

Pa told what he'd seen flying past the bay window. "Unless a course red apples has lately growed wings."

"Oh. That's different," Ma said.

Ma gave Free a look to show how disappointed she was in him.

The worst was, Free dearly loved pear preserve.

Free ❦ 27

SHORTLY BEFORE SCHOOL started again, the neighbors, Mr. and Mrs. George Bowman, Jr., came over one evening. They'd called on the telephone at suppertime. With them came their little girl.

One look at Mrs. Bowman's clothes and Ma conducted the company into the parlor. Pa quick put on new overalls and Ma knotted on a new gray apron with red trimming. The boys were sent out under the trees to play. The little girl stayed in the parlor with the older people.

Pretty soon Ma called Free into the house. She pushed him into the parlor ahead of her. "Here's our son, Free. Free, say hello to the company."

"Hello."

"Good evening," Mrs. Bowman said. Mr. Bowman smiled like an important man. He had a red face.

Ma said, "Our boy isn't the neatest at the moment, playing outside, you know."

"Oh, we understand," Mrs. Bowman said. She smiled with a town lady smile that was meant to win one over. She had black eyes that sparkled, just like the little black winking beads on her waist. Her hair was done up fancier than Ma's. Mrs. Bowman had her arm around her little girl's middle. "Free, this is my daughter Constance. Constance, say hello."

Constance wouldn't look up. "Hello." She had sleek black hair that made her look like a swallow. She kept stirring around in her blue velvet dress. She had black eyes too.

"Hello," Free said, short. The girl was pretty but he liked Larry Grey better.

Mrs. Bowman said, "Free, we came over to ask if our Constance couldn't walk along to school with you this fall."

Free knew instantly he wasn't going to like that. The kids at school would rag him about it all day long. Free scowled.

"Why, Free," Ma said, "what a face you draw. Aren't you glad you've got a pretty girl to walk to school with?"

"Yeh, boy," Pa said, "just think of how lucky you are." With a laugh Pa added, "I know I never was that lucky."

Mr. Bowman laughed too. "By gosh, Alfred, I don't think I had that privilege either."

Free knew that if he said no he'd get an awful scolding later on. It was the law that one had to get along with one's neighbors. Free thought of something. "Don't she belong to Rock No. 3 like I once did? When we lived on their place?"

Mrs. Bowman smiled. "Yes, she does, Free. But we're not sure we want our Constance to walk with those Horsberg boys."

That was different. Free knew what Mrs. Bowman meant. She didn't want those Horsberg boys to do to Constance what they were doing to the Windmiller girls.

"What do you say, Master Free?" Mrs. Bowman gave him a most winning mother smile.

Free hesitated. "Well, all right. Though I don't want to take the long-cut around by the road. Everett and me most generally take the pasture."

"Whatever you say, Free. We'd like it very much if Constance could walk to school with you. We think you're a responsible boy and that you'll know enough not to start home from school when it's storming. And so on."

"Teacher most generally keeps us in school if it's storming bad."

"That's sensible of her. And sensible of you to listen to her."

Ma had the same winning smile for him. "Then you think it will be all right, son?"

"I guess so."

"Good. That's settled then."

"Constance better be on time though. I like to get to school early so's I can have more time to play ball before the teacher rings the bell."

"Constance will be here on time, that I promise you." Mrs. Bowman said to Ma, "I'll see to it that she's here at least five minutes early."

Ma smiled. "I'm sure she'll be on time. Though Free does go into a fit if Everett is slow getting ready. I've never known a boy so anxious to get to school in the morning."

Mr. Bowman cleared his voice. "Good sign, that."
"Yep," Pa said.

Free was crabby with Constance the first while. She arrived on the yard on time, so he couldn't complain about that. But she couldn't walk fast enough to school to suit him. When he'd help her over the stile, she'd lean on him like she was family. It got so he could hardly stand to have her touch him. And the more he'd growl at her the more she'd try to please him. It was then that her black eyes shone like flowers.

When it got colder she began to wear a black fur coat and a white stocking cap. It made her look all the more like a swallow.

The minute they arrived on the school grounds, and she was safe under the teacher's wing, Free pretended he didn't know her. The first couple of weeks she tagged along wherever he and Larry played. Larry was inclined to be nice to her. Her people went to the same church his people did. But Larry soon saw how Free felt about her and then began to ignore her too.

The more Constance showed how much she liked Free, the more he knew what a great friend Larry was. Saturdays and Sundays at home he held all sorts of pretend talks with him, some of them so real that when he saw Larry again on Monday he had trouble remembering the talks hadn't been real.

A fellow couldn't talk to a girl about playing burn-out. Or stand side by side with her and open up their petcocks together. Or dream about the day when they'd run a threshing rig together.

Finally by Thanksgiving Day, Constance gave up trying to be his friend. On the way to school she walked off to one side a little and spent as much time smiling shyly at Everett as she did at Free. Free liked that much better.

Walking apart they began to trade stories. Constance told about how her mother wanted to take the train to Florida right after Christmas Day for vacation and how her father said absolutely not. So her mother wouldn't let her father smoke his cigars in the house anymore. At last her father said, all right, they could go, but for goshsakes don't ask me to play tennis there. Please. Free in turn told her about his little brother Albert and a cute remark of his. Pa'd bought the family a new Edison phonograph and Albert would always beg Ma to please play him a record before he took his nap at noon. One day Ma played him a record called, "Brighten the Corner Where You Are." When the record was over, Albert began singing the song. "Papa and Mama drinding coffee, right in the corner where you are."

One February day a blizzard came up while they were all eating their lunch at noon. Teacher quick closed school and sent the kids home before it got too bad. Larry had gotten permission from his folks to stay over with Free that night. All four, Free and Larry, Everett and Constance, one by one, ducked under the fence by the culvert and hurried down the pasture together. The strong wind burned on their right cheeks.

By the time they crossed the creek, they could hardly see each other. The wind kept pushing them south toward the fence. Pretty soon Constance caught her new fur coat in the barbwire and tore it a little. Her ma was going to be mad about that. Free stopped them all and gathered them in a circle. They leaned their heads together.

"We got to do something," Free said.

"I guess we do," Larry said.

"Tell you what. Constance, you give me your coat belt."

Constance had trouble unbuckling her leather belt with her mittens on. Free helped her. Flying snow melted on their red cheeks.

Free undid his long gray shawl and tied it to the belt. It made a rope some eight feet long.

"Now look, you guys." To make himself heard against the wind Free had to shout. "I'll hold the front end and lead the way. The rest of you grab hold behind and hang on."

"All right."

"Larry, you be the caboose at the end there and make sure nobody lets go. If they do, sing out and jerk on the rope."

Larry nodded. It was serious.

"Constance, you walk behind me. And Everett, you behind her."

Constance said, "But won't you freeze without your shawl?"

"Naw. I'm the leader. All right, let's head for home."

They moved out.

Free knew every tussock and clump of slough grass in the Walker pasture. Leaning forward, bucking into the wind, stocking cap pulled down, he led them single file all the way to the stile.

"Now," Free said. "Get over this safe and we'll have the wind on our backs until we hit the pasture windmill below our barn."

Free climbed over halfway, then reached down a hand to help them over, first Constance, then Everett, last Larry.

"All right, grab hold of the lifeline again, kids."

Free led them across the creek and then kept the line of tussocks in sight on his right. Tussocks always meant they were near the creek and the creek meant they would eventually come out by their windmill.

Sometimes the storm blew so hard it flipped their coats up over their heads, especially when they leaned over a little. Without her belt it was the worst for Constance. Everett, when he could, kept pulling it down behind for her.

They filed along, following the snake track of the creek. It got darker out.

Free began to wonder if the pasture windmill would ever show up. Could they have missed it in the flying snow?

Constance began to cry. "We're lost."

"Not so long's you can see me, you ain't."

Everett cried next.

Free snarled over his shoulder, "Shut up and follow the leader."

"My poopet's froze and I can't walk any more."

"Oh, good grief. Did you wet in your pants again?"

"It's the wind coming under my coat doing it."

Larry at the end of the line jollied Everett. "You should feel my behind. It's the first to get hit by the wind."

They had to yell to make themselves heard. Their clothes became so plakked with flying snow all they could make out of each other was their red faces.

Then Free saw an outline in snowy gloom ahead. That had to be the pasture windmill.

But the outline moved. It swayed from side to side. It came toward them.

"Pa!" Free yelled, suddenly very happy. "It's Pa."

"Yep," Pa laughed down at them. "And thank God it's you too." Pa was all bundled up in his long sheepskin coat and black storm cap and long lambskin-lined mittens. "Hey, what's that you got between you?"

"It's our lifeline," Free said.

"I'll be doggoned. Who thought of that?"

"Free did," Constance said. She was happy to see Pa too.

"Good boy." Pa shook his head at how good an idea he thought that was. Then Pa grabbed hold of the lifeline and led them up the lane, past the barn, past the cobshed, and at last safe into the warm snug kitchen where Ma had some bread baking in the oven. Oh! that bread smelled like heaven.

Ma was so happy to see them that she gave them all a kiss on their red cheeks.

Constance and Larry thought of wiping off Ma's kiss, but at the last second decided she was pretty nice.

Ma called up the Bowmans and the Greys to let them know the children had all arrived safe. Then Pa walked Constance home.

That night Larry slept with Free in the same bed. Everett was moved in with Albert. Every time Free woke up he'd hear the wind howling in the orchard. And when he fell asleep again, it was funny, but he'd dream, not of flying snow, but of red perfume flowing out of a patch of wild roses.

Free ❦ 28

MA WASN'T TOO happy with the kind of schooling her children were getting. A public school was not a Christian school, and Ma wished with all her heart that they lived closer to town so her children could go to the church school.

One Saturday morning the Kasper Gores drove onto the yard. That the Gores should visit them at all was a surprise. That friendly Pa and Ma had never been with them. Pa and Ma tended to sit about halfway down in the middle section of church, and always came early, while the Gores sat in front just inside the south door, and always arrived just as the domeny was ascending the pulpit. It was just coffee time. Of course Ma invited the Gores into the house.

Kasper Gore was a runt. He was bald down the center of his head like a striped skunk. His little brown eyes were always rolling and circling, and his mean little mouth leaked tobacco juice at both corners. His wife, Maude Gore, was at least twice his size, and walked with her legs apart like a champion wrestler.

Pa had a half smile for Kasper but for Maude he had a careful eye.

Ma turned to her kids, who were gawking at the Gores. "All right, you kids, under the trees. This company is not for you."

"But Ma," Free said, "it's still freezing outside."

"That's right. I forgot about that. Well, then upstairs with you. Go play school up in the storeroom."

"Aw, Ma—"

"Here's an oatmeal cookie with raisins for each of you. Now go. We don't want you underfoot just now."

All three went upstairs.

Free missed the first part of whatever it was the folks and the Gores were talking about, but the minute he finished his cookie, he crept halfway down the stairs until he could hear what the older people were saying in the living room.

The older people were clicking their cups in their saucers, when Maude cleared her throat and said, "Kasper?"

Kasper hitched up his chair an inch. "Ya. Well, Alfred, I hear you're thinking of moving."

"What?" Pa said. "That's news to me. We like it here."

"That ain't what we heard. Maude?"

The rocker under Maude cracked. "That's funny. We heard you folks were real anxious to move closer to the Christian School in Bonnie. So your children could get religious instruction there."

"That's true," Ma said. "But it was really only a wish on my part. Because our landlord has been good to us."

"But if you could find a place nearer town, you'd move there, wouldn't you?"

"Yes, I suppose we would. But I've already asked Domeny if he knew of anybody and he said he didn't."

"Oh," Maude said, "that's where we got it from then."

Ma said, "But I still don't understand what this has got to do—"

"Kasper and I," Maude broke in, hitching up closer in her rocker, "Kasper and I have been thinking a little that we'd like to move to California. You see, all of our relations have moved there, and we're beginning to feel cut off. So, well, to make a long story short, we thought maybe you people could take over our place. We rent, you know."

Pa said, "Jess, your brother, is still here though."

"Yes, he is," Kasper said. "But he plans to move too as soon as he gets married. To that Buwulf girl."

Free's eyes sparked in the dark as he listened. If these Gores wanted to go to California, why didn't they just pick up and go?

Pa said, "Don't you folks live on that Hamilton place about three and a half miles east of town?"

"That's right."

"My sister Karen was raised by the Gordon Hamiltons."

"Oh, was she?"

"The old folks are dead now, ain't they?"

"Yes. Horace runs the Hamilton estate for the three heirs. For Joyce, Sylvester, and himself."

"That's right. Horace is the one that became a lawyer. I knew him the best back then," Pa said.

"You did? He lives in Cedar Rapids now, you know."

"So I heard."

"Well, Alfred, with Horace being a lawyer, it ain't going to be easy for us to just vacate that lease."

"I can see that," Pa said. "But how will my kids get to school from your place, those three and a half miles?"

Maude said, "It isn't that far but what your children can't drive it with a horse."

"We'd have to buy a horse then of course," Pa said.

Ma cleared her throat. "Our boy Free drive a horse to school so young, Alfred?"

"Oh, he can drive a horse all right," Pa said. "He's good around animals. I don't worry about that none."

"But that's quite a responsibility, Alfred."

"So was quick saving Albert from those crazy sows that time."

Ma said nothing.

Maude said, "It sounds like he can handle a horse then."

Ma still said nothing.

"Well now," Maude said, "like Kasper says, it's going to be hard to vacate that lease. Especially since we just signed a new one. It's going to be pretty sticky."

"Oh."

"But, if we can get someone to take over the lease, and pay us a little for vacating the premises, for all our trouble, why then, maybe . . ."

"What kind of money would you expect for your trouble?" Pa asked.

"Kasper?" Maude said.

Kasper hitched up his chair another inch. "Well, it ain't really a good thing to break a lease, Alfred."

"What would your trouble be worth?"

"Five hundred dollar."

"Five hundred dollars?" Pa said. "Tain't worth it."

Free thought in the dark: "Good old Pa. He's got the better sense. Because I don't want to leave Larry Grey and Rock No. 4."

The rocker under Maude creaked a couple of times. "Well, think about it. It won't hurt to do that."

Ma said, "No, I guess it won't."

"Well, we thought that we could at least let you know that there was a chance for you to move closer to town." Maude got to her feet. "Well, Kasper, I think we better go now."

Ma got up too. "It was kind of you to tell us."

Pa got to his feet too. "Say, that reminds me. I've got most of the fall plowing done here. How much have you got done on your place?"

Kasper didn't right away answer. When he did, he spoke slow, as if he were figuring out how Maude would answer the question. "Well, Alfred, um . . . the last couple of year I been doing all my plowing in the spring."

"Oh. Ain't you a bit crowded for time then? Me, if I find extra time in the spring, I haul manure. To keep that barnyard clean."

"Well, I got two boys to help me. Hib and Hankie are fourteen and twelve, you know."

"That's right." Pa scratched his beard, loud. "Wal, if we do move, I'll just have to try and get the next renter to pay me for my time plowing here. Or lose my work."

Kasper said, "By the way, I suppose you've already signed your lease for next year here?"

"Kasper," Maude said.

"Yeh, that's right," Kasper said.

"No, we haven't," Pa said. "But the landlord and me shook hands on it last fall that we'd renew it this spring. I expect Haines to come out with the new lease any day now."

"Oh, well, then you're in the clear," Kasper said. "A handshake ain't legal."

Ma said, "With us it is though."

"Well, think about it," Maude said. "And let us know. Maybe at church sometime you can."

"We'll do that," Ma said. "We'll take it up with the Lord in prayer and see what He says."

"Good."

Free crept upstairs again before Pa or Ma could catch him sitting there.

What Pa and Ma were thinking of doing was awful. He couldn't leave Larry Grey, the best friend he had in the whole world. And who would walk to school with Constance Bowman?

Free sat on a box by the south window in the storeroom. He looked out at the bare trees in the orchard and at the bare hill beyond in Horsberg's pasture. In three months the apple trees would be clouds of blossoms again and the hill would be white with just-popped mayflowers. O my. The raw wood of the sloped ceiling above him smelled like an empty salt barrel.

A couple of days later Pa and Ma went to have a look at the Hamilton place.

When they came back the evening, Free knew the worst.

Not much was said at supper. Pa was busy thinking hard about something and Ma looked like she was communing with God.

Around eight o'clock Pa said, "Wal, son, ain't it about time for you to go to bed too?" Everett and Albert had long ago gone upstairs.

"I don't care if I never go to bed."

"I know, son. But just remember we're doing it for your good. So you'll get a good Christian education."

"But I don't want a good Christian education if it means I can't play with Larry Grey anymore."

"You'll find new friends in the new place fast enough."

"But I don't like those liar Christian kids in Bonnie."

Ma was shocked. "Why, Free!"

"No, I don't. The kids at Rock No. 4 are a whole lot better than the kids I see at the Christian School."

"Don't you like your cousins Johnny and Bert? And Johnny Westing? You'll be going to the same school with them."

Free thought they maybe were all right, but he liked Larry Grey better. "Besides, won't Pa have to dig a new privy hole again? Like he always does when we move?"

Pa laughed. "Yeh, this one we'll have to dig for sure. The hole they've been using won't take but one or two more sittings by that fat mare Maude Gore and it'll be full."

Ma sighed. "Yes, and your mother will want to clean and redecorate the whole house too. So you have a point there."

Free gave Pa a direct look. "When's our ship ever gonna come in? So we can own our own place once? Like the Bowmans, who never have to move?"

A sad look came into Pa's eyes. And Ma looked like she was going to commune with God again.

Free had himself a dipper of rainwater to drink. Then he headed for the stair door.

Ma got up and came over and put her arms around him. She kissed him on the neck.

"Everything's going to be all right, boy. We want you to grow up to be a good Christian boy."

Free submitted to her hug and kiss. Usually he hated it when womenfolk tried to get him to do things their way by loving him up. But Ma had honest tears in her eyes.

"Besides," Pa said, "just think, son, you'll be driving a horse to school every day. Not every boy gets that chance. Your very own horse, son."

"I'd rather have Larry Grey, Pa."

Free ❦ 29

MA'S COUSIN GARRETT came to help them, riding his favorite horse, Lady. Lady was a lively chestnut pacer, but Garrett had also trained her to be a good cow pony. Hooked onto his brown saddle was a hemp rope lariat. When Garrett drove the cattle up the lane and headed them for the new place, he looked exactly like a hero in a Western magazine.

As soon as the last wagonload left the yard, Pa got out their new Buick and loaded in the dishes, the forks and knives, the clocks, and the glass frame pictures, all in the back seat. Ma and the kids had to pack into the front seat beside Pa. Ma was so smothered with kids she looked like a mama cat moving her family to a new place, one kitten in her mouth and the rest hanging onto her titties.

Pa drove slow to keep the plates in back from banging together. He took the King of Trails Highway to Bonnie, then at the churchyard took the east road out of town. They crossed the Little Rock near where Great John Engleking had died from the hiccups. They drove past Arlo Barth's place, and at last rolled onto the yard of their new place.

The place had a good grove on the west and north sides, willows on the outside and ash on the inside. There were four apple trees. The house had never been painted and looked awful. The machine shed had a fallen backbone. The barn was old but it was the best painted. There were only two good buildings on the whole place, the corncrib and the hog house, but they too, like the house, had never been painted.

Junk stood everywhere. Of course the Gores hadn't quite finished moving out yet, and the Alfredson stuff that'd just been brought onto the yard still hadn't been put in its place, but it could easy be seen that the Gores always had a messy yard. There were four big fat manure piles in the barnyard, the feed bunks looked like they hadn't been cleaned out all winter, the chicken coop was full of dead chickens, tin cans and broken fork handles lay everywhere. Worst was the house; it was dirty and unpainted both. Free saw all this and looked at his folks in wonder. Was his going to the Christian School all that important?

"Yes, son," Pa said, noticing his look, "when your ma gets the religious bee in her bonnet, the horse has to run her way."

The two Gore boys, Hib and Hankie, hung around watching the Alfredson stuff being unloaded. They kept laughing to themselves about all the funny furniture the Alfredsons had. Their pa called them several times to help him move their own things, but they wouldn't do it. Hib was fat like his ma and had his pa's mean little mouth. Hankie was skinny and kept laughing like a soft-running little engine. Both wore their overalls over their sweaters with their side buttons left open.

Pretty soon Hib and Hankie began to tease Free about his big feet and his two cowlicks.

Free didn't know how to handle it at first. If these boys were prize examples of Little Church people, man, when he grew up he was going to leave the church and attend instead Larry Grey's church in Rock Falls.

Everett and Albert were wiser. They began climbing the tallest trees on the place.

Hib spotted something in a box his mother Maude Gore was carrying out of the house. "Hey, Ma, just a minute." He reached in and pulled out an air rifle. "Gimme that."

"Put it back."

"No."

"What? Kasper, order that boy of yours to put his gun back."

Kasper Gore moved his blue cap up and down a couple of times. He repositioned the chew in his cheek. "You better listen to your ma, Hib."

"No."

Free was amazed. Boy, if he'd ever have smarted off like that he'd have gotten a licking.

Hib led Free to the machine shed. He handled his nickel-shiny air rifle like he was an expert hunter. "Would you like to shoot it once? It's a real Daisy air rifle."

Free said nothing. He took the air rifle.

"You got to pump the lever to get the beebee into the barrel," Hib said. "And if you'll leave the lever hanging down as you pull the trigger, it'll shoot further that way."

Free pumped the lever, let it hang.

Hankie held his hand over his mouth to hide a laugh. It was as though he thought Free the dumbest sucker he'd ever seen.

Free handed the air rifle back to Hib. "I don't care to."

"Go ahead. You want to shoot it, don't you?"

"No," Free said.

"Aw, g'wan, it won't hurt you. And Hankie, you shut up."

Reluctantly Free took the air rifle again.

"Shoot at that tin can there."

Free aimed and pulled the trigger. There was a hard cough from the air rifle, the tin can pinged where the beebee hit it, and the lever snapped up and cut Free across his long finger.

"Did you get hurt?" Hib asked.

He'd been made a fool of, trusting those rascals. "That was a dirty trick!" Free threw the air rifle on the ground. He refused to look at his finger, though he could feel blood trickling down the end of it.

"Oh, so you're going to be a sorehead instead of just having a sore finger, huh?"

Free thought of taking a club to Hib. But finally he decided to have nothing more to do with the Gore boys. They were worse than the Horsberg boys.

He wandered into the grove to look for Everett and Albert. He found the grove an even worse mess than the yard. Throwaway junk lay everywhere. It looked like hell with the door left open.

Free came out on the west edge of the grove. Ahead downhill sloped an alfalfa field. A dry run snaked through a pasture below that. The run headed north down to the Little Rock River.

Hey. A river. And not more than a half mile away. That might make up for a lot of things. Swimming. Skating.

He heard voices above him. Looking up, he saw Albert in the tippy top of a cottonwood. It was much taller than the willows and the ash trees around. Everett had quit climbing halfway up. That Albert. He was getting ahead of Everett.

Albert spotted Free and called down. "Hey, Free, you ought to see what I see from up here. I can see all the way to the water tower in Bonnie. And there's farms everywhere, on both sides of the river. Man alive, you can see far from up here."

Looking west, Free counted seventeen farms between their new high hill and town. If all of them had three kids there'd sure be a lot of kids to play with in that part of the country.

"Children?" It was Ma calling from the new house. It meant she had some kind of lunch for them.

Albert started climbing down right away. He was always ready for a meal no matter what time of the day it was.

When the three of them got to the front porch, they found the Gores gone. Good. Free hoped he'd never see them again.

They stepped onto the enclosed porch. The bare cement stank of sour milk. Free could see where the Gore cream separator had been screwed to the floor near the cellar door. The wood walls looked like they'd been smoked they were so dark. There were fly specks everywhere. Ma was surely going to have to do a lot of painting to make it into a homey entrance.

The kitchen smelled better. Ma had a cob fire going in their own stove. She was cutting slices of bread on the cabinet counter. Pa and Garrett were still pushing things around in a far room, banging against the wall, cussing a little, with Garrett sometimes laughing.

"We won't have time to sit down today, children," Ma said, "so you better just step up . . . say, what happened to your hand?"

Free looked at the cut in his finger. The tip of the finger was coated with dried black blood. As he looked at it, it began to hurt again. Those Gore rascals. He decided not to tell Ma about them. Ma and Pa had enough troubles. "I must've hooked it on some barbed wire."

"We've just moved here and already you've had an accident." Ma reached into a box she hadn't unpacked yet. "Here, put some peroxide on it. Later I'll tear up a rag for a bandage."

Albert was eyeing things over. "In the other house, the kitchen was on that side."

"Yes, this house lies east and west, with the bay window facing south. That means the house will be that much more sunny."

"But everything is so unpainted, Ma."

"Yes, boy, once again your mother has been called upon to improve a landlord's property."

Free said, "I wish we didn't have to move all the time."

"We won't, son," Pa said, coming out of the living room. "We're going to ask the landlord if we can somehow buy this place."

"That wouldn't be such a bad idea," Garrett said, following Pa and taking a chair by the north window. With his fingers Garrett combed back his sunny pompadour. He had a quick smile. "The land is good. And these buildings are basically sound. They just need a couple of coats of paint, is all."

"That was my thought." Pa picked up a thick sandwich. "Or I wouldn't've moved here even if the angel Gabriel was principal at our church school."

Garrett had to laugh. "Our present principal, Harold Holly, is hardly Gabriel. He likes to lick the boys too well for that."

Ma said, "If we are to gossip, let's at least see what good we can say about Mr. Holly."

Pa said, "Free, you take your two brothers and go pick the cob box full of cobs from the hog yard."

"Gore hog cobs?" Free cried.

"Son," Pa said, trying to be kind about it, "it's got to be done."

After the boys got the cobs, they went to see what the barn was like. The stanchions for the milk cows were on the west side and the gutter behind them was full of manure. The feed rack for the fatteners was on the east side and behind it the manure was a yard deep. A lean-to with stalls for horses was on the north side and there the manure was so deep the hind ends of the horses stood higher than their ears. Boy, to make up for all that manure the Christian School in town had better really be good.

There was no hay up in the mow, only dust and treacherous floor boards. The hay carrier had jumped the rail near the mow door and hung like a car wreck on the edge of a bridge. There were no cupola and no pigeons. But mice? There were so many that their tails made a fringe along the two main cross supports.

Pa had put the calves in the night yard. After their long trip from the old place, they were having fun, bucking each other, banging into the strange fences, circling around four big cottonwood trees, and just generally bellering around. The new Shorthorn bull didn't know what to make of his calves and their crazy stunts. He stood by the biggest cottonwood tree. He lowered his head and let some syrupy spit drip to the ground.

With so much junk and dirt everywhere, the chickens had the best time. They flew and ran all over the place not knowing what to peck at first. There was spilled grain on the floor of the alley in the granary. There was spilled shelled corn on the ground on the west side of the corncrib. And all the cowpies and horsebiscuits were full of swollen kernels of corn like cookies with raisins.

Everybody hurried and did the chores even though things and animals were in the wrong places. Some of the chickens didn't know where to lay their eggs. Free found some nests full of rotten eggs laid by the Gore hens. Those Gore boys were not only rascals, they were poor egg-getters. The calves weren't sure they wanted skim milk. They kept jerking their heads up out of the pail and looking around, sometimes coming up so hard they spilled milk over Free's shoes.

Supper wasn't much that night. "You'll just have to forgive me this one time," Ma said.

"Just so the grub has got the gaff," Pa said from his new corner by the south window. "That's all we ask."

Garrett ate neat like a domeny. "Ade, your worst meals are better than Fat Ett's best." Garrett's teeth showed as he laughed about his sister-in-law Etta. "It's no wonder those two are as big as lard cans, eating all that half-done fatty meat three times a day." Garrett allowed himself another short laugh. "Those two are so fat, I can't figure out how they manage to make kids."

"Hold the thought," Ma said, "it's too awful to think about. And all pots . . ."

Garrett nodded. He was smart enough not to even glance at the kids.

When they were finished eating, Ma asked Free to get the Bible. In the orange lamplight the old black leather Bible shone a little from all the handling. A smile came over Ma's face. "You know, I've been thinking, Alfred, now that we've moved to a new place, we ought to also turn over a new leaf in another matter. You know how I've always believed that the man of the house should lead in family worship. Well, Alfred, you already lead us in the word of prayer. Now I propose that our oldest son, who, according to his teachers, is quite a reader, should read from the Bible at family worship."

For a second Pa's eyes began to shine.

Albert and Everett gave Free jealous looks.

"Well, Alfred?" Ma said.

Pa selected a toothpick from the holder. He worked the toothpick around in his teeth like a man picking weeds out of a sickle bar. "Mmm. That about the man of the house being the proper one to lead in such things I agree with."

"It does not behoove a woman to read at the table, you know."

"Just so it don't make the kid stuck-up."

It could be seen that Garrett thought it might give Free the bighead too. "You can always fix a steel clamp around Free's head, Alf."

"Reading God's Word shouldn't make anyone vain," Ma said. "If anything it should make him more humble."

"All right," Pa said, "we'll do it."

"Good," Ma said. She opened the Bible and moved the silk marker to the first chapter of Genesis. "And I also propose that he start from the beginning. That way, reading the whole Bible through from chapter one, he'll get a good grounding in God's Word." She handed the open book to Free.

Free trembled. Only nine years old and already reading the Bible at the table like a father?

"Read, boy."

"In the beginning God created the heaven and the earth." Free read steadily. In the whole chapter he stumbled only three times, once over the word "abundantly," once over "dominion," and once over "herb." Ma helped him. He was aware that everybody—Pa, Garrett, Ma, his little brothers—was listening closely as they worked their toothpicks to see how he'd do.

He read the last paragraph with a flourish. "And God saw everything that He had made: and behold, it was very good. And the evening and the morning were the sixth day."

Pleased with himself, Free decided he'd do as Ma always did upon finishing the reading. He looked firmly at Everett and Albert. "And who can tell us what was the last word read?"

"Day," Everett said promptly. For once he'd listened carefully.

Ma acted like she didn't know whether to laugh or to get mad.

Pa looked at Ma. "See what I mean?"

"Well," Ma said, "I don't think Free meant any harm by it." Then Ma held her head a little sideways. "Though I think, Free, that for a while at least, your father, or I, should be the one to ask about the last word read."

Free slid the blue silk marker in place and closed the Good Book. "All right, Ma."

"That's better," Pa said. And closing his eyes, Pa placed his folded hands over his face and gave thanks.

Free was still feeling so good about being the second head of the house that right after Pa said "Amen" he hurried through his little prayer. "Lord's'food'am."

Everett and Albert followed him. "Lord's'food'am."

Pa opened his eyes. "Here, here. Let's do that over. Maybe the Good Lord can understand you, but I surely can't. All of you pray over."

"Yes," Ma said, "we should always show respect when we pray to Him. Speak clearly and with proper reverence."

Free colored. But he folded his hands and closed his eyes again. "Lord, we thank Thee for this food. Amen."

Everett and Albert did it over too.

"That's much better."

After a while, Free selected a toothpick for himself and worked the flattest end of it in and out of his teeth. Meat always got caught in his tight teeth and he had to be careful how he went at digging it out or the toothpick would break off and part of it would be left in his teeth. Then it would feel even worse. He never had any trouble with the two top front biters though. There was a small opening between those two, almost big enough to whistle through, and little spaces to either side of them. He'd inherited that from Ma. She could put a match end between her two front teeth.

Free ❦ 30

THE NEXT MORNING Ma hustled Free and Everett off to the Garfield No. 2 country school a half mile up the road to the east. They would have to go there until Pa found a safe horse for them.

Garrett left that morning too. He promised Pa he'd build the kids an enclosed cab on a buggy running rear. In an enclosed cab they could go to school in any kind of weather.

There were only ten kids in the Garfield No. 2 school. Most of them came from the Albert Moss family. Mr. Moss farmed three eighties to the east. The oldest Moss kid, Minnie, was like a mother to the rest of them, fighting for them when the DeGreate kids played tricks on them. Rosie, the youngest Moss, was a sweetheart. Minnie kept making a doll out of Rosie, braiding her gold pigtails perfect and tying her ribbons in big flat bows. Minnie was always pushing her into the arms of the little Goff kid, Sylvester. Sylvester was an over-petted creature too and went around with his thick lips puffed out. Minnie would make Sylvester and Rosie put their arms around each other and kiss each other. Then Minnie would cry, "Ain't they just the cutest pair though. Just like on a valentine. Someday they're going to get married."

Free cast the two baby lovers a wondering eye. He remembered the Horsberg boys with the Windmiller girls.

Of course the teacher knew about Rosie and Sylvester. She also thought the baby sweethearts were just too cute for words and had them sit in the same double seat up front near her desk. When the two kewpies kissed in class, teacher looked out of the window and smiled at the cottonwoods on the Peterson place across the road.

The teacher couldn't wait to get married in June. She went around lost in a cloud most of the day. Everett didn't learn a thing. It would've been a waste for Free too if there hadn't been some reading books in school. There were four he hadn't seen before, and after he finished doing his lessons, he started in on them. He read them all within a week. The next week to keep Free busy the teacher gave him a hard history book to read. The book looked interesting and Free took it home. By the next morning he had that read too. Teacher couldn't believe it, and gasped, and started talking about how smart her fiancé was.

Sometimes at noon, the teacher got so moony she let the kids have a two-hour recess to play while she took a stroll by herself out to a forsaken graveyard an eighth of a mile south up on a hill. She'd sit on a gravestone and comb her curly black hair in the sun until it sparked and jumped up at the ends.

After school Free had to get Pa and Ma's mail from the mailbox under the Peterson cottonwoods. He liked getting the mail because he kept hoping he'd get a letter from Larry Grey. But Larry Grey never wrote him.

By the end of two weeks Free was awfully tired of waiting for Pa to get that new horse. When Garrett brought over their new cab, Free really began to make a fuss about how he hated that Garfield No. 2 school with all its crazy sweethearts. The cab was a beauty. It was painted a nice gray and the new wood inside smelled like a pitcher full of warm sage milk.

One day Free came home and right away knew something was different by the way the horses were behaving in the night yard.

Free changed into his yard clothes and got the eggs first. He was a good egg detective. Brood hens hated him and tried to outwit him, but the law was the law, and all eggs belonged to Ma.

His pail was about full when he entered the horse barn to search through the mangers. And there it was. A new horse stood in the stall near the door, a bay, with a black mane and tail. Free set his egg pail down.

The minute the hay in the alley crackled under Free's feet the new horse reared up its head.

Pa'd always said to move slow around an animal. "Sing out and let the critter know you're around. Then, when you get near the critter, don't make any fast moves. And talk low like you love 'm."

The bay had a narrow blaze down the front of its head. It had sly brown eyes. It had a gray rubbery nose.

Free kept shuffling slow until he stood directly in front of the bay. He looked into its feedbox and manger. Yep. Pa had given it a little hay. But not nearly enough.

Free had to feed the horses anyway later on so he decided to do it now. Quickly he put some slough hay in the new horse's manger, and then filled all the other mangers down the line. Next he got a bushel of ear corn and gave the new horse twelve ears like he always gave the other horses. When he finished parceling out the corn he had two ears left over. He gave them to the new horse.

The new horse bit into the corn like it was sticks of peppermint candy.

Free decided the horse might like to be curried. He got the curry comb and horse brush from the medicine cabinet. He approached the new horse quietly, slowly, like Pa said, letting it know he was behind it. "Whoa, there." The new horse looked around at him, curving its long neck. It pranced around a little. It lifted its tail. It was then that Free saw it was a she. From the loose look of things she'd once had a colt.

Free spoke to her lovingly gruff. "Whoa now, girl. Whoa." He angled in on her from the side, staying well out of her kicking range. He placed his hand gently on her shoulder.

She rolled her brown eyes, rippled her bay hide; decided she liked him.

Free breathed easier. So far so good. He curried and brushed her down, the sleek neck, the withers, the backbone. He found a witches' bridle in her black mane and untangled it, careful not to pull out any hairs.

When he got to her rump, he spotted a brand on the right side. Hey. A wild bronc. He wondered if the brand belonged to the cattle outfit Grampa once had a fight with in the Dakotas.

She was touchy about letting him curry the brand, swinging her butt away from him. He ran the brush over the brand, tenderly.

The big door opened behind him and there was suddenly a lot of light in the stall. It was Pa.

The horse looked up from her corn.

''Wal,'' Pa said, ''I see you've already got acquainted with her.''

''Gee, Pa, she's a beauty.''

''Her name is Tip, in case you want to know.''

''I wonder why Tip?''

''I dunno. It's what the man told me at the Cannonball yards.''

Free stroked her withers. ''Hi, Tip.''

Tip decided neither the father nor the son meant her any harm. She went back to eating corn.

''Am I driving her to school tomorrow morning then?''

''Your ma says you've got to get used to her first.''

''Shucks.''

''Be careful Tip doesn't kick you. She just might be full of tricks.''

''Can I ride her horseback sometime?''

''That's what she was in the first place. A cow pony.''

Free spotted a fairly new harness and bridle hanging from a peg behind Tip. ''Is that hers?''

''Yep. It was part of the price.'' Then Pa went outdoors to do his chores.

Free brushed out Tip's black tail until it shone.

The next Saturday, after Tip had her breakfast, Free got her bridle and slipped in beside her to put it on. When he reached up to take off her halter, Tip snapped around at him.

''Hey, you.'' With the flat of his hand Free whacked her lightly over the withers. Then he said in a firm boss voice, ''You cut that out.'' He decided he'd better keep the halter headstrap looped around her neck while he put on the bridle. She just might trick him and get away.

He slipped her nose out of the halter, rehooked the headstrap, then went to open her mouth.

Tip refused to open her jaws for the bridle bit.

"Well, we'll see about that." Free slipped his fingers into the back part of her mouth, and then Tip gave in. She recognized the mouth-opening trick. At the same time she released a long wet tongue. Click, and the bit went in, and the headstall of the bridle slipped over her head and caught snugly behind her ears. Free buckled the throatstrap in place, then finished taking off the halter.

He led her outside to the water tank. She appeared to know who was boss. As she drank he stroked her withers.

Albert and Everett came tumbling out of the house.

''Are you going to hitch her up to the cab?'' Albert asked.

''Don't get too close. A horse can kick plenty far behind her.''

Albert and Everett backed off a few steps.

Tip stood sideways to the tank. Here was a good chance to hop on. Free threw the two lines over her back, got up on the edge of the tank, swung a leg over her, and slid aboard. She sat good, a perfect fit for his seat and long legs.

Albert and Everett fell back a few more steps in awe.

Free waited until she'd finished drinking, then nudged her with his right knee. ''Okay, girl, let's go for a little ride.'' He tugged on her right line at the same time. She listened more to his knee than to the line. She walked across the yard, turned by the little unpainted garage, headed back again. He nudged her more than drove her. After he rode her a half dozen times across the yard, he reined up in front of the water tank again.

''Can we ride her too, Free?'' Albert asked.

''No. Too dangerous. She's a wild bronc, you know.''

''But me and Everett want to ride her too.''

Free looked down at his two brothers. He felt like an emperor. ''I think I'll go get the mail on horseback. Instead of walking.''

''Ma'll get after you,'' Albert said.

''What she don't know won't hurt her,'' Free said.

''Unless I tell her,'' Albert said.

Free reached back and gave Tip a light whack on her behind. ''Giddap, let's go get the mail, Tip.''

Tip set herself in motion. She wagged her head up and down.

Free walked her all the way to the Peterson cottonwoods. It took a while but it was easy. Man, it was fun to ride a bronc.

He had some trouble getting the mail out of the mailbox. Every time he reached down to open the lid, Tip would shy away. At last, though, he managed to get out the packet of mail; even managed to close the box by kicking the lid shut with his heel.

He turned Tip for home. Tip liked that. She walked faster.

Curious to see what was in the mail, he opened the packet. There was Ma's weekly *The Watchman*, a letter from Grandma, a flyer announcing the summer schedule of the new Bonnie baseball team.

The team picture on the flyer caught his eye. He recognized most of the players. He'd seen them up town on Saturday nights. Too bad Pa didn't play on the town team. Free kept looking at the picture. He examined the bats stacked in front of the team. Someday he was going to have a man's bat too.

He was so lost in the flyer that he was only partly aware, out of the corner of his eye, that Tip had arched her neck around and was looking at him past her blinders. The next thing he knew—eenyenk! Tip bucked and sent him flying over her head. He made a complete somersault in the air before landing on his butt. Luckily he didn't land on the hard road but on the grass alongside. He sat stunned for a moment. In his mind he checked over his body to see if he'd been hurt anywhere. Then, seeing that all he was going to suffer was a good jarring in his teeth, he got mad and jumped to his feet. "You goldarn sneak you! So that's why they call you Tip. When a fellow ain't looking, you tip him off."

Tip didn't seem to hear him. She'd spotted a little bunch of fresh grass poking through some old roadside grass, and trailing her lines went over and began to crop it.

Just in time Free remembered Pa's rule never to rush an animal. Moving almost as if he wasn't interested in her, he got close enough to suddenly grab her lines.

He gave her a couple of hard yanks on the mouth, cussed her with some mean Horsberg words, then, still mad and knowing he couldn't very well show up on the yard unhorsed, stuck the mail in his back pocket, grabbed hold of her mane above the withers and by a miracle swung himself aboard.

His hopping aboard helped Free make up his mind. Back on the yard he led Tip into the barn and put the mail aside. He got down Tip's harness and then, like Pa, said, "Whoa, girl," and swept the harness up over her back. Again Tip swung her head around at him. But he knew her trick and ducked her bite.

He lifted up her tail, slipped her crupper under, then buckled on the rest of the harness.

Free led her out to the gray cab. He swung her around in front of the buggy shafts to back her into them.

Tip shied her rear off to one side of the shaft tips.

"Here, you. Get your butt in there. Back. Back up, you!"

Tip swung her rear the other way.

"Well, there's more than one way to skin a cat." Holding onto the hitching strap with one hand, with the other hand Free reached back for the near shaft tip, and by sheer arm muscle pulled the cab forward until he had her caught in the shafts. He hooked on her tugs. "There. Ready to roll."

Albert and Everett came running up. "Can we go along?"

Free acted like Pa. "Wal, if you're good boys, I guess so."

"Goody." The two climbed in through the little door in back.

Free poked the ends of the lines through the two driving holes. "Grab hold of them in there, will you, Albert?"

Albert pulled the lines through.

Free climbed in too and took the driver's seat, a crossboard caught onto the benches to either side. Albert sat on the right-hand bench and Everett on the left-hand bench.

"Aint you gonna tell Ma we're going somewhere?" Everett said.

"No."

"We're gonna get a licking," Everett said. "You better let me out."

Free picked up the lines. "Giddap, Tip, let's go."

Tip didn't move.

"Better open the front window," Albert said. "So she can hear you."

Free hooked the little window up to an eye screw in the roof. "All right, you. Giddap." He sawed on the lines a little.

For a miracle Tip began to amble ahead. The wheels rolled.

Free aimed Tip for the road. The springs gave the cab a soft rolling motion. Albert and Everett watched the yard fence pass by through the little window in the rear door. They really were out riding by themselves.

Free turned Tip east toward the Garfield No. 2 school. Tip didn't seem to mind. She went at a walk. They slowly rode up and over the three little hills, going past the Hopkins place.

When they reached the corner, Free turned Tip north past the Peterson cottonwoods and the row of mailboxes. A half mile down the road they saw Sylvester Goff sitting in a swing on the Goff yard.

Everything went fine. Tip didn't mind pulling the cab as long as she could walk.

At the next corner Free pulled east . The hill ahead was a stiff one going up. It was even steeper going down. The cab began to push against Tip's breeching, almost making her trot. But Tip didn't want to run. She set her legs against it.

Albert said, "This is going to take all day."

"Yeh," Free said, "maybe now is a good time to make her trot once." He sawed on the lines, trying to make them snap through the driving holes onto her back. "C'mon, Tip, let's get a move on."

Sighing, like an old man who needed twenty steps to loosen up, Tip finally broke into a slow trot.

Albert smiled and watched a cornfield go by.

About halfway down the steep hill the cab pushing into the breeching made Tip go at a merry clip.

"Wow! Now we're really flying," Albert said. He laughed for joy.

Everett sat on his hands. "Boy, are we gonna get it."

Warmed up, Tip kept right on trotting, up the next long slope and around the next corner south.

Tip was still going at a lively clip when Free turned her at the next corner going west. They rolled past the Besters' and the Mosses'.

When Tip spotted the Garfield No. 2 school coming up, she really put the socks into it. Home and ear corn lay ahead. They spun over the three little hills and whirled onto their own yard. Tip could sure fly when she was of a mind to.

Free pulled up in front of their house-yard gate in triumph.

Ma came sailing out of the house. "Where have you kids been?"

Albert and Everett climbed out of the cab right away. Albert began to look where Pa might be and Everett held his behind.

Free decided not to climb out of the cab. He'd answer Ma through the little front window. "We just took a little ride around the section, Ma."

"Yes, that I know. Because I put out a general ring to alert the neighborhood that my boys had run away."

A general ring? That always meant a calamity was on hand. Free could feel his face turn white.

Ma had to work at her breathing. "So at least I always knew just about where you were. People along the route kept calling me up just after you'd gone by." Ma shook her head. "How did you dare to do it, Free? Weren't you afraid?"

"I'm not afraid of Tip."

Ma sighed a tremendous sigh. "Dear me. So bold. Well, in that case then you can begin driving to the Christian School."

Free ❦ 31

FREE ROLLED OUT of bed the minute Pa called up the stairwell. He climbed into his clothes and ran outside into the pink dawn. He rounded up the cows from the night yard and drove them into the barn. He fed Tip and the rest of the horses. He curried and harnessed Tip. He milked his two cows. He helped Pa separate the milk. He ran into the house a minute to hurry Everett out of bed, then ran out and fed the calves their skim milk.

He hardly had time for breakfast. "Lunch buckets ready, Ma?"

Ma had to smile. "Just about, boy."

Pa said, "When it suits him he can surely go, can't he?"

Ma nodded with another smile.

Right after Albert's amen, Free rushed into his school clothes, knickers and sweater and stocking cap, gave Everett a black look to hurry him up, and ran out to get Tip.

Tip wasn't quite through eating her corn and didn't want to take the bit. But Free snuck it in anyway. Tip sneered, and some corn fell out of her mouth. He led her out and watered her, and that she liked, taking her time.

He led her in front of the shafts, tried backing her into them. Again she shied off, first one way, then the other. Once more he had to hold her with one hand while he pulled up the cab with his other hand. He'd just about got the shafts slid into the leather holders, when Tip suddenly reached around and caught his left arm between her teeth. He had no chance to defend himself. She almost bit through his sweater.

"Why you slick son of a bitch you!"

"Here, here," Pa called from the machine shed.

"But she bit me," Free raged, holding his left arm.

"Yeh, I know. I saw it. But cussing does not behoove a pupil going to the Christian School."

Once more Free went about pulling the shafts up around Tip. This time she stood quietly.

''If that Everett ain't ready in two shakes of a lamb's tail,'' Free said, ''I'm leaving without him.''

Pa said, ''Did you take along some ear corn for the horse?''

''No.''

''A horse likes to have his dinner too, you know.''

Free got a gunnysack and put in a dozen ears. By the time he threw the corn onto the floor of the cab, Everett was standing ready with both their dinner buckets.

Free and Everett climbed in and closed the door. Free opened the little window up front. ''All right, old girl, let's get high behind.'' He snapped the lines hard enough through the driving holes to make them ripple across Tip's back. Tip started up and headed for the road.

Ma stood on the front steps, waving good-bye. ''Free, did you scrub your fingernails? Get those milk rings off?''

Free looked at his hands. Darn. "I'll get 'em at school, Ma."

''I don't want it said that one of Ada's boys had funeral rings on his fingernails.''

Tip walked the first ways again. She even walked down the first hill with the cab riding pretty hard into her breeching.

''We're gonna be late if I let her walk all the way,'' Free thought. ''I've got to speed her up.''

Free pulled up at the bottom of the hill. He asked Everett to hold the lines a minute, then clambered out and ran down to some willows growing in the ditch. He broke off a live green branch, a slim one, and snapped off the little twigs. He flicked it up and down a couple of times. It whistled like a good whip. He crawled back into the cab and took the lines again. ''Now watch our speed.'' He reached through the little window and snapped the willow over Tip's butt. ''Giddap, you. Get!''

Tip jerked up her head, she was so surprised, and bucked once, eengk, and then started up and fell into a good steady trot.

''You funny old maid you,'' Free said. ''You first have to complain before you do anything.''

By the time they topped the next rise the sun was a glowing pink behind them. While ahead lay a magic thing. The town of Bonnie hung spread out like a pink dream city on a slim fallen cloud. The whole town looked like a heavenly city on Judgment Day. No wonder Ma liked to talk about heaven on Sunday.

It was downhill all the way to the Little Rock River and Tip went along at a good clip. But when the road leveled off near the approach to the bridge she slackened off to a walk. No matter how Free scolded her, or hit her with the willow switch, she wouldn't go any faster.

She went so slow across the bridge each plank cracked separately. Old Daise would have made that bridge sing like a band.

Free cussed. ''We're gonna be late sure as the dickens now.''

''Try sticking her in the behind once with your whip,'' Everett said. There was a sharp look around his nose. ''Tickle her there where she's touchy.''

''Good idea.'' Free jabbed Tip in the buttocks.

Tip hardly noticed. The tender end of the whip bent too easily.

"Stick her in the poopet under the tail there."

Free waited until Tip lifted her tail a little between winders, then quick pricked her.

Tip reared, eengk, kicked back at the cab, just missing it, and then broke into a good steady trot again.

The mud road was full of wriggling buggy tracks. A deep mudhole shone where Big John Engleking's lane came in.

Free let Tip have her head. She could pick out her way the best. From the Shields lane on, the road was higher and drier.

The pink town slowly became a white town. Some of the houses high on Prospect Hill were yellow and brown.

Over the rippling suck of the buggy wheels came the sound of a bell tolling. Free hoped it wasn't the nine o'clock bell. They crested a steep rise. Looking ahead Free saw kids playing on the Christian School grounds. Good. They were plenty on time.

Free drove Tip onto the churchyard next to the school. Other cabs, one black, one white, and one regular buggy, were already parked by the long red church barn.

Free pulled up. "Everett, you stick close to the cab while I put the horse away."

Some boys were standing in the wide entrance to the barn, among them Johnny Engleking and Johnny Westing, Free's second cousins. They drove a cab to school too.

Free unhitched Tip and led her into the barn. Pa said to use any open stall. Free picked one halfway down. He slipped off Tip's bridle, replaced it with her halter, tied her to the feedbox. The stalls had a lot of manure in them and Tip had to stand with her rear end high.

Free joined the other boys standing in the barn entrance.

"Quite a horse you got there," Johnny Engleking said. He stood with his head tipped forward a little like he was ashamed of being related to Free yet felt he had to say something.

"She's a wild bronc," Free said.

"My Fly's faster," Johnny Engleking said, trembling a little.

Free thought the trembling a sign of weakness. Johnny Westing was much better. He always looked cool. Free said to Johnny Westing, "I'm in the fourth grade. What room do I go to?"

"You go to Miss Herman's room. That's where we go too."

"Everett's in the second grade."

"He goes to Miss Goslin's room. C'mon, get your dinner buckets and I'll show you."

Johnny Westing led the way into the cement-block schoolhouse. He first took Everett to Miss Goslin's room, then Free to Miss Herman's room.

Free liked Miss Amelia Herman right away. She had light blue eyes, shy and sharp by turns. Her brown hair was done up with a knot in back. She had dogteeth a little, catching her lip where it was dry. But her smile was wonderful like Ma's.

"Yes," Miss Herman said, "your mother called the principal this morning and told us to expect you. You're joining us a little late in the year, so the only seat I have for you is one at the very back of the room. I hope that will be all right?"

Free nodded. Sitting there would keep the other kids from staring at him. It was against the rules to look around.

There was still plenty of time to play outdoors so they all played King's Base. Johnny Engleking said that since Free was a newcomer he should be It. Free agreed. He wanted to win them over. Right away the other Englekings thought that a good joke. They laughed that they'd put one over on him. The front steps on the south side of the school were King's Base. They all ran like the wind. Free was a fast runner and soon had them all prisoner except Johnny Westing. Johnny Westing really could go. It was like he had a fast fanning mill in his butt. He didn't need to claim King's X, he knew how to dodge and get away. Some kids didn't know that it was no fairs to be crying out King's X all the time. But finally Free outran Johnny Westing from the boy's toilet to the schoolhouse and tagged him with two more steps to go.

The second cousin Englekings soon saw they couldn't shame Free in running games. So they took to ragging Everett. They said Everett was as dumb as a post. All Everett did was smile.

A boy named Cornie Tollhouse began to rag Everett pretty hard. He called Everett names. He spat on him. Cornie had a mean smile with a sharp chin. He wore his overall suspenders so tight his crack could be seen as plain as day.

Free didn't say anything at first. But he kept an eye on what Cornie was doing to Everett.

Just before the school bell rang, Cornie stepped up to Everett and stuck his fist under Everett's chin, hard. "Mmrr! Mmrr! For two cents I'd have you for breakfast."

In a flash Free jumped over and pushed Cornie to one side. "You leave my brother alone."

Cornie fell back a step, surprised. Then he got fierce. He rushed at Free, stuck his fist under Free's chin, hard. "Mmrr. And for one cent I'd have you for breakfast."

Everybody laughed nervous.

Free didn't back an inch. All of a sudden he punched Cornie an awful crack in the belly, so hard Cornie fell doubled to the ground.

Everybody jumped off King's Base to get away from the fight.

Somebody grown-up cleared his throat behind them. "Hrr-rump."

"Principal Holly!" a little girl whispered in shock.

Free turned. A man wearing black patent leather shoes, gray suit with black tie, black hair combed back to hide a bald spot in back, was looking at them. One gold tooth shone in the corner of his lips. "Well now," he said, rubbing his hands together, "what do we have here? Fighting on the Christian School grounds?"

Cornie quick scrambled to his feet. He forgot all about the punch in his belly. He put on a Christian School look.

Principal Holly stepped toward them. He had a stiff right leg and moved like a spider. He stopped in front of Free. "Aren't you the new Alfredson boy?"

"Yes sir."

"And already you've managed to get into a fight?"

"Cornie started it. He teased—"

''Enough! I don't like tattletales.'' Principal Holly next looked at Cornie, his eyes as black as his patent leather shoes. ''And you, you seem to have a gift for getting into trouble too, don't you?''

''But this new kid—''

''Enough. I said I don't like tattletales.'' Principal Holly lifted a gold watch from his vest pocket. Then he smiled. ''Yes. We just have time before the bell.'' Principal Holly grabbed both Free and Cornie by the collar. ''Come, you two culprits, we're going to the basement and put an end to this fighting once and for all." He gave them both a shove up the steps ahead of him. He followed them, swinging his right leg up a step at a time.

Free felt ashamed of himself.

Cornie, Free, then Principal Holly trudged down the hallway. They clattered down some wooden steps into the darkness of the basement. It was like a dungeon until Principal Holly snapped on a light.

Principal Holly picked up a small club, a tie board taken from a pack of shingles, an inch thick and about two feet long. He whacked it into the palm of his hand a couple of times. ''I think this is about the right weight. To make the punishment fit the crime.'' He smiled. ''Now we'll ask Master Tollhouse to bend over that chair there. The one without the back."

Cornie trembled. His eyes were like a scared mouse's."Please don't lick me on my bare behind, Mr. Holly.''

"We won't ask you to drop your pants today."

Cornie bent himself over the chair. He reached back and covered his behind with his palms up. He craned his head around. "You gonna lick the new kid too?"

Principal Holly raised the club over his head. ''Remove your hands.''

Cornie began to bellow even before he got hit. Albert at home always did that. It made Pa let up a little on the spanking.

Principal Holly got madder. ''Remove your hands. Or I shall have to break every bone in them.''

''No.''

Principal Holly let Cornie have it over the hands. Whack! whack!

Cornie couldn't stand it and took his hands away. After a second he couldn't stand it on the tight overalls over his crack either so he put his hands back again.

Whack whack whack! Principal Holly could swing that stick pretty good. He'd have made a first-class rug beater.

''Owwhh! I'm gonna tell my paaa.''

Whack whack whack. ''Eighteen. Nineteen. Twenty.''

Principal Holly let up on the licking. His face was red. ''All right, get up.''

Cornie quit crying and jumped to his feet all at the same time. He hardly looked flushed. ''Now the new kid. I wanna see that.''

''You go right on upstairs. Get! Or it'll be another twenty for you.'' Principal Holly made a jump like a spider toward Cornie.

Cornie skedaddled up the basement steps.

Principal Holly turned toward Free. He didn't appear to be quite as mad as before. "Aren't you a little ashamed of yourself to get into trouble on your very first day at the new school?"

Free decided it'd be no use to explain to this fellow that he had a perfect right to protect his dumb brother Everett. He'd let it be the principal's fault for not knowing any better.

"All right, bend over the chair."

Free lay himself over the chair. Too bad he wasn't wearing winter underwear. He made up his mind he wasn't going to cover his behind with his hands or beller out like Cornie.

Whack. Whack. Whack.

It hurt all right. Especially on the tailbone.

Whack. Whack. Whack.

Boy, it sure was getting hot back there.

Nine. Ten.

Principal Holly paused. "Well, a little Spartan, I see. Not even a whimper. Good. That I like to see. You may get up."

Free pushed himself upright.

Principal Holly shook his head a little. "What are your parents going to say tonight when you tell them about this?"

So this is what it meant to go to the Christian School. He'd been much better off to have kept on going to Garfield No. 2 with that loony teacher who liked to sit on a gravestone and comb her curly black hair.

"Aren't you ashamed of having dishonored your parents?"

Free remembered the horsewhipping he'd once got from Pa by the Horsberg mailbox. That had been awful all right. But now he was bigger and a horsewhipping wouldn't hurt as much. The licking he'd just had, while still warm on his sitter, was already fading away. "No."

"What? You don't honor your father and mother?"

"The heck with my pa and ma when I get a licking for nothing."

Principal Holly was shocked. "Well, I see we shall have to resort to another form of punishment." He grabbed Free by the shoulder and held him like a vise. "Young man, do you know the fifth commandment?"

"Yes."

"Recite it for me."

"Honor thy father and thy mother that thy days may be long upon the land which the Lord thy God giveth thee."

"Well, at least you have a good memory. I want you to write that commandment one hundred times for me. And you're to do it at home, tonight, in the presence of your father and mother. So that you will hereafter never forget to honor your father and mother. And I want those hundred lines handed in to me, personally, upstairs in my room, tomorrow morning before school starts. You hear?"

"Yes."

"All right." Principal Holly let go of him. Then Principal Holly looked at his gold watch. "Past time for the bell. Upstairs you go. Ahead of me. Directly to your room."

Free climbed the stairs. He heard Principal Holly clamber up behind him with his stiff leg.

Miss Herman was standing in the doorway to her room. She gave Free a wide smile as he walked in past her. Her smile caught her dogteeth in a cute way. He was the first one to sit down.

The school bell began to clang in the tower outside. In a minute the kids streamed in. The Engleking cousins for once didn't hold their noses high at him. He was a real hero.

The bell quit ringing. Principal Holly stopped to talk with Miss Herman. As she listened her wide smile slowly closed up. She turned a hurt look over at where Free sat.

Free lowered his head. That darn principal.

The last straggler came in and the door was closed.

Miss Herman led in prayer. They sang the national anthem.

Classes started with Biblical History, with Miss Herman reading a portion from the Good Book. Then came reading and language in strange Christian School textbooks, then arithmetic and penmanship.

Spelling came just before the noon hour recess. The speller they used was much tougher than the one he'd had in Rock No. 4. He only had a few minutes to go over the lesson. Meanwhile Miss Herman started recitation down the third-grade row. Each kid had to stand up to spell out the word. Most kids managed to do all right.

It was the turn of the boy sitting across the aisle from Free. "William Tollhouse, 'believe.' "

The boy was a younger brother of Cornie. He was so shy he began to shake in his seat.

A girl behind William whispered under her hand. "Get to your feet, Wimp. At least try it. It starts with b and then comes e."

"No whispering please, Rena Tollhouse. And no helping."

Wimp shook some more.

"Master Tollhouse?"

At last Wimp got up and stood beside his desk, scared. He started in. "B-e-l . . ."

"Go on." Miss Herman shaped her lips to give him a little hint as to what letter came next. "Yes?"

There was a sound of trickling.

Free looked. For godsakes. Wimp was wetting in his overalls. It was running down his pants leg to the floor.

Miss Herman saw it too. "All right, William, you can sit down. Quiet, everyone." Her blue eyes swung toward Free. "All right, Master Alfredson, since you seem to be so interested in what's going on in the third grade, suppose you spell 'believe' for us."

Free turned red.

"Go on."

Free knew the rule for ie. "B-e-l-i-e-v-e."

Miss Herman studied him for a moment. Her face began to look pleased with him again.

When the fourth grade spelled their words, Free did all right there too. He spelled "revolutionary" and "nostalgia" correctly.

That noon, after they'd finished off their dinner buckets, the boys gathered east of the church barn to play Duck on the Rock. It was a new game for Free. Everybody found himself a stone about the size of a baseball in the ditch between the church and the school, then went over to a post and threw at it. The one whose stone landed closest was made the guard. He took his stone and put it on top of the post. Putting it on the post made it a duck on the rock. The rest of the kids made a line in the grass and threw from behind it at the duck on the rock, trying to knock it off. After one threw at the duck one had to run and get his stone and then run back behind the line before the guard could catch him. If the guard got to close while one was chasing after his stone, one could stand on it and then the guard couldn't tag him. If the duck was knocked off the rock, the guard couldn't catch anybody until he'd placed the duck back on the rock again.

Everett surprised everybody. He was the last to try his throw and he hit it on the first crack. Wow, all the boys said, and they looked at Free's brother with more respect.

Cornie had another brother named Maynard who was in the fifth grade. Maynard was the best one of them. He made a game out of everything. Cornie had to be the guard, of course, and that made Maynard put out all the more. "All right, fellas, let's all dock the rock at the same time. One, two, three, fire!" And they all threw at the duck. It looked like the Revolutionaires firing at the Redcoats on Bunker Hill. Cornie got so mixed up at all the rocks flying around him that he bowed over, putting his head between his knees. This made Maynard laugh all the more, and he led the way to retrieve the rocks. They ran back to the throwing line and they all roared together. "Dock the rock!" And once again they threw at the duck on the rock.

Just when they were having the best time, yelping, running back and forth like happy pups, Principal Holly rang the bell.

Going home that night was a sad time. There were all those lines Free had to write yet that night. Free made Everett promise to let him tell about it first.

The minute Free was done with his chores, he hurried to the toolshed. He'd thought of an invention that might help him.

He got a piece of baling wire and bent it into a shape that would fit his fingers as well as hold two pencils at the same time. When he made a practice run at writing on a smooth clean board, the baling wire invention wouldn't hold its shape. Too soft. He had to find something stiffer.

He rummaged through an old pail of odds and ends under the workbench. At last he came upon a broken door spring. That was better. It was stiff at the same time that it was springy. He bent it into the shape he wanted and tried writing the lines on the board again. It worked.

Instead of going to the barn to play cob war with Everett and Albert, he went to the house instead. Pa was sitting in his swivel chair with his feet up on the reservoir of the stove, sipping coffee, smoking his pipe. Pa was almost asleep. Ma was getting supper ready on the cabinet counter.

Free went about it quietly. He got a wide tablet with lined sheets. He sat at the table by the light of the south window. The fifth commandment was too long to fit into one line, so he had to open up his invention to make it write every other line. He wrote one word and found he had to bend his invention a little more to make the two rows of writing fit the first and third lines.

He worked away at it. After some ten double lines he noticed that his invention worked a little like a two-row cultivator in a cornfield. One could always tell when a two-row was at work and not a one-row. Principal Holly would spot the trick right away.

He turned the invention over in his hand. If a fellow was to bend the spring a little every other line or so, first parting the two pencils a little, then closing them a little, and then leaving them as they were to begin with, it would be hard to spot that the lines hadn't been written one at a time. Sure. It would be like a pitcher mixing up his pitches, drop, upshoot, knuckle ball.

"What are you doing there, son?"

Free jumped. He looked up.

Pa was staring at the invention as he put his pipe away in his bib pocket. "What've you made there?"

Free tried to shield the invention in such a way that it wouldn't look like he was hiding it. "Nothing. Just some schoolwork."

Ma looked up from where she was slicing potatoes. "Is the Christian School that hard that you've got homework?"

Free saw Everett looking slyly at him. Everett was playing with Albert and the baby on the floor by the sink.

Pa leaned over for a closer look. "What is that thing you got there? Two pencils in it."

"I'm just trying something out, Pa."

Ma stepped over, hands white with flour up to her wrists. She looked over Free's shoulder at the tablet. "Honor thy father and thy mother. . . . Boy, are you writing lines of some kind?"

This was awful.

"Boy?"

When Ma went after a fellow in her sweet severe way a fellow didn't have a chance. It was best to knuckle under and confess.

"Son?" Pa demanded next.

"I guess it is."

"A punishment?"

Free wondered if he should tell them that he didn't deserve either the licking or the lines. He decided not to. They'd take the part of the principal every time.

Everett spoke up from the middle of the city he was building. "Cornie was teasing me, and spitting in my face, and so then Free stuck up for me and hit Cornie in the belly. Then the principal came and grabbed Free and Cornie by the collar and hauled them into the basement and licked them. We could hear Cornie bellering from where we stood outside. But not Free."

"What?" Pa cried, standing up.

"Did you ever hear the like?" Ma cried, sitting down.

"All that on your first day of school there?" Pa cried.

"Free, I'm ashamed of you," Ma cried.

Free threw Everett a look of thanks.

Pa pointed at the tablet. "How many must you write?"

"I have to write the fifth commandment one hundred times."

"But why that commandment?"

"Because I'd said the heck with my pa and ma if I was to get a licking for nothing."

Pa stared at him. "Oho. Now a light goes up. All right, young fellow, just for that I'm adding another hundred lines on top of the principal's. And you're also going to hand them in so the principal will know we're backing him up one hundred percent."

"You mean, I got to write two hundred in all now?"

"Yep. And give me that invention." Pa snatched it away from Free. "You're going to write those lines one at a time with one pencil. Tonight yet. Before you go to bed. Even if it takes all night."

"But, Pa, I wasn't even guilty. You heard what Everett said."

"I don't care. The principal must've had a reason."

Ma said, "Besides, son, when someone strikes thee on the cheek, thou must learn to turn the other cheek."

Free almost let go with a snort. He'd turned two cheeks. And Principal Holly had promptly struck both of them.

Pa next picked up the tablet and tore off the sheet with the lines Free had writeen so far. "It's cheating to use a double-row rig like that. Start over from scratch with one pencil."

Free muttered, "Trouble with you people is, you believe the other guy before you believe your very own child."

"What!" Pa cried.

"Boy," Ma said, "a good Christian first tries to see if maybe his neighbor isn't right. To begin with. And only after he's made sure that his neighbor isn't right, then he considers whether or not he himself might be right. That way, when you finally do decide you're right, the Lord will be on your side."

"Then the Cornies will always be spitting on us," Free said.

"No," Ma said. "Because after we've made sure that we're truly in the right, then we pursue the enemy with the sword of truth."

"Suppose our enemy kills us first?"

"Listen, boy." Ma was turning hard like Pa. "How many licks did Principal Holly give you?"

"Ten."

"Consider yourself fortunate then that we don't give you ten more of those too, besides the extra hundred lines you got."

If he could have chosen between the licks and the lines, he'd have chosen the licks. Licks only took a minute. But it looked like he was going to have to do the two hundred lines no matter what, so he'd better shut up before he made it any worse for himself.

Sighing, picking up a single pencil, he started a fresh page.

He managed to write thirty-seven lines before milking. Later while Pa and the kids were washing up at the sink, he pinched in another thirteen lines. The minute Albert said the last amen at supper, Free pushed his plate aside and went at it again. Gradually the count mounted. Sixty lines. Seventy lines. The more he wrote the more his hand began to tremble and his penmanship to break up. Older people sure knew what punishment to dole out to make little children suffer.

He set goals for himself. When he got to eighty he'd have himself a drink of fresh soft water. When he got to ninety he'd ask Ma if he couldn't play her favorite record, "Beautiful Ohio," on the Edison phonograph.

When he finally hit the hundredth line, he had a question to ask. "Pa, if I'd gone straight to you on coming home tonight and told you what happened today, would you have added your one hundred lines anyway?"

"You've got the principal's share done?"

"Yes."

Pa puffed on his pipe a couple of times. "Wal, son, I still think it's a good idee for you to write that hundred more. Parents have got to go along with the teachers or you have revolution."

Doggone. Pa'd almost let him off. "Can I do your hundred tomorrow night though?"

Pa puffed some more on his pipe. "Naw, you better do 'em yet tonight. Tomorrow night I might change my mind and that wouldn't be right."

Doggone again. Sighing, Free started in on the second hundred honor-thy-father-and-thy-mothers.

Ma did the dishes. When she got to the pans, she found that the milk had burned onto the bottom of one of them and she had to scrape it off with a paring knife. The scratching sound was so piercing Free had to cover his ears. Ma was bound and determined to make each pot and pan lick clean. After a while the scratching was like a hot needle in his ear, all the way into his brain.

Free finally couldn't stand it any longer. He jumped up. "Ma, if I'm going to write all my lines tonight, you've got to cut out scraping that pan. It's driving me crazy."

Pa said, "Yeh, wife, it's been getting into me too."

Ma paused. A soft look came over her face. "All right. I can let this pan soak overnight." And she filled the pan with sudsy dishwater and set it on the back of the stove.

Ma went to bed at ten-thirty. By then Free had reached one hundred and sixty lines.

Pa continued to sit up with him. Pa smoked his pipe, feet up on the reservoir of the stove. The clocked ticked slow.

Free liked it that Pa kept him company. Pa was beginning to have a lot of gray hair. Where the light caught it over the top, it was as white as moonlight. Someday Pa would look exactly like Abe Lincoln. He already was as tall.

Finally at eleven-thirty, fingers aching like they might be an old man's, Free finished.

"Good boy," Pa said. "Now to bed. You've got the gaff and that I like to see."

The next day, the moment he arrived on the schoolyard, Free went straight to the principal's room and handed in all two hundred lines.

Principal Holly checked the numbering of the lines, then stared at Free. "But I only assigned you one hundred lines, young man."

Free looked him straight in the eye. "Pa assigned the second hundred and said I had to turn them in too."

Principal Holly's eyes opened very black. "Well now, isn't that just splendid. Parents like that make teaching a pleasure."

That day school went pretty good. Physiology was like watching Pa butcher a hog. In geography he drew a map of North and South America from memory so accurate Miss Herman pinned it up above the blackboard as an example for all three grades to look at.

The Christian reader and the American history book he'd never seen before. There was a Christian message at the end of each chapter but if one skipped the messages the books were interesting. The two books were brand-new and looked so nice Free asked Miss Herman if he could take them home with him.

Miss Herman had another gentle wolf smile for him. "Ah, you're one of those who doesn't mind doing a little homework, eh?"

"No, it's just that I thought I'd like to read in 'em a little. From the beginning. Which I missed because I didn't go to school here until now."

She gave him a puzzled look. "Well, all right. But take good care of them."

Free loved the battles of the Revolutionary War. He'd studied them before, but it was fun to read about them again. And there were two stories in the Christian reader that made him wish Pa and Ma were rich so he could travel to foreign lands. One story told about Nestor, who lived in a stone house high on a hill. The etching at the beginning of the Nestor story showed a wise old man looking out to sea wondering if his ships would come in. The other story told about a fight to the death between a knight of the Crusades and a Saracen. They were both on horseback and they fought it out on the plains below Damascus. The knight won, but just barely.

The next morning Miss Herman saw him come in carrying the two books wrapped in a copy of *The Bonnie Review*. "Did you manage to get a couple of chapters read?" she asked with a bright smile.

"I finished them."

"You mean, the whole book? Both of them?"

"Yes, Teacher."

Her eyes narrowed. Her smile became fond.

When his report card came out at the end of the month, Free was sure he'd have a

"Poor" in deportment. But to his surprise Miss Herman had given him a "Fair."

Ma didn't like that "Fair." But Pa said it was all right. Any boy with some grit and gaff to him was bound to do things now and then that the old hens wouldn't like.

Free ✤ 32

THE NEXT SUMMER was a great one. Gramma and the new grampa and Sherm came to live with them for a month. Gramma and the new grampa, Garland Stanhorse, slept in the guest room over the parlor. Sherm slept with Free in one bed in the boy's room, while Everett and Albert slept in the other bed across the carpet.

The new grampa came because he was an expert painter. Pa wanted him instead of a stranger to paint the rusty house. And Gramma came because she wanted to enjoy her grandchildren before it was too late.

Grampa Stanhorse turned out to be a jokey man. He had a nose like a sweet potato, and when he pulled your leg his mouth wouldn't smile at all but his nose would. When he wasn't painting he was dressed up like a domeny in a black suit and a heavy gold watch chain. He always had the exact correct time and could always tell when the moon and the sun were a couple of seconds off. When he was painting he wore roomy white coveralls and a painter's white cap. He was an expert too with ladders and how to set them so he could even paint up in the peak of the gable. He was so slick with the way he dipped his brush into the paint and flished it on that hardly any paint fell on the ground. In the evenings he sometimes asked Pa to play the Edison phonograph. When a record was finished he'd say, "Majestic!" and fumble with his watch chain, and roll his brown eyes, while his big nose quivered. Gramma loved him very much and would start laughing already at his jokes even before he got the first word out. His best joke was about his own name, Stanhorse. He said his pa once had a horse so well-trained that on his milk route all he had to do to make it stand on a certain spot until he got back was to say, "Stand, horse!" and the horse would stand.

Gramma couldn't get over how much Free had grown since she'd last seen him. "We're going to have to tie a stone on your head."

"Yeh," Pa said, "and the worst is, try and keep him in shoes and clothes. It's a good thing he's hard on 'em or we'd have the attic full of things he'd outgrow."

Sherm helped Free get his chores done quick so they'd have more time to play. Sherm even asked Pa if there wasn't something he could do for him, so as to stay on the good side of him. Pa gave him a couple of cows to milk.

They played farming. Sherm always did things like it was a story.

First they cleared spaces in the grove for their two houses. They used fallen branches to mark off the rooms, and little boards from the junkpile for doors and windows. They made lines in the dirt to show where the tables and chairs and beds were. They got some twine and strung up a telephone line between their two houses, using the tree trunks for telephone poles. They invented themselves each a telephone in Pa's toolshed and hooked them onto their lines. The phones worked the very first time, though they had to talk loud over it like Gramma always did.

Next they cleared spaces for their barns. That was easier. With the outbuildings they didn't have to be so neat. For pigs they used the curved staves of a herring tub. For cows they used the staves of a salt barrel. For horses they cut themselves good stout willow branches. And for harnesses they used braided twine.

Pa overheard them talking at breakfast about how maybe they could play they were cultivating corn by marching up and down the corn rows with their stick horses.

''Say, you kids, while you're busy marching up and down doing nothing, how about watching out for cockleburs for me? I don't seem to get them all with my cultivator no matter how I set the shovels.''

Work for Pa during their own free time?

''There won't be that many,'' Pa said. ''Just here and there one.''

Gramma cleared her throat. ''Look at those lips, hanging all the way down to the third button. My, my.''

Ma had to smile. ''Those lips are better than bibs, the way they hang down so far.''

Grampa Stanhorse knew how they felt. He smiled at Pa. ''Alfred, why don't you give a prize for the one who picks the most cockleburs.''

''Wal,'' Pa said, slow, ''just so the prize don't come too high.''

''A double-dip ice-cream cone next Saturday night.''

''All right,'' Pa said, ''but I want to see results.''

''You mean, we got to show you all we pick?'' Free wondered.

''That's all right,'' Sherm said. ''We'll manage. We'll get us each a gunnysack, sling it over our shoulder, and stuff 'em in there."

''Now you're talking,'' Pa said.

They went at it. Each took a corn row like Pa did with his cultivator. They watched carefully under the arching green leaves. It was like walking down rows and rows of parlor ferns. All they could see of each other was their heads moving along.

That noon Free had thirty-one cockleburs and Sherm twenty-eight.

Pa was amazed. ''That's fifty-nine my cultivator missed.''

They made the rounds through Pa's two cornfields for the rest of the week. By Saturday evening when they finished, they'd pulled up four hundred and twenty-two cockleburs, exactly two hundred eleven each.

Pa had to laugh at supper table. ''Boys, boys, you've given me a wonderful conundrum. What am I going to do with your tie?''

''Flip a coin,'' Sherm said.

''Fooey,'' Gramma said. ''that's gambling.''

''But it's all right though if we pull straws?'' Sherm asked, shrewd.

Gramma threw up her hands to God. ''Now you're being the wise snot-nose again.''

''Calm, calm,'' Grampa Stanhorse said. ''I have a suggestion.''

''Fire away,'' Pa said, still happy that all his cockleburs had been picked.

''I have two bits, Alfred,'' Grampa Stanhorse said, selecting a quarter from some loose change in his vest pocket, "and if you have two bits, we can let them buy a quart of ice cream in town tonight and divide it between them."

"Done," Pa said.

Sherm took his jackknife along to town that night and he cut the paper carton of Hello ice cream in half. Using the little wooden spoons that came with it, they had themselves a great treat. They sat on the front steps of Highmire's Hardware as they licked away. All the kids uptown that night watched them, jealous.

Next Free and Sherm played they were married and had children. When they were in the privacy of their own homes, they'd talk and gossip with their imaginary wives, and scold their children, though loud enough of course so the other one could hear it; otherwise it was for nothing. Sometimes they took the part of their wives and children, changing their voices for each one. Free's wife's name was Fredrika, because he was kind of thinking of Uncle Great John's daughter, who might ride along with him to school next fall. Sherm's wife's name was Frances Simmons, because he used to play with her during the time when her mother Ada was divorced from that comical Barry Simmons. Barry and Ada Simmons were now remarried.

Sherm said to his Frances at his supper table, "You know, wife, it's time we had another kid. I always wanted six."

His wife Frances said, "Well, I haven't been too tired lately."

"Good. Then when we go to bed we'll do it." Sherm kind of looked over at where Free was having supper in his house to see if maybe Free didn't think he should play the same thing.

Free wondered how Sherm was going to make a baby with a pretend wife. It might be as tough to do as making a centaur. He watched out of the corner of his eye while he ate pretend potatoes with his wife Fredrika.

Pretty soon Sherm read out of his pretend Bible, prayed to God, and then, because he wanted something out of his wife, a favor in bed, he helped her wash dishes. He jollied her a little, hugging her around her waist, goosing her too, and sneaking kisses up around her cheek. Frances didn't seem to fight back too hard.

Free decided to do the same thing with his Fredrika.

Sherm threw out the dishwater for his wife Frances and then led her to his dirt bed. He played they undressed, blew out the night lamp, and then crept under the covers.

Free was puzzled as to what one did next under the covers. He kept looking over at Sherm.

Sherm happened to glance over at where Free was in his pretend bed. "Hey. You ain't supposed to be able to watch me."

Free made a quick motion with his hand at their twine telephone line to hint that they couldn't really talk across like that, it was a mile from Sherm's place to his, that if he was going to tell him something he should call him up.

Sherm understood. With a sigh he got out of bed, saying, "I'll be back in a minute, wife," and then went over to his phone and called Free up.

Free heard his phone ringing two shorts and a long. He got up and answered it. "Hello?"

"Say there, my short-peckered friend, quit peeking at me and my wife."

"Well, I don't know how to make babies."

"Where did you get your other kids then?"

"I dunno," Free said.

"Well, you can be sure the stork didn't bring them."

"Is it like with stallions?"

"It sure is, bud."

"Well," Free said, "I guess I won't have any more kids."

Sherm happened to look through the leaves of the trees and saw where the sun was. "Hey, it's time for dinner. We better scramble or we'll miss eating again like we did at the other house."

A couple of days later, Grampa Stanhorse announced at supper that he was done painting. Then they all marched outdoors to have a look—Pa, Ma, Gramma, the kids—and there she was, a brand-new white house to live in. At last it was respectable to say they lived on that Hamilton quarter three and a half miles east of Bonnie.

Pa drove Grampa Stanhorse, Gramma, and Sherm to the depot, where they caught the Cannonball for Gramma's town.

Ada 33

WHEN ADA AWOKE she found her face beaded over with sweat. Another hot July day. She stirred her legs and found she was already tired. She rolled over on her side, only to be reminded of that new weight in her belly. Come cornpicking time there'd be a fifth mouth to feed.

She could hear Alfred lighting the kerosene stove on the front proch and setting on the coffee pot. Summers they tried not to use the range in the kitchen.

One thing made her feel good though. The house outside was painted a beautiful white and the floors inside were varnished a luminous gold. Once more they'd fixed up a landlord's shack into a country palace. With the children trained to take their footwear off on the porch, and all of them having fairly neat habits, it was worthwhile being alive after all.

There was something the matter with the coming child. It felt heavy on one side. At first she'd thought it was only a side ache, which she sometimes got when she worked too fast. But as her belly swelled the feeling gradually became more and more pronounced.

She got out of bed slowly and she dressed slowly. If she could remain calm and composed from the start, she'd be all right for the rest of the day. She wouldn't sweat so much either. She hated feeling sweaty, especially on the insides of her legs.

By the time she got to the kitchen, Alfred and Free had already gone out into the warm dawn, Alfred to feed the stock and the boy to get the cows.

She decided to make a cool breakfast that morning: hard-boiled eggs from yesterday, sliced cold ham, bread and butter, skim milk from the cooler. She took her time setting the table.

The sticky flypaper hanging over the table began to gyrate. Looking, she saw that the curtain in the south window had begun to ripple a little. Good. A person could at least breathe when there was some wind.

She called Everett, Albert, and Jonathan, and had them washed up by breakfast time.

Everybody ate slowly that morning.

Not much was said until Alfred announced after the thanks that Free had better help him get up the last couple of loads of alfalfa hay that morning.

Free immediately had a black look. "All that chaff in my neck always."

"I know how you hate that, son. I hate it too. But, it's got to be done. With you driving the horses, and tromping down the load, I can get it up in four loads. That'll save me a lot of time."

Free continued to look black. "Shucks."

Alfred gave his nose a pull. "My joints ache like rusty hinges this morning and that means it's bound to rain this weekend. With tomorrow being Sunday, we've specially got to get it in today."

Ada felt sorry for Free. But she decided not to interfere. It was time the boy learned one had to work hard to survive in this world. Besides he was tall and strong and it shouldn't hurt him any.

Alfred got to his feet. "All right, son, let's make hay while the sun shines."

"You always say that," Free said with a shudder.

"None of your high airs now."

Clapping on straw hats, man and boy went out to tackle the day.

Ada smiled down at Everett and Albert and Jonathan. "And what will you boys be doing today?"

"Can we stay in the house today, Ma?"

"What? When we've got a whole grove of trees for you to play under? I should say not. Get your straw hats and go. Ftt."

"But it's so hot outside, Ma," Albert said.

"Look. Later on I'll set out a tub of water in the sun, and then this evening you can splash around it to your heart's content."

Grumbling to themselves, the little kids left for the trees.

Ada washed the breakfast dishes. She peeled potatoes for dinner. She made all the beds. She emptied out the boys' chamber pot as well as her own. She dusted the parlor for Sunday. She washed the cream separator tins and milk pails.

She looked at the clock. There was just time to quick feed the chickens before lunch. She got a pail of cracked corn from the bin in the barn. The white chickens nearest her knew right away what she was up to and came shrilling toward her, wings lifted, beaks agape. "Chick chick," she called to the chickens who'd wandered out into the hog pasture. She scattered the corn in a wide circle, going slowly. A white flood of wings engulfed her feet, sometimes surging up under her blue dress.

Finished, she turned the pail over and sat down on it in the middle of the yard.

Her flock had grown over the years. She had around four hundred—two hundred forty layers, a dozen active roosters, and the rest capons.

Egg production had fallen off lately. Her eye moved from comb to comb, critically, on the alert for disease and pest. As long as the combs remained a bright red the chickens were healthy.

A hen near her lifted its wing and pecked at something on the pink flesh under her pinfeathers. The hen did it several times. Lice?

Ada watched the flock narrowly.

There it was again. Another hen lifted a wing to peck at something itching her.

''Dear Lord,'' Ada said aloud. ''I hope I don't have to go through a delousing program again. That powder was guaranteed.''

She fixed her eye on an older hen. Its comb was a sick pink instead of a bright red. Ada leaned over, slowly brought her hands forward, and, willing swiftness into her hands, pounced. She caught the old hen solidly around its breast.

''Yeacckk!'' went the old hen.

''I'm not going to hurt you.'' Ada held the hen well down into her dress between her knees. She ruffled her fingers through the pinfeathers under the wings. And there they were. The moment light appeared, lice scurried for the darkness of the long feathers.

''Fooey!'' Ada brushed the hen out of her lap, then jumped up and brushed off her dress in case some lice had fallen on her.

''How I hate to treat creatures for lice.'' She looked up at the blue heaven. ''I know You have a reason for the things You've put here on earth—but of what earthly good are lice?''

She picked up the pail and tossed it into the feed bin.

''The boys can help me douse 'em Monday."

Around eleven o'clock she got out three washtubs and set them out in the sun on the grass. She cranked up rainwater from the cistern. The cup-and-chain pump splashed water irregularly into the pail. When a round tub was full the rainwater took on the color of pale tea.

Dinner was a torment. Everybody and the water pitcher sweated. There wasn't much talk. Ada asked Free to read a short psalm, instead of from the Pentateuch, where the chapters were long.

Alfred retired for a nap on the sofa in the darkened living room.

The children sailed outside to take advantage of the light breeze moving under the trees.

Ada washed the dishes. The smell of green corn in the milk stage came through the window. When she finished, she stepped as quietly as possible past the sleeping Alfred, and lay down in their dark bedroom.

She fell asleep with sweat running off her forehead. She dreamt she was taking a bath in a tub of dishwater with just her nose sticking out. In a minute she was going to drown. She snutched her nose clear, waking up to find that sweat had run into her nose.

Everybody rested until two o'clock, then gradually house and yard began to stir with activity again. Ada prepared extra food for the next day. The Sabbath was intended to be a day of rest and worship.

They ate an early light supper.

While Alfred and Free milked, Ada laid out fresh underwear for everyone, placing it in a neat row on the cement stoop. She tested the water in the tubs. It was body warm from standing in the sun since eleven. "All right, you kids, you can begin your splashing now."

Everett, Albert, and Jonathan hurried in from the trees, shedding clothes as they ran. They resembled pullets, wings spread, running for the feeding ground. Everett and Albert finished getting off their clothes at about the same time and each jumped into a tub with a scream of delight. Water splashed up over their bellies and faces. Jonathan was last in and he more fell in than jumped in.

Ada got herself a chair, a bar of soap, and a washrag. She caught Jonathan first and pulled him out of the tub. Sitting down, she soaped up his whole body, partly by hand and partly with the washrag. When she began to scrub his face and neck, he resisted the washrag, squirming and squeaking. When she'd finished scrubbing him thoroughly, she lifted him into the tub again and with cupped hands spilled water all over him. He cried with joy.

Albert was next. He too resisted the washrag, hating the accidental soap in the eye, the prying finger in the ear. Ada had a good hold on the back of his long head and held him to it. "Now, now, it isn't all that bad. You'll feel a lot better when it's over. Clean as an angel. Here now, let's rinse you off." She spilled handfuls of water over him too.

Everett was different. He accepted the washrag placidly. And because he did, Ada was gentle with him. He also smelled different. Where the other boys smelled like green corn, Everett smelled like a haycock. She also spilled water over him.

Albert, as naked as a plucked pullet, came legging by and tagged Everett. "You're It."

That woke Everett up and he jumped out of the tub and began chasing Albert around the house.

Alfred and Free came walking up from the barn carrying the milk just then. Alfred laughed at the sight of his pink sons running naked around the white house on the green grass, and when he got to the stoop he set down his two milk cans to watch a moment.

"Can I quick take a bath too, Pa?" Free asked. "I can feed the calves later."

"Sure, go ahead and wash out your canyon, son."

Free shed his clothes on the spot and ran for the near tub. Two jumps and he was in with a big splash. "Yow."

Ada grabbed him. "First a little suds, boy." He laughed in her hands. In a moment he was too slippery with soap to hold. He managed to duck out from under her prying washrag. "You're getting to be too big for these nature-boy baths." She threw handfuls of water over him too. He cried in pleasure.

Everett came by and gave Free a whack on the butty. "You're It."
"No fair," Free cried. Then he leaped out of the tub, drops of water flying like silver beebees, and took out after Albert.
Albert shrieked, curved around Ada, and headed for the privy.
"No fair," Free shouted. "You ain't allowed to lock yourself in there. Unless you really got to do number two."
Albert veered off for the lilac bushes, and, stooping low, squirted through them without a scratch. He yelled in one long continuous sweet scream of joy.
Free dodged around the lilacs and once more took out after Albert.
In a moment they came flying around the other side of the house, chest first, little pintles flipping back and forth, bare feet barely touching earth. Their bare arms and necks were dark with summer, the rest of them pearl white.
Free caught Albert just as they reached the front gate.
Alfred smiled a wide smile at his flying sons. "By golly, they run a little like my champ brother Abbott did."
Ada loved them with a thick smile. Just bathed, and shouting happily for the sheer joy of just playing, how could they be otherwise but pure in heart? "Oh to be ten again and as free as the wind."
The sound of a motor came to Ada. That would be the three Hopkins boys heading for town. On Saturday nights they paraded into town like all the other boys of the valley did. In a moment they came over the last little hill and cruised by in their black roadster. All three stared at the flying naked boys.
"I wonder what they were thinking," Alfred said with a laugh.
"Yes," Ada said, "we'll probably be the scandal of Bonnie tonight."
"Oh, they don't gossip much. They only think it to themselves."
"Well," Ada said, "if the Supreme Court calls us next week, why, we'll just have to say that at that age little boys running around like that, full of joy, are innocent of any sin."
"Unless'n one of them was a daughter."
"I wonder at that age."
Alfred fell silent.
"Once I might have thought it wrong, innocent puppies sporting in the evening sun, but now that I've seen a little of life, I've changed my mind. I can't see how God can object."
Alfred watched Free sail by; still said nothing.
The unborn baby kicked in her belly. Ada thought: "Why, it's as if he's jealous of them." Then she sighed. "I'm so used to having boys I don't even think anymore it might be a girl."
Alfred picked up the milk cans and began separating.
Later, after the children had gone to bed, first Ada, then Alfred, took their baths in what was left of the sun-warmed water. Just enough light came up off the grass for them to see themselves by.
"A bank's come up in the northwest there," Ada observed.

"The way my rusty joints ached this morning, I told you it was working up to something. And with the wind in that quarter for three days, southeast, it's just got to bust loose sometime."

Alfred offered to towel her back, but she declined it. "Tonight I'm just going to let the warm air dry me off."

A vast clap of thunder awoke her. She sat up in bed with such a start that even the baby in her stiffened, straightening out its legs in fright.

"Alfred! There's a storm."

"Nrrm." Alfred rolled over and pulled a pillow over his head.

Ada got up and lighted the night lamp. It was just midnight on the clock. She moved through the house in her white nightgown. Just as she entered the kitchen lightning dazzled down west of the grove. Thunder cracked instantly after, as if coming out of the depths of eternity. The lightning lit up the whole countryside, so that through the north window she caught a glimpse of a low roll of clouds rushing toward their farmstead. That decided her. Still carrying the night lamp, she climbed the stairs. "C'mon, you kids. It looks like a wild one coming up. Hurry. We may have to go down into the cellar."

"Cyclone?" Free asked from his bed.

"It's hanging awful low out there, boy." Ada went over and shook the others awake. "Hurry now, you kids."

All four tumbled out of bed. They had slept naked and the yellow lamplight made their skins glow like fresh milk.

"Better slip on your shirt and overalls at least."

Numbly they hustled themselves into their clothes.

It became very still outside. Ada didn't like it. Old pioneers often talked about how stillness usually preceded terrible summer storms. She felt the start of tremors in her legs. "Hurry, now."

They stumbled down the stairs, Ada following with the lamp. Once in the kitchen they looked around for a spot to lie down in.

"Why don't you lay down on the cellar door out on the porch? Then should the house start going, you can quick flip down the cellar."

The four disappeared into the dark of the enclosed porch.

Ada set the lamp on the table.

A few huge drops hit the roof; then stopped.

Through the window, in the quick moment of lightning, she caught yet another glimpse of the sky. My God. The clouds were almost level with the treetops. And wild? They looked like great whirling horsetails.

"Alfred!" she called as she ran toward their bedroom. "Alfred! now you for sure've got to get up."

Without opening his eyes, Alfred asked, "Which way is the storm coming from?"

"The northwest."

"No cyclone then." He turned and nuzzled his nose into his pillow again.

"Alfred, you get out of that bed! You hear? I don't think I'm called upon to handle this storm alone.'' She gave him a shake. She thought: ''Dear Lord, but his thighs are hard.''

''Free can help you hold down the house.''

Just then rain and wind hit the roof. It was as if a whole lake had been dropped on the roof.

Alfred sat up out of his sheets. ''Gotske!'' He swung his lank legs out of bed. ''Okay. I'm up. I'll be right there.''

''Thank God.''

The noise of the storm was fearful. The whole house shuddered. Windows on the north and west sides rattled, almost broke.

Ada's heart beat like a hummingbird's. ''It's going to squash us, Alfred!'' Still carrying the night light, she ran through the kitchen out to the enclosed proch. ''Get in the cellar, you kids!''

Alfred loomed up beside her, barefoot and just in his overalls. "Wait. I think . . ." He listened. "It's just a straight hard wind. With a lot of water in it. It'll be over in a minute."

''You mean the whole storm?''

''No, the wind. Afterwards it'll just trickle all night long. Become a soaker.''

''How would you know that?''

''Shh. Wait. Listen, now. Calm.''

Then the wind let up with a snap. The window panes fell silent. The sides of the house quit shuddering. And the hard rain let up, became a gentle pittering on the porch roof.

Ada held her belly with one hand while she held the night lamp with the other. All their faces looked like bland moons in the dark of the porch. ''I don't understand how you knew what God's intentions were. Because I thought surely there was going to be a cyclone.''

''But, wife, not out of the northwest corner.''

''You mean, not even God can order a cyclone to come out of the northwest?''

''Nature wouldn't let Him.''

"Alfred, that'd be blasphemy if it weren't that nature is already part of God."

''Whatever it is, it just ain't possible for a cyclone to come out of the northwest. Now, you kids, back to bed with you.''

Ada took her time going back to bed.

She was thankful for having such a sure-minded husband in their wilderness of a world. She remembered how her father Alfred always got so excited when a storm came up. There certainly was a world of difference between the two Alfreds. Had her father been more like her husband, she too might have been calmer when storms descended upon them.

Free ❦ 34

THEY WERE OUT on the cement stoop after supper and Pa was giving Free a haircut. Pa had already lowered the ears of the other boys. The apron pinned around Free's shoulders and the stoop were littered with blond hair. Pa was handy with the clippers and could give haircuts almost as good as the barber in town.

The phone rang inside: two shorts and a long.

Free tried to turn his head a little to catch from the tone of Ma's voice who it might be calling. He hoped company was coming. It had been pretty dead around home lately.

"Hold your head still." Pa gave Free a push with his hip.

Free stilled. Sometimes when Pa stood too close Free could feel where Pa hung soft inside his overalls. It always made Free feel nervous.

In a moment Ma came out on the stoop. "That was Hal Haber."

"What did he want?" Pa pulled down Free's ear as he clipped neatly over and around it.

"They asked if we'd be home tonight. They'd like to drop around."

Free held his ear up as high as he could to keep Pa from hurting him. Free asked around the corner of Pa's hand, "Are their kids coming too?"

"The whole family is coming," Ma said.

"Hooray, the Habers are coming!" In his joy Free jerked his ear free of Pa's grip. "Ow!" His jerk so startled Pa that Pa hadn't been able to bite through quick enough with the clipper's teeth and Free's blond hair had got wedged between them.

Pa pushed him back down on the chair. "Now look what you've done." Pa worked the clippers several times but couldn't quite make it cut through. "Your hair is as tough as piano wire. I'll have to get a screwdriver and open up the teeth, I guess. Ada, get me that screwdriver there on the window ledge by the separator."

Free held his head very carefully up and sideways toward Pa. It hurt like the dickens when one's hair got hooked in the clippers.

The kids came running up. "Are the Hal Habers really coming?"

"They sure are," Free said sideways toward them.

"Goody. Now we can have some real fun."

Hal Haber's oldest boy, Floris, was born the same month Free was. Floris drove a cab to school too and they'd become friends while feeding their horses at noon. The Habers had a lot of other kids besides—Benjamin, Willard, and Hubert. Hal Haber was also the uncle of the Catherine Haber that Free had gone to school with at Rock No. 3.

Pa finally got Free's hair untangled from the clippers. "Now you sit still on your one-spot there until I'm done, you hear?" Pa took Free by the shoulders and gave him a good shake.

The kids ran in circles around on the grass. "The Habers are coming, the Habers are coming!"

Even Pa finally had to smile. "I wish I could get that worked up over company coming."

"Now, Alfred, Hal is smart and makes good company," Ma said.

"Sometimes a little lazy though," Pa said.

"For a grown man, yes, he does like that children's game a little too much." Ma couldn't help but stick it into Pa a little about baseball, though she did it with a smile.

Pa humphed. Then he stood back to give the haircut the once-over. ''Okay, that's good enough.'' Pa unpinned the apron from Free's shoulders. Lifting it, he gave the apron a shake. Tufts of light hair floated off across the green grass. Then Pa swept off the stoop and put away the chair and clippers.

Free joined his brothers frolicking on the grass. It was summertime and it would stay light a long time yet and afterwards Ma would give everybody a treat. A great time was coming.

Every now and then Free and the kids would look east to see if the company was coming past the Hopkinses over the three little hills.

But the Habers took their time coming.

Finally Free ran up to the kitchen window and called inside. "Ma, are you sure they said they were coming tonight?"

Ma smiled from inside the dusky kitchen. ''Son, you know how the Habers are. Always a little late. Even to church.''

Free saw where the sun was setting through the grove. ''If they don't hurry up it'll soon be too dark to play ball.''

''You'll just have to be patient a little while longer, boy.''

Once there was a rising plume of dust on the other side of the first of the three little hills. That had to be the Habers. But when the car came into view it only turned out to be Mr. Bester.

Pa called over from his seat on the stoop. ''Free, while we're waiting, why don't you run down and shut off the mill for me a minute. The tank's full. I can see the rising edge of the water from here.''

''Shucks.''

''Git, now. You can easy be back before they come.''

Free shuffled off to do it. He went down the hog pasture to the windmill slowly; came back in a hard run.

Still no company. Free cussed. And his brothers got tired of waiting and went back to the grove to play. Free sat down beside Pa on the stoop.

Slanting sunlight raised blue shadows behind the trees and the buildings. The evening began to cool pleasantly.

''We're going to have clear weather for a while,'' Pa mused.

Free jumped up. ''There they come.''

An old Dodge came whining over the first of the three little hills. It gained speed going down each one and lost it going back up. Rolling over the last culvert opposite the hog pasture, the old Dodge geared down, and curved onto their yard.

Pa got to his feet too. The kids came running up.

A big dark-haired man with a smile as wide as a currycomb manhandled the car around on the yard. Besides him sat his thick wife Hattie also smiling wide. The back seat was full of heads, all staring at the stoop where Pa and Free were standing. The dog barked something fierce at the turning front wheels and almost got run over. Mr. Haber pulled up on the handbrake and the old Dodge stopped exactly even with the gate.

Ma came out of the kitchen. She stood smiling in the doorway, a kind openhearted angel in an open house.

Hal and Hattie Haber got out of the car on opposite sides. Hal said, ''Hi. How's every little thing with the Alfredsons?''

Pa smiled. ''Very well, thank you.''

Hattie shook her head, at the same time that she spotted Ma's big stomach. ''Sorry we're late. But I forgot that I hadn't tightened the jars. I canned some tomatoes today.''

''Oh, that's all right,'' Ma said. ''I was busy myself until just now.''

The two sets of kids stared at each other.

Hal had to smile at his kids still sitting in the back of the car. ''For goodness sakes, you kids, the way you act a man'd almost think you'd never seen each other before.''

''It's like raising a crop of bull calves,'' Pa said. ''All of 'em scared of each other until they've butted heads a couple of times.''

''Yeh,'' Hal laughed. ''All right, c'mon, we're here now. Out.''

That broke the ice, and out the Haber kids tumbled. In a few minutes both sets of kids were playing work-up baseball in the hog pasture. Floris was a hard runner and a good-looking kid. The next Haber boy, Benjamin, could be stubborn, but that night he was full of smiles. He knew how to be the boss of Everett. Willard and Hubert were like Albert and Jonathan, pups who didn't know what to do next in baseball until someone told them.

Pa got out some folding chairs and the older people sat out on the grass watching the kids run in the sunset.

The kids played hard, hitting and running and sliding in the grass, until they were covered with dirt.

When it got dark, Ma called them all inside to have a glass of sage milk, sweetened, and a slice of chocolate-raisin cake.

Free loved milk treated with sage leaves, especially the smell of it as one sipped it. But it was his luck that as Ma filled his glass some of the slag floating on the boiling milk slipped into his glass. Slag he didn't like, so he made a sieve of his teeth to keep the slag out and managed to suck up the warm milk anyway. What a spicy sting there was in sage milk. It always made him think of young colts, just born, running in circles around their mothers.

Pa and Ma and Hal and Hattie talked at a prettty good clip about the new dissension in church. It had to do with the thousand-year reign of Jesus Christ that was to come after Judgment Day. Pa thought the whole thing ridiculous. Who cared about that future so far off when they were all still back here on the farm along the Little Rock River near Bonnie? Pa said the real truth was the Coopers and the Ardmans just didn't like the Englekings. Hal smiled and said it was a case of six of one and a half dozen of the other. Besides, if the church was going to split up, it was going to be tough on both halves financially, since they'd have to pay the salaries of two domenys instead of one. Hattie didn't think much of the Englekings, and said so. Hattie didn't mention, of course, that Fat Sherm Engleking had once asked her to marry him, and that Hattie had turned him down, so that now the two families, the

Hal Haber family and the Fat Sherm family, hated each other right down to the last kid. Ma sat under the light of the pulldown lamp frowning at what she was hearing. All that talk was close to gossip, which she abhorred.

Pa said, "There's something about that Big John branch of the Engleking family that grinds one all right. Who at the same time can't leave it alone. You know how they're always having to stand up in front of church confessing they've transgressed the Seventh again. It's in them like the brown-spot rot."

"Alfred," Ma warned.

"Wal, it's the truth, wife," Pa said. "I'm not saying it's in your branch of the family, you know." Then Pa added with a laugh, "Though sometimes I wish a little of it was."

Hattie looked like they'd been talking about God's hinder parts. She rolled her eyes.

Hal rolled his dark eyes too and smiled his big currycomb smile.

A quiet smile came over Ma's face. "Alfred, I wonder, couldn't we first see what good we can say of people before we harp on their bad points?"

Pa held the thought a minute. Then he stroked his face with his big hand. "You're right, wife. All pots have ears."

The younger pots, though, were sound asleep. The warm milk and the talk about church affairs worked like a double sleeping pill. They lay stretched out everywhere on the kitchen floor.

Free and Floris were still awake. Free had been telling Floris about a new pencil box Uncle Kon and Aunt Karen had given him for school. Floris wanted to see it. Free gave Floris a look to go quietly so as not to wake the kids, and then they crept up the stairs in the dark. Free lit the night lamp and got out the pencil box from the commode.

They sat down on Free's bed to look at it. The pencil box had three parts. The little sliding door on top opened onto four brand-new yellow pencils. The side panel opened onto a space for two erasers. Last there was the part which, if pushed, opened the whole thing into two halves, showing a ruler, colors, paper clips, and two indelible pencils.

"Wowie," Floris said softly. He took the pencil box from Free and began to play with it, opening and shutting it, taking out the colors one by one to see if they were real colors and not just wax ones.

Free got nervous over the way Floris was handling his prize pencil box. He looked around for something to draw Floris's attention away from it.

Floris began to squirm. "Say, you got a pisspot up here?"

Free thought of the pot under the boys' bed; finally decided Floris had better go downstairs and outdoors. That way he'd also get Floris away from his new pencil box.

Floris threw the pencil box on the bed and jumped to his feet. "Oe, I gotta go so bad I can taste it." He grabbed for the front of his pants. "Say, how about letting me go out through the window there?"

"We never pee out of the window in our family."

"Not in an emergency?" Floris opened his pants and grabbed his tool and held on tight. "Open the window, or I'll let fly in here." His tool swelled up from the pressure inside it.

"Go down and do it outside in the grass."

"I can't go down this way. I can't let go of it. It's already right to the end. Your mother would faint."

"Okay." Free checked the south window. The bottom half of it was open but the screen was held in place by four catches on the outside. No use trying to go through that. Free next examined the little square window at the foot of the boys' bed. It faced east just past the edge of the roof of the kitchen. It had no screen. If he could open it Floris could use that. Free got down on his knees, pulled at the two spring bolts, then heaved up. Luckily the window wasn't stuck and it came up. The spring bolts caught in the next slot.

"Ahh," Floris groaned. He immediately knelt against the low sill and let fly through the opening. The darkness below was cut by lamplight shining out of the kitchen window.

By that time Free had to go too. So he knelt beside Floris and let fly in turn. It was against the rules, yes. But when one had to go one had to go. Besides, it was kind of fun.

"Say, Free, have you ever played with it until you got so hot inside you fainted?"

"No."

"Well, Brut Weatherly, our hired man, showed me once."

"How?"

"We were still in bed one morning waiting for Pa to call us, and we'd both woke up with a hard-on, and Brut asked me if I'd ever squirted juice yet and I said no. He was surprised and then he took hold of mine and played with it and showed me how."

Free watched his stream sail out and down toward the shaft of light shining out of the kitchen window.

"Brut said once you start playing with yourself, you can't quit. And it gets even worse, he said, when you start doing it with girls. It gets to be like a disease, he said."

Free stared down at their two streams. Sometimes their streams accidentally crossed and then both streams broke up into a little shower of shattered drops. Every once in a while too the south wind carried some of the shattered drops against the lighted kitchen window. To make sure that his stream didn't hit the kitchen window Free aimed his more out over the grass.

Floris laughed when he saw how some of the drops splattered on the kitchen window. He aimed his directly for it.

Before Free could warn him not to, the grown-ups downstairs began to talk loud. Free could hear them clearly.

Hal said, "Gollies, look. Ain't that rain on the window?"

"Naw," Pa said, after a second, "it can't be raining. It was as clear as a crystal out when we came in a little while ago."

"Well, but just look there. It's raining at a pretty good clip." Hal pushed his chair back with a loud scraping noise and stood up. ''Hattie, wake up the kids. We've got five miles of dirt road to travel on and that ain't fun when it gets wet.''

Ma was watching the window too. ''It seems to be raining in spurts though. Like it's only going to be a little bit of a dust settler.''

''We're not taking any chances,'' Hal said. ''To, wife, get a hurry on. I hate fighting muddy roads with a carful of squealing kids.''

Everybody downstairs got up and began waking up the kids.

''Hey,'' Hattie said, ''Where's Floris?''

''Yes,'' Ma said, ''and where's Free?''

Floris and Free had by then reached the end of their streams, and quit. They buttoned up.

''You know what,'' Floris said, ''Pa and Ma are going home because of us.''

''Yeh,'' Free said.

Pa's voice came booming up the stairs. ''Free?''

''Yes, Pa.''

''Come on down. Floris too. Company's going home.''

The minute all the Habers got outside, with Pa carrying a lighted lantern, Hal looked up at the sky. ''Gollies, look. There's stars out. That sure was a quick shower. A dust settler, just like Ada said.''

Pa looked around at all the horizons. "Why, you can't even tell where that bank went."

Ma said, "If you want to, you can come back in the house and finish that sage milk. There's a whole pitcherful left.''

''Naw,'' Hal said, ruffling the hairs of his sleepy kids as they climbed past him into the rear of the car, ''we'll just keep on going here. Now that we've got all these young colts corralled we better take advantage of it."

As soon as Hal was sure all his family was aboard, he cranked his car, climbed in, and let out the brake. ''Bye,'' he called out. Then with a wave of the hand they were off.

Ma called after them, ''Say hello to everybody that knows us.''

Free ❦ 35

THERE WAS SOMETHING going on in the house the kids weren't supposed to know about. That morning at breakfast Pa said it was too bad it was Saturday because now they had the doggone kids underfoot. Also, right after breakfast, Ma went back to bed. She had a look on her face like she was going to prophesy.

Free and his three brothers played cob war in the haymow. They got cobs out of the horse mangers. They filled their pockets with them, front and back, and then started out. The best cobs to fire were the heavy wet ones, with horse slobber still on them. The four brothers crept through the dark mow, and when they came upon the enemy they roared like lions and threw their cobs like King David throwing javelins.

Around ten o'clock Dr. Fairlamb drove onto the yard in his Essex. Free barely caught a glimpse of him as he rushed into the house with his black bag.

The kids next played wink. Someone was always It and someone was always Caught, with the rest hiding somewhere. The one who was Caught waited to get a little signal, a wiggling finger, or a real wink from an eye, which Caught could see but not It, and then, when It was looking the other way, Caught escaped and hid.

Around eleven Uncle John drove on the yard in his touring model Ford. He went into the house on the run.

Free wanted to sneak past the lilacs and have a look in Ma's window to see what was going on. But Albert got mad and said he had to play wink with them.

"If you only knew," Free said.

"That Ma's going to have another baby?" Everett said.

"Oh." Free hadn't thought Everett knew about such things yet.

Around noon Uncle John and Pa went to the toolshed. They did some hammering in there and then pretty soon came out carrying a little box about the size of a coaster wagon. They took the box into the house.

Albert complained to Free, "I wish you'd play better. And not always stand there looking out of the calf-pen window."

A little later, Uncle John came out of the house again carrying the little box carefully. Uncle John had a sad face. Uncle John placed the box on the back seat of his touring model Ford and got in and then drove off slow like his car was a hearse.

"Will you please play good?" Albert yanked at Free.

Everett rubbed his belly. "I'm hungry."

Next thing they knew there was Pa in the barn door. He had dark corners in his eyes. He was carrying two little pails. "Here, you kids. I brought you something to eat. Warm sage milk and some dried-beef sandwiches."

Little Jonathan had his stocking cap half turned around on his head. "Is Ma sick?"

"Yes, son. Now here, you kids can each sit on a milking stool and eat. I can't let you in the house quite now."

Everett held his head sideways a little. "Are we supposed to pray before we eat in the cow barn here?"

Pa thought a moment. "Na, you don't really need to." Pa thought some more. He had trouble thinking he was so sad. "You ain't sitting around a table, for one thing."

Albert said, "I guess we're just mostly sitting around a cow pie." Pa didn't like jokes just then. "You kids get busy and eat now, hear?" Pa straightened out Jonathan's cap. Then Pa left in a rush.

The kids had to chaw their way through the stiff dried-beef.

Pa didn't know how to make a sandwich. He was too stingy with the butter, just like he always was with the sugar.

Around two o'clock Dr. Fairlamb came out of the house. He set his black bag in his Essex like he was mad at God. He drove off with a jerk, digging a little hole in the ground with the left rear wheel.

Around three o'clock Pa came out to the barn again and said now they could come into the house. But they had to play quiet or else.

The kids galloped into the house. They were cold and ringed around the kitchen stove and held their hands over the warm lids. Free put in some more cobs.

Pretty soon Ma called from the bedroom. "Free?"

"Yes, Ma?"

"Come here a minute."

Free quick spit-combed his hair in place, and then went through the living room into her bedroom. "Yes, Ma."

Ma was lying back against two pillows. Her face hung sagged under her ears like she'd been laughing too much. Her eyes were like broken bits of ice. "Boy, a sad thing happened here today."

Free waited. He stood at the foot of her bed.

"Come closer, boy. By me here."

Free stepped up.

Ma placed her hand on his wrist. Ma liked to touch people, especially children. She couldn't walk past one of her children at the table but what she had to place a loving hand on his shoulder. She stroked Free's arm several times. "I had hoped the good Lord would at last bless us with a daughter. But it seems that in His infinite wisdom He saw fit to visit us with a sorrow instead."

Free like her stroking hand.

"Yes, boy, a baby boy was born to us today. But he died shortly after he arrived. The Lord giveth, the Lord taketh away, blessed be the name of the Lord."

Free thought: "The baby was in that box Uncle John carried off." Free said aloud. "Did you bury our brother next to Grampa?"

Ma was surprised. "You catch on quick, I see. Yes, boy, we did."

"Why did he die, Ma?"

"His head was too big. He had what is known as a waterhead." Ma had trouble moving even the littlest bit in bed. She talked into herself. "Oh, I don't think I'm ever going to get over this one."

Jonathan called from the kitchen. "Ma, can I come too?"

Ma tried to raise herself up in bed. But she couldn't make it. She whispered, "Free, will you tell him to shush, please?"

Free leaned around and let out a fair-sized roar toward the kitchen. "Jonathan, you shut up out there. We're still busy talking."

"Not so rough always, Free," Ma whispered. "He's your own dear brother." Ma was getting weaker. "Can you help around the house a little today, boy? We can't afford a maid this time. And Pa's about to begin picking corn, so he's up to his ears in his own work."

"Yes, Ma."

"You might begin by giving your brothers each a spoon of Gramma's Harlem oil. Yourself included."

"Oh, Ma, that awful stuff tastes terrible."

"Give yourselves each a cracker with it. With butter on."

''You can still taste that oil afters for hours.''

''But Harlem oil is good for you. For your bones and lungs.'' Ma could hardly whisper. ''And while you're at it, bring me some too.''

Free got the brown bottle and silver spoon and handed them over.

Ma sat up a couple of inches and poured herself a spoonful and sipped it up. She took it like she liked it. "Now you take one."

"Now?"

"Yes."

Free had in mind taking only a drop while going through the living room before he got to where his brothers were in the kitchen. But now he had to take a whole spoonful. He poured some of the yellow stuff into the spoon. He looked down at it cross-eyed. Then bllawth, he threw it into the back of his throat and quick swallowed. "Uck." Then he ran to the kitchen for a cracker.

Ma had to laugh behind him.

Free fed his brothers their oil plus a cracker with butter.

He wondered what to do next. His eye fell on the Bible where it lay on the sewing machine. Reading the Bible alone by himself he got more out of it than when he read it in family worship. With Ma and Pa listening, he was too busy trying to read it correct.

"Ma," he called to her, "may I read in the Bible a while?"

"Why sure, boy," Ma said surprised. "Just be careful with it."

Free sat by the light of the south window. Paging around, he came across the story of King David and his son Absalom. Free hadn't understood it before. That crazy Absalom had killed his brother Amnon because Amnon had made their sister Tamar lie down with him. Free wondered if that was fair. Amnon had only been sick. A brother shouldn't go around killing his brother because he was only sick. Free's brother Jonathan was sometimes sick too, but that didn't mean one had a right to kill him.

Free read the whole story again, seven chapters long. And his eyes were at last opened as to what the story was about. That Amnon had made his sister Tamar lie down with him so he could make a baby with her. No wonder Absalom was mad. The way Domeny talked about Absalom, a man would think Absalom was a bad guy. But Absalom had his side of it too. He shouldn't have killed all those other brothers, though; just that Amnon, that bastard. And no wonder King David wept over Absalom: "O my son Absalom! My son, my son Absalom! Would God I had died for thee, O Absalom, my son, my son!"

Ma called from the bedroom. "It's so quiet out there. What are you kids doing?"

"I'm reading about King David," Free said. "And the kids are playing city behind the stove."

"That's good."

Free said, "Do you want something, Ma?"

"Yes, boy, I do. Would you play a record for me?"

"Sure, Ma. Which one?"

" 'Beautiful Ohio.' I need something to cheer me up."

Free put the record on and carefully placed the diamond-point needle in the first groove. The Edison phonograph shone amber in the dusky room. The diamond needle began to make a light noise and then a woman began to sing. She sang like Ma:

"Seeming in a paradise of love divine,
Dreaming of a pair of eyes that looked in mine,
Beautiful Ohio, in dreams again I see
Visions of what used to be."

Tears came into Free's eyes. As he looked out of the window the tears made the three little hills past the Hopkins lane tremble.

When the record was finished, Ma said, "Thanks, boy." It was so beautiful she was crying too. "And now I'll take a little nap."

"Yes, Ma."

Free went back to the kitchen, closing the door quietly behind him. He picked up the Bible and sat down by the window again.

He had trouble getting the story of Absalom out of his mind. What he really couldn't understand was how that Amnon could have such a sudden change of heart about his sister Tamar. First Amnon couldn't do without her; then he hated her exceedingly. So that the hatred wherewith he had hated her was greater than the love wherewith he had loved her. What could've got into him so suddenly to make him flipflop so?

After a while Free went to the barn to curry Tip.

Pa went to town for Ma. When he returned, he had a crate of groceries and a new wooden box. The kids, their work done, followed Pa into the house. There was going to be something good after all that day, despite all they'd gone through. Pa first put the groceries where they belonged, in the pantry and the kitchen cabinet. Then he picked up the new wooden box and set it on some old newspapers on the table. He got a hammer and pried the top laths off. He took out some excelsior and then lifted out a shiny new nickel lamp.

"Wow," the kids cried.

Pa poured some gas into the bottom of the lamp and then pumped in some air. Pa tied on two little gray sacks near the top and put a match to them. The sacks turned into little shrunken bags of hanging white ash. Then Pa opened a little petcock and the lamp began to hiss. "Back up, you kids, in case she explodes." Pa struck another match on his pants leg and held it to the two little bags of shrunken white ash, and, blick! the kitchen was full of bright light, so sharp the mirror over the sink became a second light.

"Hey," the kids said.

"What's going on out there?" Ma called from her bed.

Pa gave the kids a wink, then picked up the sharp sizzing light and carried it into the bedroom, the kids following.

"Oh, my," Ma cried, putting up a hand to her eyes, "can this be Judgment Day?"

"I thought I'd brighten things up a little."

"A gas mantle lamp. It isn't dangerous, is it?"

"Naw. Not if you're careful."

Ma looked past her hand at it. "It's got a hook on top too I see, so we can hang it from the ceiling."

"The clear thing," Pa said.

Ma touched Pa's hairy wrist. "How thoughtful of you, Alfred."

Free liked the lamp too. It would make for easier reading.

That fall Free had to pick up two riders on the way to school, first Hankie Barth and then later Fredrika Engleking.

Hankie Barth was in the primary grade with Albert and had only a little ways to walk to the cab. The first couple of times Mr. Arlo Barth took Hankie by the hand to the road. Hankie had dark brown hair, brown eyes like a pup, skin even a little brown, and good red lips. His ma, who Pa said had a screw missing, dressed Hankie in Old Country pantaloons. Hankie looked a sight. His pa asked Free to protect Hankie at school so the kids wouldn't tease him too much. Hankie was as scared as a mouse of everybody.

Fredrika had a long ways to walk up her wriggling lane. But Fredrika didn't need anybody to come with her. She was an Engleking. She had two silver pigtails and robin-egg eyes and shiny pink skin. She generally wore a red dress and could run like a new colt.

Free, Everett, Albert, Hankie, and Fredrika got along good the first month. No mean words to speak of. Fredrika was a little bossy with Free at first, but Free knew what to do about Fredrika. He just stared at her until she looked down. When she saw she couldn't boss Free around, she went after Everett. But Everett looked at her sideways and then up above her head to the left. So she decided Everett was too dumb to be worth bossing. She next went after Albert. Albert slowly got dark in the face. She didn't know what to do about black faces and finally went after Hankie Barth. She kept telling him to blow his nose. "For catsake, you don't have to let your snot drip all over me." If anybody had married her right then and there he would've had a wife worse than Aunt Karen.

Free finally had to tell Fredrika to lay off. "If you must pick on someone younger than you, go pick on one of your cats at home."

Fredrika pouted all day.

It got cold for a couple of days and Pa got Free three bricks to keep their feet warm. Free put the bricks in the oven at night and then just before they pulled out in the morning carried them into the cab each wrapped in a gunnysack. One heated brick was for the driver up front and the other two were for Everett and Albert in back. When Hankie came aboard, Albert shared his brick with him. But when they picked up Fredrika she right away kicked Everett off his brick and wouldn't share it with him. My, she was a boss. She was worse even than that Alvina Horsberg back at Rock No. 3.

That Friday after Thanksgiving there was no school. Pa and Ma made plans to go see Gramma and Grampa Stanhorse, taking Everett and Jonathan along. Ma was still pretty weak, but she thought she could bear up now that they lived some eleven miles closer to Gramma.

Ma called up Tante Engleking and asked if Free and Albert could play with Fredrika while they were away. Tante said that was fine. So Pa brought Free and Albert over first before heading for Gramma.

It turned out to be a warm day and Tante said the children should play outside.

Fredrika first showed them a hog skeleton with a baby pig skeleton still inside it. The hog skeleton reminded Free of the time he'd visited her place with Ma and he'd spotted those hogs by the milkshed eating another hog. It was when Fredrika's pa was dying of the hiccups. Free felt sick to his stomach remembering.

Fredrika said, "You look like something the cat just dragged in."

Fredrika next took them to the barn. They decided to play farmer and his wife. They found an old broom and cleaned out an empty bin for their living room. They decided to make a horse stall their bedroom with the manger their bed. They told Albert he was their hired man and that at night he had to sleep upstairs in the guest room, which was the haymow. The guest room was awful big, yes, but it was the best they could do for now.

Next Fredrika decided it was such a great day they should have a family picnic on the river beach. Hired man Albert could take off from work and come along. They got some bread and wieners from Tante, and some matches, and then took the stepping stones across the river to the better beach. They built a little fire. The wieners tasted good except for sand getting into the bread. Albert was cute the way he sat on his heels and held his willow stick with a wiener on it in the fire.

"It's enough to make the cat laugh, he's so comical," Fredrika said.

When they were full to the brim, Fredrika rubbed her stomach. "I feel so funny. Like I've had too much catnip." She laughed silly.

Free said, "You probably only need a little catnap."

Fredrika pushed her lips way out, like she was thinking hard like a wife. "We've been married long enough now so people won't talk when we have our baby nine months from now."

"You mean it's time to go to our bed?"

"If you wanna."

"Sure."

They covered up the fire with sand like they promised Tante. Then they skipped across the stepping stones and ran to the barn.

Albert followed them with his slow fat legs.

In the barn, Fredrika ordered Albert to bed up in the big guest room. Then she pretended she went to the privy before going to bed, and ordered Free to do the same.

Free was happy to take orders for once.

First Fredrika climbed into their horse manger bed, then Free. The manger narrowed toward the bottom and they lay cozy together on some old smelly hay.

"You got a bump there," Fredrika said.

"Sure."

"Is it always there?"

"Just sometimes."

"Well, I was going to say. I don't have one there."

Free's belly began to feel like he had a hornet in it. He didn't know where to put his hands. They were in the way no matter how he lay beside her.

"Well, I guess we better start making our baby then." Fredrika reached under her dress and pulled her pants down. "You get ready too."

Free got his tool out. He got on top of her.

"Not there, you silly. I pee out of there." Fredrika pushed him off and then rolled over on her belly. "You put the seed in my number two."

Free wondered if he should tell Fredrika what Maynard Tollhouse had once told him. Maynard said he'd seen Fredrika and that Jeanette Westing in the basement of school do something once. Maynard was hiding down there, when all of a sudden Fredrika and Jeanette came tripping down the steps, looking for a place to hide too. They looked around to all sides, saw no one, then sure they were alone, they all of a sudden hugged each other and began bumping their bellies hard together. So Fredrika had to know that men put the seed in number one. Free said, "The man don't put the seed in the behind, you silly."

"Yes, he does. The other place is too small for the baby to come out of."

Lying on his side, Free's eye caught movement above them. He looked up. Gotske. There was fat Albert leaning over a crosspiece and looking down at them.

Fredrika rolled back and forth. "Don't you want to make a baby?"

"You better look up towards heaven. Somebody is watching us."

"You mean God is watching us?"

"No, our hired man."

Fredrika pulled up her pants and whipped around like a flash. She stared up at Albert. She was going to get mad, but then after a minute started to laugh. "Oh, shucks, he don't know what he's looking at."

"He saw me have mine out and you with your poopet showing."

Fredrika glanced down at the fly of Free's overalls. "That thing of yours sure got soft all of a sudden."

Free drew his seat back and buttoned up.

Fredrika smiled to herself. "You sure got a little one yet. My brothers've got great big ones."

"How would you know?"

"I catch them doing number one around the corner of the barn sometimes when I'm getting eggs."

"Have you got dominoes in the house?"

"For catsake, why? Sure we do."

"Let's go play that a while."

"All right. But on the porch. Ma'll say the weather's too nice for us to play inside."

"C'mon, Albert," Free said, "you better come with. We can't leave you sleeping up there in the guest room."

Free ❦ 36

THE NEXT SPRING Pa hired Dick Buwulf to help him. Dick was a fifteen-year-old neighbor boy living a mile to the north. Dick owned a .22 Winchester rifle. When Dick walked over from his father's place he sometimes hunted in the connecting pastures.

One Sunday evening, as Free was getting the cows, he saw Dick coming with his rifle. Just as Dick came up to the line fence, Dick spotted something. A jackrabbit. It was slowly zigzagging in long even bounds across last year's broken-down cornfield. Dick set himself; took careful aim; fired. The rabbit doubled up at the top of its next jump, and hit the ground nose first. Dead.

Dick ejected the shell, climbed over the line fence, and quietly walked over and picked up the jack. It was a big fellow.

Free finished rounding up the milk cows and waited for Dick to catch up. "Boy, I wish I could have a gun like that."

Dick had the quiet smile of a domeny who'd just hit a home run at a church picnic. "You're too young for a gun yet." Dick slung the jack over his shoulder. Several drops of pink blood showed on the jack's white underbelly.

"Well, maybe Pa'll let me have one early."

"Your dad maybe would. But not your ma."

"Is it hard to hit a jack on the run?"

"You bet." Dick pushed back his tan cap, letting loose some blond hair. "You got to guess in what direction he's going to jump next. And you aim the gun ahead of him so he meets the bullet when it gets there."

"You mean like a train and a car meeting at a railroad crossing at the same time?"

"That's it."

They followed the cows home up the wriggling trail. The grass had just turned a soft tender green. One of the cows spotted the first dandelion of the year and swung her head over and cropped it. Free and Dick had to watch out for fresh cow droppings.

Free admired the shining blue .22 rifle.

"Better not get your mind too set on having one," Dick warned.

While they were milking, Free had to ask Pa. Could he have a rifle like Dick Buwulf someday? When he grew up a little?

Pa finished his cow and got up and dropped his stool in the straw. "I should say not." Pa emptied his milk into the five-gallon milk can. "One gun on the place is enough."

"Shucks," Free said. "I'd sure like to have a gun someday. Look at all the meat I could bring home. Like Dick did tonight. That jack is sure going to taste good for supper."

Dick said nothing from behind his cow.

The next night, after Free finished his chores, he went to the old Gore junkpile in back of the grove. He was hoping to find a couple of little wheels with which to make a toy car. Just as he pushed through some dead ragweeds, he spotted gray movement. He froze. A bunny rabbit. It was partly hidden under an old rusty pail. It had heard him coming and it had scrunched itself up into a tight ball hoping he wouldn't spot it.

There was something he could shoot for Ma's table. And show that Dick Buwulf that he could hunt too. It wasn't as big as Dick's rabbit, but it still was a rabbit.

Free carefully backed out of the tall ragweeds. He made sure the rabbit stayed sittting.

The thing to do was to get Pa's .410. Somehow. It was on the enclosed porch.

Free looked toward the west forty. Pa and Dick were still busy getting the corn in, the one planting and the other dragging. Free next looked to see where the kids were. He found them busy under the trees. Good. The only problem would be Ma.

Pretending he was going to start milking by himself, in case Ma should happen to be watching out of the kitchen window, Free lolled over to the rack by the gate and took down the milk pails. Then he pretended to have forgotten something on the enclosed porch and went in to get it.

There was the gun hanging on its nail over the separator. The blue barrel was shiny with oil. The red-brown stock shone. Free dared it. He reached up and took the gun down. He broke the .410 open and looked inside the barrel. Empty. That's right. Pa kept the shells on top of Ma's cabinet.

He closed the gun and lay it on the milk table under the window. Again pretending to be getting something important, in case Ma was curious as to why he was in the house, he lolled into the kitchen. She'd started the supper and it had just begun to steam on the stove. Ma herself wasn't around; probably in back of the house somewhere. Good. Quickly he climbed up on a chair and reached for the box of shells. The box was almost full. Only two red shells were missing. If he took one more it would be easy to spot that three shells were missing. Those two empty spaces already looked like two front teeth missing. He thought so hard he sweat. He remembered he had a nickel hidden upstairs under the bed. He'd put it there in case of an emergency. Well, here was the emergency. Tomorrow at noon he'd go to Highmire's Hardware and buy one shell and as soon as he got the chance he'd slip it into the place of the one he'd take now. He took a shell from the center of the box. He stuffed it into his pocket, closed the box and put it back, and got down quietly. He slipped out to the porch again, picked up the gun, and hurried out to the junkpile.

He broke the .410 open again and slipped the shell in. The brass part of the shell shone brighter than the primer. As he closed the gun carefully, it clicked shut with a snap.

He carried the gun with the barrel pointing well ahead of his feet. He began to feel like a hunter. He was careful to avoid twigs. He pushed through the tall ragweeds again, careful to take the same path as before. Dusk was coming on fast and he had some trouble making out the rabbit under its pail house. Finally though, leaning forward, he made it out. It had heard him coming again and had once more scrunched itself up into as small a ball as possible. It appeared to be shivering a little.

Free lifted the gun to his shoulder; aimed, catching the bead at the end of the barrel in the V near his nose; pulled the trigger.

Nothing happened. Not even a click.

He lowered the gun and looked at it. Then he smiled. He'd forgotten to cock it.

He thumbed back the hammer; aimed again. The bead first wavered on the head of the bunny; then on its fluff of a tail; then back on its head. When he got it centered on its heart, he pulled the trigger.

Bam. The stock of the .410 gave him a good whack on the cheekbone.

He looked across at the west forty. Pa and Dick were still sailing back and forth across the field. They hadn't heard the gun go off. Good.

The blast of bird shot had completely knocked the rabbit over. Free set his gun down and went over and knelt down beside the rabbit. Blood was oozing out of its gray fur in a dozen places. There was the sweet smell of the rabbit's insides.

One of the rabbit's rear legs pumped a few times. Then, dead.

He picked it up by its ears. It wasn't nearly as heavy as Dick's jackrabbit. But it would still make a good meal.

It then hit him he couldn't give the rabbit to Ma for her to fix for supper. He'd have to explain how he got it. For one thing it'd be full of birdshot, so he couldn't say he'd killed it with a slingshot. Too bad he hadn't thought of that ahead of time. Darn. That was sure dumb.

Slowly he put the rabbit back in its nest of leaves under the old rusty pail. As he did so one of the rabbit's eyes opened a second; then, like a wink, closed. The rabbit was telling him he'd killed it for nothing. It hadn't been doing him any harm. It had been just going along minding its own business, eating alfalfa leaves, when all of a sudden like a bolt of lightning it was full of birdshot.

Free began to feel sick to his stomach.

He broke the .410 open and the empty shell jumped out. There was a whiff of fired powder. He looked inside the barrel. It was speckled with bits of powder and dirt. He'd better clean that out or Pa would know someone had shot with it.

He went back to the toolshed. He found a piece of wire and a corner of a sack and cleaned out the barrel. He worked at it until the inside of the barrel shone.

By the time he brought the gun back to its nail above the cream separator he had the shakes. But he got it back safely. Neither Ma nor the kids had seen him. All he had to do now was to buy one shell from Highmire's Hardware and put it in the box on the cabinet and no one would know.

He had trouble sleeping that night. In dream he kept seeing a rabbit winking at him with one eye, and then, flop, dying. The winking eye slowly got bigger, and more fierce and mocking with each dream, until it became a nightmare, with him yelling a strangled cry. Once Dick, his new bed partner, had to shake him out of it, he was caught so deep and stiff in the nightmare.

In the morning he woke up all tired out. The day ahead was going to be rough. He had to pull off the stunt just right or he was really going to get it.

It was a beautiful morning all the way to school. The city of Bonnie lay like a pink candy castle on the far misty slope. The eight o'clock high school bell rang as sweet as the chimes of a mantel clock.

School was fine all morning long. Teacher didn't ask him any questions. All the while the emergency nickel burned in his pocket.

At noon recess he threw Tip her dozen ears of corn and then hurried to town. He ran past Grampa Alfredson's old house, past the Shatswell house, and finally the Corner Cafe. Across the street, behind the fountain on the corner, stood Highmire's Hardware.

Mr. Highmire was in. Free had been afraid he'd be closed for noon.

Free spotted the gun department halfway down the east wall. A dozen shotguns stood gleaming in a gun rack. Stacked below them were boxes of shells. There were different kinds of oil smells in the place, from the floor, from the guns, from the tools.

"Mr. Highmire?"

"Yeh." Mr. Highmire had been lounging against a shiny new black kitchen range. He was a heavy man in tan shirt and trousers. He had a naturally mean mouth, drawn back and down at the corners. He had cold blue eyes. His uncle was the church elder with all those unmarried daughters.

"How much does one shell cost?" Free had his hand in his pocket holding the emergency nickel. The nickel felt wet. "A .410."

"One shell?"

"Yes."

Mr. Highmire went over behind the gun department counter. "What do you want with only one shell, kid?"

"Well, you see . . . uhh." Free couldn't look Mr. Highmire in the eye. "Pa wants to see if his .410 still works before he throws it away. So he told me to buy just one shell to see if it does. No use'n buying a whole box of shells."

"I can't sell you a single shell, kid. If I was to take one shell out of a box I'd have to sell it as a used box and I'd lose money."

"Oh."

Mr. Highmire spat a juicy brown bulls-eye into a cuspidor at his feet. "You say your dad just wants one shell? To see if his .410 still works? Before he throws it away?"

Free couldn't get over how easy he could lie. Lies showed up in his head like mice in an attic. And the way Mr. Highmire was looking at him with those close-set eyes meant Mr. Highmire didn't believe a word of what he said. The best thing to do was to get out of there as fast as possible. Free began to back toward the door.

"Kid?"

Free felt around behind him until he found the door handle. He tried not to look nervous. "I guess I better be going then, Mr. Highmire. I don't have much time at noon recess." And, turning, he escaped. Whew.

But the worst was he hadn't got that shell.

He made it back to school just as the bell rang.

He wasn't on the yard at home more than a minute before he knew that the folks knew. It was in the way Ma was hanging out the wash on the line behind the house.

He hustled into his yard clothes and did the chores extra special good. He worried that he would have to go to bed without supper.

He wasn't too surprised when Pa called him into the house just before milking. It was Pa's pet time for a cup of coffee.

"Wal, son, what's this about a shell for my gun that I'm about to throw away?"

That darn Mr. Highmire. He'd called Pa up and told him. Free tried to look mad but couldn't get his cheeks to do it.

Pa dropped his feet to the floor. "Hah?"

Free weighed the tone of Pa's voice. It didn't sound like he was too mad. Free also checked to see how Ma looked. She didn't look mad either. Free decided to risk it. He told Pa the whole truth.

Pa sipped his coffee. "Why didn't you tell me you felt that way about Dick and his gun? I'd have made him leave it t'home."

"I was scairt to."

"And besides, son, you never shoot a sitting animal like that. 'Tain't fair to it. You always give it a chance to get away."

Free knew he was never going to forget how that poor rabbit winked its eye after it was dead.

"After this, talk to me first before you get into trouble, son."

"Ya, Pa."

Later on, Free grumbled to himself that he could see no harm in him actually having some kind of a little gun. Shucks.

Ma overheard him. "Listen here, boy. You better count your blessings while you can. When Mr. Highmire told your Pa about it over the phone this noon, your Pa was all for driving to town right then and there and giving you a good tromping in front of the whole school." Ma let out a deep sigh. "Yes, this noon I frankly didn't know who to save; you from death or your father from hell."

Wow.

"Boy, boy, what are we going to do with you? We block one hole and out you pop through another."

Free felt quite ashamed.

Pretty soon Ma came over and stroked his hair back from his forehead. "Boy. Boy."

Free ❦ 37

ALLIE WESTING, GOSSIPPING on the phone with Hattie Haber, happened to let slip that she thought a certain neighbor lady of theirs, Matilda of Uncle John, was a pretty careless housekeeper. "Even Ada of Alfred agrees as to that." The Habers were on an eight-party line and one of the eight was Uncle John. As luck would have it that morning, Matilda had heard the Haber ring, three shorts, and had laid aside her dusting rag and rubbernecked in.

That really set the dolls to dancing. Aunt Matilda served Uncle John burnt potatoes that noon, along with giving him a blistering attack on what a witch his sister Ada was.

"That sister of yours tells lies about me. She had the gall to tell your cousin Allie Westing that your wife, yes, the Matilda Westraw you married, is a pretty careless housekeeper. When your sister Ada herself, proud and vain as she is, with her big feet, is pretty careless herself. Especially about where she throws her draining rags. And who is she, this lumpen sister Ada of yours, who married that dumbbell Alfred, a fellow who can't even read or write . . . who is she to hold her head so high on Sundays? When the truth is, it was me who stooped low when I married you, loafer that you are!"

"Loafer?"

"Am I a pretty careless housekeeper?"

"When I'm always first in the field in the spring?" Uncle John yelled back. "And first to get cultivating done in the summer?"

"I askt you, am I a pretty careless housekeeper?"

"No, you ain't. And I'm going to do something about that right now." Uncle John jumped up from his burnt potatoes and called up Ada on the telephone, two shorts and a long.

Ma and Pa had just started eating their noon meal when the phone rang on the wall behind Pa.

"You better see who that is," Ma said.

"Yeh." Pa reached a hand back over his head and took down the receiver. "Yeh?" Pa listened a minute, then looked at Ma. "It's for you. It's your brother John and he's mad about something."

Ma got up with a wondering look. She took the receiver. "John?" She listened a minute too. "What?" She listened some more and slowly turned red. "Why, John, that's not true!" She listened still more and started to turn white. "John, I don't think we should talk like this over the phone. I just heard two receivers go off the hook." She hung on still more. "John, Alfred is not a dumbbell, and I didn't say any such thing about Matilda. It's all a mistake somehow."

Pa sat up very straight. "Who says I'm a dumbbell? That stuck-up John of those trembling Englekings, for godsakes?"

Ma turned real white. "John, that's not so."

John began to talk so loud on his end of the line that Ma had to hold the receiver away from her ear a little and then everybody in the kitchen could hear him. "Are you calling me a liar, Ada?"

Pa stood up. "That's enough of that." With a sure hand he firmly took the receiver from Ma and hung it up on its hook with a good sharp click. "It's not good to fight while you're eating." With a funny smile he led Ma back to her chair and sat her down.

"Well, I can't eat now," Ma said.

Pa himself sat down. "Wal, I can." And Pa calmly picked up his knife and fork and once more went at it.

The kids stared. Uncle John mad at Pa and Ma? They couldn't eat either. When the big grown-ups started to fight the whole world was about to come to an end.

A funny laugh bubbled up out of Ma. "For a minute there, with John roaring at me over the phone, and you exploding behind me, I thought of David, where he says, 'I am ringed about by mine enemies.' "

"It's that darn telephone," Pa said. "It was a clear mistake when that thing was invented. The telephone is the perfect invention for gossips."

"I wonder who started that all now," Ma said to herself.

"Wal, let's postpone talking about it until I've had my nap," Pa said. "Besides, all pots."

"Yes. That's right."

But the telephone call bothered Ma all afternoon and finally, after she'd made lunch for Pa, she called up Matilda to ask where she'd heard all that gossip. Free was on the porch looking for some pitch thread for their baseball and he heard Ma's end of it.

"Matilda, if what you heard is anything like John told me over the phone, I deny it. And if beyond that I've been remiss in anything, I ask you to forgive me. . . . You mean you prefer to believe idle gossip? . . . Matilda, I find this hard to believe . . . . No, I'm not calling you a liar. It's just that there's been some kind of misunderstanding. . . . What? John? You home from the field so soon? . . . John, I don't like it that you interrupt Matilda and me. We were trying to iron out a few wrinkles between us. . . . Yes, I agree it was probably wrong to iron it out over the phone, but I couldn't rest until . . . Ochh!"

Ma jiggled the receiver hook. "John? John?" She listened some more. "Oh dear, he hung up on me." She hung up the receiver.

That evening upon finishing supper, Ma asked Free to read from the Epistle of Paul the Apostle to the Ephesians, Chapter Four, instead of their usual place.

Free read smoothly, though on the alert for the key verse Ma might have in mind. About two-thirds of the way through he spotted it.

"Wherefore, putting away lying, speak every man truth with his neighbor: for we are members of one another. Be ye angry, and sin not: let not the sun go down on your wrath. . . . Let all bitterness, and wrath, and anger, and clamor, and evil-speaking, be put away from you, with all malice: and be ye kind to one another, even as God for Christ's sake hath forgiven you." Free paused.

Ma looked at Free. "Well, boy, why do you think I asked you to read from Ephesians?"

"Verse 26. Let not the sun go down on your wrath."

"Exactly." Ma turned to Pa. "Alfred, right after thanks, we're going over to John's to get this cleared up before the sun sets."

Pa was tired, and hated to agree, but he finally did. "Though the kids don't need to go, do they?"

"Of course they do," Ma said. "I want them to witness this."

They didn't put on their best clothes, just clean overalls. Ma put on a fresh apron. Then they got into the Buick and went. Something serious was about to happen.

As they rolled past the box elders onto Uncle John's yard, Uncle John was just going across the green grass carrying a pail of skim milk. With him was his boy Alfie. Alfie was five years younger than Free and still not much to play with. Uncle John stopped in his tracks and stared at them, looking mad. A pair of pliers gleamed in his plier pocket. Pa pulled up at the front walk.

Ma got out on her side and started walking toward Uncle John. She held out her hand to Uncle John.

Uncle John set the pail of skim milk down. He raised his hand, holding it palm out against her. ''Ade, you can stop right there if you think you can smooth this over with your pious smoochies.''

Ma kept walking, her hand still out in love to him. There was a noise behind Ma, and Uncle John looked past her. Aunt Matilda had come out on the stoop to listen to what might be said.

Ma stopped. But she kept smiling. ''John, we came here tonight after having read Ephesians 4:26.''

''Don't throw the Bible at me,'' Uncle John said, ''because that'll make me even madder.''

''In front of our little children, John?''

Pa got out of the car. ''John, watch out what you say there.''

Uncle John stared at Pa for a minute. ''I declare, if finally this ain't a case of where marriage is thicker than blood.''

''But more than that,'' Ma said, ''it should be a case of where the love of God is thicker than all.'' Ma stood very quiet on the green grass in the middle of the yard. The new green leaves on all the trees in the grove hung shiny and still.

Uncle John studied Ma's remark. The old carbuncle bump on the corner of his neck turned red. His boy Alfie hung onto his hand.

Free sat very still in the car. Maybe the earth was really going to open up in a big crack and the sky fall down.

Albert got tired of waiting to get permission to play with his cousin Alfie. He opened the door on his side and ran toward Alfie and Uncle John. ''Hi.''

''Hi,'' Alfie said, starting to smile. Then Alfie looked up at his father to see if it was all right.

''Hyar!'' Pa roared after Albert. ''You get back in the car.''

Albert stopped in his tracks.

Uncle John's old carbuncle got redder. ''I suppose a boy born to a father who can't read or write is too good for my boy to play with?''

Pa took two steps toward Uncle John.

Free thought: ''Here we go. The world is coming to an end.''

Ma held out both her hands to Uncle John. ''Remember our father.''

Uncle John looked past Ma to where Aunt Matilda stood on the stoop.

Alfie kept looking at Albert. He liked Albert. All of a sudden he couldn't hold it back any longer. ''Say, Pa gave me a whole calf to raise. All my own. You wanna help me feed him some skim milk?''

''Sure.'' Albert again broke into a run toward Alfie.

Pa and Uncle John watched the two little kids come together. The two little kids had big pleased smiles for each other.

'' 'Course,'' Alfie said, ''if the calf dies it'll be my own fault because I didn't take care of him right.''

''Is he a real baby calf?''

''Sure. About this high. And boy, does he like to suck. If you ain't careful he'll suck the pants right off your butt, suspenders and all.''

''My grampa once had a calf that sucked some green dollar bills right out of his pocket.''

"Yeh, they'll suck anything that sticks out. A man dassent take a leak around 'em much."

Albert said, "They'd surely pretty quick know that wasn't milk."

"Ulk, yeh, I suppose they would."

Ma looked at first like she was going to scold the little kids for their dirty barnyard talk. But then, bowing her head, hiding her face, she burst out laughing and let her hands fall to her sides.

Uncle John burst out laughing then too.

And Pa slowly began to smile.

Aunt Matilda came around the side of the Buick. "Yes, out of the mouth of babes and sucklings hast thou ordained strength."

Ma looked around surprised.

Aunt Matilda said, "Yes, I know my Bible too, you know. That stands there in Psalm 8:2."

Albert said, "Let's go." He grabbed hold of the handle of the pail of skim milk.

"Okay." Alfie helped him lift the pail.

Together the two trudged off, carrying the pail between them, inner shoulders down, outer hands raised.

Uncle John said, "I suppose we all better kiss and make up." Uncle John bent down to look under the trees. "I see we'll be able to just get it done before the sun hits the horizon. Ephesians 4:26."

Ada ❦ 38

GOD SURELY TESTED the Alfredsons during the next summer. First, the Northwest Harness Company of Minneapolis, in which the Alfredsons had invested seven hundred fifty dollars, filed bankruptcy papers. Next, a fire destroyed the Lakewood Grocery Store and there went yet another seven hundred fifty dollars they'd invested. Alfred and Ada had earlier thought of using that money, fifteen hundred dollars, as a down payment on a farm, but had been talked into investing it in the harness company and the store instead, where they were told they could expect to double their money in a year's time. Gone was their old dream of someday owning their own place.

To pay their various debts in town, Alfred had to sell his share in Grampa Alfredson's cement-block home in town. So there went even that chance to own a house in town for their old age.

As if to impress upon them how much He abhorred speculation, the Lord God visited the land with a scorching drought all through July and August. Oats just barely went ten bushels to the acre and the corn didn't even form ears. And then, worse yet, in the middle of the awful drought, the Depression of 1922 set in. Nobody had any money to buy things with.

As the land turned drier and drier, and the rising dust turned as ever more ashen gray, the wrinkles around Alfred's eyes became deeper and his hair turned whiter.

Sometimes Alfred said bitter things. The day the cistern ran dry he remarked that now they'd all have to spit in a cup if they wanted a drink.

When the cash rent for pasture and hay land was due, Alfred told Ada she'd better write the landlord a letter to say that they didn't have the money to pay him. "Not even one red cent."

A few days later landlord Horace Hamilton wrote to say that he'd be driving up from Cedar Rapids on business the next week and that he'd drop around to see them to discuss the severe drought. He was certain, he wrote, that something could be worked out. The letter was typed on legal stationery and was important looking. It made Ada and Alfred feel some better. It would be good to talk to him in person. Alfred said he remembered that when Horace was a little boy he was polite, neat, and always had his head in a book of some kind. Karen, who'd lived with the Hamiltons, spoke of him as being the perfect little gentleman.

Dust was blowing out of the southwest the day Horace Hamilton arrived on the yard.

Ada spotted his dusty car through the porch window. She wet a finger and touched her hair in place and quick put on a fresh apron. She paused a moment at the screen door to first have a look at him to see what manner of man he was.

Horace Hamilton got out of the car and stood quietly looking around at the white house, at the red barn and cribs and granary, at the newly painted white garage, at the whole neat yard. He appeared to like what he saw.

Alfred came out of the barn just then.

The two men advanced upon each other and shook hands.

Ada stepped through the screen door. "Hello."

Horace Hamilton looked around. He gave Ada a steady look, brown eyes measuring her. A quiet smile lay on his full lips. "Hello, Mrs. Alfredson." He came toward her. His glove was off and he held out a city hand to her. "My pleasure at last." There was a measured air about him as though he might be more of a judge than a lawyer.

Ada went much by touch. She liked him. "Yes, Mr. Hamilton, and it's good to meet you in person too."

Horace Hamilton wasn't nearly as tall as Alfred, but he was broad-shouldered and well-built. There was a look about his fleshy jowls and pink cheeks as if he might someday be a heavy man. He wore an expensive black suit, shiny black shoes, white shirt with a red tie, glinting gold tie clasp and cuff links. As his smile widened, several gold-capped teeth began to show. "You know, I'd like it if you people would just call me Horace."

"If that's what you wish."

"Your sister Karen always called me Horace."

"Yes, I guess she did," Alfred said.

Horace made another slow survey of the place. A riding veil of dust muted the colors of the buildings. "I must compliment you people. It surely looks good around here despite the drought. A vast improvement over what it used to be."

"Well, we tried our best," Alfred said.

The kids in the barn discovered there was a strange car on the yard. They came piling out. "Is it company for us too, Ma?"

Ada had to laugh. "No, not this time. It's just for the grown-ups."

"Aw, shucks."

Alfred pointed a finger. "Into the barn with you again."

Ada added, "We'll call you when it's time to eat. Where's Free?"

"Up in the haymow. Reading like always."

"All right."

The three kids stared at Horace as though he were from another world.

Ada shook her head at them. "Haven't you kids learned yet it's not polite to stare at strangers? Get. Out of sight with you." Then she said to Horace, "Our oldest is always reading when he gets a chance. He must've snuck a book out with him."

"Oh," Horace said with a lift of brows, "a good sign that."

"You think so?" Alfred said.

Horace nodded. "Yes. Very much so."

"It won't make for him becoming a very good farmer, though."

Horace laughed. "Alfred, you have three more sons, don't you, who might make farmers?"

"That's true."

Ada crossed her arms in pleasure. "Can you stay for dinner? We have our best meal at noon out in the country, you know."

"I'd be happy to. In fact," Horace added with a smile, "I was sort of counting on it. There's nothing like a good country meal."

While Alfred showed Horace the fields, Ada hurried to get that good country meal ready. She decided not to make it too special, because that would only be showing off. She would get out her best silver, but for the rest he was going to have to eat what they usually had at noon: potatoes, sausage, cabbage, beans, rice, canned peaches, and coffee.

It was twelve up when they all came in at the same time, Alfred and Horace, and Free with his younger brothers.

The children behaved like angels all through dinner. Their manners were perfect. They never once spilled on the table cloth.

Horace meanwhile seemed to enjoy the food. He asked for seconds on almost everything.

Ada was also pleased to note that Horace showed quiet respect for their form of family worship at the table. He listened carefully while Free read from Scripture. He bowed his head when Alfred asked the blessing and again when Alfred offered thanks. His smile in appreciation was just right when the children offered their little prayers. For a city lawyer who might have been cynical he showed class.

After dinner, the three littlest went back to the barn to play. Free asked if he could please stay and read in the house instead. Dust got in the pages out there, he said, and it made him shiver. Alfred said he could sit with Mr. Hamilton and himself in the living room, provided he kept still, as children should be seen, not heard.

When Ada stepped into the living room to join the menfolks, she found them comparing notes about the hard times before the turn of the century. Horace sat in their best chair, a black leather Morris near the bay window, and Alfred sat on a hardback chair beside the trembling maidenhair fern. Free lay on a throw rug reading

Tom Sawyer. Their best carpet, the brown and gold one with the sleeping lion in it, lay spread in the center of the room.

Horace told of the time when a grasshopper plague had been so bad that the green devils had eaten up the green onions right into the ground, leaving neat round holes, with the brown papery outer skin of the onion lining the walls of the holes.

"Wal," Alfred said, "at least we've been spared that."

"Did you have any kind of garden at all?" Horace asked Ada.

"Just some early radish and lettuce." Ada sank into her favorite rocker. She rocked herself. One of the blond oak runners creaked like a comfortable cricket. "But our flowers just sort of fuzzed out."

"We even lost some trees in the grove this summer," Alfred said. "In fact, most of the grove has been looking for the dog."

Horace let go with a wry laugh.

Ada had to laugh too.

"Tell you," Alfred went on, "and I'm not saying this to get my rent down, but it is a fact that our wagon wheels rattled so this summer that I twice had to reset the spokes in them and throw them into the tank."

Horace wagged his head in sympathy.

"Look." Alfred ran a finger along the sill under the bay window. He came up with a thick smudge of gray dust. "See that? And I saw Ada dusting that very sill this morning. That's how much has sifted into this house since then." Alfred winced when he gave the gritty dust a pinch between his fingers. "It gets into everything. The milk even."

Horace held up his white fingernails for review. "We'll just have to somehow hope for the best."

"Hope ain't going to help much," Alfred said.

"The Lord must have His reasons," Ada said. "Meanwhile, we'll all have to pray. And have faith that in time He'll see us through."

Alfred allowed himself a grim chuckle. "Faith we've got. At least Ada has." He chuckled again. "Two weeks ago our minister conducted a special prayer service in church to pray for rain. For once we had perfect attendance. Nobody wanted to be left out if some rain was coming." Alfred's grim smile deepened. "But that wife of mine, she went everyone one better."

Horace held still as though waiting for a witness to finish.

"She went to the meeting with an umbrella."

"Alfred," Ada said, "you didn't have to tell him that."

"Wal, at the time I thought it was a pretty good idee. So did our minister. He pointed her out as an example for the rest of us, that she was the only one there who really had true faith in prayer."

Horace nodded. "My mother had such faith."

Free looked up from the book he was reading. "Of course you know the real truth is, God has just plain forsaken us."

Ada, and Alfred and Horace, stared at the boy. Ada asked, "Why do you say that, Free?"

"Well, that special prayer day hasn't even helped us one miserable drop's worth."

Ada said quietly, "Perhaps we've sinned in some way that was grievous to the Lord, and now we're being properly punished for it."

Free's blue eyes opened a little. "Then maybe He's punishing this part of the country because of the way the Kasper Gores ruped us out of five hundred dollars."

Alfred said sharply, "What do you know about that, son?"

"Didn't we pay them something special for vacating these premises? For all their trouble when they really didn't have to move?"

Ada stared. That boy.

Free saw that he'd probably said too much. He turned to his book again, talking low to himself. "When what I wanted was to keep on going to Rock No. 4 and see Larry Grey every day."

Horace shot a look at Alfred. "Do I understand your boy to say that you gave my former renters, the Kasper Gores, five hundred dollars for vacating these premises?"

"Wal, yeh," Alfred said, reddening, and giving Free an angry look, "I guess we did."

"For all what trouble?" Horace pursued.

"Wal, to break their lease with you."

Horace sat straight in solid dignity. "To break their lease with me?" His deep brown eyes rolled as though this was about the worst he'd heard in all his life. "Why, the rascals! When I ordered them to be off the place by March first."

"You did?" Ada gasped.

"Yes."

All three stared at each other.

Free on the floor looked at Horace with amazed blue eyes.

"The dirty sonsabitches!" Alfred cried. "Them lying sneaks."

Horace's face turned dark as if he were about to curse too.

Ada could feel her face turn white. "That they, of all people, our people, Christ's special children, should do such a thing."

Free said, "I told you, Ma. The people around Rock No. 4 were a whole lot better."

Alfred jumped to his feet. "Them goldarn crooks. They ran off with five hundred of my hard-earned dollars. And I mean hard-earned. Because they were pinched-out, belt-tightened, belly-skimped five hundred dollars!"

"Christians," Ada whispered.

Alfred stomped up and down on the gold lion in the brown capet. "My dad always said to me, 'Alfred, never trust them Little Church people. Nor them Big Churchers either for that matter. They come out of a class of people in Europe where their whole life was fixed to squeeze the last possible penny of profit out of their neighbors. It's what the Frisians always felt about the Hollanders and the Norwegians about the Swedes.' And here, by God, we moved closer to town so we could have the privilege of going to church with them more often, sitting next to them hipbone to hipbone—"

"Alfred!" Ada warned.

"By God, now I wisht I had've stayed a Congregationalist. Your dad's church, Horace. You know."

"Alfred, you're swearing now," Ada said. "And you mustn't condemn a whole church because of one family."

"One rotten apple makes the whole barrel rotten."

Horace said, "I'm terribly sorry to learn about this."

Alfred said, "Supposin' we sued?"

Horace shook his head. "On what grounds?"

"Why, on the grounds that the sonsabitches cheated us."

"Fraud, you mean."

"Fraud, rotten fruit, whatever you want to call it; in any case, it's crooked cheating."

"Where are the Gores now?" Horace asked.

"They moved to California."

Horace shook his head some more. "Then we can't get at them. It's difficult to take legal action across state lines."

"You mean, we can't get back that money of ours?"

"I'm afraid not."

"Why, them sly underhanded pharisees." Alfred jumped up and down on the lion with both feet. "Them crooks. By God, if they land up in heaven, I sure as hell don't want to live there in the next life. Even if it turns out God has forgiven them for some reason or other."

Ada looked sadly out of the bay window. Gray dust still came veiling through the trees and darkening the sky. It was midday and inside the house it was almost dark enough to light the lamp.

"I really mean it," Alfred went on. "I'm not going to heaven then."

Horace put his hands together and leaned forward. "Meanwhile, I think we better just cancel the cash rent for the hay land and pasture, as well as my share of two-fifths out of the crops. If you can come up with half the taxes, we'll call it square for this year."

Alfred sat down then, considerably mollified. "Wal, now Horace, that's mighty decent of you."

Free 39

BECAUSE OF THE drought there'd be no threshing that summer, no sweet smell of steam engine, no stuffy aroma of dust riding off an oily separator. Free became so lonesome for the usual threshing time that one day he decided to make a toy rig for himself.

Free fashioned the separator to look like a real Case, with a hopper mouth, a grain spout and a blower with a little tin hood to deflect the flying straw. From the old Gore junkpile Free salvaged four bed casters and used them for the running gear. From Ma he got a handful of empty thread spools and made pulleys of them by tacking them onto the sides of the separator with six-penny nails. He made belts out of the leather fringes of fly nets. He used a large darning spool for the drive pulley. And for the drive belt between the steam engine and the separator, he cut a narrow strip from one of the binder canvases Pa had discarded.

Making the tractor was harder. He'd heard of steamers exploding and scalding the engineer, so he decided to make another kind of tractor, an Advance-Rumley. Searching through the junkpile some more he found the brass works of a discarded alarm clock. Just the thing. The spring of the clock would be the motor.

He removed the clockwork out of its rusty case. In checking it over, he discovered the spring was still wound up. Aha. The Gores had wound up the clock too tight and when it wouldn't work they'd thrown it away. He doused the clockwork with penetrating oil. Prying into it with a screwdriver, checking each sprocket wheel for dirt, he at last got the balance wheel to tick a few times. He kept rotating the works back and forth until finally the main spring began ticking merrily away.

Working carefully, he built a body around the works that pretty much resembled an Advance-Rumley. Two more bed casters were tacked on up front for the front wheels. The big rear traction wheels he made out of two-inch wide sections sawn from a cedar fence post. For lugs he drove staples into the outer rim of the big wheels at regular intervals. He used a long bolt for the axle. He cut cogs into the bolt with a chisel and cleverly fitted the cogs into the last sprocket wheel of the clock where it protruded from the brass frame. He invented a little lever to engage and disengage the sprocket wheel, and screwed it all down securely. Going to the old junkpile yet again, he found another little wheel, this time from a discarded roller skate, and made a drive pulley out of it. It took some strong thinking to figure out how to gear the pulley into the last sprocket wheel with the same little lever, but, concentrating until his brows hurt, he managed it.

Gingerly he set the new tractor on the ground outside the shop and tried it. First the pulley. He pushed the little lever forward, and, by gum, the pulley began to turn. Next the big traction wheels. He pulled the little lever back all the way, and, by jiggers, the Advance-Rumley began to bumble across the grass. It climbed over a stray cob, ran down an ant, brushed through a clump of dried foxtail. It moved like a crude beetle. It was wonderful. What a great invention. He pushed the lever to neutral to stop it.

He put all of Pa's tools back where they belonged. He made sure the various bits for the drill press, Pa's pride and joy, were back in their proper slots. He swept up the curlings from the dirt floor.

He took the rig out to the old sandpile. Within seconds his brothers were on hand to see the new wonder. They wanted to help him run it, but that he couldn't allow. He put them to work instead. First they had to rake some sand level and make it a waving field of ripe oats. Free next took a shingle, and holding it at a slant bindered their field for them. The kids came after and formed the ridges of sand into neat windrows of shocks. They next got out their hayracks, two of Pa's old cigar boxes, and filled them with shocks.

Free played he'd just finished threshing at a neighbor's place. He hooked the tractor onto the tongue of the separator, pulled the lever, and the whole rig started to tremble down the play road toward Everett's place. "Rum-te-rum-te-rum."

"Keep working," Free ordered. "Or you won't be ready when the threshing rig arrives on your yard. We threshers ain't got a minute to waste."

The kids hurried to get Everett's yard in order. They laughed funny. They could hardly believe it was true that Free's invention was really pulling its own separator along.

Free steered the great old Advance-Rumley onto Everett's yard. "Rum-te-rum-te-rum." He pulled up by the barn. "Where do you want your strawpile this year?"

Everett pointed. "Over there behind the cattle shed."

"Good. But you'll have to take down part of the hog yard fence."

"Okay."

Free pulled the Case separator into position. He unhooked the tongue. He wheeled the tractor around in a wide circle, "Rum-te-rum-te-rum," and lined its drive pulley up with the drive pulley of the separator. Next he dug four little holes in the ground and set the separator wheels into them, anchoring them, deep enough so the separator wouldn't rock out. He got out the long canvas drive belt, and crossing it, hooked it on. He played it was awful heavy to lift onto the drive pulleys. He also dug four holes behind the Advance-Rumley wheels and rolled the tractor back into them. And had real good luck. The crossed drive belt was exactly tight enough.

Everett and Albert breathed heavy with their mouths open. Jonathan just stared.

"All right, drive up a load of bundles," Free ordered.

Everett and Albert pulled up their cigar boxes full of sand, one on each side of the feeder.

"Ready?"

Albert looked puzzled. "If we throw the sand bundles into the feeder, will it really come out of the blower?"

"I'll show you." Free pushed the little lever forward on the tractor. The drive pulley began to turn and slowly the big belt flopped and moved, turning the Case separator drive pulley, which in turn set all the other little belts on the separator to flopping and running. It was a great thing to see. An invention made at home that worked. Then Free took an old soup spoon, dipped up some sand from Albert's load, and then threw it where Everett wanted the strawpile. He did it in such a manner that it actually looked like the blower was blowing it.

"Oh," Albert said, understanding what was wanted.

Both Everett and Albert went at it. They were playing with a real pretend threshing outfit. Slowly the strawpile grew into a real strawpile just like on Pa's yard, resembling George Washington's pompadour, windblown from one side. It piled higher and higher until, all bundles finally threshed, Everett had a tremendous strawpile.

They had so much fun doing it that they made strawpile after strawpile, each time pretending they were threshing out yet another neighbor's grain. They hardly had time for their chores on Pa's yard.

Every now and then they had to get out the sprinkling can and rain some water on the grain sand so that it would mold better, form real-looking shocks of grain, and pile up better in the strawstacks. Real people often had rains on their fields too so it was all right to use the sprinkling can.

Pa and Ma finally had to see for themselves.

"Wal, I declare," Pa said, staring at all the running belts.

"Well, if that isn't the limit." Ma said.

Pa slowly put on his thinking cap. "Boy, am I looking forward to the day when you can make me some man-sized inventions. It'll surely take a lot of field work off my poor tired old shoulders."

Ma said quietly, "Yes, Free, we surely must not let your talent get buried."

Of course Pa had to brag about what a smart kid he had. Pretty soon different parents started calling up the Alfredsons wondering if they'd be home that night, it was such a nice evening out, and the kids were all talking about Free's invention so . . . could they see it, please?

At first Free was happy to show them all how it worked. The Haber kids were nice about it, because when they asked Free if they could run it once, work the lever, and Free said no, they didn't get mad, but just sat back and enjoyed looking at the rig as it crawled around through the sand. But it was the Engleking second cousins who turned out to be pests. They yanked around like bawl babies, and complained to their folks that Free was stingy with his toys, and generally made such a ruckus, that finally both Pa and Ma said Free should let them play with his threshing rig a little while.

"No," Free said, "I didn't make it to be broken by dumbbells."

"Free!" Ma said, sharp. "Don't be so selfish."

"All right, let 'em play with it then. But just you wait and see."

Sure enough, Albert of Fat John was too rough on the lever, and it broke off.

Free was as mad as a wet rooster. "See! I told you."

Albert of Fat John started to tremble. "It wasn't much of an invention in the first place. I'd rather drive old Fly to school any day. That's a whole lot more clever."

Free could see that Pa wanted to cuss the Englekings too—he didn't always like them either—but couldn't because Ma was related to them. Pa finally said, "Son, why don't you put your rig away and come the next rainy day we'll fix it together."

Free liked that. "Okay, Pa."

The sack swing Pa'd made for them was getting to be pretty beaten up. The straw in the gunnysack had been pounded almost to dust. Free refilled the sack with good new straw. It was while examining where Pa had tied the other end of the rope up on the maple limb that Free got an idea. Pa could've picked a higher limb from which to hang the swing. The higher the limb the bigger the swoops up and back. Also if a fellow could take his jump onto the sack swing from another high limb, he'd really have himself a wild ride. It would take real courage.

He shinnied up the tree and untied the rope from the low limb and moved it to the higher limb. Looking down, he saw where the new arc of the swing would swoop right through the center of Everett's oats field. No harm in that so long as nobody was playing threshing. When the Engleking cousins came, he could say they couldn't play threshing because of the sack swing. He smiled. After telling them that, he'd then dare them to take the big jump onto the sack swing. That would discourage them from coming over.

Examining the next nearest tree, Free found a good high limb to jump from. He tied a twine string to a corner of the fat sack, wrapped the end of the string around his waist, and climbed the next tree. He crawled out along the high limb, hauled in the twine string until he could grab the corner of the sack swing, next got a good hold on the rope just above the sack, and then, legs apart, jumped like he was leaping aboard a mustang running underneath. The sack swing swooped toward the earth; then soared up toward the leaves of a box elder on the far side. When the sack mustang stopped rising, Free's stomach wanted to keep on going. Up and thinner and dizzy. He could smell the perfume of a wild rose. Wow.

Everett and Albert and Jonathan watched him. They were scared to death of Free's flying mustang. Good. The second cousins were sure to be scared.

After a while though, about the tenth time, jumping off the good high limb turned out to be pretty tame stuff. He looked around for something higher to jump from. Sizing up the near tree again he decided that a thinner limb higher up would be a great one to jump from. With his eye he measured the arc the swing would make. Man alive. It looked like he wouldn't be able to make the sack swing from it.

He thought it over; finally decided to try it anyway. He got a longer piece of string, tied it to the sack swing and around his waist, climbed the next tree, and bellied out along the thinner limb. He crawled out until the limb began to sink under him.

He broke out in a sweat. He saw Everett and Albert and Jonathan stare up at him. Wow, they sure were a long ways down there. If he fell he'd be smashed to bits. He began to tremble.

He rested a while to catch his breath.

At last he knew he was either going to have to try it or admit he was a coward. He began to haul in the twine string, at last managed, by stretching for every quarter inch his body could give him, to grab hold of a corner of the sack swing. Just barely. He let go of the twine string.

Now to stand up while still holding onto the corner of the sack swing. Cautiously he drew up first one knee under him, then the other, then slowly straightened up almost to his full height still hanging onto the corner with thumb and forefinger, teetering, tottering, wondering if he dared, wondering if he was a crazy fool after all, wondering what it would be like to be dead like his two grandfathers, smelling that wild rose again, bare feet beginning to sting where they gripped onto the bark of the maple limb. . . .

"You're going to break your neck," Albert said up to him. All that could be seen of Albert was his tanned face and shoulders.

"I'm. . ." And then he was losing his balance. Sparks set off behind his eyeballs. He was tipping forward. Well . . . in that case he might just as well jump and try to catch the sack swing between his knees. Sucking in a great breath, crying, "Dare to be a Daniel!" he did jump, for all he was worth. Just barely he managed to catch hold of the neck of the sack with his hands, just barely he managed to nip the corner of the sack between his knees; and down he dropped. He hung on, bitterly nipping the corner tight. His butt was mostly below the fat sack; he couldn't hunch himself up any higher nohow—and ow! oh! his butt burned as it gouged a trench through Everett's oats field. And up he zoomed, climbing, going way up into the leaves of the far maple, so that one tender notched maple leaf lay across his right eye, so close he could make out in the leaf little dark veins like the web of blood vessels he'd once seen in a setting egg. Then, at the top of the arc, the fat sack stopped and his body kept on going, and at that moment he quick opened his knees and regrabbed the sack between his legs, and then, firmly aboard his flying mustang, coasted back down, his scorched butt easily missing Everett's oats field, and then rode back up the back side of the arc, up to the limb he'd jumped off of. That was the greatest wild rose he'd ever smelled.

Free ❦ 40

ALL TOO SOON August came to an end and it was time to think of new clothes for school. After some thought Ma decided to repatch Free's and Everett's things and work up a new set for Albert out of the hand-me-downs from Everett, which were already hand-me-downs from Free. And Pa, after inspecting their shoes, decided the uppers were still pretty good, so perhaps Old Shoester could somehow still fix 'em.

On the last Saturday night of vacation they all piled into the old Buick and went to town.

Main street was packed with cars. Pa parked in front of Tillman's Mercantile. Ma preferred to trade at the Mercantile because Garrett Tillman was a member of their church.

The moment the right front tire hit the curb, the kids in back made moves to scramble out.

"Hold on there a minute," Pa said, shutting off the motor. "What I want to know is, are we going to behave tonight? Or are we going to be a bunch of rascals and sneak into the pool hall?"

"We always behave in town, Pa."

"Well, here are my orders. Free, take Everett with you and deliver that sack of shoes to Shoester."

"Yes, Pa."

"Jonathan, you go with your mother. And Albert, you come with me. No running off by yourself."

"But, Pa—" Albert began.

"Shh. Those are your marching orders for tonight."

"But I want to see Shoester's horned hoof with Free," Albert said.

"Horned hoof? Is that what the kids are saying about him now?"

Free said, "He means cloven foot."

Ma looked around at Free. "Where did you hear that?"

"The kids at school. They say Shoester is of the Devil and can call up witches to hex you if you tease him about his leg."

Ma and Pa looked at each other, and shook their heads.

Free picked up the sack and he and Everett got out of the car. Free slung the sack over his shoulders.

"Behave now," Pa called after them.

"We will."

The stoop to every store was crowded with seated men smoking their pipes. The insides of the stores were full of mothers and children milling around. Free spotted some of his second cousins sitting on the iron stoop of Highmire's Hardware, hands in their pockets. Mr. Highmire happened to be out front. Free thought he was looking at him because of that one bullet he'd tried to buy from him once. All of a sudden, with a straight face, Mr. Highmire wrung his ear with thumb and finger, turning his ear down like it might be a petcock, and out of his mouth spurted a long stream of tobacco juice. It shot between Everett's legs and splashed into the gutter near the town fountain. The Engleking cousins laughed.

Free glowered. He didn't think it very funny.

They turned the corner north. On both sides of the street stood a row of hitching posts. Some farmers still drove a horse and buggy to town. Free counted thirteen rigs. The horses were streaked with sweat. Only the colored celluloid rings, red and white and yellow and blue on the horses' bridles, looked fresh.

The first building past the alley was Old Shoester's, a low shop standing cool under a pair of maples. It was connected to a little house in back. Both were painted brown.

Everett dragged behind.

"What's the matter?"

"Just so he don't touch me with that horse hoof."

"He's got a cloven foot, not a horse hoof."

"He's got a horse's leg and that means he's got a horse's hoof."

"C'mon."

"You're scairt of him too."

"I've been in his shop before with Pa and I know he won't eat me."

Shoester's real name was Wilhelm Terpen. He was a bachelor whose only friends were two other bachelors from Rock Falls. None of the three bachelors believed in cars so they visited each other back and forth by taking the Old Omaha train. All three were fiddlers and about once a month they got together and fiddled and drank beer all night long. Sometimes they sang drinking songs so loud they kept the town up most of the night and made the marshal mad. The three never went to church. They also read a socialist newspaper that was against the President.

The smell of freshly cut leather drifted through the screen door. There was also the stink of chewing tobacco. A voice spoke. "Don't be bashful. I won't eat you."

Free stepped in, Everett dragging after him.

"Well well, what have we in that sack." Shoester was just then carving a fresh sole out of a thick side of dry leather. Shoester put his work aside.

Free upended the sack and let the shoes tumble out on the floor. There were three pairs. "Pa says new soles and heels."

Shoester leaned over his leather apron and picked up one of the shoes. "Okay. I'll fix your shoes tomorrow."

Free hesitated. "But tomorrow's Sunday."

Shoester laughed, revealing yellow teeth under a wide brown moustache. "Not for Old Shoester it ain't."

"Don't you believe in God?"

"No. I believe in the Devil."

Free stared at Shoester astounded.

Shoester had a bald head and it shone like the bullet Uncle Richard always carried in his pocket for good luck. "Sure, the Devil, boy. Who else would've given me this?" Shoester lifted his right leg. It came up off the floor like the handle of a jack. At the end of it was a special slipper with a sole shaped like a horseshoe.

Everett leaned to one side to see if the sole of Shoester's slipper was cloven or a simple horse's hoof.

Free asked, "Does the Devil have a church too?"

The smile under Shoester's brown moustache curved up like a quarter moon. "No, the Devil just believes in having a hot time in the old town tonight."

"You mean in the pool hall?"

"No no. Just two people having a good time together somewhere."

"Church people have a good time too."

"I don't mean praying, boy. I mean fiddling."

"You ought to hear my pa fiddle sometime."

"Ya, your pa is all right that way." Shoester aimed some tobacco juice at a spittoon off to one side. He hit it smack in the middle. Even the last couple of brown drops made it in.

The north wall of the shop was lined with slanted shelves full of shoes and slippers already done. The south wall behind Shoester had a bench covered with different size shoe lasts, from a little girl's to a grown man's. An iron stand stood between Shoester's legs with a girl's shoe on it getting fixed.

Shoester's brown eyes twinkled. "Did your pa give you a nickel for an ice cream cone tonight?"

"No."

"Not? And this is Saturday night? Well, we'll have to do something about that." Shoester heaved himself up off his stool, and staggering mostly on his good leg through a jumble of discarded shoes and boots, went to a shelf on the east wall. He reached into an old tobacco can and came up with two nickels. He tossed one to Free and one to Everett.

The two boys caught the nickels handily.

"Aha, I see your pa taught you kids baseball." Shoester hobbled back to his seat, the last ways leaning on his tremendous arms and swinging his body into place like an acrobat.

A breeze came through the screen of the south window. It was sweet and cool. It made the new leather and the leather soap smell like a friendly horse barn.

Free rubbed the nickel between his thumb and forefinger. From under his throw of blond hair he looked at Shoester. Shoester couldn't be such a devil after all if he gave little children ice-cream money. Free was sorry he'd believed that about his having a cloven hoof. "Thank you very much, Mister Shoester."

Everett piped up too. "Thanks, Mister Shoester."

"Don't mention it, boys." Shoester pinched his brown eyes together like Gramma sometimes did when she got excited. "Tell your pa I'll have your shoes ready

Monday." Shoester clapped his hands together hard, cupped, so that it sounded like a shotgun going off. "Now, my dear hearts, run along before I eat you up."

Free and Everett first walked, then ran, back to the corner.

They stopped at the trickling rusty fountain. They looked at each other. Should they tell their folks about the nickels Shoester had given them? If they did, Albert and Jonathan would surely begin pestering the folks for a nickel too and that would make Pa spend two nickels he hadn't intended to spend.

Everett got that butter look on his face. "I know were we can get a cone in secret."

"Where?"

"Swaim's Cafe. If you sit way in back nobody can see you."

"You'll never tell then? Even to brag about it?"

"Cross my heart and hope to die."

They stepped kitty-corner across the main intersection, dividing around the town flagpole. The ropes leading up to the silver ball on top of the flagpole rippled in the night breeze.

Swaim's Cafe was crowded. Free only needed one peek through the glass door to see that even the back booths were full of young folks having fun.

Everett wasn't about to give up. "Let's try Fraser Drugs. He's got them ice-cream chairs in back. Aunt Gerda once give me a sundae there."

The wire ice-cream chairs in Fraser Drugs were only half full. There was a smell of sweetheart perfume around.

Free and Everett edged toward the back.

Mr. Fraser had stiff blond hair but the crinkles of a kind uncle were in the corners of his blue eyes. He always acted a little like a doctor. "What can I do for you boys?"

Everett held up his nickel. "Ice-cream cone. Please."

"I'm sorry but I don't carry cones. You'll have to try Swaim's next door. Or the Corner Cafe up the street."

"Oh."

A gaudy red Western magazine caught Free's eye. It showed a man crawling on his hands and knees with Indians shooting at him. Free counted six arrows sticking out of the man's back. The man looked like Pa when he was all done in.

"Maybe you'd like a Western?" Mr. Fraser said.

"No," Everett said. "We'd rather have an ice-cream cone."

They headed west. It had become dusk out. Fleischer's Meat Market smelled of sawdust and dried meat. The open doorway of Kerber's Implement stank of axle grease. Dr. Fairlamb's office smelled of disinfectant. Old-timers rocking away on the veranda of the Bonnie Hotel smelled like old rusty pails.

Free stopped at the next corner. "I know what let's do. Let's put our nickels in the collection box for the poor next Sunday."

Everett backed away from Free a couple of steps. "I'm gonna spend my nickel on an ice-cream cone."

"Go ahead. But all them storekeepers and Pa and Ma know each other and if we try to sneak spend our nickels, they'll be sure to call Pa up tomorrow and tell him." Free remembered how miserable he'd felt getting caught trying to buy that single .410 shell.

The lamps up and down main street came on. It was like a couple dozen eggs were being candled all at the same time. The white globes lit up the signs on the high false fronts.

Everett looked at the lights in the Billards Hall across the street. "Maybe they sell ice-cream cones over there."

"That's the pool hall. And you know what Pa said about that."

The two benches in front of the Billards Hall were full of spitters. Several town bums were standing around, hands in their pockets, joking and laughing.

One man stood quiet by himself. He looked like a picture of an elegant gentleman in the Sears Roebuck catalog. It was Jack Manning, the rum runner. He knew how to let his hands hang correctly alongside his body. He was said to be the richest man in town. He carried a gold-tipped cane, gold teeth, and a wide gold watch chain. His roving eyes lighted on Free a second. For that second his eyes glowed in the dark.

"Let's go find Ma," Free said, and without waiting for what Everett might say, headed diagonally across the street.

"Wait," Everett called after him. "Let's see if we can't just find one more ice-cream place yet. There's gotta be some kind of little grocery where they sell cones to little children."

"Well, there's Bliss's Grocery. You can try him."

"Okay." Everett ran into Bliss's Grocery.

Free had heard Pa tell about Mr. Herman Bliss. In the old days Mr. Bliss had every once in a while announced that on his sixtieth birthday he was going to close up shop, dress in his Sunday best, take the Cannonball to Sioux City, rent a room, buy a bottle of rye whiskey, hire a whore for the night, and then, after a high old time, shoot himself. And Mr. Bliss had done it too. Grampa Alfredson had admired that, but Pa and Ma had thought it an awful thing to do. John Bliss, his son, ran the store now.

It didn't take but a minute for Everett to come out of Bliss's Grocery with a long face. No cones there either.

Next up the street was Hunter's Harness Shop. The door was open. All sorts of harnesses and whips and fly nets and hemp ropes hung from the ceiling. Hunter also sold shoes known as the Wear-U-Wells. Pa had once bought a pair for Free; and once only, because Free wore them out inside of a month. The soles were so flimsy.

Young men leaning against the buildings whistled at young girls parading past. Sometimes the young men catcalled after them, "Detour! detour!" It was because the girls were wearing stockings with an arrow woven into them. The arrow on the inside of the leg pointed straight up.

Two of the Cooper boys were sitting in the red stone entrance of Rexroth's Department Store. They had been drinking.

The older Cooper boy said, "You know, that Jenny Porter, if she was to have as many pricks outside her as she's had in her, she'd be a porcupine."

The younger Cooper boy laughed. "Yeh, she's the one they tell about, that if you should happen to see two sets of shoes in the tall grass somewhere, one set of them is sure to be Jennie's, with the toes turned up, like a dead man's, while the other set of shoes is sure to be Brut Weatherly's, with the toes turned down, like a man leaning over to vomit."

They were about to cross over to Highmire's Hardware again, when they heard a commotion across the main intersection near the Corner Cafe. Somebody was shouting mean. Everybody had turned to look. People inside the stores hurried outside to see what it was all about.

"C'mon." Free grabbed Everett by the hand. "A fight."

They ran past the flagpole and then hopped up onto the trunk of a Ford roadster to see over the crowd.

The man doing all the roaring was Henry Hiller, king of the local yellow gold, who owned all the gravel pits in the valley west and south of Bonnie. He drove a very fast red pony hitched to a funny democrat wagon. The democrat had bright red wheels and a red seat. People said he was meaner than a cat with a mouse. He was so tight that to get him to part with a penny was like asking him to give up a drop of his own red blood.

The other man was Milo Kerber, the implement dealer. Milo was also the town mayor. Milo was known as a man who spoke his mind, and who in a quiet way, once he'd said what he had to say, never backed down. Pa once said of him he was a man of steel inside.

Mr. Hiller was doing a little jig in his democrat, and waving and snapping his horsewhip around, he was so mad. "And I say you're a goddam Bolshevik, interfering with the way I handle my workers."

Milo was smiling. He stood with both hands in the pockets of his green coveralls suit.

Mr. Hiller had no lips, just a saw-mark between his sharp chin and sharp nose. "When I fired Pete Durlo I meant for him to be fired out of town too. I don't want him around Bonnie any more."

Milo placed his hand on the dashboard of the jiggling democrat.

"Get your hands off my prop'ty," Mr. Hiller cried.

Milo withdrew his hand. "As I was about to say, Henry, Pete Durlo worked for me once, and he can work for me again. He's a good man."

"But I want him run out of town. So you fire him, or else. I want him blacklisted."

"But why?"

"I caught him fornicating with the Brewster girl. In one of my sandpits. Mine, you understand, mine. The country is going to hell because of the likes of him."

Milo managed to smile. "Pete stays."

"God damn you, I say he goes. And if you don't get rid of him, by God and by Jesus, I'll take this horsewhip to you myself."

"Pete stays."

Mr. Hiller jumped up and down. Then, foaming at the corners of his mouth, he swung his horsewhip up.

The lash of the horsewhip never made it. Milo suddenly surged halfway up into the democrat, over a red wheel, grabbed the whip by the stock next to Mr. Hiller's hand, gave the stock a hard jerk, and had the whip. Then Milo dropped the whip to the ground. He spoke quietly. "Henry, we'll talk about this sometime after you've cooled down." Milo turned and headed for his implement shop down the street.

"Where's the marshal?" a woman cried.

Mr. Hiller looked at her for a crazy second. Then he cried after Milo, "Milo, I'm the king of Bonnie and I want you to know you're going to do as I say." Mr. Hiller leaped off his democrat, pushed through the crowd, ran straight for Highmire's Hardware. Before anybody could do anything about it, he emerged carrying one of Highmire's new double-barreled shotguns. He was loading it with new shells as he ran. He headed diagonally past the flagpole, spotted Milo, who still had a dozen steps to go to the entrance to his shop, dropped to one knee, and fired. Birdshot rattled across the false front of Milo's shop. People scattered, either jumping inside the stores or diving for the gutter.

Milo himself didn't turn to see who might be shooting. He kept right on going toward the entrance of his shop.

Mr. Hiller fired the other barrel. The second swarm of birdshot sprayed all around Milo.

Milo fell to his knees. It was as though someone had cuffed him across the shoulder. Milo shook himself, once. Then, a hand to each knee, he stood up. He still didn't bother to turn around. Instead he angled himself past the entrance to his shop and headed for the door of Dr. Fairlamb's office. He disappeared inside not even limping.

"That'll teach him to keep his nose out of my business," Mr. Hiller cried. He threw the shotgun on the ground and said over his shoulder in the direction of Highmire's Hardware, "You can send me the bill for the use of your gun and shells." Then waving people out of the way with his right hand, he picked up his horsewhip, climbed aboard his red democrat, and still standing picked up the lines and shook the red pony into action. He disappeared around the Corner Cafe.

People picked themselves up out of the gutters and emerged from the stores.

"Somebody ought to get after that Henry Hiller," fat Mrs. Sudaberry cried. "Even though his business is good for the town, he can't go around shooting at our mayor."

"Where's the marshal?" a woman cried.

"Marshal Coltoff's got the gout."

Rexroth with his bristle-white hair and black beard came roaring out of his store. "What happened?"

"Oh, Henry Hiller took a notion to shoot up the town."

"Did he hit anybody?"

"Just Milo Kerber. But he was too far away. You got to be pretty close up for birdshot to hit a vital part. No, I think Milo's just been spiced up a little. He had on his heavy green coveralls."

Just then the town band struck up a tune from the bandstand in the open lot north of Mable's Millinery Shop. They played a jolly Sousa march. The drums in the band soothed the crowd. Everybody went back to their own business again.

Free and Everett got down off the turtle of the Ford roadster. Both were numb from all the things they'd seen.

Ma spotted them just as they were having themselves a drink at the town fountain. "Where have you kids been?"

Both remembered their damp nickels. They said nothing.

"Come, you can help carry the groceries out to the car."

They followed Ma into Tillman's Mercantile. The store was full of people still cackling about the shooting.

Garrett Tillman was fitting the lid onto the Alfredson egg crate into which he'd put their groceries. There was a wise look in his wide-set blue eyes. "Well, Ada, what do you think we ought to do with our local Napoleon Bonaparte?"

"I fear a house visitation wouldn't do him much good."

A smile opened Tillman's broad face. "No, it wouldn't." He had a high forehead and wore his blond hair slicked back.

"Won't Milo sue that wild beast for assault and battery?"

"Not Milo. No, it'll have to be someone else along main street who'll have to make the complaint."

"Poor man," Ma said.

Free caught all kinds of wonderful whiffs in the store: bacon, ham, woolen blankets, salt crackers, oranges, rubber pants for babies, overripe bananas. But it was the smell of chocolate-covered cream drops that was the best. Free peeked through the slats of their egg crate to see if Tillman had remembered the Alfredson kids.

Tillman smiled. "Looking for something?"

Free turned a little red. "Not really."

"It's on the bottom. I put it in first."

"Good thing too," Ma said. "That way I can dole them out at home for dessert. Candy between meals can rot the teeth so."

"A little candy won't hurt them, Ada."

Free picked up the egg crate. "Shall I carry this out to the car?"

Ma nodded. "Yes, Everett and I can carry the rest."

Outside a crowd had gathered around the bandstand. Some of the shoppers had reparked their cars near the stand so they could sit in comfort while they listened. Some people settled on the grass.

"Ma, can we go up close and listen?" Everett asked. Everett always livened up when there was band music.

"Yes, go ahead, you two. Jonathan and I will stay here in the car. I think we can hear it good enough from here."

"Oh boy."

Free and Everett pushed their way to the front of the crowd.

There were two drums, two slide trombones, two cornets, one piccolo, one bass horn, and one trumpet in the band. The man with the cornet, Wiley Cobb, played the loudest. Red face dark, he directed by motioning with his shoulders. When the drums came on the whole bandstand quivered. Some of the big nails at the corners worked in and out a little and made noises like crickets. Some of the fresh planks had bled rosin and looked like someone had spilled Karo syrup over them. The players sat on the chairs and took turns standing up and tootling a little solo. The piccolo player was the best. When he soloed it was like a thrush opening up its pipes in a grove.

The men listened with their hands in their pockets and the women listened with their arms crossed over their bellies.

Free noticed Floris and Willard Haber darting in and out of the crowd, doing some kind of stunt, and then going off to one side and laughing to themselves. A couple of times some of the grown-up men whirled around on the Haber kids, and snarled at them. "Why, you goddam little twerps you!" They were having so much fun Free had to find out what they were doing. He caught Floris by the belt. "What you up to?"

"Cracking nuts." Floris laughed so hard it was like he was leaking water all over. "We look around for a fellow blowing about what a great crop he's got this year. We always make sure he's got both hands in his pockets. It takes him a second or two to get 'em out and by that time we're gone. We sneak up behind him and reach in under his butt and grab him by the nuts and give 'em a yank. Then we jump sideways and disappear into the crowd."

Everett had overheard them. He looked up at the stars and thought that over. Then he said, "You better not do that to my pa."

"Your dad? Never. His arms are too long."

"It's kind of a lowdown dirty trick," Free said.

"Yeh, some are dirty, and some are lowdown." Floris thought that the greatest joke ever. He laughed and laughed. "What fun. Especially when they let out a yell and then grab for their crotch."

The Haber kids were almost as bad as those Horsberg boys.

Pa stood over them all of a sudden. "Boys, time to go home."

"But the band ain't done playing yet," Everett said. Everett still had his other hand around that damp nickel in his pocket.

"Ma is tired. C'mon, home we go. No ifs, ands, or buts."

They were in the car and riding for home, the car headlights poking along ahead in the dark like a pair of silver knitting needles, when Pa asked, "What did Shoester have to say?"

Free said, "He said he'd have them ready on Monday."

Pa nodded over the steering wheel. "Good."

The old Buick rumbled on for a couple of miles.

As they crossed the rattling plank bridge, Free felt of his damp nickel and finally decided he better tell Pa about how good Shoester had been to them. "Shoester gave us each a nickel."

"What?"

"Yes. He told us to go buy ourselves an ice-cream cone."

Everett gave Free a dirty look.

"Did you get ourself an ice-cream cone then?"

"No. We was afraid it wouldn't be fair to Albert and Jonathan."

Ma turned around in her seat and looked back at them. "Well, that was thoughtful of you."

Pa asked, "What are you going to do with that nickel?"

Free thought a while. "I think I'm going to put mine in the Sunday collection for the poor."

Pa and Ma didn't say anything for a while.

Then, as they turned into their own lane, Ma said, watching out for where Pa was driving from the shadow of her eyes, "Husband, at last I see evidence that our children are being Christianized a little. Thank the Lord."

"Yeh," Pa said. "As long as it lasts."

Free ❦ 41

IT WAS GOOD to be going to school again. Turning out of the lane and heading west, it was always a thrill to see up ahead the city of Bonnie gleaming pink in the rosy morning sun. Somewhere behind those shining windows four miles away lived people with libraries full of gold-and-red books, doctor and domeny and banker. Some day he'd find a beautiful girl in one of those gold-and-green parlors, a pretty girl who'd have gold hair like Ma, who'd like to read adventure stories in bed, and who'd be happy to roam the high hills west of town with him.

The way Free felt soon made everybody else in the cab feel good. Hankie Barth smiled even though things were sad in his house, and Fredrika began giving cheerful orders a mile a minute, and Albert, often glum, laughed out loud when Tip popped her tail because Free wanted her to run faster.

School was easy. One look at a tough word like "reciprocate" and he knew it for keeps. One reading of the Battle of Bunker Hill and he knew it down to the last Revolutionary bullet. One good look at the map of a country and he knew where all the rivers ran.

He liked to sit hidden behind his big wide geography book and wonder about things. That palace of Montezuma, were its walls really made of solid gold? And those Mayas, did they really wear feather clothes instead of cloth clothes?

Free was glad that he'd been promoted to the sixth grade and could at last climb the steps to the top floor, where Mr. Ardman, the new principal, taught in a big sunny room. Free was now one of the older kids and could act important in school if he wanted to. Mr. Ardman liked him too and always turned to him for the answer if the others didn't know it. Free sometimes pretended he didn't know it so he wouldn't get those dark looks from his cousins. But Mr. Ardman was wise to him. Free like Obert Ardman.

Mr. Ardman had ears to match his given name. They stuck out like he might be sleeping on them folded over against his head. Mr. Ardman was built a lot like Pa, even walking like him. He usually wore blue trousers, brown knit jacket, blue socks and brown shoes, and a white shirt with a blue knitted tie. His fingernails were scrubbed pink. He wore his brown hair slicked back, with some Vaseline worked in to keep his rooster tail down. He kept order in the room without having to roar at the kids. When he wasn't happy about something, he'd just stand and stare at the kids, until everybody hid behind a book.

One noon Mr. Ardman asked Free to remain in his seat.

After all the kids had gone down to get their lunch buckets and had scattered out over the schoolyard to eat, Mr. Ardman waved Free up to his desk.

Free couldn't remember having done anything wrong. Unless it was that time he'd peeked through the hole Clarence Etten had drilled into the back of the girl's privy and had seen Nelda Brewster pee. But that was more than a month ago.

"Free, are you happy in school?"

"I think so. Sure."

"You're always dreaming behind that geography book of yours."

Free put his hands in the pockets of his brown knickers.

"Free, it's a bad habit to get into, dreaming like that. So I've decided to give you more work to do. I'm going to have you take both the sixth and seventh grades at the same time."

Sparks sailed around in Free's head. Hey. What would Pa think? Pa was already a little jealous of him that he could read the Bible without a mistake.

"Think it'll be too hard for you?"

"No."

"All right, we'll start you in both grades this afternoon. And now you better go down and eat your lunch."

After the noon recess, Principal Ardman moved Free to a desk at the back of the seventh-grade row. There were only four other seventh-graders: Maynard Tollhouse, Nelda Brewster, Ruby Young, and Jessie Dykeman.

His Engleking cousins were so jealous that during the afternoon recess they wouldn't play with him. They said he was a teacher's pet. They said he cheated and that was why he always knew his lessons. They sneered so hard their eyes almost disappeared.

Ma was pleased to read the note Principal Ardman sent home with Free. And Pa, well, one minute he was all smiles, as though he was going to break out and brag, and the next minute he was sober, as though he'd just heard about a crop failure.

Two boys in school were even more jealous than the Englekings. They were Clarence Etten and Tommy Holtup. They were the big goofs who for two years had been too dumb to graduate out of the eighth grade. They were now sixteen. When they heard Principal Ardman announce that Free was going to take two grades at once, they let out snorts like disgusted horses.

One noon recess the two big lummoxes played a dirty trick on Free. They threw his stocking cap down the girl's privy and laughed their heads off while he spent an hour fishing it out with a teacher's pointer and a hairpin and then had to wash it in the basement of the school. "Ho ho," they roared, "I guess you're not so smart after all."

Coming home late, Pa asked him what the matter was.

Free told Pa what had happened.

"Is that so," Pa said.

All through chores Free talked about how he was beginning to hate school because he'd been moved up a grade.

At supper table Pa finally had enough. "What do you want me to do, go over and beat up on them two lummoxes for you? Why don't you go after those two guys yourself?"

"But they're so much bigger than me, Pa."

"I don't care. Let them know that if they pester you too much you get mad. Wild mad, see?" Pa's eyes turned into carbide lights like in the old days. Even though you know you may get licked, tie into them luffers. They'll think twice before trying it again."

Ma gave Pa a disappointed look. "Are you trying to make a brawler out of our son?"

Pa stuck out his famous chin. "You bet. A fighter. If it means defending his rights. I don't want him to grow up a sissy."

Ma shook her head. "I don't know if I approve of that."

Pa said, " 'Course, at the same time, son, I don't want you to start any fights either. If I ever hear of you starting a fight, then I start a fight with you. On your bare ass. But if the other guy starts the fight, and you're sure you're right, then I want you to defend yourself. Fight fierce. And no matter who the guy is, even if it's the President of these United States, fight him until one of you drops. You hear? And if you get beat up, then I'll step in and help you. That's the way a true Frisian handles it."

"Alfred," Ma said, "now."

"I mean that," Pa said. "Handle your own fights, son."

A couple of noons later Free was a little late getting out to the horse barn to feed Tip her dozen ears of corn. The other drivers had already fed their horses. Just as Free entered the west door of the barn, he heard a horse rearing and kicking in her stall and then heard someone laughing in high glee.

Free's eyes slowly adjusted to the dusky interior. After a moment he saw who it was. Those two big dumb goofs, Clarence Etten and Tommy Holtup. And they were tormenting Tip. They were sitting up in the rafters above Tip, each with a long stick, and they were taking turns teasing their stick into Tip's behind, under her black tail, until Tip would finally rear up and kick out long and high. Every time she reared up she made a great sad honk of a sound.

Free got wild mad. He ran to Tip's stall, dumped the dozen ears of corn into her feedbox, turned and grabbed her bridle from its hook, and started to climb up the rafters after the two devils. The bridle had a heavy breaker bit. It was of solid steel and was about as heavy as a coal chisel.

Clarence and Tommy were so surprised at seeing him come after them they let go of their sticks and dropped to the soft carpet of dried manure below. Half laughing, half scared, they started to run for the open door.

Free was too quick for them. Bawling, snarling, he dropped to the carpet of manure too and jumped forward to block their path. Then he piled into them, swinging the heavy breaker bit. He caught Tommy, the shorter of the two, over the head, hit him so hard his stocking cap flew off. Tommy almost fell down.

"You dirty mean rotten sonsabitches," Free raged.

Tommy bellowed in agony and ducked for the back of the barn.

Free next caught Clarence between the shoulder blades, an awful crunching blow.

"Owwh!" Clarence yowled. And he too almost fell down. Then, stumbling, wobbling, Clarence followed Tommy toward the back.

Free raced after them, blowing like a mad stud, flailing his heavy breaker bit.

Tommy and Clarence dug into it. They banged into the east door, clawed at it trying to roll it open. When they found it nailed shut, they jumped left into a dark empty stall. They clawed up the wall and tried to escape through a little window over the manger. But the window was small. With Free flailing away at them they couldn't take their time to worm their way through. They next tried to scale up the wall to the rafters above, scrabbling up a ways, then losing their hold and falling down again.

Free flailed and swung and flailed. The breaker bit hit them sideways and flatways and endways. Free sobbed in black rage. "You mean sonsabitches, tormenting a poor creature like that, tied to a manger and can't get back at you fair. You sonsabitches, I'm gonna kill you for that."

Tommy and Clarence finally crumped down in the darkest corner of the stall, trying to make themselves as small as possible.

In the middle if it all, Ma suddenly appeared in Free's mind. "Boy, boy, is this what I raised you to be? A killer? Ada's boy?"

Free let up. Ma was right. He couldn't go around killing people. Pa said to beat 'em up if he was sure he was in the right. But Pa hadn't said anything about killing them. Free backed off, and turned his back on Tommy and Clarence.

Free went back to Tip's stall. He hung up her bridle.

Sobbing to himself, he slid in beside Tip to pet her over the shoulder, even giving her nose a hug.

The corn was good. Tip had already forgotten about the poking into her behind and wasn't very interested in having her mouth hugged. She shrugged her withers, making the harness rattle.

Alfred ❦ 42

ALFRED WAS HAVING a cup of coffee at three in the afternoon when the phone rang above his head. It was Domeny Donker.

"Alfredson?"

"Yes?"

"Could you come to the consistory meeting tonight?"

"Sure. What time?"

"Oh, we generally start the meeting at eight. Suppose you be there at eight-thirty?"

"I'll be there." Alfred hung up.

Ada, also having a cup of coffee, looked at Alfred wonderingly. "What was that all about?"

Alfred rung his ear. "I don't know."

"Are we behind in our church budget payments?"

"Nope. We're all caught up. Meantime, my conscience is clear, and I've got a pasture fence to fix." Alfred wrung his ear again. "That darn Sam Young is the poorest excuse for a farmer I ever saw. He just never worries about his half of the fence."

On the way over to the consistory meeting that night, Alfred found himself mulling over something that had nothing to do with Domeny's call. His hair, once crow black, had turned almost white, and yet here he was only thirty-six. When he looked in a mirror he saw the face of a young man, smooth forehead, no crow's-feet around the eyes, no wrinkles off the corners of the mouth. Except for that darned white hair, he could easy pass for twenty-five. And he felt like twenty-five too.

Did all middle-aged men wonder about such things? Perhaps other men thought themselves young too, and while looking in a mirror saw themselves as still pink-skinned, when in actual fact and in the eyes of others they looked exactly as old as they were. If thirty-six, they looked thirty-six. If sixty, as Pa was when he died, then sixty.

Alfred wondered if Pa had felt sixty when he'd shocked grain for him that summer. Pa'd shocked like a young man.

The test would be if Ada should happen to die. She easy could with that unsteady heart of hers. God forbid that she would, of course. But supposing she did? Would he feel like marrying another woman his own age? One as old as Ada?

"Naw," Alfred said aloud as he turned into the church yard, "naw, I think I'd go for some young woman. I'd feel more at home with one of around twenty-two." All the women friends of Ada's age looked like over-full grain sacks.

The consistory met in a narrow room just off the church entry. Domeny Donker sat at the head of a long table, six deacons ranged along one side and six elders along the other. Domeny had on his usual black suit. He was jingling his watch chain. Most of the men were smoking cigars, a few their favorite pipe. The air in the room was hazy with tobacco smoke. Only Elder Etten chewed tobacco.

There was one woman in the room, Mrs. Holtup, and she was sitting to one side in a hardback chair.

"Close the door, Alfred," Domeny said with a nod, "and you can take a chair along the wall there beside Mrs. Holtup."

"Is it going to take very long?"

"No."

"Then I'll stand up. I've some chores to do yet."

"As you wish."

"What can I do for you people?"

There was some honking of throats, several uneasy glances, and one very odd angry look from Elder Etten.

Domeny brushed back his straight-up heinie haircut. "Well, Alfred, both Elder Etten here and Mrs. Holtup here have"—Domeny threw in a gold-tooth smile—"made a complaint to the consistory about your boy Free."

"What could he have done now, for godsakes?"

Domeny placed both of his hands on the brown tabletop. "Plenty, it seems." The Domeny recited the facts about how young Alfred Alfredson, a baptized member of the church, had beaten up Clarence Etten and Tommy Holtup, also baptized members of the church, on the church grounds, in the back end of the church barn, using a devilish weapon known as a breaker bit, and that finally he had gone berserk, declaring he wanted to kill the aforementioned Clarence Etten and Tommy Holtup.

Alfred's heart gave a leap. His boy had beat up on those two big lummoxes? Man alive. "May I ask what Clarence and Tommy did to make my boy do this?" Alfred looked directly at Elder Etten.

Elder Etten tongued his cud of tobacco from one cheek to the other. "They were only boys playing a little in the barn."

"How playing?"

"They were only teasing your boy's horse. A little."

"Ya," Mrs. Holtup sniffed, "my boy was only having some boy's fun. It certainly wasn't anything that called for the terrible beating he got." Mrs. Holtup tolled her old gray head with its tiny black hat. "Och, he's got such terrible bumps over—"

Domeny broke in. "Alfred, actually both admit that their boys were tormenting your boy's horse, but—"

"How tormenting?"

Domeny turned to Elder Etten. "Well, John, suppose you tell him."

Reluctantly, tonguing his cud of tobacco around in his mouth several times, Elder Etten told a little more.

"Hm," Alfred said. "Domeny, do I have the right to make one statement?"

"Certainly you do."

"And do I have the right to ask Mrs. Holtup and Old John Etten here each one question?"

"You do."

"All right. Look, my boy is ten years old. That's my statement. Now, my question is this: Mrs. Holtup, how old is your Tommy?"

"Well, you know, he's sixteen."

"And, John, your boy?"

"Well, like her boy, sixteen."

Alfred turned to Domeny. "One boy of ten against two boys of sixteen. Domeny, that's all I have to say in reply to your complaint. Good night, gentlemen. If you need me for anything else, you know where I live."

Free ❦ 43

ONE EVENING THE Wilmer Youngmans came over for company.

Mr. Youngman was Aunt Josephine's first child by her first husband and not really Ma's cousin. But he was kind of a relative. Mr. Youngman could ask sharp questions and often made Ma laugh. As for Mrs. Youngman, she never said boo or bah and she always had a look in her brown eyes like she knew a secret about her husband.

The Youngmans had two kids, Wilma, who was a year younger than Free, and Joseph, who was Albert's age.

It happened Albert and Everett already had quite a city built on the floor in the pantry. Once in a while Ma let them play there to get them out of Pa's way. She herself knew how to step around their towers and skyscrapers. She'd gotten used to stepping over babies and puppies and kittens and pullets. It turned out that Joseph was a good player with blocks. He understood how to drive a car through the streets and he could rebuild a tower if it fell down. Albert and Everett let him play with them.

That left Free and Wilma to play by themselves. The older folks sat in the living room with the ferns.

Free decided to be nice to his company. Since she was probably only going to grow up to be a cook like her ma, he showed her how Ma's kitchen cabinet worked and where Ma kept her recipes.

Wilma didn't say a thing. All she did was follow him around. Wilma had on a green velvet dress. Her hair was black and it made her brown eyes shine like a lapdog's. She was as slim as Constance Bowman.

Free next took her out on the enclosed porch to show her Ma's jelly. Ma liked to put dates on the jars, along with a little saying of some kind, about what the weather was like when she made the jelly, and so on. Sometimes Ma wrote some pretty clever things.

Wilma still didn't say a thing. She just stood on the slanting cellar door and leaned against the wall with her velvet belly curved out a little.

Some light from the gas lamp in the kitchen came through the window by the cream separator. It was just enough to touch up Wilma's green velvet dress with a little silver over the belly.

Free reached out lackadaisical and put his hand on her belly and stroked it like he might a kitty. Wilma seemed to like it that he stroked her belly. "It sure is smooth," he said. "Like cat fur."

Wilma finally said something. She spoke in a low whisper. "Ma made it from an old dress of hers."

Free decided this company wasn't so bad after all. Nobody in the house, neither the older people nor the kids, were paying them any attention. He and Wilma could do anything they wanted to. He kept stroking her belly. After each stroke she'd curve out her belly a little like a cat pushing up its tail.

"It sure is nice." Free was surprised to hear how husky his voice had become.

"Yes."

Free's hand wandered down to where her legs joined. He wondered what Wilma's pussy was like. Since Wilma liked what he was doing so far, he lifted up her velvet dress and slipped his hand inside her bloomers and reached down. The minute he did that she opened her legs and curved up her hips. She had two low ridges of skin there.

Wilma began to show spirit. She moved her pussy around like it couldn't get enough petting. After another minute she grabbed his arm, the one that was stroking her, and hugged it like she wanted to marry it.

Meanwhile Free discovered that more company had come, this time in his pants. It was the kind of company that didn't mind standing up for its rights either. All of a sudden Free clamped himself onto her like a bumblebee dipping down for nectar in a tomato blossom.

Just then Free heard Pa talking in the kitchen, on the other side of the wall. Scared stiff, he managed to lean to his left and look in through the window. The Youngmans were going home. They were looking around for their coats. Darn. If only he'd come out on the porch sooner with Wilma. Well, next time.

Wilma got scared too. She jerked away from him and gave him a look like they'd been fighting a little. The look cooled off the company in his overalls. By the time they stepped into the kitchen together they looked like a couple of innocent little children.

A couple of weeks later, Principal Ardman began practice for the Christmas program. The three upper grades were to give the program. Some kids had to recite a

Christian poem, some took part in a morality play, and all took part in the chorus.

Free was asked to recite a long poem called "The Blind Child's Prayer." It turned out that Ma had recited the poem when she was a young girl and that on the quiet she'd specially asked Mr. Obert Ardman if her boy couldn't recite it. Ma still had the copy, a piece of hard cardboard with the poem pasted on in her handwriting. Her handwriting was a lot like Free's.

Free memorized a couple of verses a day until he knew all thirteen perfect. Ma helped him sometimes while she ironed. There was something in the way Ma acted that made him pay attention to the story in the poem. There was a death in the poem.

Principal Ardman decided the chorus should sing a hymn and a carol. They began to practice first on the hymn, "It Came Upon The Midnight Clear." He placed the boys in the back two rows and the girls in the front two. Some of the girls could sing alto so he separated them from the sopranos. But the boys were still all sopranos.

Principal Ardman kept three boys out of the chorus. One of them was Billy Donker, who sang too loud. Principal Ardman asked him to sing a solo—that way he couldn't complain. The other two boys were Tommy Holtup and Clarence Etten. When they sang it sounded like a hollow fence post whooing in a hard wind. Besides, they stuck out above the others and spoiled the nice rank-on-rank look of the chorus.

The first time through the hymn everything went fine.

"Well," Principal Ardman said, "it looks like we won't have to practice much on this one. There's some flatting going on, and Fredrika, our leading soprano there, is coming through a little too fierce. If she keeps that up we're going to have to ask her to sing a duet with Billy Donker. But all in all, not bad, not bad." He bent a warm smile on the altos, Nelda Brewster and Ruby Young. "And our altos are perfect."

Free noticed he had a frog in his throat that day. After the first couple of notes, the frog cleared up and he once again sailed up there with all the other boy sopranos around him.

"All right. Let's go through it once more." Principal Ardman blew on his silver pitch pipe, and then began to beat out the tune using the silver pipe as a baton. It glittered in his right hand as he waved it up and down and around.

They sang with all their hearts, mouths open, a bunch of baby robins tonguing for their worms:

"Peace on earth, good will to men,
From heaven's all gracious king."

All of a sudden, just as Free hit the word "will," his frog came back and he let out a loud croak. Free quick coughed to clear it up. Swallowing, he joined in again on the word "heaven." To his astonishment the frog came back even worse. He then tried to blast through it, harsh, thinking he might blow the frog out. But his voice stayed down there where Pa usually sang. And the worst was, it wasn't even singing true down there. It was out of pitch.

"Hold up," Principal Ardman cried, raising his hand. "There's something wrong here." He looked the chorus over. "I think I heard it over there. You girls keep quiet a minute while the boys try a stanza alone." He raised his right hand. "All right, one, two, three, 'It came' "—and he waved them on.

Free knew whose voice it was. Free gave his throat a hard scraping gargling clearing cough. Since no phlegm came up he decided his voice was now all right. He tried singing again. "To touch their harps with gold." Darn! The frog was still there. And it was baying away worse than ever.

"Hold it." Principal Ardman held up his silver baton. "I think I've got it located. Free, suppose you sing the stanza alone."

"Me?"

"Yes. I'll give you the pitch." Principal Ardman blew on his silver pitch pipe. "It came"—and he waved Free on.

Free turned red; trembled that he had to sing alone in front of everybody; at last let go:

"—upon a midnight clear."

The frog was gone. But in its place was the voice of a grown-up, a pure baritone like Pa's.

"Hold it."

All the kids laughed, especially his second cousins.

"All right, let's have no levity on such a serious matter as a Christmas program, please." Principal Ardman thought to himself a minute. He wrung his ear like Pa did sometimes. "Free, how old are you?"

"Ten, going on eleven. I'll be eleven next month."

"Free, I'm afraid you're having what they call a change of voice. So your voice is going to be unsteady for a while. We won't be able to trust it." Principal Ardman smiled especially kind at Free, as though he admired what Free's voice had become. "At the same time your father and mother will be disappointed not to see you up on the platform with the rest of your chums. So this is what we'll do. You just mouth the words silently and do it so it looks like you're singing with the rest of them. That way nobody will be able to tell that today you suddenly became a man."

A large snort rose from Free's second cousins.

Free wondered if it was fair to Tommy Holtup and Clarence Etten. They'd been booted out of the chorus for having a low croaking voice. But they weren't around to complain and Free decided not to say anything. He wasn't sure he liked being different from the rest.

Principal Ardman bent a hard look at the Engleking cousins. "Well, I've heard of people being able to hum a tune, but here we actually have a case of where jealous people can actually sneer a tune." He looked at Free especially kind again. "Never mind them, Free. You be the bigger man. And concentrate on doing a first-rate job on your recitation."

Christmas turned out to be a great day. A sharp gold sun shone on ten inches of fresh snow. Pa got out the bobsled, filled the bottom with thick yellow straw, threw in a pair of sweat blankets for Polly and Nell the grays, and pulled up in front of the house gate. Everybody piled in wearing their Sunday best. All wore scarves over their noses.

"Giddap."

There was no wind out and so long as their feet remained warm nobody got cold. Pa stood up in front in his great fur coat. He broke the wind for Ma standing behind him. The kids stood in the middle. The tug links jingled a steady tune. Sometimes the bobsled hit patches of ridged ice and then it slid sideways and the kids yelled. There was so much snow on the bridge over the Little Rock that the planks for once were silent. Some black crows flew out of the Tamming cottonwoods and headed toward the maples along the river.

When they arrived on the churchyard, Free helped Pa throw the sweat blankets on Polly and Nell and put the horses in the barn, while Ma and the kids hurried into church to their favorite bench halfway down the north aisle. Most people came in their bobsled or in their cutter. It didn't take long to flatten out the snow on the churchyard. The wide doorway of the horse barn was full of fathers standing around in long fur coats having a last smoke before going inside. Pa's coonskin coat was the longest and darkest. The smell of tobacco smoke and the aroma of pulverized horse manure made for a cozy man feeling.

Free left Pa to take his place with Mr. Ardman's grade-school kids in the front benches. The church was packed. Little kids and babies were glad to get in where it was warm and for once shut up. People were watching each other where they were going to sit and looking for where their kids in grade school were sitting up front.

At exactly one o'clock Domeny Donker stood up in the audience and opened the program with prayer. His pulpit had been removed from the platform and set to one side. By the time he got to the amen the fathers had filed in from the barn and had found where their families were seated. Domeny turned the program over to Principal Ardman, with God's blessing.

All the kids behaved letter perfect. They took turns marching up onto the platform and singing and reciting their pieces. Fathers, and mothers especially, looked past each other's heads to see how their children were doing. They swelled up proud if their kids did real well.

Free mouthed the words of the hymn and the carol silently while the others sang. He wasn't too sure he liked the idea. It really was cheating, though it was well-meant.

Twice Principal Ardman asked the audience and the children's chorus to sing together, once "O Little Town Of Bethlehem," and the other time "Silent Night." There was a wonderful lot of stirring around, and a ruffling of clothes as the people rose to sing each time and then settled down again. Some of the heavy ladies in church could sing like organs and they liked it that they could stand up and let go.

Free's recitation was the last piece, coming just before the benediction and the handing out of presents. Principal Ardman got up and announced him. "And now we shall hear 'The Blind Child's Prayer' as recited by Master Alfred Alfredson."

Free stood up, banged down the bench past the knees of kids, marched up the aisle and then up onto the platform. He faced the audience exactly from the center of the platform and started in:

"They tell me, father, that tonight
You wed another bride,
That you will clasp her in your arms
Where my dear mother died."

It was like everything had turned blank in front of him. It was like he was facing a heavy silver fog inside the church. He couldn't make out a single face. He couldn't even see the rows or aisles. Part of it was because the bright afternoon sun struck directly upon him through the circular colored window high in the south apse.

"They say her name is Mary too,
The name my mother bore.
But, Father, is she kind and true
Like the one you loved before?

"Please, Father, do not bid me come
To greet your lovely bride,
I could not meet her in the room
Where my dear mother died."

The sharp beam of the sun seemed to dim, then to light up very sharp in his eyes. He tried to pierce through the fog just off the edge of the platform. He wanted to find Ma's face in the crowd. He knew exactly where Pa and Ma sat, yet for the life of him couldn't make them out.

"But when I've cried myself to sleep
As now I often do,
Then softly to my chamber creep
My new mama and you."

He listened to how his voice was sounding. It seemed to be all right. Clear. Steady. He became aware that it was very quiet in church. That meant people, wherever they were sitting out there, were listening respectfully.

He put in a few gestures in the right places, as Principal Ardman had instructed him, his right hand pointing to the first mother and his left hand pointing to the new mama.

"And bid her gently press a kiss
Upon my throbbing brow
Just as my own dear mother would . . .
Father! You're weeping now."

Free was careful to back a step upon the exclamation, "Father!" as if he truly had been startled to see a father cry.

"Now let me kneel by your side
And to the Savior pray,
That God's right hand may give you both"—

Free raised his right hand dramatically—

"Strength through life's long weary way."

"The prayer was softly murmured; then,
'I'm weary now,' she said.
He gently raised her in his arms
And laid her on the bed."

The people in church became really quiet. The sun moved an inch across the circular colored window. For a second a sunbeam shown gold in Free's eyelashes; then flickered off. Like magic the silver fog disappeared and there before him sat row upon row of the multitudes. Hosts of them. It was hard to believe there could be that many faces in the world.

One of the faces moved. It was Ma. She was smiling up at him, tears in her eyes. Next to her sat Pa, head sticking out with his bold nose shining. Little Jonathan sat between them, with Everett and Albert on either side of them.

He almost forgot the last stanza. He could feel fright gathering in the back of his throat. Lord. He better not forget his lines now.

He remembered the look of Ma's handwriting on the cardboard. She had a way of writing her capital T like an F, of writing her little l's separate in the middle of a word, and of cutting off each word without a tail. A picture of the whole poem came back to him then and in his mind's eye he ran his finger down the stanzas until he came to the last one.

"Then, as he turned to leave the room,
One joyful cry was given.
He turned, to catch that last glad smile—
His blind child was in heaven."

It was over. He moved out of the slanting sun and stepped down off the platform and went back to his seat.

Domeny led the congregation in the singing of the doxology.

Free didn't sing. He listened as he enjoyed being famous.

Afterwards everybody was jolly. People stood up where they were and gossiped and smiled. Pretty soon they came over and complimented each of the children for a real good program.

Three deacons carrying grain sacks over their shoulder distributed an apple, an orange, and a sack of candy to each child. The babies got presents too, a stick of colored peppermint candy.

Free couldn't get over how big the oranges were. They were almost as big as a baby's head. It would take a while to eat them. He decided to save his and eat it slowly at home, section by section. That way Christmas would last longer. It was one way to make up for Pa and Ma being poor and not being able to give presents any more.

Free ❦ 44

IN APRIL when the weather turned warm Ma asked Free, "How would you like to visit Johnny Engleking overnight sometime?"

"Why him? He don't think much of me."

"Oh come now. He means you all right."

"Besides, both his pa and ma are lazy."

"Now, now, Johnny's father is a very good man. Really. Fat John is actually a smart man even."

"Oh, Ma."

"It's true. I respect him. He can sometimes stump Domeny with his sharp questions."

Free had to admit Fat John was quite a character. Fat John was probably the strongest man around. Pa liked to tell about how Fat John once pulled a hay rope apart with his bare hands. Free himself had once seen Fat John quiet down Con Etten, the brother of Clarence Etten. Con Etten sometimes had the fits and at the last Decoration Day picnic he'd all of a sudden started tearing a buggy apart with his hands. Fat John just put his arms around Con Etten and hugged him until he quieted down. Fat John also had a funny side to him. In church, if he knew some boy sitting behind him was watching him, he'd make his whole scalp wriggle back and forth, like he was nodding when in actual fact his head itself wasn't moving at all. He could make a kid choke with laughter in church while he himself kept staring at Domeny with solemn blue eyes.

Ma said, "There's no school tomorrow and your father's going over to Fat John to have our last butchering made into sausage. So you can go along. We'll pick you up Saturday."

"But why all of a sudden must I visit Johnny? He's always got his nose up in the air when it comes to me. Especially since last week."

"What happened then?"

"Oh, nothing really. We were playing work-up and I hit him in the belly with a line drive. He turned red in the face, started to tremble all over, and then picked up the ball and wouldn't let us play any more. It was his ball. He made all the kids mad at me."

"Maybe that's all the more reason you should go. Make up."

"Must I?"

"Yes. His mother, Etta, called today to ask if you couldn't come. Johnny and Albert both asked if you couldn't stay overnight once."

Free's eyes opened. Hey, maybe he'd made a mistake in thinking they didn't like him.

Free agreed to go. Ma made him wear his in-between clothes.

Pa rolled onto Fat John's yard around four o'clock.

Fat John had just built a new house painted yellow. He'd also painted the old barn a fresh red with white trim. But the rest of the place was still pretty junky. Fat John had the bad habit of leaving a disk or a rake stand anywhichway on the yard when he'd finished using it, instead of putting it away in the machine shed.

"What a mess," Pa said as he steered the car around through the scattered implements. "It's a wonder they know enough to use asswipe."

Johnny and Albert came smiling out of the yellow house. They had red cheeks and their hair shone white-gold from under the bills of their caps. They trudged to the house gate.

Pa said, "Where's your pa, boys?"

"You're to go in and have a cup of coffee with him," Johnny said.

"Fine. That I'll do." Pa shut off the motor and went into the house.

Johnny started to tremble. "Wanna play ball?"

Free gave him a clear look. "I didn't bring my glove along."

"We got a couple."

"Got a bat?"

"Yeh. One of Dad's cracked ones."

"Is that the one he hit the home run with Decoration Day?"

"Yeh. The one he hit over the river."

"Pa says your dad makes a great catcher. Your dad squats down low and makes a great target to pitch to."

"My dad says your pa can really throw a curve. It comes in like a crochet hook."

"Okay. Let's play."

They played in the night pasture behind the barn. Johnny and Albert didn't have any tricks in mind. They just played plain work-up and hit the ball as hard as they could. They could swing a bat okay but couldn't hang onto a ball. Their hands always closed one second too late around the ball and of course they always made an error.

When chores time came they got the cows together. They got the eggs. They hauled in the cobs for the cookstove. They fed the dry cows in the cattle shed. The Engleking chores were just like Pa's.

When they went up in the haymow to throw down some hay for the horses, Johnny asked Free if he'd ever played with it until he fainted.

Floris Haber had asked him that same question. "No."

"You ought to try it sometime."

"Have you?"

"Sure. We both have. Albert can't faint yet. But I can. Man. First it's just fun. You know. Then the next thing you know you start looking at it real hard, so that you forget where you are, and then it turns real hot and you just faint away. Most fun in the world."

The faded slough hay smelled of a horse in heat. The sinking sun outside made the air inside the high-domed haymow turn rosy.

There was a sound of beating wings overhead. The wings beat so hard puffs of air whuffed against the shingles on the barn. There were also long floating single honks of big birds, sometimes twice in a row. "Whounk. Whounk."

"Hey," Johnny said, "there's the snow geese again. C'mon, that's something to see."

They slid down out of the haymow and ran out past the hog barn. Johnny shaded his eyes against the red sun. He pointed to a silver pond across the road in the neighbor's pasture. Several V's of geese were sliding down out of the red sky toward the long pond. And every time a goose hit the silver surface, it churned up like it was blood.

"Those are big fellows," Free said.

"You bet." Johnny watched them floating down out of the south. "Too bad they don't taste good in the spring."

As the birds continued to settle in, the whole silver pond turned a beaten red for a couple of minutes. Then the pond turned silver again and on top of it rode hundreds and hundreds of snow geese. The birds formed bunches and then it was like there were long white snowdrifts stretched across the silver-blue water.

Fat John called from the barn. "John? Time to milk now."

Fat John's did their milking just like Pa did. Fat John took the best cows, and of course the tough heifers, while Johnny and Albert took the cows that were being dried up.

Fat John sitting beside a cow was something to see. He was so wide across the butt that the one-legged stool he sat on looked like a turd coming out. His belly stood so far out it touched the cow's belly and he hardly had room to reach the tits. There was no room for the pail between his knees at all and he had to set the pail on the cement floor under the bag. His hands were so wide he had to milk a tit with his thumb and upper two fingers. With his ring finger and pinkie sticking out, he looked like a milker who'd made up a fancy way of doing it. A little straw hat sat on his huge head of blond curly hair. He looked a little like a fat snowman milking a cow.

When they all sat down to supper, Fat John prayed a blessing much shorter than Pa's. He skipped over some of the sins. The strangest thing was how Fat John sat at the table with his little straw hat on. Ma surely wouldn't have liked that.

While Fat John prayed, Free looked between his fingers at what they were going to have for supper. There was a lot of meat, fried steak, fried pork chops, fried bacon, sliced baloney, sliced smoked beef. There was a bowl of beets. And there was no bread nor butter and jelly that he could see, and no dessert.

"Free?"

Free opened his fingers farther and looked up.

"It's your turn."

Free turned red. They'd finished praying, even the kids, and they'd caught him peeking during prayer. "Lord bless this food. Amen."

For once Johnny and Albert didn't laugh at him. They felt for him and wanted their pa and ma to think him good company.

Fat Etta at her end of the table by the stove swung her slow blue eyes at Fat John. "That lid, Fat. We have company."

Fat John pushed out his heavy red lips. "You know I wear it at the table, company or not."

"Don't wear it now. Be a little mannerly. This is Ada's kid."

Fat John took off his pet hat and set it on the Bible beside him on the windowsill. He didn't seem to get mad like Pa might have.

Food started being passed around. Free took some of the dried beef and a pork chop, as well as some of the beets. For gravy they used straight melted beef suet. Free passed it by. Ma always said the Big John branch of the Englekings were heavy meat-eaters. Some of the West Frisians spoke of Big John's family as beefeaters and beer drinkers and that they really were greasy Saxons and not East Frisians at all.

Free went after the pork chop first. It was getting cold and he couldn't stand cold fat. Biting into cold fat always made him want to vomit.

The Engleking kids heaped their plates with big portions of the different meats. They each took one beet. Fat John and Fat Etta had plates such as Free had never seen, as wide as a meat platter, and they heaped on the meat too. All the Englekings ate with juicy sounds.

All of a sudden Free remembered the time Ma went to visit Big John when he was dying and there were those hogs eating that dead sow lying in the mud. Luckily Free had just finished his pork chop.

Fat John had hold of a thick T-bone steak, a hand on either end, gnawing away at it, when he noticed Free's plate was empty. He lowered his T-bone a little and pushed a hunk of meat he'd just bitten off into his cheek. "Help yourself to seconds, boy."

"No, thanks. I've had sufficient."

"What? No wonder you're so skinny. Being fat is a blessing, boy. Especially in cold weather."

"No, thanks."

Fat Etta said, "Maybe Free don't like our food."

Free wanted to please them. But he knew that if he ate more of their kind of meat, he'd vomit all over the place and then they'd really know what he thought.

Fat Etta said again, "Maybe Free don't like our food."

Free could see how mortified Johnny and Albert were about him. But Free's stomach was the stronger, and again he shook his head. "No, thanks. I don't generally eat much in the evenings. Our big meal at home is at noons." Free hoped that in the morning Fat Etta would somehow serve pancakes or johnnycake so he could show them that it was true he ate lightly only at supper.

"It is here too, boy," Fat John said, hunk of meat still caught in his cheek.

Free was amazed. "You mean, you eat even more at noons?"

"Yes."

Free blurted, "A case of pigs being hogs over a platter of pork chops." Free quickly added, "That's what Pa said, not me."

Fat John's eyes opened big and blue and wondering. His belly jerked like it was going to have a convulsion. His swallowing machine worked once. And then he began to choke.

Free pinkened. "Pa didn't mean you, of course."

Choking, Fat John began to tremble so that the whole table shook.

"Fat!" Fat Etta cried. "Spit it out."

Free couldn't make out if Fat John had misswallowed because he'd suddenly got mad or because he had to laugh so.

Fat John slowly turned red, then purple. He pointed to show that the hunk of meat in his cheek had popped into his Sunday pipe. He tried to clear his throat, hard. "C-ha! C-ha!"

Fat Etta jumped to her feet. "Lean over, Fat. Quick, quick!"

Fat John pushed himself away from the table and leaned his big head down between his knees.

Fat Etta came around the table and with her hands began beating on his broad back. Whump. Whump.

Fat John turned blue-black. With his thumb and two fingers he reached up into his throat, ringfinger and pinkie wiggling around stylish near his nose. But his hand was too broad.

"Fat, we're going to have to upend you again!" Fat Etta cried. "Boys, help me. Free, you too." She gave Fat John a hard push, and he toppled out of his chair onto his broad nose, his great butt rearing up. Fat Etta threw her arms around one of Fat John's huge legs while Johnny and Bert, trembling, grabbed the other one, and together, straining, grunting, they managed to get him to stand on his head. "Free, you help too. Hit him on his back."

Free quick gave Fat John a couple of whacks on his spine.

"Harder. Kick him in the back with your foot if you must."

That Free wouldn't do.

"Oh my God," Fat Etta cried. "Here." She threw Fat John's leg at Free. "You hold that up then."

Free found himself suddenly staggering under the weight of what felt like a cottonwood log. Free almost fell down.

Below near the floor Fat John's upside-down head gagged and gagged.

Fat Etta kicked off her shoe and with the flat of her wide foot gave Fat John a thunderous kick square in the middle of his back.

Out flew the hunk of meat onto the linoleum.

"Ahhh," Fat John's upside-down head gargled near the floor in relief. "That's much better. You can let me up now."

Fat Etta leaned over head down for easier talking with her husband. "Are you all right now?"

"Let me up," Fat John said again. Then he jerked his stump legs free, retracted them, and with the rolling motion of a barrel suspended between wheels righted himself.

Everybody stood back and surveyed Fat John. Quickly black blood rinsed out of his cheeks. Within a few seconds, except for around his eyes where he looked like he'd been crying, he looked all right again. Greatly relieved, rolling their eyes and shaking their heads, everybody sat down to the table again.

Fat Etta saw that she better explain something to Free. "You probably didn't know that the Englekings are chokers."

Fat John picked up his small straw hat from where he'd placed it on the Bible and perched it on his head again. "That's what comes of it. I eat better with it on."

"Fat," Fat Etta said, "that had nothing to do with it."

"Well, I wear the hat, so I should know."

Free said, "My Uncle John ain't a choker."

Fat John picked up his T-bone again. "You're right, boy." He gave Fat Etta a mild look. "It isn't in the Engleking blood at all. It comes from my mother Sarah's people, the Rigging family. They all had throats as if they weren't put together right."

Free decided to please Fat John a little. Poor man. Free held out his plate. "Could I have some more dried beef please?" Free thought he could somehow manage to swallow some of that.

Later on when they went to bed Free got another jolt. Fat John's didn't use sheets. They slept in khaki blankets that didn't seem to have been aired out for a month. They smelled like old mouse nests.

The worst was the blankets were prickly. Free wondered if Fat John's had lice. He lay between Johnny and Albert. They both wanted the privilege of sleeping next to their guest. He waited for bites. But none came. After a while he relaxed.

He remembered the time he'd spotted lice in the hair of Maynard Tollhouse. Maynard was reciting his lesson, when his eye picked up movement in Maynard's brown hair. Narrowing his eyes, Free spotted a red louse crawling out to the end of one of Maynard's hairs; saw it stop, wiggle around; and then saw it turn around and crawl back and disappear into where the hair was thicker. Later on Free decided he'd better warn Maynard about it. Maynard was kind of a friend and he didn't want him to be caught with lice by Principal Ardman. But Maynard had only laughed at Free and said it was cow lice and that it came from leaning his head against a cow's flank while milking her. Maynard said cow lice never stayed on a human being very long. They couldn't stand the human being smell.

Free fell asleep at last. He dreamt about lice all night long.

The next morning at breakfast Fat Etta served pancakes with homemade butter and dark syrup. There were two platters of meat on the table too, beef and pork, but Free politely passed them by. Fat Etta set out milk to drink. The milk was still warm. It had come straight from the cow without having been run through the separator. Free passed that by too. He added a little extra syrup on his pancakes for moisture. He loved homemade butter melted in syrup. He ate until his stomach hurt, ten pancakes.

When he got home that evening, at supper table, Ma asked Free if he'd had a good time visiting his cousins.

Free said slowly, with a quiet look at Pa, "Fat John almost choked to death."

Ma looked at him peculiar. "Are you pulling my leg, boy?"

Pa knew something good was coming and got set to laugh.

"It's true," Free said. Free cut a piece of lean ham neatly with his knife and fork and ate it. There was nothing like eating at home. "We all had to help Fat John stand on his head and hit him on his back."

"Dear Lord," Ma said.

Free told about it.

Everybody laughed, Ma hardest of all.

Pa shook his head. "Yeh, he's some comical guy all right."

When they finished their potatoes and ham and home-canned beans, Ma got up and began slicing some balkebrea she'd made. It was what Pa sometimes called Frisian bulk bread. In the Old Country, Pa said, it was what the poor people ate and made them strong. But the rich, Pa said, heh heh, liked white bread better, which was why they were always so paffy fat and short-lived. "In fact," Pa said, "every once in a while the King would feel so hungry he'd go out in the country and ask a peasant's wife if she couldn't serve him some balkebrea."

Free liked balkebrea even better than pancakes. Sometimes he helped Ma make it. They always had it after butchering a hog. Free knew the recipe by heart. One took two pounds of cracklings, a pint of meat juice, three quarts of water, a tablespoon of salt, stirred it all thoroughly, and let it all come to a boil. Next one added enough buckwheat flour to make it pasty thick and then poured it into a loaf mold and let it cool. One sliced it then, fried the slices on a hot griddle until they were a crispy brown, and served them with butter and syrup. That crispy brown crust soaked in butter-laced syrup really was too good for most people.

The balkebrea was so delicious that night, smothered in its puddle of dark syrup and melted butter, that by the time Free had his third slice the skin under his eyes began to flush, as if the sweet-soaked brea was too rich for his blood.

Free was properly thankful that when Ma did use fat, she was always careful to use hog lard and not beef suet. Even as he ate the balkebrea, he was already looking forward to breakfast, when they'd have fat-with-syrup, clear hog fat so boiling hot that it spit a little, poured into a soup bowl to make a little lake, with in the middle of it, smaller, a pond of dark syrup. Breaking off a piece of bread and dipping it expertly in the clear hot lake and dark pond to catch up a little of both, man, that was food fit for the President himself. Free ate six slices.

Free ❦ 45

IT WAS THE LAST DAY OF May, a Saturday, and school was out and ahead lay a whole summer of play and wonderful times to come. Even Pa knew he was going to have a great year. There'd been plenty of rain in late April and the grain stood blue deep and the corn ran in perfect check over the hills. Cows and horses couldn't keep up with the grass. And birds? The willows were full of song sparrows and cardinals sang high in the cottonwoods and meadowlarks told the whole world all was well in the sloughs.

It was as if even Ma was feeling her oats. It all started at supper table when Pa caught Albert sprinkling two spoons of sugar on his barley soup.

"Here, here," Pa said, "one spoon per serving, young fellow. I guess we better go back to me doling out the sugar again." Pa gave everybody his piercing look. "Even Free." Pa skimmed some of the sugar off Albert's barley and dumped it on Everett's.

Albert first looked black, then began to suck his thumb.

Ma smiled at Albert. "Shame, shame." Ma had a way of smiling like she belonged to the New Testament. She shamed one finger off another at him. "Only girls suck their thumbs."

Albert withdrew his thumb. He looked at it and pouted.

Ma smiled some more. "Look at whose lip is hanging all the way down to the third button."

Free remembered how Fat John could make them laugh by making his scalp move. Hoping he could do the same for Albert, Free tried it. To Free's surprise, his scalp did move.

Ma was startled. "I didn't know you could do that, Free."

"I didn't know I could do it either," Free said.

Pa tried to move his scalp, but no matter what kind of face he made his white hair stayed locked in place.

Everett also tried it, but all he moved was his eyebrows.

Free tried other things then. "Hey. Look. I can make my ears wiggle like a mule's." Then he made his nose do stunts. "See? Like a rabbit."

Ma laughed. "For goodness sakes. That's an Engleking trait, all right. It was said Great John could do all those things."

"Huh, puh," Pa said.

"It's nothing to brag about," Ma added. "You get that gift from God."

"Well, me," Pa said, "at least I got good teeth." Pa opened his mouth and showed everything he had all the way back to his throat. For a second he looked like a wolf.

"Goodness," Ma said, "that's enough to scare me into the next life."

It was fun to be able to do special things and Free continued to slide his scalp back and forth and wiggle his ears and quiver his nose.

A look of mischief showed up around Ma's nose. "I bet none of you can do this though." She stuck her tongue way out and made the tip of it curl up and reach for the point of her nose. Her tongue tip wiggled back and forth, as far as it could go, like an inchworm looking for the next place to land, and finally managed to touch her nose. The underside of her tongue was covered with blue angleworm veins. "See?"

Pa tried it; and couldn't even come within an inch of his nose. "I suppose you inherited that from Great John too?"

"No," Ma said, "that's only peculiar to me." She looked at Free. "Unless he can."

Free pushed his tongue way out; narrowed it to a searching point; touched his nose.

"Pots before kettles," Pa said.

"Watch me," Albert said. He thought all the stunts fun and had sat up straight again. He arched up his tongue tip and easy touched his nose.

Pa laughed. "In God's name, it looks like I've sired me a batch of nose-lickers by way of a champeen dam. Why, you're all as bad as that cow that could reach around and drink her own milk."

Ma and the kids laughed loud and merry at that. And Albert finally ate his barley pap with its one spoon of sugar.

The next morning, just before Pa got up, Free heard Pa downstairs urging Ma to do something for him. Free was about to turn over and get in a few more winks, when he

heard Ma say, plainly, through the hot air register, "Not on Sunday morning."
"Aw, love, you really want to though, don't you?"
"Well, a little. But it's wrong today."
"I'll take the blame, love."
"Do you need it that bad then?"
"Love."
"Oh, all right, if you must."

Some bed noises followed, creaking springs, rustling sheets. It sounded like two people getting set to wrestle. After a minute their bedsprings began to creak regular. After another minute Pa groaned as if he was the happiest man on earth.

Pretty soon Pa swung out of bed and got into his clothes. He didn't say good morning to Ma or nothing. He stomped in his socks through the living room. In the kitchen he first washed his hands in the sink. Then he set on the coffee and pulled on his shoes.

All too soon Pa called up the stairs. "Free?"
"Mmm."
"Time to get up, son."
"All right."
"Got to get ready for church."

Free ❦ 46

FREE WAS IN BED about an hour when he remembered he hadn't kissed Pa and Ma good night. He flipped back the sheet and in his B.V.D.s went downstairs. Pa had his feet in the open window to cool them off and was having a last cup of coffee, and Ma was darning some socks under the sharp gas lamp. Ma was nearest and Free kissed her first, "Good night, Ma," and then went over and kissed Pa on the whiskers near the corner of his mouth where it was moist, "Good night, Pa."

Free thought they acted kind of strange, but went back upstairs to bed and thought nothing more of it.

He had some trouble finding the right spot to curl up in. He tossed and turned back and forth several times. On one of his turns he bounced a little too hard and the mattress collapsed under him and there was a loud slam on the floor below the bed. Darn. One of the slats had slipped out again. Good thing the pot was under the other bed.

Groaning, he slipped under the bed and pushed the slat back in place.

Albert woke up. "What's going on around here?"

"Flip, you guys must've been rousing around when you went to bed. That middle slat slid out again." The kids lately had given Albert the nickname of Flip. He had a funny way of flipping over in sleep sometimes, sudden-like, and still not waking up.

Flip said nothing.

Free climbed back in bed.

Free must've napped. Because for a second he didn't know where he was. He followed his thoughts about for a time, one thing after another, about Fredrika and her bossy ways, about Wilma and her velvet belly, about Johnny and his snow geese.

After a while it came to him he'd forgotten to kiss Pa and Ma when he went to bed that night.

At least he couldn't remember that he had.

He went back over the evening. Nope, he couldn't remember that he had. It was the night before last that he'd gotten out of bed late and had gone down and kissed them.

After a while, sure that he'd forgotten again, he got out of bed and on bare feet went downstairs. Pa had his feet in the open window to cool them off and was having a last cup of coffee and Ma was darning some socks under the sharp light.

Free kissed Ma first. "Good night, Ma."

Ma smiled funny at him. "Good night, boy."

Free next went over and kissed Pa. "Good night, Pa."

And Pa said, "Goodness, son, what have you done? This is the third time you've come downstairs to kiss us good night."

Free was dumbfounded. "Maybe I fell asleep so fast I forgot."

"Three times, son?"

Free blushed. That night at the table he'd read the last half of Chapter 26, from Matthew, where three times Peter had denied he knew Jesus of Galilee. "I know not that man," and immediately the cock had crowed.

"It's all right, boy," Ma said. "You might not have kissed us at all. At least you're not mad at us."

Free looked down at the floor. He wondered what was wrong that he should have forgotten he'd kissed them twice before. It was kind of like denying them all right. "I'm sorry."

Ma smiled. "Kisses from one's own boy a mother can never have enough of."

Free went back to bed.

Apostle Peter had gone outside to weep bitterly. Free himself didn't quite feel the need to go outside to weep, certainly not bitterly. But he sure felt sheepish.

Free 47

THE LITTLE CHURCH in Sioux Center had quite a baseball team. They beat everybody around. The way they bragged about their team was hard to take. Finally Garrett, Pa's new hired hand, formed his own church team in Bonnie and challenged the Sioux Center bunch to a game on the Fourth of July at Bosch's grove near Hello.

The Bonnie church team practiced in Tante Josephine's pasture. Garrett caught, Pa worked out at third base, Uncle John played at first base, Sherm, now a hired hand at Uncle John's, played shortstop. The older Etten boy, John, played centerfield. Ed van Driel, the underhander, was the pitcher. Garrett's three younger brothers made up the rest of the team, Alfred at second, Robert in right, and Rich in left. All the men on the team were good hitters and all except Pa could run like the dickens.

Free went along the nights Pa practiced with the team. Free chased foul balls and wild throws. He ran across the green grass in the cool evening air. Once Free managed to run a long ways and catch a foul ball over his shoulder.

For two weeks before the Fourth, after he'd finished his chores, Free played baseball with Everett, pretending he was the great Ed van Driel pitching the Bonnie church team to victory over the Sioux Center bunch. Everett batted for the whole Sioux Center team and at first Ed van Driel struck them out one two three every inning.

Free didn't know the names of the Sioux Center players and after a while he and Everett switched to playing major league games. When Free got the mail each day he also picked up Mr. Hopkins's mail. Mr. Hopkins took the *Sioux City Journal* and Free figured out a way to peek into the sports section for the major league box scores without making it seem he'd opened the paper. Mr. Hopkins liked his newspaper crisp and tight. The *Journal* favored the Chicago Cubs—it was the nearest major league city—and always had them in the headlines. "Cubs Blank Pirates, 4-0." Free became the Cubs and Everett the Pirates.

Everett batted for each of the Pirates, Little Poison Lloyd Waner, Big Poison Paul Waner, and the great Pie Traynor, right down the batting order; and when it was the Cubs' turn at bat, Free swung for each of the Cubs, Cliff Heathcote, Riggs Stephenson, and Charlie Grimm. Both Everett and Free tried to bat in the style of the man they stood in for, closed stance, wide stance, close to the plate, deep in the box.

It didn't take long before Everett, working at all the batting styles, became a good sticker. And he did it even though his left arm, still weak from infantile paralysis and a bad burn, was only half as strong as his right arm.

Free asked Pa to show him how to throw a good curve.

The great Joe Melette himself had shown Pa how to throw a hook. You threw it off the front finger with a snap of the wrist and elbow. Free soon learned that to make it really hook, the spin of the ball had better be flat like the spin of the earth around the sun. He also discovered that if he held the ball so all four seams caught the air, the ball really slid off and down, away from the plate.

They played on the yard, using the corner of the chicken house for a backstop. If they threw the ball hard enough against the chicken house, it would bounce halfway back to the pitcher. Batting right-handed a fellow had to be careful not to swing late because of all the windows in the house. But if a fellow swung early there was the whole long yard to hit across, all the way to the sack swing. And to hit it over the trees, not even Babe Ruth could do that. The only real worry they had was after a rain. Then that dratted Gil the cream-hauler rooted up the yard with his cream truck, leaving ruts sometimes four inches deep, all because he wanted to claim he never got stuck.

Everett made a pretty good pitcher too, learning how to throw to a batter's weak spot. Though he had trouble catching line drives above his chest. He couldn't get his lame left arm up fast enough. Everett even learned how to throw a curve.

When Free batted as Cliff Heathcote he tried to hit the pitcher and get singles up the middle. When he was Riggs Stephenson he leaned low over the plate and tried to hit singles over the shortstop's head. When he batted like Charlie Grimm he hit smashes over first base.

One day Free decided he needed a home-run hitter so he traded his right fielder and a bench warmer for Cy Williams of the St. Louis Browns. To be fair, he let Everett trade for a long-ball hitter too, getting Harry Heilman from the Tigers.

It took a while to hit the first home run. It had to be into the trees where the sack swing hung. Free swung, and swung, and hit dribblers and pop-ups, or struck out when Everett threw him the curve. But one day Garrett gave Free a new bat for a boy just his size. It swung smooth, like a cow's tail going after a fly. And instead of a big swing, he learned that the quicker he swung the farther the ball sailed. Finally one day while batting as Cy Williams he caught one on the meat part of the bat, and away she went.

"There she goes! there she goes!"

Everett turned his curly head to watch it go.

The ball kept rising, and going, and reached a height as high as a cottonwood, and sailed on and on, and at last slowly sank, and, miracle of miracles, cleared the trees and landed on the road.

"Wow!" Free cried. "Cy Williams's first home run as a Cub."

Everett looked like he was going to quit playing.

Free quick praised Everett for the pitch he'd thrown him. "I tell you, Everett, that was your best curve yet. I was lucky to hit it."

"You was?"

"Sure." Then Free couldn't help but jump up and down some more. "Wow." And he ran to get the ball for Everett. Usually it was the pitcher who retrieved the ball.

Everett appeared to be grateful for that.

The morning of the Fourth bloomed like a coneflower, big and wide and pinkish. Free and the boys rushed through the chores. Pa helped Ma get the picnic food ready. Jake Young was hired to do the evening chores so they could stay over for supper and see the fireworks at Hello.

On the way over to Bosch's grove Pa and Ma had a short fight. It started just as the old Buick rolled under the first viaduct of the Cannonball railroad and ended when they passed under the second one. The kids in the back seat had never heard the folks fight before and they started to laugh they were so scared. Ma was quite upset to learn that Pa was going to play third base in a real ball game at just about the time that her favorite missionary, Reverend Merle Babcock, was going to give a report on how many souls he'd been able to save on the Zuni Indian Reservation.

"It's only a game for little boys," Ma said. "Not for grown men."

"But baseball is at its best when it's played by grown men," Pa said. "It takes brains to play the game right."

"Fooey," Ma said. "It's just some throwing of a leather ball back and forth between bags of straw."

"You got to hit it too. And there's not more'n a half dozen men in the world that can do it right. Babe Ruth. Ty Cobb."

"Babe, yeh," Ma said. "It's a game for babes all right."

Pa gave the steering wheel one pound with his fist. "Wife, that Mister Merle Petcock is too much of a pretty bird for me."

"His name is the Reverend Merle Babcock."

"Wal, whatever it is, I'd rather play baseball. So I tell you what I'm going to do. I'll listen to your missionary fellow for a half hour and then I'm going to play ball with the Bonnie boys."

Ma shut up then. Whenever Pa said, "I tell you what I'm going to do," he meant it and a person had better give up trying to get their way with him.

Bosch's grove lay on a slope a mile east of Chokecherry Corner. A person knew they were getting near the grove because of all the firecrackers going off. Pa parked their Buick under the west edge of the trees.

Cars and horses and buggies stood scattered all along the road and into the pasture south of the trees. The trees in the grove were mostly cottonwoods, with here and there a hackberry and a maple. It was cool under the tall trees and the womenfolk and their little babies liked it. Old men favored it too.

Pa gave Free a quarter. "That's all you're gonna get today. So you better spend it wisely. And as for the rest of you littler tykes, your ma will buy you what you deserve."

Ma said, "Now remember, you kids, we're having lunch right after when you hear the doxology being sung by the whole crowd, you hear?"

"Ya, Ma."

Pa went one way into the grove to join the men talking and Ma headed for the plank benches where a fine crowd was already sitting. Everett and Flip and Jonathan went with her.

Free spotted some kind of love affair going on in a roadster two cars over from their Buick. A young man with white-gold hair was talking to a young girl with brown hair. Free decided to hang around a while.

He slipped behind Pa's steering wheel to watch.

The young man was trying to persuade the girl to do something she didn't want to do. She kept saying, "No, I can't," and shaking her head. She sat with her head bowed a little, looking down at where her fingers were twisting through each other. Once she threw a wild look at the grove as though she was afraid somebody might have heard what he said. Once the young man gave his steering wheel a single pound, like Pa had, as though he was giving her only one more chance. Another time the young man picked up her hand and folded it into his hands and played with it generally and at last placed his thumb in her palm. She didn't like the way his big thumb lay in her palm and she jerked it back. Free made out only two words, "elope" and "rape." "Elope" meant to run away and get married, and "rape" meant a kind of cabbage without a head in it like Barry Simmons grew for his cows. Finally the girl nodded, and said, "Yes," and the young man immediately smiled like a big red moon just coming up. He started his roadster, backed up in a wild curving turn, and was off on two wheels.

Free ran into the grove. Thousands of people were sitting on row after row of planks. Some of the planks had oozing knots. The multitudes were listening to a minister from Zion, Michigan, and he was giving them hell for liking it here on earth when they really should be getting ready to go to heaven. The minister had a blue mouth. Free couldn't stand to see all the bulging behinds of women hanging over the edges of the planks. Some of the mothers had thrown their babies up on their shoulders and the babies were drooling watery cottage cheese on the mothers' dresses.

Free couldn't find any friends. So he looked up the concession stands set deeper under the trees. Some raw planks had been nailed to the trunks of four trees to form square stands. The knots in the nailed-up planks oozed resin too and a fellow had to be careful where he placed his hands as he leaned in to see what there was to buy. Free got out his quarter. Everything sold mostly for a nickel: pop, cones, Cracker Jack, big long all-day suckers.

Free pondered what to buy. The quarter turned damp in his hand.

Finally he decided on a cream soda. But no more than that before lunch. Better to spread that quarter over the whole day.

"Something, little boy?" a jolly man with a bald head asked. The bald man wore a butcher's apron over his white shirt and Sunday trousers.

Free stared at a cattle tank full of water where various kinds of pop were floating around in it along with some chunks of ice.

Free placed his quarter on the plank counter. "A cream soda."

"Cream soda coming up." The man plunged his bare arm into the icy water, came up with a dark bottle. He uncapped it, handed it over. He gave Free back two dimes in change.

"Thank you."

Free went and hid behind a wide tree to make sure his brothers couldn't see him drinking the cream soda.

He smelled his pop. Mmm. It crackled bubbles up into his nose. He took a sip. Mmm. It tasted even better than it smelled. It was like green tea flavored with brown sugar and citron.

He took another very small sip and then placed his thumb over the mouth of the bottle to keep the pop cool.

It was very noisy under the cool trees. Bawling babies, young kids playing tag, girls screaming when a firecracker blew up near their feet, young men horsing around, someone blowing the horn of a car, and the minister from Zion preaching away a blue streak.

Free took another small sip, swirling it around the tip of his tongue. Wow, was it ever good. He swilled it around from one cheek to the other to get every last bit of sweetness out of it.

Two fathers with brown beards stood talking by a fat maple. One of the fathers had his little girl by the hand. She was looking at all the kids playing tag nearby. She had brown wavy hair and dark brown eyes. There was a dimple in her cheek like the eye of an Idaho potato. She was wearing a white blouse and a red dress and white slippers. She was pretty.

Somebody yelled something behind Free. The girl looked his way and her eyes crossed with his. For a minute.

Her father at last finished talking with the other father, and smiling, gave her a tug, and started to lead her away. She looked back at Free and gave him another good look and disappeared into the crowd.

Free had trouble breathing for a moment. He took a big sip of his cream soda. He filled his mouth too full and couldn't swish it around to get the full benefit of it.

He felt a push in his behind. He looked around for the privies usually set up special for the Fourth. At last he found them inside a little cluster of plum trees. A couple of old women were just then stepping out of the girls' privy. They pulled down their corsets at the same time that they threw a sad look up at heaven.

Left hand already unbuttoning his blue knickers, while with his right hand he held onto his cream soda, Free pushed open the boys' privy and stepped inside. And almost fell down from the terrible stench. Holy-ka-boly. People had pissed all over the sides of the holes and over the wood floor. Some had even missed the biggest hole pooping. And down in the big hole itself on what once had been green grass, were all kinds of colored poops, every color imaginable, all the way from chalk to axle grease.

It was too much. He backed out of the privy and pinched back the push in his behind. He'd wait until the family got home that night. Then he could sit in a decent privy.

He heard a quartet singing. Sure enough, the Zion preacher had finished and four fellows in tails from Christian College in Zion were harmonizing in "Swing Low, Sweet Chariot."

Pa and Ma had said the Christian College quartet was a great one. Free hurried over to hear them. He found a spot beside a tree not too far from where Ma was sitting. He was careful to hold his cream soda behind his leg, thumb still pressed over the mouth of it.

Three of the men in the quartet were tall, and they sang all right, but whenever they made gestures to go along with the message they were kind of clumsy. The fourth fellow, a tenor, was different. His name was Timothy Stor. He was a dapper fellow and his gestures were always just right. The women in the crowd hung on his every note, and he sometimes added a couple of notes to give them a little thrill. He had the good sense to be solemn when singing a religious song. During "Come Where My Love Lies Dreaming," when he held his head to one side on folded hands, and closed his eyes, some of the women sobbed right out loud.

Free quick looked to see how Ma was taking it. Hey. There was a tear twinkling on her near cheek. Looking farther down the bench, Free was surprised to see that Pa had also come over to hear the quartet. Like Ma, he too had a tear sparkling on his cheek.

When the whole multitude finally rose to sing the doxology, Free saw he had only an inch left of his cream soda. He sang the first three lines of the doxology and then, while everybody sang the last line, he finished off the sweet soda in one big swallow.

They ate on the grass beside the old Buick: potato salad, bread and sliced ham, pie, and a drink of lemonade out of Pa's harvest jug.

After they gave thanks, the whole family went back to the seats in the grove. Pa made Ma sit on the back bench, so in case the missionary rambled on too long, Pa could escape unnoticed and head for his baseball game. Ma was smart enough to select an old plank to sit on. Old planks didn't bleed resin. Ma almost had a fit any time she found a stain in the clothes she couldn't get out.

The people sang a couple of psalms, and then Reverend Merle Babcock, the famous missionary to the Zuni Indians, got up to give his address.

Free studied the missionary carefully to see why Pa called him that Mister Merle Petcock fellow. Missionary Babcock was tall and his brown wavy hair was combed back pompadour. His shiny black eyes could one minute be tender and the next minute cruel. And his voice was even more winning than Uncle John's when Uncle John specially wanted you to do something for him. He'd lived with Indians so long he acted a little like one, quick dark looks to the right and left. He wore a light gray suit. He had a blue watch fob made of beads with a yellow lightning zigzag in it.

Missionary Merle Babcock said the Zuni had their own religion. They'd worked it out themselves. It was a pretty good religion too, with a heaven and a hell, a good and an evil, a day when the world was created and then a Judgment Day yet to come. But they had no notion of a Savior and they didn't believe in sin. They didn't think it a sin to kill a Navaho. When the funny thing was they always apologized to an animal before they killed it for meat.

"Now what kind of religion is that . . . when we white Christians know that we are all prone to sin and that we need Christ Jesus so that we can be saved? Thus these poor ignorant benighted unenlightened creatures are souls lost to Satan. There are presently 2,563 of them on the reservation, of which we've managed to save two souls, leaving 2,561 doomed to everlasting destruction. These people, who in some respects are even more democratic and liberty-loving than we Americans are—yes, that's true—they actually celebrate a ritual in late December on almost the very same day we observe our Christmas Day. The only trouble is, this ritual takes the form of a lewd dance they call the Shalako dance. Imagine! Yes, they are totally lost!"

Missionary Babcock took a handkerchief from his lapel pocket and brushed tears from his eyes. His voice began to purr.

"O poor red man doomed to hell, living in your dusty bug-infested adobe pueblos in New Mexico, don't you realize that if you do not believe on Christ as your Savior you'll disappear into the darkness forever, much as a snowflake, for a moment beautiful as it drifts down from heaven, will disappear, vanish"—Missionary Merle Babcock snapped his fingers—"forever once it falls into the waters of a raging river? Forever?"

A cold shiver swept down Free's back. What a great speaker.

Missionary Babcock moved to the very edge of the podium. His eyes glowed like Ma's sometimes did when she wanted to touch a person. "You who have children of your own . . . listen. When a brown-skinned Zuni boy looks at his father, this is what he sees: a grossly fat man drunk most of the time, who still believes that his dusty pueblo is the center of the universe. Is it hardly a wonder the little brown boy grows up to be another no-good loafer? Both father and son lost to everlasting perdition. Never, never, will they know the loving glory of heaven."

Another cold shiver swept down Free's back. A tear tickled in his eyelids. He looked at where Pa was sitting. Pa was listening so hard his mouth had fallen open a little.

"Or take the little brown-skinned girl. When she looks at her mother, this is what she sees: a creature who at twenty is already wrinkled, prematurely old, and saddened beyond all repair of soul, vermin-infested, superstition-ridden. Is it hardly a wonder the little girl grows up to be another wanton heathen, a reservation whore? The poor dear beautiful brown children. O poor lost mortals. O lost, lost."

Free thought of that special face he'd seen that day, the pretty girl hanging onto her father's hand. Suppose she had to live in a pueblo full of bedbugs with a set of drunk fat parents?

"So I plead with you, people with a glorious heritage, members of the church of our Lord Jesus Christ, listen, when you are asked to help us save the souls of those remaining 2,561 heathen Zuni, will you not give generously? Give and give until it hurts? As you can? Will you not share a portion of your bread with them? At least a tithing of that which by all rights already belongs to the Lord?" Missionary Babcock paused, and held out both hands in a sweet begging manner. "Give. Give." Then Missionary Babcock's voice turned hoarse. "Give!"

Free looked at the two damp dimes in the palm of his hand.

Missionary Babcock wiped his brow with his handkerchief, then sat down, crossed his long legs, and bowed his head as if waiting for a verdict.

A potbellied minister from Middleburg rose to his feet. "A collection will now be taken up. Will the deacons present from the churches of Bonnie, Hello, Middleburg, Sioux Center, and Rock Falls please step forward, and then pass the hat through the crowd? Meanwhile, we'll all sing, 'Bringing In The Sheaves,' as we remain seated."

When the hat came by, Free was first of a mind to give both dimes to help bring those poor little brown-skinned kids to Christ. But then he remembered that a tithing meant only a tenth of one's personal crop for the year. He decided that one dime would be more than enough. That'd leave him a dime for himself to buy two more cream sodas. So with a happy smile he dropped one of the dimes into the collection hat.

He felt so good about it that after the singing he went over and gave Ma a kiss in front of everybody. "You know what, Ma?"

"No, boy. What?"

"I'm gonna be a missionary too someday. And I'm gonna give an address on the plight of the red man, better than Merle Babcock's even."

"That'll be wonderful, boy." Ma placed her hand on his head. "Perhaps I haven't lived in vain after all. To see my own flesh and blood go out and save souls for our dear gentle Jesus will be a wonderful thing to witness."

Pa kept shaking his head over what he'd just witnessed. Pa'd changed his mind about that Mister Merle Petcock bird. "Man oh boy, I surely heard a great sermon today. That missionary was better by far than I ever expected. He gave us the before, the what-for, and the therefore of why we should support our mission work amongst the red heathen. Man, man."

Just then Sherm came running up. "Say, Alf, ain't you gonna play third base for us today?" Sherm was carrying his glove and he was pounding in it with his fist. "It's our turn next for infield warm-up."

Pa got to his feet. "You know, I plumb forgot about that ball game." Pa said down to Ma, "That's how good your missionary friend is."

Sherm looked kind of disgusted. "We've been playing catch for hours already." He pounded in his glove some more.

Free looked. Sure enough, a lot of men in shirt sleeves were running around in the pasture across the road.

A firecracker exploded under the bench Ma sat on. She jumped up and grabbed for her heart. "Oh." Her blue eyes rolled. "Those terrible inventions of the devil. Ohch. And then at a Christian Fourth yet."

Sherm smiled a little. "It's just some kids having fun, Ade."

"They keep going off all day long."

"C'mon, Alf." Sherm said it like it was an order. Then he turned and ran off. His sneakers flittered a clean white in the blue shadows under the trees.

Pa gave Ma a look as if to say, "You see how it is."

Free said, "I'm gonna watch them play, Ma."

Ma sighed. She'd already had her way in part. "Oh, all right. Go, then. The both of you."

Free looked at the damp dime in his hand. Quickly he made up his mind to get himself a cream soda. Watching Bonnie beat Sioux Center while sipping his favorite pop would be heaven.

By the time Free ran through the pasture gate, the big noisy crowd had divided into two camps, the Bonnie fans along the third-base line and the Sioux Center supporters along the first-base line. Behind them the owner of the pasture had rolled out a hayrack apiece for each group of ladies to sit on as a kind of bleachers. The owner had also put up some chicken wire between two tall poles for a backstop. Some volunteers had earlier gone over the pasture with some scoops to pick up all the cow pats, dried or fresh. Someone had set up a cattle tank behind the backstop and filled it with ice and pop. Insults and jeers sailed back and forth between the two camps.

Free sat on the grass just behind third base. From there he could easy watch Pa play third and Sherm play short.

Bonnie was taking infield practice. Pitcher Ed van Driel hit Pa grounders to help him catch up with the others. Pa bobbled the first couple. He lobbed the balls back to Garrett the catcher and made faces to show how it hurt to throw with the old soupbone. But gradually Pa got better. Finally Ed van Driel hit a wicked grass cutter to him and Pa caught it on the short hop and fired a perfect peg across the diamond to Uncle John on first base. Then Garrett the manager knew Pa was ready.

Free shook his cream soda a little to make it fizz and then took a sip. Bubbles spitting out of the dark of the drink crinkled in his nose. The taste of it reminded him of the dark-haired pretty girl he'd spotted that morning. Then, just as he thought of her, as though his eyes had been pulled by a magnet, he saw the pretty girl on the Sioux Center side, right behind first base, still holding onto her pa's hand. Her pa was smiling—he looked like a nice man—and she was looking through the crowd as though trying to find someone.

Another cold shiver swept down Free's spine. Was she looking for him? He watched closely. Too bad she was part of the enemy. Maybe the game could end in a tie and then both could be happy.

An umpire walked out into the middle of the pasture diamond. Somebody behind

Free said it was the minister from Matlock, Reverend Erpelding, who loved baseball. He was as old as Pa and wore a dark suit.

"Batteries for today," Umpire Erpelding bawled in a loud domeny voice, "for Bonnie, van Driel and Engleking, for Sioux Center, Gath and Tinklenberg. Will the two managers please step forward?" Umpire Erpelding waggled a bat over his head. "We'll see who gets first bats."

Garrett and Tinklenberg came over from opposite base lines. Some players from both sides also gathered around to make sure all was fair.

"Nubs," Garrett said quick.

"All right," Umpire Erpelding said. "Then Sioux Center gets the first grab." He threw the bat handle up in the air toward Tinklenberg. Tinklenberg caught the bat with his right hand just below the trademark. Garrett then placed his right hand above Tinklenberg's, Tinklenberg placed his left hand above Garrett's right hand, Garrett placed his left hand above Tinklenberg's left hand, and so on until they reached the end of the bat handle. Tinklenberg was the last to be able to place a full hand on the handle. He tried to make his hand as broad as possible to make it reach to the knob, but couldn't quite do it. Umpire Erpelding leaned in to watch it all carefully. He had quick black eyes and a smile that curved up at the corners in a clever way.

Garrett let his free hand come down like a bird claw on the knob and caught hold of it. There was just room for his fingertips. "Nubs," Garrett said with a smile.

"Right you are," Umpire Erpelding agreed. "What's your choice, take the field or bat first?"

"We take the field," Garrett said.

"Play ball!" Umpire Erpelding bawled, and he walked over to take up his position behind the mound in the middle of the diamond.

The Bonnie team ran out on the field. They chirped encouragements to each other. The Bonnie crowd let out such a loud cheer that in their excitement they surged across the third-base line. The umpire shooed them back.

Right-hander Ed van Driel strode to the mound. He took a few warm-up pitches. He threw a hard submarine ball that seemed to come out of his ankle. He couldn't throw a curve. His pitches came up like rising white bullets. Each pitch came faster. Finally he said he was ready.

"Batter up!" Umpire Erpelding cried.

The first man up for Sioux Center was a shorty, right-handed. Van Driel put his right foot in a little hole, wound up, and let fly. Just as he let go of the white ball he flashed a big wide white smile. It let the batter know a wicked one was coming.

"Strike." And the game was on.

The Bonnie bunch roared; the Sioux Center fans booed.

Free didn't cheer much. There was too much to watch. Free wondered how people found time to cheer at all.

The first five innings van Driel kept mowing 'em down with his submarine ball. Twice he struck out the side. Each time he struck out a batter his white wicked smile made the Sioux Center swinger so mad he beat the ground with his bat.

Meanwhile Gath was having trouble getting his outdrop over. It was as big as a hoop. But the Bonnie batters waited until he got behind and then went after his fast ball. He appeared to grove it right into the meat of the Bonnie bats. Line drives shot all over the field.

Pa got a walk, a pop-up, and a double. His double was hit so sharply it went on a line all the way to the fence by the road.

"Atta boy, Alf," Sherm cried from the Bonnie sideline. "Your wife could've hung her week's wash on that one."

All the shelling of Gath made the Bonnie girls up on their hayrack shriek and dance for joy. While the Sioux Center girls in shock fell silent on their hayrack.

When Sioux Center came to bat in the top of the sixth the score was 10 to 0 in favor of Bonnie. But from then on the tune of the game changed. Van Driel began to tire and the Sioux Center boys began to time his pitches better. Soon enemy line drives began squirting all over the field. The three outs that half of the inning came tough. Uncle John made a great play at first, leaping high in the air for a wild throw, and then, as he came down, throwing his body at the bag to tag it just in time. "You betcha! that's why he plays first for me!" Garrett cried. Van Driel managed to strike out the second batter when he accidentally threw a hook for the third strike. And Sherm made, as Pa said afterwards, "an unpossible catch" over his shoulder while running away from the infield down the left-field foul line. The bases were full at the time with one run already in. Sioux Center at first couldn't believe it and said Sherm must have caught the ball on the bounce. But the Reverend Merle Babcock, just then coming through the gate by the road, saw it, and said Sherm caught it, and they could hardly gainsay him. Score: 10 to 1.

In the last half of the sixth, Gath suddenly got control of his outdrop and started getting it over the outside corner low. Then it became Bonnie's turn to flail the air. They looked like butterfly hunters the way they swung. Gath had the big white teeth to go with his outdrop too, and he in turn let the Bonnie bunch have his wide wicked smile. The Sioux Center supporters went wild. The ladies up in the hayrack yelled and danced. While the Bonnie fans sat tight, hoping their boys would somehow pinch through to victory.

Pa struck out for the last out in the bottom of the sixth.

"C'mon, Pa," Free cried. "Hit that ball."

Pa gave Free a sheepish smile as he came by to take up his position at third base. "It's easy to say, hit that ball. But that curve of his is worse than an emery ball. It's like he's smeared it with invisible ink."

The Sioux Center swatters came up with three runs in the top of the seventh, then four more in the top of the eighth; while the Bonnie bums scored none, six men in a row striking out. Not even Garrett or Sherm could hit the dazzler Gath was throwing up there.

Free became so nervous he forgot his pop, as well as the dark-eyed girl behind first base. After leading 10 to 0, it hadn't seemed possible that Bonnie could lose. Yet there it was, Bonnie, 10, Sioux Center, 8.

In the top of the ninth, with Sioux Center batting, van Driel kept rubbing his elbow after each pitch. His smile was sick. Eight pitches and van Driel had walked two men. With Sioux Center's home-run slugger, Sam van Gelder, up next, it looked like the end for Bonnie. Van Gelder waved his bat around like it was a whisk broom. If van

Gelder ever got ahold of one of van Driel's tired pitches, look out, good-bye, that'd be the ball game.

Garrett took off his mask and called time out. He walked slowly up to the mound to have a talk with van Driel. He kept rubbing the ball, blue eyes going every which way. Van Driel hung his head.

"Let's play ball!" the Sioux Center nuts cried. "Quit stalling around. We got chores to do yet tonight."

The sun for a fact was low in the sky.

"Play ball," Umpire Erpelding cried.

Garrett turned and with his finger called Pa over to the mound.

"Me?" Pa said.

"Yeh, you."

"Okay." And Pa stepped over.

Sherm and Uncle John came running over too. All five conferred. Then all of a sudden there was Garrett walking back behind the plate again and there was Pa sticking his right toe in the pitching hole and throwing a few warm-up tosses. Van Driel took Pa's place at third base.

"Alfredson now pitching for Bonnie," Umpire Erpelding announced.

Free's belly drew up tight. Pa was going to pitch.

The Sioux Center players along the first-base sideline baited Pa about his long legs and his big nose.

"Play ball!"

The big clean-up hitter, Sam van Gelder, stepped into the batter's box. He took Pa's first two pitches for strikes. Van Gelder didn't mind. He was looking for a certain fat pitch. Pa couldn't throw very hard any more, but he could get the ball over. At home sometimes Pa could hit a cow on the tail with a cob every time he threw.

The Bonnie ladies cheered the two strikes like they thought them two outs.

Pa leaned in to get the next signal.

Garrett gave it, careful to hide it in his pud between his knees.

Pa nodded. A big sly smile curved across his face.

Free groaned. That famous smile meant a curve. Pa could throw a curve all right, but it wasn't like Gath's big outdrop.

Free thought: "Van Gelder's going to hit a home run." Then Free, to save the game, jumped to his feet and yelled, "Pa, throw him your fast ball. You know, that dark fast upshoot." Free hoped Van Gelder would hear him and so get fooled after all despite Pa's big give-away smile.

Pa wound up, his arm and his important nose came around, and then the gray ball streaked toward home plate. Garrett stiffened himself to catch it no matter what.

For a moment from the way Garrett stared at the coming ball it looked like he thought sure it was going to hit van Gelder.

Van Gelder thought the ball was going to hit him too. He hadn't seen a curve all day and expected a fast ball.

All of a sudden, about a dozen feet from the plate, the ball stuttered, and then like one of Pa's big smiles it curved right over the plate.

"Strike three!"

Wow! The Bonnie crowd roared, and the Bonnie ladies up in their bleachers began hugging and kissing each other like crazy.

Van Gelder looked like he'd just got notice that somebody in his family had died.

Garrett came out from behind the plate holding up the ball and shaking it at his team telling them to hold hard now for two more outs.

The next batter wasn't going to wait to get struck out by Pa's smiling curve. He went after the first pitch and hit it on one bounce right smack at van Driel. Everybody held his breath knowing that van Driel's arm was gone and that he probably couldn't throw the ball all the way across the diamond to first base. But van Driel smiled his big white smile and ran over and stepped on third for a force.

The next batter, Bert van Citters, was one of those pesky swingers from the left side. He let Pa's first two pitches go by figuring Pa wasn't used to pitching to left-handers. Both pitches were balls. For Pa it was like milking a cow from the wrong side.

Garrett frowned so hard inside his mask he looked like a gorilla with a headache. He thought things over and then gave the next sign.

Pa studied the sign. Again he flashed his famous smile.

"Oh," Free groaned to himself as he got down on his knees, "I wish Pa wouldn't give himself away so like that."

It was a curve all right. But the batter took it thinking it was going to be outside. It curved over.

"Strike one."

Again Garrett gave the sign, and again Pa leaned in and nodded and then wound up with his big smile, and again the pesky van Citters took it.

"Strike two!"

On the next sign, a sly smile showed up on Garrett's face inside the mask. The batter couldn't see it of course.

Pa saw the sign and showed surprise.

Free knew what that meant. Garrett was calling for a fast ball right down the middle. If only Pa would really be sly and act like he was going to throw the curve again. For Pa to show surprise was to tip his mitt.

Some mean boys from Sioux Center just then lighted a giant firecracker and threw it out onto the middle of the diamond. When it first landed it looked a little like a corncob. But then it exploded about four feet behind Pa with the blast of a Civil War cannon. Pa came up off the ground like he was an old-time acrobat.

Pa came down stomping mad.

Free thought: "Oh oh. Now they did it. When Pa gets mad he can do anything. They made a mistake there, thank God."

After the smoke cleared away, the umpire called for everybody to get back to the game. The batter stepped in. Pa wound up and let fly. He didn't smile. But his jaw stuck out like the hard toe of a blucher shoe.

As the ball streaked toward Bert van Citters, it could be seen that he really didn't know what to expect. His bat kind of jiggled. He set himself to hit the curve, then unset himself a little in case it was a fast ball. It was right down the pipe with everything Pa could get on it. Van Citters had to swing. And he swung late.

Crack. It was a handle hit, a soft-liner with just enough umph in it to start sailing over Sherm's head out at shortstop.

Sherm took off after it, going so fast with his head tipped back looking at the ball that his cap fell off. His gold hair streamed out behind him. At first the ball gained on him and led him by a couple of steps. But after a couple dozen yards the ball began to die and then Sherm began to catch up to it. Meanwhile with two out both runners on base were rounding the bases for home. Just as the ball was about to hit the green grass, Sherm made an all-out stretch for it, turning his glove over backhanded, at the same time that he put down his right hand to break his fall. The ball landed exactly in the middle of his glove. The moment it hit the glove, Sherm let his shoulder and neck hit the ground, and then made a complete somersault in the air and landed flat on his back. He held up his glove to show he still had the ball. Sherm was some shortstop.

"The batter is out!" Umpire Erpelding cried.

The Bonnie fans roared onto the field.

Afterwards all Uncle John could do was stand there and shake his head. "That Sherm. He held onto that ball like it was his own soul."

Free knew somebody else was also a hero. He ran across the diamond and hugged Pa around the waist. "That was a great relief job, Pa."

A little later Free remembered he was still carrying his cream soda. His thumb was white where it clamped down on the mouth of the bottle. Great. He still had a lot left to drink to celebrate the victory.

Taste of the dark drink reminded him of the dark pretty girl. He looked around for her special face, over at where the Sioux Center supporters were slinking away. He soon spotted her. She still had her hand in her dad's hand, and she was crying and looking sad because her town had lost.

After a moment Free felt sad too. A fellow couldn't have everything, a victory, a drink, and a girl. He let her disappear into the crowd.

Free lingered behind to go over the game again. He toed the hole from where Pa had thrown his fooler of a fast ball. He pretended he was Sherm catching a soft-liner over his shoulder on the dead run. He leaned ahead faster than he ran and fell on his belly, spilling part of his drink.

All in all a great day. Bonnie, 10; Sioux Center, 8.

Back in the grove, when they sat down to picnic supper, Ma asked Pa, "Well, Alfred, did playing that ball game advance the kingdom of God any?" Ma asked it with a smile, but there was still a stinger in it.

Pa bit into a radish. "Wal, that missionary fellow, Merle Babcock, must have thought so."

"Oh?"

"Yeh, he was in the crowd enjoying the game like everybody else. In fact, I think he was a little on our side."

"Oh, come now, Alfred. He wouldn't take sides in a child's game."

Free got mad. "Ma, Pa was a great hero today and the missionary had to see that. Pa came into the game in the top of the ninth with nobody out and saved the game with his great pitching. It takes a hero to be a great pitcher, Ma. He even surprised me."

Pa appreciated it that Free stuck up for him and gave Free a sly smile in thanks.

Ma still shook her head. She was stubborn about that baseball.

That evening everybody headed for the Hello baseball diamond on the west edge of town to see the fireworks. The playing field was surrounded by people standing a dozen rows deep. Faces and light summer shirts glowed under the sparkling light from all the skyrockets.

Sitting with his head back, gullet stretched, watching the umbrella rockets explode high above, Free couldn't help but belch a couple of times. Each time cream soda fumes from his stomach rose in his nostrils. The fumes reminded him of the dark pretty girl and wistfully he yearned to see her just once more.

It was when several cannon crackers went off, trailing bluish streamers and casting a bright Judgment Day-like light over everything, that he caught sight of that special face. She wasn't more than a dozen steps away. And it hadn't been an accident either that he'd spotted her. She was looking at him. She'd been looking at him for some time even. Because the minute he caught eyes with her she had to work to break free of him. Slowly she turned her head and looked the other way. Ah. Then she knew he'd been trying to catch her eye all day. Better yet she must've liked him a little too. The proof of that would be if after a while she'd shyly turn her head and look at him again.

He decided to fasten his eyes on some face to one side of her, at the same time that out of the corner of his eye he could still be half-watching her.

Sure enough, a minute or so later her head slowly wried around, and after she'd made sure he wasn't looking directly at her, she looked at him like before. The strange girl was in love with him.

It couldn't be more wonderful. Because he loved her.

And he loved Ma, and loved his brothers, and loved Pa, and loved God and Jesus and the Holy Ghost. He even loved Satan a little bit. It was a grand Fourth of July.

Free ❦ 48

JAKE YOUNG WAS a couple of years older than Free. He wasn't very bright, and he blundered around some, but he had so much pep that his friends tended to forgive him.

Free and Jake sometimes met when they both went to get the cows on Sunday afternoon. Jake's people, the Sam Youngs, had taken over the Buwulf farm where Dick Buwulf used to live.

One Sunday Jake asked Free why he and his brothers didn't go swimming with him and his brother and sister sometime.

"You go swimming in the river?"

"Sure. Below the cliff there."

Free had seen the river one evening where it curved dark and green and silent under the trees below the yellow clay cliff. It had looked awful deep to him. "Ain't there some drop-off holes in it? Or whirlpools?"

"Nope. Not one. It's nice and sandy and pecker deep there. You couldn't drown if you tried." Jake's brown eyes jumped with fun. His thick red lips curved all the way back to his loose ears. "Why don't you and your brothers come tomorrow? Floris and Willard Haber are coming too."

"But we don't have bathing suits."

"We don't either. We swim naked."

Free's eyes opened. Jake's sister Gertie swam naked with them? That he had to see. "What time?"

"Right after dinner at noon. We always sneak off while Pa is taking a nap."

Free and Everett stole off too while their pa was taking a nap. They ran barefoot most of the way. Only when they topped the last hill did they slow down. On the slope below them gooseberries grew as thick as bristles on a boar. Beyond the next ravine where the river kept cutting away stood the yellow clay cliff.

Sure enough, the Youngs and the Habers were already having a high old time. They were leaping around in the green water. With their elbows and knees sticking out, they looked like a bunch of white frogs at play.

Free and Everett slid down through the gooseberries, then pushed through a fringe of willows onto a sandy beach. Clothes of the kids lay scattered around on the sand. Free and Everett hurried to get out of their clothes too, shirts and overalls and underwear. Then they skipped to the edge of the riverbank and plopped in. They sprayed up white explosions in the flowing green water.

The water was cold. Yow. Free had to work at getting his breath. But he dove under again and when he came up for air the second time it was all right.

The Young kids and the Haber kids were so busy splashing each other in a water fight they didn't notice Free and Everett at first. When they did, they let out shouts of welcome. "So you made it after all. Great." Then they began another water fight.

Free thought the noisy slewing around in the water was the most wonderful fun he'd ever had. He soon learned that if he held his hand half-cupped with the fingers crooked over at an angle, and if he skimmed the heel of his hand about an inch deep in the water, he could shoot water like a fire hose at the enemy, even twenty feet off. He began to shoot water with both hands.

In the middle of a bunch of different water battles, he finally found himself spraying water at Gertie. He recognized her by her long clay-red hair. Otherwise from what showed above the water she looked like a boy. Her eyes were pinched shut. She was holding one hand over her nose while fighting with the other hand. Free hit her in her sucking mouth with a shot of water, short and hard like hail. She had to turn and duck. He kept after her and she had to dive into the water to get away. She dove so deep she upended herself, keyholes showing.

Floris hit Free with a side-shot of water and Free had to turn away and defend that side of himself. Gertie got away.

The swimming appeared to wake up Everett. He hopped around in the shallows on the far side like a wild idiot. He swam under water in the deep part and snuck up on people and tripped them backwards into the water. The kids were all glad Everett was at last part of the bunch.

Big horsey Jake climbed up on the riverbank and then shinnied partway up a thick willow. The willow bent over like a whip. "Well, here goes nothing," he cried as the willow waved up and down. Holding his nose with one hand, he sprang for the deepest part of the river, his petcock lifting up while he went down. He disappeared squatting, making a big volcano of a splash, then after a moment rose to the surface, red mouth opening first, then brown eyes.

Pete Young tried it next. He was much smaller than Jake, and neater looking. He was covered with a rash of rusty freckles. When he sprang in he looked like a folded cricket.

Everybody had to try diving then. Pointing his hands straight out in front of his nose, Free half sprang, half tipped off into the gently streaming green water. He slipped in like a spear. Only trouble was his nose filled up and stung green.

The bottom of the river was soft sand. Free could feel grains of sand eddying over his toes. It was like minnows were tickling him.

Floris was almost as horsey rough as Jake. Only he was handsomer. He decided to back up a ways and take a flying jump off the bank. Floris ran loose-jointed but he could really go, and when he sailed off the edge of the black riverbank his feet were still churning the air. He hit the water like a skipping stone, then sank in, one hand straight up.

Gertie had to try it next. Clay-red hair tossed back, arms flinging around, she ran with her knees high right off her hips like a boy. A fellow hardly noticed she was made different. She sailed off the bank like she meant to run across the surface of the water. But of course she wasn't Jesus and finally went under like everybody else.

Willard Haber had to try flying in too. He was short-legged and ran like the front set legs of a pony. When he hit the water it was like someone had thrown a sack of cement into it.

They hardly talked. They yelled. There was so much to do in the wonderful slow-flowing green river. The taste of green water deep up in the nose was better by far than all the cream sodas in the world.

Pretty soon they heard someone calling them from a long ways away. "Jake? Gertie? Time to do the chores. Get the eggs."

That broke it up. They crawled out. Their cheeks were blue and their fingertips a weathered white. They dressed on the riverbank partly turned away from each other. The clay cliff glowed like a big egg yolk above them. They agreed to come back the next day and then, waving to each other, hurried home. Free and Everett took the cows home with them. That saved one trip down the pasture.

That night it came out about Garrett. Free heard Ma and Pa talk about it after he'd gone to bed. He had trouble hearing them clearly from where he lay, so he snuck into the attic over the kitchen and heard the whole thing word for word. Garrett had knocked up Laura Pipp and had to marry her. Garrett? Who'd been a great hero on the Fourth.

The next morning Free heard Pa scold Garrett in a kind way. But Garrett hadn't liked it and had shown his teeth. "Well, Alf, what do you want me to do, gnaw off my balls?"

When Free and Everett arrived at the swimming hole that afternoon, Jake and Floris and Gertie had heard what Garrett had done too and were talking about adultery. They dog-paddled around in the water. The littler kids were too busy playing in the shallows to worry about adultery.

Just as Free was about to step into the water, he spotted a dead crab lying on the sand. It was crimped up into a tight circle. Crabs in the river? With their awful purple pinchers around? The thought of one of them grabbing him by the big toe made him shiver. If it wasn't that swimming was a lot of fun he'd never think of going in with those things lurking around in the shadows of the waters. He got into the water slowly.

Everett hurried in ahead of Free and joined the littler kids.

Jake swam a little ways with only his head sticking out and his hands underwater. "Everybody does it before they get married."

Floris swam a little ways, then said, "Well, I ain't yet."

Gertie didn't like the way Jake and Floris were talking. She sank down neck deep and crab-walked over to where the littler kids were playing in the shallows. She made her face blank.

Jake said, "Well, I have."

Floris said, "You have? With who?"

"Me and Pete do it to Gertie every Sunday morning while the folks're in church."

"You do?"

"Sure. We wait until the folks are for sure gone to church and then we go upstairs to Gertie's bed."

Floris rolled his eyes. "Man."

Jake began to play with himself underwater. It could be seen through the green water that he had a big one. He also had a little hair, more than Floris. Jake's patch was reddish like Gertie's long clay-red hair. Jake grinned funny. "Ham and eggs between your legs, my machine and your machine will make a baby. C'mon, Floris, Free. You try it too. The Palmer method of penmanship."

Floris said, "I couldn't in cold water."

Jake said, "Did you ever dream about it in your sleep and then wake up with it already too late and you grabbed hold of it to enjoy the last of it, so that you both did it and yet didn't do it?"

"No."

"Not? Well, me, I think maybe I'm gonna marry my right hand."

All of a sudden Jake's eyes closed and he moaned and bent over backwards.

Floris admired what Jake had done. His thick dark brows crossed together. "Man, and you did it in cold water."

Free wished he had more hair. Like Gertie he carefully stayed neck deep in the water so Jake and Floris couldn't examine him.

Floris said, "I'm gonna ask my folks to visit your folks some night, and then Gertie and me can run off together when we play hide-and-go-seek and then I'll finally get to do it once too."

Jake didn't have much to say for a minute. He'd become as sober as a deacon. "Gertie won't do it except on Sunday mornings upstairs in her bed."

"Why not somewheres else?"

"I dunno." Then Jake said, "C'mon let's horse around like we did yesterday."

But Floris and Free somehow couldn't get into the spirit of it again. Not even the green sting of water in their noses was the same. Both kept trying to catch a glimpse of Gertie out of the water, and Gertie kept herself down neck deep the rest of the afternoon. Nor did Gertie come out of the water and dress with them when it was time to go home. She waited until they were all out of sight.

On the way home, driving the cows up ahead of them, Free got to thinking about Garrett again. Garrett was always talking about it. Like that time when Free brought Pa and Garrett lunch one afternoon where they were cultivating the west forty. Free hadn't paid much attention to what Pa and Garrett were talking about while they ate their sandwiches and drank their chilled tea, until Garrett said, "He was so clumsy she finally had to tell him he had it in the wrong hole. That's as dumb as he was." Pa had grunted, and had the funniest look on his face, like he'd gotten something down his Sunday pipe.

When Free and Everett got back to the yard, Free right away knew something was wrong. Ma had just come out of the garden carrying a handful of beets by their heads. She broke off the heads with a snap and threw the beets into a pail. "Where've you kids been all afternoon?"

It was no use lying. Ma already knew. "Swimming."

Ma placed her hands on her hips like a general. "Where?"

"In the river."

"You could've drowned. The river is deep in some places."

"Where we went it was only so deep." Free turned to Everett. "Wasn't it?"

Everett looked to one side, away from both Free and Ma.

"Well, anyway, who was it you were swimming with today?"

"The Habers and the Youngs." What was Ma after?

Ma reset her hands on her hips. Her face was a little red. Her eyes were blue and square. She bit on her tongue a couple of times. It could be seen she was trying to figure out how to ask a tricky question. "Was there anything funny about your swimming together today?"

Everett stared at Ma wall-eyed.

Ma kept after them. "Different? You know?"

Free thought of what Jake had done. If that was what she was after she'd never find out from him. That was for a boy to know and have to himself. "Just guys playing around in the water."

"Was there anything peculiar about any one of the guys?"

Everett woke up to what was wanted. "Yeh, one of them was a girl."

"Ah." Ma shook her head. "Then it's true then."

Somebody had called up Ma on the telephone. Drat that invention, like Pa said. Gertie must've told her Ma that Jake and Floris were talking dirty about adultery. That was a laugh after what Gertie had done with her brothers on Sunday morning while her folks were in church. Though Free could see how that might have happened without them meaning anything bad by it. There was something about Sunday morning when you were home alone that made you think of doing something special and hot. Anyway, Mrs. Sam Young must have got hysterical about her poor innocent daughter Gertie swimming with all those boys and started calling up all the other mothers about it.

Ma let her hands fall. "Well, what's done is done. And from your behavior I can see that it must have been innocent enough." Yet Ma waggled a finger at Free, gently. "After this though, young man, you ask for permission first before you go swimming. You hear? And with whom."

"Yes, Ma."

"Now, we won't say any more about it. Go do your chores." Ma turned to go into the house, muttering to herself, "Lord, Lord, when sex rears its ugly head, one never knows what's gonna happen next."

It was four o'clock the next Sunday and they were driving home from church. The old Buick had just rolled across the plank bridge over the Little Rock River, when Pa thought he heard an odd noise. He let up on the footfeed a little to hear the better.

Free happened to be looking up the river toward the sandy beach where he and Fredrika had once roasted some wieners. All of a sudden he was surprised to see the sandy beach disappear under a rushing tumbling wall of brown water. The wall of water was as high as a grove and it was sticking full of tree trunks, fence posts, old decayed logs. It looked like a wide pincushion was rolling downriver lickety-split.

"Pa!" Free cried. "Look. Towards Tante Josephine's there."

"Gotske!" Pa tromped on the footfeed. "We've got to get out of here. Get to higher ground."

The old Buick zoomed up and in a minute they climbed to the next rise of land. Pa pulled up at the corner and jumped out to look back at the river valley. So did Ma and the kids.

The wall of water rushed on past Tante Josephine's yard. It didn't quite reach to the foot of her house. There were a lot of sucking noises in the roaring wall. There was no stopping it. The east edge of the wall of water sudsed across the lower pasture. The brown flood was the highest in the middle where the water rolled the fastest.

The high center of the brown flood rushed under the plank bridge. The water rose so high that a few somersaulting trees hooked in the bridge supports. After a moment the running flood pulled them free again.

Pa said, "A cloudburst up the river somewhere I betcha."

Everybody looked to the northeast. All they saw in the way of clouds was the wisp of a drained-out thunderhead.

The sides of the brown flood soon lapped up into the ditches, then quickly rose until it began flowing over the road. Just watching it do all that was a hard thing to believe.

"There goes a cow," Flip cried, "tumbling over and over."

Ma said, "Let's hope no poor human being got caught in it."

"There goes a chicken coop," Everett cried. "With all the chickens still sitting on the roof."

"Man," Flip said, "God must've got out of bed on the wrong side this morning."

"Albert," Ma said, ruffling up Flip's white hair a little, "Don't talk like that about God. That's blasphemy."

Cars and buggies began to pile up on the other side of the bridge. They were families who'd left the churchyard a little late.

Pa said, "All of a sudden the river looks like the Missouri."

Free watched where the water had edged toward them in the roadside ditch. "I think it's quit coming up though now, Pa."

Pa watched then too. "Yep. In fact it's already going down."

Pretty soon some of the bigger trees across from Tante Josephine's yard began to emerge. All kinds of junk hung caught in their branches.

A peculiar odor came off the brown flood. It was like the smell of an old strawpile butt that somebody had just stirred up with a fork.

"Well," Pa said, "that's it, kids. Let's go home and do the chores."

The next morning at breakfast there was a general ring on the telephone, ten shorts. That always meant trouble somewhere.

Pa reached back over his head and took down the receiver. "Yeh?"

A voice crackled in the receiver. It was so sharp Pa had to hold the receiver away from his ear a little. They could all hear it in the kitchen. ". . . the body is somewhere down below the clay cliff there."

Pa broke in, speaking up loud at the mouthpiece. "Say, Sheriff, this is Alfredson. Where did all that water come from so fast?"

"They had a cloudburst up near Yellow Smoke yesterday afternoon. Seven inches of rain in twenty minutes."

"Great shining stones."

"Yeh, it came awfully unexpected." Sheriff Rexwinkle's breath ruckled in the phone. "Say, now that I got hold of you, Alfredson, are you very busy?"

"Got a couple of jags of hay to get up."

"Could it wait?"

"What do you want me to do?"

"Hunt for the body on your side of the river there. Below your pasture. We could sure use an extra set of eyes."

"All right." Pa hung up.

Ma was white over the nose. "Who drowned?"

"That little Hoffman girl."

The kids all quit eating.

Pa said, "You know how that Pete Hoffman always drives a horse and buggy to church? And won't buy a car? Wal, yesterday he hardly gets onto that bridge west of Sam Young there, when that wall of water hit them broadside, dumping him and his wife and the little girl into the river. Pete and his wife grabbed hold of a tree and hung on. And the horse made it too, to the other bank, with the buggy. But the little girl got washed away."

"Little Tena."

"Yeh."

"That poor little kid."

Pa swung his swivel chair around. "Free, you're coming with me and help look."

"All right, Pa."

Ma said, "Yes. Daily we are surrounded by a thousand dangers."

Nobody could eat much after the sheriff's general ring.

Free read a passage from the Bible and Pa added a couple of words about the Hoffman girl in his prayer of thanks.

Free put on his straw hat and followed Pa outdoors.

Pa decided to take a four-tine fork along in case they had to fish around for the body in the deeper holes.

The floodwaters had backed up into their pasture the day before. Halfway up the draw they'd floated a big log against a line fence post and had cracked it off. Pa temporarily braced up the broken post with a dead limb.

When they emerged from the ravine, they found floated junk left everywhere: soaked dead chickens, bloated hogs, tobacco cans, rusted cream cans, a wagon box half full of mud. Each one of the dead bodies had its own powerful putrefying smell. The overall stink was awful.

Some of the floated stuff up on the grassy bank moved.

"Look, Pa."

"Yeh, son. Snapping turtles."

"Big ones, Pa."

"You bet." Pa stopped to stare down at the turtles. "I didn't know we had any that big around here. They must've been washed down out of some mudhole above."

"They're all tipped over, Dad."

"Yeh, they got tumbled over by the flood and now they're left high and dry."

"Some of the tipped-over ones look dead."

"Naw, they've just pulled their heads in out of the sun."

"Will they die upside down like that?"

"They're apt to."

Their yellow bellies and their dwarf wrinkled legs looked ugly. Their little alligator tails gave them the look of a monster.

"Wal, son. let's get on with the hunting for that poor girl."

Free lingered behind. "I think we ought to tip them over onto their bellies again Pa. I feel sorry for them."

"You know what a snapping turtle can do to you in the water, don't you? Snap your toe off just like that. They've got jaws powerful enough to cut a bone in two."

"I still think we ought to turn 'em right side up. 'Tain't right to leave them this way. They're God's creatures too."

"Maybe we better kill one and take it home with us for soup."

"Ullk, Pa."

"If you were hungry enough you wouldn't say that."

Free caught hold of the edge of the shell of the nearest snapping turtle and heaved. It was heavy, and very greasy, and his fingers slipped off. Close up the creature smelled like a wet slough.

"Don't get your fingers too close to its head there. It'll snap at you."

Free tried again and, grunting, managed to tip it over on its belly.

The turtle lay very still for a moment. Its long head, half-turned around from its efforts to turn itself over, slowly began to unwind back to its natural position.

Free tipped over several more of the dull brown land monsters. He hated their slimy touch, their awful rotted-grass smell, but a person couldn't let the poor creatures suffer either.

"For goodness sake, son, suppose we hadn't come along here?"

"I still think we ought to help them, Pa."

"Wal, if that's your mind, I guess then I better help you be a good Samaritan."

Free and Pa tipped over a good dozen as they went along the south bank of the river. Most of them were too stunned to move at first.

The river was still up a little. It ran brown and dirty. Small dead creatures were still coming down it, floating on the surface—mice, beetles, grasshoppers. All the trees on the south bank had flotsam hanging in their branches up to a certain height. A fellow could tell exactly how high the flood had come.

They were just entering the curve above Uncle John's swimming hole, in his acre of wild land, when they heard a shout. It came from somewhere ahead.

"Shh," Pa said, stopping, holding up a hand.

Free cocked an ear too.

"I've found her," a voice said. "She's over here."

"All right. Coming," another voice said.

Pa said, "That's Arlo Barth and your Uncle John. Come."

Pa and Free hurried down along the sandy beach. The flood had torn out the line fence on both sides of Uncle John's corner of land. The little woods of wild willows on their left lay bent down almost to the ground, full of wet straw and dirt. The older willows looked like haystacks up on stumps. Still carrying his fork, Pa climbed a black bank. Free followed him.

Uncle John and Arlo Barth were standing under a tall plum tree looking up. Free recognized it as the only wild yellow plum tree left along that part of the river. All the rest of the wild plum trees were of the hard red kind that turned sweet only after a hard frost. The year before he and Everett and Sherm had picked six big milk pails full of yellow plums. The wild yellow plum was a sweet plum and the sweetest ones were always those that had a little touch of red on the sun side. It was the tree's off year and there were no plums to be seen in its prickly branches.

What looked like a store dummy from Rexroth's Department Store lay hooked in the upper branches some eight feet off the ground. A white Sunday dress was soaked to it.

Pa stared up at it a while. "Reminds me of an Indian burial."

"Shh, God forbid," Barth said. "That's heathen."

"She never had a chance," Uncle John said.

"Wal, how're we gonna get her down?" Pa said, leaning on his fork.

"We better get an axe and chop down the tree," Barth said.

Free spoke up. "Not that plum tree. That's the only one left around like it."

Barth looked at Free funny. "But the body's got to come down."

"Yeh," Uncle John said. "I think it's commencing to smell already."

"Maybe I can reach her with this fork." Pa reached up after her with his four-tine like she might be a bundle up on a hayrack.

"Don't!" Free cried. "Not with a fork, Pa."

"How else are we gonna get her down if you want to save that tree?"

"I'll climb up and unhook her for you."

"Ain't that pretty grisly work for a boy?" Pa said.

"I want to save that tree, Pa."

"Okay. It's your stomach. Here, I'll give you a boost." Pa set his knee out so Free could use it as a first step up into the plum tree.

Uncle John held Free by his back until he could grab the first limb. From there Free shinnied up until the limbs became prickly.

Free maneuvered himself past a spiny limb without hooking his shirt or overalls. Though he finally had to take off his straw hat and let it sail to the ground.

He got his foot set in the crotch of the limb and gave himself a push up. His head brushed through a branch of thick leaves and there she was. He found himself face to face with the body. Her head hung thrown back and her long gold hair was caught on the prickles of a slender branch. Her hair was smooth. There wasn't a tangle in it. The water washing through it had combed it as perfectly as though her mother had just brushed it for church. The eyes were partly open, circles of blue showing through tiny slits. For a second Free thought there was life in them and that some kind of brain was watching him. But then he noted the pupils were fixed in a wide last terror. She was dead all right. Her lips were parted and her teeth showed like the tips of two rows of chalk crayons. Her cheeks had the color of blue milk. Her nose was blue, flared open like a pair of washed-up seashells. She looked a little like Ma when Ma was dead tired.

"Can you loosen her?" Uncle John called up.

The body didn't smell of maggots so much, like that rabbit in the junkpile, as it did of rotted grass overheated in the sun.

"Can you loosen her?" Uncle John repeated.

"I think so." Free couldn't get himself to touch her right away. He examined how the body hung caught. "I think it's only her hair holding her in place. Like Absalom in the Bible."

"Don't blaspheme, boy."

"You'd blaspheme too if you could see and smell what I do."

"Told you," Pa said.

Free worked at loosening her gold hair. The hair felt as soft as a colt's tail. The flood had taken one turn of her hair around the slender branch. It didn't take but a moment for him to free it.

Free was shifting around in the tree to see what else was holding her up, when abruptly there was the sound of cloth tearing. It was the white dress. As it tore the body slowly turned over; then the body, naked except for a pair of little blue bloomers, slipped down through the branches of the plum tree.

Uncle John saw the slim naked body coming and set himself in the right place and caught it before it hit the ground. He did it with a half jump and a flourish. The body acted like a springy quarter of beef. He placed it on the grass.

Free almost fainted out of the tree.

"Are you all right up there, son?"

After a moment, Free said, "Coming." Free pulled the torn dress free of the prickles. He balled it up and dropped it to the ground. Then he dropped out of the tree.

Uncle John tenderly wrapped the white dress around the girl's stiff body.

Nobody said anything.

Uncle John picked her up and carried her across the shallows in the river. The still risen river almost came to the top of his red hip boots. There weren't any jokey expressions on his face. He had driven his Ford down his pasture to his swimming hole and he carried the body toward it. He placed the body in the back seat. Then he cranked up, got in, and slowly drove home across the bumpy grass.

Arlo Barth slowly went his way down the river to his pasture. Pa and Free trudged their way back up to their pasture.

Nobody had said good-bye.

As they walked along the muddy bank Free saw that all the turtles had crawled off. He could see where their wriggling trails disappeared into the brown river.

For a second Free saw his own body dead some day.

When he thought of how Uncle John would handle his body, deft and sure, and carry it home to Ma, he cried a little.

Free ❦ 49

THAT FALL the Coopers and the Ardmans finally had enough of the high and mighty ways of the Englekings.

When Domeny Donker accepted a call from a richer congregation in the Big Church near Pella, the Bonnie church had to find a new minister. Candidates nominated were just-graduated seminarian Melvin Dusseldorf, Reverend Tiller from Plato, South Dakota, and an old domeny living in Canada. All three were invited to conduct a service in the Bonnie church. The old domeny in Canada said it was too far for him to come, but the other two came.

Dusseldorf was a slim fellow with very red hair. Two minutes into the sermon and he was already foaming at the mouth and leaping from one side of the pulpit to the other pointing everybody straight to hell. The Coopers and the Ardmans took a liking to him. He'd be just the fellow to put the Englekings in their place.

The Englekings favored Reverend Tiller. He was about forty, had brown curly hair, blue eyes, and humorous lips. He had a fine domeny style about him. He could smile and look tough at the same time. God had touched him. The Englekings respected that in him.

After a lot of loud angry debate, lasting until one o'clock in the morning, a vote was taken. Each of the eighty-three families had one vote apiece. The final tally, as announced by gnarly Deacon Abt, was fifty-three votes for Tiller, thirty for Dusseldorf. When Elder Etten called for a unanimous vote so that Tiller would know the whole congregation was behind him, the Coopers and the Ardmans, galled to the heart, all got up in a bunch and walked out.

At school the kids broke up into two gangs too. The Engleking kids said the Cooper and the Ardman kids were a bunch of wild rascals and called them the Katzenjammers, after a comic strip. The Coopers and the Ardmans said the Englekings had the big head and called them the Big Shots. The first name stuck; the second didn't.

The kids gossiped like fiends about each other. One week the Katzenjammers claimed it was one of the Englekings who'd knocked up the telephone operator above Tillman's Mercantile. The Englekings came back and said, no siree, it actually was one of the storekeepers along main street who'd done that, a man both sides traded with. The next week the Englekings shamed their fingers at the Katzenjammers because their leader, John Cooper, had declared bankruptcy, and so had neatly got out of paying all his true and just debts. John Cooper was a moral leper. The Katzenjammers said, not so, most of the money he owed was to the estate of Big John Engleking, and Big John had trapped John Cooper when he loaned him some money for which he'd charged excessive interest. It was Big John's family who were moral lepers because they practiced usury, and the Bible was flat out against usury.

One day the kids came to school talking about the terrible fight there'd been between Willie Alfredson and Wayne Haber. Willie was Pa's cousin. Willie'd once done something wrong to Johnny Westing's mother up in a haymow. Willie hated the Englekings and always voted with the Katzenjammers. Wayne was a brother of Hal Haber. Where Hal had a great smile and could catch about as good as Johnny Kling of the Cubs, Wayne had a perpetual mad-on and had the bad habit of wanting to pass everybody on the road. He liked to leave other people behind in a cloud of dust. Wayne hated the Katzenjammers and voted with the Englekings.

It happened that Willie's and Wayne's farm bordered each other. Willie's bull jumped the fence one day and bred several of Wayne's cows. Wayne went after Willie's bull with a pitchfork, saying he'd be damned to hell first before he'd let any of that mongrel Alfredson seed get into any of his prize stock. Willie overheard Wayne and ran to get his own pitchfork, saying he'd be damned to hell first too before he'd let a dummed post of a neighbor insult his prize bull. More words passed. The wives of the two men hurried outside to calm them down, but by the time they got on the scene, it was too late. The two-legged old boars were at it, trying to jab each other in the belly. Wayne managed to nick Willie's arm and Willie managed to rip Wayne's fly open, exposing his tool for both wives to see. The two men kept circling and jabbing each other, and swearing that this time they were not going to quit until a certain somebody's set of guts lay raveled out on the ground.

Finally Willie's wife, who had the better sense, took off all her clothes, got herself a wheelbarrow, and announced that when the two maniacs got done gutting each other, she'd be happy to shovel up their guts into the wheelbarrow and parade down main street with them, she still stark flour-white naked, all the way to the depot, and then ship their guts off to the Sioux City stockyards to make chitlins out of them. Because that's what they were, a pair of dumb boars who ought to be butchered. Wayne's wife, who was already naturally walleyed, promptly became cockeyed. Because of the various directions her eyes were looking in, she didn't even have to turn around not to see it. When Willie's naked wife rolled the wheelbarrow between the two, both Willie and Wayne lowered their weapons. Willie finally went over and gave his wife a clap on the bare butt, and told her to pick up her clothes for godsakes and go back to the kitchen and cook. Meanwhile Wayne gave his wife a cuff over the ears, which straightened out her eyes, and sent her back to the kitchen too. That ended the fight.

The two gangs of kids next got into a boil over the Dempsey-Firpo fight, which had just taken place, September 14, 1923. The Katzenjammers claimed Jack Dempsey hadn't won it fair because he'd been helped back into the ring after Firpo, the Wild Bull of the Pampas, had knocked him out of it. The Englekings claimed it wasn't Jack Dempsey's fault if he somehow tumbled back into the ring. And anyway, Dempsey had knocked Firpo down six times just before that, so he was on the way to victory. Which was proven when Dempsey knocked Firpo down three more times, the last time for the KO.

At first Free didn't know what side to take. His father was an Alfredson and his mother was an Engleking. The Alfredson relatives tended to vote with the Katzenjammers; the Englekings, of course, voted with the Englekings. But gradually, because he liked Ma a little bit better than Pa, and loved his Uncle John and Uncle Sherm, Free took the Engleking side of it.

Then one Sunday their new minister, Reverend Tiller, decided to preach on the subject of "a house divided against itself cannot stand."

The church was packed for the morning service. Janitor Knave had to bring in some of the chairs from the consistory room. The aged as well as the very young were there.

Pa and Ma sat in their usual place, about halfway down in the center section, with Pa on the right end of the bench, Ma in the middle, and Free on the left end. Everett sat between Free and Ma, and Albert and Jonathan sat between Ma and Pa. Free was finally tall enough so that if he angled his body just right, and pretended to be looking up at the vault above as though he was thinking over what the preacher had just said, he could also catch a little catnap now and then.

A fellow had to be careful though how he dozed off because if Ma caught him at it she had a clever way of removing a hatpin from her wide blue hat and of quietly reaching across Everett to jab a guy a light prick with it. Lately, because Ma was in a family way again, a fellow had to be extra careful because she was on the edgy side.

At nine-twenty-nine Janitor Knave, a bent old man, came down the aisle carrying a glass of water. He set it on the right ledge of the pulpit handy for the preacher.

At nine-thirty on the dot, Reverend Tiller emerged from the consistory room and headed down the aisle, followed by the twelve, six elders and six deacons. The thirteen formed a procession, until at the foot of the rostrum Reverend Tiller turned to ascend the black leather chair behind the pulpit, while the consistory turned to file into two pews, the six elders in the front pew and the six deacons in the second pew. The consistory was lucky. They could sit on a padded black runner.

The organist played a prelude. Then Reverend Tiller rose and lifted up his hands and blessed the congregation, one and all, in Jesus' name.

Church was strangely solemn all through the reading from Scripture, Revelations 22, and the taking up of the collection, and through long prayer. Even the singing of psalms was subdued.

Reverend Tiller usually began his sermons quietly, as though he were only passing the time of day with a couple of old friends. He went over the main articles of faith of the Little Church. He pointed out that the Little Church wasn't just called the Little Church because it had the littler tower, and the Big Church wasn't just called the Big Church because it had the bigger tower, but that it was called the Little Church because it believed in special grace while the Big Church believed in common grace. There just were fewer people believing in special grace and that was why they were the smaller church. He said that most all Christians agreed about the main articles of faith. It was only when the fine points were being considered that trouble started. He said the Lord wasn't going to send somebody to hell because he didn't always agree with his neighbor about the fine points. But what really counted were three things: 1) that the Christian admitted he was a sinner, 2) that the Christian needed saving, and 3) that Christ the Lord Jesus was the only and sole instrument for the salvation of such a sinner. Thus, if there was disagreement amongst the members over certain fine points, it shouldn't at all be considered a stumbling block. It certainly shouldn't be something to split the church down the middle over anyway.

Reverend Tiller took a sip of water. His gold ring flashed when he raised the glass; flashed again when he set it down.

The congregation waited. Now it was coming. There were no sleepers.

Reverend Tiller took up a stance to the left of the pulpit. He placed one hand on the open Bible.

"But split this church is. There is no denying it. All one has to do is look where certain families sit Sunday after Sunday to realize that. You Ardmans and you Coopers and your friends sit over on my right there; you Englekings and your friends sit over on my left there. Even in our four back rows, where our beloved rascals like to sit, where they think they can hide during long prayer leaning their foreheads on the bench ahead and get in a little catnap, even there in those four rows, I notice our boys sit in two separate groups, the Katzenjammer gang on my right there and the Engleking gang on my left there."

Reverend Tiller took another sip.

A few oldsters in church couldn't help but look around to see how the young folks were taking it. Even Pa had a notion to have a look around, but Ma ever so little shook her head at him not to.

"We all know that there is more to it than just some little disagreement over a fine point, like, say, as to whether or not there is to be a thousand-year reign ruled by Jesus after Judgment Day. Such an issue would only be an excuse for something bigger. Such a bone of contention would be ridiculous and petty. And as to whether or not the Englekings like to put on airs because of a supposed noble ancestry in the Old Country, or as to whether or not the Englekings are always standing up in front of the church confessing their breaking of the Seventh Commandment, adultery, or as to whether or not the Englekings like to lay in bed on Sunday mornings . . . to wrangle over all such matters is utterly petty and ridiculous when you remember what the real purpose of our church on earth is."

That Domeny should mention some of those items out loud was a shock.

"Or, by the same token, as to whether or not the Coopers duck their honest debts by declaring bankruptcy, or as to whether or not the Ardmans come from people of humble birth in the Old Country, ard-men or earth-men, or as to whether or not old Peter Hooks should have been read out of the church for hiding his son John from the draft board during the last World War . . . to fight over such things is absolutely ridiculous." Reverend Tiller whacked the open Bible with the flat of his right hand, so hard it sounded like a gunshot. "It's all petty of you. Small."

In the bench ahead of Pa and Ma sat another large family, the Doake Dykemans. Jessie, the oldest, was in Free's class. Their children were all blonds and good-looking. Ma often said of them that the Dykemans had the prettiest children in church. The Dykemans sided with the Ardmans and the Coopers and usually sat on their side of church. But they'd arrived late and thus wound up in the row ahead of Pa and Ma. When they'd filed in and taken their seats, neither the mister, an owly fellow with a heinie haircut, nor the missus, a silent woman with her hair done up in a tight knot in back, would look at Pa and Ma and nod and smile at them as was the custom in church.

All the while that Ma was following the sermon carefully, her eye was now and then caught by the cute behavior of the little Dykeman baby. It kept standing up in its mother's lap to look over its mother's shoulder at Ma. Ma smiled at it a couple of times but it only stared back, its big blue eyes flat and blank. Pretty soon its mother noticed what was going on and she took hold of the baby and sat it down hard on her lap. This happened several times. Twice the mother even turned the baby's head around sharply with her hand and made it face the domeny. But after a bit the mother would get lost in the tremendous sermon Domeny was preaching, and the little tyke with a sly baby frown would gradually work itself onto its mother's shoulder again. Watching all this, Ma couldn't help but smile at the baby. Though no matter how warm and kind Ma smiled at the baby, it just would not smile back.

Finally Ma let go of listening to the sermon a minute, and with an even warmer kind smile reached out a hand and gave the baby's hand a sweet pinch. The baby had a widow's peak and Ma next gently stroked the whorl of silky gold hair in place. Ma just naturally couldn't help but touch and soothe live things.

The baby looked down at Ma's stroking hand, then back at Ma's eyes. Slowly its eyes clouded over. And then, just like that, the baby opened its mouth and let go. In the packed listening church it sounded like a lost soul crying for help. The mother woke up from the sermon and jerked the baby back down into her lap. Then, when the baby didn't right away shut up, the mother opened her blouse and lifted out a sloping white breast the size of a strip of fresh dough and gave the baby titty.

Ma made a gentle mouth at herself for having caused the commotion in the first place.

While the Dykeman mother was quieting her baby, Reverend Tiller paused to take another sip of water. He set the glass down thoughtfully. Then he moved to the right side of the pulpit. He looked from face to face below him as if he meant to look every person in church in the eye.

"Now I didn't come here today to stand here in God's stead and threaten you with everlasting hellfire. As you've all probably observed already, I am a little reluctant to preach damnation. The fact is, I prefer to preach love. So I am not going to say that the Katzenjammers are going to heaven and the Englekings are going to hell. Or vice versa. The notion of there being rival gangs in this church is abhorrent to God. Suppose all of you poor souls wind up in heaven, for some fortunate reason or other? Do you think God will permit you to have rival gangs up in heaven? And fights between gangs?"

All of a sudden Reverend Tiller lifted his hands over his head, so high half of his forearms showed. His eyes bloomed a wide blue.

"And he shewed me a pure river of the water of life, clear as a crystal, proceeding out of the throne of God and the Lamb. In the midst of the street of it, and on either side of the river, was there the tree of life, which bare twelve manner of fruits, and yielded her fruit every month"—Reverend Tiller opened his arms wide to embrace them all—"and the leaves of the trees were for the healing of nations." Reverend Tiller made another grand embracing motion. "For the healing of nations."

Reverend Tiller first pointed a single finger at the Katzenjammer side of the church, and then a single finger at the Engleking side of the church.

"For the healing of the warring factions of this church!"

Reverend Tiller paused for what seemed a long time. Then, with a flourish, he pointed a single finger at a far distance, at the single colored window high in the back of the church.

"And there shall be no more night there. And they need no candle, neither the light of the sun; for the Lord God giveth them light: and they shall reign forever and ever. And I, John, saw all these things, and heard them."

Reverend Tiller once more threw wide his arms, to hug the whole church to his bosom, so that the Katzenjammers and the Englekings, at last full of love, would never fight again.

"And behold, I come quickly. Blessed are they that do my commandments, that they may have right to the tree of life, and may enter in through the gates into the city. For without are dogs, and sorcerers, and whoremongers, and murderers, and idolators, and whatsoever loveth and maketh a lie. I am the root, and the bright and morning star! Surely I come quickly: amen."

Reverend Tiller's eyes opened an even wider blue.

"Even so, come, Lord Jesus. The grace of our Lord Jesus be with you all. Amen."

Free ❦ 50

IT WAS THE twenty-eighth of February, 1924. All day long Ma had been hoping something would happen before midnight. The next day was Leap Year's Day. No child would want a birthday every four years.

Ma would look at the clock and sigh. "My, my, it seems to have a mind of its own." Then she'd sigh again, and say, "Well, at least my heart hasn't been acting up this time. For which thank God."

It was dark when Free awoke. He raised himself up on his elbows. There was a woman downstairs talking with Ma. She was making sour remarks. It made Ma laugh in a sour way herself.

It had to be Ada Simmons, Ma's cousin. Ada Engleking Simmons had never gotten over how her husband Barry had once left her. There had been bad blood between them, and even though a minister and Big John Engleking had somehow cemented them together again, it had not improved her nature. Why Ma ever bothered to be friends with her was something Free could never understand. That Pa and Barry got along was different. Barry was a great storyteller. He could tell stretchers that a fellow couldn't help enjoying.

Ada Simmons's voice all of a sudden sounded loud and clear up through the register. "So you've come around to liking Alf then."

"Yes, I have," Ma said.

"And you've completely forgotten Alvin Ravenhorse?"

"I never think about him anymore."

"Now, you're lying, Ada. I remember how you once felt about him."

Ma said nothing.

Free's eyes sparked in the dark. Ma let that Ada Simmons call her a liar? And who was Alvin Ravenhorse? Had Ma once gone with another boyfriend besides Pa? Hey. Maybe Pa wasn't his real pa after all then. Maybe this Ravenhorse fellow was. It was like a piece of knitting had suddenly unraveled very fast in his intestines. He could feel a big gap in his belly.

All these years Pa and Ma had been fooling him into thinking Pa was his pa. The sneaks. They hadn't even given him the tiniest hint of it. Just think . . . every day Pa and Ma had got out of bed in the morning knowing that their firstborn son Free was not Pa's son. How terrible it must have been for them to pretend in front of him all those years. They'd played the hypocrite, when they went to church, when they went to town, when they went visiting. Everywhere.

Free almost cried out Ma's name. Involuntarily he got up out of bed and stood still in the dark. Ma. Pa.

It was cold in the upstairs bedroom. His winter woolen underwear made his goose pimples itch.

Free heard someone walking in the kitchen. A man's walk.

Pa. Pa was tending the stove, keeping the water hot for Ma as well as making coffee. Good old Pa, sitting on guard in the kitchen, with those strong eyes of his, with his great tall strength. Things were bound to turn out all right with him down there. Pa was a great man even if he wasn't the father of his oldest boy.

"Pa and I can at least be friends," Free whispered to himself. Though it was going to take some getting used to, that he, Alfred Alfredson VII, was not really the son of Alfred VI and Ada, but of Alvin and Ada.

Shivering, Free got back into bed. He pulled his quilts close up around his neck. Flip lying next to him was lost in sleep. Flip twitched around several times as though he were dreaming of running. Flip had a warm body. It was like having a little stove in bed.

Again Ma and Ada Simmons down in Ma's bedroom talked loud enough for him to hear. Ada Simmons had a scolding way of talking. "I suppose you're still desperate to have a little girl made in your own image."

"If God wills."

"Why, for catsake? Life for a woman on this earth is a plain hell. You've got all those holes to get poked into. Your womb isn't your own because your lord and master has the say of it. A woman can't even take a good crap and feel she has the right to it. Let alone your bowels needing to. No, it's not worth it to be born a girl. Gladly would I have it that I'd never been born at all. That my mother would've died before I was conceived."

Ma gasped. "But it was the Lord's will that you were born."

"A woman's lot is the shits."

Pa's voice suddenly broke in. Pa had come up on the womenfolk without their hearing him. "Here, here," he growled, "I won't have that kind of talk in my house." He went on. "Ada Simmons, we're glad you're able to come help us, of course. But don't bring any of your Engleking sour milk into our house. Or, by golly, I'll have to throw you out."

The women said nothing.

"I come to ask how everything is. Any sign yet?"

"No, Alfred, not really," Ma said, cowed a little.

"Wal, I called Doc's home twice, but he's still gone somewhere."

"Thanks, Alfred."

Pa stomped back to the kitchen.

Free had been holding his breath while Pa talked and now he let it go. Good old Pa. Pa was afraid of nothing.

Free drifted off to sleep.

Free dreamt of tangled things. His dream made no sense at all. It was about some turtles crawling into a river on one side while on the other side a dead little girl wearing a white shroud was crawling out. There were two fathers in the dream, one on each side of the river. Each father had a four-tine fork. The one on the near side was poking the turtles in their behinds to hurry them into the river, and the one on the far bank was making motions as if to stick his tines into the girl to throw her higher up on the bank. The turtles all made it into the river on their side, but the little girl had trouble getting out on her side. So when Pa on the other side stuck his fork tines into her, she let out an awful ow.

Free jerked awake in bed.

"Ohhh!" the voice screamed again. "Oooee."

That wasn't the girl in the dream. That was Ma downstairs.

"Oooee."

Free could feel his peter retreating.

"Ohhh!"

"Once more," Ada Simmons said. For once she sounded kind.

Ma gathered herself together in one more great breath and gave a great push. "Ahhh!" The bed creaked under her. "Ahhh. There. At last!"

"Good girl," Ada Simmons said. "You did fine without the doctor. No complications." Ada Simmons called out to the kitchen. "Alfred, bring the hot water and the carbolic acid."

"Coming."

Ma lay breathing hard.

Pa came stomping fast carrying things. "What is it?"

"A boy. A spanking baby boy." Ada Simmons gave the baby's wet body a light slap.

The little baby got mad and started to bellow. "Aaaa!"

"Gotske," Pa said. "What a lively looking fellow."

"It isn't a girl then?" Ma asked.

"No, Ada," Pa said. "It's a boy."

"Ohh," Ma said. "Ohh."

"And he's all there too."

"Thy will," Ma whispered. "Not my will but Thy will. Blessed be the name of the Lord. But I am so disappointed."

Free and Pa were milking. The lantern light shone red on the Shorthorn cows.

It was cozy in the barn. Outside it was ten below. The baby was a week old.

"Say, that's right," Pa said from behind his cow. "I forgot to tell you but I think I got a job for you."

Free groaned to himself. He thought he already had enough jobs.

"Did you hear me?"

"Ya, Pa."

"Reverend Tiller wants you to pump the organ on Sunday. He noticed we had a perfect attendance record at church and thought he could depend on us to always get you there on time."

Free rebalanced himself on his one-legged milking stool. The smell of fresh cow plop was sweet in the gutter near his left foot.

"They pay fifty cents a Sunday."

Free grumbled to himself.

"Don't you want to earn two dollars a month for your family? We can surely use it, son. And keep milking there. You should know by now that when you interrupt your milking the cow tends to dry up."

Free went back to squeezing.

"It'll help pay for the clothes for your new little brother Abbott."

Free thought: "Why should I help buy clothes for him? He's only half my brother. That is, if Alvin Ravenhorse is my real pa."

"Son?"

"Well, I guess if I have to I have to."

"Don't you like the idea of earning fifty cents every Sunday?"

"I don't like marching up in front of the whole church."

"Here I thought you'd figure it'd be an honor to do this."

"I'd rather hit a home run for our church."

"Ha. Against who? The pigs in our hog pasture? Don't be such a dreamer. It won't get you anywhere. Except in trouble."

"We're not getting anywhere fast this way either."

"Boy, boy," Pa said, finishing his cow and getting up and throwing his milk stool in the straw. Pa emptied his pail into the tall milk can. "You're almost smarting off now, you know that?"

Free finished his cow too and got up and emptied his pail into the tall milk can.

Pa grabbed Free by the front of his sheepskin coat. "Listen. I'm going to tell you something now. I've already told Domeny you'd take it. We need that money. Because I tell you, son, I've hardly got enough money left to be called mister anymore."

The sheepskin coat pulled tight across Free's shoulders. He looked Pa in the eye. "If you say so."

Pa let go of Free.

Free settled beside his next cow. One of the cow's tits had a crust of dirt on the end of it and he had to crinkle it off gently. Cows were touchy about what one did with their tits when their bags were tight with milk. Also if one didn't clean off the tits good, dirt formed lines along the backs of one's fingers. When Ma saw those dirt marks she always went wild about the family having dirty milk to drink. She sometimes boiled the milk during a muddy spring. For himself Free liked boiled milk best.

The first Sunday he pumped the organ everything went fine. He didn't pump too fast or too slow. The organist always had just the right amount of air pressure to draw on. Ma complimented him on how well mannered he carried himself up and down the three steps to the organ door. She took great pride in the fact that her oldest son had grown up enough to take part in the church service.

But the second Sunday it was different.

Domeny was into long prayer and was listing all the things wrong with the world for God to fix. Sitting up front for all the people to see, Free had an awful time staying awake, and managed it only by making up an imaginary ball game in his head, how he'd make a triple play unassisted—the first ever for a pitcher to make in the whole history of baseball. He noticed too that organist Joyce Engleking, Ma's cousin, was also having her hands full to stay awake. She kept wiggling around, and jerking back and forth in her bench ahead of him, like she might have a beetle in her pants.

Opening his eyes a crack to see what Joyce was up to, Free was startled to see, looking past her, that his swimming pal Gertie Young was sitting across from him. She was with her parents in the middle curved section. Free right away saw her naked in their swimming hole again. Beside Gertie sat Jake. Hey. Maybe her folks had got wised up to what Jake was doing to Gertie on Sunday mornings.

Gertie must have felt someone looking at her, because her brown eyes swam open and she looked straight at Free. They stared at each other a couple of seconds before Gertie broke into a soft smile. Then she looked at something in her lap.

Free's nose thickened. He thought: "Maybe someday next summer, after she's brought lunch to her pa west across the river there, I can catch her as she comes home across the bridge. I'll hide in the weeds until Gertie comes into sight, and then I'll call to her, 'Let's go swimming a while,' and she'll say, 'Okay, let's,' and we'll sneak along the riverbank, until we get to the swimming hole below the clay cliff, and then we'll undress on the grass, sort of sideways to each other, and then we'll slip into the water. After a while we'll try to duck each other under, and then I'll accidentally catch her there, and she'll smile to herself and look down at where my hand is touching her, and then we'll climb up onto the bank and lay down on the soft grass—"

Organist Joyce gave herself another sharp wiggle. Her bench cracked so loud it made Reverend Tiller pause for a moment.

Free quick closed his eyes in case anybody should look up out of long prayer and catch him looking at Gertie.

Reverend Tiller prayed on. "Oh Lord, we realize that some of us lust after our neighbor's wife, that some of us are guilty of adultery in thought if not in deed.

Nevertheless, oh Lord, despite all our backsliding, do look upon us in mercy."

Free noticed he had a warm bump in his knickerbockers. Thinking those sticky summer thoughts about Gertie had stirred up his little fellow. He moved his folded hands over a little to push it down. It was so hard it hurt. It was like a bone.

Domeny wound up the long prayer. "We pray that Thou wilt help him who will preach Thy word today. May what he will say be truly Thy wish and will. May it prove uplifting. In Jesus' name we ask it, Amen."

Silence and a few sighs.

Reverend Tiller opened a psalmbook. "Now let us sing Psalm One, verses one and three."

Organist Joyce got up, quietly slid out of her bench, and started for the rostrum steps. The console of the organ was directly behind where Domeny sat when he wasn't preaching.

Free almost cried out for Joyce to wait. He couldn't go up those steps just then with a big bump showing in his checkered brown knickerbockers. People would laugh at him for weeks to come. He made a motion to stand up, then, knowing he couldn't, quick sagged down again. His eyes for a second were cockeyed.

He thought: "What in God's name am I going to do?" He thought: "Whatever it is, I better do it quick."

Reverend Tiller started to read the psalm aloud. "Blessed is the man that walketh not in the counsel of the ungodly, nor standeth in the way of sinners, nor sitteth in the seat of the scornful."

Just in time Free remembered Pa had given him a new belt that morning as a present. It had a fine brown color, matching Free's brown knickerbockers to a T, and the buckle was a dandy, leather-covered. Free first pulled his pants down over his hips a ways. Then, through the fabric of his knickerbockers he maneuvered his hard fellow out of the left pants leg, around and up, and then hooked it under his belt. It was just long enough. Then he stood up casual-like, careful to keep his hips tipped up a little, at the same time trying not to make it appear there was something awkward about his gait, and stepped toward the three rostrum steps, and mounted them, and pivoted to his right at the same time that he pushed open a narrow little door, and stepped into the raw wood insides of the great organ. Safe! He'd made it.

He saw movement in the insides of the organ. A long lever kept jerking. It took him a moment to understand that organist Joyce was trying to play. There was no air so there could be no sound. Quickly he grabbed the long wooden handle and began to work it up and down. A half dozen strokes and the bellows filled up to their proper level. A pumper had to be careful not to get the bellows too full or the organ would begin to shriek on its own. The organist tried again, and then the music purled out of the long cigar tubes. The prelude began spreading beautifully throughout the whole church.

When he looked down, the bump in his knickerbockers was gone. Just that quick it had retreated.

Church was out. People were standing around saying good-bye and talking about the good sermon they'd heard. Free and his brothers had climbed into their Buick, but Pa was still talking to Barry Simmons in the doorway of the horse barn, and Ma was still talking to Mrs. Ytta Hardman on the steps of the south door of the church.

Free was in a hurry to get home. A good book was waiting for him, *The Speedwell Boys and Their New Racer*. He'd just gotten it from Sherm. Free kept looking over at where Ma stood talking, knowing that if she made a move toward the car, Pa would come then too.

Free sat in the car wishing Reverend Tiller had won out in his argument to have the horse barn removed. Domeny said it was difficult to preach about paradise in the next world on a hot summer day when the wind was south. What good was the barn now that most everybody drove a car to church instead of the old horse and buggy? The womenfolk in the congregation agreed with Domeny one hundred percent. But they didn't have the vote. Only men could vote, and the men liked to have the barn right where it was. But had Domeny won out, maybe by then Pa would've called Ma to come and go home.

Mrs. Ytta Yardman was wound up about something. She was waving her free hand around while with her other hand she was holding down her wide black fur hat. Ma was smiling. Mrs. Ytta Yardman was also wearing a long black fur coat which reached down to her three-buckle arctics. Ma was wearing a long oxford gray raglan.

A stronger gust of wind than usual came along. Ma up on the steps had to bend into it for a second to keep her balance.

Mrs. Ytta Yardman had just then removed her hand from her head to make a point with both hands. The gust of wind caught her hat just right and lifted it from her head as slick as if a store clerk had removed it, and sent it sailing galley-west. When Mrs. Ytta Yardman clapped her hand back to her head, her hand landed on bare pink skin.

Ma stared, mouth open, at the totally bald woman standing in front of her.

Free, sitting in the car, stared too. He hadn't known that Herm Yardman's ma was bald and wore a wig. She'd apparently pinned her hat down to her wig just like all other women pinned their hats down to their real hair.

Other people couldn't believe it either. They stared. It was a sight. Bald naked to her neck, from there on down Mrs. Ytta Yardman was covered by fur. She looked like a condor. The funniest part was she made only one grab for her hat as it sailed away from her and then when she saw that it was no use went right on waving both hands.

Mrs. Ytta Yardman's hat hit the frozen earth on its edge, bounced lightly once, then began rolling and dipsy-doing and making figure eights around on the churchyard.

Her husband, Jelt Yardman, busy talking hogs with Lemuel Willems, had his back to his wife. Jelt had never pretended he wasn't bald. Jelt and Ytta usually sat by the south, he with his pink skull showing for all to see, on which there weren't even eyebrows, and she with her wonderful bunned-up thick pile of red-brown hair.

The first figure eight his wife's hat made brought it within plain view of where Jelt was counting on his fingers the number of new little pigs born to him that week. He stopped the count with the forefinger of his right hand set on the long finger of his left hand; and stared. Anyone looking at him at that moment could see it was taking his brain some little time to adjust to what he was looking at. He saw it all right but his brain didn't believe it.

At last though his brain did believe it. He cursed, once; then sprang after the hat. He chased it like he was quartering after a tricky critter, a pullet which might dart in any direction.

The wide fur hat kept rolling in circles and figure eights through the crowd. It curled toward the barn and then away from it. Twice Jelt almost caught up with it, only to have it roll under a car. The third time he got his fingers on it. But, almost cornered, the hat did a clever thing. It shed the red-brown wig. Of course Jelt Yardman, very embarrassed, had to stop and quick pick up his wife's wig. It was true that by now everybody knew about the wig, but still he couldn't just let it lie there either. He stuffed it into his overcoat pocket, then took out after the hat again.

The fourth time he came real close. At that point though the wind interfered. It jerked Jelt's hat off and sent it sailing across the churchyard.

Jelt paused. He had to consider which hat to catch first. He teetered a second on his toes. Finally he decided which one. It would be his wife's hat. It was the decent thing to do.

What a spectacle. A totally bald man chasing after two tricky hats on the churchyard while his equally bald wife stood talking away to a ma on the church steps. Some people laughed. Some people cried. Some people bent over to hide their faces.

Finally Jelt caught up with his wife's hat. He stopped. He took his wife's wig out of his pocket and gently placed it in the hat like he was lining a nest with straw. Then, silently, with a maroon face, he stepped over and gave it to his wife.

Ytta Yardman, still deep in her discussion with Ma, paused. She stared at the wig and the hat a second. Then with a funny involuntary shiver, she grabbed them both, clapped them onto her bald scalp, and went on gesturing and talking with Ma, hardly missing a stroke in her pointing out.

Jelt, face all wriggled up like a can of worms, bowed, then took out after his own hat.

After a hard run he caught his hat just as the wind headed it for the open barn door. He clapped it onto his head and went on into the barn to do his duty in a horse stall.

The last couple of months of the eighth grade went by like a streak.

There was the ball game the Christian Schoolers played with the town high school team one noon recess. In just two innings the Christian School got swamped by those big fellows Gene Bunch and Spud Hodges, 10 to 1. Free'd had a bad stomach that morning, with cramps, sometimes so severe he couldn't recite in class, and that noon pitched poorly. Free should have called off the game, but he hated to give excuses.

There'd been really only one thing to cheer about. That came when those big town boys began mocking Free with the nickname Frycake. It made Free burn. The next time at bat Free swung with all his might at one of Gene Bunch's slants and sent it soaring over the privies all the way into the roadside ditch for a home run, their only run.

Later, after Principal Ardman rang the bell, and after they'd all filed into their seats, with Free bent double over his bad stomach, Principal Ardman couldn't help but make a remark about a boy they all knew who was too sick to recite in class but who was not too sick to play ball. But Free didn't care. He'd shown those town bums.

There was the day when the whole school was dismissed so the eighth-graders could take their state examinations. Jessie Dykeman had the miseries that day—she was often absent with them—and couldn't come. But Maynard Tollhouse, Ruby Young, Nelda Brewster, and Free came. They'd take an exam for thirty minutes, then go outside for a breath of fresh air for ten minutes. Free was kind of disgusted with Ruby and Nelda. During their fresh air breaks, they kept talking dirty about Principal Obert Ardman, saying that they'd say yes if he ever were to ask them to do it with them. Maynard thought it kind of fun and asked if he and Free wouldn't do instead. Ruby and Nelda considered the proposal and argued between themselves about who'd get who. For the rest of the day Free hurried through the exams as though it was an insult to take them. He did pretty well though, getting 100's and 99's in civics, history, geography, spelling. But he stumbled in grammar, just barely passing with a 76.

And last there were the graduation exercises held in church. Free had to give a recitation from Emerson, something about self-reliance, and left out about a third of it, mostly because he was mad that he didn't have a decent pair of dress shoes. He felt embarrassed that he had to wear a pair of steel-shod brown work shoes specially blacked over for the occasion. Pa said he was not going to buy his boy Sunday shoes until the boy's feet settled down.

"Boy, boy," Pa said, "Here you are, barely twelve, and already the size of your foot is thirteen, bigger than your age. Now that's got to stop. When are you ever gonna catch up with the size of your shoe, boy?"

Pa's remarks made Ma smile. She tried to smooth things over by saying that at least the boy had a great understanding. But Ma's talk didn't change the fact that Free had to wear his brown work shoes specially blacked over.

Free was still looking black two days later when Principal Ardman took the whole class to Rock Falls and had their graduation picture taken. Principal Ardman had to lecture Free all the way to the Mart Studio to get rid of that scowl. Luckily the photographer was a funny fellow and Free managed to make his lips level. Also luckily the photographer shot the picture in such a way that their feet didn't show.

There was one fine bonus. The Christian School board gave each graduate a brand-new black leather Bible. The good book was trimmed in gold and had a blue silk bookmark. Free loved the feel and smell of the new Bible. Now he could read about King David's wars and invasions and adulteries in his own book.

Free ❦ 51

THAT JUNE FREE learned to operate a single-row cultivator. The first couple times across the field he had no trouble. Pa cultivated every other row ahead of Free, as this made for easier turning at the end of the field. Free took up the rows Pa skipped. As they steadily gained on the field it was great to see the tan land turn black, ribbon after ribbon every other row.

They were cultivating the west forty lengthwise and after a while they edged into a swale. Here the land was gucky, sticky when wet, hard when dry. The least pressure on the shovels, feet in the steel stirrups, and the cultivator shovels dug in, throwing black clods in all directions. What was worst of all, the clods buried the tender corn. The corn was only a couple of inches tall. From where Free sat on his steel seat, the little green shoots looked like young ferns. If he held the shovels down with just the wooden handles, he barely left scratches behind him in the ground. If he went back to pushing down on them with his feet, they dug down into the ground again, too deep.

"Dargang it," Free cried. "Whoa."

Pa was a little ahead of him in the eighth row over. Pa pulled up too. He had the lines fastened in a knot around his shoulders and stopped his horses by just leaning back into the lines. "What's the matter, son?"

"This dummed thing either plows too deep or too shallow."

Pa tied his lines to a handle of his cultivator and stepped over. He looked back at the row Free had just plowed. In one spot the tender green corn was completely buried. "That'll never do. We won't have a corn crop." Pa looked at where the shovels had barely cut the surface. "And there we'd been better off pulling a hen backwards across the field." Pa studied Free's cultivator.

Free wanted to love his cultivator. It was a new one with yellow wheels and a green frame.

"Tell you what, son. While I try out your cultivator a little here, you go back down the row and uncover that young corn."

"Okay."

Pa didn't have to go more than a dozen feet before he saw what the trouble was. "Whoa." Pa got off. "The springs controlling the set of the shovels ain't tight enough." Pa went over to his old red cultivator and got several wrenches from a toolbox. "We'll tighten this set of screws a little." Pa grunted several times. "There. Now try it."

Free climbed aboard, adjusted the lines around his shoulders, set his feet in the steel stirrups. "Giddap."

The grays leaned into it and the shovels went merrily to work.

Pa watched. "Whoa a minute. I ought to make one more little adjustment. Those shields should be set a little lower. The dirt still wants to sneak under them and get at the young corn."

Again Free tried it through the gucky swale. It went swell.

Because Polly was a little lazy and didn't keep up her end of the evener, Free's gray team was a little slower than Pa's bay team, Dick and Fan. But the grays were steady and at the end of the day Free wound up plowing as many rows as Pa.

Pa was proud of Free and at supper bragged about him. Pa told Ma, "With the boy helping out, we ain't going to be too far behind that early-bird brother of yours."

Ma said with a smile. "Yes, our oldest is growing up, taking part in both church service and field work."

Free took the praise with a little shrug.

The next Monday Ma didn't feel good. Pa elected to stay home and did the washing for her. Free went out alone to the north twenty.

Everything went fine. Polly and Nell pulled steadily round after round. At the ends Free got them to turn carefully to miss stepping on the young corn. Free rested the grays at the ends when they began to look a little gaunt, always facing them into a light southwest breeze.

Redwings and meadowlarks sang in the east slough.

Pretty soon Free's mind made up an imaginary ball game in which his Christian School team finally beat the high school team. He played the game in his head pitch for pitch. He gripped the ball across the seams and threw the ball from between his long finger and his ring finger for an upshoot. The ball screwed toward the big batter, breaking up and in on his fists, and he swung with all his might for nothing. Strike one. Next Free turned the palm of his hand over as he came around. Again the ball spun toward the batter, this time for an outshoot. Strike two. Next he threw a knuckleball. The ball went dipsy-doing like a butterfly. The big batter swung too early and was down on one knee when the ball came by. Strike three. Pitch after pitch Free speared past those big lummoxes. And, miracle of miracles, he struck 'em all out through the whole game. They only got five fouls off him all day. Man, what a game. Why, even the Chicago Cubs's scout in the area heard about it and called Pa up to ask when his son would pitch again so he could scout him and maybe sign him up for the Cubs and have him report for spring training next year at Avalon on Santa Catalina Island. Meanwhile, as a batter, he usually took the Rogers Hornsby stance, deep and back in the batter's box, feet together. When the high school pitcher, Gene Bunch, wound up, Free rose up on his back leg; when Gene Bunch strode forward and threw, Free strode forward and swung. He tried to hit the fast ball over the second baseman's head up the alley in right center and the curve over the shortstop's head into left center. He saw the ball twirl toward him, white and fast like a planet around the sun; as he came around himself saw it hit his bat and hesitate; then saw it jump into a slow rising drive, the white thing getting smaller and smaller as it rode away from him; saw it reach a proper height, at last sink into the right-field bleachers for a home run. At the end of a long and wonderful game he'd beaten the high schoolers, 14 to 0. He had to have that many runs to fit in two grand-slam home runs and two three-run homers.

Automatically watching the endless row of tender corn passing underneath his spread legs, lines around his back, grays pulling steadily and breaking wind now and then, his eyes spotted an old cornstalk coming up. It lay across the row.

He woke up. His shovels would catch it crossways. It would break off all the corn shoots coming along. He thought he could edge off his seat while hanging on with one leg and snatch up the cornstalk. It'd be the same thing as stunt-riding on old Tip, picking up a handkerchief off the ground on the dead run. He swung off on the left side, reached down, and got the cornstalk.

He shouldn't have kept the lines around his shoulders. Polly was a little lazy but she also had a touchy mouth. She had a sore in the corners where the bit worked. A fellow had to drive with slack lines with her. The line on her side caught her hard in the mouth, and she instantly yeenked, and then kicked with her butt high in the air, and took off. Nell lifted her head and stopped. This made Polly yaw around to the right. Polly's sudden jump made Free slip off his steel seat and the next thing he knew he had fallen into the moiling shovels below. This made the lines jerk even harder on Polly's mouth, as well as Nell's and it set them off. They broke into a gallop, veering in a curving path across the rows. Tender shoots of corn erupted into the air.

"Oh my God."

Somehow one of the shovels on the left side caught into Free's left leg, the tip of it stabbing him like a sword. Free managed to shake the lines from around his shoulders, freeing the upper part of his body. But by that time the horses were going so fast he couldn't jerk his leg free. The shiny sharp point of the shovel was set into his leg like an ice pick. It began to drag him along. He closed his eyes.

"Whoa! Whoa!!"

But the horses kept running and he kept being dragged across the cornfield. His pants legs and hair filled with boiling earth.

Pa would kill him for wrecking the neat cornfield. Pa was famous for planting his corn in a perfect cross-check. And Pa would double-kill him for destroying all those tender corn shoots. A whole wagon load of future ear corn was being destroyed. And on top of that his own dandy yellowwheel cultivator was going to kill him if he didn't get his leg unhooked from that sharp-pointed shovel.

"Halp!"

He could feel the point of the shovel cutting crisply into his left leg some five inches above the ankle, slowly. It cut until it hit bone, cracking.

Meantime the shovels on the right side of the balanced springing were suddenly free to dig all the way to China. The faster the horses ran, the deeper the right set of shovels buried themselves. Finally the shovels went down so deep the horses began to pant; then struggle; and then just plain quit because it was too hard to pull the rig.

Silence. Free opened his eyes. He was still alive.

The horses stood breathing hard and switching their tails excited.

Free eased himself up to have a look. Wow. The sharp point had really dug into him all right. It didn't hurt. It just looked awful. He gave himself a hunch along the ground. He heard the iron point cracking a little in wet bone. He took a deep breath and then with a sudden forward motion of his leg jerked it free.

He drew up his leg for a closer look. What a cut. Deep. About two inches long.

He wiggled his toes, then his whole foot. It all still worked. No real damage done. He'd been lucky.

He pinched the new slit to see if he couldn't make it bleed. Instead some fat bubbled up in it. It was a strange place to have such a cut. He pinched it some more. It still wouldn't bleed. He saw some black dirt in the lower part of the cut and brushed it out with a fingertip.

He got out his red handkerchief and bound the wound snugly. Soon it would be blood poison time. It had better be healed before those dog days came along.

He stood up. He looked at the path the cultivator had cut across the rows of corn. A regular devastation. Well, there was nothing for it but to uncover all the little tender corns and replant them, making sure they were all set in Pa's perfect cross check.

It took him a half hour to get them all back in place.

"And they better not die now," he muttered to himself, "or Pa'll be sure to spot it."

By the time he got the horses headed up the right row again, the sun was almost straight overhead. By that time too his leg began to ache like the Sam Hill, more in the bone than in the flesh. He took a peek under the red handkerchief. The fatty stuff still looked funny.

Two rounds later he heard Pa's thumb-and-finger whistle. Time to come home. Pa must've got the washing done and had dinner ready. The piercing whistle lingered in Free's ears like the whistle of a train.

He stalled the grays and fed them.

He hobbled toward the house. His lucky brothers were playing under the trees. Pa was hanging out the last of dark clothes on the line south of the house.

Free went directly to the medicine cabinet over the sink, got out the peroxide bottle. He went back outside and seated himself on the cement stoop. He removed the red handkerchief. The cut still hadn't bled any. He splashed on some peroxide. Instantly the long wound began to sizz, then boil up in a thick froth.

He could feel the foaming medicine go to work. What an awful cut it really was.

A shadow touched his cheek. "Wal, that'll clean it out good." It was Pa. He was carrying a basketful of dried clothes.

"Nnn."

Pa stared at the wound some more. Then he made a lifting motion with his head. "Nope, by golly, I'm not going to ask where you got that." Pa turned toward the sandpile. "Kids! C'mon. Time to fill that hole in your belly again."

When the wound quit sizzing, Free got himself a fresh white bandage. Ma kept a supply of them, torn up from old sheets, in a bag under the staircase.

One morning early Pa told Free to get the horses up with the cows. They would begin harvesting ripe oats that day.

The sun was barely up and the meadow was red with lilies. The horses were grazing in the farthest corner of the pasture. The cows might be anywhere in the pasture at dawn, and usually weren't too much trouble to get. But the horses were always as far in the back as they could get, especially on the day they had to work. It was as if the horses had a spy in the house and overheard Pa as he gave the orders for the day.

It was warm. All Free had on was a pair of overalls. He ran a ways. Pa might complain about the size of his shoes, but barefoot his feet felt as light as a bird's.

The six horses cropped busily until he was almost upon them. With one eye on him, lips sly, they kept ripping sideways at the grass. Finally when he was only a half dozen steps away, the gelding Dick ripped off a last mouthful, and up came his head. He snorted; popped his tail, alerting the other horses; and took off.

At first the whole bunch appeared to be heading for home. But at the head of the ravine, Dick suddenly swerved left, black mane lifting, black tail flourishing, and started to lead them all around to the far east corner of the pasture.

Free thought: "If I don't head them off right now, they'll give me a merry chase all morning long, running from one corner of the pasture to the other, and I'll never get them up."

He leaned left and headed straight for the ravine below. He was sure he could jump it. It didn't look too wide. His stride lengthened downhill. Soon he was going lickety-split. Wind fanned his face. He looked across to see where the horses were. Good. He had the angle and was gaining on them. That devil Dick was going to be a mighty surprised horse in a second.

The ravine was wider than he'd thought. My God, he was never going to be able to clear that. He'd land short of the other bank, right where those couple of rocks stuck out. Memory of the time when he wasn't sure whether or not he could make the jump onto the sack swing flashed through his mind. But he'd jumped anyway and made it. Well, why not now? Take a chance, what the heck.

Two more leaps to go. He put everything he had into the two leaps. Then he heaved his body up. Here goes nothing. As high and as far as it would go. Hup!

And up! As he rose, his insides gathered himself up even more, pulling his weight up into his shoulders. Somehow he had to make himself float. Stars crackled all along the edges of his eyes.

Then, by God, having willed it, he actually did float a ways. For a few seconds he was actually hanging in the air. The seconds stretched. Out of the corner of his eye he saw that the horses appeared to slow down, hung in the air like he did, pendulums of a clock slowly stilling in a numbing dream.

At last he let one toe tip down, and glided to earth. He landed on the green turf on the other side of the ravine. His jump carried him into a leaning run, gave him momentum up the east hill. Up he sailed, short steps. and beat the horses by a dozen yards.

Waving his arms he roared at Dick in the lead. "Back, you bastard! Back!" He'd done such a great thing in leaping across the wide ravine that he'd at last come to know he could even take on a horse alone if he felt like it and alone wrestle it to the ground. He veered slightly and charged straight at Dick's violin head. He bellowed a challenge. "All right, you son of a bitch, I'm gonna knock you down."

Dick, shocked, set down on all fours; skidded to a stop in front of Free. The other horses piled up behind him.

Free swung at Dick's nose; landed a punch. "Back, you bastard!"

Dick broke. And wheeled around. Then Dick, mad, popping his tail, gathered himself together again. From the way his eye looked back over his black mane, and the way he ran swiftly and slightly sideways, ears down, tail flourishing, it was easy to see he was going to try to sweep back to the west hill again. The other horses raced to catch up with him.

"The bugger!"

Free leaned into it, and running downhill once more took the ravine. He cleared it by at least two good yards. Again he beat Dick to the hill by a good dozen steps. "Back, you bastard!"

Dick skidded to a stop a second time. He reared. He whinnied, shrill, very high, like a woman almost. Then, lowering his tail, Dick gave up. He turned around; started for home. The other horses trailed after him, going up the pasture and then up the lane to the barnyard.

The second day shocking behind Pa's binder, Free gradually became aware of a sore spot on his left wrist. Looking, he found an angry red bump.

At lunchtime he showed it to Pa.

"Hmm," Pa said through a bite of dried-beef sandwich, "you got yourself a boil."

Free fingered the tip of it. "Then I better pinch it out."

"Don't. We'll slap a poultice on it and get it to come to a head."

"How will I know when it's come to a head?"

"It'll look like an oversized ripe pimple."

But Free couldn't help but bump it a little now and then. It became so sore he had trouble holding onto a bundle with his left hand. And by late afternoon a knot formed inside the red swelling. The knot felt like a coat button.

Pa got a slab of unsalted bacon and led Free out to the cement stoop. "Now let's have a look at that wrist of yours." Pa took Free's left arm and placed it across his knee.

The sun set on a gold world. The smell of harvesting was thick in the air.

Pa placed the raw bacon gently over the boil. "This'll make it come to a head. If not suck out the core." Pa secured the bacon with a bandage and fastened it neatly above the wrist.

"When will we know?"

"By tomorrow morning. And try not to get yourself scratched up for the next while. These are dog days now, you know, and with your blood bad you just might be in for a lot of trouble."

Free dreamed wild all night.

By dawn the bandage had worked off. When it was light enough to see, he found the boil had come to a head all right. A white point like a grain of rice stuck up out of the angry swelling. His arm felt like it was going to explode. It was stiff with poison.

Later down in the kitchen Pa looked at it. "Wal, I see you had the sense not to pick at it." Pa got another slab of white bacon and a fresh white bandage. "We'll wrap this one tighter. And you can go back to bed. I don't want you milking with that. And no shocking."

"But you'll get so far behind, Pa."

Pa give him a little smile. "Wal, you may have a lot of bad blood in you, boy, but at least your heart's in the right place."

It was mid-morning and Free was about to bring some lunch out to where Pa was bindering, when, all of a sudden, as he picked up the little lunch bucket, his arm felt easy and free. And his wrist felt like heaven.

He took a peek under the bandage. His boil looked like a volcano. Reddish matter was running out of the hole. When he lifted up the slab of white bacon, a worm, or what looked like a grubworm, came up out of the hole. It was stuck to the slab of bacon.

He showed it to Ma.

"Ah," she said, "The core came out. Now it'll heal up in a hurry."

Pa was right about his blood being bad. Before Pa finished cutting the oats, more hot sores appeared, one on the back of his left ringfinger, one on his forearm, finally two on his right arm. And before he and Pa finished shocking the grain, boils also showed up on both his knees. One day he counted twenty-eight active boils on his body. Six were on his left knee, all within an area of a few square inches. He ached all over. He knew exactly how Job felt with all his boils.

A couple of nights later he woke up with a bad bellyache. More sign of bad blood. He groaned to himself. When was it going to end?

Lately he'd been constipated a lot. He'd be loose one day; then nothing for three-four days. He hoped he wasn't going to be loose again. He hated to get up in the dark and go out to the privy. And he couldn't very well use the white owl under Everett's bed either. Everett had let the lid drop on the cement stoop one day, breaking it, and so now the pot had no cover. If he did number two in it at night the room would shortly stink to high heaven.

He ran his hand lightly over his belly. Lord, it was as if a huge boil had formed in his belly, with a core as big as a saucer, located just under the skin in the lower right-hand corner.

He lay breathing shallow a while.

All of sudden, boy, did he have to go. Groaning, he swung out of bed. As he did so, the saucer in his belly got mad and turned itself into a crab and gave him an awful bite. Worse yet, a freight train started to come around the last curve of his intestines. Where it was forcing its way it hurt like the dickens. It was going to be awful. He crawled on hands and knees to the pot under the other bed. He pulled it out and dropping his underwear hoisted himself aboard.

He'd barely got himself balanced, knees up on either side of his cheeks, when the freight train arrived. It almost split him apart. His bowels churned. In a moment his stool changed from hard to loose. It became a first-class case of the runs. It was as though once the plug had been removed, his bowels went wild. His one-spot turned into a repeating rifle. Lord, it was terrible. Terrible.

"Pee-uu!" Flip cried from across the room. "Did you die?"

"You awake?"

"After all that racket?"

Free groaned. That very moment had to be the worst he'd ever lived on earth so far. It was misery complete.

"Couldn't you bring that out to the privy?"

"I was lucky to make it here."

"Pee-uu."

"It's just as hard on me as it is on you."

"Bullshit."

If anything the lower right corner of his belly hurt worse than before. It was as though someone had jabbed a sickle-edged hay knife into him.

Free rested as quietly as he could on the cold pot.

"I can't sleep in this awful stink!" Flip wailed.

Free agreed it was pretty bad. "As soon as my one-spot quiets down, I'll haul it out to the privy." Free had begun to worry a little that it was piling up pretty high under him.

A warm wind breathed in through the south screen. It was almost like a dream touching him.

There was more firing of his repeating rifle. His buttocks turned numb where they rested on the cold rim of the old white crock.

"My God," he moaned, "maybe I'm unraveling."

"There ought to be a law against this," Flip cried muffled from under his pillow.

At last Free's repeating rifle quieted down and he could get up. His belly felt hollow. The stabbing pain was still awful. He wondered how in the world he was going to make it to the privy carrying the heavy pot. He was hardly strong enough for that.

But it had to be done. Bent over, he buttoned only one button of his underwear in case of an emergency. He picked up the pot with both hands. He felt his way in the dark with his toes. He straddled down the stairs so carefully they for once didn't crack. He set the full pot down on the last step and turned to open the bottom stair door. He maneuvered himself into the kitchen and, with his butt, closed the stair door behind him. He toed his way across the kitchen, across the still darker enclosed porch, then outside onto the stoop.

The south breeze soothed his hot face. Stars by the millions sparkled overhead. A meteor seared across his eyeballs. All that eternity up there and here he was with a terrible bellyache.

He made it in the dark to the privy okay. He emptied the pot.

He got about halfway back to the house, when the miseries hit him again. He set the pot down in the grass and bending low scooted back to the privy.

He sat in the privy astonished. He couldn't have eaten that much the day before. Perhaps he truly was unraveling.

His innards quieted down just as light began to spread over the horizon beyond the roof of the hog barn. He pulled up his underwear and set out for the house again. He found the white pot on the green lawn and went to the cistern pump and rinsed it out.

Both he and Pa were somewhat startled to spot each other coming through opposite doors into the kitchen, he on his way back to bed and Pa on his way to make his morning cup of coffee.

Pa looked at the pot he was carrying. "You've got troubles?"

"Oh, Pa, I got the misery trots. Bad."

"Humm. We better give you some cinnamon."

"I couldn't eat anything now. My stomach's as sour as a swill barrel." Free was about to take hold of the stair doorknob when yet another push started up in him. He set the pot on the floor, doubled himself over, and on the dead run headed for the outside. "I'll never make it this time."

But he did. Just. As he swung into position he managed to curve the wild stream into the first hole.

Pa stepped outside after a while and came to the privy door. "I don't suppose you can get the cows and milk this morning."

"No, Pa. Not a chance."

"It's that bad, huh."

"I'm making water out of the wrong hole. It's like my private parts have changed places."

"Okay. Just wanted to know so I could allow for it."

Free was still in the privy when the family ate breakfast.

Ma came out to see how he was doing around nine o'clock. She looked in through the door. "Why, boy, you're as white as a ghost."

"Oh, Ma, my belly hurts so."

"Well, I guess we better get the doctor."

"No, no doctor." Pa and Ma were too poor to spend doctor money on him. "I just got a bad case of the summer complaint, is all."

Ma brought him a warm glass of cinnamon water.

The cinnamon didn't help much. If anything it made it worse. He hardly dared to swallow saliva for fear it would start something.

Pa peered in through the privy door when he came home from the field at noon. "Boy, boy, you've really got it bad, ain't you?"

"The pain is awful, Pa."

"Hasn't it quieted down yet at all?"

"Nope."

Free sat in the privy all afternoon. He had to hold his right side carefully in his hands. He had to breathe shallow to keep from stirring up that giant crab of pain. "Boy, will I be glad when I can go back to making straight ordinary posts again."

Around five o'clock his belly quieted down once more and the pain seemed to ease off. He was emptied out to the last drop. He felt cold. He took several steps toward the house; saw the grass dip under him; fell flat on his belly.

Pa came running across the yard. Pa had a close worried look. Pa picked him up and carried him into the kitchen. "Wife, this boy is really sick. Carrying him is like carrying a limp worm."

Free stirred in Pa's arms. It felt good to have Pa's powerful arms around him. "Put me down behind the stove, Pa. Where Rover sleeps in the winter. I'm cold."

Ma stroked his brow. "His face is hot, all right. I'll get him a pillow."

A big crock behind the stove was plumb full of fermenting grape juice. Free and Pa had picked two gunnysacks of wild grapes a couple of weeks earlier. The sweet smell of the troubling juice was almost enough to make Free vomit. The warmth of the stove was comforting though, and after a time he got used to the making wine. He kept falling asleep on the hard floor while the rest of the family ate supper and while Ma read the Bible in his place.

It was dark when Pa picked him up. Pa's beard touched him on the bare shoulder for a moment. Pa said, "I better take you up to bed."

Free liked that.

"Sleep well, boy," Ma called after them.

Pa carried him up to his room and tucked him in. "Now if for any reason you need us, sing out, will you? We'll get the doctor if we have to."

"I'll be all right."

Pa went downstairs somewhat slowly.

Free ran a hand over his belly. He was so gaunt he could almost count the points of his backbone from the front. The hard place on his lower right side was still there. He ran a fingertip over it. It felt like he'd swallowed a whole plate and it'd got stuck in one of the turns of his bowels. His guts seemed to have rallied around the hard place. There were occasional darting pains all around the spot. The pains felt oddly like dogs barking at an intruder.

He awoke with Ma's hand on his brow. The sun was very bright in his room.

"Would you like something warm to eat?"

"What time is it?"

"Ten o'clock. Your brothers've just left to bring your father his lunch."

"No."

"You don't want anything? Not even a glass of cold water?"

"A glass of hot water maybe."

Ma got him the hot water.

Within a couple of minutes he had to trot off to the privy. "Ma," he cried as he ran outside, "how can water turn into poop so fast?"

He soon saw why. He was bleeding inside.

There were no more drinks of water for him.

He kept fading in and out all day.

Pa checked him just before he went to bed. "Hurt you bad in your right side yet, son?"

"Not really any more. It's like there's been some warm water spilled over my intestines now."

"Hmm. Well, you be sure to call us if the pain comes back. The next time off to the doctor you go."

Free lay in bed all day. He ate nothing. He drank nothing.

The fourth day he finally had a little hunger. Ma gave him a dish of mint tea. It didn't fly through him.

The fifth day he had two dishes of mint tea as well as a small bowl of warm rice. He sprinkled some sugar and cinnamon on the rice along with a little slab of butter. He liked that. He was pleased to notice that his taste had come back. He kept that food aboard too.

The sixth day he sat at the table mealtimes. The hard place in his side had shrunk to the size of a saucer. The world no longer buzzed.

On the seventh day he happened to look at his knees. He showed them to Pa when he got downstairs. "Look. The boils are gone. All I have left is some purple scars."

"Wal," Pa said, "maybe the boy poison has finally worked itself through you."

It was ten days before he was strong enough to milk again.

The Frank Westings came over for company.

For a while Free wasn't sure if he could play. The hard spot in his side was still there, about the size of a walnut, so he began easy.

It was when he was running for base that he discovered he couldn't run fast any more. Johnny Westing caught him easy. In the old days he'd always beat Johnny Westing in foot races.

Several days later Free offered to get the horses for Pa. He was stunned to see Dick outmaneuver him easily in the back part of the pasture. He didn't have a chance to stop him. Dick went by him like he was almost standing still. Worse yet, Free's knees hurt.

Pa finally had to come and help him. As they walked up behind the horses together, Pa noticed him limping. "You walk like an old man with gingersnap knees."

"That boy poison seems to have gone to all my joints."

"Wal, growing boys often have growing pains. You'll get over it."

"But I'll never beat Johnny Westing again, Pa."

Ma was digging up some potatoes in the patch north of the grove. She overheard them. "I had growing pains too when I was your age, boy."

"Did it take you long to get over them?"

"About a year. It was very painful."

Barry Simmons and Pa agreed to help each other stack grain that summer. Barry's oldest daughter, Frances, and Free got the job of loading the hayracks, and Pa pitched off and Barry stacked.

Pa was every bit as good a stacker as Barry, but Barry could argue all around Pa, and so it wound up with Barry as chief up on the stack. Stacking was by far the easiest. The stacker could act the gentleman if he wanted to. The bundle pitcher meanwhile not only had to fork up the bundle from the rack but also had to heave it across to where the stacker wanted it on the stack. And the bundle had better land just right too, on the dot in front of the stacker, with the butt facing out and the head in. All the stacker had to do then was push it in place with his three-tine fork and step down on it.

When Pa stacked, his finished stacks looked exactly like an egg sitting on its fat end. When Pa finally put the last bundle in place on top, neither wind nor rain could damage the stack much. As he built it, Pa kept the center high. That way the heads of the oats, set to the inside, always stayed cork dry. They'd also sweat just right and would cure perfect and later on taste sweet to the horses and cows.

Barry built his stacks the same way except that his wound up looking more like a pyramid. His could take the weather too.

Pa and Barry made quite a pair. Pa was lanky and long-armed; Barry was tubby and short-coupled. Pa was all for getting up the stacks pronto; Barry liked to take short rests now and then, and to make sure he got them told clever dirty stories which made Pa so weak from laughing he couldn't pitch bundles for a few seconds.

There was even a difference in the home-brew beer the two made for harvest time. Pa's beer was as clear as rainwater, no settlings in the bottle, and after it was poured into a mug it kept a fine-bubbled head, while Barry's beer was apt to be capped green, with at least an inch of yellow settlings, and that would cause all kinds of problems when a bottle was opened. In fact, a fellow sometimes even had to uncap a brown bottle of his beer inside a cream can, where it could safely explode. Luckily Barry's beer didn't hold its head very long and a fellow could soon pour the settled beer into a mug and drink it. Pa's beer made a fellow's eyes wimmer at the corners a little, but one could still work steady on it. While Barry's beer was apt to make the horizon wobble like a top for a while.

The stories Barry told were mostly stretchers. "There was this drunk. One night just as he started for home a heavy rainstorm came up. It rained so hard that before he'd gone a block the gutters were running full. Shaking his head he staggered on through the rainstorm. He had a block yet to go when it came over him he'd better stop and take a leak. He'd never make it. So he unlimbered his tool and let fly right there on the street. Well sir, it happened he'd stopped to take his leak next to a waterspout off a grocery store. Of course, long after he'd finished making water, the waterspout next to him kept running. He stood there puzzled. Here he thought he was done but according to the sound of falling water he was still urinating. Shaking his head some more, he waited and waited for it to finish. But finally, getting sick and tired of it, he at last looked up at the dripping heavens and said, 'Oh, Lord, do I have to stand here pissing into all eternity just because I got drunk tonight?' "

Pa had to lean on his fork and laugh. Barry of course got in another short little rest.

Barry liked to brag about his horse Colonel, a black Percheron. Colonel, he said, could outpull any horse in the valley. "I tell you. Last fall I decided to remove a big red boulder from my south forty. My plow kept catching on it and breaking off the point, and I got sick of it. So I dug all around it, hooked a log chain around it, and then got Colonel to pull it out for me. Alf, that red boulder was just too big to move. Because before Colonel could budge it a quarter of an inch even, he'd break the singletree. In fact he broke three singletrees on me. Finally I made him an extra thick singletree out of an ash limb, one I was sure he couldn't break. It was about so thick. Well sir, Colonel pulled, and pulled. He lay down so flat pulling that you could've stretched a chalk line from the tip of his ears along his spine all the way to his back hocks. Pull? Why, he pulled so hard his asshole stuck out far enough for me to have cut off a dozen washers from it. If I'd have wanted to, that is."

"Oh, come on now," Pa exploded.

Barry stopped work and stared at Pa with his peculiar comical stance as if he were daring Pa to disbelieve it.

At that Pa finally had to break down and laugh. "Barry, Barry."

They first stacked the early oats at both places, then the late oats. By the time they got to Barry's place for the last of the late oats, Pa and Barry, and Free and Frances, all four had become part of a smooth working team. Free and Frances always managed to be driving the next load onto the yard as Pa was throwing up the last bundle from the rack he was on.

In the beginning Free hadn't been too sure Frances could keep up her end of it. She was a girl. But Frances surprised him. Her dad had made a tomboy out of her. She knew how to handle a pitchfork. When he and Frances started down a windrow, Free usually worked ahead and threw up the first four bundles of a shock of grain, and Frances came along behind and threw up the last two bundles of the shock.

In imitation of Pa and Barry, Free and Frances told stories too. Frances's stories always ended up with a hint that she might like to do what Gertie Young did with her brothers. Free's stories were mostly about baseball. The hints Frances threw out weren't wasted on Free and he sometimes wondered just how he should go about doing it with her. Perhaps sometime after they had crawled on top of the load to drive home, he could slip on a bundle and fall on her, and then in the musty-smelling oats they could do it. No one could see them up there on the load.

Free liked working at Barry's place best. For one thing Ma and the kids did the chores then and he and Pa got out of that. But the best was the apples. Barry had a lot of crabs growing in his grove and they had just begun to ripen, still a little green with a touch of red on them. Crab apples canned were better than pears canned. But eaten raw they were puckery sweet. In another week they'd be mushy. As Free and Frances drove through the grove sitting together on top of the load of golden bundles, Free would hand over the lines to Frances and then'd crouch up and grab a good handful of crab apples, enough to fill his pockets.

One day, in addition to the already big harvest-time meals, Free ate fifty-six crabs, chewing up everything but the stem. He'd pop the small apple into his mouth while pitching so's not to lose any time. It was a world's record.

Frances thought the record a joke. She told Pa about it.

Pa shook his head. "What? You're eating all those apples right after that awful bellyache you just had? You're asking for trouble."

"I feel fine, Pa. Everything's working first-rate again." It was true. Even the hard walnut lump in his right side had disappeared.

On the last day Barry and Pa had only one bottle of Barry's wild home brew left. They decided to save it until they'd thrown up the last bundle. Then they'll all have a sip in celebration.

Pa set up a ladder so Barry could put the last several bundles in place by hand. Putting the cap on a stack was always a tippy business.

Barry stood on the top rung and moved with the careful motions of a deacon reaching for the church offering down a long bench. Then, the last bundle spread-eagled in place, Barry anchored it all down with long strings of twine weighted with a pair of bundles.

"Now," Barry said, "to get down without breaking a leg."

Pa reached up a hand and placed it on Barry's behind to steady him down the rungs of the ladder. Barry had a broad butt and short thin legs. Pa guided Barry's last step onto the railing of the hayrack, and then all was safe.

Down on the ground, Barry jabbed his three-tine into the ground. He wiped his brow. "Whew!" He rolled his merry brown eyes around. "All right, Frances, go get us four beer mugs while I get that final bottle of home brew from the cooler. And Free, you go to the house and ask the Missus for a cream can."

Free came running back after a minute to say that all the cream cans were full waiting for the cream hauler.

"Shucks." Barry looked toward the drying rack. "Hmm. I see that the Missus has set out the washtub to dry. Go get that then, Free."

"Washtub?" Pa said. "Where you people take your baths in?"

"Well, Alf, the Missus may be a bit crabby, but one thing she ain't, and that's dirty."

Free got the washtub. It was galvanized and big.

Barry took the brown bottle from Frances, got out his combination pocket-knife, snapped out the bottle opener. Face averted, a smile curving up one side of his sunburnt chubby cheeks, Barry pointed the bottle down into the washtub. "Stand back, folks, here she blows."

Pa, Free, and Frances backed off a step.

Barry set the opener, yanked it up. Whoosh! A jet of foam hit the bottom of the washtub, then frothed up like a vicious whirlpool

"Gotske!" Pa cried. "That stuff sure is wild all right."

Barry laughed. He shook out the last few flecks of foam. The tub was level full of jumping writhing foam. It was a sight. The smell of the home brew was sweet.

Barry picked up one of the beer mugs with a flourish. He pretended to be a barkeep in a saloon. "Well, Alf, old boy, how much do you want? Surely a full glass if it's on the house, eh?"

Pa wiped a smile off his face. "I'll take an inch."

"An inch?"

"Yeh. An inch in a washtub."

Barry laughed so hard he had to bend over.

Pa finally had to fill his own mug, pouring it out of the washtub on a slant.

About then Gramma came for a visit. Grampa Stanhorse couldn't come. He had to stay home and run the church.

Ma decided Gramma should sleep with Free. Gramma said she wasn't going to sleep in the guest room alone. She had to have somebody in the same room with her at night. Free liked Gramma all right and so couldn't very well say no. But sleeping with her was a trial. She snored.

The second night of Gramma's stay, Free woke up with a jump and a start. It took him a while to understand that Gramma wasn't breathing. Hey. He was sleeping with a dead person. It was her dying that had awakened him. The hair on his arms stuck out. He quit breathing himself. He lay stiff for a minute. Gramma dead?

Then before he could unfreeze himself and call downstairs for help, Gramma's bulk heaved once, shuddered, started to breathe again. She breathed real fast for a couple of dozen breaths, sucking in gulps of air. She sounded exactly like Pa's old four-horse engine.

Free relaxed, and began breathing again.

What was wrong with Gramma that she should have a stoppage of breath? Did she have a bad heart? Maybe her first husband Alfred, Grampa Engleking, had come back to haunt her in her sleep, telling her that he didn't like it she'd married their old church janitor, Garland Stanhorse, that the fellow was beneath her station, that she came from a better class of people. It would serve her right if Grampa Engleking taunted her with that. Though the new grampa was a good sport.

Free lay listening to her huge breathing beside him. There was no rhyme nor reason to it. She jerked and wiggled worse than even Rover did in sleep after he'd been chasing rabbits. A dozen times Free was sure she'd died. She'd quit breathing for such a long time that he'd finally think to himself: "Yep. That's it. She's finally gone and done it. Grampa Engleking is right now welcoming her at the pearly gates. I better call Ma." But then, once again, Gramma's great bulk would heave once, and shudder, and start to breathe.

What a comical character Gramma really was. He probably had the most peculiar and most wonderful gramma in all of Siouxland.

As he lay smiling to himself in the dark, Gramma went into yet another one of her spells. He thought he'd count his own breath against hers to see how long she could go without hers. Five. Ten. Fifteen. Hey, wow. Twenty. Her bulk slowly swelled up beside him. It also seemed to turn hot, like a base burner throwing out heat. When he got to thirty, his smile faded. No one could go without breath that long and live. As Pa would say, it was unpossible.

The school book on how to rescue the drowning said that five minutes was the limit for a human being to live without breath.

He kept counting his breath. Forty. Fifty. Now she'd really gone and done it. Quit breathing long enough to suffocate. My God.

He swung his feet out over the edge of the bed.

His motion triggered something in her. Her fat lips suddenly sucked wet air. "Echuuh." Then a vast shudder shook her. Then she bounced up and down like she was a horse bucking off a rider.

Wham wham! The bed gave out from under them and Free was sucked back into bed and down they both went. Their bottoms hit the floor together.

"What! what!" Gramma cried out, waking up. "What's happening here? Good Gertie, I haven't fallen into the privy, have I? With my knees up around my head like this?"

"Gramma, Gramma," Free cried. He tried to climb out of the depression they'd fallen into; couldn't quite make it. "Are you all right?"

"What's happened to us here, grandson?"

"I think it's the slats. They broke under us. Or fell out."

"Oh, Lord, what next? And here I was dreaming I was in the afterlife singing psalms with Alfred and living in a state of final exultation."

Pa sounded up the staircase. "What's going on up there?"

Gramma caught her breath; then quick whispered. "Shh. Don't say nothing."

Free whispered back, "Why not?"

"I don't want your father to come up here and see me sitting all doubled up like this."

"Hey you people up there, are you all right?" Pa called again.

"Shh," Gramma whispered again. "Don't say nothing now. We'll fix this bed ourselves."

Pa wasn't satisfied with the silence. He came upstairs carrying a lamp. The moment he saw what had happened he burst out laughing.

Gramma was mad. Without her glasses on she couldn't see very well and she kept blinking her eyes up at the lamp Pa held. She looked like a great fat ewe that'd just been caught in the feed bin.

The other kids woke up too. They sat up in bed, blinking at where Free and Gramma were sitting collapsed in a big hole in their bed.

Pa finally got control of himself. "Wal, you both better climb out of there so we can put the slats back in place."

Free swung his feet up and managed to get out.

It was different with Gramma. She was wedged in too deep to get out by herself. She started to scold Pa. "Nah, can't you see I'm caught here helpless, you lummox? Reach out a hand and help a poor creature up."

Pa laughed another wild laugh. He backed off to study the situation.

Ma came upstairs then too. "What in freedom's name . . . " She stared. Slowly her eyes opened very wide and blue in the lamplight. "Ma!"

Free laughed.

Gramma didn't laugh. She held out both her fat hands. "To, you two, Ada, Alfred, grab hold and help me out of this awful predicament."

Finally, puffing and hauling away, and with some luck, they managed to help Gramma out of the depression in the bed.

After he'd laughed some more, Pa crawled under the bed and put the slats back in place. To make sure the bed wouldn't collapse under Gramma again, Pa got their old trunk and shoved it under the bed. It just fit. It made the bed a little harder, but it was safer.

Free lay on the grass on his favorite hill in the pasture. He took to watching cumulus clouds drift in from the west. They were sky ships from another world.

As he often did, Free fell into an old daydream of his, in which he'd set out to conquer the world. He and the neighbor boys would first conquer their own township, then conquer the neighboring townships, then hit the county seat, Rock Falls. Once they had a county in control, they would go on to conquer the state of Iowa county by county, until finally they'd march on the state capital, Des Moines. Man oh man, wouldn't the governor of Iowa be surprised one morning to see two wings of a country boy army standing on the capital steps demanding his surrender. The governor would stare and stare at Emperor Alfredson VII. The corners of his eyes would wibble a little and it would be seen that he was trying to think of some way yet to let the President of our country know about the new threat—

"So here you are. Son, son, I've been looking all over for you."

Free put up a hand and looked past it. There was Pa standing between him and the sun. Pa looked like a monument. "Something the matter?"

"Matter? A lot of manure needs to be hauled out of the calf pen. And you're just the man to do it."

Free remembered some talk that morning about him cleaning out the calf pen. It made him sick to think about it.

"Son, son, I can't be having a big fellow like you lollygagging on his back all day looking up at the sky doing nothing. You're twelve years old now, and it's time for you to pull your share of the load."

Free slowly sat up. He hugged his knees.

"When I was your age, boy, I was practically managing a farm alone for Charlie Pullman."

"That was them days, Pa."

"Get to your feet and let's go. I've got your horses all hitched up to the manure spreader. All you have to do is pick up the fork and start pitching."

"Why can't you do it?"

Pa shivered a little in his tracks. "What!"

Free got to his feet.

"Son, if you was born in Fat John's family, you'd be putting in ten-twelve hours a day of real hard work. Those boys of his are already first-class hired hands. You know darn well he'd never've let you lay in the grass dreaming the whole day away like this."

Free lowered his head.

"And you better dig out your work shoes. That calf manure comes pretty sharp. It'll chew up your bare feet worse than battery acid."

Free started walking home.

Pa followed a few steps behind. "Man, man. I had a time finding you. What were you doing there all alone in the grass?" Pa asked the question as if he expected to catch him at some kind of sorry deed.

"Well, if you must know, I was out conquering the whole world."

"On your back?"

"Yes."

"Wal. You and your grampa with your crazy wild notions."

"Grampa Alfredson was a great man."

"And not your father?"

Free fell silent. He lowered his head a little more as he trudged up ahead of Pa. He hugged his chest.

The calf manure was tough to pull apart. Hay in the calf manger usually spilled over into the pen, and when the manure was allowed to build up and get tromped on by the calves all winter long, it became as tough as old wine leather.

Free first used a four-tine fork. He jabbed at the yellow matted stuff, tugged at it, tore at it, but couldn't dig up much. All he managed to pry loose were several strands of stinky straw along the edges of the pen. After a half hour he still only had the manure spreader about a fourth full. He was wringing wet with sweat.

Meanwhile, the grays Polly and Nell, stood outside switching at flies.

He next tried the potato fork with its knife-sharp points. It did cut the matted mess a little better, but at the same time it made lumps almost too heavy for him to throw into the spreader. He had to shag the lumps along the floor and then, with all his might, heave them in. It was back-breaking.

He shagged six big lumps into the spreader and then had enough. He threw the potato fork into the alley.

He got Pa's hay knife next. But it didn't work good either. The point of the hay knife was too round.

"Goddammit, I'm gonna go and get me the axe. Even if it means chopping off my toes and so never play baseball again. Let alone conquer all of Iowa."

The axe helped in cutting the matted manure into sections. But he still had to pry each section loose from the cement floor, and that was like trying to scrape burnt gravy off a frying pan.

After an hour of grunting and struggling, he still had only half of a load on. "Goddammit, this is worse than what the jailbirds have to do in the state pen."

"Is it really all that hard?" Pa said suddenly beside him.

Free almost jumped a foot.

Pa picked up the four-tine fork and tried it. Pa did pretty well with the sections Free had already cut with the axe. But when Pa tackled the uncut part, he didn't do much better than Free. After a couple of minutes Pa began to sweat and then to cuss. "By dab, I plumb forgot how tough it was."

Free wanted to say, "Yeh," but didn't quite dare.

Pa grunted and struggled. He tore at the calf manure like a mad bulldog pulling at an old cowhide. He managed to separate several hunks of it and heaved them onto the spreader.

Free stood watching. Soaked with sweat, he still puffed a little.

Finally Pa threw the four-tine aside and went at it with the potato fork. "This calf manure is going to be removed or my name ain't Greate Pier."

Pa did better with the potato fork. Pa was powerful enough to make it work. It took a strong back and mighty arms. Pa managed to throw out a dozen forkfuls in short order. Soon the spreader was full.

Free was grateful for the help.

"There, dagnab it," Pa said. "Haul it away. And when you get back, call me, and I'll help you with the next load. I can see that this is too tough for you. Not even Johnny Engleking could've loaded this stuff." Pa wiped sweat from his face with a red handkerchief. "And pee-uu. What a smell. In all the world there ain't no smell as awful as old calfshit."

Grunting and cutting, and tearing at it, Free and Pa finished cleaning out the calf pen by three o'clock.

They had some dried-beef sandwiches and cool lemonade together.

Then right after that Ma had a job for Free. It was time to churn again, Ma said, and if Pa could use their oldest boy for barn work, she could use him for some housework.

More hard work yet that day?

Gramma was fanning herself in the lawn chair under the apple trees. "What? A big boy like you looking black because of a little work he has to do? Come, you're almost a man now, and real men never complain about a little job like churning."

Ma had already set out the barrel churn under the nearest maple tree. At least the barrel churn was easier to operate than the old stomp churn. But it was such a doggone tiresome chore. A fellow cranked, and cranked, until it seemed a whole age had passed before the cream turned to butter.

He'd worked about ten minutes, with the cream still slopping loose back and forth inside, when it came to him what he should do. He gave the idea several more turns through his head as he cranked away. Then, short off, he announced it to the world, including Gramma. "I'm gonna run away."

Gramma stopped fanning herself. "Good. Run away to the Old Country and I'll go with you."

Free was startled. "What about Grampa Stanhorse?"

"Of course we'll take him with us."

Free fiddled with the loose wooden handle of the crank. "Well, anyway, whether you come with or not, I'm running away."

Gramma let her purple Japanese fan fall to her bosom. "Why?"

"It's all work and no play around here. With bellyaches and diarrhea thrown in. And I want to go to a place where the work can be fun. Like Uncle John makes his work for himself. So that it's sport."

"And your father doesn't?"

Free opened the churn and looked in. The cream hadn't even come close to having little clots of butter. "All Pa does is give orders."

"Yes, your father is not your Uncle John. Your father's hurt my feelings many times." Gramma sucked up an old sigh. "He was not my first choice for a son-in-law."

"Anyway, when I get done with this churning I'm pulling out."

"I wouldn't say that too loud, boy. The Lord still and all wants you to be an obedient child, you know."

"I don't care if He does hear me. I'm done living here."

"Where will you go?"

"I'm going to try to find me an island somewhere. Old Willems the trapper says there's a nice island in the wild Missouri near Devil's Nest. Really wild."

"A wilderness full of wild boars then."

"I guess so."

Gramma resumed her fanning. "Well, for now I think you better finish that churning first."

"There's nothing to look forward to around here, Gramma."

"That's what I've said all along." The bags under Gramma's eyes turned pink. She began to remember sad times. "But your Grandfather Alfred, oh yes, he knew better. Removing me from all my dear ones and all my appointments, oh yes, he knew better." She fanned herself slowly.

"Well, me, Gramma, I like America all right. It's just that I don't like it here in this particular place. Besides, Pa probably ain't my real pa anyway."

The bags under Gramma's eyes tightened. "Who told you that?"

Free drilled a look right through Gramma. "Alvin Ravenhorse ain't my father then?"

Gramma made a heavy funny motion with her big bosom. "Alfred, boy, how long have you been thinking such thoughts?"

"Well, Gramma, I just think it sometimes." He grunted a short laugh. "When I get mad."

Gramma fixed him with a lifted look. First she shook her head to herself and then she nodded to herself.

Free took hold of the handle again and began to churn.

That night at the supper table, as Pa was chortling happily that it was beginning to look like they were going to have a pretty good summer after all, Gramma broke in to say, "Ya, ya, Alfred, you can build up your material wealth all you want to, but that won't make you any better in the eyes of the Lord so long as you have a son who's thinking of running away."

Forks dropped on plates, Pa's loudest of all.

Free threw Gramma a hurt look. He had just taken a large bite out of a slice of bread with fresh butter and chokecherry jelly on it. How could she blab on him after admitting she didn't like Pa either? She had betrayed him.

"Our Free is thinking of running away?" Pa said.

Gramma nodded. "So he told me."

Ma placed both her hands silently beside her plate. She brushed back her gold hair. "Was it too much to ask you to make a little butter for me?"

"Yeh," Pa said, "butter that just a minute ago you got through smearing on your bread there? Doesn't the butter taste better knowing that you churned it yourself?"

Gramma tolled her head. "Grandson, grandson, better parents God could not have given you—even if you could've prayed for them."

Free glared at Gramma. That old fat traitor. After all he'd endured sleeping with her, all that deathlike stoppage of the breath, was that what he got for it?

Ma looked at him sadly. "Well, I won't ask you to do anything for me again. I'll try to get along without your help from now on."

The large bite of bread in his mouth lay like a leather mitten across the back of his tongue.

"Yes," Ma went on, "after I'm gone, then you'll miss me. And then maybe you'll finally be sorry you didn't go out of your way to do things for your mother while she was still alive. Maybe then you'll remember that it wasn't such a bother after all."

Free wished Ma wouldn't talk like that. He tried to swallow the chunk of bread, but it just would not go down.

Ma closed her eyes and inside her head looked up. "Oh, Lord, any time now. I am ready if you are."

Pa picked it up again. "Did this boy of ours really say he was thinking of running away?"

"Och," Gramma said, finally throwing Free a look as if to say she was sorry she'd blabbed. "It was really only just boy talk. You know how it is at that age." Gramma threw Pa one of her bold looks. "When you were a boy, you once thought of running away too, didn't you?"

"Wal, but maybe I had more reason to, what with my mother dead, and my dad so wild with grief he didn't know what he was doing."

"So you did think of it once then?"

"Do I have to admit it?" Pa said.

On the third try, Free managed to swallow the chunk of bread.

Free had seen an occasional airplane fly over their farm. Usually it was a biplane taking a passenger from Sioux City to Sioux Falls. Everybody stopped work when they heard a plane coming. Pa marveled at them sailing along up there like a floating hawk. Ma shook her head and said she thought that if human beings were meant to fly the good Lord would've given them wings to fly with in the first place.

Free thought them wonderful. He already envied all the birds. He wished he could get close to an airplane once to see how it worked.

One Saturday early in the morning Pa took Free with him to Sioux Falls to get some parts for their old McCormick-Deering binder.

They finished buying the parts in short order.

It was then that Pa got to wondering if maybe they shouldn't just for the heck of it stop in and see an air show for an hour or so.

"Hey. Can we, Pa?"

Pa gave Free an old-time pa smile. "Sure we can."

They rolled south out of Sioux Falls, crossed the Big Sioux, and zigzagged up a steep bluff past a big-shot country estate partly hidden by lilacs and tall pines. Presently they came to a big sign on a corner.

Free read the sign aloud for Pa. "Air Show. See The Famous Clarence Chamberlin Risk His Life Flying Upside Down."

"That's it," Pa said.

Looking west, they saw it. A country road ran toward an open pasture. There were some grandstands already full of people, and along the edge of a dirt runway four airplanes stood ready to go.

Pa parked the Buick along the country road. They got out and paid their admission at a gate and hurried to join a crowd of men and boys lined up behind a rope. The stands were mostly filled with ladies holding onto big wide hats. Many of the ladies wore white dresses with dark sash belts. The men and boys mostly wore dark Sunday clothes, with the men cocking back their bowlers so they could look up into the sky.

Pa spoke to a man in a soldier suit. "When's it supposed to begin?"

The old soldier pointed to the airplanes across the pasture.

A man wearing leggings just then climbed into a blue biplane. He adjusted his helmet and goggles. Then another man came out of a small shed and walked around to the front of the biplane and grabbed hold of the propeller.

The second man called out sharp and clear. "Contact?"

The pilot nodded. "Contact."

The man on the ground gave the propeller blade several hard pulls. At last there were some pop-pop sounds. The man jumped back and then the propeller blade began to jerk around on its own. The pop-pop-pop grew into a steady roar and the propeller blade vanished into a shimmering blur. The biplane began to move, bouncing across old wagon ruts. Some brown dust whizzed up as the propeller passed along.

The extra man helped start the other three planes too, two biplanes and a monoplane. The monoplane had its wing fastened on overhead. Together the four engines made a tremendous roar. Soon the four planes were moving across the pasture. They looked like heavy wasps wobbling along the ground.

After a moment the first plane began to wobble faster across the rough pasture, then something in the tail set at a different angle, and up she went, off the ground, and slowly floated onto a light wind.

A loudspeaker above the grandstands awoke: "Clarence Chamberlin, in the blue plane, will make the first dive."

Chamberlin floated his plane up higher than any heron Free had ever seen flying south. His plane became a tiny speck in the sky. It was hard to make out against the blue sky.

The crowd waited, buzzing.

Chamberlin's plane fluttered; turned up on its side; then, curving, started down. It came straight toward them. Head on it looked like a bullet with wings. As it got bigger its engine could be heard again; became a rattling blast of a sound. It kept diving toward them. Everybody backed up a step; then a couple of more steps. People kept separating into different flocks, making different alleys for the plane to pass through, first here, first there, in case it went out of control. Then the people got all mixed up and sagged down a little, heads on their necks sinking down too a little like swans dippling on a pond. The bullet with wings became as big as a steam boiler. At last Chamberlin's head could be seen, goggles flashing. Then the goggles turned over, the plane with them, and in a moment the goggles lowered to earth, down, down, until at last Chamberlin's helmet almost touched the ground.

Free thought: "If that plane don't lift up, the top barbwire's gonna slice off his head."

The biplane veered to fly alongside the stands. Women screamed. Boys squeaked. Men sank to their heels.

Chamberlin turned his face to the crowd. He gave them all a quick flash of a smile. His goggles blinked in the sunlight.

The biplane headed straight for the line fence at the end of the pasture.

Free thought: "If that plane don't lift up, the top barbwire's gonna slice off his head."

Then, at the last second, something moved up in the tail, wrong side to it seemed, and the plane lifted up. It rolled over and began to climb. Chamberlin was safe.

"Gotske!" Pa exploded. "What a daredevil. Man."

"He easy did it though, Pa."

"Yeh, with luck."

Soon the other three planes made a pass at the field flying upside down. It was a great sight. But everybody could see that none of the other pilots had Chamberlin's daring. The closest any one of them flew upside down along the ground was twelve feet. When they dove by the women didn't shriek nearly as loud.

Pa and Free watched the stunts for about an hour; and then Pa said they had work to do at home.

Free left the air show reluctantly. He wished they lived nearer to Sioux Falls so he could watch them fly longer.

Free decided to make an airplane. Instead of running away, he'd fly away. Riding up there in the sky it'd be easier to find the island he wanted.

Pa didn't have much work for him the next several days. Free rode Tip down to the yellow cliff and cut down two young willow saplings for the wing. He made sure they were straight by rolling them on the ground like the billiard players in town rolled their cues on the flat green billiard table. He tied a rope around the thick ends and shagged them home behind Tip. With Pa's saw and sawhorse, working in the open door of Pa's machine shed, he cut the ends off neatly.

He found four two-by-fours ten feet long. He checked them for knots and other weak spots. He built them into a long slender frame. After some thought he decided to invent a new kind of monoplane. Instead of having the body hang underneath the wing, he'd have the body set on top of the wing. That way, as he flew along, he'd always have the wing in view when he looked down at the earth. He stretched heavy gunnysacks across the two willow poles, and painted them with some white paint left over from painting the house.

Frame and wings built, he dug out a pair of iron wheels from the old Gore junkpile. The wheels were about a foot in diameter and still attached to an axle. They were somewhat rusted but a liberal squirt of oil soon put them in perfect running order. He attached them under the frame. He also built a landing point under the tail out of a piece of strap iron. The moment he got the frame up on three points it began to look like a bird.

Next came the tricky part, the making of the tail assembly. He found some sheet iron in the junkpile and cut it into two pieces, a horizontal part to move up and down, and an upright part to move from side to side. He fixed in two levers, one to be run by foot pedals and the other to be run by a control stick in his hand. The pedals would make the plane dip left or right and the stick would make it go up or down. He connected the levers to the tail assembly with four pieces of store rope. When he sat down on the crosspiece inside the frame and looked back over his shoulder and worked the stick and pedals, he was overjoyed to see how good the whole invention worked.

"Wow, is that slick."

But getting an engine was going to be a problem. For the first time the Gore junkpile failed him. It had all kinds of old clockworks in it, but no discarded engines. One forenoon while Ma was in the garden he dared to use the telephone and called the Bonnie dump man to ask if he had any old small engines. The dump man said he didn't, but that even if he did, he'd never give it to a kid to put into a fool airplane.

Ma's Fairbanks-Morse engine was much smaller. That might just fit. The only trouble with that was that if he flew off with Ma's engine and stayed on his island for a while, Ma wouldn't be able to do her washing Monday mornings.

Besides, the Fairbanks-Morse was a cranky engine. It didn't always like to start. Two weeks before, Ma had the hot water and the soap and the clothes in the washing machine, only to discover that the engine didn't feel like starting that morning. Ma tried choking it, setting the spark in different positions, setting the clutch in and then out, everything. No matter how long she cranked, once for two straight minutes at a stretch, until her face turned purple, it wouldn't fire, not even one pop. A couple of times between crankings Ma looked out toward where Pa was mowing alfalfa and spoke at the skies like a despairing prophet, "Oh, Alfred, what have you led me into," and then went at it again. Free also cranked, until blisters as big as bloodsuckers popped out on the palm of his hand.

Finally Ma sent Free to get Pa. Pa came on a dead trot with his horses. He listened to Ma's complaint with his head held to one side. Then he gave the engine a hard look, cussed it once, which Ma approved of, and then, grabbing hold of the iron handle roughly, cranked it. He cranked and cranked. He put his hand over the intake pipe; took his hand off the intake pipe. But not a pop was heard. Pa too looked up once and stared at a faraway place, and cried out like a prophet in the desert, "Oh, Mister Fairbanks and Mister Morse, you super plutocrats wherever you are, your fetch-sticking engine ain't worth the powder to blow it up with, let alone a widow's fart on Old Year's Night." Nothing helped. And at last Pa said Ma had better give up the idea of washing that day. The engine, he said, was just plain not in the mood to work that day.

But Ma wouldn't. She was finally mad. She kicked the belt off the engine. Then she picked up the whole engine, tongue and four wheels and running gear, and hurled it over the fence into Pa's yard, and cried, "I don't ever want to see that dratted engine near my washing machine again. You take it."

Pa looked at the toppled engine across the fence, then at Ma, and his eyes swelled wide, and he said, "Gotske." Then he went around through the gate and set the engine up on all fours again, and pulled it back into the houseyard into place in front of the washing machine. Just for the heck of it, before heading back to the alfalfa field, he gave the heavy iron crank one more whirl. And by cracky, it started. And Ma got her washing done after all that day.

The thought struck Free that since Ma wasn't too hot about the old engine, maybe it wouldn't really hurt if he took the engine for his airplane. Ma and Pa would be mad at him for a couple of days, but they'd soon see that Ma would be better off with a dependable engine.

Free got the old blue Fairbanks-Morse out of the houseyard and pulled it up alongside his plane. He did some measuring with Pa's carpenter rule and saw that the engine would fit exactly across the frame. He unbolted the engine from its running gear and with a hoist moved it into his airplane. He set the engine with the pulley sticking out in front and the handle on the inside. He bolted the engine down securely. The plane was heavy up front and if he leaned down on the engine too much the nose wanted to dip. He figured though that when the pilot got into the cockpit the plane would be in balance again.

The next problem was the propeller blade. He first considered cutting one out of an ash limb, but the thought of having to whittle the whole thing down to its fine tapered tips made him think again. Too hard to do. Then he remembered seeing a Kenwood steel windmill lying in a ditch in the west end of neighbor Billy Peterson's pasture.

Free got aboard Tip, and getting the mail at the same time, stopped in at the Petersons to ask if he could have the windmill.

"Sure, go ahead and take it," Billy Peterson said. "But when you get your plane built, you owe me a free ride."

After some tinkering Free fixed the six sails of the wind wheel to the six spokes of the Fairbanks-Morse flywheel.

Enough of the pulley still showed through the windmill for him to put a belt on. What he could do each Monday was to taxi his airplane up to Ma's washing machine, slip on the belt, and wash the clothes for her. And with that wind fan whirling around, he could almost dry the clothes for her at the same time, maybe even as fast as she removed them from the washing machine. The picture of it in his mind was so funny he had to drop his wrench a minute and laugh out loud about it.

Albert and Jonathan came over to see what he was inventing. In their eyes Free was already a famous inventor. When they saw how big the airplane was and what he was going to do with it, they got scared and ran back to their sandpile. They didn't bother him again.

Everett was different. He watched a while from twenty feet away, head cricked to one side, a funny smile on his face.

The day Free finally got everything into shape and was set to take off, Everett showed up again.

"Well," Free said, "you're just in time. How'd you like to have a ride up there in the sky."

Everett smiled the peculiar smile he got when he hid his bread crusts. Everett hated hard black crusts, and was the best in the family at getting rid of them during a meal.

"Maybe you'd like to be the first one to fly this plane, ha?"

Everett backed up a step.

"I'll show you how." Free wasn't about to let his dumb brother wreck his great invention, but still and all, he was a little afraid to fly it himself, now that it was ready. "Come here."

Everett gazed straight up into the sky.

"Is that supposed to mean you don't want to be a hero?"

Everett continued to stare up at the high blue sky.

"All right, then I'll fly her."

After all the adventures Ma'd had trying to start the engine, Free hardly dared think it would start easy for him either. But just for the heck of it, he set the spark and the gas, checked the tail assembly to make sure that it worked up and down as well as sideways, then grabbed the iron crank handle and gave it a whirl.

It popped on the first turn; then began to bang away. Suck-suck-poch. Suck-suck-poch.

Free was so shocked he almost forgot to let go of the crank.

Thank God the cold engine didn't right away get up full speed. Even so the six-sail propeller generated so much wind it almost blew the hair off his head by the roots. He quick scrambled backwards and landed correct into the pilot's seat. His eyes were so wide open they were taking in stars.

Slowly the engine warmed up and slowly the windmill propeller buzzed faster and faster. The plane shook under him like a threshing machine.

There was a creaking sound under him. Looking down he saw that the landing wheels had begun to roll. He was actually moving. The plane was actually beginning to taxi across the yard.

He waved to Everett. "Say good-bye to Ma for me, will you?"

Everett continued to gaze up at the sky.

Too late Free realized he'd forgotten to pack some sandwiches and lemonade. But then who would have thought that Ma's fetch-sticking Fairbanks-Morse engine was going to start the first time he turned it over. Well, in a minute he'd be airborne. While his hair was being blown straight back, his mind raced straight ahead. He saw, in his mind's eye, his plane slowly lifting up over the trees by the sandpile and then curving over the Hopkins cornfield and then over the housetops of Bonnie and then on west to an island in the Pacific Ocean somewhere. It was going to happen.

Ma appeared in the doorway of the porch ahead. Her face showed up blue behind the screen.

Free didn't wave. The fan propeller was blowing wind back at him too hard. He had to hang on with both hands.

The landing wheels under him began to squeal at a pretty good clip. Looking sideways he guessed he was going about ten miles an hour. He wondered if it wasn't about time to pull back on the control stick and take off. If he didn't pretty quick he'd never clear the trees by the sandpile.

Just as he drew up even with the house gate, he felt the tail of the plane lift up behind him at the same time that the nose went down. It flashed through his mind that he'd fastened the engine too flat onto the frame so that the propeller was sucking the nose down. The pitch of the propeller should have been tilted up so that it would have pulled him up.

He pulled back on the stick. Nothing. The tail kept coming up. With rising horror he saw that in another minute the blurring roaring propeller was going to bore a hole right into the earth of the yard. He was going to arrive in China looking like a badger.

He cast an agonized look around. Ma had stepped outside and stood on the stoop with one hand shaded over her eyes and the other hand over her heart. Everett had run forward a couple of steps.

Dust and sand began to pellet back at Free. He bowed his head into it at the same time that he pulled back on the stick for all he was worth.

The edge of the whirring fan caught at the grass, then at the earth, and all of a sudden the plane nosed over completely and the propeller went after the earth like it meant to pulverize it. It dug a little ways into it, about a foot. Dirt flew up in a brown explosion. Then the propeller ran stuck and the engine choked and died.

Silence. Dust settled down around Free and his monoplane.

The control stick bent down under his weight. He hung by the fronts of his toes where they were hooked behind the pedals.

Ma came stomping toward him like a general entering a scene of death and destruction on a battlefield. She looked up at where Free hung onto the stick. She looked at the wings of the monoplane. She looked at where the fan had dug a circular hole into the yard. Then she looked at her Fairbanks-Morse engine and found voice. "What next!"

From his perch Free looked down at the engine too.

Everett came running up. "Free wanted me to drive it first."

"Lucky not." Ma glared at Free. "Young man, I want that engine of mine removed from that flying contraption of yours and put back in its place in my yard immediately. And I do mean immediately. Or else I'm gonna call the sheriff and tell him to haul you off to the crazy house."

"Okay, Ma."

"Wait'll your pa sees this." Then Ma turned and slowly walked back to the house shaking her head. "That boy. Heh."

Free knew that Ma's engine was done for him.

Everett said, "Now I wisht I could've rode along. That was fun."

Free climbed down out of his plane. "Oh, go back to your sack swing."

That noon Ma told Pa about it.

Pa wasn't sure at first if he should laugh or get mad. Finally he just said, "Too bad your engine couldn't have run a while longer and've dug that hole a little deeper. You might have struck water for us."

Everett with a sly roll of eyes wanted to know if, had Free been able to fly off, would he, Everett, have been the boss of the other kids then?

At that question, Pa looked up from eating buttermilk-and-barley soup and said there was only one boss on the place and that if you knew what was good for you you'd pay close attention to who that was. "There's room for only one bull per pasture."

Free wasn't done with his plane. About that time he got hold of a book called *The Speedwell Boys and Their Flying Machine*. It told how the Speedwell boys were once flying over some river breaks when their motor conked out. They discovered they could float around on rising air currents. The cliffs and the bluffs made for upshoots of air. Thus they were able to glide ten miles before they had to land. It made Free wonder if he couldn't sail around the county a little and see the sights from the air after all. He had a cliff too and he was sure it had rising air currents. He'd many a time seen hawks hanging silently over it, sometimes for many minutes without having to dip their wings. If he could just somehow get his plane airborne maybe he too could hang over the yellow clay cliff and look down and watch things below, see when Gertie Young went swimming, or when a cloudburst was coming down the river.

The next day the wind came out of the north corner. It came strong and cool. It tipped over the chickens and blew loose straw around. Pa called it great working weather for man and beast.

Free himself thought it perfect weather to test out his idea. Why not shoot that plane off the cliff like a slingshot and then take advantage of the air currents and soar around?

No sooner thought of than done. He got Tip up from the pasture, harnessed her, hooked her onto a singletree and then onto the tail of his plane. Everett agreed to come with so long as it was understood he didn't have to ride in the contraption.

Tip pulled the plane to the little table of land above the cliff. Free took along a short post, an auger, an iron hook, Pa's long hay rope, and the hay pulley. He planted the short post deep into the earth at the very edge of the cliff so that the top of it stuck out only a half foot. He threaded the hay rope through the pulley and then tied one end of the rope to the singletree and the other end to the hook. He set the hook into the point of the plane. Next he wired the pulley onto the top of the post in such a way that when the hook came along and hit it, the hook would pop loose from the plane. He backed Tip to the post facing away from the cliff, then pulled the plane as far as he could the other way, away from the edge of the cliff, until the rope was tight.

He called Everett over from where he'd been watching from a safe distance. "Listen to me now. And listen good. I'm not asking you to ride in the plane. I know you don't like being a bird. All I'm asking of you is to ride Tip horseback for me and to make her go as fast as she can in that direction. See? Everything will happen automatic after that. You don't have to worry about a thing. Just ride the horse fast."

"Where's your suitcase?"

Free got mad. Everett for all his dumb brains could sometimes be a darn smart snotnose. One never knew what he was going to think of next. "Everett, if you don't get on top of that horse, I'm going to pound you."

"No," Everett said, and took off for home.

Free yelled for him to stop.

But it didn't help. Everett disappeared down a path through the gooseberries.

Free ran after him. "Everett, if I ever get ahold of you!"

Everett kept on running. He ran pretty fast too.

"Come back here!"

Everett popped out on the other side of the gooseberries and ran out of sight into the ravine in Pa's pasture. Free still had sore knees and so it was easy for Everett to outrun him.

Free stopped. He sat down on a stone and cussed. He cussed out everybody. Ma for being stingy with her engine, Everett for being such a poor sport, and finally That Fellow up in heaven for not making Pa richer.

Finally, after resting for about an hour from his running and his cussing, he made up his mind.

He went back to his plane. He set the stick and the rudders for takeoff; tied them down with a piece of rusty bailing wire. Next he climbed aboard Tip, jerked her head up from where she was peacefully cropping grass, gave her a whack over the butt with the end of the lines. "C'mon, old skate, let's give our great invention one last ride and then we'll be done with flying. Forever. Hup-ah. Get."

For once Tip obliged him. She leaned into it and ran like the dickens. She seemed to know that in a few minutes they'd be headed for home and her manger full of ear corn.

The monoplane scurried toward the edge of the cliff. When the hook hit the pulley on the post, it separated from the plane, and the plane took off on its own. For a good twenty feet it actually flew. Level and beautiful. It even gained in height, a foot or so. But then a cross breeze caught the near wing and slowly lifted it. The plane made a Clarence Chamberlin roll. And then it dove straight for the willows below, the very willows from which Free had once cut the poles for the wings. It vanished from sight. There was a crash.

"I guess the good Lord never meant for me to leave home."

BOOK THREE

Angel Country

To
HENRY VAN ENGEN
and
HERMAN VAN ENGEN
uncles

Free ❦ 1

A BLACK CAR with a Sioux County license plate rolled onto their yard one afternoon. Free was up in a maple tree reading *Riders of the Purple Sage*.

Pa went out to the gate to greet the visitors. From his perch in the maple Free saw that it was a stranger domeny and two other well-dressed men. Ma was right behind Pa with her good smile. Pretty soon they all went inside to talk.

Free was well lost in the purple sage, when Ma spoke to him from the foot of the tree. "Boy? Could you come down a minute?"

Free looked down at her. "What have I done now?"

"Come. There's some men here from Western Academy who'd like to meet you. Take your book with you."

Free shinnied down the sleek maple and followed her into the house. He made sure the sides of his overalls were buttoned. He noticed that his bare toes had grass stains.

The three men were sitting around the kitchen table having a cup of coffee and smoking cigars. The cigar smoke burned sweet. It reminded Free of the smell of trains. The domeny was wearing a black coat, striped vest and trousers, and a red tie. As the domeny toyed with his cigar, sliding it in and out of his thick red lips, a wide gold ring on his finger flashed in the light coming through the window. The other two men had eyes like horse traders. Their sharp eyes kept going back to the book Free was reading.

Ma said, "Son, this is Reverend Marcellus Weathers. He's president of the Western Academy Association. And this man is Principal Gary Hedges. And that man is Professor Gary Ralph. They both teach at Western Academy."

Free shook hands with all three men.

"Sit down son." Ma pointed to where she usually sat at the table.

Reverend Weathers had light gray eyes and a dark plum face. He held his cigar to one side of his face. He smiled slowly, revealing a row of gold-capped teeth. "You like to read, do you?"

Free didn't like being talked down to. He nodded.

Pa had been watching with a little smile. "That kid's always got his head in a book. And I can't understand where he gets it either."

Ma said, "Both of his grandfathers were readers."

"Wal, I guess that's right," Pa said. "I forgot. One of them knew just about everything there was to know about the Bible. And the other one was an expert on Bolsheviks."

Professor Ralph threw Principal Hedges a private look, and smiled. Professor Ralph wore a silver-blue suit. It went well with his silver-blond hair.

Principal Hedges fingered a gold medal on his watch chain. He wore a rich brown suit. It matched his hair and little moustache exactly.

Reverend Weathers tapped the ash off the end of his cigar in his saucer. "We're prepared to give you a tuition scholarship at Western Academy next year. Would you like to come?"

"If my folks can afford it," Free said.

"We'll have a brand-new building for you. Your class will be the first freshman class to begin in it. Which means you'll have new facilities all the way through high school."

Ma asked, "How is our church coming with the money for it?"

"Fine. Fine. The Lord is going to provide all right."

Pa said, "Just a minute. Not so fast here. The pocketbook is pretty flat in his house."

Reverend Weathers said, "As to board and room, it won't be much. Only four dollars a week."

"What about his books and clothes?" Ma asked.

"Well, yes, those too."

"How much will those books be?" Pa asked. Pa could never get over it that people actually spent money on books. Making books was a God-given talent and anybody having it shouldn't be allowed to charge for it.

"There'll be four textbooks. They shouldn't cost much more than ten dollars all together the first year."

"What? That's four times more than what our big black Bible cost."

The three visitors smiled.

"Can't my boy buy his books with some other kid in school and so share the cost?"

Professor Ralph spoke up. "We feel it's a good habit for a boy to own his own books. That way he can take pride in them. When you own something you're more apt to make it a part of your life." Professor Ralph looked at the book Free had been reading. "I don't mean junk like that, you understand. But true books written by masters. Books that will build a hungry fire in a young boy's mind."

Free frowned. Zane Grey read good. In fact, Zane Grey read so true and real that there were times when Free forgot where he was. He'd once almost fallen out of the maple tree reading him.

Professor Ralph quickly said, "Oh, it's all right for you to be reading Zane Grey at this stage in your life, son. Because at least you're reading something. But later on you'll want books that'll make you reach for better things. And in so doing you'll enjoy life that much more. Zane Grey will seem flat to you then."

Free caught on. It was like with that sack swing of his. Once he made himself reach further to take that first big jump off the higher tree, swinging never was better.

"Why," Pa said, "we ain't got more'n a half dozen books in the house and we're getting along all right."

"Alfred," Ma said.

Pa went on. "There's *The Black Prophet* we got. And that set of four black books you call *The Compendium of the Bible*. And our black leather Bible itself. And that book Gar Ault gave us on our wedding night . . . you know . . . "

"*Our Marriage Formulary*," Ma filled in.

"Yeh, that one." Pa continued counting on his fingers. "And then there's that doctor book with all them pictures in it of the human being you ordered from Sears Roebuck. The one you hid in our bedroom. *Dr. Hood's Plain Talks*. That's eight books."

"Alfred," Ma said.

Free hadn't heard about that doctor book. Pictures in it of the human being?

Principal Hedges had a question for Free. "What would you like to become someday?"

Free looked down at his green-stained toes. He couldn't very well tell these important men that he'd once dreamt of conquering the state of Iowa. And if he told them he wrote rhymes for the fun of it, and worse yet, gave a long poem to Principal Ardman once, they'd think him an idiot—especially when they found out he almost flunked grammar.

Principal Hedges pressed him some more. The man looked right through a fellow. "Maybe you aspire to be a governor of our fair state someday? Like my colleague here"—and he nudged Professor Ralph in the ribs—"still dreams of becoming."

Professor Ralph flashed his friend a silver smile. "Not fair, Gary."

Pa had a sly smile. "Maybe Free wants to study to be just a hired hand for his pa and help him get ahead on the farm."

Ma said, "Would anybody like to know my thoughts on the matter?"

"Of course we would, Mrs. Alfredson," Reverend Weathers said.

Ma first looked at Pa, then Ma looked down at her red thumbs where they fumbled with each other in her lap. "I would like it very much if someday our boy could do some kind of special work in the Lord's vineyard."

Reverend Weathers nodded. "That's noble of you."

Principal Hedges and Professor Ralph said nothing.

Pa looked down at his hands then too. When Ma started talking religious, and preachers chimed in with her, Pa ran out of words.

Reverend Weathers cleared his throat. "Well. So." He clapped both hands on the table. "It seems Master Alfred will be with us next fall then. Good." He looked at his two professor friends. "We have several more recruiting calls to make yet today, so I think we better be on our way." He stood up.

Pa sat shaking his head a moment longer. "Times have sure changed. In the old days the oldest boy always stayed to home and worked for the old man. If anybody went to school at all it was the youngest boy."

Reverend Weathers nodded. "Yes, that's right, Mr. Alfredson. And unfortunately all too often in the past many a brilliant first son was lost to us."

"That could mean me then," Pa said. "Because I was the oldest and I didn't finish grade school."

"Yes, it very well could."

The other two gentlemen from Western Academy stood up to go too.

Ma and Pa walked them to their car. Free lingered behind, standing near Ma's flowering pink peas.

The black car was a new Packard. It fit the grand manner of Reverend Weathers. As the reverend got behind the wheel, he placed his half-smoked cigar in a gadget perched on a special ashtray. The gadget worked like a clothespin. The two professors got in back.

Reverend Weathers threw Free one more look. "Someday, after you've graduated from Western Academy, and then Christian College in Zion, Michigan, I'll come to your church and hear you preach."

Free looked at the reverend's dark plum face, then looked down at the pink peas.

Ma laughed. "And I'll be there too, Reverend, when that great day comes."

Reverend Weathers started the car, then lifting his hand in a wave like a blessing, drove off. The two professors waved through the back window.

Ada ❦ 2

IT HAPPENED THAT the Fat Johns came over for a visit the next evening. Both sets of kids were overjoyed and ran out to the hog pasture to play ball. While Fat John and Fat Etta stumped into the parlor with Ada and Alfred.

Fat Etta settled into an easy chair by the window. She was short of breath. Fat John took a rocker across from her. Alfred seated himself by the door. Ada took a rocker next to Fat Etta.

Ada opened the west window of the parlor to catch the cool northwest breeze. After a while she could smell her garden, especially the thick cracking cabbages. The occasional breeze was just strong enough to lift the white lace curtains and the curving green arms of the big maidenhead fern by the door.

The two men talked crops for a while. The two women talked canning.

Then Fat John brought it up. "Say, I hear Western Academy wants you people to send your oldest there."

Ada looked at Alfred; Alfred looked at Ada. Ada had been thinking of asking Fat John what he thought of the idea. Fat John would give her his usual straight flat-out opinion. Domeny often worried more about what Fat John thought of his sermons than he did of anyone else in church. Ada had liked Fat John ever since the time he'd met her train in Bonnie years before. She had been down in the dumps then, trying to get over that Alvin Ravenhorse business. Fat John could be both comical and profound. There in that cousin of hers was a man who, with a better wife, might have been some kind of great person, an important man in the government or the boss of a big company in Sioux City or Sioux Falls. She looked at him with a little smile. There he sat in her strongest rocker so fat he couldn't keep the side buttons of his brand-new overalls fastened. And that odd habit of his of never removing his little hat no matter where he was, except in church of course, set him apart all the more. In only one thing was he like Alfred—he always had clean hands and well-trimmed fingernails. A woman could forgive a man many things if he had neat hands.

Fat Etta had her points too. She had a way of making her children mind without having to yell at them. She was loyal to her husband. And she never missed a church service. It was just that when it came to brains she wasn't in Fat John's class. She pulled him down.

"Well, Ada?" Fat John reminded her.

"Yes, we've given it some thought."

"What kind of malarkey did those high dudes hand out to make you people think of such a damn fool thing?" Fat John spoke with so much gravel in his voice it was almost as if the words came out of his armpits.

"They were interested in our son because of his high marks last year. As you know, God wants the best for His schools."

"Best, best," Fat John growled, "who really knows if your boy is the best? Certainly that ass of an Obert Ardman wouldn't know, coming as he does from a poor class of people."

What? It almost made Ada laugh out loud. This slothful man with his fat-eating ways, who was always deep in debt at the grocers, he still thought of himself as some sort of descendant of nobility?

Fat John saw he wasn't getting anywhere with Ada. He turned to Alfred. "Alf, I'm going to give you a piece of advice. More schooling will only turn that boy against you."

"That's true," Alfred said. "It's already bad enough that he's always reading."

"I say, make him work," Fat John said. "Like I make my oldest work."

"You're probably right," Alfred said.

"By the sweat of his brow." Fat John started to cross his legs; remembered he couldn't; reset them wide apart like the columns of a gate. "Really, you're actually not thinking of letting him go just when he's going to start earning his oats, are you?"

"I guess not."

"Him making up all those rhymes for the prinicpal last year . . . ha! what's he gonna do when he gets through high school, write books, for godsakes?"

"Yeh."

"Gat, Alf, look at how lucky you are with all those boys coming up. You can work them until they're twenty-one. With all that free labor you can be rich. You can live like a lord. You're a fool to let that opportunity pass by."

Ada began to squirm. She didn't like it that husband Alfred was agreeing with Fat John. Those two men were jealous of the boy, Alfred because he'd never been to school, Fat John because he hadn't been allowed to develop his talent.

After some thought she decided to be the wiser person. "John, cousin, the Lord will not hold us guiltless if we let the boy bury his talent in the cornfield." She looked down at her quiet thumbs. "I think it would be nice if our son could become a domeny. And if not that, then at least a teacher in our Christian School system. You know, special work in the Lord's vineyard."

Fat John finally said, "Well, for catsake."

Ada decided she should also get an outside opinion. She called up Josie Newinghouse and invited her out for the weekend. Josie was the younger friend of Free's former teacher, Amelia Herman, and was a student at Western Academy.

Josie Newinghouse drove over in a Ford roadster with her roommate, Sadie Ralph. When they arrived they were laughing about the antics of her tricky old car. Josie was almost as tall as Ada, with a sleepy blue glance. Sadie was short, red-haired, peppery. Ada put them up in the spare bedroom.

It wasn't long before the whole house, from top to bottom, was full of joyful girlish laughter. Josie and Sadie helped Ada with the dishes. They ironed for her. They tended the baby for her.

Sadie turned out to be the younger sister of Professor Gary Ralph. She'd just finished Western and was working in the Hello Drugstore. She was going to go to Christian College in Zion, Michigan, the coming fall. Ada had been impressed by Professor Ralph, but getting to know his younger sister gave her an insight into one of Free's future teachers she wouldn't have had otherwise.

Alfred also perked up with those two girls around. He tried to shine up to Josie, who was more his type than Sadie. The children too were better mannered than usual. Only Free remained the same. He was up in his maple tree reading.

Ada told the girls her problem.

Josie didn't say much at first.

But Sadie after some thought said, "I'll keep my eye on Free for the next couple of days and then I'll tell you what I think."

"Good enough."

Sunday after supper, Sadie had a question for Free. They'd all pushed back their chairs from the table, and the little ones had run out to play under the trees and Alfred had lit up one of his rare company cigars. "Free, tell me, when you're alone by yourself, like up there in your tree, what do you dream about?"

Free's eyes turned blank.

"Or when you wake up at night, what sort of hero do you dream of becoming?"

Free didn't like being asked such a question.

Ada smiled at him. She too wanted to know what his secret dreams were. Over the last months her oldest boy had been slowly shutting her out more and more. She didn't really think that was wrong. Or that he didn't like her any more. It was more that he was about to start up the path of manhood, and like her brothers John and Sherman had done with Ma for a little while, had to get out from under her thumb. She wished she could place her hand on his shoulder like in the old days, but knew that this would drive him further into silence. How sad it really was between an aging mother and a growing son.

"Free?" Sadie pressed.

"If I told you, you'd laugh," Free said.

"You really think I'd be that impolite?"

"I dunno."

"That book you're reading there, *The Arabian Nights*, do you like it?"

"It's pretty good, all right. I like the part where Sinbad the Sailor hangs onto the leg of a rukh and so flies off to strange lands."

"Just pretty good?"

"Except it ain't really real sometimes."

"How do you mean, it isn't really real?"

Free gave her a look to show that the only reason he was going along with her was because she was a guest. "Well, it keeps telling in there about how beautiful the gardens were with flowers and bushes, but it never gives any colors."

"You mean, it's vague as to details? Isn't realistic?"

"I suppose so."

Josie woke up out of her sleepy softness. "Don't you mean, Free, that you can't lose yourself in it because it isn't a true book?"

"Yeh. Like it never really happened. Like something that happened in a dream at night, not in one in the daytime." Free warmed up. Josie had hit on something interesting. "Now, if I was to write it, I'd put in more smells, and stickers like roses have, and real mud from the field. That way the flowers and the slave girls would look even prettier."

"Ah," Sadie said, and became thoughtful.

Later, just before dark as the girls were leaving, Sadie took Ada by the arm and whispered, after making sure Free couldn't hear her, "Send him to Western. He'll do."

Ada held her heart.

Free ❦ 3

EARLY IN THE morning Pa backed the Buick out of the garage and pulled up in front of the house. He honked the horn.

"Just a minute," Ma said. She looked Free over.

Free had on his brown knickerbocker suit and a new pair of brown shoes. Pa had given him one of his ties, a polka-dot red one, and to keep it from looking too long he'd made the knot high into the wide part and had tucked the narrow part into his shirt.

Pa honked the horn again.

Free started for the door with his brown leather suitcase.

"Just a minute," Ma said again.

"But Pa's waiting."

"Set that suitcase down and come here a minute. Let's you and me kneel by this chair." Ma took him by the hand and drew him over to a chair near the north window.

"Aw, Ma."

"Come." She kneeled on the floor and tugged at him to do the same. "It's always a good thing first to ask the Lord's blessing."

Free let himself be drawn down beside her.

"Fold your hands and together with me now lean on this chair."

With them both on their knees Free was at tall as Ma. He closed his eyes. He could feel Ma's elbow against his elbow. There was a smell of baking powder in her clothes.

Ma prayed. "Father in heaven. We are mother and son on our knees before Thy throne. The son is about to embark on a new heading across life's seas. Oh Lord, we look with some fear upon this venture. It is not lightly taken. We are not rich. Every penny spent on this boy will be hard-earned. His going to school will mean that the rest of the family will have to pinch by for four long years. Yet, oh Lord, we rejoice in the opportunity given us to deepen our minds in a true knowledge of Thee and Thy works, as well as to develop such talents as we have, whatever they may be. Watch over him now, Lord, as he"—the horn outside blew three times, hard—"goes into a strange new land, where he will meet new faces. We know there will be temptations along the way. Let him remember that the hand will do what the eye won't look at. We trust that Thou wilt guide him in the true path of wisdom, which is to ever seek the Good. We ask it in Jesus' name. Amen." Ma held still for a moment longer, eyes still closed.

Pa blew the horn again, this time long and hard.

Free got to his feet.

Ma sighed. As she opened her eyes, a tear rolled out. "A mother's heart is different from a father's heart all right." She put a hand to her knee and stood up beside him. She stroked him over the forehead, touching him tenderly.

Pa blew the horn once more, mad.

"I better go, Ma."

Ma made herself smile. As her eyes went over him again from head to foot, she spotted something. "Free."

"Now what?"

"Hehh. Boy. Don't you know I want you to wear your knickers buttoned above the knee?"

"Oh, Ma."

"Why not? When I wish it?"

"Because those inner-tube garters Pa made cut into me something awful just above the knee. But with the knickers buttoned below, I can wear the inner-tube garters below the knee where the leg is thinner."

"It doesn't really hurt you that much, does it?"

"It sure does." He undid his knickers and showed her what the rubber garters had done to him above the knee. They'd left what looked like rows of white rice under the skin. "See?"

"Oh," Ma said, a hand to her gold hair. "I never thought of that."

"I'll sure be glad when I can wear long pants some day."

"I never thought of that," Ma said again.

Free became brusque. "Bye, Ma." He picked up his brown leather suitcase and went out to the car.

Ma followed him to the gate, blue eyes on him loving and a little forlorn.

"About time," Pa growled. Pa waved to Ma; then snapped the Buick into gear and with a lunge drove off the yard.

Free felt he should wave one last good-bye. Ma'd be awfully hurt if he didn't. He turned and gave her a little salute.

Ma waved back.

Pa tooled the old Buick past the row of cottonwoods along Bester's pasture. It was where Garrett had once hit a mighty home run. The ball had landed clear across the ditch.

Pa wriggled his big nose. "What took you so long in there?"

"Nothing."

"Women. They always have some last-minute thing for you to do yet just as you're about to leave the yard."

Free kept silent.

Pa turned the corner to take the Hello road. They rolled down into a little wet valley. The sun shone slanting across it from the east. A white bridge spanned a quiet creek. The water was as clear as a north window. A patch of wild tobacco grew in the ditch. Some of the lower branches still showed tiny blue flowers.

They ground up a long steep hill. When they got to the top they could see the water tower of Hello on the horizon ahead.

Free had trouble believing it. He was actually going to Western Academy. Getting out from under Pa's and Ma's strict rules was going to be a relief. Once he was in Hello they couldn't always be giving him orders. He could do just what he wanted when he wanted to.

Pa still had to hand out a little more advice. "Now listen. If you're in doubt about the manners of the house you're staying at, just watch the head of the house to see how he does it, and then you do likewise."

Free squirmed. He'd heard the same thing from Ma a thousand times.

The grove of a mystery place came up on the right. The grove was so thick it was hard to see the upstairs windows of the weathered house. Had the dark place been next door back home, he and Sherm would long ago have figured out the mystery. People said the sheriff had once dug in the basement looking for the body of a missing wife. Free would have gone to the grove to look for where the twigs and leaves had been disturbed and then dug there.

They rolled past the sewer plant. It stank pretty bad.

Free spotted the house on the north end of town where an old man of sixty had knocked up a young housekeeper of eighteen and had had a nice boy by her. Free tried to imagine how it might have happened. The old man had probably caught her in the barn where he kept chickens. She was probably out looking for eggs, up in the haymow, and the old gent helped her look, and she slipped in the hay, and he caught her, and she gave him a certain sly glad look, and then he slipped his hand under her dress—

Pa turned a corner and parked beside the third house down the street. It was an orange house and the poorest-looking one. "Wal, here we are."

"How did you know where it was so easy?"

Pa nodded toward the house next door. "A relative of ours lives there. Frank Dykeman. Deputy Sheriff. His mother was an Alfredson. Your ma and me went to her funeral a couple of years ago. The Dykemans left our church and now think themselves red-blooded American Congregationalists." Pa snorted to himself. "That's the church I left to marry your mother, boy."

The Dykeman house had a wide veranda with two bay windows. A blue roof of tar shingles and cream-colored siding gave the house a rich look. Four evergreens stood at the corners of a pick-neat green lawn. Free wondered if the Dykemans had any kind of library.

"Frank and his wife never had kids, so they could afford such a place." Pa got out of the car. "Wal, let's go meet your landlady, Mrs. Fish. She's a widow and takes in boarders for a living. C'mon. Get your duds."

Free reached for his suitcase and followed Pa up the walk.

An old lady opened the door for them. Her gray hair was done up in back in a tight knot. She had on a gray-green dress and scuffed green high-heeled shoes. Her eyes were like smoke and she had a soft old smile. "So, this is the young man who's to board with us then."

"Right. I brought him here first. I think he can find his way across town to the Academy from here."

"My youngest daughter, Hattie, is starting as a freshman too this fall. She can show him."

"Say, that's fine."

"Would you care to see his room?"

"Nope. Principal Hedges said you kept a neat house."

"Your boy's roommate is coming later. John Sootman, a senior. He comes from near where those Quakers once settled."

"Good. He can show my boy the ropes then too."

"Wouldn't you really care to step in a minute for a cup of coffee?"

"Nope. I'm behind in my work. Thanks just the same." Pa got out his pocketbook and gave Free a ten-dollar bill. "That's for your study books. If there's any left over, bring it home. I don't want you to be eating candy bars when we need it so bad at home."

"He'll have enough to eat here, never fear," Mrs. Fish said.

"It's all right then that we pay you for his keep every two weeks?"

"That'll be fine."

Pa handed over eight dollars. Board and room was four dollars a week from Monday through Friday, and it was a dollar extra if one stayed over Saturday and Sunday. Pa expected Free to walk home Fridays, the whole long seven miles, and then in turn he'd bring Free back again early on Monday.

"Bye, Pa," Free said.

"Bye, son."

Mrs. Fish led Free upstairs into a narrow room. It had a peaked ceiling and only one window. She pointed to a white iron bed. "You and Sootman will have to sleep together. It'll be big enough, I think." She next pointed to two small secretary desks facing each other next to the window. "John had the one next to the closet last year, so you'll have to take the other one."

Free glanced under the bed.

Mrs. Fish caught his look. "You'll just have to use the backhouse by the woodshed. We don't have white owls for our boarders. I won't let my girls empty them."

Free nodded. He'd have to hold it until morning then.

"I'll call you when Hattie is ready to leave." Smiling a dry wrinkle, Mrs. Fish withdrew.

He sat down on the chair by his desk. There were no pictures on the walls, nothing. The wallpaper had no design, just a plain flat yellow color. The wood floor was painted a dull blue-gray. Only the quilted coverlet had some color. It looked like it might have been made out of different colored dresses, rose, blue gray, yellow. The coverlet meant he and John Sootman could sit on the bed and read sometimes. When women put a white bedspread on a bed, a fellow had to be careful to stay off it daytimes.

Free put his things away in the clothes closet and the bureau. The mirror over the bureau had some clouds in it and when he leaned down to comb his hair the clouds made his nose as big as Pa's.

Pretty soon Hattie Fish called upstairs to say she was ready.

"Okay."

Any hopes he had that Hattie might turn out to be as nice as his Fourth of July girl were doomed the minute he saw her. Hattie had a hump nose and wore black-rim glasses. And she was at least an inch taller than he was, despite being stoop-shouldered.

As they ambled toward the Academy, she kept picking at him about how many there were in his family, and how did he like it that his father was alive, because hers was dead. She finally asked him how many relatives he had, and before he could answer, she announced that as the baby in the family she probably had more relatives than anybody in the whole world—nine brothers and six sisters. All but one were married, and that one was Gert, who worked as a waitress uptown. Hattie bragged she already had twenty-one nephews and nineteen nieces.

Free could feel his bowels set against Hattie. With that hump nose and those big black-rim glasses, she looked like a cross between an owl and a parrot. She next rattled on about how many distant relatives she had, not just near ones. Her ma, she said, came from a family of twelve, while her poor departed pa came from a family of eighteen.

"Eighteen?"

"Don't you believe me?"

It was all beginning to sound pretty fishy.

"Laugh if you wanna, I don't care."

If what she said was true, her relations were worse than his own, the Big John Englekings of Bonnie. Pa'd once said that if the government didn't clamp down on the way the Englekings were breeding, they'd take over the county.

"I'm gonna become a schoolteacher. What are you gonna become?"

Hattie would. Free could just see her making life miserable for hundreds of poor little country kids somewhere.

"Didn't you hear me? What are you going to become?"

Free recalled how Fat John used to go around breeding all the mares in Leonhard County. "Well, I'm sort of leaning in the direction of becoming a stud peddler."

Hattie swung away from him, to the very edge of the walk on her side. She held her arms stiff against her sides. "I'm gonna tell Ma what you just said, smarty-pants."

Free was sorry. He liked Mrs. Fish and didn't want to get into trouble with her.

It was a long walk to the Academy. As they turned the corner on main street, heading north, a runt called over from a filling station. "Hey, Fishie, wait up. I'll walk to school with you."

Hattie glanced around. "That's John Sootman."

"My roommate?"

"Yes. He always calls me Fishie. The smarty-pants."

John Sootman wandered over. He looked to be only fifteen, though he wore long pants. He had a small head with a very tight scalp. His blond hair was parted down the middle. He was one of those who would never look grown-up. "Who's the friend?"

"Alfredson. Your new roomie."

Sootman looked Free over. Sootman didn't like it that Free, a freshie, was taller than he was. But he said nothing, only smiled down at Free's big brown shoes.

Hattie said, "And cut out calling me Fishie, will you, John?"

"Okay, Fishie. I'll try and remember." Then Sootman hooted at his own cleverness.

"Oh, you," Hattie said, and she placed both her hands on Sootman's chest and gave him a hard push.

Sootman gave her a surprised look. Then he in turn placed both his hands on her small breasts and pushed her back. "Oh you yourself."

Hattie enjoyed the push. "Oh, well, everybody's always called us Fishes that, so I guess I shouldn't complain either." She turned to Free. "What do they call you when they tease you?"

"Free."

"Well, that's kind of a nice nickname."

They continued north. The street ended in a turnaround in front of a brick building three stories high. The building had tall white-frame windows and in the sun looked red and new. Fresh black dirt lay raw around the footings.

Sootman said, "Yep, that's her. Western Academy. Spanking brand-new. We get first crack at cutting our initials in her desks."

Cars full of students began to arrive and park out front. Other students came flocking down the sidewalks from all corners of town. They formed groups of twos and threes and headed for the glass doors under a wide front archway.

Free began to feel out of place. It usually took him a while to make friends with strangers, just as it took him a while to get into a book. He loved to read, yet often found himself reluctant to start a new story. It meant getting acquainted with a whole new set of people in a new place. Of course once he knew a book was going to be good, then he couldn't have enough of it, and wished it would never end. A good book was never too long. He was choosy about who his friends should be, whether they were in a book or out in life.

Most of the older fellows wore long pants. The long pantsers all seemed to know each other and clapped each other on the back and cracked jokes and picked up the razzing where they'd left off the past May. There was a slick look about them. The few wearing knickers had to be freshies. They looked a little like puppies who'd just had their tails clipped and weren't sure where they belonged.

The older girls wore the better-looking clothes, while the young girls kept worrying if their hems hung level. The older girls compared notes about where they'd worked the past summer, who was now going steady with whom, while the freshie girls like Hattie listened with envy.

Everybody headed for the gymnasium, the boys on one side and the girls on the other. Chairs set in neat rows glistened on a golden hardwood floor. The chairs all faced the stage. The gym was used for both assembly and athletics. Up on the stage four straight-back chairs stood in a row behind a slender lectern.

Free had in mind to sit with Sootman. But Sootman had other ideas. The minute Sootman spotted an old friend he left Free like he was poor relation.

Free found himself a seat alone in the very back row at the end. He drew his knickers well down over the knee and then doubled his legs under his chair so that from above it looked like he had on long pants.

He watched Hattie looking for someone to sit with too. Finally another girl wearing glasses sat with her. The other girl had popped eyes. Every time she blinked they appeared to moisten the inside of her glasses.

Josie Newinghouse wandered in. She was smiling and laughing with some snooty girls. Soon Josie spotted him. She came over. "Well," she said, "I see you made it."

Free saw the snooty girls wondering who she was talking to. He pinkened. "I guess so."

"Hey. You don't sound very happy."

"I think I'll go home. I liked it the way it was."

"Have you seen the library yet upstairs?"

"No."

"Wait'll you see that. All those wonderful books." She gave him a good smile. It was a better smile than the one Ma sometimes gave him. And it came from a girl who was more his own age.

"All right."

"You'll soon find yourself a chum. When I first came here I din't know a soul either. Now I've almost got too many friends."

Her snooty friends began to cough behind their hands.

Josie placed a hand on his shoulder and gave him a warm shake. Again it was something like Ma would do, only better. "See you around."

Free almost had tears. "See you." He watched where she sat down with her friends.

The gym slowly filled. The older kids were having a great time visiting back and forth.

Someone tapped him on the shoulder, asking him to make room. It was another freshie wearing knickers. The fellow wanted to pass by. "That seat next to you taken?"

"No."

The freshie settled beside him. He too looked lost. He had stiff brown hair brushed tight back. His lips were shaped in a double curve. "You from around here?" he asked.

"I'm from Bonnie."

"I'm from Plato, South Dakota."

Free nodded. It was where Pa said all the dust storms started.

"You got a handle?"

Free told him. "Though they mostly call me Free."

"I'm Roy Fowler. Though they mostly call me Birdie."

Gradually a very bad smell began to spread through the gym. It was worse even than if someone had just opened the bowels of a very old cow. Free finally had to hold his nose.

Birdie's curved lips drew back in a sneer. "Boy, did someone let a rotten one." He looked at Free thinking maybe Free had done it.

Free shook his head. "He who notices it first is himself accurst."

Birdie had to laugh at that. "What we say out our way is, the first to wail has it himself in his shirttail."

Sootman had taken a seat two rows down. He heard Free and Birdie talking. He turned, laughing, and behind a hand said, in a loud whisper, "It's that Sioux Center gang again. They exploded a stink bomb to start the year off right."

"No wonder," Free said.

Soon all the students in the gym were smelling it. The girls looked ashamed over at the boys' side. Some of the girls glared mad at the boys. The boys just laughed back at them, and threw up their hands to say they weren't the guilty parties. A couple of the boys made raspberry noises at the girls. The whole place began to roar with raw noise. The hard brick walls and the iron ceiling set off a lot of cracking echoes. The funny thing was the bad smell made Free feel a little bit better about school. Everybody wasn't such a perfect angel after all.

The kids nearest the entrance stilled. Then in a moment, in marched the faculty, Principal Hedges at the head, with Professor Ralph and two other profs following. Principal Hedges took only two steps into the gym, when his nose and little brown moustache came up. His eyes almost instantly began to blaze. He slowed down a couple of steps, as though he didn't want it to be true that he was smelling what he was smelling. He snuffed twice; found it was true; then got madder'n ever and picked up speed again. By the time he reached the steps to the stage he was almost skipping.

Professor Ralph smelled it too. He couldn't make up his mind whether to laugh or get mad and after a couple of steps began to smirk. The next prof was a tall skinny fellow with a high head. He walked a little like a momma's boy. When the smell hit his high nose he began to look outraged. He tried to wave the smell away. The last prof was a short old man with faded brown hair and half-tired blue eyes. He ambled along like a little brown weathered caboose. He smiled sheepish like he'd lost the ball game once too often. His old smile didn't in the least show if he'd smelled the stink bomb. It wasn't either that he was lost in thought.

Principal Hedges headed straight for the walnut lectern. His colleagues settled on the chairs behind him. Principal Hedges gripped the slender lectern with both hands. His hands shook.

The student body became deathly still.

Principal Hedges glared back and forth across the student body as if he right then and there expected to find the culprit with the guilty face. "I see we have people in our midst who haven't been properly brought up. When here I was led to believe that anyone brought up in a Christian home would be housebroke at least."

The short old man prof rose to his feet and ambled up to Principal Hedges and whispered something in his ear. Then he turned and sat down again.

Principal Hedges slapped the lectern. "Professor Brooks thinks it's only some prankster who's exploded a stink bomb."

Giggles erupted on the boys side. The girls frowned.

Principal Hedges glared a while; finally eased off. "Well, all right, I suppose we might as well begin the school year smelling the way we do. For those of you who are new here today, I think maybe some introductions are in order. First of all the teachers. The man at the far end is Professor Peter Brooks."

The short old man nodded.

"Professor Brooks teaches Latin and German. For those of you who get homesick for the farm, he also teaches a course in Pig Latin."

Some students laughed a little.

"Professor Brooks is also our Bible instructor."

Again Professor Brooks gave a little bow while seated.

"Next to him is the ladies' favorite, Professor William Van Rill, our English instructor."

Professor Van Rill bowed from his chair, then with pale fingers tossed back his long black forelock.

"Seeing how many of you ex-farmhands have a way of systematically mutilating the English language," Principal Hedges went on, "Professor Van Rill has volunteered to assist Professor Brooks in teaching Pig Latin."

Professor Van Rill rolled his high head around as though that idea revolted him to his very soul.

"Though I want to warn you," Principal Hedges continued, "that getting a passing mark in Pig Latin doesn't mean you can graduate from this high school. You've still got to learn to use the English language correctly. Etgay the ointpay?"

Free had to laugh at the same time that he felt a little uneasy. He and his friends back home sometimes talked Pig Latin when they wanted to tell a dirty story in front of the littler kids. He also remembered he'd nearly flunked English in his state exams. He already didn't like Professor Van Rill's prissy ways. Professor Van Rill would have made a perfect match for Aunt Karen.

"Next is Professor Gary Ralph, our new instructor for the coming year. He's just graduated from Christian College. He'll teach history and civics."

Professor Ralph stood up partway and nodded with a quick smile. As he did so his silver hair slid forward. With a shake of his head he flipped his pompadour back in place.

"And last there is myself. Gary Hedges. Principal. I handle the mathematics and physics department. I teach the girls how to add up the grocery bill and the boys how to calculate interest on their bank loans. I'll also show you how to make a perpetual-motion machine out of your hired hand." He paused, still sniffing the stink bomb. "And I also might add that as principal I have the right to ferret out the rascals who have offended our olfactory nerves this morning and to expel them from school."

The students by that time had begun to relax. They laughed heartily. Principal Hedges was pretty witty all right.

The student body sang the national anthem and a hymn.

Professor Brooks read Psalm 23 and led a short prayer.

"I heard him preach at home once," Birdie whispered to Free, when they opened their eyes again.

"Him? Brooks?"

"Yeh. He graduated from the seminary but when he didn't receive a single solitary call from a church, he took up teaching. His sermons were so terrible flat."

Free stared up at the short man. Something about the man pricked his memory. He'd heard Ma or Gramma, he couldn't remember which, mention Peter Brooks several times.

"You can see what we're in for with him."

"He's kind of tenderhearted though, I bet."

"Yeh, like some old nanny." Birdie lifted his nose. "Me, I like my teachers tough. I came here to learn something."

"What're you going to become?"

"My mother wants me to become a minister."

"That's what my ma wants me to become too."

"Are you?"

"I dunno. Maybe I'll become a poet."

Birdie's blue eyes fastened on Free's big hands. Slowly his curved lips pulled down at the corners in a little sneer. "Do—you—write—poetry?"

Free didn't like the supercilious look. "Heck, I was making up poems before I started school. Before the primary grade even."

Birdie let Free know that he thought him a big bullshit artist. He moved away from Free a few inches.

Principal Hedges turned to confer with Professor Ralph a moment. While they talked the whole gym began to buzz a little.

Presently Principal Hedges held up a hand. He looked at his gold watch, returned it to his vest pocket. "All right. Let's have a little quiet. This is our first day of school in a new building, as you all well know. Originally we'd planned to have Reverend Weathers address us this morning to commemorate the occasion. But unfortunately he hasn't arrived yet. So instead we'll ask our new instructor, Professor Ralph, to say a few words." Principal Hedges turned and smiled at Professor Ralph. "It will be a good way to initiate him." Principal Hedges retired to his chair.

Professor Ralph shook his head to himself. Then he smiled and got up and stepped up to the lectern. "Well. Hello. So." He gripped the edges of the lectern. "I don't think we should start off the new school year with a long dull lecture by me. I think it would be much more instructive, and perhaps more enjoyable, if I instead told you a little story. Storytelling is still the best way to get something across. That's why I often wish I might have been born a novelist." Professor Ralph spoke in a clear lively voice. He liked what he was doing. With each shake of his head his straight silver hair began to slide forward. "But I wasn't given the gift, and instead I took up the study of history so that I might pass on to you the sum and substance of what others have recorded in diaries, in letters, in official documents and public records, the like. I am at best but a recounter of literal happenings, not imagined or created happenings. Not that there aren't good stories in literal history. Actually, history is full of dramatic stories. In fact, before this day is over, you yourself may find yourself an actor in a dramatic piece of history. What, me, you say? Me associated with some history-making event? Yes, you. Too many of us think that the heroics of great heroes are the only things worth recording. For example, Horatio's stand at the bridge. Or the valiant stand of Leonidas and his three hundred Greeks defending the pass at Thermopylae against the vast hosts of the Persian army. Those two events were important of course, and they may have helped change the course of history."

Professor Ralph seemed to look each student in the eye, one by one.

"But consider the following story as recorded by Herodotus. The ruling party at Corinth heard by way of an oracle that a little boy had been born in the city who would someday grow up to destroy them. Ten men were selected to go find the boy and kill him. The ten men found the house where the boy lived. The mother opened the door to them. She thought they'd come to pay her a friendly visit. When they asked to see the new baby, she happily went to get it, thinking they wanted to compliment her on it. She placed it in the arms of the man she knew best. Now these ten men had agreed beforehand that whoever should receive the child from her should be the one to take it and dash its brains out on the stone floor of the house. But . . . and mark you all this . . . but, it happened that the baby woke up and smiled at the man who took it. Yes. The man held it a moment, staring down at the sweet little infant, and then, shuddering, and closing his eyes, handed it on to the next man. The next man, of course, couldn't bash its brains out either, and he in turn passed it on to the next man. And so on down the line, until all ten men had held it and couldn't kill it. They gave the infant back to the mother, and left. On the way back to the palace, they all blamed each other for being softhearted, but especially the first man who'd held the child."

Chapel was quiet. The students all wondered up at the speaker. The three other professors were also enthralled.

"Just think. A little baby's smile actually changed the course of history. And who knows but what any one of you may someday do some little thing, smile at some man in the window of a passing train who turns out to be the President down in the dumps at the moment—you'll cheer him up with your smile. Or you may help a little old lady across the street who turns out to be the wife of the very banker from whom you will later try to get a loan to help save your farmer's cooperative elevator from going bankrupt. So don't think your life can't be important. It can be. Yes. Yes." Professor Ralph gave one last vigorous nod. His silver-white hair lashed down over his eyes. "Thank you."

The students clapped loud and long.

Birdie said out of the side of his mouth, "Hey, he sounds pretty good."

Chapel was dismissed. As each student walked out he was handed a schedule for the day. The freshmen had English the first period with Professor Van Rill, Civics I the second hour with Professor Ralph, Algebra I the third period with Principal Hedges, and study hour the fourth period in the assembly room. Noon recess lasted from twelve until one. They had Bible I the fifth period with Professor Brooks, Latin I the sixth period also with Professor Brooks, and finally another study hour the seventh period in the assembly room.

As they moved from room to room, Free was struck by how old most of the freshmen were, especially the boys. Some of them were at least seventeen. He mentioned it to Birdie.

"Sure. This is not the usual high school, you know, but a parochial school supported by our church. A lot of these fellows had to stay home on the farm a couple of years after graduating from the eighth grade. Help support the family. But when they discovered how easy the preacher had it, they had a change of heart." Birdie snickered. "You and I are going to school with a bunch of exhired men. Who know what they want and go straight for it."

"How old are you?"

"Thirteen. And you?"

"I'll be thirteen in January."

Birdie shook his head. "There won't be much chance for us to shine around those old bucks."

Free nodded. "It'll be like trying to play baseball with grown-ups. They can throw big curves and hit a lot farther."

The school library had very tall windows facing west. The varnished backs of the books—red, blue, gray—shone in the wide light, giving them a hallowed look. Free had never seen so many books in his life.

Josie Newinghouse was serving as librarian. She and another senior girl, Ada Seaberg, shared the job. Josie gave him a good smile as he stood in the doorway. "Don't be bashful, Free. I told you it was quite a library, didn't I?"

"Are there any books I can take out overnight?"

"You can take out a novel overnight. But not a reference book. Those you can only read either here or in study hall."

Free glanced at a couple of girls flirting with some fellows sitting under the tall windows. Free asked, "I can just walk in behind the railing and look for a book?"

"Certainly. And when you find what you want, bring it to me and I'll make out a card for you."

Free ranged through the various sections: history, poetry, fiction. There weren't many novels, and no Zane Grey or Harold Bell Wright. There were novels by Thackeray, Dickens, and Hawthorne, but they didn't look very interesting. A page in Thackeray looked like a tough essay and the talk in Hawthorne didn't sound real.

He was about to go back to the history section when a title caught his eye. *Tom Sawyer*, a book he'd already read. It was part of a set of red books. Free stared at the picture of the author, Mark Twain, in the frontispiece. Someday, Free thought, he himself would be a famous author like Twain. Free selected the volume next to it, *Huckleberry Finn*. He read a little in it. Mark Twain's talk sounded real. It was much the way he and the neighbor kids talked.

"Found something you like?" someone asked. It was Principal Hedges. He'd come quietly up behind Free.

"I think so."

Principal Hedges gave him a steady look. His little black moustache sat very still on his upper lip. He reached for the book. "Twain, eh? Yes, I suppose that's about your speed. Later on, though, when you begin reading Joseph Conrad, you'll think Mark Twain childish."

Free was a little afraid of the principal. That morning the principal had made Algebra I sound like a tough course. Also there was the look of an important man about the principal. It was in the way he tossed back his brown hair, in the style of his little sharp brown moustache, in the knife-sharp press of his brown suit and in the perfect shine of his shoes. And then after a moment it hit Free what it was. Principal Hedges resembled the picture of Mark Twain in the very book he held. Funny thing.

"But," Principal Hedges said, "go ahead, read Twain. At least you'll be reading and that's a step forward." Principal Hedges turned to Josie. "Let this boy browse in here any time he wants to. It's better than loitering." Principal Hedges threw a look at the flirts sitting under the tall windows. "Speaking of loitering . . . eh?"

The kids under the tall windows got the hint and retreated into the study hall.

School out, Free walked home alone with his new textbooks and *Huckleberry Finn*. He didn't know what he was happiest about, the smell and solid feel of the brand-new textbooks, or the Twain book to read. Smelling and reading in them was going to be something to look forward to that night.

Mrs. Fish served a fair dinner: boiled beets and potatoes, country sausage, lettuce dipped in cream-and-vinegar, flour gravy, bread, and butter and jelly. To make it taste right, though, Free had to sprinkle on quite a bit of salt and pepper. The limp white store bread, of course, didn't taste as good as Ma's homemade bread. Mrs. Fish served home-canned crab apples for dessert and they were all right. It was hard to ruin crab apples. For the beverage Mrs. Fish served green tea.

There were four of them for dinner, Mrs. Fish, Hattie, John Sootman, and himself. Except for Hattie's endless chatter, there wasn't much said. Mrs. Fish read from the Bible and gave thanks.

After dinner, and after Free and Sootman had retired to their room upstairs, Sootman announced that later on when they went to bed Free'd better sleep against the wall. Sootman said he couldn't sleep cornered up; it drove him crazy. Well. That meant that if Free had to do number one in the night he'd have to climb over Sootman.

Sootman began to dress up for the get-acquainted party for that evening. He didn't have much to say as he put on his shirt and tie. He kept humming to himself. The humming was a way of putting Free in his place.

Free finally figured out that Sootman didn't want to be seen with Free at the party. It was all right to walk to school with him in the day, since that could have been expected, but to show up with him at a party, never. The funny thing was, Free himself didn't want to be seen at the party with Hattie. He wondered how he could sneak out of the house without Hattie catching him.

After Sootman left, Free took off his shoes and stretched out on the bed and began to read *Huckleberry Finn*. It very quickly became interesting, which was a relief, since there was always that hackle in his head about starting a new book. Twenty pages into it he decided not to go to the party. It wasn't going to be very much fun anyway with all those grown-up farmhands around. Old buggers.

About a half hour after Sootman left, Hattie called upstairs. "Free? Aren't you going?"

If he answered her he'd be in for it. She'd talk him into going after all. Mouselike Free got up, and picked up his shoes, stepped into the clothes closet and pulled the door closed.

Sure enough Hattie came upstairs and knocked on the door. After a moment she peeked in. "Free, aren't you . . . Oh. He's not here." Hattie breathed to herself a moment. "Now how did he manage to get out of the house without me seeing him?" After a minute she went back downstairs.

Free stood very still amongst the hanging clothes. His eyes sparked in the dark. He knew he'd better wait until she left before he moved. If he made the floor crack and she found him, she'd never let him hear the last of it.

Minutes later, Free heard the screen door slam. On tiptoe he stole to the window. Ah, there she went. Some other girl joined her on the walk. Hattie had probably called someone on the phone and got her to walk to the party with her.

Relieved, Free stretched out on his bed again and went back to reading.

Free ❦ 4

ACROSS THE AISLE in the English class sat a pretty girl. She was seventeen and her name was Winifred Bonner.

Upon graduating from the eighth grade, Winifred stayed home for four years to help her mother keep house on a farm near Pipestone. She was the baby in the family and the only daughter. Her four older brothers doted on her. She was used to getting loved up innocently all day long. Then one day her father died and her mother, lost without her mate, decided to sell her farm and move to town. That gave Winifred her chance. Winifred made up her mind that she wasn't going to work herself to the bone for some dumb farmer husband and grow old before her time. After settling her mother in the new home, she decided to go to Western Academy and either become a teacher or catch herself a domeny husband. Old-maid teachers, contrary to what people said of them, had a way of looking slim and youngish well into their thirties, and the wives of ministers, of course, had a chance to look like handsome ladies well into their forties.

Winifred was about five foot four. She had wavy auburn hair worn brushed off to the right like a boy. Her cheeks were as ripe and as full as a pair of golden pears.

The guys down in the boys' room were in a continual buzz over her. "Have you seen the legs on that Bonner dame?"

"Yeh. I'd sure like to get my horse between those shafts."

Free himself thought of her as a nice person. Winifred always had a serene smile. She was serious about her schoolwork. And she didn't get mad when the joke was on her.

Right from the start Winifred acted like an older sister to Free. When she came into class with her quick muscled walk, she always had a warm smile for him. If he looked a little grouchy, she cheered him up with some joke she'd just heard out in the hallway. Once she even reached across the aisle and ruffled up his hair to get him to smile. She actually spent more time looking at Free, and being friends with him, than with the older guys. And the way she did it didn't mean she was in love with him either. It was just that she liked him.

She made English I sufferable. She sometimes helped him; and he, grateful, sometimes helped her. He had trouble parsing sentences; she had trouble catching the drift of various reading assignments. God had given Winifred the gift of knowing what was proper diction; and God had given him the gift of somehow being able to follow a story line no matter how cluttered up a paragraph might read.

That damned grammar was a burden all right. It was a punishment invented by mean old lady aunt teachers. One day Professor Van Rill told Free in front of the whole class that if it weren't for his ability to read, he'd long ago have sent him back to feeding pigs again.

"Why," Professor Van Rill raged in his high slender voice, "you don't have any brains at all when it comes to grammar. You can't parse a sentence any better than Sam Ruffman. And he's the limit."

Both Free and Sam Ruffman came up with red rooster combs.

Winifred raised her hand.

"Yes, Miss Bonner?"

Smiling in a way that Professor Van Rill couldn't resist, Winifred asked, "When you're just talking with your wife, are you conscious of how each sentence should be parsed as you go along? Or do you just talk along without thinking about it?"

The whole class took a breath. That Winifred. Only she would have the nerve to ask such a question.

Professor Van Rill brushed some lint off the lapel of his neat gray suit. "Good point, Miss Bonner. No, I do not consciously think about the structure of my sentences when I'm talking with my dear wife. And I do not because I've so trained myself beforehand that I can just naturally talk correctly without thinking about it, as you put it. It's a little like the game of baseball. In practice you learn to do things the right way, batting stance, pitching form, the way you field a ball on the short hop. But in a real game you forget all about that and just go out and play."

Birdie in the back seat looked surprised. Professor Van Rill knew about baseball? Birdie considered himself a potential star in baseball. Birdie had a couple of times told Free that if he couldn't be a good minister, he was going to be the best shortstop that ever lived.

Professor Van Rill caught Birdie's look. "Yes, yes. I know. With this ungainly frame of mine I hardly look like a candidate for baseball's Hall of Fame. But when I was a young man, about your age, Mr. Flowler, I dreamed of becoming another Christy Mathewson."

The next day, while reading *The Merchant of Venice*, the class hit upon a tough passage in Act One, Scene One: "Thanks, i' faith; for silence is only commendable/In a neat's tongue dried and a maid not vendible."

Professor Van Rill asked for volunteers to explain it.

Free's eye caught at the word "neat." On wet summer mornings Pa often waterproofed his shoes with a finger of grease from a round box of Rime Neat's-foot Compound. The cover on the round box showed a picture of a cow. Pa'd said neat's-foot was made by boiling the feet of butchered cattle from which a leather dressing was made that was far better than crankcase oil. The word "neat" had something to do with cows then. And the expression "maid not vendible" couldn't help but have something to do with someone like Aunt Karen. Free's brain blinked and then he had it. He raised his hand.

"Well, our plot detective seems to have come up with an explanation. Yes, Master Alfredson."

Birdie in back snickered.

"Now now," Professor Van Rill scolded, "let's hear Master Alfredson's explanation first before we vent any ridicule upon him. Go ahead, Free."

Free plunged in. "Since silence becomes an old maid, and a dead cow's tongue can't beller, the passage means that except for dried-up prunes there's no harm in talking."

Professor Van Rill's brown eyes widened. "Why! That is exactly the meaning of that passage. Free, very good." Then Professor Van Rill smiled a smile that was meant to be rueful. "You see, class, that's why I can't send that boy back to the pigsty. He is just simply uncanny when it comes to ferreting out the meaning of a given piece of reading matter." Professor Van Rill pouted his red lips a little. "I've just simply got to figure out a way to pound some grammar into that head of his. He's got to be saved for English I. And I shall, too."

One weekend there was a heavy rain and Free had to stay over at Mrs. Fish's. He spent all day Saturday in his room reading Zane Grey's *The U. P. Trail*, which he'd found in a house down the street.

The sky cleared off Sunday afternoon and in the evening by the time church let out, the walks were dry enough for the young people to promenade up and down main street.

Sootman stayed over too. His usual buddy, Orrie Overslough, the veterinarian's son next door, had a cold, and so for want of a friend, Sootman elected to show Free the sights that might be seen in Hello on Sunday night.

Sootman knew where some of the wilder town kids hung out. It was behind the high school, near the round fire escape chute. The chute leveled off the last few feet near the ground and helped brake the speed of someone sliding down. It made for a perfect place in which to neck a girl. "No one can see you in there at night," Sootman said. "If you want to go the limit."

They found four public school kids sitting on the grass near the mouth of the chute, two boys and two girls. The street light on the far corner was just strong enough to pick out the cheekbones of the four. The orange chute glowed a dark red behind them.

Sootman whispered that one of the boys was Art Cruellen. Art Cruellen was said to be harder on virgins than horseback riding. Cruellen himself was heard to say he was an old-time hard-nosed pioneer who liked to open up new territory. Cruellen had a lantern jaw, a long nose, and dark hair parted down the middle. His light gray eyes were glistening wet. He was tall, with long fingers and long feet. He fancied bell-bottom trousers and was the home-run king of the high school baseball team.

Cruellen didn't like having Sootman and Free around. He made a motion as though to get up and chase them off. Cruellen reminded Free of Pa's jealous bull back home.

Sootman spotted the motion. He settled a careful dozen feet away. Free also sat down a respectful distance away.

Cruellen was doing most of the talking. The other fellow was Cyril Sweep, the high school shortstop. Sweep kept laughing at Cruellen's remarks and generally was making a fool of himself. The girls sat sideways to the two fellows and kept picking at the grass. Every once in a while they threw a blade of grass to one side.

Finally Cruellen's voice took on the rich bass purr of a tomcat. "C'mon, Angie, let's climb into the fire chute and kiss a while. I won't hurt you. And you know you like it."

Angie spoke softly. "Oh, Art, I can't." Angie had long blond hair and a gentle sister's manner.

Cruellen gave Sweep a hard look. "Cyril, why don't you and Jeannette go take a little walk?"

Sweep said, "But I thought we would—"

"I said, go take a walk with Jeannette."

Jeannette spoke up. "But maybe I don't wanna take a walk."

"Well then, how about you crawling into the chute with me? There's no fun like conjugating a couple of verbs."

"Go to grass."

Cruellen grabbed Jeannette by her belt and gave her a shake. "Go take your walk. Don't be a spoilsport."

Jeannette jerked free. "Angie, let's go home. Before it's too late."

Angie picked another blade of grass. "Yeh. I know what he wants all right."

Jeannette said, "Well, then?"

Angie threw the blade of grass away. "Oh, I don't know what to do."

Cruellen slid his arm around Angie's waist. He cupped her breast with a gentle motion. "Aw, c'mon, honey, you love me a little, don't you?"

"Oh, Art, if I could only be sure that afterwards you wouldn't drop me like a cold potato."

"Aw, honey," Cruellen said, "you mustn't worry about such things. Tonight's tonight, and let's just think about that."

Sweep put his arm around Jeanette's waist. "Honey—?"

Jeannette threw his arm off her shoulder like she was shrugging off a shawl. "Don't."

Cruellen said, "Cyril, get. And take your dried-up sour pickle with you."

Sweep jumped to his feet. "You bet, Art. C'mon, Jeannette."

Jeannette jumped to her feet too, but for a different reason. "Coming, Angie?"

Cruellen spoke soft again, in a honey baritone. "You like me, don't you, Angie?"
"Yes, I do. Rats."
Jeannette flished her dark dress around her calves. "Coming, Angie?"
"I don't know what to do," Angie whispered to herself.
"Well, suit yourself. But I'm going." Jeannette turned and walked away.
Sweep stood puzzled a moment. He looked at Cruellen, then looked at the rotating buttocks of his disgusted Jeannette.
Cruellen pointed. "Get!"
Sweep ran after Jeannette.
Ignoring Free and Sootman, Cruellen got to his knees. "Come, hon, let's go climb into our honeymoon chute."
"You crazy old you, you."
"Nobody can see us in there. It's safe there."
Angie snapped off one last blade of grass. "Oh, all right. Though I'm not sure I should."
"Come."
The two climbed into the mouth of the orange fire escape chute. It was just wide enough to allow two bodies to lie side by side. There was the sound of bumping and some struggling.
Several times Angie said, "Don't." And for a little while Angie appeared to be putting up a stout fight. "Cut it out, Art."
"Honey."
"I said, cut it out, Art."
There was some more rough struggling, and bungling against the sheet-iron sides of the chute.
At last Cruellen had enough of her holding him off. His deep lantern-jawed voice boomed in the chute like a bullhorn. "Goddam it, Angie, you gotta lose it sometime. Why not to an expert? The way I do it, it won't hurt you anymore than a good gargle. And after a couple of times, it'll start to be a lot of fun. You'll never regret conjugating your verb with me. You'll thank me for the rest of your life for introducing you to the most wonderful fun a human being can have this side of heaven. After you get used to my grammar, you'll want to talk it every day."
There was a long silence.
"C'mon, honey. Your honeyspot feels so rich."
"Well, if you wanna then. But don't give me a baby."
"Don't worry. I know what to do with the jism." There was some more rustling, mostly of clothes, and of something like a rubber band being snapped.
"Oh, Art, please be good to me. Ohh."
Cruellen spoke in a low thick voice. "I'll be good to you, honey, never fear." After a couple of seconds Cruellen muttered, "God, but you're good. I knew you would be too."
Sootman jumped to his feet. "C'mon, this is the part I can't stand."
Free already had a sad stomach. He was glad to get away.

It was one thing for Gertie Young back home to play with her brothers on Sunday morning while her folks were in church, but it was another thing for Cruellen to really do it with that Angie. Cruellen and Angie were old enough to be married.

What he'd just heard kept coming back to him as clear as though a record were being played over and over again on Pa's Edison phonograph. He wondered how it felt for Art Cruellen to be putting it in and for Angie taking it in. People were sure anxious to conjugate their verbs. Someday, somehow he was going to find out for himself what it was like.

Sootman spotted two girls walking ahead of them. "Hey, ain't that Tena Brunstein?"

"Yeh." Free's heart leaped. "With Winifred Bonner."

"Man, that Tena, now there's one gal I could go for. She's older than the rest of you freshies. She's about my speed."

Free nodded. Tena and Winifred were the two oldest girls in his class. Tena, like Winifred, had stayed home to work for her family for four years.

"Listen, they're headed for Tena's house. She lives on the other side of the public school grounds there. If we cut across the baseball diamond we can bump into them before they get there."

Free hitched his knickers around at the waist. "Maybe we ought to go home. I still have to study my Latin yet."

"C'mon. I just want to bump into Tena a minute."

"Well . . . "

Sootman said, "After you see what I do to Tena, you can do the same to Winifred."

"You mean, conjugate her verb?"

Sootman laughed. "No, not that, you dumbbell."

"Well, I was going to say. Winifred is a nice girl."

"Yeh, she's not bad."

"Not bad? She's the prettiest girl I've ever seen."

They came upon the two girls just as they were about to turn up the Brunstein walk. The girls brightened when they saw them. Here were some boys left after all. Winifred smiled her usual bonny smile. Her quick vigorous walk slowed. Tena, a pouter, was suddenly all apple pie, and she put on the airs of a flirt.

"Watch me," Sootman whispered. He pretended he hadn't seen them, turning his head as though listening closely to what Free was saying. Sootman was on Tena's side of the walk. He headed directly for her; but then at the last second, seemingly to keep from bumping into her, put up both hands; and accidentally on purpose placed his hands full on her breasts. "Oops. Gee, I'm sorry, Tena. I guess I didn't see you."

Free meantime stopped short of Winifred.

"You did that on purpose, John Sootman," Tena cried, angry and pleased both. "I know you."

Sootman let fly with a merry haha.

Tena aimed a slap at him; missed. "I'll get even with you someday, Mister Sootman. You've got a dirty mind."

Winifred said, "Why don't you act like a man once and just plain ask for a date, John? Instead of pulling off a silly boy's stunt."

Free said, "Yeh, John, why don't you? Art Cruellen wasn't afraid to ask Angie for what he wanted."

Sootman didn't like that. He threw back his forelock with a snap of his head. He sneered up and down at Free. "Why don't you ask Winifred for a date yourself, seeing as how you think she's the prettiest girl in the world."

Free blushed.

Winifred smiled. "Did Free say that? Really?"

Sootman's smile was like a weasel's for a moment. "Yeh. Too bad he ain't man enough to follow it up."

Winifred's face darkened. "That's not being very nice."

"You ought to see him naked once," Sootman said. "Why, he ain't even got hair in his armpits yet."

Tena said, "See? You do too have a dirty mind."

Free got a little mad. "Sootman, maybe I ain't got hair in all the right places yet, but there's one thing I can do. Take you on any time you say."

Sootman sneered. "Yeh, you big overgrown Percheron, you would take advantage of a pinto."

"Hey. Color don't count if the colt don't trot."

Winifred laughed. "That's the old comeback, Free."

Encouraged, Free said, "I wouldn't put on any airs if I was you, Sootman. Not after having to take algebra over. While I'm passing it the first time."

"All right," Sootman said, "if you're so much smarter than me, let's see you ask Winifred for a date. Because I'm asking Tena here. Right now. How about it, Tena?"

Tena blinked. Her pout became a surprised smile. "Well, I don't know now, John. I'll have to see what Winifred says."

Winifred gave Free a funny smile.

In his head Free again heard Art Cruellen doing it to poor Angie in the fire escape tube. Everybody seemed to be doing it. Or thinking about it.

Sootman taunted him. "You ain't got the guts, Alfredson."

What came out of Free's mouth next astounded even him. "Winifred, how about conjugating your verb with me?"

Tena gasped.

Sootman gaped.

The gentlest, sweetest, most compassionate smile Free had ever seen in his life, one that not even his mother had ever given him, came over Winifred's face. Winifred's smile was like an opening into her. She placed a hand on his arm and gave it a little squeeze. "You're sweet to ask me, Free. But, you know, you're really a little too young for me. So will you forgive me if I say no for the present?"

Forgive her? God. When it was really he who should ask her for forgiveness? And goddam that dirty Art Cruellen for putting the words in his mouth in the first place. Free felt awful. What a terrible ass he'd made of himself. With a groaning cry, he wrenched himself around and ran home for Mrs. Fish's.

"Free," Winifred called after him, "it's all right. I understand."

Tena was still outraged. "Let the dirty bugger go."

Free wept to himself as he ran.

Footsteps came running after him. It was Sootman. "What's the rush? Wait up. The world ain't going to end just yet, you know."

"No."

Sootman grabbed him by the arm. "Wait up. I'm still your roomie and I don't mind what you did. We all make fools of ourselves some time or other."

Free slowed down. Not wanting Sootman to see him cry, he kept swallowing back sobs.

They walked together for about a block, and then Sootman said, "Well, anyway, I finally had my way. I've been wanting to feel Tena's mammets for a long time and tonight I finally got the chance. Mmm-hm. Nice and firm and plump."

When they got to the house, they found it full of Fishes. All of Mrs. Fish's married sons and their wives and children had stopped by after church for a cup of tea. The living room and the parlor beyond were packed full with fat pale women and skinny rednecked men swaying back and forth in rocking chairs. They were all working on their tea and nibbling at rusks with butter and sugar on. The Fish men all looked alike. They took after their mother. None of them had Hattie's parrot-owl nose.

Free and Sootman had trouble picking their way to the stair door.

"What's the rush?" Hattie called out. "Wouldn't you like a cup of tea?"

Sootman hesitated. "Ain't you a bit crowded?"

"There's always room for two more."

"Okay."

Hattie led them into the kitchen. It was packed with kids eating cookies. Mrs. Fish was making a fresh batch of tea. Mrs. Fish turned from the stove and gave them a tired friendly smile. Though it meant a lot of fuss, she liked it that her sons with their families had shown up after church. Hattie poured Free and Sootman each a fragile cup of hot green tea.

A mob of blond pigtails and chamber-pot haircuts milled around underfoot. Sugar and crumbs scrinched everywhere. There were no chairs for them and Free and Sootman had to brush clear a space on the green linoleum floor before they could get down on their knees by the table.

Sootman blew on his steaming tea. "Fwhew, it's hot. Well, I know it ain't polite but I guess we'll have to saucer it." With a smile at his own humor, he spilled some tea into his saucer. He lifted the saucer to his lips, stylishly balancing it between three fingers, forefinger above and thumb and long finger beneath. "Ah, great."

Free saucered his tea too for the fun of it. He was about to take a sip when he heard one of Mrs. Fish's sons say in the other room, "Go on, Minnie, you're just plain fat. Admit it." Free paused, holding the saucer of tea poised at the edge of his lips.

Daughter-in-law Minnie said, "Harry Fish, you know why I've put on weight. I'm with child."

"With child, my ass," Harry Fish growled. "It ain't any bigger in you than a small cat. You're just plain fat."

Free exploded in laughter, blowing the green tea out of his saucer. The dollop of tea fanned out and spattered over the kids ringing the kitchen table.

Sootman exploded too. Except that he had the good sense to lower his saucer first.

A sharp voice behind Free said, "The manners of some people's kids." It was Gert Fish, the other daughter, just home from working in Jensen's Cafe. She was built like a brunette kewpie doll. She was in her late twenties and had the eyes of an unhappy old maid.

She didn't like it that her mother took boarders.

Free felt twice ashamed. First that blunder with Winifred; now this blasting of tea over everybody.

"Aw, Gert, c'mon," Sootman said. "If you'd have heard what your brother Harry just said, you'd have spluttered over everybody too."

"People with manners don't drink out of saucers."

"But we only saucered our tea as a joke."

"I don't care. It's still true."

Free set his saucer down. He got to his feet. Eyes smarting so that he could hardly see, he toed through all the kids sprawled on the floor, opened the stair door against their bodies gently, and went upstairs.

"See," Sootman said. "Now you've hurt his feelings."

"I don't care. I didn't like him when he first set foot in this house."

Free undressed in the dark and hung up his clothes. He draped his stockings over his shoes under the bed so he could find them in the morning. He slid in between the sheets. He got way over on his side.

What a jackass he'd made of himself. God.

Much later he heard the company go home. The women clucked up their children and the men thanked their ma for the tea and rusks. Presently both horse and buggy and old Ford cars pulled out for the country. The house was abruptly silent.

Free lay very still in bed.

Soon Free heard Sootman laughing downstairs. Free lifted his head off the pillow and listened. He could hear him talking clearly through the hot air register.

"Yeh," Sootman said, "he sure is a greenhorn all right. The things he don't just plop out with."

"Well, he makes me nervous," Gert Fish said. "And clumsy? Why, when he walks through the house our fancy dishes shiver on their shelves. He's got the biggest feet I ever did see."

Mrs. Fish spoke in a calm way. "He's only a boy, Gertrude."

"I don't care. Boys that age drive me wild. All those dirty habits they're just beginning to learn."

Sootman laughed. "How would you know about that, Gert?"

"I don't care."

"I suppose you prefer clean boys of around thirty?"

"Sootman, you're hardly dry behind the ears yourself, so I wouldn't talk too loud if I was you."

"Now, now," Mrs. Fish said. "Free's only a boy."

Hattie said, "And I like Free."

"Well, good for you," Gert said snappishly. "He better have somebody to stick up for him."

Sootman laughed some more. He was remembering something.

Gert asked, "Now what are you laughing about?"

"I think maybe he's about ready to outgrow those dirty habits," Sootman said. "You should've heard what he asked Winifred Bonner tonight."

"Why? What did he say to her?" Hattie asked, jealous.

Sootman laughed.

"What'd he say to Winifred?" Hattie pressed.

"He asked her to conjugate her verb with him."

"He what?" Gert cried. "He didn't."

"Cross my heart and hope to die."

"He really didn't now, did he?"

"Cross my heart."

Hattie said, "What did he really ask her now, Sootman?"

Sootman said, " 'Winifred, how about conjugating your verb with me?' "

"My God," Gert cried.

Hattie said, "I wonder why he likes her better than me. She can't even sing. While me, I'm in the Apollo Club."

"My God," Gert said again.

Hattie rose to Free's defense again. "Maybe he only meant he wanted to study his Latin lesson with her."

Sootman laughed. "Not after he'd heard the way Art Cruellen was conjugating Angie Westrum's verb in the high school fire escape there."

"Disgusting." Gert jumped up and began to walk up and down. Then after a minute she asked again, "He really didn't now, did he?"

"Cross my heart."

"That's scandalous."

Listening in growing shock to what that traitor Sootman was telling them, Free could feel goose pimples of shame come out all over him.

It was scandalous all right. Ma would disown him if she ever found out. And

Pa? Pa would send him off to bed without supper.

He shuddered. And shuddered again. The shudders spread out of the center of his belly. It was like rings on water after throwing a rock in.

A belch broke out of him. It vapored up into his nose like the smell of old weeds in a roadside ditch. It was that green tea.

He'd never be able to face the Fish family the next morning at breakfast. Or even the whole school. Because as sure as shooting that Hattie would blab it to everybody.

"Oh, if only I hadn't said that to Winifred. If only somehow I'd kept my mouth shut."

Again he heard them laughing downstairs.

"Oh God," he groaned. And then, miserable, remembering what Ma would have him do, he slowly rolled out of bed and got down on his knees and leaned his head on his folded hands on the bed. "Oh Father in heaven, if it be at all possible, let this cup pass me by. Nevertheless, not as I will, but as Thou wilt." As he whispered into the bottom sheet of the bed, he realized, off to one side, that he was at last really praying, truly. He could feel a red essence reaching out of him and stretching upward toward a Purple Essence. "Yes, O Lord, as Thou wilt, yet at the same time, please, please, blot from their memory downstairs this sin that I've done. May it appear that they never heard it. And please, O Lord, also blot it from my memory. Which is really the worse of the two. So that it will be as though it had never happened. For this one time only, please forgive me this one great sin. In Jesus' name, Amen."

Slowly and piously he crawled back into bed.

Both Gert and Hattie were gone the next morning when Free and Sootman went down for breakfast. Mrs. Fish behaved around Free as she always did, calm, tired. All through the fried eggs and oatmeal it was so much like any other morning that Free began to wonder if last night had happened at all.

Mrs. Fish gave them a lunch to take along. Mrs. Fish sometimes on Monday cleaned house for a sick neighbor lady.

When Winifred discovered Free'd taken lunch along, she asked him if he wouldn't like to eat lunch with her up in the unfinished room on the top floor. It was after English I and they were standing out in the hall with everybody brushing past hurrying to get to the next class.

Free asked, "But ain't that room locked?"

"Shh." Winifred smiled at him. "I know where the Apollo Club keeps the key. For when they practice there."

He loved the way her auburn hair lay combed away from her brow, the way she kept rising on her toes as she talked. She meant him nothing but good. "All right."

"You looked so glum this morning in English."

"I'm okay."

After the next class he had to go down to the boy's room a minute. On the way back up he took the terrazzo stairs three at a time. He landed on the top step with a last long bound. He was about to hurry on when he heard someone clearing his throat. Turning, he saw Principal Hedges standing in the door to the mathematics room.

"Just a minute there, young fellow."

"Yes, Prof?"

"Come here a moment."

Had Principal Hedges heard about what he'd asked Winifred? Free advanced toward him. "Yes?"

"Did your mother teach you to take the stairs three at a time at home?"

"No." Free shifted his class books from one hand to the other.

"Then why three at a time here?"

"I was in a hurry. I had to go between classes."

"That's no excuse for acting like a billy goat. Now, let's see you go down that flight of stairs like a young gentleman."

Other kids were watching. It made Free a little angry to be made an example of. But he decided to obey. He was careful to go down them one at a time. It was embarrassing. Yet he was glad he wasn't being punished for that other thing with Winifred.

"Well, I see you can hit every step if you put your mind to it. Now try it coming up the stairs."

Free came up the stairs as casual and as everyday as possible, one step at a time.

"Well, Mister Alfredson, you hit every step again, I see. Good. And now that you know there are no steps missing, that the architect placed every one where it is supposed to be, let's see you make sure that you use them after this. Every one. Okay?"

"Yes, Prof."

"As a gentleman. Not as a billy goat."

"Yes, Prof."

The kids laughed.

Principal Hedges turned and glared at the laughers. "At least Alfredson had some drive in him to take them three at a time. What have you got to show for yourselves?"

The laughers slunk away.

That noon Free headed for the door of the unfinished room. Idly he turned the brown knob not expecting it to open. But the door did open. He stepped in. His quick eye caught a silhouette against a north window. "Hey, you're early."

"Hi. Yeh, I beat you upstairs," Winifred said.

The big room was empty. The walls and ceiling were still unplastered, with the slats showing like the ribs of a skeleton. The floor was of rough boards. The windows had big whitewash X's painted on them. It was like walking into a haunted house.

Winifred said, "Lock the door behind you." She smiled mischief. "I put the key on this side of the door."

He clicked the key over.

"Come."

He stepped slowly toward her. Trembles moved up his thighs.

"In here," she whispered, and she pushed open a door into a little side room. It also was unfinished. "There's a table in here and we can sit on that."

Free thought it odd there should be such a fine table alone in an unfinished anteroom. Then he spotted a half dozen folding chairs stacked in a corner.

Winifred set her lunch bag to one side on the table and then hoisted herself up on the edge of it. "Sometimes the faculty meets in here. When they want to get away from everybody. They have to have their secrets too, you know." Her green plum eyes were level with his. "Hop up here." She patted the tabletop beside her.

He set his lunch to one side too and in a turning jump got up beside her.

"Free." She picked up his hand and held it between her two hands. "The reason I wanted to see you . . . say, you've got long fingers, you know?"

"A little."

"Free, don't worry about what you thought you'd done last night. As the youngest child back home in a houseful of brothers, I heard just about everything there was to hear about sex. And I mean in rough language too." She laughed wholesomely. "In fact, I thought the way you said it was kind of cute. I'd never heard it put that way before."

Free's face began to sting. Winifred right beside him was actually thinking of the thing itself, of her sweet privates as well as of his, and she wasn't at all nervous about it.

She gave his hand a warm squeeze. "But I haven't done it yet. And I'm not going to do it either until I find the right man." She smiled close up, her nose almost touching his. "Oh, Free, I wish you were older. As old as Alfred Dempsey. Who thinks he's so smart."

His mind tumbled over. He couldn't see her for a moment.

"Though I might with you if you were older. Only I'd hate to have a baby right away. Though if I did it with you now I probably couldn't get a baby yet, could I? You're too young to make babies yet, aren't you?"

Make babies. He could smell wild plums in bloom.

She let go of his hand and threw her arms around him and kissed him.

He'd never before had a kiss like that. It wasn't a Ma kiss, dry and warm, or a smack like Pa gave Ma, tight and noisy. Winifred's kiss was moist and warm, and so given that her lips felt thick on his, with in the middle of them a little opening into herself. Her smile sometimes had an opening like that. His first girl kiss. He hadn't known kissing could be that good. Art Cruellen didn't bother with kisses. Old Lantern Jaw just went right to the point. But then Art Cruellen was an animal first baseman for the public school team.

Winifred then held him away from her, firm hands on his shoulders. She was flushed too, and smiled with her eyes almost closed. "Shh. Before it's too late we better sit decent. And anyway, we came up here to eat our lunch together, didn't we?"

He wondered what a guy should do next with a woman who liked him that much. He'd seen Art Cruellen go to work on Angie, but that'd been too much like a fox going after a juicy chicken. His thought was more that when a guy liked a girl he just naturally would want to be touching her all the time, and she touching him, and then they'd hug each other. Just to be close and warm together. He'd mean her no harm.

She opened her paper bag and helped herself to a cheese-and-lettuce sandwich. She took a small neat bite. "Aren't you hungry?"

He gave her a look. He opened his paper bag too and took out an egg sandwich. He was disappointed it didn't have a leaf of lettuce in it. He liked eggs with lettuce.

Free ❦ 5

WHEN MA LOOKED over his first-semester grades she noted that he'd only got a 76 in English I. "Well," she said, "what's wrong with that class?"

"Don't worry," Free said. "I won't flunk. Professor Van Rill says I'm the best reader in his class."

"What makes him give you such a low mark then?" Ma pressed. "Your other marks are good. You have an average of 81."

"I can't parse. I'm dumb in grammar."

"What's parse?" Pa said. Pa was sitting as usual with his feet up on the reservoir of the stove.

"It's where you take a sentence apart, name the parts, and then put 'em back together again."

"Like you take apart a carburetor?"

"Something like that."

"It seems to me," Pa said past the stem of his pipe, "that any fellow who can build himself a near perfect airplane ought to be able to put together an English sentence."

Free gave Pa a surprised look. Here Pa couldn't read and yet he would sometimes use pretty good language. "Reading comes easy for me, grammar don't. The way the prof talks and the way I talk are two different things."

"Hum," Pa said, "I take it you don't like Van Rill."

Free decided not to say too much about what the kids in school thought about Professor Van Rill. Free had to smile to himself when he thought about what Birdie, for example, said of him. Birdie liked to make up imaginary scenes about William Van Rill and his wife Luella in bed at night, with their little Stanley already asleep in the next room. William would have the notion and he'd start talking sweet to Luella, but fussy Luella would right away spot what he was up to and would quick change the subject. And once Luella got started on something, her tongue would rattle on like perpetual motion itself. William would sigh beside her, and wriggle around not daring to touch her, and would sigh some more, until finally Luella, feeling a teeny bit sorry for him, would decide to humor him, and she'd say, "All right, William, you may touch it. But mind, just once, once, you hear?" Then William, suddenly nervous, shaking, would reach over and touch it . . . and would faint dead away. Everybody in the crowd always laughed at Birdie's picture. And when someone in the crowd would wonder how William and Luella ever managed to have Stanley, Birdie would say, "They didn't. A stork brought Stanley."

"Son," Ma said, "you must try and do better next time."

"Sure, Ma."

In the spring, when the first warm weather blew in from the south, Free discovered Sootman liked to play ball. Soon they were playing burn-out on the lawn. When both discovered that Orrie Overslough next door and Birdie and Tony Strawman and Sam Ruffman, who all lived nearby, liked to play ball too, they marked out a diamond on Mrs. Fish's little pasture north behind the privy and played every night.

Sometimes their antics in Mrs. Fish's pasture drew a crowd along the fence, girls from the Academy, old men who a long time ago had played for the town team of Hello, and little boys looking for heroes.

Once even Principal Hedges, out for an evening stroll, stopped to watch them. Principal Hedges didn't say anything, just looked, a hand in a pocket, neither smiling nor frowning. After a while Principal Hedges continued on his stroll.

The gang played so much their classwork suffered. Sootman did all right in most classes, but in algebra, which as a senior he was taking over, he didn't. His brain just wasn't made for equations. Double plays, yes; polynomials, no. Principal Hedges told him several times that he'd better do good work his second time through algebra or he wouldn't graduate come June.

Sootman and Principal Hedges weren't meant to be friends. One day after Sootman had turned in a lesson with eight of ten algebra problems wrong, Principal Hedges asked Sootman what he would do if he were the prof and had corrected such a miserable paper.

"I dunno," Sootman said. "Send the boy home, I guess. Back to parsing Pig Latin on the farm again."

The whole class fell silent. Everybody looked out of the window as though wishing it weren't happening. The high windows faced west, and with the morning sun coming up on the other side of the building the western sky had an endless depth to it, making the blue appear to be almost purple.

"Sootman, how can any mortal be so dumb?"

"Sir, if I am truly that dense, how can you expect me to answer that?"

Principal Hedges shot a surprised look at Sootman. His little square brown moustache quivered. His sharp eyes went all over Sootman, picking him apart, finally settling on the smallness of his head and the still smaller patch of hair. "Haven't you got any brains at all up there in that tiny dome of yours?"

"I guess not. Though to say so probably means I'm making a false statement."

The whole class sat like a collection of salt pillars. That Sootman. It took a lot of nerve to sass back at a prof like that.

Then Principal Hedges's eye happened to light on Free. "And you there, Alfred Alfredson . . ." Principal Hedges stepped back to his desk and picked up another lesson he'd corrected. He waved the corrected lesson at the class. "Here's a young fellow who has got all kinds of time to play baseball, and who yet, at the same time, has the gall to turn in a paper in which he has only four correct answers. A little bit better than Sootman, it's true, but not very much better. While back home in Bonnie he has an honest father and mother who are slaving themselves to the bone, who perhaps even at this very moment are sitting at their kitchen table trying to decide what not to buy at the store, all in a valiant effort to keep this young fellow in school . . . when the said young fellow fools away his time."

Free slowly sank down.

Principal Hedges glared at Free. "Sit up."

Free moved himself up an inch.

"Tell me, what's the latest trashy book you've read?"

"*Ivanhoe*."

Principal Hedges looked at him as if he didn't believe him. "What's it about?"

"It's about a man named Ivanhoe who loves and marries Rowena, a Saxon beauty."

"Well, that's not a bad book at that." Principal Hedges's eyes softened. "But look here, Alfredson. You've got enough brains to get a better mark than 40. Turn in a couple more lessons like this last one and I'm going to have to flunk you for the course as I did Sootman once. So hit the books for me a little, will you, if not for your honest father and your earnest mother?"

"Yes, Prof."

Professor Hedges threw Free's paper back on the desk behind him and picked up Sootman's paper again. He studied it a moment. "Sootman, what a moral poser you've given me. If I pass you with a mark of 20 it'll be a mortal sin. Yet, if only to get shet of you, I've got to pass you. Lord, Lord." He shook his head. "You haven't got the brains of a teapot."

Birdie thought that a pretty funny remark and laughed out loud, getting his whole belly into it. Birdie never thought much of Sootman either. Also the Teapot Dome oil scandal of that year, 1924, had been much in the news. Birdie was one of the young pups in school who had become a bit disillusioned with the way the older generation was running things. Corruption in the government had even made cynics of such lesser brains as Orrie Overslough and Sam Ruffman. So Prof's remark had hit a laugh nerve.

Meanwhile Sootman's little ferret face drew up into a tight fierce knot. Like some cornered animal ready to defend himself to the death, he exploded. "What do you want me to do, Prof, shit in my hand? To prove I'm an ass?"

The whole class quivered. Girls snapped their knees together. Boys jerked erect. Hattie Fish took off her glasses to see if they needed cleaning.

Free's mouth dropped open in admiration. His roomie had guts. Why, he was a dangerous little fellow.

Sootman continued to face up to Principal Hedges.

Principal Hedges said suddenly, "Teapot, much as I hate to, I've got to admit it. You've finally shown me what I have been wanting to see. Nerve. You'll do. You're a man. And that allows you to graduate. No matter how poorly you do in this class from now on, you're going to get your diploma. Class dismissed."

The class jumped to its feet in relief. They swarmed out into the hallway, buzzing, in a slight state of shock. Principal Hedges followed them, heading for his office.

Sootman didn't get up right away. Nor did Free and Birdie. A wonderful rising surprised look slowly took over Sootman's face. He was going to graduate after all.

Free was glad for his roomie. He gave him a large happy smile.

But Birdie gave Sootman a sour look. He hated to change his mind about Sootman. "Teapot, wait'll this gets around school, that you talked dirty to the principal and got away with it. It's gonna make for a worse stink than the Teapot Dome scandal itself. In fact, I wouldn't be a bit surprised if the church didn't cut off its support for Western Academy."

"Bird," Sootman said, "one handful is enough for today."

That evening Free and Sootman attended the last meeting of the Beaver Club for the year. There were some twenty-one present and they met in the algebra room. Principal Hedges was their faculty sponsor.

It was Free's turn to give a reading. He'd chosen the story of the massacre of Big Foot and a band of Sioux at Wounded Knee, South Dakota. Free thought the murder of Big Foot's band a very sad story. He was first on the program and read along with what he thought was gathering indignation and excitement, only to discover after a while that there was a tittering in the room, and that in a couple of instances certain members couldn't keep from laughing out loud.

He read on for several more paragraphs before he understood why. Sootman was the only one, along with Principal Hedges, who was not laughing. So it had to be something personal, something about the reader and not the story. Sootman as roomie was considerate enough not to laugh. When Free once more mentioned the name of the chief, Big Foot, he knew. The Beavers were laughing at the reader's big feet.

Free snapped the book shut with a hard thump, sat down, and refused to read further.

Sootman clapped. "Atty old boy, Free. That's showing them."

A fellow named Cornelius Uphill was next on the program. He gave an original dissertation on the seven kinds of love. It was pretty good.

Cornelius, when excited, spit a lot as he read, and the fellows in the front row pretended he was giving them a soaking, and after a while the fellows even got out their handkerchiefs and made a show of having to wipe off their faces. When Uphill finished, the fellows in the front row pretended great relief.

Third on the program was Birdie. He'd written an original epic poem. He told about a famous baseball game between the marrieds and the singles back home which had been interrupted by a hailstorm. The game was in the bottom of the ninth, two out, bases loaded, when the hail started to fall. Nobody wanted to quit, especially not the marrieds, who were at bat with a chance to pull out the game. Finally, just as the batter swung and hit a short swinging bunt a half dozen feet down the line, a particularly large hailstone the size of a baseball fell in front of home plate. The catcher picked up the hailstone and pretended it was the baseball and stepped on home plate for the force-out. The home plate umpire, whose view was blocked by the catcher, thought that the catcher had picked up the real baseball and called the man sliding in from third out. Game over. The singles team ran off the field and ducked under the roof of a concession stand to get out of the falling hail, all laughing to themselves. Of course the marrieds raged. In vain.

"And loud was the anguish of the marrieds,
As the hailstones fell on their backs,
And loud was the joy of the singles,
As their sweethearts fell on their necks."

Free, like the others, laughed about the force-out at home plate too. He was sitting slouched in his chair, with his seat just barely caught on the edge of it.

All of sudden, too late, Free became aware of a large bubble of air in the barrel of his colon. It had descended from nowhere and had paused at the very end of his rectum, trembling before venting. It was so far along he didn't dare pinch it back for fear he'd be the inadvertent composer of a little solo. If he gave it a push, as he might have done had he been alone, it would have made just the right kind of report to make Birdie and Principal Hedges and the others think he'd done it on purpose. So he just waited. And hoped. Then, just as everybody had quieted down, the bubble decided to venture into the world. It made a neat muted squeal of a sound.

Everybody sat up a quarter of an inch in his seat, and looked surprised around at each other.

Someone said, with a half-laugh, "Well, there's another country heard from."

Instantly there was a great crescendo of laughter.

Principal Hedges was sitting to one side of Free. He glared at Free. "For godsakes, what do you call that?"

Free couldn't resist it. "An inadvertent fart."

There was another blast of laughter.

Principal Hedges shook his head. "My God, what a year this has been. We began it with an artificial fart, that stink bomb, and we end it with an inadvertent fart, Free's faux pas."

Everybody quieted down a little. They were never sure just which way Principal Hedges's wit would dart next.

"I'm sorry," Free said. "I couldn't help it."

Principal Hedges glared at Free some more. "Just watch it. One of the purposes of this Beaver Club is to learn how to be a gentleman."

Free ❦ 6

THE NEXT SUMMER Free got another chance to play man and wife with Fredrika. Pa and Ma and the kids visited Tante Engleking one evening. Uncle John and Aunt Matilda were visiting Tante too.

The moment the older folks vanished into Tante's parlor, Fredrika suggested they all play hide-and-go-seek. Free thought he knew why. She'd acted horny the minute he arrived on the yard. But he was an academy student now, had been kissed by the beautiful Winifred Bonner, and that changed things between himself and Fredrika.

Also Free had been reading *The Deerslayer* and *The Last of the Mohicans* and *The Pathfinder* that summer, and thought it more fun to play Indians and pioneers. He'd come to love the three books and was sorry that Dr. Fairlamb in town hadn't had a complete set of James Fenimore Cooper's work. The Cooper novels always started slow and hard, with sentences he couldn't have parsed for the life of him, but if a fellow trained himself to pick out the noun and the verb and skipped all the rest of the sentence, sometimes as many as a dozen words, he'd do all right. Free wanted to act out *The Deerslayer* in the willows along the draw behind Tante's house. He wanted to be Chingachgook. He didn't care who'd play Deerslayer just so whoever it was would help him stalk the hated Mingoes.

Free, Fredrika, Everett, Flip, Jonathan, Alfie, and Etta were all standing in the middle of the yard, arguing over what to play, Fredrika's game or Free's game.

Finally Free said, "Fredrika, why don't you be Deerslayer? That way you'd always be with me, since I'm Chingachgook. The rest of the kids can be the dreaded Mingoes."

Fredrika brightened. "What will I wear if I'm Deerslayer?"

"Well," Free said, "we're all supposed to be wearing leather stockings and buckskin jackets."

Everett held a finger to one nostril. "Where'll we get the bows and arrows?"

Free said, "Fredrika, has your ma got a ball of twine handy?"

"Sure. In the tool shed."

"Then we'll get us some long sticks out of Tante's willows."

They cut slender branches for the bows and straight twigs for the arrows. It wasn't long before everybody except Fredrika had a bow and a couple of arrows. Deerslayer Fredrika outfitted herself with a broom for a long rifle.

Flip became the head chief of the Mingoes. He was the bossiest and so won out. The kids vanished into the thicket of willows.

Free explained to Fredrika that as Chingachgook and Deerslayer they were supposed to walk quietly through the forest, softly and carefully so that the enemy couldn't hear them coming. They mustn't even step on a twig, because if they did and it broke, it'd make a loud cracking sound, and then the dreaded Mingoes would learn of their whereabouts and in a minute both'd look like they'd just grown feathers. They'd be riddled with arrows. Dead.

Fredrika caught on. Side by side Free and Fredrika skulked through the willows in the dusk. They stepped with their toes down first and then their heels. If their big toe felt something, they brushed whatever it was out of the way. They looked to all sides for the enemy, eyes flicking sharply back and forth.

The Mingoes did a good job of hiding.

Free and Fredrika crept out of the thicket of willows and entered the cornfield thinking the Mingoes might have hidden there. The deep cornfield made a perfect place for an ambush.

Skulk around as they might, Free and Fredrika couldn't find the Mingoes. After a while Fredrika got tired of playing Indians and pioneers. She whispered in Free's ear that she wanted to rest.

Free was disgusted. Girls had no notion at all of how to play a boy's game. And she sure didn't look like Deerslayer either carrying her gun around like it was just a broom.

Fredrika shook her gold curls out over her shoulders. The last year or so Fredrika's nose had begun to stick out so that it looked like the point of a paper airplane.

"Let's try it a while longer," Free said.

"Oh, all right."

They crawled cautiously. The pigeon grass and the underbrush got thicker and deeper. It darkened overhead. They picked up fallen corn leaves lying in their path and set them to one side. The earth smelled like ground-up oats.

They came to the end of the cornfield and still no Mingoes.

Fredrika whispered, "They never left the willows, I betcha."

"Could be. Let's go back to the forest then."

They skulked into the willows as silent as cats.

Pretty soon they came upon a nice patch of thick grass.

Fredrika was glad to see the grass. "Let's rest a while."

Their crawling together had warmed Free toward her. "All right."

"Catching them Mingoes is hard work," she said. She put her long gun aside and lay down on her back. She didn't care how much of her bare legs was showing. "Lay down too, Free."

"All right." Free put his bow and arrows aside and stretched out beside her.

The willow tips overhead moved in the evening breeze. Sometimes they blotted out the stars.

Fredrika fidgeted. "I wish we was married already."

What? "Why?"

"Well, then we could do it and wouldn't have to worry." Free remembered

Winifred's remark: "You're too young to make babies yet, aren't you?" Free said, "I don't think we really have to worry."

"Why not?"

"Because I don't think I got any jism yet."

"Don't the man just pee into his wife a little and that's the jism?"

"No." Free recalled the last time he and Fredrika played man and wife in a tight manger. "And you don't put it in your number two."

"Oh, I know that much now."

"Who told you?"

"My older sisters talk about it when they go to the privy and I hear them."

Free began to feel real good about Fredrika. He lay on his side against her. He'd suddenly grown a third leg. It felt like a sticky milkweed pod about to ooze over.

Fredrika could feel it too. She said, "I know what let's do."

"What."

"Let's play we went to bed early, and that I was tired and I went to sleep right away, but you wanted to do it, so you softly got on top of me and started doing it to me while I was asleep. And then we can play that after a while I woke up and then I said to you, 'Say, what are you doing to me?' and then you said, 'Why, honey, I'm doing it to you.' Okay?"

"Okay."

Fredrika in a whip had her bloomers off and opened her legs.

Free lifted himself on top of her.

"Not there, you dummy. It's not above the bone," Fredrika whispered.

"I thought it was above the bone like the belly button is."

"No, no."

"Where is it then?"

"It's under it. You gotta go under the bone there. Down."

But he couldn't find it. There just didn't seem to be any kind of opening under the bone, certainly not one big enough. He pushed and it bent on him. "Ow."

"That's far enough," she said. She began to wiggle under him like the dickens.

But it wasn't very good for him. Girls were sure a mystery where they had their things. "What comes after this?"

"I don't know."

It was fun, but for what? Towards what? Was that really all there was to it?

"That's sure a funny one," Flip said close by. "First they're supposed to find us and they don't. And then when we want to find them we can't."

"Yeh," Alfie said.

"It's the Mingoes!" Free whispered.

"Quick!" Fredrika whispered sharp. She pushed Free off and stuck her legs into her bloomers and snapped the bloomers up around her waist.

Free just as quick buttoned up.

Both grabbed up their weapons, Free his bow and arrows and Fredrika her broom gun.

"Here they are," Flip cried.

Free jumped up in front of Flip. "Got you! You're my prisoner now."

Fredrika fired her long gun. "Bang! Bang! Drop dead, Everett, you Mingo you."

The lower well went dry in July. Ma wrote Horace Hamilton, the landlord, about it and Horace wrote back to say Pa had better have a new well dug and to take the cost of it off the rent.

Pa knew a Herman Battles living near Chokecherry Corner who was a good well-driller. Pa called him up, and one evening Battles showed up on their yard in an old Ford runabout. Battles had a burned red face, walked with his head tilted back as though walking downhill, and chewed tobacco right through his talking.

"Where do you want your well?" Herman Battles asked.

"Close to the yard," Pa said. "If possible."

Battles reached into the front of his runabout and got out a slick-looking forked stick. It would've made a good slingshot. "This'll tell us where."

The sun was just beginning to settle behind the trees.

Battles began walking slowly back and forth across the yard. He held the stick by its forked prongs with the butt end up. He shuffled along very slowly, pushing his feet across the grass so as not to lose contact with the earth. His face looked like he'd suddenly got religion. His blue eyes shimmered like rippling water. He moved along as though he were cradling an offering.

Free asked, "What's he doing?"

Pa said, "He's witching for water."

"You don't believe in that hocus-pocus, do you?"

"I dunno. He does. And he's the well-driller."

"Good thing Ma ain't watching. She'd think it was of the devil."

"Wal, now, Battles belongs to our church." Pa got out his pipe and lit up. "Besides, what's wrong with using the devil to our advantage once? So long as we use it as Christians, I don't see any harm in it."

Battles couldn't find any water on the yard. "Alfred, how about trying the barnyard there?"

"Fine. Just so long as it's close by."

Some thirty feet east of the barn and right above where the water line came up from the dry well, Battles found it. All of a sudden a magnet in the earth pulled at the witching fork. No matter how hard Battles held against the prongs, the butt of the forked stick slowly wanted to tip over and point down at a certain spot in the ground. Battles's wrists bent over at right angles. "Alfred, come here quick and help me hold against it."

"But why? If that's the water vein we want, then that's it."

"I want you to feel the draw of it to prove it. It costs me money to drill for nothing. I guarantee my work."

Shaking his head to himself, Pa stepped behind Battles and took hold of him by both elbows. Pa's eyes popped wide open. "Gotske! It's there all right."

"It's there, ain't it? With you holding onto it too, that proves it."

Pa let go of Battles's elbows. "Has it ever happened that it's quit drawing on you when someone else held your elbows?"

"You bet."

Two days later, some twenty feet down into the earth, the rotary drill bit hit something odd. Battles immediately threw the clutch. Piles of different kinds of colored dirt lay around the new hole, black loam, yellow clay, blue gumbo, golden gravel.

"That's sure peculiar," Battles muttered to himself.

Free stepped over. "What's up?" Free had been helping out as gaffer. Pa was over in the toolshed getting the binder ready.

Battles looked up at the sky as he mulled it over to himself. "I could feel it right up through the drill rod. The rig commenced to dig as though it had hit something sticky." Battles savored the feel of the rod to himself some more. "Let's try it again." He put the clutch in gear. The big Elgin engine growled as the belt caught hold. The drill rod first turned easy and then turned hard and then easy again. "It acts a little like a cat chewing on a mouse down there."

Free placed a hand on a cross brace. Sure enough. It felt like when Ma complained that the batter for a fruitcake was too sticky to stir.

Herman Battles studied the irregularly turning drill for a full minute. He had been marking its descent with chalk every few feet and it hadn't gone down any since the last chalk mark.

Free wiped sweat out of his eyes with his sleeve. "Every now and then it hits something hard."

"You bet. Let's have a look." Battles reversed the gear and the drill rod started coming up.

Both leaned over the edge of the curbing to watch the big wide bit come up. As it rose an unearthly smell wafted up ahead of it.

A glutinous mass appeared to be caught in the bit. It came up in a huge chunk. As the bit lifted free of the thirty-inch hole, both Free and Battles, astounded by what they saw, jumped back.

"Look at that big ball of guck!" Battles cried; then he threw the machine out of gear and hauled back on the brake.

"Gotske!" Pa cried behind them. Pa had come up behind them unnoticed. "That's a critter of some kind."

"Yeh," Battles said.

"And look at that big broken bone," Free cried. "That's got to be a monster of some kind."

"Unpossible," Pa said.

It had the look of a poorly cut roast. The flesh had a macerated look and had an old purple color. The broken bone that stuck out was brownish in color and was about as thick as a stovepipe.

"What the hell is that thing doing down there, twenty feet below the surface of the earth?" Battles said.

"A mammoth," Free whispered, "like the scientists say the earth was once full of."

Battles snorted. "Don't mention scientists to me."

"But it's got to be," Free said. "What else can it be?"

"I'd rather listen to Job," Herman Battles said. "Where he says, 'Behold now Behemoth, which I made, with bones as strong as pieces of brass. Ah, canst thou draw out Leviathan with a hook into his nose? Or bore his jaw through with a thorn?' "

"Twenty feet below the surface of the earth?" Pa said.

"Well," Battles said, "whatever it is, you better get me a fork. I ain't letting any part of me touch it."

The smell wasn't strong; just strange. It wasn't a maggoty smell, or a rotten-egg smell; just a very old old smell.

Pa got a fork and Battles jerked the great mass of ancient flesh loose from the bit. It rolled lumpily over to one side of the well hole. As the air began to work on the old flesh, it slowly turned whitish before their very eyes.

The religious look in Battles's eyes deepened. He spoke down to the big chunk of ancient flesh. "My tongue clave to the roof of my mouth. Yea, behold, we know thee from of old, thou who drinkest up rivers and who pluggest the hole of the underground streams, trusting that thou canst draw up Jordan into thy mouth. The Lord saith, I will not conceal his parts, nor his power. Who can come up to him with his double bridle? His teeth are terrible round about. His scales are his pride. By his neesings a light doth shine. The flakes of his flesh are joined together; they cannot be moved. When he raiseth himself up the mighty are afraid. By reason of his breakings they purify themselves."

"Yeh," Pa breathed.

Battles closed his eyes for a moment. He blinked fiercely to himself several times; swallowed loudly. Then, opening his eyes again, calm, he said, "This is costing us money. Back to drilling."

"Wait," Free cried, "ain't you gonna call somebody up and tell them what you just found?"

"Call up who? Some domeny? When God already knows about it?"

"I mean, some scientist somewhere."

"Scientist, pientist, hell no. I've got work to do. And money to earn by the foot. I ain't got time for grown-up men who lollygag around with enlarging glasses while sitting on their asses."

"Boy," Free said, "when Principal Hedges learns nothing was done to find out what it really was, he ain't gonna like it."

"Who's Prinicpal Hedges? Does he drill wells?"

"He teaches mathematics and science at Western."

"I don't care who he is." With a harsh curse, Battles threw the clutch in. The drill bit dropped down again, lowering into the cement curbing, disappearing into the depths.

The drill bit didn't hit anything odd after that. And Pa went back to getting the binder ready for harvesting.

But they found no water, and at forty feet Battles gave up on the hole as a bad one.

"That goddamed Behemoth," Battles grumbled, "there must've been just enough moisture left in his old carcass to mix up my witching stick."

Before Battles could get started on another hole, a bristling thunderstorm came up. Bolts struck the countryside everywhere. One of the biggest bolts hit the steel mill over the dried-up well, crumpling up one of the corner struts; then crackled down into the well hole itself. It shook up the sandstone below and within hours the seam into the well ran with water again and filled the well to the brim.

The chunk of ancient flesh from Behemoth's carcass withered away within a week. It didn't rot; it just dried up and blew away. Soon all they had left of it was a big piece of chalky bone.

They got an announcement from Aunt Karen that Uncle Kon was getting his Master of Arts degree at Iowa City in early August. Aunt Karen sent along a little note wondering if maybe Pa and Ma and the children wouldn't like to attend the ceremonies.

Ma got all excited. She had to see that great thing. Ma always got a special look on her face when Uncle Kon's name was mentioned.

They were on the road to Iowa City.

Ma actually smiled a lot. Sometimes when she saw that the road ahead for the next ways was as straight as a clothesline, she relaxed and took a little nap.

Free and Flip had the back seat to themselves, along with two suitcases. It was decided to leave Jonathan and baby Abbott home as they wouldn't get much out of the graduation ceremonies. It was also decided that Everett should stay home to tell Sherm how Pa did the chores. Sherm was sixteen and he still worked for Uncle John across the river. Sherm was almost a man now, with a lot of hair under his armpits.

Uncle Kon had sent them a map of Iowa, with the trail they were to take marked in red ink on it. Ma suggested that Free be their guide and read the road map for Pa. It was easy. It was just take the old AYP Highway, now called U.S. 18, east out of Chokecherry Corner, and follow it all the way through Mason City.

The country was very flat. It was not very homelike. Their own country with its long slopes and swinging shallow valleys was better. Pa remarked that it was like living on the surface of a black kitchen range. Also much of the land was gumbo and that was hard to work if the season wasn't just right in the way the rain fell and the sun shone. Pa kept comparing the crops on either side of the road with their crops back home. Ma meanwhile checked the clothes hanging on the lines and the flowers growing by the gate. She watched to see if the curtains were hanging neat and clean in the parlor windows. Sometimes Ma checked the chickens too, and could spot which flock had lice and which not. Flip watched to see which yard had good tall trees to climb. Free watched to see which farmsteads had a nice flat hog pasture in which to play ball.

The old Buick rolled smooth at thirty per; and sometimes, when Ma was napping and Pa could ease her up to nearly forty per, she rolled along like a sack swing ride going on and on. Every time they stopped to get gas or stretch their legs, Pa went around and kicked all four tires. Except for the two-mile stretch of pavement between Chokecherry Corner and Hello, and a stretch of ten miles of pavement through Mason City, all the roads were dusty gravel. But the gravel roads were bladed daily and were mostly smooth.

At Charles City they next took 218 south.

Beyond Waterloo the country was very dry and all the leaves of the trees and all the leaves of the weeds along the road were covered with pale gray dust, so that it looked like they'd landed on another planet.

At Vinton, Ma began to act nervous. Now that they were almost there she worried they might have an accident at the last minute. The sun was almost down and the shadow of Ma's head cut exactly across the side of Pa's face.

Just as the sun set, the flat land fell away and in front of them lay a wooded valley. Down in the bottoms lay a large town. It was Iowa City.

Ma got out Uncle Kon's last letter and read it again for instructions. "We live on Kirkwood. You take 218 until you run into 6, then you turn left until you run into Linn. Then you turn right on Kirkwood."

They found it just as it began to get dark. Uncle Kon and Aunt Karen lived upstairs in a house that was built against a hill. Pa got out and climbed some white stairs. He had just barely knocked when the door burst open and Aunt Karen flew out like a hen and threw her arms around Pa and gave him a big kiss. Pa was even more surprised than the kids were.

"You've come! You've actually come," Aunt Karen kept crying. "Come in, come." She leaned down and peered down at the Buick. "Oh, Ada, what I don't have to tell you. And, oh, there's Free and that cute little chubby Albert too. Come in."

Ma got out, and then Free and Flip got out. Flip let on that he wasn't exactly pleased being called cute and chubby.

Uncle Kon came bustling out then too. His smile was as wide as Aunt Karen's. "So good of you to come." He shook Pa's hand with both of his. When Ma reached the top of the steps he gave her a kiss. Ma showed she liked the kiss by the way she blushed. Then Uncle Kon and Aunt Karen bustled them all into their apartment.

Then the first thing Aunt Karen did, right in the middle of all her loving up, was to check the soles of their shoes for dirt; and then, to make sure they didn't bring any Bonnie dirt into the house, she swept up around the door where they first stepped inside and whisked the imaginary dirt outside.

"Karen!" Uncle Kon scolded politely, like the gentleman he was, "that wasn't necessary."

"But I know children," Aunt Karen said brightly, getting her way at the same time that she kept smiling at her nephews, "after all, I taught in a country school once and I know all about the shoes of country boys."

"We didn't have a single flat on the whole trip down," Pa announced.

"Yes," Ma said, "the Lord was surely with us all the way." Ma looked at Uncle Kon as she spoke.

" 'Course, I drove careful," Pa said.

"Yes," Ma said, "Alfred is a good driver."

"But Free did the bestest," Flip said. "Free with his finger followed the map and didn't get us lost once."

Uncle Kon laughed. "He did, did he?"

After a while Pa and Uncle Kon got the suitcases out of the car, while Ma helped Aunt Karen set the table for late supper.

Aunt Karen overfed them. She set out much too much of everything: sweet potato salad, creamed lettuce, boiled sausage, buttered Kentucky wonder beans picked not an hour before, and tall glasses of lemonade with ice cubes. When it was ice-cream time, Uncle Kon couldn't help but sneak Free and Flip large second and third helpings. Uncle Kon laughed his silver uncle laugh at the way his two nephews managed to get themselves around still just a little bit more of the homemade vanilla ice cream.

That night Free and Flip slept on army cots on the screen porch off the kitchen. They fell asleep listening to the folks talking inside.

It rained once during the night. It was strange to hear rain falling on the trees just outside a porch screen in a foreign country. Free listened to it half asleep. Man, but the earth was a wide thing. They'd traveled a whole day across what looked like an absolutely flat surface. It only went to show how big the old earth really was.

Uncle Kon woke them up for breakfast. Free and Flip ate fried oatmeal and eggs and toasted bread until they were about to bust.

Uncle Kon thought it would be nice to show his guests some of the sights before the graduation ceremonies began, so they drove down to the university campus an hour early. The ceremonies were to begin at eleven o'clock outside the Administration Building.

In the University Library Uncle Kon led them through a little wicket gate and then took them into what he called the stacks. Free could hardly believe it was true, all those shelves and shelves of books reaching to the ceiling, and aisles and aisles of them going in all directions. The smell was like that of very dry straw.

"Son," Pa said down to Free after he'd looked at all the books, "do you think your brain could thresh all these stacks of books out in a year's time?" Pa houghed up a soft laugh at what he thought was pretty good humor.

"If I didn't have any chores to do, sure," Free said.

Uncle Kon let out a loud coughing laugh. Uncle Kon turned a little red. A person was supposed to be very quiet in a university library. Some of the gray-haired women librarians peeked around at Uncle Kon and his company, but they said nothing. A couple of scholars with spectacles on also peered out of the ends of the aisles to see what was going on. When they saw the children, Free and Flip, they smiled in a soft way to show they understood the noise.

Free liked the miles of books. Now he knew for sure he was never going to be a farmer or a famous baseball player.

The Zoology Building stunk like old pickles. It was full of the wildest sights Free had ever seen. There was a stuffed grizzly bear, and a stuffed chimpanzee, and a stuffed human being from a cave in Utah. In one of the big rooms stood the skeleton of a creature that was as big as their wooden windmill back home; if their mill was to lie on its side, that is.

Ma didn't walk into the big room very far. She gave the great humpnecked skeleton one look and began to be short of breath.

"What's the matter?" Uncle Kon asked, right away worried.

"That thing can't be true, can it?"

"I'm afraid so, Ada." Uncle Kon read the inscription pasted on a small boulder beneath it. " 'This skeleton was found in Como Bluff in Wyoming.' "

Free tugged at Pa's sleeve. "That thing looks like the skeleton of Behemoth, don't it? Like the one our well-driller caught into back home?"

" 'Spect so," Pa said, thinking heavy to himself.

"Well," Ma said, "there better not be too many of these Behemoth skeletons around or they're fake."

"Why not?" Uncle Kon wondered.

"Well, if a person reads Job carefully, it sounds as though God was the only one to ever see one. Just one." Ma stared at the great skeleton some more, then politely backed out of the room. "No, I mustn't see too much of such things."

Uncle Kon herded them outdoors, then led them to the temporary plank seats under the trees outside the Administration Building. He showed them where to sit in the reserved section under a huge elm. The plank seats under the trees reminded Free of the Fourth of July picnics back home in Bosch's grove.

Pretty soon Uncle Kon left to put on his gown and get ready for the procession.

Aunt Karen was so nervous about the whole affair that she laughed silly at the least thing.

Soon the plank seats were filled with the relatives and friends of the graduates. Though it was warm out a lot of people were wearing their dark Sunday clothes.

Promptly at eleven o'clock the candidates for the degrees marched in and took their seats up front. Uncle Kon was one of the last in line.

"There he is," Flip cried. "He's got a black breadboard on his head and a woman's house thing on over his suit."

"Shh," Ma whispered, smiling.

Next came the professors. They also wore flat hats and black gowns.

The main speaker, Dr. Allard Falloncock, psychologist, had invented a new way of treating hypochondria. Hypochondria was what Pa called a strong notion of I-don't-wanna-work. Dr. Falloncock started out his speech with a joke. A farmer had a wife who every now and then had a fit of hypochondria. The farmer was very patient with his wife and did all he could to ease her over the rough spots. "After he'd gotten the doctor for about the tenth time," Dr. Fallancock said, "the farmer remonstrated mildly with his wife and told her that really now, those fits were not all that necessary, were they? If she would only use a little willpower she could get rid of them. Whereupon his wife retorted, 'Lester Eberle, 'tain't no use talking. I can have fits, and I will have them.' "

Slowly the crowd laughed.

After that the speech was as dead as a dried wishbone. People settled back and began to fan themselves, the men with their straw hats and the women with their Japanese fans. Dr. Fallancock wasn't even as good as their domeny back home. Dr. Fallancock was too polite to describe real bad fits in detail. Domeny back home not only raved about sins, he told his congregation what each sin was in detail.

Free couldn't get the sight of the great skeleton in the Zoology Building out of his head. It came to him he'd forgotten to check to see if the bone in that hunk of curious purple flesh Herman Battles had dug up resembled any of the bones in the big skeleton. There'd probably be no time to visit the Zoology Building again. After the program a big celebration dinner was planned at Uncle Kon's home, and friends were going to be dropping by the rest of the day. And the next morning Pa and Ma were planning to leave for home before dawn. Shucks.

Then Free got an idea. He touched Ma on the elbow and whispered, "I gotta go to the bathroom."

Ma smiled around at him, half lost in thought. She was carefully following the speech. "Do you know where to go?"

"Sure."

"Come back right after."

Free nodded. He slipped past her where she sat on the end. He first headed for the Main Building where the bathrooms were; then, safely out of sight of the crowd, headed for the Zoology Building. He found the big room with the great skeleton.

He walked around the huge skeleton several times. He examined the bones in the various joints carefully. But look as he might, he couldn't find a bone resembling the one in the barnyard back home. Disappointed, he finally gave up.

On the way out, he spotted what looked like little curled-up pigs in bottles. They were standing in a row on a long shelf. He stepped up for a closer look. Reading the labels on the bottles, he discovered the little pigs actually were human being babies preserved in formaldehyde. They were examples of the human fetus in various stages of development. The first bottle had a very little baby in it, not much bigger than a skink. The fetus in the next bottle was about as big as a small cat. It was probably the size Harry Fish meant when he put down his wife Minnie Fish. The fetuses kept on getting bigger right on down the line. The last one was a full-size baby.

Free stared at all the pickled babies with a great wondering look. How in the world had they managed to get hold of that many fetuses with each one progressively bigger than the one before. They all had to be miscarriages.

The thought hit him that he could have been a miscarriage himself. Imagine being on exhibit like that in a bottle. He could feel his whole body turn pale. He got out of there.

On the way back to his seat beside Ma, he kept shaking his head to himself. "That waterhead baby Ma had, it could have wound up a pickled fetus. God."

That night Aunt Karen gave them each a small bunch of chilled green grapes for dessert. Free had never tasted such sweet grapes before. Delicious. Each little grape was a swallow of sweet green drink.

Free ❦ 7

A WEEK BEFORE school began, Pa and Ma called Free into the house. It was raining outside and the kids were playing cob baseball in the alley of the corncrib. Pa was sitting with his feet up on the reservoir smoking his pipe and Ma was by the window darning socks.

"What do you want?"

Pa looked at Ma. "You better tell him."

Ma was reshaping the heel of one of Pa's socks using a darning egg. As she worked she bit on her tongue a little. "No, it's for the father to say."

"But you're the one who wanted him to have more schooling."

"Well . . . all right." Ma fixed Free with troubled blue eyes. "Boy, how much does school mean to you? Really now?"

"Ain't I going this fall?"

"We've gone over the money situation and I'm afraid we can't spare the money this coming school year."

Free sat down. "Oh."

"Yes, son," Pa said, "we lost too many pigs to the hog cholera."

"But that wasn't my fault."

"We know that, son," Pa clapped out his pipe in his hand and threw the dottle into the stove.

Free thought of all the books in the school library he still hadn't read. He thought of the fun he'd had in the Beaver Club. Better yet he'd be a sophomore this coming year, not a dumb freshie. Doggone it. He was about to lose everything worthwhile in life. Man alive.

Pa began to feel for him. "Wal, son, I tell you what. If you can figure out some way to take care of your room and board, I'll dig up the money for your tuition and books. And Ma says you can wear last year's clothes again."

Free grabbed at the chance. "Do you mean that, Pa?"

"I do."

"Okay. I'll figure out something."

He went to the barn and out of habit began to curry Tip. Tip of course liked the currying and helped him by turning herself toward him.

It quit raining about the time he got an idea. He'd heard that a neighbor boy, Jack DeGreate, was driving every day to the Hello High School. Jack DeGreate lived a mile over the hill on the other road to Hello.

Free bridled Tip and led her outside and hopped aboard bareback. He kicked her in the flanks and slowly with a weary groan she galloped up the road. The road was sticky. Soon Tip's hoofs were as big as plates.

Arriving on the DeGreate yard, Free right away knew something was wrong with that family. It was something dark. He thought maybe it had something to do with Mr. DeGreate having died two years before. Mrs. DeGreate was doing yard work like a man and the kids were glum. Mrs. DeGreate was a good-looking woman who wore overalls and a pair of man's red rubber boots.

Free told her what he had in mind.

Mrs. DeGreate listened carefully. "But it'll cost you."

"How much?"

"Let's say a dollar a week. And you've got to be here on the yard on time." Mrs. DeGreate hollered across to the barn. "Jack? C'mere a minute."

Jack came out. He was wearing red rubber boots too. He'd been manuring out the calf pen and wasn't very happy about it.

Mrs. DeGreate explained what Free had in mind.

Jack didn't like the idea very much. "There ain't much room in my cab." He pointed toward the corncrib alley.

Free saw a cab half as big as the one he used to drive to the Christian School in Bonnie.

Mrs. DeGreate stood with her arms on her hips and her legs wide apart. "Jack there's plenty room for two skinny kids. Besides, we can use that buck a week."

"I'll ask Pa if he can spare me that buck," Free said. "Thanks."

When Free got back to the yard he found Pa agreeable.

"What I'll do," Pa said, "is give up half of my chewing tobacco. I should cut down on it anyway."

On September first Free found himself riding to school in a cab once more.

It was great to see all the kids in school again, even the professors. Everybody asked everybody else if they'd had a good time the past summer. Some of the stories told were real stretchers.

Free was always careful to be on time to catch his ride in the morning. After school he always made it a point to be early at the barn behind the Big Church where Jack stalled his horse. Jack drove a black mare named Topsy. Topsy ran at a good clip. She was even-tempered and could've made her way up and back without a driver. Jack sat up in front in the cab, on a cross board, and Free sat in back.

One afternoon Free heard from a neighbor what the trouble on the DeGreate yard might be. It was the hired man. The year before, during cornpicking on a

Saturday, Jack's ma decided she'd bring their hired hand some coffee out in the field. Shortly after she left the yard, the phone rang asking for Mrs. DeGreate. Jack ran out to get her. He saw the hired man's wagon at the end of the field. When he got there he couldn't find either his ma or the hired man. Finally, thinking he could get a better view of the cornfield standing on top of the load of corn, he climbed up on the wagon. He was about to step on the pile of corn, when, unbelievably, there lay his ma looking up at him from the sloping pile of corn. The hired man was on top of her.

The story made Free sick. His own ma would never have done a thing like that. A mother who prayed kneeling at a chair with her boy couldn't possibly do such a thing. Free felt sorry for Jack.

Jack wanted to leave home and begged his mother almost every day to let him stay in town so he could go out for the high school track team. The track coach had spotted him running on the school grounds one day and had asked him to come out for the team. Jack had outrun the school's fastest runner on a dare and the coach told him he could make the first team right off the bat and win a lot of track events. Jack had read about the great milers in the Sioux City *Journal* and wanted to get on the Olympic team someday. But his ma told him that if he didn't shut up he could run to school because they could use that extra horse in the field.

Jack DeGreate fussed so much about not being able to go out for the team that one day on the way home Free suggested Jack should train for the team anyway.

"How?"

"Let me drive Topsy and you run behind the cab. That way you'd build up your wind. And then maybe by next spring you could talk your ma into at least letting you stay after school for the track meets."

Jack's brown eyes began to sparkle for the first time in a long while. "Hey, that's a good idea. And we'll use my Ingersoll watch to time me. It's got a second hand."

Jack surprised Free. He really could run. Free had to whip up Topsy to full speed to keep ahead of Jack when Jack opened up. Pretty soon Jack could not only run the mile under five minutes, he could also run the two-mile in just over ten minutes.

Jack wanted to share his new-found power and he offered to take turns running with Free. Free could run while he drove.

Free knew he'd never make much of a dash man, certainly not since he'd once had that bad case of sore knees. But he surprised himself with the way he could run distance. Jack might be able to run the mile faster, but Free could run the farthest without tiring. Since Topsy knew the way, Free and Jack sometimes ran side by side for several miles. But it was always Jack who had to quit first. His face would get purple around the nose, and he'd have to pump to keep up, and then finally, about to collapse, he'd give up and call out to Topsy, "Whoa! Stop!" While Free kept on running.

By the middle of October Free could run the six miles from Hello to DeGreate's place non-stop and hardly puff. Sometimes he also ran the extra mile catercorner across the section from DeGreate's house to his house. Many times he ran both ways to school, fourteen miles a day.

Ma was the first to notice what it was doing for him. Free would pop a button now and then when he lifted heavy things. Ma also had to reset the buttons on his suit jacket.

Weekends at home Free often found himself with time on his hands. Using the excuse that he had to study, he'd go upstairs and curl up in bed and read a novel. He still liked the feel of the sharp hard corners of his new textbooks all right, but it was novels and histories that drew him.

One Friday he brought home *Tess of the D'Ubervilles*. In paging through it he'd spotted a reference to an English dairy farm. He'd also spotted a passage about Tess feeling sad about something. The description of Tess reminded him of beautiful Winifred Bonner.

That night right after supper, he plunged into the book. He sat with his back to the gas lamp and with his stocking feet up on the sewing machine in the corner.

After about an hour he vaguely heard Ma say, "I wonder what that boy is reading there. I've called him three times and he hasn't heard me."

"Free!" Pa called sharply.

Free broke away from his book. "Yes?"

"Pay attention to your mother once when she asks you a question."

"Yes, Ma?" The gaslight in their farm kitchen was much sharper than the lamplight in Tess's house.

"What are you reading there that's so interesting?"

Free had got far enough into the book to know that that dirty Alec D'Uberville had just ruined Tess. That Ma had better not know about. "Oh, just some schoolwork," he lied.

"What's it about?"

"Oh, about some farm people in England." To make up for his lie, Free read a few lines from the paragraph he'd just finished. "After Tess had settled down to her cow there was for a time no talk in the barton, and not a sound interfered with the purr of the milk-jets into the numerous pails."

Ma was amazed. "Since when have you become so interested in milking that you get lost in reading about it? Especially English milking? When we can hardly get you to help with our American milking?"

"It's just a story, Ma."

Pa said, "You mean to tell me we're paying good hard-earned money to send you to school to learn how they milk cows in England?"

"It's the story of it, Pa, that makes it important. And what it means."

"Ha," Pa said, "a cow's swift tail in your eyes will tell you what it means a whole lot better. Especially if it's a little damp."

Ma shook her head. "Shakespeare, yes. But reading about Tess milking a cow in England, no."

Pa mulled it over some more. "Though I have to say that that purr of the milk-jets into all those pails sounds pretty good."

Ma shook her head some more. "They sure must be backward in England that they still require young girls to milk. I wouldn't milk here in America for love nor money, even if I was starving to death."

Pa filled his pipe and lit it. "Wal, as to that, wife, young girls in the Old Country, Fryslân, they still milk."

Free said, "You still haven't told me what you wanted, Ma."

"Oh. That. Yes. Could you go down cellar for me a minute and bring up some jelly for breakfast tomorrow morning?"

"Sure thing."

The next Sunday, Ma decided to stay home from church for once.

When they got back from church Free right away spotted an offish look in Ma's eyes. He soon found out why. When he looked around for *Tess of the D'Ubervilles* he couldn't find it. He still had about fifty pages to go. When he asked Ma if she'd seen it, she had an answer for him.

"I put Tess away." Ma set the steaming rice cooker on the table. "Imagine, you reading that kind of stuff."

He liked warm rice with butter and sugar on it, along with a sprinkling of cinnamon, but that noon it didn't taste very good.

The next morning off to school he went as usual.

To his surprise, right after chapel, he spotted Pa and Ma being ushered into Principal Hedges's office. Ma was carrying the book *Tess of the D'Ubervilles*. The door closed behind them. Through the rippled glass in the door Free could see vague shadows moving about as the three people inside turned their chairs a little and sat down. For Pa to take off half a day from fall work, and Ma to go along with him, meant his folks were really upset.

He was working on his Latin II lesson during study hour right after school lunch, when someone tapped him on the shoulder. Looking up, he saw Principal Hedges and his little square moustache. Principal Hedges crooked a finger at him to come along with him. Free got up and quietly followed him into his office.

"Have a chair, Free."

"Yessir."

"You already know what this is all about no doubt?"

"I think so."

"What did you get out of that tale of Tess?"

"Well, I learned a lot about the way the English run their dairy farms."

Principal Hedges bent a quizzical smile upon him. "And?"

"I learned that adultery does not pay. Though that poor Tess, she couldn't help it. That devil Alec caught her sleeping in the woods and before she knew it he'd ruined her."

"Is that what you got out of it?"

"Well, but, adultery is wrong, isn't it?"

"Yes. I guess it is." Principal Hedges looked down at the wide gold ring on his left hand. "Do you think you understood, fully, what you were reading?"

"Hardy is hard to read. He writes awkward."

Principal Hedges laughed. "Now there is a bit of pretty good literary criticism. Those are exactly my sentiments about him, son. I much prefer Mark Twain." Principal Hedges often took on Mark Twain's imperial stance when he was aroused. "Well, Free, of course you know that your mother loves you. She's a fine woman. But she feels you are too young to read about sex. So she's asked me to work out an agreement with you. That you must first get my approval for any novel you want to take out of the library. Okay?"

Free looked black. Slowly he nodded.

Principal Hedges folded his hands and then formed a church steeple out of his forefingers. "For myself, I don't see any harm in your reading about poor Tess. You seem to have handled reading about her in a mature way. But you want to remember that your mother is not used to that kind of reading matter."

"Ma's pretty smart though, prof."

"I know she is. It's just that she hasn't read many novels." Principal Hedges smiled. His little black moustache thinned out. "I admire her for coming here. And I admire you for your loyalty." He got to his feet. "Now, just remember that before you can take out a novel you've got to get my approval. Okay?"

"Okay."

A couple of days later, Principal Hedges found Free in the library browsing through the fiction section. Principal Hedges seemed irritated to find him there so soon after their talk. "Got your studies done?"

"Mostly."

Some of the kids lounging under the tall windows snickered.

Principal Hedges whirled around and blazed black eyes at them. "And that question goes for you mockers too, you know."

The kids got up and moved into the study hall.

Principal Hedges turned back to Free. His eyes fell on the length of Free's shanks showing beneath his knickers. "You're beginning to shoot up, aren't you? Well, so it goes. Sometimes nature goes in for brains and sometimes for brawn."

"And sometimes she goes in for both," Free retorted.

A look of genuine surprise, even pleasure, bloomed on Principal Hedges's face. "Atty old comeback, boy. Now I know you've got something upstairs there. Good."

The cows had sores on their tits that fall, and the first thing Free knew he had a few sores on the backs of his fingers. A couple of days later sores appeared on the undersides of his wrists. And then, worst of all, sores erupted across his chin. The sores weren't the usual kind of boy's pimple. They were wide flat lesions, and had a yellowish crust. Just when it appeared they were about to heal, they'd break open and start mattering all over again.

Ma gave him some of her woman's salve, but that didn't help any. Pa gave him some of his horse salve, but that seemed to smear the sores over his face all the faster. And the more he washed with soap the worse it got.

The kids at school began to look funny at him. Birdie, who usually had time for him, began to avoid him. Orrie Overslough, when he ran into him in the bathroom, lifted his nose as though he were smelling something rotten. And Winifred Bonner, sweet womanly Winifred, also had a wrinkled look for him.

Pa had bought Free a new brown leather jacket. "It'll keep out the wind for you," Pa'd said, "and yet be nice and light to run to school in." During noon hour recess Free had to go on an errand for Ma at the Hello Drugstore. After a quick lunch, he hurried downstairs to the boys' coat room to get his leather jacket. His jacket was hanging the wrong way on its hook but he thought nothing of it. He grabbed it and shrugged his shoulders into it and ran up the stairs outside. As he passed by a cluster of girls he noted funny startled looks on their faces.

There were more startled looks for him uptown. He could see them out of the corner of his eye. The druggist in particular stared at him as he left the drugstore.

He was about halfway back to the school grounds when it came to him that there had to be something the matter with the back of his neck and not just his face. He made up his mind that when he got back to the bathroom he'd have a look at his neck in the mirror.

What he saw was a shock. His neck was all right. But someone had chalked some words on the back of his new brown leather jacket:

Unclean!
I HAVE LEPROSY
Beware!!!

So that was why.

He recognized the handwriting. Orrie's. Orrie had never liked him after all those base hits he'd got off him in Mrs. Fish's cow pasture. The son of a bitch.

Well, there was no use crying over it. Pa'd said the sores would gradually heal over and then everybody would forget he'd ever had them. Free took off his leather jacket and washed off the chalk lettering in a wash basin.

A half hour later Professor Peter Brooks touched him on the shoulder in the study hall. With a sad old smile he whispered that he'd like to see him for a moment.

Free followed him into the language room.

"Free, you've seen a doctor about those sores, haven't you?"

"No. Pa just says they come from cows."

"Hmm. Well, I think you better go get your jacket and come along with me to the doctor a minute."

"But why? We can't pay for it."

"Come, we'll go see what the doctor says. It'll be my treat. As an old favor to your mother."

Free got his leather jacket. Numbly he walked uptown with Professor Brooks.

There was an odd air, fatherly almost, in Professor Brooks's manner. Professor Brooks, a short stump of a man, toddled along more than he walked, with an odd rocking motion in his knees. He already had quite a batch of children, seven in six years. The kids in school said of him that he performed where Professor Van Rill only promised. He had the half-smile of a man who was willing to be surprised just once more.

Dr. Brander Mars had an office in the back of the hospital on the first floor. He had a purple nose. People said he drank a lot because he saw too much tragedy every day. Still he was known as a first-rate doctor. Pa had once made the remark that if a man and a boar got mixed up in an accident, and one of them was to die, Dr. Mars could fix up out of such parts as were still in working order a fairly decent hired man. Ma didn't like Dr. Mars's black brows. He was too blunt, she said. He thought of people as animals.

Dr. Mars caught up Free's problem in one swift glance. "Ah, cowpox, I see."

"So that's what it is," Professor Brooks said. "Is it contagious?"

"You might wish it were."

"How so?"

Dr. Mars wriggled his purple nose. "A case of cowpox makes the perfect vaccination for smallpox."

Frew sat up. "I can't get smallpox then?"

"No. And cowpox, unlike smallpox, leaves no scars."

Professor Brooks looked relieved. "How long will it take for his sores to heal?"

"About two weeks."

"Hmm. Well. What do we owe you?"

"Are you paying?"

"Yes."

"After all the obstetric business you've given me, nothing."

"Thanks, Brander."

On the way back to school, Free asked, "Then I can keep going to school?"

Professor Brooks took Free by the arm. "Let me have another look at you. Mmm. You know, son"—Professor Brooks swallowed as the word "son" formed on his wide lips—"you know, Master Alfred, perhaps you should stay home those two weeks while your sores heal. They're so . . . there really are a lot of them."

Free knew that. When he'd looked at himself in the mirror that morning he'd thought of Lazarus and his sores. Something in the way Professor Brooks spoke to him made Free catch his breath. People were filled to loathing at the sight of him. To the point where one of them was even reminded of leprosy.

"I'll write a note to your mother," Professor Brooks said finally, with some private satisfaction, "to explain the situation."

"All right."

That night Ma read the note with some surprise. "Well, I never," she said in a low voice. "How very nice of him. I always knew he was a nice man."

Pa was having his coffee. He took a sip and smiled to himself. "Ain't he the one who tried to date you once? The one your folks thought would make you a good match?"

"Yes, I guess it is."

"Maybe you should've married him. Then your oldest could've been a city boy and so wouldn't have had to milk cows with sore tits."

"Never mind now. That's last year's cabbage. But Peter Brooks always did have a tender heart. Though the way Mrs. Brooks is always having babies makes one wonder."

Free's mind began to chase its own tail around. So Ma could also have married Professor Peter Brooks. And his name would've been Alfred Brooks. Free tried to imagine what kind of love thoughts Professor Brooks might've had about Ma. It was very interesting that Ma should've chosen a tall handsome man who couldn't read or write over a short man who was a college graduate.

Pa finished his coffee. "So Professor Brooks wants you to stay home for a couple of weeks, ha?"

"Yes."

"Maybe we can turn that into a good thing. If you help me pick corn those two weeks we can get that corn out before the first snow flies."

"Me pick corn with all these sores?"

"Sure. Why not?"

"Well, I thought I'd keep up on my schoolwork. The profs told me what to cover during those two weeks."

"I'm not going to have you sit in comfort here by the stove while I slave out in the cold. Nobody'll see those sores out there." Pa caught Free's black look. "Listen, boy. I've let you go to school when every dummed relative of yours was agin it. At least you should be thankful for that."

The next morning Pa outfitted Free with a two-box wagon. "Fill those twenty-six inches twice a day and you'll have picked yourself fifty-two bushels." Pa gave him an old bangboard, plus a six-inch sideboard in case he should pick more than twenty-six bushels a load. "Your old school chum Floris Haber, I hear, has a couple of times picked himself sixty-five bushels in one day."

Pa dug out an extra cornhusking hook for him, a Clark Mascot model. He also gave him a pack of double-thumbed mittens. After one thumb wore out, a fellow could turn the mitten over and pick with the other thumb. The cotton mittens were covered with a nap as soft as a kitten. Next Pa painted the left leg of Free's overalls with red barn paint. The edge of a dried corn leaf could cut right through ordinary denim but not through painted cloth. And finally Ma made Free some picking sleeves out of the pants legs of some old overalls. He wore the picking sleeves over his shirt sleeves.

It was drizzling when they got up the next morning. One good sniff of the driving mist after breakfast and Pa decided not to go out into the field.

It cleared off by eleven, and at twelve-thirty after a full dinner, the two of them rattled out to the field, Pa driving the bays, Fan and Dick, and Free the grays, Polly and Nell.

Pa moved out first, taking two rows.

After a minute Free guided his grays into the two rows Pa had just picked. Like Pa, Free kept one picked row between the horses and the still standing corn.

Free started out picking slowly. Pa'd taught him how: grab the ear with the left hand, rip the hook on the right hand through the husks on the underside of the ear, finish the grab of the left hand by clutching up the remaining husks on the ear, catch the bare ear with the fingers of the right hand above the hook, jerk the ear from its stem, and, still all in one motion, throw the ear in the general direction of the bangboard. The ears rose in an arc one by one against the bangboard, then clattered to the hardwood floor of the wagon. Grab, husk, jerk, throw. Bang, bang, bang.

Dreaming ahead, he could see where he just might come in with a big load of golden corn that evening. At least thirty-two bushels. He'd show Floris Haber. And while he was at it, all those crabbing relatives too who thought school was ruining him. It would be like hitting a home run in a man's ball park. Pa himself filled a three-box wagon thirty-six inches deep twice a day. Pa in fact considered it a great day when he could come in with eighty bushels. So did Uncle John. Though crazy Sherm and that even crazier Garrett tried to pick three loads of forty bushels a day. But that kind of picking was for champs.

Looking ahead Free saw that Pa had vanished over the hill. The old man could pick at a pretty good clip. Free decided he'd better put the socks into it.

Halfway down the slope on the other side of the hill, Free saw Pa reach the end of the field. Pa climbed up on his wagon, looked back to see how far his son had come, then reached down into the wagon for his water jug and helped himself to a good swig. Pa didn't waste any time. Done drinking, Pa drove his horses across the end and turned them into the next set of rows. In a moment Pa was at it again, bang, bang, bang, coming back up the hill.

Soon Free noticed his flying corn no longer made a clattering sound when it fell in the wagon. The bottom of the wagon box was filling up. The thought thrilled him.

After a while he couldn't resist a peek to see how much he'd picked so far. He hopped up on a hub and looked in. And was disappointed. The pile under the bangboard had just barely begun to climb up against the second board, with the edges of the pile only an ear deep at the ends. He dropped to the ground again.

He began to pick like the dickens. He promised himself not to look again until he'd made the end of the field.

"Get to work, bud," he ordered himself.

When he got to the end he decided he wouldn't do what Pa did, have a swig at the same time that he had a look-see. He'd already had his look. Stoutly he led the horses by the bit to the next two rows and plunged back into the field.

Polly and Nell behaved perfectly. Each time he came up even with their butts, they moved ahead a dozen steps, until he was a couple of hills behind the back wheels. Then, while he picked to catch up again, they would nuzzle through the nearby fluttering husks to see if maybe Pa had missed an ear. Sometimes Pa left a nubbin, a short two-inch ear too tough to pick, and then Polly and Nell had themselves a little feast. Pa said it wasn't worth it to pick the nubbins. Too easy to sprain a wrist on them.

Halfway back, cresting the hill, Free became aware that his constant brushing against the leaning cornstalks, as well as straddling them sometimes, had aroused him. The creamy smell of just-snapped corn and the perfume of trampled pigeon grass underfoot also helped. He thought of Winifred, especially of that time when she'd sat with him on the table of that unfinished room at Western. Suppose a fellow was to do it to Winifred, how would he go about it? Let's see. If he did this, slipped his hand halfway up her leg, then she'd probably close her legs. And then?

It was funny, but in his mind he could never get beyond where the girl made that closing motion with her legs.

Lovely Winifred. He wondered what she was doing right that minute.

''Probably only studying Latin II,'' he said aloud.

That made him laugh. And in a moment he felt a whole lot better.

Northwest across the river he spotted two bangboards sticking out of Uncle John's cornfield. Uncle John and Uncle Sherm. They were moving toward the far end, with Uncle Sherm far in the lead. Uncle Sherm was always racing against some imaginary champ. What fun it was going to be some evening, while sipping a cup of hot chocolate in the kitchen with everybody bragging a little, to hear Pa say that, yessir, his oldest boy had come in with a colossal load of thirty-two bushels, and that, sir, on his very first try at picking alone.

He had to have a peek into his wagon. He hopped on the nearest hub and looked in. Well. That was better. The pile of orange corn had climbed to the top of the second box. By the time he got to the end of the third and fourth row he'd be able to see it from where he picked. From then on he could watch it mount with every ear he threw.

He put the socks into it again. He leaped and grabbed an ear here, jumped and grabbed an ear there. He whirled and bowed and stretched. His hands performed like revolving flywheels, smooth, sure, swift. Bang, bang, bang. He managed always to have an ear in the air. There'd be the ear falling off the bangboard, then the ear just thrown, and then the ear he was husking. It was said that Garrett could always keep two ears in the air. But the main thing was never to look to see how full the wagon was.

Free was thirsty when he got to the end. He had to climb up onto the wagon for the jug and so of course couldn't help but look at the corn in his wagon. Yes. The corn had climbed to just above the second board. The cistern water in the jug was good. Pure nectar sucked from puccoons.

He started in on his fifth and sixth rows. About then some of his yellow sores began to hurt. They'd been itching for weeks; sometimes so fierce he couldn't help but scratch them. The sore on his left wrist was the worst. It was as big as a penny, and there were times when, upon removing the bandage, he was sure he could see bone. He led with his left arm and the continual butting into the tangled cornstalks made his left wrist very tender.

It came to him that school was actually pretty wonderful. He'd be mighty glad when the ordeal of having cowpox sores and having to pick corn was over. School life was the only thing. Every now and then a corn leaf, fluttering near his nose, reminded him of the smell of his Ancient History book. Even of his dreaded Latin II book. Yes, reading about Caesar conquering all of Gaul, even unto three parts, and that in a cackling foreign tongue, was still a whole lot better than watching corn rise in a wagon on the third time across the field.

The pile mounted as he picked his way up the hill. Soon it reached the second crack in the bangboard.

He began to aim the ears for the peak of the pile. The faster that peak climbed the faster the wagon would fill. Sometimes for a dozen hills or so he'd be sure he'd have more than thirty-two bushels by the time he got to the end. Then, a dozen hills farther along, he'd despair, sure that he'd have less than thirty bushels.

Coming to the top of the hill the pile in the wagon rose high enough to begin spilling over on the near side. Time to make an adjustment. He climbed up on the wagon and lifted the sideboard off the bangboard and placed it on the near side. He had to jam the middle pair of cleats down through the corn.

He took a good pull at the water jug and went back at it again.

The pile of corn mounted. It thrilled him to think that at last he was a man picking his own load of corn. He fantasied himself someday winning the state cornpicking championship. Winning a state medal was about as great as pitching a team to victory in a World Series game. Picking his own load alone he now belonged to a certain great breed of men. Why, maybe even some year he could first pitch the Cubs to a World Series championship in early October and then later in October go out and win the National Cornpicking Championship. And so the same fall be a double hero. For a fellow who was supposed to have leprosy, not bad at that.

The sun owled down. There was no wind. Fermenting smells rose all around him. The smell of dust underfoot was as sweet as the taste of brown sugar.

The spiders of late afternoon came out. Their silver threads drifted across his face, caught on his sores. It made the sores itch like Billy Sixty. He had to rub them a little, gingerly, with the silky nap on the back of his mittens. Some of the open sores left pinkish streaks on his mittens. It was a mess.

The nap on his left thumb wore off first. It wasn't long before the sharp edges of the corn kernels were rasping the bare skin of his thumb. He picked a while with the bare thumb, until it began to redden, then decided to reverse the mittens and use the second thumbs. It involved taking off the hook but it was worth it.

The big open sore on his left wrist oozed blood.

With his teeth and left hand he strapped the hook over his reversed mitten; went back to picking.

An ear spilled over the sideboard. He climbed the load and pushed the pile of corn out to both ends, until the two-box wagon was level full. It worried him some that there wasn't more corn. It began to look as though he wasn't going to have the thirty-two bushels at the end of six rows.

He glanced down the hill to see how much he had left to pick. And, looking, he then understood why he wasn't getting out as much corn as he'd expected. It was his luck to have run onto a dead furrow. His last two rows had a stunted look about them. They couldn't help but have less corn.

He put the socks into it once again. The load slowly became heavy and the iron rims of the wheels cut deep tracks into the dry earth. The grays groaned as they pulled the wagon ahead the usual dozen steps.

It pleased him that he could hit the bangboard without looking. He was getting to be as accurate as a second baseman tossing the ball to the shortstop to start a double play.

The closer he got to the end the faster he went. The ears in the dead furrow were small and were easier to handle. Snapping out some of those big sixteen-inch ears earlier in the afternoon had been hard on the wrist.

He picked the last ear of corn just as the sun set.

He stood very still for several moments, looking at things. The cornstalks resembled tall red sunflowers. Someone had unwound a spool of pink gossamer and its single thread undulated across his vision. He was standing in a red dream.

He climbed up on the wagon. He untied the lines and turned the horses around and headed for home, going up some already picked rows. Looking back, he saw that Sherm and Uncle John across the river were heading for home too. In the scarlet dusk their wagons gleamed with fat mounds of red-gold corn. Sherm's was the biggest. Free wondered if Sherm in turn was looking across the river. Sherm was probably speculating a mile a minute wondering who was helping Pa.

He was a man. It was a sweet thing to unstrap the hook slowly from his right hand. He took the mitten off slowly. There were deep strap marks over the back of his hand. What a luxury to be done for the day. Better yet, the sores had quit itching.

Pa was waiting for him at the end near the hog pasture. Pa'd finished a full eight rows and had a whopping load, a good forty-two bushels. Pa's also had the time to pick a couple of dozen ears of seed corn in the apple box. Pa could feel a seed ear through the husks even before he picked it. The apple box was tacked onto the step on the near side.

"So," Pa said. "Pretty good." His eyes went back and forth over Free's load. "Did you get to the end?"

"Yep. But I didn't come up with thirty-two bushels."

"I know. You ran into a dead furrow."

"If it hadn't been for that I think maybe I could've even got out thirty-six."

"Son, thirty bushels is a God's plenty for a young fellow like you."

Free surveyed the load under him. "You sure that's what I got?"

"Yep. If I was to pay a hired hand for picking that load, that's what I'd call it."

Free could have kissed Pa.

"Wal, son, let's head for home. Ma and the elevator are waiting."

Two weeks later, Pa and Free finished getting out the corn.
About the same time the last of Free's sores healed up.
"I guess I can go back now and help Caesar conquer the rest of Gaul."

Free ❦ 8

THAT WINTER JACK'S mother and Free's ma decided it was too cold for their boys to be riding six miles to town in a wooden cab. January was always the below-zero month and February was the snowstorm month. It meant the end of their running for a while.

Professor Ralph found Free a room with the Henry Brunsteins.

Henry Brunstein had just quit farming. Henry was a cousin of Tena Brunstein, the girl Sootman had bumped into on purpose. Henry was in his early thirties, married, and had a little boy of eight. He'd done well as a farmer but hated every moment of it. His wife Carrie hadn't much cared for the farm smells either. But when Henry announced one day that he was going back to school instead of buying out a business on main street, Carrie began to regret she'd complained so much about farm smells. What would they live on while he went through high school? Henry told her not to worry, he planned to go through high school in two years. It would take at the most only three thousand dollars out of the fifteen thousand they'd cleared on their farm sale. Henry and Carrie rented a house across the alley from Professor Ralph. It happened that Professor Ralph became Henry's advisor, and he was delighted, and thought it splendid, that Henry wanted to save his talent.

Free liked Henry, but didn't much care for Carrie. Henry had a wide blond face and wondering blue eyes and a quiet smile. Henry loved to eat, but because he could no longer work it off, had a tendency to put on weight. Carrie hated fat men. She put Henry on a severe diet. She served a breakfast of half an orange, one ladle of oatmeal with a half glass of skim milk, and one cup of black coffee. At noon she served a lunch of a glass of skim milk, a slice of cheese, and two leaves of lettuce. And in the evening she served a dinner of one dab of mashed potatoes, a spoonful of gravy, a thin slice of roast, one thin piece of pumpernickel bread with a pat of butter and a little corner of jelly, and for dessert a half pear with a little rivulet of juice. It was hardly enough to keep a sparrow alive. But the diet did keep Henry's weight down to a respectable figure. Meanwhile wife Carrie thinned out until she looked like a strip of dried beef. And their boy Sylvester slowly shriveled up like a dried cucumber. In fact, Sylvester's boy lips became in time as pale as egg peel. The pale lips stood out vividly in the midst of his lemon freckles.

Free got the distinct impression that Carrie was feeding all four of them on his four dollars a week for board and room.

A couple of weeks of Carrie's lean fare and Free began to worry that he would soon wither away. He went home as often as possible weekends for Ma's bountiful home cooking. He didn't dare tell his folks that the Brunsteins weren't feeding him very well. He was too happy about being able to live in town again and only a few blocks from school. Ma accepted his vast weekend appetite as another sign that her boy was eating like any growing boy might.

It turned out that Henry was a Chicago Cubs fan. That made up for a lot. It was almost enough to make up for his wife Carrie. After a bird supper, Free and Henry woud often have a great time recounting to each other stories about the various Cubs, about the great curve Three-Fingered Mordecai Brown could throw because he'd lost his forefinger in an accident, and the great double-play combination of Tinker-to-Evers-to-Chance. They read all the baseball gossip of the winter stove leagues as reported in the Sioux City *Journal*. Both longed for the day in April when box scores would once again appear in the sport pages.

Henry didn't attend any classes. He was going through high school on a hurry-up schedule, taking one course at a time. He studied at home and when he thought he was about ready for a final exam, he went to the prof's house and took it. He sailed through Latin I and Latin II in six weeks. Same for German I and German II. There was a good chance that by the first of June Henry could finish both his freshman and sophomore years.

Free meanwhile took his own time. He studied just hard enough to pass and then for the rest followed his nose reading. He soon finished most of the good books in the school library and began to cast about for another library to raid.

One night the Ralphs asked Free if he'd watch over their two little boys while they went to a party in another town. Their regular girl was ill.

Free was happy to do it. Professor Ralph's house was loaded with books.

Free put the two Ralph boys to bed at eight as ordered. It wasn't much different from putting his own two brothers Jonathan and Abbott to bed. Then Free began to browse through all the books.

There were books everywhere, shelves and shelves of them on the first floor, in the hall entry, in the living room, in the parlor, even in the bathroom.

The upstairs was even more cluttered with books. Free had to pick his way carefully into Professor Ralph's study. Man alive. What a great thing it was to be a professor.

Free decided not to touch any of the books in the professor's study. Prof probably knew exactly where every book was and could right away spot if someone had been nosing around in his holy of holies.

Free went downstairs again and began to range through the stacks in the living room. All that book world yet to be explored made him feverish. It'd take him years to read even a tenth of all those books. And as sure as shooting, if he was going to be a great man someday, he'd have to read at least a good share of them. A fellow couldn't just skim through them either. If only there was some kind of magic way a person could absorb them into one's memory, say by eating them, or by some kind of hypnosis.

The Rise of the Dutch Republic by Motley caught his eye. Free remembered having once heard Professor Ralph say that Motley admired the Frisians for the way they'd resisted the Spaniards and had battled to remain a free people. Pa's people, the Frisians, were sometimes called Dutch. For several thousands of years the Frisians had persisted as one people in one place.

Free found an easy chair with a good reading lamp beside it, put up his feet on a hassock, and let himself drop into the fat brown book.

Motley's writing was dramatic, though the sentences were sometimes a little long. The description of that endless waste of ooze in the deltas of the three rivers—the Rhine, the Meuse, and the Scheld—and the story of how certain early inhabitants had managed to gain a foothold in it caught Free up as though he'd just jumped onto a wild sack swing. He read about the gigantic Celts and the huge Frisians who successfully resisted the Roman legions of Caesar. Both people had fierce blue eyes, with the Celts having long floating yellow hair and the Frisians having long locks of fiery red hair.

So that was who Pa's people were. Pa didn't have red hair, but he sure had the fierce eyes.

Free didn't hear the Ralphs come home. Suddenly there was Professor Ralph smiling down at him. Beside the professor stood his patient wife with her pale blue eyes.

"What are you reading?"

Free was afraid the professor wouldn't like it he'd raided his stacks. "It's something about the Frisians." Free closed the book and placed it on the arm of the chair.

"Motley, eh? Caught you, did he?"

"It reads like a good novel."

Professor Ralph picked up the fat brown book and leafed through it. Then he opened the book in the middle and smelled deep into its binding. "So."

Free could see that the good professor was changing his mind about him. Free hadn't been doing too well in his Ancient History class.

Mrs. Ralph set her purse to one side and shrugged out of her coat. "Did the boys give you any trouble?"

"They were easier to put to bed than my two younger brothers."

"Good."

Professor Ralph dropped the book on an end table and shrugged out of his coat too. "So Motley reads like a good novel, does he?"

"Yes." Free got to his feet. He slipped into his leather jacket. He didn't want to wear out his welcome.

"Gary," Mrs. Ralph said. "We were gone four hours."

"Oh. Yes. What do we owe you, Free?"

"What do you usually give?"

"How about fifty cents?"

That much? Plus all the wonderful reading? "Fine."

"Want to take Motley home with you?"

"Say, that'd be great. I'll guard him with my life. If there's a fire in the house he'll be the first thing I'll save."

Professor Ralph laughed. "Take him."

After that Free borrowed many books from Professor Ralph. Free was careful with them. For precious first editions he made slipcases out of newspapers.

From then on Professor Ralph had an eye out for Free in class.

They were studying Greek life before the time of Christ. Professor Ralph showed them photographs of the Parthenon, of the theatre at Epidamus, of the oracle at Delphi. He spoke of how it must have been in those olden times—a dazzling white temple set high on a rock, a crowd listening intently to a play by Sophocles, a stricken hero waiting for a verdict from the oracle. Professor Ralph dramatized the love affair of Paris and Helen. He described in detail the clever trick the Greeks used to get some of their soldiers inside Troy by means of a vast wooden horse.

Some mornings Professor Ralph couldn't wait to get to class to tell his students about those golden days. He came charging into the classroom, mouth already going, telling them about quixotic Socrates, who, while he might be considered a nuisance on the streets of Athens with his cynical questions, could at the same time be a hero saving the life of Alcibiades. Within moments Professor Ralph had the class lost in a life that'd taken place twenty-five hundred years before they were born. All their young faces glowed in the morning light. Sometimes Professor Ralph's glasses caught the forenoon light just right and made them flash like he had the eyes of Zeus himself. Professor Ralph paced back and forth, from the window to the frosted glass door. He rolled his head until his silver-blond hair fell to either side of his high forehead. And when the bell rang at the end of the hour, students filed out of his classroom floating a little off the floor.

One evening Free told Professor Ralph shyly that he had made up his mind to be a historian.

Professor Ralph was sitting in his favorite chair. "But your mother wants you to be a preacher."

"Preacher? Never. I want to travel to Greece someday and see all those places you talked about in class." Free found himself at ease. "You know, Prof, sometimes when you tell about those old days, it's like I'm really there. In the flesh. For a split second I sometimes see it all again. It's like a curtain parts for me, and there it is, people arguing over the price of vegetables in the marketplace, and donkeys crapping in the streets as they carry barrels of olive oil to the merchants. Once, the way you told it, I even saw where one of the straps on Alcibiades' sandal came loose, and how Socrates, seeing it, smiled to himself because he himself went barefooted. Really, Prof, for a minute there I really saw Athens. The sun shining on the white marble Parthenon . . . and then, blick, the vision shut off."

Professor Ralph's blue eyes glinted behind his glasses.

"Really, Prof."

"You know something, Free? You've got something most people never experience. The workings of a very good imagination."

The next time Free brought home his report card, in April, he just had to show Pa and Ma his mark in Ancient History. It had jumped from 78 to 96. Some of his other marks moved up too, geometry from 89 to 92, Latin II from 85 to 87. Though his English mark fell off a little, from 87 to 85.

That same week he went back to running to school again, seven miles up in the morning and seven miles back in the evening, though not behind Jack DeGreate's cab. Free decided he didn't need Jack's cab anymore.

Free was proud of his legs. At chapel time he'd noticed that lately the sloping muscles over his knees had filled out. His knees were at last as well shaped as those of the basketball players.

When Pa bought him a pair of tennis shoes, tan with white soles, Free began to glory in his running ability. What with his already having a wild imagination, he was being a true Greek.

Free ❦ 9

TANTE ENGLEKING DECIDED to move into town that next summer. She bought a house not too far from Grampa Alfredson's cement block house. It was painted a dark green.

One evening Pa and Ma and kids rolled into Bonnie to pay Tante a visit. The kids went along to play with Fredrika.

The first while Fredrika with her pointy nose showed them some of the things on her new place: a garden full of red tomatoes, a tiny pasture for Tante's jersey cow, the new white gate next to the barn. The barn was a little red town affair with a sliding door for the carriage. She even took them up in the haymow where up in the cupola the pigeons were cooing like soft mouth organs.

While they were up in the haymow Free looked around for some place where he might lie down with Fredrika. Fredrika caught his look and quick hurried them all down the ladder.

Just about then the neighbor's dog came over and challenged Fredrika's dog, Shep. Shep got roaring mad and chased them off his new property. Everett and Albert and Jonathan thought the dogs' roaring at each other a lot of fun and ran out to help Shep.

It gave Free a chance to ask Fredrika what was the matter.

"Nothing," Fredrika said. "Except that I know for sure I mussent do it now."

"Why not?" Free closed the white gate behind them.

"I can get a baby now."

He took hold of her hand. "How do you know that for sure?"

Fredrika let him hold her hand but she wouldn't pinch back. "My sisters told me that when you get hair there it's too dangerous."

Hair. He could just see it. A couple of weeks before his folks had taken a trip to Bigelow to visit Aunt Joan, leaving Free behind to watch over things. The moment Pa drove off the yard, Free wanted to do something special, something wild and forbidden. He remembered Ma had that secret doctor's book in her bedroom. He went into the darkened bedroom and let up the shade. He found the book, a thick green volume, in the bottom drawer of her commode under a pile of nightgowns. Paging through it he found a calendar for the whole year. It was called Schedule for Births. Below it one could make notes. He saw his own birthday circled, the sixth of January, with a question mark over the third of January. There was no circle for Everett, but there were circles for Albert and Jonathan. Looking across he saw that the fifth of April was circled too with his name written in it. Nine months. So. Ma having her babies when she did hadn't been so innocent after all. She planned doing it ahead of time. He paged further through the doctor book. At last he found what he was really looking for, pictures of a woman's business as well as of a man's tool. In the case of the woman it showed the hair like long grass on an Indian mound. It showed the long opening. There was a cross-section picture of the vagina. Free was surprised to discover the vagina was curved. Hey. When he was hard it was as straight as a ruler. He read on. The doctor book said the average length of a grown man's penis was six inches. Free remembered Sherm saying he should pull on it five minutes a day if he wanted a big one. The cross-section picture of the male penis showed hair too.

Anyway Fredrika had hair and all he had was some longish fuzz. He whispered in the dark, "Let me touch it once."

"No. Once you get your hand in my pants I'll give in."

"Please."

"No." Fredrika looked around wildly. "Let's go sit in the glider and rock a while."

Free thought, all right.

They ran across the yard and stepped onto the glider. It was darker under the trees. Free drew at her to sit on his side, but she shook him off and took the seat across from him.

"If you push with your feet," Fredrika said, "this way, on the floor of the glider, you get a nice easy ride back and forth."

The ride in the lawn swing was soothing. He helped her pump the glider until it began to rock noisily in its grasshopper frame; then quick hopped over and sat beside her.

"That ain't fair," Fredrika said.

He placed his hand on her belly. "Please."

"Oh, all right. You can feel me through my bloomers. But not inside it." Fredrika sat as quiet as a waiting cat.

After a while Free was quite surprised to find he had a pretty good one in his new overalls. "Let me," he said.

"No."

"We tried once."

"That was when we was just kids."

"I can't make seed yet."

"How do you know?"

Maybe Fredrika was right. Wouldn't that be something if he and Fredrika had to stand up before the whole congregation and confess having broken the seventh commandment, and then, after that, have their baby baptized.

They pumped the lawn swing smoothly back and forth.

"Are you sure?" Fredrika asked.

"About what?"

"What you just said, that you can't make seed."

"Unless a little pee can make babies."

Fredrika gave him a loving push. "You silly."

"Let me just lay on you at least."

"No. I know you. You'll sneak it in. Besides, the kids'll see us."

"Sit on my lap then."

"Oh, all right." She slid up into his lap.

Free hugged her.

"What a funny bump you got there," she said.

"You got a funny bump there yourself," he said.

"That must be my tailbone."

"It sure is sharp. It pokes even."

"You silly."

Free cradled her up a little higher on his lap. At the same time he managed to unbutton his fly under her. When he released his third leg, it snapped out like a jack-in-the-box.

"You're sure doing a lot of fussing under me there."

He helped her resettle on his lap. "Is that better?"

All of a sudden she got excited. "Where is it? Where have you got it? You haven't slipped it into me, have you?"

"No." Disgusted with her for being such a nervous silly, he gave her a good shake to settle her down.

"Where is it then?"

"It's standing up between your legs there."

She felt around. "Oh. All right. That's better. Now to make sure we keep him right where he is." She clamped her legs together.

Free liked it that way.

They helped each other rock the lawn swing. Every time she pushed down on the floor it felt better and better between her legs. Pretty soon the soft flesh inside her thighs began to hurt him very sweet. The happy cries of his playing brothers vanished. He felt thick. He could hardly see beyond the end of his nose. All of a sudden he felt he just had to help her rock the lawn swing harder. She seemed to know what he wanted and helped all she could. She made the movements of the insides of her legs as nice as she could for him. And it was like a horse had got under him, and then like the horse had got inside him, and then the horse made him buck up hard and high a couple of times, and then Fredrika grabbed hold of him.

"I can feel your pulse there!" she cried. "My, it's so funny."

Free fainted away for a few seconds. No wonder Gramma liked fainting. It was sweet to feel that way. Sometimes on the yard at home, after he'd been bent over for a while picking weeds, if he stood up too quick, he'd faint away for a second too. It'd been scary to feel that way those times, but it had been nice too. Yet that kind of fainting was nothing like this new kind of fainting. It was a silver honey thing.

"Nope. You can't make seed yet," Fredrika said.

Free ❦ 10

FREE HOPPED ABOARD Tip and galloped her up the road to get the mail. He was anxious to see how the Cubs came out in Old Man Hopkins's Sioux City *Journal*. For the first time in years the Cubs were in the first division and had a chance to win the pennant. Charley Root and Sheriff Blake were pitching great ball. Fat stubby Hack Wilson with his long bat was hitting home runs right and left. If they walked Hack, they had to face Old Hoss Stephenson, who was a hard man to get out. It was the campaign of 1926 and the Cubs were coming.

Free had to make several passes at their mailbox with Tip before he could get her close enough to reach down and get the mail out. Tip always kept shying away; and she did it on purpose too.

He next picked up Old Man Hopkins's *Journal*. The *Journal* favored the Cubs and when they won they always headlined the game. When there was no wind out he could safely unroll the folded paper and open it a crack for a peek at the sports section.

He parted the paper and read the sports headline backwards, slowly. "0-1, hitter-one pitches Root." Hey. "Root pitches one-hitter, 1-0." Old Charley Root had done it again.

He opened the paper further and read on. Root had struck out ten Pirates. Only Big Poison Waner had got a hit off him, a single up the middle. Too bad Gabby Hartnett had called that certain pitch. If he'd have called a curve instead of a high hard one, Root would've had a no-hitter. Free visualized how the other pitch would have gone. Just as Big Poison started to swing, the pitch would've broke in on his fists and he'd have missed it. "A no-hitter after all!" What a victory. Now the Cubs were only six games behind the St. Louis Cardinals. The Cubs still had time to catch the Cards.

"Go to it, Cubs, you can do it," Free whispered.

Tip rippled her hide under him, and he awoke to where he was. Carefully he folded up the paper again so it wouldn't look as if it had been tampered with. Old Man Hopkins was a tough old nut and if he ever found out what Free was doing, he'd tell Pa it wasn't a favor anymore to get his mail for him.

Coming up past the Hopkinses' grove and then even with their orchard, he spotted several trees full of red apples. He considered hopping over the fence and filling his pockets with them, until he spotted Old Man Hopkins rocking on the front porch. The old man was looking straight at him. Beside the old man sat his wife and daughter, also rocking away. Both women were wearing sunbonnets. Old Man Hopkins and his wife were an odd cross-grained couple. Mrs. Hopkins was almost a foot taller than the old man. But she was scared to death of him. Old Man Hopkins was worse than Napoleon. None of his three boys had ever had a date yet. He kept them home and worked them like slaves. And Pearl, the daughter there, who was pretty, had never even left the yard to go to church, where she might have met some nice young man. Pa'd said that someday that family was going to explode into a tragedy. As the three on the porch rocked away, Free could feel them looking him over. He pretended everything was all right though, and casually rode up to the auxiliary mailbox and cussed Tip when she tried her shying tricks and hooked a bare toe in her ticklish parts until she bucked over far enough for him to whip the Hopkins mail in the box. As he pushed the *Journal* in, he was pleased to see that it looked pretty much uncracked.

"Git, Tip."

In a moment Tip began to rock in her pretend gallop and they headed for home. Tip sure hated work.

When he got back to the yard Pa was waiting for him by the house gate. Pa reached for the mail.

"No letters," Free said. "Just some junk. But the Cubs won, 1-0."

Pa gave him a half smile. "They did, huh."

Free began to worry about that half smile. Something was up. It had to be about his schooling.

Pa looked through the mail himself. "No letters all right. And that's too bad. Nah, you better get down off that horse and put her away. Your Ma and I want to talk to you."

Ten minutes later Free was sitting with Pa and Ma around the kitchen table.

Ma began it. "Well, Free, we fully expected to hear from Professor Ralph in today's mail. As you know, we'd told him to look for a part-time job for you to help pay your way through school this coming year. Because again we just simply can't afford to pay board and room for you."

"But I told you I'd run to school again. Running is good for pitchers."

"Naw," Pa said, "that's not the answer. Because we can't afford to pay your board and room during January and February when its too cold for you to run to school. We're worse off than ever, son."

Ma said, "Your mark in History came up, but your other marks really haven't improved much."

"Oh, Ma."

"So we've got to wonder again if you should go to school at all."

Stay home? My God no. He wanted to be a great man someday.

"What I don't understand," Ma went on, "is how our Principal Ardman in Bonnie can say you're bright, when at Western you're only getting average marks."

"Because I got all those old farts in my class to buck," Free said, "and they run off with the top marks. Let alone all the old hens in my class."

"Old hens?" Pa cried, mouth falling open. Pa seemed a bit interested in that item.

Free said, "You know that Henry Brunstein I stayed with? Well, he's going to sail right by me this year and graduate next spring."

Ma sat with her hands folded in her lap. She was wearing a gray dress and a blue apron. She was sorely perplexed about her son. "'Old farts,' he says." For Ma to use a dirty word was worse than hearing Domeny swear from the pulpit.

Free went on. "Yes, and that Alfred Dempsey, why, he's at least five years older than I am. And he's bright to begin with."

Ma looked up. She drilled a look straight at him. "I'm going to ask you again. Remember, much will depend on your answer. Your whole life, perhaps." A deep sigh lifted her head. "Free, is it really your wish to go to school?"

"Yes."

Ma sighed once more. "All right. That settles that. Alfred?"

Pa took up the sticky thing then. "Son, you know I'm awfully busy just now. But just to make sure we're doing the right thing by you, I'm going to crank up the old Buick and you and I are going to Hello yet today to see if we can't find you a part-time job somewhere so you can still go to school this fall. Get your duds on and let's go."

They first called on Professor Ralph. Prof had no leads for them. Next they called on Reverend Lodge. Domeny couldn't help them either. Next they called on the mayor of Hello. No help there either.

Pa and Free sat in the car awhile, thinking it over, wondering where they could try next. Pa got out his pipe and lit up. His sharp teeth made grinding noises on the pipestem. "Boy, I don't know. Unless you got an idee."

Free couldn't think of anything. Instead he found himself feeling good about the great Cub 1-0 victory yesterday.

Pa refilled his pipe. "Now if I had this problem in our hometown, just who would I go see?" Pa blew out a couple of smoke rings. "Why, heck, of course." Pa's gray eyes opened that he hadn't thought of it before. "Why, go see Chauncey Mack. Bankers know everything that's going on in town. A doctor may know more about the hind end and how poorly it sometimes works, and the domeny may know more about the heart and how depraved it can be, but the banker knows even more. He has to, before he can make a loan." Pa smiled at Free. "Son, you just sit tight here a minute." Pa clapped out his pipe, and got out and strode up the street to the First National Bank of Hello.

Pa was back in ten minutes. He was smiling one of his victory smiles. "Maybe we're in luck after all. There's a fellow here by the name of Bart

Westham who runs a dairy. He's just had a bad operation and can use an extra milker. I know you ain't the best milker in the world, but if you'll just put your mind to it, you can be good enough to get by. Shall we go look him up?"

Free felt like the criminal who, after first being condemned to life imprisonment, is suddenly, miraculously, given a light sentence. "Let's go."

Bart Westham lived on the southeast edge of town with wife Emma and daughter Dodie. Bart had forty acres of land, and the house and dairy barn and the other outbuilding were all brand-new and painted white. A grove of cottonwoods stood powerful in the night pasture east of the house. It was a fancy place.

Pa pulled up at the front gate and shut off the motor. "No wonder the fellow is in hock at the bank."

A man came out of the kitchen door on the run. He was lean, had hollow temples, and flickering blue eyes. He had twisted, even brutal, lips. "Yes?" he demanded.

Pa reared back in his seat a little. Then with a look at Free, he got out of the car. Pa liked to stand up to his full height when he had something important to talk about. "I'm Alfred Alfredson of Bonnie. You Bart Westham?"

"Yes?"

"I heard you could use a part-time milker."

"I could, I could." Bart Westham looked from father to son and back again. "You mean him?" he then asked, pointing with his nose at Free.

"Yeh, my boy here. Free's going to be a junior at Western this fall, but I can't afford to send him. So he's got to work his way through. For his board and room."

"Him, huh? Yeh, I guess I can use him. But he's going to have to work. There's no room for laggards on a dairy. We milk five on five right on the dot. Twenty-six cows."

Pa whistled. "You and my boy here'll milk twenty-six cows twice a day?"

"I've got a hired man too. We get up at four-thirty in the morning. Finish milking by six, have breakfast, bottle the milk, then load it onto a flatbed truck. I always try to get the milk delivered by eight. That'll give your boy plenty of time to dress and get to school by nine."

"School's almost a mile away though," Free said.

Bart sneered. "What's a little walking."

Pa spoke up for Free. "Don't worry about him not being willing to walk." Pa's voice leveled off into near scorn. "He ran seven miles up and seven miles back from school last year."

"Oh."

"What about after school?" Pa asked.

"I want him to be home and ready to work by four. It takes an hour to feed the cows. By five on the dot we start milking. Finish by six. The Missus wants us to eat by six, sharp. Then we bottle what we've milked by seven. The Missus wants to finish up with her dishes about the same time we do. She's particular about the work load being fair for her too."

Pa was beginning to have misgivings about the job. "That's an awful lot of work for—"

"Take it or leave it."

Pa's neck turned red. Pa was the one fellow on earth a man should never interrupt. Pa glared at Bart; then remembered he had to think about his son and not his own feelings. "Course, the boy also gets a little spending money for all that work, don't he?"

"Not one red cent. Why, after my terrible operation, the hospital has its hand out ahead of the church for any kind of money I make. Let alone the bank."

Pa wheeled away from Bart. His knuckles were white. "Son, it's your game. You're pitchin' it. What do you say?"

Free looked squarely at Pa. "Ma says God gave me a talent. I'll take it."

Bart backed up a step. "Hey, wait a minute. Can you milk?"

"Try me," Free said.

"Can you start yet tonight?" Bart demanded.

"I didn't bring my overalls with."

"Well, what the hell then."

"Naw," Pa said, wheeling back toward Bart. "For now the boy comes home with me. School doesn't start until Tuesday and that's soon enough."

"If the job's still here."

"Wal, now," Pa said, "will it be? Or won't it be?"

"Well, all right. See you Tuesday then, kid. But mind. We all work hard here. Hard. Hard."

On the way home, Pa said, "I was almost of a mind to give that fellow a kick in the ass. High up."

Free was grateful for the thought. Compared to Bart Westham, Pa was a sweet man.

It was quarter to four when Free knocked on the kitchen door of the Westham house. He was carrying a suitcase.

"Come in."

Free entered. A fleshy woman with brown hair and blue eyes, wearing a green dress, stood at the sink washing some tea dishes. She had the neck of one who would be fat some day. Free said, "I'm your extra milker."

"Oh. And I'm Mrs. Westham." She examined him from head to foot, his hands the most. She was reserved in her manner. "Come, I'll show you to your room." She went up the steps sideways. She opened an oak door onto a big west room. The room was papered blue. With its white curtains tucked back it had a well-lighted cheery look. The floor was quarter-sawed oak and shone like neatly stored ingots of gold. There was a little walnut desk in a corner, a walnut commode, a huge brass bed, and a scattering of varicolored rag rugs about.

"I'm going to like this room," Free said.

"You'll be sharing it with Kaes Hinke, our hired hand."

A little girl entered the room behind them. She had the whitest blond hair Free had ever seen. And her blue eyes had the color of rainwater just barely touched with bluing.

Mrs. Westham turned around. "Dodie! My, but you scared me." Mrs. Westham laughed in apology. "Dodie has a way of sneaking up on one so silently one never knows she's there." Mrs. Westham caught herself being familiar with a stranger. "Dodie, say hello to Free, our new extra hand."

Dodie decided she liked Free and opened up like a large smiling flower. "Hello." She came forward and held out her hand.

Free was surprised at how firmly the little child gripped his fingers.

Mrs. Westham looked at an alarm clock on the stand beside the bed. "Come, Dodie. I'm afraid Free has to hurry into his work clothes. In ten minutes your father will be wanting him in the barn." Mrs. Westham gave Free a half smile and pushed Dodie out of the room ahead of her and closed the door behind them.

Free quickly emptied out his suitcase, undressed, put away his good clothes, and slipped into his work clothes.

Out in the barn Kaes was already feeding the cows ground grain. Kaes was a burly fellow with a curl of dark hair showing under the bill of his engineer's cap. He gave Free a head-on blunt look. He took a watch out of his bib pocket. "On time, I see."

"What do you want me to do?"

Kaes liked the question. "Go up in the mow and throw down some alfalfa. I'll yell when to quit."

Free climbed into a huge hall of a mow half full of alfalfa. The alfalfa had been cured to perfection and smelled like expensive tobacco. Pigeons cooed in the two white cupolas above.

Free peeled off layer after layer of alfalfa and tossed them down through the hole in the mow floor.

"Enough!" Kaes called up from below.

Free climbed down. "What next?"

"Get a pail of water and wash off the cows' tits. Bart's awful particular about having his milk clean. If he finds even as much as one speck of dirt in the felt strainer, he goes into a mortal rage."

"Where is the boss?"

"Uptown fighting off the bank. He'll be along soon enough. I for one work best with him not around."

As Free washed the cows' tits, Free noted that all but three of the twenty-six cows were black-and-white Frisian-Holsteins. The odd three were cream-colored Jerseys. The twenty-three Frisian-Holsteins had great low swaying bags while the Jerseys had tight high bags. "Kaes, why the three Jerseys?"

"The Frisians give you volume, the Jerseys give you cream. Leave it to Bart to get the most out of his feed."

Promptly at five Kaes got the milk pails and the cans. He assigned several cows to Free. "We try to milk them in the same order every night. You can sometimes get an extra month of milk out of a cow if you milk her twelve hours apart right on the dot.

"What if the cow ain't in the mood to give on that same exact dot some night?"

"On this dairy the cows are machines. They don't even have names. They have numbers."

"But suppose she's in heat some night?"

"Bart Westham's cows are never allowed to come into heat unless Bart presses a button." Kaes quirked a smile at Free as he handed him a one-legged stool. "Bart goes by the book. He keeps a breeding record and once a cow's number gets into that, she gets the bull's syringe when he says and not when she wants it." Kaes picked up his own one-legged stool and selected a cow. "And now, no more talking until we're done."

Free settled beside his first cow. She had a white flank and black shoulders. Her bag hung swollen wider than her hips. Free liked her tits. They were as big as cobs, much bigger than the tits of Pa's Shorthorns. On each pinch a long squirt of milk hit the bottom of the pail with a good firm ping. Soon a froth of foam formed and then the squirts punctured down silently. Listening he noted that Kaes's squirts came faster and sounded fuller than his. Free speeded up.

By the time he tackled his cow's back tits his forearms stung. Milking twenty-six cows twice a day with even three men was going to be a killer of a job. He stripped a while with thumb and forefinger, until the ache ebbed away. There was one consolation though. All that milking would give him powerful forearms—the better to hit home runs with. Just like with his legs. They'd developed into powerful pistons from all that running he did the year before. Someday he was going to be a great athlete. Like the great Greeks were. From there he could also go on to being a great poet. Like Homer. Though where he was going to get the story for his first Iliad he didn't know.

Kaes got up from his cow. His pail was so full of milk with its thick head of foam it looked like a huge ice-cream cone. Using a strainer Kaes emptied it into a milk can. He glanced at Free. "Not done yet?"

Free shook his head. "I'm not used to such big tits."

Kaes nodded. "You'll get used to 'em. Just do a good job. Because as sure as sunrise the boss'll check your cows afters."

When Free finished his cow his pail was brimming full too.

Kaes looked around at him past a cow's tail. "Well, at least you're getting all the milk out. That's more than Bart usually gets out of her."

"I get along with cows. Mostly."

"Just don't marry 'em though. You know what the Bible says about that. 'And if a man lie with a beast, he shall surely be put to death; and ye shall slay the beast.' "

Free almost had to laugh. "That don't sound very fair to the beast." He settled beside his second cow.

"How so?"

"Why, it's the man that should know better, not the beast."

"No talking while we milk."

"Think its ever happened?"

"Plenty of times."

Free was shocked—until he remembered Floris Haber's confessions about what he did to cows, as well as Jake Young's stories about what he did to his sister Gertie, "Yeh, I suppose."

"What I can't understand though is what it says there in Exodus. I can understand a little about doing it with a heifer. It's always around you on a farm, at about the right height, and about the right slit shape, but to do it with a woman who . . . you know where it says there in verse 18, 'And if a man shall lie with a woman having her sickness, and shall discover her fountain' . . . uhh! that I can't understand at all."

"And what I can't understand at all," a brutal voice said above them, "is why by God some people feel they have to be talking while they're milking my cows."

"Oh, hi, boss," Kaes said pertly.

"Yeh," Bart said. He pointed his lips at Free. "How's the new kid doing?"

"So far he's got more out of your cow than you get out of her. But he's doing it slower."

Bart glared at Free. "Son, speed up your rhythm a little."

Free nodded mutely. He resented being called "son" by a stranger. That was for Pa alone to do.

Bart grabbed a stool and went after a cow farther down the line. His first squirts sounded like someone drumming on a tin roof.

There was no further talking.

The cows chewed first a bite of ground feed and then a bite of alfalfa.

The three men finished milking all twenty-six cows ten minutes ahead of time. Free milked eight, Kaes milked eleven, and the boss milked seven. The boss checked several of Free's cows and found them milked clean. He was pleased. He came at Free rubbing his hands. "A little faster and I think you'll do."

Free's forearms ached like they might have appendicitis.

Supper was eaten in a rush too. Bart couldn't eat much at any one time because of his operation, and he didn't want his wife to eat too much for fear she'd get fat, but curiously enough he liked seeing his help eat. He kept urging both Kaes and Free to take seconds and thirds, potatoes, roast, sweet corn, beets, dark bread with dairy butter and homemade plum preserves. He kept their glasses filled with chilled fresh milk. Free was used to skim milk and thought the unskimmed milk almost as rich as a malted milk. He could feel the cream in it heading straight for the sore muscles in his forearms. Bart, nursing his own small portion of meat and milk, and fighting down belches, had to smile at the way Free could eat. "That's it son. The human body can't run without gas either. So the more gas you take the harder you'll work."

Later, the boss decided that now that he had an extra helper he could lie down after supper a while. That left the bottling of the milk for Kaes and Free to do. It was tedious work.

Free asked, "What kind of operation did the boss have?"

"They cut away two-thirds of his stomach."

"What for?"

"Cancer."

Oh. Like Grampa Alfred Engleking.

"Yeh," Kaes went on, "all they left him was a corner of his stomach no bigger than a teacup. That's why he eats a little every two hours or so. Though otherwise his gut seems to be all right. Excepting that he breaks wind to beat the band. Sometimes when he lets go with one and I'm sitting under a cow, I'm sure a thunderhead's come up. When it's only the boss."

Free wondered what Mrs. Westham thought about her husband's gas problems. Free recalled then he hadn't heard Bart breaking wind while they milked. Perhaps Bart was only being polite that first day. Or else worried that it might disturb his cows.

"Yeh. In the hospital the nurses told him to fart away if he felt like it. Well, that was all the boss needed, because since then he's been breaking wind like he's out to break all records.".

Free didn't laugh. Something really had to be wrong with the boss to have a belly like that.

Free was too tired to study that night and crawled into bed early. He was sleeping like a rock when Kaes crawled in at ten o'clock.

Later something woke Free. For a few moments, as he rose up through clouds of sleep, he could not for a fact figure out what it was. The sound he was hearing had all the irregularity of Gramma's breathing. Then he realized what it was. Kaes was snoring in the bed beside him. And no wonder. Kaes was lying flat on his back with his legs wide apart and his mouth open.

Holy-ka-boly. What a racket. Kaes sounded like Pa's old four-horse gas engine with the compression cock left open after it had started firing and it was still a little flooded. Then Free remembered a story Sherm'd once told him. Sherm had once slept with a hired hand at Aunt Joan's house who'd snored like a wood stove with the draft left wide open. Well, Sherm knew what to do. Close the damper. The best way to do that with a human being was to reach over and pick up the fellow's third leg and drop the head of it square over the bunghole, thus shutting off the draft between the bunghole and the mouth. Not that a human being really worked like a stove, of course. Anyone who'd had a little physiology knew that much. But the very act of picking up the fellow's third leg and letting it drop between his legs was bound to wake him up a little and so get him to roll over and quit snoring.

Kaes's engine of a chest huffed along without missing a stroke. The continuous wet ruckling in Kaes's throat was just awful to listen to. At least sleeping with Gramma a fellow got a few thrills along the way. But this Kaes now, he snored along so steadily and so serenely that the listener almost went crazy with the sameness of it.

"Doggone it," Free thought to himself, "no man has a right to rob another man of his sleep, not even if he's the President of the whole United States."

Free didn't know how come he did it, but, smiling in the dark, he snuck his hand rustling along under the sheet, guessed just about where Kaes's third leg lay, slowly dropped his hand down and found the head of it, lifted it up and then let it drop. The head of it was almost as big as a turkey heart and about as firm. Then Free quick jerked his hand back.

Both of Kaes's hands came up waving as though they knew there was an enemy about and they had to fight the bastard off but really didn't know how. "Hey! What the! Leavemealone. What?" Then, snorting, Kaes woke up and clapped both hands over his third leg to protect it from further attack.

Free smiled to himself in the dark. Kaes probably didn't realize what'd woke him up. Free could hear Kaes lick his dry lips and then swallow to himself a couple of times.

Free wondered if Kaes had ever done it with his girl.

Suddenly Kaes sat up in the dark. He tapped Free on the chest. "What the devil was that for?"

Free still couldn't resist smiling. "You were snoring so hard I couldn't sleep. So I finally thought I'd just shut off your draft."

Kaes thought this over. Then he started to laugh. "You don't really think I got a draft like a stovepipe through me, do you?"

"No. But I did figure you'd quit that way. It was just a joke."

Kaes laughed some more in the dark. "Well, I tell you kid. Yes, I do snore. And I wisht to God I didn't. And when I marry Gretch someday, she's gonna complain to beat the band. So I tell you, maybe I could use a little training not to snore. So let's make a deal. If I wake you up because of my snoring, give my nose a pull, not my cock, to make me roll over. That way we'll be friends for life. Otherwise not. Okay?"

"Okay."

Then Kaes lay down again, on his side. He laughed some more a couple of times and then fell asleep. He didn't snore.

And Free soon fell asleep too.

The next Saturday was sunny. After the morning chores, Bart came out of the house rubbing his hands. He'd just had one of his little meals and felt pretty good. "Tell you what, boys. Those cottonwoods over there"—he pointd to the night pasture across the fence east of the house—"need to be thinned out. Not enough sun is getting through to the grass below. Why don't you two fellows get the crosscut and knock over a few of those big boys."

Kaes tipped back his blue engineer's cap. He stared across at the monster cottonwoods.

Free liked the great trees. He sometimes heard their murmurous cliddering in the night wind. Their slick leaves always looked bright, sunlight or moonlight.

"Besides," Bart went on, "a cottonwood burns pretty good in a furnace."

Kaes asked, "Have you ever split cottonwood, boss?"

"What?" Bart's lips hung open and wet. "Have I got me a mutiny on my hands?"

"Not at all, boss."

"Well then?"

Kaes said grimly. "We'll do her."

"It'll be good for the kid's muscles here. When I get through with him, he'll be the strongest man around."

Free thought: "Thanks a lot."

"Tell you what though, boss," Kaes said. "You personally better mark the trees you want felled. That responsibility I don't want."

"Oh, all right," Bart snarped. "I'm really needed uptown, but I guess I can do that a minute." On the run the boss got an axe and went around in the night pasture chopping blazes on the trees he wanted dropped.

With Kaes on one end and Free on the other, the crosscut saw moved into the cottonwood pretty good the first while. But some six inches in the sawing became hard labor. Both men sweated.

Free had tough legs, and after the first few strokes, learned to rock on them for the pull rather than using just his arms.

Kaes on the other hand, whose legs were too small for his big body, and who worked his end of the saw mostly with his powerful arms, soon began to puff and to heave.

At last Kaes said, "Hold up, kid," and let go of his end of the saw. He stood back to catch his breath. He took off his cap and wiped his face on his sleeve. "It may be the middle of September, but you'd never believe it the way I'm all ganted out."

Free stood back at ease.

The sun found a hole in the canopy of slick green leaves above Free and Kaes, caught them in a downstriking shaft of golden light. A cool breeze moved under the trees from the southeast.

"Damn, kid. You don't look like much, skinny like that, yet you surprise me."

Free smiled.

After a while, breath caught, Kaes signaled for them to go at it again.

A half hour later the big tree dropped. The trimming of the tree and the cutting of it into sections was an easy thing.

But the splitting of the logs turned out to be pure hell. A cottonwood had tangled fibers. Mostly because of its height the wind had a chance to twist it about. It was like God had knitted the cottonwoods rather than grown them. A fellow could get a split started in a log all right, but to separate the chunks from each other was another matter. Kaes and Free once had four wedges buried in a chunk, so tight in they couldn't pry them back out. They'd even driven smaller split pieces of cottonwood into the cracks as pries, and still couldn't separate the pieces of the chunk.

"By God," Kaes said, "if it wouldn't be that we've got those wedges lost in there, I'd say the hell with this chunk and let the boss burn it all in one piece in his dummed furnace."

They finally had to get the block and tackle to pull the chunk apart.

Around three o'clock Kaes decided they'd cut enough wood for that day. "Kid, go get the flat truck and haul this wood home. I'll go start the chores."

The boss had converted an old Model T Ford into a handy little homemade truck. He'd cut off the back seat and replaced it with a flatbed. He used it mostly to deliver milk.

As Free started up the old Ford, Dodie, the little girl, came running out of the house. "Can I go with?" Dodie had on a white dress and a white ribbon in her hair.

"Sure, hop in."

Free for the fun of it and to give her a little ride took several figure-eight turns around and under the big trees. Dodie sat beside him like a little Mother Goose princess.

She continued to sit like royalty in the front seat while he loaded up. When the flatbed was about full Free began to show off a little with how accurate he could toss a chunk of wood onto the very tip of the pile.

But he missed once and the chunk rolled off the pile and landed in Dodie's lap.

Dodie laughed. She took the piece and crawled onto the pile to put it in place.

"Careful," Free said. And he hadn't more than said it when the pile on her side began to cascade down, she with it.

Dodie landed with her legs apart, one on each side of the door. She first looked startled; then let go with a rising shriek.

Free quick lifted her up and took her in his arms. "Dodie!"

With her hands clasped tight on her tussy Dodie shrieked and shrieked.

"Little girl," Free said sympathetically.

"Give her to me!"

Free turned around. It was Mrs. Westham.

"Give her to me!" Mrs. Westham's face was dark with mother passion. Even her blue eyes were dark.

Free handed Dodie over.

Dodie continued to scream her head off. It was a strange kind of shrieking. There was in it the hint that Dodie was also mortified to have been hurt in a modest place.

Free stood with his hands hanging. He didn't know what to do.

"What did you do to her?" Mrs. Westham demanded.

"Dodie thought she'd help me pile up the wood and then the pile on her side slid down and she landed on the door."

"I bet." Mrs. Westham looked from Free to where Dodie had her hands. Mrs. Westham turned Dodie's bare thighs away from Free. Dodie's high shrilling slowly trailed off, became a low keening that tore at the heart. Mrs. Westham demanded again. "What did you do to her?"

Something clicked in Free's mind. Mrs. Westham thought he'd done it to Dodie. His pulse began to beat in his ears. What she was thinking was serious. If only Ma were present. Ma would believe him.

"Well?"

Free decided to trust Dodie. She'd given him that strangely firm handshake that first day when they'd met. "Ask her."

Mrs. Westham sneered at him. "But she's only a child. She doesn't understand what's happened to her."

"That she fell down? It sure's making her yell enough."

Mrs. Westham turned Dodie even farther away from him, as though she feared Free might intimidate Dodie even farther to keep her from telling the truth. "Dodie?"

The crying stopped.

"Dodie, can you tell mama what happened?"

Dodie sucked up a sob. "I fell down from the pile and hurt myself."

"You're sure now?"

"Fwee gave me a ride and it was my turn to be nice."

"Oh. Well. That's different." Mrs. Westham relaxed some. Though she continued to glower at Free. "After this, young man, I want you to make sure she has permission from me to go along with you. After all, Bart never allows her to ride with him on such jobs." Then Mrs. Westham lowered Dodie to the ground, and taking hold of her little hand, slowly stalked away with her.

Dodie had trouble walking. After a dozen steps Mrs. Westham picked her up again and carried her into the house.

When Free got back to the yard he had to quick go relieve himself behind the barn. Then he thoughtfully unloaded the wood next to the garage. He loved Dodie for telling the truth. The little girl could just as easy have made up a wild story. But he made up his mind to stay shy of her from then on.

At four he went to the barn to help Kaes with the feeding.

Kaes hadn't seen what had happened to Dodie. But he did see something amiss with Free's overalls. "You got a license to sell hot dogs?"

"What?"

"Your shop is open."

Free looked down. "Oh." He turned red. He buttoned up with numb fingers.

The next Friday afternoon around two-thirty Free was studying in the session room when he overheard Principal Hedges say to Professor Ralph, "You know, it's pouring buckets out there."

"Yes. Out back the water's already rising in the creek."

The two teachers were standing by the tall windows behind Free.

"I wonder if we should dismiss school early."

"You're the doctor."

The rain fell in wavering sheets. The water gods were having a hilarious water fight upstairs.

It was still raining buckets when school let out. Free took off his shoes and along with his books bundled them under his leather jacket. Then he ran home barefoot all the way, through town and the short distance down the highway to the Westham house.

Bart had the door open for Free as he jumped onto the porch. He spotted Free's bare feet. He seemed pleased. "Good boy."

Free changed into his work clothes. Just as he was about to step outside into the rain, his boss handed him a yellow slicker.

"Can't be having you catch cold on us."

"Thanks." Free shrugged himself into the slicker.

Bart looked at Free's feet. "Still going barefoot?"

"I don't have any rubber boots."

"Hmm. I suppose your feet are too big for my extra set. Well, tell Kaes I'll be along in a jiffy."

It rained all through milking. The rain fell on the barn roof with a steady unrelenting drenching sound.

Between cows Bart had a look out through the cobwebbed windows. "By the Lord, it had better quit pretty soon or there'll be all hell to pay around here."

Kaes nodded against his cow. "Cloud's got stuck somehow and can't move on."

"She tried to rain two days ago and couldn't. And now all of a sudden she's decided she can rain and is giving us a cloudburst."

Free nuzzled his head against his black-and-white cow. His wet feet had begun to dry off. The barn was a cozy place.

"There's no place for all that water to go but through our crik here behind the barn."

"It's gonna be rough all right," Kaes agreed.

It was still pouring buckets outside when they sat down to supper.

"There's some wet spots beginning to show in the ceiling in the attic," Mrs. Westham announced.

Bart took it personal. His loose lips pushed out. "This rain is completely unnecessary so far as I'm concerned. The subsoil was already sopped to begin with."

"I'll set out some pans," Mrs. Westham said.

Bart looked at Free across his soup. "Kid, good thing we don't have to deliver milk tonight."

Free nodded. For the first time the house began to feel cozy too.

The alarm went off at 4:30. It had stopped raining during the night. They dressed and went out to the barn with lanterns. Stars were out overhead. As Free was about to step into the barn, he saw glints of reflected light riding past the end of the barn. "Look."

The boss and Kaes swung up their lanterns. A flood was swilling past the end of the barn. And then they heard something. Farther out there was the low rushing sound of driving water.

Bart's lips curved down. "There go my fences."

As they milked, the sound of the water pushing and swilling through the low pasture became louder and louder. They could hear it over the sound of their milking.

When they got up from their last cow, Kaes spotted water coming into the barn through the open end of the gutter. All three men stepped outside to have a look. Shafts of yellowish-blue sunlight struck them in the eye.

"I told you," Bart said. "Both fences completely under."

Black water stretched all the way out to some cornstalks in a field an eighth of a mile away. Raging V's of water rushed down the middle of the flood. The near edge of the water sudsed against the footings of the barn.

"Can't let the cows out today."

"I guess not."

Free and the boss came back from delivering milk. By then the water had begun to subside some. The nearest fence posts in both fences of the pasture had begun to reappear. They'd all been bent west, out of line, by the force of the flood. They resembled two lines of an army slowly giving way before the onslaught of a powerful enemy. Some of the barbwires had snapped and lay coiling and twisting like unhappy hookworms suddenly dumped out into open light. The woven wire part of the fence was packed with flotsam: hay, weeds, sticks, dead animals.

After dinner that noon all three went out to have another look. The water was going down fast. The entire line of the two fences, buckled over flat, had begun to show.

"We got to straighten out those fences yet today," Bart said.

"What?" Kaes cried. "In all that water?"

"We got to take advantage of having the kid home today. Tomorrow's Sunday. And Monday it's school for him again."

"But working in that water is going to be deathly cold, boss. I haven't got hip boots. Besides, we're gonna get all cut up in that barbwire snaking around underneath in the water there."

"No help for it. I'm still going to ask you to do it."

"What? Me barelegged too?"

"Your skin won't spring much of a leak, like a boot will."

Kaes thickened around the neck and over the shoulders.

Bart clapped his hands together. "Let's get at it, you two. I'll keep you supplied with hot coffee. Take it or leave it."

Kaes and Free first cleaned the flood debris out of the woven wire. It was picky work with a fork and it was messy to do by hand. The worst part was to remove dead pigs and chickens caught in the squares. Next they grabbed hold of the iron fence posts one by one and together pulled them back upright. They moved slowly across the moving fan of water. The water came well up over their knees. It was bone-ringing cold. Soon their bare feet felt like clubs. The feel of the mud oozing up between their cold toes was like being like a baby again. Shin-bones stung like they might have turned to iron. The noses of both men turned blue.

The more deadly work involved the goddam barbwire. The barbwire was snarled in all directions. They had to fish around with their toes in the muddy brown water for a safe place to stand. They couldn't wear gloves in water and had to handle the prickly stuff barehanded. It took time. Their numb hands soon became crude tools too. The palms of their hands became pricked over with sores.

Bart came out with some warm lunch at three o'clock.

"Heard something uptown that's hard to believe," he announced. "The flood tore out that whole new million-dollar corner they built there, you know, on the other side of Sioux Center."

Kaes spoke around a mouthful of bread and cheese. "Boss, I just can't seem to get excited about that news."

"Not if I told you that Pete Barrow and his little boy got drowned in it?"

"No."

"Yeh. He was just crossing that low spot there, when a wall of water came along and caught up with his old Ford. The engine killed. The fellows in the filling station across from the corner saw him hoist his boy onto the roof of his car and then he himself climbed up. Pretty soon the water came up there too. The fellows in the filling station had to watch helpless. Didn't have a boat. Pretty soon they saw Pete tie his boy to his back with his suspenders and then try to swim to shore. They saw their two heads go bobbing down the flood and then lost sight of them."

Free remembered when Tina Hoffman had drowned in the Little Rock back home. It was after a cloudburst too.

Bart shook his loose lips. "Too bad. Pete was a good guy. Paid his bills on time. Went to church regular. It's the good ones who always go first, you know."

Kaes snuffed. His nose was thick. "I wonder what they'll say about Free and me when we die of pneumonia."

"Goddam Kaes, I can't go into that water with my bad belly."

"It could've waited."

"I haven't got time to wait, Kaes. In another year I'll be six feet under. And I can't leave my wife behind in debt up to here." Bart held his hand level with his nose. "Who'll feed poor Dodie after I hang up my pants for the last time?"

Kaes pointed to a pair of pincers he'd left hanging on the fence. "Free, hand me them, will you? We'll see if we can't finish this up before milking."

"If you guys'll keep working till five, I'll manage to feed the cows alone somehow."

"Done," Kaes said.

They finished by five.

When they walked back to the house they clumsed along like they'd been born clubfooted. Their thighbones felt like bars of cold iron. Free couldn't tell whether the stuff between his toes was mud or cowpies.

Free went home for Christmas holidays.

He was playing cob war with his brothers in the haymow, when Pa's face showed up in the opening of the hay chute. Pa'd climbed up the ladder just high enough to spot them.

"Say, Free."

"Yes." Free was hanging from the hay-carrier rail in the peak of the roof.

Seeing Free hang upside down above him with only an arm and a leg Pa had to smile. "Why, you monkey you." He shook his head in part admiration. "Look, I gotta go to town and get Dr. Fairlamb. Will you keep an eye on things?"

"Sure, Pa."

Ma was due. Free let go of his hold and fell some fifteen feet onto the hay below. "Do you want me to sit in the kitchen and watch there?"

"Wal, you might as well. But don't go into Ma's bedroom unless she calls you."

"I won't."

It took Pa but a half hour to get Dr. Fairlamb.

As Pa and Dr. Fairlamb passed through the kitchen, Dr. Fairlamb gave Free a crinkled smile. "It looks like your mother is going to be just on time to give you all a Christmas present."

"Make it a girl, Doc, will you?" Free said. "For Ma's sake."

"I'll try my best."

Pa also had a crinkled smile for Free. "Nah, you better go out to the barn and play with your brothers."

Four hours later, Pa called the kids in from the barn. He had on a great smile. It cut all the way back to his earlobes. "Okay, you kids."

Free was the first to be allowed to go see Ma.

Ma lay pink on her pillow, surprisingly so. She was smiling.

Dr. Fairlamb was fussing with some purple flesh in the chamber pot in the near corner. After a moment he brought the chamber pot outside on the back porch. There was a strange smell of pure urine in the bedroom. It had to be the baby's.

"Son," Ma said, "you have another brother." She sighed. "Yes, for some reason the Lord saw fit again not to bless this house with a daughter." She sighed a second time, from the depths of her bowels. "He must have some reason for this."

A little red face lay in the curve of Ma's arm. It slept so deep it was frowning.

"But isn't he lovely?" Ma said.

Free recalled the many times he'd helped the cows and hogs have their little ones. "It's all right?"

"A bouncing baby boy, as they say."

"What are going to name him?"

Ma wedged her gold head down in her pillow. She smiled a wide sweet smile of pride. "I think we'll name him Sherman."

"Uncle Sherm'll like that."

"Yes. And let's hope this little Sherman takes on the best of the two Shermans Gramma had."

Free stared down at his new little brother. He tried to envision its little corrugated matted brain and what it might be sensing. If Ma'd already given it titty, the picture it had of the world probably was that of a soft red Pike's Peak with a little white drop of snow on it.

Jonathan called from the kitchen. "Ma, can we see him too?"

Ma laughed like one who had a side ache. "Sure, boys. You're all my sweethearts." Ma was beginning to feel better by the minute.

It was the twenty-third, two days before Christmas. Little baby Sherman was a nice Christmas present all right. Already Free loved the pink little wrinkled baby.

And he loved little Sherman despite the fact that the baby's coming had been the cause for his having to take that job with Bart Westham. That had been the unsaid thing that August day when Pa and Ma had called him into the kitchen to ask him again if he really wanted to continue school. There always seemed to be some further reason behind the usual reason given.

The usual week of below-zero weather came along late in January. One morning it was twenty-six below when Free and Bart set out to deliver milk through town. The boss sat behind the windshield and had a warm motor underfoot to protect him from the Arctic northwest wind. But Free had to stand on the running board as they moved from house to house, holding on with one hand while with his other hand he refilled the wire carrier with six bottles of fresh milk and got ready to make the next delivery. The boss was always rushing against what he considered record time and wanted Free to jump off on the run before he'd even gotten the open flatbed truck stopped. Free didn't mind the running since it helped keep him warm a little, but his gray stocking cap didn't quite cover his ears, and his nose had no protection at all. There weren't enough hands to cover both ears and nose at the same time. His earlobes and nose stung for a while, then turned numb. Once he saw his boss look at him closely after a delivery.

Soon the milk bottles on the open truck began to freeze. Cream that had risen to the tops of the bottles, forming a solid gold section, began to push out like jack-in-the-box ice-cream cones.

Bart kept looking back at his freezing load. "Hurry up, kid! Get going. Frozen milk don't sell."

When Free ran to deliver a single bottle to the Brunstein door, Carrie happened to see him coming as she was looking out of her kitchen window. What his former landlady saw alarmed her and she ran to open the door for him. "Free, it's froze."

Free thought she meant the bottle of milk. He nodded; then saw she was looking at his nose. Numbly he raised a hand to his face. Through his leather mitten he could feel it. His nose was solid. It felt like the top of a ball peen hammer.

"You come into the house this instant and warm up, you hear?"

"I can't. The boss."

"That man! Everybody knows about him. Cruel. You come into the house this instant."

"I can't." The way she fed her family Free thought it was a case of the kettle calling the pot black.

She was so worked up she puffed shallowly. Her white cheeks had actually turned pink. "Well then, you wait right here a second." She scurried to her bedroom.

Bart blew the horn for Free to snap it up.

Carrie reappeared with a blue flannel shawl. Her light blue eyes glittered ice at Bart sitting outside in his truck. "Here, bundle this up around your face at least. Here, swing it twice around your face and then I'll tie it up in the back."

Free let himself be engulfed up to his eyes. The warm flannel right away felt good over his cheeks.

"There. That should help your nose a little." Then feeling the cold air on her skinny legs she closed the door against him, apologetically.

Free hustled back to the truck, leaping up on the running board.

Bart gave the blue shawl an outraged look; then snorted. "That dried-up old hen, sticking her beak into my business."

They finished ten minutes ahead of time. Free helped Bart carry in the empties.

By the time he got to his room and took off Carrie's blue shawl, his nose had thawed out. It was as red as a radish. And it hurt. He had to grind his teeth to stand it.

Free ❦ 11

FREE MANAGED TO keep up his marks fairly well. But he began to look so skinny that Professor Ralph became alarmed. And when Professor Ralph heard the story about Free freezing his nose and ears from neighbor Carrie Brunstein, he didn't like it at all. He wrote a note to Free's parents.

Pa immediately drove to Hello. He talked with Free; then with Bart Westham; then with Professor Ralph.

"Your boy is being maltreated there, Alfredson," Professor Ralph said. "Get him out of there or God knows what'll happen."

It didn't take Pa long to make up his mind. He hadn't liked Bart Westham in the first place. Also the cream checks had slowly improved. When Pa learned that Carrie Brunstein would be happy to have Free as a boarder once more, he drove back to the Westham yard and called Bart outside.

"Yeh?"

"I'm taking my kid away from you."

"You gotta give me two weeks' notice. At least until I can find a replacement for him."

"I'm taking him right now."

"I'll sue you."

"You do and I'll sue you for letting my kid get his nose froze while delivering milk for you."

"Oh, hell . . . all right. I'm gonna die soon anyway."

Pa helped Free get his things.

Free's second stay at Carrie's house turned out to be great. Carrie was still tight when it came to how much her husband could eat, as well as tight with herself. But when it came to Free and her pale little Sylvester with his lemon freckles, she wasn't. She splurged when it came to them. She pushed seconds and thirds on them until it came out of their ears.

Henry looked upon his wife's sudden liberality with a private smile.

Free was by now fifteen and some of the older boys in his class had taken a liking to him. What helped win them over was the way he'd handled Sam Ruffman.

One noon hour, during a pickup game of basketball in the gym, Free startled everybody by twice breaking up Sam's dribble and stealing the ball from him. Sam fancied himself as quite a dribbler. And he especially liked to show off when a certain Mabel James was present. Mabel didn't care a rip for Sam. Instead Mabel liked Free. Sam had grown into a powerful six-footer, with heavy calves and huge sloping shoulders. Except for slightly bowed legs and a low brow, he was a handsome physical specimen. Free was almost as tall, but was mostly a long stretch of bones.

Sam was so mad at being made a fool of that later on, when they were all showering together, he struck Free in the jaw. Free happened to be standing in the far corner of the marble shower stall. It was like getting cracked on three sides of his head at the same time. Free dropped to the cement floor. For a second he was only vaguely aware that Sam was standing over him like some victorious bull, and then that Sam, suddenly scared at what he'd done, had turned and left Free lie there.

Water spraying down out of the nozzle helped Free come to. It also helped him get mad in a hurry. He jumped to his feet, and skinny-limbed, shot out of the shower for Sam, yelling, "You goddam coward!" Sam with a red-faced smile had stopped at his clothes locker. But when Free came at him enraged with his clanking skinny bones, Sam bolted. He ducked out into the hall, yelling, "But Free, I ain't dressed yet!" Free kept going after him and Sam kept running. To the consternation of the girls standing on the sidelines in the gym, including Mabel James, the two raced around the basketball court stark baby naked, pintles bobbing, one mad bull chasing another red-faced bull around and around.

Sam finally took refuge in the boys' room, where he locked himself up in a toilet.

Wild laughter broke out everywhere. The boys especially went into hysterics when Sam begged somebody to please for godsakes bring him his underwear at least.

Free let Sam beller a while in his locked toilet. Later, cooling off, and seeing the humor of it all, Free relented and finally let Sam out.

Tony Streetman and Johnny Ralph were especially gleeful to see Sam humiliated, and they invited Free to join them after supper and bat around town looking for fun. Johnny was the young brother of Professor Ralph. The three of them checked on a deserted house where rumor had it Del and Jo and Flop and Nellie went screwing every night. They checked on a certain upstairs window where the blind was never drawn and a widow could be seen undressing at ten o'clock.

The boys usually wound up their prowling about at Jansen's Cafe. Tony and John took turns buying each other treats—a candy bar or a malted milk—and they always included Free.

Free had no spending money. He knew he'd lose his new friends if he didn't soon stand them to treats once in a while.

One day Free learned from two other boys, Arthur Cage and Bert Whiffler, that it was an easy thing to swipe Eskimo Pies from an ice-cream freezer Jansen had standing out in back of his cafe.

Free went along with Art and Bert a couple of times and stood watch to make sure Mr. Jansen wasn't coming while they snuck up the alley and raided the freezer. The best time to raid was when Jansen left his kitchen in back and went out front to take an order. Afterwards, running off into the dark of the public school grounds, under the same fire escape in which Art Cruellen had done it to Angie, they shared their spoils, two Eskimo Pies each.

It was kind of a lark to raid an outdoor freezer and get away with it. It wasn't much different from raiding Ma's pantry for raisins, or swiping a watermelon from Sam Young's melon patch. It was a little like young Indian braves raiding another Indian village for their horses. Yet Free felt guilty about it.

One night Tony and Johnny didn't ask him to join them. Free knew right away why. It was not very nice of him that he never treated them back. Well, too bad. But he'd be damned first before he'd tell them how poor his folks were.

Walking the streets alone, Free wondered if he shouldn't steal some candy bars and then go around and treat his friends Tony and Johnny with them. Art and Bert sometimes bragged that they'd also stolen candy bars inside Jansen's Cafe, right under Jansen's nose. And if a man thought about it, you know, there really wasn't much difference between swiping an Eskimo Pie out back and stealing a candy bar out front. Both were done on a dare. And it would be for a good cause. He wanted to be nice to his friends. He'd been a lone wolf most of the way through Western so far. Since the days of Larry Grey at Rock No. 4 county school, he'd had no real chum to share secrets with. He hadn't even told anyone yet about that sweet fit he'd accidentally had with Fredrika in her glider. Or about the times he'd shook hands with his third leg when all by himself.

Jansen took the Sioux City *Journal* and usually had it on hand for his customers to read with their coffees. Free sometimes asked Jansen if he couldn't read it too. He wanted to keep an eye on the Cubs, Free said, to see how they were doing during spring training. Jansen told him to go ahead.

The guys liked Jansen. He was a blond fellow with graying hair, about forty, slightly bent, steady, with a kindly tolerance for any kind of story, clean or dirty. He sometimes treated a hungry student to a malted milk. It happened several times that Free was among those he treated to a candy bar. Jansen kept a very neat shop and was known to have quite a good memory for names and prices.

Free finally hit on a scheme on how to steal, no, borrow the few candy bars from Jansen, which he'd pay back later when he had the money.

Jansen usually kept his candy bars in a glass case on the left as one entered the cafe. The sliding door on the back side of the case was mostly left open. Free selected a *Journal* that was still fairly fresh and stiff. First he spread the sports page out over the candy case and pretended to be reading it as just someplace, anyplace, to be leaning on. Young fellows were always leaning over things, or against them. Presently, as though tiring of that stance, he propped the paper up on the left side by holding it up stiff from the right side with his right hand. It didn't surprise him to find that his face and his left hand were completely hidden from Jansen out in back or from anybody else in the cafe. Sure he had it arranged perfect, Free with his left hand reached over the edge of the candy case and selected two O'Henrys and pocketed them. For a couple of minutes more he pretended to be absorbed in the sports section, and then, apparently finished, folded up the paper and went over and placed it on the counter near the cash register where Jansen usually kept it. And walked out.

Overjoyed, at the same time stunned by his own daring, trembling, he began looking for his two chums Tony and Johnny. Young Indian braves must have felt the same way after they'd crept into the enemy camp and had counted coup on a sleeping chief or had stolen a chief's favorite war pony.

Free found Tony and Johnny checking out the deserted house where Del and Flop were busy polishing their canes with Jo and Nellie.

"Hi, been looking all over for you," Free said.

"Hi."

"Say, ain't it about my turn to treat?"

"No. Not really."

"Yes it is. Here." Free handed them each an O'Henry.

"Thanks." They unwrapped one end of the bar and bit off a chunk. "Where's yours?"

"I already had mine."

Tony and Johnny gave him veiled looks. But they said nothing.

Free managed to treat Tony and Johnny two more times. And they treated him to candy bars in turn. He felt he was back in their good graces again.

One Thursday evening, after Young People's Meeting, Tony and Johnny went their way while Free drifted off to Jansen's Cafe.

A dozen or so young fellows from his church were having malted milks at the main counter. They were joshing each other, and ribbing Jansen, and trying to top each other's stories.

Free said hi and after a moment went over and selected the stiffest *Journal* there. It turned out that even the freshest-looking paper was pretty limp. He was going to have trouble making it stand up on one side. He was about to spread the *Journal* out over the candy case when he was startled to see that a new advertising display had been set out on top of the candy case. Free stared at it a moment. It showed a rosy-cheeked boy eating a dish of Hello Creamery ice cream. The Hello Creamery ice cream was the best around, as rich as gold almost. After some hesitation Free decided to use what was left of the top of the candy case for his operation. He folded over a corner of the sports page and hooked it over the top of the display. It worked. It helped hold up the limp paper on that side. He stared down at the paper, making his eyes move back and forth as though reading hard about the Cub prospects for the coming year, while with his left hand he reached around the side of the candy case and dipped in and borrowed two O'Henrys and then dropped them into the near pocket of his leather jacket.

"What are you doing there?"

Free's left hand turned to stone. Instinctively, like a child that'd been caught, he said, "Nothing." Then he wished he hadn't said it. He'd been caught flat out.

Jansen was standing on the other side of the candy case and was staring at the pocket into which Free'd dropped the candy bars. "What did you just do there?"

A nervous silence spread through the cafe.

Jansen continued to stare down at Free's pocket. His blue eyes slowly turned sad.

Free decided to pretend that he was buying the candy bars. He folded up the newpaper and brought it over to the cash register. He pulled out the two candy bars and placed them on the rubber pay mat. Then he began to search through his pockets for the money. His fingers turned damp.

Jansen followed him and took up his position behind the cash register. He watched Free looking through his pockets a moment. Then he said, "You haven't got the money, have you?"

Free could feel the eyes of the young folk bombarding his left cheek. He was surprised to hear himself, his own voice, say quite firmly, "No, I haven't I see."

Jansen stared at him. After some thought, with a flick of a look at all the eyes watching them, he said, "Well, in that case we better put them candy bars back where they came from." Jansen picked them up and went around to the other counter and put them back in the candy case.

Free shrugged. "Okay."

At that the boys along the counter went back to their joshing around.

As Jansen came back past Free, heading for the back of the cafe, Jansen whispered, low and quick, "Go outside and I'll meet you around in back."

"All right."

"Do it. Now." Jansen then sauntered toward the kitchen.

Free lingered around a moment longer. He thought: "What will Ma say? Worse yet, what will Pa do? And even worse than that, what will all my cousins back home say?"

Free left then and went around in back. He had to walk past the very freezer from which Arthur Cage and Bert Whiffler had swiped their Eskimo Pies.

Jansen let him in through the back door. Jansen was careful to lead Free to the far corner of the kitchen, well out of sight of the boys out front. Jansen looked

Free in the eye, then placed both hands on his shoulders. "Just how many candy bars have you taken so far from that case?"

Free knew exactly. Six.

"You know I can call the constable and have you put in jail for this, don't you?"

"Yes."

"Well, then?"

"Six."

"Are you sure?"

"Yes."

"Why did you take them?"

Free was ashamed to tell Jansen that his folks couldn't afford to give him spending money. "I didn't eat any of those six myself, you know."

Jansen could hardly believe that.

"Yes, I gave them away. To my friends."

Jansen stared at him.

"You see, my two friends, Tony and Johnny, they're always treating me. But I couldn't treat them back. I almost lost them as friends once, until I took those six bars and gave them to 'em."

"My God." Jansen's eyes became very big and blue.

Free had the feeling that all this was happening to some other fellow. While the real Free, Alfred Alfredson VII, had departed his body and was riding in the air above it, about a dozen feet off the ground. "I'll be glad to pay you for those six. Somehow. I meant to pay you for them anyway sometime. And would've. When I got the money."

Jansen chewed to himself. "Well, all right. I'll let you work out those candy bars. You come around after school tomorrow and I'll fix you up with something to do. Six times five is thirty cents. What I'll do is give you fifteen cents an hour."

"But I can't tomorrow. Tomorrow is Friday and right after school I always run home for the weekend."

"Run? home?"

"Yes. I did that most of last year. Seven miles up and seven miles back." Free allowed himself a smile. It was only a little smile of pride though. "I had to. It was the only way I could go to school. Pa said it was that or nothing."

"I didn't know that." With his thumb and forefinger Jansen tugged at his lower lip, then doubled it up in thought. "Maybe I'm being too hard on you."

"No no. Actually, I really should work more for you than thirty cents' worth."

"You mean, you took more than six bars?"

"No no. I mean, I should also get punished a little for having borrowed them from you without your permission."

"Oh."

"I want to do double the work for you. But please, for godsakes, don't tell my folks."

Jansen gave his lower lip such a pinch it turned white over the edge of the fold. "About that now . . . Well, son, that's what I meant when I said maybe I'm being too hard on you. You see, I've already told your folks."

Free almost passed out. "You have? Oh my God."

"Yes. You see, I always know exactly what I've got in each showcase. So I keep accurate tab on how much each display makes. You're right you only took six. That's all I've missed out of that case. And I actually saw you taking them the second time you tried. And God, kid, I didn't know what to do. You, of all the kids to come in here, I never expected you to be the one. You're one of the nicest-looking kids I know. So I didn't know what to do. For one thing if I let you go on, you could very well drift into becoming a thief. Anyone can drift into thievery. Even Jesus Christ. That's why He had such patience with thieves. Even whores. So I had to figure out a way to stop you before it became too late. That's why I finally called your folks long distance."

"Long distance!"

"Yes. Your mother answered. The first thing she said was. 'Thank you very much for calling us instead of the constable.' Then she said, 'But the boy must be punished. He must be given a good stomp to get him back on the true path. So this is what I want you to do. Catch him in the act. In front of his friends even, if it can't be avoided. And then I want you to have a good heart-to-heart talk with him.' I told her I thought that a little strong, that it might drive you into being worse. Get revenge. But she said, 'No, I want him to have that stomp so as to scare him back into his senses. Meanwhile, on my end of it, I'll get down on my knees and pray to God.' "

On her knees.

"Yes, son, you've got a good mother."

"Ma knows then."

"Face up to it. And next Monday when you come back to town, drop by after school and we'll work something out."

Free ran home Friday after school. He ran hard to punish himself.

He entered the kitchen puffing. He was so pooped out he hardly had it in him to act sheepish. "Hi, Ma."

"Hello, son." Ma was leaning over the ironing board. She gave him a steady blue look. Then with a glance at the clock, she said, "I think Pa's expecting you to do the chores alone tonight. That'll give him a chance to finish the west forty and so catch up a little."

"All right, Ma."

Ma tipped up her iron a moment. "Your father doesn't know. I thought it best for now that he didn't."

Free whitened. "Thanks, Ma."

"Yes." She went back to her ironing.

Free changed clothes in a rush. He was almost wild. Pa didn't know yet. That meant his brothers didn't know either. Nor his many cousins. Nor the domeny or the people in church. Maybe it was not going to be so bad after all. He hurried to do the chores and the milking.

"Man, from now on I'm never even going to look at something that ain't mine," he whispered to the real Alfred Alfredson VII still riding in the air some dozen feet above him. "Not even if it means taking no more raisins from Ma's pantry."

The next day Ma asked him to hitch up Tip. Everett and Flip had to go to catechism and she had to get groceries.

After Ma had finished buying the groceries at Tillman's Mercantile, she went over to the millinery a minute. Free lingered behind in Tillman's Mercantile.

After a moment Tillman came around from behind his counter. His usual smiling face was strangely grave. "Free, can I talk to you a minute?"

"Sure." Free knew what that meant. Ma had talked it over with Tillman. Ma respected Tillman's judgment.

"Come with me in back then."

Free followed Tillman into a little storage room.

Tillman put his foot up on a store box. "First off, Free, let me tell you that there are only four of us who know about this. You, your mother, Mr. Jansen, and myself. I was brought into this thing by your mother. She was afraid of your dad's wrath, that he might order you to stay home and work on the farm no matter what kind of a talent you might have."

Tillman looked through the door to make sure no one had entered out front. "Also, she wanted to know if I'd ever caught you stealing a candy bar from me. Or ever suspected that you might have. I told her, never. Not once. I told her I was as shocked as she was to learn of your taking candy bars in Hello. Now tell me, honestly, just why did you take them?" Tillman reached out as though to lift up Free's chin; then, at the last second, seeing that Free was going to stubborn up against it, changed it to the friendly gesture of roughing up his shoulder a little. Tillman had wide heavy hands.

That Tillman, whom he admired so much as a great man in church, should know about this bad thing about him was almost too much to bear. Free looked down at the floor. The smell of the oiled floor mingled in with the odor of ripe bananas. The real Alfred Alfredson VII rose a couple of feet higher in the air above him. Alfred Alfredson VII was watching him with an air as if he was about to disown him.

"I understand if you don't want to talk about it, Free. In fact, I sort of like that in you. It means you have pride. Which in turn means you are, fundamentally, an honest boy. Which means further there must've been something special eating at you to make you take those candy bars."

Special, yes. All of a sudden the real Alfred Alfredson VII came down and snapped back inside the skin that was him. And he broke down and cried.

Tillman was careful not to touch him.

After a bit Free told Tillman what he'd told Jansen, that he felt he should treat his friends if they treated him.

"So that's it." Tillman whacked his right hand off his left hand. The gesture made a loud report, like someone popping a paper bag. "I knew it had to be something like that."

Free could just barely make out Tillman through his tears. What a wonderful fellow. Free wished Pa was in on this thing then too. It would have been wonderful if Pa, knowing, had said something like Tillman to show he understood too.

About then Ma came back. She didn't look at Tillman to see if he'd had a chance to talk to Free. She just simply said, "I don't like those new flapper styles at all. That Jazz Age. It's as if some nutsy street dandy created those hats. So I guess I'll just have to make do with the old one." She raised a hand to the hat she had on. It was her old blue Gainsborough. She shook her head a little at her sad lot when it came to hats. The imitation pink poppies on her hat rattled like old dried rose hips.

Tillman shook his head too and smiled. He turned to Free. "Would you do me a favor? I promised Old Lady Kolder I'd bring her groceries over this afternoon. Poor soul, she's got the rheumatism pretty bad this spring."

"Sure." Free knew Tillman wanted a word in private with Ma. "Where are they?"

Tillman picked up a heavy cardboard box from behind the counter. "You know where she lives?"

"Sure. Down the block across from Tante Engleking."

While Free delivered the groceries Ma and Tillman had their talk.

On the way home, Ma said, "Boy, boy, if I'd only known."

"I'm sorry, Ma."

"And at the same time I don't want you to feel ashamed about how poor we are."

"I'm sorry."

"All right, son, I accept that. But remember, from now on sorry is as sorry does. For all of us."

On Monday morning early, while Pa was out in the barn harnessing the horses and the kids were dressing upstairs for school, Ma said, "Free, before you go, come here with me a minute."

Free knew what she wanted. A breakfast of cornbread and syrup lay heavy on his stomach. "Aw, Ma."

"Come." She knelt by the chair under the north window. She reached back a flour dusty hand. "Come. Kneel with me a minute."

Abashed, he set his pack of books aside and knelt beside her. Ma placed her elbows on the seat of the chair and closed her eyes. Folding her hands, she lifted her gold face to God. The smell of Pa's coffee was strong in the kitchen. Just as he was about to close his eyes Free saw how wonderfully blue the sky was over the grove to the north.

"Father," Ma prayed, "a troubled mother comes to you this morning. She asks, where did she go wrong? Was she wrong to send her boy to the Academy? Would she have been wiser to have kept him home away from the temptations of a strange town? Or should she and his father have gone to the bank and borrowed some money for him to go to school with, for proper clothes and spending money? What should we have done?" Ma let go with a deep sigh. "Well, Lord, now that the worst has happened, what will become of my boy?" Ma shifted on her knees. She often complained of sore knees while polishing the kitchen floor. "Father, in his strange misguided way, this boy of ours appears to have meant well. But stealing for whatever purpose is still stealing. Father, now that he has seen the right way, and has said he is sorry, I am sure he will never do it again. Forgive him, Father, and guide him in the path of right living. We ask it in Jesus' name. Amen."

By the time the prayer ended, Free was quivering.

Ma stood up. She sighed profoundly. Then with a hand to his shoulder she raised him to his feet. "Go, son. Let's look ahead and think of tomorrow."

Free ran hard to school, punishing himself all the way.

Two weeks later it turned warm and during recess the Academy boys ran out onto the diamond west of the school building and played work-up baseball. Free played like in the old days. No one in school seemed to have found out about him and his six candy bars. Jansen had kept his word, giving Free a dishwashing job on Thursday evenings so Free could pay off what he owed Jansen as well as earn himself a little spending money.

In other years Western Academy had had a baseball team. But that year Principal Hedges couldn't coach the team. He was too busy studying for his PhD degree. All the games with the other parochial academies around—Canton, Blue Wing, Jerusalem—were canceled. It was too bad. Because for the first time in years there were a lot of good players at Western. The junior class was especially loaded.

One day Tony Streetman got the bright idea that the juniors should take on the whole school at the annual school picnic coming up May twentieth. Free and Birdie and Bert Whiffler right away thought it a great idea. So Tony, making himself manager of the juniors, issued a challenge. The seniors, mostly old bucks, and a few sophomores and freshmen promptly accepted.

The year before Sam Ruffman had done some relief pitching. Sam had good velocity and a fair curve. If he was ahead he was rough. But if the game was close he had a tendency to blow up. Actually he didn't have the hands for baseball. His fingers were too short and fat, and they were also for some curious reason bent up and back at the tips. Sam had trouble controlling the release of the ball as he came around and almost every third pitch was wild. Batters were afraid and kept bailing out. There was one easy way to beat Sam. Stand close to the plate and sure as shooting he'd walk you.

Tony worried about having Sam pitch for the juniors. Shrewd Henry Brunstein, by then a senior, would be sure to know how to take advantage of Sam's wildness. Tony made himself catcher and worked with Sam, trying to get him straightened out. But those two didn't hit it off very well and the more Tony worked with Sam the worse Sam got.

One afternoon during practice, Tony finally had enough of Sam's wildness. He called a halt, pushed up his mask on his forehead, and advanced into the middle of the diamond. With his slightly bowed legs, mask tipped up, and sharp pale nose quivering, Tony looked like a horned toad. "Free! Come over here a minute."

Free, playing first base, loped over.

"Free, you pitch a while. Sam, you take over first base."

"First base?" Sam cried. "Me?"

"Yes, Sam, first base."

"Crap, Tony, Free can't throw curves."

"I saw him fooling around with Bert the other day and what I saw looked pretty good. Somehow he's learned how to throw the big curve."

"But his fast ball, ha," Sam snorted, "why, he can't even break a spider's web with it."

"Never mind. Get over on first base."

Sam was outraged. It had been bad enough that Free had chased him stark baby naked around and around in the gym, but this, Free taking over as the junior pitcher, that was the limit. "But I'm the star Academy pitcher, now that Stiffy Vernon's graduated."

"Get!" Tony ordered. "Or you don't need to play."

Sam, rednecked, finally stomped over to first base. Sam was even more afraid of Tony than he was of Free.

Tony gave Free a searching look. "You know the signals?"

"Yes."

"Good." Tony went back behind the plate.

Free went to work on the junior subs. With two ins and a straight ball he got a one-and-two count on Timmy Johanson. Then, getting the three-finger sign from Tony, he fired a big roundhouse curve. Timmy missed it by a foot.

Tony came striding bowlegged halfway to the mound. He shook the ball at Free. "I told you you could pitch, you skinny shit from Bonnie you." The wire mask gave Tony's face the look of a fierce bear.

It didn't take long for Free to learn how to pitch with a flowing rhythmic motion. All those days of playing ball at the Christian School in Bonnie as well as those times playing ball with his brothers in the hog pasture at home were finally paying off. Free was thrilled. From thief to star pitcher was quite a climb up.

Principal Hedges chose to hold the school picnic at Oak Grove State Park along the Big Sioux River bluffs. May twentieth dawned fair and warm. For once there was no wind. The apple trees in town were all in bloom. A fellow couldn't help but be in love even if he didn't have a girl.

By eight-thirty a caravan of some twenty cars was on the road. Principal Hedges led the way in his black Dodge and Professor Ralph in his Ford took up the caboose position. The caravan stopped on the west edge of Sioux Center, where Principal Hedges checked to see if all was right; then snaked on toward the Big Sioux River.

The black land began to roll after a few miles. Soon the caravan rolled down a road between two bread-loaf bluffs. Arriving in the bottoms, all the cars pulled up on a sandy bench beside some park tables. To the north spread a wide slowly undulating meadow. The grass was still short. Patches of dandelions had just begun to show yellow. Light purple pasqueflowers grew on a nearby sandy knoll.

The Big Sioux flowed wide, dark green, full of turns with deep dangerous holes. Occasional fish slapped up out of the water. Single moths zigged over the surface, and birds darting after them also dippled the river with the tips of their wings. Beyond the far bank spread more meadows, and beyond them more farms, until in the clear yellow distance pale blue sky blended off into green blue pastures. The west horizon appeared to lie far below the bench on which the caravan came to rest.

The boys helped to unload the picnic goodies, and then got out their gloves and balls and took over the meadow. Tony cautioned Free to save his arm for the big game. Sam Ruffman, however, kept begging Free to play burn-out catch with him, but both Free and Tony were on to him.

The game started at one o'clock. Principal Hedges served as umpire. They'd brought along three sacks of straw to serve as bases and a square piece of board for home plate. Principal Hedges stepped off the distances between bases, along with a lot of talk about hypotenuses and right angles, as well as marked the little hole for the pitcher's mound, and they were set to go. The whole school gathered along the sidelines, the juniors along the third-base line and the rest of the school along the first-base line.

Free fanned the side in the first two innings. Tony kept calling for the inshoot on the first couple of pitches and then went for the outcurve until Free got his man. The first man up in the third inning hit a weak roller to Free, who threw to Sam for the out. Then the next two men fanned.

Out at shortstop Birdie kept laughing funny to himself. Every time Free let go with his big sweeping sidearm hook, Birdie would let go with another gleeful chuckle. Birdie was letting Free know that with every pitch he was beginning to think more of him.

Free pitched steady ball through the fourth and fifth innings.

In the sixth, the Old Bucks began to get to him a little, two pop-ups and a grounder. Brunstein and his boys tried to get set for either Free's curve or his inshoot, but Tony outsmarted them with his shrewd calls.

Free could hardly believe it was happening. Even Principal Hedges as umpire calling the pitches from behind the mound could hardly believe his eyes either. His moustache moved agitated all afternoon. His wondering smile gradually became a grim smile of surprise. Free's buddies on the opposing team quit razzing him too after a while. It was hard to razz a fellow who was leading 9 to 0.

Free got into trouble in the seventh. The tendons on the inside of his right elbow began to hurt. He could still throw the out, but when he threw the inshoot his trembling fingers were no longer sure of themselves. And when he threw the straight ball he was way off target. He walked the first two batters, got the next two on pop-ups with his inshoot, walked the fifth man, and finally found himself with a three-and-two count on batter Brunstein. Tony called for a curve. Luckily Henry topped it, only because Free threw it so soft, and the ball rolled a few feet in front of the plate. Free lunged in on his long legs, picked up the ball, and tagged home plate for the force-out.

Free had better luck in the eighth. He threw just three pitches, all curves, and had three outs on grounders to Birdie.

Birdie was by then ecstatic. "Keep throwing those hooks, Free. We're all behind you and can get 'em for you at first."

The Old Bucks got their first hit in the top of the ninth, a smack over third base. It went for a double, rolling all the way to a gooseberry bush. Free, unnerved, walked the next batter on four pitches. His arm was so sore the last two pitches hardly made it to the plate.

Tony pushed up his mask and called time. He strode fiercely out to the mound. Sam, thinking that he might be called on to relieve Free, also came striding up. Tony's nose was white. "We better take you out, Free."

"I can finish," Free said. "We're nine runs ahead."

"Yeh, but I want to shut those mudlucks out."

"Yeh, Free," Sam said. "I can save that shutout for you. I'll fire nine fast balls by 'em and we can go home."

"You will not," Tony said. "I'm gonna pitch."

"You? Why, you've never pitched in your life." Sam said.

"I'm still gonna pitch," Tony said.

"But who'll catch then?"

"Free."

"But he's never caught in his life."

"Free's got the hands. He'll do."

"You mean, I'm not going to pitch now? When I'm the star Academy pitcher?"

"No."

"Then I quit." Sam threw his first baseman's mitt down on the ground and started to walk off the diamond. His neck was red and his lips were white.

Umpire Hedges finally had something to say. "No you don't, Sam. Tony is your manager and he has the right to run his team as he sees fit. Pick up that mitt and get back on first."

"But—"

"—get!"

Sam picked up the mitt and slump-shouldered went back to first. Sam had trouble getting passing marks from Principal Hedges.

Free said, "What if Sam should deliberately drop the ball when we throw it to him?"

"Don't worry about him," Tony said. "I'm going to strike out the side. Here, take the mask and pud, and get behind the plate."

Free put on the catcher's paraphernalia and got behind the plate.

Tony, all business immediately, went to work. Tony was a sidearmer and had a natural inshoot that broke in on a right-handed batter. And he could throw hard.

Tony did strike the side out. On ten pitches. 9 to 0.

The next day in Algebra II, Birdie still hadn't gotten over how Free's big sweeping curve had cut down Henry Brunstein and his Old Bucks. He compared Free's curve to a complicated algebraic theorem having to do with the semicircle.

The whole class laughed and looked around with affection at where Free sat in back near the window.

Principal Hedges had a big smile for Free too. His little square black moustache almost touched his nose. "Yes, our Free was throwing a pretty good curve at that. It didn't quite come full circle."

Again there was a general laugh.

"But then, in the ninth his curve straightened out and he blew up."

"Yeh, it sure did," Sam agreed loudly.

Birdie came to Free's defense. "For a kid that's never pitched a game in his life before he did pretty good. No hits for eight innings. That's got to be some kind of record."

Principal Hedges's face became gentle. "Yes, our long bag of bones is gradually growing up to be a man all right. Who knows but what someday we'll all be glad to admit we knew him when."

Free elected to remain silent. The near no-hitter was almost enough to make up for that candy bar affair.

Free ❦ 12

SHERM HEARD ABOUT the great game Free'd pitched at the Academy picnic and was jubilant. With Free on the mound the Singles at last had a fighting chance to beat the Marrieds at the Little Church picnic on Decoration Day.

But Garrett, now married, snorted when he heard about Free's great game. Free couldn't have grown up that much. The Marrieds would hit his dinky little curve all over the place. After all it had been mostly the married men who'd beat that great Sioux Center team 10 to 8 on the Fourth of July.

After the parade in the morning, which lead from the First National Bank on main street to the Hillside Cemetery across the river, everybody drove out to Brewster's pasture. While the womenfolk set out their food on the picnic tables, and the children scared up the frogs along the soppy bank of the Big Rock River, the Marrieds and the Singles got out their balls and gloves and warmed up. Some of the young fellows played burn-out catch. A couple of the more sporty old bucks tried to take part, but it wasn't long before they were making fools of themselves, getting hit in the belly, and turning red over the nose because they hadn't run that much in years.

Free was careful not to throw much. His elbow was still a little sore and he had to save his arm for the game. He joined the outfielders and caught flies. Tillman, the storekeeper, was one of the best fungo hitters around. He could hang up a fly so high that no matter how far it was hit almost any kind of runner could get under it and catch it. Several times he hit the ball so high above where Free stood that it looked like a little brown moon slowly moving across the sky in broad daylight.

When the twelve o'clock siren blew everybody sought out their own families spread out on the grass.

Free knew it was bad to pitch over a full stomach, but he couldn't resist seconds on deviled eggs, potato salad, smoked ham, and a puddle of home-baked pork and beans. It also happened that Ma'd made one of his favorite desserts, raisin cream pie, and he felt that since this was a fun day he really had a right to have two pieces of that. And he had a generous helping of gold rich homemade ice cream heaped on top of that even. The rich food made him thirsty and he wound up drinking four glasses of lemonade. There was no fun like the fun of eating picnic food while sitting on green grass beside a river.

The game started at one-thirty. Several fellows had gone over the diamond with shovels and had cleaned off the cow plops and chopped down the dead stalks of last year's bull thistles.

It happened that the catcher for the Singles, Tom Boer, couldn't make the picnic. He'd had to go to a funeral. So the Marrieds loaned the Singles their other catcher, Hal Haber. Hal had a fine coaxing voice and his wonderful expressions seen through his catcher's mask were such that even a cripple could have thrown a pretty good game. He had only one fault. He couldn't squat on his heels but had to stand half crouched. The result was he was occasionally guilty of passed balls.

Again for three innings Free's big sweeping hook baffled the batters. The married stiffs swung where the ball wasn't. It made Free laugh to see those old fellows wind up with their big bats to knock that little baseball into the next county, only to have it at the last moment fade away from them. Free could hear their bats go swish, swish, swish, even from where he stood on the mound. Some of the old muscled bucks almost fell down after each swing. Pa was pitching for the Marrieds and he swung so hard his back cracked. While out at shortstop Sherm smiled to himself at the way his old playmate and nephew Free was pitching.

The Singles girls were going nuts on the sidelines. Their heroes were finally winning a game. Nelda Brewster, in whose father's pasture they were playing, had a smile for Free alone.

Sherm was especially up when his older brother, Uncle John, came to bat. Uncle John batted cross-handed. It was curious about Uncle John but he did other things cross-handed too. He had the terrible habit of sometimes driving down the left side of the road. That was all right so long as he didn't meet anybody. He drove okay on short drives to town, staying in the right lane, but on longer trips when he got tired he'd slowly let the car drift over onto the left lane.

Then should an oncoming car show up on the horizon he'd quick point ahead with his right arm and cry out, "Hey, look, that fellow's driving on the wrong side of the road," and only at the last second, because everybody was yelling at him to get over where he belonged, would he finally get over in the right lane. He also had a tendency to pick things up on his right side with his left hand, like say a fork or a wrench. While he buttoned up right-handed. And his humor was cross-handed. A person never really got used to the way his jokes came off. There was always an obb-ended twist to everything he said.

The first time Uncle John came to bat, Free threw him one hook and learned something about pitching to a man's power. Uncle John came around early, and because his left hand drew the bat around lower than usual, the bat followed the arc of the dipping curve exactly and, wham! there went the longest foul ball past third base that Free had ever seen. It went a mile. Sherm came running in from shortstop and Hal came stomping up from behind the plate. And the girls along the sidelines fell silent.

"Say!" Hal said, with a choked laugh, "we better not throw him one of those again."

Sherm said, "I'll say not. I'd never live it down if he got a home run off us."

Free said, "Maybe if I bent the curve more . . ."

Sherm shook his head. "Never. With your curve you're grooving it for that weird swing of his."

"Shall we just walk him then?" Hal wondered.

"What? He'd razz me until the day I died if we did that. No, not that." Sherm spat a fat gob into the pocket of his glove and greased it. "No, I got an idea. With his left hand on top like that, if we was to pitch him high and tight, he'd never be able to get at the ball no matter how he swung. He'd go fishing for it clumsy-like. So give him nothing but inshoots, high and tight."

Hal nodded, and tromped back behind the plate. Half squatting he showed Free two fingers laid across the hole of his pud.

Free fired two straight inshoots level with the shoulder and Uncle John missed them a foot.

All the girls once again went back to shrieking.

Free wondered a little about Nelda Brewster cheering for him. He'd heard lately that she'd been going out with Dennis Nabor. Dennis had a bad name. Dennis was watching the game from the turtle of his Ford Roadster. He wore his hair parted down the middle and had a wet loose-lipped smile. He always looked a little like a young bull who'd just smelled something interesting.

For seven innings Free had the old stiffs swinging at air or popping up weakly. Only Garrett and Pa got a fairly good piece of the ball. They hit grass-cutters straight at Sherm, who gobbled them up and threw them out on a line to hook-nosed Hank Tollhouse at first base.

Meanwhile the Singles built up a five-run lead. Sherm hit a long home run with two on and Tollhouse hit a lucky double to score two more. Sherm's home run landed on the railroad trestle, while Tollhouse's double rolled into a gopher hole for a ground rule two-base hit.

Then in the top of the eighth, arm tiring, Free walked two men in a row, and Tollhouse dropped a pop-up, and Uncle John got lucky and hit a long double scoring three runs, and Garrett hit a home run to tie the score.

The girls moaned.

When Free walked two more men with no outs, Sherm came running in from his shortstop position. He looked at Free in mild outrage. "Don't you care anymore?"

"Of course I care."

"So that's what going to that Academy did to you. Give you the big head instead of a good curve."

Free turned his back on Sherm. And, angry, he motioned for Hal to come up to the mound.

Hal came up and looked at Free through his wire mask. Hal didn't catch often enough to get into the habit of throwing off his mask automatically after a foul ball or when his pitcher wanted to confer with him. "Yes?"

"For the rest of this inning I want you to show me nothing but four fingers."

"You got another pitch?"

"I'm going to throw my curve straight overhand instead of sidearm. Just be sure and catch it even if it's hard for you to squat. It might hit the ground right behind the plate."

Sherm held his head to one side. "I dunno now, Free."

"Hal, can you catch such a pitch?" Free demanded.

"Try me."

With his new drop Free proceeded to strike out the side.

The Singles failed to score in the bottom of the eighth and the ninth and the game went into extra innings.

It was good old Hal Haber, the catcher borrowed from the Marrieds, who won the game for the Singles. With two out in the bottom of the eleventh, he caught one of Pa's slants and parked it in a pile of colored marbles, horse dung, deep in center field. Nicholaus Mendaring, who was fussy about such things, decided he'd first better kick the ball out of the pile of horse marbles and make it roll through the weeds to clean it off a little, before he'd pick it up. But that time Hal, the old stiff, had made it to third. Garrett, the catcher, was so disgusted that on the next pitch he missed Pa's curve. It went for a passed ball and Hal scored easily from third. The Singles won, 6 to 5. It was their first victory in years.

Even Reverend Tiller was impressed. He came up and took Free's hand in his two hands and congratulated him on his show of manly fortitude, hanging on until he won.

Looking past Reverend Tiller, Free noted soberly that Nelda Brewster and Dennis Nabor had linked arms and were starting across the pasture for home.

Free ❦ 13

WHILE PA AND MA were away an emergency arose on the yard. Kicker's heifer lay in the cow pen with her head crooked at an awkward angle. Her eyes were cloudy with dust. Her belly lay bulged up like a bloated carcass. Her bag of waters had broken and her puddle gleamed on the dirt behind her. A dry birth.

Free was about to quick go call Doc Overslough, when a cough shook the heifer. Her eyes opened bright again and her neck straightened out. She saw him. She tried to lift her head. And then a convulsion seized her belly. It was as though a giant fist had closed trying to squeeze out her calf.

He kneeled beside her and examined her. No wonder she was having trouble calving. The calf was coming out rear feet first. Two soft hoofs stuck out like a pair of rabbit ears. If he tried to help the calf out rear end first, it'd be like removing a fishhook.

He ran to the house and put in a call for Doc Overslough anyway. Doc's wife said her husband was out on call near Sioux Center, but that when he called in she'd tell him he was wanted at the Alfredson farm next. Hands sweating, Free filled a pan with warm water from the reservoir and grabbed a bar of tar soap, and ran back to the cow pen. He washed his hands and arms. Then, getting down on his knees again, he slid in a hand past the calf's protruding rear hoofs and reached inside the heifer. It was cozy inside her. Warm. A smell of slightly fermented honey came from her insides. Grunting, finally having to work inside her with both hands, he managed to get the calf turned around. He kept pushing sighs out of her. All the while she lay flat out, inert. To his surprise his fingertips came across two heads. For a moment he thought he was dealing with a two-headed calf, until, reaching in farther, he traced out two backbones. Twins. Aha. Another reason why she had trouble. What a thing for a heifer to go through the first time. Eyebrows dripping sweat, he rearranged both calves and placed them in their proper order of birth. It was a little like reaching in under a tied-down quilt on a bed and rearranging the sleeping postures of a couple of dreaming children. He withdrew his hands from her gently and cleaned off his bloodied hands and arms.

He sat back on his heels.

The heifer still lay with her head arched back unnaturally. The twin calves were still alive. Every now and then one of them kicked inside her, making the hide over her belly jump.

Finally one of the calves gave an awful kick. The other calf reacted with an equally violent kick. That seemed to stir up the heifer and her head came up off the floor. Immediately after, her belly convulsed, once. That did it. The first calf emerged up to its ears. There was another surge and the calf sluiced out onto the dirt floor. As Free drew it gently to one side, it opened its mouth and bellered wetly.

A minute later the second calf was born. When the second calf also bellered wetly the heifer lowed. Both calves were red with spots of white and both were heifers.

A half hour later when Pa and Ma drove onto the yard, Free had helped the twins to their feet and the heifer was up and licking off their backs.

Pa loomed through the door. "Wal, son, how did Kicker's heifer do?"

Free pointed.

"Twins, by dad. And heifers."

"I thought you'd like that."

"She must've been lucky." Then Pa spotted the pan of water and the bar of soap. "Oh." Pa stared down at Free. His eyes opened. "How did you know what to do?"

"You had me help you with the pigging. When I was little."

Pa shook his head admiringly. "So Kicker's a grammaw now."

Free sprayed the cows for flies at quarter to six and at six sharp Free and Pa began milking. Free always took the toughest cow first, a heifer with short thin tits. He mostly had to strip her. Pa tackled Kicker first.

The new twin calves in the pen behind the cows were already bellering for milk and mother. Kicker's heifer kept trying to peer around at her children out of her stanchion, nervously switching her bloody rear back and forth. She'd come out of it surprising lively.

The oily fly spray glistened on the backs of the cows. Frustrated flies buzzed in circles above them.

Kicker stood stock still as Pa milked her. She didn't even switch her tail at the flies buzzing above her. Kicker was a rare one. She was oddly built, resembling an angled box of bananas more than a critter. Her glowing prominent eyes made her look like she'd just been transfixed by a bull. She had one bad trait. She'd stand perfectly still while being milked for months on end, and then, one day, suddenly, when one least expected it, she'd go stark mad berserk. Pa'd once marked her berserks on his breeding calendar to get a line on when next to expect one. It didn't help much. There was no rhyme nor reason for her occasional crazy fits. But she gave the milk, a lot of it, a good big brimming pailful twice a day, and so her berserks were mostly forgiven her.

Pa said, voice muffled a little in Kicker's hair, "Them twins got a chance to suckle Kicker's heifer, didn't they?"

"Yes."

"Too bad. Once they've had tit in the mouth they're spoiled for drinking from a pail."

Whambang!

Kicker. Berserk.

Free peered past the cow behind him. There went Pa and pail and a sheet of flying milk and his stool. Pa was quick though. Even in midair he managed to right himself some and landed on his hands and knees. The flag of flying milk lashed itself around an upright post behind him. And the pail and stool tumbled all the way to the open door.

"Hey! You damned nutsy bitch you!"

Kicker kept on rearing and kicking. Her rear end went up in a series of violent arching kicks, sometimes so high her whipping tail brushed the rafters overhead. Sometimes at the top of her soaring kicks, she snapped out her rear legs so hard she lifted herself off her front feet a little, so that the only part of her still anchored to earth was her square ugly skull caught in the stanchion.

Pa didn't bother to check his joints. He got to his feet, went over and picked up his milk stool, and grabbing hold of it by its one stub leg, jumped to the attack. He timed his swings so that every time she came down, whack! he hit her over the rump with an awful crunch.

Kicker kept on kicking. She paid no attention to the smashing blows across her tail. And Pa went on cracking his stool across her butt. "You damned nutsy bitch you! I should have sold you long ago. Made glue out of you. With your crazy treacherous fitsy spells you." Umph! Whack! "Goddam your hide. I'm going to beat you until I bring the blood."

The one-legged stool finally broke. The board seat sailed over the stanchions and all Pa had left in his hand was the stub leg.

"And now you broke that!" Pa cried. So he next picked up the manure shovel.

Pa's terrible words about "bringing the blood" instantly brought back to Free that time by the mailbox when Pa'd come up in Uncle John's wagon and had jumped out and whipped him, his own boy, down the road toward school. That morning long ago Pa'd looked like Satan. Free couldn't stand it any longer. He bounced out across the gutter. "Pa."

"You damned critter you." Whack.

Kicker kept on rearing and kicking.

"You've got to have crossed wires is all I can say." Whack.

"Pa, please. Kicker don't know any better. She's only a poor old cow born wrong."

"The hell she don't know any better." Whack. "One look at those eyes of hers and you know she's a schemer."

"Oh, Pa, it's just that she was born with popped eyes."

"Nosiree. She's met the devil once, that's what." Whack.

Kicker kept on flinging her heels high and hard.

Ma spoke up from the doorway. "What in heaven's name is all this ruckus about?" She stared. "Oh, Alfred." Her voice dropped a full octave. "Surely you have more sense than to pound a poor old helpless cow who doesn't know any better. You, a member of Christ's congregation?"

Pa held up.

"Why, Alfred, you're just as insane as that cow is."

Kicker kept on kicking.

Pa still wanted to hit something. For a second Free was afraid he'd swing the manure shovel at Ma. Pa swallowed several times. Then he wiped his face with his hand, once; and got control of himself. He set the shovel to one side. "You're right, wife." His voice was oddly hoarse. "You're right. But tell me now, how do we stop that perpetual motion kicking machine so I can finish milking it?"

"Kicker'll probably quit when she's decided she's had enough of it."

"Let's hope you're right."

All three stood watching Kicker. She had begun to make a humping sound on each outward fling of her heels. Motes of dust swirled around her. Her eyes were almost closed.

At that moment both twin calves in the pen behind Kicker let go with a beller for milk. Kicker's daughter answered them with a mournful lowing sound.

Kicker instantly stopped kicking. She righted herself properly on all four legs. She stood breathing hard. Then after a few moments, she fell into her old transfixed attitude.

Without a word more, Pa picked up the parts of his one-legged stool, hammered them together on the edge of the cement gutter, and reset himself under Kicker to finish milking her.

"You aren't afraid of her after all that?" Ma wondered.

Pa buried his head deeper into Kicker's flank.

Free said, "Pa knows she won't move her tail again until next year sometime."

"And for that you beat her up so unmercifully?" Ma wondered further.

After they'd separated the milk, Free took two pails of skim milk to feed the twin heifer calves. He climbed into the pen with them and caught the nearest one. He straddled himself over her. He swung one of the pails of milk under her nose, and placing his hand on her head between her ears, pushed her nose down into the milk. The calf held her breath. He could feel her narrow chest slowly swell between his knees. Then, burbling into the milk, she blew all her breath out in a blast, at the same time that she jerked her head out of the pail. Milk flew all over Free's blue denim overalls.

"Pa's right. You've had tit and now you're spoiled. Well, there's more than one way to skin a cat." Free dipped his right long finger into the milk and then thrust it into her soft rubbery mouth. She was all too eager to suckle and in a moment she had Free's finger sucked in all the way. Free then slowly pushed her head down until her lips entered the milk, his finger still in her mouth. He let her suckle a while, in such a way that she also sucked up milk alongside his finger, and then, slyly, gradually withdrew the finger, until she was suck-drinking the milk on her own. After a dozen suck-swallows she realized the milk was coming in without the tit thing in her mouth. She bellered with a strangled burble into the milk, jerked her head up and out, almost spilling what milk was left in the pail.

Free went patiently through the routine again.

The other heifer calf meantime nosed Free over looking for something to suckle. Reaching up, she found a corner of his red handkerchief sticking out of his back pocket. In a moment Free could feel his handkerchief moving out of his pocket. It felt like the slow slither of a snake.

"Hyar you." He grabbed for his red handkerchief just in time. It was half-way down the calf's gullet. "Darn good thing I ain't feeding you naked."

He stuffed the handerkerchief deeper into his back pocket. He went back to teaching the first calf to drink from a pail.

The heifer calf bellered under the milk several times. Her mother heard her protest and called from her stanchion, swinging her sore butt back and forth, trying to catch sight of what was going on with her darling.

Finally, half sucking milk past Free's finger, half drinking, the first calf got to within an inch of the bottom of the pail.

"That's enough this time."

He got the other little pail and caught the second heifer calf between his legs. To his surprise, she caught on fast. Once started, she kept on suck-drinking on her own after he'd slowly removed his finger. He finished feeding her in a jiffy.

When he emptied what was left of the calf milk into the swill barrel, he noticed that his long finger had been sucked clean of milking rings.

Pa came home with a pair of tan jackboots for Free the next Saturday.

Free loved them on sight. He had long wanted a pair, and had pored over pictures of them in the Sears Roebuck catalog. He liked the strap and the buckles across the top and the pouch with a knife on the right boot. They fit around his ankle as snug as a firm handclasp. They made him feel surefooted as he hurried down the ruggled pasture lane to get the cows.

"Them boots is for good work done with Kicker's heifer." Pa said.

Free ❦ 14

FREE NEXT DREAMED of getting long pants. All the other fellows in his class had them. Here he was going on six feet and was about to be a senior and still had to wear knickerbockers.

Two days before school started a package arrived in the mail from Uncle Kon and Aunt Karen. Of course everybody gathered around when Ma opened it. The package was a little long to be candy, but one never knew. When Ma unfolded the last piece of tissue paper, there were some surprised faces ringing the table. It was only some clothes. A note was pinned to one of the sleeves. It was written in Uncle Kon's perfect Palmer Method hand.

> "Dear Ada,
>
> Here is a blue suit I've hardly worn. It's too big for me and it just hangs in the way in my closet. It should fit Free. At least I hope he hasn't grown that fast! I also enclose an extra pair of gray trousers. The blue suit he can wear Sundays and on special occasions; the gray trousers to school. Tell Free we're pleased to welcome him to the club of men.
>
> Uncle Kon"

"Shucks," Flip muttered. "Just some clothes for Free."

"Just some clothes nothing," Pa said. "That's going to save us a lot of money."

"Let's first see if they fit," Ma said. She lifted out the dark blue jacket and held it across the top of Free's shoulders. "It looks all right there." She next held up the dark trousers against Free's leg for length. "Mmm."

Free asked, "How come they sent these just now?"

"I wrote Aunt Karen about our trouble clothing you."

"Oh."

"Nah, ain't you glad?" Pa demanded.

"No," Free said. He liked the deep blue color of the suit all right, but the gray pants were an old man's gray. Also Free didn't want it to be known he was wearing hand-me-downs from an uncle.

The kids scattered under the trees. They wanted no part of what was coming next.

"Why, you haven't even tried them duds on yet," Pa cried. "Listen, young bozo you, you eat what the pot gives up, you hear? If we're gonna pay your board and room this coming year, we simply can't afford to buy you a new suit too."

"You're gonna pay for my board and room somewhere?"

"Yes," Ma said. "We thought it would be best if you could concentrate on your studies your last year in high school."

That put a different light on the matter. Smiling a little, grudgingly, Free stripped down to his underwear and allowed Ma to fit the new clothes on him. The jacket needed taking in at the back around the waist. And the shoulders were a little too broad, but Ma thought she could pad them out a little. Both pair of trousers were too short in the inseam and too full across the crotch, but again Ma thought she could let out the cuff all the way and take in an inch across the seat. She set to work immediately. She chalked out where she wanted the alterations made and then rolled out the Singer sewing machine in the living room.

Every little while she called Free in for a fitting.

It made Free's stomach hop to see how anxious Ma was to make the suit just right for him. She still had the wonderful habit of leaning in close to the sewing machine needle and of cutting thread off with an eyetooth. As she bent down he saw that his mother had aged over the last years. There were little wrinkles at the corners of her eyes and under her ears. Her fingers had broadened at the tips and wrinkled over the knuckles.

He glanced out of the north window and saw where Pa, too, as he worked at repairing the hay-loader, had aged. Pa's hair was barley white and his lips hardly more than a slit.

Ma never did get the suit to fit right. The padded shoulders of the jacket and the cuffless trousers suggested a Chicago gangster. The lengthened trousers were still an inch too short and had a way of flapping loosely around his ankles as he walked about. They didn't help hide his big feet either. Thank God his age, fifteen, had at last passed the size of the biggest shoe they could buy, thirteen.

The gray trousers worked out better. They hadn't been cut as roomy across the seat and as for the inseam Ma managed to eke out a narrow French cuff. The cuffs reached to his shoes and didn't flap.

Then it was time for school. But before he left, Ma had a go at his ears. She made a point of the wet washrag with her finger and pried out some dirt. She showed the dirt to him. "See?" she scolded. "Shame on you. Fifteen and here you've got enough dirt in them to plant potatoes in." Free tried to slip out of her grasp but her hold on the top of his skull was too tight. Ma had a grip like Pa sometimes.

At the Academy no one appeared to notice he was at last wearing long pants. He belonged.

He boarded at the Fat Van Arkle home on the east end of town near the Catholic Church. The Van Arkles were members of the Big Church. Fat was a trucker hauling cattle and hogs to the Sioux City stockyards. Fat was a huge laughing man, balding, with a ring of hair level with his ears like a monk, and was quite lusty in his talk. Fat's wife Gretch was tall, slightly stooped, with sly gray eyes. Gretch liked her husband's dirty stories.

Free hadn't been boarding there more than a week when Gretch began to brag about her hearty stud of an old father who'd bred and raised two families—one family of ten children in the Old Country and another family of eleven children in America. His second wife had been a maid for his first wife. He'd fallen in love with the maid and had persuaded her to run away with him across the ocean. They'd first gone to Canada and then had quietly slipped across the border into the good old U.S.A. Wasn't her father some man though? Truly, he had followed the Lord's command to be fruitful and multiply.

It was curious about Gretch, but she always found something to do in the barn-garage just when her boarders went to the privy, and would accidentally push open the privy door on them. A fellow had to hook the door with her around. The excuse she used was that she only happened to be getting some wood for the stove or some kerosene for the lamp, and thought she'd . . . She had the bad habit of not always finishing her sentences.

Fat and Gretch had one child, a girl of seven named Darleen, a blond doll and a love.

There were three other boarders: a Francis Ardman (no relative of Principal Obert Ardman of Bonnie), Jan Byer, and Lew Rogers. Francis and Jan roomed together in the south upstairs room and Lew and Free in the north room. Francis, Jan, and Lew were sophomores.

Francis Ardman had aristocratic airs. He was the only son of a rich merchant and the handsome darling of his beautiful mother. He wore his dark curly hair pompadour, with sideburns, and had blue eyes with dark arched brows. His nostrils were flared. From the first he didn't like Free much.

Jan Byer was four years older than Francis. He was one of those fellows who had worked on the farm for a while after graduating from the eighth grade, had not liked it, and longed to go on to school. His father had finally relented and let him go to Western provided he agreed to become a teacher, a worker in the Lord's vineyard. Jan had thin brown hair. Jan said jokingly that he probably had more hair in his nose than on his whole head. Jan had a quiet style about him. He was earnest, thorough, and in the long run had it in him to outlast all the flashy bright ones. He openly admired brilliance, but privately was determined to catch up and pass the smart asses. He liked

Free and defended him when Francis was disposed to sneer at him.

Lew Rogers was different. He was twenty and an emigrant from the Old Country. He too had a tale to tell about skipping the country and going to Canada, in his case to escape military draft. After a year in Canada, he'd walked all the way from Winnipeg to Pembina, crossing the border during the night through a field. He stayed off the main roads until he came to Grand Forks. From there he'd hitched a ride with Fat Van Arkle. Fat spotted Lew standing miserable and cold along the road. Lew had sloping shoulders and flipperlike arms. He walked like a goose. There was a hint of a hairlip under his considerable nose. His glittering brown eyes had a way of fixing themselves on one's Adam's apple. He had the look of a fellow who'd just heard the worst about the other fellow, stealing, adultery, cornholing. His ears protruded, mostly because he slept with them doubled over. He was above cleaning up after himself. He said he was of higher issue and didn't have to, much like Gramma Engleking always said of herself. While Free and Jan and Francis liked having an occasional bull session, Lew preferred to sit at his desk in his room reading biographies of men like Napoleon Bonaparte, or Otto von Bismarck, or Alexander the Great. The three boys often smiled about Lew's odd manners. Francis said he wouldn't be a bit surprised if the great Lew Rogers wasn't planning on raising an American army of mercenaries someday and of going back to the Old Country and of conquering it for having chased him out in disgrace in the first place.

One evening after school Gretch asked Free to help her. Husband Fat was gone on one of his trucking trips again and she'd had company all afternoon and so had gotten behind. She gave Free the basket and pail and told him it would be just sweet and dandy if he could get in the fuel for her that night, cobs for the kitchen stove and coal for the base burner in the living room.

Free was filling the basket with cobs, when little Darleen showed up beside him. He was quite startled to discover that she'd been in the woodshed all along and had been quietly observing him. She gave him a sexy look and declared, "I know what you boys do." Then she pulled down her pink pants and said, "You pee into me here and then I get a baby."

Free was astounded.

"I seen my dad do it to my ma in bed. They had so much fun."

Free remembered what had happened with him and that Dodie Westham girl. Around little girls an older boy had better be careful. Mothers had a way of going on the prod when big boys became too friendly with their little girls.

That very moment someone grabbed hold of the door handle outside the woodshed and turned it. It was locked. Someone had clicked the lock on from the inside.

Once more Free was astounded. He knew for sure he hadn't locked it. He flicked a look at Darleen. She had a naughty look on her face. She'd locked it. Why, that little dickens. She must have done it under the cover of the noise he'd made while throwing cobs into the basket. My God, now what?

"Let me in there!" Gretch cried wild outside. "Right now!" Gretch shook the door. Rattled it.

Darleen pulled up her pants. "Now maybe Ma will let me marry you."

"What's going on in there!" Gretch cried outside. With both hands she gave the door a powerful jerk.

Quick as a squirrel Free decided the best thing to do was to go along with what had actually happened. "Darleen!" he cried sharply. "How do you expect me to carry out the cobs if you keep locking the door on me?" He also decided to save Darleen's face about that pee-in-me stuff. "You quit playing tricks on me or I'll tell your mother."

It worked. After first giving him a cold blue look, Darleen went over to unlock the door.

Free quick grabbed up cobs by the double handful and finished filling the basket and picked the basket up.

Gretch burst in. She snatched at her little girl. "What are you doing in here?" Then she saw Free advancing on her. "Oh." She stepped aside to let him through. She snapped at Free. "Has she really been bothering you?"

"Well, she's a little tease, you know. But it's all right."

Gretch snapped down at Darleen. "Have you been bothering Free?"

The cold look of menace left Darleen's eyes and in a moment, pouting, she began to cry. "I didn't mean anything bad, Ma."

"Bad? Bad?"

Free said, "She means, in locking the door to tease me."

Gretch darted a storm-gray look from Free to the top of Darleen's blond head and then back to Free again. "Oh. All right. But you stay out of this barn when Free is doing errands for me. You hear?" She gave Darleen a shake.

Gretch continued to be suspicious. For supper she served old fried potatoes just barely warmed up. For dessert she served only a single half pear in a shallow dish. The other three boarders couldn't understand what was going on. Also, she rushed them through the supper, finally even reaching for the Bible and reading from it before they'd finished their desserts.

Free wouldn't hurry. He was still working on his half pear when she finished the last two verses.

"Thou preparest a table before me in the presence of mine enemies. My cup runneth over. I will dwell in the house of the Lord forever."

Free spooned up the last corner of his pear and placed his spoon across his plate.

"Well, Free," Gretch said, as she snapped the black family Bible shut, "and here I thought you knew better than to eat while the Bible is being read."

Free squared his eyes calmly into hers. "That's funny. And here I always thought it wasn't good manners to read the Bible while someone was still eating."

Gretch could have hit him with the black Bible.

Jan, Francis, and Lew looked at Free with some admiration.

"Well," Gretch said finally. "Let's pray then." She closed her eyes and folded her hands. The Van Arkles usually prayed silently at the table.

A couple of nights later Fat Van Arkle was home again and then the air cleared. Supper never was better. Fat loved to feed his fat and Gretch set out her best for him. He was a returned hero and was full of tales about his trip to Faith, South Dakota. Of course the boarders also benefited from Gretch's munificence. Baked potatoes with country butter, creamed onions, creamed peas, diced sweet pickles, homemade bread with butter and plum preserves, and home-canned whole pears three to a large cereal bowl. They all ate until their cheeks turned hot and their eyes stung.

When Jan once questioned Gretch with a roll of eyes at all the wonderful food, she said, with an equal roll of eyes, in her case at her husband, "When you work hard, you gotta feed that big toe."

Presently Fat and the boys retired to the living room, where Fat continued to tell of his exploits. With his huge bald head and large cucumber lips and lard hard belly, and huge thighs set apart showing where his well-worn trousers lay formed over a considerable pudendum, he looked like some Saxon baron returned from a raid on a land flowing milk and honey. He told of a skinny wind-withered cowboy who refused to get down off his horse and fix fence. "I ain't diggin' no holes in no dirt for no man. I don't do ground work." Ha ha.

Gretch joined Fat and the boys after she'd finished washing the dishes. She had a horny look in her glittering eyes. She kept wanting to know about the various waitresses he'd run into.

Fat waved her off with a roll of thick blue eyes and told next of running into a sheepherder who'd read Mark Twain. "Yep. A complete set of his works. Twice through." Fat thought that one of the wonders of the world. He himself barely managed to read the Hello *Index* once a week.

When Fat continued to duck her questions about waitresses, Gretch finally picked up a yardstick from her sewing machine and began poking at him to get his attention. When he still didn't respond, she leaned forward on the edge of her chair, legs apart until her under-thighs showed, and inserted the end of the yardstick between his buttocks and his chair and began to run it in and out. "Nnn, n-nn, you," she leered, lower lip wet.

Fat appeared not to notice. He kept right on regaling his boarders with yet another story, about a fellow who could recite the whole book of Job backwards. "For a fact." His bald head shone like a polished freckled apple.

The boys squirmed on their chairs at the spectacle. Free worried that the probing yardstick would connect on some vital part of Fat.

Darleen had been watching with her wise blue eyes. "Daddy, when you put your seed into Mama's wintie tonight, make sure it turns out to be a baby brother for me, will you?"

"Arrarrh," Fat Van Arkle broke out at last, waving his great arms around. "What's this? My little girl knows about such things already?"

All four boys slipped off to their rooms upstairs.

Free and Lew slept in the bedroom above the Van Arkle's bedroom. Sometime during the night both Free and Lew woke up to a steady banging sound below them. Fat had apparently got aboard Gretch's saddle and was riding the line with her, hell-bent for glory. The bedsprings were screeching, the slats were cracking, the iron casters were crinching in their glass cups. It was tremendous.

Lew whispered in the dark, "Well well, it sounds like our lord and lady are having themselves a high old time." Lew prided himself in using the very latest American vernacular.

"Yeh. From the sound of it they're making twin boys for Darleen."

Lew rustled around on his side of the bed. He made moves like he was stripping a cow. "Someday," Lew murmured, "when we get married."

"Not you to me," Free said, withdrawing from Lew as far as he could.

The whamming noises downstairs continued.

"It's sure taking Fat a long time to make that hill," Lew murmured. Lew continued to rustle around between the sheets.

The funny motions of his bedmate made Free sick to his stomach. God. "Yeh, all that rich food still hasn't quite worked its way down to Fat's big toe."

Finally there was a wonderful groan in the bedroom below them.

"God God," Lew groaned in turn, "at last the squirrel got caught in the trap." Lew walloped himself around in bed. He couldn't stand it that the Van Arkles were having themselves a great time while he was not. He seemed to be trying to strip the cow at the same time that he was pushing her away. Then in one of his anguished floppings about, his buttocks landed squarely in front of Free's nose.

Free had been giving his bedmate with his gyrations as much room as he could. He had taken up a position on the extreme edge of the bed, on the very seam of the mattress, where it was hard and cut into his hip and shoulder. And he had also been trying to pretend he wasn't noticing anything unusual. But the presentation of Lew's overfed goose of a behind to within inches of his nose was too much. Utterly disgusted, rigid with anger, Free exclaimed in the dark, "For crissake, Lew, get your goddam stinking strawberry out of my face."

"What! Oh." Stiff silence.

Free moved another quarter inch farther away. And, fell out of bed with a crash.

There was an awful silence in the bedroom below.

Lew lolloped himself back to his own side of the bed and pretended to be dead asleep.

Free decided to say nothing either. He picked up his bones and got back into bed.

The next morning, all through breakfast, Gretch kept sneaking looks at the boys. She was worried that they'd heard her and Fat going at it. But the boys went about loading their pancakes with thick syrup in an imperturbable manner. Besides, the great thick pancakes she always served the mornings her husband was home prevented anyone from saying much. And Fat of course behaved as if he'd just stepped down from the cab of his red truck, a little whoozy from a long rough ride somewhere.

On Halloween night Free and Jan and Francis decided to take a stroll around town to see what the local cut-ups might be up to. They asked Lew to come along, but he dismissed them with the remark he had better things to do, such as read the new biography of Napoleon Bonaparte that Professor Ralph had lent him.

They watched several gangs of young men put a buggy on top of the First National Bank, and a corn sheller on top of the grain elevator, and a live bellering protesting bull on top of the Hello Cooperative Creamery. Already piled up around the flagpole in the center of main street were heaps of junk hauled out of the garbage dump west of town.

As the three boys returned to their own block, they spotted the two Hogan boys sneaking down the alley toward the Van Arkle barn and privy. The Hogans lived next door to the Van Arkles.

Jan held up his hand. "Let's see what those two scalawags are up to. There's never been much love lost between those two families. Fat and Old Jim are always roaring at each other out of their kitchen windows."

All three squatted down behind a row of lilac bushes. The leaves of the lilacs were still green and shone glossy in the weak light coming from the Catholic Church front entrance.

The two Hogan boys, Sean and Pat, just graduated from high school, had also settled on their hams behind the Van Arkle privy.

Francis whispered under his hand, "Wonder what they're up to."

"I think I know," Free said. "They're waiting for Fat and his midnight deposit on the First National."

"How would you know?"

"Fat sometimes has himself a good lonesome crap just about the time I take my midnight look at the North Star." Free still had the habit of getting up once during the night to relieve himself. It went back to those days when Pa used to rouse him out of bed to help him get bed wetter Everett to pee.

"Oh boy," Francis smiled, "then maybe we are going to see some fun."

Sure enough, inside a few minutes, there came Fat Van Arkle waddling out of the house and heading for the privy. He had his own quaint way of throwing out his heavy knees as he walked. The weak light from the Catholic Church shone orange on his bald skull. He was picking his teeth and looking forward to a quiet sit by himself. He threw his toothpick away and pushed open the privy door. He had to step sideways to get inside. He didn't close the door. There was a fine sigh of relief as he settled down over the big hole.

"Now," Francis whispered, "if they're—"

At that very moment the two big Hogan boys made a run for the back of the privy on tiptoe and then, each at a corner, leaned their shoulders into it. With a strange cracking sound, a dozen reluctant spike nails let go of their hold in wood and the privy began to teeter over.

"Hey there!" Fat exclaimed in a compressed voice, "Hyar! what the hell?"

The Hogan boys heaved once more, faces contorted, silent. The privy tipped over and fell on its door side.

The Hogan boys didn't run for their house to hide in, but ran for the snowball bushes of widow Fern Daling living to the east of the Van Arkles.

There was a muffled series of roars, and a considerable amount of bumbling and scrambling about inside the fallen privy.

The three boys listened with slowly widening eyes. They were sitting in exactly the right place to look at the bottom of the overturned privy. They could see the undersides of the three holes quite clearly, the big one for papa, the middle one for mama, and the little one for Darleen. There were stains running in all directions from the edges of both the papa hole and the mama hole.

There was another series of vast grunts, and then suddenly Fat's huge bald head popped through the middle mama hole. Fat looked exactly like King Henry VIII with a stained ruff around his thick neck. Fat's mouth opened in a great bawl of sound. "You gotdam sons a bitches! If I ever get my hands . . . halp! for crissake!" Fat's right fist showed up in the papa hole and his left fist in Darleen's hole. He shook them at the world. "I'm gonna kill somebody for this!" With his fists upraised Fat next resembled some New England magistrate who'd somehow been placed in stocks and was as mad as a wet cock about it. "Because the sons a bitches deserves it after what's happened to me in here. Halloween, shit."

Free and Francis and Jan knew they had to get out of there pronto. All three had to fight off wild laughter. They crept out of the lilac bushes and then scooted across the grass of widow Fern's lawn. Leaning, they shot across the street and then jumped a fence into a cornfield. They each ran down a row, until they were sure they were out of earshot; and then they fell on the hilled earth and broke into exhausts of laughter.

About an hour later the town constable and some neighbors rescued Fat.

Free ❦ 15

GRETCH ASKED FREE to get her some pork chops from the butcher shop. It was after school and Free was reading an article in a sports magazine about Babe Ruth's having hit sixty home runs the past summer. Babe had broken his old record of fifty-nine made six years earlier in 1921. Free hated to let go of the article, but felt he owed Gretch a favor. Frowning, he took the dollar bill she gave him and without a word left to get the meat.

Just for the heck of it, and to be taking a different route downtown, he crossed the street and cut through several backyards until he came out on the street Ada Shutter lived on. Ada and Margaret Newinghouse boarded in the last house on the south side of the street. Margaret was a sister of the Josie Newinghouse who'd once come to visit Ma on the farm. Margaret always had a warm smile for Free. Free kind of liked Margaret, and sometimes did smile back at her. But he preferred Ada. The only trouble was Ada didn't even bother to give him a part interested look when he tried to meet eyes with her in school.

Ada wore her brown hair in a bob that hooded her face, with bangs that curved down to her brows. With her head tipped forward it gave her a very modest appearance. Yet she walked with a vigorous stride. She was a star forward on the girls' basketball team. She could run. She'd once raced Tony Streetman from downtown to the Academy on a dare and had won going away. She strode directly off the hips like a man. She had lovely muscular legs and a fine bosom. But the hooded look puzzled Free.

Headed for the butcher shop, deep in thought, eyes on the ground, Free scuffed along.

He passed under a double row of tall young cottonwoods. They formed a precise corridor, with the sidewalk going exactly down the center of it. Their tough leaves had just turned yellow. The sun was almost down at the far end of the street ahead and its light bloomed on the undersides of the cottonwood leaves. The yellowed light fell upon him in little rains of gold. It even made the sidewalk gold. There was also a vague tint of pink in the yellow light and it gave his swinging hands a healthy glow. The sound of the cliddering leaves in the easy evening breeze was like the accidental chords of leather wind chimes. He was aware of walking down an avenue of beauty. It was as if he'd walked in on a sonnet of Shakespeare. "That time of year thou mayst in me behold/ When yellow leaves, or none, or few, do hang/ Upon those boughs which shake against the cold,/ Bare, ruined choirs, where late the sweet birds sang." He sauntered slowly along. He seemed to be wading into a golden moment of some kind. A Judgment Day was flowering around him. Some glorious revelation was about to dawn upon him. Wondering, in a daze, he looked up to see what was about to happen.

There she was. Ada Shutter. With her modest hooded look. She was coming home from downtown, entering at the other end of the corridor of yellow cottonwood leaves. There were just the two of them in the golden avenue. Her gray eyes were looking straight at him. There was a little smile on her pink lips. It made her lips look like a pair of cherries. Luscious. She was wearing a dark blue dress and a light blue blouse. She had on brown loafing sandals. Her smile was a smile showing she was for once having pleasant thoughts about him. Her teeth showed ever so little. She too was sauntering along. Her limbs, especially her plump calves, were swinging along resilient and muscular on every step. Sunlight glancing off the undersides of the tough yellow leaves touched her brown hair. It made her brown hair look as if it had been burned blond by the summer sun.

Ada.

Saying her name was like saying a first baby word.

He scratched around in his head for something to say, desperately, anything, to make that tiny bud of a smile grow. But the only thing to pop into his mind were some words from *The Taming of the Shrew*. He'd finished reading all the books in the school library and had lately taken to reading Shakespeare. "I never yet beheld that special face which I did fancy more than any other." But those words weren't quite right.

He prayed: "Let me say something that'll be just right. I want to touch her."

His legs kept carrying him forward. He could feel the gold of the cottonwood leaves lighting up his face.

Her shapely legs kept carrying her forward too. Her eyes filled with bluing. Her little smile of interest widened. It invited him to enter her with some kind of hello. The good word.

He shaped his lips to say something.

They were only a dozen steps apart. Her head came up. Her hair swung back from her pink cheeks. She looked directly into his eyes; then shifted her look to his lips.

He knew he looked like a fool with his lips all bubbed out and no words coming forth. He bit on his lips.

She saw his teeth sink into his lips. Her bud of a smile abruptly vanished. Her head tipped forward, her hair slid around her cheeks, and the hooded impenetrable look came back into her gray eyes again.

They walked past each other.

The heels of her brown sandals made light clicking sounds.

The sun set.

A shadow rushed under the double row of yellow cottonwoods. The golden moment vanished.

He wanted to turn around and look back and call out her name. But he didn't dare.

Yet despite the shadow racing past him he was oddly, crazily, happy. He was breathing marvelous air. Now he knew what life was all about.

As he continued on to the butcher shop, he saw her again in his mind's eye, sauntering toward him, gold-touched hair thrown back, eyes very blue, calves muscling out on each step. If he'd only given back the same smile she'd given him.

Ada.

A wonderful name for a girl. Even if it was the same as his mother's. And maybe for that reason all the more so.

He got the meat from the butcher shop and started back. He took the same street. He walked down the avenue of beautiful cottonwoods. Darkness had settled a clear rust brown over the world and the yellow leaves of the cottonwoods hung a subdued gold. The evening breeze had also died down and only occasional bunches of leaves, here and there, cliddered lightly overhead.

He looked at her boarding house. It was a one-story bungalow, painted a soft yellow, with white trim windows. The roof was blue. The blinds on the street side were drawn.

Rhymed words rose to mind as he continued on to his own house: "That special face in a new place. Blue eyes, cottonwood leaves. Blue skies, oat sheaves. Ada of old Atlantis, Ada come to hant us." The words didn't make much sense, but they belled in his head like a lovely set of wind chimes.

He floated into the house. He gave Gretch her meat.

"Say. What's the matter with you? You look like you've just had the fits."

He felt sorry for Gretch Van Arkle. Compared to Ada she stank.

"Did you see a ghost or something?"

"No." He hurried up to his room. He found his roommate Lew sitting foursquare at his desk, a palm to either temple, elbows akimbo on the blotter of his desk. Lew didn't look up from his fat Modern History book.

Free settled in front of his own desk. He snapped on the desk lamp. Swiftly he wrote down the wind-chime words before he forgot them.

Free stared at the words. A second thing had happened to him that day. He was a poet. A young boy had found his girl and so had become a poet.

Free looked across at where Lew burned at his desk. Lew was no doubt dreaming of the day when he'd conquer the world. Well, Lew wasn't the only crazy dreamer in the house. While Lew in his imagination was conquering the world with a sword, he, Alfred Alfredson VII, was going to conquer the world with words.

After supper Lew and Jan got into an arguument about who was the greater, Napoleon or Alexander. They sat around a wood stove upstairs in the hallway, feet up on the nickel trim. Lew was all for Napoleon. Napoleon was not only the more brilliant tactician in battle, he also initiated the revolution and started universal democracy on its way. Jan argued for Alexander. Alexander was every bit as good a general, and in addition he also hellenized the then-known world. If it hadn't been for Alexander the Great, Napoleon and his exploits would never have been possible.

Free excused himself after a while saying he had to go out and take a look at the North Star.

Once outside, brown leather jacket pulled up around his ears and blue cap pulled down over his eyes, he trotted around the block to Ada's street.

He stopped behind some lilacs across from her house. Glancing down the line of windows on the east side of Ada's house, he saw that the blind in the last window was still up. A light was on in the room.

It was Ada's room. It had to be. He angled to the street corner to get a better look into the room. He could make out a picture on the far wall. The picture had trees in it. He moved across the street corner. Luckily there was an open lot with neither houses nor bushes to block the view. He moved down the side street a few more steps and began to make out the figure of a girl sitting at a desk. She was facing the wall under the picture. She sat like Lew always sat, palms to the temple, elbows akimbo on the desk. The posture surprised him. He'd always thought fanatics and teachers' pets studied like that.

He stopped on top of a little culvert. From there he had a clear view of the room and the sitting girl. Behind her was a bed with a white silk bedspread. A commode with a mirror stood in a corner.

Abruptly the girl threw back her hair, with a lift and toss of her head; then went back to studying. Her brown hair slid around her face and hid it again. Ada. No doubt about it.

He stared across the open lot at her. He stood as one petrified. No wonder she got nothing but A's. Like his roommate Lew. If one could believe Jan and Francis, who were classmates of Ada and Lew, those two were in deadly combat with each other for the highest marks in class. Lew never talked about Ada. But if Lew knew his roommate had fallen in love with her . . . when Lew hated, he hated.

A car headed out of downtown toward him, its headlights striking the cottonwood leaves and making them a million little yellow bells, all hanging silent in the still night air. The car hit a bump at an intersection and the beam of light sawed up and down through the cottonwoods. The car was headed for the country east of town. In a moment the full width of the beam would pick him out.

Not wanting to be caught window peeping, he dove into the grass; flattened himself out as best he could. He prayed his heels wouldn't show.

The car crushed along the graveled street, shot across the bump of the intersection, and headed on east, its headlights catching up yet more cottonwoods on a rise of land.

Close shave. Free wanted no more of that. He wormed around and examined the round culvert. It was wide enough for him to crawl into. He peered through it to make sure a skunk hadn't made it its home. It was empty. Feet first he backed into it until only his head and arms showed. A layer of soft sand about an inch thick lay in the bottom of the culvert. Tufts of grass growing around the opening were tall enough to hide his head and arms from even the brightest of headlights. Free rested his elbows in the little delta of sand and his chin on his hands.

He could see Ada even better from there. The angle was almost perfect. As long as it didn't rain he had a perfect hideout from which to watch her.

He loved the shape of her bobbed hair, from the bangs in front to the shingled curve in back. Even with her head bent in study she sat very straight. The curve of her bosom was a lot like Winifred's. Ma's were fuller.

It bothered him that she studied so hard. Lew had his reasons for studying hard. Lew needed to know history if he meant to conquer the world. But what good would Ada get out of studying so hard? Maybe Ada was just being a good dutiful girl bent on doing her best for her parents. He would have liked it better though if she'd have been lying on her stomach on her bed reading a novel with her feet tossed up and playing with each other. Studious people weren't much fun to live with. They read books to get good grades, not because they enjoyed them. When a person enjoyed studying something just for the heck of it, he could have a lot of fun with a friend talking about it, could even whomp up some new ideas.

He sighed.

It was warm inside the culvert. The leather jacket felt good over his shoulders. The sand under his elbows had the smell of a summer river in it. For a moment he thought he could smell mud turtles like those he and Pa found overturned on the riverbank after the cloudburst. That poor Hoffman girl. Drowned. He wondered what that Hoffman girl looked like in her coffin in the Bonnie Hillside Cemetery. By now the grave worms would have left only a slim string of bones, skull hollow, jaw fallen, hollow eyeholes staring up at the underside of the coffin lid.

He tried to imagine meeting Ada again somewhere. Of course he'd never be so lucky as to meet her in that corridor of golden cottonwood leaves again. No, it would be between classes maybe in the hallway, or out on the school grounds somehow.

Or down the post office maybe. The Academy kids liked to go down and meet the Thunderbolt Flyer when it wailed through town at five-thirty. Ada and Birdie sometimes went down to meet it because they expected a letter with a check in it from their home in South Dakota. Maybe he could join the bunch there sometime and so by accident fall into talk with her.

Another car came down the street past her house. When it approached the intersection it slowed and then turned and headed his way. Its bright headlights illuminated the fringe of tall grass in front of him. The driver couldn't see him, yet instinctively Free ducked. The car rolled over the culvert. A rolling boom bounced around Free in it, burst out past his ears. Gravel rattled above his grass hideout and sprayed into the ditch. It was scary.

When he looked across to Ada's window he discovered she'd left her desk. He'd missed seeing her get up. It was probably her time to go to bed.

Several minutes later she reappeared in the doorway. She stood in front of the mirror and brushed her hair for a while, so many strokes on one side, so many strokes on the other. She sure was dutiful. Like Ma. Ada put the comb down. She came to the window and dreamed out into the night. She couldn't see him but it made him shiver. She probably felt safe from peeping toms, living as she did in the last house at that end of town. She was living in the very end room of town. She heaved a huge sigh and then reached up and pulled down the blind. Her shadow on the blind thinned down to the shape of a jug; then was gone.

He tried to imagine what she would look like undressed. She would be clean-limbed. She would have an ivory body. The rough guys in school would probably lick their lips over her if they could see her naked. When here she was a pure and dutiful girl. Beautiful even. She'd be above all that. In his mind Free got mad at all the guys who might think such dirt about a nice girl. The bastards. Ada was an angel.

Her light snapped out and the whole house turned dark.

After a while he elbowed himself out of his hideout, brushed off his clothes, and headed for home.

Lew was still up, but the rest of the Van Arkle household had gone to bed. Lew sat foursquare at his desk, hands to his head, still busy with Napoleon.

"Hi."

Lew dropped one hand and looked around at Free. "Been playing with yourself out there in the privy all this time?"

Free was revolted.

"Too much of that and you'll turn blind."

Free flared up. "Yeh, and too much of your dreaming of becoming another Napoleon will land you in the nut house."

Contempt glittered in Lew's eyes. "Poor fool. You don't know what you're saying."

"I went through that Napoleon stage once. Dreaming I could conquer the world. First a township, then a county, then a state. That's little boy stuff."

"Ffft. Some day you'll remember that you scorned me and my plans. You'll remember this very moment in this very room and you'll wish you could undo it. Nut house. Huh. You fool."

"And a pantsful to you too, sir."

Free went to bed. He lay on his side facing the wall. He closed his eyes against the light reflected from Lew's lamp. He steered his thoughts around into dreaming about his beautiful Ada.

A couple of days later Free stood in the recessed opening leading down to the furnace room. It was a good spot to stand if one wanted to watch basketball practice without being observed. Ada was out on the floor with the girls. Free watched her doughty way of catching the ball with both hands despite close guarding, and then of quickly dribbling off to one side and firing up a tow-hander at the basket. She had a good eye and rarely missed. Even through her loose blouse and bloomers Free could see the flow of her slim athletic body. Free was lost in admiration of her . . . until he caught a glimer of something to one side. Quickly snapping his head around, he spotted Lew.

Lew smirked, then duckfooted off down the hall.

That night around ten, Lew looked up from his desk and directed a glittering look at Free. "When are you going to marry her?"

Free was lying in bed reading Zane Grey's *The U. P. Trail.* He knew Lew thought adventure stories junk but Free read Grey anyway. Free slowly sat up. "We know what I was doing near the furnace room today. But what were you doing there?"

"I hate her."

"You were down there to hate her?"

"Yiss! I was trying to hex her."

Free laughed a hinny laugh at his roommate.

"Listen, Alfredson. When I want something to come about, I can make it happen. By sheer willpower. And I will . . . and will . . . that she shall come to harm. Break a leg. Or have stoppage of the heart."

"But why?"

"She's of the enemy."

"But why? She means you no harm."

"Remember me by my enemies."

Francis spoke from the doorway. Neither Free nor Lew had noticed him poke his handsome head into the room. Francis was smiling "What's this? Napoleon here in love with Ada Shutter?"

Lew didn't bother to turn around. He quivered. "Ulkk."

Free fell into a watchful silence. He didn't trust a smiling Francis.

"Or is it that Alexander the Great is trying to save Free from falling in love with Lady Ada?"

Lew whipped around in his chair and looked at Francis. "Ahh, now you are closer to the mark."

Francis regarded Free with lordly gaze. His lips curled up at the corners. It made his lips look large, even brutal. "Ada would never go out with dirty Free."

Free stiffened.

"Thank God Free hasn't got the guts to ask her for a date," Francis continued.

"Because she'd really put him in his place."

Free said nothing.

Lew smiled in victory.

Later, when both were in bed, Lew said in the dark, "Free, someday you're going to understand that the wise person, one who knows what life is all about, tends to divide all life into either victory or defeat. There is no middle ground."

"Then there's no place for kindness in the world?" Free was thinking of Ma.

"None. That's what Bismarck believed too."

"I see you've found yourself another hero."

"Yes. Unlike you, I'm out to broaden my mind."

Free scratched his stomach.

"In some respects," Lew went on, "I'm more like Bismarck than Napoleon."

Bismarck. For godsakes, wasn't that the bastard who'd chased great-grampa John Engleking out of East Friesland? It was because of that bastard Bismarck that Great John Engleking had to give up all his lands and rights in Lengen, Germany, and escape across the Dollart into West Friesland. With his wife Adelheid and three children. Broke and penniless. By rights he, Alfred Alfredson VII, son of Adelheid Engleking, she who was the granddaughter of Great John Engleking, he should give this admirer of Bismarck lying in bed beside him a good swift kick in the ass to knock some sense into him. The bastard.

Lew frumped his blocky body about in bed several times trying to find the right position. Lew sighed twice.

Try as he might, though, Free couldn't find it in himself to get after Lew. Instead he started to think about Ada Shutter. He wondered if Ada's real given name was Adelheid, like Ma's.

Because of the intense cold Pa and Ma told him he didn't need to run home weekends, but could stay in town at the Van Arkles'. Free was pleased to find, when he started going to Young People's Catechism on Sunday night in the Hello church, that Ada went there too. Good.

She liked to sit at the end of the bench in the second row from the back. She always sat with Margaret Newinghouse. Free generally sat in the last row near the door. It gave him a perfect view of her silhouette. If she were to turn her head to the left, she couldn't help seeing him. He began to look forward to Sunday night.

But Ada never looked his way.

Reverend Lodge led the class. Reverend Lodge was a stocky powerful-looking fellow with wide blue roving eyes and a steep forehead. He liked to tip his head back and look down his cheeks as he asked a question, at the same time that he played with a Phi Beta Kappa key on a gold chain strung across his vest.

Reverend Lodge took a fancy to Free. The reverend loved baseball and sometimes threw Free a curve. "Tell us, Mister Alfredson, how do you explain the Truine God, the Father, the Son, and the Holy Ghost? How can three be one?"

Free scratched around in his head for some kind of answer. He wanted to impress Ada. He could see out of the corner of his eye that she wasn't looking at him. But she was listening. After some thought Free decided to throw the curve right back at the reverend. "Maybe we should first ask, how can one be three? Instead of three be one."

"Oh?" Reverend Lodge tipped back his lofty brow. "How so?"

"Well, maybe we should look at it as though God were a peapod. You know, three peas in a pod. Nature produces a whole pod intent on having the pea perpetuate itself. If only one of the three peas sprouts to start off the next generation, well, at least the pea as pea survives. So too with God. It doesn't really make much difference in the idea of salvation which one of three parts of Himself saves a soul, just so long as a soul gets saved. The main thing is—just so some part of God is believed on, because eventually then all of God will be believed on and so carried on."

Reverend Lodge's high brow elongated even more. "V-e-r-y ingenious, Mister Alfredson."

Everyone turned around and looked at Free. What a clever answer. Everyone, that is, except Ada. Ada continued to look at Reverend Lodge from under her hooded bangs.

Reverend Lodge went on. "Very ingenious. Though I don't think our church will go for that explanation of our Triune God."

A crazy memory popped into Free's head. He almost laughed out loud. Back home he'd once asked Sherm as a joke, "Well, you old son of a gun, how're they hanging?" and Sherm had cracked back, "Three in a bunch, and hot and sweaty."

Luckily Reverend Lodge didn't see the strangled expression on Free's face. He went into a little harangue and gave the Little Church position on the tricky problem of the three-in-one Godhead.

After that Reverend Lodge saved his more difficult questions for Free just to see what he'd come up with. If no one could finally give him an answer, he'd turn to where Free sat in his corner and say, "Let's ask our philosopher sitting by the door there, Mister Alfredson." Sometimes Free managed to come up with another ingenious answer.

One Young People's evening, as Free sat thinking to himself about how ridiculous it was to be in love with a girl who never once looked at him . . . it gradually dawned on him that everybody in the catechism class was staring at him. Apparently Reverend Lodge had asked him another tricky question. "What?"

Reverend Lodge tipped his head forward a little in kindness. "So. And what were you wool-gathering about just now?"

"Nothing."

"Nothing?"

Before he could turn red, Free's tongue chirped up, "Omnia vincit amor."

Reverend Lodge's head reared back. With a swift flash of eyes he looked from Free to Ada and back again. He knew. He'd obviously caught Free looking at Ada in a special way. "Really."

Free squirmed. He was afraid that one of the boys or girls would catch on what he meant by the Latin phrase.

Reverend Lodge gave him another kindly look. "I'll wager no one here knows what Mister Alfredson's Latin meant. Anyone?"

Not a hand showed.

"Well, Mister Alfredson, it looks like you and me now share a secret. And for the benefit of the rest of you, it's too good to share." He paused. "Though the strange thing is, Mister Alfredson, you're right, religiously speaking. That was the whole thrust and meaning of Christ's ordeal here on earth."

There was one fellow in catechism class Free couldn't abide. He was Duke Wangen. Duke invariably sat behind Ada, and was always looking at her and trying to catch her eye.

Duke Wangen was twenty-one, a six-footer, with curly brown hair and a lover's appealing blue eyes, and an all-confident smile on his wide sexy lips. His name Wangen back in the Old Country meant cheeks, and that's exactly what he had with the girls, cheek.

For some crazy reason all the girls in town were in a tizzy over Duke. There was hardly a girl around who didn't return Duke's leering smile with a silly smile of her own. Duke owned a Ford roadster with red wheels. The red wheels went well with his cherry cheeks. Most boys didn't have a car to date a girl in. Nor did most boys have much spending money. Duke seemed always to have a fat roll of bills in his back pocket. All the girls knew he had a terrible reputation. Yet the girls continued to risk ruining their good names by accepting a ride from him.

The boys in town called him the prick peddler. Duke worked for his father on a farm north of town, but he also went around with a bay Belgian stud and serviced the neighborhood mares. It was as a prick peddler that he'd earned the money to buy himself the sporty roadster. The boys said that it was after he'd bought the roadster that he really started knocking off the girls. He serviced more girls in his red-wheeled roadster than his stud bred mares in the barnyards around. He was successful with the girls for the same reason he was successful with the mares. He used Spanish Fly. The old men in the pool hall always laughed when someone mentioned Spanish Fly, but they'd never say why. Orrie's veterninarian father said Spanish Fly was a powder made from ground-up beetles. The beetles had a low-grade poison in them which made a mare feel toxic, and so made her that much the more receptive to the stud.

Orrie told about how Ellie Skenk once made the mistake of going out with Duke just to have the pleasure of a ride in his spanking new roadster. After she got in his car, she wouldn't let him buy her a take-out milkshake, or anything to eat or drink at all, for fear that when she wasn't looking he'd shake a little Spanish Fly powder into it and then she wouldn't be able to help herself. But she wasn't careful enough. She accepted a piece of gum from him. Gum had a little factory dust on it, but the stick of Juicy Fruit she put in her mouth was more than usually dusty. That was something she didn't realize until later. What he'd done was to shake a little of his magic Spanish Fly powder on the sticks of gum beforehand and then rewrapped them. Ellie Skenk said she'd chewed on her stick of doctored gum a couple of times, and then, just like that, she'd all of a sudden lost control of herself. She started to shake like she had the heebie-jeebies, and her arms hung out all loose, and she couldn't defend hersief, and her legs'd fallen asleep, and then . . . well, Ellie Skenk wouldn't say what happened next, except that she rolled her eyes around like a Sears Roebuck doll.

Hello girls were getting knocked up all over the place. There was a shotgun wedding every month. But the reason the girls didn't name Duke as the father was that he'd let them know beforehand he couldn't make babies. He'd had an operation, he said. He even had a scar to show for it. Janice Blye said she'd seen it. She wouldn't take his word for it when she got knocked up. She demanded proof. So he showed her the scar. Some of the more cynical guys said Duke had got the scar the time he fell out of his dad's haymow butt first into the tines of a pitchfork. Still nobody could prove he was the father. So Janice Blye had to name her steady, her regular fellow. But the cynics knew better. They'd point to all the little children in church with cherry red cheeks. The village wits spoke of them as being all part of a Duke's mixture. Duke was like the old dukes back in the Old Country, exercising first-night rights. The remark about a Duke's mixture always caused a coarse laugh. One could buy a sack of tobacco called Duke's Mixture for a dime.

Every Sunday night after catechism, just as everybody was filing outside into the cold, Duke would ask Ada if she'd like to have a little spin with him out in the country. Each time Ada would say, in a low voice, white-and-blue stocking cap pulled well down over her dark bangs, "No, thank you," and head for home with her friend Margaret Newinghouse.

But one Sunday night in February, Ada looked up strange-eyed at Duke and said, "Yes, I think I will go out for a little spin with you."

Free almost fainted.

Later, standing on the frosted sidewalk, the boys figured out what must have happened. Francis remembered noticing that Duke had been awfully liberal with his gum that night. Duke had passed out at least two packages of Juicy Fruit down the row he sat in. And Duke had also got Ham Kirk to pass on another package to the girls sitting ahead of him. The girls took the package thinking it was Ham Kirk treating them. Among the five who helped themselves to a stick of gum was Ada. It wasn't until they'd pretty well chewed the juice out of the stick that the five girls learned the gum had actually come from Duke. Francis said he remembered the girls all of a sudden giving a little gasp in class. A little later four of them began to act loose-headed, giggling at anything and everything. All except Ada. She'd kept control of herself until just as catechism let out. And that was just when Duke had asked her out.

Free went home disconsolate. He wouldn't walk home with Francis and Jan. He didn't want any kind words from them.

Terrible scenes came to mind in which Duke, right that minute, along some lover's lane somewhere, was pulling Ada's bloomers off her . . .

In his agony at the thought Free leaped straight up off the sidewalk like a cricket that had landed on a hot stove lid.

Free couldn't sleep that night. Not wanting to disturb his bedmate Lew with his tossing about, he sat in the hallway by the east window waiting for dawn.

The next day in school, he caught several glimpses of Ada, once in the hallway between classes, and once down in the gym in girls' basketball practice. She looked perfectly calm and composed. There wasn't a sign on her to show that she'd given up first-night rights to Duke.

Then sex reared its handsome head in another and most unlikely place.

Some of the old hens in church, putting one thing with another, and comparing notes, gradually came to the awful knowledge that their very own minister, Reverend Isaac Lodge, had once been guilty of adultery. His first child, a girl named Tracy, had been born in June, 1924. That was when he was a missionary to the Navaho Indians in New Mexico, where records weren't kept too accurately. They had been given to understand by the reverend's wife that she and the reverend had gotten married some time in 1923. That sounded all right. But the old hens, asking a question here, and another question there, always at cleverly different times, learned that the reverend and his wife had actually been married between Thanksgiving and Christmas, in New Mexico, in the year of our Lord 1923. So. Tracy had been born two months too soon! At least. And him a reverend yet. Scandalous.

Finally one of the elders in church tipped off Reverend Lodge to what everybody was saying behind his back. Reverend Lodge accepted the news quietly. He thanked the elder for doing his Christian duty.

Reverend Lodge after some thought decided to meet the problem head on. He announced one Sunday that on the following Sunday afternoon he was going to preach a special sermon based on The Gospel According to Saint John, Chapter Eight, verses two through eleven.

The congregation received the announcement in stiffening silence. When church let out, Free and the boys noticed that most everyone left the churchyard early. Later when they told atheist Lew about it, Lew looked up from reading a biography of Julius Caesar and snorted in laughter. "Ha! They all hurried home to read Chapter Eight to see what it was about."

Free wondered just how Reverend Lodge was going to handle that hot potato, adultery in the parsonage.

The next Sunday Free went to church early and managed to get a corner seat in the very back of church. From it he could see everybody coming in and taking their seats.

Ada and Margaret came early too and took a seat in the second row from the back, middle section. Free saw that with luck he'd be able to see that special face of Ada all afternoon.

Witse Baron, an incredibly old woman, took the end seat ahead of Free. Old Witse had some kind of disease of the nerves. Her face muscles were continually on the move and her skin was a maze of constantly wriggling wrinkles. Free wondered if her face ever quieted down in sleep. He was sure he'd never be able to fall asleep if some part of him was constantly wriggling away. He looked at her so intently that it wasn't long before a few of the nerves in his own cheeks quirked in empathy.

It was fun to watch people come into church. He understood a little why people craned their necks around to have a look at latecomers, to see what they were wearing, new clothes or odd clothes, and had any of the ladies found a new way to put up her hair.

One could usually tell what such and such a person thought of himself, or herself, by just watching how they entered church. Some people first stood in the doorway looking and gawking over the people already seated to see if their favorite bench was occupied. The womenfolk generally were fussy about where they sat. They sometimes acted like they were picking out a dress at a bargain counter. And most women, just before they started down the aisle toward a seat, quick stroked the flat of their hand down their dress over the butt. The church dandies weren't much better than the womenfolk. They always first made it a point to touch their hair in place, or check their fly, or snug up their tie a little tighter, before going to their seat. The older men weren't nearly so fussy. They sometimes just wandered in, without looking, trusting to luck as to where they might sit. Some men walked in with their cheeks set stiff and vain, some walked loose like some hired hand going down to slop the hogs, some walked apologetically with sheep-eating smiles. The business of seating oneself in church was an important ritual.

After a while a blond fellow, a hired hand named Brad Steppen, took a seat next to Free. There was a faint aroma of tar soap about Brad. His black oxfords cracked when he shifted his feet about. His blue suit smelled of a cedar clothes closet.

At one o'clock the sun began to strike in a slant through the rippled glass of the three tall windows on the west side. The rippled sunbeams made perfectly straight hair look like it had been put up in curlers.

By one-fifteen the church was packed. The janitor and a helper brought in some folding chairs and set them in the aisles. When that wasn't enough they pushed back the folding doors of the catechism classroom and allowed that to fill up. A lot of the regulars got to church too late to sit in their favorite places. Mention of that Chapter Eight in Saint John had sure stirred up interest in religion.

At one-twenty the organist, Mrs. Elizabeth Hedges, sister-in-law of Principal Hedges, slid into the seat of the great organ and began to play a series of preludes.

At one-twenty-five Mrs. Lodge came in. She carried a baby and led a little girl by the hand. Everybody looked at them as they settled in the seat reserved for the pastor's family.

Precisely at one-thirty Reverend Lodge marched out of the consistory room, followed by six elders and six deacons, and headed for the platform. He was dressed in black tails and strode forth like a stocky diplomat. The whole church took a breath. There he was, their shepherd, the one who'd broken the Seventh Commandment. What in God's name could he possibly say in his own behalf in God's own church? Reverend Lodge paused at the foot of the platform, bowed his head, folded his hands, and prayed a moment to himself. The elders and deacons seated themselves quietly in their velvet-padded benches. The organist lifted her fingers off the keys. Silence for a moment spread through the whole church. Reverend Lodge's big forehead shone. Here and there a bench in church cracked. Air coming up in waves from the hot air register directly in front of the platform made the scarlet runner draped over the edge of the pulpit ripple now and then. The cross of gold design in the runner wavered like it might have a life of its own. Finished praying, Reverend Lodge ascended the three steps of the platform and approached the pulpit.

The whole congregation stared up at their domeny silently. Even babies could feel from the way their mothers handled them that something unusual was going on. Little kids watched the reverend's every motion as he opened the Bible to the passage he wanted and slid the gold silk bookmark in place.

Soon Reverend Lodge began to read from The Gospel According to Saint John, Chapter Eight, verses two through eleven.

"And early in the morning he came again into the temple, and all the people came unto him; and he sat down and taught them. And the scribes and pharisees brought unto him a woman taken in adultery; and when they had set her in the midst, they said unto him, Master, this woman was taken in adultery, in the very act."

Reverend Lodge's voice vibrated low and clear through the nave of the church.

"Now Moses in the law commanded us, that such should be stoned: but what sayest thou? This they said, tempting him, that they might have to accuse him. But Jesus stooped down, and with his finger wrote on the ground, *as though he heard them not*. So when they continued asking him, he lifted up himself, and said unto them, He that is without sin among you, let him first cast a stone at her. And again he stooped down, and wrote in the ground."

Out of the corner of his eye Free caught movement where Ada was sitting. He quick flicked a look. Nothing. Everyone in Ada's row was sitting as still as a headstone. All were intent on The Word read.

"And they which heard it, being convicted by their own conscience, went out one by one, beginning at the eldest even unto the last: and Jesus was left alone, and the woman standing in the midst. When Jesus had lifted up himself, and saw none but the woman, he said unto her, Woman, where are those thine accusers? hath no man condemned thee? She said, No man, Lord. And Jesus said unto her, Neither do I condemn thee: go, and sin no more.' "

Reverend Lodge raised his black brows and gave the whole church a glowing look and then bowed his head in prayer.

"Our heavenly Father, we approach Thy throne on this Thy day in all humble and reverent respect, knowing full well that when we have bared our soul to Thee and to all Thy congregation, full and free, and have asked for forgiveness in Christ's name for all our sins, Thou wilt forgive us, full and free, even as Jesus said, 'Neither do I condemn thee: go, and sin no more.' "

Halfway through the long prayer, Free peeked through his fingers to have a look at Ada to see what she was doing, only to have his eye fall on Old Witse Baron instead. To his astonishment Old Witse had fallen sound asleep. She was snoring a little, just barely audible. So. She was able to fall asleep despite her endlessly wriggling face.

"Amen."

The second hand of the big clock in back of the church moved along in even severe jerks.

"We shall now sing Psalm 23."

The whole church rustled as people paged through the Psalter. Mrs. Hedges played the prelude. The church sang with a great voice, the melody lifting and falling in noble fashion:

"My soul he doth restore again
And me to walk doth make
Within the paths of righteousness
Even for his own name's sake."

The sound of the massed voices resembled the weaving of many cords into a powerful rope. The sound had a troubled edge to it at times, and came slow, but it finally mounted into a moment of grave ecstasy:

"Goodness and mercy all my life
Shall surely follow me:
And in God's house for evermore
My dwelling place shall be."

Reverend Lodge began the sermon in a low key. Word for word he repeated what the elder had told him. He spoke with his head thrown back, proud, so that his big forehead gleamed in the sunbeam-filled church. He told about how he'd afterwards talked to his wife about the matter. What should they do? Ignore it? Or bring the matter up before the whole congregation of our Lord? After much prayer, and after much wrestling with their consciences, they decided to bring it out in the open.

Reverend Lodge paused. He moved to the left side of the pulpit. He lowered his head. His forehead took on shadow. The whole congregation sat as if they'd suddenly been connected to a live electric wire of heavy voltage and couldn't move.

"Yes, we admit it, my wife and I. We did sleep together as man and wife before we were married in church. In our own minds, of course, at that time we already were one. We loved each other. We were officially engaged. And we planned that as soon as I was sure I had a call from a church, we would get married. But, nevertheless, mea culpa, there was one time when we were so overwhelmed by this great love of ours—and I can't think of any other word to describe it—we were so overwhelmed by our love for each other that before we knew it"—Reverend Lodge paused, rolling his eyes to heaven—"it happened."

The black second hand swept evenly across the big white dial of the clock in back.

The eyes of many women, even of some men, swung toward where Mrs. Lodge and her children sat in the parson's bench near the front of the church. She was looking up at her husband with pride, even with some little shining triumph in her face.

"Naturally we were sorry. At the same time, for some strange unfathomable reason, we also felt glorified by our love."

All eyes went back to staring at Reverend Lodge.

"Well, this is what we did. We, by ourselves, went to God on bended knee and begged Him for forgiveness. And further, we also went to the consistory of the church we attended at the time and confessed our sin before them. Shortly thereafter we stood up before that congregation there and before God and them confessed our mutual sin of breaking the Seventh Commandment."

Reverend Lodge heaved a huge sigh, then resumed his position behind the pulpit.

"After a time, a long time, we felt that God had forgiven us. Our firstborn, Tracy, who sits there now by the side of her mother"—Reverend Lodge gravely pointed a finger down at his family below him—"turned out to be a healthy happy obedient child. She has been everything that a father and a mother could expect. We also felt, when the call came from this congregation here in Hello, that God was showing further evidence of having forgiven us. From that point on, having been forgiven, we gave it no further thought. All the more so when our second child, a boy, Raymond, was born whole and healthy, favored of God. He sleeps there now"—again Reverend Isaac Lodge pointed down at his family—"at his mother's bosom, a lovely boy, a sweet fellow."

Reverend Lodge paused. With an elegant gesture he picked up a glass of water from the ledge of the pulpit and took a slow sip.

The congregation waited with lifted faces.

Reverend Lodge's glowing dark eyes roved over the whole church, even into the catechism wing.

The bench where the twelve men in the consistory sat cracked.

"According to Webster's Dictionary what was committed by us was not really adultery. Webster defines adultery as voluntary sexual intercourse between a married man and someone other than his wife, or between a married woman and someone other than her husband. But we here in this church are Christians and so we accept what Scripture says it is. Scripture says adultery is all manner of lewdness or unchastity as forbidden by the Seventh Commandment. So, by that definition, the Church's, we stand condemned."

Some in church were shocked that the words "voluntary sexual intercourse" had been spoken aloud in God's temple.

"Now, beloved in Christ, we ask you, after all this, what else do you want of us?"

Again Reverend Lodge let his glowing eyes rove over the faces below him. He selected several of the faces, individually, and paused to gaze penetratingly into them.

"Do you want us to retreat into the fields and go on our hands and knees like Nebuchadnezzar once did? Like unto a four-footed beast? And like him suffer the tears and groans of judgment? Is that what you want of us . . . in addition to what we've already gone through in expiation of our sin?"

The sun moved down the western heavens. Shafts of brilliant sunlight struck through the three tall windows on the west side with all the glory of Judgment Day. Bald heads gleamed golden, and dark heads glistened silver, and blond heads glowed platinum.

"All right, if that is what you want, we accept the extra punishment. You pick out the pasture, and name the hour and the day, and we'll be there to begin penance, my wife, and I, and our two children. If the need for our punishment be so strong in your hearts, then these our knees, and these our elbows, are ready." Reverend Lodge paused; then roared, "Even though! even though we have already confessed our sin before God and His congregation in another place! Once! When what you want from us is even yet a second confession? Suppose in time we get a call from another church? Must we confess yet a third time before that congregation? On and on? Ad infinitum?"

Free in his back seat could feel himself turn pale with excitement. Reverend Lodge was tremendous.

Free looked at where Ada sat. There was no way of telling if she were wondering whether or not the shoe fit her. Visions of what might have happened between Ada and that dirty adulterer Duke Wangen rose in Free's mind like glowing hants off a swamp. The visions gave him so much anguish he didn't know if he could stand to be in church a moment longer.

"Ada, my beautiful sweetheart . . . oh God, why did you do it?"

He jerked upright. Had he talked out loud in church?

He flicked a look at blond Brad Steppen sitting next to him.

Brad was staring straight ahead as usual, pink lips slightly parted, blue eyes hazed over with inner reverie.

Free let go with a slow sigh. Thank God. It was only that he'd been thinking so strong about Ada that he thought he'd talked out loud.

How silly to get so worked up over a girl who'd never so much as met eyes with him.

Reverend Lodge took up the final point of his sermon.

"Were our fall from grace singular, if we were the only couple to break the Seventh Commandment, then perhaps driving us out into the fields with the rest of your cattle might be the proper punishment. But you know, and I know, that our fall from grace is not singular, that in fact not a year goes by but what some poor unhappy couple comes before us here, standing up before this entire congregation, and confesses that they have broken the Seventh Commandment. Since I've been called here there have been exactly six. Now, you cannot tell me that such behavior on the part of our young is something new. That much better we older folk are not. We older ones like to think that our young folk are going to the dogs. But if we will reflect a moment, and think back, we all know that all older generations that ever lived have always thought that the younger generation was going to the dogs."

Reverend Lodge moved from behind the pulpit again and stepped to the very edge of the platform. He stooped down and made motions with his finger as though he were writing on the ground.

"Thus, my friends in Christ, I say this unto you. He that is without sin among you in this matter of adultery, let him be the first to cast a stone at me and my wife. A-men."

The final song, Psalm 42, was sung in a strangled manner.

Reverend Lodge though sang as if at last released from bondage. He could be heard over all the other voices. There were moments when his powerful voice was even a match for the organ:

"Like as the hart for water-brooks
His thirst doth pant and bray;
So pants my longing soul, O God,
That come to Thee I may. . . .
O why art thou cast down, my soul?
Why in me so dismayed?
Trust God, for I shall praise Him yet,
His countenance is mine aid. . . .
At the noise of thy waterspouts
Deep unto deep doth call;
Thy breaking waves pass over me,
Yea, and thy billows all."

After the benediction Reverend Lodge moved through his parishioners with his head held high, like a Napoleon smiling at hoi polloi, His wife and little baby moved out of the church like a Mary carrying the Blessed Babe. Little Tracy trailed modestly after her father and mother.

Most everyone was a little pale.

Landlady Van Arkle was silent all through Sunday supper. She was of the Big Church, but that Sunday had elected to attend the Little Church to hear Reverend Lodge. Her husband was gone on one of his trips so she asked Jan Byer to read from the Scripture when they finished eating, specifically asking him to read again the text the minister had preached from, John 8:2-11.

After they had all bowed their head in silent prayer giving thanks for the food that the good Lord had set before them, Gretch Van Arkle looked up and whispered, more to herself than to anyone in particular, "That sermon surely made me think."

It was between classes and there was a lot of general milling around in the hallway, and in the middle of it Free overheard Birdie invite Jan and Francis over to his house for a bull session that night. Some of the fellows were coming over to shoot the breeze, Birdie said, and some of the girls too, and it might be a lot of fun.

"Any girls I know?" Francis asked.

"Well, for one, Ada Shutter."

"We'll be there."

Free actually could feel his face fall. The bunch weren't inviting him over.

The thought of Ada smiling with all those fellows at Birdie's apartment upset him for the rest of the day.

Around seven that night Jan and Francis without a word to him put on their coats and disappeared into the night.

Free loafed a while on his bed with a new good book he'd found, *The Count of Monte Cristo.* But try as he might he couldn't get into it.

Free wished he had a friend with whom he might talk about Ada and how much he loved her. It burned him that Francis once said that Ada would never go out with "dirty Free." It was becoming pretty clear that Francis and Jan didn't really like him. They were friendly enough with him at the table, and when they bumped into him at school, but otherwise . . . heck, they probably even laughed about him behind his back. It was the one bad thing about going to Western Academy—he didn't have a single real friend there. Trying to be friends with Tony and Johnny had got him into trouble once. He shuddered when he thought again about that candy stealing episode.

Free made up his mind. He had to know what Birdie and his bunch were up to. He got his leather jacket from the closet and slipped it on.

Lew's head swiveled around. "Pretty cold to be lying in a ditch worshiping a shadow on a window blind, isn't it?"

Free sucked in a breath. Now how had Lew found out about that.

Lew's eyes mocked him. "Oh, I have ways of finding out about things. You know me. If I don't get to be top dog in this country, I'm going to be its head spy."

"You mean you've been sneaking around after me?"

Lew winked in derision. "My dear friend, in following you around in your adventures at love, I was just training myself to be a good detective."

"Sneak."

Lew bristled. He turned his square body around as if he meant to go for Free. "What—did—you—say?"

"Like Napoleon, I never chew my cabbage twice." Free turned his back on Lew and headed for the stairs.

Lew snickered after him, once; then with a hard scrape of his chair went back to reading his book.

Birdie lived in an old house near the water tower. It had once been a rich man's mansion. Later it had housed Western Academy in its early days, until 1924, when the new building was finished. Western still owned the old house and every year tried to get its older students to rent rooms in it. Because the rent was cheap a few students sometimes did try to live in its huge barny cold rooms. At the moment only Birdie and his current buddy, Nap Edgerton, lived in one of the first-floor rooms, while an aged caretaker known as Old Trompet bached on the second floor directly above them.

Free stopped behind a big maple north of the Little Church to reconnoiter the old house a half block away. The front of the old yellow mansion was well lighted by the lamps along the main street. There was a light on in Birdie's room but the rest of the house was dark. Old Trompet was either in bed or down in the basement. Probably down in the basement. Birdie said Old Trompet liked to sit by the big furnace and watch the flames in its open grill. Old Trompet smoked a pipe and was partly deaf. He wore his clothes until they were ready to fall off his back, like an animal shedding fur in season. He was reluctant to have his hair cut. No one knew if he had any relatives. Whatever he'd been would go to the grave with him.

Occasional shadows flitted across the blinds in Birdie's room. Once Free recognized Ada's silhouette.

Free watched until his toes turned cold.

"Well, there's nothing like knowing exactly once and for all what they're talking about."

He went around to the back of the big house. He had to push his toes carefully through a tangle of broom handles and snow shovels, as well as past several garbage pails. He noticed a small window below the back steps. A dim light was on in the basement. He squatted on his heels to have a closer look. There sat Old Trompet, smoking his corncob pipe, smiling idiotically at the flames jumping in the firepot of the furnace.

Good. That left the way clear for him to take the back stairs up to Old Trompet's room directly above Birdie's room. He took each stair as close to the wall as he could. All went well until he hit the last stair, and that one screeched like a cricket. When he let up on the stair, it screeched again. A loose nail. He stepped over it to the landing above.

The light from the main street came in through a side window and he could just make out a door at the end of a dim hallway. He took off his rubbers and shoes and set them carefully behind the balustrade, marking the spot carefully in his memory, and then on stocking feet, more sliding his toes along than going on tiptoe, he headed for Old Trompet's door. The door wasn't locked. He pushed in. He sniffed. Unwashed socks. An old man's rancid sweat. Mixed in with it was the smell of cheap tobacco. Old Trompet's tobacco was hardly better than wild slough hay.

To his surprise he spotted a weak light coming up through the floor. It shone up around a black stovepipe. Aha. The old kind of hot air register. The second-floor room was heated by way of the room below.

Free slid his stocking feet across the linoleum floor. He began to hear voices. Birdie and his bunch. He was directly above them.

He lay down on the floor, placing his ear over the register. As he did so, his fountain pen fell out of his shirt pocket and hit the linoleum with a light click.

"Say," somebody below said, "did you hear that?"

Jan said, "It was like someone dropping a pencil."

Everyone downstairs listened intently.

"Oh," Nap said, "it's probably only Old Trompet."

"If it was a pencil, it can't be Old Trompet up there," Birdie said. "Old Trompet can't read or write."

"Shh. Let's listen some more then," Nap said.

Free took shallow breaths.

After a while Nap said, "You see? It was nothing. Just an old house cracking in the cold."

Birdie said, "But a little bit before that I thought I'd heard one of the stairs creak up there."

"Naw. Just an old house creaking."

Free took more shallow breaths. He didn't dare feel around for his fountain pen.

The bunch below talked in an aimless fashion for a while. The noise had jarred them out of the mood for good talk.

Then Francis said something to Ada. "Say, I see where Duke is getting married."

"Oh?" Ada said guardedly.

"Yeh. That Ada Shutter girl we all know dared to say no to him and that so surprised him he asked her to marry him."

Ada burst out in a peal of merry laughter. "Always fishing, aren't you?"

"That's what I heard."

"Fact is, I'm never getting married. I only wish our church had nuns. I'd be the first to join up."

"What? With such a beautiful chassis?" Francis exclaimed.

"Ha! That's just what Duke said."

Birdie said, "One hears so many stories about Duke, one hardly knows what to believe. Tell us what it's really like to have a date with him, Ada."

"Well, he was very nice to me, really, after I flatly told him no and that I meant to be a nun."

"Why did you go out with him?"

"To show him that not every girl was an easy mark. Ech. I'm sick of hearing about how all the girls fall for him. As for that Spanish Fly thing, I think that's just a big hoax, and he knows it. It's all in their head."

"Ellie Skenk didn't think so."

"Her! She wanted to believe she had to do it."

"Gosh," Birdie said. "I never thought of it that way."

Free had trouble believing his ears. Ada talkative? Ada open and frank. And Ada to become a nun?

Francis said, "And to think that all along poor Free had a crush on you, Ada. Lord."

Ada said nothing. There was a titter from the others.

Free was horrified to hear himself being mentioned in that way.

Francis went on, with a laugh. "Well, I always said Free never had a chance with you."

Ada became indignant. "Meaning, you do?"

"Well, don't I? I'm willing to take you home tonight."

"Thanks, no. If anybody's to take me home, I'd liefer it'd be Free."

"What?" Francis said stiffly.

"However, not even he shall have that privilege. I'm off men forever."

Birdie snickered. "Except for that one date with Duke."

"That was done to teach him a lesson. That arrogant animal."

Margaret Newinghouse laughed. "You should've heard Ada tell about it after Duke dropped her off at our house."

"Never mind now," Ada said.

Francis said, "You sound like you kind 'f like Free."

"I do," Ada said. "I think he's interesting."

"But the clothes he wears. Nothing but hand-me-downs. Why, he looks like Ichabod Crane himself."

"Never mind now about him," Ada snapped.

"You know of course he's always looking at you, trying to meet eyes with you."

"I know he likes me. That's his privilege. And it's also my privilege that I shall never have a man nor ever get married."

Francis couldn't let go of it. "And he's getting to be so tall. Like some freak. Free the freak."

"That might endear him to me. Because that's what I feel I am. A freak. Different. And that's why I think I'll become a nun. Or a schoolteacher out in the sticks somewhere. Where there'll be no men around. Men and their dirty fingers. Ugh."

"You must be nuts."

Birdie said, "Wouldn't it be something if Free could hear all this?"

Jan said, "Well, you don't have to worry about that. Free's safe at home in bed reading."

Birdie said, "Those noises we heard up there, they could've been Free."

"Nah," Nap said. "I know Free, and that much of a detective he ain't."

Free decided he'd heard enough. He began to slither away from the hot air register. His leather coat made soft squeaking noises on the linoleum, though not loud enough for them to hear below. Just in time he remembered to feel around in the dark for his fountain pen. He found it on the first sweep of his hand. He located the doorway with his stocking feet without making a sound. He also found his shoes and rubbers by the balustrade. He stepped over the squealing stair and went on down. He sat on the bottom step and put on his shoes and rubbers.

As he went quietly through the back door and down the back steps, he threw a look down at the basement window. The light in the basement was still on. Old Trompet was still sitting smiling idiotically at the flames jumping in the furnace grill.

Free ❦ 16

IT WAS THE last day of school before Christmas vacation.

It wasn't too cold out and Free decided to run the seven miles home. When he arrived on the yard he found his brothers Everett and Flip and Jonathan doing the chores. All three were glad to see him but they had troubled faces.

"What's the matter?"

"Ma don't feel well."

Free pushed into the kitchen. Little Abbott was playing with baby Sherman under the table. There was a wonderful smell of freshly baked bread. "Ma?"

"Here I am, boy. In the bedroom."

Free took off his rubbers, cap, and leather jacket. He swung around the black horsehair sofa into the bedroom. "So. Working too hard again, huh?"

"Yes. Sometimes it gets me so right here in the chest."

Free leaned against the door. "Ma, Ma."

"How's school?" Ma gave him a bright blue look. It was the look she sometimes gave him when she expected him to tell her something exciting had happened to him.

"Fine."

"You look sort of sober though."

Free thought of Ada Shutter. "Everything's fine, Ma."

"That reminds me, son. Pretty soon you should make up your mind about church, you know."

"Yes, Ma."

"It will surely please me if you become a confessing member of our church. Though you must join only because you really want to, and not just because I want you to."

Free nodded.

Ma fingered the edge of her blue quilt. The bedroom was almost dark. The brown commode stood like a black buffalo in the near corner. "Well, I guess I better get up and make supper. Dear, dear. There's never any rest for the wicked."

"Wicked, Ma?"

"Just joking, son. Though I did agree to something today I'm not sure was right."

"What was that?"

"Your father and I signed a lease to rent the Hamilton half-section east of the water tower. Near town. The landlord was here. You knew Horace owned that land too, didn't you?"

"You mean where Boncourt rented?" Free straightened up. His hair touched the top of the doorhead. If he grew another inch he'd have to start ducking through doors. "Why, Ma, that yard is in worse shape than the way the Gores left this place when we moved here."

"I know, son. It seems to be our lot to clean up other renters' messes. But the Hamilton half-section has one thing I look forward to."

"Yeh?"

"It has electric light all over. In the house. In the barn."

Free was utterly disgusted. "Moving again."

"Nah, you better change clothes and help Pa."

When they all went into the house after chores, Ma looked better. Supper was steaming on the table. The younger kids hurry-upped and washed their cheeks and lips and combed their hair in front. The stove roared comfortably.

Even more comforting was the sound of Pa sharpening Ma's bread knife. Pa said with his ploughshare smile, "Wife, you let this knife get so dull a person can ride on it from here to New York in perfect comfort." Pa had a slick way of sharpening it. His strokes were so swift they glittered in the lamplight. They appeared to slice into the steel and Free could never figure out how that could sharpen a knife. But it did, because when Pa finished he could pull a hair from his arm and cut it in half with the fresh edge.

Free was last at the mirror. He had lately figured out that if he combed his hair like Charles Lindbergh he could get rid of one of his cowlicks. Sometimes, when his blond hair lay just right, Free thought he looked enough like Lucky Lindy to be his brother. Though a lot of good that did. Ada Shutter was lost to him forever. As he combed his forelock to make it hump up into a curl, he wondered if maybe it wasn't time to be nice to Mabel James instead. Mabel had soft gold hair and soft blue eyes.

The last couple of months between classes Mabel had been very friendly with him. She smiled, and leaned against him, and sometimes let a book drop for him to pick up. She rode to school every day with classmate Chris Jackson, the new Academy basketball star. Chris was hot to have her, but she wouldn't have anything to do with him. She hated his pimply face, she said. There were times when Mabel, catching Free alone a moment, would almost mew like a kitty. If she'd have had a tail for him to stroke she would have purred. She was always looking at Free's hands, especially his long fingers. Well, he kind of liked her, but since he didn't have a car, and she never stayed in town overnight, there wasn't much he could do about it.

Mabel wore the shortest skirts in school, which showed off her good-looking legs, and she had a way of tripping along on high heels so that she looked like a red-hot mama. There was a joke about her in *The Westerner,* the school annual.

The joke upset Mabel terribly. She came to Free with it and asked him what he thought. The joke read:

"Mabel James: 'I'd like to try on that rose dress.'
Salesman: 'Sorry, madam, that's a lampshade.' "

Mabel asked, "Free, are my dresses too short?" Free thought they were but he liked them that way. She really had great legs and it was a pleasure to see that much of them.

"Wal, young man, when you get through admiring yourself in the mirror there, maybe we can eat." It was Pa talking, bringing him back to earth.

Supper at home was always good. Afterwards, Ma handed him the Bible, saying he could read at family worship again now that he was home for a couple of weeks. The blue silk marker lay in the middle of The Song of Solomon. It always made him uneasy to read from The Song, about two breasts that were like two young roes that are twins which feed among the lilies.

After prayer, the kids dove for their Erector set on the floor by the sink, and Ma and Pa and Free sat talking easy for a while. The question of the meaning of their names came up. Free was surprised to learn that his given name as well as his family name had a very old meaning. His name wasn't just a convenient handle. It went back a long way. In the old days, Pa said, long before Napoleon even, the name used to be pronounced Alle-frede. Free's family name, if they'd have kept the old pronunciation, would have been Alle-frede-soan. It meant, Pa said, "All sons who believe in peace." But over the years the name gradually became shortened.

Ma said, "Then my father's given name meant that too. All peace."

"Could be," Pa said.

Free leaned back in his chair, musing about his family. He was careful not to tip his chair back on two legs. Ma said sitting on two legs cut holes into the linoleum. Life was sure moving on for his pa and ma. In a few weeks their oldest son, himself, would be sixteen. That meant they'd been married seventeen years. Seventeen long years together. They were rapidly becoming old people. Soon he'd be taking their place with his own family.

His brothers were growing up fast too. Everett at fourteen had shot up like a young cottonwood. At the same time Everett hadn't gotten along with the new principal, Sid Trayer, at the Christian School. When Pa found out that Sid Trayer had thrown the school globe at Everett one day when Everett didn't have an answer for one of his questions, Pa kept Everett home. "Let the truant officer come if he wants to," Pa said. "It's okay by me. I'll turn around and sic the sheriff after that bully Sid Trayer." So Everett only got through the sixth grade. Pa made Everett his hog man. Everett had to see to it that the hogs were fed plenty. He also had to keep the hogs' drinking water warm in winter and that meant he had to make sure the kerosene burner never went out under their drinking fountain. Pa was fussy about clean pens and Everett had to manure out the hog barn every day and put in fresh straw for bedding.

Albert the Flip at ten had become a sturdy fellow, very handy with tools and machinery. Pa let Flip have the run of the tool and machine shop. Pa said Flip had a talent for fixing things. Better yet, he'd become a good milker. "By gum," Pa said, "that kid can not only milk a cow faster'n me, he can get more out of her. That's why I've set him to milking Ol' Kicker. And you know what? Ol' Kicker likes him. She ain't had one of her kicking spells since."

Jonathan at nine was the funmaker, full of innocent mischief. He milked one cow and liked to sneak squirts at the cat as she drank from her pan of milk. Jonathan had a hundred good excuses for never getting enough fuel in the house for Ma. "But," Pa said, "still and all, he's the best egg-getter I've had so far." It was like Jonathan could outthink the hens where they might sneak-make a nest somewhere, up in the haymow, up on top of the corn in the crib, in the canvas roll of the binder in the shed. At the same time Jonathan was tender with Abbott, showing him how to build cities and roads and cars and trains. And with baby Sherman, Jonathan was like a nurse almost, Ma said.

Abbott was a strange one. He had a temper and could boil over in a second. Yet he already, going on four, had a streak of wisdom in him too. When he did get mad, he'd jump up and go off by himself somewhere, behind the grove, or down the pasture lane, and get rid of his rage alone. Then, cooled off, he'd come back all smiles and wet kisses.

About baby Sherman there wasn't much to be said yet. He had just learned to walk. He had fine-spun gold hair, so light it rode air like spider threads. And already it could be seen from the intent way his blue eyes looked at one that he might have a pair of brains.

The next Sunday dawned bitter cold. It was twenty-five below. Ma didn't feel well and Pa wasn't sure he could get the old Buick started in time, so it was decided they'd all stay home from church in the morning and plan on going to the afternoon service at one-thirty.

At eleven-thirty Pa said for Free to come along and help him get the car started. They bundled up in their sheepskins and woolen mittens, and then, each carrying a steaming kettle of water, went out to the old Buick. The night before Pa had covered the hood of the car with two horse blankets.

"Let's roll this thing back out into the sun," Pa said, "so we'll know what we're looking at. Besides, the sun'll help warm it some."

The wheels were mighty stiff, but with both of them pushing, using the power of their four legs by bracing them against the back wall of the garage, they managed to crack the old girl outside.

Pa threw off the blankets and opened the hood on the sun side. He picked up one of the steaming kettles and began pouring it slowly over the manifold. "It'll be too stiff to even think of using the starter."

"Funny the water don't freeze on the iron."

"The water is too hot and by the time it's cooled off it's already run off." Pa finished emptying the kettle. "Now to set the spark and gas and give her tail a twist or two. Free, reach in there and pull out the choke." But when Pa pushed in the crank and heaved, he couldn't quite turn it over. "Shucks." Pa stood up. "All right, pour over the other kettle, nice and slow."

Free poured, slowly, until the kettle was empty. It was so cold out Free had to blink his eyes to keep them clear.

"Now," Pa said, "once more." He set the crank halfway around on the right, and then pushed down and heaved up around. It turned, but just barely.

"Gotske! That thing is really cold. Wal, son, tell you what. We're gonna give her the full treatment, as though it's sixty below. We'll drain the oil out of the crankcase as well as the alcohol mix from the radiator, and we'll take both into the house and warm them up on the stove."

It took a while. They had to get a couple of small cans and crawl under the car and open a drain cock and a petcock. The oil slid out like it might be grease and the alcohol mix was slushy with ice crystals. Free's fingertips got so cold he had to get out from under the car once and wallop his arms around his chest to warm them up again.

When the two cans were almost full, Free shut off both cocks. Pa and Free each carried a can into the house. Pa set the can of oil on the front of the stove amongst the cooking pots of food and set the can of alcohol mix on the back part of the stove, as far away from the firepot as possible. Soon some strange smells began to waft around in the kitchen. Ma said the house smelled like a saloon full of drunks.

Right after dinner, Pa and Free went out to try starting the car again, Pa carrying the oil and Free the alcohol mix. Free then ran back to get two kettles with fresh hot water. Man, it was cold. His teeth felt like cold steel. They poured in the hot oil, and the warm alcohol mix, and then successively poured two kettles of hot water over the manifold. Free grabbed the crank and Pa got in behind the steering wheel to give her just the right amount of choke. Free was careful to crank with his thumb held back. "She just might kick on you," Pa had once told him, "and if you don't have your thumb held back, she'll catch your hand full and break your arm." Free heaved around on the crank. Surprisingly her tail twisted easy. He spun her four times. On the fifth revolution there was a low muttering growl in her and then away she roared. Free stood up smiling.

Pa sat inside carefully adjusting the choke as she opened up. Pa had the touch of a surgeon when it came to feeling just what an engine needed.

Clouds of gas poured out of the exhaust pipe.

Ma and the kids watched out of the clear part of the north kitchen window. Abbott had his nose pressed flat onto the green pane. When they saw the exhaust pouring smoke they all rushed off to finish dressing for church.

After the old Buick was thoroughly warmed up, Free asked Pa if he could drive the car from the garage to the front gate. Pa said he could.

Minutes later, just as they were all about to pile into the car, Pa surprised everybody by getting in back with the kids. He took the seat behind the driver. Ma, already in the front seat with baby Sherman in her lap, turned around and looked at Pa astounded. The kids sat shocked.

Pa wiped a funny smile off his face with a gloved hand. "Yeh, wal, I think it's about time Free learned how to drive to church once." Pa winked up at Free still standing with one foot on the running board. "Get in behind that wheel there, boy."

"Me?" Free cried.

"Yes, you. If you can drive it up from the garage to the gate, you can drive it four miles to church."

"But, Alfred," Ma said to Pa, "our boy drive a car? What does he know about it?"

"Heh," Pa said. "He's been watching me drive for years like he was a Buick factory inspector."

"Well!" Ma said.

Free climbed in behind the wheel. He could feel Ma eyeing him. She had the same look in her eye a cow got when a dog approached its calf. Ma huddled up Baby Sherman protectively against her breast. Baby Sherman was encapsulated in two white woolen blankets plus a dark outside horse blanket. Only a little hooded hole showed at the upper end through which he could breathe. Free could feel his brothers behind him eyeing the back of his head equally watchful.

Free was too chilled by the cold to be excited. He pushed in the clutch; shifted to low; let it out again. The old Buick cracked; and slowly rumbled off. He shifted into second as he turned onto the road to town, and then into high as they started downhill. He did it with only the least hint of the sound of gears meshing, and without a jerk.

The road was a little rutted, and in places cars had rammed through ribs of snowdrifts, but Free held the wheel steady. A bright sun picked out the trouble spots ahead. Also a very bright light had come on inside his eyeballs. He was seeing everything twice clearly. He found he had all kinds of time to look things over and get ready for emergencies. From quite a ways off he could line up the front wheels for ruts. He could drive the car to within an inch of where he wanted it to go. Going up the next hill his foot had the sense to goose her a little to keep up the speed. The footfeed felt like a tongue under his overshoe. His vision broadened. It appeared to take in a 180 degrees of the oncoming landscape, especially at the mile intersections.

Out of the corner of his eye he spotted Ma looking steadily at the speedometer. He looked at it himself. He was going just twenty-five.

He kept picking out the smoother tracks all the way to church.

It was too bad nobody important was watching when he drove onto the churchyard. He rolled into Pa's usual spot, pulling up on the brake and shutting off the motor.

"Hum," Pa said from the back seat directly behind Free. "You'll do. I can't correct you on a single thing."

Ma let out a sigh. "Yes, you drive good, boy. But how I hate to admit it that I'm the mother of a young man who can already drive a car. One grows old so fast towards the end."

"I wish I might drive the car sometime," Flip said.

"Enough of that," Ma said. "Come." She got out, and the kids got out with her. She marched toward the main door, carrying the baby, with the other four kids close behind her. She was like a Mother Israel clucking her chicks along.

Free followed Pa into the horse barn, where the men liked to go and talk a minute before church started. Free found an empty horse stall like Pa and took a leak in the powdery horse manure underfoot. He remembered the day he'd caught Clarence Etten and Tommy Holtup in the horse barn tormenting poor old Tip. Then Free accompanied Pa into church, Pa stalking down the right aisle to take his seat at the south end of their bench and Free walking down the left aisle to take up his position at the north end.

When baby Sherman put up a bit of a fuss during long prayer, Free cracked open his eyes to see if Ma wanted him to take the baby out to the consistory room until it quieted down. Instead he saw her lifting out one of her veined breasts to give baby milk, taking it between her two fingers and inserting it into little Sherman's eager mouth.

Ma could be a very hearty mother.

Free ❦ 17

EARLY IN MAY, Principal Hedges had a question to ask in chapel. Could anyone present get to use his old man's car? Five girls still didn't have a ride to the school picnic.

Free wondered what five girls. If one of them was Mabel James he might be tempted to ask Pa if he could have the Buick.

Perhaps on the way back, after he'd dropped off all the other girls, he could ask her to sing for him. Mabel had sung two solos in a spring concert given by the Apollo Club, a mixed quartet, and ever since he'd been wishing he might hear her again. She didn't have a strong voice, but it was as pure and as true as Ma's voice. As far as Free was concerned, Ma was the best. He knew. He sat but a couple of feet from Ma every Sunday and her voice was always exactly on the note the organist played, while most everybody else around was off a little. Ma sometimes sang solos too, on Old People's Night in church, and Free was always moved each time he heard her. She'd quietly sail up onto the platform in her floor-length blue dress, like a queen, and sing away. She was best when she sang her two favorites, "Beautiful Ohio," and "There Were Ninety and Nine." Pa was proud of her too. He said she sang good enough to be put on an Edison record. Ma had taught herself to read music and she sometimes practiced on their old organ in the parlor.

Free remembered all too well that time when his voice had cracked and changed in grammar school. He still had a sore spot in his memory about it, having to mouth the words and not sing them in that famous Christmas program. For a long time he had gone around believing he didn't have a speck of music in him. Even Sherm had given up on him when it came to singing. Sherm was like

Ma. Sherm could sing as sweet and as pure as a bird. He too sang solos in church. Some of the old folks had specially requested that he sing on Old People's Night with Ma. And whistle? Man. Sherm could triple-whistle. He'd curl up his tongue until it looked like a pig in a blanket, set his lips into a tight curve, and then blow. It sounded like three people warbling in harmony, a tenor, a baritone, and a bass. Sherm especially loved to whistle while milking cows.

After a long prayer, Principal Hedges asked again: could any one present possibly get his old man's car?

Free shot up his hand.

"You, Alfredson?"

"Yes."

"Good. Come to my office right after chapel."

It turned out that Mabel James was one of the five. Holy smokes. The picnic was the next day, so that night Free caught a ride home to their new place.

The mile-long west side of the Hamilton half-section lay against the east side of Bonnie. And the only way into the place was through town. Their lane was a continuation of main street, going east under a white cypress water tower, then down a slope, and then up a slight rise. The lane next turned north around a giant ash and ended in front of the house gate. The farm buildings stood on a rise in the very center of the half-section of land. There were five trees in the house yard, four maples along the south edge and a cottonwood on the west side. The single cottonwood, curiously, had the shape of a giant mushroom and cast a perfect umbrella of shade over the roof of the house. Instead of getting their mail from a country mailbox along a road, they now had to get their mail from the downtown post office a mile away.

It was a shock to see all of Pa's stock and machinery on a different yard. The chores were the same as always though. By the time they were milking in the new barn, Free began to feel at home a little.

Free waited until he'd finished his second cow before asking Pa. Free had learned that sometimes if one did something with another fellow for a while the other fellow would be in a better mood to do a person a favor.

Pa listened as Free explained how Principal Hedges had specially asked for someone to come up with an extra car. Then, when Pa finished the cow he was on, he got up, dropped his milk stool to the floor, and said, "No. You're too young."

"Shoot. Then I came home for nothing. What a waste of time."

"I'm right sorry," Pa said. "But that's it."

Free leaned disgusted against the alley partition.

"And as for wasting time," Pa said, "what about all those times I took off on Monday mornings and brought you to the Academy?"

"Shucks, Pa."

"Son, you cost me a lot of money this spring being in school, beyond what you cost me in room and board. I had to hire a man to help us move and get the crop in. So if I was you, I wouldn't be so anxious to ask for favors."

"Doggone."

By the time Pa and Free and Everett and Flip finished the milking and the separating, Pa finally got around to remembering he'd once been young too and that he'd liked girls. In a soft voice, Pa asked, "You say Principal Hedges asked you specially for the use of our car?"

"Yes, Pa."

"And you'll be driving our car in the caravan with the rest of them up and back?"

"Yes, Pa."

"Wal, all right. But mind, no fast driving now. Because I'll hear about it."

The next morning at eight Free rolled up to the front entrance of Western Academy with the old Buick. Most of the students had already arrived. They were dressed in outdoor clothes and were milling around on the front walk. Principal Hedges was busy lining up the cars. Principal Hedges's car, a Dodge, was in the lead. He saw Free coming and waved for him to join the end of the line.

Birdie was standing beside a Ford just ahead of Free, cap tipped back. Birdie had talked the local barber into letting him use his roadster. Birdie had his eye on Joletta Ditcher, Ann Ditcher's younger sister. Joletta was a freshman and everybody thought it pretty strange for a senior to be dating a freshie. Birdie had been frank to admit it too. "Sure I'd love to play drop the handkerchief with her. I'd cut across the circle to catch her. If I had to."

Free spotted Joletta standing with Mabel James and Nellie Underhill. Joletta's name hadn't been on the principal's list of those who were to ride with him. Behind Mabel and Joletta and Nellie stood Winifred Bonner, and Ellie Skenk. It came over Free that Joletta was standing with the other four girls because she was going to be riding with him. Originally a girl named Ann Dempster had been on his list. Ann Dempster, a great debater, was as ugly as a turkey. Principal Hedges must've changed the list, switching Ann Dempster and Joletta around. Man. Was Birdie going to like that.

It came over Birdie about then too that Joletta wasn't going to be riding with him. He got a little mad. He came over to Free. "Say, Free, old friend, I got a favor to ask of you."

"Shoot."

"At the last second, just as we start off, let me switch Joletta back to my car. And you take back Ann Dempster."

Free had begun to feel proud of his crew of girls. And that Nellie Underhill was no small shucks either. She not only was a brain but she had a good kind heart like Ma. He had variety in his car. There was sure to be a lot of lively talk, especially if Ellie Skenk opened up with some of her wild stories about Duke Wangen.

Birdie coaxed Free. His blue eyes came together in a little frown behind his glasses, making him look exactly like a cock robin. "You'll switch with me though, won't you? We've been such good friends for all these years."

Free smiled on one side. He recalled the time Birdie hadn't invited him over for that bull session with Jan and Francis and Ada Shutter. "No. I kind 'f like all the girls I got."

"What are you going to do with them all?"

Free was tempted to rag Birdie a little, telling him he meant to drive his girls out to some lovely pasture somewhere and breed them all and start up a whole new super race of people and then go out and conquer the world, and so make come true a boyhood dream. After turning it over in his mind, Free decided against it. Birdie didn't have the brains to understand a daydream. Birdie was better at cutting up people.

Principal Hedges came striding up. He winked his off eye at Free. "Any problems here?"

Birdie looked down at the ground. Then he kicked at the ground, making gravel spray all over Free's pants legs. "Ohh, I suppose not, really."

"Good. You know of course I put Ann Dempster in with you."

Birdie nodded. "Yeh. I know."

"I thought maybe what with the two of you being the school's champ debaters, you'd have a lot in common."

"Thanks a lot."

Principal Hedges's little square black moustache twitched. He was enjoying himself. Then, after another wink at Free, he went back to the head of the caravan. He called out in a loud voice, "All right! I think we all know what cars we've been assigned to, so let's climb aboard and on to the wilds of Canton, South Dakota!"

With a quiet smile, Winifred opened the back door and ushered herself and Joletta and Ellie Skenk inside. That left Nellie Underhill and Mabel for the front seat. Nellie knew about Mabel too and when Free opened the front door, Nellie waved Mabel in first and then took the seat by the door. By the time Free got in on his side, with Mabel in the middle, Mabel had a high pink color.

It was a tight fit for three in front. After a while Free's right leg warmed up against Mabel's thigh. She wasn't wearing picnic clothes like the rest of the girls but had on a short pink dress. Because of where the knob of the gearshift stuck up she had to straddle it with her knees. She held her knees apart about the width of a hand. Out of the corner of his eye he could see that Mabel was looking at the knob of the gearshift too and had begun to see what that would mean when he started driving. She turned even pinker. Free was aware that the other four girls were smiling to themselves in that warm way girls had when they were being happy for some other girl.

The car ahead jerked forward, and Birdie and Ann Dempster, the champ debaters, were off.

Free quick started the old Buick too and shifted into low. Sure enough, the bottom of his hand brushed across Mabel's soft knee. There was no way around it. He let out the clutch smoothly and they began to roll. He also shifted into intermediate, as Pa always called it, and into high. He took pleasure in directing the knob into its proper slots. The smooth round black knob had a familiar feel.

All five girls watched him closely to see what kind of driver he was. He kept a proper space between his car and Birdie's roadster up ahead, and stopped and started smoothly, and talked easily over the wheel like he'd been driving for years.

When they took the turn north at Chokecherry Corner, Winifred remarked, "Well, Mabel, I notice our Sam Ruffman managed to stand behind you in our mixed quartet picture."

"That pest." Mabel shuddered and turned to look back at Winifred. "Now for the rest of my life every time I look in my annual I'll see that dumb brute standing there." She shuddered again. "I just can't stand having him near me."

Winifred laughed. "It was either him standing behind me or behind you and I can't stand him either." Winifred waggled her head. "I can't imagine anyone marrying him."

Nellie said, "He'll probably wind up being one of those oily salesmen somewhere taking his commission out in trade."

All the girls laughed.

"Yes," Winifred said, "at least Duke Wangen was out in the open about what he wanted."

Ellie Skenk laughed a little, scattered. "When Duke finally does get married he's going to make a good father though."

Jolette had her eyes on the roadster ahead. "Look at the way Birdie is driving."

Birdie was purposely going slow, and was looking and smiling up into his rearview mirror at them.

Joletta said, "Free, let's pass him and then we'll drag our tail in front of him. Let him eat our dust."

Free shook his head. "Not today."

Their route led them along the west edge of Bonnie. To Free's surprise he saw Pa driving a load of grain, coming up from the white Farmers' Elevator along the Cannonball Railroad. Pa pulled up at the corner to let the Academy caravan roll by.

Pa right away recognized his old Buick, and then spotted Free behind the wheel. His gray whiskered face opened in some surprise. When he saw all those girls, his old boar eyes really lighted up.

"Hey, look," Joletta said, "look at that old man staring at us."

Free let a few seconds go by, then said, "That old man is my old man."

In the rearview mirror Free saw Winifred give Joletta a sharp elbow in the ribs.

"It's all right," Free said. "But Pa is exactly the reason why I dassent horse around with this seventy-horse buggy."

Mabel breathed gently beside him. "Your father looks just like my father,

Free." The ends of her breaths touched him lightly on the cheek. "My father is a farmer too."

Free was glad that from Pa's angle up on the spring seat of the wagon he couldn't see the way Mabel had her knees parted around the black knob of the gearshift.

Mabel looked back at the high slope where the white tower of Bonnie stood, and then around at the soft hills to the west across the Rock River. "So this is your country, Free."

Free liked her warm limb swelling against his leg.

"When where I live it's all as flat as a ballroom floor."

"Mabel," Winifred said, "say, that's pretty good, that about the ballroom floor. Worthy even of our class poet Free here."

Free thought the figure of speech pretty good too. It was the kind of thing a pretty girl would think of.

Free considered himself an expert on figures of speech. Professor Van Rill had assigned F. V. N. Painter's *Elementary Guide to Literary Criticism* as their textbook the past semester. It was a slender green volume and Free had come to love it. He liked to sniff into its spine, deep, liked its soft egg white pages, liked its precise clear type. But best of all he liked the style of the writer and all he had to say about the various figures of speech: metaphor, simile, allegory, parable, synecdoche. Only a true daydreamer could appreciate what the Painter book was all about. Birdie riding in the car ahead, for example, missed the point of it. Birdie right away wanted to categorize flights of fantasy, pigeonhole them, when what Painter had in mind was to encourage the writer to have explosions, all kinds of them, the more the merrier, all in the interest of making what one had in mind all the more clear. Painter wanted the writer to present, truly, what was really real in his imagination. A writer never started out with the thought that, well, today he'd write a paragraph with a couple of metaphors in it. A writer might tag his figure of speech after the fact, but never before. Birdie went at things from the top down, when the truth was all good explosions began from the bottom up. To dream and to make up stories was like letting an acorn grow up into a tree.

The caravan rolled on. Soon they were headed west on the Inwood road. The country began to roll, and then shortly became ruffled in aspect, and finally fell away into the Big Sioux River breaks.

"I like this country even better," Mabel said.

Free had to agree. The bluffs along the Big Sioux were tremendous. Dead ahead, on their left, reared the Canton International Ski Jump, where a Norwegian named Haugen had set several world ski jumping records. The Old AYP Highway curved into the head of a ravine and then began to wind down toward the river itself. The town of Canton glinted below. Beyond lay the flat land of Dakota going on forever. Free wished again he'd been born along the Big Sioux instead of near the Big Rock. Outlaw country lay just north of them in the deep studded hills, and Free thought the stories about the ruffian families living there more romantic than stories about the champ hog-raising families living around Bonnie.

It had been decided by the picnic committee that the girls should play baseball too. There were squeals of delight from the girls and scoffing haw-haws from the boys. The boys had to bat and throw left-handed to make it fair for the girls. It wouldn't have made any difference to Ada Shutter how the boys played. She not only could run like a boy, she could hit like a good lead-off man, spraying singles just over the infield. Mabel didn't play. She found herself a tree stump and sat for two solid hours watching Free trying to hit home runs left-handed. Wonderfully enough, the girls won, 33 to 27.

All day the sun shone yellow on the green pasture, and the wild plums were white with spilling perfume, and the potato salad and the pie à la modes were great.

Just as the caravan was about to pull out for home, Birdie managed to escape with Joletta in his roadster. Ann Dempster had decided to catch the bus home to Sioux Falls and that gave Birdie his chance to snatch Joletta. Birdie had hovered around Joletta all day, and had finally managed to talk her into ducking into his roadster when no one was looking. He'd purposely parked his roadster near the head of the caravan.

Someone hollered after Birdie and Joletta, "The sweetest way home is the longest way home, you kids."

That alerted Principal Hedges. He gave an order for Professor Peter Brooks to take over and get everyone started properly, and then alone leaped into his Dodge and sailed after Birdie and his prey. The students all thought it a great joke on Birdie. The two chasing cars disappeared behind a pillar of dust.

Mabel had little to say on the way back. It could be seen she was hoping to dear God that Free would ask her if he could take her home when they got back to the school grounds. She and Nellie had ridden to school that morning with Chris Jackson and she didn't like riding back with him at night.

Winifred partly solved the problem. She asked to be let off downtown at Jansen's Cafe, where Jack Faber would be waiting for her. Ellie Skenk decided to go with Winifred to the cafe. It could be seen she had hopes of running into Duke Wangen there.

Nellie helped too. She told Free he could drop her off at the school front door, where she'd wait until Chris came along.

"Sure thing," Free said.

Nellie got out without closing the door or looking back.

Mabel didn't move. She was trembling. With the door still open, soft clover smells from the meadow behind the Academy came in on a May breeze. It smelled like the sweetest kind of music. Mabel sat waiting, trembling.

"How far is it to your place?" Free asked.

"About twelve miles."

Free looked to see how much gas he had. "I think maybe I got enough to take you home." He smiled at her, then reached past her to close the door.

The sun was just setting over the trees of Hello. It caught Mabel's pink face from the side and made her cheekbones warm and transparent. Her eyelids trembled. Her eyes glowed at him with a blue as soft as a pair of robin eggs.

It was funny. He wasn't quite in love with her but he was almost even more nervous than she was. The sight of that round knob sticking up between her soft round knees made him sweat. He had no doubt she'd do it with him. She had such a crush on him she'd do anything for him.

"I can take you home then, Mabel?"

Her eyes closed a second. She turned red. "Yes, Free."

"Good. Like Pa says, let's get high behind and roll."

Her color returned to normal. And after a moment she exploded into a peal of merry laughter. She almost sang she laughed so loud. "What a comical thing to say, Free."

"Yeh, Pa can be pretty comical at times."

Free put the car in gear and they were off.

Mabel stayed sitting close beside him. When he shifted into high his fingertips drifted off the knob onto her knees. He withdrew his fingertips slowly.

Out in the country, going east towards Sheldon on the old AYP Highway, Mabel couldn't help but talk about Chris Jackson. "He's got such busy hands when he catches one alone." Mabel took Free's arm and pinched it to let Free know how relieved she was that she was riding home with him instead of Chris.

"Maybe he's inherited some of his dad's blood then. His pa and ma had to get married, you know."

"They did?" At the thought Mabel appeared to thicken beside him. "How do you know that?"

"My ma and his ma once were friends. Ma told me his ma was a pretty woman."

"For heaven's sake." Mabel was genuinely surprised. "When he's so pimply and pockmocked that . . . and with that awful yellow hair and yellow complexion."

Talk continued to be deliciously touchy all the way onto the James farmyard. Dark settled a deep bluing over the green land. The stars came out. The house was dark. Animal eyes glowed up in pairs in the headlights as Free took the turnaround near the house.

Free braked the car by the gate. "Looks like your folks are in bed already."

"Yes." Mabel's lips trembled. "Would you like to come in for a minute?"

"Sure." Free shut off the engine and the lights. Blue darkness engulfed them. "Couldn't we just sit in the car?" Free felt he'd rather not run the chance that her parents might get up and want to meet him.

"My father wants me to invite my young man in. And Ma says the parlor is always there for me and my friend to use."

Free nodded. Her parents knew Mabel would feel more guilty about going too far under her very own roof. "All right."

When they got to the front door, Mabel took his hand and led him into the dark kitchen and then through the dark living room and finally into the parlor. They managed to miss all the furniture. "You wait here," she whispered. Gently she pushed him down on a davenport.

He waited, heart skipping an occasional beat.

In a moment a match was scratched and then in the living room next door a lamp came on. Mabel waited until the flame steadied on the wick and then turned it down as low as it would go without going out. The light became a faint yellow blush on the window blinds.

Mabel came back. Her silk underthings rustled. She settled near him. Where they sat in the parlor it was almost dark. Free could just make out the curve of her cheeks and the flash of her eyes. Her lips were in shadow.

Mabel said, "Mother also said I had to have a light on. But I don't see any harm in having it on in the next room."

"Satan likes to work in darkness."

"So do some young men."

Free felt let down some. "Meaning me?"

"With you it's different."

Free's eyes gradually adjusted to the dim light. On their right was a phonograph and on their left two rockers and a piano. The piano looked new. No doubt her parents had bought it special for Mabel and her music.

Free sat very stiff. What did one do next?

Mabel's eyes kept opening and closing.

Free finally dared to be a Daniel. He raised his right arm over Mabel's head and let it come to rest behind her on the back of the davenport.

Mabel closed her eyes.

They sat a while, she waiting, he stiff with fear and desire.

Mabel finally nuzzled her soft gold hair against him. She didn't really want to take the lead.

Free next placed his left hand on her knee.

Mabel quivered. Her knees parted an inch; then closed.

Free thought: "My God, we're going to do it."

They sat in silence. A mantel clock in the next room tocked off the seconds. Somewhere in the house a bedspring creaked. A little later the whole house creaked, once, in the flooring. The air in the parlor was close. The smell of mothballs and mohair hung in it. There was also the sweet yeasty smell of a young girl about.

Free moved his thumb an inch above her knee.

"Looks like Mister Thumb is a drifter." Mabel's whisper was moist.

"Yes."

Mabel laughed a soft breath. "He's kind of nosy too, isn't he?"

"That's because he has a nose of his own."

Mabel nuzzled her head against him ever so little.

Pa and Ma no doubt were wondering where he was out so late.

"Free?"

"Yes?"

She was about to confess something; then didn't quite dare to go through with it.

"Free?"

He tried to whisper; couldn't. He wet his lips with his tongue; still couldn't. Here he was with a girl he liked and couldn't even whisper. Fear of breaking the Seventh was sure deep in a fellow.

"Free?" Her voice was as soft as fresh butter.

Willing it, willing it, he moved up his thumb another inch.

Her knees parted again slightly; then closed.

He could smell yet another kind of yeast rising somewhere. There was a whiff of wild roses in it. Again he moved up his thumb an inch. It touched the edge of something round. He felt a little farther. It was where she'd rolled up the top of her silk stocking. Beyond it would be bare flesh.

After a moment her hand found the back of his hand and rested on it briefly and then felt over the edge of his thumb to feel what it was feeling.

Free could feel her smile in the dark by the way her cheek moved on his. Free had to work to get his breath. She had to breathe fast too. His third leg hurt something fierce. He moaned to himself a little. It was there for him and yet he just couldn't get himself to make the next important move. He dared to all right but just couldn't unlock himself. It got awful heavy in his head. The wild rose smell and the yeast smell got so thick his nose became stopped up. He was sure he was going to pass out. He wondered if maybe he shouldn't kiss her first. That might break the ice.

She sensed his thoughts. She took a light hold of his hand and moved it to her bare thigh. Her thigh was heated. "Free," she whispered, suppliant. Then she nibbled his earlobe.

At that he exploded; then fainted for a brief moment. There were jerks in his thighs. He tried to suppress them.

She felt the jerks. She sighed. She knew what had happened.

He felt abashed and was very miserable about it.

"Next time maybe," Mabel whispered. "When we're more used to each other."

A bedspring creaked somewhere again. It creaked several times. Then a man's voice sounded from beyond the living room. "Mabel?"

"Yes, Father." Mabel spoke so clearly and sweetly innocent it was as if she hadn't been intimate with Free at all.

"Isn't it about time for your young man to go home?" Her father had the low measured voice of an important man along the main street.

"Yes, Father. He was just going."

Free moved to stand up. To his surprise he couldn't.

Mabel again sensed what was up. She rose to her feet sleekly. She reached down and took both his hands and helped him to his feet.

With the dim lamp on in the living room they made their way through the house. She took him to the front door and stepped outside with him on the stoop a moment.

He turned to say something. All he could do was mumble.

"I understand," she said. Then she reached up with both her hands and drew his head down and kissed him wet on the lips. "Good night, Free. Don't forget my address."

He stumbled out to the car. Somehow he started it. A few moments later he found himself sitting behind a set of headlights picking out the tracks on the right side of the road.

He managed to make Boyden all right. And then Hello. By the time he took the turn north at Chokecherry Corner, he'd pretty well recovered from the low sunk feeling in his belly.

He'd just rolled across the Thunderbolt Railroad tracks, when his headlights fell on what looked like two cars standing side by side blocking the road ahead. The one on the left was facing him, lights out, while the one on the right was headed the other way, red taillight glowing. Free guessed the fellow on the left had car trouble and the fellow on the right had stopped to help him. There were several flashlights wiggling around the car on the left. Free sat up straight. His eyes opened. It was as though for the moment the headlights of the old Buick were shining out of his head. He was going well over the speed Ma allowed Pa, about fifty, and the old Buick was barreling along, kicking up gravel under the fenders. He was driving so as to straddle the washboard ruts. It came to him there was only one thing to do. Take the ditch. He was going too fast in loose gravel to stop in time. His eyes flicked left, then right. But both ditches were deep. He was sure to get killed at the speed he was going.

Then he saw something. The car on the left wasn't standing opposite the car on the right. It was some thirty feet farther down the highway. Aha. He didn't have to take to the ditch. He could swerve left past the car on the right and then swerve right past the car on the left. He wasn't going to wreck Pa's wonderful Buick after all. He got a good grip on the wooden steering wheel and turned it left. He felt the loose gravel giving a little under the front wheels and allowed for it. He heard the gravel spraying out from under the rear fenders and allowed for the skidding there. Then he righted the wheel and held it for a second. Then he turned it to the right. Ah. He was going to have just enough room to sling her by. If he could keep the car from going out of control he'd be home free. Good thing he hadn't slammed on the brakes. It was best to keep an even speed and have the motor help him keep control.

But then to his horror he saw yet another car parked ahead. It was on the right side like the first car farther along. His headlights just barely picked out its red taillight.

Reason said sharply, "Take the ditch on the right."

But his hands decided otherwise. His hands took over. They whipped the wheel left, sharp, so hard he hit himself in the belly with his left elbow. The rear of the old Buick slewed right, almost slid at right angles across the road. As he passed the second car on the left his headlights picked up the figures of three boys, pink faces astonished, for a second terrorized. They were looking at a flat tire together.

"Grab!" Free cried sharply. He directed all his willpower to the car's rear wheels. If the rear wheels didn't grab, the trunk of the car would catch the rear end of the third car sideways.

Again his hands knew what was best. Carefully, as though measuring the car's weight against its velocity, his hands twisted the wheel slightly to the right, and so managed it that speed, resistance of the graveled surface, angle, shearing action, all came up even, and guided the old Buick exactly through the only slot left it.

And he was through. All he had to do was level the car out.

God. "Now that was what I call a narrow squeak."

He let the car coast a ways on its own.

"Those dumb sonsabitches, parking that way. My God, they ought to be arrested."

He rolled on yet another ways.

It came to him that in a pinch he could sure do the right thing fast. "I've got a pretty wonderful secret governor back there, you know? When it has to, it takes over and does it."

Ada 18

IT WAS JUNE FIRST, Free's graduation day.

Ada was proud of her oldest son. Only sixteen and already he was through high school. The last months he'd buckled down some and his marks had improved: a 92 in Reformed Doctrine, a 90 in both Bible and Civics, an 86 in English 4, an 81 in Physics, and a 78 in German IV. As a reward she and Alfred decided they should buy Free his first new long pants suit, a deep blue serge. They'd also bought him a new white shirt, a new red tie, a set of gold cuff links, and new black oxfords.

It was a soft June evening, just perfect, when Alfred wheeled the Buick onto the churchyard in Hello, where the commencement exercises were to be held. The sun was setting in the west and it struck all buildings, white siding or orange brick, with a lustrous citron hue. They were going up unto the house of the Lord to see their son graduate. It made Ada's heart leap up.

Free had asked if he couldn't go along with his friend Birdie Fowler to college in the fall.

Ada hadn't known what to say at first. She'd bit on her tongue as she pondered the future of her boy.

"You're biting your tongue again, Ma. And you know what happened to me once when I bumped my chin."

"Yes, son."

"Can I then? Go with Birdie?"

"We'll hold the thought for a while. We have all summer to think about it."

All the relatives of course would say it'd be ridiculous for the boy to go on to college. Who did the Alfredsons think they were that they should have a boy in college?

Ada knew she wasn't vain. Nor overly proud either. It was only that she loved her Lord Jesus and wanted to please Him by offering up her firstborn son in His service.

Alfred, in agreeing to rent the Hamilton half-section next to Bonnie, had figured on having Free home with him the next couple of years. With all those boys coming up, six of them, now was the time for Alfred to make hay. A fellow couldn't get hired men any cheaper than by raising them himself.

"We better get on inside if we want a decent seat."

Ada blinked; came to. "Yes." Alfred at the wheel was talking to her, smiling. He'd been in an especially jaunty mood that day. "Yes, I suppose we must."

"I'm looking forward to hearing the main speaker, Reverend Lodge, tonight. They say he surely can make the sparrows fly out of the rafters."

The churchyard was half full of cars. Most women had gone directly inside while the men lingered outside. The old horse barn had been torn down, now that no one drove a horse and carriage to church anymore, but the men still gathered a moment where the horse barn used to stand.

Alfred accompanied her into church. He found a seat for them halfway down the right aisle. They sat at the end of the bench. Alfred liked to sit on the aisle so he could stretch out his long legs now and then.

When the church was about filled, the consistory room door opened and the graduates of the class of 1928 filed in. They marched to the front of the church.

Alfred whispered under a cupped hand, "That kid of ours sticks out like an Abraham Lincoln."

Ada smiled. She watched the graduates seat themselves in the front two rows directly under the pulpit.

"Nice-looking bunch of kids, though."

Ada nodded. She watched where Free sat down. Even sitting the boy's blond head stuck out above the rest. She had to smile again at how his stubborn cowlick just would not stay slicked down. Her eyes filled with love for her son. He was so innocent of the world, and of all the toil and worry that lay ahead for him, such as she and Alfred had gone through. There was an odd streak in the boy she couldn't quite fathom. It was just out of her reach. And it wasn't either that he was of a different sex, but more that his mind ran to unearthly things. She hoped that side of him was not of the devil. She had once sensed it in Alfred's father and his stout way of beholding life and what he thought about it. In a way it was also like her own father's passionate search for God's truth. Free was a throwback to both grandfathers all right.

All sorts of smells drifted about in church—cologne perfume, scent of peppermints, fresh tar soap, someone's feet. The overhead lights cast a mellow lemon glow over the assembled heads.

Alfred recrossed his legs. He rubbed one knee where he'd let it rest against the bench ahead too long.

Principal Hedges marched in, followed by Reverend Lodge, the speaker, and Reverend Marcellus Weathers, the president of the Western Academy Association. In solemn pomp they took the three steps onto the platform and settled themselves in the black leather throne chairs behind the pulpit. The brass pipes of the organ stood ranked behind them. All three sat a moment contemplating the audience. At that very moment the setting sun struck level through the tall west windows. It cut three strong orange shafts into the church, piercing the soft luminance from the overhead chandeliers. It set the three men apart from the people. They were on a separate brass cloud by themselves. Then with a glance at the big clock in the back of the church, Principal Hedges rose and came forward to the pulpit and announced the audience would sing Psalm One.

"And he shall be like a tree planted by the rivers of water, that bringeth forth his fruit in his season; his leaf also shall not wither; and whatever he doth shall prosper."

Ada loved the sound of choirs. The young graduates up front sang especially lustily.

The opening remarks of Reverend Lodge's charge to the graduates turned out to be a disappointment, Ada thought. Free had told them about Reverend Lodge's be-the-first-to-cast-a-stone-at-me-and-my-wife sermon and she had expected some lively fireworks.

The general idea of be-the-first-to-cast-a-stone Ada approved of. That was why she'd made it such a point to invite cousin Garrett and his wife Laura over for coffee after they'd confessed at church. She recalled how outraged, even downright ugly, many in church had been that she'd dared to be friendly so soon with those dirty adulterers. The people wanted to exact the last drop of humiliation from those poor strayers. But they'd paid their penalty and were now to be counted among God's chosen. And of course any babies born too early to such wayward couples, those soft lovely creatures, so innocent that even their pee at birth was as pure as rainwater . . . why, who could be so cruel as to demand that they be punished too? On that one point she dared to disagree with the Little Church doctrine, where it said that the punishment for the sins of the fathers shall be visited upon the children unto the third and the fourth generation.

Her breasts were beginning to feel full again. She'd nursed little Sherman just before they left home in the hope that he could wait for his next feeding until she got back from the graduation exercises. She'd decided to go to a program just with Alfred alone for once, where she could relax, with no motherly worries. Just sit and listen and enjoy. Though she liked the full feeling in her breasts. There was no other feeling like it.

"Amen."

What? Well! Reverend Lodge had finished his charge. Dear God, except for the opening remarks, those about making sure one planted one's tree of life near a running brook, she'd missed the central theme of his address. And here she prided herself in always listening to every word a speaker had to say.

Reverend Lodge announced the commencement song, "God Be With You Until We Meet Again."

Ada thought the song most appropriate. Those sturdy youngsters soon to be dispersed to all ends of the earth to work out their appointed destinies needed to know God would be with them.

Presently the class was asked to rise. In fitting silence, so quiet one could hear an overhead arch in the church creak, Principal Hedges read off the names. One by one, separated by a dozen steps, they advanced to where Reverend Weathers, as president of the Western Academy Association, stood in tall dark gravity and handed over the diploma with his left hand and shook hands with his right hand. To each one he said the same thing. "Congratulations and Godspeed."

Free was one of the first ones. He stepped from the moving line going down the bench and walked around to the three steps of the podium. He waited for his name to be announced, "Alfred Alfredson," and then mounted the steps. He moved tall across the platform and received the diploma with one hand and the handshake with the other, and moved on.

Her son. Issue of her flesh.

Ada remembered vividly the night when she'd softened in love for her husband and received his embrace, when she'd conceived that trembling son standing out above all the other graduates like some Saul of old. That blond head there with its two stubborn moons, with its odd set of brains, with its strange mingling of innocence and mischief, that blond head had once had its start in her belly, a tiny acorn that had set its roots into her womb and pushed forth its sprout, until eventually it came to grow into an oak six feet tall. And it was still growing. Pray God it might become a mighty oak, sheltering future little sprouting acorns.

The class of 1928 continued standing as Reverend Weathers pronounced them all graduates.

"Let us bow our heads in thankful prayer on this special occasion."

Afterwards friends and relatives pressed to the front of the church to congratulate them.

Free was crying when Ada and Alfred came along to shake his hand.

Ada marveled to see the tears. They made it all worthwhile.

The house on the rise was dark when Alfred rolled up to the gate. It meant the children were in bed asleep. Good.

Ada and Free got out and moved up the walk together, while Alfred put the car away.

Ada pushed into the dark kitchen feeling around in the air above her head for the light chain. "Electricity is wonderful," she said. "Except that one still almost has to light a match to find the light cord." She felt the tickle of the chain finally and caught it. She pulled and the yellow kitchen was instantly awash with light.

Free set down his suitcases. He smiled at the swinging light. "This has been quite a year at that. I graduate from the twelfth grade and my family graduates into having electric light on the farm."

"Yes. No more stinking kerosene spilling over things." She smiled at her looming son. His new blue suit fit him perfectly. For all his size he looked dapper standing in her kitchen. "Now, can I see your diploma?"

Free dug it out of his suitcases.

Ada unrolled it on the table. "My, what an important looking document." She could feel warmth emanating from Free. It touched her.

Alfred stepped into the kitchen just as she read the elegant scroll parchment aloud: "This certifies that *Alfred Alfredson* having completed the course of study prescribed by the Board of Trustees is hereby declared a Graduate of the Western Academy and as an Honorable Testimonial of Scholarship and Character is entitled to this DIPLOMA, Given at Hello this first day of June, A.D. 1928. Gary Hedges, Principal. Reverend Marcellus Weathers, President."

Free glanced sidelong at his father.

Alfred smiled down at where the writing flowed across the opened scroll. "Wisht I'd learned to sign my checks in a hand like that. It'd make my checks look like a real bank money order."

Free laughed.

Ada smiled to see her two tall men in good spirits together.

Alfred went over to the stove and clapped out his pipe in the firepot. "Son, I was proud of you tonight. I noticed that you listened carefully to what Reverend Lodge had to say . . . all the way through."

"Thanks, Pa."

Alfred placed his pipe on the window sill. "Well, I guess its time for us to hit the hay. Tomorrow we got to get at that cultivating."

Free and Alfred got ready to go to bed.

Ada thought to herself a moment, and then smiling, went into their bedroom and picked up the sleeping baby from his crib. He wasn't wet. Good. She sat down in her favorite rocker by the open porch door. A soft breeze came up off the far valley. It brushed lightly through the screen. She opened her dress and lifted out her left breast, the one that lay over her heart. It was so full it hurt. A drop of milk welled onto the surface of the nipple. The touch of the wet nipple on Sherman's soft pink lips was like magic. Instantly the lips set out and the nipple vanished. As she rocked, Sherman's little round mouth followed her breast back and forth.

She felt the milk of life drain out of her and fill baby. She also felt, flowing the other way, against the streaming milk, a surge of life rising from the babe and entering her body. It was as if the two of them were giving each other a transfusion.

Ada smiled down at the little sucking machine. She watched its little pink fingers pinch her veined breast, lightly, involuntarily. "Yes, little fellow, you better drink while you can. Because I think it's time we weaned you. It's been almost eighteen months now, sonny, and that's longer than I breastfed the others."

The pink eyelids opened a little. Milky blue orbs volved. The eyelids closed.

"Yes, you, you cute little dickens you. You know I love you very much, don't you? And you don't mind taking advantage of it either, do you?" She gave the nipple a little playful shake in the baby's mouth. "Yes, and later on when you get old enough to step on my feet, you'll be old enough to walk on my heart." She sighed a sigh of gentle resignation. "Though perhaps that's as it should be. Each generation has its own conscience and should live in accordance with it."

The moon was up. The soft maple leaves fluttered outdoors. Horses stomped in the night yard. The long pasture below lay spread out a silvered green lake. The alfalfa field was in bloom, and its fragrance was heaven's perfume. In the summer the country was like a male pheasant, colorful and bright. Too bad that generally winter in the country was like the female pheasant. It did not say much for the female spirit. Another one of God's almost unjust mysteries.

White blood from her veins flowed into the baby.

She was going to like the new place. Perhaps with their oldest boy home now for a couple of years, they might have a happy life together after all, toiling in the sun under God's love. How sweet it was to live with Alfred these days. As they got older he bothered her less and less. She recalled how disappointed she'd been during their first years together. He had been so passionate and ardent. Every time she'd turn over in sleep she'd bump into his hard bone there. Why had God put such a strong urge to cohabit in some men, when at the same time God had also ordered that they were not to make love unless they had procreation in mind, His Procreation, since He was the Creator? It was a puzzle. Because when she didn't permit Alfred his pleasure at regular intervals he became irritable. Karen's husband Kon was much more the ideal husband. God's kind of man. Ada had once been quite jealous of Karen. God forgive, but perhaps she'd even been in love with Kon. In a spiritual kind of way, of course.

"When I was a little girl I wanted to remain a little girl all my life. I never wanted to grow up. How I hated to learn about draining rags and the like. I never wanted to grow up and bear fruit."

The suckling at her breast was pleasurable. She noticed the left breast was almost empty. She turned the baby around and let him suckle the right breast.

Presently baby's diaper felt warm against her arm.

"Why, you little rascal you. You've wet your pants."

Sometimes, when she felt especially lonesome, in need of being touched, she took up baby to let him suckle her. She loved nursing her babies. It was the one time of the day she had time to think.

Sometimes baby's ardent suckling made her swoon in pleasure. All her feelings, her whole mind, seemed to come to a point in her nipples. It would've taken but a spark, of the kind one got when one touched a light chain after walking across a thick rug, for her to explode. She wondered if that was what Alfred felt when he galloped upon her spread thighs and groaned so pleasurably at the end there.

"Yes, Kon is a sweet man, but in Alfred I've now got a husband who has also matured into a sweet man."

Those times when she'd been reading articles aloud to Alfred, and he'd fallen asleep, and she'd chided him about it—"So, you think I'm reading aloud here just to hear the sound of my own voice"—he'd pretend he'd been awake all along. He hadn't wanted her to think she'd read for nothing into thin air. Yes, he was truly "a gentle man." He was one of those who could work with wrenches and greasy machinery and never nick his fingers. He could sometimes wear his overalls the whole week, even during the manure-hauling season, and still not have them soiled. He always had clean hands. When he had a moment he'd sit and pare his nails. He had no body odor to speak of, even after sweating all day. Except for his coal-black hair, now white, he had the complexion of a Kon, white-skinned, almost womanly.

She had a sudden longing to go out into their garden and pull up a fresh onion. After a rain there wasn't a finer treat than to bite into the white end of an onion. Memory of the snap of it in her mouth made the saliva flow so that she had to swallow several times.

She was at an age when memories of other times began to come back to her more and more. A new richness was creeping into her life. Certain memories, when they came again and again, were like sudden harp notes. They came in the midst of what was sometimes a vast silence of work. The harp notes made her long to ascend to angel country.

The suckling at her breast ceased. Baby had fallen asleep.

That Karen now. Looking at her one would think Karen was innocent of guile. Not so. Ada was sure that Karen had sensed her feelings for Kon. It seemed to Ada, when Karen and Kon had visited them the summer before, that Karen had acted a little too excited, even a little too possessive of Kon.

For some reason too Karen always kept being overly curious about her relations with Alfred. There was something unhealthy about it. Karen kept wanting to know about Alfred's demands as though privately comparing them with what husband Kon demanded.

Baby in sleep gave her nipple a soft suck. After a second baby gave her a good hard suck. Then baby's mouth slid away inert again.

Her heart did the same thing. It gave a soft little beat; paused; then bounded once, big, in her chest. Then quit.

She managed to get out one sound. "Alfred!"

She came to, very gradually. Her mind worked like a sun burning off a fog.

Alfred was holding her in his arms. She could smell him in his nightshirt. Baby lay on the floor bawling his head off. Baby must've rolled off her lap and fallen to the floor.

Alfred gave her a shake, hard. "What happened?"

"I—don't—know—Alfred. My heart beat funny once and then I fainted."

"I'll say you did. When I came out here you were laying in the rocker like a sack of white flour."

"I—feel—so—funny—Alfred."

"You cried out and then I heard the baby hit the floor."

"I can't seem to get my breath. I—need—more—air."

"Here." Alfred carried her out onto the porch. "That better?"

Ada clawed at the screen door. "More air. Bring me out on the lawn."

Alfred pushed through the screen door with his elbow and carried her outside. He laid her out on the grass. "That better?"

"The baby." Ada sucked for air.

"Let him bawl. So long's he can bawl he's all right."

She sucked and sucked for air. Her brain was floating off by itself. It was a mist.

"Ada?"

"I feel so funny numb all over, Alfred."

Alfred chafed her wrists. "I better call the doctor."

She puffed. "Wait." Gradually what appeared to be drops of dew glistening on a hairnet close up, lofted up and away from her and became stars in heaven.

"I better call him."

"No. I'm beginning to feel better."

"You sure?"

"It's so expensive always, calling the doctor."

"Not when it comes to your life, Ada."

Ada gazed up at the skies. "Look at all those stars. I never before realized there were so many." She took several very deep breaths, all the way in. Her head began to clear up. "Nor so precious."

Alfred watched her.

"We better go pick up the baby before he gets the hysterics," she said.

"You're sure you're going to be all right now?"

"Yes."

"Okay." Alfred helped her to her feet.

As soon as she could she gave baby her breast again to quiet him down.

Ada ❦ 19

ALFRED CAME HOME from town with the mail. He called Free up from the barn.

Ada had just stepped outside to throw the potato peelings into the swill barrel. "Dinner isn't quite ready yet. It's only quarter to twelve."

"I know. I got a package here for him. From his aunt and uncle."

Ada placed the dishpan upside down on the drying rack. "Oh?" She wiped her hands dry in her apron and held out her hand for the package. "Let me see."

It was postmarked Whitebone all right. It was long and slender. Kon had addressed the package in his usual perfect hand: *Alfred Alfredson VII, Esq.*

Free came up with his long stride. He stopped at the gate to clean off his heels on the shoe-cleaner. The old hoe, set with its sharp end up in the cement walk, rang each time he cuffed it with his instep. "What's up?"

"I think you got a present from your Uncle Kon." Ada handed him the package. "And your Aunt Karen."

The slender package looked fragile in Free's brown hand. He smiled, surprised. "Well."

The three went into the house and sat down at the kitchen table. Table was set. Baby Sherman sat in his high chair nearby playing with a rattle.

Free unwrapped the package slowly so as to stretch out the pleasure of receiving a gift. It turned out to be a slender black watch case. On the lower right-hand corner of the box were some letters in gold. *Gruen*. Free snapped the box open and there lay a new white-gold wristwatch with black leather straps. Tucked in a corner was a little white envelope.

Ada smiled in soft love for the boy's uncle.

Free opened the envelope and read the enclosed note aloud: "For our dear nephew Free on the occasion of his graduation from high school, June 1, 1928. Aunt Karen and Uncle Kon."

Alfred's eyes in the meantime had slowly enlarged. "Wal, I declare. They didn't turn out to be such tightwads after all."

"Alfred!" Ada said. "What an awful thing to say."

Alfred's face quickly closed over. He got out his pipe and lit up the half-burnt tobacco in it. "It's a pretty watch all right."

"Well, I was going to say."

"Though it ain't gonna be of much good out in the field."

"Why not?" Ada challenged.

"It's too fine."

Ada bethought herself and fell silent.

Free got up to wash his hands, then back to fit the watch on his left wrist. It just fit in the last hole. "They remembered," Free said quietly.

"Your Uncle Kon is a very thoughtful man," Ada said.

"And I'm not, eh?" Alfred bristled.

"I didn't say that."

"I can take a hint."

Ada went over and gave Alfred a hug in front of her son. "No one can be much more thoughtful than you, my dear one."

"Wal, I was wonderin'."

Free took off the wristwatch. He set it, marking the time on the kitchen clock, and wound it carefully. Then he placed back in its black case. He looked at the watch case with dreamy eyes. "It'll be handy for when I go to college."

Ada and Alfred gave each other a look.

Free caught the look. "I take it I'm not going to college then this fall."

Ada said, "I don't think you're ready for college yet, son."

"In a couple of years I'll have forgotten all I learned in high school." Free held up his palms. Already calluses as thick as streaks of dried yellow paint lay across them. "My brains'll look like the insides of these hands pretty soon."

"Your father needs you until Everett gets older."

"I didn't rent this big farm," Free said.

Alfred came bolt upright in his swivel chair. "Are you questioning our authority?"

Free's shoulders came up. It was as though the boy was getting ready for a butting contest with his father.

"Wait, you two," Ada said. "Tonight is house visitation and we'd best prepare ourselves to meet our pastor with a clean heart."

Reverend Tiller and elder August Highmire arrived on the yard at eight o'clock. By then Ada had mopped and waxed the kitchen floor. Ada prided herself on being one of the few housewives left who still did her floors on hands and knees. It was the old way. But it was the only way to get the corners clean and get at those rings of dirt by the stove legs.

Alfred ushered the two men into the living room, offering the black rocker by the window box to the reverend and the easy chair by the phonograph to the elder. Alfred and Ada settled side by side on the black leather horsehair sofa. The two men were wearing black suits. Alfred had on his new blue work shirt and new overalls. Ada had on her usual green dress. The children were outside playing on the grass under the trees.

Reverend Tiller beamed upon them with his ruddy face. The good reverend liked to work in the garden in the summer and he looked as weathered as any of his parishioners. Elder Highmire was getting older. His hair had become a shock of sheer white, as had his eyebrows, while his cheeks had tanned to a deep old wine red. While Reverend Tiller was enjoying life to the hilt, Elder Highmire was lamenting it. He still had four daughters at home, all old maids, not one of whom had ever had so much as a single date. Worse yet, his daughters refused to help him with his fieldwork. All four sat in the house with his wife, slowly getting fatter by the day and eating him into the poorhouse.

After a couple of minutes of reverential joshing, Reverend Tiller came to the point. "Well now. Here we are." He set his elbows on the arms of his rocker and built up a temple with his fingers. "So. How goes it with the Alfredsons this glorious summer? I trust well?"

"Fine," Alfred said. Ada had always wanted him, as the man of the house, to take the lead.

"You've all been in good health?"

"Tolerable."

"And spiritually?"

"Fine. Like everybody else we have our ups and downs. But we try our best."

"There are no questions about the Godhead of Jesus Christ our Lord and Savior?"

Ada said, "On that score none in our house, thank God."

"We shall be having Lord's Supper again next Sunday. Is there anything one of you has to confess before that event? Something you may have done to cause a brother or a sister to stumble?"

"Naw," Alfred said. "Not that I know of. Though there's a couple of guys I wouldn't mind tripping up."

Ada looked at Alfred surprised. This was no time to joke.

"Are they members of our church?" Reverend Tiller asked.

Alfred hardened. "Domeny, a tattletale I ain't. But there are some fellows in our church who bet on the board of trade, and if that ain't gambling then I don't know what gambling is."

"I see." With his two forefingers Reverend Tiller formed a very sharp steeple for his temple of fingers. He rested the point of his nose on it. "That's a serious charge. Do you have any facts to back it up?"

"No, Domeny. But they sure talk about it a lot downtown. I think you know who I mean."

"Perhaps. Sooo."

Elder Highmire's thoughts were busy with something else. "Your oldest son, now. What are your plans for him?"

Ada looked at Alfred and Alfred looked at Ada.

The children could be heard outside yelling under the trees with the joy of play.

Reverend Tiller asked, "What is your son's wish?"

"He wants to go to college this fall," Alfred said.

"Rrrach!" Elder Highmire growled. "It's all cray-zy to send a big boy like him away for more schooling. Cray-zy." Elder Highmire's voice was coarse and grating. It worked on one like a whirring eggbeater. "If the boy was a weakling now, and the youngest in the family, well, that might be different. But looking at him I can see the Lord gave him a strong back and big muscles for use on the farm. I know that's what I'd use him for."

Alfred couldn't resist it. "Wal, August, maybe we should marry my boy off to one of your girls." Alfred had the good sense not to say old maids. "Or, better yet, let's you and me make a trade. You take my boy for your fieldwork, and my wife here take your girl for her housework."

Elder Highmire gave Alfred a pair of white-ringed eyes.

Reverend Tiller caught something. He pursed up his red lips behind his steepled fingers. "Mrs. Alfredson, are you still unhappy with God's decision not to give you any daughters?"

"No, Reverend. I say with Job, 'Naked I came out of my mother's womb, and naked shall I return thither. The Lord gave, and the Lord hath taken away, blessed be the name of the Lord.'"

"Good, good. And you might quote another passage from Scripture that'd be apropos. 'And it shall be said of her that she had sons, not daughters.'"

Elder Highmire backfired like an old engine. "And what shall be said of me and all my daughters?"

A wide surprised look came over Reverend Tiller's red face. "Well, now, Brother Highmire, don't be looking at things so on the down side. Just think, besides your wife, you have four extra girl friends in your house."

"Rrrach."

Ada thought: "And I suppose by the same token I should consider myself well off that I have six extra lovers in my house." Ada thought: "Domeny should see what I've noticed lately. That witches have begun to visit my oldest son." Ada was thinking of the stains she'd found in Free's sheets.

Reverend Tiller went on with the inquiry. "About your boy again, Mrs. Alfredson. Does he accept your decision to stay home?"

"He's got to," Alfred said, absolute.

"He's a good boy," Ada said, quietly, "and knows how to be obedient if need be."

Reverend Tiller let his temple of fingers collapse into his lap. "Isn't it about time he joined church?"

"Yes, it is," Ada said.

"Perhaps we ought to talk to him about it," Reverend Tiller said.

Alfred said, "I'll call him in."

"While you're at it," Ada said, "call in the others too. It's time they went to bed."

It took a few minutes to get Everett, Flip, Jonathan, and Abbott washed and upstairs to bed, as well as put the little baby in his crib in Alfred and Ada's bedroom.

When all had settled down again, and Ada had put on the coffee percolator, Reverend Tiller turned his beaming red face on Free. "So. I hear we're going to be seeing a lot of you this coming year."

Free sat on a hardback chair in the doorway to the kitchen. "I guess so."

"Well now then, perhaps in another year, after attending catechism regularly, you'll be ready to join church."

"I suppose so."

"You'll be seventeen next January, not?"

"Yes."

A squabble developed in the bedroom above them. Flip was whispering, trying to keep his voice down, but he was so fierce in what he had to say that everybody downstairs could hear him clearly. "You did too forget to empty the pisspot, Everett. We haven't pissed that much yet tonight."

"Why couldn't you have emptied it for me once?" Everett said. "If you noticed it still had something in it."

"It's your job, not mine. I got my own jobs to do."

There was a sound of a pair of folded knees hitting the floor.

"Look out!" Flip cried.

"Well, I got to piss too," Jonathan said.

"Why didn't you go behind the house a minute before you went to bed?"

"Why didn't you?"

There was some bumping of bodies.

Then came the awful sound of a crock tipping over. In fighting with each other, Flip and Jonathan had tipped the pisspot over. There was a swish of spreading liquid; then a swilling sound; and then, before the astonished eyes of Ada, Alfred, Free, and Elder Highmire, a slender yellow waterfall came down through the hot air register and splashed directly onto the back of Reverend Tiller's neck.

Reverend Tiller's eyes opened wide. He didn't say a thing. With the infinite patience of the good shepherd, he quietly moved his black rocker over a couple of feet. The rest of the yellow waterfall pittered directly to the linoleum floor. Then Reverend Tiller plucked out the white handkerchief from his lapel pocket and delicately dabbed himself dry over the back of his neck.

Alfred looked heavenward and let go with a roar. "Yarr! you kids up there. Behave!"

There was a strangled silence upstairs.

Everett got in the last word, very quietly. "See, I told you."

Elder Highmire couldn't hold himself back any longer. He let go with a crazy dry cracked laugh. "At least that my daughters don't do."

Free ❦ 20

PA GOT FREE up while it was still dark.

Free stumbled downstairs to discover it was only four in the morning. "Why so early?"

"It's going to be a corker today. So you and I are going out to the field the minute it's light and cultivate until eleven. Then we'll rest the horses until late in the evening. And around eight, say, we'll go out again and work until midnight. Flip and Everett can do the yard chores."

"Cultivate at night?"

"There'll be a full moon out the first part of the night."

"Oh."

Free had made other plans for the evening. Aunt Karen had sent them her old violin in the hopes that one of her nephews would take it up. Free wanted to give the violin a try. He thought he could teach himself. If Pa could once play it as a fiddle at square dances, he could play it the Fritz Kreisler way at concerts. Free knew just where he could practice too. Down in the pasture a ways was a curving cutbank that'd make for a little private concert hall for himself. Nobody'd hear him make mistakes there.

"We've got to think of the animals, son." Pa poured Free a cup of coffee. Pa set out the cream and sugar. "Horses are God's creatures too, you know." Even when the weather was normal Pa insisted the horses should have a two-hour rest at noon. Of course while the horses rested Pa also had himself a sweet nap.

Free fixed his coffee. He treated his tongue to a sip of it.

"And you better get up that fetch-sticking Pet too." Pa stood with one foot up on the reservoir. "Now, for a fact, there's one horse I wouldn't mind if it dropped dead in the field." Pa sipped at his coffee. "I sure did get ruped when Wilmer Youngman sold me that horse. Said Pet was a good horse. No bad habits. Gotske. When Pet's almost hopeless. As full of tricks as a lawyer. Can't trust him a second. And the less you work him the worse he gets." Pa tolled his head. "Yeh, and at the time Wilmer Youngman sold that horse to me he was an elder in our church. As well as your mother's shirttail relation." Pa took a deep sip of his coffee. "Can't feed the blame horse oats because he's got the heaves. If you do he'll fart you to death. So you got to feed him expensive corn. Why, riding behind that horse on a still day is like riding behind a foul-smelling shotgun."

Free began to laugh. He almost choked on his coffee.

"So coon-footed he walks like a man with a pair of overshoes on four sizes too big. And he's the worst darn cribber I ever did see. Why, he's half-et his manger on his side. Wood, mind you."

Free coughed to clear his eyes of tears.

"And such an ornery bastard to get up from the pasture. He walks home, not trots home. The dog dassent nip his heels because of the way he kicks. In fact, the dog almost lost his brains the other day."

A week before just as their new dog Rover reached in to nip Pet, Pet kicked at Rover in a clever way. Instead of in an arching kick, Pet had stroked his hoof flat along the ground and caught the dog full over the skull. He knocked Rover out. It took Rover two days to recover.

Done with coffee, Free stepped outside and called up the dog. Rover came out from under the front porch on Free's first call. Rover shook himself; then stood ready at Free's heels. Free reached back a hand. Rover gave Free's fingertips a single warm lick. The dog's tongue barely showed pink in the pale brown light.

The morning star hung over the roof of the barn like a great yellow period. It danced as Free footed it down the dusty pasture lane. His bare feet found the right way by themselves, fastidiously avoiding the cowplotches and horseballs. Rover padded along behind. Rover's black coat was of a piece with the darkness close to the ground; his white chest and white nose glanced like flowing milk.

The lane opened into the pasture and the path tailed off in the grass. The grass was sopping wet. The smell of the wet cloverballs was as sweet as a garden of peonies.

Dawn opened slowly. Free began to make out the weathered fence posts bordering the long zigzag pasture. The gully down the center deepened, yellow clay showing under the top layer of black earth.

He came to the turn in the pasture where he planned to practice the violin. The curving cutbank would make a nice little theatre all right. He called out, "Hey!" There was a quick echo in reply, "Hey." It was going to be perfect to practice in, like trying out one's voice in a bathroom.

His pink feet stroked through the soppy grass.

Dawn came on faster.

Around the next turn he spotted the cows. They were already up and grazing. They looked at him ruminatively with their orange glowing eyes, until they spotted Rover trotting along behind him. Then only those cows that were being milked at the time turned and headed up the trail home. Rover never chased cows; only started them up and headed them for the barn. Milk tended to leak out of a full bag when a cow was hurried along too fast.

Free strode onto the last hill. For some reason the buffaloes in the old days had dug a considerable wallow for themselves on the crest of the hill. There the grass was always the deepest and coarsest. Neither cow nor horse cared much for the coarse grass.

Free found the horses below the hill. All eleven horse heads came up. When Rover appeared at Free's heels, Fan and Nell and Maud immediately headed for home. They knew Rover. Sam and Prince, Colonel and silly old Polly lingered for one more last mouthful of grass, and then joined the procession. Highnose old Dick, and the two golden-tailed sorrels, Queen and Daise, bred out of Fan, looked around for some place to escape to. Rover read their motions and made short work of their foolish hopes. He shot swift and silent across the grass, head low, and then, just as he came within a foot of their heels, let go with a deep wolfish growl. Snorting, heads rearing, manes flying, they set off to join the parade for home.

Pet, the son-of-a-bitching bay, went right on grazing coolly by himself. He kept a quietly wary eye out to see what Rover would do about him. Pet had a beautiful coat of reddish-brown with a yellow mane and a long yellow tail.

Rover's head came up to think things over. Then, mind made up, he ran lightly across the deep grass until he'd maneuvered himself around behind Pet's heels. Ears flat along his skull, he suddenly skulked in under Pet's long trailing yellow tail and bit Pet in the heels. Almost in the same motion, Rover jumped to one side about the width of Pet's hoof. Pet snapped his hoof back low along the grass. And missed Rover. Again Rover skulked in; took a good nip; and immediately after darted to one side. Again Pet kicked low and hard. And missed.

Free smiled. "Well, Rover, you've wised up a little, eh?"

Rover took two more nips, Pet still missing.

Mystified, Pet gave up and broke into a trot to join the procession up ahead.

Free followed the moving line of horses home. Rover fell in behind Free and trotted along at his heels. Free reached back a hand and petted Rover over the top of his head. Rover reached up a single quick warm lick.

Dawn came on, a clear light blue over the deep green pasture. It flashed over the stippled oats field and the ribboned cornfields.

Walking along, feet pleasantly cool and wet, Free abruptly remembered there was something special up at the house. A hired girl. Ma had finally relented and had hired herself some help.

The hired girl was Aletha Gladjanus, a distant cousin of Ma's from Sioux Center. Aletha had been sent out to help with the family finances. She was just sixteen and pretty. But Free soon discovered he didn't have much in common with her. She never looked at a book. Ma wasn't sure she liked Aletha either. Aletha wasn't very neat and was always looking at Free. Ma tolerated her though because Ma liked her name. Ma had always wished she'd been baptized Aletha.

The milk cows ahead entered the head of the lane. Free counted them. Eighteen. They were all there.

When Dick came to within forty feet of the entrance to the lane, he reared up for a last look around to see if he couldn't still somehow escape slavery for that day.

Rover came alive at Free's heels. He first growled in warning, then ran toward

Dick a dozen swift steps, slowly lowering his head to the ground, until he looked like a snake with a bushy tail.

That was enough. Dick popped his tail in disgust, then went meekly along with the other horses.

When they all arrived in the barnyard, Pa showed up at the barn and opened the doors. The cows and the horses filed in willingly. They could smell the feed that Pa had put out for them.

The sun popped over the horizon just as the last cow swung inside.

"Man," Pa said, "it's going to be a scorcher all right."

It was six sharp when Pa and Free got out to the cornfield, Pa on the double-row with Dick and Fan and Queen and Daise, and Free on the single-row with Pet and Polly. Pa loved old Fan and her daughters, Queen and Daise, while Free hated Pet and felt sorry for nervous old Polly.

The hole over Daise's eye had only just healed. Free still shuddered sometimes when he remembered how Daise had got hurt. Pa had named the new Daise after his old beloved Daise.

The horses hadn't been worked for a couple of days, and that always gave them runaway notions. When Free and Rover brought up the horses from the pasture, Daise along with Dick had tried to shy out of the barnyard just as Pa was closing the hanging gate.

"Hyar!" Pa roared at the two.

Dick had the sense to veer off to one side.

But Daise reared straight up. And, in rearing, Daise rammed the top of her skull into one of the bolts sticking out of the top of the anchor post from which the gate hung. She rammed her skull so hard onto the bolt that she impaled herself on it. Just over the eye.

Pa instantly broke into action. He shinnied up the post, wrapping his legs around it; then very delicately lifted Daise's whole skull off the bolt; then let her down.

Free standing a little ways away couldn't believe his eyes. His father had lifted half of a horse up by its skull, and had done it while clinging to a post with his legs. God! What a person couldn't do in an emergency.

Daise stood exactly where Pa let her down. She didn't run.

Pa slid down the post. Trembling, he looked her skull over. Then on the run he shot to the house and called Dr. Overslough.

Dr. Overslough happened to be in Bonnie that afternoon, where the telephone operator happened to see him out of her window, and within twenty minutes was on the yard. Pa in the meantime had led Daise into her stall in the barn.

Dr. Overslough took one look and shook his head. "Better shoot her, Alfred, and take her out of her misery."

"There ain't no chance to save her?"

"Well, you can try doping that hole with some salve if you wanna. And stuff that hole once a day with fresh cotton. But even then . . ."

"I'll do it if you think it'll work."

"Well, I guess it won't hurt to try."

"I'll do it."

"Well, you're the doctor. But remember one thing: put a little less cotton in the hole each day."

"When will I know when I'm gaining on it?"

"When you see maggots in the hole."

Pa bent over and started to bawl.

Free got out of Pa's sight.

After a while Dr. Overslough clapped Pa lightly on the back and wished him well; and left.

About a week later Pa came into the house after supper with a smile. He had just come back from doctoring Daise. "Well, the sorrel's finally gone and done it. Raised herself a handful of maggots."

"Goodness me," Ma said. "That means death, doesn't it?"

"I was right not to shoot her," Pa said, chin set out in victory. Then Pa explained to Ma what the maggots were good for. They ate away dead tissue and so helped heal the hole.

They knocked off the cultivating at eleven. It was 101° in the shade. The sun burned straight down on man and beast and leaf. The sun appeared to oscillate. They let the horses drink for only a minute and then ushered them firmly into the barn and unharnessed them and fed them. Free got a pail of water from the tank and washed off the horses' shoulders. The horses loved it when he laved them with lukewarm water. They leaned toward him to help him. Some of the horses had worked up balls of sweaty foam behind their hind legs.

After dinner Pa retired for his nap, while the kids went out under the trees. Ma took a nap too in her bedroom, while hired girl Aletha did the dishes.

Free retired to the little west room at the head of the stairs. It was where Ma stored her sugar and flour. It was the one room in the house to get the full benefit of the shade from the umbrella cottonwood towering over the house. Free like to lie on the bare gray-painted floor and have the little window open behind his head. What little wind there was came out of the southwest. The shadow of the great tree cooled the wind before it brushed through the screen.

He picked up Jack London's *The Call of the Wild,* borrowed from Dr. Fairlamb. He had gone to the doctor's home one Sunday evening on the hunch that the good man was bound to have some kind of library. Doctor did and told Free to help himself. The first thing Free spotted was the complete works of Jack London. Free lay on his side to read. It was a good book. He read until his eyes got tired. He noticed how rusty his brain had become. After a while he slipped the bookmark in place, lay the book aside, and rolled over on his back. Lazily he stretched himself. Scent of dry sugar and dry flour drifted about the room like the odor of a sweet cigar.

Outside the breeze was just strong enough to stir up the leaves of the cottonwood. The leaves whispered, murmured. Sometimes they clappered lightly with the sound of little leather bells. It reminded him of the time he saw Ada Shutter walking toward him under a row of golden cottonwoods. For a couple of seconds the total feel and taste of that agonizingly beautiful moment came back to him. Even the gray walls of the little room he lay in for a moment turned golden. He wept. Too bad Ada had the soul of a nun. What a difference there was between Ada and Ma's maid, Aletha Gladjanus.

Speaking of the devil, Free heard the stair door open below and then heard someone coming up the stairs. Looking past his bare toes, through the open door, he saw Aletha's face appear in the stairwell. She was through with the dishes and was also going to her room. Her face was as plump as a pumpkin and her eyes as round as little blue moons. The blue in her eyes was heightened by the blue of her dress. She saw him and slowed a little and gave him a soft wondering smile. She kept coming up, slow, her sloped breasts showing, then her narrow waist, then her melon hips, then her vigorous thighs. She hesitated on the top step. She smiled fatly at him. Her eyes thickened, half closed.

He stared past his two big toes at her. He waited.

Her eye fell on the front of his overalls. She blinked. She appeared to thicken even more around the eyes. Then, knowing something, her chin came up and her eyes looked away. Slowly she tripped past his door to her own room.

He heard her moving about in her room through the closet between them. Presently he heard her bed creak.

Dream queen Ada Shutter vanished from his mind's eye. Instead all he could think of was Aletha's thickened eyes and soft fat smile. He wondered if she'd ever done it. Probably not. Her parents, the Gladjanuses, were every bit as strict as his own pa and ma. Stricter even. All the older Gladjanus children were discouraged from getting married. Aletha's oldest brother was past thirty and still hadn't left the nest. Same for her oldest sister just twenty-nine. Their parents had bred and raised them to be their hired help, without pay, as they fought to pay off the mortgage on their section of land.

Aletha's bed squeaked several times.

It didn't take him long to decide that she wanted him to hold her. He got up and tiptoed down the short hall to her door. He stuck close to the wall to make sure the floorboards wouldn't squeak. He didn't want Pa on his horsehair sofa or Ma in her bed to hear him go to Aletha's room. If they caught him visiting Aletha in her room, man, that would really set the dolls to dancing.

He pushed her door open slowly to keep it from creaking.

Aletha was lying with her knees up. Her dress having slid down, her legs were bare to her pink panties. The brown blind had been drawn down to the window sill and it gave her skin a tanned look. Her hands lay at her side. There was an air about her hands, or fingertips, that suggested that but a moment before they'd been busy.

She sensed something in the room. Her legs parted. Her face peered at him from between her knees; then, with a little squeak, she bounded out of bed. The motion of her was that of a sleek cat. Her round blue moon eyes turned squarish.

She was scared. "What do you want?" she whispered.

"I just thought maybe we both needed a little company," he whispered back.

"Oh." Again her eyes settled on the front of his overalls. "You're not s'posed to come in here."

"I just thought . . ."

"Your mother won't like this."

"A fellow can't always be worrying about what his mother thinks."

"What do you want?"

"Just to visit a little."

"Well . . ."

He advanced upon her. He slid his bare feet along the floor to avoid making the boards creak. He watched her face to make sure she wouldn't cry out. He moved very slowly.

She began to feel reassured he wasn't going to throw himself upon her like some crazy stallion. Her face softened. After a moment a soft look came over her lips again.

"Have you ever had a date?" he whispered.

"Have you?"

"No."

"Well, me neither then."

She stood a little like a meek bitch. She was the dog that was to be under and he was the dog that was to be on top. Her air made him bolder. It was funny but all of a sudden he didn't feel a bit nervous. It was the exact opposite of the way he'd felt around Ada Shutter. He was the boss. He was careful though. He made himself appear shy in a country boy way as he slid an arm around her. How lovely slim she was around the waist. His long fingers fit over her hipbone like a belt around a pulley. He looked down at her, smiling fatly with her. "Gimme a little kiss."

"No."

He pushed his lips at her anyway and she dodged him. "So you like to play games, eh?" he whispered. He slid his arm firmly around her and with his other hand cupped her chin up to him. He tried to kiss her again. She dodged once more and his smooch landed in her brown hair over her ear. She sought to break out of his embrace. He had to put both arms around her to hold her against him. They struggled. A stout visitor appeared and in their wrestling around she could feel it. One moment she resisted him fiercely and the next moment she let herself be pressed against him to make sure it was true. Her bosom slowly became firm too. When the stout visitor sometimes came upon him during the day, it was very embarrassing, especially around Ma. He groaned.

"Don't," she whispered, breathing with a thick noise.

"I don't mean you any harm."

"This is too far already."

"Please? I—"

"Free?"

It was Pa's voice calling up the stairs. "Your ma wants you to help her weed the garden. Can't waste the whole afternoon lazing around, you know."

Both Free and Aletha stiffened, petrified. Free's stout visitor withdrew. Aletha's breasts softened.

"Free?"

Free let go of Aletha; then put his finger to his lips to shush her. Quickly he skipped on bare toes to the door. He deliberately huskered down his voice to make it sound sleepy, as though he were only just then rolling over, and aimed it at the ceiling over the stairwell. He hoped it would sound as though it were coming out of the little storeroom. "Coming."

"Good. Aletha?"

It was Aletha's turn to pretend. "Yes?"

"Ada thinks maybe you could help a little too in the garden, girl."

"All right."

All three went at the weeding taking it easy. Free did the radishes, Aletha did the beans, and Ma the carrots. Free went at it on hands and knees. Aletha and Ma went at the weeds from a stooping position, hind ends up in the air, faces down and half hidden in their fallen hair. It was amazing but out in the sun Aletha's hair was the exact same color as Ma's, a blond with a vague hint of red-gold in it.

After a half hour of it, Ma's face turned a mottled red. She puffed. She had just about finished doing the carrots.

Free sat back on his heels. He didn't like Ma's looks at all. "Say, dear lady of the house, I think you better go inside. It's over 100° out here and no place for you."

Ma stood up with a groan. She brushed her hair out of her eyes. "I know. But I'd like to finish the weeding today. If we get rain tonight those weeds will race ahead of us."

"We'll finish it."

Aletha stood up too, brushing back her hair. "Yes, Ada, why don't you? Free and I can finish it easy."

"Well . . ." Ma hated to give in. "This dry air is a great killer of weeds just picked."

"Ma." Free spoke sharply, making it an order.

"Well, all right." Ma sighed. "Remember now, with those weeds that grow right next to the plant, hold the plant down in place with one hand while you pull out the weeds around it with the other hand. You must not disturb where the plant root has taken hold."

"We won't, Ma. Just go."

"All right." With a last look at her beloved garden, Ma slowly went off for the house.

Free and Aletha gave each other a look and then went back to weeding their rows.

Pretty soon with a laugh, Aletha tucked her blue dress up under her pink panties and went at the weeding on her hands and knees too.

"Isn't the ground hot on your bare knees?" Free wondered.

"Not if I stir up the crust of the earth first with my fingers ahead of where I'm going."

Free was very careful with the way he selected the tiny weeds out from between the pindling radish shoots. His thumb and forefinger slowly thickened with dirt.

On their second row back, Aletha abruptly asked, "Didn't you date in high school? Really?"

"No."

"Why not?"

"I was too young."

They weeded another row.

Free asked, "Then you ain't done it either yet?"

Aletha turned red. "No."

"Would you like to?"

"What do you think?"

Pretty soon Ma called them in for a glass of cold lemonade.

It was eight in the evening when Pa and Free went back to the field. The hollows in the horses' flanks had filled out again and they were pretty frisky for the first while.

The sun set around nine. It struck sideways across the eighty, catching the tops of the corn rows from the barn all the way to the top of the north hill. It made the cross-checked field look like a well-woven piece of green buckram.

They let the horses blow at the end of every round, while they themselves got down off their cultivators and shook out their legs. The seats of their overalls were stuck to their butts. They used folded burlap sacks for cushions on their steel seats but it didn't help to keep them dry. Sometimes Pa lit his pipe; sometimes he took a chew of tobacco. Sometimes Free dreamed about what he and Aletha might do some night; sometimes he dreamed of the home run he'd hit against Rock Falls.

The deep heat lingered on through the gathering dusk.

There was a little period before moonrise when they cultivated in the dark. What with no light and the air close, it was like working in a dusty coal cellar.

Around ten they stopped to blow the horses again. Pa was silent behind the radiant bowl of his pipe. Free had his own thoughts.

Presently a moon as big as another earth came bobbing up over the single cottonwood on the east horizon. It had the look of a fertilized egg. Bloody lines wriggled over it.

The moon shrank as it rose. Soon it began to shine brightly. It touched the whole field with yellow shellac and cast deep blue shadows under the arching green leaves. Where the earth had been freshly cultivated it took on a purple glow. Light rose from the ground. The fluttering corn leaves began to smell different.

Around eleven o'clock Aletha brought them fresh lemonade and some dried-beef sandwiches.

All three sat in the grass at the end of the field. They drank their lemonade with little lipping sounds. All three watched fireflies flitting through the draw behind the hog house.

After a while Pa began to tease Aletha about all the boyfriends she probably had back in Sioux Center.

Aletha kept throwing side-looks at Free. She wanted to flirt back a little with Pa but didn't quite dare. Her blue moon eyes kept ogling back and forth between the two men.

Pa gave her a loving push as he jollied her. When she didn't seem to mind, Pa playfully slipped his arm around her and hugged her up, catching one of her breasts in his big hand.

Free looked the other way. It wasn't very pleasant to see an old man make a fool of himself with a young girl. Especially when he belonged to Ma. Ma in turn would never think of loving up a young man somewhere. Though the family was a family of loving touchers. That Pa should sit feeling a girl up at the end of a cornfield in the moonlight . . . uggh.

Aletha saw how Free felt. After a moment she politely, even gracefully, withdrew from Pa's jollying and got to her feet. She turned and began to count the fireflies.

Pretty soon Free could look at Pa again.

When the men finished their snack, Aletha slowly traipsed home.

Around midnight Pet began to loaf. No matter how Free hit Pet over the butt with the lines or with a clod of hard dirt, Pet let Polly do most of the pulling. When Free finally broke off a branch from a chokecherry tree at the end of the field and whacked Pet with it, Pet got out his favorite weapon. Pet began to fire foul blanks. The smell became so awful that riding behind him was like wading through the cutting room of a slaughterhouse.

The next time they stopped to blow the horses, Free had an idea. He got off his cultivator and pretended to stagger over to Pa. Just as he got to Pa, he collapsed in a heap.

"What fool stunt is this now?" Pa said.

"You drive that goddam Pet for a while once."

"No swearing now."

"I don't think I was born to have to follow a farting machine around in a cornfield. A perpetual motion one yet."

Pa started to laugh. "Yeh, I know how it is."

"No, you don't know how it is, or you'd take mercy on me."

"Yeh, boy, that's our Wilmer Youngman for you. Our esteemed elder."

"You know what I'd like to do? I'd like to get that Big Bertha the Germans made in the last war and run it up Pet's behind and touch it off."

"Ha. Wal, it's only a half hour more, son, and then we can quit. It's nice for the horses to be cultivating in the cool night air, you know."

It was true. The earth no longer gave off heat. The brilliant moonlit night had slowly turned chilly. The overalls no longer stuck to their butts.

Around one they quit work. They watered the horses, unharnessed them, and let them out into the night pasture.

Free went silently off to bed.

As he took the turn at the head of the stairs, he saw that Aletha's door was open and that the moon was shining across her bed. She was lying naked on the white sheets. The moonlight made her look like a dream girl.

But he was just too pooped out to go in and visit her for a while. He went to sleep instead.

Free ❦ 21

PA AND MA drove to Le Mars for a few days. Ma was still having those odd spells and they decided maybe the famous Dr. Paul Cottman at the Le Mars Clinic might be able to help.

Around ten-thirty Free finished some chores Pa asked him to do. The first thing he thought of was the violin. He got it and went down the pasture to practice in his little private amphitheatre. He set the music stand in some loose gravel. He tuned the violin. Facing the highest part of the cutbank he sawed away.

The first while his playing grated on his nerves. It kept sounding like he was scraping the bottom of an aluminum pan, something he couldn't stand. Farm work had made his fingertips blunt. Gradually though his fingering became more accurate and his motions became smoother and he began to get a sweeter tone. He played until the echoes began to sound good in the little draw.

Coming back to the yard, he found the kids playing under the trees. He entered the house and put his violin away. The potatoes boiling on the stove smelled good. He looked around for Aletha. Not finding her in either the kitchen or the living room he climbed the stairs. He found her making the beds in the boys' room.

"Need some help?"

"I can manage." She swooped the sheets in place. Her body undulated from the neck down.

They were alone in the house. Antl upstairs. He felt thick. "Well, at least I can help you make my bed."

Her eyes thickened up too.

He felt bold. He advanced upon her and slipped his arm around her. She made a couple of more wiggles to straighten out the sheet, and then gave up.

He turned her around and pushed her down onto his bed. They landed with a whompf. The woven wire spring gave off a wrenching noise.

"Oops!" she cried softly.

He cupped her breasts like he'd seen Pa do it. He began to swell up. He pressed his swelling against her. She could feel him and didn't know what to do. Both began to breathe as if each breath was going to be their last. She lay inert. Like him she didn't know what to do next. Finally he brushed his hand down her blue dress and fumbled his fingers over where her legs divided. He could feel she had pants on by the rib of the elastic around her waist.

He reached down to unbutton himself.

"No," she cried, pushing up against his arm, managing to sit up. "The potatoes will be boiled to pieces."

He grabbed her to pull her down again, but she broke out of his grasp and jumped free. She brushed down her dress and ran from the room.

The phone rang during the noon meal. Uncle John wanted Free to come over and help him and Uncle Sherm put up the rest of his alfalfa hay that afternoon. Free reluctantly agreed to come. It was hard to refuse Uncle John. Free'd had it in mind to somehow lure Aletha into the storeroom for a nap together.

He got back from Uncle John at four-thirty and immediately set the kids to work doing the evening chores. It was important, he told them, that they did the chores early. He'd got a message while at Uncle John's that the Bonnie Gilt Edge baseball team was going to practice that night in Alfred Engleking's pasture at seven.

Free raced through his share of the chores.

Some ten minutes before their usual milking time he went to the house to get the milk pails. Curious to see what Aletha might be doing, he stepped into the kitchen a minute. He found Aletha working over the stove. She was cutting up the leftover boiled potatoes into a frying pan. She heard his step on the threshold and looked over her shoulder.

"Making supper already, I see."

"Getting it ready a little." Aletha's whole mood was different. She'd apparently decided after all that she liked what had happened that noon. "So all I have to do when I hear your boys come in to separate the milk is to put it up front."

He stepped up behind her and slipped his arms around her middle. He pressed himself against her. She could feel him and she laughed like a goose. She kept on cutting up the cold potato she had in her hand. When she finished the potato she let her head fall. The sight of the roots of her hair where it was parted in back, and flowing to either side, made him hot. His hands came up and cupped her breasts, full, firm. She backed into him. Then he knew for sure she'd changed her mind. He pressed his lips deep into the parting of her hair over her neck. She warmed in his embrace.

He slid her sideways in his arms and then, arm still around her, led her into the living room to the black horsehair sofa. She pretended not to know what he was going to do with her. She didn't resist when he pressed her down and back. He lay beside her a moment. It was going to happen. Then he reached under her dress and pulled her pink panties down. Her brush of hair was exactly like the parting in the back of her neck. When he saw how tight the elastic rib of her panties was across her legs, he slid the panties down and helped her right leg out of them. She lay with her eyes closed and rolled up under her eyelids. He unfastened his suspender and slid down his overalls. He opened her legs. She didn't resist. He rose over her and rode down at her. He missed and slid past; and she jumped.

"Oh. Not there."

"Sorry." Free tried again. The second time it went in snug and good. He didn't know what he was feeling. His mind was sparking a hundred miles a minute. He thrust several times.

"Let's quit," she said under him.

"Am I hurting you?"

"No."

"What's the matter then?"

"Let's quit."

Puzzled, he withdrew. He couldn't understand the sin-weary note in her voice. She said she'd never dated. Though of course she knew about boys, having grown up with big horsey brothers. He drew himself back into his underwear. He stood up and pulled up his overalls and fastened his suspender. Below him she slipped her leg back into her panties and snapped the panties up around her waist. Head turned to one side, she got up too. Just then there was a noise out on the porch. Quickly she hurried into the kitchen and began setting the table for supper. The noise on the porch turned out to be Flip getting his shoes.

After a minute Free called up Everett from slopping the hogs. It was time to pail the cows.

He caught a ride with Garrett Engleking out to Alfred Engleking's pasture. Garrett seemed to be doing pretty good with his second wife. There didn't seem to be any mark on him that he'd committed adultery twice, once with June Memling and once with Laura Pipp. Garrett was as funny as ever, full of assurance that now that they had one game under their belt playing in their new uniforms, given them by the Gilt Edge Paint Company in Sioux Falls, they'd really settle down and have a great town team. Both had a good laugh over the way they'd lost their first game, 11 to 7, all feeling so out of place in their new striped gray, with hated Hello scoring all their runs in the first inning. Their infield had made six errors in that inning, four by third baseman Pete Haber.

As they drove along, Free pictured himself as taking over Garrett's role as the usual Bonnie hero. He'd pitch a no-hitter, as well as hit a long home run and win 1-0. He became so lost in imagining himself pitching that next game that he unconsciously made the start of a pitching motion right there in the car beside Garrett. Then, the bottom of the ninth, with himself at bat, he saw the ball leave the enemy pitcher's hand and spin toward his waist. From its spin he could tell it was going to be an outdrop. He rocked back on his right foot; then stepped into the pitch. He caught the ball on the fat of his bat and sent it rocketing toward right center. Grandly, wonderfully, it arched far out, and actually carried over the edge of the

Hello High School roof and landed in auctioneer Meyling's yard. What a home run.

"I said, how's your arm?"

Free jerked; found himself back in Garrett's car. "Oh. That. It feels fine."

"Good. Because we depend a lot on that arm of yours, you know."

Free wondered what Garrett would think if he could've seen what he'd tried to do to Aletha on Pa's black sofa.

When they arrived at Alfred Engleking's pasture, the fellows were already out knocking up flies and hollering to each other. "I got it, I got it."

They had a great time practicing until it was almost too dark to see the ball.

They all sat around on Alfred's Engleking's cement stoop and had a bottle of home-brew beer. Alfred's beer had settlings in it. Everybody started to break wind after a while.

Pretty soon Pete Haber let go with a tremendous blast. It shook everyone up a little, including even the stoop they sat on. Playfully, Pete quick whirled on little Fritz, Robert Engleking's boy. "There he goes! Catch'm, Fritz, catch'm." Then, sighing exaggeratedly, letting down his slope shoulders, Pete said, "Oh, shucks, he got away. Why didn't you go after him, like I told you to? Now we'll never see him again."

Some of the fellows laughed coarsely.

Uncle John, Uncle Sherm, and Garrett didn't laugh. They were of the better sort.

It was dark when Garrett let Free off by the water tower. Garrett turned his car down Prospect Hill toward his house while Free walked the other way home.

The light was on in the kitchen. Aletha was still up, probably waiting for him. He wondered what mood she'd be in. Pa and Ma wouldn't be home until midnight. He and Aletha would have plenty of time to spoon a little again if she'd let him. He made up his mind he wasn't going to be so crude about it this time.

The thought of what Ma might think—her boy Free no longer innocent and pure—he pushed to one side. Ma'd been flatly wrong about baseball, so she was probably wrong about sex too.

Rover heard Free coming up the lane and pattered out to meet him. Free sat down on the cellar door and took off his shoes. Rover delicately licked his ear several times. Free in return gave Rover a massage over the top of his skull.

"Good dog."

Rover licked Free's ear once more and then trotted off for his hole under the porch.

Free set his shoes on the porch and stepped into the kitchen. "Hi. Keeping the home fires burning, I see."

Aletha looked up from Pa's swivel chair. She was reading *The Bonnie Review*. The single light bulb gave her cheeks the look of transparent porcelain. "Hi."

"Kids safe in bed?"

"Yes." She gave him a ruined look, though at the same time appeared to be glad to see him. The ruined look was an old ruined look. Her eyes were like blue quarter moons. She asked, "Are you hungry?"

"Not really."

"Would you like some sugarlary?"

"No." He stood looking down at her. It amused him that he had no qualms about what he was going to do next. He was the top dog all right; and she the underdog. "Here," he said, taking her under the arms and lifting her out of Pa's chair and sitting down in it himself, "you sit in my lap." He settled her down on himself. "There. Now."

She let her head hang. She laughed goosey and made a funny wiggling motion.

The motion made the blood rush to his eyes. It made the light in the kitchen turn pink. He set a kiss deep into the parting of her hair over her neck. She laughed like one who had given in to something.

"Here," he said, and he helped them both slide down onto the yellow linoleum floor. He laid her out beside him. When he went to strip her panties down, he discovered she didn't have them on. She'd looked forward to his coming home then. Without looking at him, eyes closed and rolled up under their lids, she parted her legs. He became all the more inflamed. The nickel on Ma's stove glittered off to one side. He pushed down his overalls. One look and he realized he'd never seen himself like that before. He had what looked like a voyageur's canoe, a lot of weight in the stern with the prow tilted up proudly. What a great ride they were going to have together. He knew he should pleasure her a little first, spoon her up, but he just couldn't wait. He rose over her. He steered his canoe around for the open part of the river. He met the waves head on with her. She moved under him like giving water. He finally knew what he was feeling with her. A geyser was getting ready to let go.

Of a sudden she lay dead under him. "Let's quit."

"Not now."

She spoke more firmly. "Let's quit."

"We haven't really started yet." He spoke through her sun-brown hair into the hard yellow linoleum floor.

She tried to push him off. "Let's quit."

"No," he cried. "Not now, for godsake."

She gave him another push. "Please. Before it's too late."

That set it off. My God. He pulsed all over her belly.

She gave the puddle of egg white stuff a look; shuddered; then gave him a glittering look. Again it was an old look, one she must've given many times before. She grabbed up her dress, holding it away from her belly, got up, and ran outside to the privy.

Free lay blinking to himself on the floor a moment. Too bad. If it weren't for that sad business of some kind in her head, the two of them could've had a lot of fun. He got up and pulled up his overalls. He went to the sink and washed his hands and face.

When Aletha came back from the privy she wouldn't look at him. She too went to the sink and washed her hands and face. Then, still not looking at him, she went upstairs to bed.

He was suddenly very hungry. He found himself lusting after one of those treats he sometimes snuck out of Ma's pantry.

Sure he was alone, the delicious sense of doing something forbidden rose in him. He got a bowl and filled it with various delicacies: cornflakes, bits of green citron, a sprinkling of shredded white coconut, a handful of raisins, several figs, four heaping spoons of brown sugar, and finally some cream from the night's separating. He fluffed up the raisins left over in the blue box to make it seem the box was as full as before.

It was good. He ate slowly. He savored all the different wonderful tastes.

When he finished, he washed the bowl and spoon under the cistern pump and put them away. Coming out of the pantry he forgot to duck and rammed his head against the top of the doorway. For a moment stars exploded in his skull. "Ow." He rubbed his scalp. He cussed the carpenter who'd made the low door.

He turned out the light and climbed the stairs. He lit a match in his room to see if everybody was in their right stall. They were. Everett, Flip, and Jonathan were packed in the south bed. Little Abbott slept on the far side the north bed. The boys all slept naked, sheets pushed down. It was a sight to see: all those innocent closed eyes and little tumbled toadstools. What a fine collection of slim pink boy bodies. He loved them all.

He waved the match out. He undressed in the dark and crept in beside Abbott. After a while Abbott woke up enough to snuggle against him.

The next morning Ma told Free that Dr. Paul Cottam in Le Mars had diagnosed her teeth as the culprits for her poor health. He said she should have them pulled.

"Are you going to then?"

Ma sighed. "I guess I have to."

Two days later Pa took Ma to Dr. Dale Moloney in Rock Falls to have her uppers pulled. She didn't look too bad with just her uppers out. It made her look a little more thoughtful than usual.

A week later Dr. Moloney pulled out the lowers.

When Pa and Ma arrived on the yard, Free could tell right away something had happened. It wasn't just that with all her teeth out Ma looked as old as Gramma; it was something else. Pa held a hand to Ma's elbow as he squired her into the house.

A little later Free went into the house. He found Ma in bed, pale as a ghost, with Aletha standing helplessly by.

"My goodness, Ma, you look like you went through a wringer."

"Yes, I guess you almost lost me." Without her teeth, and her cheeks collapsed, her speech was full of wet s's.

Pa loomed up behind Free. "Yeh, son."

"What happened?" Free could feel himself turn pale.

"Wal," Pa said, trying to smile now that it was all over, "Doc Moloney had just finished pulling the last tooth, when he noticed she wasn't breathing. So he gave her smelling salts. When that didn't bring her to, he stuck something into her with a needle. That finally revived her . . . though he had to slap her hard on the cheek a couple of times to keep her going. You see, he gave her gas to put her under when he pulled 'em."

Ma's fingers played with the edges of the colored squares of the quilt. "It was the gas that done it. I can still taste it."

"You're all right now though?"

"Yes. I'm just a little weak is all."

Free picked up Ma's wrist. He counted her pulse against his own. Her pulse seemed fairly regular. "It wasn't your heart then?" He held her wrist warmly.

"Naw," Pa said. "It was that gas."

Ma rolled her head in a wondering way to herself. "I think it stopped there for a minute though. But then that shot he gave me pulled me through. It was adrenalin, he told me." Ma smiled at where Free's hand held her wrist. She appreciated his touching her. "It was so strange, son. For a little while I was in another world. I was lying on something soft, like it was all fresh cotton, with angels sitting on the higher white tufts."

Free tried to joke about it. "You didn't happen to see your dad, Grandpa Alfred?"

"No. Him I didn't see."

"Oh, well, then," Pa said, "then you wasn't as far as heaven. Because he's sure to be in heaven."

Free had to turn away. They took it so seriously.

Free went outside and collected the milk pails and headed for the barn. Free felt pale. That's what he got for lusting after Aletha.

A couple of weeks later Ma sent Aletha home. Ma said the reason was they didn't have the money to pay her. But Free knew that Ma had spotted how odd Free and Aletha behaved around each other.

Free ❦ 22

FREE STARTED FALL plowing in the middle of August. He tackled the southeast fifty first. The old Emerson gangplow had two twelve-inch plows. One full round meant a width four feet wide had been turned over. It took many rounds to plow fifty acres of stubble field. Along the ends, with the plows withdrawn, the three-wheeled old Emerson hobble-rolled like a broken-legged horse. But once the foot trip had been kicked in and the two plows had locked themselves into the earth, it ran level and firm.

Free loved plowing. Except for fixing fence, it was just about the best job on the farm. Free used the best horses, Maud and Nell in the lead, Sam and Prince and Fan in the rear. Once he had them trained, plowing was a snap. Nell up in the lead was a great one. Most times he didn't have to drive her at the ends. She'd keep pulling straight ahead beyond the plowed strip until he'd kicked the foot trip, then she'd slowly swing to her right, stepping sideways, drawing Maud with her, also drawing the rear team with her, and go down along the width of the plowed strip, and then beyond it, until again at the exact right point, she'd swing right drawing the other horses with her until she hit the furrow, and then she'd start down the furrow at the very moment Free would kick in the plows. After each round she learned to allow for the four extra feet they'd just finished. For much of the day Free could tie up her lines to the handle of the plow and forget about her. The lines to the rear set of horses he let hang slack.

The first couple of days it was fun to observe the bank swallows sail between the horses snapping up botflies and mouthflies. Their cunning blue-black iridescent wings could fling their bodies in any direction no matter how erratically the flies tried to dart away.

Two continuous ribbons of purple soil eight inches thick curled over under Free's seat, burying gold stubbles and green pigeon grass. The just-cut soil shone like the top of a polished kitchen range. A vast procession of things appeared in the shiny cut surface: colored pebbles, white grubs, little pockets of nacreous sand, severed angleworms, gaping gopher holes, cut wild rose roots. Occasionally the plowshares upended a mouse nest, exposing a downy little home with mewling white mice babies crawling numbly out of it.

By the fourth day Free was hungry for books again. Knowing Pa abominated reading on the job, Free took to hiding a book inside his overalls just below the bib. He was always careful to keep his side buttons fastened. Carrying a book to work did make him look a little like he'd put on some weight. Each day the first couple of rounds he made sure the horses were behaving themselves, especially his lead horse Nell, then hooked the lines on the plow lever and relaxed on his seat. He always waited until he and the horses had moved out of sight over the hill and then, just as the chimney of the house disappeared from view, he'd haul out his book.

As always, he began books slowly just as he made friends slowly. Making new friends always meant he'd have to make deep changes. It always took a while to figure out who was going to make a good friend. When a stranger wanted to make friends right off the bat, it usually meant he didn't have much grit. Thus starting a new book with new characters in it was always a wonderful dilemma, almost like taking that first bite into a sharp tangy apricot. A person thought, "enhh," at the same time that he couldn't resist the apricot either. It was also a lot like going swimming. A person loved sporting around in the running water of a river, but, oh, that first jump off the bank, that was always a problem. In the end, though, a fellow always plunged in because he loved to explore, and longed to know what was going to happen around the next bend.

At the moment he was well into Jack London's *The Sea Wolf* and couldn't leave it alone. He couldn't wait to get out to the field to read it on the other side of the hill. He'd been careful to wrap the book in thick brown butcher paper to keep from staining it, sweat or grease, and was always careful to wipe his hands pick clean and page the book with the edge of the callus on his thumb.

He had a kind of natural alarm clock in his head that woke him to the world on the homestretch just as he was about to crest the hill and was within sight of the yard again. But his alarm clock failed him one afternoon. He'd become totally lost in *The Sea Wolf,* when suddenly Pa spoke up beside him.

"Wal, son, it looks like I can give old Nell your wages, seeing she's doing all your work for you."

Free snapped the book shut; and just in time did not try to hide it inside his overalls. He decided to go along with Pa's sally. "I didn't know you were paying me wages."

Pa took the book and riffled through the pages. "This yours?"

"Nope. Dr. Fairlamb's. It's from a set. So I dassent lose it."

"That why you got this paper around it?"

"Yes."

"Wal, son, I'm glad to see you're careful of other people's property. But I'm not glad to see you reading on the job."

"It ain't hurting anything. Just check the plowing. Me and Nell are doing it perfect."

Pa turned and walked up and down the end once, studying each round. He couldn't find a missed strip. He checked each horse carefully too. All five appeared to be in good shape; blowing a little but not more than would be expected. "Just the same, I'm not exactly excited about you getting all wrapped up in that bookshit."

"Bullshit, you mean, don't you? Like Grampa used to say?"

"No, bookshit, like I say. Because he read more than was good for him too." Pa stepped over to the deep grass at the end of the field and retrieved two pails. "I brought you your lunch today."

"Instead of the kids, ha, so you could check up on me."

"That's right."

Rover came running out of the grass. Rover had just had himself a good run and his tongue lolled out puffing. He came over and gave first Pa a lick on the hand and then Free.

The lick mollified Pa.

Father and son sat down in the stubbles to eat their lunch.

They were well into their sandwiches, when suddenly Rover came alive at their feet. He stood up; shook his black coat; began to bark furiously.

Free and Pa looked back up the slope. It was Butler's dog Sport, also a shepherd with the same black-and-white markings.

Pa smiled. "Get 'im, Rover."

Rover broke into a roar and took off rear end low. Sport barked back. But before he could get himself bristled up, Rover was on him and gave him a bite in the neck. Sport yipped in surprise and pain. He whirled and took off east for the Butler line fence. Rover had the momentum and kept right on Sport's tail all the way. He managed to nip Sport in the tail several times. Sport slipped through the line fence, Rover still in pursuit.

Some dozen rods into the Butler stubble field, Sport appeared to bethink himself. He was on his master's property, not the neighbor's. He was boss there, not Rover. Sport whirled around in midair and met Rover head on.

There was a terrible tangle of bared teeth and stiff tails and humped necks. There were outraged yowls. It became Rover's turn to wonder where he was.

Sport, on home ground, was suddenly fighting like a fiend. Rover finally caught on he was no longer on home ground. Instantly his tail dropped and he whirled for home. Sport took after him with a victory roar. He managed to nip Rover in the butt just as Rover was clearing himself through the line fence; got him once more as they shot past the blowing horses. The horses stood with their heads high and appeared to be just as bemused by the wrangling dogs as Free and Pa were.

Some dozen yards into Pa's pasture Rover appeared to bethink himself in turn. He was on his master's home ground, not the neighbor's. He was boss there, not Sport. Rover reversed course in midair and met Sport head on, teeth bared. Rover gave him an awful bite in the neck. Again for a moment there was a snarling whirl of black furry bodies. Together the two dogs resembled a furiously whirling eggbeater. Then Sport awoke to where he was, and dropping his tail, ducking his head, took off for safety beyond the line fence.

The two dogs chased each other back and forth four times before Sport finally gave up the game. He was a little farther away from home base than Rover was.

Rover came puffing back, tongue hanging out, and settled in the stubbles between Pa and Free. He faced toward the Butler homestead, eyes on the horizon, ready to challenge the next intrusion.

Pa took a last sip of tea and then lit his pipe. "Yep, it's always important to know who's the boss. Take how I pick the top little boar in the spring when the sows come in, and then trade him for some top little boar from Minnesota so as not to have any inbreeding." Pa took a deep puff. "When the sows start to come in, I don't get much sleep. I'm always there to make sure she's having her pigs okay. And I got to be on deck to spot the little boss pig. In every litter there's always one that's the top boar. He's the first to come out of that birthing sleep and he's the first to head for titty. He makes sure he's had his fill first too before he lets any other little pig get any. He'll root 'em away until he's had all he wants."

Free wasn't sure he liked to hear all that. "What's this got to do with me?"

"I just want you to know that in case you should have to pick him some spring."

"I don't think I want to be a farmer, Pa."

"Raah. I was thinking that in case I should drop dead suddenly, then you'd know how to run the farm for Ma."

Free said nothing.

"As all the litters grow up, keep watching for the bossiest one of all. Especially when you're swilling them. The one that still pushes everybody away from the trough until he's had his fill, wants to get it all, that's the one you trade with the other fellow's top boar."

"Picking a boar is hardly Christlike, is it?"

"No, it hain't. But then, we're talking about the hog world."

"How do you pick the top little sow pig?"

"The gilt? You don't have to worry about who she'll be. Mostly because just about all gilts make good breeding stock."

Free was shocked. "You mean to say most female pigs are good but not most male pigs?"

"Yep. Let's say you get a crop of a hundred little pigs. Fifty-three or so will be boys, forty-seven will be girls. Some six of those boys will die the first couple of days. Too poorly. They hain't got the gaff. Of the rest of those boy pigs there'll probably be only some six or so any good. The remaining forty, wal, all they're good for is to make fatteners of 'em. If you was to try to breed your sows with one of those forty, that is, if he could make connection, why, in two generations your pig stock would run downhill. You'd never get the top market for 'em even if you was to feed 'em the best corn in the world."

"That's sure a funny way for God to arrange things."

"I know. I used to think the same thing, when Old George Pullman taught me. But so it is."

"I wonder if that's true of human beings too."

"I don't know. George Pullman never talked about that. He was too much of a gentleman. And as for me, I dassent ask around of my friends."

Free picked up *The Sea Wolf*. "You know, in a way, that's what this book is about."

"Uhh. That book again."

"In fact, Pa, Jack London writes like you talk."

Pa jumped to his feet. "You and your big ideas." Pa grabbed up the lunch pails and somewhat angrily headed for home. He said over his shoulder, "Just you keep those furrows straight."

Free was careful after that to keep his book out of sight.

Free read about Jack London's struggles to become a writer, and decided that, yes, he too wanted to write. There was nothing like reading a good story to get lost in. A good story helped a person live in another world, so that for a little while he forgot who he was in real life.

The whole problem was to get down the really real. That was the trouble with most writers. They never quite managed to get into where the real was really real. Like when he himself, in daydream, saw himself playing baseball. Such a daydream game was so real he really could count the stitches on a rotating baseball as it came toward him from the pitcher, could really read the label to see whether or not it was a National League ball or an American League ball. Shaking his fist at the earth as he routinely did his chores on the yard, Free swore to himself, nodding, that someday he was going to make his stories so real, so dramatic, that when he described a dust storm the reader would think he was actually tasting dust between his teeth. The reader as he read would unconsciously wet his lips with his tongue.

One noon while the horses rested, Free made up his mind. He found himself a spot in the haymow under the sloping roof over the horse stalls where a little light came in through a small window. He cleared out the chaff and dust and constructed a small sloping desk out of an endgate and made a seat out of an old beer crate. He tacked a broken bedspring onto the wall above the desk for a pencil holder. Quietly he began to sneak butcher paper out of the house. He constructed a secret passage through the mound of alfalfa in the main part of the haymow to get to his writing room. He didn't want anybody to come upon him while he was busy writing.

He first tried writing about the Hoff girl drowning. But when he tried to show how she felt when the water was sucking her under, he didn't know how to make it real enough. He next tried to tell the story of a great game a certain Slim Fredman pitched against Alvord one Friday night. But he couldn't make that come off either. It was too easy to strike out a batter on paper.

Free finally settled on a detective story. He'd never forgotten the time when Henry Hiller tried to gun down Milo Kerber with a shotgun on the main street. Free used what he'd seen that Saturday night and then added another episode in which a Hiller-like fellow snuck up on a Kerber-like fellow later in the night and shot him through an open window as he was smoking his pipe. Detective Slim Fredman solved the crime by making a mold of the footprints under the window.

Free entitled it "The Dark of the Night." He made a fair copy of it in longhand on some of Ma's lined linen paper and sent it off to *The Iowa Homesteader*.

Sometimes in the evening, after the chores and the dishes were done, the kids liked to horse around on the grass. Free couldn't resist joining them. Duty called him to his secret desk up in the haymow, but love for his brothers called him out on the grass. His brothers were always testing his strength, especially Flip, who lately had become quietly bold. Flip kept claiming that if all five, including even the baby Sherman, were to tackle Free all at once at the same time, they could get Free down. When Free was looking the other way, Flip would signal the other brothers and then with a rush they'd jump Free. Free had no trouble handling them all. Everett had only one strong arm, as his left arm had never really recovered from infantile paralysis, and Flip though sturdy wasn't big enough, and Jonathan was still such a runt he only had a few chicken muscles to wrestle with, and Abbott was too inclined to kiss and make up. Toddling baby Sherman of course only got in the way, and when he had wet pants he was a nuisance to both sides. Tickling wasn't permitted, but it didn't take long before Free began to laugh anyway, and laughing, he was only half a man. Then at last they'd topple him to earth and swarm over him, taking turns trying to hold down an arm or a leg, sure they could lick him at last.

Pa laughed from where he sat on the cellar door. "You kids fighting there look like a bunch of potatoes quarreling in the ground."

The kids kept wrestling and grunting and laughing together.

When finally Pa saw that the five kids weren't going to get Free down after all, he couldn't resist joining the struggle.

"Hey, no fair," Free cried when he saw Pa looming over them.

"Oh, I'm not going to touch you," Pa said. "I'm just going to help your brothers use their best weapon." Pa picked up little Sherman and dropped him seat first onto Free's nose. The wet pants not only shut off all air, they almost asphyxiated Free. Free had to give up.

"Just the same, that wasn't fair," Free said, pretending he was choking to death. "You know how in the last war everybody said the dirty Huns didn't fight fair when they used gas."

Pa filled his pipe as he resettled on the cellar door. A smile cut his face in half. "I just wanted to show you that you ain't the only one with clever idees. Some of us don't

need to read a book to win a war. We get our idees out of clear air."
"Ha. You mean out of a wet diaper."

A month later Free got a rejection from *The Iowa Homesteader*.

"Please include return postage and a self-addressed envelope with your submissions.

The Editors."

Free ❦ 23

THAT FALL PA bought a secondhand corn picking machine. Once he got used to running it, Pa couldn't get over how fast the corn came out. It sure was a heck of a lot easier'n picking corn by hand.

Pa had a bumper crop that year. Within three weeks' time they'd picked ten thousand bushels. After the corncrib was full, they put up temporary cribbing outside, two huge towers of gold three tiers high.

Pa was overjoyed. With the price of corn high, he could pay off his debts. He'd gambled in the spring when he'd bought extra horses, extra cows, extra machinery; and, he'd won out. He'd taken on the Hamilton half-section because he had all those boys growing up, and by gum it was beginning to look like it was the best move he'd ever made.

Pa was in such a good mood he let Free take a job picking corn by hand for their old stack-threshing partner, Barry Simmons. Barry and wife Ada had taken over the Hamilton quarter after Pa left it and so it was somewhat like going home again for Free to pick corn on the place where he'd grown up as a boy.

Free took it easy the first day picking corn by hand. It was like in baseball; a fellow had to go through a training period or he'd sprain a wrist. So the first day Free came in with two loads of forty-five bushels each.

The second day he went at it a little harder, mostly because the fellow he picked behind, Frank Haber, cousin of Floris Haber, taunted him about being too long-geared to pick fast. Free came home with two loads of fifty bushels each.

The third day he put the socks to it. They were in the same field he'd learned to pick corn in while still a sophomore in high school. His grays, Maude and Nell, who also recognized old home ground, were right on top of Frank Haber's heels all day long. Every now and then Free would jump over and pick an ear out of Frank's next round. Finally at three in the afternoon Frank suggested Free take the lead. Free did. That night he came in with sixty-seven bushels all on one load. That sixty-seven with the fifty-eight he had in the morning gave him a day's total of one hundred fifteen. Frank's total was a hundred ten for the day. Free went to bed that night knowing he could pick with the best. Frank had won the county championship the year before. Even better, Free was hardly tired.

The next day Free and Frank got the corn out for Barry Simmons. When Free drove his grays and his rattling empty wagon home to Pa and Ma at four in the afternoon, he had a check in his pocket for $32.00. Barry paid the going price of eight cents a bushel.

After supper Pa asked Free what he was going to do with all that money. The kids were in bed and he and Pa and Ma were sitting together in the kitchen. Free was reading *Quo Vadis* for the second time. It was the one book Pa didn't mind him reading since it was approved by Domeny. Free sat with his feet in the cob box in front of the stove. Pa was sitting in his swivel chair smoking his pipe with his feet up on the corner of the table. Ma was cutting herself a new dress according to a pattern Aunt Karen had sent down. A single bulb cast yellow light over them all.

"Ain't you gonna answer me?" Pa said.

Free looked up. "I was thinking of buying myself a new overcoat."

"What's wrong with the one you got?"

"You mean my old leather jacket?"

"I don't mean that one," Pa said. "I mean that coat your Uncle Richard sent you."

"Oh, Pa." Free lifted his feet out of the cob box and swung around to face Pa. Even in his socks his heels hit the floor with a considerable thud. "That khaki thing. That was his old World War army coat."

"It was hardly wore, though," Pa said.

"It's much too short for me. I look like Ichabod Crane in it."

Pa's lips thinned out. "So you're too good to be wearing hand-me-downs any more, huh? Wal, let me tell you something, boy—"

"Alfred!" Without her teeth Ma's speech slurred together. There were blue triangles under her eyes. "You like good clothes too."

"Hey," Pa said, "are you sticking up for that kid now? When he's already too big for his britches?"

Free couldn't resist it. "You mean, for his hand-me-downs, don't you?" Free had worn Uncle Richard's army coat once, downtown, and that had been enough. He caught the lovely Brewster girl, Elizabeth, giving his coat an odd look. And no wonder. His knees stuck out like a pair of stovepipe elbows.

Pa's chin shot out. "You see? He's even smartin' off to his parents now."

Ma spoke calmly. "What do you want him to do with that money he's earned?"

"Why," Pa said, "when I was his age, all my earnings went to my pa. Until I was twenty-one."

Ma sighed. "Well, Alfred, if the boy is going on to the seminary someday, I think maybe it might be a good idea if he were to start saving for that day."

"Mrmmp," Pa went, swallowing what he was going to say next.

Ma gave Free a mother's good smile. Because she was toothless it was a horrible smile and he couldn't look at it. "What would you like to do with that money, Free? You earned it."

"Buy me a new coat."

Pa brought both feet down to the floor with a double thud, so loud it shook

Ma where she sat. "If a new coat shows up in our mailbox downtown from Sears Roebuck, you're in trouble."

Free had to work at looking into Pa's eyes but he managed it. "Otherwise though, I can do with that money as I want?"

"Wal . . ." Pa began.

"Alfred, hasn't the Lord blessed us this past year with good crops?"

"Yes, that he has."

"And hasn't our oldest boy done well by us the past year?"

"Wal, yeh, that he has. But that was what was expected of him to begin with. You don't give anybody a reward for what he's supposed to do."

Free said, "Well, if that's all I get for it I might just as well turn lazy."

Ma gave Free a warning look. The look, coupled with her collapsed cheeks and sucked in lips, made her look sinister.

Pa got up and clapped out the dottle of his pipe into the stove. He slipped into his blue denim jacket and stepped outdoors.

Free couldn't resist grumbling to himself. "That Pa. He still thinks we're back in the days when he was sixteen. He can't see that times have changed."

"Now, now." Ma patiently placed a piece of paper pattern over some purple cloth.

"I feel like I'm living in a jail here. After I've put in my share of work, I'm still not free to read when I want to. Pa's worse than the Kaiser." Free stood up and began to pace back and forth in the kitchen. He found himself taking the same kind of slinging steps Pa took when he paced up and down. That irritated him all the more. "I'm not staying around here very long."

"Son!"

"You can rot here, Ma, but I'm not."

"Your father has his side of it too."

"Like what?"

"How many husbands help their wives wash clothes like your father does? How many husbands insist that their boys help the mother set the table and wash the dishes? How many husbands are as neat as he is? And teach that neatness to their boys?"

Free had to admit it was all true. Pa was even good at ironing clothes and sewing on buttons. And Pa's manners at the table were every bit as good as Domeny's were.

"Yes, your poor father, you must not be so hard on him."

Free shot her a look.

"Perhaps I've been depriving your father all these years of something he should have had more of, seeing the Lord made him the way he is."

Free stared at his mother. The light bulb hanging from the middle of the ceiling was exactly level with his eyes and he had to look at her through its rays. Ma appeared to be surrounded by a bright glow. Did they still do it? Thinking suddenly of what he'd done with Aletha Gladjanus, almost on the very spot in which he then stood, he felt ashamed.

"One thing I would like though, son."

"What's that, Ma?"

"I've mentioned it before. I'd surely like it if you became a confessing member of our church. That would surely please me."

"Aw, Ma."

"Someday you'll be glad you did. When I'm no longer here."

"That's not fair, Ma."

"I know son. But God's will."

An hour later, turning over in his sleep, Free heard Pa and Ma talking in the dark downstairs. Free lifted an ear from his pillow. Pa was still in a swivet over Free's not wanting to wear a perfectly good warm winter coat, and Ma was her usual calm self, pointing out that the boy did look a little ridiculous in his uncle's army coat.

"What of it?" Pa bounced up and down so hard Free could clearly hear their bedsprings squealing. "I looked a little ridiculous myself wearing hand-me-downs. From the Pullmans. From the Reynolds. From the Harmings. And it didn't hurt me any. In fact, I was happy to get all those good clothes. If only to stay warm."

"Alfred, you've been a noble husband. Much better than I ever expected you to be. But, Alfred, now, in this one thing, I think you're going a little too far."

"I'm thinking about how my father raised me."

"Alfred, your son can't be to you what you were to your father."

"Free takes after your Engleking side of the family, with all those big shot ideas of his."

"Big shot? Is it wrong for him to think of becoming a minister?" Ma's voice rose a little, and in so doing her being toothless made her sound a little drunk.

"Arrch! Just like with your father, thinking the Lord was taking special pains to listen onto him with all his troubles."

"Alfred, Alfred, remember how you used to shake your head over all the strange and balky ideas your father had? I think Free takes more after your side of the family."

Pa fell silent.

After a while Ma spoke up so softly Free had to strain his ears. "Alfred, like I was saying, you're a noble husband. And I fear I haven't done my duty by you as a wife."

There was a moment's pause. Then Pa seized on what she'd said. "You mean, I can?"

"If it pleases you, my husband."

There was a sound of rustling sheets, several odd half-smothered grunts, and then the rhythmic squeaking of springs.

Free got up, slipped into his overalls and shirt, and climbed out through the window and down the drainpipe to the cellar door below.

Rover heard him and came padding silently out from under the porch. He licked Free's fingertips, once.

Free reached down and ran his hand over the back of the dog's head. He noted, as he had many times before, how the dog had an odd pointy bump on the back of his skull. It reminded him of the odd bump he had on his own head. His brothers had skulls as smooth as billiard balls. But he didn't. He probably had that bump because he was more animal than his brothers.

Free banked the thirty-two dollars at the First National. He paged through the mail order catalog for something he might buy for the sheer pleasure of having it for himself alone.

He finally settled on *The Works of Shakespeare,* complete in one volume for a dollar twenty-five. Sears Roebuck guaranteed forty-eight-hour delivery service.

The next Thursday evening on the way to Young Men's Society, Free checked the post office. The Old Bonnie Omaha had come in an hour before from the north. He could hear the postmaster distributing mail behind the bronze boxes. Free peered into their box, 124. Aha. He spotted an orange card in it, "Notice to Call at the Window." He rapped on the door.

"Yes? What is it?"

"This is Free. Is there a package for me? There's a notice in our box." There was a smell of clean new paper in the place.

"Just a moment." There was some rustling, and then the door cracked open and a hairy hand held out a package for him. "That what you looking for?"

Free spotted the name of the sender and then hit on his own name on the package. "You bet."

Tucking the package under his arm, he walked the rest of the way to church, down the main street west, then down the long girl-watching avenue. Curfew rang just as he stepped into the church.

Lately in Young Men's Society a half dozen candidates for church membership were being instructed by Reverend Tiller. They met in the consistory room. Only one large clear glass bulb, its white-hot filaments visible, burned above the long brown table. All the young faces were a bright red from having been out in the wind picking corn, and all their clothes were dark, new blue denim overalls and denim jackets. There was a strong smell of oily cleaning compound in the long room.

After a while Reverend Tiller, sitting at the head of the table, noted Free's package. "That looks like a book, Free."

"Yes. *The Works of Shakespeare.*"

Reverend Tiller's blue eyes opened, his brown brows climbed his forehead. "Shakespeare?"

"Yes."

"Shakespeare won't distract your attention from Christ Jesus as your Savior?"

"No. If anything he should improve it. I like to think that God enjoys good literature too."

"What about your other reading?"

"Most of that's all right too."

"Are there any questions you'd like to ask as the result of your reading?"

Free gathered up his shoulders to think. He chose his words carefully. He wanted to be accurate yet didn't want to show off in front of friends. "Well, I have a little trouble with the idea of eternity."

"That's something that is not for us poor mortals to worry about. That's God's province."

"I have trouble with the idea that hell is down there and heaven is up there. When what you mean by down there has got to be the center of the earth. Should people everywhere on this earth point down there they've all got to be pointing at the same spot. And heaven has got to be the everywhere away from the surface of the earth, in all imaginable directions. Which means that heaven isn't just in one place. It's all over out there in endless eternity, in all directions."

"Again, that is a problem better left to God. What you must concentrate on is—are you saved."

"Yeh, but what if such thoughts keep coming to me anyway? And when such thoughts seem noble and good to me? Which means they can only come from God. So therefore I think God wants me to consider them."

Reverend Tiller was impressed. "Tell me, are you still planning to go to college?"

"In a couple of years, yes."

"Good. Because with your inventive mind, you're going to be quite a candidate for the ministry." Reverend Tiller smiled a wide white smile. "Yes. What lively thought-provoking sermons you're going to preach someday."

The dialogue didn't set too well with Free's friends. They glared at Free.

Free ignored them. "Domeny, tell me. Suppose we could agree on what was the last and farthest star out there. What would be beyond that?"

Reverend Tiller smiled. "God knows."

"And once you've figured that out, what would lie beyond that?"

Reverend Tiller laughed, partly red-faced. "Free, now you've lost me. If I were to think about such things my brain'd crack."

Free didn't like Domeny's attitude. If Domeny really believed in God he shouldn't be afraid to inquire into anything. "But suppose there had been no God. Then there would have been no world. And if there'd been no world then there would have been no me."

"Those questions I try never to bother my head with. I let God handle them. I trust Him."

"What was there before God?"

"Free, really, those are questions for a Plato, not you."

"When did it all start? And why did it start just when it did? I mean . . . what was The Real Thing behind The First Thing?"

"Free, are you questioning God?"

"I'm questioning you, His representative."

Reverend Tiller smiled again. "Well, all that this representative can say is

. . . his Boss didn't let him in on how He started everything off. The Big Boss up there kept that a secret unto Himself."

Free rushed on. "Suppose my ma'd decided not to let my pa have his way one night some sixteen years ago, why, I wouldn't be here."

Everybody laughed. It was an uneasy laugh, loud.

Second cousin Johnny Engleking couldn't resist sticking it in a little. "Free with his big ideas. First thing you know, he's going to prove he ain't even here. For a fact."

Albert Engleking agreed. "Or just prove he's just a big bag of wind. Which we knew all along."

Reverend Tiller placed both elbows on the brown table and sloped his hands alongside his cheeks. For a moment he resembled a horse with blinders on. "All these speculations are very interesting, Free. But let's return to the main point. Do you believe in God?"

Free hesitated; then said, slowly, "Yes."

"Good. I think then that you and the other five here are ready to be examined at the next consistory meeting for membership in the congregation of God."

Free thought: "Well, why not. It won't hurt any." The other five boys might be joining church for all the right reasons. He himself was mostly joining church to please Ma. In some ways he trusted Ma to be right in such matters, much as Domeny trusted God. Besides, where else could he go? Also, he'd done some awful things. It was time to start life with a clean slate.

He found Ma still up. Pa and the boys had gone to bed. Ma was dusting the living room with some cheesecloth. Ma had on a white dust cap and looked like a queen with her crown on. Ma fancied cheesecloth for dusting because it was a good picker-up of dust.

"Ma, Ma, you shouldn't be working this late. What's a few specks of dust here and there? You know. Nobody'll ever see 'em."

Ma got to her feet. "I've just finished," she whispered. She motioned for him to go into the kitchen ahead of her so as not to wake Pa or baby Sherman.

"Really, Ma," Free whispered.

Ma closed the door behind them. The bright light in the kitchen caught her fair in the face. Work had flushed her cheeks and for once she looked like she was in the pink of health. She was having one of her better days. She spotted the package under his arm. "What have you got there?"

Free settled in Pa's chair. He got out his jackknife and cut the package open. A thick red book emerged. The title, *The Works of Shakespeare,* was stamped in gold across the spine and across the front cover. The red binding was limp, the kind Free loved. He opened it carefully. The plays were printed in double columns. The paper was thin, expensive looking, and the type was dark and quite legible. He smelled down into the half-opened book. The odor of old times was in it, as well as the smell of fresh ink and fresh glue. Then he placed the book carefully on its back on the table and began breaking it in, as Professor Ralph had once taught him to do, pressing down some twenty pages at a time on each side, until he'd worked his way through the whole book.

Ma smiled at him. "The care you show for that book tells me that someday you'll take equally good care of your soul."

Free said nothing. He loved the book and he loved her.

"What's it about?"

He pushed the book toward her across the slick white oil cloth.

"William Shakespeare. Well." Her eyes became dreamy. "Reverend Carpenter, the domeny who married us, and for whom I once worked, had a set of his works. He loved the set dearly. I always meant to read in it but never got the chance." She handled the thick book lovingly. "What a beautiful volume. Almost looks like a Bible." She pushed it back across to Free. "It goes well with your black leather Bible."

It did go well with the Bible. It was of about the same size. He resolved to carve himself a pair of bookends for the two books. It would be the start of his own library.

"Did you have a good meeting tonight?"

"I'll tell you about it later."

"Time for you to go to bed then."

"Yes." He couldn't look her in the face because of those toothless gums. "Good night, Mom."

"Night, Free."

It was the next Sunday late in the afternoon.

The little ones were out in the house yard making a snowman, and Pa was busy in the barn with the horses, and Free was about to gather up the milk pails from the drying rack by the gate, when of a sudden Free heard music in the house behind him. Free listened, hands not quite touching the pails. It was Ma playing the organ in the parlor.

Sunday was Ma's day of rest, such as it was, and she always tried to have the house to herself a few hours. She'd first walk slowly back and forth through the house, as though drifting about in a dream, looking at all the work she'd managed to get done during the week, touching things she was fond of, the mantel clock, the clear grain of the oak table, the last photograph of her father, the precise whiteness of the perfectly hung curtains. Then she'd go into the parlor, closing the door behind her. She'd stand a moment looking at her best furniture glowing in the subdued brown light and then go to each window and let up the tan blinds and permit the pink light of dusk to enter. The thing she loved the best was the old organ. Its carved oak still glowed like living wood. Only its red plush-covered foot pedals showed wear and fading. Standing a while with a hand to her gold-brown hair, soaking herself into every passing moment to enjoy it to the last drop, she'd finally settle on the organ stool, and dreamily, not a woman nor a mother anymore, but a spirit composed of the perfume of the prairie rose, slowly begin to play.

Free listened to her muse her way through "Rock of Ages," "Gathering in the Sheaves," and "There were Ninety and Nine."

Then she played "Beautiful Ohio." When she came to the chorus, she began to sing. "Drifting with the current down a moonlit stream."

For once Ma didn't seem to be short of breath. Her soprano voice climbed, rich and wide, making one summit after another with ease, and holding steady. She moved from phrase to phrase with assurance. Free noted how true her voice was, more true at times than the organ itself. Her voice always surmounted and survived the gathering flood of bass notes. She swung from one note to the other with the effortless motion of a cardinal flying from limb to limb.

Tears leaked into the corners of Free's eyes.

"In dream again I see the visions of what used to be."

Free waited until the sound of the organ died away, and then, resolutely, turned and entered the house. He kicked off his boots, and his shoes, and in his stockings tiptoed through the living room. The film in his eyes gave the pink dusk in the room unnatural radiance. He opened the parlor door and peeked in.

Ma sensed him instantly. She turned on the organ stool. She appeared to be bathed in a bright glow. "Yes?"

"I didn't want to say anything about it the other night. But now I'm telling you. I've decided to join church."

Her face turned even brighter. "I'm glad, son."

"It's Sunday and I thought you'd like to know."

"Yes, I did want to know today. Now I can rest easy."

The key moment came two Sundays later. Church was almost full. Reverend Tiller, having read through most of the "Liturgical Form for the Confessing of Faith," paused and looked around. He smiled down at the six young men sitting before him in the front bench.

"Will those who are ready to confess their faith now please rise?"

All six rose to their feet. Free stood at the end on the left. With him were Floris Haber, Frank Haber, Johnny Engleking, Maynard Tollhouse, and Jake Young. The late autumn sun struck through the round south window high above and picked out the six young men as though it were a spotlight. It was almost as though Domeny had arranged that they should stand in that exact spot at that exact time.

Free answered the several questions automatically. Despite what had happened in the parlor several Sundays ago, Free still felt he was a player in a play, not a young man in real life. He could confess his faith with a clear conscience when it came to the bad things he'd done, but he still really and finally couldn't say he believed in Jesus Christ as his Savior. But he was fairly sure that faith in Jesus Christ would come of itself later on. Free caught a glimpse of Floris standing next to him. Free could see that the reverse was true for Floris. Floris didn't feel bad about all the girls he'd done it to. Floris probably never gave a second thought to the fact that his friends liked to brag about him that he could fart a tune, a whole song, "My Country 'Tis of Thee," by lying on his back while holding his knees in a certain position which allowed his rectum to suck in air at will. At the same time, Floris no doubt really did believe that God had sacrificed His only begotten son Jesus Christ so that he, Floris Haber, might be saved for all eternity.

Just in time Free made the final response with the others. "I do."

Reverend Tiller smiled down at them. "I now pronounce you full members of this congregation in the Lord."

Free turned his head a little to look back at where Pa and Ma and the kids sat. Pa had his usual chin-out smile. The kids looked impressed. While Ma's face was illuminated from within, as though someone had just lighted a pair of gas mantles inside her head. The soft thoughtful smile on her lips was one he'd never seen before.

Free ❦ 24

ONE SUNDAY NIGHT in the Corner Cafe, Roy Wickett, the local garageman, happened to mention that he'd come across a pretty good motor in an old 1918 Ford touring car. He'd just taken the Ford in trade. Free was there having himself a malted milk. A good motor? That might be just the thing. He'd often wished they had an extra jalopy on the yard to get things from town in, especially when Pa and Ma were gone for a couple of days. After a little banter back and forth, Free bought the old Ford for eighteen dollars. Had it been a 1919 model, Free said, he'd have paid nineteen dollars for it.

When Free drove on the yard with it, Pa almost fell to the ground in mock horror.

Free pulled up on the brake and stopped in front of the house gate. It looked like Pa wasn't going to crab about his having bought the car.

"Who gave you that to get rid of it?"

Free laughed. "Roy made it out of some Tinker Toys."

"He must've."

"Get in and drive it once, Pa."

"Never in your life. I'd rather ride Tip."

The boys came running in from all points of the yard. They stared with awe at the shaking machine. The top was down and they could look in from all sides.

"C'mon. Try it once." Free slid over for Pa to get in.

Pa let down a shoulder. "I know I'm fool for doing this, but, all right, here goes nothing."

Pa climbed in. The kids stepped back, already full of mirth at what Pa might do with the old jitney. Everett stood apart from the rest, a hand to his seat, his eyes not quite focused on Pa.

"All right, stand back everybody." Pa let out the brake, and then stepped her into low. With a groan of dry clutch drums, the old Ford began to ramble. When Pa got near the tool shed he eased over the wheel and turned her around and headed back to the house gate. Since everything had gone just fine, Pa decided to make another turn around the yard. But the next time he came a little too close to the tool shed and had to haul over the wheel hard to the left. All of a sudden the front wheels cramped over, locked, and the old car shot sideways.

"Hey!" Pa hollered. "Whoa, you! Gotske!"

Before Pa could remember how to stop the old Ford, she sailed right up a huge pile of fresh red cobs. Near the top of the pile the old Ford choked to a stop.

Everybody stood with dropped mouth, including Ma in the kitchen window.

Pa erupted out of the old Ford, and jumped, then slid, down the cob pile. "Pah! Fords! You can tell Mister Henry Ford for me that his Model T is a failure."

Free leaned laughing out of the front seat. "Roy warned me she might do that if you turned too short with it."

"Wal, you just tell friend Roy that one of these days I'm gonna be short with him too." Pa stomped off for the barn.

The younger kids laughed. When they looked at the kitchen window to see how Ma was taking it and saw she'd broken out with a wide smile, they laughed even harder.

Free noticed Everett still standing with a hand to his seat, except that his head was wried around facing the cob pile. "Everett, don't tell me that you still don't know enough to go to the privy!"

"Oh." Everett turned solemn. "Yeh. I had to go but I didn't want to miss anything." He broke out of his stiff stance, and with a hand still clapped to his seat headed for the outhouse.

Free got out of the old car, then slid down the cob pile. He and Flip got Nell and with a rope and singletree pulled the old Ford down off the cob pile, no worse for its wild ride.

The next couple of days, Free and Flip put their heads together and decided to make a truck out of the old tin lizzie. It would make a handy thing to haul wood in. They cut off the back seat with a hacksaw, and replaced it with a flatbed using boards left over from when Pa and Mr. Tollhouse built an overhead granary in the corncrib. The flatbed measured seven by seven.

It paid off the very first week. Pa'd set Free to work cutting down the dying willows along the lane for firewood, and each evening after school Free and Flip hurried to do their chores and then hauled the wood onto the yard next to the cob pile. In a half hour's time they hauled in what it took Free all day to cut.

Ma got a letter from Gramma asking if Free couldn't come up for a week with Sherm to cut some firewood for them. Garland was too busy as church janitor to cut wood and they were almost out.

Sherm decided they should drive up in Free's jitney. It was a foggy morning when they started out and every few miles they had to pull over and scrape the ice off the windshield. It was too burning cold to lean around the corner of the windshield to look up ahead.

Sherm took over the wheel at Hello. Sherm liked to clown around and he made a lark out of driving the old jitney. He and Uncle John always did everything with a little curlicue to it. He'd drive with one finger a ways; then he'd goose the footfeed in tune with "Swing Low Sweet Chariot"; then he'd drive with one foot over the door. The one finger he usually drove with was the only one on his left hand. His left hand had gotten all mashed up in Uncle John's corn picker. Sherm had grown up into a handsome blond fellow, six foot one, clear blue eyes with always a little mockery in them, and gold hair neatly in place. He was going with Allie Pipp and was thinking of marrying her.

"Say, Free I got something to ask you."

"Fire away."

"Did you ever play with yourself?"

Free clammed up.

"That question too close for comfort? Well, I got another one for you. What chance do you think there'd be of me knocking up Allie if we did it just once? You know, just once?" Sherm quirked his eyes at Free for a second. "After what happened to her sister Laura, Allie is scared to death of it."

Free's legs slowly stiffened. The roar of the old Ford motor throbbed up into his hips. It made him uneasy to hear Sherm thinking of doing it with Allie.

Sherm gave Free another spearing look as they drove along. "So you claim you don't use the Palmer method, eh?"

Free pinkened.

"You better start dating girls pretty soon or the first thing you know you'll have to marry your right hand."

The windshield began to ice up pretty bad again. Sherm reached around ahead and scratched a little hole in the ice with his thumbnail. He was driving on his side of the road mostly by guess. He'd just managed to make an opening about the size of a silver dollar, when he saw something through it that made him suddenly wrench the wheel hard over to the right. The gravel was icy and the front wheels didn't take hold right away. But when they did, they cramped over, and the old jitney shot sideways into the ditch.

"Hey!" Free cried. "Watch out."

Sherm cried, "Hold her, Newt!"

The old jitney shot up the other side of the ditch, hit a snowbank which straightened out the front wheels, slewed around in the right direction again, and a second later Sherm got it back on the shoulder of the road. Just then the car that Sherm had spotted coming toward them whizzed by, horn blowing. Sherm pulled up.

"Gotske!" Free whispered. It was Pa's word but it was the only one that came to mind.

Sherm turned as white as snow. "That crazy fool." Sherm looked back; then suddenly got mad. "Why! he was driving on our side of the road. Headed right into us. Like brother John used t'."

Free didn't say anything. Sherm shouldn't have let the windshield get so iced over.

With a look at Free, and a nervous laugh, Sherm hopped out and began to clean off the windshield.

They arrived at Gramma's door without further mishap.

Gramma was happy to see them. Her life with Grampa Stanhorse was a good one. The old frown in her brow was gone. "Well, well, here come the woodcutters to the rescue." She immediately sat them down at her kitchen table and served them cups of hot coffee and black rye bread with butter and sugar on it. In a few minutes their faces were glowing like the cheeks of Saint Nick.

Soon Grampa Stanhorse came home. Marriage had been good for him too. He looked much younger and his nose didn't stick out as much as it used to. There was a merry look in his eyes, as though he'd recently learned something wonderful about himself and was very happy to have discovered it. "Well, well, here come the woodcutters to the rescue." He stood first on one leg, then on the other, fumbling with his gold watch chain.

Sherm lifted a brow at Free. "Where have we heard that before?"

Free lifted a brow in turn. "Yeh. It sounds like somebody was quite worried about their winter supply of wood."

It was five o'clock, too late to begin sawing that day, but Grampa Stanhorse did show them what he expected of them, where the tools were, where the trees were he wanted cut down, and where he wanted the chopped-up wood stored. The trees were scattered around the neighborhood.

The next morning after ten pancakes and three eggs each, they went at it. They tackled an ash tree by the water tower first. Until they got used to it, it was best to start with the easiest first. It was an old tree, a monster about four feet thick. When the cut neared the center of the tree they didn't have much leeway in which to pull the crosscut saw back and forth. But they persisted and soon they had more room again. When the backcut came to within an inch of the undercut, there was a ripping crack and the old dying ash began to topple.

"Timm—berr!" Sherm yelled, making a great show of being a lumberjack, lips turned up like a dog yowling.

Free with Sherm jerked the saw out and ran off some twenty steps.

The great old tree came down with a smash of breaking limbs. Some of the middle-sized branches jumped around on the ground like a bunch of hard snakes for a moment. Then all was silent.

Sherm surveyed the wreck. "When they're old and dry like that, a lot of your work is done for you if they hit the ground hard enough."

By noon they had the tree trimmed and all the limbs and branches cut into stove-length pieces. They used Free's flatbed to haul in a load when they went into dinner. Because Sherm always tackled any kind of job like it was a campaign in a big war, cutting wood turned out to be great fun. According to Sherm they were breaking one record after another. By five o'clock, when it got dark under a gray sky, they also finished cutting and splitting the main trunk of the tree. Ash split easy. One tap and the log opened up like a watermelon. They hauled in the last load on Free's flatbed by six o'clock.

Grampa Stanhorse was as pleased as any grampa could possibly be. He rolled his dark brown eyes at all the wood suddenly piled up on his yard. He kept checking his big gold Waltham watch as though he couldn't believe so much could happen so fast in one day. "Wife," he said, as he and the boys entered the kitchen, "you haven't forgotten that reward we had in mind for them?"

"What? I don't love our woodcutters?" Gramma tried to frown right through the middle of a big happy red sweating smile. The single electric bulb over the kitchen table shone a mellow gold.

Sherm washed up under the cistern pump. "What reward is that?"

Grampa Stanhorse rocked back and forth on his heels. Then he pointed toward the porch.

"What've you got out there?" Sherm asked, drying his hands and face. "Huh?"

Grampa Stanhorse picked up a flashlight and led the way. He shone the light on a barrel standing in the far corner. There was hand lettering on it: *North Sea Herring*. "From the Old Country," Grampa Stanhorse said. "The best. Specially ordered for you boys. Packed in ice and shipped all the way to America."

Sherm punched an elbow into Free's ribs. "Now you're gonna see some eating. I remember how good they used to be."

Free washed up next.

Soon they were sitting at the table. After the blessing, Gramma served them their first round of fried herring, along with brown fried potatoes, boiled beans, and canned red beets.

Sherm showed Free how to eat herring the easy way. "Gently prize off the top half with your fork, sideways like this, going down the backbone; then gently lift out the whole skeleton, and, presto, you're ready to eat. What you have left is some flakes of the sweetest white flesh in the whole world."

Gramma kept the fish coming until they each had six. Gramma kept throwing up her hands as though she were witnessing a miracle. "Good grutkins! You two eat enough for an army."

Sherm smiled at Free. "Well, I guess at that it would've taken a small army to keep up with us today."

Free was so muscle-tired, and so full, he could hardly smile.

As Gramma ladled the seventh fish into Free's plate, she leaned over him with her big loose bosom. "What a big fellow you've become. I still say we should've put a stone on your head to keep you from shooting up so."

"But then he would've shot out sideways," Sherm said. "When he's already wide enough as it is."

Grampa Stanhorse nodded. "He's become a real slap-up fellow all right."

As they visited together, Gramma remembered something. "One thing I mussent forget. I want you two boys to pay your respects to Tante Gertie before you leave."

Sherm balked at that. "Not on your life."

"Fooey, Sherman. Shame on you. She's your great aunt on your father's side. You should show respect for such a venerable relative."

"For Tante Toothache? Never." There was a snarl on Sherm's thin lips. He turned to Free. "Did you ever meet her?"

"Once. Years ago. You and me got some milk there. She lives on the west end of town there. Alone except for a cow."

"That's the one." Sherm shook all over, he disliked her so. "Every time I'd go there to get milk she'd have a different complaint. First it'd be an awful toothache and she'd open her mouth real wide like this"—Sherm pried one corner of his mouth back with a finger to indicate his own back molars—"to show me a big hole in her wisdom tooth. Way back to there. A brown stinking hole. The next time she'd tell me about a toothache in her belly. And the third time she'd tell me about a toothache in her behind."

"Fooey!" Gramma said. "Nobody has a toothache in their behind."

"Well, she does. If she goes to heaven when she dies, then I'm going to wonder a little about God's judgment."

"Sherman!" Gramma cried. "Blaspheme not."

Grampa Stanhorse understood. "Now, Sherman, she's had a hard life. Complaining may be her only satisfaction in life."

"All you have to do is ask one question," Sherm said. "Where are her kids? Yeh. Your Tante Toothache has driven them out of her life with all her endless complaining." Sherm threw Gramma a sharp look. "And I too hate complainers, no matter who they are."

Sherm's look didn't set too well with Gramma. She knew what he meant. She thickened up a little and her face slowly turned red.

Grampa Stanhorse knew how to smooth things over. "Well, wife, have you told our fine young gentlemen about the other surprise we have in store for them?"

Gramma swallowed several times, and finally managed to revive her joy at having the boys there. "No, I haven't."

"Well then," Grampa Stanhorse said, "after we finish here we'll show them."

"If it's ice cream," Free said, "then I got a little room left."

"You've got more room left after seven fish?" Gramma cried. She threw up her hands. "Good Grutkins, you must have a haymow for a stomach."

Grampa Stanhorse got out the Bible and opened it at the blue marker. "Let's hear from Scripture first. Uh, we've just started reading in Phillippians, boys. First chapter. So." Grampa Stanhorse read in a style that went with his high nose. There were those in church who said that the wrong man was janitor. The new minister, for all his learning, looked like a clodhopper beside Mr. Garland Stanhorse. Grampa Stanhorse meant his high style.

A third of the way into the chapter a lively verse made Free perk up. "How greatly I long after you all in the bowels of Jesus Christ." Free had never before thought of Jesus Christ as having bowels.

About two-thirds through the chapter he heard another striking verse. "For to me to live is Christ, and to die is gain." Now that was quite a statement. It made sense at the same time that it was deep. In this life one should try to live like Christ; and then, upon death, because of such a life, one could expect to gain heaven. He nodded to himself. When he got home he'd read that chapter for Ma at the table and then talk to her about it. She'd like that verse.

Grampa Stanhorse gave thanks. As usual he rolled off his favorite phrases. "This fragile crumbling shell of flesh." "The strange furies that sometimes possess us and place us at the mercy of the devil." "Oh, God, in Thy majestic mercy, be inclined to forgive us, these Thy miserable worm sinners. In Christ's name, Amen."

All four released their eyes and slowly looked around.

"Nah," Grampa Stanhorse said, getting up from his armchair, beckoning them to come with him, "follow me." He strode into the living room, the boys and Gramma following.

Behind the door, under Gramma's old picture of the Alps, stood a brand-new radio, four feet high, with a dark mahogany finish. Grampa Stanhorse opened the folding doors in front. There were two knobs. Grampa Stanhorse clicked one of them, and instantly a green light came on behind a dial. "A New Brunswick," he said proudly.

"Hey," Sherm said. "When did you get that?"

"Last week. And already Gramma and I have heard programs all the way from Pittsburg. Even from New York. As clear as if you were to hold this"—he extracted his gold watch from his vest pocket—"right against your ear for the ticking movement."

The big mahogany radio began to hum and in a moment a man's voice came cheerily into Gramma's living room. ". . . and yes, folks, it's snowing here in Cincinnati, which means we're going to have a white Christmas after all."

"Cincinnati! You hear that?" Grampa Stanhorse stomped excitedly. "I thought that was who we had last night when I turned it off. This thing can surely reach out a long ways."

Free had often wished Pa and Ma had a radio. The old Edison phonograph with its beat-up records was about done for.

"Nah," Grampa Stanhorse said, "take a chair. Tonight I've got a great program for you." He looked at his watch. "Yes, in just two minutes it begins. We're going all the way to New York to hear Walter Damrosch and his NBC Symphony Orchestra."

Sherm pulled a face. "That kind of music?"

Grampa Stanhorse held up a strong finger. "Uk. Just wait. Sit down and listen to it first before you criticize."

Free stretched out on the floor. He found a soft spot on one of Gramma's rag rugs directly below the loudspeaker. His thick forearm made a good pillow and he nuzzled his cheek on it. His forearm ached pleasantly. It felt good to rub it with his chin.

Grampa Stanhorse drew up his rocker. Slowly he began to rotate the dial. There was some screeching, and some distant crackling from the stars, and then, again, as clear as if the announcer were right there in the room, a liquid silver English voice was heard to say, "This is the National Broadcasting Company in New York. Tonight we shall hear Walter Damrosch conduct the *Tannhäuser* overture by Wagner. But first, Conductor Walter Damrosch will give us some background on the overture, as well as tell us what to look for as we listen to it. Mr. Damrosch." There was a pause, and then another voice began to speak in a foreign accent, manly, grave. "In this piece Richard Wagner's harmonic style comes to its full glory on a grand scale. The musical technique throughout is superb. Robert Schumann said of *Tannhäuser* that it represented one of the great peaks of all musical creativity. Listen carefully then as the harmonies come at you as if they were vast columns, yes, towers, of music, all in balance with each other." There was another pause. Then slowly the sound of music purled into Gramma's living room, music such as Free had never heard before, as if two slow Dutch psalms were being delicately woven together.

The music throbbed up through the floor into Free's bowels. In his mind's eye the green light on the dial lit up the vast green slopes of a mountain range. The green mountains were the tall misty Alps in Gramma's picture on the wall.

Grampa Stanhorse stopped rocking. The hand with his pipe in it gradually settled to his knee. His lips parted. His bold nose lifted. His brown eyes hazed over, became tranfixed.

Gramma in her rocker stopped rocking too. A great kettle in her was about to boil over.

Sherm slid out of his chair and lay down on the floor beside Free.

Free forgot he was bone-tired from all the sawing and chopping, as well as full of seven fish.

The music rose to a climax. A towering Samson was clutching up huge pillars, a half dozen of them, and clanging them together with great ringing stone sounds. There was a final blast of horns and drums.

There was a long moment of silence in Gramma's living room.

Then Grampa Stanhorse broke out of his trance. "Ahh. Majestic. Majestic! Ha, wife? boys?"

"If I hear that music in heaven, then I don't know," Gramma said.

Sherm said nothing. He'd heard something all right.

Free'd caught a glimpse, beyond Ada Shutter and Mabel James and Aletha Gladjanus, of a very beautiful girl, with white-gold hair, light blue eyes, and a slender athletic body. She had a sister's smile for him, tender, compassionate. He'd never had a sister. Yet the floating vision he saw was clearly his sister.

The white-gold sister was so real he sat up to see her better. As he did so his eyes cleared; and she was gone.

"Nah," Gramma said, rocking herself out of her chair with a hand to her knee and standing up, "Time for our woodcutters to go to bed. You've had a lordly day, hard work, seven fish, and God's music."

Grampa Stanhorse shut off the radio. "That Walter Damrosch, ach! What a great man. It's surely a miracle to be listening to him from so far away." He wound his watch; then went about the house winding up various clocks. He locked both the front door and the back door.

Free and Sherm went to bed in the same room they'd slept in together before. The picture of the onrushing train with its great plume of smoke still hung on the wall at the foot of the bed, and it still, if one half closed one's eyes, jumped back and forth from being first a train and then a lovely woman with her hair piled up on top of her head.

Free lay next to the wall, while Sherm lay on the open side.

Grampa Stanhorse and Gramma could be heard going to bed in the next bedroom. They talked together like a couple of great old friends. After a while Gramma let out a yip; then cried out, loud, "Pa! that's scandalous." After a moment she let out another cry. "Och, Garland, still at your age?"

Sherm rose up one one elbow. He cocked his head at Free. "Listen to 'em. I'll give you one guess what they're doing."

Free could make out Sherm's expression clearly in the blue light coming from the hard-coal burner in the other room. The look was one of leering delight.

"They're not too old for it, you know," Sherm added.

Gramma?

"Oh, yes. You'd be surprised. Some people have fun like that all the way to the edge of the grave. And the way those two get along, they may even have fun beyond the grave."

Free recalled Gramma saying once that if it should happen Grampa Stanhorse died before she did, she was going to jump into the grave with him. "Gladly."

Gramma let out one more yip and then the house fell silent.

The next day Free and Sherm ran into trouble with a cottonwood on the school grounds across the street. It was worse than the worst cottonwood on Bart Westham's place. They had to use dynamite. First they had to drill a series of holes, then tamp in the dynamite kernels carefully, then lay in the fuse. But it was sport to see the logs burst apart into split sections. By the third time around Sherm was an expert at it. He placed the drilled holes so strategically there was little splitting left to do.

They finished off the cottonwood, and finally a box elder on Gramma's yard, by noon of the fourth day. They'd chopped up a great pile of wood, higher even than the little red barn, and had all of it neatly stacked.

Grampa Stanhorse had some papers to sign at the courthouse and asked Sherm to come with him to witness them. The weather had turned strangely warm for that late in the year, and the two left wearing raincoats and rubbers.

Free sat reading in Grampa Stanhorse's armchair. He'd found an old book in Gramma's attic, *Blind Peter and the Smugglers*. It was sometimes so simple a story he had to laugh right out loud.

Gramma was peeling potatoes.

After a while Free became aware that it was getting quite dark for mid-afternoon.

"Hach," Gramma sighed. Her glasses were pushed down to the end of her fat nose. "Isn't it close in here, boy?"

"What? Oh. Yeh, I guess it is."

"Ackie weather. Like we're going to get some kind of storm."

"Yeh."

"Yes, boy, you're not really listening. Well, it's all right. Gramma don't mind talking to herself. Just so God hears me."

There was an awful clap. The whole kitchen jumped, then vibrated like a threshing machine. At the same time an explosion came down the chimney, then burrowed into the kitchen stove, then blew out through the four stove lids. Each iron lid rose about six inches above its hole, hovering on top of what appeared to be boiling white-yellow light. Then there was another snap, and the four boiling balls of light snapped together, forming a cylinder of light. The four lids fell back clattering on the stove, shedding black soot. With yet a further snap, the cylinder of light shot sideways across the kitchen and fastened itself onto the cistern pump. The cylinder of light shimmered a moment. Then, click! it dove into the pump. It gurgled down the pipe into the cistern under the house, where it blew up in a final explosion.

Gramma gasped. Terrorized, she sagged in her chair, letting the pan of potatoes slide out of her lap. Peelings, wet potatoes, dirty water spilled onto the yellow linoleum.

There was a smell of burnt air in the kitchen. It cut the nose.

Free was stiff from shock, as well as from a small charge of electricity. With difficulty he put aside his book. "Gramma?" Then he went to Gramma's aid. "Are you all right? Gramma?"

Gramma heaved a great sigh; her eyes rolled once; then she got her breath back. "Ahh. Get—me—a—heart—pill. From somewhere. I don't know."

Free helped her sit up. He chafed her hands and her cheeks.

"God heard me all right. Sending me a ball of lightening like that."

"Well, Gramma, whatever it was, it sure was a close call."

Free went over and fitted the four stove lids back in their place and then cleaned up the mess on the floor. A smile edged into his brain as he thought about the way Gramma had taken it. Old people were sure wonderful the way they reacted.

Gramma remembered something. "Oh-oh. We're going to have to re-cement the cistern walls above the water line."

"How do you know that?"

"Your Grampa Alfred had to do it once for a neighbor. A bolt of lightning exploded in their cistern too." Gramma shook her head. "I wonder what God meant by that. You can be sure he was giving us a message of some kind."

Ada ❦ 25

Bonnie
January 18, 1929

Dear Karen and Kon,

Your most welcome letter reached us on my birthday. Many thanks for your kind good wishes. May they all come true.

We also received the fat letter of Kon this week. Many thanks. I would have an's yours before, but took suddenly sick last Wed. eve the 9th. I had just nicely done up a big washing mending all except a couple pairs of stockings. Of course I planned some sewing. But very little has been done since, though I started this week Wed. once again.

I am feeling fairly well again, though this evening my stomach acts so queer. It started that way then too. I went to bed feeling so full and bloated. Rested maybe an hour and then I got up, tried to throw up, but it wouldn't work. My stomach pained so on the left side near the two lower ribs. Finally I took a dose of castor oil, walked the floor, and put a mustard poltice on the painful spot. Finally the oil worked, but no relief, and towards morning the pain went a little lower towards the side. I got up, tried to make breakfast, but soon went to bed again. The pain was so bad at times I could hardly breathe. I kept the hot water bottle on it all the time. Friday even we called the Doc. As all was in vain, he gave me some pills to stop the pain, but could not say what it could be. Thot it was my kidneys. Tested them the next day, and a couple days later again. But nothing seems wrong with them, so we don't know what it has been. To me it seemed like pleurisy, though I had very little fever. My appetite did not come back till Mon. Then it began to pick up and the pain left. I do hope to spend a better Saturday tomorrow. Last Sat. I managed to dust the bedrooms and dining room at little intervals. The rest of the work Alfred and the boys managed to do. I was glad they did it so well. I didn't care much either how it was done. I think it must have been the flu, though I didn't seem to have such a bad cold.

I felt sorry for Alfred in a way as he had planned to make a trip along with Garrett Tillman, brother John, and Case Van Driel (you know he married cousin Alice of Uncle Claus) to the sale of Mr. Westraw at Pease the past Tuesday of this week. They were going to leave Sunday eve at twelve o'clock and expected to stop in Whitebone for breakfast, where Tillman was to look after some of those hearses there for sale, and then proceed on over to Pease. But I didn't look a bit well yet Sun. eve so Alfred gave it up. He would have sure run in to see you a few moments. The other men went anyhow and started out about the said time but sure had a time of it to reach your beloved town. It was twelve noon when they did reach it and while eating dinner they tried to get you per phone but could not find your No. No wonder, your phone doesn't have a No. does it? They left soon after and had no trouble from there on to Pease, and they came back on another road, a hundred miles further west and had no trouble at all, made it within 12 hours. Your part of the country must have had a great deal more snow than we had here. They were back home at eight Wed. evening all tired out, but safe.

We are glad to hear about the enjoyment you get from your radio. It sure is nice for Karen to have and sure can't blame you folks for getting one. I believe I would like one too. Alfred is very interested but we have plenty of radios around as yet for a while. Besides we cannot afford one now. Although I'm sure it would interest the boys very much. Maybe they would learn to be more quiet with such a thing to listen in on. Radios are very nice to have the Christmas season and Old Year's eve. We, Alfred, Albert, Jonathan, and myself heard the New York bells ring in the New Year at the home of the Tillmans. We couldn't all go as Sherman wasn't well at all. He was sick for a week with a very bad cold and quite feverish. We kept him greased up good and watched the bowels, giving him cough medicine, and now he is fine, though you can see he lost in weight as he wouldn't eat at all, but little ones soon catch this up again.

Uncle Ben spent a short day with us last week Wed. He is the same as always. Aunt Gretchen looks terrible, they say, with all her teeth out. She had an awful time getting them all pulled.

I am a new woman, now, ha, ha, and sure wouldn't like to go without my teeth again. I got my new ones Old Year's morning. First it felt like a terrible big mouthful and I couldn't eat at all with those stiff things. But you can learn it all right. I wonder what Kon's mother Mrs. Harmer thought I looked like. She didn't say anything about them when we were there. Some say I do not look like myself, but I do not think there is much of a change. The boys all looked so funny at me when I stepped into the house. One said I looked like that person and another had me linked on somebody else again. And Sherman often pulls on his own and tries to get them out. He then says, "I can't, Mama. Mama can but I can't. Watch."

We had a letter of Gerda on Christmas Day for a change. A card of Richard's and a fat letter of Janet. I believe I wrote you this in our Xmas letter. Gerda's husband was in the hospital at that time with a double mastoid, which they drained through his nose. We heard from her later, stating that he was to come home on Mon. and start working on Wed. of that same week. This must be two weeks ago now. They have also bought a house up there for $5000 and are planning to pay it off on monthly installments instead of paying rent. So they must be making some headway. Good, isn't it?

Richard in Michigan was out of work a couple of weeks during the holidays and Selina had a job for them during that time for $12 a week in some shop, but she says she'd rather keep house.

Now I must close as I can't think of any more news. All have gone to roost. How about you, Kon? Still listening in? Do not let it interfere with your health. Then you better trade it in for a car. So Brant thot you folks were beginning to turn her loose. Pretty good. But I don't believe you will get one yet, unless if all are well and the beautiful summer evenings tempt you folks pretty soon.

Your mother has a very nice tan stove, she is so proud of it now, is planning to have the kitchen wall painted the same shade, pretty soon. The stove is from the same company as ours but a way different make or style.

With best and loving wishes from us all.

Alfred and Ada.

P. S. Oh, yes, Karen, I wanted to tell you, you should not have worried about your Xmas candy. I know you take great pleasure in sending it. But your family duties could have been such for many years that you could have stopped sending it long before this. The boys all love you just the same. I made them some a week after Xmas, the white kind, and it was just fine—it is quite a trick for me to get it good.

Ada ❦ 26

Bonnie
Feb. 13, 1929

Dear Karen and Kon,

Alfred wanted me to write you a few lines this evening. I first finished mending socks and stockings, so now it better be, even though it isn't very early anymore. But I can write best when most all have retired.

We were wondering whether you people received the letter we sent you some four or more weeks ago. Or wasn't the thing filled out right? Please say so. We will gladly send another. We sure hope you folks are not sick up there. Or has the radio taken complete possession of you people?

We are not in a hurry about the note, no, not at all, but if you failed to get the letter you could think we were such pokes about it.

Are you having such severe cold weather up there too? Last Saturday morning it was 30 below around here. It doesn't bother us in the house as we have plenty wood to burn. So far we haven't bought a piece of coal. But Alfred says it ought to let up a little else we will not have enough till spring and they may have to saw some more. There are lots of dead trees yet but not chopped up.

This week it is not near so cold. This noon it was 14 above zero and it does not seem much colder at present, though every day it has snowed a little. The sun is not out very long.

Alfred was on the sick list today. His stomach seems out of order. I hope he will soon be over it.

The boys all have been wonderful healthy this winter, but now the old folks are on the blink off and on. A week ago last Sunday I was way off again. It started on Saturday already, such cramps in my stomach, and they kept getting worse during the night. We tried to calm it down with hot cloths but it was of no avail. Toward six in the morning we had Doc come out as I didn't know where to go and he gave me an injection which soon stopped it. And since that I haven't been worth 2 cents to work. I'm so all in right away. I was picking up so nice off my first attack. Although this last attack is more my stomach, where the first time I believe I had a good flu. I threw up some gall which Doc thot did it and I must be more careful of what I eat for a while. That flu sure makes a person weak, doesn't it? I never had it before but it got me good and proper this time. I have lost considerable in weight. I know so many tell me I'm so thin, but that doesn't hurt. I'll soon have that back, just so my appetite returns. Doc gave me pills for it which I hope may help. It sure is no fun to have to poke it down. I can sympathize with you of olden days, Karen. My rosy face has completely disappeared but it is now slowly returning. I would like it to go much faster as there is always so much to do. Though I must not complain as Alfred and Everett sure have done their best.

We are planning to do some butchering soon. Also for the summer. We haven't had much meat at all this winter. One medium sized hog and a half one during the cornpicking season.

I sure dread to think of the job, would like to get it out of the way next week, but I'm afraid I can't do it yet. I must feel better than these last few days. I have so much bother of rheumatism, lately. First I had it in my hands and arms. The muscles would swell up and now today I have it above the ankles. This is sure painful and makes a fellow so stiff. Ha, ha, I'll bet you people think I've got it bad and it sure seems queer that I should complain, well, not a word anymore about myself if I can help it.

Say, Karen, Alfred bought me a new coat in Rock Falls last Monday, a soft shade of dark tan with a real fur collar of dark brown, French lynx, if I remember right. No fur cuffs. The cloth is a twilled broadcloth. At Brockways I had looked them over once, yes twice, when we were there fitting my teeth, but they were so high with it. Though there was none other there to fit me so well. It was one of the longest ones. I lengthened it a good inch yesterday, making it 47 inches. I could have it a little longer but they do not seem to think that tall people need any coat and of course I will not wear my skirts short as most of them do, so there you are. They first, Old Year's day, asked $49. They had dropped $10 on it then. And two weeks ago I peeked again when we were up with Alfred and Albert, they each had a tooth pulled. Then they asked $39 so that was already 20 off. But we thot 30 was plenty but they would not let it go for that. They wanted 35 or else they would store it over the summer as it was a good style, she said. I didn't think Alfred would take it for that but he did it. Sure, it is some price for me. I think I had my other one just six years this month. It sure is getting saggy looking too.

Well, just a little more news and I must stop. I read in a Zion, Michigan, paper a couple of weeks ago the wedding license of Mr. Garrett Underhill, 56, and Elizabeth Graves, 43 ys. We think that must be Edward Underhill's father. He is about that age and he also went east a couple of years back. So he has a home again.

May we hear from you soon? If I tire you with my whining about myself, burn it. About the note is the most important part. With lots of love and best wishes from us all.

Alfred, Ada, and boys.

P. S. If we could talk to you once, we could tell you how we have been blessed this past season. We cannot express our thanks enough unto the Great Giver of it all. Alfred has sold most of the hogs and was able to pay off a wonderful lot of debt and all the expenses of the past year. Although he bought a team of horses with it as we run short last year. Chauncey Mack our banker was so surprised. We milked 11 cows the last few months. During the month of Jan. the cream brought us $105. Wasn't that good? Are milking nine now as 3 more will be fresh pretty soon. The chickens stopped entirely. Too cold, we think. Although we sold a nice lot a month ago. Last week had $9.50 per hundred for the last batch of hogs, the top market that day. Of course we have 25 sows left.

Free 27

AS FREE THREW out the last scoop of cow manure, he heard the 9:11 Cannonball whistling down the valley. Looking, he saw smoke bubbling behind the river trees. In a moment a green passenger train trickled into view. It ran lightly over the Little Rock railroad bridge and then veered a little to head straight north into Bonnie. It whistled again, twice, white steam pluming up each time, its haunting echoes hooting across the valley.

He was closing the doors, both bottom and top, when he spotted a black car rolling up the lane toward the house. It was Dr. Fairlamb coming to see Ma again. Pa was helping her do the morning housework, and must've called him after breakfast.

When Free had gone in to breakfast that morning Ma was washing her face in fresh rainwater. She'd looked quite pink. Ma said cold rainwater beat all the beauty creams in the world.

The black car pulled up at the gate. Two men got out, Dr. Fairlamb and another doctorlike man. Both headed directly for the porch door.

Two doctors? Something was wrong up at the house then.

Free finished putting down fresh bedding for the cows and then went out and choused them up from the water tank. Milk cows couldn't be left outside very long in zero weather or they'd freeze their tits. After they'd all marched into their places he locked their stanchions.

He went to the house. He poured himself a cup of coffee, adding some cream and sugar, and parked himself beside the kitchen stove. He settled his feet in the cob box.

He heard them talking in Ma's bedroom. Pa wasn't saying much. Ma was responding to questions put by the two doctors.

At last Pa said, resignedly, "Wal, if that's the way the wind blows, we better sail according to it."

"But, Alfred," Ma said, "the cost! We've just barely got our head above debt."

"Debt be damned. I want a healthy wife. This is no way, Ada."

Ma sighed. "Well, if it's the Lord's wish that I be operated on, then so be it. We'll put our trust in Him."

"Don't forget the surgeon," Pa said. "He's the one who's really on the other end of the knife."

"Alfred," Ma said, "what you're saying borders on blasphemy."

The strange doctor laughed a rich downtown laugh. "Don't worry, Mrs. Alfredson. If God wants to help me, I won't mind."

Presently the two doctors came into the kitchen. Pa stayed behind with Ma. The two doctors didn't right away see Free sitting by the stove.

Dr. Fairlamb said, "That pain in her abdomen really isn't pronounced enough, is it, Tom, for us to be certain it's an inflamed appendix?"

The other doctor said, "I think it is. What else can it be? Her bowel movements are irregular. And the pain is in the lower right quadrant. It is a trifle high, but that could be deferred pain."

"Well . . ."

"If it breaks, then she's really in trouble."

"That she is."

The other doctor spotted Free. "Oh. Hello, there."

Dr. Fairlamb turned around. "Oh, Free, this is Dr. Thomas Husum. From Amen. Your father and mother decided we should get another medical opinion."

Free got up and shook hands.

"Lord, what a big fellow," Dr. Husum said. Dr. Husum was tall himself but he still had to look up at Free. "You overheard us?"

"Yes."

"Well, never fear. We've got your mother's trouble pinpointed."

Two days later Pa took Ma away to the Amen hospital for the operation. They left before six so that she could be on the operating table by eight. Ma looked pretty good. She'd almost decided not to go.

Free tried to keep his mind off of what was going on in Amen. He could see the smokestacks of Amen some seven miles down the valley where they stuck out over the trees along the winding Big Rock River. Free cleaned out the entire barn, the cow side, the horse side, the matted calf side. He carried in fresh bedding from the straw pile. He repaired two sets of harnesses. In a couple of weeks they'd be out in the field again. Finally, morning chores done, he went into the house.

He tried to read in his red Shakespeare. But soon finding himself only paging through *King Lear,* not reading it, he put it away.

He thought: "By now they've surely opened her up and found out the real trouble."

He called his brothers in from the barn, where they were playing monkey in the warm haymow. He fed them some warm rice Ma had prepared.

Dishes finished, he lay down on the horsehair sofa a while. He tried to imagine himself into Pa's shoes taking a noon nap.

He found himself aroused. He scratched his head, and felt the bump in his hair, the one like Rover had. "I'm an animal, all right." He bounced up and put on his sheepskin coat and four-bucklers and went down to the hog house. Everett was a good hog man but he was as slow as molasses when it came to throwing out the hogshit.

Free punished himself cleaning the hog house. The smell was awful, worse even than human dung when the human being was gallsick. A lot of it was frozen along the edges, both along the walls inside the hog house as well as on the cement feeding platform outside. When the edge of the shovel hit an embedded cob, it was hard on the gut. It made him grunt. At the end of two hard hours his wrists were sore.

Pa came back at three. Uncle John was with him. Both of them were somber as they got out of the car.

Uncle John smiled a crinkled smile at Free. "Got the coffee on?"

"I think Everett's made some."

"Good." Uncle John rubbed his hands. "Then I stay a minute. Sherm is coming along later anyway to pick me up."

Free tried to catch Pa's eye. But Pa wouldn't look at him.

All three went into the house. Pa set out the cups and saucers and then poured the coffee. Pa also found the cake and cut them each a generous piece. The cake was Free's favorite, dark brown with dried fruit and citron in it and brown sugar frosting.

Free had to know. "What happened?"

Pa almost bawled. "They operated on her all right."

"Was it broken?"

"No, it didn't need to be taken out, I guess."

"What!" Free dropped his cup so hard that coffee spilled in the saucer.

Pa looked down at the floor. "Wal, I guess it didn't hurt to take it out. Doc said it showed it'd been infected once."

Uncle John savored a spoonful of coffee and then laid the spoon aside. "The operation was a good thing, Alf. Because now they know what caused those odd pains." Uncle John said to Free, "She's got bumps on her aorta. Discolored blisters. As well as some pimples on her bowels." Uncle John sipped some more coffee. He always liked to take a good thing slow. "It wasn't cancer though, Doc said."

"But aren't those bumps and pimples dangerous though?"

"Doc said he thought he could give her something for them."

"You sure they were there?"

"I saw them with my own eyes. Doc let your dad and me watch the operation. We had to put on a white gown and mask. Like a doctor."

Uncle John, even Pa, saw Ma's bowels? When only the other week he'd wondered himself about how he'd lain next to them when she was carrying him?

Uncle John said, "Yes, boy, life's a tough titty."

Free said, "I'm not sure I trust that Dr. Husum fellow. He's kind of a windbag."

"That's what I think too," Pa blurted, crying down at his coffee.

Uncle John licked his lips. "Well, Alf, I tell you. Dr. Fairlamb is a good doctor, and he wouldn't lightly let any of his patients go under the knife unless he thought the surgeon was a good one."

"Wal, that's true."

"And beyond that, we've all got to trust in the Lord."

Free said, "How did her heart take it?"

Uncle John looked surprised. "You mean that part where she's always feeling so light-breathed that you wonder?"

Free nodded. He took a sip of coffee. It was getting cold.

"They never mentioned her heart," Uncle John said.

A horn sounded outside.

"Well, there's Sherm and it's time to chorse." Uncle John threw down the rest of his coffee. "Let me know if anything happens."

Pa was too upset to do chores. He sent Everett out to milk in his place. He said he'd make the supper for his boys. He said he wanted a minute alone by himself. Even toddler Sherman had to go out to the barn and play while the boys milked.

Little was said at supper. The boys had to work at chewing their meat. Pa hadn't fried it Ma's way. Pa had to cut Sherman's portion into tiny pieces; otherwise the little fellow would've been chewing until kingdom come. Pa had to cut his into fine pieces too.

Everybody was looking at everybody else chewing and chewing.

Finally Pa threw down his fork. "If you kids want to give up, you can. We'll give it to the dog. This meat is as tough as a belt."

The rest of the meal, the rice and the homemade bread Ma'd baked before she left, went down as slick as ice cream.

Free read from the Bible. Pa gave the thanks.

After the dishes were washed, and the younger kids had gone to bed, Pa got out a pencil and did some figuring on the back of a grocery bag.

Free read Shakespeare with his feet in the cob box.

Pa looked at Free. "Well, philosopher, if you're gonna have the privilege of sitting that close to the stove you better make yourself valuable there and fire up a little. It's getting cold in here. And while you're at it, throw that book in too."

Free didn't like being interrupted. Old King Lear had just rejected the one daughter, Cordelia, who loved him most. Too bad Pa and Ma with all their sons, six of them, couldn't have lived in the time of King Lear. They might've been able to arrange for the marriage of at least three of their sons. Free himself would take Cordelia.

"Fill the stove."

Free opened the stove door. Pa was right. The fire was almost out. The first red cobs to hit the collapsed pink ashes didn't burst into flames right away. He filled the stove to the brim. He picked up his red book again.

"Nah," Pa said, "put that book aside once. I got a job for you."

"This late?"

"I don't mean that kind. I want you to write a letter for me to our landlord. T' Cedar Rapids."

"Must I?"

"Wal, your mother ain't here to write it for me." Pa dug out Ma's pen and ink and her linen tablet. "Sit at the table here with me."

Frowning, Free took his usual place at the far end of the table. He opened the tablet and dipped the pen in the ink.

Pa began to dictate. "Dear Mr. Horace Hamilton." Pa watched as Free scribbled down the salutation. "Did you put the date up in the corner?"

Free filled in the date and the place.

"All right. Now. Banker Chauncey tells me he thinks hard times is just ahead again. Only worse this time. All prices are way up over what they're supposed to be." Pa watched Free scratching. "Got that?"

"Yes."

"Also, your previous renter left the pasture in bad shape. It's full of stinkweed so bad that in August nobody wants to drink the milk, not even the pigs. And the creamery has been complaining about the stink in the cream we sell them."

"Not so fast."

Pa watched Free's hand move across the page until it stopped. "Say to him next that I'll give him five dollars an acre this coming year, not seven, until I can get that pasture built up."

"Please, Pa. I'm not used to being a secretary."

"Wal, your Ma takes it down as fast as I can say it. Say to him that he can double-check with Chauncey if he wants to."

The cob fire in the stove took hold and began to roar up the chimney.

"Say to him," and then Pa's voice broke a little, and he looked down at the yellow linoleum floor, "say to him that my wife Ada is in the hospital. That'll get his attention. He always liked her. Sincerely yours. And when you got that written down, I'll sign it."

After a moment Free slid the linen table and pen and ink across the table.

Pa dipped the pin in the ink, and carefully, like he was cutting initials in a piece of leather, signed it.

Pa got Ma from the hospital the next Saturday. Ma was pale but she was smiling. Now that she knew who the enemy was she could relax.

At supper that night the children laughed more than usual.

Ma didn't seem to mind the noise for once. She sat in her place smiling. Better yet, she let Everett put the food on the table. She held her belly a lot.

Ma went to bed right after supper. Doctor's orders. He still wanted her to go slow for a while. She had to learn to just sit and do nothing. She asked Free to put on a couple of records and listened to them, smiling to herself. Then she drifted off to sleep.

Back in the kitchen, Free filled the stove with red cobs, put his stocking feet in the cob box, and read in his Shakespeare.

Pa got out his shaving set. It was Saturday night and he had a rule about never shaving on the Lord's day. He stropped his straight razor until he could cut a fuzz hair off the back of his wrist with it. He poured a flib of hot water into the mug and worked up a lather. He lathered himself twice, the last time so thick he looked like a trapper.

Quite soon now Free himself would be shaving. He already had a thin golden moustache as well as a hint of a goatee. His beard would never be as heavy as Pa's. Except for his nose Pa just about had a beard all over his face. What a powerful sight he'd make if he'd let his beard grow. With those eyes he'd look fierce.

Pa shaved steadily. S-crettch, s-crettch. Pa wiped his blade each time on a corner of a page torn from *The Bonnie Review*. S-crettch. S-crettch. Gradually little gray dabs lined the edge of the paper.

Everything was going to be all right with Ma. In another year, if they had another good crop, Ma would let him go to college. By then Pa would be able to handle the half-section with the other boys.

Pa washed up in cold water. He cleaned his straight razor and then polished it with a piece of cloth. Pa was wonderfully neat and precise.

Free was about to put more cobs in the stove, when Pa stopped him.

"Nah, don't you think it's time for bed? Tomorrow it's the Lord's day and He don't like sleepyheads in church."

"All right, Pa."

Ma looked good the next week. She sat smiling as they bustled about her. They set the food in front of her. They wrestled the dirty plates off the table into the dishpan. She laughed. "It's fun being treated like a queen for once."

On Thursday she discovered Pa and Everett had left the sheets in the clothes basket in the basement. She was one of those who liked to put her sheets away unwrinkled. A wrinkled sheet always looked a little dirty. She carried the basket up from the basement and into the living room.

Free caught her in the act. He'd just come into the house for a pair of dry mittens. "Hey, I thought you weren't supposed to go up and down stairs."

Ma smiled. "It's no fun lying there in bed hour after hour looking up at a blank ceiling."

"I'm talking about you climbing stairs, Ma."

"Here, grab hold, and help me shake out these sheets."

Free finally took hold of the sheet at two corners and helped her give it several sharp snaps. Linen washed in soap smelled good.

"That's it," Ma said.

"But what I want to know is," Free said, deciding to make a joke out of it, because privately he was glad Ma showed gumption, "what are we going to do with you?"

Ma finished folding the sheet. "I feel so guilty doing nothing in my own house."

"Read, then. I know I wish I could."

"I've read everything in this house at least a dozen times."

Free had an idea. He got his Shakespeare. "Here. Get in bed and read this.

And I know just the play for you too. *The Taming of the Shrew.*" Free took her by the arm and led her into the bedroom and half pushed, half helped her into bed.

"I can get into bed by myself," Ma protested. At the same time she liked it that Free made a fuss over her. She fluffed up her pillows. The afternoon sun glowed through the single west window and lighted up her face with good healthy gold. Light reflecting off the colored block quilt made her cheeks pink.

Free found the play for her and placed the book in her lap.

Pa came in and overheard them. "What does 'shrew' mean?"

Free winked. "It means a wife who will not follow orders. Who won't stay in bed after she's had an operation."

Pa missed the wink. "What's that play really about?"

Free gave Pa a quick synopsis of it.

Pa's mouth slowly opened as Free talked. Pa's lips imitated Free's lips, trying to mouth what Free was saying, even trying to anticipate what Free was going to say next. Sometimes Free's telling took strange twists, and then Pa missed, and in mid-lip movement had to switch. Pa's face slowly opened into a smile over the story of hard Kate.

Free's heart gave a jump as he watched his father trying to follow him. What an awful life it had to be for him not to be able to read.

When Free finished Ma asked, "And I'm a shrew like your Kate?"

"No, no. I'm only joking."

"All right." Ma shifted herself around a little so the light from the window fell across the page.

Free and Pa left.

When Free came in to say good night around ten, Ma had a smile for him. "Got another play to recommend?"

"Hey. Did you finish *The Taming* already?"

"Sure did. And you know something? I know a woman like that."

"Who?"

"That would be gossip."

"Shirttail relation?"

Ma smiled. "Recommend me another play."

"All right. Try *Romeo and Juliet*. A great love story."

"Good. I'll get after that tomorrow then. Time to sleep now." She looked over at where little Sherman lay curled up in sound sleep in his crib next to her bed. "Look at the little angel. If it weren't for the end results of having to eat, you'd have to say he was spotless."

"Yes, Mother."

The next day just before milking, Free went into the house for a cup of coffee. He sat half nodding with his feet in the cob box.

"Free?" Ma called from her bedroom.

"Yes, Ma?"

"Can you come in here a minute?"

"Sure thing."

He scuffed through the living room and took a chair by her bed.

Ma was holding the red Shakespeare in her lap. She was smiling to herself. "Ohch, if I'd only known about Shakespeare before."

"Did you like *Romeo and Juliet?*"

"It was a joy, son. So sad. So beautiful. What a wonderful love affair." She shook her head. A bright nimbus circled her golden head. "Too bad we poor common mortals can't experience a love like that."

"Didn't you and Pa?"

"Not quite that way."

"What about that other fellow you had before Pa?"

"Oh, him. He proved unworthy."

"But didn't you think you'd die if you couldn't get a little glimpse of him once in a while?"

"Not after he pulled that stunt." Ma paused. "Say, what do you know about such things? Have you been in love?"

Free thought of Ada Shutter and the time he met her under the golden cottonwood leaves. "We're talking about you now, Ma."

Ma looked at Free with frank blue eyes. "Your father made a wonderful husband. And over the years I've come to love him very much. In a different and better way."

April the eighteenth they got the oats in. Pa remarked at supper that for once he and the boys were ahead of Uncle John.

Ma had supper in bed that night. She'd felt dreamy all day.

After dessert, a dish of Ma's home-canned pears, Free got out the Bible. He read louder that usual so Ma could hear him from where she lay. It was from The Book of Ruth at Ma's special request.

"And Ruth went down unto the floor, and did according to all that her mother-in-law bade her. And when Boaz had eaten and drunk, and his heart was merry, he went to lie down at the end of the heap of corn; and she came softly, and uncovered his feet, and laid her down. And it came to pass at midnight, that the man was afraid, and turned himself: and behold, a woman lay at his feet. And he said, Who art thou? And she answered, I am Ruth thine handmaid: spread therefore thy skirt over thy handmaid; for thou art near a kinsman. And he said, Blessed be thou of the Lord, my daughter: for thou has shewed more kindness in the latter end than at the beginning, in as much as thou followedst not young men, whether poor or rich. And now, my daughter, fear not; I will do to thee all that thou requirest: for all the city of my people doth know that thou art a virtuous woman."

Pa had barely got into his prayer of thanks for all the bountiful food and all their good health, also loud enough for Ma to hear him, when there was a sudden cry in the house.

"Alf--f-r-e-d!"

The cry began weakly, as though Ma was in a nightmare and had trouble breaking out of it; then, as she broke free, it became almost a shriek.

Everybody burst up from their chairs. Little Sherman flipped the adjustable table of his high chair over his head and jumped down to the floor. Pa was the quickest. Even though he had the farthest to go he was the first in Ma's bedroom. "Ada!"

All piled in behind Pa standing beside her bed.

Pink color was just returning to Ma's face. "Ohhh. I'm still here."

"Ada?"

"It was so funny." Ma spoke dreamily. "I heard Pa start praying, and then the next thing I knew, I was in another world. And it wasn't in the right place. It was awful. So I fought to get out of there." Ma gave them a wan smile. "As you can see, I made it."

"Are you all right now though?"

Ma fumbled with the silk silver tassles on the edge of the bedspread. "I guess so." Her smile became brave. "All right, children, you can go back to the table. In a minute I'll let you have Pa and then he can finish the prayer."

The children and Free slowly retreated back to the kitchen and settled in their places. They stared at one another. They were whiter than Ma.

After a moment Pa came stepping around to his swivel chair. He kept looking back over his shoulder. He sat down and made short work of the thanks. He hardly listened to the little ones as they recited their short prayers.

Pa took up watch in Ma's bedroom.

Free told the kids to do up the dishes and to shut up with their loud playing for once. Then he joined Pa.

Pa picked up Ma's wrist and counted her pulse. After a moment he looked up in surprise at Free. "Why, it's . . ." He got out his watch and counted her pulse against the sweep of the second hand. "Why, it's . . ." His mouth clapped to. "Ada, I'm calling Doc."

Ada smiled odd and lazy to him. "Can we afford to?"

Pa's big chin stuck out. Quickly he stalked to the telephone and rang central to get Dr. Fairlamb on the line. After a moment Pa said clearly, "Doc, you better come out here. I don't like her pulse."

Free took Ma's pulse too. It was slow. It also beat erratically. It would beat twice, and miss, then beat three times, and miss.

Doc was there in fifteen minutes. He held his bristly black head of hair to one side as his dark eyes examined her critically. He took her pulse, then got out his stethoscope and listened to her chest. After a while he nodded to himself and put the stethoscope away. He dug around in his black bag and got out a small bottle of pills. He scowled a bedside smile at Ma. "Take one of these every two hours for a couple of days."

Ma placed a little white pill on the tip of her tongue, then helped herself to a swallow of water from her glass.

Pa sat on the end of the bed. "Wal, Doc?"

Dr. Fairlamb studied his hands.

Free sat near the head of the bed. He picked up Ma's wrist again. He had trouble finding her pulse. He checked his own pulse to make sure he was looking for it on the proper side of the wrist. At last he found it. It bubbled under his fingertip like a series of beebees going by.

Dr. Fairlamb counted her pulse again.

Pa spotted the kids, even little Sherman, staring in at the door. "Hey, back in the kitchen with you. We'll call you if we need you."

The children reluctantly trailed back into the kitchen.

After another minute, Dr. Fairlamb let go of her wrist and placed it in her lap. "That's better."

Pretty soon Pa asked Dr. Fairlamb if he'd like a cup of coffee.

Dr. Fairlamb thought that a good idea, and the two men went to the kitchen. While they had their coffee, Pa told the kids to head for bed.

Everett said, "But we hain't washed dishes yet."

"Never mind them. Free can do 'em later. I want to talk to the doctor alone in the kitchen a minute."

The kids came into Ma's bedroom one by one and said good night. They gave her a wet kiss, and didn't want to leave, but finally they had to.

Free helped baby Sherman out of his clothes into his nightgown and held the pot for him to pee in. Baby kept looking over his shoulder at Ma. Then he decided he had to have a second kiss before he would agree to let Free lift him up and put him in the crib.

Ma cried as she kissed little Sherman and hugged him. "Poor little fellow," she whispered.

Free thought: "But such things happen in other people's families."

Free helped little Sherman into his crib. He tucked him in and gave him a kiss.

Pa called Free into the kitchen. He and Dr. Fairlamb had been talking in a low voice. Pa looked haggard. "I don't want to scare your mother but I want you to leave the house quietly and go telephone Uncle John from Tillman's house. And then you go get your Uncle Sherm from Young Men's Society."

That's right. It was Young Men's Society night. Free had completely forgotten about it and was surprised that Pa had remembered. He put on his shoes and slipped out of the house for the Buick. An April shower had just passed over and the yard was wet. The Buick took hold on the first revolution. Free threw the car into low gear, then into high gear. He worried that Ma might die while he was gone. He made the first corner on two wheels and roared up the lane toward town. It had rained just enough to make the top inch greasy. The Buick began to slither back and forth. It was like trying to guide a snake. Luckily he'd played car shinny on that pond north of town driving an old beat-up Ford and knew how to turn into the zigs and zags.

He pulled up to the church door and shot into the consistory room, where the young men were gathered with Reverend Tiller. Mouths dropped open around the long brown table. Reverend Tiller rose to his feet.

"Pardon me, Reverend . . . Sherm, Ma is going."

Sherm came to his feet in a single fluid motion, already fastening his jacket as he came around the table. "Sorry, Reverend. Excuse us."

"That's all right." Then Reverend Tiller called after them, "Our prayers will be with you."

Free led the way outside. He described Ma's fainting spell during supper.

"Ohoh. I better go get your Gramma. She'll want to be present. With my new Model A Ford it won't take me more than an hour up and back."

"Okay. And I'll call Uncle John from Tillman's."

Free called Uncle John and then slithered down the lane home again. He turned off the ignition near the house gate. He let the dead engine chug the car to a stop by itself and leaned on the dead run into the bedroom.

Ma was sitting up in her pillows. She was smiling. She was pink. Pa was sitting on one side of her bed; Dr. Fairlamb on the other. Little Sherman was awake and telling his teddy bear that now their mama was much better.

Ma had to smile at Free. "Well, it didn't take you long, did it?"

Free shot Pa a look.

"Yeh," Pa said, "she knows. She heard the car roar off the yard."

"I'm sorry."

"It's all right," Ma said. "A little company I'll like."

Uncle John came a few minutes later. He hurried into the house and stuck his head around the corner of the door. "Ade?"

"Yes, John."

Uncle John stared down at her critically a moment; then let his shoulders down. "For goodness sakes, Ade, and here I was afraid I wouldn't get here in time to ask you to prepare the way for me."

Ma frowned. "Please, John."

"Yeh, but that call so scairt me that for a fact I couldn't tell you what road I took to get here."

"Oh, John, you always joke so."

Uncle John drew up a chair. "Well, anyway, you're feeling better now."

"Much better, I think the worst is over."

Dr. Fairlamb seemed to agree. He had been checking her pulse through all the talk and let go of Ma's wrist and placed it in her lap again. "Still feel short of breath?"

"Not now."

Dr. Fairlamb nodded. "Yes, it's pretty well stabilized itself."

"You're gonna go now, Doc?" Pa asked.

"Well . . ."

Ma said, "I don't think you need to worry about me anymore tonight, Doctor."

Dr. Fairlamb closed his black bag and got to his feet. "Well, if you get the least hint it's going to flare up again, call me. And let's hope Mrs. Harter's tenth child doesn't put in its appearance tonight."

Ma brightened. "Another baby? Well, well. And she already has six girls.

How fortunate she is." Ma played with the tassels along the edge of the bedspread. She looked within herself.

"Call me then if you need me," Dr. Fairlamb said. Then he left.

Pa and Ma and Uncle John began chatting like in the old days. Little Sherman fell asleep again.

In about an hour Uncle Sherm arrived with Gramma. Gramma started to wail even before she opened the door to the porch. It made Uncle John and Pa and Ma smile at each other. Gramma came ruckling into the bedroom with a big red nose. She'd been crying and weeping all the way over. Sherm trailed in after her, ashamed of the way she was carrying on.

Gramma at last managed to take a good look at Ma through her glasses. She paused, almost in shock. "Why, daughter! You look fine."

Ma had to laugh. "Why shouldn't I look fine?"

"Daughter. Well, at least thank God you can still laugh."

There was a pause. Then Ma looked around at all the faces as if for a few seconds she hadn't been there. She played some more with the silver tassels on the bedspread.

Gramma sat down on a chair Free got for her. She frowned at where Ada lay. "You're so thin, daughter." Gramma had long been jealous of Ma's slim figure, and was especially envious of her carriage. Ma walked more like Grampa Alfred than Gramma, and Gramma had never gotten over it.

Free sat down on the floor with a groan.

Ma looked at him. "Are your joints still sore, son?"

"No, Ma."

Ma shook her head to herself. "I surely had sore joints when I was twelve. In fact, I had them when I was nine already."

Gramma said, "Everybody has growing pains when they're young."

Uncle John nodded. "That's true. You take like Sherm here too now, he says he had them once."

Sherm nodded. "I had them my first year in high school."

It was a mistake for Sherm to mention high school. Gramma had so wanted Sherm to someday become an important man. She lamented once more that she'd let him quit high school. "Instead I let you go to work for your sister Joan and that shiftless husband of hers."

"Oh, her husband ain't shiftless," Uncle John said. "It's just that he's dumb, Ma. He's a good guy, but dumb."

Ma looked up brightly. "Let's see if we can't say something nice about them. Please?"

Sherm glanced at the little fellow sleeping in the crib. "Well, I see my little namesake ain't worrying much over the present state of affairs in this bedroom."

Ma laughed with love. She smiled over at little Sherman. "Isn't he the little angel though? Yes, spotless."

Reverend Tiller surprised them by suddenly poking his head around the corner of the door. They hadn't heard him step across the thick rug in the living room.

He beamed a smile at the circle of faces around the bed. He could always smile in the presence of trouble. "I saw a light on, so I thought I'd at least ask how Mrs. Alfredson was." His frank blue eyes examained Ma. "Well, I see you've passed the crisis."

Crisis? Domeny could've used another word.

Ma lifted her head. "Yes, I seem to be fine now." She glanced at Pa. "I wonder . . . could you help me with these pillows? So I can sit up a little straighter?"

Pa fluffed up her pillows as she leaned forward.

Reverend Tiller continued to smile. "I've missed you in church, Mrs. Alfredson. There's a big hole in church where you usually sit with your family."

"And I've missed your sermons."

"What did doctor say?"

Ma fumbled with the silk tassels again.

Uncle John gave Reverend Tiller a curving smile. "Doc wouldn't have left if he didn't think she was going to make it."

Reverend Tiller nodded. "I'm preaching on Job next Sunday. With all his tribulations. Would you like me to send a copy of the sermon home with your husband?"

"That would be so nice, Reverend."

Things became uneasy. Domeny in his dark clothes had cast a shadow into the room.

Reverend Tiller rocked on his heels. "Yes, Mrs. Alfredson, a Mother Israel. And it shall be said of you that you had sons, not daughters."

Ma shook her head, gently. "Begging your pardon, Reverend, but perhaps I wouldn't be quite so weak tonight if all these years I could have had two girls out of those six children I had. They could have helped me."

Reverend Tiller didn't quite frown. "Well, Mrs. Alfredson, I'm sure God had His reasons for giving you sons."

"Yes, Thy will, not my will."

Reverend Tiller worked his smile some more on them. Then he finally said, "Well, Mrs. Alfredson. You probably need your rest. Would you like me to offer a prayer to God?"

"Yes, Reverend," Ma said, "that would be a good thing."

Reverend Tiller folded his hands over his lean belly. He rolled his blue eyes at everyone circling the bed and then let them fall shut. "Father, forgiving one in heaven, we stand here now in the home of this Thy beloved parishioner, Ada Alfredson, and ask that Thou look kindly down upon her. Give her good health once again so that she may be restored to active life in the bosom of her family as well as in the bosom of Thy church. Forgive her, and all of us, all our sins. We ask this in Jesus' name. Amen."

"Thank you, Reverend," Ma said.

Reverend Tiller shook hands with everybody and left.

Uncle John hadn't liked some of the things Domeny had said. "Well, Ada, in his mind that man's got you well on the way. So will you be sure and give our best regards to everybody that knows us?"

"John, I wish you wouldn't always joke so about serious things." Then Ma reached for Uncle John's hand. She loved her brother. "I'm sorry. I didn't mean to criticize. It is one of your gifts that you can help us over the rough spots with your quips."

"I wonder," Uncle John mused, "if God'll have time for clowns in heaven."

Both of Ma's hands rose to her bosom. "I'm so short of breath. Always so short of breath." Ma sucked for air; sucked. Then, after a second, her face turned white over the cheeks and her eyes hazed over.

"There she goes again!" Pa cried.

Uncle John leaped up from his chair and began shaking Ma. "Ada! Don't go yet, girl. For godsakes."

Free jumped to feel for her pulse. He counted them against his own heartbeats. She had only one beat for his two.

Uncle John turned to Pa. "Got any whiskey in the house?"

Pa bethought himself. "Yeh. I guess we do. We still got that bottle of Old Taylor left. From when we was first married."

"Get it." Uncle John kept shaking Ma.

Pa dug down in the bottom of Ma's wardrobe. "Here it is." Pa held the bottle up to the light. There was about an inch left.

Uncle John took it and sat himself beside Ma and slipped his arm around her. Tipping her head back a little, he let a few drops run in between her lips.

Ma coughed. Again. The second cough was a good healthy explosion of air. Ma came to. The light blue haze in her eyes became a level blue stare. "Am I still here?"

Uncle John shook her playfully. It was wonderful to see an old brother shaking an old sister. "Where did you think you were?"

Ma made a face. She'd tasted alcohol in her mouth. She spotted the whiskey bottle in Uncle John's hand. "What? Was I given whiskey just as I was about to enter eternity?"

"Hey, you're not so slow with the quips yourself."

"Fooey." Ma tried to push the taste of the whiskey out of her mouth with her tongue. She reached for a handkerchief from the pocket of her nightgown and wiped her lips.

Uncle John laughed some more. "We had to do something to bring you back."

Free headed out of the bedroom.

"Where you going?" Pa called after him.

Free didn't answer. He was scared. Ma was going to go if they didn't do something drastic quick. He went to the wall telephone and rang central and asked her to ring Dr. Fairlamb.

Mrs. Fairlamb answered. When Free told Mrs. Fairlamb what he wanted she said her husband was out on call. "I'll try and get in touch with him, Free. Though the Harters don't have a phone out there on their farm. By the way, Free, in housecleaning I found another set of books for you. They were up in the attic. A set of James Fenimore Cooper, complete. You're welcome to come over and borrow them."

"Thanks." Didn't Mrs. Fairlamb understand there was something radically wrong with his mother? "Please tell Doc to call when he gets in, pronto, will you?"

"Yes, Free."

Pa spoke up. He'd come into the living room behind Free. "You couldn't get hold of him then?"

"No. He's out helping Mrs. Harter have her baby and they have no phone."

Pa's face had become quite hollowed out. "We better get somebody. 'Cause I don't like it either."

Free turned back to the phone. "I'll try and get Dr. Husum in Amen." He called central and told her who to get long distance. After some crackling in the receiver, a woman answered. "Miss Longwood speaking."

Free recognized the voice instantly. It was the nurse who'd come along with Dr. Husum one Saturday afternoon when the doctor had dropped by to see how Ma was getting along after her operation. Free was on the yard at the time, sharpening disk blades, and he'd caught a hint of something about the two. As Dr. Husum and Miss Longwood stepped through the house gate, Dr. Husum took her hand as though he were her boyfriend. It struck Free at the time that they hadn't come so much to see how Mrs. Alfredson was getting along as to get off by themselves. Miss Longwood was an easy-smiling beauty.

"Miss Longwood speaking," the woman repeated. "Yes?"

"This is the Alfredsons in Bonnie. My mother keeps coming and going. Fainting away." Ma and the others had fallen silent in the bedroom behind him. "Can Dr. Husum come out?"

"Isn't Mrs. Alfredson a patient of Dr. Fairlamb?"

"Yes. But Dr. Fairlamb is out on call just now."

"She is a patient of Dr. Fairlamb though, isn't she?"

Free slowly got mad. It hit him that Dr. Husum was right there beside Miss Longwood at the other end. Her voice was easy polite on the outside, but down in the middle of it was the dark purr of a woman who'd been interrupted. "If you two could drive by to see how my mother was getting along the other Saturday, why can't you come sailing out here now?"

"Why isn't your father calling if it's so serious?"

"Maybe he's too busy shaking her to keep her heart going while I make the call!"

Silence on the other end of the wire.

"Can Dr. Husum come out?"

"Why don't you try to get Dr. Fairlamb again? He's right near you while we're quite some distance off, you know." She spoke with the smoothness of an old hand in a department store. "I'm afraid Dr. Husum can't help you just now." And she hung up.

Free raged. "That bitch!" At the same time Free thought: "But who am I to rage at that horny doctor and his nurse?"

Free stomped slowly back into the bedroom.

Pa and Sherm and Gramma appeared to be some surprised that he should talk so rough with a nurse. Uncle John appeared to be pleased.

Ma was leaning forward from the hips, breathing harder than usual. There was a suggestion about her that she was uneasy about something under her.

Gramma spotted the motion. She got up and and reached in under Ma's bedclothes. "Aha."

Ma got mad at that. She clamped down on Gramma's hand through the bedclothes to keep her from investigating any farther.

Pa woke up to what had happened. "Everybody out! There's too much commotion in here for my wife," he half sobbed. "Get out!" He held a finger under Gramma's nose. "You too."

Uncle John agreed with Pa. He got up and made a motion for Sherm to lead the way. Then Uncle John grabbed Gramma by the arm and forcibly led her out into the kitchen.

Free followed them.

When they got to the kitchen, Gramma had a pronouncement to make. She was trembling. "Ya, ya, my daughter, by morning she will be with my first husband and the angels."

Uncle John was disgusted. "Sit down."

Gramma sat down. She wept into her handkerchief. "Ya, ya, but I know what's coming. Oh, I know what's coming. She passed her water that last time she fainted and that's always a sign death is at hand." Gramma knew. She herself suffered from an occasional wet bed because of an erratic heart.

Uncle John stared, "You mean, she wet her bed just now?"

Gramma nodded, sobbing into her handkerchief.

"Well," Uncle John said up at the ceiling, "I dunno now."

Sherm didn't want to believe it. "Aw, you know how Ma is. She exaggerates so. It's probably only some tea Ada spilled from supper."

Ma hadn't had tea for supper. Free stepped back into the living room. He heard Pa and Ma talking.

Ma said, sighing, "Alfred, my husband, I'm sorry if I wasn't nice to you in the past."

Pa said, "Oh, wife, let's not talk about that now."

"Perhaps in the next life, Alfred."

"Perhaps. But let's not talk about it."

"But I do want to clear my heart with you, Alfred. You see, I'm pretty sure now that my Savior is going to call me home tonight."

"Wife, don't."

"And I am ready."

"Please now, wife!"

Free was careful to breathe through his open mouth so they wouldn't hear him.

"Alfred?"

"Yes?"

"Would you call Free in here? I want to talk to him alone a minute."

"Alone?"

"Yes. And Alfred, one word of advice about that boy before I go. Whatever comes up between you two in the future, let the boy have his say once in a while. He'll feel better then. And you'll know better."

"All right. I'll call him."

Free quick skipped back into the kitchen. He didn't want Pa and Ma to know he'd overheard them.

Pa poked his head into the kitchen. He crooked a finger at Free. "Your ma wants to see you."

Free entered Ma's bedroom reluctantly.

"Sit down, son. Here. By me. Closer." Ma pointed to the near chair.

Free sat down. Behind him little baby brother Sherman slept with the soft sound of silk sliding on silk.

"Look at me, son."

Free forced himself to look her in the eye.

"I don't know how to begin this, son."

Free said nothing.

"But I shall shortly be in heaven. With my Savior. And—"

"Don't talk like that, Ma!"

Ma looked over at little Sherman. "Not so loud, Free. We mussent wake him."

Free nodded.

"I hope to go to heaven tonight, Free." Ma looked down at her fingers where they fumbled through each other in her lap. "And, son, I'd so like it if someday you could join me there and live beside me in glory."

"Ma."

"You're such a strange one. I sometimes don't understand you at all. You are not of us, really. You are not like any we have lived with."

"Oh, Ma, except that I'm too tall for doorways, I'm just like everybody else."

"You and Uncle John with your quips. No, son, I'm serious. I would very much like to have you in heaven with me and Jesus someday."

"Yes, Ma."

"At the same time, though, I don't want you to pretend to be a Christian just to please me when privately you're not. Don't pose. Don't be a hypocrite. God hates a pious fraud. In fact, God may very well have more time for the honest soul that denies Him than for the covenant member who offers Him lip service only." Ma fumbled with the silver tassels of the bedspread again. "And then there's the question of living with one's own conscience. So, son, be honest about your true feelings, no matter what the consequences may be. Be a man about them."

My God, here was Ma, on her deathbed, having forbearance for a way of thinking that was alien to hers.

"Awful as the thought is, I think I'd much rather have you in hell, an honest soul, then in heaven, a hypocrite."

A sweet sanctified smell rose from her body. It couldn't really be happening.

"So live what you are. Even if that takes you away from me and Jesus."

Free's head felt airy and aromatic, like a haymow with the doors all open.

"All this reading, this learning of yours, what are you going to do with it? And mind now, I approve of Shakespeare, you know."

Free looked down at his twisting fingers.

"What do you want to become?"

"A storyteller."

"What kind of reader do you have in mind?"

"Smart people, mostly. Doctors. Teachers like Professor Ralph."

"And not the average Christian?"

"Of course him too. If he wants to read them."

"What will your books look like? I mean, the nature of them?"

"Oh, like Jack London's. Or that Hardy you once wouldn't let me read. That kind."

"What a strange boy you are."

"Don't you like it that I want to be like them?"

Ma shook her head to herself. "Ada's boy a writer. Free, of Alfred and Ada, turned out to one of those writer fellows."

"All this crazy talk, Ma. You're going to be all right."

Ma fixed him with a different look. "Tell me, son, when you think of marriage at all, what sort of girl do you have in mind? You know, I won't be here to see you get married."

"I dunno. A kind of a sporting girl."

"A what?"

"You know. The kind that'll like to take trips with me. Climb mountains. Who'll read good books with me."

"As your father would say, you and your big ideas."

"Ma."

"All right. Let's say you do marry such a girl. Can I give you a word of advice?"

"If you must."

"Well, remember this then. There is no fun in it for the woman. Only for the man."

Free was dumbfounded. What she said was exactly what had happened when he was fumbling around on Aletha on the kitchen floor.

"All that's in it for the woman is the satisfaction of giving pleasure to her man. And of bearing his children. That's all."

"Gosh, Ma, must we be talking about such things at a time like this?"

"Yes, son. I won't be here tomorrow."

"Cut it out now, Ma."

"Oh, I know it's easy to question the Lord's doings sometimes. Because we don't understand." She picked at the bedspread sharply. "Like how I can't understand why the Lord is going to take me first, when it would have been a whole lot better for you children if he'd have taken your father first. I can't understand that."

"And the other day you were praising Pa, saying such great things about him."

"I know." Ma sighed. "But I don't know how you kids are going to get raised without me. You're not the usual brood. You're all so different. It's going to take a lot of patience and understanding." Ma heaved an immense sigh. "Yes, I hatched me five hawks and one chicken."

Free thought that pretty good.

"A person just doesn't know. Perhaps I'm just thinking selfishly, that this little me wants to stay alive, as if that was important, when something else may be a whole lot more important."

Pa stuck his head in the door. "What are you two arguing about?"

"We weren't arguing, Alfred," Ma said.

"You were too fighting," Pa said. Pa grabbed Free by the front of his overalls, gathering up the bib of it into a tight roll. "Listen, you. Lay off my wife. Getting her all stirred up like that when she ain't well."

Ma said, "Now, Alfred, temper, temper."

Pa quieted down right away. Ma had wonderfdul control over him. "But I do think there's been too much commotion here tonight." Pa let go of Free.

"Yes, perhaps so, Alfred."

Pa looked like a nervous stallion about to climb out of his stall. His fingers trembled like he might have the palsy. Pa was aware of his jumpy fingers.

Ma said, "Free, why don't you go make Gramma and your uncles some hot chocolate."

"All right."

In the kitchen Free discovered Gramma had anticipated Ma. Gramma had just put some skim milk on the stove and was setting out the cups and saucers on the table.

Free filled the stove with red cobs. Softly he let down the stove door. Then he let himself slide down on the floor. He was dead tired. It was good to lie on the floor next to the warm stove. He could use some sleep.

He heard the milk slowly rise to a simmer on the stove. Gramma and his uncles talked old family talk.

Presently Uncle John wondered if he shouldn't drive out to the Harters' and get Dr. Fairlamb anyway. Uncle Sherm wondered if they shouldn't send a veterinarian out to the Harters' to take the place of Dr. Fairlamb. Uncle John wondered next if they shouldn't call a heart specialist from Le Mars.

Free drifted off.

When Free came to, he heard them talking about him.

Gramma said, "And I still say we should have tied a heavy stone to that boy's head when he was little."

"You mean, like the Chinese women bind their feet to keep them small?"

"Something like that."

Uncle John laughed indulgent. "Look at him laying there. He practically stretches from one end of the kitchen to the other."

Uncle Sherm laughed too. "It's when you see him all stretched out like that that you realize how big he really is."

"Why," Uncle John said, "he's so tall I betcha he can't tell when his toes are cold."

Gramma breathed a soft fat laugh. "Well, thank goodness he's seventeen now and is probably all through growing."

"Yeh," Uncle John said, "and when he fills out, say at twenty-one, what a man's he's going to be then. Him lifting that wagon wheel off the ground the other day and then setting it down, not dropping it, mind you, but letting it down easy, that was something. He sure put that Marion Hubert to shame."

Uncle Sherm said, "Was the wagon full?"

"Plumb full of shelled corn. Forty-three hundred pounds on the city scale."

"That means he lifted at least a thousand pounds at that one wheel."

"That's right."

Gramma said, "Yes, but the best thing is, that when it comes to brains he takes after our little Shermie that died." Gramma had herself a little sob over that old tragedy.

Sherm laughed. "Yes, dumb Free ain't. He's pretty fast with the old come-back. When we were cutting wood for Grampa Stanhorse, a smart aleck asked Free how the weather was up there. Quicklike, between strokes of his axe, Free said, 'Why don't you grow up and find out?' "

Uncle John laughed.

Free's side hurt where he'd lain on the hard linoleum. He wanted to roll over but didn't want them to know he'd overheard them.

Gramma got up heavily. "Hoo. The milk's about to boil over. Grutkins."

Sherm beat her to it and lifted the pot off the stove.

"John!" Pa cried suddenly from the bedroom. The cry pierced them to the roots of their teeth.

Uncle John got there first. He took Ma out of Pa's hands and began to shake her. "Ade! You can't go yet. You've got a lot of work left to do here on this earth. Ade!"

Free, Sherm, and Gramma stood in the doorway transfixed.

Uncle John kept shaking her. "If we can only get her past dawn," Uncle John wept, "then we'll have her for another day."

Ma flopped between Uncle John's hands like a piece of cooling bland wax.

"Ade!"

No response.

"Where are those heart pills?" Uncle John cried.

"Here." Pa handed over the small bottle Dr. Fairlamb had left behind for Ma.

Uncle John shook a little white pill out of the bottle and stuck it under Ma's tongue.

Slowly pink came back to her neck, then to her cheeks.

Uncle John kept calling her name, winningly. He shook her a little less roughly.

At last she opened her eyes. Her eyes were like skim milk at first. Gradually they formed into blue crystals of clear sight. "Am I still here?" she whispered. "I just saw Jesus and the throne. It was so nice there." She looked at them each in turn. "I'm not sure I wanted to come back to you people. It was so peaceful there."

Uncle John let her lie back gently against her pillows. "Well, sis, if that's your mind, next time I'll just let you go."

"Now, John."

"If you prefer their company up there, why, go right ahead."

Gramma began to bawl. When everybody including Ma looked at her, Gramma pointed at the bed. A widening spot of wet began to show in the bedcover. "See! She did it again," Gramma cried. "That's the sign."

Pa ordered them all out again. "March! Get!"

Uncle John held up a hand. "Sorry, Alfred, but I'm staying with my sister."

Pa had to swallow a couple of times to accept that. "But the rest of you, get! While we clean up here."

Free, Gramma, and Sherm trudged to the kitchen. They sat down around the table. They picked at the tablecloth.

After a while Uncle John came out. "Alfred's right. We should try and let her sleep. Alfred is going to keep watch until three and then I'll keep watch until six." Uncle John at last looked sad. "If we can only get her past dawn."

"But we can't go through this every night, for heaven's sake," Sherm said.

"I know. That's why I'm going to sneak off the yard a minute and see if I can't get Dr. Fairlamb from Harters' after all."

Sherm said, "Let me do it for you. Afters I'll go home and sleep a little and then do the morning chores and come back here."

Uncle John decided that was a good idea. "All right. Then I can go take a nap on the sofa. Gram, you can sleep upstairs in the guest room."

"Is there a white owl up there, Free?" Gramma asked. "I've got to have a chamber pot at night."

"The hired girl had one up there."

"Good. That's the one comfort I must have."

Free looked at the kitchen clock. It was just midnight. He peeked into Ma's room a minute.

Pa spotted him from where he sat by the bed and signaled that Ma was asleep.

Free nodded, and faded back.

Free climbed the stairs to bed. He took off only his overalls and lay down beside Abbott.

His brothers Everett, Albert, Jonathan, and Abbott were dead to the world.

Free prayed. "Oh God, if I be the guilty one, and if it really is my fault that she keeps slipping away, forgive me, oh place the whole blame on me, but don't take her from us."

Abbott rolled over in sleep against him.

An hour later the sky cleared and moonlight streamed into the room.

Free drifted off into sleep.

There was a loud call up the stairwell. "Hurry, Free! or you'll never see your ma alive on earth again."

Free was out of bed and into the legs of his overalls in one motion. He skidded downstairs. He bumped into Pa in the semidark of the living room. They bungled into the bedroom together as they fastened their suspenders.

They were too late.

The heart had at last stopped completely. It was done. The cheeks were losing their color. Before their very eyes her spirit rinsed out of her flesh like water soaking away in sand.

Uncle John gave her yet another great shaking. Her head rolled loosely. Her gold blond hair tossed around wildly.

"Don't!" Pa cried. And he kneeled down by the bed and took Ma away from Uncle John. Pa yelled an awful piercing yell. "Ada!"

Too late.

Ten minutes later Dr. Fairlamb came hurrying into the house.

"This is a heckuva time to be showing up, Doc," Pa said.

Dr. Fairlamb gave Pa a grim look. He went into the bedroom alone.

Everybody moved out to the kitchen. Pa made coffee. He filled the stove. Dawn opened fast in the east. Just as the sun burst red over the long sloping land, Pa said, "Ada was right. It would have been a whole lot better if the Lord had taken me instead of her. She could have done a better job of raising the children."

"Oh?" Gramma cried, "oh? Now you admit that your wife was your superior? Of higher issue? Eh?"

"Oh shut up," Uncle John said.

Free couldn't stand it. He picked up his shoes and went outside and in the red sun sat down on the slanting cellar door and slowly laced on his shoes.

Ma lay dead behind him in the house. He could see again the strange white frost spreading into her cheeks, as though somehow she were freezing up from the inside.

He called up Rover to help him get the cows.

Around ten, coming back from the pasture where he had gone to mend a break in the fence, he noted a new car on the yard. It was one of those new panel trucks he'd been hearing about. As he stood examining it, a man poked his head out of the porch door. "Could you help me a minute?"

"Sure."

Pa and the children and Gramma, everybody, had gone to Uncle John's house for breakfast.

Free followed the man into Ma's bedroom. He saw Ma lying naked and girlish on her bed. Only then he understood it was the embalmer who had called him into the house. The man had inserted tubes into the big blood vessels in her armpits. The tubes were connected by thin rubber hoses to a container hanging overhead. Embalming fluid was being run into her blood vessels. Her blood, already drained, filled a small pail near the foot of her bed.

The man said, "I'm about done." He jerked the tubes out of her armpits and plugged the apertures with cotton. "Could you help me slip this dress on her?" He pointed to Ma's best purple dress draped over a chair. "Mr. Alfredson picked it out before he left."

Just before Free touched his mother, steely resolve took over, the same one that had helped him snake the Buick around through those three stalled cars a mile north of Chokecherry Corner, and then he was cool. Quite calmly, as though his mother was only a bundle of grain, he lifted her up high enough for the embalmer to slip on her dress. Free couldn't help but cast a glance at his mother's naked body, the place out of which he'd come forth. He noted too her broad long big toe. According to the kids in school, it meant she was the boss in the family.

"Now to carry her into her coffin."

"Coffin?" Free said. "Where've you got that?"

"It's already set up in the parlor. Mr. Engleking helped me a minute before they took off for his house."

"So quick," Free said.

"Yes. They ordered the make by telephone."

"I'll carry her alone," Free said.

"She's heavy."

"I can carry her."

Free carried Ma out of the bedroom into the parlor. She wasn't stiff yet. She felt a little like Flip holding himself stiff to keep from being pinned in wrestling. Free swung her over the open coffin and laid her gently on the puffed-up silver silk lining.

The embalmer reached in and helped lay her head firmly on the raised silk pillow. He got out a comb and neatly arranged her gold hair.

The beginning of a smile had crept into Ma's lips. It was stiff, though, and opened her lips a little.

"Thank you very much," the embalmer said. "Good thing you came by."

Later in the afternoon, with Pa and the boys home again, they suddenly discovered little Sherman was gone. Everybody quick began scurrying around looking for him, on the yard, in the house.

The last place to think of finding baby Sherman was in the parlor. Yet Free decided to have a peek in there just in case.

There sat little Sherman on top of the coffin looking at Ma's face. He'd drawn up a chair and had crawled on it. He looked around at Free. "Here's Mama. See?"

Free wrote the obituary for the church paper, *The Watchman,* at Pa's request. "If you're going to be a writer," Pa said, "let's see what you can do with that."

It pleased our Lord on Friday, April 19, 1929, to take from our side a beloved wife, a caretaking mother, and a loving daughter and sister,

Mrs. Alfred Alfredson,
Ada nee Engleking,

at the age of 38 years, 3 months and 16 days. We do not weep as those who have no hope. We trust that she has fallen asleep in her Lord and Savior.

Mr. Alfred Alfredson,
and children:
Alfred
Everett
Albert
Jonathan
Abbott
Sherman.

Bonnie, Siouxland

Blue Mound
Luverne, Minnesota